A Thousand Li
Books 7-9

An Omnibus Collection for a Xianxia Cultivation Series

By

Tao Wong

Copyright

A Thousand Li Books 7-9

A Starlit Publishing Book
Published by Starlit Publishing
PO Box 30035
High Park PO
Toronto, ON
M6P 3K0
Canada

www.starlitpublishing.com

Ebook ISBN: 9781778552090
Paperback ISBN: 9781778552083
Hardcover ISBN: 9781778552076

Books in A Thousand Li series

The First Step
The First Stop
The First War
The Second Expedition
The Second Sect
The Second Storm
The Third Kingdom
The Third Realm
The Third Cut
The Fourth Stage
The Fourth Fall
The Fourth Wall

A Thousand Li World Novel

The Sundering Blade

Short Stories
The Favored Son
The Storming White Clouds Sect
On Gods and Demons
Clifftop Crisis and Transformation
Imperial March
Villages & Illnesses
Descent from the Mountain
The Divine Peak
Fish Ball Quest
Ten Thousand and One Fates

Table of Contents

A Thousand Li: The Third Kingdom 11
What Happened Before 12
Chapter 1 13
Chapter 2 17
Chapter 3 23
Chapter 4 30
Chapter 5 37
Chapter 6 44
Chapter 7 52
Chapter 8 61
Chapter 9 67
Chapter 10 75
Chapter 11 81
Chapter 12 91
Chapter 13 98
Chapter 14 107
Chapter 15 121
Chapter 16 128
Chapter 17 135
Chapter 18 141
Chapter 19 148
Chapter 20 157
Chapter 21 163
Chapter 22 169
Chapter 23 179
Chapter 24 187
Chapter 25 196
Chapter 26 205
Chapter 27 211
Chapter 28 219
Chapter 29 226
Chapter 30 234
Chapter 31 239
A Thousand Li: The Third Realm 245
Chapter 1 247
Chapter 2 254
Chapter 3 259
Chapter 4 267

Chapter 5 274
Chapter 6 281
Chapter 7 286
Chapter 8 294
Chapter 9 299
Chapter 10 308
Chapter 11 315
Chapter 12 322
Chapter 13 328
Chapter 14 336
Chapter 15 343
Chapter 16 351
Chapter 17 359
Chapter 18 365
Chapter 19 372
Chapter 20 382
Chapter 21 389
Chapter 22 398
Chapter 23 404
Chapter 24 410
Chapter 25 417
Chapter 26 423
Chapter 27 432
Chapter 28 439
Chapter 29 447
Chapter 30 454
Chapter 31 461
Chapter 32 468
Chapter 33 475
Chapter 34 482
Chapter 35 488
Chapter 36 496
Chapter 37 502
Chapter 38 509
Chapter 39 518
Chapter 40 526
Chapter 41 534
A Thousand Li: The Third Cut 542
Chapter 1 543

Chapter 2 548
Chapter 3 554
Chapter 4 559
Chapter 5 566
Chapter 6 573
Chapter 7 580
Chapter 8 588
Chapter 9 592
Chapter 10 599
Chapter 11 607
Chapter 12 612
Chapter 13 618
Chapter 14 625
Chapter 15 630
Chapter 16 635
Chapter 17 642
Chapter 18 652
Chapter 19 662
Chapter 20 667
Chapter 21 675
Chapter 22 680
Chapter 23 688
Chapter 24 694
Chapter 25 699
Chapter 26 704
Chapter 27 710
Chapter 28 716
Chapter 29 722
Chapter 30 725
Chapter 31 735
Chapter 32 742
Chapter 33 748
Chapter 34 752
Chapter 35 757
Chapter 36 763
Chapter 37 770
Chapter 38 776
Chapter 39 780
Chapter 40 785

Chapter 41 789
Chapter 42 793
Chapter 43 799
Chapter 44 803
Epilogue 807
The System Apocalypse Series 809
Author's Note 810
About the Author 811
About the Publisher 812
Glossary 813

A Thousand Li:

The Third Kingdom

Book 7 of A Thousand Li Series

What Happened Before

Long Wu Ying has traveled far from his humble beginnings as a rice farmer. Since joining the prestigious Verdant Green Waters Sect in the kingdom of Shen, he has risen in the ranks to become an inner sect cultivator under the aegis of his Master. He's partaken in wars and uncovered plots by a Dark Sect, one that would see both the Verdant Green Waters and the kingdoms of Shen and Wei embroiled in war.

In their latest blow, the Dark Sect had kidnapped Wu Ying's Elder Martial Sister, the beautiful Fairy Yang. Rather than see her stay captured, subject to the whims of those who held her, Wu Ying defied the orders of the orthodox sects and mounted a rescue mission.

His friends and other brave individuals, many of whom had lost their own loved ones to the kidnappings, joined him. Journeying deep into the kingdom of Wei together, the group watched for traitors in their ranks while seeking Fairy Yang.

In the end, after overcoming significant trials, the group managed to rescue Fairy Yang, though not without loss. A last-minute appearance by Wu Ying's Master saw him injured unto death. Leaving his Master to recover—or die—within a cave, the survivors returned to the Verdant Green Waters, triumphant.

Only for the consequences of their actions to apply. Wu Ying is cast out of his sect, banished from their environs for his defiance and the loss of prestige and personnel the Sect has suffered. An example, for those who might break the rules.

Chapter 1

Wu Ying turned back one last time, wiping at tears that refused to fall. In the distance, he saw his parents clutching one another near one of the many rice fields that abutted the small village. They held on, looking older, frailer than ever. He wondered if he would ever see them again, speak with them, have dinner together.

He drew a deep breath, letting the sorrow that gripped his heart and tightened his lungs exist for a few more seconds before he made himself relax. He did not dismiss the grief or toss it aside or contain it but acknowledged its presence, allowing it to stay within him but not affect his body.

He had warned them, had spent as much time as he could with them while the Elders had deliberated. He had sent what miniscule amount of funds he had left to them and made arrangements such that any goods he sent back for resale would be theirs. Most importantly, he had spoken with his friends to ensure the village continued to see some benefit from being located so close to the Sect.

Not that they would turn their backs on the village now, not after the village had bled for them. The Verdant Green Waters was not without honor, and the attacks on their Sect had impacted the village beneath the mountain. More so, the addition of a village—one that had begun to produce rice of a higher grade than normal—would be a boon for the Sect in the future. Already, the budget for the outer sect had seen a positive outflow, one that would only increase as the village grew.

No, the Sect was not without honor, but it was a little vindictive. Refusing to bend their rules, angry at being disobeyed. Afraid of the example that such defiance might create, and yet…

And yet amused too. For defiance was the very heart of cultivation. Defiance of the natural order of things to achieve immortality. Or so some interpreted the matter at least. Others might believe that such an act was not defiance but a return, a recursion to what had been. A joining of self to the immortal moment.

Immortality or not, if he achieved it or not, his banishment was all too real.

His presence would not be welcome in these lands for many a year. Decades, maybe even centuries if he lived that long. Time enough for ire to quell, for deeds to grow such that the loss of face and defiance of their orders faded with the mists of time.

Too long, likely, before he would see his parents' faces again. If he ever did. A last goodbye then, a pressing of flesh and words of love and loss. Of thanks and apologies.

Then Wu Ying turned away and strode off, to see what his destiny held for him.

***

He could have left by boat. Had done so often enough. Yet this time, clad only in his peasant robes, he walked through the forests. Bamboo forests he had grown to know oh so well. After all, he was the *Verdant Gatherer*. Hah! He wondered if there would be a quiet campaign to change that name now, to remove association with him. Or not.

He was not exiled, just banished. A fine distinction, but an important one. The Elders had not taken his robes or his sect token, not branded him. He was just not welcome in their halls anymore.

So Wu Ying walked through the forest, feeling the wind catch and tug at his hair, whispering secrets and entreaties even as his feet glided over leaf-strewn paths, as they sank into gentle moss and danced across uneven ground.

Come North! A hint of frost, a shivering layer of air begged him to come to where the plains lay. See a land of wide vistas, a place without looming mountains where the wind ran across open ground and brought with it memories of a colder, even more desolate country.

No, go East! Salt, carried on the wind, blew across his body with it a whiff of the ocean, seaweed and dissipating wood, the smell of fish and fruit. Forget the land. Explore the deeps of the sea and what lay across the ocean. An island, one of immortals lay in the distant reaches. Reach it, and one might escape the drudgery of cultivating for immortality by supping upon a single Peach.

Foolish, foolish, foolish. Wu Ying could almost hear the taunt. The Eastern Wind promised much but drowned most who attempted to take it up on its offers. No, no bountiful promises or sudden traitorous changes on the waves. In the West, dry air, sand, and soaring, empty canyons. A stark simplicity, where beauty was hidden and showcased only to those who dared look deeper.

The South laughed at the others, bringing warmth and humidity. Pouring not entreaties or desires, for so many—too many—traveled to their bountiful lands, searching for their fortune. In the south, jade lay on the ground, waiting to be picked. To the south, gold was found in rivers, fruit on trees. The secrets of lost arts and hidden clans who stood with nature awaited.

If you could survive the Spirit Beasts that roamed those lands, rending apart cultivators and mortals alike. The south held monsters, old and ravenous; untamed even as civilization pressed upon their domains.

Wu Ying smiled a little, feeling the beckonings, the whispered entreaties and invitations as the winds danced through the bamboo forest. He knew them, those winds, those friends. They were as much a part of him, of his soul and body, as the earth he had dug his fingers into.

Wind soul, wind body. Sometimes, Wu Ying wondered, if he reached the peak, would he even be himself? Would he become nothing more than a breeze given form, as gentle as a child's caress, as raging as a typhoon? Would he break apart at the barest touch and still be strong enough to level buildings?

Would he even be… him?

Funny thoughts that. Deep ones. What lay at the end of this road that he walked? What dao did he seek? What would he—in the end—choose to embody? What would he grasp so tightly to his core that without it, he would not be himself?

He had no idea.

And perhaps that was why, through all this, even as he perched on the edge of ascending to Core Cultivation, he had not taken that last step. Uncertainty at such a step would spell doom. Too many stories started out that way for him to dare the change without understanding.

Lord Khoo, the Youngest Purple Crane, heir to the Patriarch of the Purple Crane Sect. Prodigy of Dance and Culture, as svelte and cultured as could be asked. Someone who had set the heartbeats of dozens, hundreds beating at his very presence. In three years, he went from Body Cleansing to Core—a record.

The flaws came later. When it took ever greater amounts of resources for him to build his Core, to layer understanding and chi upon it. Three decades later, when the sect had beggared itself feeding the Patriarch's son ever more precious herbs and pills, he sought to ascend to the next level.

In the throes of growth, his cultivation Core broke. Shattered under the stress of expectations and an incomplete understanding of himself and his dao. The Nascent Spirit within, fed incomplete enlightenment, tainted with other desires, other experiences anathema to its origins had bucked and twisted and broken the Core, exposed itself to the Heavens and the world.

It died.

So did the Purple Crane Sect, its treasury empty, its hopes dashed.

That had happened nearly four hundred years ago. Within living memory for some cultivators. Only a couple of generations in the past. A story held up for any to hear and understand. It was not the only one, though most were more remote—whether in terms of age or location.

And those were tales of the prestigious, the famous, failures though they may be. Individuals who had strode over mountains and streams in their youth before they crashed. How many more, how many hundreds, thousands more had failed, but their lives never made into stories?

No. Wu Ying dared not take that step. Not yet. He had an inkling of where his path lay, what he desired. The wind spoke to him, whispering secrets and promises; but it was why he walked rather than sailed this day. For there was one other he might ask for wisdom, one who had spoken to him before.

One other who lived deep in this forest, and who had perhaps seen something in Wu Ying that no others had before.

Now, if he could only find him.

***

They came out of the forest, naked and bereft of armor on their torsos. How could they, when their faces were on their chests, their heads lost long ago to the Yellow Emperor. Now, they emerged bearing shield and spear, shield and axe, their eyes flashing with malevolence and anger at the intruder they sensed within their forest.

Wu Ying froze, his body blending into the shadows of the forest. He was not crouched low, though in the shadow of the tree he stood beneath, his plain clothing faded into darkness. The monsters turned their bodies from side to side, searching for the traces of his scent, of his presence.

Aura held to his skin, Wu Ying waited, watching. His hand hovered near the hilt of his sword, but he chose not to draw or even touch it. Doing so might leak his killing intent into the air and that was not his intention, even now, hunted as he was.

He had nothing to be gained by doing battle with the monsters. There was an entire tribe living in these woods, days from the Verdant Green Waters. They had flourished as the Sect had focused on the greater threat of the Dark Sect. Flourished, growing stronger.

Driving other monsters aside.

Then a flicker of another aura. The monsters stilled, for another lurked deep within these wild lands and was the true owner of this demesne. Strut, stalk, and state their intentions to rule they might, but the xing tian knew it was the other whose forbearance guaranteed their survival.

The aura of a Nascent Soul Spirit Beast pulsed through the forest, sending the weakest of the monsters to their knees in horror. For there was a trace of bloodlust, of anger within the aura. Something had woken the great creature, and the xing tian feared it was them.

Barked orders in their own tongue and the monsters pulled back, disappearing into the undergrowth. They chose to hide rather than face the creature that ruled this land. Perhaps one day, they might dare—but that day was not today.

Wu Ying, on the other hand, smiled, waiting for long minutes until he was certain he was alone before he strode onward. Deeper into the forest, seeking the originator of the aura.

The goal of this entire diversion.

Chapter 2

Head bent, Wu Ying traced the edges of the plant's roots, sending unaspected chi to probe the ground. Not wind chi, which would dissipate within inches in the hard-packed earth. Earth chi would have been better but converting his own chi from wind to unaspected to earth was an arduous process. Easier to just do a single level conversion and send his chi into the ground and use more.

He breathed out, tracing along the lines of energy as it came into contact with the heat emanating from the roots. Flame aspected wild ginger, growing under shade in the middle of the wilderness. Easy to miss if you didn't know how to probe the wilds for such treasures. Even now, Wu Ying might have walked by it, not intent on actually gathering, his goal deeper within.

But this was too good a present, one he would add to his World Spirit Ring. The artifact had grown bigger and wider as he'd poured goods and chi within. Now, it was the size of four full rice fields, with towering trees in one corner while deep water and a pond sat in another. Balancing the flow of energy, the creation of chi within the garden was difficult.

Oh, so difficult.

Wu Ying made a mental note to spend more time reading the notes his Senior Brother had given him. Notes on natural formations, on the rotation of plants to ensure that not just soil but chi was never depleted. It wasn't enough to balance energy individually, but across the world; to flow hot fire chi into metal-oriented plants, heating them until they too shed their own chi, which leached into the ground and burrowed its way to the earth-chi oriented plants where…

Balance, but only in motion. Like a dancer perched on the edge of a cliff, flowing through the motions and tottering on the edge. Stillness would see her tumble and fall, but an errant breeze or a slick stone was adapted through improvisation and momentum.

Content he had found the limits of the plant's root system, Wu Ying drew out his tools. He dug into the ground carefully, pulling the entire clod of earth to him and into his Spirit Ring, where he guided its planting via will and aura alone. Careful minutes of manipulation, digging the hole, adding fertilizer, planting and watering. Then tamping it all down ever so gently and reviewing the flow to ensure it worked.

Satisfied at last, Wu Ying returned fully to himself. He checked his surroundings, letting the wind speak to him of greater problems that might be. Finding none, he turned to the next, sister plant. Doing his job.

Gathering.

***

He only took a few of the plants—the biggest of course, leaving the others to grow. In time, hopefully, the ginger would spread and more would be left for others to take. That was the right way to do Gathering. You took just enough, always leaving some behind so that it would replace itself.

Well, mostly. Some noxious weeds—plants that only grew for a season before they died, having already passed on their seeds and genes through other methods—could be harvested in full. Other types needed to be split or parts harvested, rather than the entire shrub. Most, bereft of a ring like his, wouldn't bother with entire trees or shrubs.

Even when Wu Ying wanted to gather everything, it was often only specific portions that were useful to the apothecarist. No reason to haul the entirety of a bush or shrub when only the buds of the newly grown moonlight vine were useful. Or to harvest all the orbs of metal aspected longan, when it was those that were taken on the eight month that had enough metal chi to actually be usable in crafting a pill. The rest of the time, the longan was just a little bitter.

And so on, so forth.

Moving on, Wu Ying tilted his head from side to side, tasting the aura in the air. He followed it toward the center of the woods, where the Spirit Beast lay. No hiding, not this one. He wondered if the others—Elder Po and Lu and the rest—had noticed the aura the first time they came, had sensed it far away. Perhaps they had even angled their expedition to meet it.

Hard to say, no way to ask. He would be surprised if they had not sensed the pixiu though. After all, he, a simple Energy Storage cultivator, could do so. Even if he did have a bent toward that kind of thing.

Hours more of tramping through the undergrowth, only to come to a stop as he entered a clearing and came face to face with the creature he hunted. Surprise registered on Wu Ying's face as he stared at the Spirit Beast, tawny golden fur with bright streaks of red and lighter yellow running along the fur of its massive cat body. On the lion's head, a pair of antlers sat; its feathered wings were folded across its abdomen, hiding portions of its body.

"Surprised to see me, little one?" the pixiu rumbled, amusement and a touch of menace in its voice.

Wu Ying dropped into a deep bow; hands clasped together. "Only that I managed to find one as illustrious as oneself so quickly, honored pixiu. I would not dream to believe that I could find such an honored being that easily."

Already, Wu Ying felt the way the aura the Spirit Beast wielded shifted, contracting a little and solidifying. Wu Ying had been tricked—the wind had been tricked, he realized—by the creature's greater command of wind and aura. Projecting its aura such that Wu Ying had believed it many hours away, informing the wind to not speak of its own presence.

A creature such as this, it had much more control of the elements than a poor cultivator like Wu Ying. Much more control.

"Mmm… and yet, you trespass on my domain." The pixiu stood, moving closer with the barest of motions.

Wu Ying could sense it now that he was here and the wind and his own spiritual sense told him where the pixiu was. Sense it, but not hear it, for the creature moved with such silence and stealth that neither ear nor nose could pick it out.

"Such daring. Such bravery. Such foolishness."

"This one humbly begs forgiveness. If the honored pixiu would allow this one, he would present the gifts he brought with him," Wu Ying said, his body still bent low, eyes to the ground. He knew there was nothing he could do if the Beast wanted him dead.

This battle would be one won with words and custom, with compliments and gifts, not with his sword.

"You may present your gifts." Low, rumbly, the pixiu sounded more amused than angry now. As though it was humoring him. It probably thought Wu Ying had nothing to offer him.

Yet, Wu Ying knew it was wrong. For over two years, ever since the germ of this idea had been born, he had been gathering, setting aside items that might interest a creature of such strength. The one who had first spoken to him of his bloodline, who might hold further clues to it.

Stepping into the center of the clearing, Wu Ying looked around and made a face. He had debated bringing a table to set the offerings upon. It would have been better, more fitting. Yet his storage rings, numerous though they might be, were all small—not suitable for carrying around furniture. So instead, he set a bolt of cloth on the ground, smoothing out the surface carefully before he laid out his offerings.

First were the spirit and beast cores. Not powerful cores—those he sadly had none of, unlike the last time they had come through. No, what he placed were the different, the rare, and the interesting. The kinds that even a Spirit Beast might find hard to locate.

A spirit core of a thousand-year-old Golden Carp.

A demonic core of a Deep Forest Air Boar.

A trio of spirit cores from the Berry Eating Monkeys of Luxu.

Rare, unusual, different. Wu Ying placed each aside, hesitating only on a few. Would the pixiu be insulted or attracted to the hunting cat core, a creature of shadows and darkness, that he had acquired? A maneater at a time, before it was slain.

Or how about the Green Spitting Venom Slug core? Did the fact that it came from a slug, even a powerful slug, matter? That was his only Core Formation core, since no apothecarist had use for it. Even then, he'd had to trade nearly a half dozen Energy Storage-level cores for it.

Hesitating, Wu Ying eventually placed the slug core down.

Next, in much more bountiful numbers, he placed the gifts he had greater confidence within. Not the monsters he had killed while traveling through the wilds for safety or sustenance, but the herbs he had gathered.

Leaves and roots that had been carefully dried—some under the moonlight, some on the summer solstice or in locations filled with elemental chi—were joined by pots of powders, all ground delicately to create teas and other supplements. Other plants, preserved in jade, stone, and wooden boxes, were also laid out, their contents alternately cooled or warmed by the tiny enscripted formations on the boxes themselves.

All those items were the ones he could carry normally—the items that were stored in secondary spirit rings, that did not break down or lose their potency over the short period of a few years or might, in some cases, even become stronger after being harvested.

Having finished with those items, Wu Ying risked a glance at the pixiu. The creature was no longer even bothering to watch Wu Ying, having turned its attention to grooming under a wing with a long tongue, angling its head carefully so that its antlers would not injure itself. When it caught sight of Wu Ying's gaze, there was a slight narrowing of eyes.

"Is that all?" rumbled the creature.

"No, honored pixiu."

Turning back to the cloth, Wu Ying set out the third series of items. Again, he pulled from his storage ring, but this time, they were not items of his own working. A series of roast pigs, carefully spliced and set on plates, came out first, then a half dozen roast ducks, a heaping plate of century eggs and another of colored red eggs, boiled soya sauce chicken…

Dish after dish emerged from his ring, purchased from the Sect itself. All filled with a trace of chi, enough food to have served a large banquet hall.

This portion of the gift had cost a significant amount of his remaining contribution points. Not just because the meats were infused with traces of chi to provide additional sustenance, but also the charm that had been laid across the entire banquet so that it could be preserved, warm and fresh, such that the succulent smells of the meal arose like the hour they had been cooked.

The moment Wu Ying started laying the banquet, he noticed the pixiu's attention return to him. Avaricious eyes danced over the food presented, more so when they landed on the whole roast pigs. Once the last dish—an oval plate of long, cooked noodles with slivers of shiitake mushrooms, chicken, bean sprouts, all cooked in a layering of soya sauce and rice wine—was placed, Wu Ying backed off and gestured.

"Honored pixiu, I have a few other small items, but would be honored if you would indulge in this small repast while I continue," he said.

A slight pause, then the pixiu strolled over. It turned, flicking over the initial dried plants, nodding approvingly a little before a paw pointed at a single set of powdered items.

"Tea," it commanded before its head dipped, snatching up a roast pig in its entirety. Retreating a short distance away, it dropped the pig on its tucked paws and tore into its meal.

Once the mythical monster had backed away, Wu Ying sprang into action. He extracted his tea pot, pulling a pouch of water from another spirit ring. Mentally reviewing the notes given to him by Tou He, he boiled the water—taken from a spring two counties away, stored in a solid jade box for transportation and costing nearly four taels—using his chi. Fire chi mixed with a trace of wind chi, poured into the pot that he held floating above his hand.

There were, obviously, certain advantages and disadvantages to the use of chi in the brewing of tea. Tou He had gotten into that in great detail before Wu Ying had cut him off, though Wu Ying had gathered it had to do with the way water boiled and the infiltration of chi into the actual drink itself.

More importantly, Wu Ying had the basics of brewing a decent cup of tea—or bowl, considering the size of the pixiu—down. He would score low with actual tea brewers, those who had taken the entirety of the act and made it a profession, but he did not need to score points with them.

Just the pixiu.

In quick order, with his free hand, Wu Ying scooped, mixed, and beat the powdered tea leaves in the bowl, slowly adding the boiling water. It was not, he knew, at the exact right temperature, nor was the consistency of the tea exactly correct. Then again, it was hard to call the tea tea. After all, it had none of the tea plant's leaves within it. The mixture he was making came from chrysanthemum petals and mixed wolfberry leaves.

On the other hand, Wu Ying wasn't going to argue with the pixiu's choice. After all, what kind of taste buds the creature had, he would not even dare to guess at. Perhaps the mixture was particularly interesting?

Another shake of his head, a swirl of the bowl as he quickly crossed the grounds to place the drink beside the pixiu with a bow. He caught a whiff of the ingredients, the lighter, fruitier tones of the wolfberry plant mixing with the floral notes of the chrysanthemum flowers making Wu Ying smile.

The pixiu bent its head, sniffed at the drink, then lapped at it a little with its long, agile tongue, much like a cat's. It drank for a few moments before lifting its head and fixing the cultivator with a long, considering look. Cold sweat broke out on Wu Ying's back as the predatory gaze focused upon him.

"Barely acceptable." The low rumble made Wu Ying shiver.

Sketching another bow, he hurried backward to the gifts and set another silk cloth on the ground. He blocked out the on-going crunch of bones being shattered and chewed upon as the creature supped on its gifted meal. Even as Wu Ying checked on the contents of the banquet, he was surprised to see another roast pig gone, along with a handful of the fowl.

Surreptitiously wiping his forehead, Wu Ying turned inward. Hopefully, the distraction of meat and tea would keep the beast from noticing the next part of what Wu Ying was to do. To provide the freshest gifts and ensure that these three final items did not lose their potency, he would be drawing them from his World Spirit Ring directly. Dangerous, since Elder Lu had informed him to keep the item secret, but less so since the pixiu was entirely unlikely to desire it.

Or so he hoped.

Firstly, the Sun Lotus in its full glory was extracted from the pond, its body and flowers still attached. Next were the deeply dug roots of a thousand-year-old mountain ginseng, the wood and earth chi mixing and twining within the root plant itself. And finally, a single glowing plum filled with an internal flame and wood chi. A plum that had been the only fruit from a plum tree that had taken Wu Ying a good two days to extract into his own ring.

As he placed the last item on the ground, ever so gently, Wu Ying realized that his concentration on the ring and the exactness of his placements had left him vulnerable. For a short period, he had entirely forgotten the Spirit Beast that lay in the clearing, but now, its predatory regard weakened his knees and dried his mouth.

Holding himself aloft and controlling himself with sheer force of will, Wu Ying stepped back and bowed. Head bent, Wu Ying awaited judgment from the mythical being as it padded over on silken paws.

Chapter 3

Snuffling, the barest rustle of fur caught on the wind, bringing with it traces of the pixiu's natural musk. Wu Ying inhaled deeply, forcing himself to calm as he cycled his chi, tasting the other's scent. Even now, even with the creature a bare hand's width away from him, he struggled to place the Spirit Beast's element.

Not one of the five main elements. Those Wu Ying felt he would have sensed and categorized immediately. Even now, he could pick traces of water and metal in the chi the pixiu let escape from its aura. More metal than water. In fact, that smell, it reminded him of…

"An eclectic selection, cultivator. Fresh herbs filled with energy and bountiful with life force. Pitifully weak cores, but rare." A paw prodded at the slug core. "Rare and mildly insulting choices…"

Wu Ying winced.

"Even more plants, dried, smoked, and otherwise prepared for consumption or burning." A noise, like something licking then swallowing.

Wu Ying wished he could see more than just tawny furred paws, but he dared not raise his head. Not yet.

"Then again, what could one expect from a thief of nature, one who raids the domains of others?"

Now, Wu Ying could not help but sweat, a spike of fear going through him as the pixiu monologued. Another lick, a slurping, and the crunch of bone. He saw it then, how the pixiu was supping on the smaller birds, its head dipping delicately between dishes to partake of the meal.

"Then again, mankind has always been the most arrogant of animals," the pixiu said. "Not content to live in nature or to tame it for their own needs, but also must alter and shape it to their designs. Before then proceeding once more into the wilds, seeking to plunder it of its riches."

Wu Ying's mouth moved, as he wanted to protest the accurate characterization. To defend himself and humanity. But in the end, he shut his mouth as the creature continued.

"On the other hand, you do make the most interesting of things with what you take…" The pixiu slurped its tea. Another loud crunch, another set of bones being chewed, meat masticated between all too sharp teeth.

Bent low, Wu Ying could not see anything but the empty dishes, the food he had spent so much to purchase floating away to where the creature continued to pile the contents near it, deftly manipulating chi and its aura. His back throbbed as the cat-seeming creature let out low, contented purrs as it consumed the food, the gifts, sating its glutinous nature.

One after the other, the dishes disappeared. Fear slowly faded to boredom to aching exhaustion and pain as he waited upon the other's pleasure. Until finally, the very last pig had been consumed, the crackling of its skin shattering sending throbbing reminders of Wu Ying's own hunger through him.

One eyeblink to another and the pixiu was before him, a giant paw coming down upon his back. It pushed, and Wu Ying was on his knees, pressed into the grass, his knees digging deep.

"Now, I thank you for the meal, little cousin, but what is it that you really want?" the pixiu rumbled, leaving its paw on Wu Ying's back but letting him rise a little so that he could turn his head and speak around the ground.

Quickly, Wu Ying spat earth from his mouth. "This one was once informed by the honored pixiu that I smelled familiar. Only later did I understand the wise wisdom imparted to him. This one—"

"Enough," the pixiu rumbled. "This foolish degree of formality grates upon me. Speak, and speak clear. I am no arrogant lord without a true deed to his own name. And get to the point."

"Of course, honored pixiu. I apologize. I just…" Wu Ying hurried on. "I was hoping you could provide guidance. Upon my bloodline and what you sensed. If there is anything you could do to aid me."

"Like a drop of my blood, or the location of another of my kind or my cousins that you might hunt and kill, to boil their bones and flesh down to make a pill?" the pixiu growled, slamming Wu Ying deeper into the ground.

Breath escaped Wu Ying's chest; his lungs compressed as ribs creaked. Automatically, he struggled, attempting to escape, pushing back at the weight upon him. Arms tucked under him attempted to lift the weight upon his back, the casual paw pushing him into the ground. Yet strain as he did, not even a hairsbreadth could he move the other.

"You desire my knowledge? My training? Better to grind you to powder and sup on your skin and muscle. Better to gnaw on your bones than to lend you information on my family. Better that than to betray them…"

Wu Ying wanted to protest, to contradict the other. He had thought nothing of the sort. He had wanted nothing of the sort. Just words of wisdom, guidance to the bloodline that throbbed within him. Blood that was pushed by a racing heart as it sought to provide what energy it could to his body, even as Wu Ying struggled to breathe as the air he once held was forced from his ribs. He fought to take a single gasping breath, to empower himself.

Air. Desperately needed air.

So required, so necessary, so empty. He sucked at it, his lips working against the ground as the monster crushed his chest, as ribs cracked. In desperation, Wu Ying threw his chi into his body, into the surroundings, energizing himself. It did nothing, his aura suppressed by the immensity of the creature's own. His attacks bounced off the paw above him, even his blade intent unable to find purchase.

"Fool. To bring such pitiful offerings, banking upon an awakened bloodline of a *wind dragon* of all things." Above him, the pixiu taunted still.

Lights flashed in Wu Ying's eyes as a rib cracked, splintering. He felt something part, tendons in the back of his body slipping free as ribs detached. Pain blossomed with each injury, but something the pixiu said caught at him.

Wind dragon.

Desperation and a glimmer of hope. Yet to do it, he needed space. Needed to create an opening. He could not push upward, but maybe…

Darkness crept in on the edges and another rib snapped.

With perhaps only seconds left to live, Wu Ying chose. He shoved upward with everything he had in a sudden explosion of energy. He failed, of course, to move the pixiu.

Then he exhaled, forcing the very last dregs of air from his lungs, using the full range of body control and cultivation techniques he had studied over the years to compress his own chest. The sudden shift downward, the tiniest of gaps was created.

Then…

Shift.

Movement techniques from the fifth wind were contained within itself, tightly controlled, circular. The motion this time was controlled even further, within the very bounds of his body. A shift that was part elemental, that embodied the very nature of the wind itself.

Wind dragon. Wind body.

The foot slammed the rest of the way down, a deep dent imprinted in the earth, one that dwarfed the earlier impression Wu Ying's crushed body had created. A few feet away, still on his front, Wu Ying lay, his body shifting and twisting for a second before it stopped.

A deep, sucking sound as air filled his lungs. Lances of pain through his torso while the cultivator breathed his first lungful of air in minutes. Desperately drinking it all in. Yet willpower and wariness drove him to roll to his knees, a hand falling to his sword as he guarded against the one who had tried to kill him.

To find the pixiu seated, licking its paw, offering him a wide, teeth-filled grin.

"You are not completely a waste of your bloodline, little cousin."

***

The pixiu had never really meant to kill him. Wu Ying could not help but marvel at the thought, so clear to him now that he was not being crushed to death. It had allowed him to gift his goods, spoke instead of acted, posing like an arrogant young master. A clue, then another, then another.

After all, Spirit or Demonic Beasts were creatures first and foremost—animals, insects, fish—enlightened but still creatures. Driven by instinct more than meandering, pensive thoughts. They rarely second-guessed their decisions, especially over something as small as whether or not to kill an irritant.

All that was what Wu Ying had concluded while he cultivated, pushing chi through his body as he sat in the clearing, driving pain and spilled blood from his body. A light coating of sweat and filth covered his bare chest as the detritus of a damaged body was exuded forcefully. The increased healing factor of a cultivator was insufficient for Wu Ying's current needs, so he was speeding up that aspect.

A minor boon for a Body cultivator was his ability to adjust his own metabolism even above that of a Soul cultivator of the same realm. There were, of course, drawbacks to such an action. Depletion of necessary minerals and nutrients in the body that sustained the cultivator required the consumption of a wide variety of meals. Healing in this manner too often could lead to overall weakness of the body, potentially misaligned and mis-healed body parts that required rebreaking or treatment and weakened overall muscle tone and strength.

None of those issues were major problems unless one chose to make use of the skill regularly. In such cases, the body stacked unstable foundation upon unstable foundation until the entirety of the body collapsed in the midst of training.

It was why Wu Ying rarely used such an ability, but multiple broken, cracked, and dislocated ribs, a herniated spine, and internal injuries in the middle of the deep wilderness were not something the cultivator could easily accept. Eventually though, the healing reached a point where dislocated bones were back in place and cracked and broken ribs were partially healed. Inflammation around the damaged tissue had reduced, such that each breath was not a multi-blow attack to his chest. Just a single knife wound. It wasn't perfect, but it would do. At least enough for a conversation.

When Wu Ying opened his eyes, he took in the quiet clearing surrounded by tall bamboo trees, the gusting wind that caught and threw leaves in the air, pushing clouds in the sky toward the looming mountains wherein his sect lay. On the ground, the pixiu lay, contemplating the barren dishes as though staring at them would make the bowls refill magically. All of his other gifts—the various herbs in their boxes and the precious materials—were gone. Whereto, the cultivator knew not.

"Done?" the pixiu rumbled.

"Yes, honored pixiu," said Wu Ying.

"Kong."

"What?"

"Honored Kong," said the pixiu. "How you should call me. I do have a name."

Wu Ying sketched another bow, using that motion to think. Spirit Beasts were not given names—not in the way humans were, obviously. They either chose them or translated them from the way they were called, though beast names were often significantly more complicated. The Honored Void was a rather worrying name to be asking favors of, but it was what it was.

"Yes, Honored Kong. I am well enough to continue your lessons." Then he added, on second thought, "Unless they are more strenuous."

"No. You are not ready for anything else. You sup on concoctions to bring out your bloodline and strengthen its bindings to your element, do you not?" At his nod, Kong continued. "Low in effectiveness, but more honorable than hunting our kind down. Unless…?"

"No, Honored Kong. I am a poor Gatherer of the bounty of nature." Kong let out a low rumble, and Wu Ying winced, switching up. "I don't fight unless I have to."

"Yet you smell of blood and violence and your body carries the numerous marks of battle." It leaned forward, staring at Wu Ying's still shirtless form. "Interesting they have not faded."

"I…" Wu Ying thought about protesting, knowing his copperish skin—darkened from the medicinal baths and his wounds, along with long hours in the sun—put him far from the human standards of fair-skinned beauty. Nor was the width of his shoulders and sculpted muscles from hours working a rice field much in demand among noble beauties. "No, they have not."

Yet, it was none of those things that interested the pixiu. And Wu Ying had to admit, the fact that many of his battle scars had not faded was interesting. The Body Cleansing process often made most scars disappear, and even afterward, the processing of chi through one's meridians should ensure a body was unmarred. He had seen the effects on others, like Tou He.

Yet his own body continued to bear the marks of past violence. And he did not know why. A fact that he proceeded to admit.

"The soul speaks to the mind, the mind to the body. At times, the only way a message may be passed for one who refuses to hear it is in the markings of a beleaguered body." A paw rose and poked at Wu Ying's skin. "And what do you think your body is trying to tell you, little cousin?"

"That violence is to be remembered?" Wu Ying said hesitatingly.

"You do not sound sure." The cultivator bowed low in acknowledgement of Kong's words. "Think of it in the future."

Another bow.

"That is not what we came to speak of. Not you, not me. You wished to know about your bloodline, about your wind body."

Wu Ying could not help but nod.

"I am the wrong creature to speak to, in many ways." Seeing the cultivator's incredulous gaze, Kong snorted. "Did you think just because I am near ascent, I have great troves of knowledge? You do, don't you?

"Ah, to be young. Us Spirit Beasts, we ascend differently. Our daos and strength come from within. Either through a progression of our bloodline or through a dao we grasp. Much like yourselves. But unlike mankind, there are no tomes for us to consult. Not that it would matter, for what we require can only be found within." A long pause, then a low chuckle. "Perhaps that too is true for you humans. For how else can you explain how few of you truly ascend?"

Wu Ying wanted to protest. The cultivation aids, the manuals and exercises the sects all partook in, were not false aids. After all, there were more mortals who ascended, who climbed the initial steps of immortality than there were beasts. The numbers only looked different because there were more creatures in the wilds than there were humans.

Then he paused, for he considered Honored Kong's words in detail. Not how many took the first steps, but how many truly ascended. That question, that answer, stymied Wu Ying, for it seemed to him that the pixiu might have the truth of it there.

How many humans joined the hosts of heaven or walked among the devils? Even at the Nascent Soul stage, rumblings spoke of how most cultivators altered their cultivation from the few manuals available. How each manual and ascension was different. And even then, so few truly broke free from the chains of immortality.

"Ah, another thought you had not considered?" Kong said, sounding all too satisfied for Wu Ying's taste. Yet he could not help but nod in thanks. "Then consider this. I might not be the most suitable, but I am certainly better than most of your mortal sources."

This time, Wu Ying jerked. "Honored Kong, I do not understand?"

"Take your elixirs. Bathe long in your medicinal baths. Progress your bloodline, what little there is within you. But know that unless you truly are fortunate once again"—Wu Ying could not help but touch the scar in the center of his chest where he had been stabbed, where he had nearly died oh so fortunately—"then you will never progress it further. The blood of a wind dragon is no small thing, and those cousins are surely the most elusive of the family."

Wu Ying winced. True dragons, even the more common dragons of cloud and rain, of lakes and rivers were all too rare. Many lived in the Heavenly Realms themselves, only choosing to descend when their duties required it. Those that lived in this realm were hard to find, their abilities more than sufficient to keep them hidden.

"And if I were to meet one…?" Wu Ying asked.

"Then, if our unpredictable cousins chose not to eat you immediately, you might perhaps beg a favor of a droplet or two. Or otherwise listen to their"—Kong's feline grin grew malicious—"other suggestions to improve your bloodline."

"Other suggestions?"

Only that malevolent feline grin was offered as an answer. Wu Ying shuddered a little, before the pixiu continued.

"On the other hand, you have achieved the beginnings of a true wind body. Stop seeking shortcuts. Train that and perhaps, just perhaps, one might become truly one with the winds."

The cultivator touched his spirit ring, his most powerful and best guarded one. The storage ring that contained all his manuals, including the copy of the Seven Winds cultivation manual. Though his soul cultivation method had progressed and taken him to the very edges of core cultivation, Wu Ying could not help but wonder how much further it could take him. He had instructions for core cultivation in it, but nothing for the Nascent Soul stage.

"Thank you, Honored Kong, for your wisdom on my bloodline."

"Good. Now, before the sun touches the horizon. Ask your questions," said Kong. "After which, I expect you gone."

Wu Ying cast a glance upward, spotting the drifting clouds and the already low-hanging sun. He knew it would not be long before his time with the Spirit Beast was done. A flicker of disappointment ran through him before he discarded it. Even this much was more than he had hoped for.

Talk and query he did, pulling what knowledge he could get from the beast. Whether through belief of kinship or just having been sufficiently bribed, the pixiu was happy to answer Wu Ying's questions. Yet, sadly, many of the answers were less enlightening.

A Spirit Beast whose greater element was rust could not teach the cultivator much of elemental conjunction. Nor did the creature understand the process of channeling chi, not the way mankind did it. Creatures of instinct and movement, whose intrinsic link to their own daos was but a question of following a lit pathway, rather than the fog-filled swamp that was mankind's journey.

Time flashed, and soon enough, the falling sun dipped below the horizon.

"Remember, little cousin, train diligently and push yourself. Find the true center of the wind, where the seven winds blow." Then, head leaning upward, its wings opened and the great beast threw itself into the sky, flapping its unfurled wings. As it left, it bellowed, "After all, that is what all beasts do to ascend."

Wu Ying watched the pixiu leave, offering a deep, clasped hand bow to the fast-disappearing dot. Already, its aura had been retracted, its presence fading from the surroundings. He watched until Kong disappeared, then sighed, looking around.

Only time would tell if this meeting would provide him the impetus he needed to continue his ascent. Time. And enlightenment.

Chapter 4

A pixiu, consuming his gifts with great delight. A conversation that Wu Ying turned over and over in his mind, to such an extent that he had committed each word, each phrase to memory. Months later, Wu Ying still considered the conversation, searching for enlightenment.

And failing.

Traversing through deep, untamed wilderness. Lands rarely set foot upon by mankind, lands dominated by spirit and demonic beasts. Under towering bamboo trees and weeping oaks, through moss-filled forest floors and slick rocks.

Contemplating words and actions whilst gliding along the water, on skiffs and boats, rafts, and once, a bare log detached from its moorings. Crossing canals and rivers, striding across streams and stopping briefly in villages, towns, and cities as he left the country.

Hounded by words of rebuke and memories of a conversation, visiting only briefly at new sects to receive words of thanks and gifts, to pass on gathered materials and receive payments. Picking up replacements for the weapons given away during his latest adventure, acquiring new storage boxes for the items he gathered, even a few precious delicacies for trade in the future.

Days that became weeks that transformed into years of travel. Though the sects he visited knew his face, he dared not wear his sect's robes. Though they knew his shame, none spoke of it, instead feting him when he arrived. For services rendered, sects and Elders opened libraries for Wu Ying's perusal. Medicinal springs were closed off for him to soak within as he tempered his body. Gratitude was repaid, for those he had saved, lofty nobles and crippled outer sect members alike.

Time passed as Wu Ying floated across the land like the wind, allowing it to take him where it would. He struggled to leave the kingdom, but the wind and duty beckoned him again and again as he traversed the kingdom. Incidents, both small and large, changed his path, though only three were significant milestones in his cultivation journey.

The first, a long overdue visit to his uncle. It was an awkward visit, for they had few things in common beyond their shared lineage. His uncle's branch of the family had long ago left their hometown, traveling to the city and dedicating themselves to the pursuit of mortal power among the kingdom's bureaucracy.

Drinks, food, sparring sessions and further discussion about the Long family jian style. Decades of divergence had seen them interpret the style differently, the shared family manuals taking on notes that sprawled in ever more divergent fashion.

His uncle was only at the Sense of the Sword. His children were worse. Ambitious scholars, burgeoning cultivators who would one day become the backbone of the kingdom of Shen. Wu Ying's first introduction saw him beat aside his first cousin with barely an exertion of strength.

Even so, blood was blood and the presence of a powerful, infamous Energy Storage cultivator brought with it intrigue and trouble galore. Asked to aid in the location of a lost shipment of gold, Wu Ying and his cousin spent weeks traversing the lower streets of Shangzhou before they located the culprits.

In reward, Wu Ying received access to and notes of his uncle's branch of the family's study of the Long family sword style. The notes differed from those his father had passed onto him, and his own; for interpretation of the same form would see divergence as philosophy and mindset altered.

Carrying the document with him, Wu Ying left, passing once more from mortal concerns in the Shen kingdom.

The second incident occurred while he traversed the high mountain passes in search of Ice Pearls, a flower only grown where the snow never left. He stumbled instead across a hidden expert, a cultivator who had chosen to withdraw from the world entirely.

For six months, Wu Ying was enslaved, forced to labor under the watchful eyes of the elder. Each attempt at escape was thwarted, for the elder was one with his mountain. So swift was his movement technique that Wu Ying only managed to make it to the first snow line before he was caught.

Six months, Wu Ying worked in snow and stone, ground granite upon alpine slopes tending to the elder's gardens and his most precious item—the Winter Pinacea whose spruce cones with their purple coloration and snow-white edging spoke of the accumulated frost chi within.

Only when the Pinacea had grown, when the first harvest was complete, was Wu Ying freed. For his involuntary employment, he was paid in a single manuscript, a cultivation technique that outlined the very same movement skill the elder had used to keep Wu Ying trapped.

Months of study would have Wu Ying expand upon his own Twelve Gales skill as he worked to piece together both movement skills and the cultivation exercise he had acquired, in search of one that made best use of his own Wind Body. New understanding, having watched an expert utilize the movement skill in close quarters alongside the chilly, mountain air and his own burgeoning study in the Twelve Gales that he cultivated, laid the foundations of Wu Ying's expanded movement technique.

In time, he knew, it would alter as he tore apart the bindings and interpretations of the Twelve Gales to replace them with his own. For now, he borrowed the inspiration to progress deeper into the style. He had much to learn there.

Finally, the third incident was a minor matter, but the one that finally took him out of the kingdom of Shen. An assassination attempt by the remnants of the Dark Sect found him late at night whilst he slept in a roadside inn. The inn itself was blocked, the windows and doors barred by enchanted talismans and a killing formation.

Only Wu Ying's liberal use of protective talismans, acquired as gifts of gratitude by the other sects, allowed him to survive the inferno. In the light of dawn, when the fire burnt itself out and his assailants came to check upon their deeds, Wu Ying exacted his revenge. Blood coated his blade that day, the trio of Energy Storage cultivators falling in short order.

Yet his vengeance did little for the victims of the arson attack. Images of the burnt bodies of the innkeeper, his wife, and their children would haunt Wu Ying, along with the half dozen travelers caught in the crossfire. Realizing that the cycle of vengeance would not end so long as he stayed within the kingdom, Wu Ying made the decision to leave once and for all.

The winds and fate themselves seemed to agree, for no other obstacles blocked his way as he journeyed north, the southern wind pushing at his back, sending him forth. By this point, he was farther west than before and passed by the lands of Li Yao, heading across the mountains. In the forest and deadlands, avoiding well-traveled routes and picking at shrubs, the cultivator traversed new paths and old, cultivating and strengthening his aura training and techniques.

***

Finally, Wu Ying stood upon a sloping hill, fall rain having soaked deep into the ground and torn land free. The landslide had pulled earth apart, taking with it numerous loosely rooted trees, shrubs, and rocks to leave the soil bare. Wu Ying stared at the natural disaster, watched as wind danced across exposed earth even as flecks of grass grew, reclaiming the open scar for nature once more.

A head turned upward as clouds high above teased the return of sunshine, only to hide it away again as they flowed ever onward. Overcast, yet something within Wu Ying soared. The wind beckoned him, speaking to him of new lands to traverse, hidden waterfalls and abandoned monasteries, wrecked villages and old ruins, people and food yet to be consumed.

"I'm here."

He said the words out loud, because the occasion was important. Somehow, deep within his soul, he knew it was true. In the last few weeks, he had trekked through the deep wilderness, where the desolate remains of a settlement long abandoned had been the only sign of civilization.

Dirt was deeply encrusted into his brown robes, the clothing washed and patched over and over again. Even his aura, layered around him to protect his clothing, could only do so much. Months of travel, of sleepless nights as he was hunted by demonic wild cats and other mythical beings as he dirtied his hands with the earth he dug into, had taken its toll.

And now, here he was.

"A new kingdom, a new land." Wu Ying spoke those words, sensing the difference.

He stood still, staring at the natural desolation before him, his gaze skipping over the forest and, in the distance, a trade road. He touched his rings, assessing their storage capacity, as he delved outward, extending his spiritual senses to feel the world around him.

A new kingdom. It was not just a marking on a map, an imaginary line argued upon by bureaucrats. One that might follow the ebb and flow of natural geography, or the whims of a general.

A new kingdom, one whose very flow of chi was different. Changed, from the kingdom he had come from. Flavored by those who lived here. Stained in a sense. Turning, Wu Ying let his senses stretch even further as he beckoned the winds to provide what hints they deigned.

Something different, something unnatural. A twisting of the energy flows, metal, fire, and water, all the kinds of chi moving in concert. Energy pulled and altered, contained and concentrated, all toward the center. The wind whispered its secrets. His eyes snapped open in disbelief.

"A kingdom-wide formation."

Now, Wu Ying wished to soar. To stand high in the sky and stare upon the land below him. If he could fly, he would be able to see it then, to judge what they had changed. Yet, eyes open, he picked out the hints before him. Memories of passages, passed over in historical documents and those of current affairs, provided background, and his eyes provided the clues.

A hill, shaped unnaturally on one side.

That road, twisting in a way that cut through land and geography rather than follow it, as it should. Minor tracks—from merchants who took a faster, less twisting road—and towers in the far distance shaped like the rocks he'd once helped his Senior Brother move.

"Audacious. Expensive." Then, grinning, Wu Ying had to admit, "Amazing."

He closed his eyes and let his senses roam. He felt the world around him and the slowly opening part of his soul. As he stood on the border between two kingdoms, between the untamed wilderness at his back and the civilized roads ahead of him. Desolation lay before his feet and growth, unchecked, rose above him.

Enlightenment arrived as he stood there.

Lands and people to learn from.

Every step of this journey, a revelation.

A kingdom changed by man's hand.

A land returned to its native state by nature.

Enlightenment of his own dao.

Amidst the Heaven's acknowledgement, Wu Ying broke through.

Having found, at last, the start of his path.

*****

How far was a thousand li? It depended on the one asked. Not much distance, in some ways. A dedicated mortal, focused on travel and naught more, might cross thirty li in a day. On a good horse, a messenger might cover a hundred li in a single day. In ten days, one could cross a thousand li on a horse. On foot, it would only take a few days over a month.

All that was if one were a mere mortal, traveling on open roads. For a cultivator spending his days and nights in the deep wilderness infested with Demonic and Spirit Beasts, intent on locating and collecting precious herbs and plants; who might hear a waterfall in the distance and stop by to take a long wash or relax in the bubbling hot springs the wind spoke of?

Well then, that thousand li as a dragon soars might take much longer.

Not much distance and yet, a world away. For those who never left their village, it might be another existence entirely. Even for merchants who had their set routes, plying their trade between major cities and small towns, a thousand li was no small thing.

Markets changed. Demand for pottery, for wines and grain, for fruit and metal all shifted. The specialty dish from one town to the next could be miles different, or so similar that only a gourmet might pick the difference. Clothing, speech, teas, and fighting styles. All unusual. All achingly similar.

An insurmountable barrier to some.

A finger's width of parchment to another.

For one cultivator, basking in the approval of the Heavens, it was but the beginning of his journey. A thousand such journeys might see him finally achieve his place in the Heavens. There was so much to see, so much to experience.

A journey that would take decades, even perhaps centuries to complete. Traversing the Middle Kingdom, dancing with the wind that blew from one corner to another.

Heavenly chi poured into his still body. Gusts of winds caught at his hair and robes, picked up dirt and leaves, whispered elusive enticements of what was to come.

Deep within Wu Ying's body, his dantian—filled to bursting—was caught in its own storm. Energy poured within, spinning, twisting, pushing. He compressed the energy he contained, tighter and tighter around the core concept of who, what he might become.

Wu Ying breathed, and air entered his lungs, sinking into his chest, bringing stinging cold and pain. Reminding him of the world he stood upon, rooted to the very earth even as the wind tugged him upward. His dantian, tight within his body, compressed further as energy poured in without end.

Together with his will, with a new understanding, Wu Ying pushed.

A memory tickled him, and Wu Ying grasped at it. A pixiu cajoling him to draw forth the heart of his own element, crushing him until he understood. His body reacted as he drew upon the energy contained within his body itself.

Wind leached from his muscles and bones, pulled from the very air and his meridians. He pushed it all in as the dantian solidified, the glowing golden core of his energy forming a tiny, compressed ball of chi.

At first, it was easy. Enlightenment gave him strength, the Heavenly chi provided power, and wind chi cared not if you squeezed. Smaller and smaller his dantian grew, compressing further than ever. Within seconds, no larger than a fist. Then a plum.

Still, it compressed. Smaller than any core that had ever been described to Wu Ying, than he had ever read about in other cultivation manuals. All but his own.

For wind could shrink, air could be compressed. After all, what care did the wind have if you reduced it for a second? It could bend, it could squeeze, it could diminish.

A mandarin orange.

That did not make the wind any less than what it was.

Time grew indistinct as Wu Ying kept squeezing, making his dantian ever smaller.

A longan[1].

Pain and exhaustion warred upon Wu Ying. His muscles throbbed, his heart raced, his chest grew labored. The Heavens had long ago left, their benediction dispersed as they moved on from the laboring mortal.

His energy refused to give way further, pouring its displeasure back at him. Wind might shrink, but it wanted to move. To expand. It would never stop pushing backward, never stop turning. It was a fool's endeavor to contain it with strength alone. As it assaulted him, his body begged for release, to layer the containment and finish this moment, to end this struggle.

Biting his lips, blood dripping from his eyes and nose, Wu Ying shook his head in stubborn refusal.

He would not give up, not now, not ever. A deep sense within Wu Ying showed him there was still more that he could contain. Knowledge, eked out from conversations and articles, spoke of the layering, the development of a Core. The more layers, the stronger the Nascent Soul.

It led, then, that the smaller the Core, the more layers one could apply. And Wu Ying had a wind core.

Gritting his teeth, blood running down pierced lips, he pushed. Harder. Ever harder, until he felt the wind give way ever so reluctantly. Diminishing, even as it pressured him to give up. His legs gave way, softened earth impacting knees, but the pain was mild, a distant note of displeasure.

Wu Ying pushed.

A longan seed.

Finally, in his mind's eye, within his body, the Core—what had been his dantian—glowed. Energy compressed and contained, wind chi churning so furiously that its very energy could not be contained in movement alone. It gleamed, shedding light in his body, as Wu Ying furiously inscribed the sigils to contain it. Layering enchantments that contained the energy,

---

[1] Chinese fruit, pale brown in color, comes in bunches. Has a white skin with a small seed within it. Slightly larger than playing marbles. Often used in dessert soups, as it is naturally sweet when ripe.

formed from his mind's eye alone within his own soul. It locked the energy in place, created the first layer of protection. The first layer of his own Core. Yet Wu Ying could sense how it was failing already.

No traditional Core formation could contain this energy. No hardened exterior of energy, supported with simple elemental enchantments. No, a wind core required more. And the Formless Realm he had studied offered him the answer.

Perhaps the pixiu had been right, that all humanity must diverge from one another eventually. Perhaps it had been correct that immortality must be achieved individually. Yet it was wrong too, for in the passing of knowledge from one generation to another, humanity stood above all others, building their edifices of greatness with each whispered word or inscribed scroll. Greatness was achieved upon the backs of all those who had gone before.

Even if, in the end, one had to adapt.

Wu Ying carved the channels, the small tunnels of power, and connected the first from one end to another in his newly made Core. Immediately, the pressure lessened a little as the restless chi found an escape. Working quickly, he carved one wind tunnel after another, such that his tiny Core no longer looked like a gleaming yellow marble in his mind's eye but a twisting puzzle of interlocking rings around a solid core. Through each tunnel, wind rushed, mixing and twisting with ever greater speed.

Finally, as the last of a dozen such channels were formed and his Core spun, Wu Ying collapsed face forward. Pressure relieved, his Core throbbed. The external walls of his dantian slowly pulled away from the spinning Core as it reformed itself.

In time, Wu Ying would refill his dantian, then compress the energy once more, creating a second layer. In time, Wu Ying would find the enlarged energy pool of his body, find that his meridians had widened, his dantian grown as he finished this great trial. In time, Wu Ying would awaken.

And truly begin his journey in the third kingdom he had ever visited.

Chapter 5

"Easy, friend, easy." The voice came gently, the warm hand pressing against his chest as he struggled upward.

Wu Ying coughed, then leaned backward, prying open gummy eyes. Not too gummy, not too bloody. He blinked a little, surprised as his eyes managed the shaded illumination that met his gaze.

Not the hillside or the landslide he had expected, not sprawled on the ground but lying on his back. On comfortable silk bedding, set upon a rustic bed. Branches that he could feel, vaguely, pressing upward into his back. And above him, a canvas tent and a smiling, genteel face. Long hair bundled upward, pale hands with a single silver ring with a chain attaching to a bracelet. Pretty, but not too pretty—just sort of feminine without betraying the masculinity. Almost good enough to be a male fairy.

Almost.

"Who are you?" Wu Ying asked, even as the wind, rustling in the closed tent, pushed against the flap. Whispering secrets, bringing scents toward him. Four horses outside, three other cultivators. Earth, fire, and wood. The one above him, another wood cultivator. All in the Energy Storage stage, ranging from mid to peak.

"I am Gao Qiu. I am honored to meet you, honored elder." A hand to the heart, then he bowed.

Wu Ying's eyes narrowed a little, surprised at the greeting. He grimaced as he pushed upward, this time not obstructed by Gao Qiu.

Already, Wu Ying was taking stock of his own condition. The other had cleaned his exterior, wiped his face, and removed the majority of the visible staining. He was not cleansed entirely. His clothing had not been removed, which meant he needed a proper bath. Still, his body had rested for a few hours—from the smell and sense he was receiving of the outside— and the majority of his injuries had healed from his ascension.

On the other hand, his dantian was empty, bereft of energy, and his body sluggish because of that. He could, of course, draw from his Core, but that would be dangerous with it having just formed. Better to spend some time reinforcing the Core walls, refilling his chi stores from the world around him.

In short, he was vulnerable, and the other man knew it.

"Not an elder," Wu Ying said, sitting up. Idly, he took a pill from a storage ring and popped it into his mouth.

Wu Ying watched the other man's eyes trace the motion, the casual use of his storage ring and the retrieval of a Chi Recovery Pill; the slight startlement as Wu Ying utilized the Never Empty Wine Pot chi recovery technique once more. All those actions, the way he dressed— slightly shabby, and from the glimpses of the others through the weave, none of the four bore similar robes, all of their clothing muted in color—lead Wu Ying to a singular conclusion.

"Of course, honored expert," Gao Qiu said, shifting forms of address with ease. He relaxed a little, even as there was a flicker of disappointment.

"You arrived quickly," Wu Ying said idly. "I had not expected anyone to find me in such a short period." Or expected to breakthrough like that, but the other man did not need to know that.

"Fortune favored us," Gao Qiu said. "We were escorting a caravan far down the road when we sensed the expert's ascension."

"Mmmm…" Wu Ying cocked his head. "You left them alone?"

"We left behind some of our brethren while they pulled over for the day," Gao Qiu said. "If the honored expert would care to join us…"

Wu Ying smiled a little, conclusions coming together. Not bandits. Not unscrupulous rogue cultivators. Just a group of wandering cultivators—maybe a small band or maybe even the beginnings of a tiny sect. Not all kingdoms were like his own. Sects came in all forms and sizes, and wandering cultivators were more common in other countries where cultivation resources were more plentiful as fewer members of the general populace were trained.

"I thank you, but I should wash myself before I visit others."

Gao Qiu bowed at Wu Ying's words, not daring to gainsay such an obvious statement.

"Though… I thank you for your consideration." Wu Ying touched a spirit ring, extracted a bottle of Energy Breaking Pills, and handed them to Gao Qiu. "A small gift."

Gao Qiu took the pills with both hands, his nose twitching a little as he smelled the sharp cinnamon and twisting coil of energy that escaped from the simple bottle. He dropped into a deep bow, extending his thanks until Wu Ying shooed him out so that he could have some privacy.

Smiling a little, Wu Ying began the process of cleaning himself even as the pill he had swallowed refilled his dantian. Outside, he knew, he was making a little bit of a commotion as the Never Empty Wine Pot drank greedily from the environment, desperate to fill the gaping emptiness that was his energy stores.

The gift would be all the more precious since Senior Sister Liu had made those pills herself. Highly refined, the pills by nature might not be rare, but their level of purity would certainly be. A good gift for wandering cultivators.

And a subtle warning, that the man they had rescued had contacts and potentially friendships that might act against those who became too greedy.

Though the fact they had not robbed and killed him while he was lying senseless probably meant they were unlikely to do that anyway. Still, a warning and the beginnings of a tale were never bad things to plant.

After all, no one in this land probably knew of the Verdant Gatherer.

***

Cleaned and dressed in new robes, Wu Ying checked his dantian and his meridians for energy. The main stores were still bare, but energy had returned to his body to some extent. He still had to test his own strength, but he could not let the others wait any longer.

Outside, Wu Ying stepped out of the tent. The wind, his spiritual senses—much expanded and still growing, Wu Ying could tell—had told him what to expect. It was such that his gaze could flick over the gathered quartet and assign the details he had already gathered to faces and demeanors.

Two were glowing with power, seated on the ground and cultivating, having immediately consumed the pills given to them. The other two—including Gao Qiu—were standing at attention, keeping an eye out for trouble. And trouble had arrived, as the gutted, skinned, and bleeding out carcass of a leopard hanging from a tree indicated.

"Drawn by me or your friends?" Wu Ying asked idly after greetings had been completed once more.

"Both, I would assume," Gao Qiu, the obvious leader of the quartet, said.

"Interesting." Wu Ying wandered over to the leopard, breathing a little deeply to taste the scent.

Even now, Wu Ying was a little surprised he had managed to survive such a dangerous moment of his life with nothing more than a few dirty pieces of clothing. Ascending— breaking through and forming his Core like that—would have been dangerous even in the middle of his Sect, but doing so while journeying in the wilds…

Foolish.

Yet, knowing what he did now of both his own dao—a dao he had had an inkling of before, but never truly put a finger to—and the circumstances, he could not see how he could have acted differently. Grasping at opportunity when it arrived was important for cultivators.

Still, perhaps he should consider purchasing some simple and quick-establishing formations so that the next time he was forced into such a situation, he had some form of protection.

"Your plans?" Wu Ying said curiously.

"We will return to our brethren once my friends are done, then we will continue our assignment," Gao Qiu said. "After which, we will journey to the tournament of the Seven Pavilions, at which point we hope to showcase our abilities."

The last made Wu Ying tilt his head in inquiry.

"It is a small tournament, organized by the Seven Pavilions merchant house. They are sponsoring the prizes directly and hope to attract a number of wandering cultivators and perhaps even a few inner sect members." The other cultivator smiled a little, eyes glinting with amusement. "Their third daughter has come of age, and they seek a groom of suitable quality for her."

"Ah," Wu Ying replied, recalling what he knew of such matters.

Such mini-tournaments were uncommon in the Kingdom of Shen but not entirely unknown. A family, with enough money or prestige, would set up a tournament, searching for a husband for their daughter. Of course, the prize was not the daughter's hand in marriage but the prizes themselves; but those who did well or attracted sufficient attention would be feted and given a chance to meet the young lady and her parents.

Such arrangements could be highly beneficial for cultivator and family alike. A powerful cultivator who was stymied in his progress due to a lack of funds could find a supporter. Or, having spent his ambition, while away the remainder of his years with a mortal family that he could shepherd through the decades or centuries. At the same time, a merchant family or political powerhouse could be assured of the martial backing of a powerful cultivator while strengthening the bloodlines of their family.

It was only, of course, Sect members in powerful organizations like Wu Ying's own Verdant Green Waters Sect who would have little use for such tournaments. The backing of a single, large organization was greater than any mortal family. Nor would the comforts available be anything like the ones provided to inner sect Elders, what with their own residences and peers to speak with.

"Is the honored expert interested in joining?" Gao Qiu asked carefully.

Wu Ying flicked his gaze toward the other man, a little smile dancing on his lips. "And what if I said yes?"

"Mmmm… my martial brothers and I would, of course, place our bets on the expert," Gao Qiu said.

"Would you still take part?" Wu Ying asked.

"Of course. Only Liu Ping would think she could win." Gao Qiu inclined his head toward a quietly seated lady clad in dark blue and brown robes.

There were a few things that set her apart, beyond her pale beauty. One was her youthful features, which Wu Ying could ascertain had little to do with cosmetics but almost entirely her age. The other was the smell of her aura.

"Prodigy and a bestial aura," Wu Ying said, having drawn a deeper breath to ascertain it. That smell, it was a little too musky, too dense for a cat. Definitely not boar either; it had not the weight of one of those creatures. Not dry enough for a snake or wet enough for any marine animal. Obviously mammalian then, but not dog or wolf. Those were easy enough to ascertain. In fact, hers was… "Bear?"

"Impressive, but to be expected from an expert," Gao Qiu said, keeping any indication of surprise out of his voice. "She has a unique bloodline that has aided her in her studies."

"Very young to be peak Energy Storage already," Wu Ying murmured, guessing that she was probably not even sixteen. "I'm surprised she has not been swept up by a sect."

"Her brother"—Gao Qiu nodded toward the older boy seated next to her, meditating and pulling the energy from the pill within—"does not have her advantages. And she is very loyal."

Wu Ying's lips pursed before he eventually nodded. He could certainly tell that her brother—who, surprisingly, only had the barest features that were similar to hers and only if one was generous with their views—was only in the low levels of Energy Storage, though he was certainly older.

Older…

Hah! Wu Ying chuckled to himself, realizing the brother was likely no older than himself. Mid-twenties then—slow, but not horrendously so. He likely would never break through, but that was not uncommon. After all, only a small percentage of individuals would ever do so.

For a second, as the pair of cultivators fell silent watching Liu Ping and her brother cultivate, Wu Ying had a moment of incongruity. What he had worked toward for so many years, he had achieved. He was a Core cultivator.

In many sects, he would be considered an Elder. Not necessarily guaranteed in a sect as prestigious as the Verdant Green Waters—he was a little too young, a little too junior to wear the black robes. They would likely send him off to cultivate quietly, reinforcing his base cultivation first. More training, in both politics and cultivation exercises, as they had done with Tou He. Eventually, Wu Ying's level of training and strength would be sufficient such that those who had reservations about his age would not dare to speak of it. That would be what the Verdant Green Waters would do.

But in a smaller sect? He would be lauded as a prodigy. His words would be considered equal with the two or three others of his own cultivation level. Wu Ying had seen many such smaller sects, places of maybe sixty or seventy cultivators in total, during his time and seen the kind of reception a Core Formation cultivator would receive.

Success, after so many years.

He had made it in a way he would never have expected.

And yet…

Wu Ying flicked his gaze toward Gao Qiu. The man was very polite. He was considerate and had acted without avarice or selfishness, aiding and watching over Wu Ying, never once asking for anything in return. He had, in fact, been highly honorable.

Yet, he had not reacted the way Wu Ying would have expected when meeting a Core Formation cultivator. Sure, he had parroted the words, but when Wu Ying had corrected him, he had gone along with Wu Ying's correction immediately. Now that Wu Ying was considering the matter, Gao Qiu's manners, the way he stood, answered, and even questioned him…

It was not right.

Rather than raise an issue—because, in truth, Wu Ying cared not—he stayed silent. He would puzzle out this problem later. For now, he retracted his senses a little, made sure he contained his aura, and smiled as the girl finally stood, having finished processing the pill before her brother.

For now, Wu Ying would watch and wait and learn. Something was happening, and he would ascertain what it was before he spoke.

***

"A small matter, merchant Teoh," Wu Ying said, bowing to the other. "I am more than pleased to be allowed to ride with you."

"No, no, great expert, we must pay for one of your standing." The Merchant Teoh was somewhat prosperous with a rotund face and had a tendency to squint.

To Wu Ying's mild surprise, he noticed that the majority of those in the caravans—all but the guards and the Merchant Teoh's own son—were bereft of chi. They were, in fact, plain mortals.

"I'm nothing special," Wu Ying protested gently, holding up his hand as he deflected the tael the Merchant Teoh was holding out to him. More importantly, as he spoke, he noticed that the Merchant Teoh was flicking glances toward Gao Qiu, as though he was checking for approval.

"No, no, I insist!" Again, another attempt by Merchant Teoh to push payment upon him.

"Expert Long, perhaps I may have a word?" Gao Qiu called, pulling Wu Ying aside while Merchant Teoh relaxed a little. Away from the group, Gao Qiu lowered his voice, putting on a slight smile. "I understand Expert Long is from the kingdom of Shen?"

"I am."

"And from your bags"—a flickering glance at Wu Ying's packs, which were filled with dried herbs and other gathered materials including a few skinned pelts and scales of Demonic Beasts sticking out the side—"you are more used to working alone?"

"True."

"Then, if the honored expert would not find it inappropriate, I might advise you?" At Wu Ying's nod, Gao Qiu relaxed. "Merchant Teoh is seeking to establish a relationship with the honored expert, such that your standing in the convoy is understood. If you were to be injured as a guest rather than a paid guard, he worries that the honored expert would seek damages from him."

"Ah…" Realization ran through the word.

"A minor token taken for the time left would set him at ease. Obviously, we would not expect the Expert to bestir himself except in the most unusual of circumstances…" Gao Qiu continued.

"Of course," Wu Ying said. "Thank you for the explanation."

Gao Qiu bowed again and stepped back, allowing Wu Ying to return to the merchant. In short order, Wu Ying was paid for his presence and took the seat offered to him by the fire, allowing him to watch over the group. In the end though, what was most telling was Gao Qiu's and the rest of the team's interactions.

In particular, the way they spoke to him and around him, the rough-handed probing at his aura by the two they had met in the caravan. Their methods of ascertaining cultivation level were lacking in elegance and specificity it seemed.

It did, however, clear up the problem. And it was Wu Ying's own fault, to some extent. His Core had been compressed, again and again, to such an extent that sensing it—even for himself—was a difficult process. It would be impossible for most others to sense it.

As for his aura—the most common method of ascertaining strength—his was obtuse and constrained. So many months spent wandering the wilds meant that Wu Ying was used to hiding his aura. Even when he slept, it was kept close to his skin.

In other words, he was, to Gao Qiu and his compatriots, an enigma. Obviously strong enough to travel the wilds alone and come out with significant items of worth—yet none of the items he carried publicly were that valuable. At the same time, his aura was non-descript, nothing that would lead them to believe he was a Core Formation cultivator.

So they treated him as a powerful expert, probably as strong if not stronger than them but only marginally. High Energy Storage perhaps. Since Wu Ying had yet to object, they grew more and more comfortable with their assumption.

One that, upon consideration, as the flames crackled around the central fireplace, Wu Ying was happy to allow to continue.

Low profile was good. He was, after all, a new cultivator in a strange land.

Chapter 6

Two days later, the impromptu group broke up at the central marketplace of the town that had been their goal. Completing the requisite paperwork had taken hours, even though they had arrived earlier in the day, long enough that an impromptu lunch had been purchased and served from roadside hawkers who knew their business.

The marketplace was a central location where the merchant caravan would split further, Merchant Teoh taking his wagons and horses to his shop while those who had paid to join the caravan headed for their own final destinations. After vigorously declining dinner and drinks from the merchant, the group of cultivators found themselves standing in the busy square.

All around them, temporary stalls displaying foodstuffs and non-perishable goods were set up, their proprietors shouting and cajoling passersby to commerce. Servants—men and women—moved through the crowds, picking at bolts of cloth, browsing dried herbs and berries for medicinal soups, and having simple household wares fixed or replaced.

Most popular in this square were the traveling merchants, their goods from far-off cities and kingdoms bringing the curious and the wealthy to their sides. Exquisite jade and marble coverings showcased multi-limbed, animal-headed gods and goddesses. Illustrated books written in strange languages sat beside incense and crushed spices, some of which could be smelled even from a distance.

Bolts of cloth—cotton and hemp, worked in a different format and colored with bright dyes that were a little too garish for Wu Ying's plain taste—were argued over and negotiated. Another merchant beside them showcased a series of exotic weapons including a flexible, whip-like sword.

Curiosity pulled Wu Ying over, the quartet following as a silent retinue. He watched as the man held the weapon in both hands, supporting the flexible blade end with one gloved hand. The entire weapon was strange, not a single blade but actually three, the whip-like elements connected to a circular hilt.

Wu Ying watched just long enough for a casual browser to move aside before stepping forward, idly noting the flicker of disappointment crossing the merchant's face before a smiling welcome was turned on him.

"What is that?" Wu Ying gestured at the weapon, bending his head a little.

"Ah… a connoisseur. This, honored sir, is an exotic weapon from the far reaches of the west! Taken from civilized barbarians[2] who live in sweltering heat all year long, this weapon takes many years to be mastered!" the merchant said. "May I present to the honored sir, the urumi!"

---

[2] So, traditionally, the Chinese had a bad tendency to call anyone who wasn't from China proper barbarians. Even though, to some extent (depending on timeframe / location / etc.) they actually knew many such civilizations were quite sophisticated. Rome, funnily enough, was considered a not-barbarian civilization.

Wu Ying eyed the weapon, watching as the flexible, inch-wide blades jiggled in the merchant's hand. Just under five feet long, the weapon was longer than his own preferred jian. He could not help but try to envision how he would use the weapon, memory flashing back to a certain enemy who wielded a dagger-and-rope combination.

Yet… it would not work that way either. Certainly, he would not look to wrap metal blades around his arm or knee.

Lips pressed together, Wu Ying continued to attempt to picture the motions required; only for a slight cough by the merchant to draw him back to the present.

"Perhaps the honored expert might wish to see the manual of instruction?" The merchant placed the blade on his table and picked up the simple, worn manual. "I apologize, but I do not have a translation of it. The merchant I purchased the set from did not speak the language himself either[3]."

Taking the manual, Wu Ying quickly flipped through the book, lowering the item enough such that Gao Qiu could look over his elbow to read it too. Numerous pictures, similar in format to his own fighting manual, were present along with lines of text. Wu Ying assumed the text explained the stances and motions, though as mentioned, none of the words were recognizable.

The script was blockish, with a dominant single line across the top and cursive strokes beneath. Different from their own script, which had been enacted by the Yellow Emperor to ensure that the kingdom could at least communicate via written text if not by speech.

"How do you expect to sell a weapon like this without a translation?" Gao Qiu said. "Surely no one would be foolish enough to purchase something this dangerous without instructions!"

The merchant offered a low bow to Gao Qiu. "This humble merchant is only displaying the wares he has acquired. The value of such items is for the honored customers to judge themselves. Surely there is, in our great kingdom, sufficient experts in both languages and skill at arms to make full use of something this… unique."

"Ah, if it's for me to judge, then I have a pair of coins for you." Smirking, Liu Jin leaned forward, holding up a pair of bronze coins. The older brother, in the early stages of Energy Storage, affable and lazy at the same time.

His sister rolled her eyes at his actions, while the merchant never lost his smile.

"Your honored expert is quite humorous. Obviously, someone with such ability and morals would not try to cheat a poor mortal like myself. Why, he obviously understands the difference between what a man says and his true intent."

"Well, I'm not sure—" Liu Jin said.

---

[3] Funny little note about the "silk road." Very few merchants actually traveled it in its entirety. Most stopped at specific cities to sell their goods before returning to their origin. As such, goods would pass through multiple hands before reaching their final destination, which is why non-perishable goods were the most common type of item distributed.

"How much?" Wu Ying cut in, placing the manual on top of the weapon. "For the urumi and manual."

"You're buying this?" Gao Qiu said, clearly surprised. "Surely you don't expect to learn this… object? It looks more like the work of a demented blacksmith than a real weapon."

"I assure the honored cultivator, it truly is a weapon used in the deep west by the most learned of weapon experts," the merchant replied.

"I doubt that." Gao Qiu's voice was filled with doubt, but the merchant had already turned away to answer Wu Ying's question. Upon the merchant naming his price, Gao Qiu could not help but raise his voice again. "Are you insane! I could purchase a half dozen usable mortal blades for that price! This is just a plain weapon, no chi, nothing enchanted. And you'd price it that much? This is highway robbery!"

Wu Ying held up a hand as he turned to Gao Qiu, smiling tightly as he murmured, "It is fine, Expert Gao. I have this." Then turning back to the merchant, he tapped the blade and manual. "You've traveled far, have you not?"

"I have, honored cultivator."

Wu Ying idly noted the way the merchant had changed his address. Curious, that he had finally picked up on this, now of all times. Wu Ying wondered what had given it away, if it mattered. Then he saw the man was rubbing a small, inset jade ring. One that Wu Ying, expanding his own senses, noticed was weakly charmed. Enough to tell him that he spoke to a cultivator.

"A long journey, for you and the weapon. A long way to carry something like this… and not sell it." Wu Ying smiled a little. "Certainly, it is unique. Fascinating in a way. The manual shows its methods of fighting are different from every style I've seen. Its flexibility, the whipping nature…" He sighed. "I cannot see many individuals, even in such a wide and great kingdom, interested in something like this."

"Perhaps. But I'm certain, for the right person, it would be valuable…"

"But how long will you wait, for that right person? When I'm right here?" Wu Ying tapped the book. He leaned forward and began to truly bargain, even as the other wandering cultivators stepped away, leaving the pair to argue in peace.

Ten minutes later, Wu Ying waved his hand over both book and weapon, depositing them in his spirit ring. He watched the merchant's flicker of surprise at the disappearing items, murmuring absent thanks to the other as Wu Ying extended his senses again.

Extended them all the way across the marketplace, gauging what was happening. He touched upon the chi flows, the way it twisted around him constantly as he drew it in, quietly cultivating and refilling his own reserves. How the pulse and auras of the four wandering cultivators he had arrived with pushed against the environment. No others though, not in this marketplace.

Wait, no. One more—a guard in the far corner. A glimpse out of the corner of his eyes showed the man wearing the helmet and insignia of a watch leader. Someone of rank then. Even then, he was barely in the first few steps of Body Cultivation.

Puzzled, Wu Ying kept extending his senses, blanketing the streets and residences around the marketplace. A truth that he had noted but dismissed became more apparent. There were more cultivators, but not even a handful of them. The majority of the cultivators were extremely low in their levels; no stronger than the people in his village before their most recent journey.

More and more, Wu Ying kept expanding his senses. The guards had a larger number of cultivators, though most were in the Body Cleansing stage. A single member—the Watch Captain, from his location in the watch headquarters—was in early Energy Storage.

Puzzled, Wu Ying kept turning, his spiritual senses fully expanded, his aura overlaying the area. He finally reached the magistrate's residence in the middle of the city. As suddenly as his aura touched upon the location, defenses sprung upward. Blades of chi erupted, cutting against his aura and senses, staggering Wu Ying as he suffered the feedback.

As quickly as his intrusion was rebuffed, another aura spread outward. It cloaked the surroundings, more powerful than Wu Ying's. At a minimum, a Core Formation cultivator's. On instinct, Wu Ying drew his aura and senses back inward, cloaking himself in such a way that he seemed no different than any other. Just another mortal, one without anything worth noting.

He felt the aura brush across his own, never stopping as it kept moving. Wu Ying felt himself exhale, then cursed.

"Hun dan…" He realized his mistake a little too late. Better to have been found out, better to have made apologies to the magistrate or his protector. Now, he looked like a thief, someone hiding from the authorities after being caught doing something he shouldn't have. Discourteous and apologetic was better than a sneaking thief.

Now the question was, should he speak up and reveal himself and apologize?

"What was that?" Gao Qiu said, coming back with his friends, all four pairs of eyes wide.

Their senses, their skills at aura reading, might be lacking in the extreme, but they'd certainly felt the seeker's intrusion into their daily lives.

"An elder," Wu Ying muttered. "Searching."

"For us?" Gao Qiu frowned. "We have done nothing wrong."

"Do you think they care?" Liu Jin snapped, the mid-twenties cultivator glancing fearfully at his sister, who was clutching her spear as she looked around warily. "We cannot be taken into custody. You know what they do with wandering cultivators."

"What do they do?" A frisson of fear ran through Wu Ying as he asked.

"It's not as bad as Liu Jin portends." Gao Qiu slapped his friend on the shoulder. "Do not deceive others with such words."

Still, Wu Ying wanted to know. "What happens?"

"The army. If you are a wandering cultivator, one who has broken a law, they enroll you into the army. Into their Everlasting Legion, which is filled with others of their kind," Liu Ping answered softly, gesturing around them. "It's why the sects are so weak in the kingdom. The army controls the majority forms of progression. They test and enroll all those with talent into their ranks at an early age."

"But they do not force," Gao Qiu said firmly. "They encourage and bribe, but they do not force."

"Unless you break the laws," Liu Jin corrected.

"We should leave," Liu Ping murmured, gesturing for the group to go. She cast flickering glances about, taking in their surroundings.

Wu Ying could not help but follow her example. He had to admit, they were beginning to draw attention. The sword merchant obviously knew Wu Ying was a cultivator, and more than a few others had noted the grouping of armed strangers. There were enough travelers that they weren't unusual, but the weapons they carried, and their general demeanor were sufficient to mark them out.

"I was looking forward to a bed…" grumbled the last member of the party. Usually silent, the man nodded when Gao Qiu looked at him.

"And you, Expert Long?" Gao Qiu said, not daring to presume.

Wu Ying cocked his head, considering. Then he shook his head. "I believe this is where we part. There are some minor business matters I have left to deal with."

Watching the cultivators glance at his bag that he carried so easily on his back, Wu Ying could not help but nod in acknowledgment at their guess. After all, many of his materials would lower in potency with age. Best to get it sold, though the lack of cultivators in the town was concerning.

Understandable, if they pushed so many of them into the army. It was a very different method, and one that Wu Ying could not help but consider short-sighted. Certainly, it was easier to rule a population that was less, overall, strong; but it meant cities and villages, even the kingdom itself, was more vulnerable to demonic beasts and other groups.

Then again, a concerted legion of cultivators, all trained to work together like an army instead of individual members like the kingdom of Shen used, that might be a frightening force to deal with. It would require different forms of formations and fighting techniques for sure. And that did not even mention the kingdom-wide formation and whatever that could do.

Watching the group move away after bidding their farewells and wishes of meeting again, Wu Ying made his way deeper into the city, bypassing the guards. He noted the way they moved, looking around, forming groups around the few cultivators in the city. More than a few of the patrols carried small hexagram mirrors, enchanted to pick up unrestricted cultivation auras.

That answered another question of his. Such items were only of use when individuals were neither good at controlling their aura or sensing others. One led to the other or vice versa. Restricting lessons and knowledge of aura control and sensing made sense then, if soldiers were expected to police normal cultivators.

Still foolish, it seemed, but it was not Wu Ying's problem. Certainly, right now, his concern was selling his goods—and knowing what he knew now, there was likely only one location to do so. Which was why he made his way toward the magistrate's residence. He kept his aura restricted as he traversed the city, not wanting to deal with the guards. He would open it once he was close. That should be more than sufficient warning, while leaving him time to greet and otherwise make apologies for his actions.

It was too bad he never managed to complete his plan.

***

The squadron of cultivators appeared around him a few blocks from the magistrate's house, forming at all points of the compass. Wu Ying had to admit, they were good. He had not noticed their presence until they were a few hundred feet from him, their auras compressed to such a level that their size was no different than a Body Cleansing cultivator; even if the density of their auras spoke of Energy Formation cultivators now that they were here.

In answer to their convergence, Wu Ying relaxed his control of his own aura. He knew why they were coming. Interesting that they'd managed to locate him as he was coming in, for he had felt nothing of their own sensing of him.

Someone in that group was very skilled.

Eyes dancing over the four before him, Wu Ying found his own lips pressed tight. They were not dressed like cultivators in the long flowing robes and highly-colored regalia of the sects—their cleanliness, their expense a mark of the cultivators' ability displayed to the world around—but in darker, tighter woven clothing with solid black breastplates and helmets. They looked like soldiers, though slightly less encumbered than those Wu Ying was used to. Breastplates, helmets, armguards, plus knee guards and long metallic skirts to cover their lower halves.

Differences in styling and the crests on each shoulder and across the tops of their helmets separated the guards sufficiently so that upon their appearance, civilians cleared the streets with haste. Wu Ying had seen that before, when the brewing storm of violence alerted bystanders to leave for another location. One that might not result in them being bisected by an errant blade or shot by a misfired bolt.

That these people—the local civilian population—had such an automatic response to the individuals surrounding him did not bode well for what was to come.

"Long Wu Ying of the…" He paused, realizing that he should not, could not perhaps, give his Sect. He had not been exiled from the Sect, he was still part of it, but he had been banished from their environs. And yet to use it... "Of the Kingdom of Shen greets the honored cultivators before him."

The group kept approaching silently, though Wu Ying idly noted how the fifth and sixth members had now taken overwatch positions on the roofs. Bow glue, the smell of carved wood and oiled strings spoke to him of ranged weapons. He focused his spiritual sense a little, understanding the outline of the weapons they wielded—crossbows, slightly larger than the handheld ones the guards sported—before he concentrated on the ones on the ground before him.

The lead guard strode toward Wu Ying, a hand on the hilt of her sword. Her features were mostly hidden by her helmet, her hair bundled up underneath the helmet such that but for a slight arch in the cheekbones, the angle of her chin, and the tilt of her lips, she might be a particularly feminine man.

"Are you the cultivator the Captain sensed?" she spoke crisply.

"It is likely, Honored Squad Leader[4]," Wu Ying replied, watching her eyes and the movements of her hands. He trusted in the wind and his other senses to tell him if the rest of her oversized squad acted, though if they were as disciplined as they seemed, they would not act without her orders.

"You will come with us."

He sensed the slight increase in tension among the others. One of the guards even forgot to breathe as Wu Ying did not answer immediately. For a second, then another, Wu Ying marveled at the increased awareness he had; but as tension crept higher, he brought his attention back to the present.

"Of course, Honored Squad Leader," Wu Ying spoke out loud, keeping his hands away from his sword. "I look forward to meeting your... superior?" An eyebrow cocked upward in inquiry.

He watched as she gestured him forward, refusing to answer. A petty power play, but he ignored it. It seemed, to him, that they were more wary of him than was warranted. Certainly, they were unlikely to believe him a Core Formation cultivator—so why an oversized squad? And a group where two of their members carried poison? The wind had spoiled that unpleasant surprise for it had carried the slightly sweet, cloying smell of nightshade and other, deadlier mixtures on the bolts of the snipers.

Wu Ying moved at her impatient hand movement, striding closer with nary a care in the world, and watched as her eyes narrowed farther. Another guard, the gentleman to Wu Ying's left, had straightened a little when Wu Ying started moving.

Instinct had him turn that way, meeting the other's upturned lips, the almost hungry look in the man's eyes. He watched as the other flicked his gaze to Wu Ying's sword then touched

---

[4] Technically, it's wǔzhǎng, which translates as corporal according to Google. Other terms I've found for it is Squad Leader, which I prefer. Literally, it's the words five and long together.

his own. There was a grin, an inviting, provocative one that broke upon the man's face when he saw Wu Ying looking at him.

"Pao Jin. No." The squad leader's voice was firm and curt, making Pao Jin drop his hand from his sword.

Realization struck in a wave. Another swordsman, potentially a self-styled swordsmaster. Probably a battle maniac, judging by the light scar on the man's jawline. Someone who wanted to test Wu Ying.

"I trust I have guest rights at this time?" Wu Ying said, flicking his gaze to Pao Jin to indicate what he meant to the squad leader.

She paused, then answered simply, "My orders are to bring you to see my Captain. However we may do so."

"Ah…" Wu Ying let that word drag out, then looked at the group that had clustered closer to him. Not so close that he could hit all of them with a single strike. Not without extending his blade with his own chi. The two crossbowmen were still above, moving across the rooftops like so many shadows. He took care to never look upward. "Well then, it was for the best that I was on the way to see your Captain."

A smile accompanied those words as Wu Ying tried to set the cultivators at ease. It did not work, but at least he'd tried.

Together, the group moved down the road, headed into the center of the city and the magistrate's office. However, when they reached the compound walls that led within, they took not the main pathway but one that led to the east.

Toward the Captain, Wu Ying assumed, and the inner compound of the magistrate's residence that blocked all his careful probing. Even the wind could tell him little of what was within, for the enchanted barrier around the building blocked all such inquiries. Even the details of the presence within.

Curiouser and curiouser.

Keeping a light smile, Wu Ying followed the group toward the second compound and their illustrious Captain. And all the while, he charted a way to leave in a hurry with the wind.

Just in case.

Chapter 7

They met under an open-air canopy, paper lanterns hanging on wooden stands and surrounding them with a soft glow as the mid-fall sun set. No demon cores being used here to give a flat, constant level of illumination, but traditional oil lamps casting the swaying trees around the courtyard in flickering light that extended their shadows into the distance. On the marble table was a small plate of snacks and fruits along with the requisite tea set in delicate white and blue porcelain.

More interesting than the furniture and carefully curated gardens was the man seated behind the table, perusing a book as he waited. Wu Ying caught a glimpse of the title as the book was closed and put away, and he was hard put to keep his face serene. Well, the *Bedroom Tales of the Green Tigress* was quite popular among certain groups…

"Long Wu Ying of the Kingdom of Shen greets the Honored Captain of the Army." Wu Ying bowed low, offering the man a clasped hand greeting before straightening.

"Please, join me. I am Zhang Po, Captain of the 14th Company of the Everlasting Army," Zhang Po replied, bowing a little from his seat. Less than Wu Ying's bow—a small mark of confidence or disrespect.

Wu Ying felt the way the surrounding chi warped around Zhang Po, down the armor he wore, along his fingers, and even his boots and sheathed sword. Enchanted items, one and all. A lot of enchanted items, more than most inner sect members would have in the state of Shen, but only marginally more than the guards standing beside Wu Ying or the squadron that had brought him in.

Wu Ying ignored the matter, unslinging his backpack and setting it aside as he took a seat at the table. Once he was comfortable, he accepted the offered teacup and plate of snacks. He held the teacup to his lips, visibly inhaling the scent and letting it tickle the backs of his nostrils. Admiring the drink while testing for poison before he sipped.

"Good tea."

"Thank you. It is a blend from the southwestern portion of the kingdom. I can have a packet sent with you, if you wish?"

Wu Ying murmured words of refusal, and after having his refusal rejected, agreed. Custom, the byplay of courtesy and manners.

All the while, the squad had spread themselves around the garden, joining the pair of silent guards in the corner. High above, Wu Ying noted the two crossbowmen had taken watch in the towers that overlooked the inner courtyard along with the usual guards. Courtesy and manners and violence.

How… quaint.

"Did you arrive recently, Cultivator Long?"

"Just today," Wu Ying replied. No reason to lie, especially since the arrival records were right under the fiction book the man had been reading. "I am, I admit, new to the kingdom itself as well."

"Yes. It's unusual for those from the Kingdom of Shen to visit the state of Zhao."

"Mmm… I have seen enough war to avoid the Kingdom of Cai. I am sure you understand."

"A pacifist who carries a jian?" Amusement lacing his words, Captain Zhang leaned forward with one elbow propped up on the table.

"Not a pacifist, just one who is tired of blood and death. I much prefer gathering…" Wu Ying tapped his backpack beside him.

"Mortal herbs? Or something more?" Captain Zhang's eyes narrowed a little.

"Items for cultivators like us. Spiritual herbs, roots, cuttings, and even a few full plants. Of course, a few demonic and spirit beast cores from those that objected to my presence in their domains," Wu Ying said. "I declared as much upon entering the city."

"Yes. With merchant Teoh, no?"

"A chance encounter," Wu Ying said. "He was willing to take this humble cultivator with him and pay for my presence while we traveled the rest of the way to your city."

Another nod. "Rare though it may be, we do get a few travelers from the States of Wei and Shen. The mountain range between us keeps such travel—and commerce—constrained for the most part, but the more adventurous do come." Captain Zhang relaxed a little, though those eyes kept boring into Wu Ying's own. Keen intelligence danced behind his eyes, searching for lies as he continued. "Many do not understand the differences between our nations, the differences in culture and courtesy."

"And I do extend my greatest apologies if I have been discourteous in any manner." Wu Ying touched his backpack again. "Perhaps I could…"

"Mmmm?" Teacup and eyebrow rose in conjunction.

"Offer some minor gift for the discourtesy."

A slight nod, though the same stern-faced regard continued to press upon him.

"To you and the magistrate of course."

Another slightly larger nod.

"And your men, including the squad tasked with bringing me in."

Now the stone face broke into a more congenial smile.

Wu Ying made sure to keep his mental sigh within himself as his bribe was accepted. While he rummaged for the appropriate gifts for the group, the Captain regaled him of the history and cultural mores of the kingdom of Zhao.

As Wu Ying had already noticed, cultivation was not heavily practiced among the general populace. Instead, army groups traveled to each village and city regularly, testing the populace for talent. They had what they called a testing crystal, which verified chi flow and gathering ability. As already related to Wu Ying, the most gifted were given a chance to progress in the ranks of the army with access to cultivation resources, manuals, and exercises.

"Yet I noticed you have a number of wandering cultivators," Wu Ying said to the now more visibly relaxed Captain. Already, the handful of herbs that was to be gifted to the squadron and magistrate had been spirited away, leaving only the small jade box beside Zhang Po.

"Mmm… dropouts, the retired, and the foolish," the Captain said with a hint of disdain in his voice. "Not everyone takes our generous offers. The sects acquire a large portion of those left behind, and the rest are taught by other wandering cultivators or attempt to advance by themselves."

Wu Ying nodded slowly. "It seems that much strength is concentrated in the army."

"As it should be," said Captain Zhang. "The army answers to His Majesty, long may he rule, and he in turn bestows his wisdom upon the kingdom. Your nation splits such benevolence, forcing the king to beg for aid from those who should give it without qualm."

Wu Ying nodded a little to show he was listening. He, of course, thought it was better the way the Kingdom of Shen did it. There, the sects were a power in themselves and checked the depredations a tyrannical king who had lost his right to rule under heaven might enact. After all, what was good for the imperial family was not always good for the general populace.

"Well, as with much, only the Heavens know which is best," Captain Zhang said, noting Wu Ying's silent disagreement.

"Of course… though I do wonder…" Wu Ying hesitated to ask.

"Yes?"

"Do many of your men ascend?"

"Ah…" Captain Zhang let that word draw out. Idly, Wu Ying felt a couple of the watching guards tense at his question, though the Captain made no motion to throw Wu Ying into jail. "You are one of those."

"Those?"

"Cultivation is to ascend and break through the bounds of mortality, is it not?" At Wu Ying's nod, the Captain snorted. "A fool's game. How many of your people ascend? Your vaunted sects and their beliefs in achieving immortality? One a century? Less?"

When he received no answer, the Captain continued. "Exactly. Even in the State of Zhao, the sects all believe in that children's lie. The army and his Imperial Majesty do not sell our men on such fools stories but on the truth—that cultivation is for the present. We have many powerful cultivators in the Core Formation and even a few in the Nascent Soul stage. And that is what gives us strength. Not having our best, our brightest try for something that so many will fail at."

"I see. So you train people in a single cultivation method…"

"We have a few, much like your sects do. A half dozen that work for the majority."

"That streamlines the kind of herbs and spiritual pills you need, while allowing for an overall increase in strength without a focus on a final breakthrough. And in so doing, you do not worry about daos." Wu Ying nodded, flicking his gaze over to the squadron standing around them.

He did not add his other thoughts. The way that the man before him—a Core Formation cultivator himself—felt weak, weaker than any other elder Wu Ying had sensed before. A fragility in his core from a dao that did not fully suit him.

Or was that his imagination? Sometimes, it was hard to tell. So much of their experiences were a matter of senses, of perception rather than hard facts. It was all too easy to deceive oneself. The mind could play tricks where the soul desired.

"Yes. You understand then," Captain Zhang said. "A gatherer like you, with your abilities…" A hand touched the jade box. "Well, if you have what we need, the army is always looking to acquire."

Wu Ying smiled then, for that had been his goal for this meeting. Not just make amends for his discourtesy but also to establish a relationship. When he'd first learned that the majority of cultivators were with the army, he had realized that they would be his biggest customer.

It was why he had not run. Better to get it over with now than to try to make amends later. After all, now he could just blame his lack of knowledge on his recent arrival.

"If you have a list…" Wu Ying tapped his backpack. "I can indicate what I might have to offer. And, of course, whilst traveling, prioritize collection."

This time, Captain Zhang smiled fully. "I will make arrangements for you to meet with my subordinate. He will provide you all those details and purchase your product."

"My thanks, honored Captain."

The man waved away the words, his eyes turning a little sharper. "Your spiritual sense is quite progressed. The way you pushed it outward from the marketplace to reach even here."

"A small matter of training," Wu Ying said, bowing his head. "I noticed—"

"It is not considered important for our people," Captain Zhang said, cutting him off.

"Of course."

"You will, of course, keep your senses contained from now on in our settlements. Especially around army encampments and other government buildings."

"Certainly."

"Good, good. And you will keep your thoughts about cultivation to yourself, especially among the mortals, yes?"

Wu Ying forced a nod, doing his best to ensure he did not tense up.

"You might not know, but the sale of cultivation items to mortals is strictly prohibited. In fact, trade in general for cultivation items is prohibited." Wu Ying's gaze flickered to the jade box, and the Captain smiled. "Minor gifts among friends are often overlooked. Such courtesies are viewed as the requirements of civilization."

Another strained nod. Even the ex-farmer could read the subtext of that line—bribes are not only acceptable but encouraged in this country. Discarding that concern, Wu Ying said, "And what denotes one as a cultivation item?"

"Mmmm, spiritual herbs, cultivation manuals and exercises, certain forms of martial arts. I'm sure the Quartermaster will be happy to provide a comprehensive list." Captain Zhang leaned in. "So, tell me how the war goes. I'm sure you have news that is more recent than ours."

Wu Ying flashed a smile, finished his tea, and murmured his thanks when another cup was poured. He took the moment to organize his thoughts, sorting the news that would be well known from the information he himself had gathered. He set aside consideration about the government and the army's tendrils, about cultivators and their entwining with the government. He had a story to tell.

When he was ready, he spoke.

A give and take of information. Just like any polite, civilized conversation.

***

Later that evening, when he had sold all his goods—all of it, at the Quartermaster's insistence, some at prices that Wu Ying would have considered outright theft in any other place or location—the cultivator stood outside the gates of the magistrate's home, hefting his empty backpack. A good thing he had kept some of the most precious and expensive herbs in his World Spirit Ring.

Then again, he had always known something like that might happen. More than once he'd had sects request to buy him out, and it had only been the strength and reputation of the Verdant Green Waters that had kept their requests from becoming demands. Now though, Wu Ying had no such backing.

It was a little frustrating, truth be told. To go from rarefied heights of privilege to becoming just another wandering cultivator with no backing, no leverage, no strength. If not for many years of learning to duck his head as a farmer, of accepting that the world could and would be unfair, he might have blown up at the Quartermaster. Acted like a petulant child complaining about doing his chores, cleaning the dishes, or feeding the chickens. He might have even revealed he was a Core Formation cultivator in an attempt to regain some degree of control and salve his pride.

That he had even been tempted to do so spoke of a growing ego problem, in his view. Something to watch out for.

A slight noise, the shifting of position from the gate guards recalled Wu Ying to where he was. Idle musing was for later.

"The Three Candles Inn, that way?" Wu Ying gestured down to the east.

He received confirmation of the directions to the location and the cultivator ambled down the street, which was ill lit by roadside restaurant stands and the reflected light of taverns, inns of ill repute and brothels starting up.

The Three Candles Inn was marked both by a name plaque outside and a sign with the aforementioned three candles, the building complex itself spanning the majority of the street. Wu Ying winced a little, but a small marking beneath the sign indicated it was one of the few locations that were rated and allowed to accept cultivators.

Within, Wu Ying flashed the first of his purchased items to the proprietor. He was quickly shown a luxurious room near the top of the building and the promise of a heated bath to be filled in short order.

"Dinner can be served here when it is ready," Wu Ying said, gesturing to the living room in the center of the open-air residence he had rented. The large, luxurious bed with its silk canopy and mosquito netting lay on a raised platform to the left of the entrance, while the bath and privy lay behind the privacy screen. Well-oiled hardwood, mother of pearl inlay, and tasteful paintings abounded, speaking to the luxurious nature of the room.

"Of course, honored cultivator," the proprietor murmured, sketching a low bow.

Further pleasantries were murmured, but the man knew when a guest wanted privacy and quickly led his servants out. Wu Ying barely paid attention to the mostly female staff, though he idly noted the addition of a handsome lad in the background.

Placing his now-empty backpack aside, Wu Ying strode over to the dining room table and touched the tea set laid upon it. He considered the set for a moment, only to be interrupted by a call from the door.

"Yes?" he called.

"Wine. Courtesy of the inn," the servant replied.

"Come in."

Smiling a little, Wu Ying watched as the young lady swept in, placing tray and warmed wine on the table. Plates of salted peanuts and other finger foods were added beside the pair of cups.

She picked up one cup for him, pouring expertly. "Is there anything more I could aid you with?"

The smile that accompanied the drink made it quite clear that she was offering more than the wine cup.

"No, I'll want silence tonight." Seeing the flicker of disappointment crossing her mortal face, Wu Ying continued. "It has been a long journey, and I have much rest to catch up on."

She nodded agreeably as she bowed and left, leaving him to regret his earlier comments. Yet, he had spoken the truth. While companionship—especially of the kind she was offering—might have been briefly entertaining, he had much to do.

First things first, he picked up the small plaque of embossed wood and gold with a tracing of spiritually empowered jade and held it before him. It was with this seal he had been able to access the inn. The same markings that adorned the plaque were showcased on the inn's sign outside. Of all the things he had purchased, this had been the most expensive. Hopefully, it would be worth every penny.

"An Authorized Vendor for the Imperial Army of Zhao."

Snorting after reading over the information, he made sure to send it into his main spirit ring. Losing it would create all kinds of problems, since every single seal was stamped and numbered. Theft of such items and improper use would lead to significant penalties, up to and including death.

"Now, I just need to find more of what they need…" Wu Ying muttered, extracting the next item from his backpack.

It was a book, one with loose pages added to it at regular intervals to amend and denote the flow of demand for the army. Still, with only a half dozen cultivation manuals in play, it was more a matter of degree of demand than lack of it.

"Though pickings might be slim." He sighed, running a finger down the information.

Over two-thirds of the items were spiritual herbs and plants that could be grown in farms like the one Senior Goh oversaw back in the Sect. The other third were items best grown in the wild, either due to the excessive elemental chi requirements or their extremely slow growth speed. Those would be his target, but the majority of the listings were in lower quantities by far, since they were meant for higher cultivation levels. Which…

"Means the pricing is a little low."

Monopolies. They cheated everyone but those who owned them.

Still, Wu Ying committed the list to memory before setting it aside. By that point, his dinner had arrived and been laid out. He took a short break to change out of his robes into another, cleaner set and offered the entirety of his stained and used wardrobe for washing. Even with his aura control and ability to push aside everything from rain to showering dirt, months of travel would eventually stain any clothing. Never mind the sweat and grime coming from within.

Well, the staining would happen with most clothing except for the really expensive enchanted robes that some cultivators wasted their contribution points upon.

Anyway, it mattered not for him, over and beyond his usual cheapness. He needed to allow the wind and dirt and scents to come in through his aura for him to smell and feel and sense the world around. Blocking oneself entirely from nature, that was not living. No more than hiding in a room, refusing to speak with another or feel the touch of the sun upon skin.

Though some might mistake the love for nature and the world outside with a discarding of worldly comfort. As Wu Ying chewed his meal, he reflected upon that and the taste breaching his mouth, overlaying multiple spices and lightly sautéed vegetables and roasted meat, a comfortable cushioned seat beneath his posterior.

Civilization and raw nature. Walk too far toward one or the other and an individual found himself trapped, cut off from a part that made humans… well, human. Mankind was not meant to walk solely in manufactured rooms and plush surroundings, never glimpsing nature; nor were they meant to prowl through the forests with naught but their feet and arms.

Or at least, that was Wu Ying's path. Perhaps some others might find a way—a dao—in the two extremes. Certainly, it felt as though all too many chose the comfort of civilization, forgetting the greater world and confining themselves to humanity's civilized redoubts. And yet, even the meanest city brought with it reminders of nature—a potted plant, weeds growing through cracks, insects sliding through open panes.

He chuckled a little, then dismissed the line of thought. Consideration of his dao—and others—was important, but there was a point where one just had to accept that individual desire played a part in an individual's focus.

More importantly, removing the next series of items Wu Ying had purchased, he had a lot to read and study. Going where the wind had brought him on whim and random desire had led him here. A kingdom whose very basis of government was inimical to his beliefs, where he might run afoul of laws and expected, civilized mores counter to his regular act of existence.

It was all too easy to acquire knowledge without end, pursuing the sweet nectar of information as though data by itself could affect the world. Scholars seated in silent libraries and debating in tea houses might speak of revolution and change; but their words were like the wayward Central Wind, spinning through the sky higher and higher before it exhausted itself, affecting nothing.

Yet stumbling through night and day, blind to the world around oneself was no better. You could choose to be willfully ignorant, but those who had knowledge and wielded it would always stand on a higher stage. If one traveled without knowing what was to come, then perhaps he might experience exactly what Wu Ying had this day, making mistakes that brought easily avoidable danger.

Knowledge was power. Or so Wu Ying had been led to believe.

Except, of course, a certain pixiu had disagreed quite strongly on that point. And perhaps its viewpoint might be true for cultivation. Threading the path of past understanding without allowing the experiences of those who had come before to cloud one's judgment was a difficult proposition.

"Why is this world all grey, the answers neither yes nor no, true nor false? If existence was simpler, would it not be easier for all to walk the proper Dao?" Wu Ying grumbled.

And sure, there were arguments that mankind once had been part of the Dao, that they had followed it intrinsically and somehow moved away from it.

Yet, he could not believe that, not really. Commentary or books that spoke of a past that had been better than the present, where existence itself had gleamed and glimmered with the light of goodness and perfect existence, always seemed to speak of a time so far past, no one present could recall it. Or that, when objectively viewed, was no better than the present.

The past lied of its glory, and the future fooled one with promises that never came true. In the present, and only the present, could one change their existence.

Finished with his dinner and his musings, Wu Ying picked up the first of many books on the history and laws of the Kingdom of Zhao, then moved over to the bath, filled by the officious and silent servants while he read.

There was, he knew, a lot more reading to do this evening.

Chapter 8

It was late afternoon, after a sumptuous lunch, when Wu Ying made his way out of the walled city. His basic errands—from cleaning his laundry to purchasing new tack, changes of clothing, replacements for camping gear, and new storage equipment among other things—happily run by the staff of the inn, Wu Ying had little to hold him in the city. His usual errands of searching for cultivation manuals and exercises had been curtailed by the local laws, leaving him naught to do but rest and relax.

Yet, instinct or perhaps unease at the constant surveillance by the army left the cultivator with little desire to stay in the luxurious building. Taking the delivered goods, Wu Ying left on foot once again via the western gate, following the road signs and maps he had acquired. Without a firm goal, he had chosen to make his way to the tournament grounds, hoping to gain a further glimpse of the cultivators in this kingdom and grasp how other wandering cultivators managed themselves here.

After perusing the laws and history of the kingdom, Wu Ying had more questions than ever. Like many others, the Kingdom of Zhao had once been ruled by the Yellow Emperor. Like Wu Ying's own homeland, they too had once been gifted the Yellow Emperor's cultivation method. Yet in the ensuing years, all traces of that book had been stripped from the mortals living here.

Reading between the lines in the official history had been enlightening, marking the shift from a society of cultivators to the present day. The spark point had been droughts and famines over multiple years that had driven "impetuous peasants" to rebel against the imperial family.

After a tempestuous decade, the rebellion had been crushed, new laws enacted, and the purges had begun. Not only of individuals but the cultivation manuals and teachers who had made the peasants such a threat.

Now, after nearly a century and a half of such actions, the Kingdom of Zhao had stabilized into its present form. One where cultivation and cultivation materials were no longer outright outlawed, as it had been in the first century, except among the army and certain sects, but was still seriously constrained. Even minor tournaments like the one he was traveling toward came about from a relatively recent shift.

All of which resulted in a kingdom with minute and major differences from the States of Wei and Shen. A world where roads were pitted and mortals worked hard at refilling sunken ground with tamped earth and broken gravel, where constant patrols of army personnel ranged along the highways to drive away the demonic beasts that were lured by the flow of humanity. A world where a true bounty lay beyond the walls of civilization, one that was rarely pillaged by wandering cultivators or sect-driven assignments.

Contemplating the land he now walked through, Wu Ying took his time traveling forward. Outside the city, he allowed his spiritual senses to relax, filling the void around him. Only a short distance, barely a full li—almost the same distance from the marketplace to the magistrate's office in fact.

It allowed him to keep track of the pair of guards trailing him, slipping along amidst the crowd of travelers moving in the wake of the patrolling guards. They would have been invisible, if not for the warping of chi around their enchanted equipment.

Wu Ying wondered how much they knew that they stood out like beacons in the night to someone with his gift. The slight burnt smell of chi as their foot bindings drew upon wind and earth chi to lighten and soften their movements, the sharp metallic twist in the wind of their armor to strengthen its bindings and afford them greater protection. No mortal had that, nor the quiet pressure that their unguarded auras displayed.

"But perhaps they don't care…" Wu Ying muttered. That too made sense, after all.

Nor were they the only ones watching him. Yet it was only as the middle of the day was passing that the guards turned back, content that Wu Ying had truly left the city. Not long afterward, the others he had sensed watching him made their appearance, waving from the roadside clearing they had set up where some cultivated and others practiced. He wondered if they knew he saw through their base deception, if they cared.

"Expert Long! You did leave at last," Gao Qiu called.

"Were you waiting for me?" Wu Ying said, a little touched. And a little paranoid. He had, after all, just left a war with the Dark Sect and these were strangers—if strangers who had proven themselves to some extent.

"Just a little while. We thought it might be best to travel together," Gao Qiu said. "We did not think you knew the way to the Seven Pavilions headquarters."

"How did you know that was my destination?" Wu Ying asked.

Gao Qiu gestured down the road. "Well, this is the way to the Seven Pavilions compound and tournament. And I assumed, since you're here…"

Wu Ying nodded, though the obvious question still lingered. "Well, if I came out this way, then obviously I know the way."

"Oh, yes. Of course," Gao Qiu said forlornly. "I see. I apologize. Of course you do not need our company."

"Need, no. However, I would not be against it," Wu Ying said. "The road can be long at times. Anyway, it seems a short enough distance and the tournament soon enough that it makes little sense for me to travel overland to the destination."

"Overland?" Liu Ping, having come closer while they spoke, sounded horrified. Then her eyes cleared up after a moment, remembering where they had found him. "Right. You're a wild gatherer."

"A wild gatherer?" Wu Ying repeated dumbly.

"A term used in our kingdom for those who travel into the wilds, searching for spiritual herbs or beast cores," Gao Qiu said. "It is a rarer occupation in our kingdom than it is in the State of Shen. Or so I hear."

"It is not common, even in my home," Wu Ying admitted.

"Hah! Liar." Liu Ping raised her chin, glaring at Wu Ying. He idly noted then that she was not much shorter than him—tall for a woman. "We've all heard the stories of the Five Illustrious Blades. The Wandering Fairy Sun. The Orange Robe Sect and the Verdant Gatherer. All of them, traveling deep into the wilds to gather."

"It's… those are mostly stories," Wu Ying said. "The Five Illustrious Blades was two decades ago. The illustrious members are now all retired as Elders in their sects." He shook his head. "The Orange Robe Sect is unorthodox, even for the unorthodox sects—"

"You can stop making excuses. We know that our kingdom is weak at gathering and dealing with demonic beasts," Liu Ping snapped, folding her arms. "You do not need to attempt to cover our failings. It is the army that does the majority of those tasks, leaving the rest of us to wander the roads."

"That's not what I was trying to do."

In reply, Liu Ping glared at him and turned away, striding off. Wu Ying's jaw dropped a little, only for Gao Qiu to snort and clap him on the shoulder.

"Worry not, Expert Long. She is like that with everyone. Liu Ping feels the burden of our lack of resources most keenly."

"Then why not just join the army?"

Gao Qiu flinched a little. Waving to the others who had finished with their current cultivation cycles or put away their weapons and unhitched the horses, he gestured down the road they were standing beside. "We should move soon, or else we will be forced to sleep under the stars tonight. And I must admit, I look forward to an actual bed myself."

Accepting the change of topic gracefully, Wu Ying nodded. "Of course. Set the pace, and I shall follow."

Sensing the minor challenge in his words, Gao Qiu smiled as he mounted his own animal. "Then we shall not hold back, Expert Long."

So saying, Gao Qiu kicked his mare to trot down the packed earth roadway.

Chuckling to himself, watching the others pass him as they urged on their own equine companions, Wu Ying drew a deep breath, tasting the air and filtering out the dust. A slight touch to the ground and he was off, crossing the distance to catch up with the others.

***

"May I ask, Expert Long, a somewhat indelicate question?" Liu Jin asked, leaning over the worn wooden table the group had taken over for dinner.

Set in a private room on the second floor, only Gao Qiu and Liu Jin were left with Wu Ying. The others had long before excused themselves to train—in Liu Ping's case—or to rest.

"It depends on the question," Wu Ying said, eyes crinkling with amusement. "But ask. I promise no answers."

"Around you, there is always a sense of…" Liu Jin frowned, searching for the right word. "Chaos is the best I can explain it."

"Not chaos. That is too… chaotic," Gao Qiu cut in. "More like a constant tide, like the river flowing toward you, but more erratic. Yet, always toward you."

"Yes, that's more like it. It's as though the world bends toward you." Then Liu Jin smiled a little. "Not the actual wind, of course, though we see that too."

Wu Ying leaned back. The pair were perceptive, of both the way the wind danced to his bidding, offering hints of the world around, but also to what he could only assume was his cultivation exercise, the Never Empty Wine Pot. He said as much, explaining briefly what the technique did in drawing environmental chi toward him at all times.

"So you cultivate while you move? While you're sitting here, eating?" Liu Jin said, sounding awed.

"Yes."

"What amazing laziness!" Liu Jin said, making Gao Qiu cough and Wu Ying smile. "I would give much to learn such a skill. To think, you can cultivate without cultivating!"

"It's not lazy. In fact, I must always keep one part of my mind on it. Like spinning a spoon around your finger, constantly, while you do everything else." Wu Ying demonstrated, picking up a ceramic soup spoon from the table and spinning the oblong object around and around.

"Why a spoon and not a chopstick?" Gao Qiu asked.

"Because it's not as simple as a straight stick."

"Oh." Liu Jin slumped backward. "Sounds like a lot more work."

"You sound disappointed."

"Liu Jin is always trying to find a shortcut, even though we tell him that cultivation has no quick ways," Gao Qiu said, glaring at his friend. "If not for his sister pushing him to keep up, he would never have made Energy Storage."

Wu Ying nodded.

"Still, that is amazing. A cultivation technique like that exists," Liu Jin said after he got over being dishonored by his own friend. "Xiao[5] Ping's right. We really are the frog in the well[6]."

"Hush," Gao Qiu said, glaring at Liu Jin. The cultivator flushed, bowing his head a little at speaking out of turn.

Wu Ying frowned, watching the byplay but choosing not to comment on it. "The wine is nearly finished. Should we order another bottle?"

---

[5] Xiǎo—literally small, or little. In this case, he's calling her "Little Ping" (Ping being her personal name); a somewhat endearing and teasing form of address. Brothers, you know.

[6] The Frog in the Well is a Chinese idiom and story. It basically refers to an individual or situation where one does not understand or grasp the greater world around them. Like a frog trapped at the bottom of the well, only able to see a sliver of sky above him. Similar to the idiom about blind men and the elephant.

Gao Qiu flashed him a smile at the change of topic, before picking up the bell left behind and ringing it to summon the mortal servant. "Another bottle!"

Bowing her head, the servant left quickly while Wu Ying smiled in agreement. It would be interesting to see how they handled an evening's revelry with a stranger.

***

Later that evening, Wu Ying deposited the two drunken cultivators in their room, Liu Ping just shaking her head a little at the state of her brother before dragging him the rest of the way in and tossing him onto his bed. Wu Ying winced as he listened to the hard thud but chose to ignore it. Best not to get in the way of two family members. Anyway, Liu Ping was a cultivator. A little rough handling would do little harm.

Alone in his room now, and reminded of his own cultivation, Wu Ying sat silently on his bed. He felt the effects of the alcohol coursing through his body, but it was minor. His greater cultivation level, along with his own Body Cultivation methods, meant that poisons—even those as innocuous as wine—did little to him these days. It would require powerful poisons, those concocted by a learned man or powerful demonic beasts, to harm him now.

That was not the only change. He had found he required fewer hours of sleep since his ascension. Having rested the night before, he knew he could spend most of this evening cultivating and still be fresh for the next day. Or he could just rise earlier in the day and spend more time practicing with his sword. He had yet to even break out the urumi, there not being a suitable location for that practice.

Maybe later. Or never. Buying it had been more an indulged whim than any practical decision. After all, it wasn't a jian. Practice with it would not progress his own journey into the Heart of the Sword.

In the meantime, he had a few hours to cultivate and review his core. It was, after even a few days, firmer now, the initial covering having been reinforced. The chi he poured into his dantian, that upheld and swirled around the wind core, patching and layering itself upon the channels he had formed, stabilizing and increasingly plating the outer edges. This, he assumed, was what the cultivation manual meant when one had to stabilize their cultivation base before moving onward.

Closing his eyes, Wu Ying reviewed his cultivation manual in his mind. He had memorized much of the relevant passages, and as such, chose not to extract the actual book. Better to keep it hidden until he was certain of his surroundings.

In any case, the process of stabilization was mostly a recurring process of drawing wind chi into his dantian, allowing it to fill and interact with his Core. At that time, the gradual process of being sustained by the wind chi and the natural growth of the first layer of his Core would allow him to truly make use of the energy contained within the Core itself.

Or so Wu Ying understood.

65

Tapping into the energy in his Core was an entirely different matter. Thus far, he had sustained himself and his current existence by using the energy in his meridians and dantian, all more than sufficient for the minor exertion of running or sensing the world around him. The widened meridians and stronger dantian that came from the process of becoming a Core cultivator, added to his Wind Body, gave him a much deeper pool of chi to draw upon than the majority of cultivators anyway. So long as they were not Core Formation opponents, Wu Ying felt he could outlast any of them.

Yet, at some point, he would have to test the Core Formation chi. Perhaps not while he was in the presence of others. Best to keep at least a few tricks up his sleeve, especially with his misgivings about the kingdom.

Still, gently handling his Core with his mind, letting it spin through his dantian as he nudged it around, Wu Ying could tell it had grown stronger. The initial brittleness that he had sensed, from cutting and patching the multi-ringed sphere, had been healed. It was still weak, but not likely to break from any minor exertion.

Satisfied, Wu Ying opened his eyes again, letting his breathing circulate as he considered his next steps. Refilling his dantian and meridians continued to be the most important step. He had no new insights into his Body Cultivation, and he still had stores of the cleansing potions left to finish his current regimen. Practice of the five winds would wait until he had consumed all those potions, though more practice never hurt.

Then another medicinal bath, another series of cleansing exercises. Trying to work out what the Heaven or Hell Winds were...

Wu Ying shook his head.

Another time. For now, he had to cultivate. Prepare himself and learn about this strange kingdom.

And maybe fight in a tournament?

Chapter 9

The sight of the mansion amidst the large rice fields being worked by serfs and protected by high walls greeted the group as they ascended the hills around the mansion. One entire set of fields nearest the mansion had been set aside, temporary buildings and dueling rings in the space.

In accordance with Wu Ying's earlier findings, he noted the presence of enchantments around each newly constructed dueling ring, meant to contain attacks and guard against accidental injury.

"There's a larger number of enchanters in your kingdom than I would expect," Wu Ying remarked idly.

"Hah! We have multiple divisions of such people in the army. Many only spend a few decades with them though, before they choose to exit the army and work as independent businessmen," Gao Qiu said.

"I'm surprised they're even allowed," Wu Ying said. "Or that it's profitable to do so."

"The army requires a set amount of work to be done annually by anyone trained by them, determined by rank and cultivation level. Whether it's working as guards or patrolling or, in the case of formation masters and enchanters, a number of hours repairing enchantments," the wandering cultivator explained. "It is paid work though, so it's a decent living if you're good at your job. Then any other contracts"—he gestured to the dueling rings they were fast closing in on—"are just additional."

"Ah…" Wu Ying acknowledged the man's words while letting his gaze roam over the cultivators who thronged the dueling rings and the fabricated village.

Even having pulled back his spiritual senses in anticipation of meeting others, Wu Ying sensed multiple powerful presences moving through the village. A pair were clustered around what he assumed was the inn, another was definitely that of an older gentleman overseeing the creation of the dueling rings, and the last lay deep inside the mansion grounds itself.

So, two Core Formation cultivators likely here for the fights—or to watch their juniors fight—and a guard deep within, who likely was here in case things got out of hand. He noticed the subtle pressure of the guard's presence, the way it was contained to the mansion grounds, yet present like a mountain range in the distance. A subtle notice to those who might think of causing trouble.

As for the formation and enchantment elder, he was a Core Formation expert, but a glance at him and the way his aura was held together was enough to let Wu Ying know that unless he hid his strength deep within, he was no martial expert.

"How many contestants do you expect?" Wu Ying said.

"Mmmm… it's a small tournament. So no more than fifty, I would assume." Gao Qiu's eyes swept over the buildings before alighting on a man in officious robes standing near the entrance of the mansion. Beside him, at a small portable podium, another man stood with a small scroll unrolled and a brush at the ready. "I believe that is where we go to register."

Wu Ying nodded, watching as the group got off their horses and led the animals over to their target. He idly followed, his half-empty backpack swinging behind him. He had not had much time to gather, though he had spent the late evenings and early mornings on brief forays away from their campsites. Still, beyond a single lucky find, the majority of his current—publicly accessible and noticeable—harvest were common materials.

On the other hand, for all the various weaponry, armors, and other enchanted items that were present and owned by the cultivators—and there were quite a few—he noticed a significant lack of spirit rings. It was quite marked. The only ones he could sense were owned by the Core Formation cultivators.

Then again, if the people of Zhao did not focus on the concept of daos as firmly, it made sense that spirit rings, which required the use and bending of the dao of space, would be lacking here. As it was, his own rather numerous spirit rings had only resulted from the clashes he had had with the Dark Sect.

Moving behind his companions, Wu Ying was surprised to find himself before the registrar before he knew it. Cold, officious brown eyes stared into his own as the shorter man tilted his head upward to meet Wu Ying's gaze.

"Name, sect if any, and weapon of choice." The words were repeated as though by rote, even as the gaze dropped, sweeping across Wu Ying's simple peasant robes. No curl of his lips, no outward signs of dismissal though.

"Ah… I had not… I'm not sure I am joining," Wu Ying said. He cursed himself quietly, realizing he had not made a decision, not since he started. To fight in another tournament, to test himself. That was good. But maybe he should try for a low profile, not showcase himself. "I was just looking to meet other cultivators."

The registrar frowned, crossing his arms. "If you are not participating, you may not stay on our land. Unless you are a registered merchant in alliance with the Seven Pavilions?"

Wu Ying shook his head. Then, remembering, he put a hand in a pouch before extracting the seal from his spirit ring and showing it to the man. "I am a registered vendor for the army. I gather—"

"Spirit herbs and the like. Yes, yes. We do buy some for the army," the registrar said, "but not here. Go visit one of the main branches in a city."

"Oh…" Wu Ying glanced back at the inn and his recent companions.

"Come, Expert Long. Join. The prize is well worth fighting for, and there is no better way to judge a man's heart than over the crossing of blades," Liu Ping cajoled him.

"I—"

"You're a swordsman, right? Jian. That's more a soldier's jian though, thick and long," the registrar said, nodding. "And your accent… it's from the State of Shen?" At Wu Ying's nod, he smiled a little. "Good, very good. We'll waive the registration fee then, if you join. It'll add prestige to the tournament to have more foreigners in it. Write it in. Expert Long, with a straight jian. A wandering cultivator too, yes?"

"I haven't—"

"Here." A hand thrust forward, and Wu Ying moved to block it. Upon contact, the registrar twisted his hand, opening and depositing the small token in Wu Ying's open palm. "This will give you a private room at the inn and meals on the Seven Pavilions. A good deal, no?"

Wu Ying, amused by the sudden change, turned the seal around. He was shooed away, sent to the inn where the uncouth foreigners were being housed, even as the registrar turned to the next group coming over the hill.

Together, the group headed for the impromptu village, Liu Jin and Gao Qiu congratulating Wu Ying and teasing him about his good fortune. Well. It would not hurt to cross blades with the martial artists here. After all, as Liu Ping mentioned, there was no better way to get to know others than over the edge of the blade.

New cultivators meant new styles. It meant new challenges, and with them, the chance of enlightenment or new understanding. After all, he still was missing something when he wielded his jian. A step away from reaching the Heart of it, even after all these years.

***

Parting ways with the group at the residence that matched the token in his hand, Wu Ying looked at the hastily built structure with a critical eye. There were minor flaws through the building, sections where the wind howled, where wooden crossbeams had not been fitted entirely tightly, loose tiles on the top and a surprising level of missing interior walls for privacy inside each room.

Yet for a building, a village, constructed, as Gao Qiu had said, for a single week-long tournament, the entire establishment was well put together. Many mortal hands must have been dedicated to this process, and though there were no deep foundations laid nor were the walls properly clay hardened, it would be more than suitable for the purpose of offering privacy and holding nature at bay.

Inside, Wu Ying was approached by an attendant who took the small token from him, read over the details, and led him up the narrow corridors to his room. As they entered the second floor, a door opened to reveal a young lady. Clad in a large, unusual triangular headdress and colorful pink, dark blue, and yellow robes of unfamiliar cut, she had a slight tan to her skin and slant to her eyes that marked her from another non-Han native tribe. She paused, one hand on the doorjamb as her gaze raked over his body.

"Greetings, Expert. Are you to take the last room?" she said, her voice a lilting singsong that altered her pronunciation of the common tongue a little. She spoke a little hesitantly, as though the words were unusual for her to voice.

"I am not sure." Wu Ying looked at the attendant.

"Yes, the honored expert will be taking the last room in the building," the attendant was quick to answer.

"Ah. I hope you do not snore then." Her nose wrinkled. "Or else I will have to spend good money on a silencing talisman."

"I do not."

"That's what all men say."

Wu Ying grinned a little, remembering the many, many days he had spent in the middle of the wilderness, tied to tree branches, hunkered in caves, or curled up in hidden tents where the slightest noise might draw powerful predators. "I have it on good authority, I do not snore. Nor talk in my sleep. Or walk in it."

"You are very confident." Another smirking smile. "She must have spent a lot of time with you, for you to be so certain."

"Something like that," Wu Ying murmured.

"Well, I shall look forward to bursting the hero's bubble." Smirking, the lady closed the door with a thump and slipped the wooden padlock in it before sauntering past Wu Ying.

She made him retreat a little to the edge of the corridor, purposely not moving all the way to the other side to force him to choose between squeezing aside so as not to touch her as custom dictated or stand there. Her eyes glittered with amusement as he edged aside, her hips swaying a little more as she left the pair alone.

"An interesting woman…" Wu Ying muttered, turning back around to the attendant. A little young for his taste though. "Not native to Zhao, is she?"

"In a way. She's part of the Zhuang enclaves, in the northwestern mountain reaches," the attendant said. "The Seven Pavilions have a number of exclusive trading agreements with the enclaves. Even so, we were surprised that she and her sisters chose to participate."

Wu Ying nodded absently, amused by the information. She and her sisters must have annoyed the attendant, for him to choose to gossip at such slight provocation.

When he was shown to his room—one much smaller than the previous inn he had stayed in—he placed his bags away without comment, ignoring the way the attendant had braced himself for a scolding. This was more than sufficient for his needs.

"If there is anything else the Expert might…" the attendant trailed off as Wu Ying took a seat on the small table, looking up expectantly. "Yes?"

"Hot water for tea. And then, if you can spare a few moments, a conversation." Wu Ying gestured around the room. "I'm new, as you can probably tell. And I'd be grateful"—his hand brushed the edge of the table, leaving a handful of coins on it—"for any news you might have."

Eyes gleaming with amusement, the attendant stepped within and bowed, his lowered hands and body sweeping outward a little early as he straightened to make coins disappear. "I will return promptly with the hot water."

"Good, very good." Watching him leave, Wu Ying smiled to himself.

Counting the number of rooms in this hallway and the mention made by the registrar, it seemed that this tournament would certainly be more interesting than he had expected.

***

Wu Ying watched as the attendant departed, smiling happily and patting the pouch where he had his bribe safely stored. Picking up the teacup by his elbow, Wu Ying could not help but go over the contents of what had been related to him.

Currently, the entire tournament was playing out as expected with only a few minor deviations. What that meant was that the majority of the participants were wandering cultivators like Gao Qiu and Liu Ping, while a smaller number were members from local sects. All the larger, more prestigious sects had chosen not to involve themselves, except in two cases. In both instances, the participants were—it was rumored—inner sect cultivators who had found themselves stymied at progressing to the next level in cultivation and had chosen the mortal road to walk.

Again, nothing too surprising in the inn attendant's view.

More interesting was the presence of Wu Ying and the young ladies from the Zhuang clan, as well as other foreigners. The three sisters had journeyed down to join the martial tournament, intent on winning the prizes and showcasing their abilities, while an additional barbarian from the northern steppes had arrived too, wielding a bow. The last member of the "foreign" dedication was a fisherman from a smaller kingdom that no one had heard of in the east. Or perhaps not kingdom but village. The fisherman's lack of fluency in the majority language, speaking only in dialect, stymied much conversation.

It didn't matter so much, since no one expected the kid—barely in the Energy Storage stage, it was rumored—to do that well. The only reason he was lumped in with the other foreigners was his much darker skin, flatter nose, and shorter limbs than your average man and the strange three-pronged weapon he wielded.

Finishing his cup of tea, Wu Ying set down the glass and poured a fresh one. For the time being, he would ready his room for his extended stay. There were two more days before the tournament would begin, and he would use the time to do his own investigations.

After all, not a single word had been said about the other two Core Formation cultivators. Whether that was due to the attendant's ignorance or discretion, Wu Ying would have to find out himself. If they were taking part in the battle, it would certainly liven things up.

***

A short while later, Wu Ying had swapped out of his travel-worn clothing for something a little more refined. Plain hemp was replaced by silk, the dull brown and grey traded for lighter, more colorful green and blue. It was not the green of his sect, but close—a minor acknowledgment of his own roots, without making a show of it.

He was still trying to work out the parameters of his banishment. In a world of unspoken rules and silent codicils, where courtesy and civility dominated and the boundaries of behavior and activities were hidden from direct observation, he often felt as if he was searching for roots by touch alone in a murky rice field. Experience helped, but sometimes, in a new field, in a new season, one could only hope that others had not dropped a blade the day before.

Having codified rules would be easier, but also perhaps more dangerous. The greater the number of laws, the greater the number of criminals. Detailed rules were either a waste of paper or the weapon of the petty tyrant.

Outside, in his new robes, Wu Ying watched the interplay of courtesy and respect among individuals who lived on the fringe of society by their very nature. Wandering cultivators walked, ate, and spoke with one another and came not to blows, for the unspoken rules of the jianghu[7] kept them in check.

The narrow pathway ran between quickly built buildings that reached up around on each side, pushing individuals close even as shadows of the setting sun shaded two-thirds of the street. Tables and chairs were pushed outward to entice cultivators to sit and drink, to catch up with old friends, while other stalls sold goods ranging from everyday mortal needs to cultivation-only items—pills, enchanted items, and scrolls among the wares.

Curiosity had Wu Ying move closer to such tables, eyes flicking over the myriad items as the raucous drone of conversations rode over him and the familiar smell of a working farm drifted by. He could not help but frown, recalling the numerous laws he had studied and the seal he had acquired at great expense. Now, here, were individuals flouting the law. Not that he agreed with the law, but it was another piece of a strange puzzle.

"Is there a problem with my merchandise, honored expert? Are you perhaps searching for a particular item?" the merchant said with a smile, his gaze flicking over Wu Ying with practiced ease as he judged the likelihood of a sale.

"My apologies. It has nothing to do with your merchandise," Wu Ying said. "I am new here"—the merchant nodded at the rather obvious fact—"and I was told that sales between cultivators of cultivation goods are not allowed."

"Ah!" the merchant exclaimed with understanding. "That is true. But the Seven Pavilions and the tournament itself has been granted special dispensation. All such tournaments are, with the Seven Pavilions having purchased the license dispensation. The rest of us but do sales for them under their banner. At the end of the tournament, we will be paying them a portion of our sales."

---

[7] Jianghu – technically, rivers and lakes. From a poem, but basically refers to the separate world that martial artists and thus cultivators exist within.

Wu Ying nodded slowly, wondering how they managed to keep track of what had been sold or not. Then he dismissed the matter. It was not as though he intended to set up a stall himself. At least not today. Still, it was good to know that there were such options in the future.

"Then is the honored expert interested in anything? If I may say so, the enchanted equipment from the State of Zhao is of better quality than what you might be used to," the merchant said with a smile, one that pulled his pencil thin mustache higher and set the trailing edges quivering.

"Mmmm… I have not much funds to my name at the moment," Wu Ying admitted readily, even as his gaze skipped over the enchanted accessories the man carried. Well, not much by the standards of cultivators. More than enough to live on comfortably if he was a farmer. "But perhaps you could speak about what it is you carry."

"Ah, many things, though few that are… dangerous." The merchant grinned. "I leave weapons and the like to my competitors. I prefer a more refined clientele." Gesturing at the various earrings, combs, pendants, soap beads, and other miscellaneous accessories and knickknacks on his table, he continued. "You might think of my wares as utility items. Meant to make everyday life a little more comfortable.

"Marble soap beads that will last for years, removing all trace of scent. Add to a bucket of water or use directly on the body." A finger tapped the aforementioned black-and-white-striped spheres. "A comb that untangles hair and smooths it out with only a few brushes."

Wu Ying perked up at that. A minor inconvenience, but long hair like they all kept did require significant upkeep, which was often less than convenient in the wilds. Even cultivator constitution and the minor alterations to aura and the like did little to stop hair from bunching and snarling after weeks on end.

Seeing his interest, the merchant picked up the comb and handed it to Wu Ying, who turned it over and over. He sensed the enchantment on the wooden comb, the way runes had been inscribed along the edges and chi embedded within, all the while aligning the comb with its new nature and purpose.

He brought it closer, sniffing surreptitiously. It was a strange chi smell, wood and water at its base, but blood in there. Something else… something similar but a little deader. Hair? There was a hair chi?

"Then, of course, we have the ever-popular pendants of shade—useful for those who spend much time in the sun to keep their complexions fair." The merchant went over those quickly when Wu Ying did not react. "Ankle bangles to soften or ring with each footstep." Another tap on a pair of ankle bracelets with tiny silver bells on them. "Earrings that dampen the noise of city living, a ring of night reading…"

Wu Ying listened, his gaze flicking over the items as they were named and, in some cases, when his interest was indicated, shown. It was a much wider array of equipment than at his own Sect it seemed, enchanted items made for everyday living, unlike the ones he had so often purchased.

A part of him marveled at the waste—of coin, of materials, of the crafter's time and expertise—but another part of him was jealous. What a marvelous world it was, to have so many minor items that eased everyday life available to even poor cultivators like him.

Yet Wu Ying could not help but think of the mortals in the city. How so few of them had any such luxuries. A steep pyramid, it seemed, this kingdom. For the lucky, the gifted, much was offered. For everyone else, the drudgery and struggle of mortal life.

Even so...

"Payment can be made in taels or beast cores," the merchant explained patiently as he set aside the comb and soap beads Wu Ying had been interested in. "We also accept script from the Seven Pavilions, obviously."

"I see." Touching his barer-than-he-liked purse, Wu Ying got ready to bargain—only for the pair to be interrupted by a heavy hand falling on Wu Ying's shoulder. Turning his head, unsurprised, Wu Ying greeted the overly friendly gentleman. "Expert Gao."

"Forget about buying today. If it's not for the tournament, buy on the last day. That's when they're desperate to sell," Gao Qiu advised, grinning a little at the fuming merchant. "Don't be like that. You know you were going to take advantage of my friend."

"Never!"

"Come, we were going to take dinner at the Seven Pavilions's main restaurant. It overlooks the dueling rings, if you care to join us." Gao Qiu said, ignoring the merchant.

Wu Ying hesitated, casting a glance at the merchant and his goods, then at Gao Qiu. In the end, the quiet thrum of a pair of presences made up his mind. After all, the merchant and his goods would be around.

Chapter 10

The two-story wooden restaurant was built with a patio significantly overhanging the ground floor, draped rain-proofed cloths above offering shelter from the elements. A short distance away lay the first of the five dueling rings. That one was fully constructed, a pair of Energy Storage cultivators sparring within under the watchful eyes of a pair of enchanters.

"Testing the rings?" Wu Ying asked, noting how the pair were unleashing flashy attacks that were easily dodged. Each attack struck the glowing, translucent barrier before dispersing while the enchanters watched and noted the changes across their formation.

"Yes," Gao Qiu said. "Mostly, the lower ranked cultivators test out the rings. It's a way for them to showcase their talents in full, knowing they won't likely win anyway."

Wu Ying nodded, turning his head upward a little. He sensed them there, seated on the patio, watching over the sparring events. The third Core Formation cultivator, the Elder in charge of the rings' construction, was working on the fourth ring, helping lay the carved stones and holding the building formation together as it was linked. Even from a distance, Wu Ying felt the gentle pull and push of chi flow.

"Come, let us eat. I reserved us a table, but as you can see"—Gao Qiu waved his hand around, including the throng of cultivators about them—"table space is at a premium."

"All but for the Elders above," Wu Ying said amusedly. After all, he had not sensed them move in the last few hours.

"The sect Elders? You caught the rumors quickly." Gao Qiu smiled a little. "Sometimes, I wonder who the newcomer here really is."

The pair smiled at the waitress who came to greet them, offering their names and being led upstairs to their table where the other wandering cultivators from their group waited. The table they received was set farther back from the edge of the patio and its view, though Wu Ying caught a glimpse of the pair of Core Formation elders as he traversed the crowded floor. Elderly, both of them, with wrinkles and white beards that reached the tops of their chests. Bushy eyebrows on one and thinning hair on the other helped differentiate the almost identical-looking pair—except, of course, for the different colored robes they wore.

"What sects are they?" Wu Ying asked after taking his seat facing the staircase and open sky.

Hints of cinnamon, cumin, ginger, and garlic rose from all around, the smell of fresh steamed fish and freshwater prawns carried from nearby dishes. A waiter walked by and deposited a whole joint of pork in a clay pot, stewed in a mixture of broth, mushrooms, and soya sauce, to the chorus of thanks from a group of lean and hungry cultivators. Unlike Wu Ying's own party, this group had not bothered to change or wash up before they came to the restaurant.

"Waiter!" Gao Qiu called, ordering swiftly from the man when he arrived. Multiple dishes of fish, prawns, vegetables, and pork were quickly ordered, along with noodles and rice for all.

Wu Ying shook his head as the cultivator splurged, though Wu Ying sensed that most of the meals were but mortal fare, without the hint of spiritual chi that would mark a better class of dish.

"I don't know the sect robes well," Liu Jin murmured, "but I think Mountain Fast? And Crimson Flowers."

No need to ask which was which. Dark grey and brown bushy eyebrows seated alongside vermillion and crimson balding Elder was answer enough.

"Are they large sects?" Wu Ying asked.

"Not the largest. Top twenty? They have a few hundred members each," Liu Ping said, wagging her hands back and forth. "Pretty good for a small tournament like this."

Wu Ying blinked. The Verdant Green Waters by themselves—admittedly, the largest by far—had a thousand or so members in the inner sect including those traveling back and forth. Even the other smaller sects were nearing a thousand total. Miniature towns, one and all.

"That's interesting," Wu Ying said, glancing at her. "So, are they one of your targets?"

"To join?" Liu Ping snorted. "Not unless they take my brother."

"Which they won't," Liu Jin said, crossing his arms. "I told you already, you should take the offers you've been given. With their resources—"

"I could ascend to the Heavens!" Liu Ping said mockingly. "What's the use of being immortal if no one I care for is there to enjoy it with me?"

"That's—"

"When I am reborn, I'll have another chance. Better to enjoy the time I have now, with the family I care for here, than to struggle and fail alone." Mimicking her brother, she crossed her arms and glared at Liu Jin. He in turn gave her a smile in return, one filled with love and tenderness.

Wu Ying watched the pair silently, a little amused, a little contemplative. After all, her words were not, in themselves, wrong. He himself had stepped aside from burgeoning relations—with Li Yao, with some others—because of the same concern. What happens if you ascend and your partner doesn't? Even crossing the threshold of Core Formation meant a hundred more years of existence, if not longer. Time enough to watch friends and family pass away if they were not able to keep up with one's own progress.

The peak was a lonely place.

He made a note to write letters to his parents and his friends. He should have done it earlier to remark upon his arrival in a new kingdom. But better late than never.

Changing the subject, Gao Qiu nodded toward the trio of cultivators seated beside the two Elders, resplendent in their sect robes. All three stared at the various wandering cultivators with a slight sneering expression.

"Those are likely to be our biggest competition," Gao Qiu said.

"Inner sect members?" Wu Ying said.

"One looks to be a core member," Liu Jin said. He gestured downward to a wooden talisman hanging off the aforementioned man's belt. "They don't give those tokens to just anyone."

His attention drawn to the three, Wu Ying let his spiritual sense focus on them. He did nothing more than concentrate it, not wanting to alert the Core Formation elders of his interest or his own, new, cultivation level. Even so, the balding Elder turned to stare at their table, lips compressed.

Wu Ying did not restrain his senses, knowing he had done nothing wrong. After all, everyone had blanketed the room with their own chi and aura, such that the overlapping brush of each other's presence made details hard to pick out. Yet he did relax his focus a little, having learned what he wanted.

Beyond the usual plethora of enchanted items that seemed so common among the cultivators of this kingdom, the token worn by the core member of the Mountain Fast sect was a powerful defensive talisman. It thrummed with restrained earth chi, a guaranteed defense against anything but a powerful Core Formation powered strike.

"What did you do?" Gao Qiu hissed at Liu Ping as the Elder continued to stare at them.

The Elder turned away once he was certain his regard had been noticed, mouthing words they could not catch to those at his table.

"Nothing! Why are you always blaming me?" she said defensively.

"Because it's almost always your fault," her brother muttered.

With the scraping of chairs being pushed back, all three younger sect cultivators stood in unison. The room grew hushed, even the waiter ascending the stairs with their meal hesitating before he made his way fully up. Together, the three sect cultivators walked over to Wu Ying's table, the eyes of everyone in the establishment following them like iron fillings to lodestone.

"Ah Ping…" Gao Qiu said under his breath with a world-weary sigh.

Wu Ying gestured at Gao Qiu to stop, even as he pushed his own chair back a little and stood, offering the group a clasped hand bow. "Greetings, honored experts."

All three sets of eyes focused on Wu Ying, and he struggled to keep his face calm and relaxed. Public speaking and spectacles were not his favorite pastime, and even now, the attention of so many was more nerve-racking than lying in a bog, body covered with mud while a Nascent Soul level Spirit Tiger prowled above him.

"Cultivator." The lead member—the core member of the Mountain Fast sect—flicked his gaze over Wu Ying's companions before returning to him. "My master mentioned that you might actually be a challenge. Unlike the others here."

Liu Ping stirred, moving to stand and object, only for her brother to yank on her arm and glare at her. She subsided with ill grace, while the other Mountain Fast inner sect member smirked at the wandering cultivator. Liu Ping was forced to bite her lip in silence.

"That is a pleasing judgment," Wu Ying said, then bowed once more a little. "I am Long Wu Ying of the State of Shen. I am a wandering Gatherer, newly arrived in your fair kingdom."

"Yes, your atrocious accent is quite clear of your foreign origins," said the leader. Arrogant young master, Wu Ying pegged him immediately. Too long nose that was held too high up.

Rolling his eyes, the other male of the three, and the only member of the Crimson Flowers, pushed forward. Slim, smiling congenially, a hand on his jian. "Oh, Ah Wen, stop being so rude and introduce yourself." Returning Wu Ying's bow, he continued. "I am Shi Fei, inner sect cultivator of the Crimson Flowers sect."

Glaring at his friend, the leader finally said, "Cui Wen, core member of the Mountain Fast sect and disciple of esteemed Elder Eng."

"And I am Kong Lai, inner sect disciple of the Mountain Fast sect." Kong Lai bowed at the end, a light smirk still on her face. She held no weapon but had angled her body aggressively towards the group. "Now, why did Elder Eng think you might be worth our time? Are you a sword cultivator perhaps?"

Her gaze flicked down to Wu Ying's blade by his side, her nose wrinkling a little. The weapon was neither enchanted nor particularly ornamental, the guard and hilt simplistic to the extreme.

Wu Ying shook his head, his fingertips touching the sword hilt absently as he answered Kong Lai. "I have a little skill with my jian, but I do not claim to be a master or a sword cultivator." Those individuals were somewhat insane, taking the way of the sword as their dao. A restrictive path, to Wu Ying's thinking, yet they were some of the most dangerous individuals to cross weapons with, as most had at least the Sense of the Sword, if not Heart or Soul. "I have, however, gained some small degree of control over my aura and senses."

Cui Wen blinked, looking Wu Ying up and down before he shook his head. "You are lying."

Gao Qiu stirred in his seat. When Cui Wen looked at him, daring him to say something, Gao Qiu lifted his chin. "Your accusation is very rude and unbecoming of a cultivator. Expert Long has given you no reason for your reaction."

"My Master would not have mentioned him if he only had some minor control over his aura and senses." Cui Wen's nose wrinkled when he looked at Gao Qiu and the other individuals at the table. "Little control is what you and your people have."

The slowly growing hubbub around them, as individuals had started to relax, grew quiet again at the insult. Some cultivators edged aside, while a few of the more practical ones ate faster in anticipation of the inevitable fight.

Liu Ping shrugged her brother's arm off her hand and stood, only to find that Kong Lai had positioned herself in opposition to Liu Ping, almost nose to nose. The sect cultivator was smiling sweetly, though Wu Ying read the unreasonable look of a battle maniac in her eyes.

Wu Ying sighed at such volume to draw attention back to himself. "I apologize. It seems I have been misunderstood." He waited a beat before continuing. "My aura control and spiritual sense control is only small when compared to the luminaries and prodigies in the State of Shen. Compared to yourself and the general abilities of the sects in this State, I fear my words are entirely too humble."

There was a long silence as everyone took in Wu Ying's words and meaning. Then the entire top floor burst into motion, the first fist coming from Cui Wen.

***

There were rules to cultivator fights in taverns. Unspoken rules, of course, but rules, nonetheless. Unless grave insults or blood enemies met, weapons were generally barred from use. As the vast majority of cultivators trained in at least one weapon, whether blunt or sharpened, the use of a weapon escalated the fight in undesirable ways.

Instead, fists and feet were the primary tools, with tables, chairs, and plates of food considered fair game to be thrown and otherwise deployed or destroyed during the brawl. On the other hand, even Energy Storage cultivators were expected to hold back from outright wanton destruction of property and the projection of chi.

After all, what was the point of a fight that destroyed the floor and walls within a half-minute of the start, leaving the group to scramble out from under the collapsed roof? No honor would be saved, no new reputation created, or level of ability staked.

As such, a brawl between cultivators in an inn or restaurant was remarkably restrained. If you considered the sheer amount of damage that such cultivators could generate if they fought seriously, that was. Of course, for the proprietor and employees of the establishment, such fights looked more like the organized chaos of scrambling mischievous monkeys.

The first punch that flew toward Wu Ying's face was easily dodged. Having such a long wind up, the attack was more a violent introduction than true threat. Slipping around the punch, Wu Ying wove forward, unleashing a flurry of jabs of his own.

Beside him, Gao Qiu and Liu Jin ganged up on the Crimson Flowers cultivator, the trio exchanging a flurry of blows. Overwhelmed by numbers and what, Wu Ying assumed, was a greater degree of familiarity with brawls, Shi Fei was retreating as he blocked punches, kicks, and a thrown rice bowl.

That bowl was the start of the all-out brawl, for its impact and spillage of rice upon a young lady's dress and her subsequent shriek led to the addition of her table. An accidental bump of an elbow as one of her tablemates led to the choking of a hastily eating stranger, which led to...

Chaos.

On the other side, near Wu Ying, Liu Ping and Kong Lai were locked in a grappling match, their bodies twisting and turning as they attempted to complete a full lock on the other's arms. Throwing herself high, a foot accidentally striking another seated gentleman, Kong Lai managed to release her arm as she landed on a table beside them. Only to have her legs swept off by an irate gentleman whose dinner of roasted duck now had a deep imprint.

Wu Ying, now beside Cui Wen, struck with quick hooking punches and elbows, shifting targets as he pushed back the other man. Using the Twelve Gales and Shen Kicking Technique, Wu Ying made sure to keep his body close to the other, never allowing Cui Wen to raise his foot to kick out without having his overall balance disrupted by a quick hip or knee bump.

Frustration grew on Cui Wen's face, his kicking techniques being spoiled regularly by Wu Ying.

"Stop doing that! Fight properly, you damn… tourist!" shouted Cui Wen.

"Are you stupid?" Wu Ying said. When he got no answer beyond another looping punch which he blocked with an elbow, he continued as he stepped in, bumping Cui Wen again and pushing him into another man behind. "This is a brawl, not the dueling ring!"

Seeing the other man who had been jolted turn around, Wu Ying grinned and faded backward, using the Twelve Gales of his sect to allow him to float between two other brawling couples. As Cui Wen surged forward to attack Wu Ying, a hand grabbed Cui Wen's shoulder and spun him around, the punch flashing outward to impact his face.

Having escaped his first opponent, Wu Ying quickly found himself targeted by another. A flurry of elbows and knees came at him, forcing Wu Ying to jump and flip onto the sprawled tables and chairs as he got away from the infighter. Idly taking note of the bushy-faced countenance of his latest opponent, the wind cultivator could not help but note what the air was telling him.

That, for all the chaos of the fight, a small quiet space around the two Elders was still being respected. Respected and enforced, as the occasional individual who stumbled too close was struck aside by pulses of solidified aura formed by the pair of Elders.

All around, the crack of breaking chairs, the grunts and shouts of fighting cultivators, the occasional shouted fighting technique split the air. In between, the smell of delectable foods mixed, as dishes and warm gravy rained upon individuals. Auras, wild with abandon, left them exposed to deployed foodstuff.

Then, he was too busy to pay attention to others, for another cultivator joined bushy-faced elbows—a sect mate or brother, judging by the similar martial styles. Forced into a corner, Wu Ying had to pay attention as he kept limbs away from body and face.

Still, the insult and chaos were rather worth it.

Even if he was missing the dinner that had been promised.

Chapter 11

The glances and studied expressions of the cultivators the next morning were grating on Wu Ying's nerves as he walked through the marketplace. More than one turned away quickly when he looked toward them, not daring to even accidentally challenge him. Others were the opposite, openly glaring at him. Most of those sported bruises or vaguely familiar features from yesterday's brawl.

The reactions of the merchants were the most frustrating however, for they were obsequious to the extreme, over-explaining their merchandise at even the slightest indication of interest. In the end, Wu Ying gave up on shopping, the experience spoiled by those very same attempts at sales, forcing the cultivator to the only other location of interest in the tiny impromptu village.

The dueling rings.

As he came out of the main—and only—thoroughfare to the rings, Wu Ying surveyed the restaurant on his left. Two familiar auras sat in the exact same spot, drinks and snacks splayed across their table. He watched as workers carried in new furniture, while others tossed broken pieces over the railing to be taken aside for reuse or the burning pit.

Already, the pile of broken fixtures was head high, broken tables, stools, and chairs all mixed in with shattered plates and cups. The quiet banging of carpenters working swiftly to shore up weakened supports and ceilings was muffled by the wooden walls, the noise only escaping from a couple of holes where a particularly enthusiastic cultivator had shattered the exterior.

Shaking his head a little, Wu Ying ignored the destruction, pushing aside the flash of guilt deep within at what his impetuous words had wrought. Instead, he eyed the rings—three of them now active, a fourth being pushed through its testing procedures—where cultivators sparred. Next to them, in the surrounding clear field, a dozen others practiced their forms and traded spoken pointers.

Wu Ying moved to the side, taking a seat a short distance away to watch the proceedings, curious to review the styles in better light. The full range of melee martial weapons were on display, from polearms like axe-halberds, spears, and guandaos to maces, axes, butterfly swords, and the usual array of daos and jians. Only a few shield users here.

A single kingdom over, and while the weapons were familiar, the martial styles on display were not. They were, of course, similar in broad form. After all, the human body had only so many variations in movement. You could have grappling, kicking, and fist styles along with variations in weapon posture and forms; and within those styles, you had hard and soft[8] variations of the same form. Even then, the variations within soft fist styles could be significant, from those that were good and those that were just bad.

---

[8] So, "hard" and "soft" styles is a relatively new set of terminology, depicting supposedly whether a style focused on "hard" penetrating, linear, and explosive attacks or "soft" internal energy and deflections.

Bad, in this case, was not effective.

Wu Ying watched a pair of cultivators face off in the second ring, using only their unarmed martial forms. The first was a softer style, using showy, spinning kicks to keep the hard fist form fighter on the other side away. Yet even though it seemed at first glimpse that the first fighter had the worse form—large, showy, spinning kicks that rotated the fighter around and around such that his back faced his opponent nearly a quarter of the time—it was actually a decent form for an Energy Storage cultivator. Unlike the hard fist fighter whose entire body and attacks were powered by his body only, the other was able to use his elemental affinity.

Flames exploded from each kick, altering the speed and trajectory of the attacks in unpredictable ways. Minor boost to fist strikes or spinning kicks that came from the ground to reach the head; the fist fighter was barely able to block each attack. His aura control was shoddy, his ability to shield himself from the flames poor. He only had his skill at arms, his body strengthened by his form, to defend himself.

"Not very good, are they?" Gao Qiu said, arms crossed. "He should get a better style."

"It's a good style," Liu Ping said softly. "At the least, an intermediate battle style. He just needs the Energy Storage side of his manual."

"True. I wouldn't want to face it at just Body Cleansing," Wu Ying replied. "It's efficient, effective, and fast."

Gao Qiu shrugged. "It's too restrictive. There's no way to make use of an element."

"Unless it's a Metal Body form," Wu Ying said. "I've seen a style like that used by a Core Formation Elder. Did not give him much additional range, but he was extremely fast, strong, and durable."

"Elements to suit the style," Liu Ping said absently. She looked Wu Ying over and snorted. "You're looking pretty well, considering last night." She rubbed her right hip, wincing a little.

Now that she had drawn his attention to the matter, Wu Ying saw the accumulated injuries all around the dueling rings and the fields. Obviously, it wasn't everyone—the restaurant had not been of sufficient size. But a good quarter of those in sight were injured, sporting a bruise here or there, a limp or bandaged arms. Nothing major. Nothing that a cultivator with sufficient training couldn't ignore for the tournament.

But certainly annoying, nonetheless.

"I heal fast," Wu Ying replied. True enough, especially since he had a Wind Body. Even the blows he had suffered had been mitigated by his rolling with the blows.

"How amazing that is," Kong Lai said mockingly as she approached from behind them. Next to her was Shi Fei, the Crimson Flowers cultivator, sporting a broken nose which had already begun to fade from the purplish coloration. "Though I noticed you were trying to avoid us later on."

Wu Ying snorted. "I go where the flow of battle sends me." He looked between the two, noted the absence above, and continued. "And your other sect mate? The thin-skinned one?"

"We have not seen him since last night," Kong Lai admitted.

"You do not seem to care," Liu Ping said.

"He disappears on his own often. Especially in a new location," Kong Lai said with a shrug. "He finds visiting in such places—the rustic barrens outside our sect—a treat."

Wu Ying sensed the humor emanating from the trio of wandering cultivators at those words, but before he could reply, another voice cut in.

"Shen-man! Are you just here to talk? Or are you going to show us what it's like to face your blade?" the Zhuang clansman called, her spear propped on her shoulder. She pointed toward the fourth ring where testing had finished, the enchantment masters moving on to the fifth and final ring.

Wu Ying stared at the Zhuang-lady, her large triangular headdress marking her and her two sisters out. The other two ladies watched their sister's antics with a trace of long-suffering bemusement on their faces, even as everyone's attention had turned to him.

Such a direct challenge was difficult to turn down without a loss of face. Doing so, even courteously, would signal a degree of cowardice that he didn't like the implications of. After all, he did have to consider his reputation—the one thing that would, eventually, give him access back to his own Sect.

On top of that, Wu Ying had to admit a quiet, arrogant part of him wondered what he had to worry about. After all, he was a Core Formation cultivator sparring with Energy Storage cultivators. Even if he had not, as yet, fully recovered his chi levels and had yet to test his Core Formation strength, he should still be significantly stronger.

Arrogance was dangerous, but pride in justifiable abilities was part of a healthy self-image. Or so Wu Ying told himself as he found himself walking over, waving goodbye to his companions. Not that they—nor the sect cultivators—intended to leave him alone.

"Thank you for your kind invitation. I will take you up on it," Wu Ying said. "I do need to limber up, after all."

In short order, the pair had climbed into the hexagram ring, its elevated surface allowing everyone to see their actions. A force wall appeared around the edges, isolating the pair within. The two enchanters in charge of the ring got ready to take their notes.

"Now remember, Shen-man. We aren't trying to win here, just test this out for them and stretch, right?" the woman said, spinning her spear around herself with casual ease. "I don't want to beat your best just yet."

"Of course. Just a minor demonstration," Wu Ying replied. He stretched a little before pulling out his jian, the simple, unornamented weapon gleaming in the morning light. "Long Wu Ying of the State of Shen. Long family sword style."

"Pan Shui of Laiban, wielding the Pan family spear." There was a minute pause before she grinned and added, "The Flower of the Northwest Hills."

There was a gasp from the sidelines emanating from one of her sisters, but before Wu Ying could determine why, Pan Shui's spear tip dipped downward, and he focused entirely on his opponent. No time to worry about anything but the fight now.

Spears. They weren't as annoying as the three-part-staff, not as tricky as the rope-dagger, not as brutal as the dao or as powerful as the guandao. However, they were considered a master's weapon due to their flexibility, their reach advantage, and the speed they offered.

In other words, they were a pain to fight.

Within the first few clashes, Wu Ying was certain of one thing. His opponent had at least the Sense of her Spear. She was fast, gifted in her movements, and crafty with her techniques. The weapon wove an impenetrable defense, flicking constantly from angle to angle to block Wu Ying's advance. Each time he stepped within range, it threatened a vital spot, and even when he managed to get past the tip, both sweeping blows from the shaft and spiraling, shortened grips allowed the tip to come back in line.

Wu Ying retreated after the first few flourishing exchanges, his movements restricted to the first form of the Long family style. It required no energy projection and was suitable for Body Cleansing cultivators. It was, however, very basic in form—not a showy style at all, with only a few feints woven into the methodology itself.

"Sense of the Sword. Not bad… but if that is all you have, you are a thousand years too soon to challenge us!" Pan Shui crowed, resetting her guard. The tip of the spear pointed toward Wu Ying's eyes. A moment later, her aura sharpened, encompassing her spear entirely as she infused energy into it. Pearl-white light formed around the edges of her aura, flickering a little before it sharpened, ringing her in a hazy outline. "You best get ready!"

"You talk like a failed opera[9] actress."

Even if he did return her taunts, Wu Ying wrapped his own aura around his blade, infusing the edges with the swirling gusts that made up his wind-chi oriented skills. Dropping a little lower into his guard, he was nearly caught by surprise when she lunged.

Fast!

The spearhead nearly punched past his guard. Only a last-minute block and sway shifted the tip from its target of his cheek to miss him by inches. Already, she was sweeping the weapon sideways and downward, forcing Wu Ying to crouch even lower and duck underneath and around the attack. By the time he rose, the weapon was on its return journey, targeted for his chest this time.

No further time to think, Wu Ying wove his favorite defense—Dragon paints the Sunset—all around himself. He flowed around each attack, combining the movement techniques he had studied to open the distance and give himself some space. Even so, even as a Wind Body with unparalleled speed and flexibility, she was keeping up with him, forcing him to the very edges of the formation.

Heart of the Spear. She had to have it. Each movement was perfectly in tune with one another, the momentum of each attack never lost entirely, transitions perfectly flowing from

---

[9] Chinese opera that is, which has a long tradition. Of course, since it's opera, the question is whether she's not bombastic enough or not convincing enough at being over the top.

one motion to another. Even his own blocks were taken into account, such that she shaved a hairsbreadth from every motion.

And in a fight, especially with a spear, small gains on her end meant the tip moved by an entire cun each time, forcing Wu Ying to take more desperate evasions. As his foot hit the edge of the barrier, another spear thrust came at him. This one would be too short, but he sensed her already gathering energy to extend the tip.

Rather than wait, Wu Ying flooded his aura with the Heavenly Soul, Earthly Body energy projection technique. It lightened his body, and he used it to allow him to run backward and up the barrier a little before exploding forward into a flying thrust.

For the first time, Pan Shui looked surprised, though her hands never stopped moving, thrusting the entire shaft upward. Wu Ying's open palm landed upon the spear's body, using the weapon's momentum to change his own as he was flung across the arena to land on his feet on the opposite end. Spinning about, he brought his weapon back to guard, surprised a little to find himself grinning at his opponent, who had turned around too.

"So, you've got some skill…" Pan Shui said, smirking. "Come. Let this big sister[10] see how good you really are."

Out of the corner of his eyes and through his spiritual sense, Wu Ying saw Pan Shui's two sisters visibly cringe at those words. Still, he could not help but grin and raise his sword in answer.

This would be fun.

***

Nearly an hour later, the pair broke apart, the call from the enchanters interrupting their match. Wu Ying was breathing a little heavily, a grin flickering across his face as he lowered his weapon. Pan Shui's spear dipped as well, then she swung it around to put it over her shoulder, her aura diminishing as she cracked her neck from side to side.

"Thank you for your instruction, Expert Pan," Wu Ying repeated the ritual words, though there was a trace of true gratitude in his voice.

The hour of sparring had clarified something within him, the difference between those with just the Sense of a weapon and its Heart. Even if he had fought others with that ability— his late Master Cheng among them—it had been the difference between weapons perhaps that made the true comparison even more stark.

Again and again, he had flirted with understanding and enlightenment. Yet the curve between Sense of the Sword and Heart rose drastically, for one was but a matter of physicality. Practice with sufficient weapons and anyone could gain the Sense of the Sword. Or so it had been explained by his father—though Wu Ying had begun to doubt even that explanation.

---

[10] Yes, she's younger. This is an insult where she is putting him beneath her by calling herself his big sister.

On the other hand, the Heart—understanding of a weapon and its very nature, its dao—was something that few could grasp. Wu Ying had achieved brief glimpses of parts of it, the nature of cutting and sharpness, the speed and weight of a jian as it moved through the air. All of it in portions, but never once had he managed to touch the true heart of his preferred weapon.

It was the same here. He had, once more, glimpsed what it meant to be flexible, to change purpose with each step, each variation of form.

The spear exemplified that, but a jian could be more than a stabbing weapon or one meant to cut via its tip. You could use the hilt to help wrap around a blade or spear shaft, pommel strike and drive the guard into pressure points. Its blade could bend and twist around attacks, turning the tip into a deadly whip, or cut into a spear shaft, slowly whittling away its durability.

More than the weapon though, Wu Ying could be more flexible. Restricting himself to only the first few forms of the Long family style had had the added benefit of making him improvise and string together movements from different forms to aid him in dodging her attacks.

Flexibility and oneness with the weapon, positioning and angles that he had never tried before for each of his attacks had opened new vistas in his mind. Sometimes, to go forward, you had to retreat.

In a true battle, one could not experiment—not without risking death. Here, in a friendly sparring match, Wu Ying could test new theories, attempt strikes, and struggle to generate power and speed from angles—low to the floor, around his back, as he skipped through the air—that he had never attempted before.

It was, after all, the reason one sparred.

"Thank you for the bout, Expert Long," Pan Shui replied. "It's a pity you're only that gifted though. If you were a little better, this would have been more interesting."

Wu Ying's eyes narrowed at her boasting, but he had to admit, he had only been able to keep up with her because of his increased speed and flexibility. The combination of a Wind Body, the various movement skills he had studied, and the flexibility of the Long family style meant that he had been able to dodge and parry her blows, even if she was more skilled. Doing that without giving away all that he could do had been rather a challenge.

Now that the barrier was down, Wu Ying descended the ring, his good cheer at having come closer to understanding the Heart of his weapon returning. It did not hurt at all that Pan Shui's sisters accosted her the moment she had descended too, with the oldest sister grabbing hold of a cheek and squeezing it tightly, tugging along the formerly arrogant woman.

The wind helpfully came along, carrying the whispered words to Wu Ying. "You dare use my title in front of everyone! And you showed off too much of our family style. You begged us for the chance to test out the rings, but then see what you have done!"

Then his good humor disappeared as the two sect cultivators pushed past Gao Qiu and his friends—who were offering praises—and bowed to Wu Ying in greeting with clasped hands. Automatically, he returned the greetings, wondering about the sudden formality.

"Expert Long, our Masters have requested your presence at their table," Shi Fei said.

Beside him, Kong Lai could not hide her dissatisfaction, but she did keep her mouth shut.

"I see," Wu Ying said, a little flash of worry running through him. Then he reminded himself that in cultivation levels at least, he was technically of equal status—or close enough. Not actual strength, of course. Not yet at least. "I will be honored to visit them."

Bowing again, Shi Fei waved Wu Ying to lead the way, with the pair following him as the group ascended to the restaurant table where the pair of Elders continued to watch over the proceedings. Wu Ying felt the gazes of the other cultivators on him, their renewed interest.

Upstairs, by their table, Wu Ying bowed to the pair of Elders. He offered them his usual greeting in this kingdom, skipping the use of his sect at the moment.

"Please, sit. I am Elder Tsui Long of the Crimson Flowers sect, and this is my companion, Elder Eng Xiang of the Mountain Fast sect." So saying, Elder Tsui poured Wu Ying a cup of tea and served it to him himself.

Wu Ying hastily took the cup, surprise registering on his face as Elder Tsui dismissed the other cultivators. When the three of them were alone, Elder Tsui then touched a small carved stone hut that had been placed on the table.

Upon its activation, Wu Ying sensed the chi that spread from the enchantment, powered by a Spirit Stone embedded within the enchanted hut itself, that formed a privacy screen. The world outside the simple screen of energy grew muted; sight, sound, and even the breeze that brought with it scents and knowledge of the world outside faded away. Even using a pre-made object like this, Wu Ying sensed Elder Tsui was manipulating the threads in a way that indicated his own mastery of formations.

For a moment, Wu Ying could not help but frown a little before dismissing his concerns that this was a trap. Too public, for one thing.

"Some discussions are unnecessary for our juniors to listen to," Elder Eng said. "After all, us seniors must have our secrets, no?"

"Us seniors?" Wu Ying repeated.

"You hide it well, but you are new to your state. And weak as your new cultivation base might be, it is not entirely hidden," Elder Eng said. "Not to those of us who can see the signs."

"Now, don't be rude to our junior, Ah Eng. We wouldn't have noticed it at all if he had not chosen to take part in that little demonstration," Elder Tsui said. "Your aura control is very advanced, for one as young as you. But even a genius requires time to consolidate his gains."

Wu Ying bowed a little at the light rebuke. "The Elders are truly generous. I am no genius. Just an individual who has been lucky on his road to cultivation."

"Hah! Lucky. The way your Core feels, you rushed ahead too fast," Elder Eng said derisively.

Wu Ying felt sudden pressure as the other man turned his spiritual senses and aura entirely upon Wu Ying, probing him without courtesy. Keeping his face smooth, Wu Ying tightened his aura and protection around himself, refusing to let the man learn more of his secrets. The swirling, twisting defense that was Wu Ying's aura barrier redirected the energy of Elder Eng's probe, shedding the energy as it sought to penetrate. The pressure kept mounting as the other cultivator, rebuffed on his first attempt, exerted even more strength.

Wu Ying's fingers tightened against his teacup a little, even as he returned Elder Eng's smirking gaze with his own, slowly angering one. Again and again, the energy pushed at Wu Ying, trying to find a gap in his defenses.

"Tell me, Elder Eng, is this the way that Elders are greeted in this kingdom?" Wu Ying said, doing his best to keep his voice serene.

"This is just a little test between friends. Surely Expert Long does not begrudge a small trial like this? After all, such matters are important for our understanding of one another."

At the end of his words, the Elder sent another wave of energy. Focused as he was, Wu Ying found himself shattering the teacup in his hand as the pressure exerted on his aura doubled.

Rather than meet the greater strength of the man before him—and refusing to tap into the Core energy within him—Wu Ying chose to allow Elder Eng's spiritual sense and aura to partly penetrate his own. The whirling tornadoes and gusts of his wind chi parted, energy seeping within to touch skin.

However, for each hairsbreadth that it entered, Wu Ying wore away at the energy, like a furious headwind bearing down on Elder Eng's exploratory craft of senses. It battered and slowed the initial impetus, driving it aside and refusing to allow the Elder to penetrate too deeply into Wu Ying's body. Certainly nowhere near his dantian.

"Wind Body and a wind aspect. How unusual," Elder Eng said.

As suddenly as the pressure had formed, it disappeared.

Only then did Elder Tsui speak. "Ah Eng, really, how rude. This is not how we deal with guests." The Elder shook his head, smiling at Wu Ying as though he had not purposely waited to speak up. "But your words and the fact that Expert Long here is a gatherer…"

Wu Ying's eyes narrowed at the casual mention of his occupation. It seemed they had done some investigating while he had been busy. Either last night or while he was dueling.

"It makes me recall some stories," Elder Tsui said. "Of a green-clad wild gatherer who did much in the State of Shen during the war. The Verdant Gatherer, was it not his name?"

"It was."

"But he was an Energy Storage cultivator, at least as of spring this year," Elder Tsui said. "And young too…"

Wu Ying sighed internally, realizing his attempts at being quiet about his background had failed. Being just another kingdom away, it seemed that the jianghu rumor mill was hard at work.

"That is a title I have been given," Wu Ying said. "And the Elders are right, I have only recently ascended."

"Rushing. Foolish," Elder Eng said, tutting a little before he waved as if dismissing the matter. Still, his voice continued to be disapproving. "It does not behoove one of our standing to win tournaments meant for those of lesser strength."

"There are no rules against my participation. Or so I have been informed," Wu Ying replied, keeping his voice light. "Surely, if what I have been told is the true goal of such tournaments, the presence of one of our standing would be beneficial."

"Only if you intend to marry into their family," Elder Eng said. "And I do not believe that is your goal, is it?"

Wu Ying shook his head, acknowledging the point.

"Then do not spoil the rankings for those of lesser strength than you," Elder Eng said reprovingly. "It is ill done, to bully your juniors."

Wu Ying snorted. "As you said, I am of the same age—"

"But not experiences," Elder Tsui cut in. "I have long said that those who have partaken in calamitous times like the wars your kingdom has experienced grow faster than those of us in our safe and stable pockets of civilization."

"It's not been that peaceful," Elder Eng muttered. "The uprisings—"

"Are dealt with by the kingdom, not us."

Cutting in, Wu Ying pointed out. "There is not much safe in the untamed wilderness, Elders."

"Perhaps. But conflict draws forth great strength from many," Elder Tsui said. "Whereas our own cultivators can only see conflict amongst the army or in such bloodless tournaments." He gestured down to where groups of fighters still struggled in the rings.

Wu Ying cast his gaze their way and he could not help but agree. The styles shown, both beginner or intermediate battle techniques, movement forms, and energy projection—it was all showy, as was the goal. Even so, it lacked an edge that Wu Ying had long grown used to among his peers.

A frisson in the fight and a focused intensity that his companions and those they had trained with bore. It came from the knowledge that all too soon, the techniques they studied would be needed in a life and death battle, that those who trained and failed would die on the battlefield. And even those who trained and succeeded might still fall.

The experiences of shedding blood amidst bloody fields and assassination attempts had given even their sparring matches an edge that those below lacked.

"Perhaps it is best that Cultivator Long has chosen to join. He can show our cultivators what they lack," Elder Tsui replied.

"Hah! If they lack understanding, that is the fault of the teacher, not the environment," Elder Eng said. "It is still unbecoming to take prizes away from those who could use them. An elder should not scrabble for colored stones in the dirt as though they were pearls."

Wu Ying took a moment to sip on his tea, studying Elder Eng and considering his motivations. Truth be told, the prizes—a bunch of pills meant for Energy Storage cultivators, a Spirit-level weapon and armor—held little interest to him. He had weapons that were stronger, armor of the same quality, and more pills leftover from his rescue. All of which did little for him in his current cultivation stage.

On the other hand, his most recent duel had been enlightening. More matches, in an environment of discovery and without the pressure of a life and death battle, might see him increase his comprehension of the jian. To set that aside because an Elder might wish for his own disciple to shine set ill with Wu Ying.

"I will take your words under advisement, Elder Eng." Wu Ying finally chose to make a neutral statement. He still had time and withdrawing even in the midst of the tournament was not impossible.

"Hmmphff."

Elder Tsui shook his head, dropping the sunflower seed he had been chewing upon on the empty table. He chose to change the topic. "Do you intend to continue your old occupation?"

Wu Ying nodded.

"Good. Then there are a number of items my sect might be interested in." Elder Tsui smiled wider, then hastened to add, when he noticed Wu Ying opening his mouth, "Of course, we cannot buy it from you, but for a suitable… visitor gift… certain benefits could be provided. Access to our sect library, for example."

Wu Ying kept himself from smirking. It made sense that the sects would find a way around the kingdom's restrictions. Trading or allowing access to cultivation libraries and exercises was important. And certainly something that Wu Ying required now that he had ascended to his new cultivation stage.

"This one would be grateful for any guidance my seniors might be able to provide," Wu Ying said.

Smiling, the pair of Elders spoke of the kinds of herbs and cores they might need. Wu Ying leaned back, paying careful attention. Sometimes, he wished other cultivators were just more upfront about what they wanted. The entire thing could have been avoided if they'd just asked him.

Even so, at least he had a lead and a greater understanding of the cultivation world in the kingdom. Now, he just had to make full use of his knowledge to his benefit.

Chapter 12

Conversation with the Elders lasted for just over twenty minutes, complete with the passing of a pair of documents detailing the kind of needs he might be able to supply. The fact that they had such documents spoke to prior preparation, a fact that made him sigh a little mentally. It was rather frustrating to find that all his attempts at being low profile had failed.

Perhaps he could try that again later, in another city or kingdom.

Perhaps.

Their talk, meandering to a general discussion about the sects, was interrupted by the presence of the two sect members and a third, hazy presence. It wasn't one Wu Ying had met as yet, and so he had trouble placing it through the interference of the privacy screen. Still, all three Core Formation cultivators within the screen could sense the agitation exhibited by those outside.

A single wave of Elder Tsui's hand disarmed the enchantment, leaving the Crimson Flowers elder to speak to those awaiting their attention. "What ails you?"

"Death and treachery!" Shi Fei spat out, then catching himself, did a clasped hand bow to his sect Elder. "My apologies, Elder Tsui."

"What do you mean by that, Cultivator Shi?" Elder Tsui asked, eyes narrowed.

Wu Ying sensed as Elder Tsui extended his aura, covering the building and the surroundings as he searched for danger. Elder Eng proceeded to do the same, while Wu Ying took a more subtle route, beckoning the winds to come to him with answers.

"Cui Wen's body has been found. Slain, last night!" Shi Fei said. "A blade was plunged into his back like a coward, his throat slit!"

The words stilled the restaurant, the patrons who had come for lunch freezing. The atmosphere grew tense and chilly as cultivators stared at one another, searching for the murderer. None of those here were innocent in the shedding of blood, after all.

"I asked that you allow me to speak with your Elder directly, Cultivator Shi." The third member of the group spoke up, drawing all their attention. "My apologies, Elder Eng."

Wu Ying turned his head to pay further attention to the most recent speaker, taking in the armor and helmet that the man wore, more to mark his position than in any hope of true protection against chi-enhanced attacks. Black and grey coated lamellar plates, the single handheld crossbow and its half dozen bolts, along with the thick, heavy soldier's sword was all indicative of the individual's position.

Curiously, Elder Eng had frozen, growing as still as the mountain his sect was named from. He sat there, his face impassive to the naked eye. But beneath that, Wu Ying felt the churn of slow-moving earth chi spreading out inexorably in all directions, like a landslide growing in speed as it fell.

A few of the more sensitive cultivators were looking at the Elder, an inkling of what was to come appearing on their faces.

"And you are?" Wu Ying could not help but ask the guardsman, hoping to gain an understanding of the ground he stood upon.

"Teng Fei, Senior Guard Captain for the Seven Pavilions," Teng Fei replied, tapping his chest in a salute. "I am honored to meet you, Cultivator Long."

Wu Ying greeted the other, only mildly curious that the other knew his name. It was not entirely surprising—Teng Fei had probably memorized the names of all the contestants. Even if there were fifty individuals, it would not be a hard task for an early level Energy Storage cultivator like Teng Fei. Especially when it was his job. Or Wu Ying assumed that was what had happened. It certainly would be what he would do if he was the guard captain.

Even as they spoke, Wu Ying rode the chi flowing outward from Elder Eng, hiding his own search underneath the man's output. Subtly as he was doing it, the Western Wind was the first to return to him, bringing with it the stench of old blood and released bowels. The all too familiar smell of death, though the beginnings of rot had yet to fully set in.

"Where did you find the body?" Elder Eng asked, his voice a low rumble of impending doom.

"To the west, Honored Elder. The body was found by some mortals, hidden in a drainage ditch amongst our fields."

Elder Eng stood, his movements swift and implacable. He stepped away from the table then leapt lightly onto the banister before leaping into the air. A second later, to the astonishment of many of the wandering cultivators, he shot out from under the restaurant patio on a podao.

The weapon was differentiated from the more iconic guandao due to its featureless clip point blade that extended a good two feet from the end of the polearm. No ornate carvings on the blade, though Wu Ying could tell this was no simple Spirit-tier weapon. The coloration of its blade, the luster of the wood spoke of something chi-infused to bring it up a tier. Or two.

Then Elder Eng was gone, carried westward.

"My apologies, Captain Teng. My companion can be impetuous at times," Elder Tsui murmured. "But the death of his disciple is a shock. Especially in a tournament that was meant to be friendly."

"My masters offer their utmost apologies for this breach of security and make assurances that we will do everything within our power to find the culprit," Teng Fei replied.

Wu Ying had to admire how calm the man was, what with facing down Core Formation cultivators and offering them bad news. Even though Wu Ying smelled the acrid stench of fear, the cold sweat from acting as the face of a failed organization pouring down hidden beneath his armor, Teng Fei still put on a polite, contrite face. One that was not quaking in fear outwardly, even if he was in truth.

"They have also invited yourself and Elder Eng to dinner in their compound this night, to speak upon this matter in more detail."

Elder Tsui sighed, finished his cup of tea, and left a couple of silver taels as payment as he stood. "Very well. It is best that we see to Elder Eng as well. Lead the way, Captain Teng."

Bowing, Teng Fei stepped back and turned, leading the slow-moving Elder Tsui down the stairs along with the remaining two inner sect cultivators.

Of the two, it was no surprise that Kong Lai was the most shaken, biting her lip and wringing her hands, a slight redness to her eyes speaking of unshed tears. At the same time, Shi Fei steamed, throwing accusing glances at everyone, searching for the culprit and daring them to show themselves.

Wu Ying, left alone at the table, hesitated. Eventually, he pushed himself to his feet and followed the group, his actions the first drop in the flood as the other cultivators in the restaurant quickly paid and followed.

After all, a crime scene and murder was good entertainment. Even more than the dueling cultivators below.

***

The body was covered with heaps of earth, the rich loamy soil a stark contrast—to Wu Ying's eyes—from the topsoil that covered the rest of the ditch. It was no surprise the farmers had spotted the difference when they walked by. The unusual mound and difference in coloration was as good as a floating lantern on a moonless night to them.

A small cordon of guards stood around the field, keeping the curious away from the body. They were about twenty feet out, the group of cultivators and passersby having carelessly tramped across growing fields from all directions to view the growing scene of interest.

Wu Ying had, of course, taken the time to move along the proper paths, not wishing to damage the remaining late-autumn crops. It was a good thing the majority had been extracted, only root plants to help contain soil and a few late harvests left. Even so, taking a longer route or not, the swiftly moving cultivator had managed to catch up with the lead group as they arrived at the scene.

Elder Eng stood over the corpse, unmoving but for a single clenched fist that trembled. He stared at the body, still covered by earth except for his face and one foot, expensive silk stained by pitiful soil. He was listening to the guardswoman nearby, the older lady murmuring explanations of the events leading up to their present circumstances. A short distance away, a shivering mortal farmer stood, ashen faced as he awaited judgment.

Even with the crowd kept back, Wu Ying noted all too many footprints leading to and from the body. Some were easily identified as those of the hard-soled boots of the guards, more used to walking on cobblestones and paved streets and courtyards than the softer earth. The soft-soled leather shoes of the farmers left less of an imprint, but still deep. Those were careful about their movements, staying to the pathways already manufactured.

Yet those were not the only footprints. He saw at least another handful of footprints from soft-soled shoes common to farmers and cultivators alike that crossed turned earth and ended near the edge of the canal, some sinking deep before turning back. Those, Wu Ying had to assume, were the work of curious cultivators who had arrived before the guards.

All of which meant, to Wu Ying, that there was little to be learned from watching the ground. He was no hunter, able to ascertain the depth and variance of all these footprints, some crossing over one another. No, he was a cultivator.

A wind cultivator.

It was of the wind that he asked his questions, having it swirl across the ground gently and carry lingering scents to him. He breathed it all in, sifting through them as he filtered remnant chi exuded from uncontrolled auras of those already present.

Fire and Metal in the air, lingering traces of cultivators. Deep, dense Earth from Elder Eng and the very field itself. Wood, crumbling and decaying as fall turned to winter and the trees grew quiescent as they conserved energy to spring forth in spring. Water, always present as carried by the wind and sky, but burnt away by the earlier traces of fire.

More importantly, the smells. Jasmine and chrysanthemum, incense, and other flower scents held aloft on droplets of oil. Dried blood, old and dark and mixed with earth, was carried from the breeze rushing along the canal edge, the hint of excrement from loosened bowels lost in the overpowering release of earth chi that the dead cultivator had released.

"We believe whoever killed him did so by surprise," Guard Captain Teng Fei murmured to Elder Tsui, indicating the body. "We are looking for the initial location of death, for the body, we believe, was brought here afterward."

"And his talisman?" the Elder murmured.

"Missing."

Wu Ying cocked his head, considering the words. Then, out of curiosity, he called for the wind, whispering his request. It helped that he had some minor elemental affinity to blood itself. By spreading his aura outward gently and beckoning the winds to work for him, it could bring traces of such chi to him.

He did not push it though, only allowing it to work passively. Perhaps he would find the location in time. Perhaps, as the guardsman had noted, it might be a little more difficult. After all, there were a number of mortals here whose regular work left minor cuts and wounds upon them, women whose time of month had arrived, and training bouts and practices which left individuals injured. Sorting life's regular mishaps with a fatal blow spreading lifeblood would be difficult.

Well, unless the killer was a fool and had left behind a large pool of blood.

"When will you be finished with your investigations?" Elder Eng rumbled, staring at the woman who had been explaining things to him. "This spectacle is unacceptable."

"I just need a few more hours," she said, tilting up her head. "It would help if all of you stopped coming here, making it harder for me to take measurements and notes."

"What use are notes? My disciple is dead!" snapped Elder Eng.

"Elder," Teng Fei hurried forward, only to receive a disapproving look from the woman. "Guardsman Investigator Chu studied under the Magistrate Di[11]."

Elder Eng paused, cocking his head to properly review Guardsman Chu. His gaze raked over the woman and the scroll clutched in her hand. To Wu Ying's surprise, the heat in his gaze died a little.

"Very well. Then we will allow the Guardsman to do her job."

Elder Eng looked around, and Wu Ying only had a second to brace himself before the Elder shoved with his chi. A single wave of energy pulsed outward from the man, one that caught the surrounding cultivators and shoved them back tens of feet. Rather than oppose it, Wu Ying let himself be carried away, floating on the pulse of power to land on his feet, unlike many others who fell or tumbled across the ground.

"You will leave the Guardsman alone and pay proper respects to the fallen," rumbled Elder Eng. "Any who fail to do so will answer to me directly."

His words, as hard as the bones of the mountain themselves, carried across the empty field. For a long moment, Elder Eng waited to see if any would object, and when all wisely did not, he jumped again. His flying weapon, the podao, floating on his back slipped beneath his feet, carrying the Elder away.

In the center of the circle, only three individuals now stood: the two guardsmen and Elder Tsui. The Guard Captain and Guardsman Chu looked a little shaken, even if they had been left out of Elder Eng's aura assault. Only Elder Tsui looked untouched.

Being one of the few still on his feet, Wu Ying drew attention from Teng Fei, who stared at him for a second. Wu Ying bowed his head in acknowledgment, though he made no move to go closer. He could have, but that would have attracted even more attention.

He still had some vague hope of being somewhat low profile.

Turning from Wu Ying, Teng Fei lowered his voice as he stepped closer to Guardsman Chu. "Get this done quickly. Then report back to me. We must make sure the body is returned to the Elder as quickly as possible."

"I want to look at the wounds more closely," Guardsman Chu murmured.

"For what?"

---

[11] So, this is a side reference to both a real and fictional individual. Real as in, the fictional portrayal is based off Di Renjei (formally Duke Wenhui of Lian) who was an official during the Tang and Zhou dynasties. He was highly respected as an individual, but these days is better known due to the detective novels written by Butizhuanren in the 18th century. He then became the infamous Detective or Judge Dee / Di and is one of the more enduring detective characters in Chinese fiction, in some ways analogous to Sherlock Holmes or Hercules Poirot.

And yes, I'm purposely mixing up timeline and chronologies to randomly throw in cool characters. This isn't actually China after all. :P

"To check the width of the blade that stabbed him, to verify the angle of the cut." She bent over to point at the body. "It looks like a typical jian, about an inch and a half thick. And the angle of the cut, it's a right-hander. See how it slopes, from the rise as they fall?"

Teng Fei nodded. "Could they not have switched hands? Or thrown a reverse cut?"

"Mmm… no, you can see the way the flesh is parted. It's definitely a left side, falling cut." A shrug. "Unless they are purposely attempting to obscure their attacks—and few think to do so—we are looking at a right-handed cultivator of around the victim's height."

"Why the height?" Elder Tsui asked.

"The Elder must know, from experience. Depending on the difference in height among opponents, a blow will twist or have to be angled differently when sparring?"

Elder Tsui nodded at the Guardsman's words.

"Well, Magistrate Di made us study the corpses of many bodies to understand how heights change the angle of attack. I will have to take full measurements later, but from what I have already seen, my estimates should be about correct."

"Fascinating." Elder Tsui ran a hand over his balding head. "The study of wounds and dead bodies. It seems… unclean to me."

"Only if one were doing it for their own pleasure," Guardsman Chu's voice grew frosty, her chin rising a little. "We study to bring justice to those slain." Her voice lowered, and she added, "Such victims are more common among the general populace, Honored Elder. Cultivators, in general, fight their battles directly."

There were nods from both Teng Fei and Elder Tsui at that. Even Wu Ying could not help but agree. He sensed the other cultivators around him moving away. Many were muttering about what they had seen, about the potential dangers to themselves and the high-handed way the Elder had acted. Those he dismissed, though he did try to listen for any further gossip about the late Cui Wen.

Just as quietly, Wu Ying was also questing for further scents. The familiar, burnt tarred sand smells of damaged cultivation bases, of hints about a Dark Sect cultivator or one who had devoted themselves to a Demon Sect. He knew, all too well, what those smelled like— and how well they could hide too.

Nor did he forget that he was still a target for those he had thwarted in the State of Wei.

"Thank you. I wish to be kept informed about anything further that you learn," Elder Tsui rumbled, getting a nod from both guardsmen.

Seeing that most of the other cultivators had moved away, Wu Ying chose to leave too. There was little else he could gather, though he absently considered looking into the reports. As he took his time walking back to the now subdued village, he weighed curiosity, his own safety, and the likelihood of making himself a target. After all, as a newcomer, he was both outside of whatever politics might have caused Cui Wen's death and also an immediate suspect.

As he reached the edges of the village, Wu Ying made up his mind.

For now, he would keep his curiosity contained and watch for changes. If he was to be targeted, he would not be caught unawares. But he would not involve himself in the kingdom's affairs if possible.

Chapter 13

They found Wu Ying in his room that evening. Training and the duels had continued but at a more subdued pace. At times, for stretches that included even hours, some of the rings lay completely untouched as cultivators gathered and gossiped. The restaurants and living rooms were filled, voices hushed as they speculated about the death.

At first, Wu Ying had joined in the meals and speculation, speaking with one group or another, introducing himself and listening more than talking. It soon wore on him though, the attitudes and words being tossed about, so he had left for the rooftops. Jealousy, paranoia, and baseless speculation turning into ugly rumors were not conversational pieces Wu Ying chose to indulge in.

To his surprise, he found himself not the only individual lounging on the clay roofs, silently watching those below or, in a couple of places, practicing their qinggong techniques. He noticed the Pan sisters seated on their residence's rooftop, murmuring to one another. Pan Shui even waved at him, a greeting he returned though he chose not to approach them.

Instead, he lay on the rooftop, allowing the wind to bring with it snatches of conversation and the scents of those below, allowing him to map the world around him. Whispered conversations of Cui Wen and where he had been after the tavern battle, a mental map of sightings—at times contradictory.

"Outside, at the dueling rings. I swear, I saw him with another cultivator. The big, hairy one from the Dan county; the one who wields that oar?… Doing? Well, their shirts were off and there was… grappling… no, of course the barriers weren't activated!"

"Stalked out of the restaurant, nursing his chest. I tell you, it was that Shen cultivator who killed him. He uses a jian too. And you saw how they fought."

"Stabbed in the back. His skin was green around the wound. Poison, I know it by sight! Just like the Fu brothers…"

"He was talking with that other Elder, the Crimson Flowers one. Late at night, on the rooftop I tell you…"

"Saw him sneaking around in the back alleys, watching three cultivators. I swear, I think he was following them…"

So many conversations, so much contradicting information. Rumors, born of mischief or conjecture, of fractured memories.

Wu Ying listened, though he asked the wind for more concrete information. It supplied it, notes of blood and spilled food. Too much, for these were wandering cultivators and they all had fought. Some failed to clean their weapons well, leaving lingering traces in sheathes and blades. Others bled and hurt from the fight beforehand.

And not once did he find the location of where the attack had happened. Whoever had slain Cui Wen had washed the blood away, cleaning earth or pavement and hiding it from all.

The day passed in that way, long hours of speculation and random fights as tensions rose. A few cultivators took to the roads, choosing to leave—only to be turned back by guards at the perimeter of the land.

That brought another round of discussion and rumor, with a small altercation quickly stymied by the sudden entrance of Elder Eng and his stern disapproval. Wu Ying noted the shift in the aura of the Core Formation Elder in the compound, that very same beacon that had sat, unmoving ever since his arrival. A presence that had begun to stir before Elder Eng subdued the wandering cultivators himself.

Evening came and Wu Ying retired to his quarters, no more knowledgeable about what had transpired but as troubled as any other cultivator.

That was when they found him, of course.

***

"Thank you for speaking with us, Cultivator Long."

Guard Captain Teng Fei and Investigator Chu were the only two individuals in the small room they had set aside for this discussion. A single room, bereft of anything but the table, three chairs that they occupied, and a tea set. Of course, Wu Ying could sense *him* there. Behind the wall, listening, watching, judging. Unseen, but his presence as clear as a candle in a dark room.

"Not at all. Your work must be difficult with so many of us here," Wu Ying answered.

Certainly, his only experience—outside of a few novels and stories—with a murder investigation had been a killing when he was a child. Enraged wife found her husband in bed with his sister and had proceeded to murder him. Not exactly a difficult case.

"Cultivators do present a unique challenge," Guardsman Chu said, though her eyes gleamed with excitement. Her hands were poised over a scroll, ready to write whatever was spoken.

Wu Ying idly considered the woman, testing her aura. Rank mortal, not even a single meridian open. Not that he needed to actually use his spiritual sense to know that, what with the slight lines across her eyes, the pimple at the edge of her hairline. Things a Body Cleansing cultivator would have cleared except in the most severe of cases.

"Have you undertaken many cases involving cultivators?" Wu Ying asked.

Teng Fei leaned forward, cutting her off before she could answer. "Honored expert, if you don't mind, we have many such interviews to conduct. If we could perhaps focus on that...?"

Wu Ying nodded.

"Then perhaps you could tell us of your interactions with Cultivator Cui," Teng Fei said.

Relating the experience of last night was simple enough. He abbreviated the fight itself, ending with, "And after things calmed down, I left for my room. I had some travel rations left over and supped on that, after which I cultivated and rested in my room until this morning."

"And you did not leave your room after you entered it?" Teng Fei asked.

Wu Ying shook his head.

"Did anyone see you return to your room? And when, roughly, did you do so? Did you ask the servants for some tea, or a washcloth, or otherwise interact with any others?"

After each question, Wu Ying answered in the negative before the next question was asked.

"I see. And the next morning…?"

Wu Ying related the remainder of his actions when he awoke, from a simple stretching routine after cleansing himself to having breakfast and then shopping. As he remarked upon each of these instances, Guardsman Chu wrote it all down.

"Thank you," Teng Fei said, leaning backward once Wu Ying was done. "That was very helpful."

"You are welcome." Wu Ying sipped from his teacup. He cocked his head, feeling a minor fluctuation in the environmental chi. He had sensed that before in the Sect, though not often. Spiritual Speech, like any cultivation technique, had to be trained.

Interesting that the Core Formation cultivator hiding in the other room knew it.

"This might be an impertinent question…" Wu Ying nodded for the guard captain to go on. "But you antagonized Cui Wen at the restaurant."

Another nod.

"Is there perhaps some hidden animosity?"

Wu Ying's eyes narrowed. He was not dumb. He knew he was a suspect, and perhaps telling the truth was not the best option. But then again, not answering might result in a fight or further suspicion. So, truth for now.

"Cui Wen annoyed me with his arrogance," Wu Ying said. Then, guessing that Teng Fei had probably learned it by now, and if not, knowing it would come out, he added, "You know of my true sect affiliation?"

"The Verdant Green Waters."

"Yes," Wu Ying said.

"However, you are not wearing their robes. Nor did you announce your affiliation on registration," Teng Fei said. "Not doing so can lead to… incidents."

"Like the one we had?" A half smile on Wu Ying's face as he waved his hand. "I am somewhat in disgrace with my sect. An issue with a recent expedition. I had hoped to travel for a while without bringing them into matters."

Guardsman Chu looked a little confused, though she smoothed out her face when she noticed Wu Ying watching her.

Teng Fei, on the other hand, had a much better political mien. "Of course. I would not look to pry into your personal business, honored expert." He paused. "Beyond the bounds of my duty, of course."

"Of course."

"But you took offense to what Cui Wen and the others said to you then? Could you not have explained matters instead of antagonizing him?"

Wu Ying considered his words, going over the night in his head once more. There was much truth to what Teng Fei had said. He had chosen the most aggressive route with Cui Wen. But...

"Even wandering cultivators should not need to bow their heads to arrogant sect members. Skill and dao enlightenment are all that matters. I decided that it was worthwhile to teach Cui Wen that."

Teng Fei rubbed at his face. "Of course."

On the other side of the wall, Wu Ying felt a slight shift in the aura around the hidden cultivator, which he could only characterize as approval. He chose not to say anything though, especially when Teng Fei returned to questioning him. Going over his statement in detail, varying his questions, and jumping around the timeline. Seeking to catch him out in a lie.

Wu Ying turned his focus fully on the Guard Captain. For now. He would find out about the hidden expert later.

***

"So, they questioned you too, eh?" Pan Shui called to Wu Ying as he ascended the stairs to their floor.

He turned, a little surprised she was talking to him. Not that he had not spotted her downstairs, but she had been speaking with her sisters when he passed by.

"Too? I assume then they spoke with you and your sisters?" he replied.

"Aye. They didn't like us saying our witnesses were each other though." She smirked before she shrugged. "But the woman guardsman, the investigator, she did agree our spears wouldn't have caused those wounds."

"You could have switched to a sword," Wu Ying said, tapping his own storage ring. "I'm sure I'm not the only one who collects weapons of multiple forms."

"Hah!" Pan Shui let out a little, raucous laugh. "Too true. Her Captain chided her for answering me and said the same." Then she narrowed her eyes, stepping closer and putting her head closer to his chest. "But we figure, they're going to ask all of us."

"Us?"

"Outsiders."

"Ah..." Wu Ying nodded. "I had no reason to kill Cui Wen though. He was..." He frowned, searching for the politick word to use.

"Inconsequential? A mewling baby whose ego was larger than his tool?"

Wu Ying blushed a little. "To-tool?"

"His sword, of course." Another smirk. "But watch yourself, Shen-man. We have our clan protecting us from being falsely accused. You—"

"Have nothing?" Wu Ying finished for her, choosing not to point out his own affiliations. After all, the Verdant Green Waters was many li away. "Surely, they would not blame the innocent?"

Pan Shui's eyes darkened, and she stepped up again, leaving only a single step between them. Bending her neck to meet his gaze, she lowered her voice. "He is the direct disciple of a sect elder. The Seven Pavilions will be desperate to cover the shame of his death. Especially before the army arrives. For if they arrive…" She shook her head.

"What of it?"

"These tournaments are a new thing. Only a decade or so. Too new to be considered permanent. Such incidents could have the kingdom banning them once more," Pan Shui replied. "This isn't the first such incident, after all. A lot of people have reason not to allow us our greater freedoms, even if the Third Prince champions this."

Wu Ying winced, already envisioning it. Perhaps the conversation and speculation among the wandering cultivators had not been entirely idle gossip but also had some elements of self-preservation.

"Thank you for the warning, Cultivator Pan." Then, out of curiosity, Wu Ying asked, "Why are you so sure that I'm not the killer?"

"We sparred, did we not?" She stepped back, giving him space. "I felt your sword. It is powerful and strong, highly energetic while being flexible. Even if you float through our battles, it is still straightforward in its strength and focus."

"You truly believe you can tell a man's character through his fighting style?" Wu Ying said, surprised. It was a theory that had as many detractors as supporters. That the depths of one's martial style showcased the truth of an individual's soul too.

"Do you not?" Pan Shui said. "A man can hide much, and we did not fight to the end where truth really does shine through, but you are not that complicated."

"I see…"

Wu Ying did agree, to some extent, that one could tell something of another via their weapon choice, the way they fought or chose to face an opponent. Someone who was aggressive and charged forward was often like that in real life. While counter-strikers were often retiring and analytical, choosing to watch and only speaking when they had to.

However, humanity was more complicated than that. A retiring young woman amongst friends might be aggressive and wrathful in battle. A boy filled with energy throughout the day could find stillness in the mastery of the sword.

Then again, Wu Ying only had the Sense of the Sword. She, the Heart of the Spear. Perhaps it was something one gained when an individual achieved that state of enlightenment. Perhaps he thought people were more complicated because he just did not see clearly enough.

There were more than a few tales of Nascent Soul cultivators able to see through aspects of their dao to the truth of a subject. A cultivator of truth, becoming the supreme judge of a small county, never making a mistaken ruling—even if not always ruling wisely. Another whose dao of painting had allowed him to pick apart dozens of fakes.

"Be careful, Shen-man." Pan Shui turned and trooped downstairs while Wu Ying debated her earlier question, leaving him alone on the staircase.

He sighed, rubbing the back of his neck. There was so much to learn about daos, martial styles, and the cultivation world he lived in. So much that was rumor and half-truth, that might work for one individual but fail for another, that sometimes he felt as if he was swimming through murky water in the deep of the night.

Then again, if cultivation and enlightenment were easy, everyone would be an immortal.

***

The disturbance at his door was respectful, willing to wait for the long minutes it took Wu Ying to safely exit his cultivation. A small part of Wu Ying was grateful he no longer sweated out impurities as he had done before. It was much better on his clothing and pocketbook.

"Gao Qiu. Liu Ping. Liu Jin." Wu Ying greeted the three, choosing to drop the honorifics. They had grown close enough that it was not an insult.

"Expert Long," Gao Qiu spoke for the three, greeting him.

Well, Wu Ying had—but his strength allowed him to step past such things, unlike them.

"Are we disturbing you?" Gao Qiu asked.

"Not at all. I was just cultivating," Wu Ying said, gesturing for them to come in. Not a big room, but it would fit all four of them, even if he did have to sit on the bed he had been cultivating on. When everyone had found a seat, he continued. "What brings you this late in the evening?"

"It is good that we did not find you asleep." Gao Qiu fell silent, looking around. The silence stretched out as he seemed to lose the nerve to say anything further.

"It is late, and even if I only require a little sleep, I do wish to be well rested for tomorrow." Wu Ying looked at the three before continuing. "And you three too."

"Bah! I can win in the preliminaries without any—" Liu Ping fell silent as her brother poked her arm. She glared at him but shut her mouth.

Gao Qiu shifted uncomfortably. "Yes. I apologize, Expert Long. I just wanted to know, did you get called in too?"

That again. Wu Ying barely managed not to roll his eyes. Not that it was surprising, but… "Yes. I assume you were interviewed because you were in the fight with me?"

"Ummm… yes." Gao Qiu shifted in his seat then sighed. "They asked us where you were and, well, we could not lie. We did not see you after the fight."

"Because I came back to my room." Then, recalling the evening, Wu Ying asked, "Where did you all go?"

"Dinner!"

"A walk!"

"To bed!"

The words were all jumbled up, spoken together. Wu Ying raised an eyebrow, turning from each member to another.

"I went to bed," Liu Jin said. "Ah Ping went to eat, and Ah Qiu…"

"Went for a walk?" Wu Ying smirked.

Gao Qiu shrugged. "I enjoy the evenings. And after a fight…"

Wu Ying did not say anything about the excuse. It was rather suspicious, but the truth was that battles between demon beasts and humans were different. Even if no one had been killed, insults and blows thrown by a human had a tendency to linger, damaging the psyche.

Nor was it really Wu Ying's place to question Gao Qiu. After all, Wu Ying could think of many reasons a man might want to take a walk alone and Gao Qiu was a good-looking man, even if he was a little too stern and old.

"Did they question you long?" Wu Ying asked instead.

"Not as long as you!" Liu Ping said, laughing a little. "They kept you in there for a while."

"You were watching?" Wu Ying said. "Then why did you ask if they had called me in?"

"Uhh…" Liu Ping flushed.

"We were being polite," Gao Qiu said, glaring at the girl. "We did not want to make you worried that we were watching you." He paused, then added sheepishly, "Even though we are."

"Why?"

"We were… well, we have two reasons. Firstly, if you are still joining the tournament, we were going to place our bets on you," Gao Qiu said.

Wu Ying was not particularly surprised there would be gambling on the tournament results. He had not seen anything as yet, but he assumed bookies would set up tomorrow. If anything, it would be more surprising to find a tournament where individuals were not gambling upon the results. And if a merchant clan was running things, he could not see them letting such a chance escape their grasp.

"Do you not have confidence in Liu Ping?" Wu Ying said, nodding toward the young girl who looked a little sullen.

"We do!" Gao Qiu said hurriedly. "But—"

"But there's no reason not to place multiple bets!" Liu Jin said, eyes glittering a little. "You see, I have a system—"

"Idiots," Liu Ping muttered so quietly that Wu Ying figured neither of the other two heard. He kept his mouth shut, not wanting to get involved in that drama.

"And the second reason?" Wu Ying asked instead.

"We have been hoping to speak with you about joining us." Gao Qiu ran a hand through his long hair, pushing it down and ensuring it was in place. "Or us joining you."

"Why?"

"It's clear you're more than a simple Energy Storage cultivator. Perhaps even Core Formation?" Gao Qiu said hesitatingly. When Wu Ying chose not to react, he continued on bravely. "That kind of strength, even if you wish to keep it hidden, is reassuring. Our missions—escorting merchant caravans, locating beast cores, and guarding camps—they will be easier. We will be stronger for it."

Wu Ying shook his head. To his surprise, there was no trace of disappointment on Gao Qiu's face, but expectation. "Where I go, where I need to go, it is not suitable for others."

"Because you wander deep into the untamed lands to gather your supplies?" Gao Qiu said.

Wu Ying nodded.

"Then perhaps we could set up a deal, perhaps request you get for us some minor items…"

Wu Ying was shaking his head already.

"Surely there is no way for the kingdom to know?"

"It isn't just that," Wu Ying said. "When I leave, I'm not entirely certain where I'll travel." He waved his hand outside. "That will make it hard for you to meet with me."

"Ah!" Gao Qiu smiled. "That is no problem."

"Oh?"

"Yes." He reached into his robes and extracted a small wooden stick with carvings and words inscribed on it. Wu Ying felt the gentlest of enchantments laid upon the stick, pushed into it so that one could verify the giver's identity if you knew it to begin with. "You need only hand this to any merchant in the White Flower Merchant Association and you may send any items to us."

"Convenient," Wu Ying said, staring at the flat stick laid upon the table. "But if you inform me what little herbs you need, I might be able to gift them to you now."

Gao Qiu smiled. "Well, it's not just for us, you see. We're part of a group…"

"Of wandering cultivators." A single eyebrow rose interrogatively. An association of wandering cultivators—what a strange thought. The White Flower Merchant Association seemed to be more than just another business.

"Among others. Think of it as a brotherhood of mutual support," Liu Jin spoke up, leaning forward. "Support and belief."

Gao Qiu shook his head as Wu Ying moved to ask further. "I had not expected to get into this conversation right now, Expert Long. We will speak on this matter later. But perhaps one last question."

Wu Ying nodded for the man to continue.

"Would you at least consider selling such goods to us?"

"Consider?" Wu Ying trailed off then nodded.

"That is all that we can ask for." Gao Qiu gestured for the other two to leave, while he stood as well. "It would be of great help to us. Strength and enlightenment should not be controlled, not by a single corrupt entity."

Wu Ying did not comment, instead leading the group to the door. After the usual words of farewell, he watched them leave before turning back to the small stick, the words White Flower Merchant Association gleaming in the setting moonlight.

How… interesting.

There had been a lot unsaid in that conversation. Hints of more than just a group of wandering cultivators attempting to acquire spiritual herbs and cores on the side. A group that had tied itself to a merchant association or controlled it from behind. One in need of significant amounts of cultivation resources, if they were willing to ask any random cultivator.

Perhaps Gao Qiu and his friends were more than just a group of wandering cultivators. Or perhaps he was reading too much into things.

Storing the wooden slat in a secondary storage ring, Wu Ying stretched his body slowly. All these unanswered questions of motive and ability, of death and murder; they could wait. Would wait. Time would tell.

As for now, tomorrow, there was a tournament.

One where he had been asked to exit.

And dangers all around.

Chapter 14

Organizing a tournament was a headache of bureaucracy and overinflated egos.

Wu Ying watched as the various contenders were allocated their positions and tournament rings, as the initial round of matches began. The contest, to ensure fairness, would take place over multiple days, with each contestant having a total of five fights. The top eight fighters with the highest number of wins would then be seeded to the quarterfinals, where an eventual winner would be found.

A fair method, Wu Ying had to agree. Much fairer than the sect tournament he had participated in, and most other tournaments. Then again, those tournaments had included hundreds of participants, forcing the more common single elimination method.

To explain away the need for fairer tournament methods, the usual excuse had been that fortune and fate were just as important for a cultivator as any minor thing like fairness. A cultivator required not just skill but luck, and if they were not fated to win, they were not.

Mostly though, Wu Ying assumed it was just easier in terms of organization. And truth be told, no vaunted son or daughter of heaven would ever complain about such rules in public. To do so would be an admission of a lack of confidence in their skills. Something none of those arrogant children of noblemen would ever dare admit.

"Huh… I guess that is one advantage of your kingdom," Wu Ying muttered to himself as he waited his turn.

Liu Jin, assigned to the same dueling ring, cocked his head. "What advantage?"

"Your nobles are few, their members lacking in the arrogance those in my kingdom contain. Here, it's hard for me to tell the difference between noble son and wandering cultivator—lacking as you all are in ability."

"Are we truly that far behind?" Liu Jin murmured.

Neither of them spoke too loudly, though Wu Ying had only a little concern about being overheard. Still, there was daring and then there was arrogance.

"If those I see here are a common example… then yes. Most battle techniques and styles here are, at best, what we would consider novice forms. A few have partial intermediate ones." Wu Ying shrugged. "Whereas the nobles of our kingdom are trained in peak or even perfected battle techniques from birth."

"And what level is your Long family style?" Liu Jin prodded, a little affronted.

"Before, I would have said an intermediate style, perhaps peak if I was being generous. Though the more I delve into it, the more I believe it was my fault in misunderstanding the text than in the form itself," Wu Ying replied unashamedly. "But it is not perfected, though it can withstand blows from those who use such techniques."

After all, he had stood against his Master, who had the Heart of the Sword and a perfected technique. Or so Wu Ying assumed. He had never asked, what with the gap between them all too stark already. Knowing the categorization of a technique—and how obscure and political the taxonomy of techniques could become—did little to help him breach the gap.

"In truth, I find myself adapting the style the more I continue my cultivation journey. Its development did not, I believe, take into account my own particular… progress." Wind Body, Twelve Gales, and the Formless Realm.

"How… nice." Liu Jin's lips pursed. "For us, the army takes away most of the talented when they are young. The nobles might be able to hire those who are retired, but any family that grows too prominent is heavily taxed the next season or required to provide a higher corvee. Standing out is a recipe for disaster. For nobles or sects."

"Then why do you all take part?" Wu Ying said, flicking his hand around at the other participants. "Is it not the same?"

"Ah, we're wandering cultivators. It's different," Liu Jin said. "We must compete for the prizes on offer. Finding or accessing good techniques or resources is difficult. Anyway, a single strong wandering cultivator is nothing, not against the might of the kingdom." Bitterly, he added, "A strong ant is still an ant after all."

Wu Ying fell silent, remembering the damage in his own Sect from the latest assault. How entire portions of the mountain had been damaged, even through the defensive arrays put in place. He recalled the immortal and dragon battle over a province and the subsequent damage as Nascent Soul elders fought for a drop of the dragon's blood. And wondered.

Did the Kingdom of Zhao truly not understand? Or were their reserves, their hidden powers, so great that even a single Nascent Soul wandering cultivator was no real concern for them?

Then again, Wu Ying had to yet see a single Core Formation wandering cultivator here. Admittedly, the prizes offered held no interest to those at that stage. It might be that reason why there were none. If not… if it was not mere coincidence, then darker tides drifted through this kingdom.

"You're up," Liu Jin said, breaking Wu Ying's contemplation.

The wind cultivator blinked. He shook his head and dismissed thoughts of the greater politics involved, instead hopping lightly to ascend the raised platform.

Standing before him was a man wielding dual dao blades, a wide grin on his face. Even from the man's basic stance, Wu Ying could tell this wouldn't be a difficult battle.

He jumped.

Wu Ying struck.

The fight ended.

***

Hours of waiting, of watching and listening. He listened and watched.

Gao Qiu, moving around the edges, always speaking with others. Making friends, making connections, passing around small slips of paper. Wu Ying had glanced at one, briefly, seeing detailed notes about the locations of the White Flower Merchant Association. He had stored it, idly.

More interesting were the others. The Northern archer, standing by the gambling table, arguing back and forth as he placed ever larger bets, having a run of luck that drew more than one envious gaze. A pickpocket, caught later in the day and strung up by the guards, choosing to be taken into custody rather than face the rough justice of the wandering cultivators.

Overheard conversations.

"You need to do well," Liu Ping was berating Liu Jin, waving a hand aggressively at the other even while she kept her voice low. "Don't just beat your opponent, win with style!"

"I'm not you, Mei Mei," Liu Jin snapped. "I'm not as good. I can't…" he shook his head. "They won't take me, not even if I do well."

"That's not true. We just need to show you have potential. Once you get in, you can get a cultivation manual that actually works for you."

"Works for me… you mean that doesn't hurt me every time I cultivate?" Liu Jin muttered.

"Yes. Maybe if we got Expert Long to help…"

"With more pills? Are you insane? We can't even afford to pay him back for what he gave us."

"It was a gift!" Liu Ping objected, glancing over to where Wu Ying stood. He had his head turned away, trusting in the wind to bring him their conversation.

"And you think that's excuse enough?" her brother grumbled, then sighed in exasperation. "What are you going to do without me? You willfully forget the unspoken courtesies we live by."

She grinned then, wide and innocent. "Good thing I don't have to, eh?" Then, lips thinned moments later. "So, win. If you want me to join a sect, win!"

"I'll try." He sighed and touched the hilt of his weapon reassuringly. "I'll try."

A presence, beside him. Wu Ying dismissed the wind, turning to the cultivator who approached, a solicitous smile on his face.

Another one, looking to probe for information and assure himself that the one before him was a Gatherer. One who might even be able to procure herbs and pills for them.

Business. Connections. Knowledge.

The point of turning up here, after all.

***

Later that evening, the small group of friends sat in the same restaurant. All of them had passed their first two fights, winning them with varying degrees of struggle. Gao Qiu, Liu Ping, and Wu Ying had won handily, while Liu Jin—the weakest of them all—had nearly lost his last bout. If not for a fortunate stumble by his opponent, he would have lost the match.

Even so, he cradled an injured arm that was slowly healing as deep bruising was rectified by his cultivation.

"You truly are gifted with that sword," Gao Qiu said. "Even knowing the forms you were using after showing them off, none of your opponents could lay a blade on you."

Wu Ying waved. "My opponents lacked movement techniques. If they were to study some, they would have been faster." He shook his head. "And I was lucky. My second opponent had not even broken through the Energy Storage stage."

"Yes. Strong though." Liu Ping grinned. "When you punched him in the mouth, I don't think anyone expected him to get back up."

"Stubborn more than strong," Liu Jin said. "And foolish. Wu Ying had to beat him so much that he might not even be able to compete tomorrow."

"But it was a good showing," Gao Qiu said. "At his level, the matchup was probably the best he could hope for. Now, anyone wanting a Body Cleansing guard would hire him. A guard who will not stop fighting for you is worth more than a stronger one who gives up at the first sign of trouble."

"Well said," Pan Shui commented as she plopped herself down on an empty seat. "Cultivator Poon did his best. We might even invite him to visit our vill—urk!" Rubbing the top of her head, Pan Shui glared at her sisters. "What was that for?"

"For speaking out of turn. Again!" her elder sister snipped. She then gestured to the remaining empty seat, the pair of them the only two of the three sisters present. "May we join you?"

Gao Qiu was quick to agree, and the older sister sat down, brushing a hair that had escaped the triangular headdress of her clan back over her ear. Closer now, Wu Ying could not only see the family resemblance but understand why she had been called the Flower of the North West Hills. Pale skin, tiny, upturned nose, beautiful cheekbones. A little more heart-shaped and soft than the preferred mode for Fairies in the Shen kingdom, but lovely still.

"I am Pan Yin of Laiban village. This is my younger sister, Pan Shui." She introduced them once more, receiving quick words of introduction from the rest of the group. As Wu Ying finished his own introduction, she bowed to him. "Of course, Expert Long. I am grateful you indulged my sister yesterday."

"Nothing to be thankful for." Wu Ying gestured toward Pan Shui. "She is talented, and I learned much."

"Told you!" Pan Shui shrank away almost immediately when Pan Yin looked over.

"Is your other sister well?" Wu Ying continued.

"She is recovering well and should be able to fight tomorrow," Pan Yin replied. "Thank you for inquiring."

"Ill luck, fighting a poison cultivator," Liu Ping said, making a face. "They should ban them from competing."

"There is no need," Pan Yin said. "Their styles are just as relevant as ours and are good training. The Seven Pavilions has already restricted the kinds of poisons they may wield and ensured that those who fight them have ample time to rest before their next bout. It is all that we can ask."

Wu Ying nodded. "It will be interesting to fight one, for sure." He rubbed his chin. "I've never had an opportunity to battle one with such low stakes. Such tournaments, they are useful for such experiences."

"What kind of experience is it? When they are restricted?" Liu Ping said. "Obviously, they will not be able to showcase their full strength."

"It is better than nothing," Gao Qiu rebutted. "After all, it's not as though Expert Long or even ourselves are showing our full skills either."

Liu Jin flushed a little, looking down into his wine cup. Of them all, Wu Ying knew, that statement was patently untrue for him.

Turning to Pan Yin, Wu Ying smiled at her. "I noticed the style of your spear is slightly different from your sister's. Are there more variations of the spear style in your family? Or just more advanced methods?"

"It's a village style," Pan Yin replied. "And there are multiple branches of it. You have a keen eye, Expert Long."

"Perhaps we could exchange pointers, in the future," Wu Ying said. He was not certain, but he felt that she too had achieved the Heart of the Spear. Though it was hard to tell, without crossing blades with her. If that was true, her family was truly blessed to have two such prodigies.

"Perhaps we can," Pan Yin said.

Gao Qiu looked around, his eyes tracking over the surroundings. Wu Ying did the same, noting how the Elders and their disciples had returned to "their" table at the front of the restaurant overlooking the dueling rings. A somber air had draped itself over the table though, leaving the tables closest to them the least desirable and those seated there hunched and twisted away from the group.

Satisfied by what he saw—or didn't see—Gao Qiu lowered his voice. "Did you all see the guards?"

"The Guard Captain and his investigator?" Pan Shui said before nodding vigorously. "They were watching everyone who was fighting."

Checking for which hand they wielded their weapons, Wu Ying could not help but think. Narrowing their list of suspects.

"They were particularly interested in the jian fighters." Pan Shui's eyes landed on Wu Ying, as though reminding him of their earlier conversation.

"Do you think they have had any further clues to who killed Cui Wen?" Liu Ping asked.

"It's a bit exciting, isn't it? Like we're in a story." Pan Yin scoffed, making the younger girl flush. "Well, it is!"

"I'd rather have excitement in my stories than live them. I'm sure Expert Long agrees. After all, he lived through a war recently, no?" Pan Yin said, looking at Wu Ying.

"Uhh… well. Sort of." Wu Ying played with the teacup before him as everyone turned their attention to him. "But I was just a Gatherer for most of it. I spent my time picking herbs, not on the front lines."

"But surely you saw some action?" Pan Yin probed. "I heard they were even attacking wandering cultivators to weaken your kingdom."

Wu Ying hesitated before he eventually nodded.

"Perhaps you could tell us a little of this…"

The cultivator flicked his gaze around the group and noticed Gao Qiu's gaze on him. Wu Ying remembered what the other man had asked and could not help but consider what Pan Yin wanted from this story. When he met her gaze, he saw her flick her gaze toward her eager younger sister.

Oh. That kind of story.

"Well, I did see a few things," Wu Ying said, running through memories of desperate battles and lost friends as he tried to recall what to say. Some losses, well, those were still too raw. Friends killed, ignominiously out of sight. Their heads tossed to him like so much garbage. Other stories weren't his…

Eventually, he found one that was… suitable.

"I was passing through the county of Xi on the way to a sect I had a delivery for. The Three Stalking Cranes. There was a small village I meant to stop at…"

Pan Yin smiled a little as Wu Ying related his experience, offering the slightest of nods. He noted it but did his best not to be distracted. This story… well, for the dead and departed, it deserved his full attention.

The other cultivators stayed silent, leaning in to listen. He even idly noted how some of the nearby tables had grown quieter as a tale of another kingdom was told.

***

Wu Ying was surprised when he stepped out of his room later that night and heard another door opening. Turning his head a little, he spotted Pan Yin watching him. Their dinner had taken a while, as drinks and attempts to top his own tale had proceeded apace.

"I wished to thank you, Expert Long," Pan Yin said, bowing a little.

"For what?"

"Your story." She smiled a little tiredly as she gestured with one hand. "Many chafe at the restrictions placed on us. They hear of the wars and battles, of the border skirmishes by the army and the riches won and believe they can do better. The stories told by the musicians, storytellers, and poets are all of the glories and moments of bravery. Not the losses, the grief and pain. The villages razed, the families torn asunder. The warriors crippled."

"You speak as though you know of it too," Wu Ying said, his voice dropping.

Memories of those she spoke of flickered across his mind. Men and women, some so damaged that their cultivation journey was utterly rent astray. Villagers, looking upon burnt fields with the knowledge of a hungry future for them and their family. Parents staring at returning sons, wondering if it was better for none to return than another crippled mouth to feed. And the loathing in their own eyes, for thinking such thoughts.

"Some of us have traveled too," Pan Yin said. There was something in her eyes, in the way she held herself that spoke of an age greater than what showed on her face. For a second, Wu Ying wondered exactly how old she was. Thirty? Forty? More?

Insight struck, one coupled with his greater spiritual sense. Pan Yin's path of cultivation was stalled, her final meridian blocked. Never stepping further and forced to accompany her prodigy of a sister on such tournaments. To babysit someone who would outstrip her in cultivation levels, but perhaps not wisdom.

The world was unfair to ask so much of another. And yet, here she was and not a word had she breathed of it.

"I see."

"My apologies. I just wanted to thank you," Pan Yin said, stepping back to her doorway. "I will not inconvenience you further in your evening."

Wu Ying bowed, wishing her well before departing. Still, he felt her gaze on his back as he left and noticed a figure in the windows. Once he was outside the boundaries of the small village, he triggered his qinggong techniques, using Twelve Gales to take him far away, past the farmed fields and into the surrounding forests.

A good half hour of moving under the waxing moon and Wu Ying finally arrived at the clearing he had been aiming for. A dimly lit location, bereft of major vegetation but a single felled and rotting log. His feet touched down lightly on the cold grass and Wu Ying smiled, letting his aura expand. Testing the surroundings, beckoning the winds to him.

They came, answering his queries.

A few Spirit Beasts: a rabbit sleeping deep in its burrow that had breached its second rank as a Body Cleanser, an owl drifting through the night on the verge of a breakthrough, a hunting fox. Nothing that would bother him.

"Good enough," Wu Ying murmured.

Next, he went around the clearing, pulling out the formation flags left over from his rescue. They would hide his aura, shielding the clearing from others who might sense his practice. It wasn't perfect, since the flags were meant to handle the chi excesses of an Energy Storage cultivator, not one who had entered Core Formation. Nor was he particularly adept at their placements, but it would do.

In truth, he had meant to wait until he had left the tournament to practice, when he was alone in the wilderness once more. But time and events had altered his plans.

It was too dangerous to wait until he left to fully test his new cultivation level. He had reinforced the first step sufficiently that he no longer worried that he would accidentally damage his newly made Core. Now, he needed to know the full extent of the changes in his body.

There were too many figures moving in the shadows at the tournament, too many layers of politics and pride and greed that he didn't understand. He felt as though he was back in the Sect again, a poor mortal coming to a land of cultivators and stumbling across lines of propriety and civility that he never knew existed.

Except this time, he was more experienced.

Now, he could sense those layers of politics even if he did not understand them. Now, he knew the one truth about the jianghu, the one aspect of the martial world that carried from kingdom to kingdom. Now, he had the strength to protect himself.

He was no shrinking Energy Storage cultivator, no matter how he chose to act. He would not swan about, believing himself better than those below him. But he would not hide from himself the extent of his progress.

Drawing his blade, Wu Ying took the first stance of the Long family sword form. He steadied his breathing, centered himself, then *moved*.

First form. Learn the blade, become the blade. Simple motions, the fundamentals of all movement from wrist cuts to straight thrusts. Drop low, explode forward.

Lunge.

Study the basic movements, for one could not build a tower on a shaky foundation.

Second form.

Specialized for the jian itself, it began to incorporate aspects that would make using energy projection viable. Less emphasis on sweeping cuts, the motions faster, more subtle. A jian was a gentleman's weapon, where skill and subtlety with blade and body were more important than raw strength and aggression.

In a duel, it was said, the jian would beat a dao, all other things being equal, so long as the jian wielder kept his composure. Of course, under the unrelenting assault of a dao wielder, the ferocious and savage attacks might break even the calmest of minds.

Already, Wu Ying could feel the difference. Calling forth the chi from his Core, the energy surged and retreated with ease, his body twisting with greater flexibility than ever, his connection to earth and air deeper than before. The energy in his blade extended and collapsed with barely a thought, moving to his whims in a way it had never done before.

Without stopping, as he came to the end of the second form, Wu Ying continued to the third.

Third form, firmly meant for those in the Energy Storage stage and those touching upon Core Formation itself. His sword hummed, the swirling winds around it cutting through the atmosphere with each swing. No longer were the blade, his energy, and his body separate items—they all moved in concordance with one another.

In his mind's eye, Wu Ying saw his opponent, the form transitioning from one manual perfect motion to another, even as the wind caught and shifted him by hair and handsbreadth. A slight sway in the hip, across his arm, and a straight thrust became a burrowing cut.

A dropping retreat, front leg splayed sideways for balance exploded the earth beneath it, throwing up dust and redirecting explosive wind to strike from below. Tricks and trouble. Around him, winds rose and formed ghostly blades of their own, leaving afterimages as he threw attacks that would hurt those who managed to evade his main assault.

Fourth form. A pure Core Formation style. One he had barely ever practiced, only memorizing the physical motions. It required too much chi, demanded the wielder be one with the jian and trust in each motion as the body spun and expended energy with each step.

He had just begun, when the attack arrived, plummeting down from above like a meteor. Murderous intent arrived seconds later, as weapon and body arrived.

***

The wind spoke of his assailant's approach, and Wu Ying parted before the plunging polearm like the breeze itself. Twelve Gales took him backward, kicking off solidified air. He flew away even as the sharpened blade tracked him, the glinting, clear reflection of his own visage staring back at him from the hooked blade that nearly cut off his nose.

Back.

The explosion of rock and earth, energy thrown into the air as the figure crashed to the ground with the dagger-axe he wielded. Choking dust arose, obscuring all sight. Wu Ying's aura caught at the burning heat and sharpened fragments of chi aura that tore out from the point of impact, intent on severing limbs by density and sharpness of the energy, the twisted, burning heat of metal parting in each breath he took.

Wu Ying's aura arose, taking sharpened jagged edges in gentle hands of air and pushing them aside, robbing them of angle and ferocity. Shards of earth and metal dropped or split away, the surrounding trees pockmarked and stripped of their leaves by the backblast.

Then, within the swirling dust, Wu Ying sensed movement. A straight thrust moving so fast that the attacker must have only taken a moment to reorient himself. Wu Ying brought his own blade upward, Dragon strokes the Painting as he parried the attack. Immediately after, Wu Ying transitioned to a counterthrust.

Around him, his aura sharpened, blades of wind forming and carrying him toward his dust-shrouded opponent. Swirling eddies of wind ran around Wu Ying's jian, a shrieking tempest that rose even higher and hurt the ears as it approached the other's weapon. Blade against haft, but the wind buffeted the other weapon, battling against his opponent's control.

Before his blade could sink into his opponent's body, shards of metal from his opponent's aura exploded. Wu Ying tossed himself sideways, switching to a defensive form as he parried the swirling blades of ill-formed metal.

They did not stop coming, even as he beat the initial attack.

Spinning, Wu Ying dodged the attacks, feet impacting a tree. He used it to change directions, charging right back into the fight, blade and cultivation aura battling his opponent's.

A further flurry of attacks, neither opponent managing to gain an upper hand. Wu Ying managed to dodge each explosive blow, only to find his counter strikes unable to penetrate the deep layers of swirling metal around his opponent. Even energy projections combined with sword intent were deflected by the sheer density of metal defense his opponent wielded.

The pair struck at one another, Wu Ying falling deeper and deeper into the fourth forms of the Long family style. Explosive dragon Breath attacks, air walking, qi-blades of wind and sword intent, it all came together. Yet…

He was losing. For his opponent was stronger, much stronger than he was—more experienced at his various martial techniques and having a deeper pool of Core Formation chi. The difference between the chi tempered from the Core and within his dantian and meridians was stark. Core tempered chi was denser, more easily manageable, and as importantly, unlikely to disperse in the environment as it was expanded.

Spikes of metal erupted from the ground, dust particles of iron cut through the air in formations, and the heavy polearm sheared through the edges of his jian when they clashed. Only exertions of his sword intent and aura managed to solidify the air between the blade and axe-head of the polearm, pushing it away such that Wu Ying's blade did not break.

Around them, the clearing widened. Trees that had stood for decades or even hundreds of years were destroyed. Grass and shrubs were cut apart, the earth rent and tossed. Even the sky above grew tempestuous, as clouds were pulled from afar to gather over them. His formation flags were ripped out of their moorings, tossed aside to reveal what was happening to all those with senses.

Each second, Wu Ying was pushed backward, his chi depleted.

The end came when Wu Ying's blade, chipped and sheared, was shattered upon a descending stroke. A piece cut across Wu Ying's cheek, tearing skin and bringing with it the first scent of blood. The final blow, barely slowed by the broken blade, fell toward Wu Ying's upraised visage, the edge catching moonlight and growing in size with each fraction of a second.

Only to stop a hairsbreadth from Wu Ying's forehead.

Time held still, in what seemed to be forever before…

Gravity pulled on Wu Ying and dumped him on the ground as his initial jerking retreat took over and the winds died.

***

"Well fought," the voice murmured, his voice distant. *Her* voice.

His opponent had backed away after stopping her attack, retreating to allow Wu Ying to recuperate and reorient his mind. The break was welcome, for Wu Ying's Core was empty. His continual cultivation methods slowly refilled his body as he sat, propped up on his arms.

Wu Ying regarded his assailant, truly taking her in for the first time. A small tug at his cultivation reserves sent the wind spinning, pushing away the last of the lingering dust. Clad in lamellar armor, dark grey and green, and a helmet with high plumes upon it, she had a long scar crossing one side of the face. A dead eye regarded him as grey hair peeked out of the corner of her helmet. The woman would have been handsome but for the scar, though those eyes were cold and hard as they regarded him.

Of more interest than her features was the weapon she wielded. The dagger-axe polearm was a single piece of enchanted steel, its body hardened through chi tempering. Even resting upon the ground, its presence twisted the chi flows around it, a sharp, biting sensation pressing upon Wu Ying's spiritual sense as it neared the weapon.

"That is a peak Saint-class weapon, is it not?" Wu Ying said.

There were many reasons for why a weapon would be regarded as another grade higher, from the method of tempering and quality of the weapon itself to its hardness; but at the highest levels, the most important aspect was the way it handled the user's chi.

Wu Ying's weapons were but Spirit-class items. The singular Saint-level jian of his Master's had been acquired by his Martial Sister, many of the shattered swords Wu Ying had given out replaced by equivalent items. Over his years of wandering, he had been unable to purchase a weapon of greater quality—either bereft of funds or connections when one came up for purchase.

"Your weapons are pitiful," his assailant said, flicking a dismissive glance at the broken hilt lying by his side. "A Core Formation cultivator should at the least have a weapon that suits him."

Wu Ying shrugged. "My ascension was recent."

No reason to lie, not after being beaten so badly. His pride was in tatters, much like his sword. He stood, brushing off his clothing and using his aura to help remove some of the stains. Not all, of course, for some had been ground in.

"Mmmm… yes. A careless prodigy, shorn from his Sect, uncaring about the natural order of things," the woman said speculatively. "Teetering on the edge of understanding and still failing."

Ignoring the insults, he put his hands together and bowed. "Long Wu Ying greets the elder. May I have the honor of your name?"

He did not need to ask her for her official identity. Her cultivation base, her aura was familiar to him. The Core Formation cultivator who had listened to his interview, who had hidden inside the Seven Pavilions compound.

She hesitated, obviously thinking about it. "You may call me Elder Cao." She flicked her hand, putting away her weapon. "Tell me, what are your intentions for the tournament?"

"Mmm… none," Wu Ying said as he switched out his empty scabbard for a filled one, strapping it into place above his robes. "I had hoped to gain a better understanding of the kingdom and make contacts with the wandering cultivators here." He turned his head toward where the other cultivators slept, noting how some lights had appeared. Their battle, short as it had been, had certainly woken others. "Winning the tournament was a consideration, though I had not intended to bully others with my cultivation."

"Then will you fight without putting your full strength on display? Mocking the efforts of my employer?" Elder Cao's voice grew colder. "Or did you have other reasons for coming?"

"Like what?" His chin rose, and a hand fell onto the newly reequipped hilt. Not that he expected to win a fight with her, but if she thought he would die easy, she would be mistaken. She had put him on the backfoot their entire fight, but this time, he would be ready.

"Greed. Demonic sacrifice. Perhaps just plain jealousy?" she said. "After all, you did have an altercation with him the night before."

Wu Ying opened his mouth to defend himself then clamped it shut. He stared at Elder Cao for a long time, a niggling feeling running through him as he swept his gaze over her all too relaxed stance. "You don't really believe that. You know I did not kill him."

Elder Cao laughed suddenly before she leaned on her grounded weapon. "Correct. It's a pity. I had hoped to tease you longer."

"Why?" Wu Ying said. "Murder is not a humorous matter, I would think."

"Ah, but your reaction to the accusation is."

"When did you realize I had nothing to do with it?"

"Investigator Chu discounted you early on. The location of the actual murder is not one we believe you had access to." Elder Cao waved her hand around. "After this, I concur."

"I do not understand."

"You might be a genius among geniuses, but even they have an upper limit. Your sword skill is remarkable for one so young, verging on the Heart. Like that child who fights with the spear. However, a single exemplary matter is of no concern. But you are also a Core Formation cultivator and have a secondary occupation—one that, I understand, you have some skill within."

"I do, but what does being a Gatherer have to do with this?"

"It is simple. A single exemplary area can be achieved via training and dedication or by a prodigy who trains little. Two such areas, a genius with discipline. Three?" Elder Cao shook her head. "Three such areas of expertise, as you have? Very commendable. But it would require a once-in-a-generation genius to excel in four professions."

Wu Ying frowned, trying to figure out what she meant. Cultivation was obviously one area—being a Core Formation cultivator before thirty marked him as special there. His knowledge of gathering, meager as it might be, was still a broad specialization that many mistook for great depths. And his own martial skill with the blade would be the third. So what fourth profession could she think he required to enact the killing?

When he moved to speak, she cut him off, continuing. "As it stands, your ability at such a young age places you among some of the greatest prospects to arise in our kingdom."

Wu Ying shook his head, thoughts diverted as he realized she might have no reason to tell him about the fourth profession. Perhaps it had to do with that missing sect token? "I am no genius, Elder Cao. I have some minor skill at arms, but I have been beaten by everyone from Cultivator Pan to yourself."

"And you feel that your bare couple of decades should allow you to stand on the same stage as myself?" Elder Cao's eyes gleamed. "I, who have fought in border wars for decades? I, who have reached the rank of youji jiangun[12]?"

He winced, bowing his head low. "I apologize. I had not meant—" He stopped when her laughter cut through his apology, and he looked up, his eyes fixing on the woman. "You were teasing me again, were you not?"

"Yes. But your skill for your age is commendable. Your strength as a Core Formation cultivator is pitiful. Wind cultivators like you all have that difficulty."

Wu Ying's eyes narrowed. "You have met others like me?"

"One—though he never made it to Core Formation. But the archives of the Imperial Army are extensive, and I perused details about his growth." Darkness flickered through her eyes for a second. "Wind cultivators have a long path, perhaps the longest amongst Core Formation cultivators. You will have to layer your Core multiple times, for the Spirit you grow will test it. A Wind Core is fragile, easy to break in the beginning."

"Thank you for your guidance, Senior."

She waved away his words, leaving Wu Ying staring at her. She fell silent too, caught up in old memories.

Finally, he was forced to ask her, "Elder, if there is nothing else…?"

"Nothing that is relevant to you." She began to turn away, only to stop and turn back. "One last thing. You may compete, but do not win the tournament. Sharpen your blade and your wiles. Watch for any who might be suspicious."

"You believe the killer to still be around?"

"Yes."

Wu Ying watched as she strolled away. Just before she disappeared into the dark, he raised his voice once more, curiosity driving the question. "Where was the murder done?"

"In the compound."

And then, she was gone, a single leap taking her into the trees.

Wu Ying turned his head from side to side, looking over the clearing and all that had been destroyed. Their battle had taken no longer than the time it took for an incense stick to burn, but trees that had stood for a decade were destroyed, leaves stripped, and branches cracked.

---

12 yóujī jiāngjūn—Guerilla General is an actual rank in the ancient Chinese military and was responsible for guerilla tactics on the battlefield, which mostly consisted of small group tactics.

In the end, Wu Ying regarded the waxing moon that stared down from the heavens, impartial to the doings of the cultivators below. Uncaring of their minor intrigues. And he was forced to wonder what else was in store for him and the tournament itself.

Chapter 15

Morning the next day. His opponent—Hao Zhi—was a fist cultivator. He stood there, arms wide, waiting for Wu Ying to make a move. His breathing was slow and easy, but so loud that it was as though bellows the size of a mountain were working. Wu Ying watched the man's feet, the way he moved, and then on a whim, recalling all that had been said, sheathed his sword.

"What is he doing?" Liu Ping, by the side of the ring, spoke, her voice rising and shrill. "Why is he putting his sword away?"

"Can I change my bet?" Pan Shui, a short distance away, cried out, turning to the bookie. He was already pulling his hands back and shaking his head.

Whispers from the crowd, all around. The morning sun cooked Wu Ying's skin, reflecting off the healthy tan. The smells of fried fish and dough mixed with congee and fresh ginger from the breakfast still being served in the restaurant floated through the air.

It made him smile. As did the voices around him.

"Does he not want to win?"

"Is he that confident?"

"This is going to be amusing…"

Wu Ying tuned them out, stalking into the center of the ring. His opponent followed a moment later, his eyes sparking with fury.

"You mock me, little man. I shall split you apart and make you understand what it means to taunt the Tiger Giant of Lushu." Hao Zhi's voice roared before he leapt, unleashing a punch at Wu Ying. "The Earth Trembles!"

Not a punch. A series of punches. Fast, but not blazingly fast. Wu Ying dodged and slipped, spun around and beneath, his arms flicking up and sideways to block when he needed to do so. Pain blossomed along his arms, bruising him even as he swayed and dodged.

Like a rockslide, almost impossible to stop, but if you were fast enough, easy enough to dodge. Twelve Gales combined with his close combat movement techniques like the Whispering Wind kicking forms. Down, right hand touching the ground, kicking at a fist. Foot connected with fist, but even on the rebound, his opponent's hand grabbed his leg. Wu Ying spun, kicking backward and hard as he projected energy and the wind at the Tiger's face.

The blast of wind made his opponent fall back, eyes squinting shut. He threw Wu Ying into the air as he flinched, and the wind cultivator spun, riding the air currents to land on the platform. Wu Ying's leg hurt, the few seconds where the man gripped it leaving bruises.

Closing was a bad idea then.

That was also what made this fun. Rather than charge directly at his opponent, Wu Ying ran around the edges of the platform, picking up speed. He used the Heavenly Body technique to lighten his body, making the explosive power of his movements even faster. Mixing in the

Whispering Wind kicking techniques, Wu Ying launched his attacks from odd and dead angles as he ran around his opponent, striking at most three times before he retreated.

Impacts like a sledgehammer striking wood rang out, Hao Zhi's Earth-chi hardened body receiving the blows well. Strikes that would have broken bone in any other left only red imprints on his bare flesh, even as Wu Ying dodged his opponent by the depth of a paper thread each time.

This was the game they played. Hao Zhi only required a few unblocked strikes to end this battle. Wu Ying's Body Cultivation, while hardening and improving his constitution overall, was not focused on durability or strength. Speed, flexibility, agility—those were his tools.

Again and again, Wu Ying struck, his kicks landing on arms, thighs, ankles, and head. He even managed to strike a few body blows, impacting just under or against floating ribs, driving energy into unprotected kidneys and liver. Those elicited small grunts of pain, but the man he was fighting kept coming.

More importantly, each moment of triggering his skills was drawing down Wu Ying's chi levels. And while he might have reserves in his Core, it would be impolitic to use that. Eventually, he made a decision, slowing down and coming to a stop in front of his opponent.

The man snorted, clashing fists together. "Finally ready to fight instead of running, eh?"

"Just softening you up." Wu Ying grinned. "Any good cook knows you need to beat the meat a little if it's too hard before you begin."

"If I am a dish, it will be one you choke on!" Having finished speaking, Hao Zhi lunged, his great strength shattering the stone plates beneath his feet as he threw himself at Wu Ying. "Mountain Breaking Punch!"

No time to mock the man for shouting his skills. Instead, Wu Ying jumped, meeting the other in mid-air. He led the way with his own leg, flooding his form with chi as he executed his technique.

Fist and leg impacted, but rather than take the impact directly, Wu Ying allowed his lead foot to fold, borrowing the energy of the impact and pushing to help spin him around. At the same time, Wu Ying extended his other leg as he let himself arc over his opponent's arm and shoulder.

The crack of his heel crushing his opponent's cheek, his point of impact shifting low just before he struck to avoid a killing blow, resounded through the field. An explosive breath exhaled from his opponent, swirling the air around Wu Ying as he began to land. But even injured and stunned, his opponent was moving, an uppercut catching Wu Ying's thigh.

Flipped up and over, Wu Ying impacted the floating barrier keeping him in the ring, his body sliding down. One leg was entirely numb with only the barest hints of radiating pain beginning to arise. Wu Ying landed in a crouch, Hao Zhi stumbling around, punch drunk.

Pushing up on one foot, Wu Ying made to continue the fight when the referee, watching from outside, spoke up. "Halt!"

Wu Ying froze, then let himself relax, breathing through his nostrils as pain radiated from his thigh—and thank god the blow had not targeted a few *cun* to the right. Otherwise, his chances of having a family would have been nullified.

"Cultivator Long would have been thrown outside the ring. As such, he has forfeited this duel!" the referee announced.

Loud murmurs rose up in objection.

"Cultivator Hao is not able to fight any longer!"

"What? No. We saw Expert Long pull his blow to not kill his opponent!"

"So did Cultivator Meng! Or do you think he'd be standing if his peaches were struck?"

"Enough!" The voice that rose up crushed all the arguments, though it had no chi infusion. It was just the skill of a man who had contended with arguing cultivators for a long time and knew how to pitch his voice. In this case, the head referee. "The rules of the tournament were laid out at the beginning. Whether or not Cultivator Long could have—or should have—won matters not. He was thrown out of the ring while his opponent is still on his feet.

"We will brook no challenges to our authority. Those who continue to do so will be dismissed from the competition."

As much as the other cultivators might want to argue, none dared do so. After all, honor and a good fight were important, but the prize on offer was more important. At least at this moment.

At the referee's gesture, the energy surrounding the barrier was cut off and friends of Cultivator Meng rushed up, gripping him by his arms and leading off the stunned fist fighter. The crushed cheek bone around his face was swelling with fluids and glowing red hot. The moment Cultivator Meng's feet impacted the earth, another cultivator was pressing an herbal compress to his face.

"Can you get down yourself?" The referee had approached Wu Ying while he watched his ex-opponent, the man's gaze on Wu Ying's injured leg.

"Yes." Pushing himself up, Wu Ying sent more chi into his body, ascertaining the damage. Bruised for certain. No tearing though. He would have trouble utilizing it fully, but it was not a crippling blow. On the other hand, even sheathed with his chi and with a solidified wind exterior, the leg he had used to kick his other opponent still throbbed.

"Then please leave. We must fix the ring before the next match."

Wu Ying turned a little, regarding the referee. His tone of voice was guarded, his entire demeanor watchful. Wu Ying sensed the other referees and guards watching him too, obviously wondering if he would throw a tantrum.

"Of course," Wu Ying replied, bowing.

He did not miss the sigh of relief as he limped down the ring.

***

"Teaches me to wager on you," Pan Shui grumbled, arms crossed as Wu Ying sat, stretching his injured leg out near the rings, watching the other combatants. "You lost me a good ten tael!"

"I never asked you to bet on me."

"No, but I knew how good you were."

"Gambling is never a sure thing," he replied easily. "If it was certain, then it would not be gambling, would it?"

"Why did you do it?" Gao Qiu asked, having come down from his own battle.

Currently, Liu Ping was fighting in the farthest ring, her brother watching over her.

"I thought I'd win," Wu Ying replied truthfully.

"You did win," Pan Shui insisted. "And if that referee—"

"He made the right call." Wu Ying sighed. "I should have formed a wind barrier to allow me to push off, but when he hit me, I lost focus."

"You could have finished the fight with that kick," she insisted, shaking her head. "What was that kick anyway?"

"There's no full name for it, but it's part of the sixth form in the Whispering Wind system," Wu Ying replied. "You know, with any other cultivator, that kick should have been enough to end the fight."

"Yes. But you were a fool anyway. Mercy is for the weak," Kong Lai replied, the female sect cultivator appearing by their sides. "Any who take part in this contest know that they risk their lives. Sacrificing a victory for mercy weakens you."

"Unless one's dao is of mercy and justice," Shi Fei, behind Kong Lai, added. "After all, the dao is myriad and the Lady Quan Yin has shown us that way too is true."

"Hah! She and her kind are an exception. Let those who follow it do so, but they should not be here." A hand waved around the tournament grounds, her brown robes flapping. "Give alms, tend the sick, pity the poor. But we are warriors. And mercy is for fools and the dead."

"Why are you bothering us?" Pan Shui asked, her arms crossing as she glared at the sect cultivator. "I would think you would not desire to lower your status to speak with us wandering cultivators."

"Elder Eng has deigned fit to speak with Cultivator Long. And anyway"—she grinned viciously—"I'm to make use of this ring next."

Kong Lai jerked her head toward where the ring was just now emptying, the pair of cultivators—dao wielders both—limped off, sporting cuts across their bodies. Nothing too deep, for they had both held back.

"Who's your opponent?" Wu Ying asked.

"Me," Liu Jin said, having returned. There was a trace of fear in his voice, though he hid it after a second and nodded to Gao Qiu. "She won. She's just making friends."

Gao Qiu smiled in relief.

"Come, boy. I want to get this over with quickly," Kong Lai said, flicking her gaze over Liu Jin before curling her nose. "If you fear being hurt, just concede."

Liu Jin bristled, even as the girl strode off.

Shi Fei raised one crimson-robed hand. "She's not kidding. I've watched her fight. She's… ummm…"

"Brutal," Pan Shui finished the sentence. "We've all seen it. Almost a good thing her Elder Brother isn't here. It's the sect's style."

The referee called for Liu Jin, and under those troubled words, he hurried over to join the girl in the ring.

***

"Enough!" The voices rose from all around the ring.

Within, the participants ignored the shouted words as blades clashed and blood dripped.

"End it!" Gao Qiu called to the referee, who shook his head.

"No outside interference. Only the participants may end a fight."

"She's killing him!"

"The rules are the rules."

Another blow, Liu Jin's dao knocked aside. Kong Lai slid in under his open guard, her paired short axes slicing into his body. Liu Jin managed to retreat, dodging the majority of the force of the cuts but not avoiding them entirely. Blood flew through the air as long cuts carved across his body and left arm, with just a singular blast of flame energy keeping her back. The injuries joined a half dozen deeper cuts.

"Liu Jin! Give it up," Gao Qiu called.

"No! I can still fight," Liu Jin replied.

Wu Ying winced, for Kong Lai had not slowed in her attacks, charging and blocking his sword with a heavy swing of one axe. She shoulder-charged Liu Jin and hit him hard under his shoulder, bouncing him backward even as he tried to backpedal more. Before he could finish flying, she finished her form by jumping and spinning, bringing down her axe.

He slammed into the floor, the blade biting deep into his chest, blood exploding from his mouth. He bounced once, then again to lie bonelessly on the dueling ring floor.

A second, screams of outrage and worry, then the ring's barrier flicked off and the surrounding group exploded into action. A water cultivator was one of the first to arrive, just behind Wu Ying, who had bandages that he lay on the open wound.

"Move," the water cultivator snapped at Wu Ying, shoving his hands aside even as the water cultivator's hands glowed. "I'll keep the blood in, but we need him to wake and close his own wounds."

Wu Ying leaned back, then backed off even more as he realized an actual healer was arriving. A wood cultivator held forth acupuncture needles that he gestured with, embedding them in Liu Jin's body with a throw. The injured cultivator's heart rate dropped, while blood that had been held back slowed as blood flow was cut off.

"Hold him still. I need to sew these wounds closed," the healer growled, then looked around. "I also need a Flickering Yang Blood Formation Pill, a Four Marrow Bone Reinforcement Pill, and an Eight Skin Domain Layer Pill."

Wu Ying shook his head, not knowing those pills. However, they sounded like basic pills meant for Body Cleansers. He quickly searched his spirit rings and found a couple that might work. Before he could speak, the referee was there, pill bottles in hand.

"We do not have an Eight Skin Domain Layer Pill, but we have the Yin-Yang Layered Skin Pill."

"That'll do." The healer pointed at the man's mouth. "Blood first, then bone. But only when I tell you to." Hands deep in Liu Jin's chest, he swore. "She cut his arteries and veins..." Hands plunged into his pouch, a curved needle and string appearing in his hand. He sewed, his wood chi burrowing into the body beneath him to hold vein and artery ends together.

"You craven worm, you pox-ridden lover of pigs and horses, you demon-infested hag!" Liu Ping was being held back by Gao Qiu and the same fist cultivator Wu Ying had fought earlier, even as Kong Lai looked down her nose and Shi Fei attempted to pull her back. "If he dies, I'll rip your guts out and feed them to you!"

"I did nothing more than win," Kong Lai said. "I warned him before the fight. He should have conceded. Someone as untalented as him is nothing more than trash."

"Trash!" Liu Ping surged forward again, a sudden musky scent rising as her cultivation aura ran unbridled.

Gao Qiu focused, pushing his own aura of water over Liu Ping, attempting to calm her bestial energy she put out.

"That's what you and the army think of us, isn't it?" Liu Ping said. "We know all about the deals you sects make with them. Taking the nobles, the rich who can afford your services!"

"*Enough!*" Gao Qiu roared, twisting Liu Ping around. "Your brother lies dying, and you are trying to pick a fight."

His words shocked the cultivator, making her shut up. He shoved her again and she stumbled away toward the ring where the healer working on Liu Jin muttered, so softly that Wu Ying only caught it barely.

"So much drama. He's a cultivator. A blow like that won't kill him..."

The healer's hands were still flying across the body, finishing up his stitching. The water cultivator who had helped initially had stepped back while the referee hovered, ready to feed pills to the delirious victim. Seeing everyone look over, the water cultivator shrugged as he pulsed his own aura, sliding blood off his skin to splatter on the ground beside him.

"What? It's true. If we left him alone, he'd probably die. Maybe if he woke up and managed to swallow some healing pills and use his chi control to aid him. But with us around?" The healer shrugged.

Wu Ying frowned, turning the man's words over in his head as he peered at Liu Jin's wound. As bloody as the wound had been, Kong Lai had not crushed his heart. She might have nicked his lungs and had certainly chopped apart and broken ribs, but those were not immediate life-ending blows.

His hand came up, touching his chest where he had been run through. His injury had been somewhat similar, though the attack had injured his heart, from what he had been informed. In addition, he had also suffered minor wounds throughout the flight… but even then…

He watched the water cultivator and healer, the referee, and the way the others reacted to their words. Some looked confused, others contemplative. Perhaps they were exaggerating their lack of reaction, but if so, it was at least calming the crowd. What could have been a disaster and a massive fight had settled. The healer finished his work, and with the aid of the referee and other cultivators, was taking away the injured Liu Jin.

Lips pressed together, Wu Ying discarded his concerns. For now, he would let their words lie without probing them. It seemed that at least a few others—Gao Qiu included—had reached the same silent conclusion.

Even so, Wu Ying watched as Shi Fei and Kong Lai were shunned, none willing to speak with them. The muttered words of recrimination brought old grudges to life once more. And Wu Ying had to wonder—how much more drama might there be in this tournament?

It was, after all, only the second day.

Chapter 16

Perhaps it was the wound done to Liu Jin. Perhaps the animosity and the grudges had been there all along, hidden beneath a veneer of courtesy and hospitality. Perhaps it was just coincidence that drove the number of injuries in the second part of the day. There was a savagery, a mercilessness in the second half of the day that had been lacking during the earlier fights.

"Hmmm?" Gao Qiu replied when Wu Ying commented on it while they waited for their turns, then chuckled. "A little, I guess. But look at the board."

Wu Ying turned his head toward where a simple wooden board had been set up. Names had been written on one end where wooden slats were inserted and another, a tally of wins. The board only carried twelve names, but it was enough to tell who the leaders were.

"I see it," Wu Ying said. "What of it?"

"Do you not notice?" Gao Qiu snorted at Wu Ying's blank look. "Only four have won every single one of their fights." He mildly glared at Wu Ying. "Might have been five if someone had put in an effort."

"Ah…" Wu Ying nodded. "They're vying for the last spots."

"Exactly." Then Gao Qiu lowered his voice, sounding a little tired. "But there are grudges being settled. It's… well. It's tough for us out here, as wandering cultivators. Not many resources, not many jobs. If you take a job from another, well, it's remembered."

"But still better than joining a sect?"

"Yes." Gao Qiu nodded firmly. "It might be different in Shen, but here…" He shook his head. "Here, it's tough. The government guards the roads and all the major settlements, so only smaller villages or traveling merchants need our help. And even then, the pay… well, you remember."

Wu Ying nodded, recalling the single tael he had been paid. It was, of course, a decent amount of coin for a merchant, but for a cultivator who needed to buy spirit stones and pills to aid them in their cultivation, it was all too small.

"So, we all compete for the better contracts when they crop up."

"You should all learn to be Gatherers or Herb Farmers then," Wu Ying said.

The look he received from Gao Qiu made him smile a little. Even here, most cultivators turned down the job. Not that he blamed them—there wasn't much money in the growing of most spirit herbs. Especially not compared to the amount of specialized knowledge one needed.

After all, spiritual herbs weren't like rice—you couldn't keep replanting the same plant, only rotating and fertilizing it as needed. Not to say rice farming was easy, but it certainly did not require knowledge of formations, chi flows, or an entire ecology of other plants to balance the overall environment.

As for Wild Gathering—that was even more specialized. After all, not only did you need to know and differentiate between hundreds of spiritual herbs, but you also needed to be willing to travel in the wilds. Many of the herbs that were most in demand didn't mature more than once every few years, if not decades.

"You know, some have tried," Gao Qiu said absently. "Most of us learn a little bit—just the basics, you know?"

Wu Ying nodded. It didn't take much to work out what Spirit Grass was or a Three-Fold Mushroom.

"But storage, finding people to make the pills afterward…" The older man shook his head. "It's not easy."

For a second, Wu Ying considered his World Spirit Ring. It continued to grow—nearly four and a half fields large now. Thankfully, the amount of work required to keep it running had decreased since he had adjusted what he grew. Now, he had multiple plants that would mature over a timespan of years, leaving him with less day-to-day management.

Rare Spirit Herbs were arrayed in fields all across his ring, many of them the herbs he required for the medicinal baths he needed to keep his Wind Body improving. Even if the pixiu had said that he needed a dragon's blood to improve most drastically, that wasn't something he could rely upon. Rather, he preferred to grind away at the blockages, slowly improving his body further.

In theory, at some point, Wu Ying would gain a true Wind Body. One that was as much mortal and physical as an aspect of the wind. He would have to master the Seven Winds, soak in the dao of Heaven and Hell. Yet, that method forward required his body to be ready.

So. Step by step.

"Why not leave then?" Wu Ying gestured around him. "Surely there are easier countries. Places where it would be easier to grow."

"Some do. Some decide it is too much and leave. But for many of us… Zhao is our home. We grew up here. The cities we see, the settlements we visit, they're familiar. We have friends, some even have family," Gao Qiu said. "And though some might preach leaving behind the ties to mortality to ascend, the kingdom is not wrong. Too few succeed—and even fewer of us wandering cultivators."

"So you form families?" Wu Ying asked.

"And associations."

"Like the White Flower Merchant Association." Wu Ying nodded. "And these other cultivators, they're part of other associations?"

"Some of them. The Brothers of Bamboo, the Prosperous Two Thousand." Gao Qiu gestured to a few groups on the edges. "Some are part of ours."

Wu Ying ran a hand through his hair, making sure it was in place. So much to learn. A world that was entirely different in a way. Now that his attention had been brought to the matter, he could see and understand the way some of them interacted with one another, the groupings.

And the way the Brothers of Bamboo were glaring at Gao Qiu and the Prosperous Two Thousand, nearly all of their own people knocked out. Or how a few of the smaller groups, not official associations but friends anyway, stared at the bigger groups.

"So, what does being in an association do for you all, anyway?" Wu Ying said. "I know you offered for me to join, but you never did elaborate."

"Ah! That…" Gao Qiu made a face. "It seems it is my turn. Another time?"

Wu Ying frowned, since it was not exactly Gao Qiu's turn. Still, he let the man go. Who knew what mental preparations another needed? Especially as things got more difficult.

Left alone, Wu Ying let out a huff, then returned to watching the fights. Yet he found himself distracted, the earlier pull of watching individuals train and improve themselves having faded. Now, the fights were more vicious, more desperate—almost like the tournaments in the kingdom of Shen. The tournament was not, at the end of the day, fun.

Then again, Wu Ying had to admit perhaps he had been the only one who had ever thought of it as entertaining. After all, he was the only one here who did not require the winnings. Who had no intention of making a connection with the Seven Pavilions.

Realization left him reeling, as the words of the Core Formation Elders clarified.

He was an adult bullying children.

Perhaps he might learn something from fighting. But just as likely, he could have learnt as much watching them. Certainly, outside of Pan Shui, none of the others exhibited the Heart of their weapons. His ascension had enforced a division, one that only now he was truly understanding.

One that, he had to admit, he was ashamed he'd taken so long to grasp. Too long, perhaps, he had considered himself the underdog. And even if he had progressed from being a mere peasant, he still had survived in the shade of those stronger about him. Those who had grown faster than him. Everyone from his martial sister, who had been lauded as a prodigy, to his own best friend, who had formed a Core two years ago.

"Cultivator Long!"

The voice pulled Wu Ying from his thoughts, the impatient referee waving to him. He offered the referee a weak wave in reply, scanning the surroundings. Lots of individuals around, but the three presences he was most concerned about were in their usual positions—balcony and compound, respectively. He shrugged and hurried over to the ring, eyes already drinking in his opponent. Well, perhaps he would consider the matter later tonight.

For now, he would fight. Even a quick glance at his opponent showed that this would not be a challenge—his opponent did not even have proper balance. A favorable duel, one no one would expect Wu Ying to lose. Tomorrow then. It would not be too late to lose, gracefully, tomorrow.

***

Wu Ying walked over to the sect Elders' table, bowing to them and taking the indicated seat. He felt the eyes of the other cultivators watching him, the quiet questioning of why he was being so honored, but he chose to ignore it. There was nothing he could do about the others, for now. Nor would declining the invitation be in his best interest. Not with the sects being a second potential source of income.

Having greeted the pair and received his tea and a portion of the snacks arrayed, the group entered into small talk even as the privacy bubble that kept their conversations muted to the outside world was left inactive. They spoke mostly about the weather and rumored incidents in various cities—conscriptions, bandit raids, rumors of demon beast appearances and subjugation. The trio of Core Formation elders and the two silent sect cultivators seated by the side all avoided the topic of the tournament itself.

Small talk. Wu Ying was grateful enough for it, for the information provided and his probing let him paint a greater picture of the kingdom. For all that the invitation had been extended by both Elders, Elder Tsui was carrying the conversation, with Elder Eng only interjecting occasionally. Elder Eng looked entirely dissatisfied, glaring about Wu Ying occasionally when his impersonal mask fell. However, in time, the talk trailed off and the point of inviting him was reached.

"Your results in the tournament today were… interesting, Cultivator Long," Elder Tsui commented leadingly.

"Having a chance to practice my unarmed styles is not something I can afford to let pass me by," Wu Ying said mildly. "After all, I do not have sect mates to test my understanding upon."

"A tournament is no place for testing! It's why you lost," Kong Lai scoffed. "As it stands, you might not even enter the semi-finals!"

"Ah, but the semi-finals do not count previous wins," Shi Fei said. "There is strategy to entering not as the chief contender, such that one might face a weaker opponent to start."

"Only if they do weaker-to-weaker pairing and not weaker-to-stronger," Kong Lai said. "Otherwise, he might face me immediately and lose."

Elder Eng snorted loudly, making Kong Lai bow her head in sudden contrition.

"Elder—" she began.

"You overestimate yourself, always. Just like my disciple… my late disciple…" For a second, Elder Eng's voice grew faint, before it firmed. "Used to. You think all this is a game, when the path to cultivation is fraught with danger. If you do not learn, you too will die."

"I was always better than him," Kong Lai said mulishly.

"Fool!" He made a small motion, a chi projection forming and slapping her across the face from his seat. She rocked backward, choosing not to dodge the obvious attack, knowing that doing so would entail greater punishment. "What good is martial prowess when you are stabbed in the back!"

"I apologize, Elder Eng. I did not think."

"Of course you didn't." Elder Eng spat to the side. "Useless. My disciple and nephew, killed. You, I'm saddled with because of my youngest sister and her lack of morals." He shook his head. "What a pitiful existence."

Wu Ying kept his mouth shut even as he watched Kong Lai bristle. It seemed that even the smallest pressure had brought out the hidden resentments among the sect members.

He could not help but remember his time in the Verdant Green Waters, the wrangling for position among certain Elders or the way they lorded it over outer sect members to make themselves feel better about their own lack of improvement in their cultivation base.

Then again, was this any better? Different certainly, but not better.

"Did you, Cultivator Long?" Elder Tsui asked.

"Did I what?" Wu Ying replied.

"Choose to lose strategically?" He even sounded mildly interested, though Wu Ying assumed most of his words were a distraction. It was certainly what he would do—if he cared about saving Elder Eng's face[13].

"I—" Before he could finish, Wu Ying sensed it.

He spun around, looking over the balcony and following the whiff of blood he had caught. Mostly fresh, a little dried, but too much of it to be a casual injury or a broken open wound. Along with the smell of iron and death was the pulsing grief, the stench of rage and grief and tears.

As quickly as he had picked up on it, he was nearly too late. The individual involved was moving too swiftly, exploding onto the scene. She ignored the stairs and main entrance, instead leaping straight up to the second floor via the patio deck, hooking an arm around the edge of the floor that jutted out. She used it to vault herself the rest of the way onto the banister, bare feet resting on the arm-width length of wood.

"Liu Ping!" Wu Ying cried.

"*I'll kill you!*" Liu Ping screamed, her swordbreaker in hand.

---

[13] Face (面子 / miànzi) is not something I use a lot, though it is obviously an important part of Chinese culture. The reason I don't mention it much is because in my experience, it's an undercurrent in everyday interactions. If you watch Chinese dramas, unless they are purposely exaggerating (to make a villain in particular), it's often not a term actively used. Phrases like "please give me some face, sir" or "you are not giving me face" can be used, but it's often in more contentious situations. Mostly, it's just a given that it is happening—sort of like saying please and thank you in Western interactions.

Her legs bunched and pushed against the banister, the wood creaking and shattering. The quad-edged steel rod was aimed to crush, her bestial aura erupting to aid her strike. The entire attack flew past Wu Ying, filled with killing intent and the sum of her energy to home in on Kong Lai.

Already alerted, Wu Ying was moving, drawing his sword from its sheath and standing. However, sword draws from a seated position, especially in an attempt to protect someone else, were highly inconvenient. It slowed him, for he had to push away from the table, draw, and reach across the distance.

Too slow.

"Enough!" The roared word from Elder Eng shook the entire building, making hastily constructed wood creak and whine.

Newly rebuilt sections trembled, nails popping out and joints stressing and fracturing as the Core Formation cultivator extended his aura. All those around felt their movements slowed, their limbs heavy as though the weight of a mountain had been added to them. Those closest to him were most affected, feeling the full weight of the unleashed aura.

The crushing strike meant for Kong Lai dipped low, digging into the chair then the floor, shattering the wooden plank. It left only the slightest scratch from the claw-like aura on the target's leg as it fell.

Crouched on the banister, Liu Ping collapsed even as the guardrail gave way. It sent her sprawling onto the floor and tottering on the edge of falling off. By dint of rage and stubbornness, she managed to scramble and keep her position. Then, edges of the same bear-bloodline and aura peeking around the pressure and aiding her, Liu Ping pushed upward against the elder's aura, attempting to finish her attack.

Wu Ying's sword, half drawn in an attempt to parry the attack, wavered as the aura combated his own. He felt the earth elemental domain of Elder Eng press upon him, trying to weigh him down. Instinctively, he shed it, letting the aura and the pressure exerted by the elder glide off him.

What was a mountain but an obstacle to move around? Did the wind care that it stood there, still and imposing? Let it stand, unmoving. It could stay for all the wind cared, for the wind was meant to travel, to see and move and gust.

Finishing his motion, Wu Ying drew and cut downward near the hilt of Liu Ping's sword. He struck hard, projecting his own aura and sword intent into the blow and beating the weapon out of straining fingers. Liu Ping's tie jian[14] fell to the floor with a clatter, even as chairs scraped, and the pair of Elders stood.

"What kind of foolishness is this? An assassination attempt on my sect member? I shall have your head!" Elder Eng roared.

---

[14] Tie jian – swordbreaker. Basically meant to destroy weapons. You see it used in Crouching Tiger, Hidden Dragon.

"She killed my brother! I'll kill her…" Liu Ping cried.

Her rage and grief gave her strength, such that she scrambled for her weapon's hilt. Only for Wu Ying to step on it, blocking her movements. A second later, Elder Tsui's fiery aura spread out, focused upon her and drawing a pained grimace.

"You traitor!" she hissed at Wu Ying even as her tears dripped from reddened eyes.

"This is not the way, Liu Ping," he murmured, sheathing his weapon. He felt more eyes watching him now, as many struggled to deal with Elder Eng's aura, and he moved without concern. He bent down, picking up the swordbreaker. "He died then?"

"He was killed!" she snarled. "He was fine when I left for my fight. But when I came back, when I came back…" She choked off a sob. "She killed him."

"Death in the tournament was always a risk," Elder Tsui said, but stopped when Wu Ying held up a hand.

Crouching beside Liu Ping, holding the tie jian in one hand in reverse grip so she could not grab it, Wu Ying raised her head with his other hand, flooding the exterior of her aura with his own, shedding a little of Elder Eng's and Tsui's auras to give her some space to move. At the same time, he pushed at her own growling aura, sending calming winds replete with memories of lazy summer days and cloying warmth to mellow her.

"You said she killed him. What do you mean?" Suspicion in his voice.

Rather than answer, she sobbed loudly. Collapsing, as though it was only fighting against the auras that had kept her moving. Now, beaten, she had no more energy.

Wu Ying's answer came from an unexpected source. The arrival of Elder Cao from the skies, coming down from up high rather than from the compound, was only preceded by a short notice as the winds murmured a warning to Wu Ying.

"He was murdered. Throat slashed while he lay in bed. We have a second murder on our hands," Elder Cao said, turning to look at all around and pitching her voice such that it carried not just through the restaurant but across the entirety of the village and the Seven Pavilions compound. "Until such time as we determine who the killer is, those who attempt to leave will be severely punished."

Pandemonium at her words. The crowd shouted. Those far away from the Elders released auras, shouting questions, gathering together, and grabbing at weapons.

Upstairs, the Elders pulled back their auras in respect of Elder Cao. Wu Ying made Liu Ping's sword disappear into his Storage Ring and he took her in his arms as she cried. Over her head, he looked up, spotted Elder Cao's troubled gaze, and winced internally.

Things had gotten even more complicated in this damn tournament.

Chapter 17

"You wanted to see me, Elder Cao?" Wu Ying murmured, standing in the narrow wooden corridor. Even from here, he could smell it—the stench of heart's blood spilled. He heard the buzz of insects that had come to feast upon the corpse and its discarded remnants. Another building, but so similar to his own in layout. Bare furnishings, just a few fresh cut flowers and paintings all around.

"Yes. You fought against the Dark Sects in your kingdom, correct?" Elder Cao said, beckoning him closer.

"Yes, Elder."

"Then what are your opinions on this?" She gestured into the room.

Within, Investigator Chu stood, measuring blood splatters as she crouched on the floor. No one else was in there. Even Elder Cao stood outside—not that the room had that much space.

Wu Ying inhaled, filtering scents and auras. Liu Jin's aura was gone, only traces of his presence still present and that, probably, from his stay in the room. Liu Ping's was much fainter, the sister having likely spent some time within. Hers was mixed with the smell of frustration, rage, and grief; the hormonal balance was stark. None of that came from the corpse though. At a guess, he probably had been killed while asleep.

There were other cultivators' essences too. Elder Cao's, the healer, the investigator, and yes, the Guard Captain. Even Gao Qiu's was part of the background, as well as maybe… Well. Quite a lot of notes floated through the background, making it hard for Wu Ying to pick them all out. But yes, there definitely was at least one more scent.

More interesting was the body itself. Liu Jin lay on his bed, his throat slit, the wounds around his chest still bandaged and dark. On the bedspread and along the floor, blood had dripped. But that was not why Elder Cao had called him in.

No, it was what had been marked on the walls. Words, a drawing. Painted in drying blood, infused with a conception by an artist, but lacking chi. The conception level of artistry – the ability to project an idea or thought or feeling by undertaking one's art. Just looking at it, Wu Ying felt his soul being attacked, the dark desires painted bringing forth feelings of anger and pride, jealousy and pain.

Wu Ying hissed, stepping away from the painting and tightening the chi around his body, protecting himself. He looked away, breathing slowly and searching the air for hints of the dark, the bitterness he had come to associate with the chi from the Dark Sect.

Yet, he could not find it.

"What do you see?" Elder Cao spoke finally, when the silence kept going.

"The painting in blood. Whoever is involved—if it's not multiple people—has gained conception in painting. Whoever killed him, they did it fast, but they took their time while painting," Wu Ying said. "This, the painting, it's an attack. A statement." He sighed. "But I cannot say if it is a Dark Sect member. I am no expert, and there are so many…"

"No signifiers to you?"

"If painting in blood can be considered that, certainly. But an individual can be twisted without joining the Dark Sects. And there is no twisting in their cultivation bases that I can recognize left behind," Wu Ying replied, looking at Investigator Chu and Elder Cao. "Perhaps others might have more to tell you, but that is all I can provide."

"Pity. I had hoped you would be more useful," Elder Cao said.

"If the Dark Sects were that easy to root out, they would not be such persistent thorns in our existence, would they?" Wu Ying said. "Even the major clues I know came from the corrupted orthodox members rather than the Dark Sect members themselves."

The Elder glared at Wu Ying, obviously unused to being chastised. Both the Guard Captain—standing outside—and Investigator Chu looked at Wu Ying with horror and surprise, that he would dare speak back. Nagging suspicion flowed across both their faces, but Wu Ying ignored it.

Instead, he continued. "I'm surprised you asked me here. Asking a suspect for their opinion is not normal procedure, no?"

"Between our conversation last night and the timing of this death, we are certain you are no longer a suspect."

"When did he die?" Wu Ying asked.

"Between the fourth and seventh hour after the midday sun reached its zenith," Investigator Chu said. "I will, I hope, be able to ascertain a more accurate timescale soon." She was eyeing the drying blood; lips curled a little.

"So accurate?" Wu Ying exclaimed, surprised.

"We spoke to Liu Ping and the healer, confirming when they left Liu Jin alone and when he was found again. That made for a very narrow window." Elder Cao was frowning as she spoke, looking a little dissatisfied.

Wu Ying could not help but ask, "What is wrong? Beyond the obvious murders."

For a second, Elder Cao pursed her lips, casting a glance at the other guardsman. At the Guard Captain's nod, she continued. "These actions, they do not make sense. So many of you were visible at the tournament, it will make our job easier. On top of that, this death…" She shook her head. "It is nothing like Cui Wen's."

"Perhaps they stopped hiding?" Wu Ying said tentatively.

"Or are trying to cast blame on another," Elder Cao replied.

Wu Ying nodded. He had no answer to that.

"Will you aid us?" Elder Cao said. When he looked surprised, she gestured to the Guard Captain Teng Fei. "You were at the tournament, watching. Tell us who you saw, when you saw them. We will be corroborating every witness statement. Even if they expect us to do so…"

"It can still provide information," Teng Fei finished.

"Of course. Anything I can do," Wu Ying replied.

Elder Cao gestured, dismissing him and Teng Fei. The pair filed away, the Captain leading the way, moving with a slow, ponderous gait that seemed weighed down by the deaths.

Wu Ying could only hope that no more deaths would occur before they located the killer.

***

Gao Qiu was waiting for Wu Ying in his own temporary residence when he finally made his way back. Wu Ying led the other to his room, and before he could even provide tea or snacks, the other man was speaking.

"Why did they call you in?" Gao Qiu asked suspiciously, leaning against the wall leading to the corridor, the thin wooden door shut beside him.

"They wanted my input on the body," Wu Ying replied. "They believed I might have some knowledge about it because of the… well, state of the room." He was uncertain how much the Elder might want him to speak on it. Not that he expected the details to stay hidden for long—cultivators were notorious gossips after all. It had something to do with the need to talk about cultivation systems, to explore daos and concepts and argue about things that made them rather talkative.

"I saw Liu Jin's body," Gao Qiu said softly. "I heard Liu Ping scream, so I came out of my room. I caught only a glimpse of her before she dashed out, and I went to look in on Liu Jin afterward. I saw the… painting."

Wu Ying nodded. "Then you can see why they thought it might be the doings of a Dark Sect member."

"Or demonic cultivator."

"No." Wu Ying shook his head.

"What do you mean? Only a demon would paint that, with another's blood!"

"Demonic cultivators find it very hard to hide, especially when utilizing their chi." Wu Ying's memory flashed back to his own encounter with the demonic Core cultivators whilst rescuing his martial sister. "They might be able to hide a little, but when they make a statement like that, they would not be able to hide their twisted cultivation. There was no hint of the demonic in the painting or the room. Or the village."

"Then what? You think someone is trying to throw suspicion away?" Gao Qiu said, pushing off the wall. "What for? Why kill both a sect cultivator and Liu Jin? What's the point of it all?"

Wu Ying shrugged. "I think if you could understand that, you would know who the killer is." His lips twisted in a rueful smile. "Though I think whoever did the killing made a mistake."

"Why?" Gao Qiu said.

"Because most of us were at the tournament," Wu Ying said. "The Guard Captain and Elder Cao were confirming alibis when I left, cross-referencing eyewitness reports. It should not be hard for them to work out who was the killer, using that."

"Ah." Gao Qiu frowned. "Who is Elder Cao?"

"She's the…" Wu Ying shrugged. "The Core Formation Elder watching over the tournament."

"You met her?" Gao Qiu said, looking surprised. "I thought she was staying within the compound?"

No surprise that he had noticed. It was not as though Elder Cao was hiding her spiritual presence. Even as light as she let it rest upon the surroundings, anyone with any awareness would have felt it. Unlike Wu Ying and the other Elders, who had their own auras retracted, Elder Cao's blanketed the surroundings in subtle warning.

"I did. Last night," Wu Ying said.

"What is she like?"

"Old. An ex-general. A guerilla general, to be exact." Wu Ying shook his head. "Important and strong. Probably in the upper tiers of Core Formation stage. She also wields her weapon well. But she seems to take her job seriously."

"Is she just here for the tournament then?" Gao Qiu asked.

Wu Ying shrugged.

"Of course. It is not as though she would tell you." Gao Qiu bit his lower lip, worrying one corner.

"What is it? Why are you worried about her?"

The other cultivator shook his head. "No. I'm not worried about her. Not really…" Seeing the doubtful look on Wu Ying's face, he shrugged. "The generals of the guerilla divisions? The divisions themselves? They're the ones who handle or deal with wandering cultivators the most. They're not well respected in the army or kingdom either, since they're all considered outcasts and irresponsible.

"They're also the ones tasked with hunting down and killing rebels when they are found."

Wu Ying fell silent, turning over the information. The White Flower Merchant Association. The number of wandering cultivators here. Gao Qiu's words and his actions. The way the sects vied for Wu Ying's attention, skirting around the rules.

"You think she might still be working for the army," Wu Ying relayed the first of his conclusions.

"Yes. And though we haven't broken any laws here…" Gao Qiu shrugged. "The kingdom is always watching over these tournaments."

"As expected," Wu Ying murmured. "No?"

"Yes. It's always dangerous to come."

"Yet you did."

"Well, of course." Gao Qiu offered a tight half-smile. "Liu Ping wanted to compete. And the prizes—"

"Were never something you expected to win," Wu Ying said, remembering his words weeks ago. "In fact, you coming here was never about the tournament. And while you've been meeting with others, you do so while speaking with multiples. To make connections, not to socialize. You haven't been buying anything much either…"

As he spoke, Wu Ying realized how suspicious the man's actions had been. Gao Qiu's whole team, in a way. They had hung out with Wu Ying, but why him? Why even come to a tournament you never expect to win? Prestige perhaps, recognition; but then would they not have tried harder?

"Why did you come, Gao Qiu?" More remembered conversations, the man's intention to set-up a relationship with him for the Association. Anger, slow to build like the wind, began to blow. "What is the Association, really?"

"This might not be the best time." Gao Qiu shook his head. "We can discuss this later."

He turned to the door, only for Wu Ying to pulse his aura. Not cold but warm, like the South Wind. Not yet blazing hot like the west. Gao Qiu dropped his hand from the door handle, turning back to face Wu Ying's displeased expression.

"Who or what is the White Flower Merchant Association, Cultivator Gao? What did you try to drag me into?"

"I wasn't going to draw you into anything that you did not understand," Gao Qiu said defensively. "I was going to explain fully."

"Explain what?"

"We're patriots. Looking to do the best for our kingdom. We believe that the current system favors the rich, the nobles, and the king too greatly. It forces everyone to join the army, to serve them—whether they are worthwhile to be served or not," Gao Qiu said in a rush, chin rising stubbornly.

"You're rebels."

"We are patriots. We serve the true kingdom—the people!"

Wu Ying stepped back and gestured toward the door. His temper, his anger, he was not sure he could control it if the other stayed. Too many secrets – and secrets killed. "I've heard enough. You should go."

"Is that it? You'll just dismiss our plight? Is that your dao then? To watch others suffer and do nothing about it? Not very heroic," Gao Qiu said, clearly incensed by the abrupt rejection. "Are you going to turn us in?"

Wu Ying shook his head. "I have no desire to get involved in your kingdom's politics. Your secret is safe with me. As for my dao…" He looked off into the distance before he continued. "I know little enough of your kingdom to ascertain who is right or wrong. Who am I to interfere in your world?"

"Another wanderer on the path! Will you look away from those in need just because their plight is not yours? Will you choose to withhold your hand because they are strangers? Of course you will. That's what you all do." Gao Qiu snorted. "I should never have expected better."

"You speak as though the choice is obvious." Wu Ying glared. "I might have reservations about your kingdom's system but aiding a group I know nothing about seems just as foolish. You could be demon worshippers, Dark Sect cultists, or just heretical cultists with a tendency to banditry."

"How dare you! You've spent days with us, and you think we would do that?"

"That's the point. I don't know you all well enough. I just learned you're rebels. What else are you hiding?" Wu Ying snapped. "Your lies might have been necessary, but they were lies. A few days means nothing, when Dark Sect cultivators spend decades being good and loyal cultivators, only to betray and kill and kidnap!"

Gao Qiu's eyes widened, and he shrank back with each sentence. At the end, he exhaled sharply, realization that perhaps his usual guilt tactics might not work against someone who had dealt with Dark Sect traitors in the all-too-recent past.

"I see. I won't bother you any further then." He pulled the door open, turned around with his hand still on the door, and frowned at Wu Ying, his voice lowering. "You know, you might have seen the worst of cultivators, but if it blinds you to the best of us—then your enemies have won even more than you think."

Before Wu Ying could reply, the door shut, leaving him alone in his room.

Chapter 18

Standing in the ring, Wu Ying stared at his opponent. Wielding a pair of maces, the man kept casting glances around, paying attention not just to Wu Ying but the referees and audience. Not that he was the only one. The entire village was subdued today, the merchants clustered closer together along the main path, wandering cultivators moving in groups.

At the invitation of the Pan sisters, Wu Ying had joined them to traverse the way to the dueling rings, braving the glares and suspicious looks the other cultivators turned on them. Strangers all, they were the obvious suspects.

As expected, rumors about what had happened to Liu Jin had spread, no matter what kind of restrictions Elder Cao and Teng Fei might have placed. Now, everyone knew not only about the second death but the bloody painting. Rumors had sprung up, brought to Wu Ying by the wind, of even more paintings found, though the lack of blood in the air spoke to the untruth of that.

"Begin!" the referee's voice rang out, dragging attention back to the ring.

The mace wielder blinked, looking abashed, and made his salutations, his words echoed soon after by Wu Ying.

A flicker of movement, then the man ran forward, casting himself in a spinning vortex of bashing, thumping weaponry. He moved in a circular form, constantly turning as each attack was blocked, rotating himself and Wu Ying in a spiral around the ring.

Gasps of amazement rang through the surroundings as partway through the initial clash, small globs of water formed around Wu Ying's opponent. Brushing up against one of the globs of water had Wu Ying hissing, for it felt like contacting vicious acid, leaving his arm throbbing and smarting.

Rather than stay close to his opponent, Wu Ying infused the surroundings with his own chi, exploding it outward into a brief gale. Using the distraction and the dust kicked up that forced his opponent to cover his eyes, Wu Ying backed off, his sword rising to project sword intent to buy time.

"Acid orbs…" Wu Ying commented. "What a unique elemental form."

"My family's style and dao is of acid and dissolution, of cleansing and destruction," the wandering cultivator boasted, even as he charged. "I'll crush and mash you, until you are nothing more than paste!"

"We shall see…"

Wu Ying met the man's charge with his sword, cutting high and low, weaving a flashing defense. He used reverse parries, cutting against the backend of the swings or catching the strikes at an angle to push maces aside. A dao wielder with their wide, cutting sabers might meet ferocity with ferocity, attempting to overwhelm their opponent with strength alone. But Wu Ying carried the jian and would not take such an obstinate form.

Subtlety and grace to meet ferocity. Open voids and positioning to ensure his opponent's second weapon could not reach him, not without losing time and power, as they turned and twisted, as weapons were sent off-line.

Pick at the open gaps, when arms crossed, when body turned and spun, cutting lightly. Water might be malleable and change to fit myriad containers, but it was still a liquid. It was slow and strong compared to the wind. For where water moved to take up space, air just compressed in on itself.

Let water be present in air, let it exist beside him. For Wu Ying need only move around it, like the breeze itself, flowing away just before it touched him, always just a little farther away. Allowing water to chase him, even as he took pieces off the other.

Wu Ying's eyes glinted as the battle frenzy took him over, as he danced with his opponent. He controlled his aura, tamped down the amount of energy he put into his attacks, prolonging the fight as he drifted around the stage.

Conserve energy, conserve chi. Fight with the least amount of energy needed, dance on the edge of his opponent and try to find the Heart of his weapon. The sword was a weapon of finesse, of elegant solutions to savage problems, a sharp compromise between civilization and the barbarian.

Eventually, the multiple cuts, the ever-increasing number of wounds slowed his opponent, forcing him into greater and greater errors. Robes were torn, sleeves shredded and stained by dripping blood. Energy drained, wasted as it was splashed about the ring with ever widening, desperate motions.

Wu Ying drifted to a stop, sword leveled at his opponent's throat.

"I concede," his opponent said, his eyes burning with resentment. He shut them for a second, the drifting trio of acidic orbs returning to his body and splashing against open wounds. They mixed with blood and open cuts before disappearing, the opponent only allowing the smallest hiss of pain to escape from his lips as flesh burnt and boiled, but wounds were burnt shut. "I have not the skill to beat you, nor the reserves to wear yours down."

"Thank you for the pointers," Wu Ying replied.

"Hah!" The man snorted. "I should thank you. Damn sword prodigies…"

Turning, the water cultivator stomped away, putting his paired maces back in his belt. His friends ran over, some murmuring angrily about the dishonorable way Wu Ying had fought. Some muted clapping occurred, even as bettors grabbed their wooden slips to receive their payout. In the corner, Gao Qiu broke away from those he spoke with, moving to another group. Before the crowd's dissatisfaction could grow, the bell sounded, alerting all of a new drama.

Because of course there was more drama.

***

The village square, almost opposite where the rings had been set up, on the other side of the makeshift settlement. That was where they found the prisoners.

Three men on their knees, enchanted manacles glinting around their hands as they were forced to bow their heads whilst trapped by the wooden pillory[15]. Each cultivator bore a long rectangle of wood, where his head and arms were fastened side by side, forcing the cultivator to carry the weight of the entire ensemble on his shoulders and neck.

Beside the prisoners in their heavy cangues, the Seven Pavilions guards stood. However, the mostly mortal guards were not the major reason the three wandering cultivators were not attempting to break free—chi-flow hampered or not—but the final figure of Elder Cao in her armor.

Many of the wandering cultivators who had gathered at the ringing of the bell were watching the Elder with ill-disguised unease. Her aura had blanketed the surroundings all this time, but this was the first time many had actually seen the Core Formation cultivator. After all, her entrance into the restaurant had been brief and without fanfare. That she wore her helmet and armor in full and stared around impassively added to her intimidation factor.

Low conversations dominated the group, even as Wu Ying reached the edge of the crowd. He briefly considered his options before making his way to Pan Shui and her sisters, a wide gap around them and the rest of the cultivators. Next to them, but not too close, was the northern archer and the fisherman, the pair of men obviously uncomfortable near the sisters. Wu Ying noted, idly, that Gao Qiu was present, having been joined by a pair of White Flower Merchant cultivators Wu Ying had noticed before, though Liu Ping's absence was notable.

"What is going on?" Wu Ying asked the ladies.

Pan Yin shrugged, placing a hand on her younger sister's arm before she could speak up. "We don't know. We're all here because of the bell."

"And them," Pan Shui said, nodding toward the prisoners.

"And them," echoed Pan Yin.

Wu Ying turned to regard all those about, breathing deeply as he drew in the scents of those around him. He remembered what Elder Cao had asked of him and took extra care to pay attention, memorizing locations and faces.

Just in case another body turned up.

"We told you, no one leaves." Elder Cao's voice cut through the hubbub, shutting down conversations. "Until the perpetrator of the murders is found, any who leave will be considered to be obstructing a royal investigation and punished accordingly."

Voices rose, but Gao Qiu's was the loudest of them all. "What does that mean?"

"The punishment is to be held here, in the cangue, for thirty days. Then five years conscription with the army," Elder Cao replied.

---

[15] The wooden pillory (known as the cangue or tcha or kea) was used on prisoners as punishment. Unable to reach their own mouths, prisoners had to be fed by friends or family or else risk starvation.

"Five years!" Gao Qiu looked at the three cultivators, two of which were in their mid-thirties and the last in his early twenties. They all bore some familial resemblance in the hair and eyes. It was obvious Gao Qiu noticed that too, for he raised his voice. "You can keep his father and the other one, but the youngster—five years as a conscript will mean he'd lose any chance of growing further. How is that fair?"

"It is not a matter of fair, but the law," Elder Cao replied. "They had a duty to stay and aid us in the investigation. And they chose to shirk that duty. This is just punishment."

"Just." Gao Qiu almost spat the word, but at the look Elder Cao turned on him, he quieted down.

That the other wandering cultivators looked unhappy at what she had pronounced was perhaps Gao Qiu's only safety. Still, Wu Ying was surprised he had dared speak out. Then again, if he did not, how would Gao Qiu recruit for his cause? Rebels who did not rebel were just loud curmudgeons.

Politics. Wu Ying scoffed internally as he listened.

Elder Cao continued. "They will be forced to stay here, under guard. Let this be warning to all of you. And if you fear delays in your continued... *wandering*, I recommend you speak with the Guard Captain and the investigator."

Having spoken her mind, the Elder stepped upward, a sword appearing beneath her feet and carrying her back to the Pavilion. Wu Ying tracked her leaving, turning her words over in his mind.

"The Sect Elders did not come," Pan Shui murmured.

"So?" Pan Yin, the middle sister, replied.

"Just an observation."

"Do you think they'll cancel the tournament?" Pan Shui frowned in deep thought. When her sisters and Wu Ying turned to stare at her, she shrugged. "What? I can't solve the murders. But I did come here for the tournament. It'd be a shame to come all this way and not win any prizes."

"Probably not," Jochi, the archer said, crossing his arms as he approached the group. "Southerners are too stubborn to change their minds. And the Seven Pavilions still needs someone to marry their daughter off to." He grinned, rubbing his chin. "I'm looking forward to the dinner."

"Dinner?" Wu Ying said, puzzled.

Pan Shui snorted. "For the shortlist. It's tonight." Her eyes narrowed. "How did you not know this?"

"I've been... distracted." Wu Ying gestured at the three cultivators and their guards.

The group grimaced, even as the remainder of the wandering cultivators dispersed, heading back to the rings to fight or to gossip. There was a lot to talk about.

"Well, it sounds like we should see if we have a chance being on this shortlist," Pan Yin said, smiling tightly. "I've heard the dinner will be pretty good."

"Good? I hear they searched a half dozen counties to find the chef who will be cooking the meal tonight." Pan Shui said, waving her hands. "If you breathe deeply, you can smell the ducks and pigs being roasted, the rice and fish that is being steamed, and the vegetables they are prepping."

"Like your food, do you?" Wu Ying replied, though he smiled a little as he breathed deeply. He could taste it on the wind, the dishes already being cooked. He heard the noisy cooks prepping vegetables and meats, washing rice and crushing soybeans to prep the tofu.

"I've seen you eat." Pan Shui waved a finger under his nose. "Too bad you might not make it."

"It will be what it will be," Wu Ying replied, shrugging unconcernedly. While the meal would be pleasant, the potential for complex political problems or awkward social situations seemed to increase exponentially with each death.

Knowing that, well…

Good food could always be found everywhere.

"Well, hopefully you will join us in the final eight," Pan Shui said. "It won't be a real tournament if the best don't fight."

Even the archer nodded at those words, leaving Wu Ying to grin weakly. Together, by unspoken decree, the group turned to head back toward the rings. If more than one of them cast a glance back at the captured and pilloried cultivators, they did not speak of it. Nor did Wu Ying mention the presence of the three White Flower Merchant Association members, arguing silently amongst themselves as they shot glances at the prisoners.

Trouble brewing there. Definitely.

***

Wu Ying stared at himself in the mirror, adjusting the fit of his robes. He let his fingers dance across the dressing room table as he looked at the multiple storage rings he had set down. A half dozen, each of them thin and nondescript, made of jade, gold, and silver and all humming with the power and dao contained within them.

Only a single ring had not left his fingers as he took his bath. His World Storage Ring never left his presence, for the danger of owning such an item continued to haunt him. He had broken with his Master once, to keep hold of it. Now, after years of use and the slow, careful feeding of his own chi and biomatter, it had grown.

Over the past few weeks, Wu Ying had noticed a subtle increase. Where it had moved perhaps a single cun[16] each day before, now, a full foot might be added on the borders. That

---

[16] Cun—Chinese inch 1.26 normal inches or 32mm. It's 1/10th a chǐ (foot) and is actually more recent. Beforehand, most things were measurement by either chǐ, bù, or li with the bù between 5 or 6 chi and 300 bu equaling a li. To make it easier, I'm using cun here instead of fractions of a chi, partly because we already have chi in multiple formats.

might not seem fast, but when it was added to the entirety of the borders in all directions, the expansion saw him owning a significant parcel of land.

Pushing his chi and awareness into the ring, he hovered over his land in his mind's eye, like a stern god staring down upon the quiet, manicured land. A touch of his energy here and there, the shifting of plants or guidance of water flows kept the trapped energy moving in an endless cycle.

Insects buzzed in the distance, snails ate leaves, and earthworms moved deep in the soil. Wu Ying could see it all, sense it all, his mind and soul infused into his domain. Yet, there on the edges, the last tens of feet, it felt different. Less vibrant. Not just bare of grass and insects, but also the chi thinner.

For a short period, Wu Ying considered what he had learned. Then understanding poured into him and he pulled at the formations, the energy pouring into the ring. He adjusted the ring instinctively, slowing the rate of growth of the world. Grow too far, too fast and the careful balance of vegetation and insects would come crashing down. He knew then that he had to spend more time, add more dirt, more vegetation to compost and herbs and trees to ground the land. Even water, to ensure the entire thing was appropriately humid.

"Why is it so complex?" Wu Ying grumbled to himself.

He still did not understand why anyone would want to steal this. Sure, it was useful for growing rare herbs and roots, for having a consistent supply of common plants like Spiritual Herbs. But it required so much time and care, knowledge of how to balance everything out, of what fauna to seed, when to rotate specific plants and where to; all of it to balance the natural chi ecosystem.

Filtering quickly through the ring, Wu Ying made a few adjustments before pulling his senses back into the real world. Over the course of his travels in the kingdom of Shen, he had tried to find more information about World Spirit Rings. No surprise that he had found little, what with their rarity as well as their specialized uses. If there was any information about the Rings, they would be within the libraries not available to visiting cultivators like him.

Dismissing his frustration, he finished getting dressed. After stretching a little, he strapped on a sword and left his room. Outside, he found Pan Shui waiting in front of his room, dressed in a purple and red silk dress, the large triangular headdress of her people on her head. This was a new one, suitable for a formal dinner. Detailed embroidery ran along the edge of the headdress, similar to the embroidery along her dress.

"What are you doing here?" Wu Ying said, his hand on the hilt of his sword.

"Do you expect me to go unaccompanied?" Pan Shui said, her youthful face breaking into a wide smile. "Elder sister said that I needed you to chaperone me and keep me in check."

Wu Ying frowned. "And you always listen to your elder sister?"

"Normally, no." Pan Shui grinned unrepentantly. Then she sobered immediately, her face growing serious. "But normally, people aren't dying in their sleep or being murdered from behind."

"A lot of trust in me." He nodded toward Pan Shui's room. "When we're the most likely culprits."

Pan Shui snorted. "The Verdant Gatherer? A demonic cultivator who kills for pleasure?" She shook her head. "Unlikely." Her voice dropped, her eyes glinting with humor. "Anyway, I'm carrying my spear. And if I die, my sisters will hunt you down anyway."

Wu Ying looked her up and down, not seeing the spear.

"You're not the only one with a spirit ring."

"You know, you're not making a good case for me to be your companion."

She grinned cheekily then fluttered her eyelashes, the movement and look on her face making her look no older than a twelve-year-old.

"Just stop." He shuddered and she laughed before he waved her to the staircase. "Come on, let's go. We don't want to be late."

"Definitely not. They might start dinner without us!"

"I really need to introduce you to a friend of mine."

"Oh, is he a good fighter too?" Pan Shui said.

"Yes. Nearly as good as me," Wu Ying said. "He also enjoys eating."

"Really? Tell me more."

Chapter 19

Entrance to the Seven Pavilions compound was through the once-barred main gates. The gate guardians looked carefully at Pan Shui and Wu Ying, verifying that they were two of the eight contestants meant to join the dinner, before they stepped aside, waving the pair within.

They walked in together on paving stones, the path lit by numerous paper lanterns. Potted plants and stone praying urns were alongside the walkway. Within the compound itself, Wu Ying spotted a half dozen buildings: the stables and wagon storage to the left, huge warehouses set along the same axis, with residences, a cafeteria, and a training ground on the right. Dominating the center though was the main hall, both the residence and bureaucratic center for the Seven Pavilions merchant center and the family that ran it.

Servants drifted along the surroundings, some hurrying back and forth with plates of food and refreshments, guiding guests, or finishing last minute tasks. Clad in simple grey and brown robes, the servants blended into the surroundings. The cultivators and the members of the Seven Pavilions group were all in the main building itself, which was where a servant guided Wu Ying and Pan Shui.

Rather than the flickering lights of candles and oil lamps, the interior of the mansion was illuminated by the use of spirit stone lamps. They provided a steadier glow, bathing the luxurious surroundings of the mansion so that the many details, from flower garlands and red silk hangings, were easily noticed. Along with that, the merchants had added exquisite wall hangings and paintings to the walls.

Passing through the outer buildings, the pair were led into the central courtyard of the mansion where the guests were currently congregated. On the opposite end from the entrance, the doors leading into the massive dining room where they were to be seated and sup were thrown open, the gleam of fine porcelain cups and dining ware spotted among the moving throng.

Wu Ying breathed deeply as they strode within, sorting through scents automatically. Plum blossoms—out of season, but still present thanks to chi formations to aid their growth—and fragrant flowers dominated the background, while the delectable smells of deep-fried finger foods and thinly wrapped rice rolls of vegetables surrounded them, all mixed with the aroma of open containers of wine.

"Cultivator Pan, the Director of the Third Northern Bureau would like to have a word with you." The servant had made his way over the moment the pair had entered.

When Pan Shui looked at the servant, he gestured a little to where an older gentleman stood, speaking with another pair of men. He was dressed in a set of understated merchant robes, the darker blue and yellow a sharp contrast to some of the more flamboyant styles present.

"Of course." Pan Shui's lips thinned a little, but she turned to Wu Ying, bowing to him. "Remember, no leaving without me! But I do need to speak with him. The director is a family friend and handles most of the trade. Making a good impression will help the village."

Wu Ying nodded, understanding. While the kingdom itself was different, being on good terms with the merchants who arrived in one's village was not that unusual. The chief of Wu Ying's and Wu Ying's father were always certain to ensure merchants were comfortable when they visited, for otherwise, their village might be taken off the trade route. In so doing, the village would have a hard few years until a new merchant decided to exploit the village.

Even then, it would take a few more years before the merchant understood the idiosyncratic needs of the village, from specific wood carvings and literature preferences to taste in wine and tea leaves. Not that Wu Ying had experienced the changeover of merchants himself, but his father had complained often enough of an incident when Wu Ying had been a toddler.

"I'll... find someone to speak to," Wu Ying said, waving her off.

Wu Ying let his gaze dance across the room, spotting the pair of sect Elders and their disciples off in one corner. The disciples might have normally been socializing, but recent events obviously saw them less enthused than normal.

Along with Shi Fei and Kong Lai, nearly all the other cultivators who had managed to make it to the quarterfinals were there—from the confident northern archer Jochi to Wu Ying and Pan Shui. Liu Ping was notably absent, but he doubted many felt that was an issue.

Elder Cao stood by herself, off in the farthest reaches of the courtyard, sipping on a drink. Teng Fei, the Guard Captain, was mingling among the various merchantmen, dressed not in his armor like the Elder but in civilian robes. He seemed to be politely enjoying himself, putting on a façade of studied interest.

It was the presence of Investigator Chu that surprised Wu Ying. Sufficiently enough that he made his way to her, catching her under the boughs of the tree where she had isolated herself.

"Are you a guest or on duty?" Wu Ying asked as he stepped under the tree too.

His words caused the young woman to jump, spinning in place a little and letting her hand drop to her sheathed short sword. "How did you notice me?"

"Ah, so the formation was meant for you and not just the tree. It's a pitiful one, if so." Wu Ying gestured down toward the crossed flags. "It would not work on any but the weakest cultivator..." Then he snorted. "But of course, you are used to dealing with mortals alone, aren't you?"

"Yes," the investigator answered reluctantly. She looked down at her formation. "That merchant swore to me that this would be effective even against cultivators."

"Did you define what level?" Wu Ying said. When she shook her head, he nodded. "It's one of the things new cultivators learn to ask. In either case, it wouldn't matter. Unless you were powering the entire formation with a Spirit Stone, formations like these require knowledge to set up. You need to take account of the local environmental chi flow and need to be integrated into it using your own chi. Not doing so, it'll mean the formation is all too limited."

The investigator nodded. "You know much about formations then?"

"A little. It's part of my training as a Gatherer and farmer. There are herbs that need formations built around them, fields and greenhouses that have to be cared for. That kind of thing." Wu Ying paused, then added, "I also took some general classes, so that I could understand the common use of formations."

"The army runs such courses too," the investigator said sadly. "They don't bother with such for the guards though."

"Or even train you to break through your first meridian," Wu Ying said disapprovingly.

"It's not necessary for our duties," she parroted some long ago authoritarian with distaste. Then she smiled a little. "If I manage to solve this case though, Elder Cao has promised to put in a word for me. Those with good references can often receive dispensation to purchase the pills needed to cultivate."

"You have a manual?" Wu Ying said, a little surprised.

"I received one from Investigator Dee while in his service. But I fear I have no talent in it," Investigator Chu said, offering a sad shrug.

Wu Ying eyed the woman again, noting the slight lines across her eyes, the fold in her neck. She was not old, but certainly not young. On the other hand, he found it hard to judge her age, since he had few experiences with pure mortals. Not until he'd come to this kingdom, actually. Someone with the signs she exhibited would be in her forties, maybe fifties. It was only when a cultivator reached the end of their lifespan that the aging process sped up.

Rather than follow up on what was obviously a sore subject, Wu Ying asked, "How goes the investigation? Did the eyewitness reports help?"

She looked around a little, verifying that no one was paying them attention before answering him. "Not at all. In fact, all of our suspects were cleared." She sighed. "We need to rebuild timelines once more. It's hard though, for even with a cultivator's memory, it was not as though you all were watching one another or paying attention to the incense clocks."

"I'm sure you'll manage."

"Oh, we will. Still, there's something about these deaths… the painting in particular…"

"Oh?"

She opened her mouth to reply, then suddenly shut it as a presence made itself known at the opened doors. The older man—easily in his late sixties, with a low-grade Body Cleansing cultivation—stood before them all whilst a small gong was rung by a servant behind him.

"Please, honored guests, dinner is served."

Wu Ying turned to the investigator who shook her head, gesturing for him to leave. Understanding that she was not invited, he abandoned her to her tree and doubts, following the group and startling a few of the mortals by seeming to appear out of thin air.

Hopefully, dinner itself was not too boring.

***

Dinner was a full ten course[17] meal, starting with simple cold appetizers of pickled vegetables and salted meat. Once that was partaken, the array of foods from the banquet were offered with ceremony by the servants, starting with the meat of the suckling pig before moving on to shrimps and scallops, crab, kailan, an egg soup dish, abalone, chicken, sea bass, then finally the long noodles to signify prosperity before dessert was served—in this case, chilled longan soup.

To Wu Ying's amusement, he was seated near the end of the table, away from the host. Obviously, his status as a foreigner with few ties presently, and likely in the future, to the merchant house had relegated him to this location. Even the northern tribal archer had a seat closer to the head, his more impressive track record in the rings offering him that courtesy.

Worse than his seating position though was the company he was forced to keep. The low-level local merchant bureaucrats who sat around Wu Ying were more than happy to attempt to ply him with drink for hints about the status of the war in Shen while tempting him with their sons and daughters. When he showed no reaction to the lusty offers, they turned to just probing him for information.

The entire affair was frustrating and tedious for Wu Ying, only relieved by the quality and quantity of food. Even his hearty appetite was a matter of commentary though, especially for the mortal young lady sitting opposite him, who shot him longing gazes each time he was served even more of the dishes brought forth.

As such, he was thankful when dinner was finally over and he was able to escape the mortals. Being polite and gracious was difficult for Wu Ying, after such long periods of isolation in the wilderness. Yet, innate politeness kept him answering questions when some of the other cultivators had dismissed the poor mortals who had gathered around them all.

Eventually, he managed to break free.

Outside in the courtyard, Wu Ying was surprised to be approached by one of the few cultivators in the Seven Pavilions employ, a man who was in the lower grades of Energy Storage. "Cultivator Long, may this undeserving one have a word?"

Wu Ying happily agreed as he spotted a new set of mortals coming for him. He was led to a less busy corner of the courtyard, slipping under the isolated pavilion with the man. Once seated, the other cultivator beckoned over one of the servants, took from him a bottle of warmed mulled wine, and personally poured a cup for Wu Ying.

"I am Cultivator Yao Zedong, honored cultivator Long," the man said.

---

[17] Ten (or sometimes eight) course meals still occur, and it used to be that the act of overfeeding attendants was considered part of the ceremony. These days, some locations "cheat" by reducing portions a bit, allowing takeout containers, and using fruits or other small desserts to make up the count.

Wu Ying bowed in greeting, waiting for the other to continue.

"I understand that Cultivator Long is a Body cultivator?"

Wu Ying frowned a little but eventually nodded.

"Ah," Zedong murmured, relaxing backward a little. "Perhaps Cultivator Long would be willing to provide a few pointers?" Zedong touched his chest, and Wu Ying noticed the way his skin glinted a little, almost as though along the lines of his visible veins, metal had been embedded.

"Metal body?"

"Yes, only the first step, however. Veins and arteries." Zedong bowed his head. "I have not the skill that Cultivator Long has."

"Skill or resources?"

There was a pause, then Zedong laughed softly. "I see Cultivator Long is sharp too, like the northern wind. I lack both."

Wu Ying sipped on his wine, letting out an appreciative noise as the expensive and fragrant drink slipped past his lips. He felt it rest on his tongue and burn a little as it slid down his throat, even as he considered his options. Options and opportunity here though…

"It seems this will be less of an exchange than a lesson. And such lessons are… expensive." Wu Ying knew there was only so much information he could provide to another Body cultivator, especially since they were of such different elements. Still, he was much further along the route.

And if all else failed, he did have some herbs and pills that might aid the other.

Zedong smiled a little. "Cultivator Long might not know, but I am something of a collector of jian."

He turned his hand and beckoned, and a mortal servant hurried over to offer a weapon case. He took the weapon case, caressing the case for a second before offering it to Wu Ying.

Taking the simple green sword case, Wu Ying placed it on his legs before opening the wooden lid. Within the soft silk and wood block housing lay an unsheathed sword and its scabbard. Even on first glance, Wu Ying could tell it was a weapon of superlative quality just from the way it affected the environment with its sheer presence. Tiny carvings on the inside of the wooden case indicated why it had not been sensed before.

"Saint tier?" Wu Ying said, not touching it just yet.

"Yes."

He hesitated before he was forced to admit, "I'm not sure if I have sufficient knowledge and materials for such a trade."

"The hallmark of a good trade is that both parties are content with what they receive." Zedong leaned forward. "Saint-tier weaponry is relatively abundant in this territory, for the right individuals. Knowledge about Body Cultivation on the other hand…" He sighed mournfully. "It is relegated only to those in the special forces."

"Special forces?" Wu Ying said and watched as Zedong turned his head, gaze landing on Elder Cao. "Oh…"

"Yes."

Wu Ying frowned as he regarded Elder Cao with new eyes. He had not noticed that with her, but then again, depending on how far she had progressed with her Body Cultivation and what kind she had undertaken, it might not be as noticeable. The in-between stages, like the cultivator before him, were most noticeable. A stage that Wu Ying had literally bypassed by spending his time in that medicinal bath and having his bloodline trigger.

As he stared at Elder Cao, memories of what she had told him rung in his ears. A weapon of sufficient quality. For a second, he stared at the sword on his lap. He let out a long breath and closed the sword case, latching it.

"Very well. As you said, if we are both happy." He tapped the case then raised it, handing it back to the other man. "But you will hold on to this, until the end."

"An honorable decision." Zedong leaned forward. "Now, the method I am working with, it consists of multiple medicinal baths I must soak within. The first three baths are simple enough to handle and acquiring the herbs has not been an issue. However, the problem is the fourth bath, which consists of the Clear Sky Liquid, the Seventh Bloom of the Purple Rink…"

Wu Ying nodded as the other man went into detail. He would see what he could do, and he would offer Zedong what herbs and suggestions he had. And perhaps, in his own journeys and collections of body cultivation, he might have suggestions for the other. Maybe Wu Ying might even learn something.

Either way, it seemed that this night was not the waste he had thought it would be.

Especially since he had an idea of one other thing he could ask.

***

"This is where he was killed," Zedong murmured, gesturing at the tiny garden. Just off to the left, inside the compound and a short distance away from where the wagons and horses were kept but hidden by the rising edges of the walls of the enclosure and other storage buildings. A rock garden rather than the greenery of the main gardens.

"Thank you," Wu Ying murmured, bending down.

That was a distraction, of course. Rather, he asked the wind to aid him, bringing forth a tiny dust devil that searched the enclosure, bringing with it the myriad scents that lingered. Mortal smells predominated, not unusually. Those could be discarded.

Some cultivators including Teng Fei, Zedong, and Elder Cao—their scents were also pushed aside. They must have investigated the murder scene, so they were unimportant. Outside of that, Elder Eng's scent dominated here. The way his chi bounced off a few locations where rocks had been crushed, he must have lost control of his dao and chi.

Again, irrelevant.

Eyes closed, Wu Ying traced the scents, the location of Cui Wen's body as it fell. He stood, neared the location, and bent, flipping some stones to find the droplet that had been missed. Or discarded. So, around here he had been killed. Struck from behind they had said…

Turning his head, he frowned. That core sect token he had, the protective one. Why had it not worked?

He bit his lips, staring around him. Whoever had struck, they must have done so quickly or with overwhelming force. Yet there was no indication of that attack—no destroyed tiles, no shattered stones other than the ones with Elder Eng's chi.

So. Powerful control, so powerful it could breach a talisman without leaking the energy elsewhere. High Core at the least. And only one such individual here fit that description. Or the killer was using impeccable aura control, which in this kingdom was unlikely.

The other, more likely option. The token had been taken. Either removed from Cui Wen before he could pick it up or stolen at some point. Which spoke of a different skillset entirely. A part of Wu Ying leaned toward that explanation, not just because it was the safer one for himself but also due to the lack of evidence of a singular, explosive attack.

After all, his own skill at sensing energy was not insignificant.

"Are you done?" Zedong asked, sounding a little nervous. "We're not really supposed to be here."

Wu Ying stood, looking around himself once more. His eyes skipped over the surroundings before he sighed. If there were more secrets to be found, it would not be by him.

"Yes, I'm done. Thank you again." A slight motion on Wu Ying's part and he extracted the bottles of pills, handing them over to Zedong along with a couple of boxes of spiritual herbs.

Zedong smiled, taking his payment. He chivvied Wu Ying back to the main party before hurrying to put aside the goods still clutched in his hands.

***

Later that night, Wu Ying found Pan Shui regaling a group of admiring young ladies with tales of her exotic hometown. Many were wide-eyed with wonder, taking in the different dress, the rougher accent of the Zhuang woman. Her occasional halting speech as she searched for the right word. Her background as a cultivator coupled with her travel across the kingdom made her an exotic, but still somewhat familiar, figure.

Wu Ying stayed on the fringes of the group, content to watch as Pan Shui answered questions about clothing and harvests, of fashion and mercantile proceedings, jumping from topic to topic with expansive gestures and a wide smile. He had to admit, she had some talent, seeming to handle the group with aplomb.

Eventually though, the lights within the compound were dimmed and the group gently ushered out. He stepped up to Pan Shui, helping her make excuses for not accompanying one of the braver merchants for the night.

Guiding her out, Wu Ying cocked his head as they left the compound. "You seemed to do well, speaking with them."

"It's among my duties in the village," Pan Shui said, shrugging elaborately. "Finding a suitable match that will strengthen the family is important." She turned her head, a small smile on her lips. "And you? You did not seem that interested in the sixth niece of the Merchant Clan. Too low class for you?"

Wu Ying shook his head. "No. I have little care for such concerns. If anything, the fact that she is but a mortal would be more of a hindrance than her profession."

"Of course. The noble Verdant Gatherer would not look down upon mere merchants but does concern himself that they are but pitiful mortals."

"Pitiful…" Wu Ying let the word linger. "Yes. Surely it is so, if cultivation and ascension, or even a longer, healthier life, is given only to the fortunate."

"Any may join the army," Pan Shui said. "Or study for the imperial examinations, joining the ranks that way."

"Really?" Wu Ying's lips thinned. "I notice that Investigator Chu continues to be mortal. Her mind is sharp, her skills undeniable. But to study for the imperial exams requires time and money, space to contemplate works that are outside her current job.

"Impossible for one who began in an environment that is not conducive to such efforts. Craftsmen and farmers alike, we have little time to study. Merchants may have the time and, of course, the nobles, but the scholarly path is not for all. As for the army…"

"And what are your thoughts on the army?" Pan Shui asked, probing quietly as they crossed through the quiet village.

Late as the night was, there were few individuals out and about. The murders had cast a grim pallor over proceedings and many no longer chose to revel late into the evening.

"That not all individuals are suitable for the army," Wu Ying said, remembering the army captain who had warned him off. After all, criticizing them, even on a quiet night, could lead to additional difficulties for him. "Physically or by temperament." He touched his chest, offering a wry smile. "I, for example, would find it hard to handle such strict strictures."

"Oh really? I find that hard to believe."

"Mmmm, not everything you've heard—or have yet to hear—is entirely true. Or wrong," Wu Ying said. Rumors might fly fast, but all too often rumors and truth had only passing kinship with one another.

"Ah Shui!" a voice called, interrupting the pair as they neared their residence. Above them, leaning out of the window, was an incensed Pan Yin. "I told you to come back earlier to rest! You have a match tomorrow! You better not have drunk too much."

Pan Shui stuck out her tongue, jutting her chin upward as she replied to her sister. "I was talking to some merchants! You're the one who told me to learn about their trading plans."

"Yes, but not too late!" Pan Yin snapped. "If you lose tomorrow…"

"I won't." Pan Shui sniffed. "I'm better than them all. You know so."

Pan Yin let out a long, theatrical groan. She then turned her head, her gaze landing on Wu Ying. Pan Shui blushed when she realized she had inadvertently insulted him.

Deciding not to ease her embarrassment, Wu Ying bowed to the ladies. "Good evening, ladies. I should get some rest. After all, I need every edge I may find."

Pan Shui's jaw dropped a little, then her eyes narrowed. Wu Ying walked toward the entrance as she called out behind him, "You're teasing me, aren't you? Aren't you?"

"May the Kitchen God[18] miss that, Ah Shui. You insulted the Verdant Gatherer. If you won't seduce him, at least try not to insult him! You know father would love him to visit our clan. They say he always has the best herbs on him," Pan Yin scolded her sister from her window.

"You know I can hear you," Wu Ying called from the open door of the entrance before he slipped in, grinning wide as he heard the gasp and spluttered outrage and the ringing peal of laughter from Pan Shui. He would leave the two to stew while he headed for his room. He really should rest after all.

And he really would miss it, when people knew of his true level of cultivation.

---

[18] The Kitchen God or Stove God (Zao Jun / Zao Shen, etc) is the god who reports on the household, so he would be the one reporting on indiscretions. It's also why he's often bribed or honey smeared on his lips to keep him silent on the day of reporting.

Chapter 20

Wu Ying was halfway down the street the next morning—having finished a simple meal of congee, fresh steamed fish with ginger, sesame oil and garlic, and fried doughnuts with the requisite cups of tea to fortify himself for his fights—when the commotion began. Brows drawn together, Wu Ying followed the group of noisemakers, knowing that he had enough time. When he came to the building involved, he had to wonder if there would be a match today at all. For the crowd had led him to the front of the guards' headquarters.

"What is going on?" Wu Ying asked the man standing beside him, one of the roadside merchants. He only received a shrug in answer.

To Wu Ying's great fortune though, another cultivator who had been in front of the crowd and had been pushing out answered his question. "Someone killed the investigator. They found her body inside."

His words sent a ripple of shock and dismay through the crowd, including Wu Ying. The cultivator went so far as to freeze entirely, his mind returning to the evening before when he had spoken to the young lady. Reflexively, Wu Ying expanded his aura, sending the wind swirling around him and toward the building only for his aura to be rebuffed by a formation.

"What?" Wu Ying's eyes narrowed. Never before had they thrown up such a formation. Why the change? Had they refused to take proper precautions until now because it was not their people dead? Or was it something more?

Pushing his way to the front, Wu Ying ignored the grumbles and protests. There was nothing to see but a cordon of guards, all of them looking nervous as they tried to reassure the angry and restless crowd.

"We demand to know what is going on!"

"You cannot keep us all here to be killed one by one."

"What are we, chickens to be slaughtered?"

Voices rang out through the crowd, all demanding answers. Fear ran rampant through the group, for stronger cultivators than most of the contestants had been killed. Even the merchants who, thus far, had felt it was a cultivator matter were afraid. For now, a mortal had been killed, and the small shred of false safety they'd had had been stripped away.

A particularly belligerent cultivator, fed up with the lack of answers the guards had to offer, strode up to the edge of the line. Wu Ying's eyes widened as he recognized Hao Zhi, who shoved aside the guard standing in his way. That started a chain reaction, as the guards standing beside the assailed had to catch their friend.

The crowd surged into the gap, led by Hao Zhi. He took a half dozen steps forward, nearing the entrance, before Wu Ying sensed it. The shift and opening in the formation, the speedy exit that was led by a single foot.

Thrown backward by the kick, Hao Zhi flew through the air, spewing pain and blood. Other cultivators and mortals were thrown away too, the group tumbling over one another as Hao Zhi's body crashed down a distance away, the sound of a foot hitting his body and his ribs snapping still echoing through the street.

Cries of pain and confusion as those bowled over stood up or nursed wounds, while Hao Zhi lay senseless. A few of his friends tried to voice their belligerence, only to clamp their mouths shut when they realized who the assailant was.

Standing on the steps, just outside the formation that had so briefly opened, was Elder Cao in her army uniform. The dark colors and militant air were perfectly paired with her cold eyes and the sneer upon her lips as she stared at the crowd. Wu Ying idly noted she was missing her dagger-axe, though her floating sword was by her side.

"I do not expect much from the mortals, but even if you might be wasted vagrants, you are still cultivators. Have some dignity," Elder Cao said scornfully. "A few deaths and you all run around like mewling babes. You have a duty—to yourselves, if not the kingdom. Do better."

None dared speak up, the aura that she blanketed the town with having grown heavier. Some of the mortals were even finding it difficult to breathe, as she choked them on the depths and heaviness of her dao. Duty, unbending, unyielding.

For long moments she stood there, crushing them all with sheer personality, before she turned about. But before she could reenter the formation, another voice cut in, cracking apart the oppressive aura as its own pushed back against it. A hard, unyielding aura that spoke of the strength of the earth and its impassivity to mere mortal concerns like duty.

"And is my concern considered petty? That the investigator into my disciple's murder lies slain?" Elder Eng rumbled, floating high above the group on his own weapon, that massive podao that warped the environment.

"Not at all," Elder Cao said, turning around and putting on a conciliatory smile. Yet her stance was still unyielding. "But such discussions can be held at a more appropriate time and place."

"No. I think a discussion here and now of what has happened is appropriate," Elder Tsui spoke up. Like his compatriot, he had chosen to make his way over via flying sword. "I would not have such knowledge kept from the others. Secrecy only breeds resentment and rumors."

Elder Cao's eyes narrowed as she regarded the two Elders. Then her gaze flicked down, landing upon the silent Wu Ying. Of those gathered, it was the three of them she could not so summarily dismiss. After all, they were her equals—in cultivation stage at the least.

"The inspector is dead. Slain by a blow to her head. We believe it happened while she worked late at night after returning from the party," Elder Cao said reluctantly. "The manner of her death indicates it is likely the same culprit. More details will follow once we finish our investigation."

Backed up by the hovering elders, Gao Qiu, who had pushed his way forward, dared to speak. "And what do you intend to do now? How will you find the murderer when your very inspectors are being killed?"

Those last words sent a murmur of agreement through the crowd. There was a tense air of expectation as they waited for the general to provide an answer. At the corner of the open doorway, Wu Ying noticed that Teng Fei was watching the proceedings but stayed within, out of sight for many.

"Because I am here," Elder Cao said intently. "Or do you believe that the murderer has avoided attacking myself or the other Core Formation cultivators but they are able to do so?"

Her confident words quieted the crowd for a second, but Gao Qiu bulled ahead. "That's fine for you and the Elders, but what about the rest of us? How will you protect us?"

Her lips curled up in disdain. "I thought you wandering cultivators were all independent souls, intent on making your way through this world alone."

"We are. And if you'd let us leave, we'd be fine," Gao Qiu said a little too smugly. His tone of voice drew a glare from the woman, but he forged onward. "But we are here by your choice. Under duress. So your *duty* would be to take care of us, under circumstances you have created."

If the air could freeze, it would have. But her aura and her dao were of duty and responsibility, not of winter or the frozen edges of snow. Even so, the regard she turned upon Gao Qiu was enough to make the man pale and tremble, as she considered what, exactly, to say.

Eventually, she spoke. "We shall consider your words. And what we may do to further preserve your lives. I would, however, recommend that none of you stay alone until additional security precautions are implemented."

Then she walked inside, leaving the group alone. She moved so fast it would almost be called a retreat if she was not so graceful in doing so. The Elders hovering above them regarded the building with narrowed eyes before turning in unison and heading back to their table at the restaurant.

For a long second, Wu Ying stood in the crowd, debating what he should do. He caught Gao Qiu's gaze, the man having regained some of his coloring now that Elder Cao was not turning her killing intent on him. The other cultivator inclined his head to the side, and Wu Ying sighed internally, nodding as he moved to follow the man.

He might as well get it over with. As much as he disliked being drawn into politics, Gao Qiu was also his only major source of knowledge and connection to the other wandering cultivators. And it seemed that the ongoing deaths were something that needed to be dealt with, not just for the sake of justice but also the necessity of keeping his head on his shoulders.

The pair rendezvoused a short distance away, each of them regarding the other with some minor trepidation. After all, their last encounter had not been the most agreeable. Eventually, Wu Ying chose to break the silence.

"How is Liu Ping?" he asked.

"Well. As well as can be."

"And how well is that?"

"Crying late into the evening. Praying to gods and immortals above and the demons below for vengeance. Lying in bed late into the day before stalking the alleyways late at night, seeking the killer," Gao Qiu clarified.

Wu Ying made a face.

"I do not know if the matches are continuing, but we should make sure. And if not…" Gao Qiu paused, then resolved himself. "If not, you should come with me. We're meeting to speak about this incident later."

"We?"

"The Association. And others interested in finding the murderer."

Wu Ying frowned. "You know I don't want to get involved in your politics."

"What you want might not matter." Gao Qiu hesitated before adding, softer, "Liu Ping has something to say. To you."

For a long second, Wu Ying hesitated. Then he nodded, acceding to the request. For the friendship he had shared with her and her brother, he would come.

***

To everyone's surprise, the tournament matches were not postponed. Or perhaps it was only to Wu Ying's and a few more empathetic individuals' surprise. Everyone else wanted the tournament over, it seemed. At the least, the gifts and prizes that would be shelled out at the end, used carefully, might provide the winners a greater chance of surviving their unknown assailant.

Or so Wu Ying assumed. It was hard to tell what some of the other contestants thought.

By action, they were hurried and ready to finish the battle; but they were also more careful and less brutal and competitive than he had expected. Even though only eight contestants and four fights remained, the other dueling rings were not in use, only the central one in play. Enchanters and other workers took apart the remaining rings, while a few addicts and those looking for a way to distract themselves from forces outside their control crowded around the betting tables.

Everyone else packed themselves around the ring. Perhaps it was the desire—and safety—of crowds that led them there. The warmth of humanity as the cold breath of death lingered on the backs of their sacrificial necks. Perhaps it was just the need for gossip, for there was a lot of that.

As for the fighters, they received short shrift. Up first was the northern archer, his bow strung, and his arrows blunted with small hide coverings. He moved and loosed, half-drawing and releasing his arrows, the chi strings on their ends and front guiding the missiles to move in ways that were impossible otherwise.

Even so, his opponent, Kong Lai, swatted the attacks away with casual disregard, her defense impenetrable. No matter what tricks he tried, she stood unshaken. Only a single line of blood where a trick shot preceded by an exploding arrow had managed to harm her caused any major issues.

The moment he ran out of arrows, Jochi gave up. Even beforehand, he had barely been able to keep ahead of Kong Lai, who had hounded him around the ring as he loosed upon her. Rather than subject himself to humiliation and a potentially crippling injury like Liu Jin, the archer chose the better part of valor. He ended the fight to some little jeering and polite applause, though Liu Ping continued to glare from the sidelines.

Even so, Kong Lai barely even sneered at the man before she stalked off to return to the side of Elder Eng to watch the next fight from the second floor of the restaurant.

Next up was Pan Shui and one of the other wandering cultivators. He was a fire-enhanced Elemental Storage cultivator who wielded a pair of jian. The man barely had a Sense of the Sword, but it allowed him to wield both weapons in such a way that he did not clash them together, which was necessary when one was dual wielding.

On the other hand, compared to Pan Shui, he was vastly outclassed. He lasted for a short while by managing to deflect her attacks with his weapons, but he was unable to enter his own measure. Pan Shui skillfully deflected his attempts at stepping in with punishing strikes of her spear.

When he grew desperate and released waves of flame, the younger cultivator retreated a little, dodging the flame-edged projectile strikes. Through scorching flames, she wove between attacks, spinning, jumping, twisting as each attack came within inches of burning her.

The battle ended abruptly, when the flame cultivator flagged after releasing a half dozen arcs of flaming energy, the movement of his fighting form complete. In that small gap before he transitioned to another attack, Pan Shui exploited the gap by extending the blade intent of her spear. It exploded forward, extending the range of her attack to pierce his shoulder.

That was all that was necessary for the cultivator to give up his attempt at winning a greater prize. The man retreated to the edge of the ring whilst calling out his defeat. Leaving the ring, there was only the slightest hint of satisfaction on Pan Shui's face, the Zhuang clanswoman slipping in amongst her sisters soon after. They made no move to leave, though the way Pan Yin glanced toward the road leading back to their temporary abode, Wu Ying had to assume they intended to.

He did not blame them. He too wanted to return to his room. There were things to be done, including increasing their defenses. Initially, he had held back due to custom and courtesy, but he no longer cared if he crossed lines of civility.

That was, however, an issue for later.

"Cultivator Long. If you will…" The ring attendant who had appeared before him was gesturing.

Wu Ying sighed internally. It seemed it was time for him to choose if he was to lose here or in the next round. Or defy the Elders and grow enmity with them over items and resources he had minimal use for.

Though winning would be pleasant.

Chapter 21

"Cultivator Long, it seems I shall have a chance to test your expertise myself," Shi Fei said, smiling widely at Wu Ying as he took his place on the ring.

The pair waited for a beat until the ring's protective enchantments were activated, a slight hum cutting off all sense of the world outside and leaving the pair trapped within.

"Cultivator Shi." Wu Ying put his hands together and offered the man a martial greeting before he drew his weapon. No point in using a sword draw to open his attacks. He could feel the thrum of power, the twisting spin of energy of the formation around him, the sun beating on his bare skin as he stood in the unshaded ring.

A small part of Wu Ying still debated losing. It would not be surprising for many if he did so. After all, a wandering cultivator being beaten by an inner sect cultivator? A story as old as time. No one cared about the actual truth when a good story was available instead.

"I look forward to exchanging pointers with you," Wu Ying finished.

"And I you. My master says that I might learn about killing intent from this match. In fact, he asked that you show me that, if you could."

"Killing intent?" Wu Ying said, puzzled. Not by the term of course. He had felt it, dealt with it, all too much.

Shi Fei smiled blandly. A flicker of something in his eyes though, hints of hidden ire there. "He says the edge of one who has seen war and death like you will be much more potent than a garden flower like myself and the rest of my sectmates."

"Ah..."

Wu Ying watched as Shi Fei finally drew his sword. He watched the man ready himself mentally, girding his paltry killing intent. As though one's enemies would give one time to compose his mind, solidify his composure.

At first, the clash was entirely physical, no energy infusing either blade. Wu Ying chose to match the other with style and intent, pitting his martial training and form against the other. Thrice they clashed, blades flashing and small sparks flickering and dying as their weapons bounced off one another before Shi Fei retreated.

Wu Ying wielded a simple Spirit-quality jian. Not the shattered jian, but one that he was more familiar with—longer, thinner, more elegant. His most recent acquisition was carefully stored away in his storage ring. Until he spent a few hours practicing with the weapon, he had no desire to wield it. Especially not in public in a tournament setting. Even if he had gained the Sense of the Sword himself, familiarity with a weapon was important.

Deeper within, Wu Ying knew he also had a peasant's fear of parading his wealth before others. Bad enough that many might notice the storage rings he owned, the World Spirit Ring, and the numerous herbs he carried. Wearing such an expensive weapon would mark him even further from his humble beginnings. And even if he knew, intellectually, that he had come far from the rice farmer he had been, he still struggled with such an acceptance emotionally.

Never mind the fact that wearing an expensive weapon in poor, peasant clothing might elicit its own brand of trouble. Accusations of theft might be the least of his concerns then. No, better to be low profile if at all possible.

For now…

"You dare!" Shi Fei's snarl brought Wu Ying back to the present, as the other man retreated with a simple push of his feet. He glided backward, moving as swiftly as flame across an oil-filled rag, his lips curling up.

"I apologize, but… I do not understand."

"You! You disgrace me with not even paying full attention to this fight." Lips curled up, the veneer of politeness and civility dropped aside as Shi Fei ranted. "Just because you were from the Verdant Green Waters, you think you can disregard our sects? You, who have been rejected by your own sect?"

"Tread carefully there. You speak of things you do not comprehend fully."

"Hah! What is there to comprehend? You are not even a martial cultivator, and you dare disrespect me and my sect by ignoring our fight." Shi Fei's aura, never the most stable to begin with, began to smoke, flames flickering on and off as he ranted at Wu Ying. "I will show you the true strength of my sect and make you grovel."

Before Wu Ying could reply, whether to calm the man or inflame his passions further, Shi Fei charged. Tiny explosions of flame and rock marked his movement as he flickered forward. It was not a direct charge, like the flight of an arrow or the fall of a stone, but the jumping, twisting path of flame which shifted and bent at the slightest gust of wind or other element.

"Steps of the Flickering Flame!"

Murmured words from outside the ring, brought to Wu Ying by the wind. Not that Wu Ying was paying that much attention to such things, instead devoting his time to dodging his opponent's cuts.

Shi Fei's jian cut and struck, thrusting and stabbing as it attempted to land a blow on Wu Ying. The man's style was all about light cuts, driven from wrist and elbow extensions at near maximum distance.

A safe, wearing series of attacks that would break down defenses as injuries accumulated. It was aided by the burning aura that surrounded Shi Fei's weapon, such that any defense that crept close to the guard or that impacted too long would leave a trail of heat on his blade.

A half dozen cuts and parries, sparks flaring higher over and over. The shimmering heat of Shi Fei's blade blended with the smell of crisping hemp robes, the dryness of the air as he robbed the moisture in the semi-isolated ring and set the very air aflame.

"Going to burn me out?" Wu Ying asked as he deflected another cut with a twist of his wrist. He felt the warmth of Shi Fei's sword as it passed within inches of his hand, but he had sat in multiple medicinal baths, being slowly boiled alive, and he could withstand a little heat.

"Heat or exhaustion, pain or fear, the Crimson Flowers sect will set it alight." Another clash, sparks flying. Shi Fei extended his blade, sending a tendril of flame licking out and forcing Wu Ying to lean aside as the living flame sought his face. "If you delay any longer, you will lose. So, show me what you truly have, Gatherer."

Wu Ying stepped and spun, kicked off the edge of the ring. He kept moving even as he sent a flicker of his blade essence outward. He had wreathed his weapon in wind chi to protect it, the tiny turbulent flames revolving around his weapon constantly. Now, he unleashed it in a small spiraling Dragon's Breath attack that forced his opponent to block.

The attack was not meant to kill or even injure. The air dispersed upon impact as Shi Fei blocked, but the diversion was sufficient for Wu Ying to put additional distance between the pair. He stared at Shi Fei, bouncing lightly on his feet as he contemplated his next action.

"Running away. I guess that's all you're really good for," Shi Fei said, smirking.

It was an unsubtle provocation. Lacking in true bite. Yet Wu Ying flicked his gaze upward toward the pair of Elders who watched. He sensed the overlying aura that pushed down upon all of them as Elder Cao continued to make her presence known.

Well, perhaps a little demonstration would not hurt. If he was to lose, he might as well do so with style.

"Killing intent, eh?" Wu Ying murmured.

Wu Ying let himself fall into the headspace, stopped taking the entire spar so lightly. He felt his mind sharpen, growing focused and cold as the North Wind. He could even feel the wind coming, sweeping at, around, and through the barrier, robbing the atmosphere of its heat.

Sparring and fighting for real were two different things. Even a duel was different from his desperate battles to survive. Some tactics, some options reared their head. Calling forth the Western Wind to pull sand from the ground to land in Shi Fei's eyes. Eastern Wind to howl and gust, to gut the flickering flames of that fiery aura and shove those delicate, intricate footsteps off course. Central Wind, with its constant course changes rising upward, tripping and pushing into his blade.

Options rose and were discarded.

He had no desire to showcase the entirety of his tricks. Instead, Wu Ying leaned into the expectation the other man had. The wind around his blade spun ever faster, becoming a keening wail. He threw cut after cut, Dragon's Breath's extension of chi energy and sword intent mixing with his winds.

Within the blade, he wove his killing intent. Honed through desperate battles, sheared clean of meaningless desires and weak aspirations. Soaked in the blood of enemies and victims alike and then washed clean in the tempest of his soul.

Death, desperation, intent, focus. The willingness to take a life, to bear the karmic burden and find oneself... altered.

Shi Fei wove himself around the half-dozen energy projections, sometimes only dodging by inches. His aura contracted and twisted, almost dying at points as the shearing wind passed all too close. Wind might make fire grow, but only if in small quantities.

Too much wind, and the fire would go out.

While Shi Fei dodged, Wu Ying closed the gap. He guided his opponent with attacks, hemming the other's options with blade strikes and energy extensions of his weapon. A searing hot blade came stabbing out in retaliation and Wu Ying, leaning aside by inches, let the all too hot weapon sear hair and clothing, bake exposed skin.

Too close for anyone without a Body Cultivation method. First- and second-degree burns would be the natural result from being even so close, the radiating heat of flame chi scorching all. Yet for all that, Wu Ying's attacks were taking their toll. Under the killing intent of Wu Ying's blade, the cold implacability of doom that arose with each clash of blade, fear began to pierce Shi Fei's demeanor. He battled not just Wu Ying's blade but fear now.

No surprise then, that when Wu Ying closed in and struck out with a fist wreathed in wind, it caught Shi Fei by surprise. Even wreathed in wind, Wu Ying's fist burnt, his opponent's aura searing skin on contact. It was one thing to come close, another to impact it directly.

Still, his attack sent Shi Fei flying back. Only a last minute save by the fire cultivator as he stabbed his sword into the floor and pivoted around it kept the cultivator in the ring. He landed and took two more blade strikes on his arm and leg, nearly tottering off the ring before he regained his feet.

And only then because Wu Ying had stopped his attacks, a smile on his lips, his blade on his shoulder.

"Daring. But you're injured. And that strike, while surprising, was not painful," Shi Fei taunted, though Wu Ying heard a trace of fear in it. "Now, I'll show you the true strength of the Crimson Flowers!"

Wu Ying's lips curled up. He shook his hand a little, feeling the tender skin of the knuckles. He had held back a little from sending too much wind into the man, such that Shi Fei was not blown off the stage entirely without any chance of recovery.

Though one had to admire Shi Fei's style. And the way the very air caught on fire as even more energy was pumped from his dantian into his aura. Tiny motes of unseen loci of flame chi erupted into blossoms of fire all around Wu Ying.

"Hell Flower Petals," Shi Fei announced, confidence returning.

For all the show he put on, Wu Ying could not help but notice Shi Fei was sweating. Judging by the sheer amount of chi he was pumping out, the strain in his eyes, and the way the flames moved, Wu Ying could not help but judge the technique an advanced one. Probably meant for Core Formation elders, not a simple Energy Storage cultivator.

In retaliation, Wu Ying poured his chi into the surroundings, strengthening his aura. A small gust of wind picked up around him, the Central Wind taking control of safeguarding the space around his body. Gusts of wind sent the petals of flame swirling away, never allowing the attack to actually impact him.

"That's it?" Wu Ying said, cocking his head.

"Fool!"

More and more energy poured into the surroundings. The temperature kept rising, overpowering the North Wind. Outside, the audience huddled close, the gusting wind that failed to enter their ring freezing those around. More than one mortal had teeth chattering, while in the distance, farmers grimaced at the unseasonable chill.

"Now, watch!"

Shi Fei raised his hands and the myriad sparks that had formed throughout the air doubled and doubled again. Caught in the Central Wind, they swirled around Wu Ying, unable to touch him. Until Shi Fei clapped his hands together, sending the flames shooting through his defenses as they were guided by Shi Fei's chi.

Inside the cyclone of flame, the Hell Flower Petals blossomed, thunder and smoke erupting, draining moisture and robbing him of energy. Wu Ying exhaled. He had treated the other man too easily. Now he was trapped, with fractions of a second to choose what to do.

Arrogance. It would be his undoing.

Just not today.

Wu Ying drew his chi in, strengthening his aura. It would not withstand a frontal attack, so rather than wait for the Hell Flowers to complete, he exploded through the flames. The Sword's Truth combined with his understanding of his body and styles, hardened around his aura, allowed him to crash through the flaming attack.

Sometimes, in battle, one had to choose how you died, not how you survived.

In this case, he chose… forward.

The heat was oppressive, and Wu Ying was forced to close his eyes as he passed through the cyclone of flame. Yet none of the petals stuck to him—thanks to his chi defenses—the attacks thrown outward as they were caught in the gullies and gusts of wind that formed the outer edges of his aura.

On the other side, Wu Ying saw Shi Fei's wide, surprised eyes. Moments before his sword plunged into the man's shoulder, exiting in a shower of blood from the back. A last-minute change of targets ensured that the attack struck the meaty, non-critical part of his opponent's shoulder.

At the last moment, Wu Ying further dispersed his wind chi. No need to widen the wound, to damage Shi Fei further. No need to cripple the other man, not to make a point. He even went so far as to break his attack, bending elbow and allowing his arm to fall behind his torso as he pulled it in, such that he impacted Shi Fei with his other, outstretched hand. Palm on chest threw his opponent off his sword and out of the ring.

Then Wu Ying skidded to a stop, blood on his sword, watching as Shi Fei bounced once then again. The wandering gatherer smiled, grimly, as he watched Shi Fei stagger to his feet, looking exhausted and incensed at losing. Behind Wu Ying, the Hell Flowers finished their attack, closing in on themselves and exploding upward, searing everything within to ash.

Looking over his shoulder, Wu Ying raised a rather bemused eyebrow. A little too fatal an attack for a friendly duel. Shaking his head, he thanked the winds and stilled them as smoke trails rose from around his body and clothing.

"You wanted to know what it was like to fight in a real war? That. A small part of that. Winning, no matter the cost. Because that's all we had," Wu Ying said.

There were a few in the audience, Shi Fei included, who could use those words of caution.

Having said his piece, Wu Ying swung his blade to shed the blood on it, sheathed the weapon, and strode off. Suddenly, he had no desire to watch any further fights.

Killer on the loose or not, he needed to be alone.

Chapter 22

mation flags around the residence, yellow talismans pasted on the door and walls of his room. Only one way to enter the building without crossing the threshold of the formation and that was the front door. The hair on the backs of his arms stood up every time he neared the boundary, reacting to the improperly placed defensive measures.

As for Wu Ying, he was seated in the dining room, a cup of tea and a bowlful of snacks on the table before him. Roasted peanuts and baked almond cookies. The tea was a little too bitter, the almond cookies a touch burnt. He still ate them.

Breathing, slow and steady, as he centered himself and cultivated. No point in wasting time, and the act of cultivation was much like meditation at times. The simple and constant act of drawing in the chi of the world and refining it, twice over from his meridians to his dantian to his core, was similar to breathing after so many years. Even if the cultivation method was different, requiring different pathways, the process of doing so was not any more difficult.

More difficult circumstances might have arisen if he had been contemplating the dao, turning over moments of enlightenment and his own experiences in his search of understanding. Or, these days, refining such understanding to feed the nascent immortal spirit within his core, supplying it with enlightenment that would define the individual he would be as an immortal.

It was strange to think that if he broke through, his very soul would be absorbed and subsumed by the spirit he was in the process of growing. That a portion of what made him, him—the mortal, fleshy, and weak parts—would be burnt away, leaving a different person behind.

A death of sorts.

For everything mortal died.

There was some atavistic fear in that. A concern that many Core Formation cultivators never managed to overcome. It was strange, in a way, that it was rarely spoken about. Then again, perhaps it was not so strange. How many would care to speak about their own death and failure?

Wu Ying turned over the words in his cultivation manual once more as he waited. Words of wisdom and reassurance, the promise that it was not true death. No more than a child growing up died, as experience and knowledge robbed innocence of its naivete and optimism.

All things changed; all things evolved. The seasons passed, mountains were worn down, and lakes froze over. There was no shame in growth, in bending to the winds of time. A soul cultivator who fed the nascent spirit within his body with the intrinsic dao of his own existence would see only a minor alteration in their personality, a refinement of mindset.

Or so it was said.

In truth, Wu Ying had yet to reconcile himself with the idea of murdering his mortal soul to step into the next portion of his immortal journey. And that was not including the difficulties of even surviving the breaking open of the core, joining his two souls, and ensuring his immortal soul—incomplete as it was when it emerged—did not immediately perish under the tribulation of Heaven's displeasure.

No, he was not ready. Then again, he didn't have to be.

He would take things one step at a time. For him, that meant replenishing his chi stores such that he might proceed with the creation of the next layer for his core. It would be a process of months, maybe even years, before he gained enough energy. Unless, of course, he managed to acquire suitable apothecarist pills.

Till then. One step at a time.

Speaking of steps, he heard the tromp of feet returning. Three gentler, more graceful ones and a fourth that had an uneven beat, as though the walker was hanging in space for a second before striking down on the second footstep. Directly behind, Wu Ying heard a pair of footsteps, more familiar than even those preceding. Missing a third, the rhythm just a little off from the familiar.

Their scents came soon after, confirming his initial impressions. Rather than barge right in though, the group stopped in front of the building. He heard them traverse the perimeter, pausing at windows and the back door before the entire circuit was complete.

Whispered words, but Wu Ying did not need to listen to their contents. After all, he knew what they likely spoke of. And if some of them might complain about the exact placement of his formations or the lack of subtlety—well, he did not need to hear that criticism either.

He was no formation master after all.

Eventually the group entered the residence, Pan Yin leading the way. Wu Ying saw the slight tension in her body when she stepped past the threshold, but realizing that there was no danger, it swiftly faded.

"Evening," Wu Ying greeted as they crowded around him. He tapped the talismans set on the table beside him. "Each resident should take one of these and imbue it with your chi. When I shut the formation later, it will be the only way to enter without breaking the formation entirely."

"It's not very good," Pan Mu said. The third sister, often silent when her boisterous younger sister or older sister were around, spoke up for once. She was frowning at Wu Ying, gesturing at the walls and the flags outside. "They're also not very well positioned. You could increase their strength by a good portion if you moved the third and seventh flag as well as—"

Pan Yin's raised hand quieted her sister, who crossed her arms, unhappily. "Why did you do this?"

"Safety, of course." Wu Ying shook his head. "Not just against the killer, but... well. The rest."

"You mean the way the other cultivators are looking at us?" Jochi, the northern archer, said. "I'm not afraid of them."

"Not individually, perhaps. But if they came as a crowd?" Wu Ying raised a single eyebrow, making Jochi frown. "Exactly. Better to take care."

"If you think your formation could stop a crowd, you're a fool," Pan Mu said. She ignored her sister's glare as she continued. "It's barely strong enough to stop an Energy Storage cultivator from breaking through. If you put it together properly…"

"The Safe and Serene Southern Breeze Campfire Formation is not strong," Wu Ying admitted, "but it has the advantage of being easy to set up and having an integrated alarm. If someone attempts to break through, we'll all be alerted."

"And then what?" Pan Shui said. The way she was frowning at him, the way she gripped her spear, Wu Ying assumed she knew what he was about to say.

"Then we run."

He watched as she frowned and opened her mouth to object, but Gao Qiu cut her off. "You think there will be more deaths."

"If the murderer could escape, they would have, I think." Wu Ying frowned a little, looking upward and staring at the wooden ceiling, letting his thoughts coalesce. "I don't know why they're killing people or what they have to gain. There's some logic to the last murder, but the other two?" He shrugged. "I don't understand it, if there is a purpose. Perhaps the killer just likes murdering others. The… painting certainly indicated as much."

"Painting?" Jochi said.

"At the second murder scene. For my brother," Liu Ping grated out, her eyes flashing with repressed fury at being reminded. "They did it in his blood. As though they were taunting us. Taunting me." Her words broke at the end, and Gao Qiu placed a hand on her arm in comfort.

"They painted in his blood?" Jochi sounded shocked, looking around and realizing no one else seemed surprised. "It must be a demonic cultivator! Why are you all not more outraged?"

Pan Yin tilted her head before shrugging. "We are worried. As is Cultivator Long." She gestured to the walls again, indicating the formation that surrounded them. "But panicking will not help us."

"Panicking? Why shouldn't I panic? I have no desire for my soul to be eaten by a demon!" Jochi replied. "Do you?"

"That's just a story. They don't actually eat souls." Then, looking around, Gao Qiu added, "Right?"

Wu Ying looked at the faces of the other cultivators, gauging their reactions. Some were nodding, obviously thinking it was an old wives' tale. Others, like Jochi's, were firmly fixed in doubt. "As I understand it, the rumors are true only for a small subset of demon cultivators. Even they find such practices abhorrent."

"And how do you know so much about them?" Jochi said suspiciously.

"The war. We had run-ins with Dark Sect cultivators who dabbled in demonic cultivation techniques," Wu Ying said. "I spent some time studying about them in my Sect vaults. However, not a lot is certain about such groups." He shrugged. "It's not as though orthodox or even heretical sects spend much time in conversation with them."

"Who would?" Gao Qiu said wryly.

"Is that why you were called in earlier?" Liu Ping said. "When my brother was murdered?" Wu Ying nodded.

"Then why weren't you asked to look over the investigator's body?" she added.

"I don't know." He sighed. "It's possible that Elder Cao decided that because I did not sense anything the last time around, there was no point in bringing me this time either. It's not as though I have that much experience with them, especially in an investigative capacity."

"More than us," Gao Qiu pointed out.

"But maybe not her," Wu Ying said. Still, he would have liked to have seen the body. To understand what had happened.

A small part of him felt guilty—irrationally so, but he had spoken to Investigator Chu the night before. Maybe if he had warned her… said something. Done something. It was why he wanted to see the body and crime scene. Not because he was a voyeur or interested in seeing another dead body. He had learned how to put aside his feelings, to see the bodies as slabs of meat instead of broken souls and lost opportunity and dreams, but it was still not pleasant.

A part of him wished he could review the corpse and crime scene. If for naught else but to put aside the nagging feeling that he could have done something.

Yet, practically, if he was not invited, what could he do? Defy the Elder? The woman looked to have grown even shorter of temper since the latest killing. Having no leads must be chaffing at her.

Core Formation cultivators grew used to being all powerful, able to deal with the majority of their problems via sheer strength. Outside of conflicts with other Core Formation cultivators, they ruled their surroundings. And Core Formation cultivator conflicts were mostly those of cutting words and angry social challenges.

Being frustrated by not having a direct solution to their conflict—or even understanding who they were in conflict with—must be making her wish for the days of leading armies and killing people on the front lines. Though considering her prior profession, perhaps she had never done that either.

"You think she has experience with demonic cultivators? Or those from the Dark Sects?" Pan Yin said curiously.

"Not really, but I don't really know much about her."

"Nor do I," Pan Yin said. "Nor do any of us, no?" She looked around, curious if anyone disagreed.

Gao Qiu was the one who spoke up, to the others' surprise. "We've learned a little about her." Wu Ying noted that he was not the only one who noticed him say we, with Jochi and the Pan sisters exchanging wary gazes. "Former guerilla general in the eastern front. She was involved in a few border skirmishes, though nothing major. Spent time in the capital, working directly under the Directorate of Armaments for a time. Well regarded and one of the strongest in her cultivation, but she was forced into retirement."

"Why?" Wu Ying asked.

"Politics. Something about a death that she caused in the process of her duties," Gao Qiu said. "The details are shrouded in rumors."

"That's a lot for a little bit of information," Pan Shui said sarcastically. "I'm surprised you managed to learn all that while we've all been stuck here."

Gao Qiu shrugged.

It was Liu Ping who answered the suspicious gazes turned upon them both. "We looked into it before we arrived. We wanted to know who was overseeing security."

"Huh." Jochi rubbed his chin. "I never even considered that as necessary."

"Nor did we. Knowing that the Seven Pavilions were arranging it all was enough for us. After all, we did not expect *this*," Pan Yin said. "Why did you?"

"It's not that we expected murders!" Liu Ping said, hurt in her voice and eyes. "Why would we? It's my brother who died!"

The others winced, falling silent while Wu Ying bit the inside of his lip. Was Liu Jin's death retaliation then? Something to do with the White Flower Merchant Association, their rebel group? Yet the rebels were against the government—not demonic cultivators.

Then again, was the painting but a distraction? Wu Ying had wondered that when he had sensed nothing from the painting, no indication of a corrupted touch. Not that all demonic cultivators had that, of course; but someone taking such blatant action, you would think so.

And why even announce yourself, especially when your first killing offered so few clues and indicated a much more methodical mind behind it? None of it made sense. If he could just make it make sense…

"Cultivator Long?" Pan Shui spoke up, breaking Wu Ying from his circular musings.

"Apologies. Just thinking of the murders," Wu Ying said, then gestured at the talismans that none had taken. "You might as well use them. I doubt we'll tease apart the murders tonight."

"Not without more information," Liu Ping said angrily.

There were a few nods, but Jochi seemed done with the conversation. He was the first to take a talisman, imbuing it with his chi before bidding the group farewell. After further unspoken communication, the three sisters copied his actions and ascended the building, leaving Wu Ying with his former companions.

After the mortal proprietor had arrived and provided further cups before hurrying to check that the other cultivators required nothing else from him, Wu Ying looked at the pair who had sat down.

"I don't trust her," Gao Qiu opened the conversation without preamble.

"Elder Cao?" At Gao Qiu's nod, Wu Ying sighed. "I told you, I don't want to get involved in your other activities."

"This has nothing to do with that," Gao Qiu replied.

"There's something strange about her," Liu Ping said. "We asked to help with my brother's murder. We asked to see the investigator's body. We have reason to be involved in all this. But she rejected it, both times."

"You're not trained," Wu Ying pointed out reasonably.

"Nor are you," Liu Ping said. "And the investigator, last night…"

"What do you mean, last night?"

"I spoke with her. After the midnight bell, when she had chosen to return from the party. She was working in her office alone and I…" Liu Ping looked down, staring at her hand. "I wanted to ask her if she had learned anything."

"And did she?"

"I think she did," Liu Ping insisted. "But she wouldn't tell me what. Said she needed to be sure."

Wu Ying frowned. "Sure, about what?"

"I don't know!" she hissed, obviously frustrated.

Gao Qiu placed a hand on her arm, calming the younger woman. He looked at Wu Ying, gesturing around him. "Do you see why we're frustrated? She learnt something, but now the Elder is hiding it."

"If Elder Cao even knows," Wu Ying pointed out. "You said yourself, Investigator Chu wanted to wait before speaking. Or perhaps Elder Cao does have a clue but is waiting to narrow down her suspects and does not wish to alert the perpetrator."

"Why bother?" Gao Qiu replied. "If she has even a rough idea of who it could be, she could drag them in and subject them to interrogation. Surely with her strength, she could pull out the truth."

"I don't think that's really her specialty. Just because she's a Core Formation cultivator doesn't mean she can beat the truth out of people," Wu Ying said. "We've all learnt how to handle pain, after all."

"There are other ways to draw out truth," Gao Qiu said darkly. "The army has taken great pains to explore them all when they're searching for traitors and rebels." His voice softened. "And a guerilla general would know them all."

"She would?"

"That's part of their other tasks," Gao Qiu said. "The Guerillas. The Directorate of Armaments."

"Really?" Wu Ying was shocked by the darker secrets of this kingdom being revealed.

"Yes." Gao Qiu shrugged. "Not all tasks are equally honorable. Some things are best done not in an official capacity but by those who understand the need for discretion."

"I see." Silence ran through the room before Wu Ying probed further. "And you expect this to happen here?"

"We'll be lucky if she doesn't do it to all of us," muttered Liu Ping.

"Strong accusations."

"It has happened before. Jiaju village. The 241st Spring uprising."

"Ah Ping." Gao Qiu shot her a look and she quieted, though sullenly.

"I'm grateful for the warning," Wu Ying said. "But why come to me? Do you expect me to pressure the Elder? She barely gave the sect Elders face. I doubt she'd speak to me."

"She's more likely to listen to you than us," Gao Qiu said. "At least she's asked your opinion once before."

Wu Ying looked down into his teacup. He downed the drink, grimacing at its tepid and bitter nature. Steeped too long, left to cool. Still, he poured himself another cup anyway. Tea was tea. "I can speak with her. That's all I can truly offer."

"That is all we can ask." Gao Qiu hesitated before he leaned in again. "Also, if things turn bad… if she does start taking people in. We intend to leave."

"We?"

"Not just the Merchant Association, but others we can trust." He exhaled roughly. "We'll free those pilloried. We already have the key for them. But when running, we could use you."

"Why me?" Again, Wu Ying played the fool, probing for more information.

"Do you think we're all fools?" Liu Ping said roughly.

"I don't understand," he replied.

"You're no ordinary Energy Storage cultivator," she replied. "And it's not just your sect, though that would have been good to know." Wu Ying frowned a little but did not cut her off, even if he did wonder how she knew what she knew. "Or the fact that you're a Spiritual Herb Gatherer. That's not enough for the Elders to speak with you the way they have. For the sect cultivators to treat you with such respect."

"Then what do you think might be happening?"

"You might be an envoy. Or a hidden expert."

"Not exactly hidden, am I?" Wu Ying said, touching his chest.

"You might be hiding your strength, playing the tiger in a goat's skin."

"Or perhaps they just truly fear my sect and my master," Wu Ying murmured.

"If that is true, that is good for us too," Gao Qiu said, cutting off Liu Ping before she could contradict Wu Ying. "When we escape, they'll try to stop us. If they will hesitate…"

Wu Ying nodded. He understood the man's point, though he was not certain if he would join them. Still, the offer and the potential to leave was one he would keep in mind. Even if running would make his time in this kingdom even more difficult.

Already, his first few weeks in this kingdom had been more complicated than he could have ever envisioned.

"Tell us if you learn anything, Cultivator Long." Gao Qiu, sensing that he had gotten all he would get from Wu Ying this night, stood, pulling Liu Ping with him.

The woman seemed sullen before she deflated suddenly, the exhaustion from the day's events and her grief robbing her of her energy. Quietly, the pair exited, leaving Wu Ying to his bitter tea and sour thoughts.

***

Wu Ying touched the edges of the formation, verifying that the building was still protected. He had spoken to the servant within, confirmed that no one else was to enter or leave the building before he shut the formation entirely. Those with talisman tokens could still move freely, but everyone else would be locked out.

Satisfied with the precautions he had taken, Wu Ying stared down the silent streets. Few dared to walk in the dark, and those who did were grouped together or moving quickly from pool of light to pool of light. Even with the added illumination of spirit lamps, the closely constructed buildings cast long shadows.

A slight shift of his chi and Wu Ying jumped, stepping upon the wind directly to take him upward, high into the sky and onto the tiled rooftops. There, he was not surprised to find watchers, guards with crossbows staring down at the hurrying cultivators and few mortal merchants.

His ascension caught the notice of the guards, and while a few took care to pay extra attention to him, Wu Ying ignored them. They were not his concern, not right now. Instead, he drew a deep breath, cycling the myriad scents of the settlement through his nostrils. He called upon the wind and a breeze answered, tearing through the streets and curling around closed doors and rattling shut windows. It stole notes and hints from those below, bringing forth their redolent gifts to their imperious friend.

Wu Ying mentally tallied the scents, placing them in a mental map of the settlement. Searching for an overabundance of blood, of hints of demonic or blood chi, for the taste of burnt tar or the tang of the otherworldly. He found nothing, though the wind spoke of windows shut tight and spheres of control that had been formed to block further investigation. Minor formations, enchanted objects deployed for privacy. Among them, the guard building, the prison.

Wu Ying turned that way, eyeing it and the group of guards who watched those who might choose to take an unhealthy interest in the prison. The trio of guards tensed, the spike of fear and wariness in their scents making him wave. Of course, that did nothing for their unease, but he chose not to tease them further.

A step and then again, and Wu Ying gusted away. Running across the rooftops, leaping between alleys, he jogged until he left behind the settlement. To his distaste, he could not return to the clearing he had trained within, for a greater formation now stood in the way, blocking egress.

Finding a fallow field at the edges of the formation, Wu Ying stopped. A small gesture drew forth the sword case, and the weapon itself was extracted from within. He exchanged weapons, belting on the new Saint-level weapon.

The jian was a thing of beauty, the sword light as a feather and still stiff enough that it would only bend when he desired it to. Turning the blade edge from side to side, Wu Ying regarded the weapon in detail once again. He drank in its intricate detailing, stared at the green jade inlay along the blade, the repeating leaf design and the water-steel pattern on the metal itself. He caressed the dark grey and green hilt, tested the weighting of the tang and the small stone in the pommel, the white jade stone gleaming with suppressed power.

No enchantment on the weapon itself, but it needed none.

Wu Ying drank in the details, swinging the weapon around to test weight and balance. He could wield it without such regard—that was part of having the Sense of the Sword. Already, he sensed the full length of the weapon, grasped the balance point, and noted the ever slightly greater width of the weapon near the hilt. He knew what his maximum lunging distance was, how easy it would be to use a tip cut, and how to balance and speed up disengages.

Yet, knowing and *knowing* was different. This moment of reflection and observation was as much spiritual as it was practical. He let himself linger over the weapon, admiring it.

Then he began.

First form. Second. Third. Fourth form.

He moved through them all, until the weapon was no more than an extension of himself. The air rippled, cut apart and shrieking with each step, each passing blow. The earth was torn and rent apart as he moved, stomping advances and floating retreats as he danced through the forms.

When he finished all four, he stopped and breathed. There was a fifth form, but it was not one he was ready to practice yet. It would take too much time, require too much careful rehearsal. Wu Ying needed to move through it slowly, so that his body remembered each position, each attack and variation that was possible from that position. How to string it all together, both sword and sword energy together.

More than that, he would need to expend a lot of chi. Enough that practicing here, now, was inappropriate. Dangerous.

Anyway, he had another reason for being here, beyond growing comfortable with his weapon. For a time, he stood still, pulling forth the memory of Elder Cao and their battle. He drew forth every moment of the duel, recalling it in its entirety. And once he was certain he had her fixed in his mind, he recreated the battle again in the physical.

Repetition of movement, repetition of attacks, starting and stopping as he chose reactions and pieced together her retaliation to his changed movements. A lunge to a cross-body block,

Dragon sweeps the Floor to take her balance. Only for her to flip through the air and unleash an explosion of energy, wielding her aura to press him down.

A thrust at his head that transitioned into a feint as the target switched to his leading leg. Cloud Hands blocked the first and second change of directions, but then she shoulder-charged him, moving into his space. Taking away his options. Failure on his part, as surprise had forced him back the last time. This time, in his mind's eye, he stepped into the charge.

The Elder Cao in his mind was surprised.

She brought her haft up and…

And…

He was not sure. Wu Ying reset his stance, reset the mental image of his opponent in his mind.

A single battle was insufficient. His image of her, unrefined. As much as he might guess, as much as he might draw inspiration from the many manuals he had read, from the general philosophy of the styles and the dao she exhibited, it was all assumptions.

Guesses of the greatest order.

Leaving him sometimes staring blankly into space as the ghostly image in his mind stuttered and stopped or chose not as she would but as he wanted her to. Which, in truth, was a failure on his part. For all this was preparation and training, practice against an opponent he might one day have to fight.

He could not shake the memory of the attack on Cui Wen, the way it might have cut through his protective token.

And if she might sense his training in the distance, his own aura blanketed the field, pushing away her spiritual senses and the light probing she and the other Elders had trained upon him. It would not stop them from physically spying upon him, but none of the three had chosen to leave the settlement this night.

Small favors as he trained long into the night. Even as the dawn broke upon the churned and trodden fields, rent from missed strikes and all-too-real retaliations against imaginary attacks, Wu Ying drifted and fought, studying.

Eventually, as the cock crowed, Wu Ying sheathed his weapon, exchanging it for his usual jian. Wondering, once more, what this day might bring.

Chapter 23

Washed and changed, Wu Ying barely made it to his match on time. The referees and the Seven Pavilions Merchant Association had pushed ahead, demanding the final quartet of quarterfinalists take part this day. The tournament, meant to showcase skill at arms and be a celebration of the Association's strength, was a subdued affair, the crowd numerous but subdued.

Stepping into the ring, Wu Ying stared at his opponent and could not help but offer the young lady a smile. Despite the dire circumstances, Pan Shui was bouncing a little in anticipation of the upcoming fight. She grinned at Wu Ying, waving her free hand at him.

"Come, Expert Long. Let us settle things once and for all!" Pan Shui said.

Wu Ying stared at the exuberant young lady, then glanced at the referee and her pair of sisters. Both sisters looked a little glum, having drawn conclusions from Wu Ying's numerous mistakes about his true standing and combat prowess. He turned his head further, meeting the gazes of impassive Elders seated at their usual table. And then farther upward, he saw the impassive mien of Elder Cao as she perched on a rooftop.

He considered them all and the surroundings, spotting the bookies who were doing brisk business. Before the referee could form the barrier around them, he held up a hand.

"I have an announcement." Wu Ying pitched his voice to resound through the square, ensuring that everyone would hear him. "I am withdrawing from the tournament."

Silence, then tumultuous shouting. None louder than the bettors who clamored for a return of their wagers.

Striding across the space separating them, Pan Shui stabbed her spearhead at Wu Ying as a pointed declaration. "No! You are not allowed to do that. Tell him he's not allowed!" she snarled at the referee.

"I cannot, honored cultivator. Attendance and participation in this event is entirely voluntary," the referee replied, sweating a little. "But honored cultivator, this is unprecedented."

"It's also your first event. There's not much of a precedent there," Wu Ying pointed out.

"Even so. This… may I ask the chief judge?" he said.

Wu Ying nodded, knowing the poor man dared not make a final pronouncement without backup. After all, he was but a sixth stage Body Cleansing cultivator, tasked with powering up and watching the fights. It would take someone like the chief judge and referee to make such a pronouncement. Or, more likely, Elder Cao, who was overlooking the entire proceedings even if she was not officially in charge.

Hushed words were exchanged in the distance, the chief judge casting glances toward where Elder Cao watched. In the meantime, Pan Shui was ranting at Wu Ying, repeating her belief that he could not just quit. It was only when she tried to poke his foot with the butt end of her spear that he regarded her once more.

"Don't."

"You weren't even paying attention to me!" Pan Shui snapped. "What? Am I really that irrelevant that you'll ignore me not just in the ring but in conversation too?"

"It's not that," Wu Ying said. "We fought once already and you're a better spear wielder. You have the Heart of your weapon in your soul, and though you might lack a little in experience, your ability more than makes up for it."

"Yet, I did not win our last duel. Not decisively," Pan Shui said.

Wu Ying shrugged. "It doesn't matter. I never came here to win the tournament but to meet others and to progress my own path of the sword." He touched the blade by his side. "Your pointers and the fights I've partaken in have helped."

"Then fight me again! This time for real. You can't have learnt everything I have to show you from a single spar. Not when we were both holding back."

"No, I couldn't. But I know what will happen if we fight for real," Wu Ying said. "Have you considered the results? What happened with Liu Jin?" He lowered his voice, gesturing around him. "Any battle between the two of us will leave us both vulnerable. And that, I'm unwilling to accept. Not right now. Not when you have a decent chance of winning the tournament."

"And the prizes?" Pan Shui said. "Do you not care?"

Wu Ying shrugged. "They are less useful for me than for many others here."

She didn't need to know that he had been warned off winning anyway. It didn't help that he had a feeling that his chances of staying hidden as a Core Formation cultivator were dropping with every passing day.

"Who, exactly, are you?" Pan Shui said, gesturing with her free hand. "You wander in, fight like a demon, lose like a fool, speak with Core Formation cultivators like you do it every day, and hold not just a rare element but soul and body cultivation methods."

Wu Ying could only shrug, unsure of what she wanted him to say. He was who he was, a poor ex-farmer turned cultivator, banished son of a prestigious sect, an apprentice wild Gatherer. A student of life and existence.

"That's not an answer!"

Before she could prod him further, the chief judge approached and raised his voice, quieting the crowd. "As participation in the tournament is voluntary and each individual may retire at any time, I hereby declare Cultivator Pan the winner of this match."

Voices rose in protest, some of the cultivators glaring at Wu Ying as he descended. A few moved to accost him but stopped as he allowed a little of the killing intent and bloodlust within his soul to escape. These wandering cultivators might see more battle than a sect cultivator who stayed in his sect, cultivating in their lofty heights. But this kingdom had been at peace, their demonic and spiritual beasts managed by the army.

He had been honed in war and competition, in the depths of the untamed wilderness and across the blades of the Dark Sect. He might as well be a slavering, blood-hungry beast to them. Even a trace of the true killing intent and bloodlust he had absorbed was enough to keep those meaning to challenge him from approaching, leaving him to stand in the crowd…

Alone.

***

Eventually Pan Shui left the stage sulkily. The remaining two contestants were escorted up to the stage, Liu Ping and Kong Lai facing one another over their weapons. Liu Ping held her tie jian in both hands, the swordbreaker no more than a sharp-edged cross-sectional metal hunk, meant to crack and break delicate weapons. Not that the paired axes Kong Lai wielded could be considered delicate.

"Interesting matchup. Good weapon mix," a mortal merchant, not far from Wu Ying, muttered to his friend.

"Axe against swordbreaker? Yes. Better than dao or jian—those would break. And it'd be boring if they wielded polearms. Good strategy, but boring fights," his friend muttered.

Beside them, a third leaned forward and added his own words even as on the stage, the referee was speaking to the contestants, almost begging them to take care to not harm one another, to fight fairly and with consideration for the tournament's good name.

"I bet there's going to be blood. You heard about the crazed wandering cultivator's actions, right? I tell you, those bestial bloodlines can't be trusted. Animals, all of them."

"I heard the Mountain Fast cultivator killed her brother," the first merchant speaker said.

"No, that was the demon cultivator. The murderer," his friend corrected.

Silence grew over the three, before the first speaker spoke. "Do you think she's the demon cultivator?"

Which she he meant, he left unconfirmed for a passing guard shot the three a disapproving look at their gossiping. The group stayed quiet even after the guard had left for the referee, who had given up on his attempt at receiving a confirmation of honorable conduct and, receiving no support from the silent Elder Cao or the chief judge, had finally left the ring.

As the referee came down, he gave the chief judge an elaborate shrug. Wu Ying did not miss the look the judge cast to where Elder Cao stood, still silent.

One had to wonder why she was watching them instead of continuing her investigation. Or perhaps she considered this—being present where nearly everyone else was—part of her inquiry. Or was she looking to head off chaos? If Wu Ying had been the killer, he would take this opportunity to sow chaos. If he was one to kill indiscriminately.

Which once more brought to mind the question of why. Motive for the killings, for the reasoning behind the killer's actions, was lacking.

His thoughts were interrupted as the protective shell covering the ring formed and the pair of contestants were protected from interference. They charged forward, intent on injury and death in a clash of arms and pent-up emotions.

Disdainful battle maniac met enraged and grieving sister in the middle of the ring, neither party willing to give a foot. Axe blades clashed with the heavy tie jian, the steel of the metal bar slamming into sharpened edges and pushing aside the lighter weapons, even as tiny wounds accumulated along Liu Ping's arms from leftover blade intent.

The injuries only seemed to fuel Liu Ping, the edges of her aura solidifying, a brown haze that softened blows and turned aside imperfectly aligned cuts. Her lips pulled apart and widened into a rictus of anger and hate, her swings growing wider and ever more powerful.

The change in Liu Ping's aura and the increased strength of her blows pushed Kong Lai back, the sect cultivator retreating every few exchanges. Chips from the edges of her axes flew through the air at each clash, metal bent and twisted as even aura-reinforcement of the weapons did little to alleviate the damage done to them.

In short order, Kong Lai had retreated to the edge of the ring. There, wounds accumulated as she transitioned to a purely defensive stance. Unlike Liu Ping's showy infusion of bloodline into aura, Kong Lai's earthen element could only be seen in the steadiness of her stance, her ability to handle her opponent's massively empowered blows.

Long seconds passed as Liu Ping thrashed Kong Lai, blood and sweat flying through the air. Yet no matter how close it seemed that Kong Lai would miss a parry and crumple under the echoing, reverberating blows, she held on. Strike after strike, disaster was turned aside by cun after cun.

Beside Wu Ying, the trio of mortals were murmuring again.

"I thought she'd do better. Not much of a sect cultivator, is she?"

"I told you. They're all false dragons and cowardly tigers. None of them are true warriors. Indolent fools, one and all."

"Who cares? It's a good fight, isn't it?"

"I hate losing money… Not as though I earned that much this time around."

"Hah! I told you, you should have brought more healing pills. That's what I did."

Wu Ying tuned out the discussion about optimal stock types, paying further attention to the battle. He did not blame the trio for missing the point, though he was surprised by how often their sentiment was echoed around the ring, even by other cultivators who should know better.

For he could sense it in her aura, in the edge of her swings.

Liu Ping was running out of energy. Her blows were growing more frantic, her attacks swung ever harder. Powered not by strength but desperate, desperate need.

And Kong Lai stood firm. She received the blows and redirected them when she could, suffered in silence when she could not. Blows hammered the edges of her weapons into her arms or chest. Even the occasional misses that struck were weathered by shifts in footwork and rolling movements of the upper body. All to keep her standing, her chi stores from draining too quickly.

A sharp spike of worry and concern, fear stench intensifying. A short distance from him, standing with his friends and allies, Gao Qiu finally noticed what Wu Ying had. His breathing slowed and tightened, and he leaned into the ring as though his focus and attention could provide Liu Ping the energy she lacked.

Interference—entrance from outside the ring—was viable, if difficult. But doing so would mean disqualifying Liu Ping. Still, Wu Ying could almost see the man considering it, weighing her displeasure with the knowledge of what Kong Lai had done to Liu Jin and the enmity the pair bore one another.

Before a decision could be made, the duel turned.

A kick, flashing upward in too large a gap between swings, caught Liu Ping in the chest. She flew backward, flipping through the air and barely managing to block the downward swing of her opponent's axes as Kong Lai followed and struck at Liu Ping while she was still in the air. The force of the block forced Liu Ping's knees to the floor, weapon held upward with both hands even as the sharpened edge of her swordbreaker bit into her open palm reinforcing her block. The smell of fresh blood mixed with the muskiness of her aura, seeping out from the ring.

"Did you really think you could win, you barbaric fool?" Kong Lai taunted, pressing down. Her chi surged, the smell of earth and loam, granite and basalt filtering outward to Wu Ying. The axes drifted closer, heavier than ever as they neared Liu Ping's chest.

"I... won't... lose." Teeth gritted, head tilted upward, even her uttered defiance was insufficient to combat the growing weight.

Cun by cun, the tie jian lowered until the edge of her swordbreaker touched the tip of her forehead, axe blades hanging over and biting a little into her collarbones as her back arched. Liu Ping struggled, the aura of the bear wavering.

Then, howling in pain, she forced her blood to burn, the caustic disruption making Wu Ying's eyes widen. His fool of a friend had done that before, burnt his very life force to win fights. Few sects taught such a method, but those with bloodlines like Liu Ping could tap into the technique instinctively it seemed. Still, even Tou He had never, ever done something like that in a tournament.

The effect was short-lived, a momentary surge of vigor that pushed the pair of axes upward by their hafts. The weapons swung down almost immediately as the strength was robbed from Kong Lai's arms as her energy petered out.

But this time, Liu Ping was ready.

She collapsed backward almost bonelessly, the momentary surge of strength allowing her to shift the position of her legs so that she could fall back and kick upward, lifting her opponent over her. Momentum changing ever so swiftly, Kong Lai tumbled over and slammed into the floor with a tile-shattering crash.

Yet that move had also robbed Liu Ping of her position and injured her body, twisting and kicking backward as she had. Blood streamed from her sides where the axes had clipped her.

She struggled to her feet moments before Kong Lai did, the earth cultivator shaking off shards of stone and dust.

Outside, Gao Qiu strained against the arms holding him back, whispered words from his compatriots telling him to keep calm. To trust in the woman. He struggled in vain even as the pair clashed once more, their movements slower, their attacks warier now as they probed for further missteps.

"You can do it, Ah Ping! Beat her until she doesn't even know her own name!" one of the men from the convoy next to Gao Qiu roared, even as he held back his leader.

Emboldened by the words, Liu Ping found a sudden surge of strength and cunning. She shifted the angle of her latest strike with the swordbreaker, managing to catch not the blade of the weapon striking at her but the haft and fingers beneath.

Crying in pain as her fingers were crushed, Kong Lai's hand spasmed open. Another swing brought the swordbreaker crashing into the now opened side of the sect cultivator's body, throwing the woman aside. Kong Lai bounced off the floor, rolling over and over until she fetched up against the edge of the ring, one leg dangling off.

Slowly, ever so slowly, she pulled herself upright.

Shouts from outside, many with their eyes locked on the sect cultivator who groggily attempted to regain her feet. Many were wondering aloud why Liu Ping stood still, unmoving as she missed the opportunity to finish the battle.

Indeed, to the visible eye, Liu Ping was trembling, her legs shaking as she struggled to stay standing.

"What is she doing? Finish it!"

"Gods above, I should never have bet on a wandering cultivator."

"Maybe the beast is taking over?"

Voices rose and fell with cries of disappointment as Kong Lai managed to stand again.

Conversations quieted as the crowd noticed the sect cultivator smiling through bloody lips, her eyes glinting in savage glee. One hand was wrapped around her side where cracked ribs were cradled, but the other was pointed at her opponent.

"Now you see the difference between a beast and a true daughter of the heavens!" Kong Lai said, sneering aloud. Then her tone changed as she chanted, waving her axe as earth chi surged. "Pursuit of the Earthen Hunter. Entomb."

Earth chi that had been gathering around the pair as they fought slammed closed. Strands of energy pulled together, trapping Liu Ping and crushing her. The crack of her knees banging into the stone tiles resounded through the ring, even as the swordbreaker fell from exhausted fingers.

Another surge of energy, this time from outside the ring. Wu Ying turned his head as Gao Qiu threw off those who held him. Only for Elder Eng to appear behind him, his hand coming down on Gao Qiu's shoulder. A minor exertion of force and Gao Qiu was forced to his knees too.

Wu Ying's eyes narrowed, but Elder Eng was not injuring Gao Qiu any more than he needed to. Choosing to keep watch and silent for now, Wu Ying turned back to the fight in the ring where Kong Lai stumbled closer to Liu Ping, absolute glee still on her face.

Standing over the trapped woman, earth chi coating Liu Ping in strands of dark chains, Kong Lai raised her axe. "I'll crush you just like your useless brother. Then you beasts will know the true strength of the sects!"

At the mention of her brother, Liu Ping released an inhuman growl. The bestial aura that had been crushed disappeared entirely for a moment before returning threefold in strength. Liu Ping threw herself forward, the earthen chains of chi holding her down exploding under the strength of her bloodline.

Kong Lai staggered backward from the backlash of her technique breaking even as Liu Ping's face twisted into an animal's, her nose and mouth seeming to lengthen and darken as her chi surged. Claws, black and shimmering, exploded from her hands as she lunged at Kong Lai, ducking under a swinging hand to claw the woman's torso. Long lines of blood and exposed ribs were drawn from the claws, but Kong Lai managed to finish her attack, burying the axe in Liu Ping's lower back.

Silence for a fraction of a second as both opponents fell, nearly on top of one another. The referee's jaw worked as his gaze darted from still form to still form.

Then, movement. Elder Eng rushed the ring, only for Elder Cao to appear and place her hand on his chest, easily stopping him from approaching.

Gao Qiu, released, staggered toward the stage, but was beaten to the two bodies by the referee and chief judge. Together, they peeled the senseless bodies apart for the healers. Wu Ying kept back, knowing there was nothing he could do for them that the healers could not.

"What a waste…"

Voices from behind, though who said it, Wu Ying could not place. For the better, probably.

"Let them work," Wu Ying said to Gao Qiu, pulling back the man as he tried to crowd the healers. The pair watched as they struggled to heal the pair of cultivators, a part of Wu Ying hoping they were well. As cultivators, it took a lot to kill one of them. "Liu Ping will be fine. She's a Body cultivator, isn't she? With that bloodline, she'd have to be."

A nod from Gao Qiu.

"Then she'll heal."

"But will she ever heal all the way?" Gao Qiu said bitterly. "She burnt her life blood. And forced her bloodline to evolve. Neither of those things…" He shook his head. "You understand."

"It won't be easy. But perhaps it might even aid her," Wu Ying said. "A bloodline evolution is hard to enact, even normally. This might have been for the best."

"The best?" Gao Qiu turned toward Wu Ying, eyes glittering with repressed fury as he shook off Wu Ying's hand on his shoulder. "You immortal cultivators truly are insane.

Anything to keep moving ahead, to ascend, no? She lost her brother, her own family. He was her everything. All that she ever wanted. And you think it's for the best!"

"That's not what I meant."

"Just leave. It's not as though you care for us, or anything but yourself." Then deliberately stepping away from Wu Ying, Gao Qiu turned his attention back to the woman.

Wu Ying stood there for a second before he turned his head. Elder Cao met his gaze, a sardonic smile on her lips even as she kept back Elder Eng and any retribution he might enact for the damage to his niece.

For a second, Wu Ying looked at the shocked faces and the looks of disgust turned on him. Between Gao Qiu's visible distaste and his own showing earlier in the day, there was no welcome for him here.

Shrugging, he left the ring and the surroundings. Whatever happened now, it was none of his business. That was what he had chosen, had he not?

Chapter 24

"This is not how I wanted to win!" Pan Shui's voice was strident as she complained to her sisters in the next room over.

Wu Ying sighed, rubbing his temples as the trio continued to shout at one another. He had been working on his World Spirit Ring on and off for the last few hours, taking care of the fields. One particular field had been laid out with new formations to concentrate the wind chi that had become inherent to his ring, drawn and fed as it was from his own energy.

He had a plan. One that he was uncertain would work—but might ease the demands on the medicinal baths he took regularly and the spirit herbs that were infused in the baths. That reminded him that he was overdue for one, but that was something he would have to undertake somewhere… safer.

Nonetheless, if he could grow a number of more common spirit herbs but infuse them with his wind chi to begin with, it was possible a competent apothecarist could substitute or modify the ingredients list for his baths further, saving him time and repetitions.

On the other hand, he did limit his experimentation to one field. It had taken him many months of pondering before he even began the growing process, though he had in the meantime prepped the location and begun the infusion of chi into the field. Part of the problem was deciding which herbs were best used.

He had to replace the ones he might need in the future while also taking into account the herbs ability to absorb wind chi. There were other concerns too, like the availability of the herbs he might replace, the price of those herbs, potential side effects and reactions between the various herbs, and any corruptive influences or byproducts.

Even speaking to a competent apothecarist for the initial trimming had not provided him with an exhaustive list. He would have to experiment, grow and harvest the herbs before a final decision could be made.

In fact, Wu Ying knew he likely had made mistakes. It might not even be possible to change out these herbs, since the delicate balance of medicinal baths—and even worse, pills—were products of years of experimentation and flashes of insight. Making a single change could lead to a lower efficacy at best, poisoning or corruption of the body at worst.

Better to limit the amount of time and space he devoted to the experiment. It was not as though his World Spirit Ring stood up to its name. It was still not even the size of his old village. Not that he could have cared for all that land himself.

It did lead him to wonder what, if anything, he should do about that. Taking care of a half dozen fields was one thing, since he could act at the speed of thought within his ring. Even a dozen fields would be no strain. But if it kept growing, what would happen when it was the size of a county? A kingdom?

Did he then create forests and lands for his herbs to grow untamed? Would it even be possible to do that, without the natural spirit beasts that helped care for the environment? If not, could he eventually sustain such creatures?

It boggled the mind that that might be possible, but there were stories…

Certainly, he had experimented with normal animals, finding it impossible to bring anything more complex than ants or bugs within. Even those, he had to be careful in regulating, for without the natural predators of the world, they had a tendency to flourish and overpopulate his ring, requiring him to cull them.

At what point would his ring be effective for animals and spirit beasts? Were they barred? If they were not, could he bring in humans? Somehow, Wu Ying doubted that—at least until he became an immortal. Still, such rings and flasks were storied items, wielded by everyone from the most common immortal to The Great Sage, Heaven's Equal.

Sadly, information was still lacking. That was the problem with cultivator society in a sense—too much knowledge was hidden from one another, such that information that might aid others was never disseminated. All too much knowledge was lost when cultivators died or ascended or were locked behind sect libraries or noble houses.

Of course, Wu Ying could not be too offended. He too kept the secret of his own ring hidden, for fear of being struck down by another who desired it. The danger of owning the ring was significant, though he had been, thankfully, untargeted as yet.

Still, he understood it was but a matter of time.

"Well, what you want doesn't matter. There's no one else to fight," Pan Yin shouted back. "So just suck it up and take the prize tomorrow."

"No!"

Wu Ying heard a door yanked open. Loud stomping feet, then his door was banged on, the door attempted to be shoved open.

There was a pause when the door did not give way, then Pan Shui hollered through it, "Come out here!"

Wincing, Wu Ying fully extracted his mind from his ring and waited for mental equilibrium to be achieved before he walked over and pulled the crossbar off the door. He stepped back swiftly as the door was thrown open, nearly hitting his foot.

"You! Fight me," Pan Shui demanded.

"No."

"I won't take a win like this! It's ridiculous," Pan Shui said. Behind her, Pan Yin and the middle sister appeared, both of them looking a little embarrassed. "At least we should fight for a proper second place."

"No. I already gave up, so it would not be fair."

"It's not fair for me to be the winner when I haven't even fought anyone!" Pan Shui said. "The entire tournament is a farce then!"

"Not my problem."

"Unless you want to make friends with the Seven Pavilions. I think they would actually be grateful if you helped them with their lackluster finale problem," Pan Yin said musingly.

"You're not helping," Wu Ying replied.

"See! Even Elder Sister thinks you should do this," Pan Shui said.

Pan Yin growled and grabbed her sister's ear, twisting it. "No. I actually think you should stop complaining and just accept the prize. What are you going to do if you lose, eh?"

"I won't lose," Pan Shui said mulishly. She let out a louder yelp when Pan Yin twisted harder. "I won't, I won't! I promise."

"You can't promise such things." Another twist before she let her sister go and turned to Wu Ying, bowing a little. "I apologize for her insult."

"It's fine," Wu Ying said, hiding his smile. "She is young."

"Oh, like you're a decrepit old hag like that Elder Cao!" Pan Shui said. Then her eyes narrowed as she leaned in to peer at Wu Ying's face, searching for lines. "You aren't, are you? I mean, Body cultivators are supposed to be able to look younger easier. Or older. Wait, are you a child?"

Wu Ying reached out with two fingers and pushed on her forehead, making Pan Shui back off. "I'm not old, and I'm not going to fight you. Now, can you leave me alone? Some of us were cultivating."

Pan Shui rolled her eyes. "At least congratulate me on winning the tournament!"

"Changed your mind fast, didn't you?" Wu Ying teased.

"You—"

Grinning, Wu Ying bowed. "Congratulations on winning, Cultivator Pan." He paused, then asked, "What happened to the other two? How bad are their injuries?"

"Serious, but not life-threatening."

Wu Ying nodded. That much he had expected, since if they had died, he would have heard of it. Even now, the wind carried snippets of conversation and a sense of what was happening through his open window. Not enough to review everything that happened, of course, but more than sufficient to alert him if something major occurred. Like another body was found or the contestants died.

"They will both recover, but neither can fight," Pan Yin added.

"Who was declared the winner?" Wu Ying asked.

"Me," Pan Shui said bitterly.

"Of the match."

"No one. It was announced as a draw," Pan Yin said.

"Huh. That must have annoyed everyone involved," Wu Ying said.

"You don't say," Pan Yin muttered. "We left before things grew even more unsettled."

Wu Ying sighed. He had picked up something of the altercation, but it was obvious that none of the angered parties had felt like testing the Elder's ire. While it was possible for Energy Storage cultivators to beat a Core Formation cultivator—he had, after all, done the same a few years ago—it required training and specialized formations. Battle techniques that empowered the individual.

Nothing that a group of wandering cultivators would have on hand.

They could still bury her in bodies if they so desired, sacrificing lives to inflict injuries upon her, building up wounds until she was forced to either retreat or risk death. However, that kind of sacrifice over disrupted wagers and a disappointing tournament was unlikely.

"Well, congratulations again, Cultivator Pan." He gestured to the door, indicating for her to leave.

"Not interested if you get a prize?" Pan Yin said curiously.

"What do you mean?"

"After all, all three of you in the quarter finals lost."

"But I gave up and was declared the loser, while the other two were considered a draw. It's obvious that I won't receive anything. There are only three prizes."

Pan Yin sighed. "But you truly don't have any desire for the prizes, do you?"

Wu Ying shrugged.

Pan Shui snorted. "Enough flirting already. The prize ceremony will be tomorrow instead of the day after. Everyone is supposed to show up. Or at least, those who can stand."

Wu Ying ignored the annoying insinuation about the flirting while Pan Yin smacked her sister in the arm.

"I'll be there," he said. Then he lowered his voice. "Any further leads?"

Pan Shui shook her head. There was no need to ask leads for what.

"Then after the ceremony, we should return here. Stay indoors, eat whatever travel rations you have, and wait."

"Till when?" Pan Yin said.

"Till they find the killer."

"And if they don't?" Pan Shui's fist tightened as she stared between the two who were speaking. "You heard some of the conversations out there. Some of those fools are already talking about taking things in their own fists and coming after us." Her voice dropped. "Or Liu Ping, because of her aura."

"They think she killed her own brother?" Pan Yin said, sounding surprised. "What fool would think that?"

"The kind who is scared and looking for an excuse, any excuse, to lash out," Pan Shui replied.

He held up a hand. "Let's worry about it later. Make it through the night, get your prizes. You make use of your prizes, get stronger. Then, if the killer hasn't been found…"

"We worry about it then?" Pan Shui said. "I don't like waiting for something to happen."

"Few do. But Elder Cao has made it clear our help is unwanted. Stepping in without her acknowledgment could mean causing more problems. Knowing when to step back is important too." Wu Ying could not help remembering his own lessons in not hurrying around.

Running from one kingdom to another, all to return and find that if he had just waited, matters would have resolved. Sometimes, the greatest wisdom was in doing nothing.

"We're to trust her? Even if she has done nothing?" Pan Shui said. "Or she's incompetent? After all, the one who had actual skill at investigating was the one killed, no?"

"Then do you have a suggestion?" Wu Ying retorted.

"I… well…" Pan Shui trailed off.

"Exactly. I'm no investigator either, and what little I've seen has shown me that none of my usual tricks work." He shrugged. "In the end, we wait. Now, if you don't mind…" He waved back at his room. "I was resting."

"Yes. You need it, after such a strenuous battle earlier." Pan Shui stuck out her tongue and hurried out before her sister could hit her again.

He snorted, then looked at Pan Yin, who had not moved. She had, in fact, a tiny smile that danced on the edges of her lips.

"What?" he asked.

"Oh, just amused at the way my sister acts when she has found someone she likes."

"A crush?" He shook his head. "I have no time for that. And she is way too childish."

"Good," Pan Yin said. "I won't have to deal with you then."

"What?"

Instead of answering, Pan Yin followed her sister, leaving Pan Mu as the last one in the hallway. The girl laughed a little at Wu Ying's face, before she chose to take pity on the man.

"It's okay. We all know you're a horrible marriage prospect. But the heart wants what it wants, no?"

She left Wu Ying to stare after the women as they returned to their room, where Pan Shui was already haranguing her sister for telling him her secret. He snorted, stepping back and closing the door.

Sisters. Devils, all of them.

***

Rather than continue to listen to the comedy trio in the other room, Wu Ying left for the same field as before. He continued his practice with his new sword, the minor privacy bubble he had put up keeping his practice a secret. Or so he hoped, at least. It was hard to tell, but with the sheer restlessness and the trio of Elders and the head of the merchant association all caught up in talks in their compound, he was fairly certain he was fine.

Hours passed before Wu Ying finished, just as the sun began to set. Practice over, Wu Ying found himself reluctant to return to his room. Instead, he took the long way around, passing through the village on his way back as he pondered the investigation. Whatever words he had spoken to the Pan sisters, he had been concerned for a while. It was why he had taken the opportunities to view the crime scenes, to listen and ask about developments.

He remembered the investigator's face, the dreams and hopes she had inadvertently told him. Liu Jin's laughing manner and the way he always tried to look out for his impetuous sister. Even the big-mouthed sect cultivator had not deserved to die.

Yet...

What could he do? He was no investigator, that was true enough. Nor did he see a reason for the deaths of Cui Wen or Liu Jin. Their murders were as different as they were sudden. The only killing that had an obvious motive had been Investigator Chu's—and that did not help him narrow his suspect list.

Whatever clue she'd had, it was obviously insufficient for Elder Cao to find the killer. Unless she was the killer. Which... well, that would be bad.

His thoughts had brought him to the guards' building, unconsciously. The only building in the entirety of the village that he could not access, that was blocked off from his senses— even the wind refusing to provide anything but the most modest of hints of what lay behind the formation.

Wu Ying's lips pursed as he wondered what secrets lay behind it all. In the end though, he turned away, for he could do nothing. Only to turn back when the door opened and a familiar Guard Captain's face was revealed.

"Cultivator Long." The man's voice was low, cutting through the quiet of the night.

"Guard Captain Teng," Wu Ying replied, offering a slight bow.

"Investigator Chu mentioned that your particular brand of cultivation and aura control is significantly different from those in our kingdom."

A nod to the man's statement.

"Yet you have found nothing?"

"Not at the previous sites. No."

"And if you saw a third, do you think you could find something then?" Teng Fei asked.

"Perhaps. Sometimes scents and clues are hard to apprise, when sensed alone," Wu Ying said.

"Yes. So Investigator Chu mentioned too." Another pause, then Teng Fei stepped aside from the door. "I'm hungry. Haven't had supper. I won't be back for another... oh... ten minutes? Perhaps you could watch over the building for me."

"Watch the building..." Wu Ying said carefully.

"To ensure no one disturbs the bodies."

"I see. Of course."

"Thank you, Cultivator Long." So saying, Teng Fei left, though not before ensuring the door was propped open.

Wu Ying made his way to the entrance, frowning a little and stopping in front of the open doorway, noting how the formation had been opened to allow entry and egress. So long as the door stayed open, the formation would too.

Feeling a little like he had sneaked out of cultivation practice as a child, Wu Ying stepped past the threshold into the building. He paused inside, his senses extended, waiting for the alarm to blare.

Nothing.

Releasing a held breath, he headed up the staircase. There was no need to work out the layout of the building—the winds had already mapped it out for him the moment he stepped within, whispering of rooms and open doors, wide passages and enclosed cupboards.

And the beginning of rot.

The room where Investigator Chu had been killed differed from where she had been laid out. The first was above, in her office. The second, down below the ground, in one of the few cellars in this temporary location. Cold stone, with secondary wards to ensure that she did not rise as a jiangshi.

First, the body. Wu Ying headed down, fast, pausing only long enough to ascertain the wards below would not trigger or be broken by his entry. Then, over to her body; a simple yellow talisman had been placed upon the forehead to preserve and protect.

The wound that killed her was ugly, half the side of her head crushed. He raised his hand, comparing the site to his own fist and memories of other wounds. Definitely a punch, delivered with such great strength that it had crushed her skull like an egg being struck by a hammer. A cultivator then, someone with good technique and in the high stages of Body Cleansing, or an Energy Storage cultivator or higher. A Body cultivator could do as much too, of course, but again—someone who was more than in the beginnings of their cultivation journey.

It did not narrow down the suspect list at all. He'd already assumed the killer had to be an Energy Storage cultivator of some sort—just from the initial murder. It was unlikely that even a hidden strike from a Body Cleansing cultivator could have ended Cui Wen. Never mind the fact that he had been snuck up upon—or chosen to give his back.

So.

Someone trusted or an Energy Storage cultivator.

And a female perhaps—or a man with small hands. The blow looked to be concentrated. Unless they used a striking technique focused on one or two knuckles—and then, it was too broad. So, probably someone with small hands.

That, at least, was useful. Surprising they had chosen to attack barehanded actually, but Investigator Chu had been mortal. Had they chosen to kill with their weapons before due to fear of being overpowered otherwise?

He wished he had seen the body initially, where she was struck. Perhaps he could find clues above, but the body, after another quick perusal, offered no further clues. Not to him, at least.

So, someone comfortable with killing with their bare hands. Someone confident enough to do so with a single attack. Either a female or someone with small hands. If it was the same killer as before, then they were confident in their use of three different weapons. A dagger for Liu Jin—or some shorter weapon to cut his throat—a jian for Cui Wen, and now, unarmed.

Unusual.

Turning aside, Wu Ying headed for Investigator Chu's office, knowing that the Guard Captain would be back soon. Even if he had allowed Wu Ying in—and that was interesting behavior, now wasn't it?—there was only so far the Captain was likely willing to bend the rules.

So best to get this done.

Upstairs, the room was filled with paper. In bookcases and cupboards, notes everywhere. The only location which was not clogged with paper was the desk, which was barren. No notes or papers there, nothing to indicate what Investigator Chu had been working on the night she died. Which, now that Wu Ying thought of it, made sense. If she had left a clue, the Captain and Elder Cao had probably wanted to find it and it would most likely be in the papers she had been reading.

So be it. He would review the scene of the murder as it was—empty but for the furnishings. Desk in front, bookcases to the side, chair behind the desk and another in front of it. Wu Ying walked around the desk, his gaze flicking across the surroundings as the wind stirred gently, ruffling parchment paper and his hair alike.

Someone had cleaned up the blood, though he still smelled the remnants of it as it rotted. On the floor, across the desk a little, and more on the back of the chair and back wall.

He traced it all, noting the largest remnant stain—where she had likely lay, bleeding from the injury—to the scattered droplets. The way it arced, the slight amount down to the right side of where he was which matched the wound on her corpse.

Right-handed then. Just like the initial killer. He assumed it was the same for Liu Jin, but he had not heard Investigator Chu's analysis of that murder. Even a small splattering on the right-side floor, where the killer must have shook off their bloody hand.

Other smells were present: the muskiness of Teng Fei's chi, Elder Cao's, and the investigator's own sharply edged chi. All of them present, and no one else's. Not too surprising—Wu Ying had never managed to pick out any additional trace chi.

The wind danced, whispering of a familiar scent, of a twist in the environment that he recognized. He went to a cupboard and opened it to find the missing seal. Cui Wen's protective talisman.

"What's it doing here?" Wu Ying muttered, his gaze darting around the surroundings. Why had he not heard about it being found?

There was some paper with the talisman, which he picked up to read. His eyes darted down the paper, the information on it neatly written.

... token returned to us by suspect Pan Mu. Suspect indicated that victim Cui Wen had left the token behind accidentally after midnight assignation. When Cui Wen's death was disseminated, suspect Pan Mu volunteered full details of their evening. See Timeline A for further details.

Below the dry text, another note was penned in, in-between lines detailing the interview in more depth.

Suspect Pan Mu cleared via multiple eyewitness reports, including sisters Pan Shui and Pan Yin. Recommended to lower probability of suspect Pan Mu being the killer by a margin of two cun.

Wu Ying read further before he sighed, realizing there was little new. At least it cleared up the question of how Cui Wen had been killed. Unfortunately, all it did was increase the suspect range again to everyone in the high Energy Storage level or whom Cui Wen would trust. Which, in truth, was probably only a half dozen.

Biting his lip, Wu Ying looked around for the suspect list and found it soon enough. He memorized the names, most of them known to him. The Pan sisters, the sect cultivators, himself, Gao Qiu, and a few other wandering cultivators.

Not many, in truth.

For a time, Wu Ying stood there, reviewing the room and memorizing what he could of the surroundings. Hoping further inspiration would spark in his mind. Nothing did, not even when he sensed the Guard Captain on the way back.

"Thank you, Cultivator Long, for watching the building." Teng Fei smiled, holding up the pair of steamed buns he had acquired. "This should last me the night."

"You're welcome," Wu Ying said, walking down the stairs and smiling to the Captain in gratitude.

"I hope it was not too much of an imposition."

"Not at all."

"It's good that we can rely on you. After all, matters are very unsettled right now. Those who are willing to step up... well, those numbers have grown ever smaller each year."

Wu Ying offered the man a tight smile, returning the intense gaze Teng Fei turned on him. There was an unspoken thought in there, one that Teng Fei was clearly unwilling to voice.

In the end, Wu Ying offered a last bow, still uncertain of what the man meant. A second later, the guardsman walked into the building and shut the door, sealing the formation once more.

Leaving Wu Ying to stare after him. With stolen knowledge perhaps, and no further ideas of what he should do.

"I wish people would just say what's on their minds!" he muttered as he wandered back to his room. Damn fools.

Chapter 25

Waking up the next morning, Wu Ying could not help but turn the night's events over in his mind. The murder itself had provided him with some little information, but Teng Fei's actions stood out. The Guard Captain had defied the Elder, something Wu Ying would never have imagined him doing. And he had done that for Wu Ying, which was another interesting wrinkle.

Was it because Wu Ying had a rather unique place among the other wandering cultivators? Because he had been asked to look at the previous deaths? Or was it that Teng Fei had hoped that Wu Ying's aura control and expanded spiritual senses might have found something they had not? Even if so, why did he ask Wu Ying to look, when the Elder had not wanted his help any further?

Unless Teng Fei thought the Elder could not be trusted to finish the investigation. Or maybe he shared Wu Ying's suspicions that she might be the killer. Then again, didn't he just disprove the fact that it had to be a Core Formation cultivator? But if that was the case, why the hesitation at bringing people in for enhanced interrogations? According to Gao Qiu, the government had done as much before.

Then again… Elder Cao was retired. She wasn't the government anymore. Was she then waiting for reinforcements? Was a group of government officials coming, and the cultivators were trapped here on purpose?

That was certainly possible.

Or, more worryingly, perhaps she knew who the killer was and was unwilling to bring them in.

That thought sent a cold shiver down his spine. There were only a couple of people whom it might be impolitic for the ex-general to deal with. Wu Ying did not know enough of either sect—beyond the fact that they were two of the larger ones in the kingdom. But size was not the only consideration. Connections—personal or family—favors, and strength could all alter the equation.

If his assumptions were true, then perhaps Elder Cao was playing politics with their lives. Trading favors or influence for her looking the other way. But the pressure of her dao, the way she spoke… he could not see it. Not unless… not unless she saw it as her duty to ensure the tournament and the Seven Pavilions were left blameless.

If that was the case, then Elder Cao must have been Investigator Chu's killer. The small fist, the location… it fit. If the Elder and whichever sect Elder were working together.

A chilling thought. Elder Eng looked too greatly bereaved by the death of his disciple for it to be him. Which meant the obvious suspects were Elder Tsui and Elder Cao. Except, of course, both sect Elders were old. And few cultivators—especially sect Elders—grew that old without learning how to lie.

Though why Elder Eng would wish his own disciple's death, Wu Ying had no answer.

Even if it was all true, what could Wu Ying do about it? What should he do about it? A single Elder he might beat. It would be risky and dangerous, but it might be something he was willing to try, given the right circumstances.

Two would be foolish in the extreme. He did not have his master around to save him.

In the end it all came back to this—what did he owe those here? What should he, as a stranger, an outsider, do?

Wu Ying was certain that when the arrows fell, he could escape.

It was not his place to dictate what a kingdom did. As an outsider, he knew little about the historical and cultural aspects in play. He did not understand what those like the White Flower Merchant Association wanted to achieve or how trustworthy they truly were in carrying out their stated objectives. Perhaps they were the culprits? Perhaps they were the killers?

After all, if the murders did not require a Core Formation cultivator, then Gao Qiu or Liu Ping might have done the initial killing. And Elder Cao could be waiting for the government to sweep in and capture the rebels. Holding them here until all could be caught.

Though why her brother then? Unless it was a cold-blooded distraction. Or competing rebel associations.

As he thought. Politics.

Deep politics.

Wu Ying had no place here. He would not be around to see the completion of any action he began, any change that might occur. He was but a traveler. Those who were rooted in place must take responsibility for their own world. It was not his place to enact his beliefs, his morality on others. Not on a kingdom-wide scale.

This, Wu Ying knew.

Yet that did not preclude him acting on minor matters like these. It was one thing to be helpless when a drought struck, knowing that one could not dictate the movement of the clouds. Yet it was a poor farmer who did not place an offering for immortals and dragons alike, beseeching their generosity in bringing the rain. It was a lazy farmer who did not dig down their wells or plan for a dropping river height.

You could lament the cruelty of the world; but if all you did was cry, you were no longer a victim of circumstances but a co-conspirator of your own tragedies.

Even so...

Wu Ying let out a long breath when he heard the striking of a gong, the Seven Pavilions tournament organizers calling all participants to the dueling rings. It was time for the presentation of prizes.

How many would attend? He doubted someone like Gao Qiu would leave Liu Ping alone, not after what had happened to her brother. And Kong Lai might be protected by wards, but even then, it was unlikely for her Elder to trust in those alone.

It would leave Pan Shui alone to take the prize, which might create even more problems. He had listened as the sisters had left earlier, other members of the foreigner residence choosing to follow. Lost in his thoughts, he had ignored their invitation.

Wu Ying let out a slow breath, his pensive musings stopping. He ceased worrying, playing out potential consequences or projections of what might or might not happen. He stilled that unquiet mind, no longer thinking about the future. And instead, for the first time, he searched his soul for the answer.

The mind was smart, the mind was knowledgeable, the mind was ethical.

The mind was not wise nor moral nor generous.

The Dao could not be found in the deep contemplation of ethics or future projections of problems. It could only be found deep within one's soul.

Wu Ying breathed in.

He might not be able to change the kingdom or alter the fate of the masses, but here and now, he could make a difference. And while he had no desire to be a champion of justice, an unrepentant wandering hero, neither would he turn away from the task before him. His father had taught him better. Plan for the future, certainly, but you still had to do the work before you.

He breathed out.

And made up his mind.

***

Wu Ying drifted upward to the second floor of the restaurant. He found them there, as expected. The general had taken her usual place on a rooftop. Showmanship, all of it. With the way she blanketed the surroundings with her aura, everyone with even a modicum of ability knew where she was at all times.

Well, so long as they were willing to extend their auras out like her. Which would be a direct challenge to her authority. An interesting thought that—was her inadvertent help to the killer(s) by enforcing the limits on everyone's aura senses accidental or on purpose?

Then again, would it have mattered? After all, Wu Ying had been unable to ascertain their aura or traces of their passing, even through all three murder scenes. Perhaps whether she blanketed the surroundings or not, the ending would have been the same.

"Cultivator Long. Are you choosing to join us?" Elder Tsui asked as Wu Ying approached their table.

"Elder Tsui. Elder Eng. If you will have me." At their agreement, Wu Ying took a seat, greeting the other two inner sect cultivators and letting his gaze dance across Kong Lai's form. She was pale and sweating, leaning against the arm of her chair, blankets and cushions padded to prop her upright. "I am glad to see that you are doing well, Cultivator Kong."

"Well enough to fight," Kong Lai said. "If they'd let me, I could show them that. Draw, my burnt meridians!"

"Ah Lai!" Elder Eng snapped. "Apologize to Cultivator Long for your behavior. It is unbecoming to protest an official ruling like a spoiled child who has been refused a sweet. If you are saddened by the draw, then next time, beat your opponent in such a way that it is impossible for your win to be contested!

"The failure is in you. Just as it was in Cui Wen!"

Kong Lai flushed and eventually bowed her head. She whispered an apology, though whether it was to Elder Eng or to Wu Ying, neither knew.

The awkward atmosphere extended for a time, only for an attendant to sweep by to offer Wu Ying tea and suggest additional dishes. After Wu Ying declined, the attendant hurried off to deal with the next table.

"I'm surprised, Cultivator Long, that you chose to sit with us. You have not chosen to do so until now," Elder Tsui said. A small gesture and he created a simple privacy bubble around them with his chi. It would do little against a dedicated probe, but more than enough for casual conversation.

Enviable ability, that. Damn formation masters.

Wu Ying had been in the midst of picking up a small fried dumpling and placing it on his plate, so he made sure to finish what he was doing before turning to Elder Tsui. Beneath them, the swell of conversation grew as more and more of the wandering cultivators arrived at the dueling ring, which was the only one that had not been taken down already.

"It seems most feel I should be up here anyway," Wu Ying said. "And with the results of the tournament, I feel it is best to give myself some space from those who might have wanted a more… exciting finish."

"We had the best fight," Kong Lai muttered, sounding somewhat pleased by that at least.

"Do you want to do midnight salutations all the way back to your sect?" Shi Fei leaned over and hissed at Kong Lai.

Thankfully, the two Elders were willing to ignore the byplay between the two younger members of their sects, as they spoke with Wu Ying.

"You should have been here since the start anyway," Elder Tsui said. "It is good that you are no longer running around with the riffraff."

"Mmm… they make decent customers and even better suppliers," Wu Ying said. "And the knowledge they have of the byways and other hidden resources are useful for someone like myself." He touched his chest then continued. "In turbulent times, you never know what you might hear."

"You mean the killings?" Shi Fei asked, breaking in.

Elder Tsui glared at him and he ducked his head, embarrassed.

"Yes. It took a long time, but I think, finally, the wind has brought me some answers."

The two Elders frowned, Elder Eng speaking fiercely. "You know who the killer is?"

"No." Wu Ying shook his head. "Not yet. But I have suspicions, and I need to check one last thing."

"The inspector's office then," Elder Eng muttered angrily. "We've not been allowed to see it either."

"Not that," Wu Ying said. "But I expect one way or the other, my suspicions will be proven by the end of the day." He glanced at the crowds, a tight smile dancing across his lips. "Probably much later in the day, truth be told."

"Why? If you need only one thing, then do it now. Cui Wen's killer has slumbered peacefully for too long!" Elder Eng ranted, his voice rising a little.

Elder Tsui shook his head, causing Elder Eng to lean back in his chair. Even then, he was almost visibly radiating his need to act.

"Less commotion, Ah Eng. Otherwise, the killer might run. But I am curious, why so long?" Elder Tsui muttered.

"Well…" Quickly, Wu Ying cast about for a reason. A memory sparked and he spoke, only realizing after he spoke how true his words were. "The Winds of the Hundred Hells rise at night, and it is those winds I must speak with."

"The winds of hell?" Kong Lai mouthed to Shi Fei, almost leaning away from Wu Ying.

"My cultivation style"—his Body Cultivation style, but they didn't need to know that—"concerns the Seven Winds. Of which hell is but one direction." Staring at Kong Lai, he grinned and added, "And heaven another."

"So not a demonic path then," Elder Tsui said, bringing attention back to him.

"No. Just unusual," Wu Ying said. "Then again, so is my element."

"True. Few enough wind elementalists. And none that I've heard of who have achieved your standard," Elder Tsui said. "Not in our kingdom at least."

Wu Ying offered a tight smile of understanding, wondering if everything he had spoken was enough. Before he could add further to the hints, the conversation was cut off by the voice of the chief judge below.

The judge coated his words with regality and formality, doing his best to make the ending of the tournament more grandiose than it was, offering praise to all the contestants. Reminding them of the most interesting battles and techniques on display.

Most stark, to Wu Ying, was the lack of mention of his own participation, though he could understand the reasoning behind that quite easily.

The ceremony droned on, the officials all insisting on taking their turn to speak and hoping that in their expulsion of meaningless words, they could somehow shore up the prestige of their tournament. An event that had been marred not just by a lousy showing in the matches but also death and murder.

"They won't recover, I think," Elder Tsui remarked. "I wonder how many more merchant associations or sects will dare host tournaments after this."

"Surely it's not that bad," Wu Ying said. "The murders are appalling, but if they are solved, the matter will be put to rest. And the fights, while dangerous, were quite entertaining."

"If it was just this tournament, it would not matter," Elder Eng muttered. "But in the last year, five of the nine tournaments have had some calamity involved. From individuals found to be using demonic verses to gain an edge, to widespread poisoning of participants, to an all-out massacre."

"Five of nine?" Wu Ying said, surprised. "Why am I only hearing of this now?"

"Because at least three of them were never to be spoken of again," Elder Tsui replied, gesturing a little to ensure that the privacy formation was still in play. The one he had created using just his chi was not meant for truly private conversations after all, just idle gossip. "Two were held by sects, the third by a merchant association that is now defunct. All of those were private events, excluding wandering cultivators like those below."

"Then knowledge of such instances has been kept quiet," Wu Ying muttered.

The two Elders nodded. "A bad sign, that so much has happened in so short a period. A third calamity for all to know of might see the end of such occasions, to the detriment of us all."

"Surely you can all still trade?" Wu Ying said.

"It's not the trading itself that is important, but the gathering and legitimacy these events impart. The connections made at a tournament held by a prestigious merchant association, or the announcement of winners to the public bolsters our reputations," Elder Tsui replied. "Even for us, meeting the few rough portions of jade that linger below"—he gestured at the crowd—"can be helpful and aid us in improving our sects."

"Never mind what we might find at the auctions. For, as you say, wandering cultivators get everywhere—and what cultivation cave or previously lost manual or spirit herb they might stumble upon, useless to them, might see a breakthrough for us," Elder Eng added.

"Thank you for enlightening me, Elders," Wu Ying replied with a courteous inclination of his head.

It seemed the burgeoning tournament and auction scenes were more important than he had thought. Looking down, his gaze drifted to a couple of cultivators, men he had seen with Gao Qiu before. Wu Ying could not help but think that such events were also great cover for the rebels. It allowed them to gather without attracting attention, to plot and recruit.

Yet before he could trace that line of thought further, there was a change in the rhythm of the speeches below. Loud clapping, too enthusiastic to be polite. Wu Ying realized that the last speaker was done, and Pan Shui was now ascending to the stage.

She was presented a small lacquer box containing the pills and technique scroll, and she exchanged words with the chief judge before taking center stage. She stared at the crowd before her, the triangular headdress that she and her sisters wore shading her from the morning sun. Something in her stance, in the glint in her eyes, forewarned Wu Ying. It was not just him though, for her elder sister was pushing toward the stage.

Too late.

"I won't take too much time. I know many of you think I don't deserve this prize. So, I'm going to give any of you who are dissatisfied with the results a chance to win it from me." Turning, Pan Shui pointed at the vacant center stage, the only one still left. "Anyone who thinks they can beat me, just meet me within and try your blade."

Grinning cockily, she put a hand on her hip and glared at the crowd. Almost everyone was too stunned to move, only Pan Yin managing to face palm herself.

Pan Yin muttered to her sister and herself, "I'm going to beat her so badly, even Mother won't be able to recognize her!"

"Let me..." Kong Lai stirred, only for Elder Eng to glare at her.

"Foolish girls. The tournament is over," Elder Tsui muttered. "This type of grandstanding is so... uncouth."

"But cool," Shi Fei muttered.

Wu Ying, on the other hand, was taking a more direct approach to the problem. Using a thread of wind, he sent his words to Pan Shui's ears and her ears alone. "You fool, at least limit the number of challengers. Otherwise, they'll beat you down by challenging you one by one."

Pan Shui's eyes widened when his words reached her, and she looked up to spot Wu Ying. Then, after a second and before the stunned crowd could fully recover, she added, "Only your three best though! I don't want to be losing to some Body Cleanser just because I fell asleep."

This time, even Wu Ying could not stop from face palming himself.

Damn fool of a girl.

Now they really were going to take her up on the challenge.

***

The arguments below grew in pace and volume, giving Pan Shui's sisters more than enough time to get her spear. Even the Seven Pavilions management were drawn in, with the merchant group eventually agreeing to fund the usage cost of the tournament ring. It was a cynical move since a good series of fights could bolster both Pan Shui's and their reputation.

After the fourth person to sneak up onto the second floor of the restaurant to ask either Wu Ying or Shi Fei to join the fight, Elder Tsui manipulated the air to form an opaque privacy ward. The not-so-subtle method of partitioning themselves away from those below discouraged their unwanted petitioners, though it did make service a little more difficult.

"I'm thinking the freshwater prawns with garlic—steamed, of course," Elder Tsui said, ignoring the ongoing conversation below.

"We had that two days ago," Elder Eng complained.

"It was good."

"It was, but I'd prefer drunken prawns instead," Elder Eng said. "They nearly managed to make it perfectly the last time."

"Fine, but we will have the catfish steamed then, with ginger and soy sauce. I won't have it fried," Elder Tsui replied immediately. "Cultivator Long?"

"Hmmm?"

"Do you have any requests?"

Wu Ying blinked at the pair of Elders, then realizing what was happening, thought for a second. "Ginger beef with gai lan."

"You like simple food too, then?" Elder Tsui remarked, smiling. "It is the best, is it not?"

"I like my food in a variety of ways, but they do their rice well here," Wu Ying admitted. "Their beef is also fresh, but the pork is a little old."

"How…?" Elder Eng began then stopped when Wu Ying tapped his nose. "Ah, your winds."

"Yes."

"A fascinating ability."

"They've been serving us rotten meat?" Elder Tsui said, sounding enraged.

"No, no. Not rotten. It's still good, but it's not as fresh." Wu Ying waved to calm the other man. "I would not eat here if they chose to do such things. And certainly, the Seven Pavilions would never do something like that voluntarily."

"Not that it matters," said Kong Lai. When everyone else looked at her, she clarified. "As cultivators, even if the food is a little rotten, it would not harm our bodies. It would have to be truly spoilt for it to cause us problems."

"And how do you know that?" said Shi Fei.

"I worked the kitchens when I was in the outer sect," Kong Lai answered.

"It's not a matter of whether it will harm us or not. It's a matter of taste. Of dignity. I will not stoop to eating rotting meat. How can one expect to progress if you stuff your body with corrupt items? Your body must be clean and pure to progress," Elder Tsui said hotly.

"The earth takes all," muttered Kong Lai.

Wu Ying chose to ignore that byplay. "Now, the other question is the fowl. Chicken or duck?"

"Roast duck of course," Elder Eng said. "It's well done here, and even I can smell it being roasted right now. There's nothing better when it's fresh and hot and the skin crispy."

"Definitely," Elder Tsui concurred.

In short order, they had a proper lunch order. Elder Tsui took it upon himself to make sure it was correctly placed with the hostess, going so far as to leave their table and the privacy bubble. In the meantime, Wu Ying noted that the group below had finally come to a conclusion as to who would be joining the battle.

Ascending the steps of the hastily built podium once more, the chief judge, looking harried, waved at the crowd to quiet down.

Well, it seemed that Pan Shui had gotten her way at least. Whatever the outcome, she would have a fight that would be spoken of by everyone who survived.

204

Chapter 26

Up first was Jochi, the man hefting his bow and grinning at Pan Shui. His fur-lined vest had been unbuttoned to give him extra mobility, while his quiver full of arrows was slung low and strapped to his back to ensure it would not bounce around too much. He carried a trio of arrows between his fingers, while a fourth rested on the strings.

"Don't be angry if I win, okay, little sister?"

"Win my foot," Pan Shui snapped. She nodded to the head judge, who triggered the protective formation around the ring.

The moment they finished their salutations and greetings, Jochi loosed his arrows. One after the other flickered across the space between them, the man managing to put three arrows into the air before the first even made its way to the woman. Faster than he had done with Kong Lai even.

It availed him naught.

Perhaps it was the words of caution already passed to Pan Shui by her sisters. Perhaps it was the knowledge that she had three such battles to fight; but the spearwoman was all fired up. She dodged the first arrow by inches, already moving when he had loosed it. The second she struck aside, and the third she dodged by flipping through the air.

As she began to descend, she cried out. "The Broken Limb!"

Rather than keep hold of her weapon, she threw the spear such that it flew away from her, boosted by her chi and weapon intent, rotating from end to end in a spinning circle. It moved faster than Jochi had anticipated.

It struck him haft-wise, hard, forcing him to stagger back. His left shoulder and ribs were cracked, making his follow-up arrow fly awry. Even then, he managed to recover and draw another arrow from his quiver, no longer having one in-hand to fast nock.

Pushing and pulling on his bow, Jochi hissed angrily as the bruised muscles protested. He still managed to aim the arrowhead at Pan Shui as she landed, targeting her chest. But before he could release the arrow, something swept his feet, throwing him to the floor.

Losing his arrow, Jochi stared as Pan Shui manipulated her spear with chi strings, pulling it back into her hand. He had missed her attaching them as she threw the weapon, allowing her to surprise him. Twice.

With the blunt end pointed at Jochi, Pan Shui struck, the capped end of the spear driving his breath from his body and disrupting the flow of his chi as he cried in pain.

"My win," Pan Shui said.

When Jochi opened his mouth, she pushed further with the weapon. Blunt and capped it might be, but the point was driving directly into his diaphragm, making the archer pant in pain. Desperately, Jochi waved his empty right hand while releasing his bow, at which point the referee called his loss.

"I wasn't going to contest it," growled Jochi as he pushed the weapon away and Pan Shui helped him up.

"Oh, sorry," the woman replied unrepentantly.

The archer grumbled, rubbing his bruised stomach. "Thank you for not stabbing me."

"We foreigners should stay together, no?" A wide grin accompanied the words.

"Yes."

"Wait, yes to the no? Or yes to us sticking together?"

"The second." Jochi rolled his eyes. Then he let out a long sigh. "I need to practice my close-range shooting more…"

"Definitely." Enthusiastic nodding.

"Damn brat." Walking to the edge of the ring, he jumped to the ground and waved to the next person in line.

The second fighter was a surprise to Wu Ying. He leaned forward, soaking in the details of the man. Big. Over six feet tall and built as if he had been born to wrestle bears. He wielded a pair of tonfa though, the long sticks with the perpendicular handles gripped in both hands. More interestingly, Wu Ying knew he had not been part of the initial tournament.

"Who's that?" Wu Ying asked.

Only grunts and shrugs were his answer from his table companions. Dissatisfied, Wu Ying pulled at the winds, asking them to bring forth the man's scent and aura. The air swirled around him for a moment, fluttering the edge of one of his loose hairs as the air worked to his request. Only to fail.

"So, what kind of element and level is he?" Elder Tsui asked. Both Elders had noticed the change in environmental chi and the shift in wind.

"I don't know. He's blocking my wind," Wu Ying said.

"Really?" Elder Eng murmured, suddenly interested. He eyed the man, raking his gaze over the figure. "That's not normal, is it?"

"No. Most people do not bother hiding their scent, even when they close off their auras," Wu Ying answered easily.

After all, the Elders would know as much. In fact, given a little training, any Core Formation cultivator could easily learn to utilize their other senses. Most would not bother, of course, since their nascent spiritual sense was stronger in most cases, but it was possible.

"Someone who blocked their scent… and who looks to be strong enough to win in a fight…" Elder Eng murmured, a hand clenching tightly in anger and suspicion.

"I am Gan Ying of the Seven Dams." The man's pronouncement was loud, easily carrying across the open air and into the restaurant. Gasps and murmured words of incredulity met his words. "I thank you for this chance to contend for the prize. I was delayed in my journey here by water bandits. Clearing them out took longer than I expected."

"Who?" Wu Ying said, looking at the Elders. Obviously, Gan Ying held some kind of notoriety in this kingdom.

"Gan Ying! How can you… Oh. Right. You're from Shen." Shi Fei paused, his excitement having made him speak up. At his hesitation, Elder Tsui waved him to continue. "Gan Ying's famous in the western region here. He fought an entire Demon Sect all by himself. He beat up the dozen members for preying on a village.

"Then the next month, he fought a Demonic Beast Snake that was the size of the building! He was bitten so badly, many believed he would die, but he still killed it. The demonic beast stone was so large, it sold for a thousand taels! And the Healing Sage himself went down to heal Gan Ying."

Nodding enthusiastically—if carefully—Kong Lai added from her slumped over position, "He's a hero of the masses. He was a mortal too, not even a wandering cultivator. He had been on a logging expedition when a Spirit Beast rose up, driving away and consuming his team. Gan Ying escaped into the wilds alone but was thought lost for a year.

"But fortune favored him and when he returned, he was a cultivator. A strong one too!"

"Energy Storage then?" Wu Ying said.

"No, that's the thing. No one knows," Shi Fei said. "He always keeps his cultivation base hidden, hiding his aura. Some think it's training. Others think that he owns a special talisman to obscure his cultivation level. Rumors are that he could be as high as Core Formation!"

"Rubbish," Elder Eng muttered, lowering a hand he had extended a while ago. "He leaks a little, even now. The earth speaks of his footsteps, and while they are heavy with import, they are no steps of a Core Formation cultivator."

"Mmm… strong though. Peak Energy Storage at least," Elder Tsui said, his eyes sharpening as he watched Gan Ying. "He burns hotly. Warps the air with his passion."

Wu Ying frowned at the two Elders, chastised by their ability to extract information where he had not. It seemed he still had a lot to learn about his new cultivation stage.

During their conversation, Pan Shui had introduced herself and the pair now circled one another. Already, a quick probing clash had occurred between the two, with Pan Shui making full use of her greater range and Gan Ying his better defense with his paired tonfas.

"Peak Energy Storage…" Wu Ying muttered, watching the air swirl around them, feeling the pulse of energy.

The two would have no choice but to reveal aspects of their cultivation as they fought, though Wu Ying had probed Pan Shui more than enough. Gan Ying though…

He was no ordinary Peak Energy Storage cultivator. In fact, Wu Ying would bet he was no soul cultivator at all. The more he probed the man, the more certain he was that Gan Ying was a Body cultivator. And only a Body cultivator.

Funny, to find four such Body cultivators in a kingdom that professed to not have many at all. Coincidence? Or was heaven pulling on fate's thread?

Another shift in energy and the two clashed again. Wu Ying's eyes narrowed as he watched the fight, judging the results. Gan Ying had—at best—the Sense of his weapons and Wu Ying was not even certain he would give him that. It was hard to tell, for he moved fluidly, more in control of his body than most martial cultivators. An aspect of Body Cultivation that benefited him in this battle.

He was also physically faster and stronger than Pan Shui, even his most casual blocks sending the tip of Pan Shui's weapon skittering aside.

At the same time, the girl was highly skilled in her spear use, as Wu Ying knew, and had adapted to the man's strength after the first clash. She pulled back, disengaged, and enveloped his arms and the tonfa on the regular, managing to avoid competing with him on strength alone. If not for the fact that he had two limbs to her single weapon, she would have overwhelmed him on the second clash.

Instead, she left him with light scratches across his torso and upper arms.

The dull *thunk* of wood on wood, wood on flesh echoed through the surroundings with each struggle. The hiss of indrawn breath and the exhalation of relief from the crowd as Pan Shui crowded and was forced back by Gan Ying echoed, even as the sour smell of waste adrenaline accumulated as the crowd grew enamored with the duel.

"She's going to lose the next fight if she doesn't finish this soon," Elder Tsui said, sounding gleeful. "Foolish girl. Challenging three people."

"You think she'll beat Gan Ying, Elder Tsui?" Shi Fei asked respectfully.

"Oh yes. He's strong. In a real fight, he might be willing to risk his body and charge her to win. But he is holding back for the tournament and that's why he'll lose," Elder Tsui said. "He's brave and strong but lacks experience and training." A hand rose, stroking his smooth chin.

"Forget it. He would not suit your sect's temperament," Elder Eng replied. He thumped his own chest. "That is a man's man. Look at those shoulders. No, we'll invite him to join the Mountain Fast."

"Just because we are mostly fire leaning…"

Below, the crowd roared, interrupting the pair.

As if sensing he was going to lose, Gan Ying had braved the danger and charged deep into Pan Shui's range. She, in turn, retreated while lashing out with her spear, scoring additional wounds against his body and legs as he attempted to deflect them. So fast were they moving that the attacks and counterattacks were all done on instinct, set patterns of defenses and assaults that were part of a form.

The end came as suddenly as it had begun. Gan Ying managed to block the majority of strikes and even the spinning butt end of her spear, such that when it came up to strike him between his legs, he caught it with both tonfas crossed. What he did not expect was for her to do a cross-legged, passing step that transitioned into a sidekick as he recovered from the block, catching him high across both crossed weapons. It slammed his arms together, throwing him backward all the way to the other side of the ring.

Feet sliding across the stone, Gan Ying managed to stabilize his position, dust kicking up as he choked and coughed. However, Pan Shui never let him rest, rushing after him to unleash a barrage of kicks. He staggered backward, blocking. The hard wood, reinforced with the man's chi, made Pan Shui wince as the tonfas bruised her legs, but she had managed to buy herself the time she needed.

Gan Ying never noticed the spear, having been flipped high in the air after her initial kick, come falling down, blunt end first to slam into the top of his head. He tottered backward for a second, eyes crossing, hands moving as his body enacted a defensive form.

However, Pan Shui had retreated rather than force the exchange, using a chi string to pull her spear back to her after its surprise assault.

As Gan Ying's eyes cleared, he stopped waving his tonfas around. For a long moment, the pair stared at one another before Gan Ying relaxed and crossed the tonfas and his arms across his body before bowing. "It is your win, Cultivator Pan. I thank you for your mercy."

Pan Shui grinned. "Thank you for exchanging pointers with me, Cultivator Gan. It was most enlightening."

Then she spun on her heels and hopped back to her side of the ring. The formation energy around the ring dispersed, allowing Gan Ying to retreat and for her to speak to those outside.

Leaning over, she called to her elder sister, who was watching, "Da jie[19]!"

"Yes?" Pan Yin said cautiously.

"Told you the Sky Striking Spear wasn't a waste of time to learn!" Pan Shui said with a smirk.

"And I told you, it's only good once! Only a fool would miss it a second time. Third Uncle should never have taught you it at all. It's a silly, showy move," Pan Yin replied.

Rather than answer directly, Pan Shui stuck out her tongue and turned away, leaving Pan Yin visibly fuming. Wu Ying smirked a little, watching the pair as Gan Ying walked off, still rubbing his head. The final contestant took the stage, the woman looking determined but perturbed by how easily Pan Shui had won thus far.

"The third contestant is always the strongest, right?" Kong Lai said curiously. "So why are they sending her?"

"Not always..." Elder Eng said, his tone taking on a teaching quality. "The Tian Ji horse racing strategy[20] is but one common example."

"But she's fighting alone. What's the point of better strategy?" Kong Lai pointed out.

To this, Elder Eng had no answer. Nor did Wu Ying.

Unfortunately, for all the theatrics and upsets the earlier fights might have had, the last one was a true disappointment. Showcasing the true strength of her ability and the full range

---

[19] Da jie—literally big (elder) sister. You don't call family members by name if they are older, as it is considered impolite. Also, each family member generally has a specific term, so that everyone understands everyone else's level of relations.

[20] A famous story from the *Records of the Grand Historian* that details Tian Ji's strategy for winning a horse race. Three horses for the king of Qi—labeled good, better, and best—are raced against another king's three horses. Tian Ji chooses to send the better horse against the good, the best horse against the better, and the good horse against his opponent's best, winning two out of three races.

of her knowledge of the spear against her fellow spear wielder, Pan Shui beat her opponent so thoroughly there was no doubt who was the true winner of the tournament.

Disappointing, but at least, as the chief judge came onto the stage to make the pronouncement of the ending of this particular diversion, no one dared challenge Pan Shui's right to the final prize.

After that, Shi Fei and a member of the White Flower Merchant Association took the prizes for the joint second and third places. The prizes had been combined then split, distributed evenly to each winner.

As abruptly as it had been lengthened, the tournament was over.

Wu Ying left soon after lunch was completed, only to find Elder Cao still standing on the roof. He found himself meeting her imperious gaze, silent accusation in her eyes. For a moment, her dao and presence pushed at him in silent disapproval, then it was gone.

Leaving him to retreat to his room ignominiously.

Chapter 27

The night had grown dark, the last light of the sun having slipped away long ago. The moon, hanging low in the day, was only just beginning to grow, the barest slip of light being offered. The stars that hung high above—a streak of white by a mad painter of light and fury—along with the light of low-hung lanterns provided illumination for the streets below.

Inside his room, Wu Ying sat, silent and still, his chest rising and falling with rhythmic monotone. In slow, hold, out slow, hold. He meditated, not cultivated, for the necessity of deep cultivation precluded the more important aspect of what he did here.

That was, waiting for the inevitable attack.

Around him, the glowing light of a spirit lamp illuminated the surroundings. Wu Ying sat on his bed. A simple cotton and hemp comforter laid across the wooden bed provided minor cushioning as he sat cross-legged, cycling his breathing. His sheathed sword rested on his lap, inches from his hand.

Wards lay across the walls, entrances, and within the room itself, while talismans waited to be recalled at the flick of a finger. Under his robes, Wu Ying wore the armor he had been given so many years ago and rarely took out now. Barely better than mortal armor, it was unlikely to do much against a Core Formation expert. He had considered leaving it off since it would weigh him down but chose to keep it after a moment's further hesitation. It could be useful.

No bow, though he could have used it. By the time he noticed his assailants, it would be too late to use the weapon. And even after all these years, he was no more than a passable archer. Good enough to take down an animal in the wild for meat. Not someone you would trust to deal with a scout.

So many years, and he had not gained any further equipment. Not for combat at least. He had a few items of utilitarian use: a pot that heated its contents without flame, a series of fire lights powered by chi that would illuminate locations around him, spirit rings and messengers. Gathering was expensive, and the numerous spirit storage boxes were probably his greatest expense.

He had his swords, but those were a hobby. And he only had two hands.

Violence had, while not disappeared, at least not been as omnipresent in his life. He had slacked on picking up items for defense and offense. Sitting here, he wondered how that would affect him tonight. Perhaps if he had dedicated some of his resources into such things…

Too late for regret. It was always too late for regret. Wu Ying drew another deep breath and watched shadows shift, listening to the whispering of the wind as it spoke of secret rendezvouses, consoling companions, and sorrowful training.

So few were awake. Even the Pan sisters, delirious in their joy and relief at their results, had trudged back to their beds and were fast asleep. Leaving Wu Ying and a few night owls to stand watch over the deepening night.

Breathe in and out. Wait.

Time passed, creeping onward to take the future slowly. In the cocoon of serenity, Wu Ying watched it pass by, counting the fading of each second by the rhythm of his breathing. When change came, it was not in the direction he had expected.

Of course, it would never be that easy.

Cries and the ringing of bells, screams of worry and concern as the sudden explosion of smells appeared. Burning wood and silk and hemp, lacquer and wax smoking and choking those who moved. All those smells and more filled the room, an explosion of scents that had been hidden until now.

Wu Ying was out of his room within moments, hopping across the street to the rooftop on the other side, exiting via his window in a flash of silken robes.

Cultivators woken from sleep rushed back and forth, forming the bucket chain required to put out the fire. Or at the least, contain it such that no further buildings were burnt. A single, familiar building, one his friends lived in. Water cultivators, channeling their chi, gestured and called forth the liquid, only to see it evaporate upon contact with the supernatural flames.

A miniscule exertion of energy, even as he pulled the wind to him and sent it swirling about to verify if an opponent was waiting. None were, but the wind brought snatches of conversation.

"Just appeared out of nowhere!"

"How many…?"

"A half dozen dead, slain in the common room. More upstairs maybe…"

"Throw more water!"

"Useless. It's not natural fire. Evacuate the other buildings. We need to contain it first…"

More words, more exclamations and shouted orders. He filtered those out, even as more and more voices added to the din as cultivators and mortals rushed to provide aid. The well was worked by a pair of water cultivators who pulled streams of water into a pair of bathtubs, where others filled the never-ending bucket chain from it.

Earthen cultivators, slower to react, called forth clay from the ground, tossing it at the flames in an attempt to suffocate them. Other fire cultivators wove a barrier, keeping sparks from jumping onto nearby wooden buildings, even as a couple of braver souls attempted to locate the living within the residence.

Further away, near the dug stream that had fed the surroundings and the pavilion, others worked to guide the stream through newly created channels while also forming a second bucket chain.

Amidst all this effort, the fire crackled with unrestrained fury. Wood cultivators focused on either side of the burning building in an attempt to reinforce the walls as the heat grew ever more stifling.

His wind swirled, bringing further knowledge and locating individuals of import. Jochi, the Pan sisters, Shi Fei, and Kong Lai, they were all easy to ascertain. Then the wind carried another conversation and he paid attention.

"Is leader Gao alive?"

"Barely…"

"Liu Ping?" Wary, worried.

"Missing."

That was what he had been waiting for. Not just the fire—that was a distraction. What he was looking for was clues, knowledge of who it was that had set the fire. The deaths, the fire, all of it was to keep others busy.

It was almost genius, if you ignored the damage done to everyone else. Smiling grimly, Wu Ying called the winds to him, sending his chi through them and connecting to the world like he had not since arriving here. He felt every twist of the air, the rising currents over the flame, the stink of sweat and tang of burning blood. Checking for traces of Liu Ping.

The wind whispered to him, bringing secrets—sweat and replete hormones on two figures, working side by side, neither looking at the other—and shame—a man, hiding in the dark of the stables, fingers caressing burn scars over and over—and finally, her scent.

She was gone, but he caught her trail. Traced her movements, the blood in the air as she raced after the killer and chased them down. The wind tugged at his hair and robes, beckoning Wu Ying to action. He had stood on that rooftop, waiting. But the time for stillness was over.

Now he moved.

***

Coincidence? Planning? Or mockery? Wu Ying was uncertain which it was, but the scent trail led him to a familiar field, one where he had trained for hours late at night, seeking to understand his new sword and the challenges he might encounter.

Fitting, perhaps.

He spotted them within, two figures. One lying prone and unconscious on the ground. Fool girl, to chase the killer alone. The other standing upright and cloaked in folds of clothing such that neither their sex nor their features could be determined.

Wu Ying stopped at the edge of the field, turning his head from side to side as he eyed the surroundings. Gusts of air flowed into the field before being rebuffed, redirected by an unseen formation. He stood there silently as his chi and spiritual sense expanded, demanding an answer. One of the truths about wind was that you could not keep it out—not entirely. Well, not unless one was underwater.

Here, now, he eventually found an entry. Moving air ruffled his robes and he drew a deep breath, but it was of little use. The cloaked figure had shuttered their aura, hiding scent and chi signature from inspection, while the formation stripped the remainder of details. Only Liu Ping's unguarded aura gave clues, and even that only informed him she was still alive.

"Afraid to finish this, Cultivator Long?" The voice was familiar but altered, twisting in the night as chi was layered across it.

"Just being careful…" Wu Ying raised his hand and gestured, once and again. He was no formation master, versed in how to break a formation with minimal exertion.

However, this was not a defensive formation, not in the traditional sense. Active as it was, it was simple enough for Wu Ying to destroy the formation flags and the ground on either side of him in long arcs of furrowed earth with projected sword intent. Earth bloomed and fell, the sound like a thousand firecrackers going off through the night. Wu Ying smiled grimly, noting how his attack had released the energy of hidden talismans as well.

Even as their trap was destroyed before their very eyes, the cloaked figure made no motion to stop Wu Ying. "Satisfied?"

"I doubt that word is even viable until… well…" Wu Ying gestured around him. "This is settled, no? But I am curious, Elder Cao, why you continue to hide your presence."

Silence, then laughter, free and unrestrained with a hint of wildness in it at the same time. Reminiscent of the woman who had attacked him so many weeks ago.

"So, you know. How?" Elder Cao said, tossing aside her cloak to reveal herself in her armor. A second later, her weapon appeared in her hand as she drew it forth from her storage ring.

The butt of her polearm came down into the side of Liu Ping's insensate form. It drew a cry of pain from her, which made the Elder frown. A second later, the general idly kicked Liu Ping away, sending the injured woman tumbling through the air. Wu Ying threw a hand out and formed wind in the direction of the woman, using his chi to help break her fall. He dared not make a bigger move, for Elder Cao watched him carefully, seeking an opening large enough to finish him.

The tumbling fall of Liu Ping's body, the involuntary groans, it all made Wu Ying's blood boil. Yet he forced calm on himself, sending his anger outward. Anger and passion could aid one in a fight, but only if it was controlled. For now…

For now, he would answer her.

"Elder Tsui and Eng are still in the village," Wu Ying said. "No one but another Core Formation cultivator would dare stand before me so arrogantly. A simple matter of deduction, when I realized that."

Elder Cao paused, then sighed. "So, all your words. It was meant to lure out one of us three."

Wu Ying nodded.

"And what? You expect to reveal my actions to the Elders now, with the way you are expanding your aura and destroying my formations? You think the three of you are enough to win?"

Wu Ying shrugged. "Win or lose, this has to end."

"Brave words. Even as you play for time, delaying me while alerting those fools with your aura." Elder Cao smirked. "That means I have to finish you off fast. Blame only yourself for what is about to occur."

So saying, she charged, the leading point of the dagger-axe polearm pointed straight at Wu Ying's body. Her aura, filled with her element of metal, the heaviness of her dao of duty and responsibility, exploded forth. It sent fragments of metal toward Wu Ying, even as her dao tried to pressure and slow his defense.

In turn, he fought back. Winds rose around him, sending metal pieces spinning away or into the ground, robbing them of their angles of impact. Small slivers twisted and escaped his grasp and impacted his robes and skin, bouncing off hidden armor where it covered him. Where it didn't, it left tiny tears along his flesh that welled with blood.

Wu Ying cut, casting ghostly blade formations of wind and blade intent, stacking them before him as he retreated. Elder Cao disregarded the wind blades, her dao and aura crashing into them long before she did, the heaviness of her aura shattering the wind containers and dispersing them.

Her dao, tempered by decades of experience and enlightenment, crashed upon Wu Ying stronger and more insistent than ever, draining him of energy. Cursing, he dismissed the thought of using external chi techniques. Even now, his nascent understanding of the Dao and the winds, of movement and freedom and knowledge struggled to aid him in slipping between the grip of an unyielding, rigid belief system.

Dragon paints the Sunset met dagger-axe, pushing the spearhead away from his chest. Immediately, Elder Cao transitioned, pulling her attack back a bit and cutting downward. The massive, heavy head of the polearm swung down, axe blade swinging at Wu Ying's right shoulder.

Rather than meet it head on, Wu Ying swayed aside.

She followed, swinging the weapon sideways even as her steps brought her closer, haft of the polearm striking him in the side as he managed to curl up his arm to take the blow and duck inward. He shifted his feet, called forth the wind and his own qinggong exercises to lighten himself as he was attacked, robbing her of her force.

After all, punching a feather might crush it a little, but the feather was just as apt to move before the fist arrived, borne away by the wind.

Elder Cao's blow sent him flying away, the crushing wheel of duty behind each blow. A portion of Wu Ying's mind tracked her attacks, blocking her movements, as he realized what had happened just now. She had felt him out, tested him on their first ever meeting. When he reused Dragon paints the Sunset against her attack, she had anticipated it.

She had been planning her attack, playing with a mental form just as he had. Except she was better at it than he was.

Luck—only luck and his own ability—had managed to save him from a grievous wound. Even then, his arm throbbed, the cold fury and relentless barrage of her attacks leaving him bruised. If he had not been a Body cultivator, he would be sporting a shattered arm and possibly shattered ribs about now.

Thoughts swirled as he flowed into his own forms, throwing a few sword strikes laced with his aura and dao. Rather than dodge them, Elder Cao bulled through, the sword chi shattering on her aura and armor. The enchanted armor took the sword chi, though each attack seemed to dull the dark metal plates.

Spinning and cutting, her polearm stabbed, chopped, and struck at Wu Ying, forcing him to employ the full extent of his martial techniques. Each parried attack sent reverberations through his arm, her powerful weapon turned aside by the Saint Sword he held.

As they fought, Wu Ying infused his will into the weapon further and further, wrapping it with small eddies of wind. The innate metal of the weapon resisted his element, but the mastery of the blacksmith and the dao the blacksmith had introduced reduced that resistance significantly. To both temper the weapon and strengthen it while reducing its own resistance to other elements was one of the ways a Saint-level sword differed from pure Spirit weapons.

Even with a proper jian, Wu Ying was being pushed back. It was not her technique, nor her innate speed or strength that was overpowering Wu Ying. Spending time fighting her in his mind had allowed Wu Ying to cross the distance between their mastery of martial styles, while being a Body cultivator gifted with wind chi allowed him to deal with her cultivation difference in speed. Even in terms of raw strength, she was not significantly stronger than him.

What he lacked was the sheer power of her cultivation, the difference between a multi-layered core and a rooted understanding in one's dao. Elder Cao had decades on him, decades honing her belief system, the structures of her personality and reality such that it could affect the world around her. Decades of wielding her dao in the wider world and growing the immortal soul within her body. It was not at the stage of a Nascent Soul wielder, where their very perception of reality began to alter the flow of the world about them, but it was enough to hamper him.

Wu Ying had just entered the Core Formation stage, his own understanding shallow and nascent. His Core, and the soul within, were tiny. Such that even those who should have known better had been unable to find it at first. In time, he knew he would progress; but against his opponent...

Against his opponent, he was outclassed. The sheer strength of her attacks, each of her blows empowered to levels he could not match, beat him down. Shards of metal flew through the air, and more and more picked at his skin, tearing lines of blood that welled up and littered the air.

Squinting around the raging maelstrom, Wu Ying fought on instinct, blocking attacks from her polearm as he attempted to retaliate, the earth around them rent apart with each attack. Eddies of wind caught this soil, gusts of freezing cold drifting forward to hamper her movements. The air was choked with earth and dust, hampering vision, and the booming noise of each narrowly dodged attack shook the air.

And still she came. Relentless, unyielding, oppressive.

Another twist, another block; another narrowly dodged chop; the Dragon turns in its Slumber, Rending the Painting, Dragon dances through the Raindrops… Sword and weapon intent flashing, extending, and retracting with each moment.

Till Wu Ying failed.

A twisting dodge that was anticipated, his movements a touch too early, such that his opponent could shift direction of her attack. Her chi-blade extended, tearing apart the mundane armor he wore as easily as wet paper and leaving a gaping wound across his chest.

The explosion of energy, along with Wu Ying's desperate surge of wind, sent dust and his body flying backward, even as he threw an empowered sword strike of his own. This one was targeted at her neck, and rather than bull through or duck away, Elder Cao blocked it, breaking the sword intent on the raised shaft of her dagger-axe polearm.

Tumbling through the air, blood leaking from his wound and coating the surroundings, Wu Ying fetched up on his feet by sheer dint of experience, long legs digging furrows into the earth. He coughed, his chest bleeding around the ragged edges of his armor.

"I'm impressed," Elder Cao murmured, "that you managed to last this long. But a false Core Formation cultivator like you is no threat to me."

She sauntered forward even as Wu Ying concentrated his chi into the tip of his sword. He did his best to hide the attack, knowing he would only have a single chance. The wind rose around him as his spiritual senses fought hers. Dust swirled through the air, hiding their surroundings and him, creating a minor dust storm and hindering Elder Cao's senses further.

"Do you think that such petty tricks will be enough?" Elder Cao said amusedly. "You are better off keeping your chi to yourself rather than wasting it."

Wu Ying's head tilted as he listened with a small smile on his lips, for she would not speak if the dust did not bother her. At least a little.

Her footsteps, steady until now, changed as she leapt forward. He felt her move in his winds, tracked her location as she pushed against the air he controlled. Rather than dodge, he waited for his opportunity to show itself.

Raised polearm swung downward—the weight of responsibility, to a kingdom and its rulers carried with it. The air quivered, rent apart by intent, and still, Wu Ying made no move to avoid the attack.

At the last second, she sensed it. The attack he had been trying to hide from her, the presence he had sensed rushing toward them. Like a boulder bouncing down a hill, picking up momentum with each falling second, the podao swung downward at Elder Cao's head. Only for her to block the attack with her own dagger-axe shaft.

The shaft of her weapon bowed inward, but the Saint-class weapon would not break; not even with the empowered attack of Elder Eng behind it. Daos strained against one another as Elder Cao stood, body twisted in place, feet sinking into freshly churned earth as she blocked the man's attack.

Open to Wu Ying's reserved strike.

The Sword's Truth drove Wu Ying forward, the lunge cutting through metal shards and aura, popping open reinforced and enchanted lamellar plate armor to bury in Elder Cao's lower ribs. It was not his most dangerous technique, but it was the most stable. The most trusted.

He kept pushing, intent on running his opponent through—only for instinct to twinge.

Reacting immediately, Wu Ying threw himself backward, forming an air shield around himself moments before the metal armor that covered Elder Cao's body erupted, sending fragments scattering through the air.

Elder Eng and Wu Ying retreated tens of steps, the Elder pockmarked with wounds from the explosive attack, his body covered in a light grey-brown armor of earth. In the silence that accompanied the initial blast, Elder Tsui arrived, landing on the ground and reviewing the scene, lips tight.

And for a moment, silence dominated the battlefield.

Chapter 28

"How annoying," Elder Cao said, the Guerilla General staring at the trio before her. "Now I'm going to have to kill you all. It's really vexing when all a person has planned comes apart, and for what? Because of a nosy cultivator who should have left things alone."

"Well, that answers my question about on whose side I should be on," Elder Tsui said, his voice light. The man stood with one arm across his stomach, the other resting over his heart and on top of his crossed hand.

"There was a decision to be made?" Elder Eng looked incensed, glaring at Elder Tsui. Only for the other Elder to give a wink that made the other man growl. Turning his full attention back to Elder Cao—who had a hand around her ribs where a light sheen of metal could be seen glowing—he spoke. "Tell me, why did you kill my disciple? Why all this… foolery?"

"Chaos," Wu Ying spoke up. His mind had put the pieces together when he first saw her, linking together conversations. "Chaos and reputation loss. She wants—they want—the tournaments and auctions to stop being held. To make them undesirable in the extreme. Isn't that right?"

Elder Cao's lips turned up slightly, her initial sardonic good humor returning. Wu Ying shivered at the changes in her demeanor, mercurial as the famed metal it seemed. "It's a good thing I have to kill you. I think you're a little too smart to be allowed to live."

"Nothing smart when the clues are as clear as day," Wu Ying replied.

"You… you never left the government, did you?" Elder Eng said, seething visibly. "This is a plot by the kingdom itself. They want to keep us weak. All their talk of relaxing restrictions, all a lie to appease us while you work behind the scenes."

"The Third Prince is a fool. Did you think the First Prince would let him weaken the government like this?" Elder Cao replied. When she took her hand away from her abdomen, Wu Ying stared at the patch of glinting material around the wound he had caused, as though she had plugged it with metal itself.

"Why?" The voice took them by surprise. Not that she was alive—they all had sensed her stirring—but that she dared speak up. Liu Ping snarled the words as she battled the combined auras of four Core Formation cultivators at once. "Why kill my brother too? Wasn't one enough?"

"Why not? The more deaths, the more chaos. The deaths of traitors like you and your brother mean nothing. You scorned the largesse of the kingdom you live in, so why cry when we take it away?"

"We took nothing from your kingdom! Everything we have, everything we gained, we earned! We slaved day and night, working for pittance to get as far as we have!" Liu Ping screamed the words, her aura trembling and twisting as she lost control. Her bloodline, triggered by her rage, overtook her and claws and fangs extended. Wu Ying could almost swear that she grew new hair, and certainly her scent grew musky and animalistic.

"You shirked your duty to the kingdom. Every one of you sect and wandering cultivators. Threw away your responsibility to us." The polearm lowered, pointing at Wu Ying. "Even you. Leaving your country, leaving your sect. None of you know the truth, the weight of duty and responsibility! But I shall show you it now."

Pressure to a level that Wu Ying had never felt before slammed onto him. He staggered and sank to his knees, wondering how this one individual could do this when the other Core Formation cultivators in his life had never done so. It hurt, as he felt something within him, the Core within his dantian, creak and twist as it experienced the full spiritual assault of Elder Cao's dao understanding.

How could she do this? A difference in training, a difference in philosophy? Or perhaps, with his master and his Elder Sister, Wu Ying had never been someone they had ever needed to fight seriously?

Then how about the Dark Sect he had fought? Did they too not take him seriously? Or had the presence of the demonic taint within led them to a different path of power?

Or was this just the case of Wu Ying never truly understanding the depths he had traveled within? Like a man searching through a cave, only able to grasp what his hands touched, what he smelled; only for a brief light to shine now to allow him a glimpse of the wider world.

Was this effect something that happened all the time, the casual intimidation factor of Core Formation cultivators given life? That someone at the heights of their understanding of their dao could physically manifest their comprehension to such an extent, impacting those about?

And if so, could he not learn to do so himself?

Even as his thoughts spun in a swirling maelstrom of doubt and conjecture, Wu Ying worked to free himself. She crushed him with her understanding, and even the earth itself compressed as she imprinted her understanding and personality upon the land. Wu Ying's dao rose about him, his understanding of the world and his body providing him the gateway to freedom.

Responsibilities were a foolish joke to the winds, a mortal failing that had little relation to the eternal storms. They blew where they wished, traveled from one end of the earth to another, seeking nothing but their own ends. Duty and responsibility, honor and burden— those were concepts for mortals. As heir to the Seven Winds, as a cultivator of the soul cultivation method of the Formless Realm, Wu Ying felt her dao press upon him.

And he shed it.

Not all the way, for the difference in cultivation strengths and enlightenment between the pair were stark. Yet their daos were, in many ways, in opposition. Not completely, for Wu Ying's path of travel and knowledge, of carrying himself where the wind willed, did not entirely shirk his ties to society. He was no ascetic, hiding from the world and refusing to acknowledge it.

But those ties that he did acknowledge were ones he chose. Not ones imposed upon him by society or family or kingdom. He was not, would not be bound by custom or tradition, in legal scripture or social mores. Under pressure of the opposing dao, Wu Ying's nascent understanding clarified and strengthened.

Under pressure, metal formed. Under pressure, diamonds grew. Under pressure, winds howled.

On his feet now, Wu Ying took in the field of battle that he had, ever so briefly, left while he struggled under Elder Cao's dao.

Three Core Formation fighters clashed, weapons, chi, and killing intent marring the land around them. Wu Ying was surprised to note a small formation of flags had been cast around him, a protection that had saved him from the effects of the battle above.

Gratitude for Elder Tsui, who must have enacted the defense for him. How much time had he been battling her dao, that Elder Tsui had managed to do this and for the battle to take itself into the sky?

Mere seconds, perhaps. But in a battle between Core Formation cultivators, seconds were enough.

High above, the trio flashed across the sky, utilizing flying swords to strike one another in passing before moving on. Elder Eng was taking on Elder Cao directly, the pair closer to the earth as Elder Eng attempted to pull energy from the earth while guarding Elder Tsui from below.

The majority of Elder Eng's attacks rained down upon the guerilla general, fist of stone and even boulders conjured to split the earth and strike down his opponent. Fighting a defensive battle as he was, his long, white beard trailing in the air, the powerful and sturdy Core Formation earth-based Elder was already bleeding. His podao under his feet, he struggled to keep Elder Cao away from the more dangerous of the pair.

Above the two, dodging the occasional shard of metal or weapon intent sent after him, was Elder Tsui. He flitted across the sky, casting formation flags into the air, building a powerful formation amidst the battle. Many of the general's attacks were targeted at Elder Tsui's formation flags, each strike tearing down a few.

Yet even though Elder Tsui struggled to keep even a third of the formation flags he threw into the air and locked in place, Wu Ying could sense the way the environmental chi accumulated, drawn into the burgeoning formation.

What kind of formation would it be?

Of that, Wu Ying was uncertain. He was no formation master, and the kinds were as numerous as there were masters; though most could be split into the kinds of effects the formation was meant to have.

Support formations—meant to grow or bolster individuals or plants. Those were the kind he was most familiar with, for obvious reasons. At the same time, support formations could be inverted to deny chi or heaven's understanding, wilting and impeding growth or individuals.

Confinement formations came in many forms—whether by illusions or hypnotic images or sounds to confuse others. These formations could also be used to hide locations and people by restricting their presence from the world around.

Killing formations were as they were named. Methods to end the life via the concentration of elemental energies or the use of mental, visual, or sound attacks. There were even rumors that high grade formations could concentrate daos.

A flicker of movement, and Wu Ying jumped aside as a giant boulder crashed into the earth close to his position. Breaking the formation that Elder Tsui had created for him, Wu Ying took to the skies, for the first time drawing fully on the Core chi within his body and engaging his qinggong methods to ascend.

"You can move…" Elder Cao snarled, dodging another attack from Elder Eng. She swung her polearm, sending killing light at Wu Ying and forcing him to ascend faster, dodging it.

Watching the pair fight, Wu Ying made a quick decision. He could not afford to fight up here like them. He had neither the energy reserves nor the skill in aerial combat the pair displayed. Even his knowledge and understanding of the winds that came with his Body Cultivation techniques were still landlocked. In time, perhaps, he would learn to dance through the air and wield weapon and killing intent with the same ability.

Time, he did not have. Then, he would have to contribute to this battle in his own way.

Decision made, he just had to enact it.

The woman might impose her beliefs, her moments of enlightenment through an over-pressuring dao. One that weighed down the body and crushed movements as it stole strength from the soul. His soul cultivation technique was of no use here, nor was his burgeoning dao. It was not something that could be imposed upon others.

Hah!

Perhaps that was the other difference. Her beliefs encompassed others, while his own master had been about stepping away from such social restrictions, cutting himself free. Just as Wu Ying himself desired freedom to travel the world, to experience and learn and grow…

And none of that was useful now.

Blocking a casual cut, Wu Ying was forced backward, skimming through the air as he darted higher. He took the imparted energy, allowing it to drive him back as he tried to clear his head. Enlightenment while fighting was important; it could be revelatory and even impactful—allowing one to breach the upper limits of one's previous self.

It also could get you killed.

Turning his attention to the pair below, Wu Ying extended the only thing he could—his understanding and connection to the wind, tapping into his bloodline. He called his connection to the world and begged them for their aid.

The wind answered.

Already, it had been tossed and turned, churned and set afire from the attacks the Core Formation elders had expended all around. It moved and twisted around the demands the other Elders imposed upon it, forced to obey as they imposed their will, their existence upon this slice of the world. And if the wind cared not for such small matters, it still—in this time, in this place—sought release.

When asked, it answered.

The air swirled and churned, growing stronger with each passing second. Energy borrowed from attacks, redirected with the barest of touches from Wu Ying's energy. Exploding rock crashed downward, throwing up dirt before the shrapnel was redirected by the metal shards surrounding Elder Cao.

Tiny needles and knives whipped through the air, growing more deadly with every second, but also less in her control. With the barest twitch of his concentration, Wu Ying created a small bubble of calm around himself and Elder Tsui, who darted about above, riding the gusts of air to his next location.

Chaos grew as their vision decreased. And still, Wu Ying urged the wind to grow in strength, his hands, his body, his chi moving to the rhythm of the Central Wind as a whirlwind rose with ever growing intensity. Beneath, in the flickering glimpses Wu Ying caught, the two Elders continued their battle. Blood flew in increasing rivulets as wounds accumulated on both sides, shards of metal lodging in earthen armor and skin alike.

A scream, a cry.

Wu Ying sensed it moments before Elder Eng exited the tornado's edge, flying backward from a strike that had shattered his earthen armor, his body pinned by a released polearm. Elder Cao's tactic of throwing her weapon away in the middle of a fight had caught her opponent by surprise.

Leaving her to ascend, like the opposite of a comet through the night sky, ignoring the gusts that attempted to blow her off course. Even as Wu Ying shifted his position, she came on, speeding up with each second. He fled to the edges of the tornado, riding the wind upward as she followed.

Till they both finally reached Elder Tsui, who had stopped moving at some point.

Darting upward with a last blast of energy, Wu Ying grinned.

"Got you," he muttered, as the ex-and-current general rose into the middle of the completed formation.

And learned why one did not anger formation masters.

Or let them prepare.

Light raced from one formation flag to another. Energy, accumulated over the bout and by the formation itself, lit the formation ablaze. Flames erupted with a choking heat that sent the wind spiraling upward even further and taking Wu Ying with it.

He floated above the formation, above the cultivator caught in the web of flames and the Elder that controlled it. He barely had to tap into his chi now, so great was the tempest that had been formed. From his prime position, Wu Ying looked down on them both. He saw it from above and could not help but note…

"A peony. A red peony." He laughed, watching as the flames grew. "A flaming red peony of doom."

Petals closed, webs of flame restricting Elder Cao's ability to dodge. She twisted and dove, rose and ducked as new tendrils grew ever faster. Shards of metal, bars, and whips struck at the flames and diverted their attention. Others twisted and melted, droplets of liquid silver and gold falling. Each moment, the heat increased in intensity as she sought to break out of the trap.

Then the petals closed and there was no more time.

Just a moment, just a fraction of a second before the flaming petals enclosed her, she seemed to shift and change. Metal that Wu Ying had thought was to free herself flowed backward, melted in the flame. It encompassed her body, enclosed her.

Then the petals closed, and a burning bulb floated where the woman had been. Elder Tsui drifted closer, drawn in by the formation and his need to control it, sweating as he controlled the formation directly.

Wu Ying rose, the choking heat drying out his tongue, leaving his skin crisped and burnt. Smoke rose from below, as well as ash, the intense heat having set even the field beneath them on fire. Wu Ying extended his energy, and high above, a channel opened that brought cool air down to him as he positioned himself in the center of his still-moving tornado.

The closed bulb raged and burnt, but as he watched, portions of the bulb bulged and twisted. Each time, Elder Tsui's face grew tight, sweat on his face evaporating as quickly as it formed. A twisted look of pain crossed his features more than once before his nose bled freely. His eyes were next, blood drying and blackening under the immense heat.

"Is she still alive?" Wu Ying could not believe it, even under the evidence of his own eyes. Was this the difference between those at the upper tiers and his own? Or were the enchanted talismans she bore, the arm guards and helmets and other protective works, aiding her survival?

Was the Verdant Green Waters, for all their vaunted strength, really not that much then? This kingdom had focused all its resources on a few rather than the many, and in so doing, had they managed to achieve greater total strength in their people?

Another twitch, all across the flame bulb. Wu Ying wished to help, but this was a fight he had no part in. He knew not about the formation being wielded, and the heat itself would damage him if he went down.

Elder Tsui coughed out blood as a hand punched through a petal. He spat blackened liquid as another arm joined it, one clad in shining silver and gold as it parted the flames. A surge of chi, of dao intent, and the formation, already fragile, shattered.

The backlash threw Elder Tsui away from the bulb, his unconscious body falling in an arc away from the battlefield. Backlash from a forcibly opened formation that one was linked to was considerable. It was why tying them to yourself in this way was never recommended.

And yet, here they were.

Beneath, Elder Cao—a living, moving statue of silver and gold—stared up at Wu Ying. He could see, he could feel, the heat radiating off the metal. Her rictus snarl of pain came from a throat scorched so dry it had no voice left. Yet she still lived, injured and floating in mid-air.

And Wu Ying, above her.

Alone.

Chapter 29

No words were exchanged as the pair stared at one another across the gulf of space between them. Everything they could discuss, everything they could speak of had been said. Now, the only dialogue that could be had was over the points of their blades.

Elder Cao pulled her chi toward her, engaging with the full strength of her body and form, and shot upward, streaking toward Wu Ying like a metallic meteorite moving in the opposite direction. She had no weapon in hand, but her fingernails elongated into blades themselves. Her mouth widened into an unending, wordless scream as hate burned in her eyes.

In turn, Wu Ying struck. Not with a sword, but with the gathered strength of the tornado he had formed. He had already expanded the cone of cold air running down the center, but now he pulled the energy and heat of the rising hot air to help channel his strike. He held the energy together for a moment, blocking the flow of energy as it built up, before he released it in a rush, allowing the accumulated energy to impact the rising Elder Cao.

The ex-general raised a hand to cover her eyes as she pushed onward, the gale winds tossing her from side to side as she struggled upward. She clamped her mouth shut, forcing her ascent even as the borrowed energy of the wind blasted into her. Shards of ice from the cold air above and remnant metal pieces pinged off her metal-encased body, but it was the air pressure itself that she struggled with.

She and Wu Ying both struggled, for to conjure the gale, to control it all, he'd had to utilize his scant reserves. He gritted his teeth, feeling his energy plummet with each passing second, until he relaxed his hold on the entire creation.

No longer under his control, the wind howled and threw them both around. Wu Ying let himself be carried into the outer vortex, pushed ever higher.

In the center, pressured from above and forced to stay still, Elder Cao struggled to close the distance. Her dao expanded, pushing against Wu Ying. Rather than fight it, he allowed himself to be taken by both the dao attack and gravity.

He fell, breaking free from the outer currents, his body arcing through the air. Soon enough, he was released even from Elder Cao's sphere of influence, his body trailing through the sky with traces of smoke and heat radiating from his skin before he impacted the ground.

Feet underneath him, Wu Ying tore a deep furrow into the land, a brief moment of reinforcement and lightening of his body ensuring he did not shatter his limbs. Even so, carefully tended fields were destroyed, drainage ditches and field walls torn open. His robes grew stained by the water, and his feet squelched in the deep mud as he burrowed into the land from the impact.

Elder Cao's final attack had disrupted the delicate balance between her and the pressing wind. She too fell, the combined weight of her dao and the wind sending her rocketing into the earth to impact and depress the ground itself. Metal skin, protective sheen of silver and gold, cracked and fell apart, even as the pair of cultivators, aching and bruised, strode out of their respective holes.

"Clever. You're very clever, Cultivator Long. Borrowing the energy of our battle to meet us on equal grounds," Elder Cao said, wiping at the trail of blood from her mouth.

As she limped closer, the layers of metal that crossed her body peeled away, shedding in the whipping wind to reveal her burnt and blackened skin. In spots, Wu Ying swore he saw weeping bone.

"Not clever enough, it seems. You still stand," Wu Ying replied.

His legs ached, and as he gauged his Core, Wu Ying could not help but wince. There was little chi left within, his extravagant overuse leaving him with the dregs. His dantian was still half-filled with normal, uncompressed, unrefined chi—but that was not enough.

"Of course. I told you, you cannot win." She grinned, her eyes sparkling with the deep-felt conviction of her beliefs. "Not even if all three of you fight together."

Another step, and thanks to a short shift beneath her clothing that had somehow managed to survive the immense heat of the battle, she was, for her modesty's sake—and Wu Ying's peace of mind—still mostly covered.

"You have not won yet," Wu Ying replied as he drew his sword from its sheath. He couldn't remember when he had put it away. Probably when he first ascended the sky.

He balanced the Saint blade in his hand. A shrieking noise, a disruption in the wind had him looking to the side. From where Elder Eng had been pinned and cast aside, General Cao's weapon flew back into her waiting hands. He was surprised enough that he did not even react as she rearmed herself, only mentally cursing himself for not acting sooner.

On the other hand, shortly afterward, Elder Eng returned, his face impassive, his body covered in the same mountainous rock armor he had worn before. Only the presence of a hasty patch down one side indicated the injury he had suffered.

"I see you brought her low," Elder Eng said, flexing his fists. He reached back, pulling the podao from where it had been locked. He hefted and swung it around, testing his balance and movement. "Good."

"We will just have to finish her," Elder Tsui murmured, his voice low and pained such that it was only with the aid of the wind that Wu Ying heard him. To Wu Ying's surprise, the man was on his feet, though streaks of blood across his face and around his eyes and ears indicated the damage he had suffered from the backlash of having his formation destroyed.

"You can barely stand, and you wish to fight me?" Elder Cao mocked.

In reply, Elder Tsui twisted his hands, pulling yellow talisman papers from his spirit ring. Wu Ying chuckled a little, amused as Elder Cao grew solemn. While talismans still required chi to wield, their effects were outsized compared to their chi investment.

"I'll lead the way," Wu Ying said, crossing the distance to right before Elder Cao as he spoke, his sword rising and pointing at the woman.

She looked a little less confident, eyeing the three of them, injured as she was. Yet it was only a little; for she was still standing and only Wu Ying was truly uninjured.

Elder Eng nodded, taking a firmer and wider stance. His chi surged then dropped, flooding the ground as he asserted his control over the earth. Rather than let him take control and dictate the battlefield, the general darted to the side, charging the Elder and attempting to avoid Wu Ying.

Wu Ying cut her off, realizing to his surprise that he was now slightly faster than her. He threw a pair of sword intent cuts at her, making the woman duck and dodge around the attacks. Another indication of the degree of her injury, as she no longer dared tank the attack. Finally, she skidded to a halt, earth and dust thrown into the sky as Wu Ying blocked her.

Her hesitation lasted a fraction of a second before she clashed with Wu Ying. Her strikes came fast and hard, and he had no time to set up his own attacks, instead forced onto the defensive once more. Each blow from her dagger-axe reverberated through his arms as he defended himself, forced back step by step as she attempted to bypass him.

This was not the kind of fight he was best at. His style, his footwork, his temperament were geared toward a flowing, mobile battle rather than staying still, battling one another until the other person fell.

A feinted thrust to her face was called. Elder Cao plunged forward and let the blade glance off her cheek, metal forming at the last moment to deflect his attack. She was within his reach then, the haft of her blade hammering into his ribs and sending him falling back a half dozen feet.

He reset as she charged.

Another cut, his blade rising to block and shed the attack. She altered the angle of her attack at the last second, aiming for the forefront of his blade, positioned to crush through the tip into his body. He shifted position in turn, taking a half step to the left, feeling the axe-head clash with his own.

He let his arm and weapon collapse, angling his body forward and arm sideways. He stepped in, even as she ripped her weapon away from the void of space he had created above his arm before she swung the polearm back, intent on crushing his ribs.

Already dropping downward, Wu Ying let himself fall the rest of the way, feeling the air stir above his head as her polearm swung through the space he had been in. He rose moments later, and his blade rose with him. Dragon salutes the Sun, sword intent pouring down his blade and flashing across the half dozen feet to his opponent as he extended the blade.

She flared her aura, pivoting her dagger-axe polearm around her wrist as she extended her chi. The extended sword intent strike clashed against her weapon, the entirety of his attack concentrating as it touched upon her defense, burrowing within before shattering on the hardened metal of her aura.

Wind against metal. It was no contest. The metal would always win in the short-term. Wu Ying's attacks could wear her down, force her to lose energy, but so long as she had that energy, he could not penetrate her defense.

Not without surprising her.

Another step, then Elder Cao jumped back. Yellow talismans landed where she had been a moment later, light forming a chi-empowered trap that reached for the skies. She twisted her weapon, throwing a blade strike of her own at Elder Tsui, only for more talismans to be employed in defense.

In the meantime, soil erupted beneath her still feet. The explosion threw her upward, forcing her to flip through the air and land, feet smoking. Blood streaks from broken vessels surrounded her now bare feet, while Elder Eng panted behind them, his chi reserves dropping precipitously.

Wu Ying glanced back, then called to the Elders, "Hold her still. I have one more trick."

Answering grunts.

Elder Cao charged, intent on Wu Ying now rather than Elder Eng. The hunger in her eyes made Wu Ying sweat even as he clashed with her weapon again, the pair dodging between talismans cast into their midst and the occasional grasping rock hand or sucking mud pile. Each motion by Elder Eng was punctuated by the haft of his polearm striking the earth.

Now that she was focused on him, Wu Ying danced. He had the ability to fight this kind of battle. Faster, he moved, calling the wind to aid him, using his chi to lighten his steps. Faster, he cut and thrust, blade sparking off flesh and metal skin, tiny traces of blood appearing across her body even as her skin cracked.

The wind might lose to metal, be forced to move around it, but the wind could wear down even the most solid of objects, given time. So long as she did not strike him, he could fight. So long as he had chi, he stood a chance of winning.

Realization tickled at the edges of his consciousness as another hard block by Elder Cao sent him spinning back, his legs flowing across the ground and digging in. His style, his technique, it had a cost. A high cost for the movement, the motions all taking their toll on his stamina and chi stores.

He needed more, and he had little left to give.

The smile she gave him as she saw his hesitation chilled him to the bone. Blood and white liquid wept from the cracked skin along her cheeks, giving her a ghastly, monstrous appearance. Hair, cut short for wearing her helmet, had burnt off. Her body was rimmed with gold and silver that shifted and faded. Even she had grown tired, the flying shards of metal no longer present.

"You see it, don't you? See—"

Her taunting never finished, as the dozen talismans cast high into the air triggered. Lightning struck the ground even as Elder Tsui slumped senseless, the last of his energy drained as he enacted the powerful attack.

Lightning strikes forced her to weave and dodge between attacks. Never truly fast enough to avoid the attacks in full, her body burned. She screamed again, voice hoarse and damaged; but the metal shield she floated above her body, the energy she redirected at Elder Eng and Wu Ying with her dagger-axe was sufficient to keep her standing.

At the end of the attack, she stood in a smoking, pockmarked land, slumped against her polearm. A hair ornament that Wu Ying had barely paid attention to shattered, its pieces falling to the ground, its defensive charges wasted. The anklets around her legs still glowed, though the bracers she had worn were gone too.

More of her enchantments destroyed. Injured. But still standing.

Wu Ying hissed, trying to raise his arm. He had caught one redirected attack on his blade, leaving his arm tingling and half-senseless. He forced chi through the injured meridians, forcibly healing himself and waking up the nerves. A strangled cry erupted from his mouth as pain, exquisite pain like a thousand superheated needles, was driven into his nerves.

Elsewhere, Elder Eng finished his preparations. He stomped, bringing his hands down together. The earthen armor around his body fell to the ground as he channeled his attack.

In a circle around Elder Cao, the land sank. A dozen feet across, with her in the epicenter, the earth turned into a bog, and a mud pool swirled as channeled chi pulled at her feet. The woman snarled, channeling her energy into the earth, pulling metal from the surroundings to form pillars of metal beneath her to stand upon.

Faces straining, the pair of Elders fought. And for once, she was still. For once, Wu Ying could concentrate.

His sword was sheathed, his body moving by rote. He fell into the breathing pattern, the mindset required. It was the first form of his own style, taken from his understanding of both the Long family jian and his master's training.

Wu Ying crossed the distance at a light run, his chi extending into his blade, into his body, into the surroundings. In his mind's eye, he knew what he had to do.

Leg. Arm. Hand. Sword. Step and cut.

So simple to say. So hard to do.

The blow rose upward as the winds shrieked and twisted.

The attack, his first, his own. Mostly. For fear, in his mind, understanding, in his heart, that he was not truly ready to wield this attack. Not in its entirety.

So.

A Wandering Dragon.

Constrained.

***

A rising cut, starting low. He cut the attack short, ending it just above his head rather than following through to the stars. The energy he released, the intent of his attack, it was all constrained. The intent was similar to the one he had first developed this movement from, the Karma Severing Cut.

However, his was altered. The dao intentions, the beliefs his master had brought to the attack had not worked with Wu Ying's own view of the world.

However, his own Wandering Dragon was broken. It infused his understanding of the winds, the attack and intentions of his Long family style, but it was incorrect, dangerous, and unconstrained. The one time he had used the attack, it had torn at the bindings and natural order of the world. While the Dao itself would change and adapt and recover, the ensuing destruction to the world from his single attack had been too wide ranging in scope. Especially for a single martial attack that had been formed while he was in the Energy Storage level of cultivation.

The Heavens had shown him what he had done wrong, what he had affected by his own misunderstanding of the world. They had rebuked him and, in their criticism, nearly destroyed him. Yet his understanding after that period had grown, changed.

There was a way to cut, to step and strike and kill and to do it without causing widespread destruction over thousands of li. There was a way to flow with the Dao, amplifying the attack while benefiting the greater world rather than disrupting it.

It was not his dao, not his goal, to destroy the world. He was no demonic or heretical cultivator. He was not looking to be part of that push and grind, the destructive aspects of the Dao and the demonic incursions.

Perhaps if he had followed those beliefs, he might have escaped Heaven's regard. Or perhaps they might have taken much stronger actions.

For two years, he had trained. He had considered and practiced and mimicked the movements. Two years, but he had not dared to unleash this attack. Knowing, deep within, that it was still incomplete. That he had not found the solution to this martial style, a way to correct the deviation.

Two years, and now he acted.

Even constrained… his movements stopped, his body seized, and he fell over. He was racked by the pain of the backlash. Blood vessels burst along his feet, his hips, his chest and arm—everywhere that focused the energy he had used. His dao, the Dao of the world, assaulted him back as Heaven's Mandate reacted. His meridians strained and the core in his body pulsed as his chi rebelled.

In pain, Wu Ying could only watch as his attack impacted, his body frozen as Elder Cao suffered.

The cut tore up the ground a little, striking along her thigh and hip and chest. The attack was edged with killing intent, concentrated wind chi, sword intent, and his dao all together. It tore apart skin, muscle, and even cracked bone itself. Even Elder Cao's concentrated chi aura and her Saint-strength weapon were not defense enough.

Her body was thrown backward, ripped out of the enclosed earth that had sucked her down. Elder Eng released her fractions of a second before Wu Ying's attack impacted, such that he would not suffer the backlash of his technique being broken. Even then, he slumped over, chi exhausted.

She flipped over and over, blood flying through the air to tumble away. Her body lay on the ground, twitching and bleeding. Elder Tsui was unconscious, blood pooling on the ground beneath his wound. Elder Eng, bereft of chi, was slumped over on his knees, breathing hard as he desperately tried to regain some semblance of energy.

As for Wu Ying, he lay on the ground, twitching, low moans venting from his chest as his body seized. The damage was reduced from the last time, the feedback lower, but the pain—oh, the pain was so much greater. It encompassed his universe, robbed him of bodily control, and left him defenseless.

Around the group, silence dominated as the battle stopped, combatants too injured to speak or move. The wind, whipped up by the attacks, began to settle, carrying the churned dirt and ash to the ground. In the distance, the voices of other cultivators, brave or foolish, approached.

Eventually, the pain from the attack faded. Wu Ying found his feet, forcing himself upward with the aid of his sword. The devastation of his attack, even restricted, was greater than when he had used the attack previously. Greater dao understanding, more powerful, concentrated chi, and a Saint-class weapon all contributed to the damage.

Standing, he looked around, trading a satisfied grin with Elder Eng.

Then Elder Cao twitched, metal flowing to constrain and seal gaping wounds. The woman staggered upward, the ex-general grinning at Wu Ying with malevolence and madness in her eyes.

"I told you, you can't beat me." She raised her hand, chi pulsing to her fallen weapon. The broken remnant of her weapon only twitched; the enchantment destroyed. "You!" Rage, thrumming through the air, hurt Wu Ying's chest and ears, just with words alone. "I was gifted that by His Highness himself. I will cut off your feet and feed them to the pigs, strip the skin from your fingers and burn the nerves. You'll rue the day you entered my kingdom!"

A gesture, one that sent a grimace of pain across her face, had her extract another weapon from her storage ring. Her fingers had been burnt to a crisp and were more bone than flesh.

What she pulled out was a beautiful weapon, a Saint-class jian rather than the guandao she had wielded before. She met Wu Ying's startled gaze, reminding him of Cui Wen's death. Though perhaps the choice to use a jian was as much to pay him back as anything else.

Elder Cao strode at Wu Ying, her right foot dragging, determination and madness dancing in her eyes.

Exhausted, his fingers and an eyelid twitching from the aftereffects of the backlash, Wu Ying readied himself.

One last clash then.

Even if both of them were injured, bereft of chi and the defenses of a Core Formation cultivator.

One last pass to end it all.

His breathing steadied, the thrum of his meridians—strained by the extrusion of energy, backlash, and regathering—filling his ears.

One last…

"*Wo cao!*" Wu Ying swore.

Forgotten by them all, a furred blur struck Elder Cao from behind, bowling her over as chi claws and furious bestial energy burnt through the air and her body. Blood flew and screams rang out as Liu Ping took her revenge. Her claws tore into soft and vulnerable flesh, flinging chunks of meat and bone into the air.

The initial surprise attack had rendered Elder Cao's right arm entirely unusable. Her weapon fell to the ground, left behind as claws tore into her chest, ripping apart her rib cage and exposing lungs and heart to the air. Chi washed out from Elder Cao's shattered body in desperate fashion, life blood burning only to be countered by the same, desperate maneuver by Liu Ping. The woman, in the full throes of her bloodline taking over, cared not for the future, only for her revenge.

Instinct held Wu Ying back as he watched the mindless, enraged woman murder Elder Cao, bringing the battle to a sudden and abrupt ending.

Hovering over the mutilated body, Liu Ping threw back her head, screaming her vengeance and satisfaction to the sky. It rang through the surroundings for long moments, reminding humanity that there were things in the dark that hungered for their lives.

Then she crumpled over the dead body.

For a long second, Wu Ying stood before he too slumped to the ground, sword still in hand as relief coursed through his blood. Voices in the distance as the rest of the cultivators arrived. But Wu Ying ignored them.

It was over.

Finally.

Chapter 30

The crowd finally arrived, guards, wandering cultivators, and sect members tumbling into the broken and destroyed fields. Perhaps they had been rushing over from the start of the fight, though if that were the case, he would have expected a bunch of broken legs.

No. Chances were they had been hampered from arriving. Perhaps by the guards, perhaps by the fire, or perhaps by common sense. Few individuals would throw themselves into the midst of a battle between Core Formation elders.

With his secret exposed, Wu Ying chose to make full use of it. He allowed his aura to blanket the surroundings, let it thrum through the air and subtly warn off those who would approach him for answers. More than a few wandering cultivators came to a stop a dozen feet from him lest they anger him.

Elder Eng had chosen not to do the same, but the respect and deference given to the sect elder kept others away from him as he sat cross-legged whilst recovering. Kong Lai stood watching over the man, only the lightest coating of sweat on her brow indicating how much such exertion cost her.

In the distance, hovering over his master, Shi Fei worked healing charms and pills into Elder Tsui's mouth whilst the Seven Pavilions's overworked healer did his best to clean and bandage the Elder's wounds. Wu Ying listened to the constant excuses the healer muttered as he tried to forestall calamity should Elder Tsui pass away, a distressing reminder of Elder Cao's prowess.

As for Elder Cao's slayer, Gao Qiu had the woman in his arms a short distance away. Surrounding him and her were the surviving members of the guard on one side and the members of the White Flower Merchant Association, the groups facing off against one another. Yet neither side dared make a move, leaving them in a silent impasse under the night sky.

"Expert Long…" Guard Captain Teng Fei spoke up, having crossed to the front of the crowd around Wu Ying. Teng Fei was breathing heavily, his voice tight and pressured as he fought against his better instincts to stand before the wind cultivator.

"Yes?" Wu Ying cracked an eyebrow then sighed. He truly did not want to get involved, but Elder Eng was in no condition to speak, nor was Elder Tsui. That just left him. And before the flood of unruly cultivators grew out of hand—which might endanger him even further, bereft of energy and wounded as he was—he needed to take steps.

So.

He dropped the aura pressure, drawing back its heaviness and repressing notes whilst allowing himself full use of his spiritual senses. He would need every second of warning if an attack was launched, after all.

Taking his unspoken invitation, Teng Fei closed the distance and stopped halfway, just outside of Wu Ying's blade reach. Not that it mattered, for the cultivator could extend his blade intent, but symbolism signified. "What happened here, Expert Long? And who, exactly, are you?"

"Elder Cao was the killer. She started the fire, took Liu Ping when she was chased down. All to draw me out. Intending to…" Wu Ying shook his head. "Intending to sow chaos. To make these tournaments and auctions unsafe, too dangerous for others to take part in. She was never retired. She still worked for the government, and all this—the killings, the injuries, the thefts—are all a government plot."

Teng Fei's lips thinned, doubt in his eyes. Even if he might have had suspicions of his own, it was one thing to be suspicious and another to have it confirmed in such a manner. "Those are serious accusations. Do you have proof?"

Wu Ying paused, considering. Did he have proof? Did he have anything to confirm what had been said or done here? Staring at the churned blood and destruction, he winced.

Seeing the answer on Wu Ying's face, Teng Fei stepped forward, lowering his voice. "The death of an ex-general… it is a serious matter."

"Speak with the other Elders when they have recovered. They will support my words." Wu Ying stared at the man, his lips compressing. "On my honor and my hopes of immortality, I have spoken no lies in this matter."

Teng Fei turned his head from side to side. His eyes drifted over to the Seven Pavilions merchants, to their servants at the edges. His employers all looked fearful and upset. Many seemed about to faint, for they could see spread before them the ends of their families, their lives as merchants.

Whether they chose to divulge the details or not, the revelation of such a plot in their tournament would see the government take action. They would not let word of a plot this damaging spread, not easily. Without evidence—and perhaps even with—the easiest way to handle matters was not to.

It was a dangerous world out there, after all.

The other wandering cultivators were slower on the uptake, but they soon realized what it meant. Some, the most fearful, the most decisive left immediately. The formation keeping them imprisoned had been destroyed in the battle between the four Core Formation cultivators.

"I… this is not something I can speak to." Teng Fei flicked his gaze over to Elder Cao's body. "I cannot… this…" Duty warred with self-preservation, as he struggled to come up with a solution.

His gaze turned to his guards, many of whom looked ill. They too understood that the government might just choose to kill them all to remove all traces of betrayal.

"Betrayal."

The word reverberated through the darkness, catching them all by surprise. It was strong and loud, and at the same time, it was accompanied by a surprisingly powerful aura. Wu Ying's eyes narrowed, realizing that Gao Qiu had been hiding his own cultivation level. He was no

Core Formation cultivator, but he did stand at the peak of Energy Storage and was maybe even a half-step into Core Formation.

Silence, and then Gao Qiu repeated the word.

"Not by us, though the kingdom will see it that way. No. The State of Zhao betrays us, stealing the best of our men and women into the Everlasting Army, declaring us free to train— but never giving us any resources to do so. And now…" Gao Qiu's voice dropped, drawing in the crowd.

"And now, they murder us. They send their generals in the middle of the night, sullying our reputations and institutions. They betray their promises of safety and comfort, their very words shown to be false. What they cannot control, they will destroy. It has always been so. It will always be so." Again, he paused.

"Until we choose otherwise."

No surprise the words caused a susurration, as whispers and startled exclamations rang through the night. Teng Fei moved away from Wu Ying, a hand dropping to his sword automatically, but then he hesitated. He knew the truth of what Gao Qiu had said and yet, he struggled with it as the binds of loyalty and understanding fought within him.

"We will not stand by and let the state take our lives without a fight. We will not stand by and allow injustice to rule the land. We deserve a life, an existence beyond the dregs the king and his corrupt advisors deign to offer us." Gao Qiu walked forward, coming close to the guards who had stood watching him and moving away from the support of his people so he could speak with the wandering cultivators.

There was a tense moment when one of the guards looked as though he might not move, before he reluctantly did at the last second. Gao Qiu never hesitated, his steps taking him past the guards so that he faced the others.

"The White Flower Merchant Association and many other groups have been growing, finding supporters among all walks of life. We will not stand by and watch as our families, our friends, our kingdom continue to be ground under the heel of the corrupt and greedy. Our loyalty is not limited to those who are rich or connected or gifted; it is extended to all who have true hearts and untarnished honor." A long pause, as he waved his hand around. "Any who wish to join us are welcome to do so. Even for a few days, to escape the watchful eye of the kingdom."

His words to the wandering cultivators were a direct challenge to Teng Fei.

The Guard Captain raised his chin before his voice rose, firm and loud. "The culprit of the murders has been found. We will report the incident and their death, after further investigation, in a week. During this time, we will not be holding any unassociated individuals in the compound." His gaze flicked to his guards, many of whom looked worried as he continued. "As the tournament is over, pay for the event will be provided this morning and all guards are dismissed."

"Captain!" A shocked voice, one of the men stepping forward. "You cannot!"

"Cannot what? I have a duty to the Seven Pavilions and the kingdom. I will see the matter reported, as fully and clearly as possible." His gaze rested on Wu Ying then jumped to the sect elders before he continued. "We will require statements from those present at the end."

Wu Ying nodded at the Captain who had firmed his stance, even knowing that he might very well be killed for his choices.

"We will not let you face this alone, Captain!" the initial guardsman speaker called. "I will not abandon you."

Teng Fei's gaze landed on the guardsman then skipped over to a few others who had stepped forward as well. For a second, Wu Ying saw the conflict within him before he nodded, accepting their decision.

Raising his voice again, Teng Fei gave orders to pass on his statements. The crowd, realizing they were being given a chance to escape, moved swiftly, their initial shock washed away. Some moved toward the village, but many others approached Gao Qiu, who had a slight satisfied glow around him.

It would not be long, Wu Ying estimated, before the Seven Pavilions temporary village and even their compound was emptied. Seated and exhausted, he pulled upon the ambient chi, refilling his dantian.

He watched as Gao Qiu, glowing with the success of his words and radiating his glowing belief in the rightness of his cause, drew rebels to him. A just cause perhaps, but Wu Ying could not help but note that Liu Ping lay discarded and forgotten now that others flocked to him. Others were caring for the injured young lady, but in this moment, Gao Qiu had moved on.

Wu Ying regarded Teng Fei, the Guard Captain choosing to stay and hold true to his promises to a regime that had already betrayed him and killed one of his subordinates. Not in a naïve hope of changing the outcome perhaps, but in the rigid belief that duty had to be honored.

Much like the torn and desecrated remains of Elder Cao. Wu Ying wished she had spoken further, explained her point of view. Perhaps clarified her anger, the dao that she wielded. How she could justify her actions and the deaths of even her subordinates.

He watched as members of the Seven Pavilions merchant cartel broke down weeping, their lives destroyed by the simple vagaries of fate. Their chances at growth and prosperity had been destroyed by the uncaring plots of those above.

Kong Lai, by the side of her Elder who breathed and cultivated, the smell of blood renewed around her wounds as she pushed herself to stand guard over her uncle who had no regard for her, who still grieved for his lost disciple that he loved more than her.

Love, lost; life, deceased; honor, shattered; duty, binding.

The wind swirled around Wu Ying, bringing with it snatches of conversation, exclamations of surprise, moments of clarity, and thrumming anger. He listened and watched as hundreds of lives and their paths diverged, as a wind blew through their midst.

The heavens demanded, punishing him for the temerity of going against their dictates of where and how the winds should blow, what rains should fall, what plains would be seeded, which forests would stand safe from the gales. The heavens dictated, and Wu Ying, having seen the damage he did, capitulated.

The kingdom of Zhao contended, guiding the development of mortals, strengthening the borders, dedicating resources to the creation of formation and enchantment masters to ensure the ongoing maintenance of the kingdom-wide formation. The creation of the Everlasting Army, the support of the rulers, and now, this plot. All for the greater good of those below. Cultivators and mortals, capitulated.

Wu Ying's eyes widened as enlightenment arrived, dancing through his mind. The Dao noticed, and his own path changed—just a little. He still believed that the heavens and their reprimand of him was not in error—the damage he had done was considerable.

Like a child who played with and broke his parents' tea set, he deserved to be chastised. The lesson was important, but the lesson was not to never touch tea sets but to have greater care. To move with deliberate focus, to serve with kindness and graciousness and to always, always be aware of one's surroundings.

It was not to punish, until one died.

Understanding grew, and Wu Ying's path changed a little. Somehow, he knew that this minor change in direction would, in a thousand li, bear great fruit.

For a moment, the world vibrated with understanding. Then it slipped away, and only a few noticed the change. It was only a small moment of enlightenment, not worth acknowledging by the heavens.

So he watched. He learned. He drew forth wisdom and experience from the events and experiences of this day. The choices others made and the way they bent to the world's will. Or stood against the forces arrayed against them.

Deep within Wu Ying's Core, a nascent soul soaked in the experiences, his thoughts and beliefs, and grew. A little differently. A little altered.

Chapter 31

The wind whistled through empty streets, picking up dirt and discarded debris, dancing along forgotten talismans and formation flags. Not so far away, stubborn mortals still worked the fields. A few lonesome servants trudged through the abandoned mansion, carrying out thankless tasks.

Wu Ying listened to the whispers the winds brought, snatches of conversations and faraway scents. The tinkle of horse gear and the howl of a demonic beast deep in the depths of the forest. From many li away, it even brought traces of those who had left, hints of their scents and their passage.

Three days had passed since Elder Cao's death, and the greater portion of the cultivators, merchants, and mortals had abandoned the location, leaving behind only a small number too proud or stubborn.

A movement nearby had Wu Ying turn his attention to where Liu Ping lay, finally waking. She let out an indelicate groan, and only after she had drunk the cup of tepid tea she was offered did she come fully conscious.

"Wu Ying?" A pause, then she blushed. "My apologies. Expert Long."

"No need," Wu Ying said, waving away the discourtesy of a slip of tongue. "You saved my life with that last attack. For a battle sister, my personal name is more than sufficient."

"I did, didn't I?" Liu Ping murmured, a little shock and a little awe in her voice as she recalled her own actions. The woman flexed her fingers, her chi stirring, and dark, insubstantial claws flickered into existence across her fingers. "I took vengeance on my brother's murderer."

Then, as though the words had broken a dam within her, huge, heaving sobs racked her body and twisted her form. She huddled into her knees, grieving for the loss of family and her past. Wu Ying watched for a moment before choosing to sit by her side on the bed, putting an arm around her.

The hourly incense marker had nearly burnt away in its entirety, requiring a change of the incense stick within, before Liu Ping calmed, pulling away from Wu Ying. He was dismissed moments later, as she sought to clean and prepare herself, leaving him to exit to the bottom floor foyer.

There sat the trio of sisters, watching with raised brows as Wu Ying descended. He related Liu Ping's wakefulness, choosing not to comment on her grief, though the watchful and knowing gaze of Pan Yin rested upon his face. Thankfully, she did not speak of it, instead sending her sisters—over the loud objections of Pan Shui—up to aid the still weak Liu Ping.

"Now that she has woken, what is your plan, Expert Long?" Pan Yin asked, putting her head on her fist consideringly.

"I am not certain." Wu Ying sighed a little. "I have invitations to visit the sects and trade with them, but after this..." He did not need to detail his thoughts. As dangerous as the situation might be for the locals, he, as a foreigner, was even more vulnerable to being disappeared. "It might be best for me to leave the kingdom entirely."

"Certainly a thought…" Pan Yin's lips pulled into a slight smile. "And if you intend to do so, then journeying with us farther west, to our clan holdings, might be best. A single traveler is more conspicuous than a group, especially one with us."

Wu Ying raised an eyebrow, choosing not to gainsay her. On the other hand, he had plans of traversing the deep wilds, places where none but other Wild Gatherers like him dared step. He would be safe enough there, for the wilds were wide and great and civilization's hold still tenuous.

"Why?"

"Well, there are many reasons…" Pan Yin smiled a little. "But in the end, it comes down to this. A good deed should be rewarded. And what you did with Elder Cao—exposing her and the government's plans—those were good deeds."

Wu Ying shook his head. "I cannot ask you to endanger your clan…"

Pan Yin laughed then. "There is no danger. They would not dare attack us, for they could not face our ire. The kingdom knows not to start wars they cannot win—and they cannot win against us, for we have a mystic kingdom to retreat to if they press us too hard. The Eternal Army cannot afford to watch over our lands for too long."

"And your trade and partners?" Wu Ying said.

"They will return. After all, what we have to offer, they cannot get anywhere else," Pan Yin said. When Wu Ying raised an eyebrow, she smirked. "You'll just have to see. But you will be interested in it… Verdant Gatherer."

Wu Ying leaned back, staring at the woman consideringly. Only for him to be interrupted by the descent of Liu Ping and the others. The wandering cultivator had cleaned herself, looking more put together via the heavy application of cosmetics. Even so, she looked thinner than ever and her eyes—even with the bags under them hidden—still contained a haunted look. No cosmetics would hide the change in outlook or the deep well of grief that had been dug within her. Only time would shore up those walls, offer some level of false succor.

After greetings had been exchanged and seats taken, Pan Yin jumped straight into matters. "And what plans do you have, Cultivator Liu?"

"Gao Qiu left, did he not?" Liu Ping said, looking around the empty interior.

Even the sect elders had abandoned the place a day ago, Teng Fei having taken their statements. It was time for them to discuss the changes with their sects, and potentially be dismissed for their part in this fiasco.

"He did. I'm sorry. I spoke to him, but he said he needed to get the new recruits to safety. That it was more important to the cause," Wu Ying said, not bothering to hide his distaste or the excuses made by the other man.

"It's okay," Liu Ping said, offering Wu Ying a half-smile. "We—I"—her voice hitched a little as she changed identifiers, remembering her brother was dead—"always knew the cause was more important than any one of us. It's what makes him so effective."

"Revolutionaries." Pan Shui's distaste was clear in her voice too. "Though if there's a kingdom that needs changing..."

"This is one," Liu Ping muttered.

"Then you're going to join him?" Pan Yin said curiously, the older sister leaning on her upraised palm as it rested on the table.

"I..." Liu Ping hesitated, doubt flashing through her eyes. It was one thing to know you were disposable; another to be discarded and expected to accept that.

"Then come with us," Pan Yin offered. "Expert Long is going to do so."

Wu Ying looked at Pan Yin, about to object to using him as bait, when Liu Ping murmured, "Is he?" He clamped his mouth shut, the other woman still somewhat distracted with exhaustion. "I do owe the Expert..."

"There are no debts. If anything, the debt is mine," Wu Ying said.

"Is that so?" Liu Ping said, a flicker of something rolling off her aura. He found himself shivering a little, a feeling of being targeted suddenly sweeping through him as her bloodline came to the fore. She even went so far as to lick her lips! "Well, I might just have to see about receiving payment."

Wu Ying stared for a long second, then shook his head a little. With her bloodline receding in prominence, Liu Ping blinked and blushed, though she did not retract her words or apologize. Something else to be worried about in his own bloodline, if it grew in prominence.

"Then that's settled." Pan Yin clapped her hands together, rising. "Since we are all awake, we should leave today. There's an extra carriage, so you can rest in there. We should be packed in the hour. Cultivator Liu, I understand most of your items were destroyed in the fire—"

"What fire?" Liu Ping said, clearly surprised.

Pan Yin ignored Liu Ping as she continued. "But that is no matter. We have enough clothing to cover for you. And Cultivator Gao did leave behind what survived. It's still packed, so you should be ready. I recommend you stay down here and eat."

As though it only needed reminding, Liu Ping's stomach rumbled, making her blush. "Is there even a cook left?"

"No." Wu Ying smiled as he stood and walked toward the kitchen. "But there is congee and some other foodstuff." Moments later, he came back with a bowl and a number of other plates of light refreshment, placing them before Liu Ping. "It's a little cold but eat up. If we're leaving, I should pack."

Leaving her startled by the speed of decisions made, Wu Ying wandered up the stairs. He was not at all surprised to see Pan Yin standing outside his room, smiling a little secretive smile.

"You planned all that," he accused.

"I did. And it worked, did it not? You cannot say that it is not better for her too though." She shook her head. "Many—if not all—of Gao Qiu's revolutionaries will be killed, even if they succeed. Revolutions are a bloody business."

"They are." Wu Ying sighed. Then curiosity poked at him, and he could not help but ask, "Those formations, the ones that cover the kingdom. I know some of it is part of a signal formation, meant to warn of approaching armies or powerful cultivators. But much of it is unknown to me."

Pan Yin frowned, looking around automatically. When she realized that no one was around, she relaxed a little, a sardonic smile pulling at her lips. "Well, if we are to associate with rebels, what's one more rule broken? But sadly, I cannot tell you. I have but rumors and conjecture, from ambient chi being focused on the royal palace, to creating a fabled land for chi cultivation, to a deadly war formation."

Wu Ying nodded. The formation might be more interesting and pressing if he were a formation master, but even if he knew the basis of it, studying a formation that encompassed an entire kingdom was outside of his purview.

"Thank you anyway. For supporting us." Pan Yin nodded toward the woman below. "It will be good for her to see a different life."

"And if she chooses to stay and join the Pan Clan, that wouldn't hurt either, would it?" Wu Ying said cynically.

Pan Yin nodded unashamedly. Waving goodbye, she headed for her own room, where she chivvied her sisters into picking up speed at packing. Wu Ying chuckled but followed her example moments later.

***

After watching the group ride off, Liu Ping inside the carriage with Pan Shui, Wu Ying turned to the man watching them all. He could not help but note the grey that had appeared, almost overnight, in the man's hair, the deep lines and shadows under his eyes. The Guard Captain was a man under siege by worries and concerns, by his impending and approaching doom. Yet he stood steadfast, and Wu Ying chose to give him the honor of not attempting to sway his mind. Too many had tried and failed.

"I'm glad you are leaving. In a few days, the messenger I sent will arrive. And then, they will come," Teng Fei said, looking into the distance and not at Wu Ying. "It will be best to be far away then."

"I wanted to thank you again." Wu Ying considered what else to say. He found that he had little to add. Mostly platitudes that the man had heard before, in the days between. Eventually, he had to ask, "What do you think will happen?"

Teng Fei shrugged. "It is hard to say. I think… I hope that most are overcautious. That the government will not kill loyal subjects to cover up a mistake. That they will choose to lay the blame on Elder Cao herself and let matters rest.

"But I do not know. No one does."

Wu Ying nodded. He understood that sentiment. People could sometimes be predictable, but governments, staffed by those desperate to keep their positions and their dignity, could react badly. Depending on how high the conspiracy went, the amount of damage this event could create was staggering. Even now, Wu Ying was certain the truth of the deaths and disasters across all the auctions and tournaments was spreading.

"The Heavens bear you fair wind, Expert Long," Teng Fei said, turning to Wu Ying. He bowed low, holding the position for a long moment before coming up and putting his clasped fists by his sides. "You honored Guardsman Chu by finding her killer. Her ghost will rest easy now."

Grief, deeper grief than Wu Ying would have expected, showed in Teng Fei's eyes. For a moment, Wu Ying wondered if there was more to the story there—a lover? Unrequited romance? Or just long companionship? He did not know and felt he could not ask. Not now.

So many stories, unspoken. So many truths, hidden. Wu Ying drifted through cities and villages, sects and kingdoms, between mortals and cultivators, and each had their own tales. Like the ruins of ancient villages and bygone kingdoms, they had stories to tell if only one could learn to speak the truth.

"Take care of yourself, Captain Teng," Wu Ying said finally as the sounds of the horses and the women drifted away.

"And yourself, Expert Long."

Wu Ying walked off, leaving the man to his fate. He could not help but feel a little unsettled, a little adrift. There was a war brewing, retribution to be meted out, moments of glory and cowardice to be enacted. And he was leaving, moving on before matters were settled.

Like the wind, bringing much needed rain to parched fields, he had wrought change in the land. Yet like the wind, he moved on before the changes he had fashioned would bear fruit. Maybe in years or decades, he would return. But it was others, the farmers and the noblemen, the cultivators who were linked to this land, who would have to care for the seeds he had planted.

Or not.

But for now, the wind blew, and Wu Ying had another land to see.

###

THE END

A Thousand Li:

The Third Realm

Book 8 of A Thousand Li Series

Chapter 1

Rolling hills with jagged caverns, newer mountains in the distance, and the remnants of old bamboo forests had been left behind a day back. In the middle of the day, twisting remnants of early morning mists swirled around the group, even as the smell of tea leaves permeated the thinner air of the mountain.

The hills were deceptive, the approaching men on their shaggy ponies concealed in dips of the earth and the mists that pervaded their surroundings. Greenery and dampness, the hint of fresh tea, and the slow fermentation of picked leaves drifted down from the peak above.

Berries and sheep, ponies and rice and falling waterfalls, the wind spoke of all those matters. It also spoke of deeper wounds in the earth, wounds that were centuries in the past but had only recently finished healing. Old blood—ancient blood—soaked the earth, and in one corner of the land, it still shrieked.

"Your lands…" Wu Ying turned his head a little, listening to the winds as they fluttered the green sleeves of his robes and tugged at his hair. "That mountain, these hills…"

"Yes?" Pan Yin asked, guiding her horse to him with slight twitches of her feet against its hindquarters, the mare well attuned to her needs. She looked down as she spoke to the standing cultivator. "What is it about our lands?"

Curiosity, from the Zhuang lady with her triangular, black hat and figure-hugging tunic and pants getup. Practical and comfortable, yet still feminine. Not that the older—late twenties, maybe even mid-thirties—cultivator seemed to pay much attention to that side of her personality. No more than the requisite social minimum at least.

"There was a battle here, was there not?" Wu Ying said. "Immortal and something else. The land, the winds, still speak of it."

"Sensitive indeed," Pan Yin said. "There's a story there, if you would hear it."

Wu Ying looked around their surroundings, then offered her a half-smile. "I'm assuming, considering the position of the sun, we aren't stopping?"

"No."

"Then speak. It will pass the time while I run," Wu Ying said.

"I still do not believe you ran all the way here," Pan Shui, the youngest sister of the trio said from her position at the back. Leaning over her saddlehorn, the sixteen-year-old peered at Wu Ying with narrowed eyes. "Are you sure you're not addled in the head? That was quite the battle, with General Cao. Isn't it tiring?"

"I'm neither. And I find the practice useful," Wu Ying said. "Where I go, horses are a burden, not an aid."

Pan Shui rolled her eyes. "Right, right. I forgot. *I'm a famous wandering cultivator.*" She mimicked his voice at the end, though she put an officious and arrogant tone to it.

"I don't sound like that."

"Of course you don't," Pan Shui said, eyes wide and innocent.

"You do know I'm your elder, right?" Wu Ying said, mildly stern.

He mostly did not mind. Weeks of travel with the group, avoiding—or finding—danger together to reach the Zhuang sisters' clan holdings had joined them all in a bond of companionship, one built around their ages and shared experiences rather than the barriers of cultivation levels. Wu Ying was having fun ribbing the youngster. She was the closest he'd ever had to a younger sister.

"Certainly. You are quite old." Pan Shui nodded firmly in agreement.

"As I was saying," Pan Yin cut the pair off before they could continue bickering. "We have a story about our land."

Noticing her irritation, the group fell silent. Even Liu Ping, though that was no different from usual. After all, the enhancement of her bloodline during the Seven Pavilions' incident had not just enhanced her strength but also given her some of the same traits of the bear she shared blood with, including a plodding, silent wariness.

"Four hundred and seventy-eight years ago—"

"Four hundred and seventy-nine. A year has passed," Pan Mu, the middle sister, corrected idly.

"Four hundred and seventy-nine years ago, a great beast ravaged this land. A White Hooded Snake, gorged on hundreds of demonic and spiritual beasts, grown strong in its blood, had formed a Nascent Soul. For hundreds of years, it dominated the surroundings, ensuring that none but a select few could reside in these lands in peace. Our clan was one of those select few. We had inhabited here before the coming of the Snake, and when it began its depredations, we came to an agreement with it. One made with little honor and great sacrifice."

Wu Ying's eyes narrowed. He knew what she meant by that last sentence, for that kind of contract was not uncommon on the far edges of civilization. It was said Nascent Soul-level beasts could only be beaten by cultivators of the same level, and often, multiple members of the same strength were required. After all, the difference between levels among Nascent Soul and Core stages grew ever higher, and beasts at that strength were often more powerful than mortals.

A minor benefit of their long cultivation and bloodline-strengthening process.

"Yet the beast did not know we were but biding our time." Pan Lin had a good voice for telling tales, knowing when to pause, when to modulate her tone. The entire party had leaned in, listening to her, and Wu Ying could tell even their hidden watchers were happy to listen. "Nor did the kingdom."

"Blundering fools, one and all," Pan Shui muttered. "I should have known they'd mess up even a tournament…"

Wu Ying offered only a half-smile at her grumbling. While he did not approve of the government's actions at the Seven Pavilions' tournament, he had done more than enough meddling by putting an end to Elder Cao.

Not that her death had been by his hand. He could not help but glance at Liu Ping, who seem enthralled by the tale. If the killing of the Elder sat heavily on her soul, it did not show. The flickers of still-healing grief that he spotted in her were more often for her murdered brother, Liu Jin, than her vengeful actions.

"They chose to showcase the strength of their Eleventh army at that time, another political play from the Royal Palace. It was the Fourth Prince—"

"Sixth," Pan Mui said.

"—who was favored to be second in line to the throne, who chose to act. Freeing up hundreds of li and thousands of people from the depredations of a Nascent Soul-level snake would do much for his standing. Deploying the full strength of his army—"

"He got his ass beaten," Pan Shui said gleefully. "Entire army wiped out, including the Nascent Soul Cultivator General and the two Core Formation Vice-Generals. You can see his resting place—right there." A finger pointed toward a larger than normal hill rising toward the north-east with a portion that seemed to have been lopped off right at the top. A small hut sat, conveniently, at the top, smoke rising from it. "Prince's Folly. We hang a light up there during the winter months, that way everyone has a guidelight if necessary."

"A rather pointed name," Wu Ying commented.

"It's not the official name in the kingdom's maps," Pan Mu corrected. "They named it General Mu's Stand."

"Ah, that makes more sense," Wu Ying said.

"I like ours better." Pan Shui stuck her tongue out at her sister. That didn't elicit the reaction she wanted, but Pan Yin cut her off.

"As I was saying, the battle between the Sixth Prince's army and the Spirit Snake saw to the devastation of the land, churning the earth, toppling hills, and creating deep canyons. Some of these ravines and mounds we ride by are named after the battle itself and the timing within—from the Cavalry's Charge, to the First, Second, and Sixth Regiment's death." Each word was punctuated by the woman pointing out the specific landmark.

"At the end, with the army devastated and in full retreat, the Core and Nascent Soul cultivators led the Spirit Snake away, destroying forests and sending waves of flame, chi swords, and lightning at it in one final, climatic act.

"All in vain, for they perished, on General Mu's Stand. The Spirit Snake rose in the sky, hissing its triumph and sending poison arcing through the air, burning away forest and grasslands alike. All hope was lost, or so it seemed.

"But their sacrifice was not in vain."

"I love this part," Pan Shui whispered to Wu Ying, only to cry out when Pan Mu pinched her upper arm.

"For the Pan Clan's Immortal Ancestor finally acted, released from his duties in the Heavens to satisfy the pleas of help from his descendants. He battled the Spirit Snake for a period of seven days and seven nights, pulling the earth up high and smashing the Snake down low, until it finally expired."

Wu Ying's eyebrows rose a little, then suspicion drove him to peer about. He eyed the hills they rode upon, sending his chi questing deep into the bones of the earth. His spiritual sense was a little truncated, battling against solid earth, but it was still the spiritual sense of one who had trained it since his Body Cultivation days.

Eyebrows drawn tight, he felt the way the earth's chi warped and twisted, how dense it was in certain areas and the shimmering curtains of energy and dense soil and rock that blocked further exploration. Head turning from side to side, Wu Ying pieced together the land within his mind from what his senses were telling him.

And wasn't that a little revelation of its own—that he had not noticed all this, even when his own senses had been extended.

"You might as well go up and see." The voice coming from a short distance away surprised Wu Ying.

His hand dropped to his jian by his side as he turned, eyes widening at the sight of the man astride a short pony. He was a nondescript older uncle, with a blackened, oiled mustache and the traditional darker figure-hugging cloth tunic and pants of the Zhuang people.

Nondescript and unremarkable, if one did not sense the Core within his body, the carefully controlled extrusion of power and the containment of it within his aura, only the mildest amount of energy leaking outward.

Next to the man were another three, ranging in strength from early to late Energy Storage. All had bows and carried the family's favorite weapon—the spear—in a spear holster by their saddle and had long, curved fighting knives in their belts.

They also all smelled the same, in a strange, almost comforting way, like the Pan sisters. The scent was more prominent now that he was in their land, surrounded by it. A tickling in the back of the throat, a hint of something different that sent the hairs on the back of his neck adrift.

"Fourth Uncle!" Pan Yin cried. She bowed to him, turning on her seat so fast that the horse beneath her stamped and huffed in discontent. "I—"

"You tell the tale well, in this language. Though it still sounds better in ours and in song," the Fourth Uncle said, smiling at Wu Ying.

"I would be honored to hear it in its original form, one day," Wu Ying chimed in, knowing his cue.

"Relax, niece. You can explain later why you spoke of it. I trust there is good reason," the Fourth Uncle said, still smiling. "In the meantime, it seems our guest has already begun to understand it." A single eyebrow rose. "Have you not?"

"I believe so…" Wu Ying gestured upward. "With your leave then."

The man nodded, and Wu Ying shifted his chi. Pulling upon the Heavenly Soul, Earthly Body technique, he lightened his weight. Then, tugging at the edges of his cultivation and borrowing the qinggong method of the Twelve Gales, he took to the skies.

Forming solid platforms of air beneath his feet, he strode upward, each step taking him multiple feet higher. The wind caught at his robes, pushing him upward as he flew, his control still a little shaky. His enhanced wind Core and the denser energy within gave him the power to fly, but strength did not equal control.

Once again, Wu Ying promised himself he would practice. If he could find the time, he would do so. But he'd spent the last few months practicing the sword with Pan Shui and her sisters, borrowing their understanding of their weapons to hone his own. Wearing away at the barrier that kept him from the Heart of the Sword.

Even if that barrier seemed to renew itself each day, for he never seemed to breach it, no matter how close he felt he was to enlightenment.

Shaking his head, he dismissed the worry and frustration. Neither would benefit him right now, and he did not want to showcase such an unbecoming attitude to the Fourth Uncle. For the man had followed him up, taking a more traditional method of flight by using his spear. It amused Wu Ying a little, since the Fourth Uncle gripped the weapon in one hand, letting it tug him upward, looking more like a monkey hanging from a branch than an elegant cultivator on his sword.

Looking down, Wu Ying stared at the trenches and the hills formed from the battle. He eyed the twisting hills across the otherwise—relatively—flat land and traced the parts that were blocked from his questing senses. Standing on air, feeling the chill of the higher altitude on the exposed skin of his cheeks, Wu Ying uttered his conviction to the Fourth Uncle.

"Some of those hills are the body of the Spirit Snake. Its bones permeate them, blocking spiritual sense and hiding the great treasure of its body and scales," Wu Ying said. "A powerful boon for your land, but one that comes with danger."

"She was right. You are discerning," the Fourth Uncle replied. "And gifted, to have ascended at such a young age."

"You do not need to flatter me, Honored Elder. I know my strength is but a minor thing compared to yourself," Wu Ying replied.

No false modesty there. While the Fourth Uncle was no peak Core Formation cultivator, he was at least in the mid-grade. Much stronger than Wu Ying's compressed, tiny beginner's Core and his progressing Wind Body.

"Pan Hai." At Wu Ying's surprise, he smiled. "And I know, of course, you are Cultivator Long of the Verdant Green Waters. The infamous Verdant Gatherer."

"I'm flattered that an Honored Elder like you would know so much of me." Contrary to his words, Wu Ying felt no true surprise that the other knew of him. Their destination had been set months ago and messages about their arrival would have been passed by Spirit Messenger as they rode.

"Pan Shui has been lavish with her praise," Pan Hai replied. Then he gestured down with his free hand. "Shall we join them? Word of your arrival has been sent ahead and I'm sure the cooks will be upset if we allow their food to cool."

"We would not want to anger them," Wu Ying said sagely. Relaxing his grip on his qinggong method, he let himself float downward, accompanied by Pan Hai.

And if Wu Ying had another, darker suspicion that a greater secret lay within the snake's body, he chose not to speak it.

After all, some secrets were worth killing for.

***

Dinner that night was lavish. The ceremonies, the songs—oh, the songs that they sung, late into the evening, both haunting and beautiful—and the accompanying dances would be carried by Wu Ying long into the future.

Succulent pig, roasted whole and over a fire, rice and fish and freshwater prawns, bamboo shoots and fried vegetables, wild mushrooms and fresh garlic—all of it presented by winsome attendants providing Wu Ying with drink and food in eye-staggering amounts.

Late into the night, the clan partied, celebrating both Pan Shui's achievements in the tournament and the safe return of the sisters. Though there might be sober and concerning reflections about the secrets revealed, tonight was not the night for such discussion.

Instead, Pan Shui regaled the clan with tales of the tournament battles. She did so from the seat of honor and spoke in excited, high-pitched tones, often standing and miming the fights. She regaled the clan members in their native tongue, Wu Ying receiving a constant translation from the young attendant assigned to him.

Eventually though, the joyous celebration ended. Men and women staggered to bed, carrying slumbering children with them or walking hand-in-hand with loved ones. Wu Ying's young attendant had long ago fallen asleep, and a quietly amused older brother scooped up the child with murmured apologies that were waved off with easy equanimity.

Inside his room, an entire small guest house set aside just for him—though markings of previous residents, along with the lingering smell of an aged body, left hints of the previous occupant—Wu Ying sat on the wooden bed, which was generously stuffed with chicken and wild bird feathers, and relaxed.

Then he inhaled.

Air filled his lungs, trickling through his nostrils as it left several moments later. Smells lingered, a veritable saga of past lives and choices made. Each breath brought additional tales, smells, and noises that spoke of sleeping children, vigorous coupling, and watchful guards.

Familiar smells of desserts and meals, the chill of mid-winter, and the turning of an older compost pile, grown a little too cold for proper breakdown. Rice and spiritual herbs, some contained in stone jars and others growing in carefully tended formations.

The tea fields, planted across nearby lands, and the sheep that the Zhuang clan raised.

The cry of a child waking, and the murmured words of consolation by a mother, nursing the hungry infant. Muffled cries as nightmares—fanciful and from the past—disturbed others, only for caring hands to placate sweaty brows.

Noises, smells, and sights all too familiar. The fabric of civilization—rough and comforting—like the hemp bedspread under his fingers.

Remembrance of things past, the constant present, and the potential future of the village and humanity itself.

The wind blew, Wu Ying breathed, and he listened as whispers of heaven on earth trickled through his soul.

Chapter 2

Morning the next day saw Wu Ying wandering the village, a new child attendant by his side to translate when required. Mostly though, in the middle of winter, there was less to do in the settlement. Upkeep of lands, repair of buildings and fences, the shoring up of drainage ditches, and the care of the tea plants as they hibernated. Thankfully, they weren't far north enough or high enough for the snow to arrive yet or last, leaving the land mostly dull green.

He wandered, listening to the unintelligible conversations, and waited. For scent and the halting explanation of his attendant had told him that the Pan sisters were meeting with the village chieftain and the council of elders, relating in detail the events surrounding the tournament.

Wu Ying was in no hurry, passing by the stock houses that surrounded the village square and the training pells where young children were shown the way of the spear by older teenagers. Many worked through the forms, thrusting, grunting, and spinning their metal-tipped mock-spears, intense concentration on their faces.

Others trained by crossing the raised plum blossom poles. Rather than the more common five poles sunk deeply into the earth in the shape of a plum blossom, the Zhuang clan used a dozen such poles. Soaring higher than the height of a man, the youngest children hopped, jumped, and skipped across, training balance and coordination in equal respects. Older children worked their way through while performing armed and unarmed forms. With two sets of a dozen poles, there was more than enough space for the half dozen advanced students to train.

For a time, he watched their training, marveling at the degree of coordination and resources devoted to them. Eventually though, he moved on. Brief observation was acceptable, but too long and it would have been considered rude. Still, as he passed another half dozen children, some as young as five, all seated with their legs crossed and meditating, he was struck by a sense of familiarity.

The Zhuang clan, for all its differences in speech, architecture, and dress, were more similar to his own village than the greater Zhao kingdom they inhabited.

At lunch, Wu Ying found himself seated alone, a single piece of fried fish offered to him along with a large helping of stir-fried vegetables and the requisite bowls of rice. A quick review of those around illuminated the degree of privilege given to him, as entire families shared the same amount of meat for their meals.

Yet he dared not protest, instead vowing silently to discuss payment and trade at a later date. After all, he was the famed Verdant Gatherer. And a few months—even months traveling with burdens like the Pan sisters—meant he had refilled his stores of herbs.

Especially since his ability to share and sell his collection had been curtailed. More from a sense of unease and wariness than any rescinding of his hard-won Authorized Vendor Seal.

He had just begun to dig into his meal when Liu Ping plopped down beside him, cradling an entire plateful of fish and a heaping soup bowl of rice. Wu Ying raised an eyebrow at the woman, whose increased appetite and sleeping patterns had led to a filling out of her muscular form. Further changes from her bloodline, it seemed.

"Which room did they put you in?" Liu Ping asked without preamble.

"The house two buildings southeast of the second well," Wu Ying replied.

"You have a full house?" she grumbled, then let out a low humph. "Damn Core Cultivator."

"That seems a little…" He paused, considering what word he should choose.

"Truthful?" She picked up an entire fried fish and bit into the head.

Wu Ying raised an eyebrow in silent reproach as the crowd watched the woman's antics.

Even so, after Liu Ping swallowed, she snorted. "What?"

"You do have manners," Wu Ying said.

"Whatever." Liu Ping waved the fish. "It's fried well enough to make the bones crunchy and tasty. It's good this way."

"And the use of your hands?"

"Chopsticks are becoming a little… fragile."

"That sounds more like a failure of control on your part than the fault of the chopsticks."

"I know, all right? Immortals above, you're as bad as my brother!" Liu Ping replied, a flash of pain crossing her face that was smothered after a second. The raw wound of her grief had scabbed over, but it was still fresh. "It's not good if I broke all their chopsticks training."

"Ah…" Wu Ying ducked his head in apology. He had not realized she had meant to be considerate—in her own way. "Your bloodline continues to strengthen?"

"Change, at least."

For a long moment, he regarded the woman. She seemed if not happy, at least accepting of the changes she was undergoing. The raw edges of her grief had blunted, hours spent weeping over her loss and abandonment late in the night trailing off, as wounds to both soul and heart healed.

More so, the changes in her physicality, while gradual, were significant. Whereas she had leaned toward the slim and graceful before, as per the usual model for cultivators, now she had a much more athletic build. Muscular, but not large, just solid. As though all the trials and her journey had given her a solidity of presence that even Pan Shui and Pan Mu, so close to her age, lacked.

"What?" she mumbled around a mouthful of fish.

"You've certainly changed." Her eyes narrowed, but Wu Ying ignored it. Teasing her was fun, but not something he needed to do. "What are your plans, now that we're here?"

"Mmm…" Liu Ping looked around, then pointed at her target. "I'm going to take a nap. Right there."

"You just woke up!" Wu Ying protested.

"Uh huh. Now I'm going to nap," Liu Ping said. "It was a long trip."

Wu Ying had to admit she wasn't wrong. Months on the trail, with few enough late wakings, had worn even on him. And he was—by temperament and experience—more used to roughing it than the others. However, the fear of the government finding and quieting them or otherwise taking revenge had driven them on, fleeing official sanctions by swift movement and rough sleeping.

Still…

Before Wu Ying could object further, an older man appeared. He bowed in greeting to the pair and, hesitantly, spoke to them in the common tongue. "Expert Long. Expert Liu. This one—Mo Heng—greets you. We offer apologies, for the tribal council continue to be busy."

"Mmmmhmmmmphhhfff…" Liu Ping acknowledged around a mouthful of rice, cheeks stuffed to the brim.

Rolling his eyes, Wu Ying stood and bowed to the other man. Only it was more an inclination of the head than an actual bow. He was, slowly, coming to understand the difference in ranks his new status required. Even if, in the future, he might hide his elevated status, there was no hiding it from this village.

"We thank you for informing us," he said.

"I am the chief? Head? Supervisor of the gardens for spirit vegetables." Mo Heng continued, touching his chest. "We understand Expert Long has vegetables too? Picked from the wilds."

Wu Ying blinked before he nodded. "Yes, I've picked some wild herbs. Maybe if you're more comfortable, we can speak through a translator?" He gestured at the kid standing respectfully by the side.

Mo Heng smiled in gratitude, then rapid-fire spoke to the translator. The youngster nodded for a time before translating for Wu Ying.

"Elder Mo cannot trade for the rarer items you might have. He does not have the right. However, your more common herbs are something he is authorized to acquire, and any that you need to plant to ensure they do not go bad, he is allowed to aid you in that too." A slight pause, then after Mo Heng blathered on, the kid added, "He's also to share pointers with you about the growing of spiritual herbs and show you our greenhouses."

"I would be happy to see them." Wu Ying glanced at his meal, still mostly unfinished, and hesitated.

"We will see you at the greenhouses. I'll show you the way," the kid quickly translated when Mo Heng noticed Wu Ying's hesitation.

"Thank you. I look forward to it."

Wu Ying watched as Mo Heng retreated, leaving the kid to watch over the group. In the meantime, Liu Ping had finished her meal, not having stopped.

Seeing Wu Ying's glance, she spoke. "What?"

"Do you want to come?" he offered.

"To listen to you drone on about vegetables?" Her eyes twinkled. "No. I'll sleep."

Snorting, Wu Ying watched as she stood and ambled away. After depositing her plate and bowl with the washing, she took a seat beneath the large tree and closed her eyes. He frowned, making a note to continue following up with her on her goals now that they had arrived.

He had not forgotten that she had left behind all she knew. And even as adroitly as she was avoiding the topic, he knew she would have to face the world at some point.

For now though, looking at his meal, he focused on finishing it with all due respect. Concerns about his friends, cultivation resources and lessons, and future plans could wait for after he ate.

After all, he was no longer dealing with one crisis after another.

***

Passage through the tea fields and the greenhouses was both enlightening and fascinating for Wu Ying. Working with his translator, Mo Heng detailed the work the clan did, happy to discuss everything from drainage, weeding, and harvesting of the tea plants to the formations that surrounded their lands and were carved into the mud-lined greenhouses.

Wu Ying perused their methods, touched the soil, and checked their compost heaps, gauging cuttings and rotations while sensing the flow of chi through their fields. He studied their formations, both large and small, and watched as gardeners flowed wood, water, and earth chi through plants and soil, carefully tending to plant after plant.

They spoke, exchanging information, professionals offering insight to other professionals. When they came to plots and formations where it suited his goods, Wu Ying unslung the bag he carried and extracted the carefully tended plants that had been held in semi-stasis in their enchanted jade boxes. He replanted the spirit herbs to ensure their longevity.

He noticed the others watching as he did so, noting the methods and the chi flows he used, the tug of power, the burying of energy and watering of the plant. He did not mind as whispered conversations passed from one to another, even going so far as to explain his actions as he worked.

In the end, they adjourned to a small building located beside the greenhouses themselves, one replete with the scent of drying, smoking, and fermenting spirit herbs. A tea was delivered, and manuals and scrolls were exchanged. The parties—elder Mo Heng, his apprentices, and a couple of elder gatherers along with Wu Ying—spoke of esoteric manuals and plants, probing one another for the cherished knowledge each party held. Mistakes in old manuals, located and corrected, methods of identification of rare or uncommon herbs, mutations and failures were spoken of.

"I'd found the white star peony in this clearing, but as I was going to collect it, I noticed a certain… scent." Wu Ying gestured with the cup of tea in hand. "Dropping, from the demonic black mountain cat. Of course, at that time, I only knew it was demonic in nature—from the rank smell of its droppings—but not its color or mutation.

"Still, it made for great fertilizer, which was why the clearing was filled with the peonies. I checked, of course, for its presence before I harvested my share. What I didn't realize was that the demonic cat had scented the clearing in a way I had not been able to sense"—and what a humbling moment that had been for him—"so when I left, I left a trail behind."

"Did it find you?" one of the apprentices asked, eyes wide with wonder. He reminded Wu Ying of his own, younger self, listening to returning soldier tales around the campfire in his village. Excited by the idea of war but knowing that he himself wanted nothing to do with it.

"Oh yes. Late at night, when I was sleeping," Wu Ying said, making a face. "Smart beast too. It avoided the formation flags I'd laid around the tree, coming in over the top. If not for the fact that I always set some talismans on the branches above too, it would have caught me out. As it was, it tore me up badly before I put it down. Still, its fur made for a good trophy for the next sect I visited."

Stories. His of derring-do and the perils of being a wandering gatherer. Theirs of frost and wind, of drought and fire and the predations of spirit insect hordes, the overabundance of rain and the lack of it and of course, the greed of merchants.

The group spoke, using manuals and scrolls for illustration, sketching new images and snacking on plates of appetizers long into the night. Professionals, regaling one another with the burdens of farming and gathering. For the first time in ages, Wu Ying found himself comforted, for even in the talk of mortal tea bushes and fields, he found a chord of familiarity and knowledge.

His people, even if a little removed. And though their struggles might be a little less dire than his own, their experience was no less real, wisdom borne of decades of toil no less profound. He learned as much from their stories as they did his own, of new plants to gather, of idiosyncrasies in cultivation and blending, of the dedication a specialized farmer might bring.

As the moon rose and set around them, they spoke; stories and memories and knowledge all blending together as tea changed to wine and snacks became full meals. The wind flowed, battering at windows and crossing thresholds, whispering its secrets to Wu Ying.

Of peace and direction and contentment and knowledge. Of the proper order of things, under Heaven.

And Wu Ying listened, learning.

Chapter 3

Morning the next day, Wu Ying was summoned before the chief and the council elders. He wasn't surprised to see that the chief was the Pan sisters' father. Such minor revelations had long ago been completed on their journey.

After the customary introductions and a period of small talk involving Wu Ying's day in the village, the group—which consisted of Chief Pan, Pan Yin, Pan Hai, and one other elder of the council—finally approached the meat of the meeting.

"My daughter speaks highly of you, your abilities, and most importantly, your character," Chief Pan said as preamble. Wu Ying inclined his head, keeping his features still even though he was shifting uncomfortably inside a little at the praise. "We are honored to have you as a guest, Expert Long."

"And I to be a guest," Wu Ying said, bowing a little from his seat. "You have a lovely village. One that is reminiscent, in its own way, of my own."

"Yes. My daughters mentioned you were a rice farmer before your ascension." Chief Pan inclined his head. "A long way to climb, as I understand it, for your kingdom."

"Longer in the majority of the State of Zhao," Wu Ying replied. "Though it seems you follow a more traditional practice."

"The Yellow Emperor decreed that all of humanity should cultivate. Why would we gainsay such a command?" Chief Pan said rhetorically.

"Especially when one receives visits from an immortal ancestor at times," Wu Ying said.

Chief Pan's gaze flicked over to where Pan Yin sat, looking entirely neutral. "Our ancestors do not visit often. After all, they have many duties in the heavens above. The last incident you've heard of, of course." He smiled a little as he continued. "But it is true that we have benefited from their guidance."

Wu Ying nodded. He would bet his World Spirit Ring that the latest Immortal to visit was a spear user.

"Now, there are many things we would like to discuss, but perhaps we should handle the commercial aspects first." As Chief Pan received Wu Ying's agreement, he gestured to the side. "Elder Mo will be handling the details, as he is much more conversant with our needs."

Of course, this Elder Mo was not the Mo Heng of the day before, though familiar familial features were present. Brothers for certain, or perhaps close cousins. Since both were only in the Energy Storage stage—middling at best—neither would have benefited over the other from a slower aging process.

"Thank you, Chief Pan." Elder Mo smiled at Wu Ying. "I must admit, I requested my brother to show you about so that we might shorten our discussion today. You have a broad understanding of what we grow, and as such, I hope perhaps we can focus on the kinds of spiritual herbs and supplements we do not have access to."

"Of course," Wu Ying said. "Obviously this will be easier with an understanding of the general items your village desires, but I noticed that you had a preponderance of flame- and earth-based spiritual herbs, lacking in some of the rarer water-based herbs like the Soaking Swamp Lotus and…"

In short order, the pair were bickering and negotiating over Wu Ying's numerous spiritual herbs, some of which he extracted to showcase there and then. In anticipation of this discussion, he had already carefully withdrawn from his World Spirit Ring the herbs that he intended to trade, not wishing to reveal its presence even to the friendly Pan clan.

The negotiations took hours, Chief Pan occasionally excusing himself to handle pressing matters for the village. Snacks and, later, lunch were served, along with a constant influx of various blends of tea after Wu Ying declined a pot of wine.

By the time the clan had passed the sixth tea blend, Wu Ying lost count entirely and chose to enjoy the event. Because the negotiation had become an event, with table banging, declarations of poverty and beggaring unto the fifth generation, and even requests for them to undertake duels of honor.

Throughout the process, Wu Ying could not help but notice the glint of amusement in Pan Yin's eyes and the exaggerated actions and bombastic words of Elder Mo. After a short while, he too fell into his part of the play, making outrageous statements and scoffing out loud with each offer. He even went so far as to grab at the various herbs, moving as though he'd take them away, though doing so in such exaggerated action and timing that it was clearly an act.

Eventually though, they came to an agreement, nearly two-thirds of Wu Ying's extensive collection of herbs that he was willing to part with claimed by the village. The biggest issue was how Wu Ying was to be paid, since the transfer of the large quantities of cash—even in paper form—was prohibitive.

Thankfully, Wu Ying was more interested in a barter, picking up rarer herbs he required for his medicinal baths, and the use of their alchemists to transform a portion of his current and newly acquired stock into pills for cultivation and medicinal bath powders.

Most importantly though, since he was in the kingdom of Zhao, he bartered for the one thing they had in abundance—comparatively. Powerful, enchanted items. Of course, the problem with acquiring Saint-level items—even in the State of Zhao—was expense. The clan, even after hundreds of years of acquisition, only had a limited number they were willing to trade.

Still, as the light grew dark, a deal was finally concluded. At least, tentatively.

"Now, I'm sure Pan Yin didn't invite me here just to acquire all my herbs," Wu Ying said, half-smiling. "What else did you have in mind?"

"Perceptive," Pan Hai intoned, his gaze taking on a grudging respect "And I assume you didn't bargain for access to our library because you expected as much?"

"In part," Wu Ying admitted but also added, to clarify, "Due to my unique element, many of the works held by others are of less use to me."

Chief Pan nodded. "Truth enough. We had our librarians review our library when Pan Yin first mentioned your particular… peculiarities. Unfortunately, we seem to be lacking in documents about your particular element. So outside of cultivation exercises and combat techniques…" He shrugged. "And of course, texts on apothecary, formations, and gathering. Outside of all that, we have little enough to offer you."

"It's no matter," Wu Ying said, waving. "I might want to browse the library anyway. You never know when inspiration and enlightenment might strike. Depending on what we discuss and what you require, of course. When we get to it eventually."

Chief Pan laughed. "It is getting late." A look outside at the fading sunlight, then at the herbs that members of his family kept taking away, now that the group had come to an agreement. "My daughter was not lying when she spoke of doing you a good turn. But as you probably realized, she had other reasons."

Wu Ying nodded, exhausted already with the constant repetition of information he already knew.

"To begin with, there is a child in our care, a member of a branch family, who has shown a degree of skill with the jian that we would like to further."

"I'm not that much of a teacher…" Wu Ying said hesitantly.

"Understood. We still wish you to showcase and teach your Long family style to him," Chief Pan said. "The child in question is… special."

Wu Ying frowned. "You're asking me to showcase my family style?"

"It is a big request," Chief Pan said, entirely unembarrassed. "However, I believe that you'll find it to your benefit." Chief Pan raised a finger. "One lesson. We'll bargain for one lesson."

Wu Ying blinked. He had an understanding of people, and the fact that Chief Pan was asking for a single lesson even after he had declined was telling. There were numerous such stories, and this one… "He's a prodigy, is he not?"

"I told you it wouldn't work," Pan Yin said, speaking up for the first time that day. Turning to Wu Ying, she bulled ahead. "My cousin is a true genius, one who has reached the Heart of the Sword already."

"Then what does he need me to teach him?" Wu Ying said, surprised.

"Experience," Pan Hai, the Fourth Uncle, said curtly. "Pan Chen is a hothouse flower, grown in perfectly groomed conditions. He is strong, vibrant—and has never had to face true adversity."

"Irrelevant. That is an unimportant point," Chief Pan said, snapping at Pan Hai. "It's not about his lack of experience that we wish for you to train him." A slight pause. "Well, perhaps if Cultivator Long stayed longer. But Ah Chen is too young for what you envision." Then he shook his head. "No. What we need now is for him to expand his knowledge base, to study as many styles as possible. To grow. You know what Grandmother said."

There were a series of nods from the group as they acknowledged the chief's words.

Frowning, Wu Ying spoke. "I don't."

"Apologies," Chief Pan replied. Still, he made no move to answer Wu Ying's question.

It was Pan Yin who, rolling her eyes, clarified. "Grandmother Pan has a minor gift of foresight. She can see the weaves of fate, prone as they are to changing. And she spoke of Ah Chen's chance at achieving the Soul of the Sword, if given proper guidance."

Wu Ying was shocked, and he chose not to hide it. Grasping the different degrees of understanding and knowledge of a weapon could help one in bypassing concerns of enlightenment and also breach the difference in strength between cultivation levels.

One who had a grasp of the Sense of their weapon stood among the peak of those in their grade. An understanding of the Heart allowed one to fight a level above—in most cases. As for the legendary levels of Soul of the Sword? Well, it was legendary for the stated reason—the degree of strength it imparted was only spoken of in fables and legends of the past. Slicing apart mountains and killing Nascent Soul cultivators as a simple sword cut were all part and parcel of such tall tales.

"And you're willing to sacrifice much for him to achieve such heights." Wu Ying nodded in understanding.

Having such an individual as part of their clan would offer great assurance, but the possibility of someone achieving those lofty heights could also bring danger. Many felt the need to prune such promising buds before they could fully flower, rather than risk a weapon pointed at them.

That led Wu Ying to another thought. "It's surprising, to know of two such prodigies from such a small clan." He left the rest unsaid.

"Not so surprising, when you understand that Pan Shui's improvement can be traced to Ah Chen's influence," Chief Pan replied, answering the unspoken question.

"Ah..." Wu Ying sat back, staring at the group.

Something was niggling at him, a memory of a conversation. He remembered Liu Ping, how the Pan sisters had mentioned being able to help her with her bloodline. Then there was the story of the Immortal. The admission of not just a single immortal from their clan. The presence of two prodigies in the Heart realm.

Bloodlines. Immortals. Prodigies.

"The blood of the immortal flows through your people, doesn't it?" Wu Ying said. "That's why you have so many prodigies." Realization hit a moment later, that perhaps he should not have spoken his assumptions aloud.

"Smart. Too smart," Pan Hai said, his voice stern and no longer half-amused. His gaze turned to Pan Yin, who returned the look with a little hint of concern as she sensed the killing intent that leaked from the Elder. "How many more secrets do you intend for him to ferret out? Give him another week and, with your daughter's help, he'll have our formations in disarray."

"Enough, Ah Hai," Chief Pan scolded the other. "Expert Long is among friends. We have extended guest rights to him, and we will not forsake our honor. My daughter has reasons for her actions, and Expert Long has already proven he is himself. In our land and his own."

"Honor matters not when loose lips and the torturer's blade exist," Pan Hai said. "The kingdom has always desired our riches."

"Which is why we must grow in strength. And we have reached the limits of our own resources," Chief Pan said.

"I'm also not going to stay in Zhao," Wu Ying added. "There's much to see in this world, and my path will take me far away." A trickle of wind, brushing against his hair, reminded Wu Ying of his destination and what he searched for.

"See?" Chief Pan replied. "My daughter chooses well. Something you should heed well in the future."

Pan Hai's lips tightened, the Fourth Uncle reluctantly bowing his head. Altercation ended, Chief Pan looked at Wu Ying, offering apologies for the brief distraction and unseemly argument. Wu Ying, of course, dismissed the matter with more polite words.

"Now, will you?" Chief Pan said, returning to the topic at hand.

"And what do I gain from offering my knowledge of the sword to your nephew?" Wu Ying asked, leaning forward. "Why would I offer up my secrets to him?" And endanger himself, it went without saying.

"Lessons. You are on the cusp of the Heart of the Sword and yet have been unable to achieve it. As you've heard, Ah Chen has a gift for enlightenment. Sword or spear, if the spark is within you, he can fan it aflame."

Hunger flashed through him, his throat growing parched. Wu Ying reached for his teacup, noting idly the smallest tremble in his fingers as he wetted his dry throat, the desperate desire almost too much to contain. Desire raced through him, and like his beating heart, Wu Ying waited.

Finally, as control returned, Wu Ying spoke. "A generous gift. But I believe, have to believe, that I can achieve much the same myself in time."

Even if he had been banging his head on the same wall for years. Then again, it could take decades to achieve that understanding. Decades, maybe even a century. Maybe never. But as he said, he had to believe he could achieve it himself. Without that belief, Wu Ying knew that such a step could never be achieved.

Mastery was as much about the heart as the hand.

"Then what else do you desire?" Chief Pan asked.

Wu Ying turned the teacup around and around, debating what else he wanted. When he spoke, it was slowly and haltingly, as he searched his heart out loud too. "Information on bloodlines. Not yours in particular, but your experiences, the changes you've seen. Improving it, if you have done so, outside of the use of spirit herbs and the like that help concentrate or develop it."

The group looked at one another, Pan Hai shaking his head and the other Elder nodding in agreement with him.

Chief Pan hesitated for a long time before he sighed. "I cannot authorize this alone. We shall have to speak of it as a council."

"Very well." Wu Ying nodded to the other Elder Mo. "I'd like to spend more time working with your gatherers, as partners. Trading further pointers."

"How long?" Chief Pan said, flicking a glance at Elder Mo, who rubbed his chin but offered the slightest of nods.

Wu Ying paused, considering. Judging by the season and timing… "Until the beginning of spring at the earliest. Perhaps until the end of the first planting season."

That would give him a lot of theoretical training around this time when the soil was still cold and not much was being grown beyond the greenhouses and the planting season, if they accepted both. More than enough time to study up on their formations and test new ideas. Maybe even go through their library further.

It was a good deal for them too, since the formations Wu Ying knew were different from theirs. They did the same thing, of course, to some extent—but any knowledge was a benefit. And his copious notes on wild herbs could be of use to them.

"We'll want your aid in planting and growing some of the wild spiritual herbs you sold us," Elder Mo said.

"Which ones?" Wu Ying said. "You understand that many will not be as potent if grown domestically?"

"Of course. But we will still want to experiment and understand the process," Elder Mo replied.

Wu Ying nodded. He could understand that. Even if none of the plants they attempted to grow were successfully cultivated, a single successful domestication of a wild spirit herb would pay for decades if not centuries of experimentation.

That in the long term, this might cause problems for someone like Wu Ying was a concern much further in the future. And frankly, from his understanding of the market, it would never entirely remove the need for gatherers. So long as they were willing to traverse the deep wilds.

"Then, it seems, we have the overall outline of an agreement for your stay, Expert Long," Chief Pan said, smiling a little.

"We do," Wu Ying said. He did not forget that they had mentioned only one of a few things but had now cut the discussion short.

Whatever it was they had wished to ask him, the chief had chosen to discard it for now. Perhaps in the future, it might be brought up. In the end, it mattered little. Wu Ying could wait and see. He was, after all, in no hurry.

***

Nearly a week later, a week of long languid days spent being shown around the hills and gullies of the land, the chief and the other Elders returned to confirm their agreement in full. Their bloodline records, their experimentations, and even access to their secret medicinal bathing areas were all part of the offer, though in turn, Wu Ying was to teach Pan Chen the Long family style in its entirety whilst parting with his collection of sword manuals.

It was a small sacrifice, since the collection would be copied by students and scholars from the Pan family before being returned to him. His travels had allowed Wu Ying to purchase a variety of such documents, but none of them were particularly secretive. Like a squirrel, Wu Ying had hoarded manuals from passing merchants, auction houses, and bookstores, acquiring them without care for origin or quality.

As such, the volumes of work he had acquired included everything from martial art manuals written by those who barely understood which side was the pointy end to the everyday martial arts manuals of the Shen army to private manuals from defunct martial art sects and fallen families.

It had become a hobby, reading them late into the night whilst gathering, practicing and laughing at the inaccurate representations. All of it in an attempt to weave together or gain enlightenment of his own family style from exposure to others.

In the secret chamber of his heart, where unspoken ambition dwelt, Wu Ying held hopes of weaving his style into a complete sword form. Building upon his understanding of the Long family style to create something powerful, something that reached beyond the manuals he had collected and been gifted, beyond the fifth form that he had only begun to practice recently.

For none of his family had ever reached the heights of Nascent Soul formation, at least not recently. And what sparse notes there were explaining forms in the fifth style, the flow of chi and the projection of energy, all came from those who had reached Core Formation. The original notes offered only the sparsest of guidance for one at his stage.

Leaving Wu Ying… bereft.

And if perhaps inspiration or understanding might come from works that were as fanciful as they were practical, so be it.

In the meantime, while Wu Ying had waited for an answer to his request, he had spent the time being a grateful guest. Even for one who had grown familiar with the rigors of travel, the long months from the Seven Pavilions residence through country roads and ill-kept inns had taken its toll.

A chance to rest, to wander through conditioned fields of tea and wild plains of sheep, to clamber across windswept lands and dance among the clouds without care was gratefully taken. Time to breathe the air, to relax the soul, and to cultivate.

Days where Wu Ying's greatest dilemma was whether he made it back in time for dinner. Hours spent cultivating on lonely hilltops and under cloudy skies, while the wind danced and he bathed in medicinal baths meant to strengthen his body and leach out impurities.

All the while feeding the Nascent Soul in his core with the glimmering touches of enlightenment, improving his body as he practiced the forms of the Seven Winds manual in the blowing western wind as he danced through the sky. Days where that nascent soul grew as the Formless Realm cultivating method fed it dao and enlightenments, and Wu Ying sought his dao.

Cultivating, filling his dantian, and waiting.

For in stillness, there too was growth.

Chapter 4

The child prodigy was truly a child. Standing four and a half feet tall, barely under Wu Ying's armpit, he was a well-proportioned kid with his hair tucked into a high hat. He had been chattering away excitedly with a girl child until Wu Ying and his escort of the Fourth Uncle arrived at the empty training courtyard. Set aside and a distance from the rest of the village, it was a perfect location to work upon new techniques—away from prying and curious eyes.

Once the children realized who had arrived, the little girl was sent away and the child prodigy—Pan Chen—transformed, maturing in the space of seconds as he straightened his back and grew a serious expression.

"Expert Long, this unworthy one looks forward to your instruction," Pan Chen said, bowing low with his hands clasped together.

Wu Ying smiled a little, noting the tiny queue the boy had tied his hair into to get it out of the way. "No need, Cultivator Pan. I am grateful for the chance to meet one so skilled at a young age."

"Student. Or apprentice," Pan Chen replied. "If you would take one as unworthy as myself as your student, that is."

Wu Ying paused, running through the options of what he should say. The role and responsibilities of official student and teacher were expansive. It was not a mere form of address, as the way the Fourth Uncle had stiffened and glowered at the youngster showcased. As the saying went, "A teacher for a day, A parent for life[21]."

On the other hand, Wu Ying had to admit, having a student reach the Soul stage of understanding of the sword would bring much prestige to him. And safety. A small, greedy part of him desired the benefits taking the youngster's overelaborate courtesy would bring. Taking advantage of his naivete…

Wu Ying regarded that small and mean and greedy part of himself. Time seemed to stretch as he considered that portion of himself, as he assessed it and his own desires. Then with a swift mental kick, he breathed out, consigning that greed back into the corner of his soul where it belonged.

Such an action, it would diminish him. Devalue his sense of worth, the hard rock of honor he had built his own ego upon. He would not grasp at such small markers of reputation, not hide under the uncertain shade of obligation.

If perhaps his choices were foolish, so be it. The journey to immortality was a fool's dream anyway. And he, a true fool.

---

21 一日为师，终身为父 - famous proverb about the importance of teachers and the gratitude one must show a teacher. There's a corollary one where to find a good teacher, one must spend a long time searching. And the teacher, the same verifying the quality of their wannabe student.

Seconds, long seconds in which the Fourth Uncle grew redder, caught in the binds of hospitality and courtesy while the blades of future disaster and foolishness closed on him. Seconds, while Pan Chen shifted from foot to foot, awaiting an answer.

And then Wu Ying spoke. "No, Cultivator Pan, I will not take you on as a student. For I am not ready to take on a student. Nor have I judged you, sufficiently, to do so." He leaned down and, deliberately, ruffled the child's carefully maintained hair. "Choosing a teacher should not be a matter of whim or courtesy but of deep and certain thought. For a bad teacher will lead you wrong and place your feet on an incorrect path. Whether deliberately or by dint of failure. I choose to do neither for you."

Pulling away from Wu Ying's hand, Pan Chen glared at the other man for a second. Shame at being rejected disappeared under the petulant rage of a child, smothered only by the hard-won control of martial arts and cultivation.

"This one apologizes for disturbing Expert Long." Pan Chen's voice was high, rough as contained emotions leaked around the edges.

Coughing into his hand, Pan Hai stepped forward and gestured to the open courtyard. "Perhaps we should start now?"

"Of course," Wu Ying said, hiding his smile from the glowering child. Irritation would go away, but shame could scar souls. "Is there a way that you prefer to learn, Cultivator Pan?"

Pan Chen glanced at Pan Hai, seeking confirmation. When he received it, he offered Wu Ying a half-smile. One that had a hint of mischief in it.

"Would Expert Long show me your style first? In its entirety?"

A good enough starting point. The bargain was for the teaching in its entirety, after all. "Of course."

Unsheathing his blade, Wu Ying strode to the center of the courtyard. Smooth paving stones lay beneath his feet, the open air courtyard allowing the winds to come in and play. Whispering secrets of dalliances and napping bear-kin. He acknowledged their words before dismissing them from his mind.

A slow, trickly exhale. Then he spoke, low but loudly enough for the others to hear. "Long family sword style—first form."

Stillness.

Then, hand on the hilt of his sword. The Dragon unsheathes its Claws. The first motion of the form, a sword draw. Step forward, twist the sheath and blade as he drew. Cut and end with the sword on the high outer line.

Thrust, transitioning forward. Twist and cut, disengage, block. Wu Ying flowed through the motions of the form. He chose to showcase the original form, as it had been taught to him by his father, without adaptations for Wind Steps or the Twelve Gales, without adding in the Shen Kicking style or any other minor variations he had created to better suit himself.

Falling into familiar patterns were easy, though Wu Ying noted the most minute of hesitations as movements or transitions he had altered caused him trouble. When he was done, he had returned to his starting position, his blade sheathed.

"Beautiful. Expert Long truly is an expert in the jian," Pan Hai praised.

Wu Ying smiled and offered a little bow but otherwise ignored the courtesy praise. Instead, he watched the slight frown on Pan Chen's face. And like a good teacher, he asked, "What is wrong, Cultivator Pan?"

"It's not very good, is it?"

"Ah Chen!" Pan Hai said, sounding scandalized. He raised a hand to strike Pan Chen on the back of the head but stilled when Wu Ying raised a hand. Remembering he was but an observer here.

"Why do you say that?" Wu Ying asked.

"That's not the style you use, not anymore. It's something you learned, but that's not your style," Pan Chen explained. "I'd like to see your real style. Not this."

"Truly, one with the Heart of the Jian," Wu Ying said, offering the kid a half-smile to show no offense had been taken.

Taking position once more in the center of the courtyard, Wu Ying half-closed his eyes. He breathed in and out. Settled his nerves and soul. Found the rhythm of the blowing wind.

And moved.

***

No hesitation, no breaks, no gaps. At least, none that he did not know of—that were still transitions that were being perfected. In the course of altering the style to suit his own body of knowledge, there were gaps, options that Wu Ying tested and discarded. Not many, of course—two or three in the entirety of the first form. The rest were smooth motions, transitions between flowing kicks, elbow and fist strikes to thrusts and cuts.

Elegance in motion, efficiency in every action. A myriad range of options opening and closing lines of attack and defense with each raise of an arm, cut, or thrust, the sinking of a foot or the tilt of the body. Angles that were created and denied, feints and false openings in equal measure that could transition to other motions.

A form was not a static thing, not in the mind's eye of an expert. Each motion was but a prelude to dozens of reactions, each action an invitation to an opponent. The final result, whether a string of cuts like the Flashing claws before Dinner to a series of circular blocks or disengages like Cloud Hands were all dependent upon an opponent's reaction.

What differentiated a good style, one that was an intermediate or peak battle technique from a poor beginner or novice one, was the range of options and reactions provided with each action—or conversely, the range of options and reactions denied to an opponent.

The sun rose, the clouds drifted, and leaves danced in the wind as Wu Ying found a peace in the sword and his forms that he had been unable to locate as a child. Hours every day spent practicing the jian long before his friends rose to see the morning. Early hours, when the sun was barely more than a sliver—for they were farmers and the day started when the dawn truly began.

Oh, how he had fought and screamed and complained, sometimes out loud and later, after learning his lessons, in his heart. He had hated his father for the strict discipline, the endless hours of repetition of each motion, each form he displayed. Talent replaced by sweat and tears, blood and blisters until he got it right. Only to do it again the very next day.

Peace, from the knowledge that he was doing a job well. Not perfect, though he chased that elusive concept. Peace from repeating actions that had been drilled into him from hours of practice, peace wrapped in the alloy of fond memories.

And then it was over and Wu Ying was standing in the same spot, sword sheathed. His audience was silent, even as Wu Ying approached the pair.

Biting his lower lip, Pan Chen was looking at Pan Hai who, after shaking himself a little, spoke softly. "Hah. I apologize, Expert Long."

"For what?" Wu Ying said, frowning.

"I had doubts about the need to have a stranger showcase his arts to Pan Chen. I did not believe that revealing our secrets to you was appropriate. And yet…" He gestured. "It seems the world is wider than even I expect."

"It was a small thing…" Wu Ying said, waving dismissively. "A minor modification of my family's style to suit me better."

"Minor perhaps, but even though I am not well-versed in the jian, I too can tell it suits you better. You truly are at the tipping point to achieving the Heart of the Sword, are you not?" The last question was more rhetorical.

"It seems so, but still, I cannot seem to find my way there."

Pan Chen, shifting from foot to foot, spoke up. "Can I?"

"Can you what?"

"Try it?" He gestured at the training ground. His fingers danced across the hilt of the jian he wore, the weapon shortened to suit his size.

"My style?" Wu Ying hesitated then shrugged. "Go ahead. Stop when you are uncertain. Don't try to push ahead or else you might learn the wrong thing."

Pan Chen was not listening as he strode into the center of the courtyard. Wu Ying sighed but knew better than to argue with the boy. He was a kid after all, literally. Better for him to learn. Prodigy or not, children were prone to rushing.

Standing in the center, Pan Chen closed his eyes for a brief second, centering himself. He breathed in and out slowly, mimicking even Wu Ying's start before he began.

At first, Wu Ying watched Pan Chen for the basics—his sense of balance, the linkage between his body and weapon, the angle of his cuts and the speed of his thrusts. In no time at all, he understood that such basic lessons—important though they might be to build the foundation of a swordsman's skills—were wasted on Pan Chen.

He was perfect. Or at least, so close to perfection that Wu Ying could not see the difference. Someone with a higher degree of combat skill, of experience, or a sense of the weapon might be able to do so. He, in the end, could not.

No, once he gave up on the idea he could teach the other anything as mundane as that, Wu Ying watched Pan Chen flow through the Long family jian style. Through the first portion, the second, the next.

He flowed through Wu Ying's variation of the form, never hesitating, never stopping. One motion after the other.

Until as suddenly as he'd started, he was done.

"Well done, Ah Chen. You copied the style perfectly." Pan Hai sounded just a little smug.

"He did not actually," Wu Ying murmured, too awed to be irritated. He had met many prodigies in his life—Gao Chen, Li Yao, Tou He, even his martial sister Fairy Yang. But this level of genius, it was on an entirely different level. "Descendent of an immortal indeed."

"What do you mean, he did not copy it perfectly?" Pan Hai replied, sounding incensed.

"I did not, Fourth Uncle," Pan Chen replied. He bowed to the other man then turned to Wu Ying, a considering look in his eyes. "Did you see?"

"I did. I saw, though I'm not sure I understood."

"I didn't." The Fourth Uncle crossed his arms, looking a little put-out. This was not his weapon, and even if he had expected his general sense of martial arts to carry him through, the pair were speaking and observing things at a level he could not catch.

"He improved on my own variations," Wu Ying said, still sounding amazed. He understood some of what had been changed, the why. Some changes had clarified ideas he had begun to explore; others were new concepts he had never considered. "Returned some to the original."

"And was it good?" Pan Chen asked, suddenly a shy child asking an adult for his approval.

"Mostly, I think," Wu Ying admitted as much, though a part of him believed that the majority were for the better. He was just uncertain.

And a little ashamed, if he dug deeply enough into his own emotions. To be shown up by a child...

"Let's talk about what you changed, shall we?" Wu Ying said, offering the boy a smile.

Wu Ying acknowledged those petty emotions, then discarded them to that same ignominious cave that greed lived in. Let them wither and die. He had much that Pan Chen did not have.

Like height.

***

Toward the end of the day, after hours of discussion with Pan Chen, Wu Ying chose to extract the urumi from his Spirit Ring. Pan Hai had wandered off not long after it was clear that the pair was ignoring him. They had already passed the Fourth Uncle's knowledge of the jian, delving deep into forms and variations, testing both theory and practice in the courtyard. The pair barely noticed being left alone, only pausing to eat and stretch.

The moment the urumi—the strange, flexible, whip-like sword Wu Ying had purchased—made its appearance, Pan Chen almost flew over to Wu Ying's side. He gripped the weapon carefully, testing the blade's weight and edge, perusing the grip and the steel's flexibility. When Wu Ying showed him the manual, Pan Chen traded weapon for document without a word and flipped through the pictures, ignoring the unknown language it was written in.

Bare minutes later, he was done and had taken the weapon away from Wu Ying as he returned to the training floor. Wu Ying hastily moved back, even as the child gave the oversized weapon—for him—a few experimental flicks.

Pan Chen started with small motions, moving his hand up and down, sending the blade rippling with each motion like a sleepy snake. Eyes narrowed, he made bigger, bolder motions, flicking the weapon so that the blade never touched the ground. Once more, he waited until he was comfortable before he switched, moving the blade sideways, then angling the attacks.

Static at first, then around his body, weaving a defensive web of swirling metal. It was familiar, in a way, as the rope-dart also moved in strange angles. But the urumi's blade was sharp, flexible metal, and it danced in silvery, angular languor with each motion.

In the web of twisting steel, Pan Chen smiled. He moved soon after, stepping outward from within the web, ducking and jumping, kicking and punching as the flexible blade moved with him. Wu Ying recognized some of the forms—pictures from the manuals given life—as Pan Chen traveled, moving faster and faster.

The air cracked and hissed as metal whip sung through the air, tiny gusts of wind broken and torn apart, while others were generated. In the cyclone of destruction, the blade end would dart outward to strike and be pulled back moments later, the wooden posts at the other end of the courtyard struck repeatedly.

Beautiful violence, a dance of destruction and grace.

Something stirred within Wu Ying as he watched a child with the Heart of the Jian interact with a weapon that was not the straight sword. He saw, in Pan Chen's motions, a beauty, an elegance that Wu Ying had removed from his own consideration. That his father had never imparted.

For them, the sword was a weapon, a tool for killing and defense. A burden to be trained in to continue their familial heritage. Wu Ying found peace, tranquility in the motions, security in his knowledge. But in the way the child moved, the joy he took in exploring and learning a new weapon, Wu Ying saw unalloyed joy and innocence. He saw beauty in the weapon.

Yes, the jian was a weapon, a tool of violence. Swords were not axes or spears, which had been created for another task and eventually turned to the killing of fellow man. A sword was meant to kill, to drive mortals and cultivators alike from their physical forms.

But even so, there was no reason there could not be beauty to the weapon, to the forms itself. There was no reason why in the act of practice, one could not find its elegant seduction.

In that moment, Wu Ying realized, he had not embraced the entirety of his weapon. In so doing, he had blocked himself from achieving the Heart of the Sword.

"You've understood something then, Expert Long?" Pan Chen said as he came to a stop before the older man, the weapon stilling by his side.

So serious, unlike the young boy he was.

"I have. And you? Have you found a new love?" Wu Ying nodded toward the weapon in Pan Chen's hands.

The child looked down, gave the weapon a little shake, then shrugged. "No. It's fun to play with, but it's not the jian." He smiled. "But there is much to learn from different weapons after all."

"So I'm beginning to understand," Wu Ying said. He offered Pan Chen the manual. "A gift, for showing me the path."

Pan Chen grinned, taking the manual without inhibition. "Thank you, Expert Long!"

"Now, it seems dinner is about to be served. And you are still young enough to need a good night's sleep."

A deep frown crossed the kid's face, going so far as to pout. He sighed deeply as he went to pack up. Not a moment too soon, as Pan Yin arrived, ready to convince the pair to come for dinner. As Wu Ying had sensed.

Smiling at her minor surprise, Wu Ying helped set the training grounds aright before they left. It seemed that this exchange of skills would be as helpful for himself as they had promised.

Perhaps even more so than they'd suspected.

Chapter 5

The next day, much to Wu Ying's and Pan Chen's disappointment, was dedicated not to further exploration of the jian but an introduction for Wu Ying to the village's archives on bloodlines. The building, to his surprise, was not located within the village itself, but a short distance away in a cave hidden behind a powerful illusion formation.

It took them nearly an hour to bypass the formation and allow Wu Ying into the first cave, where glowing spirit lamps shed light on bare stone tables. A series of books and scrolls had been laid out in anticipation of Wu Ying's arrival, each of them detailing the clan's research into bloodlines. Awaiting him was an attendant who proceeded to explain the various works set before him, even as the doors leading deeper into the library were kept sealed.

"And this section"—the attendant, a wizened old woman pointed—"is our manuals on Body Cleansing."

"I… did not ask for that," Wu Ying said.

"And yet, here they are." The attendant waved Wu Ying away before stomping back toward the other door and rapping on it sharply. "If you have trouble… don't call!"

"Thank you, elder," Wu Ying called, watching the old woman disappear through the doorway.

After a second, he laughed to himself and started browsing through the documentation. Bloodline first, since he had always found a lot of information on that area not as useful for his particular situation.

Hours passed—a serving of steamed buns allowed him to deal with the hunger—while he read. One scroll and manual after the other, long discussions about immortality, musings on changes, and dry recordings of what had happened, all mixed with lengthy notations about herbal baths, variations in spiritual herbs, pills, and even various hot springs rumored and known to have rejuvenative properties.

For the most part, Wu Ying skimmed to gain an overview. Certain manuals and scrolls, he set aside with mental notes about attempts or variations that he might look into deeper. Variations in location, in the process and conceptual ideas he absorbed and added to his understanding of bloodlines.

It was an esoteric subject matter, partly because bloodlines were rare and had a tendency to appear or form or disappear from a variety of circumstances. The dragon blood Wu Ying had provided Tou He might have enacted a bloodline change in his friend. Or it could have just improved his body and cultivation without making the kind of fundamental change required to produce a long-lasting bloodline.

Spirit Beasts who intermingled with humans, achieving a level of transformation that allowed them to procreate, were almost always guaranteed to pass along part of their heritage to their children. It was almost certain that that was what had happened with Liu Ping's ancestors.

However, bloodlines and their strength faded soon after the initial progeny. Grandchildren might only exhibit minor variations in features, chi accumulation, or physical characteristics. By the time great-grandchildren arrived, the bloodline often had faded significantly, only triggered further by circumstance or alchemy.

The process of activating a bloodline, forcing its evolution in descendants, was an interesting study and it was here that Wu Ying found the research done by the clan particularly useful. It seemed the process of bloodline strengthening came about due to two different processes.

In bestial bloodlines like Liu Ping's, a bloodline, when awakened, could evolve, growing stronger much like Spirit Beasts grew stronger through the process of living, fighting, and consuming others. The simple process of being the creatures they were, consuming other creatures and accepting the dao of their own existence, would see them evolve and ascend in time.

When individuals had such bloodlines, the goal was to create an environment, to feed the slumbering bloodline the necessary spiritual herbs to produce such an evolution. Knowing the type of bloodline and the beasts involved would, in a manner similar to Body Cleansing, see its progress. In many ways, such practices threaded the line between Body Cleansing and bloodline development, since both could evolve an individual, potentially even leading to ascension as an immortal.

This was entirely unlike the bloodline progression that happened with immortal bloodlines or those that were by themselves already highly evolved and not requiring further evolution. Humans, in many ways, could be considered such beings—not requiring an evolution of their bloodlines to grow stronger. Or at least, that could be argued. Others did not agree since what was Body Cleansing and the evolution of meridians but an evolution of the body?

Setting aside such scholarly arguments, what was important to Wu Ying was the fact that dragons were—generally—considered to be like immortals. Already highly evolved, or at the apex of immortality, they were creatures perfected by the Dao and, as such, unable to progress further. The documents theorized that the next best thing was not to attempt a bloodline evolution but instead to gather such bloodlines together.

With dragons or phoenixes or immortals, one needed to gather and refine such blood. The village had, of course, looked at arranged marriages between various branch families to do so. However, that was obviously, after so much time, insufficient.

Instead, spiritual herbs soaked in the blood of immortals or having a portion of immortality to them, alterations to Body Cultivation techniques, and the process of infusing such immortal blood—which, eventually, was reproduced within a body—was the goal. All of it to enhance the strengthening of the lineage within the body and thus the concentration and ratio of the immortal blood.

"So that's why the Body Cultivation techniques are here," Wu Ying muttered, glancing at the other pile.

Since Body Cultivation required the cleansing and replacement of parts, as one strengthened the body, turning it into a treasure or element, the very processes and techniques could be adapted to concentrate an immortal bloodline. He just had to work out which ones worked for him, how they worked with his own Body Cultivation technique—which was based upon achieving oneness with the air itself—and adapt it all.

In theory.

Exhaling, Wu Ying rubbed his eyes. More studying, more testing, more pain. More expense. Because, of course, he would definitely make mistakes. And such mistakes would hurt. Him and his pocketbook.

In truth, he was not entirely sure which would hurt more.

***

More sword practice the next day, finding the beat and rhythm of movement, finding the beauty and joy in the jian rather than elegant simplicity. Seeing the weapon as more than just a weapon. Showing and working with Pan Chen on details of his own style, improving upon it with the child, watching him leap ahead with blinding moments of brilliance as Wu Ying desperately scrambled along behind.

Manuals were tossed from his ring as distractions. While the child studied, Wu Ying practiced the new movements, discerning the dozens of options that each new change offered. Desperately practicing, varying each movement so that he could continue the conversation with the boy genius.

Learning, more than teaching, except for the occasional moment when age and experience, differences in skills and body types and hard-won experience, revealed gaps in Pan Chen's knowledge. A position that might lead to a takedown, a shoulder charge or a spit in the eye from someone all too close.

A day of training, learning and then…

Revelations.

"Exactly why do we both have to be using this at the same time?" Wu Ying grumbled.

He looked around him as the stone cavern heated by bubbling hot springs in the center, running off down one side of the sloped hollow. The water was fed into two circular wooden hot tubs—the only two of the four currently occupied—both of which smelled in terms divine and earthy and musky.

"That's because of the formations," Liu Ping said, raising one languid and much more muscular arm to point at the flags and enchantments inscribed all around the top of the cavern. "They take a lot of spirit stones to empower."

Wu Ying sighed, but he had to admit she was right. Still, it was rather disconcerting to be lounging in the bath beside the woman. Especially considering they were both in their small clothes. Or so he assumed. He certainly was. Liu Ping had been inside her tub when he had arrived, and he had made sure not to look too closely.

"So, that herbal bath. It's the same one you've always used?" Wu Ying said, casting around for a topic.

"For the most part. I had the majority of the herbs available but was missing a few items. The village was kind enough to offer me the use of their stock and suggested some replacements." She traced her fingers along the water, picked up a floating flower, and regarded it in her hand. "It feels… good."

"Good?"

"It's warm. Makes me relaxed and… hungry." There was something dark in her eyes as she stared at Wu Ying. He gulped, uncertain if she meant to eat him or… well. Eat him.

"I'm not Tou He. Don't have food for you…" He remembered what he had in his storage rings. "Well, beyond travel rations."

She made a face. Travel rations—dried and smoked sausage and jerky, dried tofu skin, compressed meat and fat and soybeans or hardened bread—were necessary for the times when you needed it. But no one wanted to eat it. Not if they had a choice. Especially after spending as long traveling as they had.

"It's fine. They'll bring food for me," Liu Ping said, waving languidly.

She swam over to one side of her big bathtub, stood, and reached over the side. Wu Ying's eyes widened a little and he turned away, since she flashed an indecent amount of skin.

"And I always bring my own." When he did not answer, she added, "Catch!"

The wind informed him of a fast-moving object coming at him. He raised a hand, not looking over since the wind had also informed him that she had stood up to throw it. The bao landed in his hand, squishing a little as the outer, soft white covering compressed. The smell of mixed steamed flour with just the hint of the bamboo container made him smile. Along with the smell of the steamed flour was a muskier, female scent that lingered on the bun, one that was enticing for a man who had been… abstinent for a while.

A long while.

"Thank you," he called.

"You're no fun."

A splash as she sat down. Not looking at her helped, but the wind had a way of letting him picture things he did not see, the flow of liquid and warmth, the rising steam from the body as she'd stood. The curves of her body, the water dripping off long hair…

"Teasing me is fun?" Wu Ying said, turning around to rest his arm and head on the edge of the tub now that she was decent.

"Why not?" She grinned. "Why deny what fun we can have? When our lives could end tomorrow?"

"Is that all then, for you? Eating, drinking, sleeping, bathing, having fun?"

"What's wrong with that?"

Remembering what he knew of her bloodline, how she could ascend further... and her own professed disinterest in immortality, he found himself without an adequate answer. "Nothing. But that's not for me."

"Of course. Immortality—or the journey toward it. Why?"

"Why do I want to be immortal?" Brows drawn together, he grew contemplative. "You know, I asked myself that when I first got the chance. Back then, it was to explore. To make the most of the opportunity that was given to me. Because, really, it was never something I had a chance at. A mere peasant becoming a full immortal? What a joke. But now..."

"Now?" Curious now, more than ever. Her voice grew lower, huskier.

"Now, I'd like to be immortal to continue doing what I've done," Wu Ying said softly.

"Meddling in kingdoms? Fighting Core Formation cultivators?"

"Seeing the world." Wu Ying raised his hand, watching water trickle off it and land in the tub. Listened to the wind as it told him the secrets that the village probably never realized he was learning. Secrets that they might not even know, for the earth, the wood, and the heat, they all spoke to him. "Experiencing it. There's so much to learn and see and do."

She made a low, deep-throated noise of encouragement.

"An immortal bloodline, hidden in a village of clansmen and..." He chose not to discuss what else he believed to be here. "Wandering cultivators, a rebellion, conspiracies, and abandoned monasteries... wonders. Large and small."

"You make it almost sound enticing," Liu Ping murmured. He heard another splash, then the burbling of water rising from the hot tub as she let it wash over her face before she pushed upward. "But sleeping and eating seems more enjoyable and less stressful."

Wu Ying snorted, but he could not help but smile a little at the girl. At least she had come to her own realization of what she wanted. Even if, perhaps, a lot of her new personality might be driven by her strengthened bloodline.

Though perhaps a portion of that was because she no longer desired to fight, to struggle, to lose those things that were precious to her. For the tendrils of grief still held her fast, refusing to release her.

"Much less stressful."

***

Day after day, step by step. Wu Ying studied, tested, and bathed. He practiced with Pan Chen, as he expanded upon his style with the aid of the prodigy. Treaded closer to the Heart of his jian and worked his fingers deep into the earth as he grew new spirit herbs and harvested others.

Everything he learned, he used to expand his skills, his world. New formations that helped secure greenhouses were added to his World Spirit Ring. Blocks of rock, taken from long sojourns across the hills beside one of the Pan sisters, were dropped into the ring and carved with new enchantments. Secured and arranged to increase the bounty within.

Wind herbs, drawn forth from his ring, added to his herbal baths as he tested new Body Cultivation mixtures. Dragon bone purchased from scammy merchants, hundred-year-old ginseng, mandrake roots… all meant to enhance the growth and development of the immortal bloodline within himself. To help concentrate and enhance its properties.

No guarantee that it'd improve and develop the wind dragon blood within himself. In fact, as the pixiu had mentioned, it was unlikely to benefit him. Yet he had to try.

And all the while, he continued his Body Cultivation practice. Though the herbal baths were only marginally useful for now. Body Cultivation, after the initial stages, was unlike Soul Cultivation in its lack of proper gradations in strength and development.

In the initial stage, to achieve an Elemental Body—or the first major stage of Body Cultivation—one had to replace portions of one's body, starting from blood, stomach and digestive organs, other organs, skin, muscle, bone, and finally nerves and meridians.

After that, once one had achieved the complete replacement, one would achieve the elemental body. Wu Ying had, mostly, skipped the process thanks to his bloodline and injury—doing the entire thing at once, and only having to refine and clear out minor portions that had not been completed properly.

Now his body was soaked through with wind energy, now he was primed. The Wind Body achieved. After that, each step after the first major milestone saw a Minor, Mid, Major, and Perfected level of perfection for each stage, for each wind.

The gradations of development varied. Just having a Perfected Elemental Body meant nothing, since it just made one receptive to the development of the aspects of the element for later. And what aspects and how far varied, depending on the type of elemental body one chose to build upon.

It was why a good Body Cultivation manual was important, and why it was so expensive. Since the next steps not only involved ensuring the body did not regress, but also enhanced the elements. The inclusion of the elemental spiritual herbs in baths, tonics, and foodstuff helped progress the body further, allowing it to slowly take on more and more aspects of the element.

In his case, due to wind formations being what they were, he needed a mixture of wood and fire aspected herbs, wind aspected herbs, and most importantly, the movement techniques that helped him gain a better understanding and immersion of the various wind chis.

However, while Wu Ying could achieve and draw in the five winds, he was as yet unable to touch upon the sixth and seventh winds—heaven and hell. It was only recently that he had found traces of the heavenly wind and, in finding those traces, absorbed it and made it part of his body.

The sixth wind's body movements were different—rigid and yet expansive. The movements took up the entirety of the space he was within, as though Heaven's wind had always meant to expand, and expand, and expand farther. Yet, rather than the circular movements of the central, or the harsh, explosive attacks of the north, or the energetic movements of the east that blew hard and soft, the Heavenly form was rigid.

Only now, glimpsing heaven on earth—the order that was required to provide rain when necessary, the rise of the sun and the turning of the seasons—for humanity to grow and prosper, did Wu Ying begin to grasp the dao. In the embodiment of the heavenly movement, mixing in with the central and western winds that were so replete here, Wu Ying grew.

The changes, now that he could incorporate the element into his body, were subtle. He grew more flexible, his attacks explosive and piercing. Lighter. Using the Earthly Body, Heavenly Soul method grew ever easier as he developed.

One day, perhaps, he would be as light as a feather, dancing along the clouds. But for now...

For now, he could but move like the winds of the Twelve Gales.

Day after day, step by step, Wu Ying grew in strength until days became weeks and then weeks, months. The world turned outside the village, and rumblings of uprisings, of army posts deserted or destroyed trickled in. Yet in their valley, their lives passed without disturbance.

Till spring finally crept forward.

And the time for growth and contemplation ended and the greater price for the Zhuang clan's aid came due.

Chapter 6

Snow on the ground. Rare, in these hills. Even if they were farther north, it was not by so much that snow would appear regularly, or so he'd been told. Not like the tales of the northern countries, where snow lay on the ground for months on end and feed was hard to come by. Still, the wind spoke of colder weather to arrive, a frost and churning, snow-laded clouds that would stay for days on end. Even the south wind could do little, only the central wind helping to warm the onrushing chill as it arrived.

Wu Ying listened to the elements as he walked, the snap and crackle of frozen grass beneath his feet and the crisp, fresh scent of northern air mixed with scent of burning wood, fresh dung, and the all-pervasive tea leaves. He made his way through well-trodden paths to the central square and the communal kitchen where he had been served his meals for the last few months.

Oh, some cooked and ate at home, but the village provided a regular set of meals for the workers during the winter month. It simplified cooking and eating during this period and ensured everyone—even those who might have had a worse year than usual—were fed.

It was a communal way of taking care of one another, something that Wu Ying's village had not undertaken except during big events. Those who had trouble feeding themselves would not be allowed to starve of course, with dishes and additional meals or caught fish, birds, or ground soya bean provided by those who were more fortunate. But nothing organized, at least—not officially.

Wu Ying knew the whisper network of women often saw to that, in ways that husbands and sons too busy with dealing the fields and woods could not be bothered to do so. Village life, where everyone knew one another. And where the effects of starvation and ignoring small evils were all too plain to see.

So unlike the big cities Wu Ying had passed through and occasionally resided within. Never staying long, for he all too soon found himself uncomfortable within them. Humanity, crowded cheek and jowl together, such that each barely had a pissing pot of their own to use.

Chief Pan found Wu Ying after he had finished his meal, appearing by Wu Ying's side with nary a whisper. Of course, Wu Ying paid attention to the flow of the winds even now, to how his extended spiritual senses spoke of everyone's location. There was no surprise when Chief Pan arrived.

Except, perhaps, in the contents of the discussion.

"Expert Long, your stay has been comfortable?" Chief Pan asked.

"It has," Wu Ying said. "I shall miss the village when I leave in the spring."

"Ah, yes. Of course." Chief Pan nodded. "Pan Chen has informed me he is enjoying the sessions with you. He notes that it has improved his understanding of the jian to fight and work with one who has studied it for as long as you."

"He is overly generous with his praise. Pan Chen's a prodigy unlike any I've ever met," Wu Ying said, true admiration in his voice. It helped that the boy was so enthusiastic and generous with his own knowledge and enlightenment of their shared weapon, such that any lingering jealousy had been squashed. "I'm sure what little I might have offered would have been something he learnt eventually."

"Perhaps," Chief Pan said. "Still, it seems that our current deal has come, mostly, to a finish."

"It has. And when the snows have melted and the flowers bloom, I shall be on my way." Wu Ying raised a single eyebrow. "Unless…?"

"Oh no, we are more than grateful to have you here." Chief Pan waved, dismissing Wu Ying's insinuation. "Your help in hunting some of the local wild beasts as another Core Formation cultivator has done much to improve our safety. Especially in such turbulent times."

"Good, good…" Wu Ying said, then fell silent.

Waiting.

"Well, there is one other thing we might want your aid in." At Wu Ying's open gesture for him to continue, Chief Pan offered a tight half smile. "You probably have an inkling of it. The land below these hills, they are not normal."

Wu Ying nodded.

"They in fact lead to a mystic realm, a place of great riches and power. One that we have safeguarded for many years. But recently…" Chief Pan looked embarrassed. "Well, we have found ourselves unable to access it to the fullest."

"How come?" Wu Ying asked.

"Evolution," Chief Pan replied. "Constant evolution."

***

Days later, Wu Ying stood before the entrance to the mystic realm. The entrance to the realm itself originated from the snake corpse's open mouth. Unlike the unsurprising opening of the entrance, the surroundings brought forth all kinds of revelations.

First was the intricate and highly developed formation that not only hid the mouth but also ensured that any who stumbled upon it would never inform others. The first layer of defenses was a subset of the illusion formation that hid the entrance, making it seem like just another bare slope. Even during the hail-ridden evening, the formation showed no sign of giving way, perfectly mimicking the flow of hail and raindrops down the grass-ridden slopes. It even created illusory water, such that an individual placing their hands against the wet earth would believe it sodden and cold.

A true immortal formation was astounding and frightening. But nowhere near as frightening as the defensive portion of the illusion, for Wu Ying had been allowed to test the defense, only to find himself wandering a three-foot-by-three-foot space, believing himself to be within a deeper, much more distant valley during that period.

The other defenses—the carnage and killing formations, the entrapment and alarm portions—he had been, of course, disallowed from experiencing for his own safety. After all, he had no chance of breaking such a powerful enchantment.

Once the group had passed the formation, Wu Ying stopped to admire the surroundings. Propping open the mouth, a golden pillar stood in the center of the room, dominating the cavern whose depths stretched into the distance, the entire cavity the size of a large mansion.

The walls of the cavern were the bleached white bones of the dead snake's skull, the hardened calcium of the floor beneath softened by a layer of moist soil. Hanging spirit lamps, powered by the remnant chi of the snake's corpse, glowed, shedding a soft yellow-white light that illuminated the surroundings, including the quartet of guards watching over Wu Ying and those destined to enter today.

"Have you satisfied yourself, Expert Long?" Pan Hai, the Fourth Uncle, said testily. The man had grown even more impatient as Wu Ying had asked—and been allowed—to study the formation and the snake corpse.

"One last thing…" Wu Ying murmured. Bending low, he ran his fingers across the earth, letting traces of it fall through his fingers before taking another handful and sniffing it. He stuck out his tongue briefly, tasting the earth too, a motion that made his companions protest.

"That's disgusting! Did your parents never teach you manners?" Liu Ping said, staring at Wu Ying's fistful of earth.

"They did. They also taught me how to gauge good soil," Wu Ying said, letting his hand fall and opening it to deposit the earth. Yet, he also pushed his hand down as he stood, surreptitiously grabbing a handful into his World Spirit Ring.

Pity he could not get more, for he wanted to test it further. Taking more than a handful would be outright theft though. He felt a little bit of guilt at stretching the bounds of hospitality like this, but curiosity drove him on.

After all, from the taste and smell, he knew the soil in this mouth was filled with an unusual chi type. Musky, animalistic—bestial. Similar in some ways to Liu Ping's chi flavor, but drier, less vibrant in a way. A matter of it being dead chi or because it was from a snake and not a bear?

Questions, so many questions.

"Does it taste good?" Pan Chen said, bending his knees and waist a little, one hand dropping toward the ground.

"Ah Chen, do you intend to give up the sword for the hoe?" Pan Yin, standing by the side, asked. The kid flushed, shaking his head. "Then do not copy Expert Long. It is unbecoming."

"For you," Wu Ying said, turning his head and winking at Pan Chen. "I, on the other hand, am just a wandering cultivator and gatherer."

"See. I told you you shouldn't work so hard," Pan Shui, who stood on Pan Chen's other side, faux-whispered to Pan Chen, all the while eyeing her uncle. "Otherwise you don't ever get to have fun. Look at my sister. She's already getting lines because she worries so much."

"Mei mei[22]!" Pan Yin barked at her sister.

Pan Shui ducked her head in chastisement, but her goal had been achieved. Pan Chen, who had begun to frown at not being allowed to do as Wu Ying had, brightened, growing even more amused at the sisters' antics.

Pan Yin and Pan Shui, Liu Ping, the prodigy, the Fourth Uncle, and two other Elders were all part of the group being tasked with this expedition. Both Pan Chen and Pan Shui were here to aid their progress and their martial understanding, a chance to test themselves in relative safety while still risking their lives.

As for Pan Hai and the other two Elders, they made up a significant portion of the village's martial arm, leaving only a few behind to guard the village in their absence. The village with Wu Ying would be fielding a total of three Core Formation cultivators, one of which was Pan Hai. The rest being brought along were at the Peak Energy Storage stage. Pan Yin was the only member who was significantly weaker, but her job was to safeguard and ensure that Pan Chen survived in the event of disaster.

"Good soil," Wu Ying said. "Your cultivators should consider using it for growing spiritual herbs. Or even growing some in here." He looked around the bare ground, frowning a little. "Something Yin-aligned though. Most Yang-oriented herbs would not survive here." Rubbing his fingers together, he raised the dirtied hand and muttered, in thought, "Though any that survived and thrived would be even stronger from the pressure."

"It has been discussed before," Pan Hai said flatly. "It was decided to not risk the mystic realm for such small gains."

"Small?" Wu Ying raised an eyebrow.

Pan Hai gestured forward, indicating the giant double doors of metal that dominated the other end of the cavern. Carvings were inscribed into the metal, enchantments that had been backed up and were part and parcel of the formations that surrounded them. The metal itself was a foreboding dark black, reflecting little light. Hints of its chi wafted through the air to Wu Ying, speaking of something cold and impervious and familiar. Only because he had caught hints of that same wind, that same energy recently.

"What lies behind is where the true treasure lies," Pan Hai elaborated. "If you are done…?"

"One last thing. Please." Wu Ying flashed a smile, walking closer to the doors. "I'm grateful for your patience. But this metal, it's strange. I sense something different about it. Something… unusual."

Pan Shui joined him, closely followed by Pan Chen. Yet it was Pan Chen who dared to touch the metal, fingers running along the raised edges in thought.

---

[22] Little sister pretty much

"This is not earthly metal. It glows, soft and gentle, like the light of the moon, purified in the heat of the sun. It is hard, unyielding in its purpose, but will shelter the world beneath its embrace." Pan Chen's voice was dreamy, as though reciting words that came from not his mind but heart. Grownup words from the nine-year-old. "This metal was forged in—"

"Heaven." Wu Ying finished the thought for the child, nodding. "This is Sky Metal." He shook his head after a moment, staring at the massive doors that were twice again his own height. "Even in the Verdant Green Waters, I have never seen such riches."

Tilting his head upward, he read the formation messages, followed the enchantments. There was something else there, another aspect of the formation beyond Carnage and Illusion and Trapping. Something…

"You need not look too long. You will not understand it," Pan Hai said, making his way to the steps next to the trio. "Our ancestor was only allowed to use so much Star Metal, to leave so much in our care, because of what you cannot read. It is an anti-necromancy formation, to ensure that the body of the snake cannot be used by others."

"Was that a danger?" Wu Ying said, surprised. Surely if it was a danger, many more such formations would be present throughout the world. Rare though it might be for a beast to rise to immortality, there would be thousands of such corpses over the course of history.

"At that time, maybe." Pan Hai shrugged. "The actions of the Heavens above are not for us to question."

Wu Ying grunted, not wanting to directly disagree. On the other hand, if he had a direct ancestor who showed up every few centuries, perhaps he too might have more reverence when questioning the Heavens above.

"Now, are you done?" Pan Hai said.

Wu Ying nodded, drawing a deeper breath, trying to make sure he memorized the smell, the feel of the metal, the hint of the world above. In the meantime, given the go-ahead, Pan Hai and the other Core Formation elder with them began the process of activating and opening the gates. Silent, Wu Ying watched the process, committing as much of what they did, what he felt, what he sensed to memory as he could. In the future, perhaps, this could become the grist for his practice of the Heavenly wind.

Long minutes of chanting and movement, of chi channeled in specific methods into the formation before slowly, locks and chambers within the door released and the doors swung open on silent hinges. So perfectly balanced, the slight breeze from within pushed them apart, moving the entire metal impediment toward Wu Ying.

As the doors opened and light streamed outward, Wu Ying caught the scent. The scent of a different realm. One set apart from the one they had walked upon until now.

A new realm. And with it, the hint of danger within.

Chapter 7

Doors swung closed as Wu Ying stepped across the threshold, slamming shut behind the group. He was the last to enter, having been caught in the process of understanding and memorizing that moment, the momentary transition between realms.

His soul—that tiny, newborn soul trapped and sheltered within his core—trembled at the smell, at the process of progressing from one realm to another. It was not enlightenment, but its close cousin, experience. Understanding, growth, knowledge all filtered within, giving nourishment to the burgeoning soul.

Only the doors closing and the prodding of the—still silent—guards had Wu Ying hurried within. After all, his presence and understanding here was part of the bargain in return for his aid in dealing with the monster that had taken over the mystical realm.

Inside, the world that spread before him was wider and larger than he would have ever believed. Stretching for hundreds of li, Wu Ying could only sense the edges of the realm due to his wind, the air flowing around him and bringing impressions of a world that ended abruptly. Beyond the realm lay nothing, a void of meaningless space that the dao of the world rejected, the earth and the air within pulling away.

Unsurprisingly, the wind was unhappy, used to flowing where it would, moving when it desired. To be constrained, even in an expansive area such as the mystic realm, made it testy, which resulted in Wu Ying's hair and robes being snapped around him.

"A problem, Expert Long?" Pan Hai could not help but ask, seeing the wind's reaction around the cultivator.

"No, not at all." He felt no desire to explain the details of his cultivation, its connection to him, and his wind body.

Head lifted a little, Wu Ying breathed. Another scent here, another wind that he was unused to. Hints of it only, too minor for him to identify it in detail. It shifted, changing from one to another, chaotic and adaptive. By virtue of elimination, it must be the last wind—hell's.

Strange that such a beautiful land, so similar to the one above, was host to the winds of hell. Then again, they were standing—even if it did not look like it—in the corpse of a half-immortal snake. Even if there were sloping, bamboo-forested hills and gullies, flowing water, and high above, a sky filled with clouds, this was not the outside world. There was no sun for illumination, but the snake's bones glowed all around them.

"Is there no day or night cycle?" Wu Ying asked.

Surely there had to be, or the plants around him would be much different. Mutated to live in constant sunlight. And they felt, to his senses, normal. Or as normal as any plant infused with the surfeit of Yin and elemental chi that pervaded this mystic realm.

It did, however, explain why the clan chose not to live here. It could not be good for the mortal form to exist in such a place for extended periods. Especially for children and their like. Even for a cultivator, it would likely pressure their cultivation base and their dao.

"The bones fade in brightness eventually, following the movement of the sun. Our alchemists believe that the bones react to the introduction of Yang energy from the sun, combating the degradation of the corpse by releasing Yin energy," Pan Yin replied, gesturing to the sky with pursed lips. "It's why the light is so much softer than the sun itself."

Wu Ying nodded, breathing in again. This new realm was different and he was adjusting to it slowly. It felt strange to be in a land that was so similar to the one before yet was different on many subtle but fundamental levels.

He wasn't the only one having problems either—Liu Ping and Pan Chen were looking around, adjusting to the world in their own ways. Pan Chen was just walking about, hand on his sword, a tightness in his young eyes. It was amusing to see him out of the context of the training grounds, unsure and uncertain of himself. Across the blade, Wu Ying forgot Pan Chen's youth and inexperience in all things but for the jian. Here, Wu Ying was struck once more that for all Pan Chen's ability and talent, he was still a child asked to take on responsibilities and experience events that none of his peers would be expected to face for at least a decade.

Liu Ping's reaction was more animalistic. She was crouched low, running her fingers across the grass, tearing up clumps and digging into the earth. She spat on the ground, mixed her saliva in it, and then seemingly dissatisfied with the change, shifted a little on her feet.

The woman looked over her shoulder and grinned widely at Wu Ying when she saw him looking. No trace of guilt there, none of the shy or reserved graces of a noblewoman. Still, he was glad she was choosing not to mark the land any further.

"Come. There is much to see and where we must go is still a distance," Pan Hai said, gesturing for the group to follow.

One of the otherwise silent companions took off, moving ahead of the team to scout the area, while the rest of the group followed at a more sedate pace.

It was time to explore the new mystic realm.

***

Travel through the forest was strange for Wu Ying. Thankfully, since they were limited by the speed of the still-in-Body-Cleansing-level Pan Chen, Wu Ying had more than enough time to ascertain the differences. More than once, he stopped to pick herbs or review the changes in the plants that had grown up in this strange environment. Yin-aspected star anise, go-go berries, fennel and lotus roots, three-eared black fungus, and flowers of every kind made its way into his ring or storage boxes.

He wasn't the only one picking the plants though. The others undertook to do some gathering too, though on a more select basis.

"We've got a list," Pan Yin replied, upon questioning. "If we succeed, we will have more than enough time to gather the rest. In the meantime, we'll be taking those items we are most in need of or are extremely rare."

"I won't be as polite," Wu Ying said with a grin.

"Wouldn't expect you to," Pan Yin replied. Then, turning her head, she looked at Pan Chen, who was being accompanied near the back by her sister. "Hurry up, you two!"

"I'm. Doing. My. Best," Pan Chen replied, panting loudly. "I've got to take two steps to your every one!"

"Mmm… more like three to two," Pan Shui said.

"Not. Helping!"

Wu Ying snorted, drew a breath, and let his senses leak out farther. In the distance, he heard a rumbling of power and movement, moments before the flash of blood and violence appeared. The scent of one of the attackers was familiar, musky and feminine, whilst the second was colder, drier. Still, there was no urgency to her scent and the battle was over within moments.

It took them another two li before she returned, the body dragging along behind her.

"Found one!" Liu Ping said, tossing the body beside their feet.

The snake was a constrictor of some form, though its body had altered from living in here so long. Now, only hints of the green of its original shading could be seen, the monster's skin and scales a light jade green that faded into the pale foliage better.

"Yin-aspected snake…" Pan Hai nodded in approval. "But this one looks young. And small."

Nearly a full score feet long and small? Wu Ying snorted a little, though he did not doubt the elder.

"Its Spirit Stone is strange too," Liu Ping replied, hefting the aforementioned crystal.

It was a faceted sphere that gleamed with a dull light instead of the vibrant energy Wu Ying was used to. On the other hand, his senses told him it was brimming with energy, close to breaching into what he would consider the Energy Storage level.

"Don't you think you should be using a weapon?" Wu Ying said as he eyed the weaponless cultivator.

"No. This feels more comfortable," Liu Ping said.

"How. Much. Longer?" Pan Chen, having caught up to the group, panted out.

"Another two days at this pace is where we last saw it," Pan Hai replied.

"Two days!" Pan Chen groaned, while Wu Ying smirked a little. Two days meant a lot more herbs for him to gather.

***

Later that evening, Pan Chen fell asleep almost immediately. Toward the end of the day, Liu Ping and Pan Yin had taken turns carrying the youngster, giving him a break from the relentless hike. Prodigy or not, he was still a child after all.

After a quick and simple meal consisting of rice, foraged herbs and mushrooms, and root vegetables along with roasted snake—the meat donated from the spirit beasts they had fought during the day—the remaining members of the group had retired. Leaving Wu Ying and Pan Shui to stand watch for the first portion of the evening.

"So, you've been avoiding me," Pan Shui said, resting a hand on his elbow and catching Wu Ying, who had been busy penning notes about his experiences, off-guard.

"What?" he said.

"You've been avoiding me," Pan Shui stated again. "What? More interested in my sister?" She put a finger to her chin, almost mockingly thoughtful. "Are you more into older women?"

"No. I've barely seen her too!" he rebutted. Then frowned. "Why am I defending myself to you? You're a child."

"Oh, so you do like older women!"

Memories of some of the older, more mature women in his life flashed through his mind. Fairy Yang, Xiang Wen, Fairy Xi and her stern sister, Liu Tsong… almost all of them older than him. Beautiful, stern, wise…

"Oooh, there's someone, isn't there?" She cackled, watching his face. "Who is it? Someone you've been dreaming about perhaps?"

"No one," Wu Ying said. "A few…" He sighed, thinking of Xiang Wen, Li Yao, the terpochorist… "A few who might have been more. But my path, it takes me far and wide, and it would be unfair to ask another to wait."

"You're an immortal, no? Or on the path to immortality?"

"Yes?"

"Then what's a decade or two?"

Wu Ying opened his mouth to explain, only to pause. She was not wrong on the face of it. It was more complex than that, of course. It was not a matter of just waiting. There were missed opportunities and heartache and longing, painful rejection and moments of burning passion that left one reeling. There was… life passing one by, no matter which way he chose.

Yet, perhaps, it was time for him to stop choosing for others. To stop ignoring the hints and subtle innuendos, the potential for something more than light flirtation. Even if it meant more heartache later on, when or if the relationship failed.

But…

"You might be right." His lips creased up a little. "But you're still too young."

Pan Shui rolled her eyes. "And my sister then?" She crinkled her nose. "I'm sure Father would not mind adding you to the family, so that removes one major objection."

"Why are you so intent in matchmaking for your sister?" Wu Ying asked. Of all the females in the clan, Pan Yin had shown the least amount of interest in him—at least in the sense of a potential mate.

"She's past thirty, you know?" she replied, frowning. "And she might, if she's lucky, make Peak Energy Storage. You know how it is when you've passed that age."

Wu Ying did. The likelihood of Pan Yin breaking through to Core Formation decreased after thirty. Something to do with the hardening of the meridians, the increased inflexibility of the dantian, which was needed in compressing the energy to form the core. Maybe even the firming up of views and insecurities of an individual as they aged, or the hardening of their souls, such that creating a new nascent soul within was more difficult.

A lot of theories, but no one knew for sure. Just that the number who managed to grow a Core after that age dropped significantly.

"I don't understand how that relates to starting a relationship with me though," Wu Ying said.

"She's Father's eldest. And normally, she'd inherit. Become the next Clan Chief. But she's not strong enough, not by herself. If she brought in—"

"Me."

"—someone with strength, then it'd firm her position."

"And love?" Wu Ying said.

Pan Shui giggled, then sobered when she realized Wu Ying wasn't joking. "What has that got to do with anything?" She shrugged. "She's beautiful—if not as beautiful as your martial sister is rumored to be, so you might have a warped sense of what beauty is, but she is beautiful. She'll be a dutiful wife. And…" She lowered her voice. "We don't mind if eyes and hands wander a little, when they're not at home."

Wu Ying's eyes bugged out. He stared at the sixteen-year-old speaking of affairs and cheating with such ease. She giggled then, after a moment, and he relaxed, thinking she was joking. Only to freeze again when she assured him she was not.

Foreign clans. They were always so different.

"I'm sorry, but if I am to marry one day, it will be for other reasons than pure necessity or safety," Wu Ying said. Because that was what would be offered. And really, having this village, this land as a safe haven he could return to… that wouldn't be a bad thing.

"Nor would I have expected you to." Pan Yin's voice caught them both by surprise. Wu Ying more, since the wind had been quiet about her waking or her approach. Even his spiritual senses, normally extended to guard against dangers had not twinged upon her. For she was no danger. Not even now, when a trace of irritation could be heard in her voice. "I can account for my own affairs, Ah Shui."

Pan Shui grinned unabashedly. "No, you can't. You nearly married that ugly lump of a Ciu, just because he was the chieftain's son." She smirked. "I got you out of that one."

"If I recall, it was more Pan Mu."

Muttering softly, Pan Shui added, "I came up with the idea!"

"I'm sorry my troublesome younger sister bothered you about this," Pan Yin said. "It was clear you were neither interested nor likely to agree. Which is why I and my father chose not to pursue the option."

Again, Wu Ying felt a little disoriented. Of course she could not choose by herself. She was, after all, the chief's daughter. Still… "And what happens to you then? If you are not able to progress your cultivation or marry someone suitable?"

"Leading the clan has never been purely about strength—"

"Though it helps," Pan Shui muttered.

"—but wisdom and foresight. Contributions." She gestured around them. "In the end, the Elders will decide, and I will abide by their decision. I can—I will—aid whoever they choose. Even if that person is too young and foolish at times."

He traced her gaze over to Pan Shui and another flower of knowledge blossomed in his mind. "That's why you're so anxious. You're trying to dodge responsibility!"

"I'm not!" Pan Shui automatically protested. Then, after a second, she shrugged. "Maybe a little. I'd make a horrible chief."

"Probably," he agreed.

"Almost certainly," her sister chimed in at the same time.

"Hey!" Offended, Pan Shui puts her hands on her hips. She had spoken out of modesty and some degree of self-knowledge, but for the pair to agree so readily still stung.

The pair glanced at one another before laughing, making the younger girl grow even more furious. Still, it was clear that the awkward conversation of marriage was over.

Though in the hours afterward, Wu Ying wondered how long it would be before Pan Chen was raised as a potential replacement.

***

What was it about monsters that looked like mortal man at a distance but were, upon closer inspection, not that twisted Wu Ying's stomach? Was it their twisted mockery of humanity and the immortals? Or the mockery of the natural order of things, for these existences were often devolved or failed evolutions of a beast?

Or was it just that every such creature had attempted to sink their talons into his flesh, rob him of his life, and sup on his immortal soul? That certainly was more than sufficient reason for him to find such creatures disturbing.

Easily deflecting a taloned finger swipe, Wu Ying riposted, sinking blade into throat. He tore his jian out with a twist of his wrist, using his greater strength and the excellent sharpness of his weapon to open its throat with contemptuous ease. As his sword left the monster's neck, he pulsed his aura and chi, leaving behind a swirling globe of air that tore through the monster's aura and widened the wound further.

Stepping back, Wu Ying watched the blood arc through the air, the familiar smell of rust and musk filling the air. Minor goblets moved to strike him, only for the wind eddies around his aura to deflect the corruption.

He held back, just like the other Core Formation elders, as the others in the retinue battled the twisted mockeries of snakes and humans. He had held back on instinct at first, but now he held back from greater understanding.

Lead without leading.

Of them all, Pan Chen struggled the greatest, having to bypass not just the absolute difference in strength of rank but also size. His attacks, laced with preternatural sharpness, still lacked the edge, the killing intent of a seasoned fighter, often leaving creatures wounded when they should be slain.

Yet for all that, the child who had the Heart of the Jian was an elusive ghost, sensing attacks before they had even begun moving, positioning himself and his weapon such that his opponents were forced to compromise speed, strength, or timing to reach him.

And if he might take two or three strikes to kill an opponent, he was as elusive and flexible as the weapon he bore.

Liu Ping, on the other hand, marked the polar opposite of his tactics. Having chosen to discard the use of any weapon, she barreled through the monsters, taking injuries by the dozen, a brownish-red glow around her as the bloodline chi of her evolved form created a defensive formation of magical fur and muscle. With strength triple, quadruple those of any cultivator at her stage, each of her blows crushed the snake-men below her black claws of bestial energy. She rampaged along one corner of the shrunken diamond formation, tossing the beasts aside with each attack.

On the other side, fighting smoothly together, the pair of sisters controlled the monsters coming at them. Spears stabbed, cut, and drove back snake-men, enforcing the distance and ensuring that none could near them without injury and a fatal wound. Though outpaced by her sister, Pan Yin held her own, her occasional slipups covered smoothly by Pan Shui.

A flick of Wu Ying's hand sent an arc of energy striking and driving back an opponent. His jian came back to defense as he and Pan Hai held the tip and sides of the diamond together, forcing the creatures to attack the others.

Alone or together, the Core Formation cultivators could have finished the war party themselves. An exertion of will, a focused series of strikes. But in doing so, they would deprive those beneath them of a chance to grow.

Standing in the center of the maelstrom, watching chi and blood and killing intent fly, Wu Ying found light shed upon his previous journeys. The battles during his first and subsequent expeditions with Core Formation Elders in formation, their actions and the strength they had exhibited.

And his own now.

How much had they held back? How much did they see, judge, and choose to happen, to allow their juniors to rise or fall by themselves? The jianghu was a harsh world, where strength spoke loudly and the weak were forced to bow their heads. Honor and courage might carry one far, but strength rose triumphant in the dark of the night.

Without testing, cultivators could never grow. Without risk, the opportunities for enlightenment faded. Without strength, the weak would run amok until karma trod upon them.

Another monster, another opponent, another strike. Hold back, watch. Save them when they needed it, if he could reach them, so that lessons may be learned and applied in the future. Watch as the saplings struggled and matured, growing stronger and fertilizing their growth with the blood of their enemies.

And if that was not a condemnation of the society that heaven, the jianghu, and fate had created, Wu Ying did not know what else it could be.

Chapter 8

Early morning mists were more common in the mystic realm, the tendrils of water cloying and seeping through clothing with casual disregard, leaving cultivators shivering in the false bone light. From the conversations Wu Ying overheard, the mist was a new phenomena in the mystic realm, a change that had happened in the last few decades. Muttered grumblings about disrupted control formations and over-abundance of water chi were the main sources of such information, but Wu Ying found himself all too lost as the elders went into greater detail.

As much as he struggled to understand the details of formation creation, the intricate minutiae of the scaffolding and strengthening of barriers in a mystic realm was on a whole other level of complexity. It was the difference between building a single-story peasant hut with mud walls and a simple roof and the multi-story pagodas that dominated cities and temples.

One required an eye for basic physics and the following of traditional forms and formats. Every farmer had helped their neighbors or family in the rebuilding or construction of such a building at least once in their lifetime. There was nothing too intricate in such work.

On the other hand, a pagoda was a multi-story affair, one requiring exacting measurements and well-cut joints. Understanding the kind of woods to use, support beams, and structural loads were an artform that no peasant was privy to.

Still, a peasant who worked on the construction of the pagoda might learn a thing or two. And Wu Ying was always good at listening and learning, borrowing pieces of knowledge that might come in use in the future. He still would not dare construct a pagoda himself, but luckily, he already owned one.

A mystic realm that was, not a pagoda.

He just needed to help control its flow.

Late at night, when the others slept, he delved into his World Spirit Ring, testing boundaries and comparing his senses. Perhaps pagodas and huts were a bad metaphor. For if the mystic realm was an edifice of formations, built upon the corpse of a half-Immortal snake, his World Spirit Ring was a nascent palace.

What he was doing was not so much adjusting the outer walls, the shoring and moorings of the mystic realm, but instead pulling down internal walls and putting up inner partitions. Dictating the flow of traffic within, breaking off portions for specific uses.

Interior design, if you would.

After nearly a week of travel, they finally reached their destination, passing through cloudy landscapes and dense foliage alike. They moved more quietly now, the presence of their prey close at hand. Over the last few days, they had sensed it, the pressure of the Nascent Soul-level monster's core exerting force upon all those present.

Conversely to base expectations, rather than having fewer monsters to battle, they found themselves beset on the regular by ever more members of the snake-men tribe. Rather than waste their members' energy, the Core Formation cultivators exerted themselves to a greater extent, striking down the monsters in greater numbers as they were attacked.

Yet eventually, the sheer numbers of snake-men drew such concern that they chose to hide their presence, the Elders and Wu Ying expanding their auras to dampen the energy surrounding the other cultivators. Along with Wu Ying's wind techniques, they actively avoided battles as they delved deeper.

Finally, they arrived in a small clearing, their prey within a couple of li. Feeling the pressure of the energy, the group triggered a series of silencing talismans before conversing.

"It's around here. A Nascent Soul snake whose birth within the mystic realm has leapfrogged its journey to immortality. A mutation, greater in strength than anything we had ever expected to deal with," Elder Pan Hai murmured, the Fourth Uncle trying to rouse their morale. "It is this monster, hidden in the depths of our birthright, wily and camouflaged, that grew without our knowledge. We learned of it only when it struck with great viciousness and drove us out of this mythic realm at great cost.

"Today, we take back what is ours. Today, we take back our heritage. Today, we take back our land!"

The last words were hissed, fury and long-held impotence dancing in his eyes.

The group acknowledged his words with nods and stamps of their feet. The snake was the entire reason for their journey here after all. If they had more time, the clan would likely have waited for Pan Cheng to breakthrough to at least Energy Storage. What was a half a decade, when they had lost their mythic realms already for half a century? But recent events including the tournament had driven them to this, and with Wu Ying's addition, the clan could attempt to take back their mythic realm while keeping guard of their territory in the real world.

"Check your Hundred Li talismans. If things grow too dangerous, retreat." Pan Hai's gaze fell on Pan Chen. "Stay close to Pan Yin. If she informs you to run, do so. You are under her command. And remember, she has a Nine Lantern Shield formation."

Pan Chen looked, briefly, angry before he calmed himself and bowed in agreement. Pan Hai nodded, then looked at Liu Ping, frowning.

"I know. I'll try to be careful and control my bloodline." The wandering cultivator grinned. "But when it gets aroused, it's hard to control. A bear, once angry, is not easily calmed."

The elders of the village snorted at her reply, but no one chose to gainsay her. Not only was she correct, in the end, she was just hired help. Her choices were her own. While they might dislike the outcome if she died, it was her path to walk. She was not family after all.

Just like Wu Ying.

"We three Core Formation fighters will pin down the monster. It will be up to the rest of you to implant the formation flags for the Nine Heavenly Spear Slaughter Formation. While we might win a straight battle, there is no reason to do so."

No further talk was required. After all, this was just a reminder of what they had discussed before.

A brief gesture, and the silencing talismans faded. Wu Ying nodded one last time to the group then took to the skies, flowing far ahead of the team. He pulled at the wind, sending it gusting out in all directions. He released his control of his aura at the same time as he searched, the curls of mist pushing away from them all to reveal the land and monster below.

Playing bait for their target.

***

It came, rising from the mists. Its head was the size of a large mansion, its body nearly half a li across and multiple li long. It was enormous, white and yellow scales that faded into the mist and the low light of the surroundings. A monstrous, powerful creature whose strength had grown with each decade, viperish fast.

Head extended, mouth wide as it stretched toward Wu Ying. No poison—it was not that kind of snake. Big, long, crushing. It would batter him aside, entrap his body, and swallow him whole if it could, but it would not poison him.

Small graces.

He floated backward, using the air it disturbed to aid him as he retreated. Sword in hand, he concentrated his attack, unleashing the projection of blade, wind, and killing intent to strike the monster as it finished its initial attack.

Scales split and blood flowed as Wu Ying's attack left a long wound along the tip of its mouth. The creature jerked back and hissed, the mist beneath boiling over as it shifted.

Already, Wu Ying formed another blade strike, darting to the side as the creature recovered. The aim of the game was not to kill, but to injure and keep its attention. Thrice more, the pair played fly and fly swatter, the monstrous head shifting and darting through the air. Blood, pale white-yellow, dripped from wounds, cast through the air in tiny rainfalls as Wu Ying's attacks wounded the monster.

Then, it paused. Pulled back.

Intuition had Wu Ying darting higher, his footsteps still a little uneasy in the air but stronger, more stable than ever. He danced on footsteps of air as his lightened body floated like a leaf.

Eyes, lidless, stared at him. Killing intent, honed over centuries, lanced outward. No dodging it, no way to avoid. Wu Ying was struck by the honed ego and soul of the creature, projected through its gaze. He froze for a moment before he dropped, his chi flow disrupted.

Paralyzed, he could only watch as the monster angled its head, tracking his fall as it waited for him to come down. Incapacitated by its soul, he waited for his death.

The snake blurred as it struck, head darting forward to swallow him. Only for the entire body to be thrown aside as a spear cast directly upward speared its head. The snake missed

Wu Ying by a dozen feet—all too close for something so big, so fast—as the Saint-level spear pierced scales and tore into the monster's body.

Killing intent disrupted, Wu Ying churned his chi, attempting to control his descent, righting himself and lightening his body. Insufficient time to stop his body from ploughing into the ground, for skin and flesh to bruise as he bounced along the grassy slopes. Time enough to ensure he was only mildly injured, not killed.

Another spear, thrown upward, caught the monster as it turned and twisted, searching its new prey. It found Pan Hai wielding a third spear, already angling forward to cast it. The snake flinched, and the spear lodged just above its eyelid. Then it lunged, even as Pan Hai extracted a fourth weapon. On his feet, Wu Ying struggled to form an attack to save the Elder.

Moments before the snake struck, earth rose. The third Core Formation Elder formed a long rise in the ground that the monster ploughed into, embedding itself, compressing loosely packed earth and slowing with each second. Its head rose, bouncing off the earth, leaving Pan Hai to sink another spear into its soft underbelly.

Earth, churned and twisted, rose farther, trapping and slowing the monster's upper body. Earth mixed with water, turning into boggy mud that pulled and sucked at the monstrous reptile, slowing it.

Wu Ying took to the air again, casting attacks from his weapon onto the monster's upper body even as the Mud-aspected Core Formation elder pulled the creature into the ground, trapping it. Pan Hai backed way, joining Wu Ying in the sky as the pair drew the snake's attention with their attacks.

Each attack was no more than a pinprick, but painful pinpricks.

Attention drawn to them, the other members of their party took to the battle, focusing their attention on the trapped portions of the body. They struck as a team, Liu Ping tearing off defensive scales with her greater strength, the pair of other Peak Energy storage elders and Pan Shui embedding formation flags in the revealed locations. And all the while, called forth to the monster's defense, snake-men rushed the team, held off by Pan Yin and Pan Chen.

All according to plan.

Wu Ying darted back and forth, wielding his sword. He dodged within a foot of the creature that attacked him and, with a push of energy, landed on the monster's scales. He ran along the body, a rushing wind holding him tight to its scales as he plunged his sword in, hardening and sharpening its edge such that it tore into the monster in a six-foot long cut.

A sudden, hard shake threw him off, then, in the air, forced to block the swinging body with his own weapon and a cushion of wind. Yet before it could attack Wu Ying again, Pan Hai was on it, driving a spear into the snake's body, all the way to where his back hand held it still.

Another hiss and scream.

The snake turned back toward Wu Ying, but he had gusted upward, higher and higher. Another spear, drawn from a spirit ring, was plunged through another scale. Unable to fight the wind cultivator, hampered in its movement, it turned on Pan Hai.

Allowing Wu Ying to ready himself. He pulled the air toward his body, building up the wind. He launched himself downward, sword trailing behind him as he cut across the lower half of the monster's body with his extended spirit blade and energy, such that he would not shatter his weapon on chi-hardened scales.

He passed within feet of his friends who fought, pulling upward even as blood gusted after him, the wake of his flight tossing snake-men into the air. Then, momentum arrested, he swooped into the air, touching upon his Core and checking on the stores of energy.

Wu Ying grimaced, for he had used too much for that showy—if effective—attack. A moment's debate, even as the Never Empty Wine Pot churned, drawing in yin-aspected chi, fire and wind and wood and more, all transforming into his own as it ran through his meridians. He cut the flow of energy to the wind, to his qinggong technique, and landed on the ground.

Footsteps, the Twelve Gales, took him forward to join the fight for a little while. It was time to conserve energy, for this was a battle of endurance rather than flashiness.

Chapter 9

Formation flags in the shape of spears were embedded in the body of the snake along its sinuous length. Drawing energy and intent from the body it was embedded within, the spears glowed with divine mortality, empowered by the snake's own chi.

Standing a short distance away from the cold, scaled form, Pan Shui clutched a broken arm, infusing the last of her chi into the activation token clasped around her neck. Beside her feet lay the broken body of the third village elder, his breathing raspy and pained.

Triggered by the enchanted trigram switch, the formation snapped into being. White lines of power blossomed from the ends of each jutting formation flag, stringing together across the lower half of the creature's body to form a powerful, energetic net.

Riding on the tip of the monster's nose, sword embedded in the monster's flesh, Wu Ying watched the proceedings. He breathed heavily, his churning dantian dragging forth energy from all around as he hid in the one place the monster could not see well.

The snake had learned not to attack him—not with its tongue at least. The fast-moving flicking appendage had been chopped and cut, parted with sword slices and almost pinned by a spear. Now, the snake paid more attention to its other assailants so long as Wu Ying stayed there, resting.

Of course, at this moment, it was more focused on the net that wrapped around its torso, constricting and burning. Instinctively, it thrust its spirit against the woven web, chi pulsing outward as it concentrated its aura.

But the spears were embedded in the monster, bypassing portions of its defense. As the final strands of power linked together, the formation flag spears drove themselves deeper into the monster, pulsing as the net tightened. Aura battled formation, holding the net apart.

"Retreat!" Pan Yin cried, grabbing hold of the elder who lay on the ground, ignoring his cries of pain.

Being so close to the monster as it thrashed would crush them all. Pan Chen led the retreat, the small boy cutting through snake-men with alacrity, pouring all the reserves of his chi into the attack.

In the distance, Pan Hai hissed and threw another spear, the weapon punching into the snake's eye as it was distracted. Half-blinded as the metal chi within the spear aided his throw, the snake twisted its head furiously in an attempt to dislodge the spear.

A pulse of energy from the formation, and the spear slid deeper as the creature was distracted. Wu Ying understood now, and he too acted. The eye, so massive, would not be completely blinded by a single spear. Still, riding the thrashing monster, Wu Ying let himself be thrown aside before he kicked off a platform of air. He no longer floated through the air, unable to endure the consumption of chi flight required. Instead, he used short-term wind platforms to allow him to maneuver.

He plunged forward toward the injured eye. He watched the creature flinch, throwing itself upward and out of range. Another kick angled him sideways and away from the twisting head, then another and he was at the eye.

It pulled backward, but Wu Ying sheathed his sword. It was not the eye he intended to use, but the spear already embedded within. He grabbed the shaft, allowing his body weight and momentum to rip it out of the eye socket, widening the wound.

Seconds before the tip exited, Wu Ying pulsed his wind chi deep into the wound, exploding the injury. The monster hissed and thrashed as he used the weapon in another strike, watching as bamboo bent and twisted, sling-shotting him off into the distance as the snake swung at him and missed.

Formation flags, pulsing with increasing rapidity, had tightened deeper and deeper into the body. Another pair of spears were embedded in the snake's sinuous form, even as giant mud hands slammed at the aura, crushing it and the formation flags.

Then…

Finally, the explosion.

A slaughter formation, empowered by the flesh and blood of a Nascent Soul-level beast, driven deep into scaled flesh. Flames and metal, the formation pulled metal chi from the air and formed blades of metal chi within the body itself. Heat increased, burning flesh as the formation burrowed deeper and deeper, giant metallic shards turning against pale-green and yellow scales.

When the extent of its contained energies, the durability of its components, gave way, the metallic hedgehog-spears of the formation flag exploded. The explosion drove chi-created metallic blades into the body of the monster, tearing flesh and muscle, scales spinning through the air.

Landing on a nearby tree branch, Wu Ying crouched, shielding his eyes from the grit blown outward. He chose not to waste his chi blocking the attacks, listening to the screams, the eruptions, and the pulse of blood to the ground, the squelch of falling meat, and smelled the mixture of iron and dry, musk of the serpent.

"Use the token, you fool!" Pan Yin's voice, coming from the distance.

Wu Ying turned his head, spotting the group hiding beneath an earthen redoubt. The injured village elder was gone, only Pan Chen and Pan Shui still standing, both of them looking exhausted. Monster corpses from the snake-men littered the surroundings, a few stirring but most senseless after the explosion had tossed them aside. Liu Ping bounced around them, looking worse for the wear but focused on finishing off their enemies before they recovered.

Merciless.

"Why? We can finish the other snakes too!" Pan Chen protested, even as his sword hand shook.

Pan Shui nodded, though she leaned heavily on her weapon.

"You promised!" Pan Yin roared, stabbing a finger at him. "Do it, or else I'll tell Father and you'll never be allowed to do this until you're… you're… eighteen!"

Pan Chen hissed but nodded, pulling out the token. Pan Shui looked just as stubborn but copied his action. Before they could act further, a sibilant hiss issued forth through the hills, fear and rage pulsing in the echoes such that the pair froze, unable to move.

Wu Ying twisted his head back toward where the snake had been shrouded by dust. Only to see it, revealed and alive.

"What does it take to kill that thing?" Pan Yin protested weakly in the distance.

Liu Ping answered with a low growl, but Wu Ying's focus was no longer on them.

The monster was injured, that was clear. Gouges in the flesh, some the size of a shield and as deep as a sword, leaked blood. Flesh and scales were scattered all around. Wounded, but the unnatural vitality of a Nascent Soul-level beast kept it alive, kept it moving.

It screamed, and its killing intent layered over its aura, slamming into everyone. Even the snake-men were affected, falling to the ground, eyes and noses and ears bleeding as their auras were crushed.

Beneath Wu Ying, the cultivators writhed on the ground, their tokens fallen. Pan Chen coughed, groaning as he suffered deeper injuries from the attack than anyone else. Instinctively, Wu Ying sought to protect him, blanketing the area below with his aura.

Wu Ying fought against the stronger aura with his own, years of practice coming to his aid. The unrelenting pressure could not be stopped entirely, but as it compressed him and his aura, it also helped strengthen his aura, making its protection stronger.

"Move!" Wu Ying snarled at the group, his knuckles white as he gripped his weapon all too tightly. Energy gushed from his Core, his body and soul buckling as he sought to protect them all. A slow dribble of blood trickled down one nostril, but he had no time to pay attention.

Pan Yin reached into her robes, extracting a series of formation flags. She threw them out, grounding the flags and activating them. A second later, the protective enchantment burst in place, the powerful single-use formation empowered by multiple beast cores embedded in the flags.

Pressure relieved, the group were able to sit up a little further. All but Pan Chen, whom Pan Shui approached, checking the child. Her eyes grew dark, her head lifting to meet her sister's gaze even as she pulled out healing pills to stuff into his mouth.

"We can't leave this place," Pan Shui said fearfully. "He's too injured. If we move him, his internal injuries…"

"Then we stay and keep him safe," Pan Yin answered. She gripped her spear tightly, lifting it in the direction of the snake that had turned baleful eyes on them.

Its attack thwarted, it looked to have changed tactics, intent on crushing them as it reared upward.

"Good…" Liu Ping, on her feet, grinned widely. Her bestial aura burst to life, covering her in faux red fur as she charged out of the formation without hesitation, picking up speed with each second.

Above, Wu Ying growled and took to the air, cursing the fool of a child. Cursing the Clan Elder for letting him come, thinking this was safe. It was a damn Nascent Soul-level spirit beast, grown strong in a mystic realm. Of course there would be problems.

Swearing under his breath, Wu Ying flew forward as swift as an arrow, passing the charging Liu Ping within seconds. They were not the only fighters still in the battle. A giant pillar of stone shot upward, catching the snake as it darted downward. Its massive form shadowed the group as it fell, the pillar like a staff thrust into an opponent's mid-section.

The pillar caught the monster as it dropped, chi-reinforced granite and clay smashing deeply into the monster's body. The attack was sufficient to bounce the monster upward and aside.

Buffeted by the winds stirred into chaos by the formation, the giant snake, and the suddenly formed pillar, Wu Ying rode the winds and changed direction easily. Liu Ping chose to rush up the twenty-foot column even as it cracked, searching for greater height. Nearby, the elder who had formed it fell backward, resting against the ground as his Core guttered low with chi.

Flitting forward, Wu Ying darted toward the monster. He spotted an eye, still open, still seeing, and zipped toward it. Still stunned from the earthen attack, the snake reacted too slowly as Wu Ying passed by, dragging his sword across the gleaming orb and sending tendrils of air within the cut, bursting the orb.

Spinning around, he landed on a column of solidified air and threw himself at the body, seeking an open wound to continue the attack. Even as he flew forward, a cry arose from beneath his leaping form.

"Heaven Splitting Spear!" Elder Pan Hai, having taken the time and distraction offered, flew upward, gripping a new weapon. He struck an open wound, the formed energy of his spear intent thrusting deeply into the gaping injury, widening as he burrowed deeper within. Then with a twist of weapon and body, Pan Hai exerted his energy to explode the chi and flesh outward, tearing away chunks of skin and scale from the inside.

Letting out another sibilant, angered hiss, rearing backward unsteadily on its deeply wounded torso, the snake uncoiled its tail briefly to strike the falling elder in the side. It sent him spinning in the distance, the snake's center of gravity disrupted from its movement.

And for a moment, it revealed the widened, opened wound to Wu Ying.

No choice, no other protectors left for the child. Knowing he had to do it, Wu Ying chose to unleash his last, reserved attack. The first cut of his self-made style.

A Wandering Dragon.

The first form was a cut meant to part, to sever heaven from earth, to banish the pathways blocking the passage of the dragon that chose to travel. It contained his understanding of the winds, their strength, their purpose, their fury.

And it was incomplete, even now.

Pain racked his body, the lack of completion of his dao, of his understanding of his own form punishing him as the heaven's leftover chi attack reminded him of his failings.

Still, incomplete or not, the attack was sufficient.

The projection of dao and sword intent tore most of the way through the softened, injured torso. Burrowed within, it severed spine and nerves to leave the Nascent Soul snake to fall, unable to control its body any longer. It lay bleeding, its lower body thrashing in pained instinct. Its head and upper body fell downward, injured eyes sightless as its long tongue flickered in impotent fury.

Liu Ping pounced from the pillar, falling onto the top portion of the snake, crushing its nose before she pounded on the skull. Unable to retaliate, the monster could only thrash weakly as she finished the job, ending the already dying beast.

Wu Ying, landing on a tree to watch Liu Ping, could not help but comment. "Kill-stealer. It was already dead, you know."

Of course, Liu Ping never answered him, reveling in the death of the monster, soaking herself in its blood. That she let out low, happy growls through the entire process was not at all disturbing.

Not at all.

***

Wu Ying alighted on the ground not far from the talismans, staring through the shimmering curtain of energy. He couldn't enter the defensive hexagon, so he was forced to watch helplessly as the sisters cared for the injured Pan Chen. They fussed over his body, carefully shifting him after ascertaining doing so would not injure him further. They applied warmed cups[23] across his skin to draw the bad blood and blocked chi to the surface and then warm compresses to extract it entirely.

Biting her lip, the other elder applied acupuncture needles into the body, a small scroll by Pan Chen's side that she referred to continuously. Occasional muttered curses erupted from the group as Pan Chen thrashed, surging chi from the pills he had been forced to consume washing through his injured body, healing and damaging at the same time.

---

23 Reference is to "cupping," a traditional Chinese medicine where warmed ceramic or glass cups are heated on the inside, then applied to bare skin. The warmed cup creates a minor suction element, drawing "bad blood" to the surface of the body and leaving big red marks across it.

Robbed of movement and tiny intensity, the boy looked like the child he was. Tears leaked from his eyes, uncontrolled as he choked back moans of pain. All the while, the girls murmured words of encouragement and instruction to cultivate the pill.

Staring from outside, Wu Ying tapped his foot impatiently. He wanted to be in there, though in truth, beyond proximity, he had nothing to offer to the proceedings. After all, he was no physician.

It took nearly a half dozen minutes before Pan Hai came to Wu Ying's side, the man covered in dirt and sap, favoring one side as he limped. Surveying the damage, the man hissed.

"Da Ge[24]'s going to kill me if he dies," Pan Hai muttered. "Or if his cultivation is damaged."

Wu Ying turned his head, distastefully regarding the man. The child was injured, and all Pan Hai could think was how it affected him?

"Don't look at me like that. You were happy to have him here too."

Wu Ying's eyes narrowed, and he shrugged.

"Or at least didn't protest too loudly. He needed to be blooded. And we needed the help."

"Did we? Did we really?" Wu Ying gestured back toward the body. "The carnage formation was of great aid, but if we had taken another trio of Energy Storage cultivators, they could have protected the women while they planted the flags."

"I think you downplay his contribution too much," Pan Hai said. "Look at the girls. They're exhausted, and they are some of our best. One who has the Heart of the Sword requires much less energy to deal the damage he did." Another gesture at the corpses of snake-men all around. The few alive had slunk off, leaving only the heavily wounded and dead remaining. "Maybe if we had brought a half dozen others, but you know why we didn't."

Wu Ying sighed but nodded. Truth was, the clan had been deadly worried they might be attacked. Securing the future was of no use if, in the present, all had been destroyed.

In the end, the past was full of regrets. He bundled them up, pulling them from the corners of his mind, and sliced them away before throwing them into the wind with an exhaled breath. By the time he had settled his mind, the earth cultivator had made his way over, looking utterly miserable but at least on his feet.

The group offered one another simple greetings, while Wu Ying, with nothing better to do, manipulated the wind. Using his sword intent and the winds, he tore open the snake-men corpses chests and extracted their spirit stones, bundling them in unsteady globes of wind.

The process was slow and painful, costly in terms of energy, but he chose not to leave this area yet. Not while the child still breathed and the sisters treated him. After what seemed like long minutes, as Wu Ying realized that careful control and guidance of the wind was a losing

---

[24] Da Ge – Big brother directly translated. Older brother in general. Formal form of address to the eldest brother. Sometimes also laodage.

subject, at least with his current level of cultivation, Pan Yin approached the edge of the formation.

"He's stable," Pan Yin said.

"And his cultivation base?" Pan Hai asked.

"It seems undamaged," Pan Yin said. "But we're not physicians. Until he awakens, we won't know for sure. Still… the fact that he was in Body Cleansing might have actually been good."

Pan Hai raised an eyebrow.

It was the other elder who nodded thoughtfully and spoke. "If he had a Core or was in the process of growing his dantian, he might have damaged either. But Body Cleansing is the lowest form, and clearing his meridians is unlikely to be damaged by the spiritual pressure our opponent asserted."

"Then the only other worry is mental demons," Wu Ying said, eyes hooded.

Mental demons, nightmares, psychic damage. Call it what you would, but he had seen the effects over the years, when once-promising cultivators were so damaged by events that they no longer dared tread the path. After all, the journey to higher cultivation levels was one of constant struggle and pain.

"Pan Chen's strong. He won't have any," Pan Hai said dismissively.

The other elder nodded in agreement. On the other hand, Pan Yin was much more subdued, a fact that Wu Ying noted in silence. The elders of the village were so excited, so enthused by the idea of a potential Sword Saint, they forgot all too often that the child prodigy was still a child.

"I could take the formation down," Pan Yin said, choosing to ignore the two elders and waving at the flags, "but we should let the medicines and ointments work in peace. Now that he is stable, there's no point in moving Pan Chen."

The group nodded, eyes flicking over the flags that still glowed. It was powerful enough to protect against a Nascent Soul Spirit Beast; it would be powerful enough to protect against any other beasts that lurked in this mystic realm.

Even as their thoughts reached that point, Liu Ping wandered over, blood dripping from the sleeves and hem of her robes, her face streaked with dark red, drying liquid and splatters of white and grey matter. She held in one hand a glittering, faceted, rough orb. The spirit stone of the snake throbbed, pulling and twisting at the environmental chi as it lay in her hand.

"I took it out. But we should collect some of its meat too. It's quite tasty," Liu Ping said, entirely unself-conscious about the state she was in. She bounced the stone in her hand. "So who has the storage box for this?"

"I do," Wu Ying said, extracting the jade storage container. He inserted the stone within, sealing away its presence and its effect on the world.

Pan Hai met the gaze of the other elder, the two communicating silently through shared understanding. After a few widened eyes, flicking glances, and subtle nods, Pan Hai turned to Wu Ying and Liu Ping. He smiled genially.

"It seems we have some hours left. There are numerous corpses that still need to be processed, however," Pan Hai said. "And we do not wish those remaining monsters to grow stronger. If you can process those slain, we will hunt down the remainder snake-men."

Wu Ying could not help but snort mentally. He knew what they were doing. Semi-intelligent creatures often had lairs, treasures they kept. If they could find it—without Liu Ping or Wu Ying—they could keep it for themselves.

On the other hand…

"Of course," Wu Ying said, looking at Liu Ping for confirmation.

She grinned. "If someone lends me a storage ring, I'll process the snake. Even if you left large holes across it, I'm sure some of its scales could still be used. And the meat."

Wu Ying nodded, handing over one of the many rings he had collected over the years. One of the few advantages of having the dark sect targeting him.

Liu Ping happily trundled away, stopping only long enough to form black claws to tear open corpses and extract their spirit stones, now that she had a proper place to store the materials.

Not to be outdone, the pair of elders disappeared, leaving with a nod to Wu Ying.

Now alone, Pan Yin spoke up from inside the ring, eyes glittering with amusement. "You're being very accommodating."

"My agreement didn't cover treasures other than what I gather myself." He grinned, gesturing at the corpses. "And there's quite a bit to gather."

"Hey!" Pan Shui shouted, wandering over and waving her hands. "I killed those!"

"I?" Pan Yin said dangerously.

"We. We…" Pan Shui ducked away before her sister could hit her. "But you're not stealing all that. Are you?" She hefted her spear, eyeing Wu Ying with an evil grin. Of course, he knew—as did she—that the threat was not serious. After all, his secret of his cultivation base had long ago been revealed.

"Not all." He gestured around him. "But many fell because of the snake itself. I'll leave you… hmm… half?" He grinned, nodding to himself. "Yes. Half that I collect."

"Half!" Pan Shui yelped, stepping forward and stopping at the edge of the formation. She hopped from one foot to the other, torn between watching over Pan Chen and stopping Wu Ying from stealing her rightful loot.

"Go. I can watch over him," Pan Yin said. "There's little else to be done right now anyway."

Pan Shui required no other encouragement, darting out immediately, the shimmering curtain of energy allowing her to exit. Laughing to himself, Wu Ying let the wind carry him toward the first corpse, dagger in hand, and he began the gruesome process of extracting the spirit stones.

And if in the process, he took apart the corpse of the monster and seeded his World Spirit Ring with the blood, bones, and viscera of a Nascent Soul-level Spirit Beast, well, none needed to know that, did they?

Chapter 10

The formation flags died off late in the day as evening set in the mystic realm. Rather than move onward and to allow Pan Chen to recuperate, the team set up more stable—if less powerful—formations to guard the camp. The village personnel took turns watching the recuperating Pan Chen, the child alternating between sleeping and cultivating to process the numerous healing tonics and pills provided to him.

Liu Ping took great joy in carving up the giant snake, working with a pair of short swords as butchering knives, stripping away scales, flesh, and muscles to reveal the snake's spine. The bones she retrieved, along with the nervous system, giant earth pots with constantly boiling water used to clean the remnants. The water itself was changed regularly, clay pots of the waste product set aside for later use.

The corpse of a Nascent Soul-level beast was of great use, which was why the team took the time to extract the full portion of resources possible. In the meantime, a message and messenger had been sent to the village. Help would come eventually.

All of which Wu Ying had little to do with. He was taking full advantage of the mystic realm, gusting from one location to another, fighting the occasional spirit beast and gathering herbs—many yin-aspected, though some highly concentrated and strong yang-aspected vegetation was found—to his heart's content. He even occasionally picked up some mineral or jade-infused item, though those only when their presence impacted deeply upon his spiritual sense.

It was only when a Spirit Messenger, the tiny paper spirit floating through the air to alight on his shoulder, found him days later than he made his way back to the encampment. There, to his surprise, he found Pan Shui and Pan Chen seated, meditating with the remainder of the party absent. Taking a seat not far away, he waited.

A short while later, Pan Chen opened his eyes, his current cycle complete. He fixed Wu Ying with a considering look, a degree of maturity now present in his youthful gaze. That first brush of mortality, days of unrelenting pain and healing, had matured the boy beyond his years.

"You are well, I see," Wu Ying said to fill the silence. Pan Chen was not. Not really. But he would be, which was the important aspect.

"Pan Shui told me tales of you. How do you do it?" Pan Chen said.

"What do you speak of, Ah Chen?"

"Fighting. Killing. Risking your life," Pan Chen said the last softer, more hesitant than ever.

Wu Ying rotated the knife he had been caring for around in his hand, working the softer side of his whetstone against its edge to remove minor burrs. A tragedy of his own chi, that he was not able to get the precise cutting edges a metal blade had. Not yet, at least. Most of the time, it did not matter—but sometimes, with metal chi-infused plants, that extra edge was necessary.

"You ask how, but I ask you, is there a difference between my life and yours?" Wu Ying said. "You speak as though such decisions, such incidents, are unique."

"Fighting a Nascent Spirit beast is!" Pan Chen said insistently.

"Yet I've already fought four… and been in the presence of many more." Wu Ying held up a hand before the child jumped on his words as though he was admitting truth. "You hope for me to explain that the danger I've faced is unusual. Yet your family has at least one Peak Core Formation master in its rank. If they wished you dead, would it matter?"

"No. But they wouldn't do that."

"Perhaps," Wu Ying replied. "Right now, even though your family has not attacked or otherwise chosen to act against the kingdom, the kingdom might send an army—or assassins—to end the lives of those of you in the village. Destroy it and your loved ones. End your line."

"They won't though," Pan Chen said stubbornly. "We're just being careful. They wouldn't dare!"

"Yet they did before. And might again," Wu Ying said. "A few years ago, when I traveled through the kingdoms of Shen, there was a battle between an immortal and a dragon. You heard of it?"

Pan Chen nodded. Such news traveled far, though details might have been obscured.

"I was in the vicinity when it began, and they reshaped the land." Wu Ying put down his whetstone and picked up a nearby stone. He flicked it into the air and cut, splitting the stone apart smoothly with his newly sharpened blade and a little of his blade intent. Watching as the rock fell in pieces, he continued to speak. "The earth was rent apart as easily as I parted the stone. The town that bisected the path of their battle, destroyed. New channels formed, farmlands made fertile from falling blood and wept tears."

"A tragedy," Pan Chen said. "I'm not stupid. You're trying to say that danger is all around. That choosing or not choosing doesn't matter, there's still danger."

"Oh, choice matters. Decisions matter." Wu Ying tested the edge of his blade and grimaced as he realized he'd blunted the blade again, He returned to sharpening it. "But worrying about the future is a fool's game. The gravest choices you face will often be the most surprising."

"I don't understand!" Pan Chen said, clearly frustrated. "You're as bad as my father. Why won't you just tell me what you're trying to say!"

"I am," Wu Ying replied. Then seeing the growing frustration, he sighed. "You ask me how I keep endangering myself and my future. But to me, I am not. What risk there was is past. What risk might come, might never arise. In between, I exist. Living the life I wish to live. And if circumstances arise again where my life might be in danger… then so be it. I'll make my choices then."

"Just be? Don't worry about the future?" Pan Chen scoffed. "That'd be like cutting without watching the line of your cut."

"Yet when you move through your forms, each motion leads to another and a thousand others. Retreat, advance, attack, defend, feint. Some are awkward, some are nearly impossible to complete. Each motion always has myriad options, and you would never say that any single motion is completely out-of-bounds, would you?" At Pan Chen's hesitation, Wu Ying continued. "The options are in the moment, for when the time comes when you need to make them truth. And only when you face your opponent's blade will you choose. And strike true.

"Without hesitation, with full commitment. Even a feint must be committed to entirely or be considered lacking. So be the form. Practice and train until you are as supple and changeable as the wind, such that when the time comes, you can choose and choose well."

Silence filled the camp for a time as Pan Chen considered Wu Ying's words, broken only by the noise of whetstone grating on steel. When he had replaced the edge on the blade, Wu Ying closed his eyes and turned to meditation even as Pan Shui exited her cultivation.

Later, perhaps, he would speak with them. For now, something in what he had said— thoughts and concepts he had known but only now put into words—had sparked a change, a clarification within. Chasing that unsteady candle of insight deep into his own mind, he meditated, seeking enlightenment.

***

They traveled to exit the mystic realm the next morning, their party significantly reduced in size. Aid from the village had arrived at their camp to finish extracting the resources from the snake, leaving the original team—sans the earth elemental elder—to return to the village. Traveling back was faster and significantly less hazardous, as both Core Formation cultivators spread their auras across the surroundings in silent warning to potential predators.

Their return was celebrated with a stupendous feast, the meat of the Nascent Soul snake made into multiple dishes, from stews to steaks. Portions were handed out with only the barest modicum of care, though more than once Wu Ying noted the presence of heaven's chi traversing through the gathering as youngsters broke through under the chi-heavy diet of spirit meat.

To save appetites, small wards were set up, blocking off the stench of Body Cleansing cultivators clearing their second, third, or fourth meridians. Large wooden tubs were extracted, set to boil a distance away, and the fortunate and newly empowered cultivators were sent to cleanse themselves more fully.

In the midst of all the revelry and food, songs accompanied by flute and stringed instruments, overturned pots and simple hand drums arose. Pan Shui and Pan Yin were the highlight of those circles, singing, dancing, and showing off their growing accomplishments with the spear to the delight of the village.

Wu Ying, as guest of honor, sat beside Chief Pan himself, speaking with the man long into the night. He repeated the story of their battle multiple times at different intervals, always sure to praise the villagers for their bravery and abilities while downplaying his own role. In turn, news about this kingdom and the Shen kingdom was passed to him.

"The rebels rose up in the Meitan county, killing the administrative commander and his military advisor. Supposedly, the army major in charge was assassinated at night by his second-in-command," Chief Pan said, shaking his head. "They evacuated before the army could send reinforcements, disappearing into the wilderness."

Glancing around a little automatically, Chief Pan continued. "They could not find the ringleaders, so they hung the city leaders who stayed behind and the sub-magistrate who had taken over as an example. Chopped off their heads and limbs and displayed them on the city walls."

Wu Ying winced. He did not need Chief Pan's weighted and knowing glance to tell him how bad a decision that was. It might quell any immediate thought of rebellions, but it would engender deep resentment among the populace, especially those who had known the innocent.

"Bad tidings all around. Supposedly there were two more attempts. Failed ones. But those rumors are more…" Chief Pan searched for a word. "Well, unknown. Information is scarce on that and conflicting."

Wu Ying nodded in understanding.

"But good news for you! The Wei and Shen kingdoms are to sit down and negotiate a cease-fire. Well, they're probably negotiating one right now—for it was to start in spring. I understand an exchange of princesses and some other noble house marriages will be occurring."

"That is good tidings." Wu Ying smiled. The only winners in a war were the weapons merchants and crows. "But will the sects be coming to the table too?"

The chief could only shrug at that question. They might get news, but it was slow. The negotiations to have negotiations likely had begun all the way in the fall of the year before, perhaps winter if things had progressed quickly.

Still, it was good news. An end to the war would see fewer lives lost and more time to focus on more important things, like immortal ascension.

For a moment, Wu Ying wondered about his friends. His sister. Tou He, Fairy Yang, Liu Tsong, Li Yao, even Yin Xue and the others he had met along the way. He hoped they were well. His parents too, though he had less concern about them falling in battle.

Then another shout, another song, and Pan Shui was before him, a hand held out, beckoning him to join their dances. Wu Ying chose to cast aside his thoughts, to rejoice in being alive after another close fight. To delight in being around people who reminded him so much of his own village, if stronger and stranger in some ways.

And all the while, leaving traces of itself, the sweet, sharp, cold smell of the heavens drifted down, touching upon the lucky few, binding the village close.

***

The fires had died down, the music had stopped. The last musician had fallen asleep, still strumming his guzheng[25] and been pulled away from the fire before he fell within by an amused Wu Ying. Pan Shui, by Wu Ying's side, banked the fire, leaving the coals to glow and warm the sleeping villagers piled around the remaining fire.

After one last glance around to ensure none of the children—all too young, all too vulnerable to the nip in the air to be left to sleep outside—were present, she looked consideringly at Wu Ying. Then, eyes glinting with mischief, she beckoned him to follow.

An eyebrow rose, but Wu Ying walked behind the woman who left the circle of fire quickly. They traversed through slumbering individuals and tables set outside for the feast, heading for the houses that dotted the slopes of the hill that the village was set upon. When he tried to speak, Pan Shui raised a finger to her lips, eyes glinting.

After traversing through small alleys and behind buildings, the drifting noises of sleeping animals and the animal with two backs accompanying their silent trip, they ended up before a hut. The building was similar to so many others within the village, built for guests and those still single but requiring privacy. Not connected to the main family homes but set aside for the independent or those looking for such independence.

Pan Shui stopped at the door, smiling at Wu Ying.

He looked at the building then at her and shook his head. "Cultivator Pan, I hold you in high regard—"

"Oh gods! No!" Pan Shui visibly shuddered. "That'd be like... like sleeping with Third Uncle." Again, another more theatrical shudder. Then swiftly shaking off the nerves, she knocked on the door before skipping away.

Puzzled by her actions, Wu Ying stared after the quickly departing figure, the woman going so far as to trigger a movement skill. By the time he shook off his shock, Pan Shui was too far away to call out to without waking others—at least without using some communication skills.

More importantly, the door that had been knocked upon had been opened, Pan Yin glaring out of it, speaking before the door had fully swung open. "Ah Shui, I swear, if this is a prank... Cultivator Long!"

"Cultivator Pan." Wu Ying bowed automatically. As he finished his greeting and came up, he could not help but let his gaze trek over her body, clad in light sleeping robes and

---

[25] Chinese zither—laid horizontally, it is around 1.63m long and has between 21 to 26 strings, with each string plucked by the musician. Often played by women, but not always.

highlighted by the spirit lamp from within her hut. "I'm sorry. I had not known you, this…" He gestured after where Pan Shui had disappeared.

"So it was her voice I heard. I was not mistaken," Pan Yin said, eyes narrowing. "That damn imp."

"I'll leave you to your rest…" Wu Ying said, stepping backward. "I apologize for the disturbance."

"It is fine," Pan Yin said. "A small matter." She smiled a little, leaning against the door as she watched Wu Ying retreat.

"Good evening. Again," Wu Ying said.

"Well, Cultivator Long, since you're here…" Pan Yin said, suggestively inching the door open.

"Cultivator Pan…" Wu Ying stopped, hesitating. His gaze flew to her body, highlighted as it was, before he yanked it back up to her face. "This is not…"

"Political. At all. I understand you'll be leaving. As does my father," Pan Yin said. "Knowing that, and knowing that I seek nothing…"

"Appropriate," Wu Ying pointed out.

"Perhaps for your kingdom." She smiled. "But you're not there. You are here. A Core cultivator with the wind and a spiritual sense. You could have known where you went if you wished. Yet you did not. Or say you do not." When he moved to protest his innocence, she shook her head. "It matters not. You are here. And I am willing." She took a deeper breath, her body pressing against the thin silks. "I will not ask again."

Wu Ying hesitated a moment more. There were many reasons not to. Midnight assignations—even in as liberal a clan as the Zhuang—always had political and personal entanglements. He was significantly stronger than Pan Yin, which led to another concern. And, of course, the fact that he would be leaving always prevented such dalliances from growing serious.

Numerous reasons to turn her down. But he was still a man after all.

He stepped forward, crossed the threshold, and gripped her waist, laying a passionate kiss on her. Pushing her back indoors, he kicked the door closed and forgot about greater concerns. At least for the night.

***

That night was never discussed again by the parties involved. It was a single evening of passion and energy before the pair slunk apart. Yet as though the evening was a bellwether, Wu Ying could feel that his time with the Zhuang clan was coming to an end. The spring planting season was nearly over and what he could extract from the village, nearly finished.

Pan Chen, forced to recuperate slowly, could no longer train with him. In the sparring arena, Wu Ying moved through the motions of his forms, finding a smoothness and an integrity to the motions that he had missed before.

When enlightenment came, it did not arrive with thundering uproar or the crashing of heavenly chi, but the gentle breaking of power and the crystallization of hours of practice. He did not need to stop, he did not need to ponder further, for he had done the work before. And now the sword sang in his hand as he heard its true voice and what it desired.

A sword was a weapon, a killing device. A weapon of war and battle and death. It was never designed to be a tool like an axe, never meant for hunting to feed a family. It was a weapon to kill beasts and other humans.

He had known that, understood that portion of what a sword was. It was a tool and weapon to Wu Ying, always had been. What he had missed, what had been revealed to him, was that the sword was not just its final utility.

A sword had been crafted by a blacksmith. Sometimes tiredly, sometimes angrily, but often for the weapons he wielded, with great care, love, and precision. A sword was not just a tool. It could be a work of art. It could be used to create beauty in dance, on the wall, in the forms he moved through.

It might kill, but it could also desire to be more than that. A weapon could take lives, but in the right hands, it could save them too.

In the movement of his blade, Wu Ying found the Heart of the Sword and finally broke through. A journey he had stepped upon so long ago, and perhaps, the final stage for now.

Chapter 11

For all his preparations, his planned departure was pre-empted by the flow of life and politics. Chief Pan found Wu Ying working in the fields, finishing up the planting of the rice that the village required. They did not have extensive fields, not like his village. The tea leaves that covered the hills took up most of their time, but still, no village would be without rice.

Stretching his back, feeling the flow of wind across his body; Wu Ying smiled at the chief as he neared. Then his smile faded, seeing the other man's demeanor. Wu Ying shifted position, leapt lightly onto the earth embankment around the sunken, submerged field, and walked over to greet the other, offering the man a courteous bow as he neared.

"You truly are—were—a rice farmer," Pan Hai, following behind the chief, said.

"I am," Wu Ying said. "But I fear that was not what you were here to speak of."

"No," Chief Pan said, his gaze heavy and regretful. "You must leave. Now."

"Trouble?" Wu Ying said, his hand falling to his side where his sword would normally be. Finding it empty, he turned and opened his hand, the wind working to his commands and casting the sword into his hand from where it rested.

"Not the kind that can be solved with a blade," Chief Pan replied. "The government has sent a representative to discuss the events at the tournament. It would be… simpler… if you were not here to speak with them. If you were never here."

Wu Ying arced an eyebrow at the blatant lie but nodded. "So be it."

He flexed his aura, pushing it outward from his skin. It was the latest trick he had picked up, and as he did so, the mud that clung to his legs, to his pants shifted and dropped to the ground. It did not clear the water soaked into his pants, nor the earth ground into his cloth shoes, but at least it kept his skin mostly clean.

"Thank you," Chief Pan murmured, bowing to Wu Ying. "I regret the circumstances of our parting. I had hoped…"

Wu Ying shook his head, cutting off the chief. "You have given me more than enough with the hospitality shown to me and the companionship offered."

After offering the man one last bow and murmuring a quick goodbye to Pan Hai, Wu Ying kicked off the ground, flitting through the air quickly. He chose not to go too high, staying just above the ground but moving much faster as he cut a direct line to the village and his temporary abode.

There would be no discussion of where he would go now. Such questions were dangerous—both for the chief who might be forced to lie and be caught in doing so and for Wu Ying if they chose to chase him.

Packing was a simple matter, with only a few scrolls and his manuals, articles of clothing, and a couple of swords swept into his spirit rings. He regarded his temporary residence, eyeing the place for anything he'd missed. A few keepsakes had been offered to him, but he had stored those already—the small, simple things that marked an individual's greater regard than the depth of their wallet. A wooden carving of a horse by a child, a string of garlands, the detailed instructions to replicate a family recipe of stewed, soya sauce pork belly.

One last look as he took in the room, knowing he would never see it again. He picked up his backpack, the one he used to store spirit herbs and other, mundane items, and slung it over his back, settling the weight with an easy shrug. He could store it in his storage ring but saw no reason. Not at the moment.

Done, he walked outside, ready to depart the village. Only to come up short as a gaggle of youngsters stood before him, arms crossed.

"Trying to leave without saying goodbye?" Pan Shui said, looking affronted. "Who taught you those manners?"

"My parents. But they would happily tell you that I bring them shame for such things all the time anyway," Wu Ying replied with a smile. "But it is good to see you all."

"Father sent word," Pan Yin said, bowing to Wu Ying. "We wished to bid you farewell. We too will be departing soon, for the mystic realm."

"Oh?"

"I'm inconvenient," Pan Shui muttered disconsolately. "I made too much of a splash, winning. Now they'll want to talk to me."

"And I'm forced to follow her." Pan Mui harumphed.

Pan Yin waved her sisters down, her gaze somber. "If it is suitable…"

"Suitable?" Wu Ying said, a tremor of anticipation running through him.

"She wants your permission to say we're going with you," Pan Shui replied, waving at herself and Liu Ping. "When they ask."

"But you won't be," Wu Ying said, with a hint of a question at the end.

"No," Liu Ping said, looking conflicted. She stared at him from under her lashes, letting out a little growl after a moment. "You're not going to take the main roads, after all. Where you go… it's not a place for the rest of us, is it?"

Wu Ying hesitated, knowing that she was asking in an indirect way if she could join him. Instinctively, he wanted to reject her request. Yet before he spoke, he chose to consider his reaction and the reasons of it.

Did he dislike Liu Ping? No. She was a little foolhardy and, with her newly awakened bloodline, perhaps a little dangerous. She still grieved for her brother, though the long months of convalescence and training had seen her grief lessen.

More, she was a good friend. Reliable in a fight. She could be useful, perhaps…

But she was not wrong. Where he traveled, where he intended to travel, bringing someone not even at the Core Formation level would be a liability. Nor was her control of her aura sufficient even for the normal regions he traversed, the edges of the deep, deep wilderness.

Bringing another with him…

"It would be your death. And mine too," Wu Ying said, putting words to his thoughts.

"I thought as much." Liu Ping bowed to Wu Ying. "Thank you. For saving me. For guiding me to a new place. And for showing me a path higher."

"You would look to ascend?" Wu Ying said, surprised.

"I would." Liu Ping shrugged a broad shoulder. "He will be born again, one day. And perhaps if I'm stronger then, perhaps I could save him."

There was no need to ask which him she meant. The group fell silent in shared memory and recollection, only for Pan Chen, patient until now, to step forward. The child looked up at Wu Ying, offering him a rolled-up scroll in both hands.

Wu Ying received the scroll with both hands, bowing to the boy even as Pan Chen spoke. "I wrote some thoughts. About your attack. The one you used against the snake." He hesitated, blushing a little. "I'm sorry it took so long. I had... well, it took me a while to remember everything properly."

"I was not aware you were even conscious," Wu Ying admitted.

Pan Chen shrugged, embarrassed, and stepped back. Then, just as suddenly, he lunged forward and wrapped Wu Ying in a hug, burying his face in his robes. His words, murmured around the fabric, were muffled and filled with emotion. "Come back, dage[26], promise? These others, they are all lousy with the blade."

Wu Ying blinked, then returned the hug. The child's tone of voice, the way he held Wu Ying tightly, it brought back memories of his own childhood, a time when he too had felt a little alone, for hours when he had wanted to spend playing had been taken up by the sword. He had been lonely, a little, without a brother or sister, without a friend who understood. And he, at least, had had some time to play with others.

How much worse was it for Pan Chen, who had no peers among his own age group? Whose joy came in an art that no others could understand. Even Wu Ying could barely glimpse the heights the child would climb. His heart ached for the child, for the realization.

So Wu Ying spoke, offering what little assurance he could. "One day. I promise. It might not be for many years..." The winds tickled his face, murmuring their promises of distant lands and further adventures. "But I'll return. One day." Now, his eyes twinkled. "And you best have progressed your cultivation. Otherwise, it won't be a challenge for me to beat you."

"You know that expertise beats strength anytime, right, senior?" Pan Chen said, withdrawing from his hug.

Wu Ying let him go, smiling at the teasing tone. "We shall see."

"Do we have your agreement?" Pan Yin said, speaking up again.

"Your father never mentioned this," Wu Ying remarked.

"He would never ask. It would be too much of an imposition for him to do so," Pan Yin said.

---

[26] Pan Chen is calling Wu Ying 'dage' or 'older brother' here, not because he's his actual older brother but because he's accepted him as family. It's an indicator of closeness between the two.

Now, Wu Ying understood. It was more politick, easier for him to turn down Pan Yin. Though, eyeing the woman, he wondered if this plan was hers entirely, unmentioned to her father, to safeguard the village. Again and again, Pan Yin had put the village ahead of herself, a village that had already chosen to bypass her. All for her lack of cultivation success.

What a foolish world, where wisdom and duty were cast aside for strength.

"I wish you the best, Cultivator Pan. In ascension and all your wishes," Wu Ying replied. At her frown, he gestured idly. "If you find it necessary, you may do so. I doubt it will inconvenience me greatly."

"Thank you again, Expert Long. We are—I am—in your debt," Pan Yin said.

"Among friends, there are no debts."

"And friends, that is what we are?" she said.

Before Wu Ying could reply, Pan Shui inched ahead and added, "Or more than friends?"

Pan Shui smirked suggestively, only to yelp as Pan Mui grabbed hold of her younger sister and yanked her back by the flesh at the side of her waist. Pan Chen, watching the entire incident, just looked confused.

Liu Ping, on the other hand, muttered, "Too late, eh? I should have marked him…"

Wu Ying glared at Liu Ping. He was not a piece of meat to be traded. Or a tree to be climbed. However, before he could reply, Pan Hai appeared, looking upset.

"Elder Pan?" Wu Ying turned to the other.

"I… see you're still here."

"My apologies. I was just saying goodbye."

"None required. But the envoy will be here in less than an hour. And it will take some time to remove your chi presence from the environment," Elder Pan said leadingly.

"Thank you, again, Expert Long," Pan Yin repeated herself, bowing low.

This time around, there were no interruptions as the others copied her actions.

Wu Ying bowed back, nodded goodbye to Elder Pan, and turned, departing quickly. Knowing they wanted him gone, he triggered the Twelve Gales, using the movement technique to exit the village, heading up the hill into the surroundings.

South and east, the wind howled, taking him with it as he gusted to the north and west. Leaving behind friends and memories. And though he lamented the parting, a part of him soared at the idea of new lands, new horizons, and new people to meet.

***

A day and dozens of li, traveling through rolling hills and the burgeoning forests, heading deeper as he danced upon the Twelve Gales. He moved faster than ever, yet was careful not to overuse his chi. For the first time, he would have a chance to test the full extent of his Core while traveling, unburdened by others. He would take it slowly, as was appropriate.

Signs of civilization gave way as formerly tilled and farmed lands were abandoned, civilization pulling back. He came across the ruins of a village a day's ride from the Zhuang clan's. Perhaps a branch village, perhaps just a competing one. It mattered not, for decades of wear had seen houses crumble, walls fall, and roads overgrow.

Beast spoor, large and infused with chi, spoke of traveling Demonic Spirits. He paused then, judging size and volume, noting the variety and quantity—a sounder of demonic boars could be dangerous. He considered hunting them for their cores, for the safety of the village. For the exercise.

Wu Ying drew a deep breath, prodded at the refuse with a finger. He touched his rings which were a little empty, for he had not gathered properly for months now. What little he had acquired in the mystic realm was of a different variety and form from the normal spirit herbs out here. And while his World Spirit Ring saw continued growth, it was better to let most such herbs mature.

And anyway… he recalled the first ever Demonic Beast he had fought. He remembered the fight, the danger, his fear. He considered it for a moment, then he chose to move.

Finding the trail was simple, following it even simpler. Demonic boars weren't the most subtle of creatures , defecating and tearing up the ground whenever some bush or herb caught their attention. Or in a few cases, some unfortunate creature was located, its body torn apart and mostly consumed. Splotches of blood, refuse, and hardened horns or hooves were the only indication of the boars' presence.

Two hours of travel, flitting through the rolling plains of grass and shrubbery, and he found them. The wind warned him long before he saw his prey, and a simple flexing of his Core and a beckoning of the winds took him to the sky.

The sounder was nearly a score in size, two-thirds of them adults while piglets, each of which were the size of a normal boar, ran between the creatures. The demonic boars were each about the size and width of a peasant's house, the entire group a moving calamity. The largest Demonic Boar radiated the power of a peak-Energy Storage creature, on the verge of breaking through to Core.

Even with Wu Ying's presence hidden, his aura retracted and the winds certain to keep his scent away, the lead boar noticed him. It turned its massive head, its tusks glowing with a dark yellow-green malevolent light that set Wu Ying's hair standing on end.

"Now, how'd you sense me?" Wu Ying wondered aloud.

His opponent offered no answer, instead unleashing a triumphant and challenging snort. It reared a little on its back legs, exhaling a loud huff. Noxious fumes rolled from its mouth, the poisonous gas matching the color of its horn. As it struck the ground, the greenery around its feet sickened and died, only the other members of its sounder seemingly unaffected.

"Demon in truth." Wu Ying gestured with his hand, energy pouring into the winds around him. It swirled around the sounder, containing the beasts and the exhaled fumes. That would ensure their battle would be contained.

Next, he drew his Saint-jian. Powerful though he might have been, Wu Ying did not have the strength to kill the monsters with just his command of the wind. Not without wasting too much of his chi, leaving him tired and vulnerable to other potential threats.

In the wild, such actions were foolish in the extreme.

Anyway, he had his new blade and his understanding of the weapon. It was time to test it. First, he cast a series of sword light, striking the air as he sent blade intent at the demonic animals. The first few strikes, aimed at the largest monster, were blocked by the creature's tusks. They shattered, breaking apart without harming the powerful creature.

On the other hand, Wu Ying's attacks were much more successful upon the younger members of the sounder. Piglets were split apart, and the youngest and weakest members were either killed or seriously injured.

Not content to be left alone, a group of the older demonic boars grouped together, forming a killing release of chi that flew directly at Wu Ying. Sensing a mild level of danger, he swung his sword and projected blade and killing intent, turning the strength of his cultivation upon the attack.

The formed energy was a crescent of white light, with flickering, shifting edges of wind chi at the boundaries of the attack. It struck the beam of demonic yellow light, tearing through the center with barely any hesitation before splitting apart the energy and continuing until it struck the gathered nexus point of energy and the boars forming it.

The group trotted backward, backlash from the attack leaving the boars injured and in pain.

In the meantime, seeing that its brethren's attempts had done little to Wu Ying and its own initial attack contained, the lead boar bent its stubby legs and exploded forward. Yellow-green energy spun around its body as it flew through the air, headed directly for Wu Ying.

"Well, that's a surprise. You can fly," Wu Ying muttered. "Or is that a leap?"

Yet, he was still not worried. The attack was more dangerous than the previous chi beam, but it was insufficient to concern him. Rather than dodge the clumsy leaping strike, he chose to meet the boar head-on, calling the wind to his back and throwing himself forward with his sword extended.

The boar twisted its head at the last second, seeking to interpose its natural weapon against Wu Ying's sword. The pair unleashed their energies, chi surging backward and forward. However, unlike Wu Ying who was held aloft by the winds and his chi techniques, the boar had no way to combat the call of the earth.

Momentum stopped dead, gravity called the boar and it slipped downward, falling away from Wu Ying as the cultivator let out another surge of energy. The blade strike was blocked by the tusk, the beleaguered horn cracking and breaking to fall away even as the boar was redirected into its brethren.

The fall reverberated through the hills, bodies crushed and injured and dying boars squealing as the lead boar rolled over and over. Even shocked by the attack, the beast managed to push itself upward, long lacerations from where the tusks of its own sounder crisscrossed its body.

High above, Wu Ying had stabilized his flight and had taken his sword in his other hand, shaking out his arm. "Strong, but not that strong. I need at least another layer or two to my Core before I can just power my way through."

Chuckling to himself as the boars snorted and growled their anger, he idly dodged a few lashes and thrown clods of earth as the boars attempted to reach him in the sky.

"I best stop acting like a Metal or Earth affinitied individual," he muttered, taking his sword back in hand. Still, strength and intent had been tested. Which left… "Forms."

Wu Ying shot downward, moving faster than ever. He passed the smaller boars, ignoring them as he struck at the largest beast. He danced through the air, dodging attacks by inches as his blade carved into the monster, sword light extending his weapon to tear through tough exterior skin.

Noxious yellow-green gas boiled up from the monster's mouth, but Wu Ying kept a bubble of clean air surrounding him at all times, robbing the monster of its greatest weapon. In short order, he left the injured and dying alpha on its last legs—literally—and landed amongst the rest of the sounder.

Raising his sword to his forehead, he gestured at the monsters. "Come."

As though they understood his speech, the demonic beasts charged him. Moving in their midst, Wu Ying ran through his forms, extending his blade and sword intent as he fought them. He restricted himself to the first three forms, content to sense the difference in the Heart of the Sword.

It was minor in external appearance. Such improvements were always slight. But the sharpening of his killing intent by a small margin was more than sufficient to make his sword a razor that cut through the toughest skin. Dodging a blow by millimeters still meant that one had dodged it, while altering the course of an attack as it started by inches meant that when it reached one's torso, it had veered away by feet.

Positioning, strength, sharpness, leverage. Everything had improved by the slightest margin. In a battle where inches meant death and injury, the improvements were staggering in depth. More than that, Wu Ying instinctively knew which form to take now, which would benefit him most in the swirling cloud of dust, in the battling scrum.

He did not drag out the fight. He struck to maim and kill, moving with a hunter's swiftness. Though nature might be cruel in its efficiency, humanity could be swift in its mercy. In less than a minute, the last of the demonic boars had been slain.

Leaving Wu Ying to disperse the poisons high into the sky and with the corpses and their treasures for him to acquire.

Messy business though that might be.

Chapter 12

A day and a night later, Wu Ying left behind the remnants of the sounder. His lips were upraised in distaste as he flitted away, piles of bones, innards, flesh, and hair left behind. Poisoned and twisted was the flesh of the majority, such that the meat was of little use to Wu Ying. Other animals—those immune to the toxins within the creatures' flesh—would consume the remnants of the sounder.

Only a small amount—a mountainside from the head pig—had been placed within World Spirit Ring, to breakdown in a compost pile set aside for its use. That poisoned, toxic soil would be of use for certain poisonous plants, their extracted seeds, leaves, and roots used for medicine by trained physicians.

In addition, Wu Ying left with the skin—stripped, cleaned, and cured and set aside in his World Spirit Ring—the demonic cores of all the creatures, and the two damaged tusks of the largest animal. The remainder were of little use to him—for sale or to enhance his Ring.

Even leaving so much behind, Wu Ying had been thorough, testing everything he came across, hoping for potential uses. The skinning of the creatures had taken much time, forcing him to leave later than he had preferred. Yet an innate stinginess from long years of want as a peasant blocked him from leaving until he had done his utmost, even if the resulting amounts taken would be of little use.

A lesson learned. In affecting the world and stamping on those beneath his current level.

Guided by the northern wind, Wu Ying reached an abandoned temple a dozen li from the fight. The perimeter walls—for even a temple must have such in the wilds, where beasts had little respect for places of worship—stretched on all sides, their grey bricks shattered and leaving gaping holes. A carpet of green vines and flowering creepers lay across the ruins.

As for the main building, once lofty ceilings had fallen, time and age having taken its toll, along with the ever-encroaching pull of nature. There was, perhaps, a lesson there—about the transience of civilization and the supremacy of nature.

It was a lesson Wu Ying had little mind for as he traced the smell of fresh water to the remnants of the temple's inner well. No guarding wall, no sheltered top, but he could sense the fresh water below. Casting about and manipulating wood and earth chi, he formed a circular bathing area nearby. Then it was but a matter of hard work—made easier with a cultivator's enhanced strength and a bucket and rope from his own stores—to fill the newly made bath.

Water and metal were hardest for him to manipulate. A pity that, for one who had a dao or affinity for the liquid might have guided it forth from the well itself. Instead, Wu Ying substituted strength and hard work for chi, throwing a trio of fire-inscribed heating rocks into the bathtub.

In less than an hour, he lounged within, having scrubbed off the last of the dirt and blood before clambering within. Eyes closed, legs spread, he relaxed, letting the wind dance through the fallen building, bringing with it hints of its past.

Incense, a mixture he had never smelled before. It was a little more floral than he was used to, many of the flowers picked from the surroundings. But there was the usual frankincense and makko ingredients in there too, along with the musky, ashy taste of burnt-out sticks.

Books—rotten, waterlogged, slowly crumbling. He was rather surprised to smell any at all, but it was mostly hints, remnants of what had been—scrolls and parchment caught between gaps, crumbling away.

Metal, rusted and fading. Stone, broken and shattered. The thrum of old chi, enchantments broken but sparking, moving in circles and never released, breaking down as the passing of years and decades wore away at the material.

The temple had been abandoned long ago, too long for the secrets and mysteries to haunt him. So Wu Ying let himself relax further, his aura draped over the hillside as warning to those beasts who might consider trying their luck. Few would, he knew, and he kept the aura contained such that only those passing by a short distance away would sense it.

No need to offer a beacon for the true powers of the deep wilderness to find him.

Eyes closed, he rested for a long while before his mind turned to the battle today. It had surprised him, in some ways. In the fight against the Nascent Soul snake, he had been careful to control his chi expenditure. That battle had not been one that could be won fast, so he had conserved much of his chi.

This fight, he had outmatched the creatures by significant margins. He had been improving every step of the way for weeks, but his control over the winds had grown by levels that surprised even him. Though perhaps control was not the right word.

The wind was a fickle friend, one which listened to him because he was, in his own way, slowly becoming wind. So it was no more an imposition to do what he requested than it would be for one's arm to move. Yet he knew instinctively if he pushed it too hard, drew too strongly, like an arm bent out of shape, it would break and injure him. The battle had not even stretched his control, the sphere of clean air, his ability to fly and flit through the air...

He still needed experience and training in air battles. He'd still had to reorient himself constantly, but it was becoming more and more instinctive to know where the sky was, where the ground was, and where his enemies were at all times. The sphere of air that he'd moved within had kept him constantly fed with information, scents and movements and changes in pressure.

All this was the result of his progress with the Seven Winds Body Cultivation manual. He was realizing he was not just transforming his body but also becoming part of the element, making it part of himself. Understanding it, accepting it.

It helped that his Soul Cultivation technique was the Formless Body. It made sense now that it had been part of the works held by the Double Body, Double Soul Sect. The Formless

Body was a somewhat strange soul cultivation technique, for it did not enforce or attempt to guide the soul into any particular shape or dao. Instead, it provided space for a soul to take on the dao or, in his case, the Body Cultivation form that he used to bolster itself. It was both perfectly suited for a powerful Body Cultivation technique like the Seven Winds, but also left a glaring weakness when a dao was not strong enough to fill up that gap.

It combined well with the Seven Winds, strengthening his soul without forcing him to combine his dao enlightenment. When he did choose to input his own dao thoughts into the forming Nascent Soul, the Formless Body strengthened the very core, developing the layers as he grew.

All in all, Wu Ying found himself content with the direction of his growth. For a moment, he considered if he should change his current course, travel not to another kingdom but to his old home. See his parents, see his friends. Partake in wine and drink, soak in their companionship.

Regain his place in the Sect as a Core Formation elder.

Then the wind shifted, and he sensed something else as a pure and cold, imperious—if a wind could be considered imperious—feeling pervaded him. It drove him to dismiss those thoughts. The winds of the north, west, east, south, and the heavens beckoned, in lands past the horizon. He had glimpsed his fate at the village. He knew if he walked this path, he would find it somewhere else.

Somewhere in the thousands of li he was to travel, the months of cultivation to fill his dantian and then, a series of compressions to build the layers of his Core. The future beckoned. In the months and years and perhaps even decades to come, but he would find that wind and grow.

***

His rest was interrupted by the movement of water, the sound of liquid splashing. He opened his eyes, a single eyebrow rising in surprise as he noticed his unexpected guest. She was no willowy beauty, one of great fame, though perhaps in her youth she might have had a shouting chance of being in the same room. Now, she was more likely to be seen in the background, gossiping with the rest of the aunties and plotting the lives of their children and the demise of their husbands and enemies alike.

"Please, join me," Wu Ying said, only mildly sarcastic.

Hair knotted and held up by a pair of chopsticks, only the slight bubbles and mild murkiness of the water, along with the dark, hid her modesty. Not that she seemed to mind, as she stretched, the peaks of her shapely body peeking out of the water.

"I have." She cocked her head a little to the side, her lips tugging up on one side as though she found great humor in their situation. "Are you, perhaps, slow?"

"I am not, auntie[27]," Wu Ying said, not at all annoyed by her biting comment. "Some might consider slipping into the bath of another rather foolish though."

"It's been many years since I've been concerned about decency."

"More the shame. For you are still a rare beauty."

"I would hope so." Again that smile, twisting to be half-mocking.

Wu Ying inclined his head in acknowledgment of her point. He drew in a slight breath, the night scents flowing toward him. Metal, wood, earth, and grass. Fallen masonry and, in the distance, the carcasses of the demonic boars. Howls, yips, and other noises echoed in the distance as animals fought over the remains—or died, having overestimated their ability to handle the poison.

"It has been many years since one has come here. Many more since there was a proper bath," she said, breaking the silence.

"Well, I am grateful to provide some minor comfort."

Her smile twisted, going from mocking to genuine. The pair soaked longer, Wu Ying allowing his chi to flow through the water to sink into the heating stones and recharge them. Neither spoke for a time as the moon and stars turned in the sky.

Eventually though, all good things must end.

"You are a pleasant young boy. One who is slightly rude, to build in another's residence." A hand came up, stopping him before he could continue. "But also cognizant of his place when spoken to."

"Thank you, auntie."

"Would you perhaps be willing to do me another minor favor?"

And finally, they came to it. He stood and stepped clear of the bath, using the smoke and the rising steam, along with his wind chi, to cloak his body and preserve some modesty. By the time he was dressed, wet hair wicking against silk robes, the woman was standing beside him, fully dressed and dry.

"Of course, auntie. I am yours to command," Wu Ying said. "Within bounds of propriety, morality, and honor."

"Of course." Again that mocking smile. "Come with me."

She turned, moving away from Wu Ying as though she floated across the ground, so graceful was her movement. He walked after her, but even as graceful and light as he was on the land, he ruffled the grass, unlike his companion.

In short order, they came to the tower, crossing to where the doors had once stood. Now, only the broken stubs lay before him, the once strong gates rotted away. Before them, covered in ivy and shrubs, stood piles of masonry.

---

[27] She is, obviously, not his aunt. The use of uncle or aunt is a title of respect for those older than you and is used widely when someone has not been introduced. Or you've forgotten their name or specific familial designation.

"Dig deep. Dig hard. And beneath, you'll find what you seek. I trust you'll know what to do when you find it."

Wu Ying regarded the pile of stone that stood multiple times the height of his own head. He turned at her words, yet swift as he was, by the time he looked over, she was gone.

"Typical."

Wu Ying stared at the stone, at the night sky, at the empty grounds. He snorted and walked aside to pitch his tent. It would be a long day tomorrow. An even longer week probably, even with the might of a Core Formation cultivator.

***

Stone, ivy, and dirt. Old masonry, rotten wood, and shards of metal. He found it all as he dug. The wind helped, aiding him as he lifted stone. It scoured the rock clean, tore greenery free, and sent loose soil gusting away. Yet it was the strength of a cultivator and his years building houses alongside the village that gave him what he truly needed to disassemble the crumbled building.

He worked from the first dawn until the stars stood high ahead. Never again did he see the lady, though he bathed each night, pulling forth new water from the well and scouring himself free of sweat and dirt.

Day and night, he cleared the rubble. As though his father and Uncle Liu stood beside him, he set aside the still usable stone, the clean and unrotten logs of wood, and the twisted shards of metal he found. On occasion, he came across boxes and cupboards, items of furniture, and personal belongings that were enchanted with runes of preservation, durability, and storage. Six such remaining items in the week of labor he spent. A week until he had cleared the way.

Those he extracted with care, picking the locks until the lockers sprung open. Often, what he found was of little use—documents speaking of long-lost clans and sects, of food and drink stores. Jewelry, precious for reasons of wealth and coin and sometimes sentiment. Herbs, dried out so long ago that they were of little use to apothecarists.

All these items, Wu Ying stored or set aside. The furniture and cupboards, the boxes were of little use. He could not carry them in his storage rings. The competing daos of space that the creators had envisioned would see them destroy one another. Instead, he took what was of value, stored the remaining contents, and composted the rest.

Taels of gold were just as common as jewelry, and though out of fashion for one and minted in another time for another, the gold and silver could be reused. Those too he took, storing them for when he found civilization once more.

Most useful, he found some pills. He knew not their providence or kind, the smell, the color, the shape escaping his meager knowledge. Taking care to touch them through a cloth, he reviewed them carefully and ascertained them to be no stronger than the pills he already carried. Energy Storage at best then. A flick of his fingers and they were stored away in the bottles they had originated from.

A lot of work for no great gain. The gold was more than sufficient riches for a mortal or a Body Cleanser, ample wealth to purchase multiple fields, to set his children to a time of indolence if they so chose. Sufficient to buy a few pills for an Energy Storage cultivator.

But most of all, what he had found were bones. Crushed, shattered, myriad in number. Bones, bleached and aged, cracked and trapped under broken masonry. Many had been scattered, limbs and legs torn apart, head shattered, torso and legs split. There was but one body, mostly untouched, in the far corner. Slight of shape and size, compared to the others.

Female.

Deep in the cracked ground, he read the tracks and patterns of an old tragedy. A monstrous creature, moving on four legs, had arrived at the temple. It had hungered, and the mortals within the temple had slaked its thirst.

These monks were not like his old friend, trained for battle and peace. These were men of peace and tranquility, individuals who sought to retire from the world. They had tilled their fields, raised their chickens, and in the end, died violently and painfully.

A monster, strong and powerful. It came, it killed, it ate. Sometimes not in that order.

And she, final member and corpse—cook, matron, herbalist, refugee? Who knew. Her story had been lost long ago, and the monks were not speaking.

The bones he arranged, digging a single grave for such was the slaughter that he could not discern the origins of the bodies. He dug deep and laid them to rest, leaving only the final body. Hers was the only one not savaged, a single line carved along one arm bone speaking of how she had died.

Hers, he laid to rest in a lone grave. He built a cairn of rocks from the rubble for both. And then he burned for them joss paper, the copper-colored paper that was for unknown spirits. He offered what little he carried, reserving only a small amount for future instances.

When he was done, the wind whispered and he turned.

A stone, unturned until now, lay exposed. Beneath, a jade box. Its contents, he assumed, were his payment.

Wu Ying turned, seeking but not finding his benefactor, though he had not expected to. Hopefully she was content, laid to rest with her companions, headstone and joss paper burned, talismans laid out to ensure the animals would not disturb them.

He took the jade box, breathed deeply, and closed his eyes. And for a moment, heaven's wind blew and his mind opened. All things in their place. Lives taken, deaths venerated. There was a lesson here, in the doing and his presence.

But what it was eluded him still.

Chapter 13

The smell in the apothecarist's room was familiar, pulling shards of memory from Wu Ying's past. How many hours had he practiced under the watchful eyes of Senior Li? She had been a patient, kind teacher who was more likely to show him the proper way of doing things than beat him with a stick until he achieved the right position.

The apothecarist whose room they stood within smelled like his room, even with brand new robes. The scent of cooking pills, strong herbs, and delicate flowers along with the sharp, acrid smell of mixing metals was familiar in content, though not in ratio.

As for the room itself, it was dominated by the apothecarist's brazier, so big that Wu Ying would fail to put his arms around the largest central portion. Gold and brass, with multiple vents to allow and control the flow of air, the brazier was at least in the Spirit, if not Saint-level of crafting items. Shelves with earthen urns and clear jars covered the walls, labels across each container indicating their contents.

Yet it was at the table near the entrance that the pair had gathered, the herbs and pills Wu Ying had provided for the man set aside, along with the Core Formation strengthening pills he had bargained for on the opposite end.

However, the final box sitting between the pair had both their attention. The pill he had located so many months ago, dragged over a thousand li as he had traveled across the border, through the depths of the wilds, and now, finally, brought here to this man and his sect.

"Do you know what it is or not?" Wu Ying said. Payment for the process of identification had been bargained for, resulting in fewer pills to aid him in his cultivation and the continued process of altering his body. All to get an answer. "You have stood there, silently, for the entirety of a joss stick, Apothecarist Cai."

"Of course I do." Apothecarist Cai sniffed and raised his nose to stare at Wu Ying. "This is just a variant of the Thousand Striation Pill."

Wu Ying could not help but raise an eyebrow. The pill itself had two bands of color, jade green and red, that slowly blended into one another.

"Variant. Also…" Apothecarist Cai raised his hand, forming a flame above it. He picked up the pill with a pair of wooden tongs, raising the pill closer to the fire so that the flames could reflect off the pill. In the brighter light, gradations between the colors, tiny bands that formed the bands of color, were revealed. "As I said, a variation. Normally it's more dispersed. This type of work… it's an ancient formula."

"Is it still good?" Wu Ying asked.

Apothecarist Cai hesitated. "It is. The ingredients in the pill, the process—it only grows stronger when left aside to mix and concentrate." He cocked his head. "How did you say you found this again?"

"I didn't." Wu Ying watched as Apothecarist Cai released the flame and placed the pill back down, hands hovering near it. "What does the pill do?"

"Well, I can tell you what the current Thousand Striation Pill does…" the apothecarist hedged, making Wu Ying gesture for him to continue speaking. "It's a pill for a Core Formation specialist like you. It reinforces the Core walls. Each layer of the pill, as it breaks down, will refine and strengthen the walls between Core layers. The pills are much sought after for those nearing or close to the Peak of the stage, to increase the strength of their Core."

Wu Ying frowned. That sounded good—strength, after all, was good. But… "Does the Nascent Soul not need to break free, during ascension?"

"It does. But before that, it must be purified by Heavenly Tribulation," Apothecarist Cai explained. "To survive the tribulation, to survive purification, your walls must be strong. After you survive the initial purification period, then the Core is weakened anyway, and the Nascent Soul can emerge. Stronger."

Wu Ying bowed his head in acknowledgement of the information and thanks. Apothecarist Cai just waved, dismissing the unspoken words. He tapped the table, his fingers edging toward the box before returning after a moment.

"This pill. As I said, it's a variant. An old variant, one I've only read of before. Such variants, such lost knowledge, it is of value to one like myself." He cocked his head, eyeing Wu Ying. "Would you consider selling this as well?"

Wu Ying paused, not surprised by the request but hesitant about his own response. The pill was valuable, that was certain, and its potency was likely unmatched. Who knew how long it had lain there, under the stone? Safeguarded for an eventual ascension that had never happened. He might never find such a potent pill ever again.

Then again, the pill only gave some form of benefit in the future. Years, maybe decades of travel. Through dangerous lands, seeing and seeking powerful creatures, gathering dangerous herbs. And all the while, he would have to safeguard this treasure. Or he could trade it now for pills that he could use in short order to speed up his cultivation journey.

"That is a significant request," Wu Ying said, his gaze tracking over to the pills he had already acquired. He sent his spiritual sense inside his body, testing his dantian. Months of meditation, months of training, and he believed, he felt, he could form another layer if he had a few more months.

"It is."

"It is not one I can make a decision on, not so easily." Mind spinning, Wu Ying gestured to the pill. "Is there much that you could learn, studying the pill without destroying it?" He knew part of this answer from his own studies, but best to ask.

"A little. In the greater degree of things, not much. But a little," Apothecarist Cai said. "What is it that you are considering, Cultivator Long?"

"A trade. I require a cultivation chamber, a place to contemplate my travels and to make use of your wares." A gesture by Wu Ying to the pills he had purchased.

"And in that time, if you were to make use of our sect facilities as a visiting Elder, I could study this pill."

Wu Ying inclined his head in agreement.

Apothecarist Cai's lips thinned for a second, then he nodded. "A moment. I must speak with the Sect Head."

Wu Ying nodded, taking the proffered seat and the tea set before Apothecarist Cai hurried away. He nibbled on the snacks brought to him by the apothecarist's disciple, making idle conversation about sect life. Or trying to, for the disciple's answers were less than enthusiastic or elaborate. Eventually, Wu Ying fell silent and chose to enjoy the moment of relaxation.

When Apothecarist Cai returned, he was all smiles. "Arrangements have been made, Honorary Elder Long."

"Very good. And there were no problems?" Wu Ying asked.

"Nothing at all. We're honored to have such a prestigious visitor," Apothecarist Cai replied.

Wu Ying chose not to pursue the matter, though his nose wrinkled a little at the acrid, tense, and fearful smell that rose from the apothecarist.

"I should pay respect to the Sect Head then," Wu Ying murmured after he finished packing the pills he had purchased.

"No need, no need!" The apothecarist waved his hands around, gesturing for Wu Ying to come with him. "The Sect Head is a busy, busy woman. She has not time to see you at this time. After you exit your closed-door cultivation, then we shall meet her."

Wu Ying frowned, but sensing no treachery, he followed. He was in a different country, a different sect. Manners and customs wouldn't be the same. More likely however, there were sect politics in play, and he had learned to leave that well enough alone.

Travel from the apothecarists' building where Apothecarist Cai worked—by himself and with a half dozen apprentices—to the cultivation chambers took them across the entirety of the sect. It was a large orthodox sect, though not nearly as populous as the Verdant Green Waters, with just over a thousand members traversing the manicured, open grounds.

The entire sect was built on a flat plane, a nearby lake providing fresh water and a river that bisected the sect itself. On the opposite side of the downriver apothecarists' hall stood the sect hall, its sprawling compound containing the residences of the main branch family and their training halls. Right opposite the hall, on the other side of the river, the gathering and training grounds were built, the paved stones regularly replaced to ensure a smooth journey.

Dotted through the grounds, amidst paved walkways and manicured lawns, were free-standing pagodas, areas for the sect members to lounge, converse, and contemplate the numerous cultivation works. On the far end, directly opposite the apothecarists' guild was the cultivation tower, formations surrounding it to help provide the additional environmental chi required for its working.

The pair were headed toward to this building, crossing the grounds as sect members bowed and greeted them. The apothecarist cordially greeted the various sect members who approached them. More than once, he had a word or two about a pending order, going so far as to be willing to speak to even lowly Body Cleansing cultivators.

Wu Ying, carrying his goods over one shoulder, idly watched the interactions and the area, drinking in the new sights and socialization.

Only for Apothecarist Cai to come to a stop, their way barred by a quintet of glowering cultivators. The two in the lead were Elders, clad in the silver and gold Wu Ying had come to associate with the sect but with significantly more elaborate designs and stitching to mark their position as Elders.

"Little Yu[28]. Who is this ruffian you bring along?" the lead Elder, a man with a thin mustache and well-maintained, thick eyebrows asked the apothecarist, all with a smile that never reached his eyes.

"Cousin Yao," Cai Yu said, offering the man a placating smile. "This is Expert Long, now an Honored Guest Elder. He is a visiting cultivator who will be making use of our facilities to progress his cultivation."

Wu Ying bowed to the group, offering them a martial bow with his hands clasped together. The bag on his back threatened to fall off, so he rose a little faster, adjusting it with his elbow. At the same time, the wind picked up a little, pulling their scents to him.

Core Formation cultivators, the Elders, one and all. He knew that this clan held its place in the kingdom due to the number of Core Formation cultivators in its ranks, though it only had two Nascent Soul cultivators heading it. Or at least, only two that were known—who knew how many hidden Elders, attempting to breakthrough, were secreted away?

"Honored Elders. I am grateful to be here," Wu Ying said.

"A foreigner," Elder Cai Yao said, lips twisting in disgust. "You would let a foreigner and outsider use our clan cultivation tower?"

"The Sect Leader has agreed," Apothecarist Cai Yu said hastily.

Wu Ying's eyes darted between the group, watching the way they stood, the tone of their words and the intent behind them. The large sects in the kingdom of Jin were clan-based sects, with family cultivation and martial techniques dominating the landscape. A total of seven clans dominated the Jin kingdom, of which the Cai clan was one of the largest—and conveniently, the one most closely located to where Wu Ying had exited the wilderness.

The entire power structure of the clans was fascinating to him, since most clans had main branch families, side branch families, and ancillary or allied clans that were considered part of the main branch to some extent. All of which were tied together by bonds of duty, promises, and specific cultivation techniques.

---

[28] The usage of "big" or "little (small if directly translated)" is a form of address from one that is close or trying to emphasize closeness. You might call someone "Big Brother" or "Big Boss" as a sign of respect, but almost never "Little Brother" or "Little Boss" without a pre-existing relationship since that would denote superiority over the individual.

All of which led to this—a level of internal sect politics that were vicious to the extreme as individuals attempted to climb higher, breaching ceilings of propriety and tradition by virtue and renown and deeds of service.

"Well, if the Sect Leader has agreed…" Elder Cai Yao replied. "It does make me wonder what it is that you traded with this… *Expert* to give him such access."

Apothecarist Cai's smile grew strained, but he chose not to answer. The silence grew tense while the crowd around slowed, watching the group with ill-concealed interest. As they stood there, the wind picked up a little, throwing leaves around the group.

"If Cousin Yao will excuse us," the apothecarist murmured, bowing low, "I should send Expert Long to his cultivation chamber."

"Of course… I look forward to speaking with the expert when he exits." Again that slight sneer to Cai Yao's words.

Wu Ying could not blame him much. Wu Ying was, as usual, suppressing his aura such that it would be difficult for most to gauge his strength. If anything, he probably felt no stronger than a mid-grade Energy Storage cultivator, and that was only because removing his aura entirely would be considered rude.

The pair offered their final thanks, skirting past the group that chose to continue to take up the majority of the walkway. As they passed, one of the other cultivators shifted his position at the last second, intent on bumping Wu Ying with his shoulder. Yet reading his intent long before he moved, Wu Ying let himself flit around the man's shoulder, hiding his dodging as he adjusted his backpack with an elaborate shrug.

Snorting a little to himself at the childish play for violence, Wu Ying hurried after the apothecarist. They ascended to the top of the tower with minimal fuss. The room that was opened for him was a plain and empty abode, the raised dais in the center perfectly positioned among the chi collecting arrays to provide the greatest benefit.

In short order, Wu Ying was alone, Cai Yu in a hurry to return to his studies and Wu Ying happy to be left alone to cultivate. After placing a couple of talismans on the inside of the room for added safety, he took a seat on the dais to begin his period of closed-door cultivation.

He would not need much to ascend.

As for what lay for him outside when he exited… well, he would deal with clan politics afterward. If he was fortunate, he would be gone long before matters came to a head.

***

Hours into days, days into weeks, weeks into months.

Wu Ying sat on the raised dais, meal pills under his tongue to help stave off hunger. Even so, full meals were delivered once a week through a slot built for such a need. Environmental chi swirled around him, feeding energy into his body as he cultivated, passing the chi through his meridians before it entered his dantian. Some of it eventually seeped into his Core, refined even further while the main energy of his dantian continued to fill.

Months of travel beforehand, his time in the Zhuang clan village, and the constant consumption of pills and herbs had seen his smaller-than-normal Core filled with Core-refined energy. In addition, two-thirds of his dantian was now filled, a prospect that had taken him years before his ascension to Core Formation. Now, the expansion of his meridians and the use of new Soul Cultivation techniques at Core Formation allowed him to grow faster than ever.

His time within the chamber became one of routine and concentration, the intense focus only viable by entering a semi-trance, meditative state of mind. Wu Ying's consciousness floated on the pool of serenity, bobbing into silent meditation before exiting to cultivate, passing between the two states of pure thought and emptiness.

Even with years of practice and the rigorous discipline of a decades-long martial artist, Wu Ying found himself unable at times to conjure the necessary stillness and discipline to cultivate. During those periods, often after he had taken a break to consume much needed repast, he would train with his sword or practice the physical Body Cultivation forms.

Flowing from form to form, alternately cutting at imaginary foes or replicating the movements of the wind, he passed the hours until exhaustion robbed him of his physical strength. Then for hours he would sleep, waking to a clearer mind to begin the process of cultivating once more.

Months later, his dantian filled to the core, Wu Ying took a few days' break. He chose to spend his time resting, reading a few novels he had purchased along the way. Perhaps it was because of his recent experiences, but the fictional accounts of Judge Di filled his leisure time, along with continued practice of his forms.

Only when he believed his mind and emotions were fully stabilized did Wu Ying choose to take the next step. He picked out the Core Formation pills he had purchased, the trio of pill bottles laid out before him. Each pill had its own effect, and he read over the written instructions again.

First, consume the Heavenly Desert Pill. The pill was beige, similar to the midnight of the deserts—or so Wu Ying had been told, having never been to one before. Upon consumption, the pill drew chi from the outer meridians of the body, "drying" out the meridians and concentrating energy in the dantian in preparation for the formation of the next layer of the Core.

Then, having intensified the amount of chi in the dantian—an amount that even now made Wu Ying feel as if he were a water pouch filled to bursting—he was to consume the Black and White Tortoise Shell Pill. Similar to the creation of the Core layer, the pill thickened the chi within his dantian, making the process of compressing the new layer of his Core easier.

Lastly, the final pill was to be consumed. The Twice-Cooked Dog Kidney and Wolf Liver Pill would provide additional chi to help fill the newly made Core and replenish the empty dantian Wu Ying would suffer from upon the next layering. That pill was the one that made Wu Ying hesitate the most, since the name of the pill and its purchase had come with a very strongly worded warning from Apothecarist Cai that it had been named by its originator due to the taste of the pill, rather than its effects.

Still, hesitant or not, Wu Ying knew he needed it. He had suffered once already from the effect of having insufficient chi in his dantian and Core. He would not make the same mistake again.

In fact, because the pill was a popular beginner pill for apothecarist venturing into the Core Formation pill-making business due to its simplicity in construction and, conversely, extremely low in demand, it had been the cheapest pill by far. For the same cost as his other two pills, he had managed to acquire five Twice-Cooked Dog Kidney and Wolf Liver Pills for his future usage.

Mind calm, soul serene, Wu Ying picked up the Heavenly Desert Pill and consumed it. He entered a state of meditation, drawing the environmental chi into his body as he waited for the pill to take effect. It was a gradual process, beginning at first with a sensation of dry mouth—except throughout his entire body. Ignoring the uncomfortable sensation, he kept focused, continuing to fill and stuff his dantian.

An hour later, his body withered, his eyes bloodshot, Wu Ying wondered if Apothecarist Cai should have, perhaps, mentioned the side effects of this pill too. And if he had chosen to not do so, how bad was the third pill in truth?

Pushing aside idle thoughts, he took the next pill. Almost immediately, Wu Ying felt its effects, the remaining chi in his body growing sluggish, even that drawn in from the environment slowing.

Still, Wu Ying forced himself to circulate the energy, pushing it through him, churning his chi as he waited for the full effects. When he could no longer contain himself any further, Wu Ying began the process of compressing his dantian, shoving the energy downward toward his existing Core.

This was the most dangerous time—for a badly built Core could fracture. Without being sufficiently reinforced during this period, without it being packed full of refined Core energy and the Nascent Soul given sufficient strength, he could fail.

Fear, for a moment, ran through Wu Ying as he compressed the energy. Yet his Core held without issue, the wind chi within rushing around, compressing even in its sluggish state, buffeting the Core as he pushed downward.

Each breath in, he relaxed a little; each breath out, he squeezed mentally. He shrank the size of his dantian, the thickened wind chi conforming to the walls of the Core, until such time that it could no longer compress itself. Then began the process of hardening the outer shell, of forming the Core, with just enough space for more refined chi to seep in to nurture the Nascent Soul.

Time crawled on as Wu Ying built his Core. Unlike the smooth-edged Cores of other elements, a wind core like his required tunnels where the compressed energy could flow, where the never-ending blowing of the wind could continue. The shaping of such took time and effort, leaving Wu Ying mentally worn out when he was done and the effects of the pills ended.

Finally, Wu Ying opened his eyes, his new layer of his Core formed. He had but one last trial left—and it was the most daunting of all.

Staring at the pill, Wu Ying girded his loins and swallowed the muddy black-green sphere, condemning himself to another cultivation session.

All to improve himself, one tired step at a time on the road to immortality.

Chapter 14

There were things that immortals, demons, and humans alike were not meant to experience. Such instances were why Grandmother Meng served her soup on the Bridge of Forgetfulness[29], driving away nightmares that would plague an individual if allowed to fester. The consumption of the Twice-Cooked Dog Kidney and Wolf Liver Pill was one such experience.

It wasn't just the taste on the tongue when one swallowed it. At least its presence in the mouth was brief, a transitory affair. One would expect it gone after sufficient drink was imbibed. No, it was that the lingering taste and the smell of the pill when the protective outer coating had broken down seemed alive, clawing its way free.

It wriggled out of his stomach, breached his lungs and throat, became close companions with his taste buds and nostrils. There was no way to describe the taste, the smell for one who had yet to experience the horror—drinking raw, rotting sewage from the bottom of a badly cared for waste bin was significantly better.

Refusing to disappear, the sensation of the pill overtook the remainder of his nerves through his body, consuming his attention, so powerful was its presence. Nerves meant to transmit movement, pain, and sensation on skin and organs were twisted as the sensations of taste and smell took over, opening Wu Ying's mind to new degrees of terror.

Worst of all—it worked.

Chi flooded his body, his cultivation method circulating faster than ever as though it too was revolted by the sensations, intent on breaking down the pill and dispersing its effects in a deluge of energy. Empty meridians and a nearly empty dantian were filled as the chi-gathering formation in the room strained, struggling to keep up with the howling abyss that was Wu Ying's cultivating presence. The pill released additional energy with each pulse. Energy poured through his aura, no longer sieved aside for the most appropriate portions, entering his meridians in a rush of cold and heat that made his body ache.

The pain was a minor matter, a footnote to his existence. Once more, Wu Ying lost track of time as he rode the wave of cultivation, drawing in energy again and again, refining it within his meridians before it entered his dantian, where it was processed once more as it passed into his Core.

Eventually though, the period of cultivation madness ended and Wu Ying, released from the sticky, clammy grip of the pill, collapsed to the side, exhausted mentally and physically. Even so, he could not help but smile a small, contented smile at the new Core layer and his half-filled reserves.

---

[29] After serving one's time in the many hells for past sins, souls are supposedly sent for reincarnation. On the way, they are served soup by Grandmother Meng to make them forget their past lives before crossing the bridge to a new life. From general Chinese religious beliefs.

***

Cleansed, fed, and sorted, Wu Ying left the cultivation chamber a changed man. No need to spend weeks, even months working on filling the next layer of his Core. Instead, the disgusting, godsforsaken pill had taken care of the majority of the work in a few days of cultivation, leaving him ready to face the outside world. It would not be always like this—the efficacy of the pill would decrease as he used it more, along with the corresponding size of his own Core—but it was a marked advantage.

There were disadvantages to using pills heavily in one's cultivation journey of course. Pill corruption and remnants needed to be purged. He had less to worry about that as a Body Cultivator—the repeated cleansing of his body in medicinal baths had helped curtail that issue early on—but it was still easy to overcompensate.

More difficult for most was cost and availability. Strong, talented apothecarists were hard to find. Even worse was the bottleneck in spiritual herbs. Locating the ingredients grew in difficulty as greater proportions of wild spiritual herbs were required for Core Formation and stronger pills.

The first breath of air as he stepped out of the cultivation tower was clear and clean, fresh in a way that the recycled, enchanted, and cleansed air of the tower failed to achieve. The wind, long hidden away in its greater part, gusted around Wu Ying, causing his robes to flutter, bringing with it reminders of the world.

He smiled, looking up at the sky, feeling the warmth of the sun on his face. He basked in the tranquility of nature for a long moment, his remade Core thrumming, the Never Empty Wine Pot swirling at ever greater speeds as it reacted to the change in environment and the winds streaming around him.

He breathed, settled his mind, and straightened his robes and jian.

Then, and only then, did he pay attention to the approaching greeting party. A familiar quintet headed by a pair of Elders, while far behind, Apothecarist Cai had just emerged from his workshop.

Wu Ying sighed, knowing he had no choice but meet them. If he failed to do so, he would be breaching the bounds of etiquette, especially since he would need to speak with the Sect Head to take his leave and thank her for the use of the cultivation tower.

Better to confront the problem head-on.

"Cultivator Long," Elder Cai Yao, the one who had confronted him and Apothecarist Cai, spoke when they arrived. "I see your secluded cultivation session was successful."

"It was. Thank you for asking." Wu Ying bowed in acknowledgement. "Thank you for meeting me upon my exit."

"Not at all. I see you have changed your dress to more appropriate wear," Elder Cai said, flicking his gaze over Wu Ying's dark green robes.

Not the Verdant Green Waters Sect robes, but reminiscent of them at least. More formal than what he would normally choose, but this was likely going to fast become a formal event. He watched as Elder Cai's gaze tracked down to the sword Wu Ying wore, belted at his side.

"One tries, though travel means that my wardrobe is, hopefully understandably, limited," Wu Ying said. "I take it the Sect Head desires to speak with me?"

"Oh yes, she does." Elder Cai's smile widened a little.

"Cousins, there was no need to greet my guest yourself. I would be certain to bring him to speak with the Sect Head." Apothecarist Cai arrived with a flap of his robes, his movement a little too loud, a little too hasty to be considered elegant. No surprise then that the quartet gave the apothecarist scandalized and scornful looks when they turned to him. The apothecarist flushed a little but chose to turn to Wu Ying. "Congratulations, Expert Long, on your successful cultivation session."

"You're welcome. And thank you for the pills," Wu Ying said. "They were highly effective."

"Even those dogshit pills he makes," one of the younger members of the quintet spoke, his hair slicked back, his lips twisted in a smirk. He was in the early Energy Storage stage of cultivation but had the baby face of a newborn teen. A treasured prodigy probably.

"Children should not speak when Elders are talking," Wu Ying said, then turned back to Apothecarist Cai. "Shall we go? I would not want to keep your Sect Head waiting any longer than we have to."

The youngster moved to interject, only for Elder Cai to raise a hand and cut him off.

"Of course," Apothecarist Cai said, bowing. "I have already arranged for word of your exit. Hopefully the Sect Head has time to see us."

"I'm sure she will," Elder Cai interjected, again with that self-satisfied smirk.

None of that escaped Wu Ying or Apothecarist Cai from the way his eyes narrowed, but their course was set. He led Wu Ying along the paved walkways to the main Sect headquarters, and this time, none of the sect members—close family or branch members—dared to approach the group. It had as much to do with the people behind, glowering at those around, as a new tension in the air that had been missing before.

Ascending the steps to the raised home, Wu Ying was surprised to sense a peak Core Formation cultivator approaching the entrance. He slowed instinctively, followed by the apothecarist. Within moments, a towering figure with a masculine, handsome face, lustrous hair, and deep-set opal eyes was staring down at them from her position atop the stairs.

Behind the woman were three pairs of Elders. They were all in the Core Formation stage of varying degrees of strength, though only a single member of the six behind was a female— the oldest of them all. The others were men ranging from middle-aged to an older, white-haired and balding, whiskered individual.

"Sect Head." Apothecarist Cai dropped to a knee, lowering his head as he offered a clasped hand bow to the woman.

"Clan head," Elder Cai echoed, copying the bow of the other. He made sure to move to the side so that he was on the same level as Apothecarist Cai before doing so.

Wu Ying, a step behind the pair, was certain to put his hands together and bow, offering his own greeting. "Honored Sect Head. Honored Elders. I, Long Wu Ying, a wandering cultivator, greet you."

It was a little stilted and formal, but overly courteous was what he deemed appropriate in the situation. Once more, he chose to avoid using his sect affiliation.

"Expert Long, I understand you used our cultivation chambers to progress your cultivation base," the Sect Head said, flicking her gaze over to the apothecarist. "Was the attempt successful?"

Wu Ying nodded, bowing again in thanks.

"Interesting." The Sect Head tilted her head. "Do you know that it is considered rude to restrain your aura in this kingdom? Hiding one's strength is a sign of a deceitful individual."

"Ah…" Wu Ying replied, inclining his head. "My apologies." He relaxed his control, allowing his aura to expand. He kept it constrained to only a hundred feet around him, but he no longer tried to hide it from those around. "It is an old habit and precaution. I travel in the deep wilds, as Apothecarist Cai might have mentioned."

"He did. He also spoke of the Thousand Striation pill you brought." The Sect Head's eyes glinted with ill-concealed avarice.

Now Wu Ying understood the greeting. Meeting him on the steps rather than inside, which custom would normally dictate. Out here, damage from a fight would be less noticeable, easier to clean up. The presence of not just a few Elders of the Sect but nine others—the six behind, the two by his side, and the apothecarist—in addition to the Sect Head was an obvious show of force.

He was just grateful the Sect Patriarch and the other Nascent Soul cultivator had not shown up. Then again, that might be too much, even for a show of force for a single Core Formation cultivator.

"A lucky find that fate brought me," Wu Ying replied. He was uncertain how much they cared about fate and fortune, about karmic ties. Some—like his Master—would be wary of interrupting the movement of fate. Others would pay no heed to such superstitious considerations.

On the other hand, the best part of him calling attention to his fortune was that he was telling the truth. It was fate, good fortune, and the well wishes of a ghost that had brought him the pill. If the Sect members had chosen to go there themselves, they might have had the same luck.

Or not.

Not everyone could meet a ghost and not react. He might have responded worse himself, if not for the clear feeling from the wind that while she might be present to his sight, she was not there physically. There was only so much she could do to harm him.

Or so he'd believed. Perhaps ignorance and arrogance had lent him undeserved confidence in his own superiority. It was hard to tell sometimes, when one dealt with the supernatural and ghosts.

"Such a pill… it holds great value to our Sect." Wu Ying glanced over as the Sect Head continued to speak, seeing the apothecarist refuse to meet his eyes. He wondered if it was shame at letting this knowledge and this confrontation to occur, or shame at attempting to acquire it himself. "We would consider it a great favor if you were to sell it to us."

For a second, Wu Ying felt it. That twinning of fate and events. It was not the same, Master Li asking him to give up the World Spirit Ring. It was not the same for the other had right, beyond force and desire. Yet he felt it, the twisting of time and fortune.

Perhaps he had spent too much time with his own Master, to notice such an event. Perhaps he just saw it in his mind and, in believing, made it real.

"I see," Wu Ying murmured as he tried to buy time. Tried to sense the shift of karma, as fate and fortune twisted. The wind blew, and with it, a hint of the heavens, of the elusive wind he had followed across so many lands.

"Come now, you've taken much, putting a great strain on our cultivation tower. Surely a small gift in return is no small matter," Elder Cai said, that smirking grin stretching across his face.

Wu Ying turned, his brown eyes meeting the others'. He saw the tension in Elder Cai's shoulders, even as he gloated. The arrogant fool, to be so blatant…

Ah.

Of course.

It would suit Elder Cai if Wu Ying chose to refuse. Wu Ying was not certain the game they played, but some of it was becoming clear. Still, his anger had his mind spin through the possibilities. He could leave, running from them. They could not catch him once he made his way clear. They might have greater strengths, greater overall power, but he was the wind.

The most dangerous moment was here, now. Before he resolved himself, one way or the other. In the gap of time when he made a decision and moved, they could suppress him, injure him, and finish the fight before he could create the space he needed to flee.

Running would leave the pill in their hands though. But it might see his other treasures safe.

Winds blew, pulling at robes, disturbing robes and hair, tugging at sleeves and bringing with it scents and smells. Reacting to his emotions. His mind cleared, and Wu Ying shifted his weight, twisting one foot so that he was facing Elder Cai fully. The movement was deliberate, elaborate. A clear signal to any martial cultivator.

It was enough.

Elder Cai sprang back, sword appearing in his hand. His closest companion, a step below, drew his sword too, and the other hangers-on did so a beat later.

Wu Ying chose to react by raising an eyebrow. Then, deliberately, he turned and shifted his weight back to neutral to speak to the Sect Head, filling his voice with scorn. "Is this how you treat guests, Sect Head of the Cai Clan? To greet my words with swords?"

"You… you… you were about to—" Elder Cai stuttered.

"Answer your question. You did want an answer, did you not?" Wu Ying said smoothly.

"I…"

But Wu Ying was ignoring the man, facing the Sect Head who was watching him with a bemused look. He shifted his hand, noted how the crowd tensed. He turned it upward, empty, and sighed. "Well, I had forgotten I'd left the Thousand Striation Pill with Apothecarist Cai. Or I would present it to you, Sect Head. A gift, for the hospitality shown to me." Then his gaze flicked to Elder Cai and his subordinates, all of whom still held swords. "By most."

The rebuke drew a sudden intake of breath from the Elders behind the Sect Head. The old woman even went so far as to cackle with glee.

The apothecarist smiled a little, quick to hide it a moment later. Then, realizing his role, he bowed low. "I shall, with the Sect Head's permission, retrieve the pill?"

The Sect Head's lips pursed at Wu Ying, then at the bared blades. Her brows drew down as she glared at Elder Cai, who hastily sheathed his weapon. The loss of face from drawing against a guest was significant.

"I… well, yes." She nodded to the apothecarist. Then looking at Wu Ying, who stood utterly at ease, she stepped to the side and gestured. "Shall we wait within? I shall have refreshments brought forth."

"I would be delighted," Wu Ying replied.

He did not, as they entered the building, miss the fact that Elder Cai and his friends were barred from coming in, even as the other Elders peeled away, leaving him alone with the Sect Head and two others.

***

Four hours later, Wu Ying left the building burdened with a large amount of travel rations, some minor pills, enchanted talismans, and everyday equipment, along with a trio of robes in the dark green and browns he favored cut in the local fashion. All minor gifts, as signs of hospitality. Nothing that was worth even a tenth of what he had given away, even if one included the items in their entirety.

Even so, as he left after having declined to stay for dinner, Wu Ying found that he felt lighter. The pill might have been of use to him in the future but holding on to it would have caused a scene. It would have created enemies he did not need in a kingdom he had just arrived in.

He had done that once before. For better reasons than a pill he could not use.

Perhaps he was learning. Material burdens, want, and desire, they held one down. It was why hermits left civilization to live in the mountains on their way to ascension.

Perhaps he had been a fool to give up his good fortune. But after an hour's travel along the main roads and no sign of pursuit, he chose to believe his actions were honorable. Whatever enmity he had generated with Elder Cai, it was insufficient for the man to hunt him down and attack him.

A situation that Wu Ying could not entirely be certain would have happened if he had not chosen to give up the pill without a fuss.

He chose to believe what he had done was right. And if the scent of the heavens, so clear and clean and crisp, had faded, he could not find it in himself to care. He would find it again, and learning—or not—to trace it was sufficient for him.

After all, he had a kingdom to explore.

Chapter 15

Travel through the deep wilds was both intimately familiar and a new adventure every day. Trekking farther west with each step, Wu Ying traversed the longitudinally elongated kingdom of Jin, lush forests slowly giving way to drier, more temperate climates.

Even as the climate changed, so did the herbs he found. More than once, he returned to civilization to purchase books on herbology, or trading herbs, coin, and at times, expertise for glimpses into Sect libraries. Not into the restricted sections on cultivation manuals or exercises, but the dusty, unused corners where books on gathering lay, hidden behind the more well-known and trekked sections of apothecarist scrolls on the care and feeding of plants and herbs.

Days and weeks spent in well-lit libraries, pouring over notes and transcribing them into his journals, expanding upon the documentation and knowledge he had acquired. Correcting or amending mistakes, drawing new illustrations or making minor amendments to the ones he had drawn. Sometimes, he went so far as to replicate multiple pages of the same herb so that he could locate and verify for himself.

More than once, he cursed lousy artists, bad handwriting, and works ill-kept and worn away by the rigors of time and mistreatment.

Tedious work, but necessary.

Along with that came experimentation and verification. Growing plans espoused by one author or another, gardens that were carefully tended in one sect or left to run wild in another, Wu Ying viewed them all and tested the methods in his World Spirit Ring. Entire fields were set apart to verify the most promising examples—and some truly strange scribblings.

Did it make a difference if you used ground-up dog or cat bones? Was watering plants only from water collected on the eleventh day of each month significantly different? Or did the springs of the Chu hills truly have restorative properties for plants and people?

In the midst of such work, Wu Ying cultivated. Nights passed in guest rooms, eyes half-closed, pulling energy into his body. Twilights, as the sun set and the temperature changed, when the winds came rushing through the buildings, were spent stretching and going through his forms.

And always, always, the Never Empty Wine Pot method rotated in his center. Yet as time went on, he modified the exercise. He had already done so when he gained his Wind Body—his aura, not an impervious barrier against attacks or chi, but a series of gullies and cyclones. Drawing forth energy and rejecting it, searching for wind chi.

Amusingly, in the height of summer, came a blessing. A small by-product of his work—a constant circulation of wind about him that kept him cool, contained such that it never disturbed the environment around him unless he so chose. After all, it made little sense to hide from beasts if one had a dust devil giving away one's location.

More though, it was his dantian and the constant suction of energy within that he altered. Instead of a whirlpool, he drew from his battle with the Guerilla General and formed an internal cyclone. There was no heat in his dantian, but it did not preclude his ability to form the cyclone. A whirlpool of energy from the wind chi in his center swirled at his command, rising and dropping, pulling energy into his dantian in a never-ending cycle. At the bottom, anchored to the end of the twister, was his Core.

The altered Never Empty Wine Pot method, empowered by Core Formation energy, was more powerful than ever. His broader, stronger meridians strained at first under the new burden placed upon it, leaving Wu Ying sore and exhausted the first few weeks.

Days of practice with his Wind Forms and soaking in medicinal baths aided his adjustment, allowing Wu Ying to cleanse and personalize the environmental chi that came through his body. Wind chi flowed, soaking into bones and muscles, altering them ever so slightly, offering him strength and speed even as the majority entered his dantian.

It was still slower, much slower, than staying still and meditating. Finding the proper location, cultivating in desolate mountains and pounding waterfalls or cultivation chambers still provided the greatest results; but trapped in study rooms and dusty libraries, arms elbow deep in soil and compost, Wu Ying had no such luxury.

Spring turned into summer, summer into fall and leaves fell as Wu Ying wandered the state of Jin. Visiting sects, providing herbs and pills, learning and training in equal measure. Occasionally he was drawn into minor squabbles, but for the most part, Wu Ying found himself left alone.

Just another nameless wandering cultivator.

In time, what he could learn from the central wind dissipated, the western wind taking over in its entreaties. He had progressed far in his wind body forms, in his search for the heavenly wind. He found traces now, more often leading toward the west.

Green rolling landscapes turned into light brown clay hills, desert lands, and deep canyons. Moisture disappeared and the sea was but a distant memory on the wind. The western wind howled, speaking of vast lands of sand, thriving oases, and clay-built villages where the travels of industrious merchants crisscrossed.

From one night to the next, fall turned to winter. The lightest dusting of snow appeared after a cold desert night, catching Wu Ying by surprise. Days grew colder, nights freezing, and the wildlife faded away.

A simple decision then, to head toward the beckoning lights of civilization in the distance and the complex, spicy scents of cooked food.

***

The boy was panting as he ran, one hand holding the sword by his side in a white-knuckled grip. His clothing was dirty and unkempt, the threads worn and the style of the everyday

344

laborers who encompassed the morass of civilization. He tore down the hard-packed earth that made up the outpost's attempt at a road, the evening's crescent moon staring down at him as he ran for his life.

Behind him, men and dogs chased the boy. The pursuers were laughing, releasing their grip on the dogs' leashes and letting them near the teenager before pulling backward, the snap of terrible jaws closing on his heels. They ran with easy strides, their higher cultivation allowing them to keep up with the poor child with ease.

The boy stumbled, his sandal catching on an uneven part of the road. An arm shot out, taking the brunt of the fall even as he tucked his head to stare at his stomach moments before his shoulders struck the ground. Rolling with the fall, the boy managed to rise halfway before a dog clamped down on his leg, yanking hard.

"Damn it, Ah Keong! Why did you let Hei Gui[30] catch him? Now the fun is over." Cursing, the smallest member of the group, his tunic open to showcase the emaciated chest he sported, swaggered over to the boy, cuffing the dog to make it let go.

Hei Gui whined but released the boy, who backed off immediately. Pushing himself to his feet while favoring his wounded leg, the boy glared at the man, one hand falling to the hilt of the sword he had held onto through all this.

The cruel eyes of the leader narrowed. "You don't want to do that, boy. Stealing our Master's sword was one thing, but drawing it on us… well, we won't just beat you now."

"It's not his sword!" the boy screamed, pulling out the blade and pointing the tip at the other man. "It's my family's! He stole it from my father when he cut him down."

Leaning back a little from the point, the thin leader smirked. "He should have paid the protection fees. He thought just because he was an Energy Storage cultivator, he was something special. Wasn't that special, was he, bleeding, legless in the street?"

Screaming in rage, the boy launched himself forward and swung. He cut and cut, rage and injury marring his form. Almost disdainfully, the other man backed away, leading the boy into the encirclement of his other men before he gestured.

The child never saw the strike coming from one of the others, the stick cracking across the back of his knuckles and forcing the jian to fall to the ground. He cried, clutching at the injury, bones shattered by the casual attack.

"Now, don't say I didn't warn you, boy…"

Nodding to the others, the leader stepped back as the other thugs closed in on the child who had dropped to his knees, attempting to grab the weapon with his uninjured arm. A foot on the blade stopped his desperate attempts, even as fists were raised.

A sudden wind ripped through the surroundings, throwing dust and sand across the pounded earth road, forcing the group to shield their eyes. When the wind died down, a man was standing beside them, regarding the scene with cold brown eyes.

---

[30] Hei Gui (黑鬼)—Black ghost.

***

Wu Ying had impassively watched the entire scene from a distance as he had journeyed toward the outpost. Only when he noticed the imminent beating and demise had he chosen to act, allowing the wind to carry him forward.

At the same time, he relaxed his control of his aura so his presence would leak outward. Otherwise, he would come off as no more than another mere mortal—albeit a well-dressed one. Now, he would register as a late or peak Energy Storage cultivator, with potentially deeper reserves of energy—depending on the quality of their aura senses.

Unlike the previous kingdom, aura-sensing seemed to be particularly strong here. The techniques he had seen used varied significantly, though spiritual senses, visual- and audio-sensing techniques seemed to be favored. He assumed it had something to do with the desolate environment—so many of the spirit beasts here were ambush predators.

He had even purchased a couple of scrolls on improving his physical senses to study during quiet evenings. There were, unsurprisingly, no scrolls on spiritual sense improvement available to a mere wandering cultivator. Still, it never hurt to supplement one's existing education, even as he came to rely on the winds and his spiritual senses more and more.

Idle thoughts, as the group reoriented to his presence. They moved with surprising alacrity and discipline, a single member keeping a foot on the boy, a sword drawn and pressed against the tiny back to ensure he tried nothing. The other thugs spread out to face Wu Ying, even as they probed at his aura.

Wu Ying idly rebuffed their advances once they pushed past the initial impression he intended to give off, content to leave them guessing. As it stood, even normally, his small Core—layered twice over by now—was still smaller than most beginning Cores.

"Who are you?" The swaggering, thin leader stepped forward, glaring at Wu Ying. Even so, he made sure to stay out of Wu Ying's sword range, overconfident or not.

"A passing stranger," Wu Ying replied.

"Senior, help me!" the boy on the ground cried. Any further words were choked out as his face was ground into the earth and the point of the sword dipped deeper into his back.

"Don't think I won't kill you, boy!" The man standing on the child had a surprisingly high pitch for the intimidating, muscular demeanor he sported.

"It's a small thing, Expert. A private matter. If you don't hurry though, the doors of the outpost will close," the leader said with an ingratiating smile. He gestured to the side and his men shuffled out of the way for Wu Ying to pass by. Watching Wu Ying, searching his impassive face for a clue which way he would act.

Wu Ying nodded a little and took the bait, walking into the group. He noticed them tense, many in the group going so far as to stop breathing. Hands tightly gripped their weapons as he passed by the opened formation. The boy struggled a little, muffled noises as he tried to say something. The blade pushed deeper, stilling the child as blade bit into flesh and set free blood.

Tension ratcheted up further as Wu Ying, having passed through the front of the group, stopped as he was perpendicular to the boy and his captor.

"Expert…" the leader said hesitantly from behind Wu Ying. It was enough for his men to tighten the circle and pull out weapons.

"Your form was contemptible. Your grip was decent, but you let your emotions control your actions. You have reached the Minor Achievement, but your mind needs to be strengthened," Wu Ying said, not even looking at the two he spoke to. "That weapon is good though. Too good for you at your stage of cultivation and learning."

A Saint-jian? No, way too much for a child.

The boy forced himself upward, driving the sword into his own back just so he could get enough space to speak. "Please, help me!"

A shove, the boot slamming the boy's face into the ground. The blade was ripped outward, blood fountaining as the thug repositioned it to finish the child.

Wu Ying's finger flicked, a sliver of solidified sword intent striking the man's hand. The weapon flew from it as the sword was struck away, and a second later, another sliver of sword intent—blunted this time and more chi than intent—struck the man in his chest, driving him off the child.

"You don't know who you are challenging!" the leader snarled.

The boy tried to stand, his back pouring blood from the wound.

Wu Ying snorted. "Stay down. Also, eat this and cultivate."

The pill bottle flew through the air, striking the boy in the chest as he missed the initial toss before catching the bottle as it bounced off him. He pulled open the pill bottle, the smell of its contents drifting outward so suddenly that the entire group froze. The Energy Storage level Gecko's Body Pill was a rare healing pill, meant to restore wounds of greater import than a simple stab in the back.

It was, by its presence and simple gifting, a declaration of strength and intent.

Also, coincidentally, the least powerful healing pill Wu Ying had. Being a Body Cultivator came with a lot of advantages, but it also came with the drawback that it required powerful healing pills to even begin the process of fixing him, especially at the Wind Body stage.

"Thank you, Expert." The words came out wheezily, and the boy crossed his legs with trouble, downing the pill without further complaint.

Another gesture by that skinny, bare-chested leader. Down low, as though he was trying to be subtle. The men reacted, launching themselves at Wu Ying, weapons singing in the air.

He was mildly amused to notice they were using a formation to attack him. Crude, sloppy in execution, but still a fighting formation. Meant to distract, strike at his blind spots, and beat a cultivator of greater strength. Good enough, in its execution, to deal with any normal Energy Storage expert.

The wind gusted, whispering of their movements as it passed them by. Wu Ying did not bother to draw his jian, blocking and striking with his bare hands. Occasionally he released a blade of sword intent from his open hands, striking his attackers and sending them flying away.

After achieving the Heart of the Sword, he no longer needed a weapon in hand to conjure a sword either. Not for something like this, not to block a weapon as it passed him, not to strike with the knife edge as he swung it to send one or the other flying back. Not to beat the half dozen fighters in the Body Cleansing or Energy Storage stage, to leave them bleeding on the ground. The fight was as simple as turning over his hand.

A dozen breaths and the fight was over.

"Leave. I've been merciful thus far," Wu Ying said. "Do not test me again."

The leader stared from where he had staggered upright once more. Stared at Wu Ying, at the boy whose consumption of the pill had begun to strip away the bruises on his face and stopped the flow of blood from his back. He trembled, anger and jealousy warring on his face, then he smoothed it out with a force of will.

"I will inform my Master of this. You will regret having crossed the Broken Earth and Sky Gang!" the leader snapped, waving his people to come with him. He edged off the road, gathering his groaning, limping, and injured thugs, and led them back toward the outpost.

Wu Ying impassively watched them go before letting out a sigh.

"You do not need to watch over me, Honored Benefactor." The boy opened his eyes and broke out of his cultivation. "I can handle myself from here."

"If you waste my pill, I will beat you until you wish they had caught you," Wu Ying snapped at the kid.

The boy's eyes widened then snapped shut, as the killing intent Wu Ying let leak out frightened him into submission.

Of course Wu Ying would not do that. But the pill was so over-powered for the child, if he was smart and grasped the opportunity, he might even cleanse another meridian as a Body Cultivator. Even if he did not, the danger of overflowing chi was present.

As for the stumbling, running away gang? Well, he would handle them when it came to it. However, Wu Ying did extend his spiritual senses a little more, made a request of the wind, and watched as the area before them was shrouded in sand the winds picked up. Choking and shrouding the gang as they ran.

No need to make it easy on child-beaters after all.

***

Twenty minutes later, Wu Ying nodded as he watched the boy sweat. A small exertion of will had the wind take hold of the smell exuding from the child, pulling the stench away from Wu

Ying. He knew that odor all too well and saw no point in suffering it. Instead, he waited as the child exuded the black, sticky impurities of a breakthrough.

Time passed, Wu Ying content to wait and watch. He listened to conversations brought to him as the gang finally made it back to the outpost, the creaking of the doors opening, and finally, their entrance to a building. One covered by talismans blocking any subtle spying.

Of course he could break them—but he had done enough so far. Perhaps in the future… Well.

This was a fascinating new predicament.

He waited, considering his options. Entrance to the outpost would be difficult. He did not need the outpost, though selling some of his herbs and the demon and spirit stones he had collected would have been convenient. Fighting the gang for the boy was possible, but it would not solve the child's long-term problems.

Wu Ying closed his eyes for a moment, letting his thoughts and soul still. He waited, curious to see what would happen when the boy finished his cultivation, curious if the gang would exit the settlement. Curious to see where the wind would blow.

Eventually, the child exhaled a mouthful of turbid air, eyes opening. Or attempting to. Blood and waste products had gummed shut his eyelids, leaving him struggling as he wiped them clear. Or attempted to, failing as he just spread the filth further.

Laughing to himself, Wu Ying extracted a water pouch and emptied it in the air, willing the wind to give the boy an impromptu shower. The pouch was enchanted, meant to draw water from the surroundings and purify it—much like the item he had once acquired in his sect.

A useful spiritual tool for the desert.

Spluttering, the boy wiped and cleaned himself, tearing a rag free of his own shirt to finish the job. It left his face streaked, but at least clean enough to pry his eyes open.

"Honorable Benefactor, my thanks. I apologize for the late greetings. I am Li Shi Min," the boy said, his young face earnest with gratitude but also touched with a hint of suspicion.

Those words… something resounded in Wu Ying's memory. And he smiled as a decision was made. "Clean yourself."

The boy hesitated, but sniffing at his own body, understood. He bent down, grabbed handfuls of the fast cooling sand, and shucking his shirt aside, rubbed it on his skin, scouring himself clean. Again and again, he repeated the process on his chest, his face, and his legs until he was finally done. It was not a perfect effort, but it cleansed the majority of the filth, even if it left him red-faced and bleeding a little.

Then Wu Ying spoke. "Come."

Silence behind him as Wu Ying retraced his steps down the road toward the mountains. He did not look back, content to keep walking. Content to allow the boy to choose. He could almost feel the boy's apprehension and hesitation before he chased after Wu Ying's retreating figure.

By the time Shi Min caught up to Wu Ying, he had his sword sheathed and belted by his side. Glancing at his new companion, Wu Ying deliberately shifted his hand, placing it on the hilt of his own sword and adjusting its angle a little to move the sheath on his belt.

Nothing.

No reaction from the child staring at his back. Instead, Shi Min opened his mouth to speak. "Honored Benefactor…"

Right. A little slow then.

Smiling a little, Wu Ying sped up. And then again, forcing the boy to first hurry then lope after him before eventually turning into a full run, his breath spent on drawing in air rather than asking foolish questions.

Adjusting his speed and simplifying the movement technique of the Wind Steps, Wu Ying ensured he was always just ahead of the boy, the wind pushing backward from him to take away the child's stench.

Into the desert and the broken canyons, along a pounded, dusty earth road under a crescent moon the pair ran, leaving behind the past.

Chapter 16

It took the demonic wolves an hour to find them in the grey-white foothills of the desert. The demonic beasts had tracked them in the shadows, flitting from outcropping to outcropping as they stalked the pair. It took the boy until the wolves were nearly on them before he realized they were being stalked, and another fifteen minutes to locate the first shadowy shape. The spike of fear, the stench of his anxiety mixed with the smell of the impurities he still wore, was an enticing lure for the demonic beasts.

Especially as Wu Ying had suppressed his aura once more, fading into the background and becoming even less than a mortal.

The pack caught them as they descended the latest foothill and faced another long climb, the demonic wolves slinking out of the darkness. Bristly fur, colored in shadows and the orange of the desert night, grown pale and stark on that ill-lit night. Three stood at the front, two at their sides, and Wu Ying sensed two more in the shadows directly behind them.

Shi Min fumbled his sword out of his sheath, his breathing heavy and labored from their progress. With every breath, he swayed a little as exhaustion threatened to take him. Still, he turned around to face the darkened shadows, enough of a huntsman to know that the wolves would encircle their tiny group. Gambit failed, the two from behind slunk out of the shadows as the animals yipped and growled, threatening the pair.

"Straighten your spine. Breathe through your diaphragm," Wu Ying murmured. "Loosen your grip on the top two fingers a little more and shift down one cun."

"What?" Shi Min said.

"Your front foot is too close. Move it to the outside by three cun and angle it outward a little more. Do not look down!" Wu Ying snapped the last sentence. "Always watch your opponents."

"Yes, Master!"

"I'm not your Master," Wu Ying reiterated.

"Yes, Senior! But is this the time?"

"If not now, when?"

The momentary hesitation on Shi Min's part as the answer arrived was noticed by the wolves, who chose that moment to pounce on him. They surged to the boy who chose—correctly—to meet the first one by stepping forward, putting himself farther away from the second monster. However, his cut strayed at the last second, the blade turning a little as it impacted the monster's body. Rather than cutting deeply, the blade tore a little into the skin and skipped, even the ultra-sharp Saint-jian useless when not utilized properly.

"Slow down. Every attack should be perfect, or as close as you can get it." Wu Ying frowned, then extracted a jian of his own from his storage ring.

He shifted quickly, using the Northern Shen circular kicking style and movement techniques to pass before the boy and boot the second animal aside. He flared his killing aura at the first monster, causing it to scramble back. Meanwhile, Wu Ying gripped the surprised Shi Min's blade and disarmed him.

"What…?" The boy's eyes widened, confusion turning quickly into anger, especially when Wu Ying made the jian disappear into his storage ring. "That's mine!"

"It's a crutch." Wu Ying thrust the sheathed jian into the boy's hand. "Use this."

The boy took the weapon, frowning as he drew the weapon. Idly, Wu Ying stepped around the child and booted another monster away, the creatures growing more wary as they realized perhaps their prey was not as defenseless as they had thought.

"This is… a poor weapon," Shi Min stared at the unsheathed blade. It was a simple mortal blade, one that Wu Ying had purchased a while ago because of the fine filigree pattern on the blade rather than for the metal itself.

"You're a poor swordsman. Now, try again." Wu Ying gestured at the monsters.

"You cannot mean for me to practice against them. They'll kill me!"

"Then I suggest you improve fast."

No more time to talk, especially as a trio of wolves chose to attack. One—the Alpha— moved to keep Wu Ying busy while the other two launched themselves at Shi Min, one of the monster's bleeding from the shallow cut the Saint-jian had inflicted.

This time, Shi Min chose to thrust, moving sideways and attempting to slip the attack through the creature's defenses as it lunged at him. It pierced the monster's skin, the tip sliding in then out as the creature landed and retreated, whimpering. The movement almost forced the boy to lose his grip and he had to scramble closer to Wu Ying as the second beast came for him.

Wu Ying, having idly dodged the Alpha's attack, grabbed it by the scruff of the neck and tossed it away. "Focus on the spot where you intend to hit. The smaller your focus point, the more accuracy you will achieve. Aim to kill with one blow, rather than injure."

The growl that erupted from Shi Min's lips was similar to the wolves, making Wu Ying smile a little. Now, he began to understand why Elder Hsu enjoyed teaching in this way. It was highly amusing.

And at least he was not asking Shi Min to wrestle the beasts, half-naked and oily.

***

Nearly forty minutes later, the last of the demonic wolves lay on the ground, blood pouring from its slashed throat. Wu Ying eyed Shi Min, who was wavering on his feet, though both his stance and his sword hand were steady. The older cultivator considered that final slashing attack before he spoke.

"Adequate. You must, however, focus on more thrusts. You are wielding a jian, not a dao. While cutting is feasible, it is not the most effective means of wielding your weapon."

"I… you… you monster!" Shi Min spluttered. Even as he spoke, the boy looked around to ensure each of the animals were truly dead.

About a few minutes into the fight, the demonic beasts had attempted to flee, but Wu Ying had easily caught them and thrown them back into the ring, leaving them with little choice but to attempt to take down Shi Min. Of course, he had also kept the boy alive, sometimes cowing the creatures until the boy caught his breath.

"Breathe properly. And care for that blade well. You'll be using it for the next while," Wu Ying said.

"You're not giving me back my weapon?" Shi Min said angrily.

"Not until you have achieved some skill. This fight should not have taken so long," Wu Ying gestured around him. "This was a pitiful showing."

"With my weapon, I could have—"

"Maybe. That's why you will not receive it back. Now, care for the one you have, then extract the cores." Wu Ying walked over to a nearby rock, took a seat, and watched the boy struggle with his emotions.

In the end, the child tore his robes further and cleaned the weapon properly, returning it to the discarded sheath. He took a moment to offer Wu Ying the Saint-jian's sheath after settling the newly acquired jian in its place on his belt before proceeding to extract the stones.

"Also, skin and bleed them. We'll want their meat for the winter," Wu Ying murmured when the boy was done, the demon beast stones piled in the center of the road. Eyeing the pile, Wu Ying extracted a pouch and tossed it into the center of the stones, watching as Shi Min muttered and cursed, doing as he asked.

The monsters were hung up, their innards extracted and stored away by Wu Ying for later consumption, blood left to be collected in a series of bowls. Once the preparations were done, Shi Min stuffed the demon stones into the pouch and walked over to Wu Ying challengingly.

He thrust the pouch at Wu Ying, mulish stubbornness warring with gratitude. "Here."

"Why are you giving me that?" Wu Ying raised a single eyebrow. "They are your kills."

"I…" Shi Min hesitated, then retracted his hand. "Master…"

"I'm not your Master," Wu Ying said, flicking the boy between his brows with a finger. "I am correcting basic form because it hurts my pride as a jian-wielder to see one wielded so badly. I will not teach you anything of note. Understood?"

Shi Min winced, holding onto his head but nodded reluctantly. Wu Ying could see his emotions, his thoughts play across his face. As much as he might dislike Wu Ying's methods, it was obvious that even the pointers already given were aiding his martial prowess. A powerful cultivator like Wu Ying could offer great help to a simple child like him. At the same time, if he was not an official student, what could he learn?

As much as he could grasp.

"Sit and meditate on the fight. Once the beasts have finished draining, we will leave."

The boy nodded, following Wu Ying's orders. Once he was seated and his breathing had evened out, his consciousness faded into his center, where he mulled over the recent battle and drew in chi for his empty dantian. Wu Ying walked off, murmuring a request to the winds as he went.

There was much to do if the future played out as he expected.

***

The group exiting the outpost had taken much longer to put together than Wu Ying had expected. It worked well for him, for he met them where the road rose in the distance, where the crags and canyons began, where the desert met the scrubland.

The party riding out of the outpost was nearly twenty members strong, the strongest on a half dozen steeds, only two of which were worth their names. The others rode upon short-legged, barrel-chested horses meant for pulling wagons and hoes rather than being ridden. None were badly taken care of, though only the lead mare and its rider spoke of any great respect taken in their care.

Wu Ying breathed deeply, sifting their scents, confirming what his spiritual senses had told him. So few people bothered to hide their scents, even if they sought to hide their cultivation bases from other more obvious sensing methods like spiritual sense.

A prime example—the man who rode to the left of the leader on a bedraggled mare, whose side sported blood from a switch taken to its back. He wore a bracer that kept his energy constrained while charging the bracer, pulling the excess energy into itself to be unleashed. In Wu Ying's spiritual sense, the man burned with the soft light of a Body Cleansing cultivator, but his scent was that of a mid-stage Energy Storage cultivator. More dangerous, the bracer could unleash an attack at the stage of a Core Formation cultivator.

Once.

As for their leader… Wu Ying's lips pressed tightly. A Core Formation cultivator was a concern, even if none of the others were. Yet his scent was wrong, his soul uneven in Wu Ying's senses. His scent held a touch of rot that the wind cultivator assumed came from the twisted and broken core that ground in his dantian. He was one whose journey to immortality had been cut short and now lorded over others in this far-flung outpost.

Where did those who fail go? Some, to hide in Sect halls. Others, to travel in search of a miraculous cure. And others like the one before Wu Ying, to the corners of the earth to hide their shame.

The wind picked up, and for a moment, Wu Ying felt the winds of heaven whisper to him. Speaking of wrongs to be righted, a world gone askew. Heaven's rules thwarted by those who had defied them once before. And now, again.

"So you are the fool daring to stand in my way," the leader said, sure to stop his horse over twenty feet away.

Enough distance that Wu Ying would have to exert himself to strike, if he so chose. Even from here, Wu Ying could see the man's eyes narrow in thought, feel the way his spiritual senses pressed down upon Wu Ying's aura in an attempt to ascertain his cultivation level.

A cautious man then. Good thing Wu Ying had retracted his aura entirely, making himself feel like a pure mortal. While he was certain the others had already spoken of his supposed strength, removing his aura now was certain to make his opponent wary.

When Wu Ying chose not to respond to the man's challenge, he snorted. "You obviously don't know who I am. I am Ching Lau, the Fist of the North!"

The man clenched his fist tightly then punched toward Wu Ying's side, a surge of power and killing intent flowing from him to tear up the ground a half dozen feet beside the wind cultivator.

Still, Wu Ying chose not to say anything, the wind that had been born from the attack swirling around him before depositing the dirt by his side, neither the pelting stones nor the dust touching his still form. He continued to stare at the other man, waiting.

A small motion by the increasingly frustrated cracked Core Formation cultivator to one of his minions. That man spoke, his voice warbling between terror and outrage. "You fool! You dare to disrespect the Master. Tell us, which foolish wandering hero chooses to dig his grave here today?"

"My name doesn't matter. What matters is that you will not be taking the boy today," Wu Ying said, altering his voice such that the pitch was a little lower, the words carried by the wind to make it seem like it came from around them.

"You think too highly of yourself," that same minion snapped.

Then another small gesture from Ching Lau, and a pair of crossbows were raised and loosed. The arrows winged toward Wu Ying's heart, only to crumple in mid-air and fall. The wind shield Wu Ying conjured would have failed against a true attack by a cultivator, one with killing intent and chi within. For a pair of measly crossbow arrows without either?

Child's play.

"You think tricks will be enough to stop us all?" the minion spoke again, but now a greater degree of fear was in his voice.

Ching Lau seemed happy to see how this played out, allowing the other to lose face as his first attempt at intimidation had failed. A cautious man, wary and testing Wu Ying's patience and abilities. He would not act, it seemed, until he was certain he could win. On the other hand, the way he glanced at the others in his retinue, the fact that he was unwilling to let the matter go spoke to either a stubborn greed or a need to keep face.

"It does not matter. The cost of forcing the issue will not be worth the reward of a single Saint-jian." Wu Ying replied, a plan coming together now that he had assessed the others. Face, honor, and the future, all balanced on the tip of a sword. "If we were to fight, one of us would walk away injured. And the other, not at all." He saw Ching Lau tense and continued unhurriedly. "Or you could wait for spring."

"And what happens in spring?" Ching Lau asked.

"A duel. Your best against the boy. Whoever wins keeps the jian," Wu Ying said. "Much less wasteful."

"To the death?"

Wu Ying inclined his head. "Or surrender."

"Still, it feels like a loss for me. We could take what I desire now. Letting him train for a season is truly disadvantageous, do you not think so?" Ching Lau murmured.

"Three," Wu Ying said. "He'll fight your three best."

"Three… why, training by an expert—"

"Three." Wu Ying cut him off firmly. "No more. Or you try now."

For a long moment, Ching Lau and Wu Ying stared at one another, one angry and considering, the other placid and calm.

In the end, Ching Lau nodded. "A season's passing. On the first day of spring, we meet and the boy fights."

Wu Ying nodded and the group turned, leaving him to stand on that barren road under the crescent moon. He watched them ride off, ignoring the single watcher they left behind until their members had crossed over a few li.

Then he moved, drifting like the wind to the man's hiding space and rendering him unconscious with a single strike. No need to let them know where he would take the boy. As payment and warning for the inconvenience, he took the man's weapons—a dao, a crossbow and its bolts—and his coin purse.

Then and only then did he return to Shi Min.

***

The boy had not moved since Wu Ying had left. On the other hand, he could see that the animals were drained of blood, only isolated drops dripping into the bowls. Insects buzzed around the bowls and corpses, some landing inside the sticky liquid, most on the rim or the animals themselves.

A click of his tongue alerted Shi Min, the boy jumping to his feet and scanning the surroundings, his hand on the hilt of the sword. When he confirmed the noise had emanated from Wu Ying, he took the nod toward the animals as indication of his job. In short order, the wolves were lowered, at which point Wu Ying stored all but a pair.

"Expert?" Shi Min asked doubtfully as he looked at the two large wolf bodies. Each probably weighed as much as he did.

"Pick them up and follow me." After asserting his requirements, Wu Ying took off, choosing not to detail his thoughts any further. There was, at the moment, no point.

He listened to the grunts, the twitches and huffs as the pair of bodies were slipped over Shi Min's shoulders, their legs tied close. Then another harder grunt as the boy stood all the way and began the slow, laborious walk to the path that ascended the next hill.

Wu Ying drifted ahead, keeping his pace slow enough that the boy eventually managed to catch up. Then Wu Ying spoke. His words were not particularly important, not yet, just rote repetitions and corrections. "Breathe deeply through your stomach. Tuck your pelvis in. Use the front of your feet when you land, not the heel. You are running—or should be running—not walking. Spring forward, using the momentum of your first step. Never stop moving. Breathe fully."

Words, droning onward. Mixing commentary on body mechanics, breathing and meditation, the Wind steps movement techniques, and the first steps toward achieving moving cultivation techniques. There was too much to try to train the boy in, and Wu Ying needed to improve Shi Min's fundamentals to see the boy's true talent.

After all, while the boy might have some skill with the sword, that did not necessarily translate to talent in cultivation. If he was a prodigy, this was the time to lay the basic foundation. If he was not, a solid foundation could not hurt.

Though, Wu Ying had to admit, he was not entirely certain how it was that he was the one to lay that foundation. Life was strange that way.

A circle, one that he found himself repeating. Words drawn from Senior Yang as Wu Ying journeyed to the Sect, from his Master as he was trained in the mist-laden, waterfall-filled sect. Even from his father. All of it distilled into words of wisdom and training to suit the situation.

An hour, and Shi Min's posture had improved, his breathing and basic body mechanics strengthening. He was making use of the fundamentals of the movement technique Wu Ying had begun to teach him, with the boy even expanding upon the knowledge instinctively. Their pace had increased as he learned how best to move, but in the last few minutes, he had begun to flag.

For there was one minor issue.

"You're terrible at cultivating," Wu Ying stated.

"You're telling me to try to pull the energy while moving!" Shi Min protested. "That's dangerous and painful and destructive."

"It's called moving cultivation and can shorten the time you require to strengthen yourself." Cocking his head, Wu Ying considered what he'd seen while the boy had partaken of the pill. How the powerful pill had moved through him, the gains Shi Min had experienced. "Have you mostly relied on pills to breakthrough?"

Silence. Another dozen steps. Wu Ying was patient as they walked along the top of the canyon walls, heading away from town and off the pathway now. He led them, and the wind led him.

Eventually, a slow, reluctant nod was pulled from Shi Min.

"So, truly lousy." Wu Ying nodded. "Stop attempting the moving cultivation. Focus on the movement technique."

"Yes." A loud, tired grunt.

Silence for another dozen steps, then a loud thud. Wu Ying turned his head sideways, raising an eyebrow as the boy had collapsed. The child released the wolf corpses, pushing them off his prone form, and staggered to wobbly feet, breathing hard as exhaustion was evidenced through every trembling limb. Still, he reached for the corpses.

Wu Ying chose not to say anything, curious to see how far Shi Min would push himself.

The answer, as it turned out, was nearly an hour and five other collapses, the last two within minutes of one another. That final time, Shi Min lay on the ground, so exhausted he was unable to even pry the corpses off his own back as he suffocated between dirt and cold flesh.

Snorting, Wu Ying removed the bodies with a wave, depositing them in his Spirit Ring. He took a seat a distance away and turned his thoughts inward even as the Never Empty Wine Pot howled, cultivating cold wind energy for him.

Eventually, the boy recovered and sat up, looking around with fear in his eyes. Upon seeing the boy awake, Wu Ying reconjured the animals and walked off.

"Sadist," Shi Min grunted from behind. But he followed after picking up the corpses.

Of course he did.

Chapter 17

Late at night, under the crescent moon, the desert canyons were a stark gray and white painting. Deep shadowy ravines were a steep drop along the unmarked pathway they strode upon, beasts prowling along the edges. Not many beasts—the desert was too stark, too difficult to survive to be replete with animals and monsters. Not, at least, in comparison to the bountiful southern kingdoms and forests Wu Ying was used too.

Even so, he heard the little skitters as scorpions and other nocturnal creatures crawled across the ground, the beat of wings and the silent glide of a flying predator seeking its dinner. Sparse clouds, too wispy and bare to offer rain, crawled across the horizon, the temperature lowering quickly as the wind danced across the sky.

When Wu Ying turned away from the edge of the canyon, taking a steep and narrow path, he stopped at the edge. Turning, he eyed the boy stumbling after him and gestured him closer. A hand reached out, touching the wolves' flesh as he drew the pair of animals into his storage ring, forcing aside the boy's weak aura to take control of the corpses and store them.

Shi Min let out a loud gasp of relief, his back straightening abruptly at the sudden release of weight. He nearly stumbled off his feet, so great was the change. For a long few seconds, he concentrated only on breathing and empowering his body. Wu Ying waited until the boy was ready before he turned and descended the trail.

Another twenty-five minutes and finally, they reached their destination. A cave, expansive in size and warmer than the chill of the surroundings. Once, it had been used by a bear, and previous to that, by a cultivator seeking solace. Now, with the trail to it treacherous and concealed by brush and an overhang, it lay abandoned.

Standing in the cave's entrance, Wu Ying looked upward, watching as Shi Min, his face hugging the wall, shuffled his way downward. Never once did the boy look down or aside into the canyon itself, at times half his feet hanging off the wall. The stink of fear surrounded the teenager, even as he shuffled resolutely toward Wu Ying.

Only when the boy was past the most dangerous passages, fingers tightly gripping the cracked wall, did Wu Ying turn into the cultivation cave. He summoned spirit lamps from his ring, directing the wind and his spiritual aura to place them against the wall, lighting the area.

Another gust of wind, more controlled, pulled at the dirt and refuse. He sucked it toward him, storing it all in his World Spirit Ring, for the droppings of the bear that had lived here before, strong and powerful in its primacy, would do well in his fields.

Wu Ying regarded their temporary abode, now cleaned and illuminated. The floor was mostly smoothed, a cleared area near the front and center dug deep into the earth, where the remnants of old ash and dung were to be found. The rusted remains of a spit lay fallen by the side, a remnant of the cultivator and his cooking fire.

Deeper within, a stone bed had been carved into the side of the cave, while a natural depression collected water farther within. It was only quarter-filled at this time, long stalactites hanging above where moisture collected and dripped away as temperatures changed.

There was no smell of fresh guano, the cave having been left alone by the bats that occupied many other such locations. It was a bare bones location, but for their purposes, more than suitable. The large open space near the entrance was sufficient for the boy to train. The pool of water sparked further consideration as well.

As Shi Min finally shuffled in, his breathing easing the moment he was away from the deadly plunge, Wu Ying walked over to the entrance and extracted a wolf corpse. He held the beast aloft as he drove a spike deep into the ceiling, hanging the beast on it a moment later.

"Butcher the beast," Wu Ying said. "I'll prepare the rice and water."

Shi Min licked his lips, attempted to reply, then croaked, his throat dry. Frowning, Wu Ying shook his head and pulled out his water bottle, handing it to the boy. As both a Core formation cultivator and a Body Cultivator, he sometimes forgot minor physical discomforts.

A failing to be corrected.

Wu Ying wandered over to the fire pit, which he cleaned out with a chi projection and wind before embedding new metal stands. From within his spirit rings, he also extracted batches of dried wood and the cooking implements he required. Others might use dried dung, but he had an entire world at his beck and call. He had no desire to stoop to that level when a little forward planning was all that was required. All the while, he paid attention to the boy as Shi Min began the process of skinning and butchering the beast.

"Stop cutting the bones," Wu Ying spoke up. "And sharpen your knife before you begin. Pay attention and focus on the empty spaces, the places where the body desires to be separated, rather than focusing on where you want to cut. In the gaps, the voids, that is where your blade should go."

"Like here?" Shi Min asked, slicing farther up at the shoulder joint.

"Better. Remember to cut gently. Hold the joint apart if necessary. In the space between, there are tendons and ligaments, but those will part with ease if you angle correctly. Remember how the beast moved, the angles and direction of its movement," Wu Ying continued. "Follow those lines, and in so doing, save your energy and your weapon."

Shi Min nodded, pulling at the leg, studying the line of muscle on the animal. Occasionally, Wu Ying reprimanded him again, asking him to cut with more firmness and less hesitation or to shift the angle of his blade or to draw harder or deeper. By the time the first haunch was separated and trimmed, the fire was burning well and coals were ready on one side of the large fire pit.

Taking the meat, Wu Ying set it on the spit and began the process of cooking their meal. Vegetables were easy enough to extract from his World Spirit Ring, along with some flat, igneous rocks, all of which he added to the pot and fire respectively.

In the meantime, Wu Ying wandered over to the pool of water and bent to taste it. He nodded to himself, grateful it was not diseased though it was stagnant. Probably best not to consume it, but he had other uses for the pool anyway. Lowering his hand beneath the pool, out of sight of the boy, he began the process of extracting water from his World Spirit Ring, refilling it.

"Expert, is a bath truly the right choice right now?" Shi Min asked, pausing in his butchering and wiping at his face. "Hot sand and a bucket would be sufficient for me."

"You will be using both," Wu Ying said, the small bubble of air he had used to keep the smell around the boy contained still in place. Scoured clean with hot sand or not, he was still filthy. "Then you will be soaking in the bath."

"Expert…" Finding no answer from Wu Ying, Shi Min sighed and focused on finishing up the butchering. "As you say."

Wu Ying snorted a little to himself as he added more spiritual herbs to the bath water, letting the herbs soak. He would need to warm the water with the stones and his chi—aspected to the flame variant—or else the entire procedure would be of little use.

If the boy wasn't going to be a particularly strong soul cultivator, then Wu Ying would find another path for the child to cross the distance between him and his opponents. He would show the path, but it would be Shi Min's choice to walk it.

***

"And all I'm supposed to do is soak in here?" Shi Min said later.

Midnight had come and gone, the deep of early morning on them. Dinner had been finished, the meal consumed with the remnants set aside. Wu Ying had cautioned the boy to eat lightly, but young as he was, he had chosen to ignore that. Now, replete with nourishment, Shi Min stared at the pool, herbs and flowers floating within, clouds of steam rising.

"Soak and cultivate," Wu Ying replied. "Just a little differently. You'll be pulling the energies within the bath into you, pushing out further impurities."

"Body Cultivation," Shi Min replied. "I heard it's… it's…"

"Painful?"

"Agonizing. That you can be driven mad by the pain, as the process pulls you apart from within."

"It can be." Wu Ying offered the boy a scroll, which Shi Min hesitantly took and unrolled, frowning as he read it over. "The Immortal Mortal Body Cultivation technique rewrites you from within. It is the most expensive technique, and it only has a dozen steps listed in the scroll you see before you. There are rumored to be additional steps, but that was all I found. It does have one advantage though. It will work with any elemental type."

Shi Min looked over the scroll for a moment more before he offered a tight smile. "May I finish reading this?"

"Oh, no need." Wu Ying waved at the pool. "The first soaking will just accustom your body to the process and pull out any surface concerns. You won't be able to cultivate until you are used to it."

"I'm stronger than you think." Shi Min's chin rose, the mulish stubbornness of a teenager rising to the fore. "I can do it."

"Then show me. Get in and cultivate. Once you are able to do so, then ask for the scroll again."

Chin jutting out, the boy disrobed to his underclothing, the threadbare and ripped peasant clothing barely hanging on anyway. At Wu Ying's behest, he scrambled to the exit and scoured his flesh again, including hard-to-reach parts of his body to finish the job he had begun earlier. As he cleaned, Wu Ying spoke of the physical exercises he would need to complete, if he survived the bath.

Once Shi Min was done, it was only then that he was allowed to climb into the bath, hissing a little as his feet entered the warm water. Breath held, Shi Min sank all the way to his upper chest. He stayed inside for a moment before looking up at Wu Ying triumphantly. "See, it's not so bad."

Wu Ying continued smiling, waiting. He watched as the boy shifted a little, as the herbs seeped through his skin, acting on his nerves and tendons, digging through his flesh. The boy's breathing grew a little constrained, his eyes pinching in pain.

"It only gets worse," Wu Ying murmured kindly enough. "Cultivate if you can, focus on breathing if you cannot. Eventually you will need to do more than just soak. The exercises to pull chi through your body, to energize the herbs and make full use of them, will be a future endeavor. For today, bear with the pain. If you fail, you will die."

Shi Min jerked, his only acknowledgment of what had been spoken. His mouth opened as he let out an agonized whimper, and Wu Ying stepped away, extracting and tossing silencing talismans around the stone tub. Leaving the child to scream his head off, a sound that was muffled but not entirely robbed of its volume by the talismans, Wu Ying returned to the front of the cave.

The boy would have to choose now, if he was willing to do what it took to grow strong. He had no talent, but that did not matter. Not in the beginning stages. Hard work, discipline, and a willingness to face the hard choices and sacrifices were what was required to succeed to begin with.

Well, that and a little luck.

Now, Shi Min had it all. Whether he walked the path was his to choose.

***

Sunlight from a new dawn was beginning to peek around the horizon, lightening the sky in varied orange and red palettes. It wasn't a spectacular morning, not as compared to other sunrises Wu Ying had experienced. Yet as before, whether he was working the fields or sitting at the edge of a former cultivation cave, he took the moment to acknowledge and savor its unique beauty.

Every sunrise the same, every sunrise different—just like humanity.

A small gesture and a coaxing of the wind drew the boy from the tub. The child was senseless, his skin wrinkled from soaking for such a length. The body bobbed and weaved as the wind carried it to the Core Formation cultivator, depositing its heavy burden with a sodden thump on the cold stone floor. Water pooled on the ground under the senseless body.

For a second, Wu Ying considered trying to guide the water in the tub into his ring but discarded the idea almost as quickly as it arrived. His control of the winds had grown, but it had not done so sufficiently to guide unwilling water across a cave to his World Spirit Ring. That level of control was something a water-aspected cultivator might have for a similar task. Or perhaps one in the Nascent Soul formation stage.

Eyeing the still senseless boy, Wu Ying wandered back to the tub, stuck his hand into the concoction, and drained the water into his ring. The impurities the boy had expunged would not be added directly to a field, but he had a number of settling ponds and other sections where impurities could be broken down by the earth and turned into fine fertilizer.

It would be a poor showing to turn up his nose at such a bounty, especially when it but required a little additional time.

As he processed the water, Wu Ying played with the wind, feeling his control and his spiritual aura extend around him, coating the surroundings with his understanding and his chi. It had been a task and a half, learning to work with the wind, to make use of it for more than carrying or containing scents.

There were two portions to his control. The first was the soft power, the indirect control he exerted. It had come to him naturally when he had begun this journey, as the winds laughed and danced around, speaking to him as one of them. The dao, the integral connection of his Wind Body, and the process of imbuing it into his very essence had given him the senses to hear them.

In so doing, the ability to speak with them as well.

To request their aid, to build upon their strengths. The results in the beginning had been elusive and troublesome, for only as Wu Ying truly began to understand the winds did his entreaties bear fruit. One did not ask the north wind for warmth or mercy, nor the south to blow steadily.

Even with understanding though, such entreaties might fall upon deaf ears, for the winds were fickle at the best of times. Even for a sworn brother, they might turn a deaf ear, listening instead to the keening of the midnight ghost or the wail of a newborn.

It was there that Wu Ying's second portion of control came forth. One he had built upon from his studies of his aura, his spiritual sense, and the projection of his chi and killing intent.

There, his studies with the blade had borne the most fruit. His Wandering Dragon strike had been based upon—in part—his projection of wind chi. An exertion of his cultivation and understanding upon the world and the winds themselves.

Wherein the first part, he asked, in the second, he demanded.

But such demands were only as strong as his control and the energy in his dantian. Such willful twisting of the world required him to dominate the conversation, to exert his presence. And like any tyrant, pushing too far might see a vast rebellion that even he could not stem.

As such, Wu Ying studied and explored both methods.

It was not enough to control the wind directly or entreat its help indirectly, but to learn the when, the why, and the how to wield both together or separately. At least here, guidance could be found in the Seven Winds manual. It spoke of twisting the winds together, to tie them tight and true, to being the paramount force.

His fingers touched the bottom of the tub, Wu Ying having leaned over and lost track of time in his contemplation of his path. The wind—the winds—were laughing at him again, tugging at stray locks of hair, at the edges of his robe. Controlling such a force that even the heavens only laid the barest of precepts upon?

A foolish thought.

Good thing he was a fool.

Standing, Wu Ying returned to the boy to find him not at the entrance but near the fire, tearing chunks of cold meat from the roast and stuffing it down his throat. He ate greedily and with little manners, not even noticing Wu Ying for long minutes in his hunger.

"Expert!" Shi Min said, popping to his feet when he finally registered Wu Ying's presence. "My thanks for the... bath."

Wu Ying inclined his head. "Do not forget to exercise before you rest."

Enthusiastic as the boy might be, exhaustion was tugging at the boy's control. He swayed a little on his feet, hunger having abated his weariness only for a little. Shi Min managed a nod, wiping his hands on his grubby pants that he had put back on before, stumbling to the front of the cave. Referring to the scroll that Wu Ying helpfully floated over, he began the series of physical exercises that would help disperse the nutrients from the bath deeper through his body.

Wu Ying watched for a time, choosing not to correct the boy's form. Not today. Sloppy as his movements might be, there was little point in correction, for the boy stumbled through each motion half-asleep. Thirty minutes later, Shi Min finished the routine and collapsed into his bedroll, snoring loudly the moment he lay down.

At the front of the cave mouth, Wu Ying set up a few simple talismans to alert him if anyone attempted to enter the cave. Then, finally, he closed his eyes. Tomorrow would be the start of their real training.

Chapter 18

Morning began with a run that traversed the narrow pathway up and down the canyon walls, from one edge to the next, before returning in a long circuitous route. Rather than have Shi Min chase Wu Ying, the wind cultivator chose to practice his own control, sending a small shuttlecock bouncing through the canyon walls and forcing the teenager to follow.

Extending his control of the wind across the land, focusing and watching over the boy, was difficult for Wu Ying, requiring utmost concentration. If anything, his greatest problem was that the wind had little desire to be controlled as it found the game alternately entirely hilarious and amusing—sending Shi Min skittering up rocks and down tight canyon walls after the target—and boring, having completed its moments of whim and whimsy.

A full two hours later, the boy stumbled back to quaff a full jug of water before being directed to stretch then relax in the medicinal bath. Pain eroded at Shi Min's control as the herbs soaked into his skin, his breathing shallow and hurried as he panted. For an hour, he soaked, then he was sent to complete the basic stretches and consume a meal of demonic wolf meat, stored and pickled vegetables, and rice. Only after he had finished eating and completed a second round of slow stretches and the beginning of the wind form was a short period of rest and cultivation enforced.

"Too slow. Run faster tomorrow," Wu Ying chided the boy when he had finished his cultivation. "Do not just run but practice the Wind Steps."

Shi Min nodded dumbly, not daring—yet—to talk back to the exacting taskmaster Wu Ying had become. He had neither the time nor the inclination toward coddling, not with the boy's future and life at stake.

Only when Shi Min had cleared his mind did instruction in the weapon arts begin. The jian was a gentleman's weapon, one of subtle nuances and maneuvers. Positioning, feints, control of the blade, and distance between oneself and their opponent was all part of the art. But without the basics, even the most powerful sword form was but a child's mud painting of the sunset in a water-logged field.

It was in the basics that Wu Ying trained the boy relentlessly.

"Lunge. Reset. Lunge."

A sheath, bereft of the weapon it once held, was used to adjust the other, lifting the lead arm a cun here, the back arm a half-cun there. A knee was tapped on the side to push inward to close a line and strengthen the body, weight was transferred backward or forward. Alterations made by miniscule amounts.

"Lunge. Hold. Correct your form."

A push here.

"Recover. Correct your form."

A pull there.

"Lunge. Hold. Correct your form."

Pressure on the ankle.

"Recover."

"Again."

"Again."

And again. until hours later, the boy was allowed to relax, collapsing on the spot as muscles—traitorous muscles—twitched and spasmed from exhaustion.

"Cultivate and consider your mistakes," Wu Ying remarked, before he too took his seat to do the same.

In teaching, he illuminated mistakes in his own form. The minor corrections he made highlighting other areas he found wanting in his own stances. In showing, in aiding, he grew.

"Take the first form," Wu Ying said when they were done.

They moved to the boy's form, the one he had been taught by his father. Wu Ying would watch, he would learn, he would correct the other's basics. As for the heart of the form, he believed he would grasp it soon enough—for was that not what the Heart of the Sword was for too?

Training, hours upon hours, before it was time to bathe. Exercise tired and receptive muscles, consume additional sustenance, then repeat one's forms until sleep called once again and the cycle could begin anew on a new day.

*****

Winter arrived with a vengeance, the cultivators' routine ruined by snow and ice on the regular. No longer did Shi Min crawl, stumble, and run across loose rocks and sand but instead he traversed snow and ice, falling and scraping his hands raw, nearly plunging to his death more than once as the cold north wind laughed.

More than once, Wu Ying gently sent the wind to nudge the boy back onto the right path, to offer him unseen purchase when he required it. There was tough training and then there was murderous training—and while the line between the two was slight in their case, he strove to stay on the right one.

With winter taking its primacy in the seasons, the pair took longer on their morning runs, their cave a warm respite where cultivation, cleansing, and forms were trained all hours of the day. Only when Wu Ying was sufficiently satisfied with the boy's basics did they begin sparring, shifting formats.

Memories flooded Wu Ying, of days and hours training with his father in the early morning hours or during such cold days in the winter—though their winters were much milder. He ran through the options, from full speed, full contact exchanges to more cautious probings, single movement rote practices, to paired simultaneous motions and finally, slow work, where opponents fought and moved at a fraction of their speed.

Each format offered different advantages. Slow work focused upon positioning and reading an opponent, of finding that golden move which allowed one to strike, dodge, and position oneself advantageously against one's opponent's retaliation.

Turn based, single move sparring forms focused upon optimal motions, lines of attack, and weapon positioning. If you chose to step, you were not blocking. If you chose to strike, you had to control your opponent's sword or risk being struck in turn. It taught patience and positioning, caution and defense, an elegance of motion that most new fighters lacked.

Full speed sparring mimicked combat, but it was ruinous upon body and weapons. It was the least useful for their purposes, for most of its advantages could be replicated using blunted tips and slowed motion, allowing one the full extension of body, the sensation of pushing weapons off-line or forcing one's opponents to retreat from a very real threat.

But without restraint, sparring with full contact with weapons saw but injuries and the true height of Mount Tai. Yet it was required, to allow the boy to control his nerves, to calm his breathing when the adrenaline pounded, to face the blade as it spun through the air toward one's pupil, knowing one's end was near.

Learning to accept death.

And then learning to move anyway.

Even when failure was all but guaranteed because to fail to move so was to give up. In the trying, success could be found, no matter how slim.

Lessons taught at the end of a blade, by father, by son.

Through the long winter months, the pair trained. And words were sparingly exchanged, outside the bounds of their training. All too often, Shi Min would collapse, exhausted at the end of each evening or between sessions, cultivating to pull what little energy he could into him.

"Expert… why do you do this?" Shi Min asked, one long winter night. He had a bowl in hand, heaped full of rice and vegetables and, of course, the seemingly never-ending supply of demonic wolf meat.

"Hunger must be fed. Or else how is the body to develop?" Wu Ying said, purposely being obtuse.

"Not the meal. The training. The herbs…" He gestured backward. "My father might have been a poor cultivator, but even he taught me about Body Cultivation. It is too expensive for one such as me."

"Yet you soak in it every day."

"That's my point!" Shi Min said, exasperated. Then, belatedly, added, "My apologies, Expert."

"And my point as well."

Narrowed eyes at the damn evasion. Shi Min's lips thinned, but he gave up. It was always like that, after all.

Then it was another day, and the boy threw himself into all those lessons, into the baths that scoured his flesh and bone and meridians, tearing them apart and rebuilding them, refining him in minutes and then hours of agony once more.

Another night, another day, and across their blades.

"Those forms of yours, a family style?" Wu Ying asked as he idly parried an attack, shifting Shi Min's arm a little to better the angle.

"My father's." Shi Min ducked his head low. "He was, we were, once a cultivating family. My great-great-great-grandfather a scion of the Wudang Sect. Then he left, for he fell in love."

Wu Ying nodded. The ascetics of Wudang would not be willing to accept such an event. It was not their way.

"He took with him what he learned and trained his son. We were—are—caravan guards, traveling where work takes us, but we trained. Over time, the style changed, adapted."

"There is some skill in there. Otherwise, imperfections." Wu Ying watched as the boy did not bristle at the mention. A lack of pride or just understanding?

"I want to be worthy of it. To be a true cultivator," Shi Min whispered.

"That path for you is blocked," Wu Ying said mercilessly as he caught an overhand strike and kicked the boy away.

Tumbling head over heels, the boy rolled and bounced to his feet. The kick had been focused on pushing—energy imparted after contact had been made—so he was not injured beyond minor bruising. "I cannot be an immortal. But being a cultivator is more than that! To be worthy of blade and honor, of the respect given. I want to protect, rather than take."

Wu Ying nodded, then flicked the tip of his blade toward the boy and back toward himself. "Then you have to grow stronger."

The wind took Shi Min's whispered words of resolution to him as the boy charged forward.

"I will."

***

Days of routine, of training. Shi Min stretched and exercised and ate, feeding spiritual herbs and chi into his very bones to give himself an edge.

Alongside the boy, Wu Ying trained and cultivated without stop. The winds howled outside the cave, throwing snow and sand without end, birthing whispers of angered ghosts and spirits to the nearby villages. He flowed through the motions of the Long family style and the other sword manuals he studied, integrating their motions into his body, into his new understanding of the jian.

At times, Wu Ying discarded his weapon, choosing instead to form a sword from chi and body alone. The Heart of the Sword required no weapon, for one became the jian. Hands as sharp as a razor-edged blade, body as tough as steel and as flexible as a blade. Whiplike in motion, deadly in its stillness.

A winter of quiet cultivation, of desperate training and progress.

When the winter winds died and the snows began to melt, Wu Ying stared at the boy and nodded to himself.

It was time. Time for a final test.

A final lesson.

***

Up above on the bare cliff, footing treacherous as black snow made cloth-covered feet slip and slide as it melted and reformed in the night. The pair journeyed upward through the narrow passageway, the boy having adapted and taken to Wind Steps with alacrity after so many months of constant, abusive training.

Wu Ying took position on the crackling ground, slushy snow breaking under his weight. He could have floated above it—would have normally—no heavier than a feather on the snow, but this was a test for the child. He suppressed his cultivation, his skills all the way down to the start of the Energy Storage stage. His aura did not need suppressing, he did that automatically; but the rest…

Shi Min took his place across from Wu Ying, his father's sword finally in his hand. The first time he had held it since they had begun training, his fingers finding the familiar grip with ease. Wu Ying tilted his head, watching as the boy shifted his stance without thought to adjust for the different length, different weight of the blade.

So close… another six months of training and he might have achieved the Sense of the Sword. As it stood, the boy had the Greater Achievement of the jian already, progressing from the Minor Achievement he'd had when Wu Ying had first seen him.

The boy had a gift. Not a bright burning one like Pan Chen but a slower, quieter one that might carry him far given enough guidance and training.

Not the heights of cultivation. No immortality for this child. But not everyone had to climb that unforgiving peak. Not everyone should.

After all, cultivation at its height, at its apex broke the very bounds of the heavens, shattered their precepts to enforce the individual's ascendance upon the natural order. In the wake of transformation, chaos arrived, and with chaos, loss and pain and revolution.

Heaven's wind howled, whispering rules and requirements, cold and cruel laws that sought order before justice, with only the barest margins given to mercy and kindness. And in that gap, a darker, cloying wind arrived, one that smelled of the dark, deep places of the earth, of the musky smell of a well-kept compost pile. It murmured of change, of the necessity of transformation, of chaos…

Before it disappeared, driven away by a sudden gust of the heavenly wind and the approaching tip of a sword.

Wu Ying turned ever so slightly, letting the blade pass by his face. His hand came up, a pair of fingers pushing against the edge and traveling with the motion of the weapon, never allowing the blade to cut his fingers. A tricky technique, the bare-handed block.

Then Shi Min was before him, recovering close and sweeping his blade backward, spinning the blade around his back and head as he built speed. Only to be met by a single step, elbow flaring upward to strike and throw the boy away.

Shi Min stumbled, recovering while executing a series of quick cuts to protect himself against a potential counter-attack that never came. He stabilized himself on cracking ice, the crisp sound drifting through the air, and he glared over the tip of his sword at Wu Ying.

"Are we not practicing swords?" Shi Min challenged.

"We are practicing survival," Wu Ying replied. "We are testing your improvements. Never forget that the blade is but a tool. The weapon is yourself."

Then with a slight shrug, Wu Ying withdrew his jian. The tip rose and retreated, beckoning the other.

The clash of blades that followed was an energetic and violent affair, one bereft of the extensions of chi blades and the expulsions of sword intent that had been so common among Wu Ying's most recent battles. The wind was still around the pair, only picking up at the edges as Wu Ying's request, neither aiding nor hindering his opponent. Their struggle was mundane, all too mortal, and reminiscent in a way that brought a grin to Wu Ying's lips.

There was a beauty in the simple clash of steel, where neither chi nor sword intent marred the intentions of the other. Here, in the passage of blade and the crossing of forms, was a conversation of metal that stripped away outward pretenses.

A thrust—desperate need.

A twist of the hand—casual disregard.

Forward recovery—aggressive demand.

Angled, triangle step sideways—measured refusal.

Sweeping shoulder cut—violent entreaty.

Angled parry to drive tip into blade—careful agreement.

Forms played across the landscape as the pair fought, the Dragon parts the Painting meeting Grass sways across the Land, the Cloud Hands circular deflection beaten aside by the Tree trunk Falling. Across the clifftop they fought, feet stamping onto crackling ice, snow and hidden rocks flying through the air as they battled for supremacy.

Shi Min had grown in skill. His stances were firmer, his grip both tighter and more flexible than ever. His basic forms, while not perfect, had improved. So much that the widest, largest flaws in his defense had shrunk, forcing Wu Ying to work to find the gaps. Blade tips teased and whispered as he offered pointed rebuke and the boy learned.

Till finally, sensing the culmination of their conversation, Wu Ying chose to end it. The same way another teacher had once ended their own—bloodier—battle.

A retreating parry to give him space. To give the child time.

A lunge that carried Wu Ying forward, the Sword's Truth exploding forth as he crossed the distance.

The boy's stumbling retreat, as careful and considered strategy fell apart under one last lesson—that strength, at its extreme, had an intensity all of its own.

Blade tip arced forward, piercing hasty defense, pushing flat of blade against body as arms collapsed backward. Shi Min's blade edges pressed into clothed flesh, dimpling skin before the pressure was relieved just as suddenly, forcible momentum sending the boy tumbling head over heels to fetch up near the edge of the cliff.

Long silence as the boy groaned in wet snow, before he clambered to his sodden feet, sword held in hand at guard. Only to find Wu Ying standing, sword sheathed, winds swirling around him as they carried traces of the fading winter and hints of the coming spring.

"Thank you for your instruction, Expert!" Shi Min intoned ritually as he bowed low to Wu Ying. Rather than raise his head, he kept it lowered, sword held backward along his arm in front of his head.

"You have studied well," Wu Ying said. "Rest. Mediate upon the battle. Tomorrow, we meet your assailants, and you have your honor to regain."

A slight shudder from the boy as he thought of what awaited him. Wu Ying watched as Shi Min fought down the fear, the atavistic knowledge of his potential death. He watched the internal struggle before the boy accepted his fate, chose to face his challenge head-on rather than beg Wu Ying for aid.

Shi Min straightened then bowed again. "Thank you, Expert. For everything."

And then, as requested, he walked to the cliff's edge to begin the long trek back to their abode. Already, Wu Ying could see the boy's mind turning to the fight ahead, to readying himself for the battle. He could not help but approve.

Even as a part of him wished for it to be different. But all seasons pass, and the wind could not stay still. It blew on, ever onward. And so too must he follow.

Chapter 19

Did it surprise Wu Ying that instead of a simple bare spot on the ground outside the town, there was now a crowd and a cleared circular location for the fight? A little. Not in the actuality of the event, for the wind and his spiritual senses had picked out the changes long before the pair of them arrived. But more in the presence of the gawkers, the curious, and the bettors.

Really, the ever-present bookies could almost be considered as much a part of cultivation life as the apothecarists and blacksmiths and talisman masters that provided actually necessary equipment. Somehow, wherever there was a fight, the bookies appeared.

Then again, in a world bereft of greater entertainment, as the winter transformed into spring but the ground was still too hard to work, what other form of recreation was there? Villagers and city people were used to making their own pleasure, from long poetry sessions to the more common play of music and tall tales. But songs and voices grew familiar, tales grew boring, and the introduction of new events was an exciting prospect.

The crowd spotted them long before they arrived, Wu Ying choosing not to cloak his cultivation. At least, not all the way. He had sensed and evaluated their opposition. Ching Lau and a Peak Energy Storage City Guard Captain were the only members of concern. The Guard Captain was a surprise, an older matronly female whose armor barely contained her wide hips, sporting a pair of crossed daos across her back.

Perhaps, somewhere deeper, a more powerful cultivator watched over matters, but Wu Ying doubted it. This outpost was but a way-stop, of little use to anyone but the residents. The fort a handful of li away was more important to the kingdom, and there, a true Core Formation cultivator resided.

Shi Min led the way, his movements smoother than before he left. Yet Wu Ying noted the angle of Shi Min's shoulder, the tightness in his core, and the jerkiness in his steps. The slightly acrid smell of sweat and fear rose from him, a constant reminder of the stakes at play.

"Cycle breathe, boy. Straighten that back and relax those hips. Move like you own this street and the only one who could stand in your way is the Yellow Emperor himself," Wu Ying commanded, his voice low and firm. "Your battle begins now, not in the arena. Conquer their minds before you beat their bodies and you might never need to raise your blade."

Shi Min slowed for a fraction of a second, his first breath a thin and thready thing. Then he breathed out the tension, the incipient panic, and went for a deeper breath. One after the other, he inhaled and exhaled, his spine lengthening as he straightened himself and his muscles relaxed. There was an arrogance to his walk now, a strut that spoke of a confidence earned through blood and tears.

The crowd sensed it, moving instinctively like the herd of animals they were. They parted on both sides of the crushed earth road, allowing the pair to stride in without interference, trampling melting snow with their muddy feet as they edged away from the predators in their mix.

Funny how they reacted to real cultivators, as though they were the real dangers, when they easily accepted the thugs who lived among them. An orthodox Sect member like Wu Ying would never touch them, these mortals whose lives only intersected his in the barest of times.

"So you came. I was beginning to think you'd run," Ching Lau called.

Then again, with such an upstanding member of the world of cultivation arrayed before them, perhaps the mortals had a reason to be wary.

Ching Lau stood across from the pair, his minions arrayed around him. Wu Ying's gaze skipped from the leader to his followers, reading and judging, trying to foretell the future. Then he stilled his mind and his caution, even as he sensed Shi Min doing the same.

Silence dragged on as Wu Ying chose not to respond. Shi Min, having led the way so far, turned to stare at Wu Ying, expecting him to speak. Only for Wu Ying to shake his head a little, declining the offer of leadership.

This was the boy's fight. His turn to shine.

Ching Lau and their audience did not miss the byplay. The broken Core Formation cultivator grinned a little, reveling in his expected victory.

Shi Min spoke, cutting off his surging feelings. "Three. I fight and beat three of your people, then this incident is over."

"Three." Ching Lau grinned, waving his first member forward.

To Wu Ying's surprise, it was a woman—small, tightly coiled, with hate in her eyes and a scar along the top of her hairline that was bereft of hair. She moved with a jerky grace, a bisected circle her weapon of choice.

Surprise on Wu Ying's side, for women generally had the good sense to avoid the thug life. It was short, brutal, and generally had no future. Then again, Wu Ying could sense the girl was probably at the end of her road too. Her body smelled off, damaged. Her last push— to get into the first stage of Energy Storage—had been too much. Too fast.

So be it then.

"Yue Qin. Finish him fast. My dinner grows cold," Ching Lau ordered.

She gave a jerky nod, moving to the center of the ring. The crowd fell back a few more steps, instinctively. Shi Min approached, hand falling to his weapon as the pair took their beginning stances. He opened his mouth to announce the challenge, and his opponent blurred forward.

"Li Shi—urk!"

He dodged, Wind Steps taking him to the side. Shi Min's sword came out of its sheath instinctively, cutting sideways to meet the sharpened circular edges of his opponent's weapon. She thrust forward, her fingers guarded by the edge of her weapon, attempting to trap his blade. Shi Min disengaged adroitly, flicking weapon sideways and around, even as he pulled his weapon backward to give him more of the strength of his blade to work with.

Then as his opponent stepped deeper, he slammed his blade forward. Hilt and edge caught on circled weapon, his body straining and pushing to the side so that the weapons were pointed away from their bodies. He stepped close and brought his head down fast. The headbutt saw his forehead impact her nose, forcing her back. Surprised by the sudden ferocity and change of pace, her fingers drifted open.

Another twist of the sword followed by a sideways motion had her weapon extracted from her fingers. Then Shi Min spun, throwing a sidekick into her lower ribs, the sound of ribs cracking sounding through the winter afternoon as the woman flew through the air. No Greater Achievement of the Sword required, just a brutal training regimen against an opponent who was more focused on winning—and training his sparring partner to win—to finish the first fight.

By the time Yue Qin managed to stand, the jian was pushing against the dimple in the base of her throat and the fight was over.

"Disappointing…" Ching Lau's voice was dark, filled with a promise of violence later as he spoke to Yue Qin.

She struggled upward, glaring at Shi Min, who had so easily dispatched her, and retrieved her weapon before limping back to her side, clutching her ribs.

"Your best lacks, it seems," Shi Min spoke, voice loud and arrogant. He backed off to his side of the ring, not bothering to sheathe his sword.

"A few months of training and you've grown arrogant. Just like your father. You going to whine and beg like him too when I cut you up?" So speaking, the second contender stepped forward, his paired daggers bedecked in jewels along the hilt. He raised one dagger to his face and licked the edges, leaving a tiny trail of saliva on it before repeating the action with the other weapon.

Shi Min was trembling, fighting to control his emotions as he had been taught.

Weaving his voice through the air and embedding his chi within, Wu Ying spoke to the boy in confidence, "Win the fight and honor your father. Beware the blades, they're poisoned."

"Time to scream." Shi Min's second opponent loped forward, body bent so low that he was almost parallel to the ground, daggers held out to his sides.

He was a fool of a poison Body Cultivator. Their kind was unusual, heretical cultivators who soaked in tubs of poison and drank it as though it was breakfast. Shi Min's new opponent might have only opened five meridians, but he had the strength of a Body Cultivator and the advantages of poison coursing through his blood.

The boy, shaken from his emotions and the memory of a strong man tortured, resolved his stance, firming his grip. His jian blocked one blade then another, his feet never stopping as he circled to keep his opponent's off-hand weapon away from him. Shi Min cut and swept, targeting fingers and wrists, seeking the closest targets he could find.

Nothing graceful or honorable in his fight, just efficient.

Body Cultivator fought Body Cultivator, and in the first half dozen passes, the poison-wielder was surprised as the boy kept up with his speed. Dual-wielding fighter or not, positioning and the greater length of the jian, along with a substantial difference in skill, made up for minor differences in speed and additional weapons.

"You fight like a coward!" Shi Min's second opponent hissed as he jerked fingers away from seeking blade, another long line scoring skin on knuckles. "Stop dancing around and face me!"

"No."

Poisoned blade disengaged and circled hand, round and round then cut upward. This time around, it only made its way a few inches high before the boy cut sideways, catching the second blade and elbow as the poison user sought to exploit the opening. Blood blossomed in the air, the boy sensibly backing off before the poisoned blood could strike him.

Cursing, the poison wielder clutched his arm, his dagger fallen to the ground beside him as injured muscles spasmed. After that, the battle became rote, almost entirely without surprise. Hemmed in by the longer weapon, Shi Min's opponent was now the one scrambling away.

Until the man, bleeding from a half dozen cuts, chose to sacrifice a shoulder. He stepped in close into a thrust, taking the pain and injury to get his blade aimed at Shi Min's chest.

The boy knew better. His hand flashed outward to catch the blade, his arm angling so that the flat lay against his muscles. It was not a guarantee from being cut, but it was the best he could do in that short moment. Even so, his focus on the weapon angling toward him and intent on stripping it, Shi Min was left open, for the dagger wasn't the poison user's main objective. These were not sect fighters, with rules and traditions, but individuals grown up in a much harder arena.

Blood dripping from a bitten tongue, pooling in his mouth and burning his own skin a little, the poisoner spat that dangerous liquid into Shi Min's face. Retreating, wiping his face as the greenish-reddish blood seeped into his eyes, eyes already reddening and skin swelling, Shi Min released the dagger hand. He felt the weapon cut, once, twice, a third time before he could back off, his weapon moving through old forms, blocking the remainder of the attacks and even returning a cut or two.

"Got you now…" The poison user burbled around his injured tongue as blood welled down from his mouth.

Eyes closed, Shi Min struck. Viper-fast, a modification of a familiar attack. The lunge took the boy across the intervening space faster than anyone but Wu Ying could have expected, his blade punching into the throat of his assailant. A savage twisting motion tore the blade from the man's throat, nearly beheading him.

Silence filled the road, the audience stunned by the sudden end of the battle and the savagery displayed. For the first time, some realized that this was no mere moment of indulgent entertainment, that lives were at stake. None moved to leave though.

Theirs was not a simple existence, one filled with tranquil moments. No, violence was not unknown to them, though to see it played out so close to one another could still be shocking.

"This is growing expensive," Ching Lau said, his voice thrumming with anger.

Many of the audience staggered back, wincing as the Core Formation cultivator displayed his ire, layering his presence upon them all.

With a minor flex of his own will, Wu Ying covered himself and Shi Min. Only the Guard Captain seemed to be handling the pressure well, and even her gaze was strained.

"Let us finish this," Ching Lau said, gesturing to the man standing by his right.

Long and lean, the cultivator was well-trimmed and put-together, resplendent silk compared to the rough hemp the others wore. Court fashion, Wu Ying assumed, though the thug's clothing bore marks of long use. It must be hard, being fashionable in the outskirts.

"I shall endeavor to make this quick, boy." A genteel voice, an accent Wu Ying did not recognize, but one that was not native to this land.

"Perhaps. But it will be later," Wu Ying spoke up at last. He strode forward into the arena as Shi Min, having managed to make his way back to his starting position, was wiping at his eyes. "A minor break. He has fought two battles already, without pause."

"You dare…!" Ching Lau snarled.

"I do." Wu Ying cocked his head, glancing at the body that still lay in the arena. "If nothing else, we need to deal with some filth."

Ching Lau bristled, but Wu Ying offered Shi Min a cloth and his water flask. He nodded slightly in approval as the boy managed to sheath his weapon sightless, though the blade and its sheath would need proper cleaning afterward.

"Fine. The passing of an incense stick…" Ching Lau gestured.

One of his thugs pulled out a container and a stick, lighting the incense stick and placing it on the ground. Wu Ying's eyes narrowed, noting how the morning breeze flowed, speeding up the burning.

Watching the boy clean his face of the poisonous blood, he took Shi Min's other hand, testing his pulse as he sent his chi questing for answers. Wu Ying was no physician to discern the vagaries of poison and healing. All he could do was verify that the other was functional and the danger was not fast progressing.

What did poison smell like? A little bit of rot, a little acrid, a little sweet, and very much alien to the body. Blood began to clot, the body slowing as the poison reacted to Shi Min's body, his aura curdling with each second.

"Take this and cultivate. It will not heal the entirety, but you may regain some of your sight," Wu Ying said, pushing a pill bottle into the boy's hand and guiding him to a seat opposite Ching Lau. Watching as Shi Min took to his instructions, Wu Ying turned his gaze back to the proceedings.

In the meantime, other members of the gang had used wrappings around their hands to limit the amount of the corpse they touched as they towed the dead body aside. A quick argument with the Guard Captain had the body eventually wrapped in additional bolts of cloth and propped upward. At the captain's orders, a guard went running back to the outpost while shovels were taken to the contaminated soil, the pile formed next to the dead body.

Eyeing the burning incense stick, Wu Ying extended his senses and his wishes to the wind. Around the incense brazier, a small wall of wind rose, the smoke drifting upward now and not sideways as he shielded the burning stick. It would not extend the time by much, but any small advantage would help the boy.

The Four Sages Poison Cleanser Pill was a fast-acting pill meant for Body Cultivators. It would not strain the boy's meridians too much as its energies pulsed through him, even if it was vigorous in its deployment. If he had not been a Body Cultivator, Wu Ying would not have chanced its use.

Well, perhaps he would have. For time was running short.

Ching Lau glanced at the incense stick then Wu Ying, the man's eyes narrowing. He chose not to comment, such petty grievances above his supposed dignity. Wu Ying had to hide a small smile, even as the nose-scrunching intensity of Shi Min's poisoned scent burned brighter as the pill pushed toxins from his skin.

Now, it was just a race to see if the boy could regain enough of his strength in time.

***

"Ready?" Wu Ying asked as Shi Min stood, the incense stick burnt down to a tiny nub.

"I have to be, no?" Shi Min replied, pupils mere slits as the skin around his eyes had flushed and expanded. "I have my sight back at least." Under his breath, he added, "Mostly."

Wu Ying nodded, stepping aside. There was nothing else he could do. Intervening as he had done was more than he had thought he would have in the beginning. Pushing Ching Lau was a delicate thing, and while Wu Ying might be able to win such a battle for the boy himself, leaving a power vacuum in its place could cause just as much trouble. Never mind the devastation a pair of Core Formation cultivators could do during a battle.

"I must admit, I am grateful for this opportunity to do battle properly," Shi Min's third and final opponent said, his sword drawn. He raised it upward, touching the blade to the tip of his forehead. "Chu Ming Yu of the Muddy Waters Pavilion."

"Li Shi Min, a wandering cultivator." Salute returned.

The start of the fight was much less vigorous than before. They probed one another, blades flicking back and forth at the maximum extent of their reach, each of them striking and parrying as openings were sought. They sought openings amidst a series of forms, grace rather than brutality.

Wu Ying soon understood the heart of Ming Yu's form, the way the other sought to win the fight. The style was of misdirection and feints, of illusions and hidden attacks woven behind a screen of long sleeves. This was but the first few forms of the style, a mundane representation of a martial style which required, at minimum, Energy Storage to shine.

A half dozen passes and Shi Min pressed his advantage. His family style was more direct, built for those at his stage of speed and strength. No chi projection, no extended blade strikes or dao intentions marred the style or were built into it. It was a killing style for a Body Cleanser, and his attacks pushed back his opponent.

The first wound appeared on a deflecting arm, blood blossoming on pale blue silk. Then another cut against a calf that turned trailing trousers red. Shi Min grew bolder, pressing his attacks even as the pit of dread Wu Ying felt grew.

For neither Ming Yu or Ching Lau looked concerned, both serene in their countenance and defense. Another two passes, and a flick of long sleeves drove Shi Min back as he cut apart the cloth marring his sight lines, retreating in an abundance of caution.

In that fraction of time, Ming Yu acted. A talisman glowed, mist boiling outward. It struck the ground around the impromptu arena, minor markings and dropped talismans containing the surging muddy brown mist that blocked vision from outside.

Eyes narrowing in concern, Wu Ying sent his spiritual sense forward only to be blocked by a twisted, acrid, and rotting aura. It pushed back Wu Ying, stymying his senses whilst staying outside the now-hidden arena.

"Let them finish this themselves, yes?" Ching Lau said. "Or do you intend to continue to fight the boy's battles?"

From within, the clash of blades. The clink and clatter as the pair fought, sight muted or not. Wu Ying's ears strained, but other than the occasional shuffle of feet and the metallic meeting of jian, he could not discern what was happening within.

"Very well. So long as we all stay outside," Wu Ying said. He allowed his aura to expand, blanketing the surroundings in light wind as they waited.

Shuffle of feet against soil and tough ground. The swirl of opaque mist and the swish of cloth, even the tap of blades against one another and the occasional meatier strike of limb against flesh. The audience muttered and growled in disappointment, their entertainment shrouded.

Still, none chose to complain directly.

A minute, then two. Wu Ying grew surprised as Ching Lau grew irate. A sharp sound broke from within, a cracking of metal that Wu Ying was all too familiar with.

Ching Lau shifted in anger and impatience, but his own words held them both back. Finally, the talismans gave way. Yellow smoke boiled outward and Wu Ying called the wind, catching the smoke and sending it skyward with a minor flex of will.

Revealed within was a bloody and injured Shi Min straddling his opponent. His sword was pressed across the other man's neck, the hilt of Ming Yu's sword pressed against Shi Min's side, blood welling from the shallow wound. Glittering pieces of Ming Yu's broken blade lay across one side of the battlefield, the turning point of the battle within obvious.

"He has conceded. I have won, yes?" Shi Min demanded, pushing his blade a little against his opponent's neck as he glared at Ching Lau.

The Core Formation cultivator's lips thinned, anger warring with good sense. He glanced at Wu Ying and the Captain of the Guard, at the surrounding audience, then forced himself to relax. He threw his hands wide, speaking as he did so. "Of course! Who would dare say Ching Lau, the Fist of the North, breaks his words? All quarrels are resolved, all debts settled." A pause, as the Guard Captain stared on, and he smiled. "I will even throw a celebration at the Golden Duck for the winner tonight."

Shi Min frowned but nodded. Ming Yu's sword hand had already dropped, leaving the sword hilt embedded in the boy's side as he struggled to his feet and stepped away. Wu Ying watched as the boy staggered a little before straightening himself and limping over to his side, recalling the previous warning about presence.

Continuing to regale the audience with bombastic words of his generosity, Ching Lau led the crowd back to the outpost, leaving his lieutenant to lie on the ground, defeated. A pair of gang members grabbed the man, helping him stand, while Wu Ying regarded the boy's wounds and, fatalistically, proffered another pill bottle.

"Thank you, Honored Benefactor." Shi Min glanced at where Ching Lau led the audience away, lowered his voice, and added, "I think, I know, I should leave now, right?"

"No." Wu Ying shook his head. "We have blunted his attentions and injured his pride. Let him regain it by serving you dinner. Then leave on the morrow."

"And I should trust he won't poison me?" Shi Min said, sounding surprised.

"Being the godfather of a border city is not just about strength," the Guard Captain, having made her way over, said softly. "It's about compromise and face. Attacking you—even having you injured—so soon after losing so publicly? It would harm his other relationships. No one would dare trust him." She touched her chest, her voice growing colder. "Even us."

"You! You let him run riot. You let him kill my father!" Shi Min accused.

She shrugged. "He died in a duel. Such things happen, among cultivators. It was insufficient reason to break the peace." The woman hesitated, before adding, "Being a Guard Captain of a border city is not just about the strict boundaries of justice. Compromise is required too."

Shi Min's lips curled up before he strode away, back the way they had come, unwilling to argue further. Wu Ying considered asking if he would come to the dinner but chose to leave it. The boy would make his choices. Their time was over.

In turn, the Guard Captain looked at Wu Ying, searching his face for understanding.

Wu Ying offered her a small nod, giving her the acknowledgment she wanted. Then, before she could settle, he added, "Be careful not to compromise too far. Or else one day, you will not be able to tell the difference between yourself and him."

"Of course, Honored Elder."

What else was there to say? Nothing. He left her to deal with the corpse, the poisoned ground, the dispersing crowd, and the incipient fight between gamblers and bookies. He left for the outpost. Perhaps now, he could finally sell his Cores and his other assorted goods.

***

After dinner, many toasts, and even more food, Wu Ying walked out of the restaurant's doors, smoothing his robes down as he did so. A new pot of wine was in one hand, yet to be stored away in a storage ring.

Clouds floated high above, the cold of the desert air mixing with the memory of heat from the oppressive sun and the ever-present smell of sand. The western wind danced across Wu Ying's skin, reminding him, teaching him, showing him of its origins, of its presence. Enlightening him further, as he breathed in.

"Honored Benefactor… you are leaving?" Shi Min, hurrying after him, caught Wu Ying as he was about to leave.

"I am," Wu Ying replied, turning his hand sideways to deposit the drink in his storage ring. "You have employment, yes?"

"The Merchant Qiu," Shi Min acknowledged. "They leave in two days when the snow melts a little more."

"Then your troubles with the Fist of the North are over. He even blessed your journey," Wu Ying said. "And so, my time here is done."

"I…" Shi Min hesitated, unsure of what more to say. Then, overcome with emotion, he threw himself to the ground and kowtowed to Wu Ying. "I thank you, Honored Benefactor, for all you have done."

Wu Ying cocked his head, watching the boy. He wanted to ask him to stand, to tell him to stop treating him like a respectable Elder. He was not that, no towering figure like Elder Cheng, Librarian Ko, or Guardian Lu.

"Enough. I was but acting on a whim," Wu Ying said.

"And this unworthy cultivator benefited from it." Still, Shi Min stood, looking at Wu Ying with fervent eyes filled with awe and gratitude.

Realization struck Wu Ying that to the boy, he might as well be a true benefactor. A towering master, like Elder Dun his own. He had played a little at the storied figure, teaching and withholding methods as he had wished. He had acted on a whim, choosing to aid the child to build upon his own skills while teaching. Most of all, he had sought to wile away the winter and set a minor injustice aright.

In so doing, he had altered the course of Shi Min's fate.

Threads of karma had woven between him and the boy.

"Walk tall. Uphold your virtues. Wield your sword with honor," Wu Ying murmured as the wind—a stern, unyielding, all-too-obscure wind—fluttered around his robes, played with his hair. Spoke in his ear, telling him what he needed to say, to do. "Heaven watches, even if it chooses not to intervene directly. Let your blade be its presence on this earth."

"I hear and understand, Honored Benefactor." Again Shi Min bowed, head bent and touching the ground. Three times, he bowed, knocking his head against the ground.

By the time he looked up, Wu Ying was gone. In his place were a pair of weapons—a familiar training sword and a spirit jian similar in design to his parent's weapon—a bundle of herbs for his Body Cultivation baths, and a bottle of healing pills.

Final gifts, in payment for a moment of enlightenment on Wu Ying's part.

The western wind blew hot and harsh, merciless in its nature. But there was bounty to be found, an oasis of calm and peace and civilization. Like nature, so must man—if they followed the Dao.

Chapter 20

Heaven's wind. It blew everywhere, from the tallest and coldest peaks to the lowest valleys that flooded with each spring. Wu Ying followed the wind that gusted through the dry western desert north, letting it take him to the steppes where the snow had yet to loosen its grasp.

Along the way, he met other cultivators, other clans and mortals.

Some meetings were amicable.

Drinks in a wayfarer inn, suckling pig, pan fried noodles, and warmed peach wine over wandering, philosophical conversations about daos, duty and responsibility and personal honor with a disparate group of orthodox, heretical, and wandering cultivators.

An invitation into a noble lord's mansion and personal library where Wu Ying perused and was gifted a new cultivation exercise—the Whispering Winds—that would help guide his voice to receptive ears across forested li and ringing battle. All for a handful of gifted fresh herbs and an hour's instruction on the sword given to a budding swordsman.

Others, less so.

A trio of wandering cultivators, seeing Wu Ying's wealth, stalking him. Three days of travel through the rolling plains, where hills were plentiful but trees sparse. Stalked, hunted, and finally, cornered. Blood, wet upon the ground as tender mercy was revealed to hide the darkest of fangs and bodies were left behind to rot as greed met the edge of blade.

In the remnants of a destroyed village, corpses and grieving mortals alike surrounding him, Wu Ying met the failure of soldiers and cultivators. Demonic beasts, allowed to roam and grow as a corrupt magistrate stole the funds necessary to equip the army and strengthen protective talismans around villages, now run rampant. Leaving behind naught but death and despair.

A small sect, seven members large, who had taken to buying children from nearby villages to train in their harsh, unrelenting methods. The cemetery lay beside the sect grounds with a half dozen small graves, for those who'd failed to meet the grade.

Through it all, the wind blew. Offering Wu Ying little lessons about the world and the demands of heaven and the chaos of civilization. Showing him the disappointments of humanity as they failed to enact heaven's will, as order broke down to chaos and mortals and sects alike suffered.

Until such time as he was standing upon the steppes of the north, where spring dawned late and fast-growing grass and herds of thundering goats, cattle, and sheep traveled, guided by the herdsmen and nomadic tribes that called such land their home.

In their midst, Wu Ying, still clad in his thin silk robes, head bare to the weather as his Wind Body ignored the vagaries of the cold weather, was crouched. He had paused in his journey, following the scent of a rare plant to this spot. Before the herd could reach the Purple Thunder Thistle, he scooped it up, pulling it from the earth to deposit in his World Spirit Ring.

Better stored in his ring than eaten by the hungry goat before him. Or so he believed. There were, after all, sufficient other plants for the Thunder Goat before him to consume. All of which he tried to communicate to the obnoxious creature staring at him as he crouched on his knees, meeting its baleful eyes.

"Chi khen be? Chi end yuu khiij baigaa yum[31]?" The buzzing noise, a language that was familiar yet far from his own, caught at his attention. Seconds later, a rough hand landed on the goat's neck, fractions of a moment before it lunged at Wu Ying.

Startled by the sudden shift to violence, Wu Ying pushed backward, drifting off the ground in retreat. He alighted on top of another animal, riding the creature's movements as it twitched at the sudden presence before it stilled, realizing that Wu Ying was no heavier than a leaf.

"Yamaany novsh chi tendees buu!" Again, more unknown words.

Rather than answer, Wu Ying studied the speaker.

The first thing that struck Wu Ying was the speaker's height. A good foot taller than Wu Ying, muscular and clad in fur obviously derived from the animals around them, the speaker had his hair kept in place via a simple leather headband which peeked out from under the flat fur cap he wore. There was a darkness in the other's gaze, an anger that rose as Wu Ying regarded him, even as his own aura spiked.

High Energy Storage then, missing but one Energy Storage Meridian before reaching Peak. Powerful, and as Wu Ying's gaze flicked sideways, not alone. Another half dozen or so herders, men he had noticed but dismissed soon after arriving.

Their auras—all of their auras—had been hidden. Like his, but now all of them unveiled. Energy Storage cultivators one and all, a staggering amount of force to be faced with all of a sudden. He idly noted the curved wooden bows in half their hands, the ways fingers found arrow shafts without drawing them.

Yet.

"My apologies," Wu Ying spoke then, choosing to use the language he was most familiar with. So many dialects, so many languages. He had studied some, learned others, his greater memory as a cultivator offering some aid. Yet this one was new, so he wandered blind. "I do not speak your language."

No recognition in their eyes, though a few of the herders slowed. It would have been comforting if those members were not also the ones with bows.

"I mean no harm." Wu Ying raised his arms sideways, showing that his hand was empty of weapons. "I was but gathering some plants when I found myself between your herd."

"Yamar teneg ni yamaan deer garch zogsdog bainaa?" the initial speaker called, though this time he seemed less like he was talking to Wu Ying directly.

Still, no one was drawing a weapon.

---

[31] I am borrowing Mongolian here for the language used. And this part does not require you to know what is happening, so here we go. Travis will have fun with this part.

"Ingej erguutej baigaad tsahilgaand tsohiulj sharagdaj uhehee meddeg baigaa?" Another voice, this one filled with humor.

Wu Ying turned and smiled at the speaker.

"Irj ene soliottoi yari gej Munkhbat-d hel."

More voices, before one of the bowmen turned and ran away. Beneath Wu Ying's feet, the goat had shifted a few times, trying to get him off. Failing to do so, the goat's horns glowed, a charge dancing back and forth. Out of the corner of his eyes, Wu Ying watched the herdsmen fall back, and instinct warned him to beware.

A tap of his foot took him into the sky moments before the built-up charge around the Thundering Goat released, sparking into lightning. It arced between goats, jumping between each of them as the roar of thunder filled the steppe before tendrils of electricity reached Wu Ying. They struck him, sending shocks dancing through his body before more tendrils were grounded.

Letting out a series of satisfied bleats, the goats moved away from the falling cultivator, allowing him to thump to the ground to the satisfied laughter of the herdsmen.

"Oh… that was what they were saying," Wu Ying said as he lay on the ground, staring at the sky. Well, he guessed he'd deserved that. He'd be a little annoyed too if some random stranger stood on him. Little arcs of lightning danced across his flesh and he sighed, eyes drifting closed. "I think I'm just going to lie here for a bit." Turning his head sideways, he stared at the nearest goat. "If you don't mind."

Another bleat and dip of the head was all that answered Wu Ying, so he just lay there. Waiting, for the presence that the wind spoke of another coming to the herd and himself. Hopefully they spoke a common language. Otherwise, he could only hope playing the fool was sufficient payment for trespassing on their territory.

He really was not looking forward to fighting his way out otherwise.

***

Wu Ying had sat up by the time the slow-moving thunder cloud that was the newcomer arrived. The woman's presence was similar to a high pressure front, pushing upon Wu Ying's aura with the strength of her own, a loud and brazen warning about what might happen if he chose to act out. That the aura dwarfed his Core Formation one was humbling, the difference in strength speaking of at least an entire variation.

When the woman finally arrived, Wu Ying made sure to be on his feet, his robes cleaned from the grass stains. He had, briefly, considered changing into something a little more appropriate—but then again, what might be appropriate? Considering the dress of the herdsmen around him, a more rustic look might aid his case more.

In the end, he met the newcomer in what he had worn before, bowing low as he regarded the other with all his senses. Wind shifted and swirled around the other, brushing ever so gently against her. It was clear, from what whispers he could gather, that the Nascent Soul cultivator before him had a similar dao; one of thunder and lightning rather than wind, but a weather-borne one anyway.

Her scent spoke of that all too easily, the sweet, pungent odor just before the start of a thunderstorm, the smell of fresh rain falling on grass. Her aura rumbled, pushing against Wu Ying's but not on purpose, more like a disturbed animal shifting in its containment.

Like the powerful aura emanating from her figure, to Wu Ying's bare sight, the Nascent Soul cultivator was a tall, imperious woman who looked to be in the later stages of her life, with wrinkles along her eyes and brows. She was clad in a singular piece of dress, the colorful cloth wrapped around her crossways and held together with a highly ornamental leather belt. Entirely unlike the free-flowing robes he wore, hers were a colorfully woven bright blue like the summer sky, with tight sleeves and a long skirt worn over the top of what he assumed were trousers. Long leather boots with a flat heel adorned her legs.

Unlike the other herdsmen in their sheepskin coats and cloaks, wool facing inward, the cultivator before him wore nothing of the sort, her body—or her dao—more than sufficient to handle minor vagaries of temperature and rain.

"Greetings, Honored Cultivator," Wu Ying intoned, offering a low martial bow befitting her rank and strength. "I am Long Wu Ying, a minor wandering cultivator and herb gatherer."

Silence greeted his words, and he looked up as he straightened slowly. The woman was staring at him, stormy grey eyes regarding him imperiously.

"I apologize for any intrusion and inconvenience I might have caused." Pausing, Wu Ying considered and chose to tell the truth. "I was but following the wind and the trail of herbs when I encountered your flock."

"And stole from the land," she spoke at last, cutting off his excuses. Her voice was deep for a female's, husky and aged and with little amusement in it. Her accent was atrocious, but at least understandable.

"Stole?" Wu Ying said, frowning. "What I took will either regrow or was about to be eaten." He gestured at the goats, many of which were being led away quietly by the herdsmen. "It seems like there was not much theft there."

"Without making an offering, all such actions are theft," she said, stepping closer. "Then again, I would not expect otherwise from a southerner."

Her words cut at Wu Ying, much like the aura she used to suppress his own. He raised his chi and spiritual strength in return, unwilling to bow to her actions immediately.

"If you have specific rituals, I am more than willing to learn them," Wu Ying said, offering her a clasped hand bow. "I will undertake whatever ritual actions of forgiveness might be required, for the taking of these plants." He inclined his head. "I look forward to instruction from the Honored Elder."

"No Elder of yours," the woman said, snorting. "We do not hold to the strictures of your false clans, as though such bonds are not fragile things that will break during the depths of a harsh winter."

Wu Ying's eyes narrowed, but this time, he chose not to answer.

"You may call me Khan Erdene[32]," she finally said.

Wu Ying smiled then, a small one, as he bowed to her again in greeting. Well, whatever they had planned, whatever she wanted from him—and he had a feeling this was a matter of want rather than need, because no weapons were being drawn—it seemed they were willing to do so civilly. And that was a good thing.

Speech was always better than war. Only children, whose egos overwhelmed reason, sought war as the first alternative.

***

Some things, even when you noticed it via one's spiritual and other senses, still required sight, in-person and nearby, to truly grasp. In this case, the moving gers – the circular, tent-like residences of these people – on top of the broad backs of the massive stone turtles[33] plodding along the steppes was a sight to behold. Wu Ying's eyes widened as he took in the creatures, a half dozen of them, their backs wide enough that at least four gers could sit on the smallest. Their heads were the size of the circular buildings themselves, but even then, it was insufficient accommodation for the tribe.

Which was why more people were riding along on horses, cattle pulling wagons trundling beside the turtles with full accommodations set up on them. Herds of goat and sheep moved at the edges of the entire entourage, lightning sparking from their heads occasionally.

The entire procession was at least a few li long, spread out to give one another sufficient space and for the herds to graze. So when they came up and over the rise, everyone but Wu Ying riding a horse, the entire display was spread out for him to see.

"Come, southern runner. We have much to discuss," Khan Erdene spoke, waving Wu Ying down into the throng and pointing at the stone turtle in the center, the largest of its kind. The central ger she pointed to was massive, with multiple chimneys sprouting from it to help dissipate the smoke from the stoves within.

"Of course." Wu Ying nodded amicably, jogging alongside the group.

He had no guards—what need was there when she was powerful enough to squash him? Never mind the fact that the famed northern horses could likely run even cultivators down eventually, if he chose to make a break of it.

---

[32] Yes, I'm drawing from Mongol culture, but not fully. After all, when women can be Nascent Soul cultivators and beat up men, there's no reason they can't be the chiefs either.

[33] I'm making a reference to the stone turtles of Karakorum, the ancient capital of the Mongol Empire.

Then again, Wu Ying wasn't exactly an average cultivator. He gave himself decent odds of escaping the horses. Lousy ones of escaping Erdene. When daos so close to one another came into conflict, the one who had the greater cultivation base was bound to win. All of his usual tricks, his advantages with the wind would be stymied by her.

Down, down, they went. More than a few glanced at Wu Ying as he ran, their lips turning up in amusement as they watched him jog along. That he was easily keeping up with the cantering horses, even unassisted as he was by the winds, was a minor matter. It was obvious no one actually ran, not here.

Not where everyone had horses.

Then again, they probably had lousy movement techniques. He wasn't even showcasing the modifications in the Twelve Gales he had created, content to keep to the basic structure as taught in the sect. Over the years, he'd progressed his understanding and adaptation, making it his own.

In truth, he was not even certain what he used now could truly be called the Twelve Gales technique. Between combining the Heavenly Spirit, Earthly Body techniques, the esoteric movement technique of the elder who had trapped him, and his own Wind Body, the resulting movement method was significantly stronger than the Twelve Gales was meant to be.

For now though, he had no reason to showcase it. Even if it meant he was ridiculed a little by others.

Soon enough, the group arrived at the base of the slow-moving stone turtle. On closer inspection, Wu Ying noticed what had been hidden at a distance—ropes hanging down the edge of the turtle shell. One after another of the herdsmen had peeled away as they neared, leaving only two guardsmen, who had appeared when the group had entered the moving village.

The guards rode ahead, grabbed hold of the ropes, and swung themselves upward and off their horses, the animals moving at a light trot to keep up with the slow turtle before they peeled away, guided by the calls of other herders a distance away.

Swiftly clambering hand-over-hand, the pair of guards ascended the turtle with the ease of long practice. Turning his head slightly, Wu Ying watched as Erdene chose to skip the entire process and jumped, pushing gently against her horse such that she did not injure it but somehow still managed to make the leap to the top of the turtle in one movement.

Not that she probably even needed to push, what with her control of her dao and chi. She probably could have flown up now that Wu Ying thought about it. Left on the ground, jogging and losing ground now that he was side by side with the massive stone turtle, he sighed at another test.

Do it like a regular cultivator or show off his skills? If he chose the latter, he would be making the woman wait, a minor insult when she probably knew he could jump it. On the other hand…

Shaking his head and discarding thoughts of greater or lesser social import, Wu Ying chose to act on his desires. Sometimes, trying to find the most correct solution just meant you delayed any action at all and failed in the lack of choice. Sometimes, acting—any action—was better than nothing.

Leaping upward, Wu Ying angled his jump such that he struck the side of the massive turtle's shell, feet sliding along the smooth shell for a moment before he pushed again. He called forth a touch of the wind, lightened his form with the Heavenly Soul, Earthly Body technique, and rose again, bounding higher with each movement until he alighted next to the waiting Khan.

As he landed silently, Erdene looked at Wu Ying before turning away and striding toward the large ger in the center, choosing to not comment. No indication if he had chosen right or not, it seemed. Forcing him to flounder in ignorance once again.

Good thing Wu Ying had practice being the ignorant fool.

Following her, he braced for what was to come. Whatever that might be.

Chapter 21

The inside of the massive ger, meant to host the Khan, was both warmer and more comfortable than what Wu Ying had expected and more rustic for what was, in effect, a permanent building. Very few pieces of furniture within, only a series of furs for sitting on the chilly, smooth shell. A pair of large chests sat next to the only, short-statured, reclining chair in the room, enchantments spiraling outward from the chair to touch upon the walls of the ger, indicating its own importance.

Warmth for the ger was provided by a trio of wood stoves spaced around the building, each of which warmed the surroundings via their pot-bellied nature. Meat, fried on massive circular pans, was being cooked alongside a bubbling stew. As he strode within, the slightly rancid smell of fermented mare milk rose from open bowls a trio of lounging older men held in their hands, each of them providing only the barest of nods to the Khan as she entered.

Wu Ying's gaze rested upon the elders before he greeted them, only to find they ignored his presence. Interestingly enough, of the three, two were Core Formation cultivators in the mid and late stages and the third a mere mid-Energy Storage cultivator. One of the Core Formation cultivators was different, the ball of energy that was his Core less dense, more diffuse than the other. If he had more time, Wu Ying would have wanted to study it.

Pushing those thoughts aside for now, Wu Ying studied the individuals, searching for clues about the upcoming discussion. Body language between the group seemed to indicate no lack of respect between the trio as they returned to their conversation in their foreign—or well, local to them—language.

Wu Ying contained the sigh that threatened to rise within him, ambling forward instead to join Erdene as she took a seat in the only chair, leaning backward as a servant scuttled over from one of the corners and brought her a drink.

"Long Wu Ying, a wandering cultivator and spiritual herb gatherer," Khan Erdene said when he had taken his seat from across her, crossing his legs. She made a small gesture, and a moment later, one of the servants arrived with a cup of tea for him too. "You have trespassed on our land, taken from it without permission, and have offered restitution."

Wu Ying inclined his head in agreement before raising the tea, pausing briefly to inhale deeply. It was a darker, fermented drink, rather than the lighter teas that he personally preferred. Still, he sipped on it without protest, idly noting that the bitter concoction had been steeped all too long. Not that he was going to mention it.

Neither did Khan Erdene as she drank hers, then held her hand out for more. "There are three methods of balancing the scales here."

Wu Ying nodded, straightening a little to indicate he was listening.

"The first is the simplest. We kill you, place your body on the land, and let it take back what it was owed. Some of my people would prefer that."

A barked laugh from behind Wu Ying indicated at least one of the Core Formation elders was one of those.

"I would prefer another method than that," Wu Ying said gently.

"As would I. Killing outsiders for transgressions has a tendency to eventually anger the southern states. Then, there are letters"—a slight shudder at that—"diplomacy, and eventually, war. A lot of waste, though it does help to sharpen the youngsters."

A titter of amusement from the three behind. But no braying or requests for her to take that path, so it seemed they were not, at this time, looking forward to war.

"The second method is one of trade and service." She glanced at Wu Ying's fingers, eyes resting on the World Spirit Ring. "Someone as gifted with fortune as you would surely be able to provide sufficient recompense in resources and time."

Making no move to cover his ring—if she knew, she knew by now—Wu Ying could not help but nod. He had, after a time, given up on the backpack he once wore. Nowadays, his World Spirit Ring was large enough that containing most herbs there was simple enough. And he had sufficient other spatial rings for his disparate other goods.

"And the third method?" Wu Ying asked.

"The third option is only available for those who are part of the clan," Erdene said. "It is also, of course, the easiest."

"Of course." Wu Ying inclined his head. "A pity then. I fear I have bonds that otherwise preclude such a method." He could understand their reasoning. An individual who had not only a World Spirit Ring but a Core Formation cultivation would be a benefit to any clan. Even one as strong as this.

"A pity," Erdene said. "Then, the second option?"

"It seems I have little choice." He leaned forward, waiting to hear what she wanted. Really, different culture or not, it was not so different from some of his other interactions with greedy sects.

A small smile then, before she turned to the side and gestured. The servants arrived, bearing cups of that fermented milky drink drawn from the open leather sack that had been propped up via a wooden vertical slat at the edge of the ger.

Wu Ying took the cup, tilting it from side to side as he stared at the drink. "Not tea?"

"Airag. Better than the southern tepid leaf water." She raised her cup and sipped on it, watching as Wu Ying shrugged and did the same.

His nose wrinkled a little at the mild alcoholic smell before he sipped on the drink. A little sour, the taste of the grass and milk still present, but also slightly sweet. Not disagreeable, though a little different. Another mouthful after the initial sip, then he placed the cup on the small table.

"Tell me then, what herbs do you require? What acts of service will suffice?"

Was the smile she offered a little wide, a little too mercenary?

Probably. Then again, for all the courtesy shown to him, he'd known from the start that he was a prisoner, held hostage by her strength. When disparities in strength abounded, only the courtesies and mores of civilization stymied outright tyranny.

Even then, there was always a price.

***

Morning the next day, he was standing before a group of students, a mixture of children and adults. None had brush or paper, nothing to take notes, but he saw a few of the older members leafing through the books he had deposited in the front of the classroom. In the ger they had set aside for him, a stone turtle over from the central one, he rode the gentle rise and fall of the turtle's movements with casual ease.

Sometimes, he did wonder about his profession. That it was valuable was without doubt. Perhaps, if anything, gathering was a tad too valuable. This was not the first or second or third time he had found himself imprisoned for his skills. That the first time was via a sect's trapped war of manners, and the second by a willful Nascent Soul hermit mattered little.

Till he had the strength to escape and make his own decisions, until he could assert control of his own destiny, he would always be at the whims of a Nascent Soul cultivator. The only advantage he had against most of those individuals was that few could—or would—take the time to imprison another for any true length of time.

After all, they had better things to do than play watchdog. In addition, from what he had begun to understand in his own studies, the press and pressure of their immortal souls, the daos they had embraced and the—often—inherent conflict in imprisoning others was a problem. Eventually, such differences had to be resolved.

Which led to him here, teaching a class on herbology and gathering. Of course, the tribesmen needed nothing from him in terms of the plants of the steppe. But herbs from the south? The kinds that could grow in modified greenhouses resting upon warm turtle shells or which might arrive via the itinerant traders?

Well, that was another thing entirely.

"It looks like everyone is here," Wu Ying said as he watched the last child scamper in, hair in disarray, tugging her dress down with a slip of meat still stuck between her teeth from breakfast.

She grinned unrepentantly as she slid into a spot near the front, prodding one of the boys to the side until she had enough space.

"I am Cultivator Long. I shall be your teacher for the next... while." Wu Ying held back an internal sigh. He had no idea how long he would be here, though if he got away with a season, he would count it lucky. "My lessons will be on the plants and spiritual herbs of the southern countries, with a specific eye toward items that may grow in this climate—with some modification—or that might be transported with minimal loss of efficacy."

He paused, waiting for the translator to finish speaking. He kept an ear out, listening to the way the man spoke, the intonation and phrases. At least, among the bargain he had made was lessons on their language. In time, he would be able to speak without a translator and spy.

"What is efficacy?" the little girl who had been late piped up through the translator.

Wu Ying could not help but wince at himself. It seemed he had spent too much time in the Sect, listening to Elders orate. He had taken their intonations, their obtuse language for himself when he too began lecturing. Which, eyeing the children before him, was probably the worst idea possible.

Well, lesson learned.

"Well?"

He did not need the translator for that word, or to understand the impatient look on the girl's face as she waited for his answer. A few others tried to hush her, but most of the other students looked resigned.

So. Troublemaker, that one.

"Potency. The strength of the herb," he said. Then, collecting his thoughts and pushing aside any others, he continued. "Before you are a number of tomes on herbs. I have annotated many of them myself, marking truth and mistakes, but these documents are the most common ones found in the south. It will be the grounding of our learning, for it is impossible to understand the differences between certain plants without understanding the others surrounding them or the environment they live within."

Two hours later, Wu Ying wrapped up the lecture after spending the last ten minutes answering questions. To his surprise, rather than disappearing or standing respectfully to be acknowledged before asking further questions, a number of his students swarmed him. Their questions were pointed and telling, calling out gaps in his explanation or, in some cases, attempting to explain why a specific northern plant was better than his southern ones.

Wu Ying answered and rebutted arguments as best he could. The fact that the entire conversation had to be done through his tired translator made the arguments both less frenzied and more heated, as parties waited for their point to be made via an intermediary.

In the end, Wu Ying clapped his hands together after glancing at the tired and strained translator. His movement startled the remaining students, drawing their attention to him. "Enough. Bring examples of the plants you describe tomorrow. We will review and compare then." He considered and added, "Live and cut, both!"

After the translator was finished, Wu Ying chased the others away before turning to the man in gratitude and expressing it.

"You're welcome, Cultivator Long. If you will give me a few minutes, we can begin your next lesson."

Wu Ying sighed but nodded. This one he had asked for, after all. And really, learning a new language wasn't bad. Even if learning this one would involve a lot fewer kisses and words of endearment.

***

That afternoon, after a hasty meal of vegetables, unleavened bread, and more airag, he was on another turtle, working in the sheltered greenhouse. Smoky glass—the only glass he had seen in the entirety of the village and each piece only a couple of hands long, with branches and mud making up the rest of the space—allowed a filtering of sunlight within. He was listening to the gardener speak as they turned over the compost pile which was kept within the greenhouse, its presence helping to increase the warmth within.

"Light, that's the hardest. Glass is expensive, and in the midst of winter, it doesn't help so much. Not when the days are clouded and short," the head gardener said. "We have to use enchantments and ask the spirits for their aid, or else what we grow dies. Even then, we rotate often." Gesturing deeper, the man continued. "Not easy, this. But fresh vegetables, good herbs… worth it. It's the wealth of our clan, a new wealth, that is above the thunder goats."

Wu Ying nodded, eyeing the runes etched on the inside of the building. He felt the flow of chi within, understood a little of their uses because of it, but there was also a dao conception embedded deep within the unfamiliar runes that he had no hope of understanding.

When the gardener ran out of mundane tasks for the two of them, Wu Ying asked, "So, what can I do to aid you then?"

"Plants! Experiments. We have a list of the kind of things we need. Plants with daos embedded in them, plants with elements. Water, swamp, marsh! Any element. If we can grow them through a winter, then we can grow stronger. Make better pills."

"Through the winter…" Wu Ying said carefully.

"And the summer too!" the gardener said cheerfully. "Got to test all the seasons, don't you think? And make sure it's worth the space." He gestured around once more. Even if the greenhouse was large, it was still only a couple hundred feet all in. Vastly constrained, when one considered how many villagers there were.

"Of course," Wu Ying agreed.

Well, now he was beginning to see the shape of Khan Erdene's vision. Why not make use of the Gatherer that had blown himself to your doorstep? Use him to strengthen your tribe for this generation and the next thirteen levels down.

A man could rage about the unfairness of it all, or…

"Do you have that list then? And a list of everything you grow already? And have tried?" Wu Ying said, smiling genially. "Best not double our workload by trying the same thing again."

Smirking, as though he knew exactly what Wu Ying was thinking, the gardener gestured for them to take a seat a short distance away. He beckoned to a nearby servant, and tea arrived as he faced Wu Ying. "No list. We do not waste paper or trees like you southerners." He snorted. "But worry not, I remember it all as related by my father, Elder Daginaa, and my own experiments."

Then, without hesitation, he launched into a spiel, his voice taking a slight sing-song capacity. That he had to stop often for the translator to finish and catch up was annoying. But it did give Wu Ying more time to record the information.

They might not use brush and paper. He would.

He jotted down the list, in exact order. Hoping the translator was right in the long list of plants detailed. Learning, even if much of it lacked further context. That, he knew, would come too.

***

Sparring. Of course there would be. Though…

"Wrestling?" Wu Ying said, eyeing the shirtless, oiled men—and a few women—squaring off against one another on the pounded earth after the herds had come to a stop for the day. "I thought you'd want…" He touched his sword.

"Hah!" The boisterous tribesman who was Wu Ying's guide for this part of the day laughed. "None of that. We have no reason to learn such a delicate weapon."

Wu Ying snorted, choosing not to rise to the challenge. He had known these were all dao wielders—though they might not call them that—and it made sense. Riding on horses as they did, the swinging, chopping motions of the dao benefited from the additional height offered by their rides. Still, to deride his weapon…

"And you think I have something to teach there?" Wu Ying nodded toward the simple arenas where fighters contested.

"That's what we're here to find out, no?" The man grinned, slapping Wu Ying on the shoulder and, not removing his hand, used that leverage to propel him toward an empty arena. He barked out commands that the translator chose not to translate, and the pair sparring within broke apart, one backing away to give room for Wu Ying.

"Why do I feel like I'm being set up?" Wu Ying muttered to himself, even as he waved for the man to wait. Then before anyone could say anything else—like calling him a coward—he stripped off his robes. No reason to get them dirty and oily.

Once he was clad in his pants alone, he made his robes disappear into his storage rings, along with his sword. It was only when he was halfway into the ring that he heard the translator's voice.

"Cultivator Long! Cultivator Long!"

"Yes?" Wu Ying said.

"Your rings. They should not be worn while wrestling."

Wu Ying blinked, then nodded. Of course. Between their sharp edges and their tendency to catch on flesh or fingers, wearing them was a bad idea. He knew that. Heck, unarmed sparring in general required you to take them off, at least when people were going full speed.

Except…

For the first time, Wu Ying hesitated. Mentally, if not physically. Handing the man the half dozen rings he carried, including the one he wore on his small toe, was simple enough. There were a few amused looks at his use of a toe ring, but what was he to do? The dark sect members he had taken them from had them worn there, and while the rings had minor resize enchantments, it was insufficient to redo them entirely for fingers.

Also, keeping an emergency ring on his toe was just useful. Emergency funds, including a few secreted Core-level Spirit Beast stones, additional weaponry and clothing, a second copy of his gathering book, and cultivation manuals were all in there.

No, giving all those rings was a small matter compared to his World Sprit Ring. That had barely left his finger since he had acquired it. And while he took his time giving all the other rings, this one… this one was important. Looking up as he placed his finger on the ring, preparing to pull it off, he met the translator's placid gaze.

"You have my word and the Khan's that none of your belongings will be touched. Such an action would be highly dishonorable and punished by her directly."

Wu Ying winced, realizing how easily he had been read. For a second time now, he felt as though he had failed an unspoken test. Greed, a desire for material goods… He had little enough in most things. But this one item, this ring…

Well. It was probably the most important and valuable he had ever owned.

"Thank you. And the Khan," Wu Ying said, removing the ring and handing it over.

Free of accessories, Wu Ying traversed back to the ring and offered a bow to the massive, well-thewed man before him. As his opponent regarded Wu Ying's slimmer—hah! when was the last time he had felt slim, especially among the elegant cultivators he was so used to being compared to?—form, he smirked and spread his hands wide in welcome.

A sharp bark from the martial arts instructor, and his opponent launched himself at Wu Ying, catching the other by mild surprise. Hands grabbed at Wu Ying, holding him tightly as he was borne to the ground. The slow envelopment and aggressive, oiled, and muscular struggles of men had begun.

In truth, Wu Ying had not practiced wrestling in years. Not since his early years in the Sect, scrabbling for Sect points. His time with Elder Hsu, battling the powerful snail style Elder whose method of fighting involved a much less energetic form of wrestling, had left him with some degree of trepidation.

The villagers' form of grappling was much less physically close. Most of the battle happened on their splayed feet, as opponents wrestled for dominance before a throw or trip was completed. At that point, fast movement and proper positioning allowed the individual on top to control the battle and blows rained down from above. Unlike Elder Mo's style, which pulled one down and then fought for dominance, theirs emphasized a degree of freedom in case the wrestler needed to disengage to deal with another attacker.

All of which meant that Wu Ying found himself flipped through the air, pulled down, and otherwise tripped repeatedly. While he had neither the knowledge nor skill to stop his opponent, he had a few advantages.

Firstly, the Seven Winds Body Cultivation methods included a series of stretching, contorting, and movement exercises meant to embody the wind itself. And such practices meant that not only was holding on to Wu Ying to execute a proper throw incredibly difficult, but so was keeping him from landing on his feet.

On top of that, as a Body Cultivator with a Core within—small as it might be—Wu Ying was stronger than his opponents. And in any battle of strength—which wrestling, at the end of the day, was—relied upon strength to some degree.

After a dozen passes and flips, the majority of which Wu Ying managed to stall or finish by landing easily on his feet, his opponent grew angry. His temper flared as did his cultivation base, roots of wood chi erupting from his feet and grounding Wu Ying. The next time they engaged, he felt his opponent's chi grip against his arm and aura, attempting to constrict his motions.

His opponent's arm closed on Wu Ying's tricep, attempting to drag Wu Ying close and tuck the arm across his own body. Feeling his opponent rooting himself to Wu Ying's body, the wind cultivator chose to go with the movements, twisting into the pull and nearly dislocating his own shoulder as he dropped and turned, placing his other shoulder against his opponent, bending his head such that he was almost parallel to the other's chest.

Then Wu Ying straightened, feeling his shoulder throb a little as wood chi reached for the ground, searching for a grip. Yet surprise had taken his opponent as Wu Ying chose to be aggressive for the first time, his feet lifted from the earth before his opponent could root himself properly. A twist was enough to throw his opponent over Wu Ying's shoulder and come crashing down, Wu Ying's trapped arm released in the midst of all this.

After that, it was just a matter of dropping onto his opponent and controlling the neck, a series of twists and moves that Wu Ying was all too intimately familiar with—if on the other side of the tricks.

When his opponent finally tapped out, Wu Ying stood, breathing a little heavily.

"Good, good!" the martial art instructor said.

Those words, Wu Ying did not need translated. Nor the way the man started shouting and gesticulating as he called others over, and his opponent's original partner hurried to take the defeated man's place across from Wu Ying.

It seemed he was going to have a busy late afternoon after all.

***

Evening and a dinner held on the ground as the stone turtles lowered their shells and campfires were set up. Most meals consisted of rice and vegetables supplemented with small strips of meat from demonic beasts hunted on the fly and the never-ending cups of airag.

Music afterward, as the tribesmen sang. Entertainment on the steppes was hard to come by, and always, always generated from within. Music, dance, tall tales. It was, if unfamiliar in detail, recognizable in overall form.

Wu Ying watched and listened for hours, until the moon had risen high and those with lower cultivations had headed to bed. Only then did he leave, his translator having left him after dinner. Wu Ying's place of rest was on the ground, a tiny, lined tent located in the center of the sprawling herds, near Khan Erdene's stone turtle yet on the ground and not in any true place of honor.

A fact driven into him by the lingering smell of sickness and death and mustiness in the tent. If he had to guess, the enclosure was usually used to separate the dead and dying from the healthy, a medical tent that offered mild comfort before old age or sickness consumed the occupant.

"Sick dog, am I?" Wu Ying muttered, eyeing the interior. At least his rings had been returned to him without fuss. Empty of all but the meanest furnishings, the small tent also lacked the altar to the spirits he had seen and sensed in every dwelling.

And wasn't that the biggest difference? All through the day, he had felt it. The silent watchers, the twisting of his wind chi as he went about his day, his spiritual senses spread apart. Unseen spirits, creatures of wind and air, of grass and earth and water.

Not that there was much water use around. The steppe was rather dry, so water was hoarded, used when necessary for drink and gardening and not other more common, southerner things. Like big baths. Not that they eschewed bathing entirely, but the use of a single bucket among many was rather penurious. Wu Ying had no intention of copying them, what with his access to a rather large source of water in his ring.

Shaking his head, Wu Ying pushed out his aura, erecting a simple but effective barrier against observation and entry. The spirits that flowed outside moved at the edges, touching upon his aura, teasing it and pressing against it before eventually drifting off.

Leaving Wu Ying, for the first time, alone.

He would learn more about them, about the role he would play and the lessons this tribe had to offer. He would, of course, look for an escape. Yet for the time being, he was content enough. After all, his journey thus far had blown him from one corner of the middle kingdom to the other...

And yet, at present, the wind was not howling. Not at all.

Chapter 22

Days blended together. Wu Ying rarely saw Khan Erdene. She spent many of her days in her ger high above. He had no reason to ask what she was doing, for the constant pull of chi toward the ger spoke of her cultivation. Such was the strength of her soul that it created a minor storm that followed them, always threatening rain but rarely gifting it. Beneath, the stone turtles trundled along, additional massive gers taken apart and put together every sunrise and sunset with startling efficiency.

Weeks passed, his days varying only mildly in routine. In time, when even Wu Ying's prodigious memory strained at the sheer amount of new information fed to him—new words, new plants, new fighting techniques, new ways of living—the translator arrived with a simple document.

Surprised at the presence of the sheepskin scroll, Wu Ying took care while pulling it open. Within, he found a cultivation exercise written in his own tongue with only a few grammatical mistakes.

"This is for me?" Wu Ying said.

"Yes. My apologies for taking so long, Cultivator Long. Transcribing the exercise into your language was a little more of a challenge than I expected. Your language is… complex," the translator, Oktai, murmured. "Many words, saying the same thing."

"True enough." Amused, Wu Ying added, "Whereas you all just add to your words to make them easier[34]."

"Of course, that is how it is best done!" Oktai said.

While they had been speaking, Wu Ying had been reading, reviewing the scroll. He got to the end and frowned, turning it slightly to show Oktai as he spoke. "This exercise…"

"Common among our children," Oktai said. "We do not have the luxury of your paper. And even you are running out, yes?"

"Among other things, yes…" Wu Ying admitted. He did not keep much paper with him. It was not, after all, his dao to be a scholar. "Is this how you all remember so well?"

Oktai nodded. "Partly. But also, you southerners are lazy. What you write, you think paper can remember for you. And so you forget. We do not have the luxury. What is said, we must remember. What has happened, we hold dear within our mind. In that way, our ancestors, the spirits of the past, and the land live."

Smiling a little, staring at the document, Wu Ying could not help but wonder if the man— their people—had it right. How much better would it be to remember all the good things that

---

[34] Mongolian is an agglutinative morphology in which a variety of suffixes are added to a word, changing its meaning. Korean, Japanese, some indigenous languages in America, and Turkic languages are similar, where words add on to change the meaning. It can make words easier to understand by breaking down the word individually, but also leads to very long words. And can be complex for those not used to such construction.

had happened? To pass on the stories from one generation to the next and know it would be remembered properly?

How much of the knowledge of his own style had been lost or changed, as their only history came from the documents passed from one generation to the next? How much had been forgotten during nights of revelry or altered through imperfect understanding? So much he'd had—his father had—to recreate. Their heritage, broken.

And then, Wu Ying recalled other things. Of desperate battles against dark sect members. Of lying in medicinal baths, his skin, bones, and muscles sloughing away, being replaced by the minerals and materials within. The transcendent pain, the terrifying fear of a Nascent Soul beast stalking him through weeks in the wild.

Perhaps memory, littered with sharp edges and broken as it might be, was also a gift.

"I shall leave you to practice, yes?" Oktai said, drawing Wu Ying back to the present. "No class today. For we arrive."

"Arrive?" Wu Ying said, surprised.

"To summer pastures." Oktai frowned. "Did you think we traveled constantly?"

Embarrassed, Wu Ying chose not to answer. He had thought, with the moving giant turtles and the efficiency with which they packed and unpacked every day, that the tribe was truly nomadic.

Laughing at the foolish southerner, Oktai walked away, leaving a rueful cultivator with a new cultivation exercise to practice. One that would improve his memory and recall when properly attuned.

***

Squinting at Oktai, Wu Ying let out a low growl as he was led through the cluster of huts to lunch hours later. The tribe had reached their summer pasture grounds and was now a flurry of activity. Old fences, left alone for a season, had to be checked and repaired, gers had to be set up in their appropriate positions, and stone turtles had to be chivied to move to rest in their allocated positions before food, stored in storage rings and trundling wagons, was brought out to appease them.

All around, men, women, and children hurried. The vast herds that made up the livelihood of the tribe were being driven to graze a distance away as their fields were checked over. Grass was cut down and bushes pulled apart while fences were ridden, double-checked. Old planting fields, meant for the summer plants, were also inspected, and it was in that direction Wu Ying was sent.

A few cookfires were lit, but for the most part, the tribe was eating on the move; wind-dried meat, wrapped in warmed bread, was held in one hand as holes were dug, posts were tested, and goods carried. Dust churned through the air, spotty tufts of grass and weeds kicked apart as the clan moved through their resting grounds.

In the fields, far less extensive than what Wu Ying was used to, the smell of old compost, left over the seasons to care for itself, was rich. Tribesmen and women turned over the compost pile, checking to ensure it was well kept, while others tore into the earth, pulling apart stubborn weeds and breaking hard soil.

"Your help has been requested here, Cultivator Long. You were once a farmer, no?" Oktai said, gesturing at the workers then pointing at a plot of land left all by its lonesome. "The tribe could use another field."

Wu Ying snorted. He did not bother asking for tools from the tribe as he wandered over to the plot, eyeing the ground. He ensured there was sufficient space to walk—or lead cattle or a horse—between the fields before he began, conjuring a hoe from his spirit ring.

If he smiled a little when others noticed the quality of the equipment he used, it was minor and petty on his part. Then again, so was asking him to break in new ground. It was the most backbreaking work, for with each swing, new rocks and old roots got in the way. Breaking the earth, pulling stones, and breaking apart rooted plants was all laborious work.

Breathing slowly, letting his chi circulate through him and down his hoe, Wu Ying worked the land. He projected a tiny thread of sword intent into the hoe, using his chi to wrap it in protective energy and allowing the sharpness of the blade held in his heart to enter it.

Each swing cut through earth and roots with ease, no more difficult than flesh. Ripping out the soil, multiple feet deep as his movements projected his chi into the land, Wu Ying churned and turned the earth. He knew he would have to return and break up the chunks of earth he tore free, clear out roots and rocks, but that was for later.

For now, he dug, his mind and body one.

Doing what he knew, what he had been taught to do. Growing and treating the earth, altering the world, one swing at a time. And if the wind blew harder, the cold north wind giving way to a more imperious one, he only barely noticed.

***

Late evening, the sun finally setting on the early summer day, Wu Ying edged backward on hands and knees. His fingers plunged again and again into the soil, striking and breaking apart clumps and ripping out roots and rocks. Each was tossed aside, forming a small pile as they landed in the heap he had started.

An entire li had been cleared, from one side to another, an outsized field. Yet without the need to worry about drainage and flooding, Wu Ying had chosen to clear it on a larger basis. Eventually, of course, it would need to be watered, but such concerns were for later.

Perhaps an Earth Cultivator, a true farming prodigy could have done better and faster work. Wu Ying understood his Senior had the ability to sink his chi within a field, to find the problem spots and twist them apart, pulling aside root and earth through spirit and energy alone. That way was barred for Wu Ying, through lack of experience and knowledge and base

400

nature. Yet he would not have it any other way. Digging his hands into the earth, pulling and sorting with his bare fingers, it was a reminder of who he had been—and who he was.

All the while, the Never Empty Wine Pot method—modified—worked, pulling at the chi around him. Earth and wood and wind—oh, the ever-present wind in the steppes that never stopped gusting, no matter what time of day it was—churned through and around his aura, drawn within and processed to become his own. His chi reserves grew, his dantian filling such that Wu Ying knew, soon enough, he might be ready for another layer.

"The sun has nearly set, Cultivator Long," Oktai spoke up, interrupting the cultivator.

Wu Ying blinked, extracting his hands from the earth and rocking back on his heels to stare at the translator. The man offered a grin, bushy mustache rising a little as he gestured back to where the clearing had transformed, the village appearing as though by magic. More buildings, more gers than ever seemed to have been built, such that it was very much a small village. The herds had been led into their fields, some uncomfortably crowded as broken fences were still to be fixed.

"So it has," Wu Ying said, staring at the multi-colored sunset. He drew a deep breath, the strong hint of churned earth and dust, the whiff of unwashed bodies and a herd of animals ever present. Certainly more noticeable than the rice fields he was so used to…

But familiar in its own way.

"And dinner?"

"Served. They slaughtered a few injured sheep, so there is much meat to be had. Or there was." Amusement glittered in Oktai's eyes. "Now there are but scraps."

Wu Ying laughed ruefully. "I might have gotten lost in the work."

"And the stonemasons will thank you for it tomorrow," Oktai replied, his gaze tracing over the high pile of rocks that Wu Ying had created in the process of clearing the ground. "Though perhaps we need not locate such small stones."

A shrug answered his words. "My father always said if you do something, do it well. Then you need not do it again."

Oktai smiled. "My father had a similar saying too." Grim amusement dances in his eyes as he added, "Though it involved more swearing and hitting."

Wu Ying nodded. There had not been much corporal punishment in his home, though it was not unusual to see others walking gingerly after a caning. Mostly though, Wu Ying had ended up being put through an extra hour or two of sword practice. After all his chores were done.

Admittedly, looking back at it, Wu Ying was not certain he would not have preferred a quick caning. He might have benefited from the hours of study with the weapon, but it also meant he'd lost out on many nights of catching tadpoles, chasing down grasshoppers, and just lounging near the river with a fishing pole with his friends on those few times where none of them had chores or cultivation practice.

"Tell me, tomorrow. What are the plans?" Wu Ying asked, his head turning a little as he felt a shift in the flow of external chi. His eyes narrowed at the largest turtle, at the ger he could barely see from his position and the small series of clouds that had formed around the animal, all while he had been caught up in his own actions.

"The Khan enters her summer of secluded cultivation once more," Oktai replied. Then, a little flicker of a smile on his lips as he continued. "Elder Ogdai asks that I mention that she can still sense us all, and all attempts at escape or violence."

Wu Ying snorted, recalling the trio of elders hard at work attempting to deplete the stores of airag by themselves. He could not recall which one was Ogdai, but it wasn't as though Wu Ying had planned on running. He had much to learn here still, even if he was being held captive against his will.

Gesturing for Wu Ying to follow, Oktai led the way back. After a moment, he answered Wu Ying's initial question. "More of the same. The fences must be repaired, the fields tilled and prepared for planting. We will want to put to seed as much as we can. There is much to do, for protective enchantments must be refreshed and the spirits appeased. There will be little time for frivolities." He gestured back to the field. "There, you will be best." A little smile. "After all, running southerner, you cannot ride."

"Ah, but I kept up well enough with your riders, no?"

"Only so long as they chose not to call upon the spirits."

Oktai's words were an answer to a glimmering question, one that had slowly been pieced together over the weeks. The spirits the tribe spoke of, that lived among them. They were as real as the demonic beasts and spirit beasts Wu Ying was used to, though lesser in their strength. In this land, they clustered and grew strong, floating in the nether.

"Tell me, Oktai. Why the lack of spirits in the south? I sense them here, everywhere." Wu Ying gestured around him. He could swear he could feel them laughing at him as the wind stirred. "Why not where I'm from?"

Oktai pursed his lips, not answering for long moments. Eventually, after they had crossed another field, he spoke up, his voice hesitant. "There are as many answers as there are seeds on the wind. Some believe that you southerners are the true barbarians, having killed or driven out the spirits from your lands. Others feel that we are blessed, and thus you are not to be derided but pitied." He turned toward the lead turtle for a second, before he continued, slower. "The Khan once said she believes that the spirits are but different in your land. Instead of moving alongside your people, they hide in the bodies of the beasts and plants of your land. It is why your books are so filled with plants, and why our land is missing so many such items."

Wu Ying listened, but in the end, he could not help but ask, "And what do you believe?"

Oktai shrugged. "I think it matters not. The world is as it is. We have our spirits, and you have your lands. Such concerns are for cultivators above me."

Nodding to a passing couple, Wu Ying considered the answer. He debated, for a moment, trying to test the theories. Perhaps capturing a spirit or bargaining with one to speak with him. There were tales, sung late in the night, of spirits who had the mind, the strength to speak directly to cultivators. Similar, in a way, to his own connection to the wind, though more directed and available even to those without a dao and body connection.

Then again, did he care? Curiosity was important, but angering creatures that were existing without harm seemed foolish. Was there a point to such knowledge? And if there was no point, what was the goal of such pursuit?

He was no scholar after all. The furthest thing from it, he sometimes felt. The knowledge he searched for could not be found in any hidebound book or dusty scroll. The wind blew and Wu Ying followed, and in that travel, his dao and his path became clearer.

"Come, think later. Enjoy, for boodog is a rare treat![35]"

A hand shoved a plate, piled with meat, rice, and vegetables, at Wu Ying. He was surprised, though only a little, that so much time had passed while he contemplated his options.

Automatically, Wu Ying took the plate, inhaling the smell of roasted and stewed meat. The hot stones that had been shoved into the inner cavity of the animal had steamed and cooked the meat on the inside while fur was burnt off on the outside before it crisped, fat embedding in the meat, along with the organs of the goat that had been reinserted. The resulting stewed meat was a highly flavorful product, having been cooked in the animal's fat and juices. Smell alone set Wu Ying's stomach rumbling as he took a seat with a smile.

Perhaps it was time to put aside such thoughts. At least for the next few days. He was learning much from just listening to the tales told late at night or in gers as children sought the blessed return of the nightly void. Better to wait and study rather than rush ahead.

After all, he was in no hurry. And the wind that blew through the steppes whispered of a world yet unseen.

---

[35] These days, boodog is made with potatoes, onions, and other herbs. Modifying the recipe here, just 'cause potatoes really don't show up in China until much later.

Chapter 23

Recognition of what you could not change. Acceptance of the world as it was. Embracing an individual's circumstances. And, finally, a stubborn refusal to bow to the tragedies one might encounter. All were hallmarks of one who had accepted the greater Dao in their soul.

Pity it was so difficult to achieve.

Hands dug into the earth of the field he was clearing, a quartet of farmers hauling compost pails to spread across the cleared land, Wu Ying fell into routines. He sought to push aside thoughts of freedom, of movement without constraint, of the watchers at night and the overbearing presence above.

In the movement of fingers in earth, searching out rocks and roots, Wu Ying sought to enter the tranquil space of meditative movement. In the distance, voices rose with the sound of women at work, weaving and dying wool long stored for this very moment. Their voices turned and twisted, eventually blending into a song.

Wu Ying paused then, rocking back on his feet to listen, the music carried on the back of the wind. He understood not a word, even familiar words learnt in the last few weeks, but the music still spoke to his soul. He half-closed his eyes, listening until a single voice rose above others, a deep, thrumming note that was formed in the throat, the voice rumbling through the steppes.

The song was no simple piece of music, for within the bounds of its notes was a dao. Budding within the voice of a singer whose cultivation was bordering on the Core Formation stage, it took the emotions inherent in the song—a song of joy in the work and the community, the recognition of another summer's arrival and the lifting of spirits as life returned to the steppes in abundance—and raised it to another level.

Tears of joy fell unbidden from Wu Ying's eyes even as a smile etched itself upon his face. He breathed in deeper, filling his lungs with the fresh air of the steppes, the overturned earth beside him, and the musky scent of the goats and sheep of the herd, all interlaced with the slight cackle of ozone, and smiled.

For a moment, he was at peace. The song continued on and on, taking him with it. As though moving to the unspoken demands of the music, his hands plunged into the earth again, acting of their own accord in accordance to the music. He sorted and tossed, crushed earth, and sent his own chi, wind and wood and a touch of fire, into the earth itself as he cleared the land foot by foot.

When the song finally ended, his eyes opened and the smile on his lips was light. A feeling of quiet interest stole over him, as though something great and good and stern watched over him. Then he stood and that feeling went away.

Leaving him with a field that had been churned and turned, where compost was being brought over and mixed with the hard earth to further nourish it. He drew in a deep breath and blinked, surprised at the fullness he felt deep within in his dantian.

Well, perhaps that song had done more than just encourage him in completing his task.

***

"A break?" Oktai said, eyes narrowed.

"Yes. I have reached a culmination point in my cultivation and require some time to consolidate my cultivation," Wu Ying said.

Again, Oktai's lips thinned. "I do not know about this."

Wu Ying shrugged, wiping at the remaining stew with the bread he had been given, the hard bread soaking up the juices admirably. The spring season foraging, along with the moving greenhouses, had supplied the tribe well with fresh vegetables, but even those were beginning to run out. The next few weeks would be a lean period, as winter stores were finished and the plants they grew still sprouted and grew.

If anything, Wu Ying wondered why it had taken them so long to arrive in their summer domicile. It seemed the timing was a little off, what with the early growing season having been missed. A routine choice, for reasons he knew not? Or something more dire?

"If I'm cultivating, I won't be eating," Wu Ying teased. "All I ask is that you ask the elders. I understand you can't make such a decision yourself."

Oktai looked relieved. "I shall speak with them this evening."

"Thank you."

Meal finished, Wu Ying wiped his hand on a cloth he'd extracted from his spirit ring and returned the plate to a nearby female tribesmember. She was tall, slightly taller than Wu Ying, with a brilliant smile, light brown hair, and startingly unusual green eyes. When she smiled at Wu Ying, her eyelids fluttered a little and she frankly eyed him up and down. He purposely looked away, moving away before she could try to strike up a conversation, only for Oktai to fall into step soon after.

"Are you, perhaps, one of those who do not like women?" Oktai asked.

"What?"

"Women. Are you not attracted to them?" At Wu Ying's frown, the translator grinned. "Good, good. Then perhaps you need some encouragement. Narangerel rides nearly as well as a man. And you know what they say about good riders."

Wu Ying frowned. "What do they say?"

"They know how best to move their hips!" Braying with laughter, Oktai slapped Wu Ying's shoulder. The cultivator sighed, allowing the translator his burst of amusement as he kept walking, only stopping when the other man caught up. "But she is healthy, her hips are wide and will carry a baby well. And, of course, she has no husband to be angry if you were to bed her."

"And bedding a southerner like me is acceptable?" Wu Ying said, a touch scandalized. Even though he had such experiences himself, to speak of it so crudely… It still shocked his

Shen heart. He knew mores were different, from culture to culture. Still, a single female, willingly and blatantly throwing herself at a stranger? Unspeakable at home.

Even with the more relaxed mores of cultivators, it was just not done.

"Why not? Your blood is strong, your cultivation even stronger. You might fight like a southerner, but you fight well. What woman would not want to offer her child such advantages?"

"And her future husband? What would he think?" Wu Ying asked.

Oktai shrugged. "It is not his place to think anything but to bed her and raise his own! The raising of children are a woman's job and the village, in that order. What skills the child needs to learn, the village will teach. And any husband worth marrying will care for her son as his own anyway." Oktai squinted at Wu Ying dubiously. "What kind of man in the south would have any thoughts, anyway, about a child? What fault has the child made?"

Wu Ying sighed. That was a discussion that would take all too long. Even those women who were known to indulge themselves outside their marital bonds were careful not to conceive a child. Inheritance laws, the splitting of the farmland or wealth in a merchant, the primary heir for a noble—those were complex matters.

When he tried to explain that, Oktai laughed. The tribe were not fools. They too had inheritance laws and issues. Herds—and grazing rights—were a matter of prestige and inheritance, the location and distance that one must drive their herd to graze a complex dance undertaken each day. Yet no single tribesmen wanted to care for their herd alone, both because of the onery nature of the thunder goats and the blazing sheep, but also due to demonic spirits, raiding tribes, and other calamities.

Better to work with others, marking one's sheep as necessary, but grazing and moving them as a group. In this way, those of the same social standing also formed bonds. Nonetheless, a child born out of wedlock was as accepted in the village and by the father as any other. The point was not the child's origins but their actions.[36]

"And so, Cultivator Long, do not run from the desires of your loins! Narangerel is willing, desirable, and frankly, if she keeps eyeing you and does not receive relief, she'll never turn her eyes to the rest of us," Oktai finished.

Wu Ying's lips tightened at the teasing, but no word escaped them. Even as Oktai badgered him for more of an answer, he chose to avoid the question. He might not be an ascetic like the Wudan Sects, but neither did he feel the need to spread his seed around without care. Desire could be sated in many ways, but a false move could set chains of parentage and fate resonating throughout the decades.

***

---

[36] Author note for people reading this and going, "Ooh, Mongol culture is amazing." I'm taking from the little bit of actual Mongol culture I know of and mixing with other known cultures. Because this is a fantasy world. Please don't finish the book thinking you read anything even close to their actual culture.

The newly created field had to be watered from a small pond located a couple of li from the settlement, a walk that had to be repeated over and over as Wu Ying used the simple storage baskets of woven leather, enchanted to contain the dao of space. Baskets the tribe had provided him. It made the watering process so much simpler than using mundane casks or pots. Even if it took time to carefully extract the water without wasting the precious liquid.

It was a pity that storage items were so rare that such implements were not provided to peasants everywhere. How much easier would it have been to be able to water fields far from rivers. How much time, how much effort, had Wu Ying and his family, his village, spent in the production of drainage lanes and runoff locations? How many canals did the kingdom create to help regulate the flow of water to reduce the amount of flooding?

Yet each storage ring had to be created by someone with a spatial dao. An understanding of the way realms and dimensions interacted with this world and the next. Only someone at the Core Foundation or Nascent Soul stage could create such items. And of course, who would they provide such items to other than cultivators? Who else could provide what else they needed to ascend? Who else but their peers?

And it was not as though such items lasted forever. Spatial rings and domains wore down, the daos embedded within them slowly being subsumed under the greater Dao. Such breakdowns often led to the disappearance of the items held within the rings, which was partly why a World Spirit Ring like his own, that could repair itself and even grow the spatial domain, was so valued.

Of course, there were rumors of violent explosions when rings broke down, but such events were just rumors. Well… outside of the Scar of the Fourth Wall. Or more correctly, what used to be part of the fourth wall of the capital in Shen.

Even with the aid of the storage baskets, the process of properly watering the field took most of the day. It was, Wu Ying had to admit, one of the setbacks of his dao and path. The wind might be great at many things—such as carrying him far, dispersing seeds, and cutting through obstacles—but a proper watering, one that did not waste the precious liquid, had to be completed much more slowly.

By the time he was done every day, the sun had once again begun to set. Wu Ying's lessons in the language had continued apace, leaving him able to—barely—converse with the others. It helped that the new cultivation exercise from the Dorben clan aided his memory.

And hadn't that been an exercise and a half? Thankfully, since it was an exercise that was taught even to children, it had not been dangerous. Just frustrating, as he'd worked chi flows through his body, strengthening mind and memory as he played games of recall, memorization, and recitation with children.

Though… now that Wu Ying thought of it, such games had also taught him a decent amount of the language. Which, perhaps, was the entire point of the way the clan did it. Even if it robbed him of his dignity over and over as seven-year-old children paraded their victories before him.

"Is this what I'm supposed to learn?" Wu Ying asked quietly to the silent night around him. "That there are worlds, kingdoms that defy my current knowledge?"

No surprise that the wind had no answer. It never did. When it spoke to him, it was with gestures and intent, with the brushing of wind across his face, the plucking at his sleeves, the scents of locations and worlds gone by.

The minor understandings that he had, they were not like words on a paper. They were not clear cut or obtuse as a writer might make them, but flashes of ideas and concepts. Then again, was that not the Dao itself? Something that could only be understood by experiencing, and when explained, it paled in comparison, becoming but a shadow of itself.

If the Dao was easy to explain, so simple as to be named and understood, then every cultivator, ever mortal would be immortal.

And then there would be no need for the heavens or the hells.

A wind, cold and calculating, pressed upon his skin. He smelled sheets of paper, the rustle of ropes and old irons, the whisper of heads knocking on the floor as one kowtowed as a judge's pronouncement arrived. Cold and hard and unyielding.

"Ah, you disagree," Wu Ying murmured, eyes closed. He waited, and understanding arrived a moment later. "For man, in heaven's view, is flawed. And so, immortal or not, one with the Dao or not, heaven and hell is required.

"Though it seems you might believe that the Dao itself is wrong. And I know a few cultivators who might argue against that." A meat-loving monk and a quietly angry, lonely Master another.

No answer from the wind this time, no rebuke or argument. Or perhaps if there was one, he missed it. For he was still but a student of the universe.

Eyes opening, Wu Ying found that another thing rumbled, much lower and closer to his heart. He put a hand to his stomach and sighed.

Dinner had been served long ago, but at least he had travel rations. He always had travel rations. And truth be told, with his World Spirit Ring, he could acquire vegetables and other forms of sustenance too. After all, spiritual herbs might be best processed, but consuming some raw or mixed would be enough.

"It's a beautiful night, is it not?" The voice that interrupted him was familiar, strong, and seductive. Her long strides took her toward him, a plate of food and a cup of airag in hand. Narangerel smiled as Wu Ying looked over. "You missed dinner, Cultivator Long. We would not wish for you to starve in our care."

"Thank you," Wu Ying said, taking the dishes from her and offering a slight bow. He automatically checked her cultivation with his spiritual sense. None of the tribe controlled their auras, all of them allowing it to blare outward. She was the same as earlier in the day, a water aspected upper-ranked Body Cultivator. "I am grateful for your concern."

"Well, if you are so grateful, perhaps you could help me with a small matter," Narangerel said, stepping closer to Wu Ying. This forced him to look up, an amusing and unusual proposition.

"And what could this poor cultivator help you with?" As if he could not guess.

A hand came up, resting on his chest. Her eyes glowed a little. "Well, I have an itch that needs to be scratched. And a breast that needs warming."

Wu Ying blushed then, for she was much more than forward. Yet he did not move away. After all, he was not his Master. And if this was the way of their tribe… well, he was here to learn, was he not?

***

The next morning, Oktai found Wu Ying before he left for the fields. The man had a smirk on his face, though the flat look Wu Ying offered the translator meant that only a hand was clapped on his shoulder, before the translator got to business.

"They said yes," Oktai said. "Your work on the field has done much for the clan. We will watch over your tent while you cultivate."

"I did not—"

"It does not matter. You are a guest. Any harm done to you would be a mark of dishonor upon us all," Oktai said.

When Wu Ying hesitated, the man, using the same hand that had clapped Wu Ying on the shoulder, shoved him in the direction of his tent.

"Go. There's no good reason to delay a breakthrough. Not when enlightenment is almost upon one, no?"

Wu Ying had to smile, bowing to Oktai before striding back to his tent. For all that they were keeping him here against his will, this was the most comfortable prison he could have found, it seemed.

One that even gave him an opportunity to advance.

Chapter 24

Weeks of cultivation, not just to compress and create the necessary Core layer within his body, but also to consolidate his cultivation afterward. Weeks to draw in the ever-present wind chi from around him, to layer it in his dantian so that he had energy to progress, all of it aided by simple cultivation aids—even the Twice-Cooked Dog Kidney and Wolf Liver Pill.

Cultivation this time was simple. His experiences in the last few years, of teaching and training, of the governments and cultures he had studied and learned from, of the whispered moments of enlightenment had been fed within even as he created another layer in his Core.

When he finished the consolidation process, the new Core layer was hard and clarified, stronger than anything he had ever felt. His dantian was not filled to the same extent, the lack of a cultivation tower robbing him of easy access to abundant chi, yet he was much better off than he could have hoped.

Still, Wu Ying would have stayed within for at least a few more days, to enjoy the respite from conversation, to study and practice and wash himself. He would have, if he'd had a say in it.

If not for the wind and the warning it brought.

Emerging from his tent as the day neared noon, he cast his gaze over those present in the village. At the same time, he expanded his spiritual senses aggressively, sweeping through the camp without any subtlety. The new Core layer within his body offered even greater fidelity to his senses, where everything within a hundred feet of him was noticed to the finest detail with his senses unfurled to this extent. It was not, of course, sustainable—no mortal mind could handle all this input without end. Still, it was a marked degree of strength.

More than that, after multiple progressions, his Core was now the same size as those who had just started the journey, perhaps a little larger. Even though that was the case, Wu Ying understood that he had, in the process of compressing the wind chi and layering it, gained greater stores and a greater degree of refined strength than another with the same Core size.

And that did not even include his skill with his jian.

"Cultivator Long! Congratulations on your successful cultivation. However, we ask that you work on your control of your new strength a little more." The guard who hurried over to Wu Ying from a nearby tent was clad in the hide armor of the tribes. At a glance, Wu Ying could tell he was in the upper edges of Energy Storage and had the Sense of the Sword.

"There are two score fully armed and armored individuals riding on horses coming from the southeast. They smell of blood and death and are using talismans to suppress their auras. Three Core Formation cultivators are in the retinue and they too are working to suppress the presence of the others," Wu Ying said curtly. His mind was flowing fast, picking out words from those half-heard, replacing them when he could not remember the right ones. Intent was enough, at least. "I doubt they are coming for a drink, with all that preparation."

The guard paled and stood stunned for a second before he spoke. "Ho-how do you know all this?"

"They smell. Very badly," Wu Ying said, grinning viciously. "They have not washed for at least a month."

"Borjigin…" A grimace crossed the guard's face.

He hesitated, though Wu Ying's domineering presence over the tribe was raising alarm all across the tribe. Women were calling children close, those with weapons close on hand went to check on their draw or gripped it tightly, cooks looked up from their stove pots, setting some to simmer. Farther afield, tribesmen were turning toward the village, a few moving to corral their herds and bring them closer.

Yet for all his new strength, he could not alert those in the farthest reaches. Not with any clarity. The herds sprawled across multiple li, some driven hours away. Those, Wu Ying hoped, would just be out of the way.

"Go! Alert them," Wu Ying snapped, seeing the guard still frozen.

A jerky nod, the steel in Wu Ying's command and the trace of killing intent leaking through sending the guard sprinting away. Set throughout the camp were simple metal shields, propped up or kept near the front of gers for sunning. Grabbing one of those—perhaps even his own—the guard slammed his drawn sword into it.

Nearby tribesmen stared at the guard, their jaws dropping. They might not have overheard the stilted conversation, might not have understood it, but the ringing was warning enough.

Rather than wait, Wu Ying took to the skies, calling forth the wind. He floated upward, ascending above the ger tops, rotating in mid-air as fingers of wind plucked at sleeves and hems, tickling his face as it whispered of a darker, bloodier future.

Idly, he noted how simple it was to float through the air now. The trickle of power required from his Core was negligible for his current reserves, the wind feeling firmer under his feet even as his body was lighter like the wind. The only issue with his current technique was that he was no imposing, unmoving figure on a sword but a drifting leaf.

From on top of a turtle, two figures emerged from a massive ger. They approached Wu Ying, leaping through the air; one riding a floating shield, another being carried by a ghostly horse.

"Cultivator Long, what are you doing?" Elder Daginaa, the first of the Core Formation elders in the tribe, said as he rode up on his metal shield. Light glinted off his armor as metal filings in the air were pulled toward him in a constant stream, plating his body and clothing in a gleaming layer.

"In the distance, two score riders and three Core Formation cultivators approaching with the smell of blood and death on their breaths." Wu Ying gestured in the correct direction.

Frowning, Elder Daginaa waited for a moment for Elder Ogdai to arrive on his spirit steed before Daginaa turned his attention away. At the same time, Ogdai took over careful watch over Wu Ying, though he stayed a distance away. No need to close the distance when one's favored weapon was a bow. The fact that the bow seemed to shimmer with the suppressed energy of a Saint-class weapon and had an arrow imbued with that same energy laid against it did not escape Wu Ying. Just as much, the steed Ogdai sat upon was stronger, denser than any spirit Wu Ying had ever sensed. In the meantime, Ogdai himself felt weaker, as though the Core within himself had diffused.

"Ancient ancestors and embattled spirits," Daginaa said when his focus came back to the present. "How did they know?"

"Luck? They always try at least once," Ogdai replied.

"With one Core Formation elder though. Never three." Eyes narrowed, Daginaa looked at Wu Ying before he shook his head. "They must have cast the bones or asked the spirits."

"Bad timing. She is at a sensitive point," Ogdai replied. "If she is interrupted…"

"Yes."

The pair shared a long look before they turned toward Wu Ying directly.

"I hope that we can speak with them first," Wu Ying said. "I will not attack them for no reason. Nor will I take part in an ambush."

The pair frowned, but it was Daginaa who spoke up, his voice troubled. "You tie our hands. For we know the Borjigin and their enmity with us is long."

"Nonetheless. I will not attack them first." Wu Ying gestured at the tribe below. "The most I can offer in that regard is to protect the non-combatants." His lips quirked up a little as he sensed Narangerel stride out of a tent, bow in hand, arrows on her hip to join a group of other women and elderly similarly armed. "Or at least, the ones here."

The pair of Elders exchanged another unreadable glance before they nodded in unison.

Ogdai turned back to Wu Ying, gesturing in the air around. "Stay here then. Do you mind a little deception?" When Wu Ying shook his head, he grinned. "Good. Then do not fear them."

"What them?" Wu Ying said, but it was to empty air.

Ogdai had already turned away, his spirit horse crossing the distance with long steps, even as a song rose from the Elder's lips. It was deep and low, a throat-sung song that sent shivers down Wu Ying's bones and which conjured spirits into being, or perhaps drew them in. In moments, he found himself surrounded by ethereal figures that were barely there to his senses, yet undoubtedly real.

"Oh. That them." Wu Ying exhaled a long, slow breath, doing his best to calm his pounding heart. The magic he was seeing, the spirits and the daos and the cultivation methods, it was different from what he was used to.

Ogdai rose into the sky while Daginaa rode his shield lower, waving as he gathered tribesmen to him. He placed himself and his recruits directly in the way of any assault, the gathered tribesmen and their horses pawing impatiently at the ground.

In the distance, the assaulting Borjigin continued their approach, not having sped up. One disadvantage of containing one's spiritual aura was that unless you had a dao or an element like Wu Ying's that contributed to the sensing otherwise, you were highly constrained. Not that they wouldn't notice the reception awaiting them, but it would take a few more li at least. Enough time perhaps for them to turn aside. Yet Wu Ying doubted such a reasonable course of action was about to occur.

For now, he could only wait as those below him readied themselves for war, locating bows and arrows, pulling children and elderly to the tops of the stone turtles, and otherwise arming themselves. Some teens, too young to take part in the fight, readied for the battle in other ways. Pails of water and sand were placed near the sides of ger. Other pots were set to boil, while campfires along the ground were banked.

Preparations for death and battle and healing, perhaps.

Wu Ying watched it all and could not help but look at the spirits that rose. Some, a rare few, were humanoid in shape. Many came from shrines, ancestral spirits that might have been but the personification of the duty and allegiance or perhaps the very souls of their ancestors themselves. Most though were spirits of hearth and home, of land and sky, of ghostly herds like those clustered around him or the thunderous goats below.

"Are you truly nothing but spirit beasts lacking form and substance? Developing in a different route? Or are you something different, inherent to this land and people because of their beliefs?" Wu Ying asked the spirits. He did not expect an answer and did not get one.

Yet he could not help but wonder.

In the distance, the Borjigin finally slowed. The three Core Formation elders briefly had a discussion, their conversation too fast, too fluid for Wu Ying to understand, not with the distance and his lack of fluency.

Not that it was necessary. Their decision was clear enough, as they relaxed their auras a little and guided their steeds forward. They moved faster, no longer attempting to hide from discovery and choosing speed over stealth.

High above, Ogdai watched over the proceedings, his horse and presence hidden in a cloak of chi and a warping of the air around him by additional spirits. So many spirits were clustered around him, but translucent. They hid the Core Formation elder, even as Daginaa approached the others below.

Silently, Wu Ying watched, his aura retracted now. He no longer felt the need to alert the tribe and so he kept his aura contained to the level of a weak Core, perhaps a half-step Core Formation cultivator. That should be enough to deceive and announce at the same time.

A presence, a pressure, spiritual senses playing across the surroundings. Wu Ying's lips turned upward as it attempted to probe his aura at a distance. He formed his sword intent and lashed out, careful not to apply too much energy. Even so, the attack cut at the extended spirit sense and forced it back, which made the wanderer smile grimly.

Probe him without consent, would they? Perhaps they would learn to keep their slimy hands away. And slimy it was, for the presence had an oiliness he did not like. A burnt tang that reminded him of an all-too-distasteful run-in with the dark sect cultivators.

At least it was not the infernal. Those were worse.

"I do not understand the point of all this," Wu Ying murmured to the spirits. "Why attack their own people?" Then he shook his head. "No, that's wrong. They're not the same people, even if we think them that. They are the Borjigin and this is the…" Wu Ying frowned, realizing he was not sure.

Why would the tribe have a name for themselves, call themselves anything? And if they had offered their name upon meeting him, he had not understood it.

"So, different tribes, raiding and fighting one another. For herds? For women and riches?" Wu Ying shook his head. "No, even if I put it that way, I still don't understand it. This land might not be abundant, but it certainly isn't so scarce that blood and death is the only way forward."

Silence greeted him once more. More importantly, the first clash was about to occur.

To Wu Ying's chagrin, his initial assumption that they would rush one another like cultivators in the south, where melee weapons were more common, was disrupted almost immediately. Rather than a direct approach, arrows were loosed at one another from a distance. The groups peeled apart, splitting at right angles to their initial approach so that they could continue the attack.

All, that is, but the quartet of Core Formation cultivators. Wu Ying frowned, though there was little he could do about the result even if he wanted to. Daginaa facing against three Core Formation elders, each of whom easily swatted aside, using aura or weapon, even cultivator-empowered, enchanted arrows.

"They're splitting up. I wonder why?" Wu Ying muttered, surprised to see that the trio weren't about to group up and attack Daginaa himself.

At least, not directly, for there was significant space now between the trio, with the split ends of each of the tribe's teams curving away and toward each other. It was like the ends of a bow, fully strung with each grouping as one end of the curved bow.

Then, no more time to think about such things as the clash happened between the three. Daginaa, flying forward on his shield, had conjured a dao in one hand, the huge, curved sabre wielded in a spinning, twisting projection as he rode his shield and sent a stream of glittering chi at his opponents. It was so broad that if the trio had not split apart, all three would have been struck.

As it was, the elder in the middle rode right through the attack, her body and her steed fading into insubstantial mist for a moment, the attack passing through without damage.

Curses rang out from Daginaa at that action. "Mahah, you damnable sneak…" Then a string of words Wu Ying had yet to learn. However, from the invective and tone, Wu Ying was certain he understood its intent. "Fight me properly!"

"Only a fool fights like their opponent wishes them to!" Mahah's voice was high and clear, filled with amusement.

A flicker of movement as the other two attackers took the opportunity to lash out at the distracted Daginaa. An arrow blurred through the air, narrowly dodged by the elder to impact the ground. It exploded when it struck the earth, a deep furrow carved into the land as the expanded energy contained within the projectile unleashed itself.

The other attack though did not miss, the whip wrapping around Daginaa's arm. It yanked backward, the elder pulled toward his opponent as the barbed whip tore into his metallic body. Yet even as Daginaa was pulled away, his silvery shield stuck to his feet and kept him aloft.

Caught and off-balance, he was pulled along as the other two elders readied their attacks. Only for Ogdai to finally make his move. An arrow from high above came arcing down, hidden in the clouds and dropping almost directly horizontally.

Then the arrow blossomed, one becoming a dozen, becoming hundreds. A rain of arrows that would have made an army proud slammed into the earth, targeting Mahah and the other archer. Mahah shifted insubstantial, but unlike before, she let out a hiss of pain, the arrows taking a trail of wispy mist out of her body as they exited.

"Interesting," Wu Ying muttered, the wind continuing to whisper its impressions to him. Her mist defense, while powerful, was obviously not all-encompassing. A part of him wondered why Ogdai had managed to hurt her and not Daginaa.

On the other end, the Borjigin archer had ripped a pair of arrows from his shoulder and leg that had managed to pierce his hide. His horse had fallen to the attacks, peppered with a couple of arrows including one lucky blow that had entered the top of its head.

Jumping off the dying horse, the archer rapidly drew and fired into the sky. He ran along the ground, arrows forming in the air as he touched the bow body and down to the string as he drew. Chi-formed arrows arced through the sky even as Ogdai returned the favor. Less numerous in number, only a score hitting the ground near the running attacker.

"I wonder why they do not attack the other riders?" Wu Ying frowned. That shower of arrows could have wiped out one entire wing of the Borjigin. Then after a moment, he answered the question for himself. "Because then the other Core Formation cultivators would attack their own people, and it would be a slaughter."

This, this entire fight was unlike the wars of his home. There was a ritual here, unspoken rules. Unlike the battles of his kingdom, where tens of thousands struggled against another equally vast army of faceless mortals. Where Core Formation cultivators were rare and sect members tore into the ranks of the opposition when left unopposed, coating the ground with blood and guts as battlefields rang with the screams of the dying.

Here the battle was less focused on ensuring a complete and final victory for one side. Neither side was attempting to crush all opposition, for that just begged retaliatory attacks of similar form. Even now, in the distance, Wu Ying noted how the weaker members, bereft of their horses from the missile exchange or injured, had turned aside from the clash and were left unmolested.

"Battle as a ritual?" Wu Ying shook his head, lips turned up in slight disgust. He could not help it, for he sensed the few unmoving bodies on the turf.

It was their way perhaps, but he could not agree with it. Even if, perhaps, it was the way they progressed. After all, he too had benefitted from battle, from the pressure of life and death.

Then his attention was drawn back to the fight among his peers. It seemed to be reaching the next step as Daginaa, having managed to regain his footing, had torn himself free. Now, the pair of Core cultivators dashed at one another, one on a horse, the other on his flying shield. The whip sparked and hummed as it struck at Daginaa, blocked by raised arm and cutting saber, while curved energy from blade strikes erupted in waves of formless energy.

On the other end, the archers fired at one another, explosive arrows disappearing into the high horizon. So far away was Ogdai that Wu Ying found it hard to keep track of him with his senses, leaving only the wind to whisper of his location. Accompanying the dropping arrows from above were spirits, each of them seeming to have melded with the arrows as they helped guide the falling projectiles to their target. On the other hand, injured or not, it seemed the other archer healed at a terrifying rate, arrows popping free from body as he attacked.

It seemed, at least for now, those two were balanced.

Leaving the third and final attacker to ride unmolested upon her misty horse toward the village.

Chapter 25

Wu Ying drifted down, letting the wind carry him to the edge of the encampment and a little farther. As he moved, the spirits of the horses that had obscured his image rode upward, rejoining Ogdai high above.

To his surprise, as he passed the outer boundaries of the village campgrounds, he felt a prickling of his aura. Then a stronger defense appeared behind him as ghostly stone turtles moved toward embedded flags, empowering the last failsafe defense of the tribe.

"That won't hold…" Wu Ying muttered to himself. Even empowered by the living stone turtles behind it, the spiritual barrier would fail. Even so, it was impressive looking, the pale blue dome formed in the image of the creatures' shells.

The cantering of the approaching horse drew his attention back, Wu Ying's lips peeling upward in a slight, agreeable smile. He kept his hands away from his sword as he floated on the wind and Mahah arrived.

"Who are you, southerner? Why do you stand with the filthy Sakhait? Have they allied with our enemies and betrayed the great steppes?" Mahah snarled, pulling her horse to a stop.

"Nothing of the sort. I'm an involuntary guest for the moment," Wu Ying said, the smile still on his lips even after the insults. "I am Long Wu Ying, a mere wandering gatherer."

"Then stand aside, Cultivator Long. You owe these people nothing," Mahah said. "I will not take much, just a few women and some gold. Maybe a few lives, if they dare shoot at me." The look she gave the crowd of elders and women who had gathered at the edges of the shielding was highly dismissive.

"Don't believe her! She's here to take revenge for the death of her son," Narangerel shouted, her voice trembling with fear. "She won't just take a few. She wants blood. That's all the Borjigin ever want." Then, a beat before she added, "Don't think that Khan Erdene will not act if you go too far!"

"Let her! She will face the wrath of our Khan and understand her storm is nothing to his own," Mahah snapped. Her eyes burning, the initial politeness having faded away, she kicked her horse to drive it closer to Wu Ying. "Now, stand aside, southerner!"

"It's Cultivator Long," Wu Ying murmured in gentle rebuke. "And I fear I cannot. I gave my word that I would safeguard those behind me." He tilted his head. "Whatever grudges you might have, let it be for this day. There is no need for more blood to be spilled."

Rather than bandy further words with Wu Ying, she kicked the sides of her horse. The creature started trotting even as Mahah raised her bow, her lips moving as she chanted a spell.

Instinct twinged, and as the arrow was loosed, Wu Ying called forth the winds. They pushed the arrow aside, the missile flying with such speed it passed within a cun of Wu Ying's swaying form before it struck the dome, releasing a ball of cloying mist that hissed.

"Dangerous…" Wu Ying muttered as he kept the wind blowing in random patterns before him. He too drifted from side to side as more arrows crossed the distance and cloying mist rose from the ground, masking distance, vision, and sound.

Wu Ying drew his weapon, holding it down by his side as he waited. Muffled hoofbeats as Mahah rode not in a straight line but pivoted around him, taking the opportunity to pepper him with arrows. None reached him, his wind diverting their path.

Eventually, growing frustrated by the ineffectiveness of her tactics, the arrows stopped flying. As equals of the Core Formation tier, the likelihood of significant and lasting damage from random attacks was low. To finish this, she would need to empower her attacks further.

Sometimes, it seemed that no matter how high the mountain one climbed, another mountain just as steep rose up ahead on the road to immortality. Hundreds of Body Cleansing cultivators might be nothing, yet still, the same amount of effort, of danger repeated, when one was forced to fight another Core Formation cultivator.

It might make a man despair. Probably had, if Wu Ying was truthful to himself. That no matter how far one traveled, the journey still stretched. Onward and onward, without end until one reached the heavens. And perhaps not even then?

The gods certainly were not saying.

Movement in the mist. Wu Ying let his body turn in that direction, twisting in the wind. Then he kept turning, whipping around entirely as Mahah attempted to sneak up on him, her curved saber crashing down on him as she rode close, her body reforming entirely.

Wu Ying's jian rose and thrust upward, taking the full force of the blow on the lower end of his guard. He could not stop-thrust at her face, the angle was all wrong even if he was floating off the ground to give him height. Instead, he absorbed the energy of her attack by allowing his body to float away, detaching his weapon from hers. In doing so, he spun and cut downward, unleashing a Dragon's Breath attack. In the attack, he imbued a little of his dao, a little of his killing intent.

It tore into her already dissipating body, seeming to clash with the remnants of the armor she wore before tearing through. Misty trails parted from her body and Mahah let out a startled gasp, even as she finished disappearing into the mist again.

Wu Ying's senses spread out further, spiritual senses offering him a hazy understanding of the world about. It was not that he could not sense her but that she was everywhere in the mist. Her chi, her aura permeated the mist entirely, hiding the concentration that was her being. Unless she was the mist itself…

No. That would be too much, too strong for someone at their level. Perhaps if she ascended to the Nascent Soul stage, where immortal soul and body began to merge with the dao of the soul itself, then perhaps. For now, these were but tricks, methods to deceive.

Another movement, another cutting attempt. She rode past him, slicing upward, and he tucked his body close, raising his feet to his chest as he floated higher. The attack ripped at him, the humming weapon in her hand missing by inches.

Then as she slowed, he felt it. A tugging at his body as the mist gripped his form and yanked him down. Mist and wind fought, but so caught out was he that he was pulled downward before he stabilized. His attention on the ghostly hands gripping him, Wu Ying never realized she still had one more trick to play.

Rearing up on its front legs, the horse kicked backward. Surprise, then impact. Crushing impact, striking Wu Ying in the chest, in the shoulder as shod hooves landed and tore him free from ghostly hands.

Coughing hard, Wu Ying rolled and rolled before coming to his feet. The horse neighed, and a derisive laugh rose from all around him in the mist.

"Teaches me for taking her lightly," Wu Ying cursed, his chest throbbing, ribs protesting from the assault. Right shoulder injured, the movement in his arm sluggish as it lay stunned. He switched grips, transferring the sword to his left hand. He was no ambidextrous hero of lore, able to fight with left nearly as well as right, but years of practice to ensure he was balanced out meant he could do well enough. "Enough with this mist."

Echoing words with intent, he pushed outward with his aura even as the wind rose, from breeze to gale. Unnatural spiritual pressure keeping the mist together was torn apart as Wu Ying imbued the full killing intent of his weapon into his aura. Blade intent tore at his opponent's aura and she fell backward, spirit bleeding. The edges of her mist were plucked apart by the wind, torn from her control as Mahah was forced to contain and strengthen the aura around herself or be cut apart.

"You wish to fight? Then let us do so." Wu Ying raised the blade to his forehead, offering her a curt salute. Dust and leaves, grass clippings, and even the manure from nearby fields clogged the air. As he brought his hand down, the wind died with it.

"A wind dao. You might think yourself unique, but we know the wind here," Mahah taunted. "It comes, it goes, but it has no edge."

Wu Ying smirked and stalked forward. He rose a little with each step, the air beneath his feet firming. When his head was at the same height as Mahah, who was busy conjuring a series of small misty orbs, he stopped rising.

A half dozen steps away, Wu Ying unleashed his killing intent. They might play at war, doing battle and raiding one another, but he had fought the dark sect—and in a real war. He had seen thousands fall, listened to the screams and cries of the injured, watched as life slowly bled away or was robbed in delirious fevers. A blood wind rose, pushing Wu Ying forward with each step, and Mahah's mare, trained and raised alongside her as it might have been, reacted. Just like any other beast, it backed away in instinctive fear.

Her preparations foiled, Mahah had no time to release the orbs that floated alongside her. Wu Ying's blade sought her life and only a desperate parry pushed the tip away from her heart. Instead, the jian sunk into a meaty then misty shoulder, ripping outward in a spray of white smoke as Wu Ying flowed forward.

Normally, he would push her back, staying close and laying into her with a series of pommel strikes and elbows, but he was wary of the horse and its hooves. Instead he swung his jian, staying to her off-hand side as he cut at her leg and then, slipping around the defending dao she had drawn, thrust upward at her torso.

Again, his blade sank into misty form. Before he could extract it, an orb came flashing toward Wu Ying. He ducked its attempt at striking his face directly, but the ball of mist exploded near him nonetheless. That explosion was sufficient to throw him, wind and his reactive retreat carrying him steps away. Even so, the expansion of air and… acid?… clung to his body as he fled.

Hissing, he called the wind to himself, the breeze tugging at the stubbornly clinging liquid before it dispersed, leaving his clothing holey and the side of his face red and pock-marked.

More misty orbs flew toward Wu Ying and he dodged the attacks, eyes narrowing as he threw a series of energetic blade strikes. Each strike that struck the orbs of mist caused them to erupt, spilling their contents across a dozen feet before his wind dispersed it. Grass, blackened and bubbling from the acid, died beneath each attack, even as the acid was dispersed into the sky.

A dozen orbs, then her attack stopped, leaving Wu Ying to stare at the woman. Her shoulder and torso wound smoked, little trails of mist floating from the wounds. The angry enemy cultivator breathed hard from the exertion of her attack, but in corners of her shifting shape, where the mist leaked, more orbs formed.

"You cannot win," Wu Ying said calmly. "Your surprise was learnt of early. The shielding will hold, even if you try to flee within to wreak havoc. Your friends do battle, but it seems that battle, like this one, will take a while. And as for the men you brought along…" The wind whispered and he shrugged. "Well, that seems to be going even less well."

Mahah snarled, the arm around her stomach moving away. A little more mist leaked before it trailed to a stop as she raised her dao. "I am no coward, southerner. This fight is not finished. Not yet. I will have vengeance for my xyy[37]."

Wu Ying sighed in disappointment. Kicking her beast into a gallop, Mahah let out a shrill, pain-filled battle cry.

***

Another dozen passes, and no true winner revealed. After grasping that this entire encounter was ritualized, after noting how much the others held back, Wu Ying did as well. On top of that, of course, was the concern of killing someone and the resulting vendetta that might grow from it. After all, he had no clan to offer surety and cry vengeance for his loss.

---

[37] Xyy—son in Mongol.

In the end, streaming tiny wisps of mist, Mahah was forced to retreat when Ogdai returned, preceding his newfound attention on their fight with a single dark arrow that plunged into the earth beside the woman. It hummed as it lay on the ground, swirling spirits arising from it and spooking Mahah's horse. Rather than fight it, she left with curses trailing after her fleeing figure.

In a short while, Daginaa returned too, a grim smile on his face while the silvery metal around his body flaked away in the wind. Beneath, deep bruises ran down his arms and along his neck. When he spoke, his voice was damaged and raspy. "Taught them a lesson, we did."

"And yet none of the elders were killed. Or badly injured," Wu Ying said. "Ogdai stopped when his opponent ran out of energy to conjure his arrows anymore."

"Are you upset at the lack of death, Cultivator Long?" Daginaa said, a trace of a sneer appearing in his voice.

"No, I would prefer none die." Wu Ying's lips curled up a little in wry distaste as he added, "But that wasn't to be, now was it?"

In the distance, he could still sense them. Tribesmen ferrying the limp corpses of their friends, aiding the injured back to the village. Two dead, another three injured badly enough that they would likely be useless for anything but light work for a month at least.

"Ah, of course. The southerner disapproves of our methods," Daginaa said. "You think we're barbarians, for our raids. You disdain our blood feuds. You think we should just act like your people, sending envoys and pieces of paper with lies written bold. Promises of peace that will be broken when it's convenient."

"Unfair. I said nothing of the sort. But I cannot say I enjoy violence for the sake of violence," Wu Ying said.

"You think this is what it is?" Another voice this time, from behind Wu Ying. To his surprise, it was the third elder, Ganbold, the final member of their tribal council. The one who was but a middling Energy Storage cultivator.

"If not, please enlighten me," Wu Ying replied.

"It is violence to train our men. Theirs. It is to keep the blade sharp, to hone our warriors and allow them to grow."

Wu Ying nodded, having realized that bit. But... "Why? There are other ways. Tournaments and competitions. Sparring and martial exchanges."

"Other ways, certainly. Yet the edge would not be as fine." The old man sighed, his head turning toward where the tribesmen were still on their way back. "Yet you are right. It is wasteful. It is inefficient. And if we had the time, the place, and the peace to grow, perhaps we would take up some of your softer methods. We used to once.

"Then your armies came north. Your envoys provided herbs and weapons to one clan, then another. Goading them with dreams of conquest and dominion over one another. And when both sides had been sufficiently weakened, you came. With your armies and your sects to take our land."

"Not my kingdom," Wu Ying said defensively.

"All you southerners are the same to us," Daginaa said savagely. "Just as we are to you."

"Daginaa!" Ogdai snapped, guiding his spirit horse to put himself in front of the other man. He glared at his friend, his voice dropping lower. "Stow your bow. You lash out at the wrong person."

Daginaa's lips curled, then he turned his head, spitting at the ground pointedly before stalking away. Wu Ying frowned, watching the elder leave.

"Daginaa might have said it impoliticly, but in the end, he is not wrong. Many see you as just another of those who have attacked us, pitted us against each other. And if we have to train our sons and daughters in a way that sees some perish, it is necessary too. For we never know when another army might come and all of us will be required to see them off." Ganbold's voice held a deep weariness. Hidden beneath the exhaustion though was a trace of longing, as though he wished for a world that was not as callous.

"I… see." Wu Ying closed his eyes for a moment. He did not know what else he could say, about the reality they had lived, how their culture, their worlds had changed because of the southern kingdoms' strategies. Then again… "And the raids conducted on the south? The peasants killed, the herds and goods stolen? Is that just retaliation? Or part of all this…?"

To his surprise, Ganbold grinned. "Well, that might have been done in good fun. Taking a few books, a few women, a few head of cattle from rich southerners who can afford it, it's not that much of a thing, is it?"

"Not to you perhaps, but for the peasants so affected? I think they might argue."

Ganbold nodded. "Perhaps there is pain enough to go around."

Silence fell over the trio before Ogdai, seeming uncomfortable with it suddenly, spoke up, almost making Wu Ying jump.

"Congratulations, Cultivator Long! On your closed-door success. We must celebrate it tonight." Eyes crinkling a little, Ogdai added as he watched Wu Ying look uncomfortable at the praise, "It'll be good to have something to celebrate other than the battle."

And with that kind of lead-in, how could Wu Ying reject the suggestion?

Chapter 26

Weeks flew by, the planted herbs and crops grown to their full extent before being harvested. Vegetables and root products were taken from the land, the remnants chopped and tilled back into the earth. Fields all around the village had been cropped down to the barest nubs by the grazing herds, such that the herdsmen were forced to take their flock farther and farther afield each day.

Each day, the tension grew. More than once, Wu Ying noted tribesmen glancing toward where the largest stone turtle napped, up to the ger that few could see. Even those without a sensitivity to environmental chi could see the effects of their Khan's cultivation, as swirling clouds lay over the turtles constantly. Occasionally, sudden showers came, but mostly, the clouds hovered, ominous and dark.

Overheard whispered conversations spoke of increasingly concerned citizens. Staying in these lands, overburdening them to the extent they were, could cause issues in future years. Patches of bare grass, a pond that had drained farther than most in living memory.

Few spoke to him about it, not even Oktai. Every time Wu Ying brought it up, the translator would divert his attention, bring up another conversation. Yet there was no hiding the increasing anxiety, the worry and concern, the frayed tempers in all the tribe members.

And then, one day, late in the afternoon as Wu Ying exited the greenhouse after improving the rotation and the insulation while studying the enchantments used for such things, the clouds parted. A soundless thunder, pressure without motion, a stern, overbearing presence that watched over them all. Lightning and ozone on the lips, pain in the ears and sinuses.

Then, nothing.

Silence.

Wu Ying turned toward the giant stone turtle, frowning as he watched the clouds that had been present there since their arrival disperse. The flow of chi to the top of the turtle shell had stopped, the constant tug of environmental chi ending.

"So, it's done." Wu Ying extended his senses a little, feeling the energy pour out of him and reaching toward the top of the turtle. It never even reached the turtle as it bounced off a domain of dao enlightenment. It was a sphere of absolute control, a world where her dao, her beliefs held utter sway and Wu Ying's paltry understanding was useless.

Retracting his spiritual aura, Wu Ying tilted his head as a voice roared outward. The spiritual voice was both too loud and yet right inside his mind, bypassing the need for such pitiful things like voices and ears.

"I am awoken, children. My apologies for taking so long. Pack up immediately. We leave as soon as possible." A slight hesitation, then the voice continued. "Elders. Cultivator Long, I shall require your presence."

Wu Ying frowned. He stepped forward, letting himself grow lighter as he poured chi through his meridians and activated his Twelve Gales movement technique. One moment, he was half a li away, the next he had crossed half the distance. And then another step and he was there, outside the tent opening.

A breath, then again, and another, and Ogdai rode up on his spiritual steed, landing beside Wu Ying. He frowned at Wu Ying.

"I was just over there…" Wu Ying said, waving toward the previous stone turtle. "Elder Daginaa?"

"He and Ganbold are within," Daginaa said, gesturing at the ger. "Ganbold does not like moving that much, not anymore. And we wanted at least one of us keeping an eye on her at all times."

Wu Ying nodded. In normal circumstances, most would want some form of protection and safety against being interrupted. Depending on the interruption and stage, effects could range from lost time and effort to a missed opportunity at enlightenment to massive backlash. If he was interrupted while layering his Core, it could, at worst, end with previous layers damaged.

Gesturing for the man to precede him, Wu Ying entered soon after. Within, he was amused to find the tent empty but for the two other elders and Daginaa, the Khan not present.

"She's changing," Elder Ganbold said at Wu Ying's curious look. "Come. Sit, drink."

Wu Ying hesitated but walked over and joined their little circle. He took the offered cup of airag and sipped on the drink lightly. After weeks of staying with them, he had acquired a degree of enjoyment for the drink, even if he still preferred less sour and stronger wines. Peach wine in particular was a personal favorite, though he had few enough opportunities to drink it.

"So, the Gansukh herd, did we manage the foot rot problem?" Ganbold asked Ogdai when the man sat down.

"When the Khan called, it was decided to slaughter the affected animals. We'll feast on them on the road tonight," Ogdai replied.

"Right, because we can't…" Ganbold trailed off. "Cultivator Long, about the bee hives. You said you believe you could seed a new field with wildflowers?"

"That was planned for tomorrow."

"Ahhhh."

None of them would be here tomorrow.

Silence fell over the group before Daginaa grunted. "Well, Sarnia promised us a new dance next week. I am looking forward to it. Cultivator Long, you've only seen her perform once, no?"

"Yes. It was very impressive," Wu Ying said. He had been so admiring of her skill that Narangerel had chosen not to visit his tent for an entire week.

"She won't do it though," Ogdai said.

"What?" Daginaa replied.

"You know she refuses to showcase anything without sufficient time to practice," Ogdai said. "With all this travel…"

Daginaa groaned.

"Is it not just a small delay?" Wu Ying said.

That brought laughter from the trio. Eventually, it was Ogdai who explained. "Sarnia is an artist. When inspiration strikes, she will bring a new dance. If the dance, when it is done, does not meet her standards, she will never show it again. And if she is interrupted and loses her inspiration…"

"Gone. Bah!" Daginaa said.

That brought another long moment of silence. Conversation after that grew even more stilted before movement in the shadows at the end of the ger caught their attention. Wu Ying frowned a little for he had little warning, his spiritual sense greatly suppressed within the ger. Even the winds were mostly still and very silent, refusing to speak to him.

"Thank you for your patience," Khan Erdene said as she sauntered over to her seat.

Wu Ying regarded the woman, curious to see what he could ascertain of her ascension. She was the first Nascent Soul cultivator he had knowingly, and regularly, interacted with.

Beyond the strength of her dao, which easily suppressed his minor dao of the wind, she also held a core of strength. Unlike Core Formation cultivators whose core of power in their dantian was a solid ball of energy—or the more diffuse forms of lesser cultivators—the Nascent Soul cultivator before him was a solid barrier of energy.

At first, Wu Ying had thought it was but a natural form of suppression. A method of hiding her actual strength. Yet now, with her ascension and a previous iteration to compare, Wu Ying was concluding that the solid intensity of chi that coursed through her body was a part of the Nascent Soul stage.

It made sense, if he considered it. After all, the Nascent Soul stage was the breaking out from the core formed in the dantian, the emergence of the immortal soul from within. The Nascent Soul then embedded itself in the mortal body housing it, slowly burning it away at each stage until it was time to ascend. The solidification of the cultivator's dao and embodiment of it was the necessary step.

So of course the body would be more powerful. Of course there would be less of a focus on meridians, the dantian, and the core. The soul now was the source of power, not some pot of energy held within the cultivator's body.

"Cultivator Long," Khan Erdene's voice interrupted his thoughts. Wu Ying bowed to her, covering his surprise with courtesy as he sought to recall the last few moments. Nothing of import had been said, just greetings. He did not, however, breathe out in gratitude at that. "Your aid in dealing with the Borjigin was an unexpected and welcome kindness."

"It was a small matter," Wu Ying said.

"Not for us. Fighting for a tribe not your own is not something that is expected. Especially from a soft southerner," Erdene said.

Wu Ying inclined his head in acknowledgement, ignoring the idle insult.

"We will speak more about this. And your presence in our camp," she said.

Again, he nodded.

Then she turned to her elders, speaking to them about what had transpired while she cultivated. A part of Wu Ying wondered how she knew all that had happened. Still, even that thought was soon drowned out by the continuing consideration of his earlier musings. After all, nothing that was being said was new to him, nor of great import to his being.

If a Nascent Soul cultivator was an immortal soul—or soon-to-be immortal soul—wrapped in a mortal body, Body Cultivation took the opposite tack. From the transformation of the mortal body to the secondary element, Body Cultivation was the eventual conversion of a mortal body into an immortal elemental concept. In his case, a body of wind. At this time, he would have judged himself in the major level of perfection of the five mortal winds. And, perhaps, beginning or maybe even a minor level of understanding for the heavenly wind.

Not for the first time, Wu Ying tried to conceptualize what a true wind body was like. Already he was faster, more flexible, lighter than any mortal cultivator. The simple Heavenly Soul, Earthly Body technique had never been meant to be used entirely by itself as a flying movement technique. In fact, few other cultivators could directly fly through the air—at least not at the Core Formation level.

Yet here he was. Gusting through the air, borrowing the wind to aid his movements, dancing through battle with nary a thought or movement technique to his name. And of course, such techniques—weapon, movement, battle—were all but expressions of motions that were inherent in humanity. They were just well-practiced, efficient utilization of body and chi.

With an infinite variety of elemental chi combinations and an unending, exhaustive amount of flows through a meridian, a wide series of techniques—many similar in process to one another—could be created. Add in individual idiosyncrasies and it was no surprise that there were so many techniques through the world.

Yet in the end, there was nothing stopping a well-practiced, well-read individual from creating their own techniques. Just as a swordsmaster might pick up a new weapon like the urumi and learn to wield it with minimal guidance, so could a cultivator who knew his own body and other techniques in general make up his own.

Which, after all, was what Wu Ying was doing. Inefficiently perhaps—but how many wind movement techniques were there?

Another thought, and one that struck Wu Ying and made him ache to return to his ger to check his manuals and notes. Was a bloodline important because it was but a head start on the process of Body Cultivation? Or was it perhaps only for certain bloodlines? Certainly it was something he recalled being asserted by a number of writers—and yet he'd also read works on gathering that were highly insistent that seawater was a powerful method of weed killing.

"Cultivator Long. Cultivator Long?" Another call, rousing Wu Ying from his thoughts. He blinked, staring as Daginaa, who could not help but grin. "Thinking of Narangerel, are we?"

"No!" Wu Ying said heatedly. "Now, what were you calling me for?"

"I was," Khan Erdene said, quelling his momentary impulsive temper. After all, having her angry at him was highly unhealthy. "You seem distracted."

"My apologies, Khan Erdene." Wu Ying bowed. "I had a thought. About my cultivation journey."

"Ah…" She raised one thin, liver-spotted hand and waved him away. Was it less liver-spotted? He could not help but consider and think perhaps it was. "Well then, let us not keep you. You may go."

"I…" Wu Ying hesitated.

"Go. If matters about the tribal management and where we go do not hold your interest, you need not stay." A slight smile. "Your presence was but a courtesy for your aid."

"Then I shall take my leave," Wu Ying said, standing and bowing to the group. "Thank you again for your consideration."

He barely heard their remarks before hurrying off. He definitely needed to write down these thoughts and look over his notes.

***

It was two days before he emerged from his tent. Well, he had—briefly—exited his housing to pack it away and set it up once more on the Khan's turtle at their behest before he returned to studying, pursuing that line of research as the turtle moved below him.

More than once, he cursed his lack of a proper library or his own incomplete notes. Yet for all that, years of travel had resulted in numerous purchases and visits to sect libraries, resulting in a small but decent collection of works. Everything from low-grade cultivation manuals to treatises on Body Cultivation were part of his library these days, and all of it was read over once again as he searched for those elusive single lines, throwaway thoughts by authors that might shed further light.

In the end, having exhausted what little studies he had on hand, Wu Ying was forced to accept that whatever further inquiries he might have would have to await the future. One where soaring libraries held remarks and manuals from cultivators who were willing to put their own thoughts to paper.

Unlike the tribesmen he lived among now.

Their own cultivation techniques were alien to him. Some, like the Khan's, seemed at first blush to follow similar lines. No spirits, just herbs and alchemical pills, dao enlightenment, and the concentration of energy within. Others though, like Ogdai's, revolved around the spirits that surrounded them all. Esoteric rituals, entreaties late into the night, worship and embodiment all earmarked that form of progression.

At times, Wu Ying believed their cultivation methods might be similar in structure, if not form. Yet other times, when Ogdai shed blood or lay upon the grass, rolling along the earth as he did so, Wu Ying was not so sure. What was the point of such activities? How did they help with the flow of chi through one's body? How did they even open meridians? At least the cultivation session he had watched where children had allowed spirits to roam through their bodies, guided by the barest touches to help cleanse and free clogged meridians made some sense.

Some.

In the end, Wu Ying could only emerge from his tent, knowing he had much more to learn. It was possible that nothing with regard to the spirits, to the way the Sakhait cultivated, would be of use to him. He could only speak with others and explore their differences in hope that some form of understanding might shed enlightenment on his own path.

It was after a meager lunch on the move that Wu Ying was called once more to Khan Erdene's tent. Entering it, he was surprised to note it was empty but for the Khan, the elders missing from their usual spots.

"Cultivator Long, sit." A gesture to a seat on the floor, where a cup of airag was already present along with some strips of wind-dried meat and nuts.

"Thank you, Khan Erdene," Wu Ying said.

"Your research, has it borne fruit as you wished?" Khan Erdene said after Wu Ying had his first polite sip of his drink.

"Not as much as I'd hoped," Wu Ying said. "I lack the proper materials for my current line of inquiry. I have more questions than answers, I fear."

"About our cultivation methods. And the Yellow Emperor's?" the Khan said. "Of spirits, the Nascent Soul, Body Cultivation, and your next steps?"

"Yes."

No need to ask how she knew. If he could sense across the camp with little effort, how much more could she, a full tier above him, do? Admittedly, much of his senses were passive, ignored—but if he were her, he would have looked into his own tent too.

"A difficult question. Many scholars have delved into such discussions. Some have even treated with us and the other tribes, searching for an answer and an easier path. Seeking to cheat the heavens as they sought a shortcut in the long road to immortality." She cocked her head. "Do you seek the same?"

Wu Ying shook his head. "Just answers and understanding."

A pause, then the Khan smiled. "That is a good answer. Let me answer then, some of your questions. Cultivation with spirits is different from the type of cultivation espoused by the Yellow Emperor. It is as different as Body Cultivation is from Soul Cultivation. Call it, if you will, Spirit Cultivation. It is closer, in effect, to what Spirit Beasts do in your southern lands."

Wu Ying blinked, his mind spinning at her casual revelation. Not a new line of thought obviously, but for her to agree and confirm it…

Before he could find words to ask the questions that were beginning to sprout within his mind, the Khan continued. "It is not, of course, the same. Our methods, the methods of the tribes in the north, are a mixture. A hodgepodge of cultivation methods in the beginning, learned by study and practice and guidance, unique for each individual." She picked up a cup and sipped on the milky white drink within before setting it down. "Our members are more unique, in that sense. Yet we must clear meridians too, work with the dantian for strength like a Soul Cultivator. At least, in the beginning."

"There is a change later? When?" Wu Ying asked.

"It varies for the individual. But often, the Core Formation stage is where we see a separation," Erdene said. "Those like Ogdai who feel the calling of the spirits grow their connection, sometimes to many, sometimes singularly. They embed their own understanding in the spirit, taking the spirit's beliefs as their own. When you sense the Core within him, what you sense instead is the spirit he has bound with and the connection between the two of them.

"Others, like myself, take a more familiar method. We form a Core, develop our soul, borrowing knowledge from the spirits that abound. Eventually, we might become a spirit ourselves or an immortal of the kind you expect."

"Ahhh… and Body Cultivation?" Wu Ying said tentatively.

"It is not something we study," the Khan said. "But as we understand it, you seek to become a spirit too, in your own way. It's just instead of learning from a spirit beforehand, you blithely transform yourself in hopes that you are doing so correctly. Following the instructions left behind by your predecessors. Many of whom have never succeeded."

Wu Ying winced at her scathing commentary. Most soul and body cultivation manuals weren't left behind by the actual immortals. More so with Body Cultivation, especially since it was rarer. Even in kingdoms where Body Cultivation was more important, successful cultivators were rare.

Was it because, as Erdene mentioned, of a missing link? Or was it just the vagaries of a near-impossible task?

"Are the Sakhait more successful then?" Wu Ying said quietly. "It seems not…" He inclined his head toward the side of the ger and the tribe outside. Of which only she was a Nascent Soul cultivator.

Erdene stared at him for a long moment in silence, long enough that Wu Ying wondered if he had insulted the Khan. Then she laughed, slapping her thigh. He could not help but shift in discomfort as the Khan roared with laughter, wiping at tears before she calmed.

"Ah, to be young again. Brave and foolhardy, without a care in the world of who you insult."

He winced at her words but did not apologize.

"Still, you are not wrong. The path of cultivation is difficult, and our methods are no more guaranteed to work than any others. If we were both scholars, perhaps we could argue further. But even for me, the final steps are long and arduous."

He let out a breath of relief, seeing that she was not angry. Or not too much. Still, her point about Body Cultivation, along with his own conclusion about how Soul and Body cultivation were, in the end, the same thing in different forms, had him wondering about the veracity of all these methods.

Perhaps, in truth, no one really knew. The Dao was infinite, and so the path to immortality was infinite too. Perhaps each method was but an approximation of the Dao, a way of achieving the same small portion of the greater whole. His search for the heavenly wind that had brought him, the progress he had made with the other five winds was as much a question of seeking an understanding of the element itself as it was the physical exercises and the supplements he drank.

"Perhaps, young fool, you might want to explore such relationships in more detail. Rather than eavesdropping on lessons, actually partake in them?" She raised a hand when Wu Ying began to protest. "Not as a practitioner, of course. That would but lead to a deviation. But as a scholarly student?"

Wu Ying considered the offer. He was not sure how much additional help it would be to sit in on a class for children. Then again, the wind had not blown and he had not felt the urge to move on.

"And my debt?" he asked.

"Already paid for with your prior actions," Khan Erdene said. "However, there is much that we want from you still. There is much, I think, you can still learn from us." A little smile crossed the woman's face. "Also, my niece is quite intent on acquiring a child from you."

"Your... niece?" Wu Ying choked. "A child?"

"Well, did you think your midnight assignations would not lead to such an outcome? You are young, but surely not that young or ignorant."

Wu Ying shook his head. "I... well. No, I'm not. But there are techniques that one may use. Breathing and muscle control techniques, that allow ummm..."

"Pleasure without ejaculation[38]?"

"Yes..." Wu Ying said, his voice almost a whisper.

He was not a very shy man, but something about talking about sexual relations with this brazen grandaunt made him feel like a teenager being sat down by the aunties. Something in the way she sat, her tone of voice, the look on her face, the pressure in the air...

Ah.

He strengthened his aura, forcing chi through his meridians. He gripped his Core, pulling at his dao understanding to strengthen his aura and banish the spiritual pressure. Almost

---

[38] Actual real world qigong technique. Supposed to increase pleasure and lengthen the process too.

immediately, he felt the tiny tendrils that had entered his mind shatter. He straightened, the rising blush fading.

"Hmmphhfff…" Erdene said. "Well. I guess I must be blunter."

"Blunter?" Wu Ying said, his voice cold and remote.

"Did you think your nightly sessions—"

"Not every night."

"—had no price? She seeks a child, and you are denying her that while using her body like a cheap southern whore."

"I had not… I had believed she wanted to spend time with me because of who I am. Not because of what she could gain."

"And Oktai had not alluded to the fact that our desire is for new blood? That we seek to strengthen the child with those not of our clan?" Erdene said. "Do not shame yourself by lying. And do not speak of a child as though it is a mercenary transaction. Children are a gift."

"One that I will not be around to watch grow up," Wu Ying said. "I have no intention of staying in your tribe. Or being trapped here."

"Trapped!" Erdene slapped the table. Wu Ying had to swallow thickly as pressure built up around his ears. "There is no desire to trap one such as you. Leave, if you will. The child— my grandnephew—will not lack for anything without you here. We do not abandon our own." She lowered her voice. "Or do you think we—I—would allow either to be looked down upon because my niece liked your eyes?"

Wu Ying was smart enough to shake his head.

"Then shed yourself of your weak excuses. Choose—honor her desires or stop your foolish actions. In either case, you are welcome to stay or go now." A slight push with the front of her hand, a motion that never even came close to touching him.

Yet the air pressure, the force of chi that struck him took Wu Ying by the chest and threw him out of the tent into the air. He tumbled for a good couple of li through the open air.

He could have aborted his flight a lot earlier, but perhaps some time away from clan and Khan was for the best. After all, her anger in the end had not been feigned. Unlike, perhaps, her earlier largesse. Also, if he was a few li away, it would take them a little longer to catch him if he chose to run.

Chapter 27

Running away was an option. Running away was easy. Running away might even be wise. The demands from the tribe if he stayed spiraled into a series of circumstances that might see him rooted there. A child, a wife, friends and family that had to be protected, a feud with other northerners. Studies about spirits, new spiritual herbs to catalogue and gather. A decent life, a quiet one—in relation to his previous hectic one.

A life dissimilar to the one he had aimed for so far.

So, run.

Leave before he was rooted, forced to stay. Leave before he truncated his cultivation path for another's needs. Leave, for the wind was not still. Even the central wind moved, circumscribed as it might be by mountains, by the other winds, by the rise and fall of the air itself.

Yet every decision made, every action chosen was a furrow ploughed into the field of his soul. From such channels did water flow and plants grow, forming the biome of his spirit. No action failed to leave a mark, and actions taken repeatedly would deepen the pathways of the soul, allowing more rooted vegetation to sprout. Sometimes in infertile and hard soil, sometimes in the moistest, richest earth.

To uproot such plants, to alter the course of one's focus, required significant work. No competent landowner began a field without considering such factors. No experienced farmer grew their crops without judging the quality of the soil and its effects.

Leaving now was the easiest choice. Running from confrontations and responsibilities. It could be the right thing to do, yet Wu Ying was wary. To carve that option into one's soul too often, to choose ease over discomfort and challenge. Soon enough, it was that route all future decisions would follow.

Avoidance was infertile soil to plant the crops of one's actions, prone to being overrun with weeds and bearing tart, measly harvests.

"And is running what I want to do?" Wu Ying murmured to himself and the wind, his head raised. He walked on the ground, feet brushing the earth as he traversed the land on an intercept course with the rest of the tribe. He had time—a lot of it—to make a decision one way or the other.

The wind had no answer for him. Had not spoken to him for days, not since Khan Erdene had woken. Was it afraid? Was it controlled? Was it screaming in the distance and Wu Ying could not hear it over the drumbeat of her dao?

Or was it silent, knowing the choices before him were of import? That such decisions would plough a new field in his path?

"There are more options than just leave or stay forever," Wu Ying said to the silent wind. "I could do as they say. Stop the breathing exercises, stop holding back. Allow fate to choose."

After all, neither party had formed a child before. All too often, Wu Ying had experienced a family's sorrow, farmlands going fallow and returned to the Lord or a close family member as children failed to conceive. Or perished all too young. Children were all too vulnerable, before they learned to cultivate.

And even after, for cultivation was no shield to sword or accident.

There was no guarantee a child would come from their efforts, no matter how strenuous. It would be up to fate to decide. Moreso, with his bloodline and wind body cultivation factored in, the entire process might be more complicated than he could imagine.

If the child died… Wu Ying's breath hitched a little, his chest constricting at the thought. Such scenarios, even in the landscape of future possibilities, were painful.

And wasn't that fascinating? Wu Ying turned the thought and feelings over in his mind, delving into his preconceptions and understandings. What cause for such concern, over an imaginary future. What brought such consternation to him? Was it the simple anchor of humanity, the concern any human would have over the loss of innocence? Or was there something else?

And if so, what did it mean?

As he ruminated on his reactions, Wu Ying's steps slowed and turned. He found himself moving with the curve of the land, traversing the gentle slope of the steppes. Most would consider this land flat. Compared to his home, it was. Yet there were gentle rises and falls in it, curving paths formed by streams and the twists of the earth.

Few enough monsters, compared to the lush greenery of the kingdoms to the south. Those that were present stayed far away, leaving Wu Ying only the company of the spirits that gusted around him. Yet even they seemed subdued, as though sensing his churning thoughts.

Long into the day, Wu Ying walked. His feet brushed the ground, ankle-high grasses tracing across worn robes as the wind rippled, bringing with it the refreshing chill of the north, yet silent in all other ways. Clouds roamed the skies, a flock of birds winging their way south. Eventually, the sky darkened as the sun gradually set.

Only when the stars were twinkling and the warmth of the summer day had fled did Wu Ying come to a conclusion. Not so much a conscious decision but a resolution to choose. Sometimes, when all options seemed equally unknown and fraught with uncertainty, wisdom came in listening to one's heart.

He poured his chi into his body, lightening his body and strengthening his soul, to cast himself upon the wind. He called it to him and floated away, taken to his destination.

***

"Wu Ying. My grandaunt told me she spoke with you," Narangerel said when Wu Ying finally reached the camp. His tent—the tent they had assigned to him—had been set up, to his surprise. Her presence was an additional surprise, only in the fact that she had been waiting this late. "You must believe me, I had no say in that. I did not ask her to speak with you!"

Wu Ying stared at the woman, a small smile creeping up his lips at her beauty. Not like his martial sister—har! How many were?—but striking in her own way, with darker and smoother skin, greater heights, and a piercing pair of eyes that spoke of intelligence and mischief.

"I believe you," Wu Ying said, allowing himself to alight on the ground. She smiled, stepping closer, but he backed off. He could not help but notice the flash of pain in her eyes. "But the Khan was right."

"About what? Having children?" Now Narangerel looked angry at him. "Do you think that is what I was looking for when I went to your furs?"

"Khan Erdene said—"

"My grandaunt is over a hundred years old. Multiple generations have passed," she said. "And still she thinks she knows our mind. Did she ask me? Did she ask you? No. She sits in her ger on her stone turtle, watching over everything but understanding nothing." Spinning on her heels, she shouted in direction of the turtle, "Nothing! Stop messing with my life."

Wu Ying winced, stepping back. Instinct screamed at him that he was now delving in even more dangerous waters than kingdom politics. More treacherous than any sect plot. No, these waters were deep and perilous and would pull down the unsuspecting within moments, never to be let up.

Family affairs. Dark waters indeed.

"Now, you. You think I want a mewling brat scrabbling at my feet?" Narangerel said, stalking up to Wu Ying, finger waggling in his face. "I wanted your body, your experience. Excitement! I wanted the stories you told me when we lay in bed, the paintings and sketches you showed me of lands beyond ours. I wanted to travel in the only way I could ever. Mewling brat. As if!"

Wu Ying stared at the shaking finger, then he firmed his stance. The initial retreat had been instinctive, coming from a time when having a woman angry at you was a deep concern, an atavistic fear of a mother and a cane. Now though, he stopped retreating as he remembered who he was and what he signified.

"Enough, Narangerel. I apologize for my assumption, but do not take your anger at your grandaunt out on me." He gestured sideways a little. "Furthermore, your grandaunt did raise a valid point." Her eyes narrowed, and Wu Ying continued before she could blow up further. "I never spoke to you about your desires. And for that, I apologize further." His lips turned up slightly. "Though you never did me either."

Narangerel hesitated at his second apology, before she snorted at his last sentence. "Oh, and were you looking for a child?"

"It doesn't matter. You never asked me either way. I assume you've been taking some herbs then, to ensure you are unlikely to conceive?" Wu Ying said.

Narangerel hesitated then nodded. "Yes."

Her words were marked by a sharp punctuation of thunder rumbling through the encampment and making tents shudder and dance. The pair cast a glance upward, reminded that at least one person was less than impressed with that admission.

Silence lingered between the pair as the thunder rumbled, lightning flashing overhead as storm clouds rolled in. Eventually, when no lightning struck them, Wu Ying found himself speaking.

"Well, it seems we are here and a discussion that should have been held has." Glancing around at the myriad members of the tribe who watched, some openly like the children and an older man outside his tent, others surreptitiously, he added, "If somewhat more public than I think would have preferred."

"Yes. It has," Narangerel said, then glared about her. "Well, if they've had their *entertainment*." She stepped toward Wu Ying, saw that he did not shrink away, and stepped closer. "Now what? Are you going to discard me because I refuse to have the child you want? Or are you running away because my grandaunt wants a child I will not give her?"

When put that way…

"I am not running, but it seems there are more conversations to be had." Wu Ying nodded toward the turtle. "After all, my debt to the clan is over, but I would not wish to incur additional debt. Nor see you injured in any way."

Narangerel's lips thinned as her eyes followed his gaze to the turtle shell and the ger above. As they watched, the stone turtle turned its head and stared at the pair, its eyes the size of dinner tables. There was a quiet, placid wisdom in them, though Wu Ying could have sworn he saw a hint of laughter too.

He had to admit, their situation was a little funny. Perhaps he should have found the matter a little more serious, but he found that he could not. Under the turtle's gaze, his lips pulled upward, and soon enough, Narangerel was smiling too. Moments later, the pair broke out laughing at the absurdity of the situation.

"Do you want to stay with me? Am I anything more than a window into another world?" Wu Ying asked, after he was done chuckling.

Narangerel tapped her lips, then she shook her head. "You are strong. Handsome enough. And you know much of the world outside. But you're a little too short for my taste and too ignorant about our customs. My husband—when I marry—will be a true man of the north."

Wu Ying nodded. "Then my question stands."

"Can we not go back to what we were? Bed companions, no expectations, no concerns," Narangerel said almost plaintively.

Wu Ying hesitated, then eventually shook his head. "No. That field has been ploughed. There is no return."

"Then can we at least be friends?"

"I don't think we will ever not be." Wu Ying looked at the tribe. Gauging the world, the wind. There were things he could learn from them, a new cultivation form, a new pathway.

Yet it was not his path. He had a clue, knowledge of perhaps something that might drive further research and development of his wind body. A way to take him to the next level as a Core Formation cultivator and Body Cultivator.

To understand it though, he needed more. More than just the methods here, more than esoteric teachings of a Spirit Cultivation method he could not use, might not even understand. He needed a sect library, the scrolls and manuals that the tribe scorned. More than one library, most likely. Perhaps it was their way, but it was not his.

That thought clarified the resolve within Wu Ying. There might be more to be learned in these plains, but it would not be with the Sakhait. Not after all that had happened.

"Yet, it is time for me to leave," Wu Ying said.

His words echoed through the tribe, causing Narangerel's face to fall and the clouds above to darken even further. At the same time, Wu Ying felt the northern wind laugh, dancing across his body, entreating him to keep exploring, to learn more of its land. It spoke of lands farther north, of plains that never grew warm. Icefields that ran for multiple li and creatures he had never seen before. A place devoid of all humans and vegetation.

A strange world, but it pulled at Wu Ying. At his curiosity, his need to know, to experience.

"You will not change your mind?" Narangerel said, her voice holding a small hurt.

"No. Too much has happened." He frowned, turning his head in the direction the Borjigin had come from. That fight, that play… "And I think, staying with you, it will compromise my own presence in the north further."

"Not worried that you'll take the wrong thing then?" Another voice. This time, it was Oktai, the translator finally having made his way down. There was something a little playful in his voice, but it was mostly grim. "The Sakhait are more forgiving than some others."

"So I've heard." Wu Ying sighed. "But at least I've learned a little more of the clans by now. Of the way of your people. Fate and luck will see me through, or not."

Oktai snorted, but in the end, he stepped forward and wrapped Wu Ying in a hug. The pair exchanged their farewells before breaking apart. A more subdued farewell was offered to Narangerel, then he was done. No need to say goodbye to the Khan. He had no desire to see her, nor she him, he assumed.

Then there was no more reason to delay. He glanced at the large stone turtle, the gathered clouds high above that twisted and rolled like a spiral of dreadful omniscience. He pulled at his chi, poured it into his body and soul, and took to the sky.

Time to go.

A step kicked him off through the air, pushing him forward. He stepped again as the wind gathered behind him and pushed him forward. Then another step that shoved him northward. He crossed the outer bounds of the encampment in two steps, no longer bothering to hide his cultivation, the speed he could achieve when he chose to travel.

Not that he was trying to run. Movement there would be at a different level. But his usual movement speed, the modified Twelve Gales technique? That did not need to be hidden.

Not anymore.

***

An hour later, his breathing was slow and relaxed. He had his small tent set up, the one he used to use when there was no place to sleep and no reason to hide. It was hemp, oiled and woven tight, and it smelled a little of mold and a little of himself. It was, in the end, familiar.

Wu Ying's eyes were drifting closed from the lengthy day, the constant pressure of choices, and the emotional interaction at the end. The surprising, twisted conversation that had sent him scrambling and setting his own expectations alight. If he had known her intentions, if they had talked, he could have saved himself heartache and worry.

Yet to his surprise, Wu Ying found that he could not find it within himself to regret the day. Futile as his day's musings had been, they had also forced him to look within himself. To ask not just what he wanted from this trip, but also from the future and those he might see in the future.

Thus far, his flings after Li Yao had never lasted more than a few days or a week at most. All too often he would be on his way, his partners knowing that a wandering gatherer was at best suitable for a moment's indulgence.

For the first time, he had been forced to discern his own desires. Whether he desired a dao companion, an individual to walk with him all the way to immortality. Once, briefly, as a youngster, he had considered perhaps he and Li Yao…

But no. Theirs were different paths, his a twisted, fickle route that carried him from kingdom to kingdom, sect to wilderness. What could he offer to another? A presence every few years, every few months? A brief lingering moment before he was pulled away once more?

What kind of dao companion would he be? Perhaps if they too were a wanderer, someone who could travel with him. But his wanderings had shown him that his travels were farther, broader than most. Most wandering cultivators traveled within a kingdom, perhaps visiting a neighboring one before returning to familiar haunts.

And here he was, lying beneath a worn tarp, on grass that was but a tall tale to those he had once called sect mates. The surge of resentment, of anger, he felt toward the patriarch, the elders who had banished him rose within his soul and choked him, catching him by surprise. Pushed down, ignored for so long.

He had done everything right, saved his martial sister, lost his Master, even rescued others. Over a score of cultivators, taken from their sects and returned safely after the cold calculus of war had deemed them dispensable. Injured, weak, traumatized, and all of them, all of them, angry.

To be abandoned, tossed away by an organization one had given so much? To be considered supplementary to their requirements? How could they not resent the very same sects to which they returned? For all that Wu Ying's banishment was but a small reflection of the Verdant Green Waters Sect's need for face, it was also entirely unfair.

Resentment rose in his throat, tasting sour and biting, acid churning and rising from his stomach. His eyes snapped open, and he stared above him. For a time, Wu Ying let the bitterness burn, his anger taking the unfairness of it all and fueling itself.

Outside, the northern wind howled, combining with the passionate southern wind, forming a cyclone around his tent. Joining together in their own ways to form the central wind, which sought stability or destruction in equal measure, bending only to the whim of timing and fate.

Wu Ying lay on his back and his chest rose and fell as he breathed, bitterness and rage combining until his body trembled. He let himself feel the emotions, experience them in full, watched as ideas and dreams of purposeful revenge flowed through him. He dwelled not on them but allowed them to pass by.

Time passed as he tasted the emotions he had not realized he harbored. He let them rise and burn and then, just as suddenly, those emotions faded.

Leaving him… empty.

Alone.

And if that was not the exact same conclusion he had come to while staring at Narangerel, hearing her words, feeling the ache in his soul and heart, he could not think of a better example. His path, his desires, his dao—it would leave him alone.

And it might be lonely, it might be empty of kin and companion at times. But it was his path.

Eventually he would go home.

Eventually he would see friends and family.

Till then, he would not tie himself to another sect, clan, tribe, or woman.

There were many paths to the Dao. Many ways to ascend to immortality. His path, lonely though it might be, was his. And his alone.

Enlightened and resolved, peace washed over Wu Ying. He closed his eyes and slept, knowing tomorrow would bring new challenges. That too was his path.

Chapter 28

Winter in the north was a different beast. It was, perhaps, a good thing that Wu Ying was a Body Cultivator with a wind body. The colder it grew, the easier it was to tap into the north wind, to understand it and the howling mass of snow and ice it brought. He felt his understanding of the form and the wind grow with each moment, enlightenment dancing on the edges as he lounged in ice-cold pools, their top crust broken with a single kick, or forged his way forward through the winds.

Through it all, unlike the howling northern wind rushing to the south, another breeze pulled him north. Pulling him farther and farther, to lands where snow dominated for months and the vegetation changed, growing sparser and shrubbier. Moss, small arctic trees whose trunks were barely a handspan across and leaves that hung on throughout the year.

More interesting to Wu Ying's particular interest than the stunted and hardy trees—though he did collect a few for his World Spirit Ring and its towering mountains—were the herbs and flowers he located. Rare though they might be, the ones that still glimmered and glowed, that drew in the cold and made it their own or burned so harshly against the oncoming winter were his greatest finds.

Flitting from location to location, trekking to hidden grottos, hot springs, and the occasional abandoned residence, Wu Ying gathered these herbs. He took them with care, planting them when possible in his World Spirit Ring. A Seven Winter, Eight Pillar Ginseng variant, the Blazing Buddha's Fireweed, and the Angel Roseroot were just a few of his many finds.

Furthermore, the cultivator was amused as his understanding fed into the ring, improving its dao, the formation of the world itself. Bare mountains rose high above his fields, and eventually rain turned to snow as it climbed the mountains and shed its encumbrance. Newly formed snow fields appeared, packed down further with each iteration of the weather cycle.

He drew in the snow then, the water around him, aiding the World Spirit Ring. Growing it by necessity, even as he adjusted his fields and lands, deepened the river and added another pond and lake above and below. Managing the flow of water within the ever-more-complex system.

No surprise that across multiple li, there were often areas and instances that changed without prior review. Boggy land became unnatural swamps, a desert formed in the lee of the mountain as rain failed to reach the earth.

The ring reacted to the world outside, the days within growing longer. No longer able to draw upon the heat of the world outside, no longer shedding sunlight within for hours on end. Plants withered and husbanded their resources. No deep winter, not like the miles of snow and biting wind he walked within, but a harsher one than his ring had experienced before.

More changes, more fixes, minor and major alterations. He found himself building storage within the ground, cold rooms whose temperature would not fluctuate much, to care for his plants. Building greenhouses to maximize the heat for more sensitive plants, moving some around to concentrate and benefit from the presence of others.

The Seven Sun Flower with its radiant petals, placed on all four corners of the greenhouse, forcibly warmed the inside. The Dripping Marsh Willow, down at one corner, ensured high humidity even as the small pool it formed beneath its eaves nourished the Singing Marsh Reeds of Liu. Hundred-Year-Old Desert Ginger beside the Seven Flowers where ground was dry and warm, basking in their radiance.

And then the formations, inscriptions taken from the Sakhait, formation flags marked around the land, stone carvings and winter statues, all repositioned for the new season. Each change was meant to aid the development of the fields, even as the majority were left to go fallow for now.

Months in the north, bypassing other tribes and clans. As he traveled, the groups became smaller, the numbers fewer. His appearance became more unique, from the delicate silk robes he wore that protected him against the cold to his features and long hair. Up here, the tribesmen cropped theirs shorter and wore thick beards that covered their faces, providing warmth under thick fur headdresses. Up here, the tribes were but a half dozen families at most, many having encamped for the winter rather than travel.

In such places, rare were the individuals in the Core Formation stage. Many of the tribe were spirit cultivators, individuals sharing the strength of the northern winds and spirits. These creatures of ice and cold sometimes walked amongst the tribes like people, long, angular, and beautiful or alien and strange, glittering cold and white.

Wu Ying found the tribes were wary of the strange cultivator who walked through the snows in nothing but a thin silk robe. Eventually, after one too many tense meetings, he traded fresh vegetables and dried meat for extra clothing, treated fur coats and warm leather shirts and pants, equipping himself with more sensible garments.

His next meeting was less tense, and relations thawed even faster when he freely shared the food he had available. Though his stores of meat might be limited in the short term, between the wind and his spiritual sense, locating additional resources was a matter of intent rather than luck. Whether it was diving into ice-cold lakes to pluck fish from the depths or locating demonic deer, the treacherous north yielded to him its scarce bounty with minimal danger.

After all, few enough creatures could challenge a Core Formation cultivator. Not one with both a powerful Body Cultivation and the Heart of the Sword. After he beat aside a powerful Core Formation tiger, a creature with long fangs in its mouth and pale, striped fur, he grew bolder in his wanderings and pushed farther north.

The wind whispered warnings then, murmuring of dangers ahead. When Wu Ying ignored the tugs upon his robes—for he wore the furs only amongst others—the wind grew even more insistent. It brought ice that lingered upon his clothing, froze Wu Ying's tongue, and crusted his hair. Ice that refused to melt upon touch and drained not just warmth but his chi as well.

Yet along with the snow, Wu Ying sensed more in the wind. A palace of ice rising in a land that never knew the touch of summer. No warmth, no mercy. And something more... the smell of flowers, blooming roses, honey from a heliotrope bush, and tiny floating lilies with their delicate floral touch.

No surprise then that the wandering gatherer pushed on.

Evenings grew longer, the wide expanse of the paint brush of the gods glittering across the dark canvas of the night. At times, under the clear gaze of the celestial denizens above, the chill grew such that every breath bit at the lungs and burnt the nostrils.

Time lost meaning.

Days flickered past faster than ever, it seemed, the night stretching onward. When the days lengthened again, Wu Ying found himself still drawn onward. The same serene landscape stretched before him as far as he could sense, dotted with minor mounds and icy depths. The earth gave way to ice and ice alone, and still, Wu Ying strode onward.

Pushed to its furthest extent, Wu Ying's spiritual sense picked out fewer and fewer living creatures. Spirits grew clustered, distracting motions at the edge of his spiritual perception. The chill stole warmth and motivation from all, leaving Wu Ying to drift forward under his own strength. Even the winds no longer aided him, his control robbed by an overpowering dao ahead.

For an indeterminate time, he strode through this colorless world, his dark brown peasant robes cracking with each motion. And then one day, at the edges of his perception, he sensed it. Kicking off into the air, he drifted higher and higher to see the ice palace glittering like a crystal.

Moments later, another spiritual sense brushed against his extended one. It shoved his senses aside like a wagon might a child, never even noticing him as it expanded. Retracting his chi and spiritual aura, Wu Ying plummeted from the skies as the powerful presence washed over him.

Domineering and harsh, it pounded his aura into the ground. The might of the creature was massive, greater than anything Wu Ying had ever sensed, tearing aside any paltry defenses and leaving Wu Ying naked.

Before it retracted, concerns about a true assault assuaged, Wu Ying felt its attention turn to him briefly. Primal fear drove Wu Ying to his knees, head bowed low. The cold and silent regard lasted only for a moment before it retracted, but it was one of the longest moments of his life, for in that instant, Wu Ying understood the extent of his importance.

Arrogant as he had grown, passing through these lands without concern, he was nothing but a bug beneath this creature's existence. These lands were quiet not because of the lack of powerful beasts but the knowledge that anything that grew too strong must leave—or attract the attention of the one who had stayed.

"Dragon King," Wu Ying said when the monster's presence was gone. "I woke the Dragon King of the North."

He found himself trembling, unable to draw a deep enough breath as his body shuddered.

Eventually, he found control by moving through the motions of his Body Cultivation forms in his mind, achieving a forced serenity that allowed him to regain control of his body. Standing, he began the movements in truth, each step, each shift jerky and untrained. Yet he proceeded with the forms, each moment slowly regaining control of himself as he danced in the snow.

All five forms, the movements that he knew best, completed. Then on pure instinct, Wu Ying started the sixth—the heaven's wind. Sharp and commanding, abrupt and explosive without the circular lines common in the central wind or the abrupt shifts in motion of the eastern. The heaven's wind form had always been one he'd struggled with, and yet at this moment, Wu Ying felt himself finding the rhythm.

Commanding and powerful, perceptive to the highest degree, but indifferent to the inconsequential. To which so many below were. It was a kind of viewpoint that Wu Ying, a farmer with his feet in the ground who was only higher than those disgusting merchants, found difficult to understand.

Until now. Until he had experienced that very same disregard.

Motion by motion, moment by moment, Wu Ying poured through the form, and a small portion of the chi from the heavens seeped into his veins and bones as the Body Cultivation form pulled it within. Eventually, Wu Ying finished, his breath slow and deep with every rise and fall of his chest. Eventually, his mind and chi stilled.

And then, he looked upward—and saw the silent regard of a celestial creature, the floating presence of a northern dragon, its scales glinting blue and a cloudy white.

***

"Explain yourself, mortal." The dragon's voice was powerful, though not overwhelming like the other presence. If the Dragon King of the North was a landslide of power, this dragon was but a minor rockfall. Still dangerous, still guaranteed to end one if you stood in its way, but still lesser.

Without hesitation, Wu Ying kowtowed to the dragon. An immortal celestial being was not someone you chose to anger. The consequences of arrogance was death at the best, destruction of one's family and friends and the village you lived in at worse.

"My deepest apologies, oh powerful and magnificent Celestial One. This unworthy mortal had sensed a change in the dao as he traveled north, and not understanding the local language and customs, found himself too close. I beg forgiveness for my impertinence," Wu Ying said.

A part of him was surprised the pair could understand one another, and only on further examination did he realize that the dragon was not speaking a mortal tongue. It just seemed that way, for understanding entered his mind even as the words themselves buzzed within his ears.

A heavenly language. How fascinating.

"You came because of curiosity and disturbed my liege's rest?" Displeasure rumbled through the words, making Wu Ying quail a little.

His knees were growing cold, the snow beneath his feet refusing to melt but drawing forth all the heat it could. Even the northern wind and his refined body could only handle so much, not when the one above him had full control of the nature of the north.

Once more, Wu Ying felt how his dao was the lesser of the two. Dragons were not practitioners of the Dao so much as creatures of them, inherently part of it. They controlled the world around them just by existing, having been born on the celestial plane. Wu Ying's control was but a paltry thing.

"I apologize once more," Wu Ying said, knocking his head on the ground three times. "I have no other excuse than ignorance."

"Ignorance is no excuse in the eyes of the law." Again that low rumbling. Silence.

Wu Ying bit his lips, debating if he should say anything further. He could beg for his life, but he had said what he could. He was no raconteur of words. No poet who could charm a king and stay his execution with but a few well-chosen phrases. He was but an honest farmer, and all he could offer was the truth.

So he lay there in silence, the cold leaching into his body, knees bent, head resting on the ground while his hands were splayed outward. Time ticked on, his body shivering and the tips of his fingers growing white. Frostbite began to settle in, but the dragon still said nothing.

Realizing he might perish before the creature above him had finished its contemplation— if this was not just an elaborate method of killing him—Wu Ying pulled chi from his core. The energy warmed him, bringing back a tingling numbness to his extremities. It was dangerous, using chi at all if the creature thought Wu Ying was gathering an attack.

In the meantime, Wu Ying gripped at the wind, his understanding of it, and the depths of the northern and heavenly chi he had recently cultivated. He poured his energy into it, trying to push the paired elements forward and make them grow, concentrating his focus on achieving control over his body and his own temperature if he could.

Wu Ying struggled as best he could, slowing down the loss of heat. After a time, the dragon sniffed. Once, loudly. The noise made Wu Ying jerk in surprise, his body exploding into pain as the lack of movement after so long triggered cramps and pins and needles.

"You… you cultivated the heaven's chi. Not just as a gift for enlightenment, but directly. Taking it from the very world around you," the dragon said.

"I apologize if I have overstepped my place," Wu Ying said, wincing with his head pressed to the ground. He just knew he was going to get eaten for what he was doing. "It is the path I follow."

"Heavenly chi abounds in this world. Its presence ties together the three planes and drives mortals and beasts alike into following the correct path. It is the chi of the celestials and immortals, of the gods above, gifted to those below." A slight pause before the rumbling shrugged. "Who am I to say if one foolish mortal chooses to take more than another?"

Wu Ying had tensed through the earlier discussion but found himself relaxing at the end. He exhaled raggedly, waiting.

"But it's curious. For one who draws from the heavens, your path is much more… winding." A long-clawed finger extended, pushing at Wu Ying. He found himself sprawled, the casual movement forcing him onto his back. "Who are you, mortal, and what is this path?"

"I cultivate the Seven Winds method, oh great Celestial One," Wu Ying said, sprawled on the ground inelegantly. He would move, but the claw hovered above his heart, not pressing, not even touching him. Just… hanging there.

"Do you now?" Amusement in the voice above. "And stop calling me by that stuffy name. I am Qianlian."

Wu Ying hesitated. High above, the monster glared at him, making the mortal gulp. "Honored Qianlian, I seek the seven winds, the heavenly one being my present goal. In the presence of the great King Dragon of the North, I found a further hint of it."

"I see…" Qianlian hovered above Wu Ying for a time, then removed its finger.

Wu Ying, after eyeing the dragon, scrambled to his knees, looking upward.

A clawed finger moved, beckoning him to stand all the way. "Well, if your goal, if your point is to grow closer to the heavens… then perhaps your minor transgression may be allowed to pass. After all, mercy is heavenly too."

"Thank you, Honored Qianlian." Wu Ying bowed low. "If it is acceptable, then I shall take my leave and no longer take any of your precious time."

"Hold." A claw raised and though Wu Ying had not moved, waiting for his banishment first, he froze entirely rather than chance angering the all-too-reasonable dragon. "I have not dismissed you. There is something else I wish to ask of you."

"Yes, Honored Qianlian?" Wu Ying had a guess, though he dared not speak of it himself. One did not presume to bother a celestial being.

"Your scent. You're one of my lustrous brethren's descendants, are you not? An offspring of a dragon and a human." Wu Ying was now treated to the sight of a dragon shuddering in pure repulsion at that thought, an act that started from the top of its long, sinuous body and carried down to its tail before returning the other way. "Why did you not claim kinship rights then?"

Wu Ying bowed low. "I have but the merest drop of a drop. One such as myself would not dare to presume to place oneself even on the lowest tiers of kinship with creatures of such great might and power." If nothing else, flattery always worked. Seeded with truth, of course.

"You speak with honeyed words." A pause, then disdain in Qianlian's voice. "You do it poorly. The immortals do it much better when they come to beg favor from my liege. Speak plainly, mortal."

"I dare not claim kinship for fear of giving insult," Wu Ying said, rapidly choosing to do as the dragon said.

The dragon's rumbling laughter made the snow on the ground jump and tremble and falling snow to swirl around in little eddies. It laughed and laughed, leaving Wu Ying to smile weakly. Eventually, the dragon stopped, eyes still glittering with amusement.

"A good choice. If you had, I would have eaten you." A wide, toothy grin. "For a dragon that dared do as you did would have challenged my liege. And in so doing, sacrificed his life."

Wu Ying bowed in thanks for the information and to hide the look of relief he knew was on his face. Not that he doubted, even for a second, that Qianlian missed a single thing. Even now, he felt the creature's aura pressing down on him, the way its spiritual sense danced along the edges of his aura, seeking entrance.

"Still. You have a touch of it. Did you perhaps come thinking my liege was asleep? Seeking to draw forth a touch of blood to strengthen your own paltry connection?" Just as suddenly as its humor came, it was banished.

"No! I had no idea what was here." Then he added, after a thought struck him, "Nor would I ever even consider doing that. Theft in such a manner would be discourteous and dishonorable to the extreme."

The wind gusted, pulling and tugging at Wu Ying's robes, making the floating frills dance. Qianlian shifted, listening. Wu Ying picked up the edges of a murmured conversation. No words, just intent.

"And yet you have stolen as much before. From another of my foolish brethren," Qianlian said.

Traitorous wind! Wu Ying wanted to curse the southern wind that had brought forth the news, the damnable fool thing that had placed him there. Yet he could not do so. Fickle as the wind, they said, and obviously the wind had no favorites. How could it?

"It was shed in battle. Cast aside, unwanted." Wu Ying bowed his head. "I sought an advantage, and if it was wrong, I can only apologize now. Still, I see a difference in picking up those items shed aside, unwanted, and taking directly, without asking." A hesitation, then he pushed on. "Do you not?"

"Mmmm… you speak better when you have tossed aside those useless refineries of polite culture that you ape," Qianlian said. "You are not wrong. Though my cousin might see it otherwise, if he were to find you. Or your friend."

Wu Ying nodded in acknowledgement of that point.

"Very well. I have judged the truth of your words." Qianlian floated away, his entire body retreating a little though he himself had not moved, as though tugged to the sky by an invisible spring. "You may leave."

Wu Ying bowed low, murmuring his thanks. He stayed low, waiting until the dragon was gone before he hurried away. The moment he turned from the palace, the wind worked again for him, helping to carry him away at speed.

Not without a touch of regret. A part of Wu Ying cursed his cowardice at not asking for blood from the dragon. Even if Qianlian was no wind dragon, surely even a drop from it would be sufficient to improve his bloodline. Increase his connection.

Yet instinct and fear had held him back. There were deep waters there, in the declaration of intent to grow his bloodline. It was a treacherous path and one he had chosen to discard. He would walk the path of Body Cultivation, not bloodline growth. He would not become a dragon, for they had a society he knew nothing of.

Politics and hierarchies and danger.

Perhaps he had given up on a true opportunity. But that was life. Opportunities abounded if but one looked. Sometimes opportunities turned into tragedies; other times they were a true boon. It but required wisdom, perseverance, and willingness to locate the correct ones and discard the others.

As Wu Ying fled the north, he could not help but think that this opportunity was one he would have to accept was not for him.

Chapter 29

Hours of flying through the air, of fleeing through the night sky, the wind at his back. He ran for three days, leaving behind the ice palace he had spotted, the dragon, and the wisps of heavenly chi he had sensed.

Three days without eating, without sleep. He fled from fear, from shame, from chastisement, from his own failure, while headed toward a future of his own choosing. And then it was over and the chi within his dantian had dropped to a level that it could no longer sustain his movement.

The landscape before him was a brilliant white speckled with streaks of blue and green, the packed ice beneath the snow appearing and disappearing as the wind blew. A desolate tundra of frozen water, shaped into hills and gullies, pressed tight over centuries of snowfall.

Seeing no difference between one spot and the next, Wu Ying fell to the earth behind a slight rise in the ground. A flicker of his hands had formation flags planted around him, heavier landscape totems drawn from his World Spirit Ring a moment later as the flags were blown off course. Two rings then. One of the totems, then another of the flags to stabilize the foundations and environment around him.

Seated in the center in the ocean of calm that his formations created, Wu Ying extracted simple travel rations and consumed his first meal in days. Water taken from the snow around him dealt with his parched throat, the unnatural cold of the Dragon King's dao no longer permeating the ground.

Bodily requirements dealt with, Wu Ying began the process of cultivating. Again and again, he turned over his experiences in his mind, focusing upon the cold of the wind, the dao of the Dragon King he had glimpsed, and the traces of the celestial that he had noticed.

In time, when his dantian had filled, he stood. He moved, performing the four forms of the other winds by rote before focusing upon the final primal wind. The north wind, his attachment to it and to the lands around, the sights of the massive creatures that padded through the frozen tundra, the herds of antlered deer and the monstrous beasts that stalked them.

A land that was primordial in its making, unchanged for millennia at its heart. Closer in conception to the earliest formations of the Dao, a time when man had yet to set foot in the north. And yet, venture within they had. Tribes eked out their existence in this harsh environment, growing close to it, growing strong within it. Forming their own nations, cultures, languages, and custom.

Wu Ying moved and drew forth the cold, merciless wind and let it sink deep into his bones.

Snow packed around the formations that ringed him, the drifts collecting higher and higher, eventually blotting out the sun as days went by. Wu Ying meditated, moved, and eventually soaked within the ice itself, carving a tub made of ice with formation markers to hold it together. Then in the ice-cold water, water that threatened to freeze solid with each moment, he added armfuls of herbs, many of them herbs and vegetation taken from these very plains.

The cold became a facet of his existence, soaking deep into his bones and marrow. It warred with the warmth of the southern wind, the tempest of the east, forcing a stillness that threatened death. Only the ever-present whirlwind of chi within his dantian, within his meridians, kept him warm. Kept the chi that was drawn within and then expelled from stilling even his mighty heart.

Days turned into weeks, weeks into months. Occasionally, explosive winds generated from Wu Ying's movements, his practice of the wind body forms, threw aside the accumulated snow, exposing him to the raw elements and sun once again.

He lost track of time as he fell into a cultivation frenzy, eking the barest scraps of knowledge from his encounter. Eventually, his movements, like his mind, grew sluggish, his progress slowing. Still, he persisted, his mind and will so frozen and entrenched in its routine that he could not break free, the subtle traces of an omnipresent dao seeping within.

In the end, it was the lack of sustenance that broke him free. Even the vast stores found in his storage rings, aided by the World Spirit Ring, could not sustain him forever. The World Spirit Ring itself, still in its nascent stage of growth, had begun to wilt, the sun and warmth within dimming. Winter—a true winter—had arrived all across the land and many of his plants fell to it.

Without food, Wu Ying was forced south by the unbearable harshness of the north. In leaving, he departed with an almost perfected understanding of the northern wind, one driven deep into the marrow and organs of his body. No longer would he feel even a trace of the cold, no longer did he need to waste chi to bear that climate.

Unbeknownst to him, Wu Ying left behind a tale among the northern tribes. Of a demon from the south that came north, wearing naught but silken rags and the furs of his slain enemies. A demon that visited the Dragon King of the North and was imprisoned for his temerity. Stories of a location that was cursed, the demon trapped by the great dragon king and where it attempted, again and again, to free itself, sending ice and snow flying through the air.

You could tell this location from the others by the way the winds moved irregularly, unstably. You could sense its presence as warmth from the south and a harsh dryness that sucked all moisture from one's face robbed you of your footing. And most of all, by the smells—unusual, floral, and pungent. A reminder of a warmer, alien world.

***

Never-ending winter gave way to summer, ice retreating before green grass and rocky lands. The wind blew, and Wu Ying traced his way south, the wind guiding him east with each gust.

The western wind, laughing at him all the way, pushed him onward during the day, and the eastern wind beckoned him at night. Ocean wind, the taste of salt and sand, seaweed and fish.

Disparate nomadic tribes, all of them tied together by bonds of blood and familiarity, became city states filled with individuals, their control only extending a few dozen li from their walls. Fields, golden with stalks of wheat, swayed as Wu Ying passed, farmers working them diligently.

Travel south came with certain perks. The wilds offered him replenishment of his depleted stores, the warmer temperature and sunlight restoring some of his plants in his World Spirit Ring. Others, too many others, were lost.

Forced to treat with others, Wu Ying sought the jianghu, sought familiar cultivation resources, bookstores and libraries where manuals, scrolls, and treatises on soul and body cultivation might be present. His long-delayed research into the intersection of body and soul cultivation resumed once more.

Here, the cities he found were dominated not by sects but by clans and families. Pulled together into temporary, shifting alliances to rule a city, a region, a people and as likely to part and crumble at the most minor of pressures. With each group, Wu Ying interacted as befitted their station.

Families which held themselves to the standards of the jianghu that he knew, living, training, and cultivating at a remove from mortal society. Protectors for the cities against demonic and spirit beasts as well as antagonistic tribes, bandits, and the occasional city state.

Those, he treated with fairly.

Other families, clans that acted like merchants, seeking only the greatest profit from each transaction, Wu Ying treaded warily amongst. All too often, he would outline the deal and find, in their presentation of the goods, a lacking on their part.

Those deals, he took, with protest, and left. Only to return late at night the next day, flitting between formation markers into libraries and training grounds. Into badly tamed gardens, where a few scrolls or herbs might disappear.

And then, he would leave, having put aright the deal.

And rarely, all too rarely, he met another kind of clan. Those who might be labeled dark sect, creatures of savagery and death, who oppressed the mortals beneath them and traded not with honeyed words or clear eyes but poisoned daggers and razor wires at night.

Those, he left burning behind him.

Li after li, Wu Ying descended.

Meeting clans anew, creating temporary arrangements to acquire or trade scarce resources for the creation of alchemical pills for the family patriarch and their members. Access to their private libraries, each of which contained the details of the lower levels of their family's styles and treatises about body and soul cultivation. Lessons on family sword styles and sparring partners to hone the edge of his blade.

In the meeting of weapons, Wu Ying learned a lot about those who controlled these mini-kingdoms. Their family styles dipped deeply into the elemental features of cultivation with strange, esoteric elements in play. Blood, bone, ash, and clay were among the elements that made their presence known in his travels.

And a few such instances were truly memorable.

***

A new opponent stood before him, crouched low. Hands were held wide, much like the wrestling men of the north had once stood, barehanded. The cultivator before Wu Ying was no wrestler though. Instead, green-tipped claws shone against darkened, scaled skin.

A slight twitch in the back foot, muscles bunching beneath loose silk trousers, was all the warning that Wu Ying received. His opponent lunged, claws arcing upward to strike at the blade of Wu Ying's jian. A shift of his blade brought the shaft of the jian out of reach, even as the tip stayed on line to pierce his opponent's body.

Twisting in mid-motion, Wu Ying's opponent slid under the point as though he lacked bones. Scuttling forward with the aid of a lowered hand, the cultivator pivoted on its lowered hand, throwing a dual-kick at Wu Ying.

Forced to move, Wu Ying sidestepped the attack, his blade coming in a retaliatory strike against the exposed legs. Blade bit into silk, parting the cloth with ease before it struck chi-hardened scales beneath. Bouncing off the protected body, Wu Ying's jian whipped around with the momentum to parry a follow-up claw strike.

The pair dueled, the scaled-cultivator's superior defenses allowing him to take risks that Wu Ying dared not. Instead, Wu Ying met the challenge with superior positioning and speed, attacking constantly and punishing mistakes with bruising blows and the occasional whipping kick.

Neither party leaked killing intent, their daos held close within their souls. Nor did they wield the greater, more concentrated chi of their cores. Not only was the training grounds they were within not rated for such violence, the terms of their spar precluded it.

Another half dozen passes, Wu Ying's breathing slow and even. A smile lit his face, for while he detested combat, the violence and the killing, the art of the blade itself held a strange joy for him. Not for the art itself but for the motion, the memories it engendered within him.

Long hours with his father beside their residence, copying his motions as a child and basking in his approval. The bloody and exhausting work to eke out a clean touch, the matches against other members of his village. Even the time he'd spent in the Sect, crossing blades with his Master and winning an approving nod or facing his blade again and again through sheer stubbornness.

The memories, both good and bad, provided delight to Wu Ying. Oh, there was a simple joy in the physicality of the motions, in competition that he would never discount; yet he had seen true obsession and genius in Pan Chen. And in that blinding light, all else were but shadow puppets.

Another parry, this time followed by a close envelopment. Wu Ying caught the wrist with his blade, pulling it close and levering it downward. At the same time, he stepped backward, the point of his blade sneaking under the armpit as he did so, his opponent's balance disrupted for a moment. The motion came to an end with the blade tip against the soft, vulnerable tissue, his opponent balanced precariously on one foot.

The pair froze, yellow pupiled eyes meeting Wu Ying's placid brown ones. The cultivator snorted and then, with a quick shudder and twist, tore his hand free from the grip. Core energy leaked as he did so, leaving Wu Ying gripping green scales that shattered and dispersed as the chi broke apart, his opponent retreating to a safe and respectful distance.

Then he bowed. "The point is yours, Cultivator Long."

"Only by merest thread of fortune, Patriarch Ding," Wu Ying replied, bowing. He watched as the faux-scales broke apart, the green skin fading back into the patriarch's pale features, revealing a much younger man than would be expected. He looked barely in his forties, though age was a tricky subject with cultivators.

In this case, Wu Ying knew the patriarch was just over ninety years, stalled in the middle stages of Cultivation, his outer Core layers patchy and fragile.

"You are too humble, Cultivator Long. Few are the students of the jian who have advanced as you," the patriarch replied. "Your jian is nimble as your feet, a silverfish darting through the corals." He grinned wide, and if his teeth were a little sharper than normal, so were his entire clan's. "You have left me much to think about on my own poor techniques."

Wu Ying murmured further bland assurances, the pair layering words of praise and dissension until courtesy was satisfied.

"Your style is still in its infancy, but it is remarkable still," Patriarch Ding said. "What did you call it again?"

"A Wandering Dragon," Wu Ying said, a little embarrassed. He had named it in a moment of enlightenment and dared not change it. Yet to call it that out loud…

"A good name. Powerful techniques, subtle and elusive but striking and fast when necessary," the patriarch said. "You showcased the first major strike earlier when you arrived. But the second…"

"Is not done," Wu Ying murmured. He had to admit, the first movement, the first strike, the one he had borrowed inspiration from was complete. Or as complete as he could make it now. There were portions of it that he could not grasp, but he had learned, in his time in the far north, to contain it. To hold the damage to only a small area and thus reduce heaven's rebuke as well.

"When it is, I am certain it will be worth observing," Patriarch Ding murmured.

As they took their seats at the table set aside for them, midday sweets and snacks displayed for their pleasure, Wu Ying considered how best to broach the question.

In the end, Patriarch Ding did it for him. "You have been extremely courteous to have held back your curiosity until the day of your leaving. But ask."

"Sir…"

"Ask. All our guests do eventually."

"Then, at your behest. A lizard? It is… a strange and unusual elemental affinity." Wu Ying shook his head. "A bloodline, I could understand. A bloodline is easily understood. But you were insistent it was an elemental affinity, not a bloodline. How is… lizardy an element?"

The patriarch smiled and picked up his cup. It was not tea, but a drink made from the delicate petals of local flowers and sweetened by the addition of honey. It was, Wu Ying had to admit, an acquired taste and so he only copied the motion a little.

Funny, that he should miss good tea.

"For the courtesies you've shown and for the herbs you provided for my son, let me relate it to you as my father did me," Patriarch Ding said, before he raised a finger. "Indulge me, yes?" When Wu Ying nodded in agreement, the patriarch continued. "Tell me, what are elements?"

"The elements, they are… they are the things, the objects that make up existence," Wu Ying said, caught off-guard. "They are the keys to existence. All things are made up of the elements, and in their interactions, all things can be explained."

"A very classical answer," Patriarch Ding said. "Did you know that some hold that the five classic elements are the only elements there are? That all others, like your wind and our lizard, are but interactions between the five elements?"

Wu Ying nodded. He had read that. In fact… "Isn't that generally accepted? My wind is but fire and wood, interacting and consuming one another. Heat, another elemental by-product."

"Yes. Every element is explainable by the interaction of the five. Yet we label and parse it out, the families vying for control and for dominance with their styles and the elements. Blood being weaker than water, except when dealing with the living. Cloud and mist, arguing with steam, for which is truer and stronger? When one or another is but a matter of… temperature." Wu Ying blinked as Patriarch Ding grew heated. "We argue and debate and write stern letters to one another, and when it's not enough, we fight for real in arenas like the one we left. And when that is still not enough, we send our children to settle scores.

"Yet."

"Yet?" Wu Ying said.

"Yet is this not all but parts of the Dao?" Wu Ying could hear the capital letter in the final word. "We struggle and grasp at the Dao, seeking to break it apart, such that we might but ascend."

"Because no mortal can grasp the Dao. Not in its entirety." Wu Ying quoted, "'The Dao that can be named is not the Dao. The Dao that can be explained is not the true Dao.'"

"Exactly! Even brief moments of enlightenment have been known to drive some, the unprepared, the young, the fragile, mad. What more could grasping the entirety of existence do?" Patriarch Ding continued. "And if the Dao is all things and all things are the Dao, then the elements are of the Dao. Yes?"

Wu Ying nodded, understanding of the man's point arriving before it was spoken. Even so, he stayed silent out of respect.

"If the elements are of the Dao, and all are within, then cannot all things be an element?" Patriarch Ding said finally, triumphantly.

Even though Wu Ying had arrived ahead of the patriarch to the conclusion he was being led to, he was unable to refute the man. Perhaps a more studied scholar might have been able to do so. Perhaps by calling into question the definition of elements. Or naming some esoteric concept, like time.

Yet Wu Ying was no scholar. He might play at it, but in his heart of hearts, he was but a simple farmer. And a farmer saw the world as it was, not as he wished it to be. The earth gave of its bounty or not, and the tax collector cared not for finely tuned definitions of what wealth was when they came to take their share.

"And so, an element of the lizard," Wu Ying said. "The results are… impressive." And he meant that, for the results were. A strange fighting method, a skillset and cultivation tomes that were perfect for a family. Even if… "But it also challenges the common beliefs."

"Truth." Patriarch Ding grimaced. "I thank you again. Few are willing to treat with us, for fear of angering the other families. And though few would take our *heretical* manuals, if we grow too weak, our demise is guaranteed. Survival for me and my family is balanced on the knife's edge of cultivation."

An old sorrow, a buried grief flickered across the man's face. And suddenly, Wu Ying understood. How a man who was as smart, as dedicated to improvement as the patriarch had shown himself to be could have made the mistake of pushing his Core into its current state.

Sometimes, the things you did for family, you would never do for yourself.

"A fair trade," Wu Ying said. His hand raised, pointing toward where the library stood. "Knowledge for herbs. A fair trade, in all viewpoints."

Patriarch Ding chose to accept Wu Ying's words at face value. "Where do you go now, Cultivator Long? Where does the wind blow you?"

Wu Ying considered his words, lifting his head a little to feel the wind on his skin. In the end, he gave the only answer he could.

"Wherever the wind wills."

Chapter 30

The wind blew him east, until he found himself before a sight he had never imagined. Even the largest lake he had witnessed was nothing like this. The waves were higher, frothing with whitecaps under the insistent hand of the wind. Seaweed and kelp and salt stained his lips even as he stared into a blue-green horizon that stretched for as far as the eye could see and still continued. Sea birds wheeled above the liquid horizon as tiny islands dotted the sight before him.

The ocean.

An endless body of water, where monsters and mystical creatures lived. Across numerous villages and cities along the coast, fishing fleets braved these waters, casting nets and lines to draw forth the bounty of the ocean.

Brave individuals dove deep, seeking pearls, shellfish, oceanic marine life, and other delectables to feed the ravenous population inland. In shallower basins, villages planted long bamboo poles into the mudflats, kelp and laver grown beneath the shifting waters to be harvested when they had grown sufficiently. Alongside the water, held in simple woven trays and placed near houses, the seaweed so taken was left to dry before being stored and shipped west.

Storage equipment, specially crafted to ensure the freshness of the catch, aided in the transportation of the harvest. Glass and wooden storage containers, filled with water taken from the sea, saw to the transportation of live seafood, carefully built formations ensuring stability and durability of the construction even as new air was piped into the tanks.

It was with one such caravan, on its way back to a nearby city, that Wu Ying had hitched a ride. During long nights, as he rested in the warmth of the ocean wind, formations and guards patrolling the perimeter to keep away monsters that preyed upon the caravans, the intricacies of the commercial network had been explained to Wu Ying.

"Entire families of noblemen have grown in strength from the movement of such goods," the caravan master, an older gentleman in the upper stages of Energy Storage, explained to Wu Ying. "Those of us in the branch families take on the task of commerce and transportation, while the main families deal with the fishing fleet and the catch. They also, of course, handle the lumber in the nearby forest that dominates the shipbuilding industry."

"And the guards?" Wu Ying inclined his head toward the constant patrols.

"A necessity. Even with the forts and the inns, the demonic beasts and spirits know that there's an easy meal if we slacken our watch." The caravan master let out a gusty sigh. "With the Eastern Dragon King's attitude toward dealing with his many progeny, many of the creatures here can trace their descent to one of his children, the commensurate strength within them too."

"Is slaying them not… dangerous?" Wu Ying said carefully. He was remembering his travels, the beasts he had slain at the edge of his blade. Some had been stronger than he had expected. Now, he worried that the beast cores he held within his storage rings might see him in danger from another dragon king.

"Not a concern. Thankfully, that same attitude means that whichever great-grandchild or other fool descendant attacks us is considered too foolish to live." The man laughed. "Not as though any proper dragon of the east would even consider anything but a full-blooded beast a true member of the family. Even those few that ascend to Nascent Soul level are barely considered more than distant cousins."

"Are there that many then, out here? Nascent Soul spirit beasts?" Wu Ying said. He had sensed a few presences deep in the wilds while he'd traveled. Creatures with an aura that chilled him to the bone and sent him fleeing carefully for safer environs.

The caravan master nodded. "Aye. Compared to the central lands, many. Not like the south though, where those immortal beasts live amongst their descendants. But here? Here, we have many. Eventually though, they either go into the sea or are driven away by the king."

Another gust, a spray of water that carried itself all the way to Wu Ying and wet his cheeks as he stood on the small cliff overlooking the water. He exhaled, returning to the present, and stared at the water. Somewhere out there, past the waves, out of sight, an island floated, or so it was said.

Even farther afield than the Dragon King of the East's underwater palace was the fabled island of the immortals. Where a storied group of immortals lived and the peaches of immortality—that all-too-infamous shortcut—grew.

The stories of those who tried to make it to that island were numerous. They were a favorite of passing entertainers, for you could do much with that plot thread. Comedy—like Ah Roh the Pilgrim, who took a raft with his rooster and rat and ended up shipwrecked. Tragedy—the three sisters of Xin who sacrificed their hearts, their limbs, and their futures. War and drama—when the King of Bu sailed his fleet and lost them, one after another, before he sank with the flagship, setting off a chain of dynastic quarrels back home.

What all those stories lacked, what all those tales never offered, was a glimpse of hope. Success at actually gaining a peach. And yet fools tried, one after the other, year after year.

And even as the shui gui[39] increased, lamenting their deaths, hope drew on the foolish and brave alike.

****

The city had walls that rose three times Wu Ying's height, a ringed series of curtain walls that surrounded a city sitting upon the heights of a cliff, overlooking the peaceful bay and the harbor. The inlet into the harbor was overlooked by a pair of forts with imposing watchtowers, flat courtyards nearby where well-worn artillery pieces watched over the

---

[39] Ghosts of the drowned

approach. Additional walls cut off the harbor from the main city and fortress, a wide paved road allowing the easy approach and routing of the day's catch into the lower city.

Scores of boats moved within the massive harbor, jockeying for position at the docks. Small gusts of wind, water, and wood chi blew across the waves, cultivators at the Energy Storage stage guiding the movement of boats with chi and skill alike. Smaller sampans and tugs darted between the ships docked at the edges of the circular bay, armored guards standing on the boats and boarding newly arrived vessels to conduct checks and receive the city's taxes and duties.

Wu Ying watched all this commotion with a bemused expression, the sight new and unique. Never had he seen a port town this busy, for even the port towns along rivers and lakes inland were but a fraction of the size. The cries of numerous voices were muted by distance, but they formed a dull roar of civilization. The smells of the city were more prominent, the harbor clogged with refuse.

He stood there, marveling and drinking in the new sight for so long that a patrol was sent to speak with him. A lone wanderer, bereft of a discernible aura, approaching from the deep wilds by himself off the main roads was an anomaly, and the nobleman who ran the city cared little for anomalies.

Anomalies were how you were assaulted by a dragon in disguise or surprised by a visiting immortal, bored of the heavens.

The patrol that came for Wu Ying was a large group—more than double the size of their regular number of their squads. It made sense since the leader who stood before him was a low-grade Core Formation cultivator. The captain—for who else could he be—stank, his scent a mixture of rotting seaweed and an open wound. Extending his spiritual sense a little, Wu Ying's breath caught as he traced the outline of the man before him. The captain sported a damaged Core, a single rent leaking chi and the agony of an exposed immortal soul, its protective covering broken.

Smoothing out his expression, even as the horror of what had happened to the captain throbbed within Wu Ying, he waited for the group to reach him. He took in details as he did so, everything from the shorter legs of the horses that were being ridden, the slight unfamiliarity of the men—especially compared to the experienced horsemen of the north—astride their beasts of burden. A quick assessment gave away their cultivation bases. An even split between those in the upper end of Body Cultivation and the five who were in the middle stages of Energy Storage.

Weapons were interesting, each of them carrying not bows or crossbows but throwing javelins that were seated in specialized sheaths on their saddles. Considering the rolling hills, he assumed it was due to the shorter ranges of combat. Their swords were short, double-edged jian that were barely longer than a big knife. Their primary weaponry though was not the sword or javelins but the polearms they held, hook bills on the end of each meant to punch through armor or hook and drag their victims behind them.

Or off boats into the water.

Armor was missing on the horses themselves, the guards sporting lighter, thinner leather protection that had been made supple with oil rather than hardened and stiffened in ovens. In addition, rather than hooked clasps or buckles, the armor was tied together by string, the knots hidden beneath the few overlapping plates on the shoulder or around the neck.

Idly, Wu Ying let his senses trace the knots, surprised at the variation among the guards. More than that, he knew not these knots, though he soon gleaned most were variations of a friction knot, all threaded to allow for a fast release with a single, well-placed tug.

Poor defense against a man who wielded a mischievous wind dao. But the eastern wind spoke of other tales, of sailors pulling off armor to slip into tossing waves to rescue brethren, of falling guards and the cold embrace of the ocean.

"The sea's blessings on you, honored visitor," the captain said when the group was close enough. Much like his soul, the captain's voice was frazzled, hoarse, damaged, and grating with each word. A sharp contrast to his smooth mien, light brown hair, and sparkling eyes. "I am Captain of the Guards Ren Xue of the Ba Province."

Five of their members split apart, the Energy Storage cultivators riding their horses to place themselves at the points of a pentagram. The start of a combat formation, Wu Ying would assume. The other five were behind the captain and to the side, each of them with a clear angle to toss the javelins they held so idly, tips pointed down.

"A fair day to you as well, captain," Wu Ying replied easily. "This one is Long Wu Ying, a wandering cultivator and spiritual herb gatherer."

The captain relaxed a little as Wu Ying announced himself politely, more so when he named his occupation. It was no surprise his control over his aura if he was a gatherer. A quick flick of the man's gaze ran down Wu Ying's robes. After due consideration, Wu Ying had changed into replicas of the Verdant Green Waters inner sect robes, ones he'd had others recreate. Sadly, without the special silk to provide additional protection and durability of his treasured originals. Still, if he was to visit and present himself, these new robes would do.

"I apologize, Cultivator Long, but I am unfamiliar with the sect you hail from."

Wu Ying wondered if the man was just fishing, or if he had truly guessed that Wu Ying was part of a sect. After all, Wu Ying understood his accent marked him as a stranger. His rounded words were a sharp contrast to the clipped, sharp notes of the natives here.

"No offense is taken. I have traveled far, and I would not expect such knowledge to have traveled as well," Wu Ying said. He touched his robes, a half-smile on his lips. "I am currently on leave from the Verdant Green Waters Sect."

"Based in the Shen kingdom," Captain Ren supplied before Wu Ying could. "No minor sect, that is. My master would be honored to host one of such renowned lineage."

Wu Ying hid the internal wince at the man's words. Not that it was surprising that the nobleman in charge of the city—and province, it seemed—would want to fete him. Still, it meant a series of dinners, drinks, speeches, and carefully worded conversations. Long, polite days.

On the other hand, it also meant, potentially, access to his library and connections, which depending on the makeup of the kingdom, might be of utmost importance. Certain kingdoms and sects restricted access to everyone from apothecarists to martial trainers, forcing Wu Ying to treat with them.

Hopefully, he would not have to decline—yet again—another insistent invitation that he join their sect or government.

"I would be honored to meet your master, Master…?"

"Viscount Khao."

"Honored to meet Viscount Khao," Wu Ying said, inclining his head in acceptance of the correction.

A small gesture from Captain Ren and the guards relaxed. The captain then invited Wu Ying to join him, surprise registering briefly when Wu Ying chose to walk over on air, rising to meet the man's height on the horse.

In that way, one man striding across the sky, the other riding his steed at a slow pace, guards surrounding them both, they returned to the city. More than a few glances were cast their way, children pointing at the unusual sight while adults, dulled by expectations, would jerk around to confirm what they had seen. All this commotion, Wu Ying studiously ignored, as did the captain.

In fact, the captain seemed intent on relating the history of the kingdom and province to Wu Ying as they traveled. His voice was grating and harsh, the words spoken almost by rote, as though he'd pronounced such words many times before.

"Baisha is the capital of the eight provinces, established by the first Viscount of Ba four hundred eighteen years ago. He built the initial harbor and the first Fang"—a gesture to the tower on the north side of the bay—"while it was the sixth Viscount—Viscount Khao's own father—who built the second Fang."

"Impressive forts," Wu Ying murmured, happy to let the man tell his tale.

"They are. The city has never been taken because of them," Captain Ren said, his nose wrinkling a little as he continued. "Though many have tried, including the fool Wakoku[40]."

"How about from land?" Wu Ying said curiously.

"Hah! We are the easternmost province of the Jiang kingdom." The captain gestured to the west. "All that way lie our people, so who would attack us?" He sniffed. "Any who try to bring an army along the imperial roads would be spotted and dealt with long before. And few dare the deeper wilds." He glanced at Wu Ying, a slight smile crossing his face. "Except, of course, individuals like yourself."

---

[40] Very old, slightly offensive name for Japan. Obviously, not actually Japan since this is not actually China; but the transliteration and offensive use is on purpose for this character.

"Then why the many walls?"

Captain Ren looked at Wu Ying consideringly. Due to the way the walls were built, only the large outer wall and a single inner wall could have been seen from their earlier position. Of course, Wu Ying might have managed to spy upon it before—after all, as he'd amply demonstrated, he could fly—but it was still an interesting revelation. One that Wu Ying had deliberately let loose.

Over the years—and how many, Wu Ying disliked to consider—the cultivator had learned that hiding the entirety of one's abilities was rather self-defeating. As a wandering gatherer, it was presumed he had goods worthy of acquisition. If others presumed him too weak to hold on to his belongings, he invited attack at a later date.

If, however, he revealed the full extent of his skills, the degree of attention he received was often distracting. More than once, he'd had to depart a city or province at speed, losing his watchers in the deep wilds. Even then, divination and other forms of remote observation would be wielded, for concerns about a powerful, sectless, unbound cultivator stoked the paranoia of the powerful.

Better to showcase allegiance and his strength—at least, some portions of it. Flight, without the use of a sword, spoke of high degrees of mobility. A powerful spiritual sense or other forms of perception that were missed by those in charge spoke of a watchful and paranoid individual. His flawless aura control that evaded even the most vigorous of probings, a mark of his skill as a gatherer and ability to escape into the wild.

All of which led one to presume that any action against him would result in, at the least, his successful escape.

And if the Verdant Green Waters had an issue with his use of the sect robes, they should have expelled him entirely from the sect. They could, also, come and find him and discuss the matter directly. Until then, better to act in his best interest and ask forgiveness later.

Or not at all.

"Imperial edict," Captain Ren explained stiffly. "No city is allowed to have more than a few licensed buildings built outside the wall." He gestured to the scattering of small stalls and inns set outside, many of which looked rather ramshackle and prone to being torn down. "These are illegal. In a day, a few at most, they will be demolished. You see, all buildings within the city are taxed. Those outside are not. King Yu the Magnificent, two hundred eighteen years ago, issued the imperial edict to combat further tax evasion."

Nearby, one of the men working an impromptu inn spat to the side. He made sure not to do so on the road itself or anywhere near the group, but his distaste was obvious. It must be a strange life, to have your business destroyed every few days at the whims of the guards within. Yet they still persisted in such endeavors.

"Is there a lot of business then, to make it worthwhile?" Wu Ying asked. Surely waiting a little longer to enter the city was no major concern, no matter how long the travel. Even now, in the height of the day, the line to enter the city was only a dozen or so wagons long.

Of course, the guard captain and himself cut past the line for the massive gates, the waiting squadron of guards nodding to the captain as he passed.

"Of the distasteful kind, yes." Captain Ren's nose wrinkled. "Some have no desire to pay the entrance tax. Others bring restricted goods or pass on such restricted goods to those with the proper licenses outside." He lowered his voice as he continued. "Then there's the clansmen. We still get them from the north or the marshes, and those we don't allow into the city. So they do business out there."

Once inside, the captain became significantly less loquacious. No wonder, since the volume from the crowd was enough to drown out any but the loudest voices. On top of that, the man watched as Wu Ying took in the sights and sounds, floating the occasional coin to a vendor or food stall.

"Hungry?" Captain Ren asked when Wu Ying picked up his eighth snack on their short trip, this one a leaf-wrapped roll of deep-fried beancurds stuffed with minced tenderloin and bamboo shoots.

Wu Ying gobbled down the roll, wiping at his mouth with a thumb. "I find myself missing food cooked by others after spending so much time in the wilds." Gesturing down the main road they traversed, their horses picking their way sedately upward to the massive fort and nobleman's residence, he continued. "I also find that food and entertainment are the hallmarks of many kingdoms."

Captain Ren smiled. "Yes, the Viscount is justly proud of our chefs. We emphasize the freshness of our ingredients, the speed and the lightness of touch required to prepare a proper dish so as not to mar the ingredients." Gesturing back to the harbor, he continued. "More so, we're fortunate to have access to some of the best locations for such ingredients."

Wu Ying nodded, eyeing Captain Ren sideways. He had to ask. "A connoisseur yourself, then?"

Captain Ren laughed a little. "One must, in my master's employ."

"Ah…"

And wasn't that an interesting tidbit. Suddenly, Wu Ying was interested in meeting this redoubtable Viscount. What kind of man hired a broken Core Formation cultivator and yet engendered such loyalty and devotion from a man who seemed so dour otherwise?

Chapter 31

The Viscount defied a number of Wu Ying's expectations. Firstly, the fact that she should have been named Viscountess, though the use of non-gendered terminology might have been a peculiarity of the kingdom's traditions. Secondly, the artful method the fort and its internal layout had employed to block his spiritual and wind senses, with the suppression strengthening as they reached the internal court room itself which had leaked not an iota of her presence.

And lastly, the simple fact that the Viscount was a child. Nine years old, with the serious demeanor of one who had had a burden placed upon them all too young. Her hair was piled up, held back by the headdress she was forced to wear, her clothing stiff and layered to force her to sit upright.

"Viscount Khao. I present to you Cultivator Long Wu Ying of the Verdant Green Waters Sect." A deep bow from the captain that Wu Ying copied—though not as deeply. There were, of course, certain degrees of courtesy and subtleties of allegiances that had to be maintained and conveyed by the depth of one's obeisance to another.

"The Verdant Gatherer?" Viscount Khao said, eyes shining brightly. "Oh, my. So they were right!"

Wu Ying hesitated, surprised. "That… is not a title I have heard in many years."

Viscount Khao smiled. "Your coming was foretold."

"By who?" Wu Ying said, on guard.

If she noticed, the Viscount showed no sign. Captain Ren, on the other hand, let his hand drop to the short sword he still carried, as did the quartet of guards in the court room. Two directly beside the Viscount, two at the doors. And another four, hidden above in alcoves with javelins—enchanted and empowered—ready to throw if necessary.

"Mmm… one moment." She reached downward, finding the delicate porcelain white-and-blue bell on the table beside her. She rang it, the sound echoing through the pillared court room, the entire location barely forty feet long. It followed much of the design of the fort itself, where space was at a premium and the furnishings, while luxurious and of the finest quality, were sparse.

From a side door, an official clad in the black robes of a scholar appeared. She leaned over to whisper her instructions before the man scurried out, leaving Wu Ying to ponder the words the wind had brought him.

"*Bring the scroll,*" she had said.

What scroll indeed? Still, unless it had been enchanted and imbued with a killing dao, it was unlikely to be too dangerous.

He eyed the Viscount, who looked all too satisfied with herself, and decided that asking would not get him the answers he needed. So that only left fleeing before the scroll was brought, or patience.

In that sense, there was little to be said. He would do what was necessary and see what they had to say, because he was tired of running. Anyway, the scroll was unlikely to be directly dangerous. Curiosity pulled at him, and when the scroll was carried forth on a pillow by the black-clad servant, Wu Ying lifted the paper with a touch of wind to carry it over to spin before him.

Ignoring the considering looks of the others, Wu Ying turned the scroll over and over. His spiritual senses probed it too, verifying that it was no more than the piece of parchment paper it seemed. The only object of surprise, in fact, was the seal. A familiar seal of the Verdant Green Waters Sect, a design only meant for use by the Elders. Personalized further by the name of the owner along the edges.

Elder Sister.

Wu Ying blinked, a sudden lump in his throat and unshed tears in his eyes. His hands drifted upward and caught the still-floating document, turning it such that the seal was facing him. His finger traced the red wax, feeling at the edges and verifying its contents. Touching it brought him closer to her and to his friends, closer than he had been in years.

He fought down the surging emotions, doing his best to keep his face serene. He knew he had failed, revealed a weakness to be exploited perhaps. He could not find the energy to care at the moment.

Still, rather than open the scroll, he placed it within one of his storage rings.

"My thanks for conveying the message to myself," Wu Ying said. "It is… fortunate… that the divinations brought it to me. I look forward to reading the contents."

"But you won't now," Viscount Khao said disappointedly. She pouted at Wu Ying, looking put out at not learning the contents.

"I wish to savor the news within, if possible," Wu Ying said. "News from the Sect is rare, for myself."

Viscount Khao made a face, but then her gaze darted to the side. Captain Ren was giving her a stern look, which made the Viscount straighten her posture and smoothen out her features. "Of course. Well, I offer you residence within our fort. I understand you have spent much time in the deep wilds. I am certain you wish to rest and cleanse oneself. Perhaps we can speak further, when you've rested?"

Fascinating. Obviously, there was something they wanted from him. Yet they were polite about it. Whatever they needed from him—and he could guess, being a gatherer—was not urgent.

"My thanks, Viscount Khao, for your consideration," Wu Ying said. "I am a little weary and would be grateful for a bath and a place to lay my burdens down."

"Then rest you shall." She rang the bell again and instructed the servant to show Wu Ying to his quarters. No mention of getting them ready though, which meant this was all planned.

Curiouser and curiouser.

***

In the privacy of his rooms—located in the northwest corner of the fort and thus leading to open air and the plains beyond—Wu Ying finished setting up the simple protective talismans he carried. He stared at the half dozen talismans he had left, knowing he would need to go shopping soon. Even though his preference was the reusable defensive formation flags he had acquired, talismans were easy to set up, quick to take down, and most importantly, more flexible. Perfect, for example, to create a ward against eavesdropping and to alert him if someone entered his room without notice.

Of course, there were significant disadvantages. Talismans were, by nature of the material used for most, less powerful than formation flags. Subtle and skilled use of senses or daos could bypass a series of talisman-created wards, and it required little effort to break them. The simpler and more focused the use of a talisman, the more powerful it was.

They were also, by their very nature, a disposable item. It was why in general, purchasing talismans was easier and often cheaper than purchasing formation flags.

In this case, Wu Ying had deployed a paired series of talismans to ward his room. They could not stop someone from entering, but if either were tripped, Wu Ying would be alerted.

Even that much, he had to admit, was an over-paranoid reaction. His host had done nothing to make him suspect treachery. Yet as a lone cultivator with neither the backing of his Sect close at hand nor the aid of companions, Wu Ying had learnt to exercise caution.

The room was spartan and small. A portion of the room, partitioned away by a silk privacy screen, contained the oval wooden bath, already filled and steaming. Small runes, powered by a tiny demonic spirit core, kept the water warm and clean. The wooden bed in the other corner had a stuffed silk futon to provide comfort, a lighter silk blanket folded at the bottom of the bed. Delicate embroidery covered both futon sheet and blanket, the serene scene depicted reminiscent of the world outside. Fishing fleet, gentle waves, and the fish they sought to haul, all delicately and well embroidered.

The only other pieces of equipment were a desk, pushed up against the window, and a chair. Calligraphy brush and paper were supplied for use if Wu Ying so wished it.

Meager but high quality work. Just like the rest of the fort.

Taking the seat beside the table, Wu Ying summoned the scroll to hand. He turned it over once more, verifying that the seal had neither been tampered with nor trapped. After long perusal, he deemed it safe and untouched. Or done by one who had much more skill than him.

A depressing, paranoid, but necessary thought.

Then he had delayed enough. His finger slid under the wax seal and he broke it open, the smooth parchment playing across his fingers.

Dear Junior Brother,

It has been many years since we last communicated. I am assured by Elder Tan that you are well at the time of the receipt of this message. They tell me that you have grown strong in your cultivation path, that you have formed a Core and that you continue to grow, embracing the wind and developing your Body Cultivation.

Stories of your travels and your activity have filtered to us, of the mysterious gatherer clad in green robes who has fought spirit beasts, defeated corrupt noblemen, and seen off bandits, all while somehow having the right spirit herb to save the princess or detoxify a village.

Obviously, stories have a tendency to be exaggerated. Still, congratulations on all your successes and commiserations on your fame.

I apologize further on the delay in getting this message to you. As you know, I was in secluded cultivation for a time, and additional complications arose in the Sect that precluded contact. It was only recently that it was possible, and at that time, your success in embracing the wind as deeply as you have clouded divination attempts significantly.

The wind is fickle and so is your future.

Understand that this is the third message sent by myself as divined by Elder Tan.

Know that the Sect and myself look forward to your return. That your parents are in good health, though aging like all mortals do. Your friends continue to grow in strength, some in startling directions.

Most of all, know that you are where you need to be at this moment in time.

May you be guided by the Dao in all your decisions.

Your Senior Sister;

Yang Fa Yuan

Wu Ying stared at the message for a long moment, reading it over and over. A part of him found it amusing, the way it was both highly personal and yet impartial. It was very much a letter only his Elder Sister could write, he felt.

Still, his gaze lingered on a few spots. The acknowledgement that his banishment was over, as far as the Sect was concerned. That his parents were well, though likely missing him. It would not be said, of course, for they would never wish to intrude upon his path. That they were aging gracefully, but nonetheless like all mortals do.

He breathed deeply, trying to shake away the pain that clutched at his chest. The tears that gathered around his eyes. He missed them, missed his family, his friends, and even the familiar routine and sights of the Sect.

Travel was important, travel was central to who, what he had become. Yet he was human. All too mortal, all too prone to heartache and loneliness and loss. Too often, his time was spent in the wilderness, bereft of mortal companionship. Beset on all sides by unseen threats, such that nary a word might pass his lips for days.

He missed them and, on the worst days, ached for the familiar, for those he had once considered bond mates. Almost, almost, the letter was his undoing, as a desire to return home, to rest and to stop traveling for a time, rose within him. A feeling that was nearly impossible to stem.

He stepped closer toward the window, wishing to let himself pass through it, to enter the skies and fly away. To return home and see parents and friends, to abandon his path.

Yet a single line held him back. Perhaps she had known what would happen when he received the letter. Perhaps his reaction had been divined. Or perhaps it was but happenstance.

But the reassurance that he was where he needed to be held him in place.

Need and want warred within his soul.

The deep, soul ache of loneliness and homesickness throbbed in his chest. Tears dripped as he felt the depths of his isolation, his otherness. In a city so unlike any other, whose sights and smells were alien to him, Wu Ying teetered on the edge of abandoning his journey.

Eventually though, that faded. Eventually, he looked down and noted that the scroll had further length to unroll and a tiny arrow pointing to the left[41]. He frowned, unrolling the scroll to find another message.

It's been boring since you left. Come back when you can but don't forget to bring some snacks!

Tou He

The laughter started from his stomach, bubbling up through his chest before breaching his throat and spilling outward. He ended up dropping the scroll, clutching the table as he laughed and laughed, the final message from his friend, his best friend, breaking through the aching melancholy that had settled over him.

From the corner of his room, Wu Ying laughed and remembered that all things passed. In the end, even the wind returned to where it had been. He would trust in his friends, in his family, that they would still be there when he returned.

***

"My thanks, Viscount Khao, for your patience," Wu Ying said later that evening. The group had reconvened after a pleasant dinner, where conversation had revolved around local delicacies, spirit beasts, and other details about the city and province itself. In other words,

---

[41] Reminder that Chinese is written vertically, from right to left. So to reveal more, you would unroll additional lines to the left in a scroll.

nothing of import. Only now, in the private study of the Viscount, did the conversation turn to more serious concerns.

"Not at all. It's easy to get tired after a lot of travel," the Viscount replied, hiding a slight yawn beneath a hastily raised cup of mung bean juice. The boiled water from fresh mung beans was meant to be good for the stomach, and the young Viscount had been sipping on the drink the entire dinner. "Not that I've had a chance to travel much."

"Viscount, you know—" Captain Ren began.

"I know," she cut him off waspishly, then stopped and shook her head. "I'm sorry. I didn't mean that. It's…"

"I understand," Captain Ren said, glancing at Wu Ying and making the Viscount blush.

"Cultivator Long," she began, sweetly and brightly, "I understand you're a wandering gatherer of some skill and fame."

"Some little skill, yes."

Still brightly, the Viscount continued. "Have you done much aquatic gathering?"

"In lakes and ponds, yes," Wu Ying replied. "Lotuses have quite the variety of elemental types, along with their nutritional value and use in medicinal baths. They are the most common, though the least of the items I've gathered."

"But nothing from the ocean?"

"This is the first time I've journeyed to it," Wu Ying said. "I have done some minor collecting of seaweed that has washed against the shores and spoken with some villagers of the process. But nothing of great value."

He had learned that lesson well enough. Best to find out what local governments felt about a wandering cultivator picking his way through their lands. Either that or avoid them entirely. In this case, with larger kingdoms making an appearance, making himself known and understanding the basic laws involved was useful. Gathering in the wilds was one thing, but along the oceans in sight of others? Better to be careful.

Their laws likely—he believed—followed the old laws set forth by the Yellow Emperor, but it was always best to ascertain such facts for oneself.

Viscount Khao nodded, looking at Captain Ren. There was a question in her eyes that he answered with a short nod.

"Then perhaps we can come to a deal," she said with a smile. "If you're willing, that is."

"A deal?" Wu Ying said.

"We are in need of a gatherer to acquire certain items. However, these items are not on land but within the ocean." She smiled grimly, pain dancing in the depth of her eyes. "I will not lie to you. The last two gatherers we sent, the ones normally tasked with the process of acquiring the items, died in their attempt."

"It seems this must be an item of great consequence," Wu Ying said slowly.

"It is. It is the bedrock of my family's wealth and our existence in this land." She touched her chest. "Without providing this tithe to the king, our very existence as a noble house is at jeopardy."

"Why tell me all this?" Wu Ying asked. "Surely you know that it will make your position more difficult when we negotiate my price."

For the first time, a clearly mischievous look crossed the young girl's face. She looked at Wu Ying, her eyes widening. "But Auntie Yang said that you're a real hero of justice and would not let a poor child be sent to be executed. Was she wrong?"

Wu Ying reared back a little, caught off-guard by the swift change in decorum and emotion. "She—she—she did not say that!"

Giggling, the Viscount pulled her legs upward, wrapping her calves in a tight embrace. Captain Ren frowned as she did so but chose not to speak. "She didn't. But the stories of the Verdant Gatherer all agree on that point."

"They do not," Wu Ying said, his chin rising. "I've heard some of them too. About how I'm a demon who steals a merchant's hard-earned goods. Or destroyed a sect, leaving their patriarch crippled and their Elders injured, all for daring to cheat me."

"Did you do that?" Captain Ren asked.

"No," Wu Ying said. "I did fight my way out of a heretical sect once, and some members were injured during the process." He rubbed his chin. "And I did have a challenge with the patriarch of a small sect, only a dozen members strong, and in the battle I did cripple him."

The captain's eyes narrowed. Wu Ying held out a hand, stalling his question to explain further.

"He and his sect were trying to rob me. They made up a challenge then forced me to duel him," Wu Ying said. "It was a lucky blow anyway."

Remembering the all-too-brief fight, Wu Ying could not help but smile. The patriarch, a wood-aspected fighter, had not expected Wu Ying to use his wind aspect to shove the man forward. The fact that the wind had, for its own reasons, come roaring forward with greater strength than normal had caught them both with surprise. The cut, meant to injure, had ended with the patriarch crippled and nearly dead.

That was the unfortunate fact of battle though. Sometimes, no matter how good you were, no matter your intentions, injuries—bad injuries—occurred. Stepping into the ring, raising one's fist, refusing to turn aside and control one's ego meant that you accepted all outcomes.

Dire and crippling as well as victorious and happy.

"As you said," Viscount Khao said, her voice muffled behind her knees. "Distorted stories. Most of them speak of a man who will aid those who need it. Will you aid me then?" Softer now, more desperate. "Please?"

Really, when asked so directly and in such a manner, what was he to do?

Chapter 32

The next morning, Wu Ying met his new teacher below the fort itself, in a deep pool dug into the earth itself by the initial builders. Multiple floors had to be crossed to enter the reservoir, long chains of buckets set aside behind a gated entrance, while glowing spirit stones and enchantments kept the entire emergency water reservoir both fresh and clean.

The man who waited for Wu Ying was half-dressed, only a pair of wrapped cloths covering his lower body as he stretched against the cold stone floor. His hair, unlike the common standards, was short, barely covering the nape of his neck, and his skin was deeply bronzed all over. A testament to long days spent so dressed.

When the bobbing spirit lamp Wu Ying carried announced his presence, the man stood and arched his back into a full stretch. Captain Ren, leading Wu Ying down the passageway, made the introductions.

"Cultivator Long, this is Master Diver Wang Feng Mei. He will be your teacher," Captain Ren said, introducing the man.

A simple extension of Wu Ying's spiritual sense was enough to ascertain that Master Diver Wang Ren was no more than a high Body Cleansing cultivator. Stronger than the majority of mortals, but nothing special at all. Yet he moved with lithesome grace as he bowed, hands clasped.

"Thank you, captain. I am honored to meet you, Cultivator Long. I understand that I am to provide some small instruction in the ways of the ocean?" Master Diver Wang said. His voice was cultured and smooth, relaxed even as he interacted with Wu Ying and the captain.

"Yes." Wu Ying grinned. "I can swim, but I must admit, my skills are likely significantly below your lowest worker." He shrugged. "The rivers are strong, but the ocean, I hear, is truly treacherous."

"She can be," Feng Mei said, then gestured at Wu Ying. "If you'll prepare yourself, we will begin by testing your current standards." He indicated the reservoir that stretched into the distance, smiling. "Afterward, we shall practice diving and work on your ability to hold your breath, all of which will be necessary."

"And what is the minimum time required, do you think, for our task?" Wu Ying said. "What did my predecessors do?"

Feng Mei hesitated, looking at Captain Ren. Only when the captain nodded did he dare answer truthfully. "A Master Diver can hold their breath for twenty minutes[42] at a time while working. Your predecessors managed to stay underwater for an hour at least."

"At least?" Wu Ying said, probing.

---

[42] Human divers have held their breath for a record twenty-five minutes. Oyster divers routinely do so for two minutes at a time, while working hard and doing hundred of dives a day. Since these are all cultivators, I extended the timing a little.

"Yes. One of those lost, the previous Master Gatherer of the Seas, had an elemental water body and a dao of the sea. He was known to spend months meditating under the water to consolidate his own path," Feng Mei replied.

Wu Ying turned fully to Captain Ren, crossing his arms in annoyance. "You would have thought someone would have mentioned this last night."

"It slipped my mind," Captain Ren said.

"Mmmm...." Wu Ying walked over to the edge of the reservoir, staring at the inky blackness of the shadowed waters in thought. Eventually, he turned to the others, his lips pressed tight. "It seems that the acquisition of the seven Lesser Serpent Pearls will be difficult indeed."

"We will, as promised, provide you what aid we can," Captain Ren replied smoothly. "Including full access to the Provincial Armory and the family library."

Wu Ying grunted in acknowledgement of the captain's words. The opportunity to receive training in the methods utilized in the province, along with access to their library, was just too good to pass up. Though it was likely something truly dangerous had taken residence near the Lesser Serpent Oysters, Wu Ying assumed he could do what he did whenever he was faced with overwhelming strength watching over something he wished to acquire.

He'd just sneak in and steal it.

To do that, he would need to acquire the skills to traverse the ocean smoothly. Considering the entire process was happening underwater, that meant training.

Shrugging off his robes, Wu Ying committed himself to hours of training. Once he was dressed similarly to the Dive Master, he listened to the man's instructions before entering the reservoir, beginning the process of familiarizing himself with the water properly.

First, swimming. Then, diving. Then, underwater movement. And finally, at the end, gathering itself.

***

"Welcome to the library." The old woman who greeted Wu Ying and the captain as they entered the darkened rooms deep within the fortress wielded a cane in one hand, using it more to point and gesture than as a walking aid. "The first section consists of a series of cultivation and martial works meant for Body Cleansing and Energy Storage cultivators. Most of the works collected by the family have been focused on dark, deep, and water elements, with some minor dabbling into beast taming—of the aquatic variety—and spirit conjuration. Nothing of interest to you."

Wu Ying inclined his head, though he let his spiritual sense extend to read titles as he passed. As the librarian had related, none of it was particularly interesting. There were some combat manuals, but many were sword and shield arts that were familiar to him, being manuals in popular circulation among cultivators. Others—like the harpoon, trident, or the rowing oar—were of little interest.

She led the way through the multiple shelves, holding the spirit lantern before her as she reached the end of the room and the doorway before it. The solid wood door was reinforced with dark iron bands and required a series of keys to open, two of which the librarian held and the third by Captain Ren.

Curious that the captain had a key. After all, if he was sent to deal with matters, how were they to access the room? Or if he was slain? Dismissing the impracticalities of their security arrangements, Wu Ying let his senses delve deeper into the room.

Unlike the much larger—if narrower—room they had exited, this room barely held a half dozen bookcases. Each bookcase was stacked with documents, though they were often grouped and separated via small, carved bookends.

Following the librarian dutifully, Wu Ying tilted his head from side to side as she walked around the walls of the room, activating the enchantments that illuminated the room from above. When she was done, she stood before Wu Ying, letting the bottom of her cane tap the floor in impatience.

"Finished prying?" she said waspishly.

"Not yet, but you can continue," Wu Ying said, refusing to be intimidated.

She sniffed, before indicating with her free hand. "These works are the pride of the family. Meant for loyal servants and direct members of the main line, it includes the family martial techniques as well as cultivation manuals for the Core Formation and Nascent Soul stages."

Wu Ying considered pointing out that her reaction to him was a little overdone, especially when the Viscount herself had ordered the librarian—her grandaunt—to show him the library. Yet Wu Ying chose not to. There was little gain in such a confrontation.

"And the cultivation exercises and techniques for deep water navigation and movement?" Wu Ying said, searching the shelves.

"This way." Stomping over to a shelf, she waved her hand up and down. "You can find all the better forms here." A beat, then she pointed farther into the room, where a lone table sat. "You are not allowed to remove any work from this location. I will be watching. It will be opened to you every day in the afternoon for the next two months. At which point, you will either have succeeded or failed. Questions?"

Wu Ying shook his head and watched as she took a seat at the table, arms crossed. Looking around him at the mounds of works available, he began the process of sieving through the documents. He could have asked for help, but considering the relative size of the location and her antagonistic nature, he felt no desire to open himself up to potential problems.

As he went through the stacks of manuals, scrolls, and other documents, Wu Ying soon realized that the sorting process would be faster than he had expected. Powerful as the family might have been, they were not a sect and the volume of information they possessed was limited. Each stack, separated by the carved bookends, pertained to a single technique, with the majority of the other documents being treatises, similar and supporting works, or observations and journals of past practitioners.

The library was, in effect, a perfect showcase of a family that had delved deeply into a single technique, unlike the sects he was used to, which often went much broader. Similar, then, to other northeastern clans, which was no surprise. After all, this kingdom had originated from a singular family gaining in strength sufficiently to impose their dominion over others.

Since then, the nobles had been cultivators and overlords, with the cultivation sects nearly nonexistent. Instead, cultivation academies had been created and sponsored by the nobles, of which the largest and most prestigious was within the capital itself.

What it meant was that instead of over a hundred-plus techniques to scan through, he only had about two score. Many he could discard immediately, like Core Formation and the pair of Nascent Soul cultivation techniques. He did make note to review those Nascent Soul techniques for later, wanting to review them in greater detail to expand upon his understanding of the process. But in those cases, it was likely the bare dozen or so journals and treatises would offer greater enlightenment than the actual manual itself.

Same with the dozen or so works on Body Cultivation. After flipping through the manuals, Wu Ying's nose wrinkled. Split across the common elemental types among the clan, they were even more useless to him as they ended mostly in the elemental body stage. Afterward, the discussion grew more esoteric, an exhortation to continue delving into the dao of the specific elements with only minor guideposts on further medicinal baths that the particular author had found useful.

A common thread, in some ways, for works in what could be considered the Nascent Soul level. Once one gained a Greater or Peak understanding of the element, the next step often grew vague as the transition into the specific elemental body was badly recorded. It delved into the daos of the element, of a painful process of subsuming oneself into the specific elemental body and embodying it. A process that had varying results depending on the individual and cultivation method.

Overall, useless.

So too the martial techniques. There were not many. In fact, he found only four works. Of interest was the Khao family sword technique known as the Breaking Wave. The others, wielding an oar—really, just a staff with a heavy weight at the end—or a harpoon was of little interest to Wu Ying, nor was the spear technique.

In the end, Wu Ying found most useful the soul cultivation exercises and myriad water movement techniques. He wondered briefly if, knowing this, that was why the Viscount had allowed his victory in gaining access. Perhaps not her own idea, but an advisor's. It boggled the mind that a nine-year-old might be that conniving.

The Graceful Turtle, Friends of the Ocean, Silverfish Darts… movement techniques were abundant, all of which consisted of swimming techniques. Many supplemented their strength from the elemental or dao understandings of their user, presuming a dark or water element. Useless, again, for Wu Ying.

Yet they were not the only techniques. Of the nine or so techniques, two required no dao or corresponding element to use, and those he set aside for further perusal. The Sea Serpent's Grace and the innocuous sounding Floating Leaf both seemed appropriate for his needs.

Then, fighting techniques. Those were more numerous, though he faced the same issues. After culling those techniques that presumed a dao or element of use within the water, Wu Ying found himself with a half dozen fighting techniques that might suit his situation.

Bringing the documents to the table, Wu Ying settled himself beside the silent, unhappy librarian for a long night of reading.

***

If anything, studying gathering and harvesting from the myriad fishermen, kelp gatherers, shellfish and pearl gatherers, and other professionals was the least arduous part of his preparations. Wu Ying only managed to begin such lessons a week after his initial agreement with the Viscount, after the Dive Master had deemed Wu Ying no longer a constant embarrassment in the water.

Wu Ying found the Dive Master a little reminiscent of Master Cheng, where adequate was insufficient and excellence the minimum. Hours of perfecting swimming strokes back and forth across the large reservoir with minor corrections every moment. Then once the man was happy with Wu Ying's basic swimming technique, they progressed to diving.

Up and down the reservoir, diving as deep as he could with a single breath before he was forced to ascend. At first, he was unable to reach the bottom of the reservoir, little glints of light at the bottom beckoning him onward. Only when he could reach the swaying lights— surprise registering as he spotted the luminescent kelp that illuminated the bottom—did Feng Mei allow him to begin his other studies.

Wu Ying started by learning the basics of kelp growing, harvesting, and preparation. He walked the mudflats with the fishermen during the low tide, striding between the sunken bamboo poles, lines affixed with living kelp strung between the rows. They showed him the barely immersed seaweed, how to cut the branches, and when to replace the older kelp with newer, fresher plants, as well as common diseases to watch for.

Then after harvesting, it was the process of drying the seaweed. He was shown the methods most often used by the residents, the wooden slats where the seaweed was laid out to dry in the air. They also showed him other methods to complete the same tasks. Poles where the harvest was hung up to be blown dry. Coconut, banana, or lotus leaves the seaweed was dried upon, soaking up the ambient smell and taste of the vegetation. Even the faster methods of warming over kilns and apothecarists' cauldrons, where pills and other herbs boiled to convey taste and the benefits of the spiritual herbs.

They spent a good portion of the first week of his lessons on just the kelp and other seaweed, the flora within the oceans varied and fascinating to the young cultivator. Hours late in the night were spent poring over documents, much of it copied into his journal as he learned about an ecology he had never before experienced.

His days were filled with constant study, from speaking with apothecarists about substitutions for new spirit herbs and the creation of new recipes, trading pointers and ingredients with gardeners and harvesters to further studies, and practice with Feng Mei and the aquatic gatherers. The deluge of information was constant, and only the clear mind offered to him by greater cultivation levels and the reduction in hours required for rest allowed him to keep ahead of the constant demands. Long into the night he would study the tomes, when work in the ocean was no longer viable and his trainers required sleep.

Then when the librarian finally chased him out, Wu Ying would take a turn along the top of the tower, practicing the techniques he had studied. On the open tower roof, where the wind howled, he performed the movements and the chi flows of the Viscount's techniques.

The Sea Serpent's Grace was the first cultivation exercise he practiced, knowing ease of motion was important. It was an arduous process since the core of the movement technique focused upon the control of the ocean in proximity to an individual. To do so, Wu Ying had to convert his chi into water chi—a process that was doubly taxing, since he had to first convert his chi into neutral chi then aspect it to water—before exuding it into his aura.

The greatest point of conflict, however, was the Never Empty Wine Pot method. His adjustments to the aura technique had created a twisting, tornado defense and suction to his aura, a process that had badly interacted with the new requirements of the Sea Serpent's Grace.

Multiple times Wu Ying found himself flinching as he scoured his skin clear of flesh or was fed a backlash of water or wind chi into his meridians. More than once, the smarting pain from an overstrained cultivation base forced him to put a hold to his practice, turning to other forms of training while he waited for his body to heal.

Most often, he turned to practicing the fighting techniques. The majority of the manuals began with an introduction to fighting underwater, the vagaries and complexities that moving within a liquid brought about. In this case, due to his ascension to Core Formation and thus access to the sky, many of the concepts were not foreign. Others, however, were of import, as crutches he had used while battling or traveling through the sky were no longer available underwater.

Chief among them, the lack of strong footing. In the sky, Wu Ying would conjure steps of solid air when necessary to provide grounding and pivot points for his attacks, allowing him to do battle almost as though he were on the ground. The wind danced to his whims, but the water would refuse to do his bidding. He could not pivot, thrust, or otherwise bear down on his attacks.

Indeed, many of the fighting techniques spoke of maneuverability, grappling close to provide a firm point of contact before unleashing a strike. Crushing motions, techniques that mimicked the biting techniques of fish and other serpents, and less common, deadly thrusts from built-up momentum were the preferred forms of fatal assaults.

Even basic techniques that Wu Ying had relied upon were of lesser use. Projected blades of chi were drowned out by the ever-present water chi, the attacks fading within a short distance. On the other hand, his sword intent, the ability to sharpen his blade and hand by reforming his chi and coating his attacks in intent, were not diminished.

Such theorems and theories, he soaked in and later would put to test within the reservoir. Once Wu Ying chose to concentrate only upon the Sea Serpent's Grace movement technique, no longer employing the modified Never Empty Wine Pot method, he found himself progressing at a blistering pace.

In fact, the first time he employed the technique fully within the water was also the first time he managed to land a strike upon Feng Mei, his sudden burst of acceleration catching the Dive Master by surprise. Reducing the pull of water upon his body, making him quicker with each powerful stroke, benefited Wu Ying immensely. The greater strength and speed of a Core Formation and Body Cultivator finally made itself known as poor technique fell aside.

Soon after, as Wu Ying's progress with the technique grew, Feng Mei no longer posed a threat individually. At that time, their training was taken outdoors into the ocean, where multiple members of the guard and other divers took part in the newly created game of "tagging" Wu Ying.

In such a way, studying, learning, and progressing his skills in the ocean, days became weeks and then months. Soon enough, the deadline loomed and the time for preparations was over.

Chapter 33

"They arrive in six days," Viscount Khao said to Wu Ying over breakfast, eyes gleaming with worry. Even seated, she seemed to vibrate with concern. "I know you understand how important it is to send the Pearls back to the king but—"

"It will be done. Today," Wu Ying said, holding up a hand. "If the weather had permitted, we would have left two days ago. But the storm that came in made it impossible."

"Not impossible, just much more dangerous," Captain Ren said easily. "I would not risk our men to the ocean when it churned like that. Nor would our master ask that of us."

The Viscount made a little moue before flopping back against her chair and its cushions, staring at Wu Ying over the edges of her robe that had begun to ride up as she slumped. "And you're sure you can do it?"

"Nothing in this world is certain." Sensing her rising tension, Wu Ying continued. "However, I expect that it should be viable. It would be best if we knew what had happened before…"

"My diviners continue to offer nothing of import." Viscount Khao's voice rose, mimicking a stilted way of speaking. "'Dark shadows, myriad tails that overshadow the world. It slumbers and wakes, swallowing the light of the heavens… 'ware the approach. 'Ware your departure.'"

"Serpent?" Wu Ying said. Why did it have to be snakes?

"It's diviners. It could be a real serpent, poetic language, or just a shadow," Captain Ren pointed out.

"Or betrayal!" Viscount Khao said, her voice rising in an attempt to sound ominous.

"Viscount!" Captain Ren said, sounding scandalized.

Wu Ying chuckled, shaking his head. Over the few months he had been present, the Viscount had slowly thawed, her initial formality giving way to the natural exuberance of a child and added familiarity. Waving a hand to calm the captain, he leaned forward and whispered, "Yes, betrayal. By me."

She gasped theatrically, then grew serious, her eyes wide. Her lower lip quivered as emotions threatened her control. "You wouldn't, would you?"

"He would not," Captain Ren assured her, pushing his plate aside and crossing his arms. "This is why we do not joke about such matters. It leads to misunderstandings and hurt feelings. Understand?"

Viscount Khao lowered her head, chastised, and tried to hide a little sniffle. Wu Ying winced, but other than assuring her he really would not, he could do little else.

The remainder of breakfast was more subdued and soon complete, with Wu Ying swallowing the last of the fish congee before standing.

"With your leave, Viscount."

"Go. The sea's blessing on you," Viscount Khao said solemnly.

Captain Ren stood too, following Wu Ying. He, three squads of his best men, and the same number of divers would accompany Wu Ying on this last, desperate attempt to retrieve the Lesser Serpent Pearls.

***

The group that gathered at the harbor was large and myriad. Three squads of Captain Ren's best guard, himself included. Another dozen divers, the best that the province had to offer. Five captains and their vice-captains, all of whom represented the junks they would set forth upon. And, of course, numerous sailors, many of whom were on the ships themselves, making ready.

"The tide is going out, so I shall make this quick," Captain Ren said. "You've all heard this before, but I will emphasize, our mission is vital to our province. Without the pearls, the Viscount has no standing in court. Another will be assigned this land, and we all know who wants it."

Grumbles arose from all around, cut off quickly by Captain Ren's raised hand. Wu Ying had a vague idea too, though he had paid only a little attention to the matter. He had thrown in his lot with the Viscount, so it mattered not who he angered beyond the most cursory of findings.

Anyway, he was but a contractor doing a job. Surely no reasonable person would get angry over such a thing? Even in his own mind, Wu Ying could not help but smirk at that thought.

"It will take two days to arrive at our destination. In that time, train if you can, but do not overexert yourself. None of you are replaceable." Captain Ren turned, meeting each person's gaze. "When we arrive, the ships will separate to set up the sea-calming formation and the wider beast-trapping formation. The positioning and safety of the vessels will be the responsibility of the captains"—multiple nods in agreement—"while the creation and care of the formations will be the guards'."

Feet stamped the ground, along with a low growl from the guards.

Captain Ren smiled in approval at their enthusiastic response. "We cannot rely on those being sufficient, which is why the divers will take to the water and deal with any spirit beasts. Once they have cleared the upper depths, Cultivator Long will begin his dive. He—and he alone—will enter the deep. The divers will hold the rafts, awaiting his signal if he requires aid."

This time, there was no outward sign of approval. The opposite in fact, for the divers were unhappy, arms crossed, some glaring at Wu Ying. Though they all had practiced with him, taught him the things that Wu Ying would put to use, none were happy at being relegated to the role of observers. Yet none objected, for such discussions had been completed over the preceding weeks. For all their strength, not a single one was a Core Formation cultivator.

"Cultivator Long will swim to the depths, acquire the pearls from the oysters—a minimum of seven are necessary to meet our quota—and then he will return. We will set sail and return with all due speed, neither dragon nor serpent the wiser."

"And if they learn of it," one captain said, smiling grimly, "it will be all the worse for them. Our harpoons are sharpened, our ballistae loaded. The killing formation will shred their scales and dry their gills, and then we will feast on serpent and dragon alike!"

Roars of approval rose from the group. Wu Ying met Captain Ren's more somber look as the crowd cheered, both realizing the likelihood of death if there was a dragon or serpent beneath. Morale was important, even if such words had likely been spoken by the two previous expeditions.

Whatever awaited them was likely to be more complicated and dangerous than they knew.

And if Wu Ying's heart sped up a little, a thrill chasing down his spine at the thought? If a gleam had entered his eye, well, it was to be expected. He was a wild gatherer after all. If he did not seek the challenge a little, he would not be who he was.

***

Captain Ren found Wu Ying later that day standing at the prow of the flagship, the wind blowing from shore at an angle to their destination. The sails had been trimmed, allowing the ship to tack into the wind to provide them the greatest speed, even as sailors below stood ready to deploy oar and elemental chi if necessary.

"What say the winds, Cultivator Long? Will they aid us in this journey?" Captain Ren asked, leaning against the railing beside Wu Ying.

No surprise, after all this time, that the captain knew of Wu Ying's element. Though perhaps the full details of his cultivation—Body and Soul—were still a puzzle to the captain. At least, Wu Ying hoped so.

"They will," Wu Ying said, tilting his head. "They might even bring us back rapidly. If we need it."

"Your element, the way you interact with it…" Ren Fei trailed off.

"Yes?"

"It's different. From what I have seen others do. The way I do it myself. Others I've seen dictate, control, demand, or become; they are all just part of it. You, you interact as though the winds are separate but not of you."

"Ah…" Wu Ying was caught by surprise. "It, the winds… they are part of me. But not. I can't hope to encompass them, not really." He turned one hand sideways, gesturing at the world around. "It is all of this. How can one man, one person, be all that?"

"Isn't that true of any of our daos? Thinking like that, is that not a guarantee for us to fail?" Ren Fei looked down, touching his stomach just above where his dantian was, and sighed. "Though some of us stumbled earlier than others."

Wu Ying's lips tightened, his gaze following Ren Fei's motion. "I'm sorry. About…" He was uncertain of what to say. His failure? His lack of timing or patience? "About it all."

"No need," Ren Fei said. "I knew I could not ascend, but we needed—the family needed another Core Formation cultivator. It was a risk I took for the province, and I'd do it again. Not all of us were meant for the heights of cultivation anyway." He laughed suddenly, depreciatingly. "What is the point of my criticizing your cultivation methods when I have never had a chance myself?"

Wu Ying shook his head. "No, you're not wrong to question me." He rubbed a hand along the railing, consideringly. "In truth, no matter how many cultivation manuals we read, the treatises and the scrolls and the learned words that we attempt to comprehend, all our ways, all our methods, they're just attempts at discerning the undiscernible. Every cultivation method is unique, every cultivator taking a different path to reach the top, and no matter how much we believe we are in the right, most will fail."

"Then why try?" Ren Fei said. "If you think you're wrong, if you are to fail anyway and don't believe you are pursuing the dao correctly, why go on? Why not be content with what you have?"

Wu Ying closed his eyes, hearing the wind whisper, brush its fingers along his hair and his skin, tug at his robes and remind him of its presence. He heard the soft susurration of a heavenly tune, the murmur of the southern wind and the places he had yet to see. Lands, far and wide; people, strangers and friends; experiences, weird and unique.

He opened his eyes and smiled at Ren Fei, holding a hand out to the wind and letting it run through his fingers. "Why ever not? If I have no conviction, the Dao doesn't require it. If I have no confidence, the Dao does not demand it. It is no taskmaster, no disapproving parent. It makes no claims on our actions. It desires no outcomes. Choose or choose not, it will be.

"And so, in choosing to do what we desire, when we desire, for the right reasons in the right time; how can we then be wrong? If no path is right, then no path can be wrong either."

Ren Fei's lips thinned as he listened. Then turning to face Wu Ying fully, he put his hands together and bowed. "Thank you, Cultivator Long. You have left me much to think about."

Wu Ying watched the man retreat, then turned back to face the water. He closed his eyes again, feeling the wind on his face as they cut through the ocean, and smiled, for the eastern wind laughed in his ears. His dantian churned, traces of the heavenly chi called forth from the surroundings and spreading through his body. Strengthening it and his connection.

One step, one li at a time. He would find his way. No matter the obstacles or the doubts.

***

The gull came from high above, stooping in a dive from the sunward direction. Its shadow, small at first, increased in size at an alarming rate. Below it, little figures scrambled, alerted all too late in an attempt to run or hide from the predator.

No screech, no scream from the spirit beast arose as it descended, its target shifting a little as the helmsmen threw their weight behind the tiller, edging the junk aside. It was too little, too late, for even as the sailors trimmed and adjusted the sail so as to catch the wind right, the bird was nearly on them.

Then from below, something rose. Bestial instincts triggered and the gull opened its wing a little, curving aside at the last minute. A twist of light and solid air tore through the space where it had been, even as light glittered off the metal talon of the figure below. Its new opponent was clad in green and white feathers, flying through the air without beating his wings.

Now, the gull cried, unleashing its anger and frustration. Its positioning had been perfect, its prey unaware. No scent, no sight, nothing should have given it away. It had sensed nothing, no threat. None of those leaking, smelly, unsightly pink fleshy things should have been a challenge. All the morning it had stalked them, ever since it first caught sight of the boat.

Now this one was here. And he would pay.

Below, the figure seemed to stagger a little, the noise the gull unleashed leaving it wobbly. The gull banked, rolling around as it flapped its wings, gaining a little more altitude. If it missed the meal below, another meal had served itself to her. Even if it carried a metal talon, it only glowed a little, pulsing like the wind that streamed through its feathers.

The wind…

Again, another shriek, this time of understanding as it dove. It was the one who beckoned the wind to him, who rode it to the sky as though he was its master that had spoilt its plan. Rotting plans, like week-old fish; gone too bad even for the gull to eat.

It dove, white wings pressed tightly against its body, long beak lowered. Wind cut and pulled away as the bird dropped. Below, the little figure stopped rising, seeming to hold still. It swung its talon again, once and then once more, that twisted warping of intent and wind rising to meet the gull.

Futile.

The attack crashed against the gull's aura and its hardened feathers. Though a pair of feathers were lost and a minor cut accrued, it was insufficient to penetrate its defenses. More importantly, the cuts healed over within moments, the blood clotting as the wood gull's chi worked overtime.

Then it was the gull's turn, and wings deployed, cutting its speed as it turned a dive into a swoop at the last minute. No beak attack but talons from below, ready to snatch and grab. Legs rotated forward, its chest rising a little as claws reached.

Only to meet a shield of hardened wind. The shield cracked and compressed, slowing the bird even more, making its steep dive alter course a little as another errant wind struck it.

Then pain as that metal talon entered its chest. The talon tore upward and sideways, and the bird watched as the green and pink bug flew away, gleaming talon now darkened by its own blood. Pain as blood beat, once, twice, then the wound began to close and muscles stitched shut.

Another turn, as the bird flapped its wings, chasing the bug. Now it had him, for they might be on the same level, but the pink fleshy thing was in its domain! It would show the creature who truly ruled the skies!

***

The captain found Ren Fei staring upward, watching the pair of aerial duelists. Wu Ying was nearly impossible to spot, so far up were he and the bird; he a fast-moving speck, the bird a massive moving creature the size of the captain's fist.

"Will the cultivator be okay?" the captain murmured.

"He will be," Ren Fei said, though his voice was uncertain.

"I told him not to. You heard me, yes?" the captain said, looking at Ren Fei with a fixed, almost desperate gaze. "He should not have gone up. If we had lost a man or two, it would not be worth his death."

"I will tell the Viscount you tried to stop him, if it comes to that," Ren Fei said. "But it will not."

"That is the Fisherman's Tragedy up there," the captain said. "It has preyed on our people for decades. Even the old Viscount could not kill it."

"Nor did the old Viscount fall to it." Ren Fei clutched the spear in his hand. He looked longingly upward, to that space he was forever barred from because of his cracked Core. "Cultivator Long is a powerful fighter."

"Your words to the sea goddess's ears," the captain muttered the blessing before he moved away. He had gained what reassurance he had looked for, and now he chivied the sailors to load the ballistae and ready them. Just in case the cultivator did fail.

Dismissing the captain from his mind, Ren Fei watched, hand gripping his enchanted spear. It was nearly an hour, the pair moving farther and closer, swooping at times nearly to skim the waves before rising again, before the fight ended. Wu Ying landed on the junk, stumbling a little as exhaustion threatened to take away his balance. He righted himself, controlling his movements as the junk rolled with the waves, and nodded once to Ren Fei and the captain, both of whom rushed to him.

In the distance, the similarly exhausted massive spirit beast winged away, flapping its wings as it glided back to its nest. It was bloody and tired, feathers scattered across myriad li, patches of torn skin marring its body.

"Cultivator Long!" Ren Fei said, coming up to Wu Ying.

As Wu Ying straightened and conjured a flask of water and drank deeply from it, Ren Fei scanned the man for injuries. There were a few, scrapes along the arms, along one side of his body. They leaked a little, the metallic taste of blood mixing with salt air as the other man stood firmly.

"I am fine," Wu Ying said, putting down his flask . "Tired, but alive. I could not slay it. Its wood aspect is too strong. It kept healing its wounds, no matter how I struck it. I apologize."

"The Fisherman's Tragedy is an old, a very old, problem," the captain said, making a face. "Its mother was a powerful dragon, its cultivation grown stronger on the blood of our people. None have managed to slay it." Then he snorted. "Obviously."

"The captain is right," Ren Fei murmured. "You owe us no apology. The monster is old. We are but lucky that it has not managed to ascend, or else it would be a true terror."

All around, sailors hocked and spat over their shoulder. More than a few made additional warding signs, and all glared at the guard captain for daring to name such an ill omen. The man looked abashed, repeating the gesture himself.

Wu Ying kept from reacting, though he found the entire process a little disgusting. Once they were done, he gestured to the front of the junk. "I understand there is a bath here?"

The captain nodded.

"I'll require its use. You may use seawater for its contents, but I shall need it." Touching his wounds, Wu Ying could not help but wince. "If I am not to go into the water bleeding, much needs to be done."

Both captains could not help but wince, the ship's captain shouting orders and sending his men to scurry.

In the meantime, Ren Fei stepped a little closer, dropping his voice. "Can you dive? You look… tired."

Wu Ying nodded tightly. "What must be done must be done. Now, I should begin cultivating."

Ren Fei's lips tightened at the non-answer. Wu Ying moved aside, taking a cross-legged seat on the deck, the minor pull of environmental chi that was always around him increasing that even the Guard Captain could sense it now. Before, the tug was so gentle that it could have been but the shift of ethereal winds. Now, it was typhoon, focused upon the cultivator with his legs crossed and blood slowly leaking from his wounds.

Staring at the other man, Ren Fei could only lower his head in acknowledgement. Perhaps this was what truly was needed to ascend to immortality. A nature so uncompromising, no matter the uncertainties of the future or the pain in the present, it forged ahead.

If so, he understood why he had never ascended. Or would ever ascend.

Perhaps in the next life.

Chapter 34

The midday sun beat down upon the junks, their anchors deployed to keep them in place. Sails furled, the ballistae had been rolled out, the massive harpoons on the ships angled downward at the ocean itself while others were trained toward the outside of the ring. On small buoys all along the edges, formation flags bobbed, containing the details of what was happening. Additional rafts had been deployed, many with smaller catapults set up to throw furled nets on them, volunteer sailors floating in the dead space between the ships.

In the front of each junk, the guards stood in formation, three in the formation center while the other two in the squad stood watch with javelins and spears at the ready. On the floor, carefully painted formation markers surrounded the three guards within, while formation flags were deployed at the edges, a single massive one in the center of the group.

Chi flowed from the environment, circling the formation flags then flowing through the markers before entering fully to be guided by the guards. There, the chi was gathered as the formation grew in strength, powering itself up to unleash a massive strike when necessary.

In the meantime, in the center of the water, green and blue blood floated, staining the water itself. Occasionally, a limb—human or aquatic—would bob to the surface as the divers fought a desperate battle against the sea life.

Wu Ying watched the proceedings silently, hands clasped behind his back, eyes tracking the limbs and the water. He could not sense what lay within, his spiritual sense falling short as the sheer volume of life—plankton, tiny fish, and massive demonic beasts alike—blanketed his senses.

Beside him, Ren Fei stood dressed in his armor, his enchanted spear resting in his hand. He shifted impatiently, looking at Wu Ying, the captain of the ship, and the water in turn; before finally impatience won out.

"What is taking so wrecking long?" Ren Fei said.

"They said already," Wu Ying murmured. He idly tugged at the emerald-green armor he wore, the skin-tight protection covered by his night robe. He did his best to ignore exactly how exposed he was, for the armor outlined every inch of his muscular form. Even if the Saint-grade armor was a prize of the province's armory and another part of his payment, a part of Wu Ying wished it was not so scandalous. "There are more demonic beasts than usual."

"But why?" Ren Fei growled.

"I'd assume an overabundance of food," the captain murmured. He gestured downward, his voice taking on a tinge of fear. "After all, at least two fleets have fallen here."

"Just one," Ren Fei corrected. "The first expedition only had a single ship, for Master Hue had not expected trouble."

"More fool him," muttered the captain. Ren Fei glared at the captain and the man offered a tight smile, running a hand along the railing and spitting to the side. "No captain worth his salt ever expects anything but trouble from the ocean."

"I think they're done," Wu Ying said, cutting in before the two could continue their bickering. He understood it was a way of relieving tension but arguing amongst themselves was foolish. Anyway, the bubbles which had been rising occasionally seemed to be coming up faster now, and within moments, heads bobbed to the top of the water.

Almost like gasping fish, the divers all opened their mouths when they rose. Yet no hard exhalation of air occurred, each diver trained to allow the air within to escape by itself to preserve energy. As expected, the divers bobbed for a few moments before swimming toward the waiting rafts. Once all divers were aboard, a single man waved to the flagship, making signs that they were ready. Already, guards scrambled among the divers, binding wounds and patching holes in armor and flesh alike.

Wu Ying waved back, then began the process of deep breathing for his journey under the water. As he did so, he removed the robe, touching the blade at his side. It was not his Saint-jian but another weapon taken from the stores, a short sword that would be easier to wield under the water. Though the dive master and Ren Fei had pressed him to switch to other weapons, Wu Ying had chosen to keep to the blade.

After all, it was not the Heart of the Harpoon that he had learned.

Anyway, the shorter blade would be easy enough to wield, and he could project his blade intent through it with the same alacrity as his jian. And if he truly required his original weapon, he had it at hand.

Idly, he touched the rest of his gear. A trio of storage rings including his World Spirit ring. He had discarded the rest, leaving them with his belongings beneath deck, secured against potential loss. A pair of Fifty Jin Water flasks, the enchantments within stuffing twenty and twenty-three jin worth of water in the flasks themselves. Wu Ying was amused that they were called Fifty Jin Water flasks when they carried significantly less—but names were like that. Either way, the flasks would help bring him down quickly and, if properly used, were potential weapons below the water.

Goggles, enchanted for clear sight. They would also magnify the amount of light available, allowing Wu Ying to see a little deeper, though they wouldn't work at the depths he was expecting to journey to. He even had a few simple light talismans, stored within clear glass orbs to shed light around him if he so chose; but for the most part, he intended to dive using only his spiritual sense to guide him.

Being blindfolded and gathering while sightless had taken some getting used to. Utilizing nothing more than his sense of touch and his spiritual senses. The months of work had expanded his skill with his spiritual sense, strengthening it significantly as he utilized the teachings of the noble house and the captain. In truth, Wu Ying had to admit that he might have been ignoring his spiritual senses in favor of his connection to the wind, smell, and sight. After all, those had been more reliable by far.

Outside of that, Wu Ying had no tools beyond his gathering equipment. Talismans wouldn't work underwater, not unless they were properly set up like the glowballs. And his goal was to locate the oysters and open them, extracting the pearls while whatever was below was left clueless.

Though looking at the churning water, replete with the blood of human and aquatic animals alike, he wondered how likely it was to remain oblivious.

"Cultivator Long?" Ren Fei's spoke gently.

"I'm ready. Watch the water for me."

With a light leap, Wu Ying threw himself into the air. One last time, he called upon the wind to send him upward and forward into the center of the ring. He rose high before he dropped almost straight down, tucking arms and legs tightly. His entry was fast and smooth, barely rippling the water as he plunged into the deep, disappearing from view of those above.

***

Diving was such a strange phenomena. Immediately, Wu Ying was cut off from the wind chi he drew upon. The constant circulation of the Never Empty Wine Pot had been turned off, the Sea Serpent's Grace taking over even before he struck the water, helping him to plunge deeper. His body fell through the ocean, the weight of the Fifty Jin Water flasks dragging him down with alacrity, leaving the sunlit surface behind.

Light, at first so clear and bright, disappeared with every moment, every foot downward. Darkness closed in on him as color bleached itself from the surroundings. First went the vibrancy of the world, the brighter colors stained with dark blues and greens.

Then, eventually, even those colors faded until only black and greys were available. What little light from above faded even as the water pressed in upon Wu Ying's body. He swallowed and blew out, holding his nose as he had been trained, again and again, clearing the pressure differential within his sinuses as he dropped.

A slight current took him sideways even as the momentum of his initial drop faded, ground away by the pressure of the water all around him. He kicked ever so gently, his body moving in a sinuous motion trained by the cultivation exercise as he angled downward headfirst.

Claustrophobic, the deeper waters of the ocean. Cold too, and growing colder with each moment. Occasional crosscurrents caught at him, but he fought them, always allowing himself to sink deeper, sight fading away and leaving him only his spiritual sense to find his way.

Now the disorientation of the water became ever more apparent. Without light, without sight, Wu Ying only had his body to guide his spatial sense. Up and down fought for control within his mind, the pull and turn of crosscurrents threatening to turn him about. Only the inexorable drag of gravity and the unceasing kick of his legs gave him any sense of the world about.

That, and his spiritual sense. Deep in the water, it expanded to its fullest extent as gently as Wu Ying could do so. It touched upon the forms and pressure of the beings living below, so much fewer in the deeps.

The ocean was barren, in some ways, in comparison to the thriving forest of the deep wilds. There, plants, insects, floating seeds, and larger animals surrounded him at all times. While numerous things grew in the water, most were so small, so trivial that his spiritual sense could discard their presence without issue. Smaller fish were abundant at the top of the ocean, but the deeper he went, the fewer there were.

Density dropped too, an issue with some of the plankton-flooded areas above. Not a problem here. Not in the deep.

In the dark, fish were less abundant, though other creatures took up Wu Ying's senses. Jellyfish, krill, shrimp, anemone, and rays all passed by within Wu Ying's senses, blips he often struggled to name and understand. Yet none burned too brightly, none were a danger to his senses.

Deeper he fell, until the earth itself rose up around him. He adjusted his angle again, blowing his nose to equalize the pressure. The need for that had decreased as he went deeper, the pressure changes fewer. Wu Ying spotted the underwater canyon that was his target toward his right.

All around him, he faintly sensed the anchors the ships had dropped, specially crafted and brought along for this expedition. Too few of their ships were geared for such an oceanic exploration, certainly not to drop anchor in the middle of the ocean.

Now, he noted the remains of the previous expeditions. Broken hulls, shattered planks, and stripped corpses, remnant flesh preserved by the cold but their bodies torn asunder by the aquatic life. Not a single body had been left unmolested. Limbs and weapons were scattered about across the seabed, ballista bolts and cracked pottery lying abandoned at the bottom of the ocean.

Each of those hulls were shattered, as though something large and powerful had gripped them tightly and crushed the vessels before they sank. Other parts, near the front of the ships, had been torn off, the masts snapped as though bitten by a titanic beast who savored wood as much as flesh.

The fates of the previous ships were here, revealed in all their shattered glory. Destroyed by something powerful enough to pull even a ship from the ocean itself. Wu Ying's skin prickled further, goosebumps running along already chilled flesh, and he forced himself to swallow the air that threatened to escape his lungs.

He would need every iota of air he kept in his lungs.

In the canyon, darkness consumed him entirely, the water temperature dropping even further. He shivered a little, for the cold of the water was unlike the cold of the northern wind, a void that sucked from his skin, his core in an attempt to rob him of movement and sense.

His spiritual sense contracted, the chi domain within the water combatting his soul's extension, shutting it down. Something slithered at the edges of his consciousness, forcing Wu Ying to draw his spiritual sense in closer for fear of alerting those below. Or worse, leaving himself vulnerable.

For the spiritual sense was but the overlaying of an individual's spirit and domain into the outside world. It was why the extension of one's spiritual sense occurred most significantly at the jumps between stages, as one's soul expanded.

In truth, the argument of exactly what the spiritual sense was and how it tied into cultivation was broad and extensive. Like most things to do with cultivation and the Dao, there were many theories with few true facts. But that a spiritual attack could be launched by another against a too widely stretched spiritual sense was well-known. Even if such attacks—and creatures that could lash out in that way—were rare and the attack generally considered to be a "dark" art.

Well, outside of the use of sword intent. Strange that such an obvious—and commonly used—method of attacking a soul was acceptable. Hypocrisy…

Wu Ying pinched his eyes closed under the goggles, biting a lip. His mind was wandering. A side effect of the depths. He circulated some chi within him to clear his mind, forcing it clear.

In the canyon that he plunged within, coral dotted the sides, clinging to the edges. Eels slept within the gaps, poking their heads out occasionally as a fish wandered too close before they were struck and pulled back into the rocks to be consumed. Sea slugs crawled along the canyon walls, their sides glowing with a luminescent light. Yet for all the variety, there were fewer animals than he expected.

Even the slugs, the eels, the shellfish, and crustaceans that lingered moved slowly and with great care, cautiously verifying their surroundings before darting from hiding space to hiding space. Wu Ying knew those movements, for they were the movements of the fearful. Prey and even predators that knew that another, larger, and more dangerous hunter was close by.

As he grew closer to his destination, Wu Ying sensed the oysters. They glowed like a beacon that drew chi to themselves, and their souls burned all too brightly. Angling himself a little, Wu Ying kicked, heading for the oysters. Noticing no dangers in the surroundings, he allowed himself to touch down on the sandy floor.

The oysters were each nearly ten feet across and closed shut. The first oyster he touched, Wu Ying knew immediately he could harvest. He extracted the harvesting tool he had brought along, inserted it into the edge of the oyster's shell, and pried it open to peer within.

Nothing. No bulge, no extrusion in the flesh to showcase the location of a pearl. The older oyster had rejected the irritant placed within by the previous gatherer. He dropped the irritant—a portion of oyster meat from another creature previously harvested—from his storage ring into its mouth.

Disappointed, Wu Ying let the shell close. With a few flicks of his hand, he cut the muscle gripping the oyster to the ocean floor and stored the oyster in his World Spirit Ring. He could do the same for all the oysters, but doing so would leave the kingdom without a bounty for the future.

He moved on, checking oyster after oyster. Those close to their expiry dates were extracted, stored away in his World Spirit ring. If he was lucky, perhaps he might even be able to form a oyster bed in the salt water lake he had created for this very purpose.

One by one, Wu Ying searched the oysters for pearls. The first one he located, he extracted the multi-colored, lustrous pearl with swift movements of his dagger. To his surprise, upon being revealed, the pearl shone with a bright light that illuminated the surroundings, encompassing him and making Wu Ying's eyes water. He pulled the pearl into his ring immediately, cutting off the light but leaving a tingling feeling in his fingers.

The sheer volume of chi stored within the pearl had flooded forth, dancing across his fingers, along his arms, and through his aura. For a time, his aura burned with the strong yang-aspected energy before it guttered out.

Out of the dozens of oysters, only one in four had a pearl within. He added slices of oyster meat to those empty shellfish, as he had been instructed to prepare them for future production. Then he let the oyster shells close, hoping they would survive. It was lucky for the province that these oysters mostly survived the act of being pried open, for the oyster bed itself grew slowly in size.

He worked quickly and smoothly as his time slowly ran down. The process of holding his breath was easy at first. The tightness in his chest grew at a rate he could easily ignore in the beginning. As he pushed onward, extracting oyster, meat, and pearls alike, the burning grew harder to overlook.

He was running out of time, but after hitting the fifth oyster in a row without pearls, he realized he had to make a choice. He required two more pearls to meet the minimum number, but he had at most a minute left where he could hold his breath. Ascending would be faster than descending, but it would still be tight even if he left now. If he ran into any problems…

On the other hand, the oppressive feeling that surrounded him continued to pulse through his body, making his skin prickle and his body shiver. He could ascend, but he wondered if he might have already alerted the creature below. If he had, leaving now might mean risking a battle upon his return.

Kicking over to the next oyster, Wu Ying placed his hand upon it, debating his best course of action. Risk running out of air while prying open oysters, or ascend now and risk alerting whatever creature waited below?

In the end, it was all risk.

Chapter 35

A moment of debate, then Wu Ying acted. He pulled himself closer to the oyster and pried it open, resolved to keep going. He would have to work faster and hope that his luck held. He only needed two more pearls, after all. He had other options, in the worst-case scenario of running out of air, though he would prefer not to enact them.

As he pushed off the latest oyster, he noticed that oppressive feeling had grown stronger. Eyes darting around the surroundings futilely, his spiritual sense doing its best to outline the world, he still found no trace of an enemy.

Something was coming, instinct told him. Instinct he had honed over a decade of moving through the wilds, the places where nature and spirit beasts still held sway. Places where man rarely set foot, for the creatures that lived there were numerous and powerful and jealous of intruders. That instinct screamed that his time was running out.

But he could not move, could not work any faster. He could but try to smooth out his movements to increase his efficiency and shift from oyster to oyster a little more hurriedly. Another shell pried open, a suspicious bulge within. A flicker of his hand, cutting open the flesh and depositing more irritant within the shell, even as he swiped the glowing treasure.

For a moment, his senses expanded outward as the bright light illuminated the surroundings and his aura grew overcharged. He again sensed something dark and slithery at the edges of his perception, then felt the expanded vision slam shut as the energy from the pearl dissipated.

Hurrying now, words of prophecy ringing in his ears, Wu Ying churned energy through his aura as he fought against the tug of current. He raged within at the clumsiness of this work. Another gatherer, specialized in this, might have been able to sense the pearls within. That was how the previous gatherers, the previous victims, had worked.

He had not the skills or the element suited for this environment. Above, where light lived and his senses were fully his own, he could have looked for clues, asked the wind or probed the edges of the flower or the soil. Yet the water and the oysters were anathema to him, even his connection to the wood element insufficient to pry apart the water-aspected oysters' secrets.

Instead, he had to do it this way, the hardest way. Spike went into the edge of the oyster shell, cultivator-enhanced strength prizing apart the flesh. He moved more hastily now, even as a part of him noted the curious absences in the oysters. Certain parts, certain portions of the rocky field he moved upon were devoid of the shellfish. Rubble lay close by, as did the scattered, broken shells.

Conclusions were drawn, and none of them were happy. He wondered briefly if he should confront the creature preying upon the oyster bed. Yet Wu Ying discarded the idea just as he discarded the latest oyster, moving on to the next.

The water was not his element, and the monster that lay within would not be his choice. Let the Viscount find another hero to do his bidding. Perhaps in the intervening seven years, one of greater stature and ability would arrive.

A strike, a twist, a push, and the latest oyster opened. Wu Ying sensed within the bulge and could not help but smile, working quickly to slice open the flesh. He gripped the oyster, beginning to will it to him.

Only to stop as his spiritual sense told him a much less satisfying piece of information. The pearl was extracted, held aloft in one hand, as its light illuminated the surroundings and the monster that stalked Wu Ying. The creature's main body alone was twice the size of the flagship he had sailed upon, its baleful eyes shrinking as its pupils reacted to the light.

Wu Ying threw himself backward even as he willed the pearl into his storage ring, knowing that the ship-killer had come. He was out of time.

And breath.

***

Wu Ying jetted to the side, expelling chi through his feet and to the side to dodge the grasping tentacles coming for him. One, two, three, four tentacles… six tentacles and two stumps. He spun around and twisted, kicking quickly as he tried to rise above the head of the spirit beast coming for him. He sensed the moving tentacles, their large suckers nearly dwarfing his body.

So many tentacles, each of them moving like a serpent, twisting and grasping at him. Dark skin lightened as the camouflage the beast had used to sneak up on Wu Ying faded away to reveal the monstrous visage.

Big oval eyes, a bulbous head, and a massive body behind the grasping tentacles. As the head reared backward, flowing in a strange, sinuous, boneless motion, the beaked mouth of the creature was revealed. It opened its mouth wide, chi gathering within as the creature began its attack. Wu Ying reacted, slicing downward with the Saint-level short sword he had drawn.

He projected his attack as best he could, pouring chi and sword intent into the motion, but as fast as he was, the water slowed his motions. The projectile ball of condensed water, filled with chi and dark intent by the spirit beast octopus, struck his own attack and was only disrupted a little.

The octopus's water ball container was damaged, the contained energy within the attack exploding outward. It threw Wu Ying away as the compressed water and the force of the attack struck his body. Precious air was forcibly expelled from Wu Ying's body, bubbles trailing upward even as his eardrums ruptured, leaving him with a blinding earache and headache.

Realizing how badly outmaneuvered he was, Wu Ying kicked his feet, rising as quickly as he could. He could not breathe, could not afford to stay down here, fighting the spirit octopus.

Instead, with his free hand, he touched one of the remaining unbroken bulbs hanging on his belt and triggered the seal within, letting the glowing light fall behind him as he rose.

Tentacles, reaching for Wu Ying, halted for a moment, the suddenly brighter light drawing the monster's attention. In the meantime, Wu Ying grasped one of the Fifty Jin Flasks and threw it sideways, piercing the flask with the edge of his thumb as he did so, the motion aided by the Heart of the Sword.

Integrity of the flask broken, the enchantment unraveled slowly at first but speeding up. The brown flask bobbled and drifted downward, only to be struck by another reaching tentacle. It was enough to break the final seal, and another explosion of compressed water erupted within the ocean.

Swimming away, Wu Ying was cast aside once more, forced higher and higher by the explosion. Beneath him, the spirit beast octopus jerked, the tentacle that had struck the flask crushed and a small rip appearing along the rubbery flesh. Yet for the most part, the creature was unhurt by all of Wu Ying's antics and was reaching for him once more.

His plan having failed to injure the creature, Wu Ying cut free the last flask, repeating his actions as he let it drop beneath him. Within seconds, it exploded, thrusting him upward and putting his body under further strain. He felt himself almost black out, the pain in his ears growing.

Yet this time, the Spirit Beast was ready. Controlling the flow of water with its chi, it rode the attack higher like the cultivator. It grasped at him with a half dozen tentacles, each seeming to have a mind of their own.

Wu Ying snarled, his nose trailing purple-looking blood under the darkened sea. He waved his sword around, projecting the blade with his chi as killing and sword intent cleaved through the water. His attacks cut through bulbous flesh like a razor, leaving the octopus to leak blue blood into the water. The pair dueled in an ascending spiral, Wu Ying's greatest advantage being the sheer size of the tentacles grabbing at his smaller form, each tentacle having to battle the others for proximity to his body.

But for all his attacks, all his preparation with the Serpent's Grace, he was unable to make it to the surface. A bare two dozen feet from air, his flailing, dodging, parrying efforts failed him. An unseen tentacle rose from behind, gripping his arm first. Then another closed on his body as his movements stilled, tightening around his legs and sliding upward to grasp his lower body.

So close to freedom, he was yanked back, the tentacles closing on him and pulling him down, back into the depth, only his improved constitution keeping his arm from being simply torn from his body. Mouth opened into a wordless, soundless scream, air bubbles escaping, Wu Ying was drawn toward the open mouth. Bulbous eyes glinted with malice beneath him.

***

No more tricks, no more air, weapon-hand held tight. Unlike normal octopuses, the creature's mouth was large and rimmed with fangs meant for tearing. As Wu Ying was pulled closer, he felt the pulsing of contained chi inside the sharp teeth, a twisted, cold, and slow chi that chilled his blood. Poison chi embedded inside the fangs. A single bite and, Wu Ying knew, he would never be able to fight off the effects before he was killed.

He twisted and pulled at the gripping tentacles, attempting to free himself but unable to do so. The strength of those slimy arms was more than he could overcome. It was only luck that he managed to keep one hand free to protect his neck and ensure he was not violently beheaded.

Chest burning, his vision darkened at the edges as he struggled, burning more and more energy with each motion. The mouth edged closer to him, aiming to bite off his legs. Wu Ying pulled, tugging with every inch of his strength to curl his legs inward. He could not free himself, but he managed to bring his upper body closer at the cost of dislocating his sword arm.

Enough to bring his other hand close enough to stick his hand forward. The hand that held his World Spirit ring. A storage ring with special properties, including his backup plan. Channeling his will and chi into the ring, he poured energy into it and pulled, extracting from within the ring. Not sand, not earth, not even herbs—nothing so prosaic.

Just air. Just wind.

A typhoon of air, of energy and power, roared from his hand. Locking his hand and arm in position, he channeled that energy directly into the creature's mouth, forcing out water and pushing himself back with each moment. Inside the cyclone of wind, Wu Ying poured the full killing and sword intent of his soul, the attack leaving bloody tracks inside the tender mouth.

Surprised, the creature spasmed, pulling Wu Ying's arm and body and damaging him further. Then it spasmodically threw him away in blind rage even as it expelled a cloud of ink.

Splashing in the deep, his body flopping bonelessly in the pressure of the throw, Wu Ying groaned and swallowed a mouthful of brackish water. He coughed and spasmed even as he cut off the flow of air from his ring, hoping the damage done to his ring was not too great.

Below him, in the inky gloom he could barely see into and not sense at all, the beast awaited. Rather than stay, he kicked feebly once more for the lighted surface. To his surprise and gratitude, in all this, they had managed to stay close to the surface.

A few moments later, as his chest burned and unconsciousness threatened to take him, he broke free of the ocean. He opened his mouth and, forgetting all his training, gulped at the air, desperate to fill his lungs. Darkness that encroached against his consciousness faded with each breath, each moment. Before him, Wu Ying spotted the ships. The back of a ship.

Eyes wide, he realized he had been thrown outside the ring, away from the center of the formation. And deep beneath the water, the spirit octopus was emerging, its shock at being attacked discarded. Realization of the choices to be made ran through Wu Ying: take to the air and safety, or swim into the center, leading the monster into it.

Not much of a choice there.

Wu Ying swam, pushing the Serpent's Grace to the maximum, lowering his head as he pulled with his still-functioning arm. Each movement sent a jolt of pain down his dislocated shoulder, an ankle throbbing from being twisted. Somewhere along the way, he had lost the short sword he had been given, the Saint-class weapon dropped deep below the water.

After a half dozen strokes, with the pain of a wrenched lower back and dislocated shoulder throwing off his stroke, Wu Ying realized he had to change his tactics. He twisted his body around, kicking so that he could tread water. Then as long tentacles reached for him, he kicked hard within the water, pouring more chi into the motion as he flapped his hand downward. He exploded out of the water even as tentacles rose from below.

The moment he breached the surface with his body, his senses, his domain, and his dao snapped back in full force. No longer trapped by the overflowing spiritual power of the creature that had permeated the water, blocking off his control, Wu Ying called the wind to himself. Immediately, he blocked one tentacle with a shearing wall of wind and dodged another attack with a simple sidestep.

Like a leaf on the wind, Wu Ying drifted between the grasping tentacles, his uninjured hand moved toward his shoulder. He needed both hands, both arms for this fight. Positioning it carefully, he gripped his shoulder and, with a scream that echoed through the open sea, he yanked it back into position.

Searing agony shot through his shoulder into his arm and body. His concentration wavered for a moment, time enough for a slimy tentacle to grip his leg and yank him down. Yet before it could drag him down too far, a ballista bolt slammed into the creature's tentacle at the base sprouting out of the water.

Moments later, the ballista bolt exploded, leaving behind a wide, fleshy hole that leaked blue blood. In the spasm as it released him, Wu Ying flew away, darting toward the center of the formation once again.

A wet tearing sound erupted from the bleeding limb as its continued movements pulled the flesh apart. Driven by anger, the octopus sent a couple of tentacles reaching for the boat, even as more ballista bolts from ships positioned farther away landed in the water. Most missed, though the eruptions filled the air with water and a painful cacophony. Not that Wu Ying could hear any of it.

A single blazing spear followed as Ren Fei threw his weapon. The weapon did not miss, cutting through the tip of a tentacle as it attempted to grip a junk.

Wu Ying only caught sight of the entire battle, for the majority of the tentacles continued to chase him. Dancing between the attacks, he conjured two swords, simple Spirit-level weapons that he sharpened with his blade intent. Rubbery flesh was sliced apart with each parry and swing. The attacks only agitated the creature more, and from his location high above, Wu Ying saw the pair of globular eyes focusing upon him angrily.

"Protect the ships! We need it in the center of the formation," Wu Ying cried, using the wind to project his voice to the nearby ships.

Ren Fei had been shouting the same thing while waiting for his spear to return, but without Wu Ying's command of the wind, even his booming voice had struggled to reach the farthest ships over the chaos of the battle.

Anchor ropes snapped and twisted, and a mast was torn off a junk as a tentacle swung. With a sudden pop, Wu Ying's hearing returned, in time to hear the creak and hiss of ballista bolts being fired and the screams of the injured filling the air. Across the beleaguered ships, blue and red blood mingled on decks, making for treacherous footing, while the ocean's salty air grew tinged with iron.

Hovering a bare dozen feet above the ocean, flowing backward and chased by the spirit beast octopus, Wu Ying led the monster into the center of the circle. He could not tell how strong the octopus was, not via his spiritual sense; the monster's ability to camouflage itself was still well in effect. It had to be at least Core level, though Wu Ying suspected Nascent Soul.

Otherwise, this battle would have been a lot simpler.

A ballista bolt hissed past him, flying from one of the ships before sinking into the water and exploding. Wu Ying watched the tentacles pause for a second, wiping his face as he was showered with saltwater. He reflexively rose into the sky.

Then the monster twisted around, as though it suddenly realized the danger it was in. It pulled its tentacles close, giving up on harrying the junks. Its attacks had not failed entirely, for one was half-broken and sinking, only held aloft by the power of the enchantments and its captain's dao and chi.

"Fools. NOW!" Wu Ying roared the last word, projecting it across the surroundings.

Perhaps the beast was running. Perhaps it was truly leaving them alone. However, he—they—could not risk it. If the monster held a grudge as some creatures did, they would be hunted across hundreds of li as they traveled back to port.

Or perhaps even more dangerously, the creature would come to the port city itself in the deep of the night, harrying the city, destroying ships, and crawling onto paved streets before slinking away. Its camouflage was more than sufficient to do that. What a disaster that would be.

No, they had to kill it and kill it now.

All around Wu Ying, the formations lit up as the channeled and contained energy linked one ship to another. Remembering the danger he was in, Wu Ying raised his hand and called the wind to him, pulling on it as he rose vertically rather than risk being caught in the attack.

Down the keels of the boats, the lines of chi ran, linking boat to boat via the water. The Five Binding, Seven Bells, and Eleven Seas formation was powerful, powered not just by the chi of the individuals who activated it but the dao intent and stored energy embedded in the formation flags. Once activated, the formation would need to rest for decades to recharge, but in the meantime, the trap worked, sending conjured lightning racing between the boats.

Once the boats were linked, requiring only a blink of an eye, Ren Fei took action. He hefted a new spear and threw it, infusing the attack with everything he had. The spear lanced through the air and plunged through the water to strike the bulbous flesh between the spirit beast's eyes even as it dived into the water. Ren Fei, having expended a large amount of chi in that one action, fell to the deck, gripping his stomach and dantian.

Even so, the attack was sufficient. The spear was the fulcrum for the formation, the guide for the energy that had been gathered. Energy arced from all five ships toward the spear, chi pouring down the connection that had been created to burn into the monster itself.

Lightning arced and danced, the smell of ozone and burnt flesh infusing the surroundings. Wu Ying floated above, watching as clouds of steam rose as the energetic chi boiled off the water on its way to striking the monster. A light mist rose even as Wu Ying guided it away. The creature thrashed and twitched, a soundless scream echoing from its body.

"Fire! Finish it," Ren Fei screamed, waving at the others from where he had pushed himself up against the railing.

The heavy *thunk* and release of ballista bolts signaled the resumption of attacks, the large bolts winging through the sky to sink into tentacles and, occasionally, the body. The bolts exploded, sending shrapnel and flesh flying. Some attacks never even made it, lightning flicking upward from the ocean to trigger the talismans long before the bolts could arrive.

Wu Ying watched the chaos and carnage as sailors scrambled to reload the ballistae whilst the formation dumped the stored chi into the spirit beast octopus. Eventually, the stored energy was depleted, the dancing blue and green lights fading away.

The octopus sank a little, then one still-moving, uninjured tentacle ripped the spear from between its eyes. It cast the spear away, jetting upward a little as the remainder of its tentacles waved about. It had three tentacles left, one undamaged, the others streaked black and grey.

The flesh across the monster's face was burnt, scars of blackened flesh racing outward from the wound. One branch reached all the way into a bulbous eye, now white and blind. Spilled ink flowed outward from the monster's mouth, released by accident during its electrocution.

Cries of dismay rose from the group as the sight of the still-living monster, followed closely by the shouts of the captains and first mates to keep loading. Wu Ying snarled, making his weapons disappear and conjuring his Saint-jian.

Always, it seemed, it was up to him.

He cut the flow of air, building up momentum as he angled himself downward. He fell, picking up speed with each fraction of a second, even as Wu Ying crouched and formed a platform of air beneath his feet such that he had a place to stand.

The Dragon Rises.

First movement of the Wandering Dragon. The world rushed up toward Wu Ying, and for a moment, he thought he could feel the earth itself rotate as the octopus, arching back, met his attack with its own ball of exploding water.

Wind and blade intent met water and killing focus in an explosion that sprayed the surroundings, the water moving so energetically that it cut and tore apart sails and skin alike. Yet for all the creature's strength, it had been injured and lured out of its domain and was competing with Wu Ying in the air now.

Here, in the space between water and sky, Wu Ying dominated. His attack split apart the water, burrowing deep within to impact burnt and wounded skin. The spirit beast screamed, thrashing as fresh blood flowed, and twisted aside, seeking to escape again.

Too late.

Falling still, Wu Ying tucked his body and legs together, sword hand leading the way. The Sword's Truth, that lunge he knew so well, combined with the fall, and the wind beckoned to him as it combined to speed his descent until he moved faster than a stooping dragon. He slammed into the water, the blade intent projected from his sword parting the ocean, wind meeting water to pierce into the dodging but slow beast.

The second form of the Wandering Dragon struck, and the Dragon's Truth pierced the spirit octopus. Warm flesh surrounded Wu Ying for a moment, his spinning aura throwing aside the blood and viscera that threatened to coat him as he plunged through the monster, exiting the other side in a welter of gore, spreading the explosion of skin and muscle through the bloody ocean.

He tucked in his legs, eyes gleaming with a tight smile as he watched the second movement of the Wandering Dragon, finally complete, take effect. The spirit beast was still alive, but gravely wounded, its massive and unnatural constitution bearing it upward even now. Though the second form was not perfected yet, the attack was everything he had hoped for. There was not even a backlash from the imperfect form, for he had combined his knowledge of the Sword's Truth with his wind body to create the much more focused attack.

As the monster twitched again, flailing limbs seeking to grab Wu Ying, he shook aside his elation and turned back to the battle. It wasn't over yet, though the outcome now was certain. The spirit octopus was dead, it just had to be convinced.

By sword point if necessary.

Chapter 36

"He did not look happy," Wu Ying observed, staring down from the tower into the courtyard below.

Beside him, Captain Ren Fei laughed a little before clutching his stomach, the minor motion enough to send paroxysms of pain through his body. "I would not think so. One could almost believe they had been hoping we might fail. But who would weaken the kingdom like that? Or lure a spirit beast to our oyster fields?"

Wu Ying glanced at the man before he shook his head, refusing to be drawn in. Once the octopus had been killed, Wu Ying and the remaining divers had gone into the water to extract the creature's spirit stone as well as much of the body as they could. In the depths, without a timer, Wu Ying also managed to sweep up a number of treasures among the sunken ships, only to find a series of formation flags sunk deep into the sea floor. Extracting them had destroyed the still-functioning formation, though Captain Ren believed them to be lures of some kind.

In the end, it was not a matter that Wu Ying wanted to concern himself with. While he had been allowed to keep both the short sword he had located and the Nascent Soul spirit beast core of the octopus, most of the other treasures had been taken from him.

That had left Wu Ying feeling a little aggrieved, though their negotiation had not included looting the wrecks. In the end, he understood that the Viscount would need all the resources she could acquire to train a new gatherer in the future for their next delivery in seven years. Still, it left Wu Ying somewhat dissatisfied, even if he was leaving with significantly greater resources, gear, and knowledge than he had arrived.

Perhaps he was just growing greedy.

Or perhaps he still bled in his heart for the destruction experienced by the orchards and fields in his World Spirit Ring. The forced expulsion of air had done significant damage to the ring, tearing apart fields, destroying embedded formations, and ruining carefully tended plants. It would take months, if not years, to set all the work aright, especially after the losses from his prolonged period in the north.

"Where does the wind take you next, Cultivator Long?" Captain Ren asked, cocking his head.

"I know not. Perhaps I'll stay for a little while longer," Wu Ying said, a small smile on his lips.

The captain said nothing, refusing to rise to the bait.

Giving in to the silence, Wu Ying shrugged. "I mean to explore the eastern coast for a while longer. See a few provinces, visit some villages. Perhaps spend some time on the ocean itself."

"Really?" the captain said, sounding surprised. "Not that one who controls the wind like yourself would ever be unwanted, but I had not expected you to join the fishing fleets."

Wu Ying smiled a little before deciding to clarify. "I was thinking of more than the fleets. I heard rumor of lands farther afield. Not just the land of the immortals, but lands where other races live. To the east and to the south."

"Ah, the far merchants," Captain Ren said, nodding in understanding. "We do not cater to them much, for our harbor has not the depth needed for those vessels."

Wu Ying nodded, having come to some understanding about the junks that plied the waters. Bigger ships with deeper keels were more stable on the high seas, which were important when one ventured far from sight of land.

"Be careful though, Cultivator Long." He grinned. "Some say that once the sea has taken your heart, no land will ever truly satisfy you."

Wu Ying turned away from the courtyard to stare at the ocean. His lips curled upward a little before he shook his head. "It is beautiful, and quiet, and lonely. But I think my heart will always be where my feet can touch the earth."

"Understandable. At least, for a land-lover, you have some appreciation of the true mistress of our hearts," Captain Ren pushed off from the railing, nodding to Wu Ying. "I should inform the Viscount of your intentions then. I'm sure arrangements will be made to see you off in proper fashion."

Wu Ying grimaced but nodded. After all he had done, it would be unkind and unbecoming of him to slip away in the middle of the day. The celebration tonight, for successfully providing their tithe, would be long and raucous. Tomorrow was more than early enough for him to leave.

After all, there was still much to be seen in this land.

***

Strange how things turned. From being feted at a Viscount's table to working the nets for a meal and a bed in a fisherman's hut. Hauling up the net cast over the side of the boat, Wu Ying eyed the half-empty net as he dropped the contents into the boat. His companion worked quickly, grabbing and tossing certain fish and other bycatch that he did not want, leaving the bottom of the boat filled with only what he desired.

While he did that, Wu Ying was rolling up the net, getting it out of the way and storing it, careful not to let the hooks or the net's weights catch on his skin. Like the fisherman, he was wearing a simple sleeveless cross-tied tunic stained with blood and guts from other fish they had gutted and cleaned.

"That's the last," the fisherman said, eyeing the bottom of the boat with distaste. "You sure you're not bad luck?"

Wu Ying chuckled weakly, offering a little shrug. The fisherman snorted and gestured to the oars. Wu Ying took them hastily, then paused before dipping the oars into the water and pulling. He did not exert his full strength—or even most of it—since neither the oar nor the boat would handle that well. It also had a tendency to scare the fish, which the fisherman had pointed out to Wu Ying rather loudly the first time.

Running a thumb along the wood of the left oar, newly carved with just a hint of sap left in the wood, Wu Ying guided the boat back to the small inlet they had left from earlier in the day. As they coasted in, the fisherman gutted and cleaned the fish, his fingers nimble as he wielded the gutting knife. Each gutted fish was dropped into a clear pail of water, washed quickly, and stored in a wooden basket for later.

"Maybe you're not all bad luck," Goh Ping, the fisherman, muttered as he held up one of the largest oceanic catfish Wu Ying had seen. The fisherman's hand exited the body cavity, a small demonic stone in his fist before he dropped the catfish into the water bucket. "I can sell those to foolish cultivators for some good money."

"Foolish?" Wu Ying murmured.

"Always hurrying, always rushing. They buy it all, grind it up, make pills, and eat it," Goh Ping said, wrinkling his nose. "Makes them strong, makes them sick, helps them grow more powerful. Rushing around, getting money and cores and favors and risking their lives, all to be 'better.'"

Wu Ying inclined his head, remembering another conversation with another heretic.

Except this time, the old man continued with a scoffing addition, offering Wu Ying a sidelong glance. "Then they travel the world and come sit by my side, hauling nets. Might as well have just stayed and hauled nets in the first place."

Wu Ying snorted. "Maybe I just want to become a better fisherman. Uncle Goh is quite skilled."

"I am, but there are better." Goh Ping stared at the fish in his hand before depositing it in the basket beside him. "But really, I think you just want me to show you my wife's manual."

"That obvious, eh?" Wu Ying said.

"You're not the first cultivator to come learn from her. Used to have quite a few come by when she was alive." Goh Ping looked sad then, his head turned away to stare at the lapping water beside the boat. "Fewer now. And you're not very good at hiding your strength."

Wu Ying looked at the new oar, the one he had to carve to replace the one he had broken and found himself smiling a little. He was so used to hiding from spirit and demonic beasts that he forgot there were other things, other tells a mortal could use to read him. Especially since he had progressed so far, gaining strength from Body Cultivation aspects that imbued themselves in his body.

"I guess I'm not," Wu Ying said.

"My wife used to say a gatherer who can't control their presence is a lousy gatherer," Goh Ping said. "And I certainly have no intention of giving her work to an incompetent."

Wu Ying chose not to answer, instead dipping the oars into the water and pulling. He eyed the crab trap buoy they passed, the little flutter of color on the top indicating that they were coming up on the beach. Turning his head, he judged the distance expertly and dipped the oars into the water once more to allow them to glide in.

"Switch," Wu Ying announced after finishing that pull and offering the oars to Goh Ping.

Once the ends had been taken, Wu Ying stood and waited, watching as the boat glided to the beach. As it crunched on the sand, sliding upward, Wu Ying jumped off. He poured chi into his footing, standing on the water rather than letting himself sink as he skipped to the front of the boat. Gripping it with one hand, he lifted the boat a little off the ground as he slid the entire vessel up the beach, far enough for it to be grounded properly.

Goh Ping watched without a word before he stepped out, water lapping at his sandals and toes. He bent low, grabbed one of the baskets, and hauled it to his shoulders before gesturing up the beach to where the wooden dry dock awaited.

"Well, if you're done hiding, put the boat on the dock and make sure to clean it fully," the man growled before stomping off, calling additional instructions over his shoulder. "And take care of the guts properly."

Wu Ying snorted, lifting the boat higher with one hand before he lifted it over his shoulder, balancing the boat in the middle. He stalked over to the wooden stands, placed the boat as instructed, and grabbed the metallic scraper.

Obviously, winning the man's approval would take longer than Wu Ying had expected. Turning his head upward as the eastern wind played with his hair, he listened to it before shaking his head. Whether the book that lay in the man's hut was the real thing or not, Wu Ying would not take it without permission. That was not his way.

"Hurry up, boy. The fish isn't going to walk itself to market!"

The shout from Goh Ping made Wu Ying sigh, but he moved faster. With swifter and more certain movements than anyone but a cultivator could replicate, he scraped the bottom of the boat. If the mussels and other debris that had accumulated were shaved off with the slightest hint of blade intent, well...

A blade was used for many things, not just killing.

***

"Ah, Cultivator Long, you still with that old grouch?" Merchant Chu said, leaning against the side of her wagon in the village. She was one of many traders who took the village's afternoon catch to the nearby city, traveling through the night to bring it to the city the next morning, then turning around and coming back in the afternoon to do it all over again. Mild enchantments and a lot of salt kept the catch from spoiling in the summer heat, though haste was always desirable.

"It would seem so," Wu Ying replied, hefting the basket and placing it on the side of the wagon.

The merchant's sons took to weighing and counting the fish, moving with efficient motions while she led Wu Ying a little way away. Not so far that he could not watch their proceedings, but such that they were no longer directly beside the wagon.

"You've lasted longer than most, but you know he won't let you see it, no matter how much fish you haul for him," Merchant Chu said. "He just likes to hold it over you cultivators' heads."

Wu Ying nodded. Somehow, he was not surprised that even she had figured out his true origins. "Yet many try."

"Of course. Auntie Goh had even the king sending his gatherer applicants to her to learn," Merchant Chu said, holding up her head.

Wu Ying chose not to correct her, knowing that it was not the king but the Viscount. Still, the difference was marginal for one like her.

"It's surprising she never passed it on," Wu Ying murmured. "Beyond the gatherers she trained, that is."

"Ah…" Auntie Goh cocked her head. "That's why you're so stubborn. You don't know." At Wu Ying's blank stare, she continued. "She did. Auntie and uncle had three children. The men went into fishing at first, with uncle. The first was lost to a typhoon, the second to the wasting sickness."

Wu Ying winced. That kind of illness was known to strike down anyone not in the Core Formation level at the least, their bodies unable to bear the burden. It was worse for cultivators in fact, for it used the chi within a cultivator's body and turned it on them. Entire provinces had been quarantined to stop the spread of such diseases.

"It was a small outbreak, just unlucky." She sighed. "The daughter trained with the mother, alongside the cultivators who came. And then one day, another beautiful cultivator came along and well…" Auntie Goh lowered her voice, causing Wu Ying to lean in a little. "They fell in love. But Uncle Goh was always a stickler for tradition. He would not hear of it."

"What happened?" Wu Ying asked.

Sadly, such circumstances were all too common. Whereas some might not care—like the Pans, or even his own sect—other kingdoms and villages, worried about inheritances and the passing on of family names and heritages, had banned such casual dalliances outright. He had not, Wu Ying had to admit, checked into the local customs or laws.

"They left. Both of them," Auntie Goh said. "She came back as a full cultivator like you, at her mother's death. But Uncle Goh would not even see her and chased her away. Wouldn't give her her mother's book either."

"So he takes out his anger on cultivators, making us work for him. Humbling us," Wu Ying said, drawing the conclusion she had obviously led him to.

The auntie nodded then gestured to the cart where her children had finished counting and marked down the amount owed. "We can send the money onward, if you wish." At Wu Ying's silence, she continued. "No one will cheat Uncle Goh here. It wouldn't be worth my reputation." She nodded toward the fishermen and women who stood about, waiting their turn.

Already, the boys were working on another haul, sorting and weighing, though the youngest was perched, casting glances at Wu Ying. It was clear which son would be sent on that errand.

"Thank you, but no." Wu Ying stepped toward the wagon, and when Merchant Chu stepped with him, he picked up the pace. "I'll take it back."

"It's good to finish what you start," the merchant said, smiling. "And you, of course, have things to pick up."

"Oh, I'm not leaving. Not yet," Wu Ying said. Surprise flashed across the merchant's face. When she did not ask but obviously wanted to, Wu Ying took pity on her. "It's not time to move on."

"And when will it?"

"When the wind wills." It amused Wu Ying a little that there was a similar saying among the fishermen here.

"So you'll do all his scutwork and errands?" Merchant Chu said incredulously. "Knowing there's no reward?"

"No one promises you a reward, not in this life. Not at the end of it or even when hauling up your nets." Wu Ying shrugged. "We can only sow our seeds and do the work. If the gods will it, the harvest will be plentiful. And if not, the work itself can be reward enough." A slight twinkle in Wu Ying's eye at the end. "So long as one has enough to feed oneself, at least."

His words gained a few approving nods from the fishermen, though the merchant rolled her eyes. She dropped the owed coins into Wu Ying's outstretched hand and waved him off, turning to the next customer.

Smiling a little, Wu Ying walked off, his aura still tightly constrained. Eyeing the village and the night sky, he made a decision to do a little more shopping. Perhaps Uncle Goh might enjoy fish without many vegetables and a meager ration of salt and rice, but Wu Ying was a cultivator with a cultivator's appetite.

And if he was no longer trying to hide his status—even if none knew the extent of his strength—then he might as well spend like a cultivator too. Humming to himself, Wu Ying made his way to the shops, already putting together tonight's dinner in his mind.

Chapter 37

Days turned into weeks. The once modest and rundown house had been modified, old maintenance chores long put off finished. The roof had been redone entirely, new rushes placed alongside clay tiles. Whitewash had been added to the walls, clay patches added to the wooden timbers to reduce draftiness, and a couple of worn windows and their sills replaced.

More importantly, a larger free-standing structure rose nearby, dug deep into the earth with foundations sunk even deeper and the exterior sealed to contain the smoke. A hearth had been set in the center, while ceiling beams were left free standing to allow fish to be hung, or fish could be inserted into flat shelving all around. The smoking shed even had a small section to partition and allow wood to dry off within, while a small coal fire burnt down the wood within a hooded corner.

Much of the surroundings had changed as well, old bushes trimmed back, the garden that had laid overrun with weeds and overgrown plants renewed. A new compost pile had been started, the contents carefully turned, while the older pile had been distributed across the garden beds.

Wu Ying could not help but look at the surroundings with a smile as dawn slowly lit it all. It had been such a long time since he had worked on such a small project, building things with his hands and spending long days and late nights working simple, mundane tasks. It was fulfilling in a way that even cultivating was not, for the actions he undertook were not just for himself but for others.

"Hurry up! The fish aren't going to catch themselves, you fool," Goh Ping shouted from the doorway, placing a hat on his head. Over the course of the months, the old man had yet to change his behavior, alternating from outright hostility to passive aggressive scorn as the wind turned.

Wu Ying snorted, having been awake for hours already. He was no mortal who needed a good eight hours of oblivion each night. Still, he chose not to reply, joining the man near the boat. As he did so, he felt the wind on his face, more energetic and insistent than ever.

He raised his head, abruptly coming to a stop. The wind pulled at his hair, whispering in his ears as it tugged at his clothing. He frowned, turning his head from side to side, then going so far as to breathe deep and noisily. The smell of fresh sea water, of growing winds and lands far away, of thundering waves and a storm about to arrive made him blink.

"Stop delaying, boy. Just because you've done some good doesn't mean it's enough to take a day's break," Goh Ping said.

"Stop." Wu Ying raised his hand. "Something's coming."

"Yes, the tide at this rate. That, and the fish's full bellies."

"No. Something more, something a lot worse." Another deep breath, as he tried to hear the words the wind was whispering. It was hard to comprehend. There were impressions he could not understand, images and sensations he struggled to grasp.

Yet the feeling it gave off made him shudder, his breathing tightening. Portents of doom that set his body shivering.

"There's always something coming. It's the ocean, after all."

"It's not the ocean that is in danger," Wu Ying said, eyes widening. "It's coming to land. Winds that can tear roots free from the earth, topples trees, and blow away buildings. Winds that churn the ocean and raise waves a half li high."

"Typhoon," Goh Ping murmured, dread in his voice. "How strong?"

"Very." Wu Ying turned from the ocean, staring upward at the cliff that rose behind them, then at the hills that kept rolling onward and onward. He searched for the highest one before he pointed. "There."

"There?" Goh Ping said.

"Go there," Wu Ying said. "Quickly. Don't take anything, just go. You'll need all the time to get there and be safe."

Goh Ping stared at the hill, eyes narrowing as he gauged the location and distance before frowning. "That's Sheep Top hill. It's nearly four li away, as the crow flies."

"Yes. Now, go!"

Having said his piece, Wu Ying chose to leave Goh Ping. The warning was late, the amount of time he had available all too little. He chose to fly, each step throwing him hundreds of feet across the sky as he raced toward the nearby village.

Shouts of surprise and amazement accompanied his landing in the square. Wu Ying pushed his chi outward, catching the nearby wind with it as he amplified his voice to carry to the water and the few boats that had already left.

"Come back! Typhoon incoming. Evacuate immediately, to Sheep Top hill at the least."

His voice made the shutters rattle and villagers rushing toward him clap hands over their ears. A couple of children started crying, while a baby let out a long wail as it was awoken. Nearby flocks of chickens scattered, startled by his words.

"Cultivator…" The village chief ran up to Wu Ying, hands wringing and eyes wide. Others were already rushing away, taking heed of his words. "I-is it true?"

"Every word," Wu Ying said, looking back at the water where some of the boats were coming back. A couple had refused to turn away, continuing to row outward against the incoming wind. "You need to sound the alarm, chief."

"I-if you're wrong," the chief dithered, and Wu Ying glared at him.

"What point is there for me to lie? The winds have spoken, and they whisper of a coming storm full of energy and fury. Save your people, chieftain. The houses and boats can be rebuilt." Wu Ying drew a deep breath, already plotting the next place he had to travel to.

"If the winds speak to you, cultivator, can you not stop it? Can you not use a formation or protect our people otherwise?" the chief pleaded, gesturing at the houses. "This is all we have. If it is destroyed…"

"The heavens have decreed the coming and no mere mortal can stand in its way," Wu Ying said, realizing even as he spoke how true his words were. The eastern wind that blew, it held not just its normal fury but it had combined with a wind from up high. This was a wind of reckoning, and it blew with an objective, bringing rain, thunder, and judgment. "There is no standing before it, only sheltering and waiting for it to pass. Survive, chieftain. And save your people."

So saying, Wu Ying kicked off from the ground again, leaping into the air. He had no more time, darting instead down the coast. There were other villages to warn, other lone fishermen and their families who lived away from the hustle and bustle. There were even a few farming villages that were in danger, though those he sent messages to via spirit messengers.

Village after village, he blew through. His fingers never stopped working, as spirit messengers flew toward the individual houses while he gusted farther south. Every moment, the wind whispered of the incoming storm, the sky darkening as rainclouds gathered.

Eventually, he made it to the nearby city. He noticed the arrows pointed at him, the crossbow and ballistae that were focused as he flew in. Even before he landed on the nearest tower, the Captain of the Guard had arrived, staring at Wu Ying.

When Wu Ying tried to provide a report, the captain cut him off.

"Of course we know of it. Which daft fool would be unable to see the incoming typhoon? Our diviners also warned us, not long ago," the captain said. "None of that is reason for alarming the city."

Wu Ying bowed and murmured an apology. "If you had divined the storm, why was a warning not sent?"

"Why would we? Divination is never clear, nor did we know what day the storm would arrive. Once we are certain, then we send out the warning. Warnings beforehand that are mistaken just create confusion and even more destruction," the captain said. "You might think we are fools, but we have lived on this coast all our lives."

Wu Ying winced and bowed low, accepting the rebuke.

"Now, go. We have no need of you on the walls."

Wu Ying hesitated before he exhaled and kicked upward. He floated in the air, heading away from the city and back toward the villages he had passed. There was more he could do to aid them. And while the captain might have his duties to the city and considerations for the greater good, Wu Ying was just a wandering cultivator. He could do what he desired, in the here and now.

***

The typhoon had arrived, the massive cyclone lashing the coast. Wu Ying deposited the child he was holding behind the redoubt on the hill that another cultivator had created, forming the earth high on one end and creating a shallow scooped depression on the other. The half dozen villagers who hid behind it had been too slow at leaving, putting them too close to the edge of the coastline when the hurricane arrived. Now, they could only wait and endure.

Stepping away, Wu Ying looked at the redoubt and the child who had reluctantly released him before nodding goodbye. He stepped into the fury of the storm, feeling the wind tugging his clothing and body as it threatened to tear him into the sky. He ignored the cries of confusion and surprise from those he'd left in the safety of the shelter.

Wu Ying chose not to resist the wind, allowing himself to be picked up and thrown into the air. He let his head turn skyward, his spiritual sense extended to the fullest extent as he idly batted away a flying branch that nearly impaled him.

In the skies high above, he was thrown around like so much debris, no more worthwhile of concern to the storm than a leaf or a boat. He saw both fly past, along with terracotta tiles, boulders, and fishing nets. Sand blasted his skin, droplets of water soaked his robes, and thunder shook his bones.

He should have been terrified, afraid for his life as he was cast in the sky and taken li away within minutes. His heart pounded a constant, heavy tempo, threatening to tear itself free, while his breath struggled to come as the air whipped around him. His hair had torn free of the simple ties he had set, flying chaotically around him.

He should have been terrified. But his lips could not stretch any wider as he grinned, his eyes sparkling as he danced in the storm, wind chi surging through his body in symphony with the typhoon.

Wu Ying's spiritual sense had blossomed further than ever, his mind straining to sift through the myriad traces of information it provided to him. The glowing bonfires of souls of huddling mortals and animals beneath his feet, the smell of the churned ocean, and the pounding of the wind at the city's protective formation. He sensed it all.

He spun through the air, taking control of the wind around him, flowing with it as he was thrown ever farther from the coast. Wu Ying laughed, controlling his movements with the barest touches of his chi, the Never Empty Wine Pot spinning its own cyclone within his dantian and drawing the energy to him. As he spun through the air, his breathing grew easier, the sand scoured his skin less, and even the droplets grew gentle, washing away the dirt that carried itself on his flesh.

In the typhoon, the wind cultivator danced and found others accompanying his movements.

Spirits of air and wind flitted at the edges of his senses, their whispery, silver flesh and ghostly forms passing nearby. Birds of the air and wind, creatures of the heavens, and even flying fish that glided upon wings of chi joined him in the sky. Wu Ying marveled at the ecosystem around him, hidden from those below by the churning, overpowering wind and water chi that made up the thundering storm.

"Little cousin, you dance well."

The voice caught Wu Ying by surprise, the presence of the speaker something he had not even noticed until he spun around to see it. Then his jaw dropped, for the speaker was another dragon. Long, sleek, its sinuous body gliding along in the winds as its eggshell white and crystalline blue scales glinted.

More astounding were its half dozen companions, all in varying shades of blue and green, their sizes ranging from a couple li long—as best as Wu Ying could guess—to just over a hundred feet. Full-sized dragons, their long whiskers and kind eyes dancing with amusement as they looked upon the cultivator who did his best to bow deeply while spinning through the air.

"I am honored, Oh Mighty and Magnificent Dragon of the East," Wu Ying said, forcing himself not to stutter. The monstrous pressure from the closest dragon was sufficient to make him quail, his minor understanding of the wind, of the greater Dao dwarfed by the dragon's strength. His heart thudded, the bloodline within him subdued as it faced a true inheritor of draconic strength. "This one is Long Wu Ying, a minor cultivator of the sect in the Shen Kingdom in the heartlands of the continent."

"Did you hear that, brothers and sisters?" the dragon cried, letting out a wheezing cackle as he spun his body in a rotating circle, keeping up with Wu Ying as he continued to be blown away. "I am mighty and magnificent!"

"Oh, if he's mighty and magnificent, then what am I?" Another dragon, one with long eyelashes and a beautiful, glittering emerald and coral blue pattern on its scales, came flying up, shoving aside her brother with a controlled gust of wind. "Tell me, tell me."

"You are magnificent and beautiful, like the rising sun striking the ocean water," Wu Ying said, his mind scurrying down old paths. Limpid courtesies thrown at his elder sister, the praise suitors had showered her with at every greeting.

"Ooooh! A rising sun on the ocean." The eyelashes fluttered over big draconic eyes before Wu Ying found himself spun around and tugged away, another dragon pulling him close.

Another female, demanding her own praise. He had barely a moment to regard her in full detail, to find a proper compliment, before he was pulled away by a golden-blue dragon, steam rising from his mouth as he demanded Wu Ying's opinion of his claws.

Like a doll, a plaything, Wu Ying was passed from one demanding wind and water dragon to the next, the creatures vying for a compliment and unique observation to stroke their egos. A couple of times, Wu Ying feared for his life when a compliment was ill-received.

Only the mercurial, tempestuous nature of the dragons kept him alive, as scorching breath or slicing wind was blocked or turned aside by another's whim or, in two cases, Wu Ying's desperate attempts at survival.

One arm hung limp after he had blocked an irritated slap of a tail, but the demands of tribute kept arriving, uninterrupted. There might have been a bare half dozen or so of them, but they kept seeking greater and greater words of admiration.

Wu Ying's mind spun, words spilling from his mouth without thought after a time, as the toil of keeping himself aloft and watching for the next fit of pique or change in wind currents that might send him spiraling into one of the lofty draconic lords drained him.

Time immemorial passed, moments grinding on in flashes of white, green, and blue, as the sky darkened and the night sky regarded each word, motion, and phrase weighed and judged in his terrifying ordeal. A plaything for creatures greater than himself, a spinning top for mocking and bored children. The moon stared mercilessly upon his dilemma, offering no succor. Catching sight of the heavenly sights that grew in prominence each moment, Wu Ying drew further inspiration as he drifted lower and lower, exhaustion taking energy and altitude in equal measure.

As dawn rose, the summer nights short and brief, the dragons tired of their play. The wind holding Wu Ying aloft was abandoned. His body spiraled downward as the dragons withdrew their beneficence. Plummeting at the sudden absence of the winds, the cultivator barely managed to assert his energy and dao upon the winds to slow his fall. He crashed into the ground, skipping along the earth until he came to a stop against the edge of a stubborn oak tree.

Propped against the rough bark, one arm bloody and broken, a wound along his thigh leaking blood, Wu Ying found himself staring at the long furrow he had carved across the earth. He smelled the deep, dank aroma of turned and muddy earth, and watched the dawning day. Nary a breeze stirred.

Wu Ying found himself laughing, gratitude for surviving his much-anticipated meeting with a wind dragon.

Sometimes dragons arrived when you least expected them and left you a bloody but living mess.

***

A day later, Wu Ying had set up a location inside the hill, digging himself a cultivation cave and hiding it with formations and simple alterations to the environment. Deep within the temporary abode that smelled of turned earth and compressed clay, Wu Ying sat with his legs crossed. His breathing was slow and steady, his intent to cultivate the dao understandings he had gained while in the typhoon. Sadly, his hope of filling his dantian to the brim in the typhoon had been waylaid by the dragons, leaving him unable to layer his Core.

Instead, he spent his time considering his experiences. The moment when his spiritual sense had expanded, offering him a view of the world below him that was farther and wider than before.

The shift of the winds, the tug and pull, the ferocious power and strength of the typhoon as it battered the land and tossed and twirled him around. The many layers of air currents that made up the wall of wind that had poured energy through the ocean, coast, and surroundings.

His expanded understanding of the typhoon and the way it had formed, from air currents not just high above but also below as hot and cold air mixed, forming the vortex across hundreds of li that would shake provinces and kingdoms.

He sat, breathing slowly as he took in his experiences, teasing apart the presence of the eastern and heavenly winds, the vortex of the central wind, and the influences of the cold northern and warm southern winds. He meditated upon his experiences, allowing those understandings to soak into his bones, appraising them in accordance with the body forms he'd trained.

Days turned into weeks before he'd fully digested that understanding, no longer standing but moving. Eventually, he was done, the memories embedded though not entirely subsumed. Then he moved on.

For the typhoon was only one encounter. The wind dragons might not have offered their blood. A laughable thought, considering how they had seen him as nothing more than a passing fancy, barely worth consideration beyond a series of kind words. He expected that their choice not to kill him had been more than enough consideration in their view.

Even so, they had not left him without a boon, though it was not one that they perhaps had even considered. Instead, their casual use of the wind, the way they'd manipulated their chi and let it course through the surroundings, the pull and shove and their myriad dao understandings and the bloodlines they had showcased was a true jade mine of knowledge.

If he chose to dig for it.

And he so did.

Chapter 38

Inside the unchanging darkness of the cave, Wu Ying found his ability to sense the passing of time fading away. Caught up in the contemplation of that long evening, he replayed each moment over and over in his mind, teasing apart that long evening of discourse, compliments, and wind daos. He recalled the way his bloodline had reacted to both the proximity of the dragons and their dominance.

At times, he would stand, breaking away from the stillness required for his usual cross-legged meditation, and move through the forms of the Seven Winds manual. The eastern wind forms were powerful and explosive, each twisting blow and motion pouring chi through his limbs and extremities. Areas deep in his bones and his organs that had resisted cleansing and the influence of his wind chi gave way, as Wu Ying felt the deeper understanding he had gained allow him to work around those areas.

It was not just the eastern wind though, for the influence of the other winds on the cyclone had shifted his understanding further. It was not just a single wind that affected his body; it was all seven of them. It was the combination of the winds that influenced the world, even if one might hold dominance at any one time.

With that understanding came further enlightenment and progress, as he worked his way around additional blockages. Shifting from the eastern wind to the western one, to north and south and central forms all contributed as he found his chi flowing through his body, coursing through bone, marrow, and arteries, along reinforced flesh and skin, and making him lighter and faster than ever.

Once he had wondered, at the greatest stages of enlightenment and assimilation, would he become a wind itself? No more real than the breeze? Forced to give up his humanity to become nothing more than just a portion of the world below?

Now, his understanding had clarified.

Exposed to numerous daos and conceptions, his bloodline throbbed and thinned, absorbed into his body and amplifying the effects of his enlightenment. He marveled at the genius of the initial Patriarch of the Seven Winds, the formation and creation of the manual and his foretelling of the future to include both the winds of heaven and hell.

For it was that inclusion, the grounding aspect of both celestial and base needs. that ensured that Wu Ying would become naught but air itself, a moving figment of energy—unless he so chose. Instead, heaven pulled him forth and hell kept him grounded, and in that duality of nature and its inherent conflict and concord, his own mortal form was anchored.

Between heaven above and hell below, mankind existed. Souls made of the firmament of the heavens and bodies born of the wind[43].

---

[43] Chinese creation myths are myriad. You have the esoteric like the Taoist, where everything forms from the Tao and then splits apart into two, threes, and "the myriad things." You have Nuwa's creation myth and her use

Heaven was order and objective understanding, morality and celestial rights; but hell was no burning place of despair, though the punishments of diyu[44] were necessary to cleanse the soul. It was not enough to drink the soup of forgetfulness, for a soul stained by the sins of the past would carry that weight into its next life, marring learning and interactions in the future. Instead, hell was a place of cleansing and a promise of future potential, for what was the cycle of death and rebirth but the cycle of hope itself?

Wu Ying would neither be an aspect of the wind nor a mortal plodding the ground, an avatar of the winds' tempestuousness in physical form. His body lightened, flesh, bones, and organs soaked deep with wind chi. On the one hand, he felt more tied into the world around himself, for the five winds that he progressed in were of the earth. On the other, he felt torn apart, a wispy creation that could part at the barest hint of a gale.

Only the barest traces of heavenly wind chi floated through his body, mingling with the seeping cloudiness of hell chi. His journey through the kingdoms had given him a sense of the heavenly, the myriad ways the celestial bureaucracy twisted and changed, dictated to the humans below, and was guided by those above.

More difficult for Wu Ying was locating the winds of hell, of which he had only grasped the barest threads. No more had he noticed it, even as his ability to sense and trace the movements of the heavenly wind had grown.

Somehow, Wu Ying knew that his next trip to the south would see a much deeper, more powerful connection to both. In the south, Wu Ying believed, he would find the heavenly wind he had sought so far. And if heaven existed, so too did hell.

***

Meditation, movement, body forms, and eventually, a tub made of compressed clay filled with the water from his World Spirit Ring. A tub where he lay in medicinal baths, leaching impurities and pouring wind chi into his bones, forcing adaptation where his stubborn body refused to yield.

In time, the cave grew cold, the temperature dropped. He was forced to shatter the ice forming on his bath each time he came back to it, the environment leaching warmth from the shallow cultivation cave. Yet for all the turning of the seasons above, Wu Ying stayed within, soaking in the depths of his understanding of the storm that had arrived.

Once more, during this period of closed door cultivation, he felt the tearing tempest above him. Its fury and strength had reduced significantly by the time it reached his location, yet with Wu Ying's expanded senses, he felt its swirling movements and faded glory.

---

of clay to create men. And the one I refer to here is the one based off Pangu who, during his death, became the world. Then we, the mites of his body, are touched by the wind and made into people.

[44] Chinese word for hell

To Wu Ying's surprise, buried beneath the earth as he was, he found himself caught in another moment of enlightenment. The experience, both beneath the ground and amongst those mortals who moved along the earth, sheltering in place and quivering as nature's fury pounded above them, cast a new light upon the typhoon.

Rain pouring down soaked into the earth, nourishing plant matter and seeping into groundwater. Trickles of water turned into streams, joining together to form rivers on their final trip toward the sea from which they had come.

Winds broke rotten branches and uprooted older trees, opening up the canopy to allow newer, younger, and more vibrant plants an opportunity to grow. Plant seeds were thrown many li from their origins, drifting dandelion tendrils and barbed seeds alike spreading across the plains and forests.

And yes, tragedies grew. Lightning crashed, starting fires in too dry plots of land. Burrows and trees were broken, leaving animals' residences exposed, and insects perished by the score as the winds blew through. Humans were no less subjected to the vagaries of chance and the fury of the storm, ill-cared-for walls blowing down and broken beams pinning mortals.

Yet this too was necessary. All things grew old and died. Even the immortals that Wu Ying strived to emulate could perish. Immortality was but a state of never-ending youth, of improved healing and the opportunity to live for millennia.

All things died, and their deaths nourished the young and the growing.

To seek true immortality, an unaging, undying, impossible dream, was a perversion of the Dao only the demons and the dark sects would dare consider.

When the storm passed and Wu Ying's moment of enlightenment ended, he found himself extending his stay in his cultivation cave, contemplating what he had learned and feeding the understanding that he had gained to the Nascent Soul within his Core. Using that understanding to progress and combine the flowing body forms of the Seven Winds with his martial style, as the beginning edges of the third strike were created.

Understanding grew, as did the soul within, and rather than blowing onward, shut away as he was in his cave, Wu Ying cultivated and drew deeply of the wind chi around him. He rebuilt his stores in his dantian, knowing that he required another layer.

Taking the pills he had acquired, Wu Ying sped up the process, shifting away from Body Cultivation for a time. Cross-legged, he drew in chi, and around him, the winds above the hill his cultivation cave existed within grew strange and erratic. Stories grew of the altered landscape and the outpouring of chi that some sensed, unaspected, fire, and metal that benefited those of the correct alignment.

In time, local cultivators arrived to train above the hill, drawing in the complex energies below. It was of marginal benefit, but for those in the early stages of cultivation, even that marginal benefit was dearly desired.

Battles were fought, body cleansing cultivators struggling against one another and vying for a spot at the top of the hill where the chi grew more numerous. Holding forth until Energy

Storage cultivators arrived, throwing those individuals away and relegating them below. It was only good fortune that the energy gathered was too paltry for a Core Formation cultivator to care for.

And all this time, plants drawn by the wind sprouted on the hills and landslides, content to grow in the altered environment. In time, the energy in the atmosphere grew stronger and more focused, metal and earth chi growing abundant, mixing with the water chi from above and the energy that Wu Ying drew and rejected.

Months turned into years as Wu Ying resided within, existing upon the stores in his rings and the pills of nourishment they contained. Fresh vegetables, ground tofu, beans, and handfuls of rice sustained him. As his Body Cultivation progressed, his physical needs decreased. All so that he could continue his growth, chasing the moment of enlightenment and understanding, rebuilding his chi reserves.

Until finally, another layer for his Core had been formed.

***

The earth shook as ground that had long lay covered broke apart. Grass and roots split, tracts of earth rising, dark loamy soil revealed to the sun. Rocks clattered soon after as boulders that had been used to keep the cave's entrance covered and hidden rolled down the slope. Clouds of dust drifted through the air, even as a warm wind blew from within the cave, expelling humid and rotten air.

Nine individuals, the majority wandering cultivators, jumped to their feet at the sudden change in the atmosphere. In the past few weeks, the energy that had formed around the hill had peaked and grown stronger, additional chi billowing forth. Only the acquisition and deployment of a chi containment and enrichment formation had kept the change in energy flows from being noticed by others.

The fortunate nine stared at the dust cloud, automatically gathering near the peak and around the strongest, a female cultivator who wielded a pair of shortened sickles. She strode forward a little, eyes narrowed as they waited to see what might emerge.

Wu Ying, squinting a little at the light, emerged from the cave, his exit preceded by the wind to keep the dust away from his body. He frowned as he exited, his spiritual sense expanding quickly to blanket the surroundings, lips tightening as he came across both cultivators and the formation.

Quickly enough, he sensed and ascertained the details of the formation via the flow of energy. His lips compressed further, dissatisfaction flowing across his mien as he realized the effects of his cultivation. Ignoring the nine cultivators, some of whom were murmuring words of surprise and daring, he kicked into the air to survey the flow of chi.

"*Hun dan*, I'm a real fool," Wu Ying said, realizing the effects his unsheltered, unconstrained cultivation had created. "The stronger I grow, the easier it is to track me. I'm really going to need to buy some proper concealment formations."

It was just chance that he had found a spot far enough away that no cultivator of sufficient strength had come to check on it. Even more luck that the cultivators who had learned of the changes he had wrought had been greedy enough to keep the matter to themselves, leaving the information to spread locally. And lastly, even more fortunate that none of those locals had had the strength or knowledge to locate the entrance to his cultivation cave.

Below, the cultivators had grown silent. His simple act of floating in the sky was sufficient to showcase the vast difference in their cultivation strengths. Between the layering in his Core and the improvement in his wind cultivation, Wu Ying was stronger than ever. Certainly stronger than any normal middling Core Formation cultivator. Perhaps even rivaling those at the peak.

Though, he had to admit, he was not certain of that. Strength was not just a matter of chi reserves and physical ability but also dao understanding, weapons, and martial skills. It would require a contestation of blades to ascertain his true standing.

"I wonder if there's a tournament about..." Wu Ying said idly to himself.

Then he laughed a little. What kind of kingdom or sect would have the funds to organize a tournament for Core Formation cultivators? What locale could withstand a group of Core Formation cultivators battling in unison with determination? Only a true fool would invite walking calamities like that to their shores. And what cultivator with an overweening ego would actually partake in such a tournament?

Dismissing such idle thoughts, Wu Ying cut the flow of chi holding him aloft and let himself fall. It seemed that he owed those below some minor consideration. After all, they had kept the secret of his cultivation cave, even if it was a matter of self-interest. Some might think that the scales were balanced, but Wu Ying had been raised by Master Cheng. And though he might not have his Master's or Fairy Yang's ascertainment of karma, he still had picked up some semblance of understanding.

"You're the leader?" Wu Ying said, landing near the group. A bare dozen feet away, far enough to keep the group from feeling crowded and afraid.

"Honored Cultivator..." A glance backward, the woman's lips tightening as the group all stepped back, leaving her alone. She offered Wu Ying a martial bow that kept her weapons out, even if they laid on the backs of her forearms. "I am so *honored*. This one is Xia Tung Mei."

"Winter plums?" Wu Ying had to suppress the smile that crossed his face. It seemed her parents had a sense of humor.

"So my parents named me," Tung Mei said, staying bowed and speaking over her clasped hands.

"Rise. I see no point in those formalities," Wu Ying said.

"Thank you, Honored Cultivator. However, we have benefited greatly—"

"If unknowingly," one of the cultivators in the back muttered.

"—from your presence and cultivation. We would name you our benefactor, if you would."

"None of that. I have benefited as well." His eyes narrowed briefly before he pointed at three of the individuals in the back. "You three. You've stepped on the road to Body Cultivation. There is a pool within that has some dregs remaining. Use it if it suits the forms you have chosen. The liquid is potent, even if diminished, so take great care." Ignoring the three as they bowed low, he pointed to another man on the far right. "Your study of the jian might benefit from the sword imprint I've left on the walls within. Study it well, though remember, my style is not your own."

Another deep bow. Five more left to go. Two were Body Cultivators, neither with any real talent, seeing that they were both in their early twenties and had barely broken through their third and fourth Body Cleansing meridians.

He spoke to the one with the fourth meridian open first. "Your fourth meridian and dantian are damaged from your latest attempt at a breakthrough. Consume this"—a flicker of his hand sent a small pill bottle flying over—"rest, relax, and recuperate. And stop pushing. You might, if you are fortunate, achieve another cleansed meridian, but you have reached your limit."

"No! That cannot be. Please, Honored Cultivator. I need, I have to, breakthrough," the man pleaded, putting his hands together. For such a big man, a man whose broad shoulders and tanned skin—along with the axe by his side—spoke of his occupation, to plead in this manner, his need must be desperate.

"Why?"

"There's a man… the Lord's cousin. He came by. I…" the big man slowed, choking on his words.

"Need to avenge someone?" Wu Ying finished for him.

"No!" the forester cried in surprise. "No. I just need to be worthy of him."

"Oh." Wu Ying blinked, the thread of an old story thrown awry. He took a moment to recalibrate as more than a few others glanced at the man, one person muttering about bunny lovers. "I… well. I have nothing to offer other than a suggestion that perhaps if you are not sufficient as you are, perhaps he might not be the best partner for you."

The forester frowned, but Wu Ying moved on determinedly. There were some things he could not fix, not in the brief moments he had here. So.

"As for you." Wu Ying eyed the last Body Cleanser before he sighed. "Give it up. You've left it too long. This path, it is not for you. Not in this life."

The man gritted his teeth, fuming at the blunt assessment. Yet he dared not contradict it, not in public. And perhaps, Wu Ying hoped, deep in his soul he knew that he had been given the truth others had refused to speak.

"As for you three…" Wu Ying flicked his gaze over them, all in the Energy Storage stage. All of them holding weapons with the surety of martial specialists. "With me. I require a sparring partner, and you three shall do."

Unspoken was the command that they would need to take what understanding they could from the sparring match. Just as he too had once been the sparring partner of a Core Formation cultivator, oh so long ago.

***

Push down on the sickle with the left hand, hand against the flat of the blade, changing angle and direction so that it would miss. Not just his body, but his robes. No reason to damage his clothing. In the other hand, his jian parried in high guard a guan dao sweeping down, his extended arm rotated around and nearly fully extended to let the structure of his body take the force of the blow, allowing it to dissipate through his feet. Proper form, even if he could have beaten it aside with pure strength.

Bring back left leg upward straight ahead before he kicked, extending forward and pushing with his hips upon contact. It was not a proper blow, for such an attack would kill—or at least, badly injure—his sparring partners, but more a push to send Tung Mei tumbling backward. She struck out with her other sickle as she fell, a movement that almost caught his foot as he retracted it.

Then the third opponent approached, unleashing a series of blows with his paired maces. The heavy weights on the weapons threatened to damage and chip away at any lesser weapon, crushing paltry defenses beneath the surging might of an earth cultivator.

Wu Ying chose to dodge, for earth might be mighty, but it was slow. Even having lowered his cultivation by significant degrees, his opponents were slow. Only fighting three of them allowed them to provide the challenge Wu Ying sought, as he worked to finish refining his understanding.

The Wandering Dragon, a progression and adaptation of the Long family style, was a work in progress. He had based the form in the familiar but had, over time, combined the movement forms of the Seven Winds, the expanded movement set and distance, the almost preternatural ability to shift in space.

It was that ability he made most use of now, exploding from stillness to motion, crossing space so that it seemed he had appeared at his objective. The movement techniques crossed intervening space in ways that seemed to defy normal physics, like now.

A swinging mace came down from the right. Wu Ying shifted, seeming to move through the swinging mace itself to emerge on the other side, pass the mace wielder to stand before the polearm owner. A palm lifted, lowered to touch the chest, then pushed downward. The guan dao wielder flew backward and into the ground, bouncing off the earth as Wu Ying

515

stepped back again, once more shifting through the mace wielder's attack, blowing through him to emerge behind.

Then another strike with the same raised palm, hammering between shoulder blades, sent opponent sprawling forward. To the cultivators watching, Wu Ying might have been the breeze, but to Wu Ying himself, he continued to fail.

For the steps between the shifts, the act of passing through another was but a trick. He could not become the wind—that way was barred to him for now. Perhaps forever. All he did was move so swiftly, bending and contorting limbs and body parts to dodge attacks by the barest margins, that it seemed he had passed through the attack.

The three cultivators struggled to their feet once again, breathing with labored and painful lungs. Standing alone, Wu Ying glanced toward the sky once more. Judging the time, the season, the moment. Then he lowered his weapon and sheathed it.

"One last form. Watch carefully. And guard well," Wu Ying murmured softly, yet his voice was pitched that they all heard it.

The third form, still in its nascent stages. He would not use the blade itself, instead intent on the motions. Hand down by his side, he stepped to the right, opening his hips with the motion as his foot landed sideways. His right hand came flashing upward, robes flickering in the wind as he followed the motion of his foot, turning the rest of the way. Foot, hip, shoulder, arm, other foot touching down not just once but three times in quick succession, each time pushing him to spin faster.

The Dragon Turns.

Wind, beckoned by the barest application of dao and chi, came rushing in to fulfill his commands. Air surged forward, a looping wind that caught the trio as they braced. The attack, rather than hitting straight-on as expected, threw them sideways, causing the trio to tumble into one another.

Wu Ying knew he could keep turning, spinning and alternating his footsteps, the movement of his arm. Combining his arm movements with a leaping attack, staying still to form the cutting winds that chewed into ground and flesh alone. Instead, he stopped moving, letting the wind die down. He felt his breathing burn, his skin churn as the heavenly chi within him throbbed.

No, no further movement.

Another incomplete form, his understanding shallow. The damage he sought to contain escaped, the placement of his feet and the location of his attack precarious. The world turned on the smallest moment, and yet was infinitely adaptive.

Nature cared not for heaven's designs, for the orderly dictates it demanded for the way the world should exist. Nature was but part of the Dao itself, and that was silent and immutable, infinite and all-encompassing. It could not be changed, and yet encompassing all, change was ever present. Nature cared not if one attempted to dominate it, for nature was forever out of control[45].

In the conflicting dictates between heaven and the Dao, Wu Ying's style had to traverse. Seeking a guiding path that would escape heavenly tribulation and nature's whims.

Exhaling slowly, Wu Ying came back to the present. Around him, the cultivators clambered to their feet, some with awe and worship on their faces, others with fear and respect etched deep in their hearts.

His head turned toward the east, where a lonely, heartbroken fisherman had been abandoned.

And felt the tug of another wind, one more insistent than ever. It called to him, demanding his attention, his presence. It blew from the north, but its heart belonged to the south. The final direction that he had not explored.

Wu Ying cast one last glance toward the east, letting go of the tendrils of desire in his heart. Some things were not fated to be.

Then before the children could ask more of him, he leapt into the sky and let the wind take him. To the south.

---

[45] Paraphrasing verses 29 and 30 of the Tao Teh Ching

Chapter 39

The temple that sat upon the mountain loomed over the lush green surroundings. The edifice was not tall enough for mountain mist to reach it, nor were there significant sources of water or waterfalls to provide an overabundance of humidity to obscure it. Instead, the temple was serene in its standing, a silent sentinel that watched over the surrounding farms and villages.

The Temple to the Merciful Goddess was famed for the beauty of its surroundings, but also for the forty-foot statue of the goddess in the courtyard. Stories abounded about the temple and the statue that stood before it. How a marauding Nascent Soul-level fox spirit had torn up the surroundings, chasing the remaining villagers to the safety of the temple. When it was about to devour the survivors, the statue had shone with a bright light that had healed the injuries of the villagers and calmed the fox spirit. Placated, the fox spirit walked over to the feet of the statue and bowed low before curling up around the base of the figure, never to harm the villages again.

Some said the fox spirit passed that day, others that it became the guardian of the temple, and still others spoke of how the spirit would eventually die, either leaving its bones to rot while still guarding the statute and surroundings or ascending to the heavens.

The myriad tales, as recounted on the way south to Wu Ying, had piqued his interest. More so, the tales of the current guardians of the locale, who ran an inn and trading post outside the temple itself. A place where goods and wonders sufficient even for a Core Formation cultivator abounded, where commerce and a neutral meeting spot could be found under the watchful eye of the proprietors.

Passing along the road to the temple, it was impossible to miss the aforementioned establishment, for it had been built and added to such that the entire structure rivaled some public buildings. The wooden front had two major entrances—one for the inn, the other for the trading post. While the trading post was thronged with customers, the doorway and insides of the inn were silent and dark, a sharp contrast to the inn on the opposite side of the road.

Joining the flow of pilgrims and villagers, Wu Ying made the ascent to the temple, pausing with others to marvel at the beauty of the building, to soak in the silence and views before entering. Even with the dozens of other worshippers within, a quiet and contemplative hush surrounded the building and its grounds.

The towering statue of Guan Yin rose to meet Wu Ying as he entered the courtyard, an immense praying urn set before it. Steps to permit individuals to walk around and insert their joss sticks allowed worshippers to constantly add to the urn, while additional buildings immediately behind and to the left and right of the statue contained other heavenly gods.

Taking his place behind the worshippers, Wu Ying acquired a trio of joss sticks from the waiting box, dropping in a handful of coins as payment before lighting the sticks. Holding the joss sticks in both hands, he bowed three times to the goddess, murmuring a silent prayer for her intercession for all those he had lost and all those he killed or harmed in any way.

For a moment, his mind grew in turmoil, memories of the battles he had been involved in, the lives he had taken surging forward and breaking the peaceful harmony of the temple. He felt the hot breath escaping his lips as he panted, attempting to block another attack while pressed against Li Yao as they escaped, the cutting wind and sand as he danced in a storm of winds while a crazed general stood above, and the desperate, last-minute attempts at saving his friends even as the acrid, rotten smell of a demonic worshipper filled his nose.

He lived those moments again, one after the other. Felt the sting of sweat on his brow, the trembling in his muscles from exhaustion, the killing intent that threatened to tear him apart. Wu Ying unconsciously leaked his own, so caught up in his memories, before a light filled him.

For a moment, Wu Ying's mind recoiled, fighting the gentle pressure that beckoned him out of his past. Then, as though plucking a blossom from a crowded tree, it pulled him awake once more, his killing intent subdued, his mind returned. As suddenly as the presence had arrived, it left, leaving Wu Ying in the present with a crowd of worshippers eyeing him askance.

Wu Ying could only offer a deep bow in apology. Straightening, his eyes narrowed as he regarded the goddess's statue. So few of the pantheon above interacted with the mortal world. Even the kitchen god, he who watched over the hearth and home and spied upon mortals, took little action, only bearing his whispered secrets to those above.

Few immortals acted upon the mortal plane, perhaps to save them the heartache of watching the same mistakes carried out over and over. Perhaps because a child could not grow to their full strength under the constant watchful and ever-cautious eyes of their parents. Or perhaps, having once walked among humanity themselves, they sought not to repeat the mistakes of the past.

Yet the Goddess of Mercy defied such considerations. She stood between the planes of heaven and earth, a constant intercession between the pitiless judgment of fortune and mortal failings. Of all the immortals who strode the heavenly halls, she was perhaps the most beloved because of that.

He breathed in the smell of the incense, the frankincense, sandalwood, and cinnamon that made up this particular brand. Stepping forward when there was room, he inserted the joss sticks in the brazier before bowing once more to the statue and taking his leave.

Leaving the other worshippers to their thoughts, the stifled sobs of a mother and her husband resounding behind him, he turned left to the temple of the gods of hell. There, he repeated his actions, burning joss sticks and asking for their mercy.

The only difference was that when he stopped beside an immense stone brazier, Wu Ying made sure to purchase and burn a large amount of paper money. He made an offering to his ancestors, then to his Master and Yu Kun in particular. He made sure to burn more for those he might have forgotten, for the ghosts of those who failed to have someone care for them. Wu Ying watched the silver paper burn in hopes that it would pay down their spiritual debt.

An easing of suffering, for the many, for the lost.

Then, having done his duty as a filial son and friend, he moved on. There were many temples to visit, and one last location afterward on this day. It suited him, this place, in its silent regard of all passing things, in its belief in mercy for all those who had passed and those who still struggled.

This day of all days.

***

The inside of the inn was as silent as it had looked, slivers of light entering through open slat windows and the wide-open door. Yet unconsciously or consciously, none of the other worshippers chose to enter the building, choosing to partake in the refreshments in the inn on the other side of the road.

Silent it might have been, but the inn was not empty. As Wu Ying searched for the proprietor as he stepped within, his spiritual senses spoke to him of the other occupants. Two were seated together, supping on bowls of noodle soup, their heads bent over a scroll of poetry. The third sat at a diagonal to the door, hidden in the shadows and opposite the kitchens on Wu Ying's left, near the adjoining entrance to the trading post. That figure had a large, woven bamboo hat pulled low over their bowed head, a sword propped against their shoulder.

A quiet, contemplative group. All gave off the air of danger, their control over their auras so impeccable that the winds gently blowing through skirted around the figures. Three figures, and each and every single individual within that room a Core Formation cultivator.

"Ah! My apologies for making you wait, dear customer. Come, come. Sit anywhere you wish." The proprietor appeared from the kitchen, pushing the doors open with his back before spinning around, a bowl of beef noodle soup in one hand and a bowl of boiled pig intestines in the other.

"Thank you, laoban[46]." Wu Ying glanced at the dishes the man held easily, then nodded to them. "The same. And tea."

"Of course, of course!" The proprietor nodded, a big grin breaking out on his slightly florid face. He walked over to serve the dishes to the lone swordsman in the corner, and Wu Ying could not help but note the way the laoban moved, the easy gliding motion he used to cross the floor, every step perfectly balanced and not a single drop of soup spilled.

Choosing not to comment, Wu Ying took a seat just past the center of the room, such that he might watch the various entrances. There were quite a few – the door he came into, the open sliding door between the connected trading post and the inn itself and the kitchen door.

---

[46] Chinese term for "boss" or "proprietor." Often used as a form of endearment and familiarity with shopkeepers and the like.

The entrance to the trading post continued to be busy, the merchant and her servants speaking with and supplying their customers with brisk efficiency. They barely stepped within the storage area behind the counter before they emerged with the requested goods, always moving.

Something about the two attendants, the shopkeeper and the laoban, niggled at Wu Ying's perceptions, making him frown a little as he regarded them. He was still considering what it was when the laoban arrived with his bowls of beef noodle soup and pig intestines, a third plate of steamed and fried pork dumplings balanced on the edge of his hand.

"Truly beautiful, are they not?" the laoban said with good cheer. Wu Ying moved back a little, offering the man more room to place the dishes down while inhaling the aroma of the pork buns. His gaze skipped to the buns, but his thoughts were interrupted as the owner continued. "My wife and my daughters."

"That they are, laoban. Very beautiful and graceful." Wu Ying smiled, both for having the niggling detail cleared up and also to show that he meant no harm. For he had heard the warning the other had offered in his words. "You are fortunate indeed to have been blessed."

Lowering his voice, the laoban muttered, "Better if I had a son, eh? But no such fortune." He grinned again suddenly. "Then again, I don't expect to have much to offer them anytime soon to inherit. So perhaps this is the best, eh?"

Wu Ying nodded dumbly. Laughing at his own joke, the jolly owner wandered away to deposit the plate of dumplings with the other pair of cultivators, leaving Wu Ying to his food. A strange man, but then again, that was why he had come here.

Hours later, when the trading post finally closed their doors and the worshippers had hurried back to nearby inns and places of rest, the shopkeeper entered the inn. Wu Ying was nursing a pot of wine by himself, sipping on the drink as he waited.

The shopkeeper drifted in, closing the doors to her trading post and leaving her daughters to finish taking inventory, sorting the items they had purchased, and otherwise handling the mundane tasks of running the business. She walked to the lone swordsman, sat beside him, and held a low-voiced conversation.

Wu Ying's wind stirred a little, intent on bringing the shopkeeper's words to his ears without asking, only to be rebuffed. It was as though a wall had formed, one of will and dao alike, forcing the winds to swirl along the edges of the room futilely.

Sipping on his wine, Wu Ying pushed against the errant wind, calling it to heel. There was no honor in eavesdropping, especially over idle curiosity, though the wind cared not for such mortal manners. As the wind quieted, Wu Ying noticed the proprietress flicker a glance at him, sharp-eyed and intent. A shiver of disquiet ran through him, and Wu Ying once more eyed the doors and windows before her regard turned away.

"More wine, honored customer?" The laoban arrived moments later, smiling widely. "Or perhaps dinner?"

"Dinner," Wu Ying said. "What is it that you have prepared and would recommend?"

"Ah, well. We have more dumplings, of course. But for dinner today, we just received a delivery of fresh carp and freshwater prawns. I'd recommend that, a serving of our gai lan from the gardens, and steamed bamboo rice," the man said enthusiastically.

"The fish. Steamed or fried?" Wu Ying asked.

"Either," the laoban replied. "But steamed is my recommendation. It is very fresh. Wasteful to fry it if your taste is for fresh fish. And to compliment it all, drunken prawns."

Wu Ying nodded in agreement and the man grinned, bustling over to the pair of other cultivators. To his disappointment, they rejected his overtures and instead settled their bill, their eyes still fixed upon his wife. The woman had just finished her business with the swordsman, handing over a small package that had appeared in her hands, before rising and strolling over to the pair.

Taking a seat before the two, blocking their view of the swordsman leaving the building, the proprietress smiled at the pair. "Honored customers. I must ask, but you know our rules?" The way she pitched her voice, she made sure Wu Ying could hear her too.

"Of course, Great One." The first cultivator scrambled to his feet, closely followed by his friend, and the pair bowed low. "We intended no insult. We have but a small question for yourself and were but anxious."

"Good. Harm to those coming or going from our property is dearly frowned upon," the woman said easily, her voice filled with good humor. Moments later, she glanced at the scroll the pair had been poring over all afternoon, quietly arguing about the passages. "Is this what concerns you?"

"No, no. This is but an idle discussion," the second scholar interrupted, bowing again. "If I may…" At her nod, he gestured over the scroll, making it disappear and replacing it with another document. "It is this map and treatise. We believe…"

The rest of his words were drowned out, cut off suddenly as the proprietress flexed her dao and muted the conversation. Wu Ying turned away, not wanting to be caught watching or listening. After all, the warning had been quite clear.

Picking up his wine cup, he swirled it and sipped on it, frowning as he tasted its lukewarm nature. He gestured downward at the bottle of wine that lay in the warm bath, channeling fire chi to warm the water once more to boiling. The simple act of altering his chi and using it in such an undirected manner was no longer difficult, not at his current level of cultivation. Even the wasted chi—and that was a significant amount—meant little at this stage. What would have exhausted him as an Energy Storage cultivator was but the barest pouring of energy now.

Night had come fully by the time the conversation between the proprietress and the two cultivators had finished, Wu Ying's dinner having been served and mostly finished. During that time, the daughters had arrived and taken dinner with their father before exiting into the back gardens. Wu Ying sensed the flow of chi as they began their evening cultivation session.

Finally, when the pair left, bowing and thanking the woman with every other sentence, she turned to Wu Ying. He sat up a little, only for the front door to be thrown open. Reactively, Wu Ying leaned back, his hand dropping to his sword's hilt as the newcomer stumbled within.

***

"Laoban, Laobaniang[47] Yang, long time no see." The man who stumbled in was dressed in rags, deep dirt and oil stains across the torn and tattered peasant tunic he wore. A large dirty hat covered his face, bamboo strips missing along one corner but still managing to hide the majority of his face.

Wu Ying's eyes narrowed, for the man's stench filled the room, pervading everything. A slight push of Wu Ying's dao and control of the winds sent the air from him, keeping the stench away from his meal.

"Beggar Soh," Proprietress Yang said, turning easily to smile at the man. She twitched her fingers a little, and suddenly the pressure that Wu Ying felt keeping the man's stench aside disappeared, the woman taking over the burden. "You come again."

"Of course. You are still married too, I see."

"And you haven't bathed either," Laoban Yang said, emerging from the kitchen. "If we are done stating the obvious, you know I don't like it when you come without bathing."

"Ah, there was no rain! Dry as a desert this past week."

Wu Ying's eyebrow twitched. If the man had seen a bathtub in the last year, Wu Ying would have been surprised. Still, he chose not to speak, for he could sense the unseen battle of daos and wills being conducted in the environment and a world above his own. His skin prickled, the hair on his body standing on end, and an unseen pressure tightened his chest, making breathing difficult.

It was surprising that a single individual could vie with both Nascent Soul cultivators in their own domain. Beggar Soh was no common Nascent Soul cultivator it seemed, even if he was one who uncommonly needed a wash.

The silent pressure increased, forcing Wu Ying to shrink back. He exerted his dao, pouring energy into his aura in such a way as to reinforce his defenses. Unfortunately, the difference between a full Nascent Soul and a Core Formation cultivator in the mid-stages was significant, and much of the pressure pushed past his aura into his body. The pounding headache increased and a trace of warmth touched the top of his lip.

When he touched his nose and the lip, Wu Ying's eyes widened with surprise at the blood flow. Tilting his head back, he squeezed the bridge of his nose, putting pressure on the minor wound even as he kept swallowing, for the tension around his ears, around his head continued to build. He knew that this was no air pressure differential, nothing so mundane. This was a

---

47 Laobanniang—female proprietress / shopkeeper's wife.

clash of daos. One that was slowly killing him. Would have killed him already if he was not both Body and Soul Cultivator.

"Seniors…" He croaked, head still bent backward, eyes throbbing. The thread of his voice was too low, the words barely escaping his throat. He tried again, louder, calling on his dao to aid him and calling on the winds.

Three heads whipped around, spotting Wu Ying's increasingly desperate expression and the blood leaking through his fingers. Two heads focused upon the interloper, fury blossoming. The slow pressure that had been building rose again, and blood now seeped from Wu Ying's eyes.

"Enough!" A hand extended sideways, and from the kitchen, a chef's cleaver flew and landed in Laoban Yang's hand.

The beggar eyed the cleaver and the folding fan that had appeared in the proprietress's hand, then he bobbed his head, the pressure suddenly disappearing. He let out a little grunt of pain, his shoulders hunching as though a sudden weight had landed on his shoulders.

"My apologies. It seems I have been truly rude," Beggar Soh said, pushing up the worn hat. Under the hat, Wu Ying was surprised to note dark, kindly eyes looking at him, ruddy red and dirt-stained cheeks, and long grey whiskers falling down the sides of his face.

"Go bathe," Proprietress Yang said, her formerly professionally cheerful demeanor cold. "You know where the trough is. When you're back, then we will talk."

Beggar Soh made a face before he bowed his head, backing out of the room and taking his stench with him. A wind—not in Wu Ying's control—stirred to life, sending the noxious remnants outward, while she spoke over her shoulder to her husband.

"Check on our daughters, dear. I shall look after our guest."

"Our daughters!" Letting out a little yelp, Laoban Yang disappeared through the kitchen doorway and out the back door in a flash of movement.

Looking indulgently at where her husband had disappeared, Proprietress Yang sauntered over to Wu Ying, who was recovering his sense of stability, the unseen, uncomfortable pressure gone now. Still, a thrill of fear ran through him, for he understood that it was just in abeyance, not gone.

"He is such a fool. Our daughters would have known to activate a defensive formation when Beggar Soh arrived. After all, it is not the first time he has overindulged before arriving," Proprietress Yang muttered as she pulled Wu Ying's hand away from his nose. To Wu Ying's horror, she dipped a cloth handkerchief in the wine and cleaned his face, the blood already having stopped seeping out. "Sometimes men feel they should face things that they need not, thinking it is beneath them to run." Proprietress Yang's tone was pointed. "Don't you think so?"

"I do," Wu Ying said, grateful when she took her hand away.

She smiled at him, muttering, "All better," before she sat down beside him, gently pushing the now-cold plates aside with the tips of her fingers.

"I also must apologize for being in the way. If I had known…"

"You would have left?" A single, elegant eyebrow rose.

"Yes."

"Good, though it would have been rude to leave without paying your bill." When Wu Ying spluttered, trying to backtrack, she let out a peal of laughter that reassured him she was teasing him. "It was our fault for indulging in an old argument while we had a guest."

"I—"

Wu Ying was interrupted by the returning laoban, the man stomping back in without his cleaver, the dark clouds of his earlier countenance mostly gone.

Instead, he eyed Wu Ying before turning to his wife. "Our daughters are safe. They activated the formations in the back. Our eldest even scolded me for interrupting their cultivation session." He made a face. "You knew that, didn't you?"

"I did."

"Then—"

"And I know you wouldn't have rested easy until you checked yourself," she said with a teasing smile. "Overly indulgent father that you are."

"I am not." Laoban Yang crossed his arms and pouted.

"Who was it who bought Yang Mu her first jian at two?"

"But she was crying…"

Turning to Wu Ying, eyes dancing with amusement, the proprietress said, "Now, what is it that such an intriguing young man wants with us?"

"Well, your fame—"

"Hush. We do not need words of praise—"

"I do!" Laoban Yang muttered.

"—but your needs. What can we do, boy, to aid in your cultivation journey?"

Drawing a deeper breath, feeling the slight sting in his nostrils and comforted already from his initial fear by her motherly, persuasive tone, Wu Ying spoke. Even knowing that part of his comfort was from her dao. The very same dao that had nearly crushed him.

Chapter 40

Beggar Soh arrived a good hour later, grumbling about having to change out the water a couple of times. Somehow, even having washed, he still managed to look scruffy and unkempt with traces of dirt still on his face, hands, and bare feet. Still, his stench was significantly reduced and the rags he wore now were less malodorous, just stained.

Wu Ying and the proprietress were hunched over the table, the dishes cleared away, with a fresh pot of wine warmed up next to them. On the table was a series of pills, talismans, and formation flags that the proprietress had collected after listening to Wu Ying's request, her hands moving over the items as she described them to the cultivator.

"… obscuring formations from the Rainbow Scarf Sect. They're better known for illusory formations, but they recently had a lower member rank up to Master level and they've been expanding their customer base with obscuring formations. It's why we're letting it go at a significant discount compared to others."

"Effectiveness at the same level?" Wu Ying said.

"Of course. Is it suitable?" At his nod, she continued. "Now, the pills you've asked for are all common." At Wu Ying's incredulous look, she continued. "For a Core Formation cultivator. Your Soul Cultivation method is not particularly obtuse, so your requirements are simple enough. However, your Body Cultivation needs…"

Wu Ying smiled a little grimly. "I understand. I had to ask."

"I'm grateful of your understanding. It's rare that we don't have something available for a customer, but in this case, for a Wind Body at your level, well, I would not call it unprecedented but—"

"Close enough that I can barely recall the last time I met one like you," Beggar Soh supplied as he strolled up, glancing over Wu Ying's pile of stuff and sniffing disdainfully.

"Is there a problem with my purchases, sir?" Wu Ying asked curiously. After the battle of wills, he was more than willing to overlook any potential insult the man might be offering in search of a pearl of wisdom. After all, strength came with knowledge all too often.

"A waste of money," Beggar Soh said, sitting down without prompting and pouring himself a cup of wine. Holding onto the pot, he downed his first cup, poured himself a second, downed that, then poured himself a third before putting the pot in the warm water. "Sleep under the stars. Trust in your instincts to keep the monsters away, or yourself to wake before they arrive. Don't pollute your body to strengthen your soul, then pollute it further—just in a different way—to cleanse and strengthen your body, only to repeat the cycle again."

Wu Ying cocked his head. "That is true, but what other choice is there?"

"The only reason there is no choice is because you children are always rushing, rushing, rushing," Beggar Soh said. "Rushing to cleanse your meridians, to build your Core, to grow your soul. Rushing to gain strength, never spending time to actually learn anything."

"You're a heretic then?" Wu Ying asked.

Beggar Soh snorted. "Only someone from the orthodox sects would call those who refuse to follow their constrained rules a heretic." His gaze flicked over Wu Ying's robes and body before he continued. "Though I'm surprised to see someone with your experiences slavishly following their doctrine."

"My experiences?"

"The wind and earth speak of your past, the travels you've been on. The trip you intend to pursue," the beggar said. "Inadvisable though that may be."

"Inadvisable?" Laoban Yang said, coming over to stand by his wife, a hand landing on her shoulder by reflex.

"He intends to go south," Beggar Soh said.

"Ah," the laoban muttered while the proprietress's lips thinned.

Caught out by the switch in topics, Wu Ying frowned between the trio. Two things in what the beggar had said had surprised him, the first… "You speak to wind and earth?"

"Wind, earth, clouds, sky, rain…" The beggar smirked. "Did you think yourself unique? I walk under the heavens, with the world around me. Why would I not listen to my closest and dearest friends?"

Wu Ying had no answer. He knew he was not unique, though few worked with the elements in the same way. Still, to hear a heretic speak of the same and accuse him of being too orthodox… it made Wu Ying reflect. He had spent so much time traveling outside the sects, working for them, yet he had been banished for defying their orders. Even his own path as a Body Cultivator was not the orthodox method of ascension.

Into the silence, the laoban spoke. "Heretic or orthodox or wandering, it's all the same. We walk the path of ascension all, and each path is as unique or similar as the one before it."

"So say the dual cultivators," Beggar Soh said. "Many would call your path a perversion too, having stepped off the direct route to raise a family and run an inn."

"Most of those who said as much have been left far behind or passed away," Proprietress Yang said. "Dual cultivation might not be accepted by most orthodox sects, but it is just as valid."

Wu Ying frowned, recalling a few sects that had pushed for dual cultivation as their mainstay method of ascension. Less common even than sword cultivators—what with the need for finding a suitable partner—it was still considered an orthodox method.

"Don't frown so, child," Beggar Soh said. "Just because you learned things one way does not mean it's valid all through the kingdoms."

"But dual cultivation is practiced in multiple kingdoms," Wu Ying commented. "How can it be not as accepted?"

"It's an argument among those of us at the highest stages," Beggar Soh replied, smirking a little. "You see, many of us think that those who espouse dual cultivation do so in a way that cuts off the cultivation path of others."

Wu Ying glanced at the pair, who looked on with quiet patience.

Beggar Soh continued. "It only requires a moment of consideration to see the issues with dual cultivation. You probably were warned of it too when you started. Many forms of dual cultivation require a willing, lifelong partner. How easy is it to find one?

"Then of course, there're concerns when said cultivating partner falls behind—or dies or otherwise leaves. What happens then? Do you raise another child to your level? Or search around for another who had lost as much as you did?" Beggar Soh snorted. "If it is hard— nearly impossible—to ascend to the highest levels of cultivation alone, how much harder is it when you have two souls doing so at once?"

"But is not dual cultivation stronger? Faster?" Wu Ying pointed out.

That was the common refrain after all, for the Yin and Yang properties of both cultivators balanced one another, the cultivation paths and flow of chi with paired partners ensuring that the same amount of time and energy was more efficiently used. The effects were supposed to be more than double that of any normal cultivation method.

"And there we have your orthodox sect's perspective. Speed! Efficiency! The rush to the top, to fall ever faster to the bottom."

Wu Ying's lips pursed tightly at the biting words. Looking at the pair, he could not help but ask, "And what do you think?"

"Beggar Soh is not wrong." The aforementioned man began to smirk, only to stop when the laoban continued. "We are not the best example. Dual cultivation was efficient, it was effective for us. It allowed us to grow stronger than our competition… but we have also chosen to stop pursuing ascension with the same fervor." He grinned then, a little. "Though sometimes, I think the Mistress who created our style meant for it to be used in this manner. To live together, to pursue cultivation as one, in peace and harmony with a family."

"Dual cultivation is strong, and I could not think I would have ascended this far without my husband." She leaned into his hand for a second, making Wu Ying blink at the casual display of affection. "Still, it's not perfect, and it's not ideal. Dual cultivation is prone to abuse in sects and among others. Ah Soh might complain about the orthodox sects, but because they're so strict, it leads to fewer abuses. Few heretical dual cultivation sects last long due to the opportunities for abuse."

"Except the more promiscuous ones…" Beggar Soh said, grinning lewdly. He leaned over, fixing Wu Ying with a conspiratory gaze. "Have you visited them? I bet you'd be quite popular. You've got good Yang chi, and with your fire and wood secondary aspects, you could work well with many of their members."

"Just be ready to run," Laoban Yang said, laughing a little. "Sometimes they get overenthusiastic with their requests. It's fun being tied down at first, but… oof!" He groaned, gripping his stomach where his wife had elbowed him. "Yes, dear. I apologize for being rude." Lowering his voice as he stepped away, he added, "But still, be ready to run."

"Such places are rarely as difficult as my husband likes to make them out—"

"Only takes one…"

"—and can be quite fun. Why, in my youth—"

"You were quite in demand," Beggar Soh said. "You had dozens of suitors and regular visitors; your lantern never dimmed. But when you met Old Man Yang, you chose to give it all up." He snorted. "There's no reason to bore the child with old history."

Proprietress Yang glared at Beggar Soh, who refused to look away, eventually forcing her to turn aside to speak to Wu Ying rather than repeat the earlier incident. "In the end, dual cultivation is a matter of fate. If you find one who makes your heart soar, then you'll not want to ascend and lose them. That is what we feel our progenitors, those who created the methods for dual cultivation, truly sought. A way to ascend with those you love. Because without it, what is the point of heaven?"

Before those profound words could soak in, Beggar Soh broke the atmosphere by laughing. The proprietress sighed, putting the side of her head on one hand as she waited for the man to finish.

He cut it off soon enough. "Pretty words." He paused, inclining his head. "And for those who do find their true loved ones, perhaps true."

Laoban Yang nodded, acknowledging the other man's kind words.

"But for most of us, grasping the sliver of the Dao itself is more than enough. We need not have another to fill our lives, for the Dao itself is infinite. My companions are the sun and rain, the moon and stars and the earth that I walk. I need nothing else."

"And have nothing else," Laoban Yang said.

Beggar Soh smirked before downing his cup of wine and pouring himself another. "What I need, the Dao—and fellow friends like you—supply. What more can I ask for?" A beat, then he waved at the empty wine pot. "Other than more wine!"

Wu Ying watched as the trio fell into what seemed to be a familiar argument, squabbling over the disparate paths even as bottles of plum wine floated out from the kitchen. It was fascinating to listen as they discussed the Dao, their own paths forward and how those paths had played out. And while it brought no flashes of enlightenment nor broke him into another layer, he found himself entranced nonetheless. Only occasionally did he interject, not daring to interrupt too often, understanding his grasp was shallow compared to these seniors.

Yet...

For the first time in a long time, Wu Ying found himself at peace, listening and learning at the feet of others who had so much more experience than him.

***

Unsurprisingly, talk of daos and philosophies and elements dragged on late into the night, with bottles of warmed wine added in ever-increasing amounts. Even though the lights from the inn glowed steadily, long after the inn across the road had closed and the mortal occupants had left, none disturbed their conversation. The subtle pressure of the presence of not one or two but three Nascent Soul cultivators was sufficient to keep even the most obtuse mortal away.

Eventually, the conversation petered toward the end, old ground having been retreaded not once but thrice again. With the fifth pot of the Soul and Memory Destroying Poison Wine having been consumed— tentatively and mildly by Wu Ying—the trio of Nascent Soul cultivators sat in silence, enjoying each other's presence. The smell of roasted peanuts, deep fried bean curd skin soaked in spirits and spices before being steamed, and the remnants of fresh baked buns mixed with the strong scent of the poisoned plum wine, enticing Wu Ying to take another sip.

Resolutely, he pushed the cup away. Already, his head was spinning, his chi churning as it fought against the poison.

"Done already?" Beggar Soh, who had provided the poisoned wine from his personal stock, smirked at Wu Ying. "You barely touched your third cup."

"I apologize, Senior. Some of us are not lushes," Wu Ying slurred. "Your drink is too strong. It burns a hole in the table, never mind my guts."

"Hah! That's how you know it's good wine."

"Be nice, Ah Soh," Proprietress Yang chided. "He's only Core. If he was not a Body Cultivator as well, I would not even let him sip it. This wine is for those at our level, not his."

"If he were a poison cultivator, he would be able to handle this minor drink without a problem." Hiccupping, Beggar Soh added, "And contribute even better!"

"If he were a poison cultivator, I might not even serve him," Landlord Yang said with a sniff. "Most of them can't control what they exude! The last one we had in here, I had to store the table, his chair, and all the utensils and lock my private room from use for a whole month, while the cleansing formation worked."

"But he paid for it all with a dozen of those bottles you refuse to share," Beggar Soh said, a trace of whining in his voice. "Do you know how hard it is to get a proper drink?"

"Not very hard for you, with your Never Empty Wine Gourd!"

Wu Ying jerked a little, surprised. Then when he saw Beggar Soh clutching the wine gourd by his side, he realized that they were not talking about Beggar Soh's cultivation method. Still, his reaction did not go unnoticed, and he was forced to explain.

When he was done, Beggar Soh broke out laughing, pounding the table. "You, you, you made my wine gourd into a cultivation method, then made it into a wind technique? Really?"

"I didn't make it into a cultivation method; it was already one," Wu Ying said stiffly.

"Show me, show me!"

"I…" Wu Ying hesitated, which caused Beggar Soh to glare at him. "I cannot. We do not allow others to see the cultivation slips we acquire."

"Foolish orthodox and their foolish rules!" Beggar Soh said. "Show me what you recorded. In turn, I'll improve on it. You can give the improved version to your Sect when—if—you return."

Still, Wu Ying hesitated.

"It is a good deal," Proprietress Yang said, placing a hand on his arm. "For all his looks, Ah Soh is a genius among geniuses." She made a face. "He would be even greater, if he stopped drinking."

"My genius comes from my drink!" Beggar Soh stated, pounding his fist on the table.

"No, you're just a drunk."

"Quickly. Before they get into it," Landlord Yang implored Wu Ying. "Rebuilding is always such a chore."

Already, the pressure was growing as the pair conflicted not just with words but with daos. Rather than get caught up in a battle between the two, since the ache from their initial greeting still throbbed, Wu Ying pulled out the bamboo scroll he had written the details—and his alterations—upon.

Immediately, the pressure disappeared, Beggar Soh grabbing the scroll and unrolling the document across the table. The remnants of their meal and drinks were swept up by Landlord Yang just in time. Without asking, Proprietress Yang had stood and walked over to the other side to read over Beggar Soh's shoulder, her lips pursed.

"Oh, that's ingenious! Using the whirlwind instead of the whirlpool. And there's indications of turning it instead into a cyclone... Broader area," she muttered, reading. "Less control, but harder to track. Yes, that might work better, but why is it only focused in one direction?"

"My pot draws in water from the surroundings, tapping into the elemental idea of water and liquor itself," Beggar Soh said, tracing a dirty—how did it get so dirty, so fast?—finger along the early lines. "This writer never understood that the barrier was the bottle itself and the dao conceptions. Look, here, he makes the aura do all the work. Waste of time."

Within moments, a pair of ink brushes were acquired, the two writing over one another and the document, adding and changing without asking Wu Ying. Sometimes, the pair held a loud argument about which change was better, while the two bemused men watched.

"Will that... work?" Wu Ying said, never having seen two cultivators argue like that.

"Of course. It's my wife!" Landlord Yang said, mock offended. After a moment, he shrugged. "It's fine. She'll make me test it first, then refine it further." At Wu Ying's look of incredulity, he grinned. "It's part of my own gift. I can create a... hmmm... clone of myself. A shadow form that can test many things for me before I commit."

Wu Ying's eyes glowed with admiration, watching the trio. He had come so far, yet it seemed the journey ahead stretched on so much further. And though these three were unusual, perhaps the peak itself was not as lonely as it might seem. Nor devoid of kindness.

"Done!"

The scroll flapped through the air, tossed toward the laoban who caught it with deft hands. His eyes skimmed over the words quickly, frowning only at a few parts before he nodded and set it aside. A moment later, he seemed to shift, as though there was a second image of him superimposed over the first, translucent but slightly off-center.

A single breath later, Wu Ying felt the tug and pull of chi. It smoothed out within seconds, disappearing from his senses as the flow of environmental chi returned to normal. It was only if he extended his senses further and paid attention that he could feel the slow but powerful flow, where energy streamed toward the laoban from multiple li. Taken from such a wide distance, it slipped past his senses even if the chi flow concentrated upon the man.

However, the flow was not entirely smooth. At times there were bumps, sudden speedups or slowdowns that made the shift of chi more noticeable. Even more alarming was the blood that had begun to drip from the nose of the shadow form, then a few minutes later, a racking, bloody cough.

Eventually the laoban stopped, picked up a brush, and sketched his notes on a new piece of paper, the initial bamboo slip too dense with words to add his commentary. Beggar Soh ignored all this as he drank from his wine pot directly while the proprietress watched the words being written, eventually nodding.

"Oh, I see. Yes, the sixth and eleventh meridian being crossed in such short order to flow the chi can cause problems… Why did we make use of the stomach meridian there? Right, because some stubborn geezer forgets this is not a wine gourd but a body!"

Muttering to herself, she drew forth a new slip and wrote, her words incorporating all the insights generated by the group. While Wu Ying watched, he felt a finger poke him in his side, with the Beggar Soh staring directly at him. His face was all too close and his breath so powerful, Wu Ying felt his head grow lighter and a light drip of blood flow from his nose as the poisoned, corrosive breath pounded his face.

"Yes, Senior?" Wu Ying said, edging back.

"You're wondering why, right?"

"I…"

"It's fine. I would too. For me, I was bored." He pointed at the couple arguing quietly. "I do what I want, when I want. That is my way, you see?" When Wu Ying nodded, having somewhat recognized that for a man who refused to be chained down even by small things like a roof over his head, personal belongings, or hygiene, whim was not an unexpected reason. "Those two, they walk a more generous path. A dangerous one, no?"

Wu Ying could not help but nod. After all, being generous was well and good, but there were those who would take and take without reason. And more who would be angered when generosity ended, demanding ever more.

"Few who reach our stage are as giving. They cannot be, for they let their daos constrain them, narrowing their vision and chaining down their souls with rules and regulations," Beggar Soh said. "Yet these two continue to give. Generosity without expectation is its own reward. Yes?"

The last statement was asked with burning intensity. Normally bloodshot, red eyes clouded with alcohol were suddenly piercing. Wu Ying sensed it, the unseen weight of judgment, the sharpened edge of an executioner's blade hovering over him. His mind flashed forward, intuition speaking of an evening one day when he would close his eyes to sleep and never wake if he answered wrong.

For a man who had nothing, who craved no material possessions, that man would clutch ever harder those immaterial things he did own. Like friendship and warm nights spent under another's roof, wiling away the hours drinking and speaking.

Yet for all the threat that Wu Ying sensed, he felt an inexorable draw from within, a pull in his soul that forced words of truth from him. The words that spilled from his mouth were his own, but not consciously chosen. "Without expectation perhaps, but a debt is still incurred. The threads of karma and courtesy bind all, whether we seek their gift or not. Only those who eschew all such threads might escape such attachments, and in doing so, live as hermits high above. Or fail in their goal, compelled by plain human emotion."

"Hah! Out of the mouth of babes." Leaning back, Beggar Soh released Wu Ying from the soul spell he had laid upon him, bypassing Wu Ying's guards with such ease that he had not even noticed until now.

Wu Ying's intuition spoke of deeper contrivances, of a poisoned wine plied upon him that had been the first step past his safeguards. Reeling backward, unconsciously reinforcing his aura and shutting down the pull of energy, Wu Ying's dao and the wind churned anew around him in protection. Too late of course, the rice having rotted on the stalk, but he did so nevertheless.

"Ah Soh! Stop bullying the boy," Laoban Yang said, looking up from where he was still writing his commentary. Or, now that Wu Ying was watching, actually drawing the flow of chi and the meridian points where energy had to be concentrated. "He's a good one. Or have you not heard the tales of the Verdant Gatherer?"

"Stories have a tendency to be exaggerated," Beggar Soh said. "Look how they speak of me."

"Smelly, uncouth, penniless." Proprietress Yang paused then smiled. "I see no untruth."

"Sharp-tongued woman."

"Smelly beggar."

"Money-hungry wench."

"Alcoholic fool."

Wu Ying cried out, the pair turning to see him clutching his head. They paused, wincing in simultaneous guilt at unleashing their spiritual pressure again, and both retracted their energy. However, this time, their combined strength, his prior injuries, and the vast quantities of alcohol—chi-reinforced and poisoned—consumed was too much.

Head bouncing off the table before he slipped the rest of the way, shouts of alarm ringing through his damaged ears, Wu Ying fell unconscious at last.

Chapter 41

"You've done well," Laoban Yang said, eyeing Wu Ying as he exited his cultivation daze. The older man was seated on one of the many boulders that made up the rock garden, perched cross-legged on the sharp tip.

A few days had passed since Wu Ying had lost consciousness. Since then, he had been forcibly commanded to recuperate and train the newly reorganized Never Empty Wine Pot method at the inn. Thankfully, no additional fights had occurred, Beggar Soh having left the next morning, absconding with a half dozen plucked and stewed chickens and a pot of cooked rice.

"Thank you, Senior." Wu Ying exhaled a lungful of turbid air, watching it float away, carried off by a gust of wind, and stood smoothly. "The new technique is profoundly stronger than the original. I must admit, I am still troubled by Master Soh's missive."

"Hah! Still can't come up with a proper name?" Laoban Yang slapped his right thigh, his movements never causing even a minor wobble as he perched on his peculiar seat. "Surely you have named techniques before."

"Only one," Wu Ying said.

"Huh," Laoban Yang said. "I guess you are still young…"

"And busy cultivating," Wu Ying said, flashing back to Beggar Soh's assertion. "Creating and naming techniques has been low on my priority list." He shrugged. "I fear I have no talent for it."

"There is nothing wrong with following the footsteps of seniors. Technique creation is but an accumulation of knowledge mixed with flashes of insight." He gestured into the empty inn and the busy trading post. "Some are more gifted at it than others. I, myself, have only authored a half dozen or so."

Wu Ying bobbed his head in acknowledgment, though he chose not to note that a half dozen was not a small number. Then again, comparison was the thief of joy and living with a genius like his wife and being friends with the infamous Beggar Soh was likely to create concern for any.

"But on the subject at hand…" Putting his head in a propped-up hand, the laoban hummed in thought. "How about the Dragon's Cultivating Cyclone?"

"I fear I might overuse such a tenuous connection," Wu Ying said. "Anyway, there are so many dragon titled texts, it will easily be forgotten."

"Right, right. So no plum blossoms, lotuses, phoenixes, rainfall, fires, or waterfalls then. Or anything to do with heaven or hell or overthrowing it."

Wu Ying nodded firmly.

"Difficult, difficult. I just named mine after me…" Laoban Yang grinned. "Yang family techniques is more than sufficient!"

"Yang family fist. Yang family foot. Yang family throw. Yang family swallowing dumplings!"

"Yes, yes, yes, yes… wait!" Laoban Yang turned in his seat, moving too fast and tipping off to land on the ground.

"Yang family alcohol swilling. Yang family cleaning the bowels."

"That was an important technique!" the flustered father protested, waving helplessly from where he lay.

"Yang family flame control," finished Yang Mu - the eldest daughter – as she strode out of the inn. "Did I forget any, Father?"

"You shouldn't be telling a stranger our techniques," the laoban protested, standing and dusting himself off.

"Our guest will not tell anyone. He is well-mannered, well-spoken, and highly regarded among the tribes, the sects, and wandering cultivators," the girl said, hands on her hips as she glared at her father. "Unlike someone who runs an inn that drains all his wife's profits!"

Letting out a long groan, the man clutched his heart. Turning to Wu Ying, he spoke. "You see what happens when your children grow? They turn on you. Why, I remember a time when my little Mu used to run to me, her bare butt swinging in the wind, and climbed up my leg even before her mother had finished dressing her! Now, all she can do is accuse me of cheating the heart of my soul."

Flushing red, the daughter flicked a hand, sending a metal dart at her father. He caught it easily, but not before Yang Mu had turned on her heels and stalked off.

"I hesitate to comment, but perhaps your words are part of the reason she is so against you?" Wu Ying said softly. He had no desire to step between the family, but they had been more than generous with him, such that he felt some obligation.

"Oh, for certain! But Yang Mu has been stymied in her cultivation for months. She must walk a new road to gain enlightenment but refuses to do so. She is bound here by loving-kindness and consideration, and so I must agitate her to leave." He cocked his head, eyeing Wu Ying sideways. "Unlike someone who cannot stay still. You are ready to depart already, are you not?"

"I…" Wu Ying hesitated, before nodding. "I am. I have mastered the basics of the Cyclone's Breath technique. The rest may be trained as I go."

"The Cyclone's Breath. You came up with that just now?" At Wu Ying's nod, the man nodded. "I like it."

Wu Ying acknowledged his words even as he sent his senses within to check on the technique. There was no longer a deep spiral that pulled energy toward him, not in his dantian or in his meridians. Instead, the cyclone originated far out from himself, touching upon the external environment via the smallest traces of his chi and dao intent.

The environmental wind energy that he touched in this manner moved to his command, forming a vortex that was many li wide, such that the movement was imperceptible to others unless one knew what to search for. The end of the vortex was Wu Ying, but it would be perceived instead as a minor increase in cultivation speed as each step closer to him, the environmental wind chi would grow more and more attuned to him.

In this way, when it flowed toward Wu Ying, it was imperceptible to most and entered his form in its entirety, flowing through his aura and body without impediment. No longer did he have to reject other forms of chi, since the kind he required was already on its way to him.

Just like the actual gourd, the new Cyclone's Breath was as subtle as it was powerful, increasing Wu Ying's moving, never-ending cultivation speed by a factor of two or three times compared to his previous technique.

More importantly, unlike the previous method which Wu Ying had often to stop using in the deep wilds for fear of Core or Nascent Soul beasts noticing him, this new method was undetectable. Theoretically, at least. After all, he had yet to put it to a real test.

"Where will you go?" the laoban asked.

"South," Wu Ying said with a small smile. "The wind beckons."

"Ah." The laoban made a face. "The rumors of what is happening in the Dai kingdom are troubling."

"I know little of them, I must admit," Wu Ying said. He had intended to acquire more information as he went farther south, visiting local bookstores and libraries to learn more. He had, after all, learned that lesson. However, the proprietress was not the correct individual to acquire such mundane information from.

Or so he had thought.

"Our history with them is complex. Some consider them naught more than another splintered kingdom from the time of the Yellow Emperor. Others, however, see them as barbarians. Their customs are not our own, though they share many similarities." The laoban waved, dismissing the topic. "All those things matter little to one like you. More importantly, they are a kingdom only in name, but actually an amalgamation of cities who control the land around them while beating back a rampant forest. A forest that breeds demonic and spirit beasts in greater numbers than many would consider natural."

Wu Ying recalled now the discussion of how many beast stones flowed northward from the monsters that had taken over the edges of more civilized locations. Tales of forests that regrew overnight, and logging villages that went silent, only for traveling merchants to find them empty, the remnant buildings bloodstained.

"You recall the stories then."

"Yes. I had always imagined them much farther than the Dai though…" Wu Ying admitted.

"Hah! Only a wanderer like you would think a few thousand li a small distance."

There was no suitable answer to such an accusation, so Wu Ying shrugged.

"Well, in any case, it is the border—and the enchanted forests that lie close to it—that see a significant number of stones. It has made the kingdoms close to the border wealthy and arrogant," Laoban Yang said. "But even that is no matter to us."

"Then what is, Senior?"

"Rumors of something darker growing in the forest to the south. Something dangerous. My wife has seen it in the types of stones we get from the south. More demonic stones than before. Larger and even more corrupted. Twisted, in a way. Useless but for powering the most basic formations." He shook his head. "Normally, I would not even speak of such rumors. Most of our guests will never travel that far south or, if they did, have a chance to see it for themselves. But…"

"I'm a gatherer. And where the demonic beasts go, I do too."

"Yes."

Wu Ying inclined his head and murmured a word in thanks, only to stop when the laoban raised a hand.

"I have one last request."

Wu Ying's guts clenched, for he knew what the man would ask. His mind spun, wondering if all the generosity, all the care offered to him, even the deals had been a long-laid plan. Then he pushed those uncharitable thoughts aside to listen.

"Keep an eye out for the problems. If what we see is an unnatural alteration, a tilting toward the demonic, then we ask that you do what you can."

Wu Ying exhaled a little, hearing the words he had dreaded. Yet at the same time, he felt the heavenly wind gust, bringing with it that sharp, merciless texture. It pushed upon his robes, entered his body, pressured his soul with its demands.

Heaven's orders, brought by the winds of those above. A command to seek something foul, something dark in the south. And perhaps, a final reward—an understanding of the wind he had sought for so long, a grasping of its complexity.

For how could you chase the heavens, and yet not bow toward their commands?

Noticing Wu Ying's hesitation, the laoban continued. "Rotten meat should be cut off and thrown aside long before it spoils the dish. Left alone, it will grow worse. Best to cook the meat properly immediately, before it corrupts the rest of your larder."

"Of course. Root rot is the same," Wu Ying said. "I will go, and if fate places me upon the right path, if the wind blows in such a way…"

"Good man." A big hand came down on Wu Ying's shoulder, before the laoban stepped away and headed back inside. "I'll let my wife know you'll be leaving us soon. She'll be sad to see you go, but grateful to you for looking into it. Hard to run a store when all the product that arrives is sub-par."

Wu Ying snorted, watching the man put on a mercenary face once more. Perhaps he and his wife might not be part of any orthodox sect—though Wu Ying had doubts of that too— but they certainly were more than just a pair of merchants.

An unusual pair that drew an unusual clientele. But that was why he had come, after all.

***

"I am thankful for you being willing to look into my minor issues of getting an adequate supply of untainted cores," Proprietress Yang said, not even an hour later. The pair were seated in a private room, the wares that Wu Ying had been reviewing spread out before them. "But you understand, of course, that business is business?"

"I do." Wu Ying swept his gaze over the formations before them. He had set aside the obscuration formation to allow him to rest. They'd also discussed and agreed upon a simple earth-aspected protective formation—The Earth's Embrace—to guard over him. It was an ugly formation, pulling upon the earth itself to form a dome of protection, but it had the advantage of being cheap—due to its features—and reusable. Now, they argued over the last formation Wu Ying intended to purchase. "However, surely you can do better on the price."

"For a slaughter formation, one created from the dao conceptions of a Heart-level dao wielder who walked the path of blood and carnage?" Proprietress Yang shook her head firmly. "Do you think such formations are easy to create or acquire? That it is not in high demand?"

"Of course not. But how effective is it if he has only achieved the Heart of the Dao?" Wu Ying said. "I myself have achieved the Heart of the Jian. It is not that rare…"

"So speaks the sword genius! Not one in a thousand martial cultivators reach the Heart of their weapon. And you speak as though it's as easy as finding gold under a rock."

"You just have to lift enough of them, after all."

"Then carve your own jian-based slaughter formation!"

"Perhaps I will."

Her fingers touched the edge of the formation flag, the woman looking hesitant at his biting retort. "Do you understand what you ask for? This formation can kill even one in the Nascent Soul stage. It has only a single use, but deployed properly by a formation master, it will definitely kill the one caught in its center." Cocking her head, she added, "For you to use it, it might only injure them greatly. But still, it can be a lifesaving item to hold in reserve. If you were not who you are, if your heart was not as pure… I would never let this item go. As it is, I have deep concerns."

Wu Ying inclined his head in acknowledgement. Good deeds, sown far and wide, had a tendency to sprout surprising seeds. Though it also had seen him flee in the night as others tried to steal from him. So. And so.

"I understand, Proprietress Yang. But I refuse to enter the south, do your bidding without at least a few assurances of my survival."

"We could provide an escape talisman," Proprietress Yang said. "We have numerous Spirit Horses—a Moonlight Rider one even. And then there are the Ten Thousand Step Earth Channels, or if you choose the wooden path, the One Tree, One Root talisman."

"Tell me more."

Wu Ying listened, quickly garnering an understanding. The Moonlight Rider spirit talisman was but a variation of the basic spirit horse talisman, most powerful at night. It allowed one to move as fast as moonlight itself, or so the creator liked to say. In reality, the Moonlit Spirit Horse that the talisman conjured was only three times as fast as a regular Spirit Horse. Or just about as fast as Wu Ying when he chose to step with the wind.

The earth escape talisman worked via the control of the creator's dao conceptions, pulling Wu Ying along the ground for ten thousand or so steps. It would take him out of immediate danger so long as he stood upon the earth, sucking him within and transferring him in the direction of his intent.

The One Tree, One Root talisman was similar, though its eventual exit point was more random due to the requirements that the plants be connected via a root or branch system of some form. Minor gaps could be jumped, though that did drain the energy in the talisman.

"Those are good. I'd take the Ten Thousand Step Earth Channels escape talisman. And maybe the One Root talisman, if it is not too expensive." Sadly, both talismans would degrade a little in effectiveness when used by one with a wind body. However, because no one would expect one with such an ability to own such talismans, he found them worthwhile. "But I still want the slaughter formation."

Letting out a long huff of frustration, the proprietress nodded. "Oh, very well then. I'll still charge you for it at my full price, you understand."

At Wu Ying's nod, she smiled a little. The price was staggering—a large number of the cores he had acquired while traveling, as well as many of his rarer plants. Even the years spent in closed door cultivation had only allowed him to regrow what had been lost before, leaving him rather penniless after this transaction. At least, until another few years had passed and he had regrown his stock or found some rarer stock.

Which, in truth, the journey to the south could be of great benefit.

"What else do you desire, Cultivator Long? Another sword?"

Wu Ying glanced at the only Saint-level jian he carried. It had been worn away over the years of use but was still in good repair. Thankfully, he had not tried to use it on anything too hard—like the scales of a dragon. Other than the shorter straight sword he had acquired from the Viscount, he actually lacked appropriately leveled weapons. "A jian of the same quality if you have one. Two, if the price is right."

"And a bow?'

Wu Ying shook his head. He had, once again, put aside the use of the bow. Ever since he had grown stronger and faster, he no longer needed a ranged weapon. Attempting to match a Core Formation user who specialized in the bow was a fool's errand, or so he had learned while in the north. Better to concentrate one's training.

"Of course. Why would the wind require a bow?" She nodded. "I know you do not require armor, for we glimpsed what you wear underneath."

Surprisingly, the emerald armor he had acquired was quite well-suited for regular wear, easily concealed beneath his robes. Unless, of course, one fainted from repeated dao clashes of Nascent Soul cultivators and poisoning.

"The Coral Dragon Scales will do me quite well," Wu Ying acknowledged. Of course, they were not actual dragon scales, just a popular name for the fine scalemail production. "I am grateful for its presence."

"As you should be. A Saint-jian… I have three with me, but I will only be willing to release one to you. A merchant must have stock for all their customers, and if you intend to take my slaughter formation…" Proprietress Yang said with a small secret smile.

Wu Ying smiled, shaking his head. "I enjoy collecting blades, it is true, Senior Yang. But I am no sword saint, nor a sword fanatic. You cannot bribe me with more blades, not if it means giving up a life-saving measure."

She laughed, leaning back. "Am I that easy to see through? A babe in swaddling robes reads me like a master merchant. All my years of experience are but ashes before your eyes."

"And now you play the fool." Wu Ying's lips still quirked into a smile though. "Perhaps if I had not watched you do the same with Senior Soh and your husband, I might perhaps be tricked." He nodded toward her hand, which she had removed from the slaughter formation flag in the interim. "Nor do you truly not wish me to leave without this formation. I think, like me, you have an intuition I shall need it. Or something more powerful."

Silence greeted his bold words, before the woman sighed. "You speak truth. There is a foreboding in me that we ask you to journey into the tiger's lair, slathered in pig fat."

"All the better to draw the tiger out, no?"

"And yet, you have yet to breakthrough."

"I'm a Body Cultivator, Senior. I grow differently," Wu Ying said, touching his chest. "Though I cultivate the soul too."

"As we all do. You are wise, to grow both. But what might come…" She closed her eyes then opened them, pushing the flags over. "Sit. I'll gather the jian, then we will discuss the final price."

Wu Ying nodded, watching her leave. He could not help but pull the slaughter formation closer. Intuition perhaps, a foretelling offered by the Dao, or a hint from the heavens. He knew not but that he would need it on his journey.

And more.

***

Behind his back, the temple rose. He had visited it and the statue of the Goddess of Mercy once more, though his visit had been brief. The winds of heaven blew heavy in that place, pushing him south even as the wind whispered of darker secrets to be learned. In the presence of heavenly commands and dire omens, Wu Ying found himself finding enlightenment once again, his sense of the heaven's wind finally growing strong enough that he could trace its presence.

Not understand it, not grasp it, not fully. But for the first time, he had the sense of it, the traces of the wind in his mind and soul. Here, where a family of cultivators broke with the common parlance, where they lived and laughed and cared for one another like mortals, he had found heaven's will.

Now, he strode down the walkway, choosing to begin this journey on the ground. He paused as he began to turn the corner, casting a long look behind him. He touched his new storage ring—much larger, much lighter, as he had traded away many of the smaller ones acquired over years of battle. Within sat the formations and escape talismans and pills he had purchased.

He caressed the World Spirit Ring on his other hand, his first, his earliest momentous find. He would train with the newly acquired jian later, to give it its proper due. To extend his understanding of the weapon, to work on his forms.

Exhaling, Wu Ying looked into the sky, blocking out the voices coming from the trading post and the worshippers that passed him, listening instead to the wind. He sensed the change in the air, the heavy pressure that pressed upon his shoulders, the urgent whispers that were not whispers. He even caught a sniff of something rank, spoiled like burnt oil and diseased meat, as the southern wind brought it forth. Ethereal fingers brushed across his face and along his neck. A small hint of what was to come.

Just enough to alert him.

Wu Ying felt the sun beat down upon his face. He had grown strong over the decade plus since he had left the Sect. He had layered his Core, gained understanding and acceptance of the five mortal winds. He had progressed with the heavenly wind and begun the process of grasping the final immortal wind.

His personal sword form grew every day, with a single movement perfected and two others in budding development. He had tools and weapons in abundance, glistening armor, and cultivation techniques and exercises that allowed him to dance with the wind and pass unseen among the darkest woods.

He had gained much in these years.

And now, it seemed, his vacation from the troubles of heaven and hell was over. He would journey south and seek the problem, no matter his words to the laoban. He would learn of the troubling rise of demonic beasts and see to their eradication and those who might have cause to create them. He would set the world aright.

For heaven commanded, and man obeyed. Or all things would twist and rot.

###

THE END

A Thousand Li:

The Third Cut

Book 9 of A Thousand Li Series

Chapter 1

Long Wu Ying, the famed Verdant Gatherer, member of the illustrious Verdant Green Waters sect of the Shen kingdom, Core Formation cultivator, and Heart of the Sword prodigy stood before his greatest trial since leaving his sect to wander the Middle Kingdom[48].

Greater than the guard of the northern dragon king's palace, greater than the Nascent Soul spirit snake he'd fought, greater even than the swarm of wind and water dragons that coaxed him into a night long dance amidst a typhoon.

Long Wu Ying, scourge of the dark sect in the states of Shen and Wei, faced his greatest trial and failed.

"Fine!" He threw his hands up, long sleeves on his green robes slipping down his tanned arms. So close to civilization, he still wore the formal clothing of his sect. Unlike the peasant robes—the *shuhe*—that he preferred to wear, these robes with their long sleeves and multiple layers made movement through the forest more difficult.

Not that a cultivator at his level found such concerns more than a trivial annoyance, what with the almost supernatural level of control over his body he had gained, along with strength and speed that defied mortal limits. But strong as he was, able to layer his aura over his clothing and self as he could, over the course of weeks, even the greatest care could not stop staining and dirtying when traipsing through the wilds of the world.

Another fact that the woman he had been speaking to would be wise to understand. Not that she was listening. Hadn't listened at all, in the last three hours of arguing.

"You'll let me come then, Honored Cultivator Long?" With an impish glint of humor in her eyes, Yang Mu put her hands together and asked ever so politely. Even if she had won his concession through argument and sheer stubbornness.

"I won't be responsible for your life though. And I will be journeying through the wilds, Cultivator Yang," Wu Ying said.

Her eyes glinted with repressed mirth—and perhaps even anger—as she answered, just before she sketched a bow. "I would not think of putting such an illustrious Elder out of his important work."

"I'm not much older than you," Wu Ying said grumpily. Elder! Hah. He might be in his mid-thirties now, but he still felt like a twenty-year-old. Maybe even younger. One of the side effects of cultivation was it extended the physicality—and sometimes, he felt, the temperament—of youth.

"Of course not, Honored Long." Even if her tone and words were polite, Wu Ying doubted that was the true intention of her words. "Shall we continue our journey then?"

"Our journey?"

---

[48] Probably unneeded, but Middle Kingdom is how China is still called (directly translated); but it's also just a general description of Earth itself, lying between the heavens above and the hells below.

Again, that demure smile that had thoroughly no give. If the wind had not told him of her presence, he was sure she would have trailed him for days longer.

Wu Ying shook his head. "Before we do, I need to know this. How much danger am I in from your parents? Two Nascent Soul cultivators angry at me for stealing away their daughter is more trouble than it's worth. If necessary, I'll travel right back to their inn."

"You would not dare…" Yang Mu trailed off, seeing the firm look in Wu Ying's eyes. "I left a note explaining my leaving. And anyway, did you think they did not notice my departure from their domain? What kind of fools do you think my parents are?"

Wu Ying sighed. "My apologies to your parents." Definitely not to the infuriating woman. She had been so much more polite when he had stayed as a guest in their inn. Much less aggravating for sure. "But you understand my concerns, yes?"

"That you fear my parents?" She shrugged. "Of course. Cowardly, but wise."

"Are you choosing to aggravate me on purpose or are you just this blunt when your parents are not around?" he said.

"I speak the truth where I see it."

"Then try speaking less. Your parents are not here to protect you, and if you try the patience of someone stronger than you, your head might just roll." He shook his head. "Courtesy is important out here."

Yang Mu smirked, and he found himself gritting his teeth. Once again, he considered just sitting here and cultivating. He had another layer of his core to build after all, so why not? Well, beyond the fact that he was missing any form of enlightenment to feed the Nascent Soul within him. The layer he formed without such enlightenment would be fragile. Also, his journey to understanding the southern wind and the winds of heaven and hell required him to continue onward.

Still.

Regardless of those minor considerations, annoying her would be satisfying.

But Long Wu Ying was an adult, unlike the petty child. If she thought she could keep up with him in the wilds, then so be it.

"Very well." He strode off into the undergrowth, wending his way between trees and bushes with easy familiarity. He managed a dozen steps before she caught up.

"The way south is that way." A finger raised, pointing about thirty degrees farther east than his current trajectory.

"I know," Wu Ying replied, gritting his teeth. He did not stop moving or change direction though.

"So are you going to change direction?"

"No."

"Ah. You're one of those."

"You know that speaking can draw unwanted attention, yes?" Wu Ying snapped.

"I sense nothing."

"That's the point."

Silence greeted his final sentence. For a few minutes, he managed to travel in peace, heading for his goal. Maybe, just maybe, she could be taught.

***

Wu Ying bent low, running a hand along the ground. He brushed the garlic shoots with his fingers, running fingers along the leaves before ripping off a small portion of a leaf. He sniffed the leaf, his sense technique working at full strength as he judged the texture and nature of the herb. The Hundred Delights and a Thousand Miseries sensory technique was one that his Master had taught him, a strange technique for a swordmaster to have. Master Cheng had never explained why he had such a unique technique, but it was perfect for a Gatherer like Wu Ying.

Seven Chives Rainbow Garlic. A rare plant that he had only sensed by exerting the full force of the sensory technique. He had almost missed it, with the highly disturbing, light floral perfume that his new companion wore masking the delicate scent of the growing garlic. The scented water she carried inside her storage ring was quite noticeable, mixing with her natural feminine aroma in ways that attracted his attention, especially in contrast to the natural odors out here in the wilds.

"Are you gathering?" Yang Mu's voice rose, slightly incredulous as she stood behind him.

"Yes. That is my profession after all," Wu Ying said. "Now, quiet please. If you must do something, watch for potential threats."

Again, his fingers brushed over the shoots, counting the number in his mind. He mentally mapped the garlic bulbs under the ground, noting placement and sending a small surge of unaspected chi into the earth. It took a little bit of work to change his chi from the wind chi that permeated his body and dantian, but it was necessary for proper mapping. He had noticed, in the last few years as his Body Cultivation progressed, that shifting his chi from wind chi to another form had grown more difficult.

An adverse aspect of growing stronger and going deeper into his cultivation practices.

Fingers dug into the ground, gently pushing aside earth. Using just a trace of his chi and strength, he pierced the earth easily to pluck out the garlic bulb. He repeated the process, taking only a third of the total number of bulbs in this patch before storing them in a white jade box that he extracted from his storage ring.

Once he was done, he patted down the earth, making sure not to compress it too much. Then, eyeing the woman beside him, he extracted and deposited some of the compost from his World Spirit Ring as was his habit, offering a small bounty to the remaining garlic shoots.

"Are you done yet?" Yang Mu said impatiently. "Can we go?"

"Not yet," Wu Ying said.

He moved away from the newly tamped down ground and took a seat, withdrawing a scroll and unrolling it. He quickly marked their location, drawing on the map to add in more details of the surroundings before setting the map aside and extracting a notebook. He wrote in it additional observations about the plant he had found, drawing a simple sketch of the garlic itself and its surroundings, including the plants that had grown around it. When he was done, he extracted a third book while storing away the now-dry map.

That was when Yang Mu lost all patience. "What are you doing now? Noting the time and day that you picked it? The color of the birds feasting on the plant? Or are you recording a personal journal and how many times you've shat yourself?"

Wu Ying stared at Yang Mu in silence, brush hovering in mid-air. A tiny drop almost dripped onto his notebook before he caught it with his other hand. While speaking to her, he wrote a few lines in his journal before setting it aside to dry.

"I'm adding to my inventory list." Wu Ying tapped the still-open book. He noted how her gaze sharpened, reading over the lines of text. It was no concern to him, since the open pages were mostly filled with notations of what items had been traded to her very own mother. "I thought a shopkeeper like yourself would understand such matters."

"I…" Yang Mu hesitated before nodding firmly. "It's a good habit. But I'm no shopkeeper!"

"My apologies. Shopkeeper's daughter."

She glared, a lip curling up in disdain as he needled her.

Smiling a little on the inside, he continued. "If you wish to continue this journey and follow me, you should resign yourself to more of the same. Also, to being quieter. While we are still in the outskirts of the wild, such outbursts are harmless. Mostly. Deeper within, you could attract attention that neither of us desires."

"You act as though I don't know something so simple!" Yang Mu's chin lifted. "You're not the only Core cultivator here. I can sense up to ten li around us, and I can tell you, there is nothing for us to fear."

Wu Ying blinked slowly. A spiritual sense that could extend ten li around her was staggering. Especially when he was certain she was not telling the full truth. No cultivator at the Core Formation stage would inform a potential opponent of their true strength. As such, she likely had a much larger sensing range. One that overshadowed his own five or six li. Admittedly, he supplemented his spiritual sense with the Thousand Miseries sensing technique, which allowed him to pick out monsters who were able to veil their presence from a simple spiritual survey, but…

"Impressive. But can your techniques pierce the shroud utilized by Nascent Soul monsters? Spirit beasts of shadow, darkness, and nature roam the deep wilds, whose very nature allows them to blend within. Others have learned to veil themselves from spiritual sense to stalk their prey or hide from the predators." Wu Ying held a hand up before she could answer. "Though they rarely are seen in the outskirts here, for there is little sustenance for them in these forests, rare is not never."

"Is this how you live your life out here? Gathering herbs, hiding from those creatures above you and only seeing other cultivators when your storage rings are full?" she said scornfully. "I would have thought, with all the stories of the Verdant Gatherer that abound, that your existence was more exciting."

"Exciting?" Wu Ying frowned at the woman. "Is that what you are searching for? Excitement? The thrill of the outside world, now that you have escaped your parents?"

"Is there anything wrong with that?" She sighed mournfully. "I have spent most of my life with family, having them watch over me. Hearing stories of faraway lands, of exciting battles and interesting events from the travelers who visited. And not once have I experienced it myself. How am I to grow? Stifled and hidden away in a cave?"

"Not all plants need direct sunlight to grow. Some do better shaded. Others, like mushrooms, thrive in the gloom." He could have added the other things mushrooms required, but Yang Mu was already glowering at him.

"Are you comparing me to a mushroom?" she said, her voice rising.

"No. Just expanding upon your agricultural knowledge."

"You… you…" A vein pulsed on her forehead.

"Also, I warned you to keep your voice down." Wu Ying gestured upward even as he collected the documents he had laid out to dry. He could have sprinkled sand or sesame seeds on them to speed up the process but had chosen to wait. After all, their new visitors were a good lesson to wield against his unexpected companion.

Yang Mu looked upward at his movement, eyes widening a little as she spotted the creatures waiting above. Four shadow leopards had sneaked over, each of them having blended in so well with the shadows of the undergrowth that they had bypassed her sensory ability. Wu Ying would have missed them if not for the wind alerting him of their musky aroma.

That they had been stalking them for the last hour was something he had noted, as well as the fact that her continued loud exclamations had provoked the creatures. Now, it was unlikely they would just allow the pair to depart in peace.

"You take the two on the left, I'll deal with the two on the right," Yang Mu said.

Then, looking backward, she blinked. For in the moment while she had been looking at the quartet, Wu Ying had suppressed his aura further, such that he disappeared from all their senses before using his wind technique to shift him away.

The cats looked a little non-plussed to have one of their targets disappear on them, but then turned their full attention on the cultivator still around.

"Damn you, Cultivator Long!" she cursed, moments before the spirit beasts attacked.

Chapter 2

Wu Ying watched the battle below him with mild interest, standing on the swaying branch of the tallest tree near the fight. In most Core Formation battles, such a perch would have been vastly insufficient, as Core Formation cultivators had a tendency to wreck the nearby environment. However, even though two of the four Spirit Beasts stalking them had been at an equivalent level, their techniques focused on movement, hidden attacks, and defense. Not widespread, destructive techniques.

As for Yang Mu…

She spun on her bottom foot, a fan in either hand twirling as she dodged a leaping shadow, her movements erratic as she shifted. At a glance, it seemed like she was entirely open. Yet as Wu Ying watched, she swung a fan with one hand, the tips of her weapon scoring against the hide of the leaping cat. The creature yowled moments before it landed and plunged into a shadow, disappearing entirely.

Simultaneously, another shadow leopard bunched its feet and sprang at the cultivator from the side. Yet even as it leapt at her, Yang Mu allowed her body to collapse the rest of the way to the earth to dodge the leopard. The other fan swung up, striking at the undefended belly.

"Drunken fairy…" Wu Ying muttered as he watched her. He had seen portions of such a technique in use before, amongst cultivators who leaned into the unpredictable martial style. Such techniques emphasized unpredictability, flexibility, and strikes from unusual locations, enforcing a constant state of reassessment and surprise on its opponents.

It was—mostly—favored by men, so seeing a young lady wield such a technique and wield it with a pair of metal-bladed fans was a surprise. Even more of a surprise was the lack of dao, killing, or blade intent infused into her attacks. It left the wounds she dealt to the monsters superficial and light.

"Are you holding back because of me, I wonder?" Rubbing his chin, Wu Ying noted the growing annoyance among the spirit beasts. Not being able to land an attack on their prey was leaving them frustrated, and being leopards, their energy levels were fast being exhausted.

Soon, they would either go all out to finish her or leave to hunt something simpler.

He had to admit, he was rather impressed. Four spirit beasts, used to working together, two at the equivalent Core Formation realm—even if near the beginning—were powerful enough a force to overcome the majority of cultivators.

Yang Mu flipped through the air and landed on top of a beast, riding it down as it submerged into the shadow of a nearby tree before she rolled to the side. Her fan opened with a snap, forming a glimmering shield of jade and gold over the same shadow as she rolled away. It forced another beast that had attempted to leap through it backward with a scream, the creature falling off the branch high above and to the left of her.

Wu Ying shook his head a little. "What are those? Saint? Immortal fans?"

He had never seen immortal-level weapons, which meant he had no idea how powerful they were or how they functioned. Not in reality, though he had learned about them in seminars offered by the Verdant Green Waters. Unfortunately, due to the amount of time he'd spent outside of the Sect, he had only the most basic of courses and information to draw upon.

At the Immortal level of weaponry, the weapons no longer were just hardened and strengthened to handle massive amounts of chi but were also able to absorb chi itself. Such weapons accumulated energy from the surroundings, bolstering the techniques utilized by their owners. In this way, weapons like Nezha's Wind Fire Wheels and the Heavenly Sage's pole were able to overcome the base limitations of the materials they were made from.

Then again, staring at the weapons she wielded, Wu Ying realized perhaps he had his answer. Below, Yang Mu swung one fan down, wind forming at the edge of the fan and blasting outward to throw another leopard away as it stalked to the side. For all their strength, these fans were not the storied weapons of the immortals.

So…

"I wonder how she got them to do that?" Wu Ying murmured. He touched his sword by his side, a simple Saint weapon that had no abilities like hers. It cut well, it was incredibly strong, and using it with his wind chi allowed him to send blade strikes of combined wind and blade intent that could topple trees and kill beasts.

Fans snapped shut, her hand sweeping upward as she struck with the closed fan at a biting mouth that leaned down from a branch. Then the fan snapped open when the lunging body stopped, slicing open a wound along its retracting neck, fur falling to the ground as the creature yowled.

Another cry, then another, as the quartet retreated in grumbling assent. Yang Mu chose not to follow, instead standing beside the tree she had used for protection, sharpening her senses. Wu Ying could feel as she concentrated her spiritual senses into the nearby locale, retracting her aura such that she could track the four leopards as they ran away, blending into and through shadows as they fled.

She stood watching for a long time, her eyes narrowed in thought. Long enough for Wu Ying to carefully make his way down, check on the damaged garlic shoots, pick out two more for use later in their dinner, and pat back the rest. When he stood up, she was beside him, a closed fan pointed at his nose.

"What did you think you were doing, leaving me to fight them alone?" she snarled.

"Exactly what I told you I would do," Wu Ying said. "Letting you handle your problems alone."

"Is this how the Verdant Green Waters treat other cultivators? Abandoning them in their time of need?"

"You did not seem to be in much need, from what I could see." He gestured upward at the fan she still had leveled at him as though it were a sword. "Not with those. And better to learn the standards you were trained to now rather than later when it truly matters."

"Four shadow leopards were not a real threat?"

"Not to you."

For some reason, she actually looked mollified by that statement. Yang Mu lowered her fan, then with a flick of her hands, they both disappeared back into the storage rings they had been held within.

Perhaps if she stopped reacting, she would also grasp the other lessons he had hoped to impart. Lessons about silence and the dangers of the journey they faced. While she might cover her aura well, more than plain woodcraft and aura control was required to survive in such places. His way of moving silently was for the best.

If he could get her to understand it.

"Now, shall we get going?" Wu Ying gestured in a new direction, then suited action to words.

She followed after a brief hesitation, falling into line beside him. The man cocked his head, eyeing her as she unconsciously flexed her wood chi, transmitting her energy into the surroundings and bending nearby undergrowth around her as she moved to make travel easier.

"What kind of movement technique is that?" he asked.

"A good one."

"Really, are we back to that now?"

Silence greeted his words and he sighed. The woman was pricklier than a cactus. And weren't those desert plants a revelation. He had an entire section in his World Spirit Ring for the hardy vegetation, though he had yet to ascertain their uses. Perhaps a proper alchemist might find the answer to that question for him.

Now, if he could find a use for his companion…

***

Twice more, they stopped for Wu Ying to gather. Once, it was from a tree, where he dug deep amidst its roots before extracting a single root and refilling the hole. The second time, he tapped a tree, cutting deep lines along the trunk before placing a small bucket by its side. At that point, Wu Ying also set up their encampment, placing formation flags to conceal their presence. To Wu Ying's contentment, Yang Mu did not stand around sullenly or shirk her share of the work, instead joining him once she had ascertained his purpose.

Of course, that did not stop her from questioning him. "Why stop now? There are a few hours left of light that we could travel under."

"The tap will take hours to finish."

"I could hurry the process along," Yang Mu offered. "Coax the sap to pour out faster."

"And damage the tree?" He shuddered. "No. We are in no hurry."

"I would think my mother would object to that characterization."

"Perhaps, but I think she knew what to expect when she charged me with her goal."

A thoughtful pause at that comment.

"Still, would it not be better to cover more ground?" Yang Mu finally said. "While we might cut short some distance by traveling directly through the deep wilds, surely a li traveled is a li traveled, no?"

"It would be. But haste makes waste and would defeat the purpose of our visit."

"Purpose?" Yang Mu said, throwing her hands up from where she had been gathering bundles of leaves for the pair to lay their sleeping rolls upon. "We go south, locate the source of the corrupted beast stones, and put a stop to it."

"Yes. And exactly how did you think we'd locate the source?" Wu Ying said.

"We ask around, of course."

"Attracting unwanted attention at best, sending our prey to ground at worst."

"Then what is your plan?" she challenged.

"Trade."

"Huh?"

"I shall do what the Verdant Gatherer does. Gather supplies and trade with the sects in the south. If the corrupted cores are as common as your mother said"—that got a firm nod of confirmation from the woman—"then we shall gather some immediately. Innocent questions about the provenance of such stones will lead us toward the source, while I ply my trade."

"And then?"

"Well, then we shall see, shall we not?" Wu Ying finished planting the last formation flag, then placed his hand on the control flag in the center and poured in his chi to trigger the formation. "I know not the source of these stones, but it seems to me that they are either a manmade calamity—at which point, we might have to fight the individuals involved—or a natural calamity. At which point, we might have to cleanse the corruption."

"You're good at that," Yang Mu said.

"What?" Wu Ying said, surprised.

"Your chi control." This time she gestured toward him and the control flag, where his energy continued to flow into the flag. Her comments made him aware of what he was doing, how tightly bound his control had grown. "It's still easy to sense a short distance away, but ever since Uncle Song taught you the proper Cyclone's Breath method, you're much less noticeable. It's not like metal chi, which flows in a straight line and under rigid control, but something more natural. It's good. Interesting."

Wu Ying was silent before he managed a subdued, "Thank you."

"No need. It's but the truth." Yang Mu finished weaving her chi into the leaves and underbrush she had gathered, then pulled out her bedroll and placed it upon the vegetation. Looking upward, she hummed idly in thought. "Is it going to rain, you think?"

Wu Ying drew a deep breath, then whispered the question to the winds. They blew away from him in a slight gust, coming back soon with the answer of hints of moisture and clouds from around him, from the east wind that would take over soon enough.

"No. Not this night."

"Good. I like sleeping under the stars." She flopped on her bed, which to Wu Ying's surprise did not collapse under her weight. He raised an eyebrow, while she grinned and placed her hands behind her head. "It's not my first trip away, Cultivator Long."

"So I see." Wu Ying walked over to the center of their encampment, conjuring a spade, and began digging their fire pit. "Could use some wood though."

Yang Mu grinned, raising a finger and floating over a bunch of wood from nearby. As she did so, Wu Ying could see how the wood itself was shriveling a little, water and sap flowing out as she pulled it to him.

"I… see." He hesitated then glanced at the wood, before pulling out some metal pit sticks to place around the fire along with a pot. "You do seem to have a few tricks, it seems."

"I do."

"Good. We'll take turns cooking from now on." He grinned. "Unless you want to do it all?"

"Because I'm the woman?" she said, sitting upward and staring at Wu Ying, weighing his answer.

"You're the daughter of an innkeeper, are you not? Or are you telling me he didn't teach you to cook?"

"I did. And what are you doing with that herb?" She stared as Wu Ying finished peeling the garlic, pulling out individual bulbs. "You're not going to add that to our meal, are you?"

"Of course."

"Raw?" she said, as she watched him toss the garlic bulbs into the pot that had yet to boil. "What are you doing? What are you making?" She watched wide-eyed as Wu Ying pulled out some dried black fungus mushrooms and threw them into the pot.

"What's wrong? Once I add the rice and cook it together, it'll be fine." Next, he conjured a bag of rice, dropping it beside him. "So, garlic, fungus, rice? I'll roast some meat on the spit too." He untied the knot around the bag. "I have some chicken I bought from your parents."

"Are you just going to throw the rice into the pot?" He nodded, and her eyes widened further. "Are you serious? You haven't even washed it." Her voice grew ever more horrified by the moment. "Is this how you cook?"

"What's wrong with it?" Wu Ying said. It tasted fine. Not as good as a restaurant of course, but that was the point. It was not as though he needed that much sustenance now, as a Core

Formation cultivator. In fact, he could go for weeks without eating, if necessary. Though the drain on his Core energy made that less than ideal unless he was cultivating too.

"I… you…" Yang Mu stared at Wu Ying then blurred across the space when he was about to tip the rice into the water. She grabbed the rice bag just before it tipped over, pulling it out of his hand. "Just… I'll cook. You wash. And finish setting up the camp, will you?"

Wu Ying stared at what she held before he sighed. "Fine. It's still fine, you know."

"Just… wait. You'll see."

Hours later, when she was done, he had to admit she was right. Her way was better. And tastier.

Chapter 3

The next morning, Wu Ying really began to stretch his legs. Whereas they had been moving at just over twice as fast as any unascended human could have, now secure in the knowledge that Yang Mu's aura control was sufficient, he sped up gradually.

Wind Steps—the modified movement technique endemic to his Sect—allowed him to traverse the land in steps that covered dozens of feet with each motion. He had to shorten the distance each step could take though, so as to avoid running into the dense vegetation. As he traveled, Wu Ying took pains to continue his practice and familiarization of his wind body where he shifted portions of his body into wind chi, allowing him to bypass smaller impediments like a breeze blowing through the leaves.

Yang Mu, on the other hand, had a different movement technique. Or, in truth, it seemed she had three that she combined effortlessly. The first and most utilized empowered her steps, allowing her to cross more ground with each movement. It was similar to the initial parts of the Wind Steps technique, a more physical expression of her chi that Wu Ying could sense had hidden depths she had not activated as yet.

The second movement technique blended seamlessly into the first, utilizing her wood chi nature. It was an all-encompassing environmental and movement technique that altered the vegetation around her or in her path. Where Wu Ying might have to stop before a tree or drift around or over or through dense vegetation, she made the vegetation part themselves. At times, it seemed like she even used branches and trees to propel her forward, increasing her speed. As such, while Wu Ying often traveled a circuitous route to get to his destination, she instead traveled in a straight line, borrowing the aid of nature itself in her journey.

Finally, there was a third technique she kept well hidden, one that Wu Ying only glimpsed twice throughout that day. The first time when they came across a wide river. The second, a long gully that they had to traverse. She bypassed the very space she crossed, compressing the intervening distance with the utilization of a high-level spatial movement technique. It utilized a high-level space and time dao in its underpinnings, he was certain.

As such, it was completely incomprehensible to Wu Ying in anything but its results. He had—briefly—attempted to understand the twinned daos of space and time, and neither had made much sense to him. How some individuals could not only grasp time in its entirety, or space as existing in multiple dimensions as showcased by the dimensional storages he carried, he could not comprehend.

At least, not in the deep-seated, soul-bound level that was required.

After all, that was the difference between knowledge and understanding. He could understand that space could be made of a myriad of things. A man could be seen, he could be touched, he could be smelled and heard. An existence in more than one dimension. And so, space itself could be said to exist in more than one dimension, being felt, being seen, even being heard if it consisted of a person.

But he could not understand how that translated to movement, to compressing or expanding it, to piercing or making that space all one. How a cultivator with the appropriate understanding could pinch off space and set it aside for a storage ring. It did not, of course, help that many of those who did understand such dao peculiarities were obtuse hermits, protected from outside interference by the fiercest of sect guardians.

So.

Three movement techniques combined to become one technique in itself, all of them blending together with such ease that it seemed she was using a single technique, if one had not significant time to study her. In fact, Wu Ying was certain, in another decade or so, they would form a single technique and she would become a veritable ghost, impossible to hold down in the forest or area of lush vegetation.

On the other hand…

Wu Ying came to a stop at his latest acquisition. The fourth of the day, a simple rose flower bush. He set his chi to cutting and digging, tiny whirlwinds burrowing into the ground. Not as much care was required, for the hardy, carnivorous, wood-aligned plant would spring back without issue once it was replanted.

Better than leaving it here to continually leach the nutrients from the other plants around. The markings of its hunger were all around, in the sickly pallor of the trees and the formations of mosses and other fungi on their bark, the rotting wooden corpses on the ground.

"You move well. But your aura control could use more work when you switch between your techniques," Wu Ying remarked.

Yang Mu's eyes narrowed a little. "My aura control is impeccable."

"When you are not moving, it is. Better than mine even," Wu Ying acknowledged. His nature did not allow for his aura or his presence to disappear entirely. Instead, he controlled its presence and blended the portions of chi that escaped, such that he seemed entirely natural to outward senses. Perfect for hiding from spirit beasts or demonic creatures. To those with the knowledge or the right kind of techniques, he was more easily spotted, however. "But you have to focus to change your movement technique and the flows, and you are leaking a little when you do so."

She glared at him before turning away, leaving Wu Ying to finish his work. He wrapped his chi around the bush, pulling it into his World Spirit Ring where he had carved a similar hole. Then, using the soil he had dug up in the real world, he refilled the earth around the carnivorous wood plant, locating it near the strand of fast-growing spirit weeds to help control their spread in his World Spirit Ring.

The ring was perhaps his greatest treasure, a mini-world that grew everyday as it leached energy from his core. As he grew stronger, the ring grew too. In theory, one day, there might even be a minor world within. For now, it was multiple li across with valleys, rivers, and even mountains in the distance.

After pulling water from the clouds and dampening the soil, the process of replanting was over, leaving a gaping hole in the earth as the only mark of their presence. Wu Ying did not concern himself about that sign, instead moving on to the next target.

Their entire journey that day and over the next few was a wending one that took them south through the deep woods, skirting along the edges of untamed wilderness before working deeper. There was—of course—no actual boundary between what might be considered more civilized forests and the deep wilds, no visible markings beyond signs of travel and the presence—or lack—of other spirit and demonic beasts.

Still, years of practice had gifted Wu Ying an understanding of the invisible boundaries that were formed by the movements of powerful spirit and demonic beasts, the subtle signs in the shift of environmental chi and the markings they created to delineate their territory.

Gliding along such edges, Wu Ying picked at the bountiful spirit herbs available. He took the rarest items, the ones meant for Energy Storage and Core Formation cultivators, but always sought to leave the area he traveled within better off. Sometimes that meant removing encroaching or destructive vegetation. Other times it was trimming away dead or overhanging shrubbery to allow the blossoming of herbs in his wake. In some cases, he would even subtly alter the natural geography, shifting the natural flow of chi to better benefit one or another plant.

By the third day, Yang Mu had taken an overt interest in his gathering. Her curiosity was of a more mercantile nature, eyeing the herbs he acquired with an assessing eye that tallied up the income he generated. After the second herb on that day, she could not help but ask.

"Why are you taking that? There's little value in green schisandra berries. Don't you have to wait for them to ripen further?" Yang Mu said.

"Normally, yes. If we were trying to sell it for consumption or as an addition to alchemical forgings." Wu Ying tapped the tree they were under. "However, this tree is water-based." He gestured at the pool of water it sat beside, the small trickle of liquid flowing from the tree to join a nearby stream. "Not many uses for it among apothecarists, since most schisandra berries are best for fire and metal applications."

Yang Mu nodded. Through her study with her parents, she had gained a wider base of knowledge than most, a deeper understanding of what goods were needed for which client. If anything, her knowledge was even broader than Wu Ying's, covering enchanted equipment and formations of all forms, unlike the gatherer and his dabbling in apothecary.

"These are more for myself, for my baths as a Body Cultivator." Wu Ying finished pouring the last of the berries into the jar he had extracted before sealing it with a cork stopper. "I'll soak it in some rice wine and use it in the bath later on when it's ready."

"Oh…" Yang Mu fell silent, though there was an inquiring look in her eyes.

"You have questions?" Wu Ying said.

"Curiosities." Yang Mu gestured at the bottle he held. "My parents were adamant I should not attempt body cultivation. That it could affect my advancement in soul cultivation. And yet, it has not stopped your progress."

He nodded. "No, not really. I've been fortunate to be able to progress both my dao and locate a wind body cultivation manual that works for me."

"Exactly. I don't understand why my parents were so worried."

Wu Ying smiled a little, making the jar disappear into his storage ring. Then he turned deliberately in the direction he intended to travel before taking a step. They moved together while Wu Ying continued the conversation, manipulating the wind around them both to hide their words.

"You've met a lot of cultivators. Those in the Core Formation realm mostly, I think. Some Energy Formation cultivators, of course, but your family caters toward those at the higher stage. Is that not right?"

"Yes."

"And you and your sisters, you've all progressed relatively smoothly. A few hiccups, a few moments where you've had troubles, but generally you progressed upward without issue."

Another grunted agreement came from her.

"So you've never seen the struggles of the less fortunate."

"We've struggled. It has never been easy."

"Cultivation has never been easy," Wu Ying agreed. "But you had your parents, Nascent Soul cultivators. Direct teaching and experience to bypass the hardest parts of the earliest stages of cultivation. Access to resources, cultivation techniques that were suited for each of you beyond the basic Yellow Emperor technique that most have to use. Even in sects like mine, finding a technique that is compatible, that can help an individual breakthrough is hard. I had to leave the Verdant Green Waters to locate my own technique.

"But that's because a sect must consider what is best for the sect as a whole. Only those with the personal attention of an Elder can hope to skip that requirement."

"So you're saying I'm lucky?" Yang Mu said, irritated at the long-winded cultivator.

"Yes. And that you've never seen how hard a struggle it has been for others." Wu Ying dodged under a tree branch, coming to rest on top of a boulder. "Body Cultivation tears your body apart. The pain that you experience is unlike anything you've ever felt. It digs deep into your physique, into your blood vessels and bones. It has broken many, made them stop cultivating entirely in fear of the process. Because that's the other thing. Many Body Cultivation techniques… you can't stop."

"What?" Yang Mu said, cocking her head. "Why have I not heard that before?"

"Because it's not something most consider." He shrugged, stepping away to continue their trek, feeling the wind blowing across his skin. "The process of altering your body is painful. If you stop before the process is complete, your body wants to revert. That process is painful too, and the reversion process can be…"

"Can be what?" Yang Mu said eventually.

"Fatal in some cases. Impossible in others. A Body Cultivator who stops could be caught in a never-ending, painful process of changing back and forth as one side or another of his body battles within him."

Wu Ying watched as she grew quiet, contemplative. He liked that about her, that she was willing to take in new viewpoints and weigh them against her prior assumptions.

In time, the Gatherer chose a new direction, headed for a new herb. He noticed that Yang Mu's control of her aura had improved, reducing the flare of chi as she switched between techniques. It had caused her to stumble a little, her movements no longer as smooth as before.

A decent trade-off in his estimation. In time she'd get better, and if she was not as swift as before, it was more than acceptable for this portion of their journey. A necessary step, if they were to cut down on the time taken to reach their destination.

Time to head into the deep wilds, where dragons and demons lay.

Chapter 4

The deep wilds was a strange place to be. So called because few humans dared cross the land, for Nascent Soul and even immortal creatures resided within. Tall branches blocked out the sun above the pair as they traversed the ground, trees that had not been touched since the scattering of humans after the flood.

In this place, mortal man held no sway. Unlike the ebb and flow of civilization at the edges, where an outpost, a village, or even a city might form before eventually falling, here, man had never emplaced themselves. Here, the Dao ran deep and the creatures all moved to an unheard beat.

Wonders never ceased to pass by, as the pair traversed these lands. There, a pool at night, so clear and calm that the moon and clouds were perfectly reflected, untouched as though a celestial mirror had been brought forward. Around this midnight water feature, spirits gathered and immortal beauties might bathe, casting aside their silken raiment for but a moment.

Here, a deep cave that glowed with hidden light. Wandering within, the pair were treated to a sight unseen by mortal man—a cluster of glow worms that bathed the insides of the cave in a myriad of colors, shifting from pale blue and green to bright yellows and oranges. In this magical land, a mushroom field that supported immortal glow worms grew.

For a dozen mushroom cuttings, the pair traded an evening of stories and warmth, bringing forth hot tea and mulled wine to the introverted immortals. When they left the next day, it was with a dozen glowing mushrooms and a tale that few would believe.

Days passed in such a manner, in quiet travel and soft-spoken evenings. Cultivation resources were bountiful in their natural form, but so was danger. More than once, the pair crouched, hidden under formation flags and within caverns, forced to wait and cultivate as dangers greater than the pair crossed nearby.

In such an environment, Wu Ying grew even more circumspect in his gathering. Oftentimes, they would come to a stop and watch a location for hours as the Gatherer ascertained that no traps lay in wait for them. Such traps came in a variety of manners, from plants that defended with poisonous sap, strangling vines that draped over the neck innocuously, or lulling flower scents that put cultivators and other vermin to sleep for the insects, reptiles, and arachnids that lay in wait for the greedy.

Nearly a week into their journey, after Wu Ying had carefully extracted a handful of berries from a bush whose branches were covered by a crawling vine that snapped and tore at any creature lured in by the enticing sight, Yang Mu chose to break their silence, drifting over to land on the sturdy branch Wu Ying perched upon above the bush.

"I never knew there were so many varieties of dangerous plants," Yang Mu said. "Or creatures seeking to stop the harvesting of such plants."

Wu Ying grunted, unsure of her point but acknowledging her statement either way. He breathed in slowly and deeply through his nose, sifting through the smells the wind brought to him as he sought his next destination. There was a particularly alluring scent, waterlogged and metallic, that came from the northwest. He knew it to be from a lotus of some form, likely a metallic lotus mutation. A rare variation, only available in lakes and ponds that had run-off from a mine or some other heavily mineralized content.

Near to him, of course, was the wood-aligned cultivator. Her scent had been withdrawn, kept focused, and, after some pointed discussion, no longer floral-scented. Now, she smelled of clean skin and that underlying mortal odor.

Farther east, there was an acrid, almost rotting scent. Either a dead animal or one of the plants that mimicked the process of decomposition to lure prey toward it. The first might offer a beast core and scavengers that might be slain for their spirit stones. The second might allow him to locate fallen equipment and gather such plants for his World Spirit Ring. Such plants' necrotic properties could be useful for creating poisons and medicines.

"I do not, however, understand why there are so few that are useful for our purposes," she had continued speaking while he was sifting out the scents. She gestured at the lush greenery around them. "Surely there must be more."

"Ah…" Wu Ying hesitated, looking at the woman. She returned his look, patiently waiting for his answer. Realizing she was not idly asking and wanted him to elaborate, he continued. "It's a matter of time, dissemination of knowledge, and training."

"Go on."

Wu Ying nodded, then flicked his hand sideways. In doing so, he conjured a small barricade of wind that sent their scent and words upward while he kept his voice low.

"Firstly, improper knowledge. Did you know that many books are not particularly well-written? Even the seminal work, the Shen Nong *Ben Cao Jing*[49], is replete with errors. Because of that, various individuals have attempted to fix the errors. Sometimes doing a good job, but just as often, introducing their own mistakes. As such, while the works available on various herbs and vegetation is significant, they must be individually verified unless one knows the author well." Wu Ying paused, then offered a slight grin. "And even then, in such instances, one must take into account the author's own flaws.

"On top of that, it's worth realizing that even the Shen Nong's work covers only 365 works." He gestured all around him. "How many plants can you see?"

"A lot."

"Exactly."

Yang Mu frowned, looking around now with new eyes.

---

[49] The "Classic of the Materia Medica" is an actual work with three volumes and 365 entries on medicants and descriptions.

"After that, we come to the issue of seclusion of knowledge. While I can sense a dozen powerful herbs around us, I have specific knowledge of only three. The others are unknown in their use, even though they burn with power. I could collect them, but I do not have the knowledge, the tools, or the market for such herbs. Another Gatherer might know three such herbs too—but a different three."

Yang Mu made a face. "Yes. Sometimes cultivators would arrive with unknown herbs or minerals or talismans, insisting they were of use. However, if we have no customer in mind for many of those wares, my mother would either refuse or offer them a much lower price than what they desired. It's no use storing items that might degrade eventually if we cannot sell them." Another deeper frown. "Or worse, we cannot define the providence of such items."

"Exactly," Wu Ying said. "Every sect has their own knowledge, their own needs. That we keep much of it from each other means that what is desired in one region is worthless in the next. Some items and herbs are, of course, widely used, like the base Spirit Grass. But those are often grown in-house. As Gatherers, we—I—specialize in the esoteric and rare."

"Ah…" Yang Mu nodded. "Which is why you avoid picking some of the things even I recognize. Because there's no point."

"Exactly. I only have so much storage space," Wu Ying said. Of course, he had a lot more than she likely knew—though he wondered how much she had ascertained or been told of his World Spirit Ring by her parents—but it still made little sense to pick much of it from the wild. He was no roving locust swarm. Better to leave what he did not require or held little value to him and allow it to grow, supporting the wildlife around.

After all, he had his own world to supply him with much of those needs.

"So that is knowledge. You said time and, I assume, training falls above too."

"Exactly, though training also of those apothecarists and cultivators we must work with." He gestured at the surroundings. "If I bring a new plant to an apothecarist, would they recognize it? Are they trained to experiment on such plants to bring about a positive reaction? Or will they, accidentally, create a poison? Are they willing to risk making a harmful product that might injure an individual in the future? It is why physicians and apothecarists are leery of experimenting, yet hunger to do so. It is a path to both vast riches and penury."

"And that's what you mean by time and training." Yang Mu waved Wu Ying quiet as he moved to correct her. "There's obviously more, with the amount of time needed to find more of the same kind of plant, the training to process and gather it properly, time taken to learn all that, and so forth."

"Exactly."

"Very well. We may go then."

Wu Ying snorted a little at her casual dismissal of the topic and her sudden impatience. Still, he had ascertained their best route for now, so he took off once more. Those metallic lotuses intrigued him. They were rare, and he hoped, by spending some time there, he might learn how to replicate the process in his World Spirit Ring.

***

Three hours later, as Wu Ying walked the surroundings, poking and prodding at trees, digging up the mud, and regarding the inflow of water from the river to the pond that held the copper lotuses, Yang Mu made an announcement.

"I shall go find us dinner." Gesturing upstream, she added, "You'll find me farther up that way." Her head tilted a little, taking in the sloping, mist-shrouded hill. "Unless you are done?"

"It will be a few hours at the least." Wu Ying hesitated, eyeing the ground and rubbing his chin. "I'd prefer the rest of the day in fact. I believe there might be a change in the energy flows when the moon rises, when yang gives way to yin. I would set some formation flags and talismans to help me record and understand the changes."

Huffing a little, Yang Mu left without another word. Wu Ying forgot about her within moments, already rubbing the earth between his fingers and raising the soil to his lips to taste it. Metallic, a little acidic too, and clean with just a touch of sulphur. Taking out an eight-sided compass, a brush, and paper, he charted the flow of environmental chi in the surroundings.

If he was right, the inflow into the pond was not just influenced by the higher metallic content within the water itself, but also a feature of the concentration of yin energy in the surroundings. Along with the growth of supporting plants around the body of water, the pond had intensified in the amount of metallic yin energy it contained, allowing the copper lotuses in the center to flourish.

The lotuses were few, numbering just over two dozen, of which more than half were normal—mortal—lotuses, with just a tinge of the copper element within them. The other half dozen were a mix, most in the spirit range and two in the saint level of progress. Wu Ying debated what to do even as he took additional readings, tested and sampled the water and earth, and sketched details about the pond, the vegetation surrounding it, and the rocks that formed this natural formation.

In particular, he debated taking or leaving one saint-level copper lotus. The strongest lotus might have a chance at progressing, becoming an immortal copper lotus in a hundred years. In a decade, the copper lotus might have grown in strength, becoming more potent. It would sell better then, be more useful for those at a higher stage of cultivation. And, of course, such individuals were wealthier.

On the other hand, Wu Ying could vaguely sense the movement of carp and catfish within the pond. Some were large and potent, their energy brushing against his spiritual senses. Others were but mortal or body cleansing level carp, not at all a concern.

Good eating perhaps, though it was obvious that Yang Mu had other plans for dinner. Perhaps she did not enjoy the taste of fish? Or she had sensed the denizens within the water and had chosen not to bother them. For at least the largest within, a creature that lurked at the bottom of the pond, was potent, its presence a watery shadow in Wu Ying's mind. And even that much was only available to his senses due to the training and experience he had gained diving in the eastern ocean.

No. Leaving the lotuses behind might be a mistake, for there was no guarantee the creature below would not consume the plants in the interim period. Of course, normally such fish were not consumers of vegetation, but certain rules bent as one gained in strength and cultivation level.

If he could ascertain the aspect of the creatures within the pond and the potent creature at the bottom, he might be able to verify if the creature was safeguarding the lotuses or cared little for them. While most creatures grew in harmony with the environment, gaining the elemental aspect that was most prominent, some might develop in direct opposition. Those creatures were often the most powerful variety, for in their struggles, they had gained strength.

It was, perhaps, a metaphor of existence. It was easy to go with the flow of social existence, choosing the occupations, the residences, and even the loves that one's parents and society dictated of them. Harder though to oppose such heavenly dictates and rise above.

Heroes of the norm, individuals who rose to prominence within such structures were common. From the three brothers of the Eastern Han dynasty to Judge Bao and his upright sense of justice, striking down the corrupt and criminal. Heroes of the society that had brought them up, that worked within the confines of their societal restrictions…

Yet there were those who stood in entire opposition to such societal precepts that inspired as well. Sun Wukong[50] was, of course, the most prominent of these rebels who set themselves apart from society. His punishments—from being trapped and cooked alive to imprisonment for five hundred years under a mountain—were legendary. Then there were those like Fan Li Hua who defied traditional roles and their very kingdom to marry those they loved and paid in the death of their clan.

Tragedy, punishment, and pain dogged the steps of those who defied the dictates of society. Much like it dogged the steps of cultivators who defied the rule of heaven. There was no easy path, yet these heroes continued their struggles against a world and a society that stood in opposition to their sense of honor and morals. They fought, till tragedy finally consumed them or they rose above it all.

A fitting allegory then.

Hours were spent at the pond, readings taken and the camp prepared. Wu Ying's contemplations of the dao were interrupted only by the return of Yang Mu, the woman proffering a brace of slain ground birds for Wu Ying to cook for their dinner.

Over the dinner of fire-roasted birds, a medley of pickled vegetables, and rice, Yang Mu broke the silence, dropping a small rock in the space between the pair.

---

[50] The Monkey King, aka the Great Sage, Heaven's Equal

"You should head north later," Yang Mu said.

Wu Ying glanced at the rock, noting the reflections arising from the object. "Why?"

"Can you not see?"

"Metal of some form, yes." He shrugged.

Her eyes narrowed and she pointed her chopsticks at the rock. "Not just any rock. That's high-grade iron ore, infused with additional metal chi. I also saw some fire garnets in the striations, though I did not have time to investigate their quality."

Again, another shrug.

"Do you not care? My family would have bought properly mined ore for dozens of tael." She snorted. "Or just traded for high quality beast cores."

"Did you bring a pick?"

"What?"

"Did you bring a pick?" Wu Ying mimed the action of breaking the rock apart by swinging a pickaxe over his shoulder with his right hand. "A shovel and pails?"

"No. Of course not."

"Neither did I."

"Why not?" Yang Mu said, sounding frustrated.

"Why didn't you?"

"Because I'm not the gatherer!"

Wu Ying finished chewing on the drumstick he had pulled from the bird laid before him, extracting the meat from the bone with his teeth before tossing the bone into the fire and swallowing the meat. Then, and only then, did he answer her. "And I don't gather rocks."

"Why not?" she repeated.

"Too much to learn."

That answer made Yang Mu hesitate. She looked at the rock, then picked it up and turned it around before she shrugged. "It's not that hard. There aren't that many variations of metals and rocks out there. And while I wouldn't expect you to mine the earth itself, there should be no reason to not extract those on the surface."

"If I knew the difference in grades and types, it might make sense," Wu Ying said. "But it always seemed to me that there was more work involved in that than it was worth. I remember crushing, tossing, and melting down a significant amount of ore each time we needed to purify the metals coming in. Herbs are easier."

"You worked as a blacksmith?" She cocked her head at that, eyeing his arms.

He had not the massive thews of a blacksmith, though he was not in any way slender. His days working as a farmer and martial artist before progressing far on the path to cultivation had ensured he would never fit the slim, slender build so common among their peers.

"A little. I had no real skill. It was enlightening, but sufficient enough for me to learn not to bother with mining." He grinned. "Anyway, how deep a seam did you find? Where would I carry these rocks? Am I expected to carry them with me till I find another sect? Who would buy them? All problems if I started moving into something new. Better to specialize and study what I can."

Yang Mu's eyes narrowed once more, then she let out one long huff. She gestured at the rock. "Fine. But we're going by the seam tomorrow. I'll gather the metal if you are too lazy to do so."

"You should have done so earlier today, then we wouldn't be delayed." She growled a little under her breath, and Wu Ying grinned. "But because you were trying to be considerate for me, we'll just do that."

Silence greeted his words, and he debated briefly about prodding her further to thank him. That fleeting mischievous thought disappeared soon though as he turned his attention back to dinner. Time enough to test her further later.

After all, they had many li left.

Chapter 5

Cross-legged, Wu Ying cultivated on the mountain slope. Winds swirled around him, bringing notice of the nearby environment and those beasts that might be paying too close attention to the pair. A Nascent Soul beetle crawled across the ground a li away, searching for new prey for its pincers of rot and decay. A flock of Energy Storage sparrows flew overhead, led by their Core Formation leader, enjoying the increased updraft Wu Ying's presence brought. And more, so many more creatures, traversed the ground around them. All of whom might object to their presence. Certainly, after the first powerful strike by his companion, Wu Ying had had to emplace a swirling defense around the cave entrance to deaden the noise of her mining.

Even now, he could not help but wonder why she had such a massive hammer in her spatial storage, or why anyone would create spirit equipment like that. At first glance, when she had extracted the hammer with its oversized head from her storage ring, he had been mildly curious. It was, after all, a work of art, with enameled green and yellow copper banding and a dark, water-marked steel head. Then it had expanded such that when placed shaft down, the head stood over Yang Mu by a good foot and the striking surface was easily larger than a large man's torso.

When she proceeded to wield the weapon against her own fans, slammed into the corners of the mountain to provide her spikes to crack apart the surface seam, he had been astounded. That her fans looked no worse for wear was just as miraculous in its own way.

Even now, Wu Ying found his light meditation disturbed by each ringing impact as he wondered about the status and condition of her equipment.

In truth, he too experienced some mild feelings of greed for what she mined. He could sense the deep-seated chi within the metals themselves, the powerful resonance they exhibited. The winds had blown around the stone dust Yang Mu was creating, pulling it together into a ball of slowly compacting metal. Entirely too small and miniscule for her use, but scattered across his World Spirit Ring?

Definitely useful.

As for the larger pieces she kept on shattering and pulling apart, well, that was hers. In fact…

"Been quiet for the last while," Wu Ying said, cocking his head.

He extended his senses to the nearly formed cave to find Yang Mu scooping shattered rocks into a small canvas bag. Something was happening around the top of the bag that his spiritual sense could not correctly perceive.

Curiosity dragged Wu Ying over to stare at the newly created shadowed cave where Yang Mu continued to toss stones twice the size of a wine pot into the much smaller opening. Each time the rocks came close, the boulders would twist and shrink, their dimensions warping before they plopped into the storage sack.

"How…?" Wu Ying said, shaking his head. "I've never seen that effect before."

"It's not a common enhancement," Yang Mu said, her voice mildly strained as she spoke. "It requires an understanding of spatial daos and theory to enact. I have to manipulate the dimensional storage and my own understanding at the same time."

Her words made Wu Ying stare more carefully and allow his spiritual senses to pick at the chi she was exuding into the atmosphere. Now that he was paying attention, he could sense the energy she was directing from her core toward the dimensional bag, the way she wrapped the area above the bag and the bag itself in the chi and her own dao understandings.

Wu Ying watched for long minutes as Yang Mu finished clearing out the space of the broken rocks. Then, to his surprise, she walked out to pick at additional rocks at the front of the cliff face. The rocks here were more carefully perused, as she sorted through them and tossed aside nearly two-thirds of those left behind.

Not once did she ask for his help, instead processing the rocks in silence. Wu Ying moved away after a time, paying attention to the storage bag and her actions, trying to gain a glimpse of the spatial daos in play. He sought to grasp enlightenment and understanding.

And failed.

In the end, Yang Mu straightened and brushed her hands clean, peeling off the gloves she had been utilizing and storing them away. Both her fans and the massive hammer had been slipped into the ring before she had begun processing the rocks, leaving naught but the massive cave and the crumbled, undesired rocks as indication of her passage.

"Done?" Wu Ying asked.

"Yes." She rolled her neck, then gestured at her bag. It floated back up to her hands, then she strapped it to the side of her robes via a simple cloth belt. She regarded the miniature cave she had created, before shrugging. "Thank you. For forming the wind wall to muffle my actions."

"You're welcome." He cocked his head and listened to the wind that had just gusted over to him, bringing a new scent. "Time to go, unless you want to start a fight."

Yang Mu hesitated, then to Wu Ying's pleasure, she shook her head. Together, the pair left the surroundings, the Gatherer taking a moment once they reached the tree line to scatter a few yellow talismans behind them. Those talismans would activate and obscure their trail, making it more difficult for the beasts tracking them.

Better safe than sorry.

***

The pair hunkered down low, broken tree branches, decomposing leaves, and mud covering their bodies. Two weeks and deep into the untamed wilds and Yang Mu no longer questioned Wu Ying's occasional impertinent actions. In this case, tackling her to the ground, rolling both of them through the nearest mud pit, and wielding his wind to pull debris over them both.

She had even gone so far as to aid him, pulling at the nearby vegetation to provide them additional cover.

Now, they lay on their fronts, their eyes small slits in the gloom of the deep undergrowth as the Nascent Soul spirit beast that Wu Ying had sensed prowled the forest. The creature was no massive monster like the last Nascent Soul beast Wu Ying had fought, but a normal-sized creature of its kind. That still left it larger and heavier than the pair put together, the beast's darkened fur flashing as deeper shades of black adjusted to the gloom within, massive paws touching down upon the ground with the barest whisper of noise.

Occasionally, the Black Tiger let out a low chuff, having drawn in the scent of creatures nearby before releasing the air from its nostrils. Its tail swished lazily behind it as the undoubted king of the jungle prowled its territory, searching for the intrusive pair of presences it had sensed.

A wind arose, brushing the treetops and swaying branches, scattering leaves, flowers, and fruit. A bird shifted its weight as the branch it sat upon swayed, and the tiger turned yellow eyes upon it. A flicker of movement, and the creature had the bird in its jaws before bounding off the same branch again to land on the ground not far away.

Jaw working once, then again, the Core Formation-level core of the bird cracked in its sharp teeth as a burst of yang-aspected water chi was released into the air. Head turned upward, the creature swallowed its victim in a single gulp, the split pieces sliding down its gullet.

Beside him, the trembles of Yang Mu's body increased. Fear locked the woman in place under the paltry defense of brush and mud. Shifting ever so slowly when the predator looked aside, Wu Ying clutched her hand and squeezed, offering unspoken comfort.

He understood her fear. Remembered it all too well. The first time he had encountered a Nascent Soul monster, the first time he had faced one alone without the aid of another more powerful cultivator came rushing back to him. The casual, predatory killing intent that the Black Tiger exuded into the air, its mastery of stealth, and its blindingly fast movements showcased how far ahead it was from them.

Even among Nascent Soul beasts, there were gradations of strength. And this one, this creature that roamed the deep wilds was powerful beyond belief. If Wu Ying did not know better—and he was not certain he did—he would have named the monster an immortal. As fabled as the White Tiger of the West. Perhaps, one day, it would become a true immortal and challenge the White Tiger for supremacy.

Till then, it prowled these forests.

And they had, inadvertently, drawn its attention in their passage. Now it stalked them, searching for their presence. Wu Ying could only be grateful that their combined abilities, layering wood and wind chi to cover their scent and obscure their tracks, had given them some degree of safety. Alone, he was uncertain he would have been able to dodge the creature's predatory gaze.

Slow breaths, taken with great care and wide spaces between each intake. As cultivators, they required little air. Wu Ying had trained to hold his breath for long minutes not so long ago. His companion had not, but even she required little enough air that she mimicked his breathing, alternating carefully so as not to alert the monster crouched all too close to them.

Her trembling had slowed a little, the involuntary fear response fading. The grip of her hand on his did not relent. If anything, she pressed a little more into his shoulder. Not enough to obscure movement but seeking comfort in his warmth and presence.

Long moments, as the creature stayed crouched over its forelegs, cleaning them of the traces of blood that had escaped while snacking. Then, lazily, the monster stood and stretched, turning its head slowly.

There was a look in the creature's yellow eyes, one that was both dismissive and malicious. As though it were informing them that their luck had held out. That they had managed to evade its attention and could live.

Today.

But one day, it would find them. It would stalk them. And then, it would feast upon their corpses.

Then, between slow blinks, the creature was gone. As swiftly as it had arrived, it departed, without a hint of noise, having crossed hundreds of feet within moments. Bypassing the trees and bushes around it, a ghostly predator of the gloom.

Even so, neither cultivator chose to move. It was nearly a half day before the pair rose from their impromptu hiding spot, their trembling subsided, the fear controlled. Without a word, Wu Ying led them away, treading in the opposite direction of their arrival. Out from the depths of the woods, no longer stopping to gather even as the wind whispered the secrets of the master of the forest to the wind cultivator.

For there were beasts that prowled this land that it was best not to encounter, nor intrude upon. For whatever gain one might acquire by traversing the depths of the wilderness, it paled upon understanding that most important of factors.

That one could not spend coin when one was dead.

***

Days later, the pair exited the depths of the forest to alight upon a much-trampled road. Now on a packed dirt road, with shards of sunlight seeping through the opened vegetation, tension escaped with each breath and tense muscles relaxed. Wu Ying rolled his shoulders, releasing them before twisting from side to side, emitting a series of loud cracks and pops as his spine shifted. Beside him, Yang Mu too stretched, a smile blossoming upon her face as relief rose.

Only for it to tighten moments later as she regarded her companion.

"Are we done then, with your testing?" she said testily.

"Testing?" he replied, shifting his stance to meet her accusing gaze face-on. He idly noted that there were no people on this road, not for a few li on either side. This was not a heavily traversed passage, for it only passed by a couple of smaller villages and a middling sized town.

"We're both Core formation cultivators. We could have easily flown to the south by now, bypassing much of these issues. And as for your excuse of needing to gather…" She glanced at his ring, raising a single, suggestive eyebrow. "Do I need to say it?"

"I do carry some items that are useful for trade, and I grow a lot of other rarer items, but your supposition is wrong. To some extent," Wu Ying said, rubbing the edge of the simple metal ring with his thumb.

That it was a plain ring, with neither inset gem or marks except for the lettering on the inside, helped with its disguise. On the other hand, at their levels of cultivation and dao understanding, it was easy enough to notice the twisting of chi around the ring. Worse, for Wu Ying's desire for anonymity, as the World Spirit Ring had grown stronger and repaired itself, the amount of chi it drew from the surroundings had increased.

There were ways to reduce the consumption of external, environmental chi, to alter the exchange between the surroundings and the tiny, twisted dimension within. Most of that was on him, to create a world that balanced the needs of the plants and the ring within itself, such that the enchantment was not required to balance itself by pulling energy from outside.

But he had not yet reached that level of understanding or grasp of the greater Dao to remove its needs completely.

It also was a concern that as Wu Ying grew further in his own cultivation, the aura and energy the ring could draw from him was tainted with his wind chi. To a certain extent, the World Spirit Ring could alter such chi to balance out its own needs as the energy passed through its internal formations. Furthermore, Wu Ying had taken the time to create internal formations and plant vegetation that would do the same. But in the end, only so much could be done.

All of which meant that, unlike in its earlier years, the World Spirit Ring had grown ever more prominent to those who had both the knowledge and the senses to watch for such things. That he had to fight duels or escape from those seeking to acquire the ring was not, in itself, new to Wu Ying.

"The items within my storage are limited in number," Wu Ying said. "And much space is set aside for the herbs for my cultivation baths."

"But we could have bypassed much of these problems already, could we not?" Yang Mu said grumpily. "If not for the fact that you wished to test me."

"It was necessary," he admitted. "I know little of you, even less of what your intentions might be. Better to understand such matters in an environment I can control, rather than when disaster strikes in a land I know little of."

"And that Nascent Soul Black Tiger? That was considered controlled?" Yang Mu said angrily. "Did you expect to manage that creature?"

"Why, is your control of yourself that bad?" Wu Ying said bitingly. "Do you have so little faith in yourself that you feared hiding from it?"

"Don't tell me you were not afraid as well. I was there."

He nodded. "Yes, you were. And being afraid and wary is part of my job. Or did you think that traversing the deep wilds was easy?"

"Of course I knew it wasn't. But that creature—"

"Was more dangerous than most." Wu Ying shrugged. "Such things happen. It is why I am careful and quiet. But so are most Gatherers. Sometimes, luck and fate are against you." He smiled a little wryly. "As my martial sister would say, it is good to know if the scales must be balanced in your companion's fate."

"What does that even mean?"

"That some people are unluckier than others in this life."

Yang Mu growled before stalking off, leaving Wu Ying to stare at her back. He ran a hand through his hair and considered maybe leaving now, before she could notice that he was gone. But there was only one path on this road unless he wanted to enter the wilds again. And even he was not willing to risk the tiger's wrath once again.

Still, he did shape the wind to carry his words to her. "You know, you're going the wrong way."

She froze, turned around, and stalked back the way she had come. As she passed Wu Ying, she glared at him, daring him to say anything.

He let her get a few feet farther away before he added, "I thought you wanted to fly?"

Again, she stopped. Now, Wu Ying conjured his winds, lightening himself with the Heavenly Soul, Earthly Body qinggong method and floated over to her under the guidance of his chi and the winds.

He smiled as he drifted closer, adding, "There's a middling sized town down that way, about sixty li or so. We can rest there, I can conduct a cleansing ritual for my body, then we can finish the journey." He cocked his head, eyeing the very still woman whose fist was clenched. "If that is acceptable, of course."

"Why should you care what I think?" she growled.

"Well, you did pass the test."

Silence from the woman, while Wu Ying bobbed in place next to her. The wind spun dust in a small circle around him, pulling him upward and downward, spinning him from side to side. Not like the impressive stillness that some cultivators managed with their flying weapons, but still, he floated serenely beside her.

"You... you..." She drew a deep breath, then let it out slowly. "You are an infuriating man."

"And one used to traveling alone." Wu Ying shrugged. "Shall we?"

In answer, Yang Mu conjured one of her fans. It expanded as it hovered before her, forming the same green jade energy shield she had used before. Stepping onto the platform it created, she directed a touch of her chi to chase after Wu Ying, who was already drifting away on the wind, ascending above the roadway and gaining speed.

Still, he did keep an eye on her, knowing that the speed he could attain was not easily achieved by others. After all, they were not the wind like he was.

Chapter 6

A day and a night, the pair resided in that small town. There were no complications during their stay, even if the appearance of a pair of Core Formation cultivators had them both feted by the local magistrate at his residence. While Wu Ying bathed in the Body Cultivation herbal bath that stripped his bones and muscles raw, tearing them apart to better allow wind chi to permeate his form, Yang Mu completed a minor task for the city lord as a favor.

Over dinner that evening—one that, thankfully, they were able to host without the now terrified city lord—Yang Mu related the day's events to Wu Ying.

"After hunting through the entirety of the mansion and its buildings, I'd still found no traces of what was causing the deaths and calamities of the Xi family. It was only when I started emplacing the formation flags that the maid who had been assigned to me chose to act." Yang Mu gestured with her chopsticks as she spoke, too excited to care about proper manners. "It was her all along."

"And what was she?"

"A fox spirit!"

"You met one?" Wu Ying said, surprised.

"I did. Met and banished her too." Then she made a face. "Horrible fight though."

"How so?"

"Illusion magic," Yang Mu explained, her nose scrunched up cutely. "I hate illusion magic. Spent nearly two hours caught in her trap, chasing her around. Thankfully, she was just mischievous rather than vicious. When I finally managed to exhaust her, she chose to leave."

"And you're sure she's gone?"

"The city at least." She raised her left hand, showing the dangling bracelet on it. Wu Ying watched as one of the jade beads glowed, flickering a little with hidden light. "I marked her before she left, so that she will not be able to return to the city without me knowing. The mark on her aura will last for at least a few years, until she changes substantially. I've passed notice of the mark to the formation master in charge of the city as well, to ensure they adjust their protections against her."

Wu Ying blinked, cocking his head. "That's possible?"

"Of course. How do you think the formations around most sects are created? They link your sect token to your aura and then both to the formation itself. Or did you think that the penalties for losing your sect token were for nothing?"

"Huh." Wu Ying hummed to himself, before raising the last of the fried rice dish to his mouth. He could smell the sesame oil and dried pork and chicken sausage that had been fried into the dish, along with multiple helpings of eggs and scallions. His tongue salivated as he chewed, noting the light spice and herbs they had used, which were new. One of the wonders of travel—new cuisine each time. "How do you know so much about sect tokens and formations then? I do not believe you've ever joined one."

"Of course not." She laughed at the thought, her hair dancing behind her as she shook her head. "Could you see my parents letting me do so?"

"They did seem a tad protective," he acknowledged.

"What a fine and politick understatement. No, I have never joined a sect. But I have perused more than a few lost tokens, taken from the slain and sold to us. I've visited a few of the nearby sects too, with my mother. She travels there to give lectures and sell or buy goods, and I started going with her in later years." She smiled in fond remembrance. "She used to take me and my sisters to watch their tournaments and take part in their auctions. When we were much younger, she sometimes even let us take part."

"Really?"

"Oh yes. Until we started winning more often than not. Then she banned us. Said there was nothing else for us to learn from them." Yang Mu's nose wrinkled as she frowned. "I think she just didn't want us embarrassing her customers anymore."

"That seems… wise."

"Mother always cared more about what we could earn than any prizes anyway," she replied. If there was still a hint of bitterness in her voice, it was much subdued. "Anyway. That was what I was doing this day, outside of perusing the wares in town. Not much to buy, all mortal goods, though I did send some knickknacks back home."

Wu Ying winced, realizing he had never even thought to do something like that. Not in years. Of course, he also had been very far from home back then. But perhaps he should look into that.

"What about you?" she asked, throwing Wu Ying's focus back into the present.

He could not help but shrug. "As I said, I had neglected the cleansing baths and Body Cultivation training lately. All of which I had to undertake today."

"More stretching and twisting?" she teased.

"Always."

Softer, gentler, she glanced over his robed body, as though she could see the injuries and the damage the cleansing baths did to him. "Does it still hurt?"

He could only shrug. It did, but the lingering ache was more soul deep than physical. A side effect of, well, body cultivation.

"I'm sorry."

"It's a small thing."

She shook her head at his reply but fell silent, allowing the pair to finish their meal. Once the servants brought in dessert—sesame balls in a sweetened soup base—the pair were done with their meal, the latter portion completed in comfortable silence. Of course, that led to the next topic.

"Are we flying then tomorrow?" Yang Mu asked. "No more delays?"

Wu Ying waggled his hand a little, then glanced at the table still filled with plates and cups. Finding no place to extract his map, he sketched in the air, attempting to communicate the problem. "Only for a short while. The mountain range is a known residence of a phoenix, so we cannot fly over it. Between it and the courting dragons and the various other winged creatures that shelter under the phoenix's benevolent domain, we will need to take a longer route southward." He gestured with his finger, tracing the route south from where they were and the mountain range that bisected their journey.

"We can either walk through the range—or ride—and travel as a mortal, or we can cross farther west first." This time, he traced their way across some portions of the deeper wild before he stopped. "There's a small mercantile town along the river there. We can take a boat down the river that crosses around the mountain range, growing deeper and wider as it is fed by the waters from the mountain."

"Which route are we taking?" Yang Mu asked.

"I'd recommend the western river route," Wu Ying replied. "Flight across the wilds is always tricky, as you know. Especially as we head to the south."

There was a reason why Core Formation cultivators did not travel through the air over large tracts of untamed wilderness. Nascent Soul and even Core level beasts lay below, and some took deep offense at such invasions. The kind of offense that had such creatures track cultivators across hundreds of li, pull them from their beds in the middle of the night, and lay wreck to the houses and cities they resided within.

On top of that, the occasional flying spirit beast dominated the skies, easily outmaneuvering the vast majority of flying cultivators. Not Wu Ying of course, but not everyone was gifted with the dao of the wind. Only in the areas around their sects or in the tamed, civilized lands of the inner kingdoms were such travel methods wielded. Or, of course, they could travel along the roads, flying low to them. But at that point, it would make as much sense to just run. As fast, less tiring, but significantly less elegant.

Even then…

Flying, for most cultivators, required a significant amount of energy. Few cultivators could hold themselves aloft for an entire day, and the energy expenditure of doing so could be better dedicated to the formation of one's core. As such, few Core Formation cultivators chose to fly everywhere, instead preferring the slower methods of mortal travel.

"You recommend?" Yang Mu said softly. "Do I then get to have an opinion on our journey, Cultivator Long?"

"You do." He shrugged. "As you said, you have passed my test. And since I cannot convince you to leave, it is best to have your agreement."

"How magnanimous," she said sarcastically.

"I am, am I not?" Wu Ying smirked good-naturedly.

"Fool. But you were right on one thing. I should rest. There is much ground to cover."

***

It took a single day and night of travel for the pair to fly to the river city, a place whose entire commerce and livelihood revolved around the loading and unloading of grain and fishing barges. After landing a short distance from the walls, the pair walked in through the massive raised-earth impediments and the wooden gates. Wu Ying let his gaze sweep over the formations that guarded the walls, noting their power and presence.

The pair moved quickly through the town, finding the harbor where trade ships stood. Yang Mu stepped aside to allow Wu Ying to negotiate their passage with the harbormaster and captains in turn, a small smile on her lips as she watched the interaction. It was not a complicated journey to negotiate, especially since there were no major forks southward from the river. As such, the majority of the ships leaving were headed to their final destination.

In short order, the pair were upon a grain ship and traveling downstream. To Yang Mu's surprise, Wu Ying declined a berth inside the ship itself, preferring to sleep under the stars like the crew. Food was plentiful and fresh, the grain ship supplementing their meals with vegetables from passing villages and fish caught as they drifted south.

In the mornings, Wu Ying practiced his Body Cultivation movements, flowing through the seven forms for each of the winds. He twisted and turned, stretched and exploded into motion, the flow of wind and chi sending gusts of air through the ship. More than once, as their destination neared, Wu Ying caught a whiff of an acrid aroma, the same one that had driven him to take Lady Yang's assignment. A rotted, twisted thing that set the small hairs on his arms and the back of his head standing.

After his Body Cultivation exercises, Wu Ying began his sword practice. First, the forms he knew all too well, the Long family style. He flowed from form to form, tapping in the movements and the energy of each rotation and twist, submerging himself in the familiar and recognizing the deep intricacies of the system created by his ancestor.

Yet now that he had gained the Heart of the Sword, now that he had studied and learned and experienced additional styles, all the way from the hot desert sands of the west to the flowing forms of eastern swordmasters, from the acrobatic north and even those of the explosive southern masters, he noted gaps in the style.

He understood the flaws in the system, the ways it did not suit him.

He understood, more than anything, why it could not be his any longer.

Finally, he understood that such differences and improvements he might create were as much a matter of preference and compatibility than true flaws.

And so, after the Long family style was complete, he moved on to the real work of the day.

Each morning, he took the flaws in the base style and flowed through them, improving upon the movements to suit his own. He borrowed liberally from past masters and foolish peasants alike, combining them into a style of his own.

A style which had been further perfected by another who had the Heart of the Sword, from the treatises and documents Wu Ying had acquired and studied and from the myriad experiences he had faced. Battles with Spirit and Demonic beasts, dark sect cultivators, and tournaments with the orthodox and heretics.

Still, the Long family style was the heart of the Wandering Dragon.

Much of the style was still being formed, the techniques individually perfected but a singular flowing form unfinished. There was no staircase of progression to allow those of lower strength, poorer flexibility, or of a different dao than his own wind cultivation to progress and utilize what he did. Though some methods were meant for use on the ground, just as many were adapted to borrow the wind and Wu Ying's ability to float through the air and command the winds.

In the end, the Wandering Dragon was a martial art that was entirely his own, that continued to adapt as Wu Ying grew more adept in his wind body. Strikes and cuts, dao understandings, and physical strength all lent to greater strength.

Blade strikes that sent cuts of sword intent and chi through the air in crescent arcs, lunging strikes that combined the Sword's Truth and exuded wind chi to form a spinning, vertical attack that crossed tens of feet in the blink of an eye.

And of course, the movements of the Wandering Dragon's various cuts. The first he had perfected—as far as he could, with his own limited dao. The second, forming in his mind and based off the simple passing lunge he had once been exposed to combined with the Sword's Truth. And the third cut…

The third was only a glimmer in his consciousness.

A spinning attack that combined a cyclone's ferocity and a typhoon's fury.

Each morning, he trained. Yang Mu joined him many days. Coming upstairs as the early light of dawn broke, she would take a seat at the prow of the ship and cultivate, drawing chi toward her. Wu Ying could see how it was slower for the woman, as they floated upon the river away from the forest and vegetation that created and concentrated the wood chi she required.

Yet it was only a mild hindrance at their level. She drew in chi from the surroundings, pulling at it across the broad river and from the lingering vegetation on the riverbanks and further, her aura splashed across the surroundings in a rather unsubtle way.

At first, Wu Ying had worried that her actions might draw additional trouble to them, but casting his senses wide, he noted the lack of concentrated chi. Whether it was the constant pruning by nearby villagers or the care and movement of the kingdom's army, the waterways were more civilized and had few creatures of concern. A word with the captain told of river dragons that patrolled the rivers too, appeased by gifts and tribute periodically.

The deep valleys of chi, the spirit herbs, and the powerful creatures required to feed a Nascent Soul beast were claimed by these dragons, and, as such, not present for utilization by others. Certainly, a few Core Formation demonic beasts might lurk in the distance, myriad Energy Storage creatures—or their equivalent—but they were rare enough. And with Yang

Mu's presence flowing outward, claiming the environmental chi all about, it would be as a direct challenge if such a creature came.

In the early mornings, she cultivated. It was only when he began working on his sword forms that she joined him, flowing through her own martial techniques. Fans would flick open and be thrown, cast through dangling rope lines to spin and return, caught as she spun, twisted, and leapt. Her movements were a combination of athletic display and dance, a martial art given grace and physicality.

To Wu Ying's surprise on the first day, not all of Yang Mu's forms were the drunken fairy. In fact, unlike him, who had mastered a single form to the exclusion of others—dabbling only in other styles to better progress his understanding of his main sword form—Yang Mu practiced a variety of disparate forms to a journeyman level of understanding.

From willowy seductress to cold and arrogant fairy, from stiff and unyielding dancer to drunken sotte, Yang Mu wielded her fans, snapping them open and casting them away, slicing through the air to return, a surfeit of personalities and martial styles showcased.

Wu Ying found himself, a week later, finished with his practice of his techniques and took a seat to watch Yang Mu. This was the seventh form that she used, as different as the ones preceding it each day. Like the majority, it was all grace and beauty, timed flourishes, staggered footsteps, and angled strikes of deadly steel and chi.

Watching her, he could not help but think of an elderly spinstress, careful but efficient with her movements, unthinking grace borne of years of practice and experience, with a surfeit of feints and hidden techniques to make up for a lack of strength. He found himself musing about the form itself, the way he would counter it, caught up in the beauty of her dance.

"Are you done watching?" Yang Mu said as she came to a standstill, one fan held open before her lips, the other low against her hip, ready to guard or deflect. Her legs were twisted like a spring, ready to throw her into a spinning leap or disengage or to crouch lower. Her chest moved up and down lightly, her diaphanous robes shifting with each breath, pressing against lightly sweating skin to cling to unmarked flesh. "Did you enjoy what you saw?"

Wu Ying blinked, returning to present to smile widely. "I very much did, Mistress Yang." He ignored the loud sniff she made as she straightened herself and put away her fans. "I note that you have many styles of the fan dance that you utilize."

A raised eyebrow was the only answer to his statement.

"Do you have many more then?" he said.

"As many as I need," she answered, smiling. "My parents were always advocates of quantity having a quality of its own. Learning and understanding the various forms that would best suit any individual encounter allowed us paramount flexibility."

"But yet, you forsake a deeper understanding of each style."

"A hammer is useful when one must break wood or lock joints within, but it is useless if you are looking to whittle down a plank."

"True, but I wield a sword. And a dexterous blade can whittle or hammer, crush or trim. It but requires practice."

"Or you could just pick up a cleaver to cook with. An axe to chop your wood down. A mace to crush." She flicked her hand, pulling a fan outward and opening it with a snap to flutter the item before her face, hiding all but those piercing black eyes that seemed to see so much of him. With such a simple motion, she caught his gaze and held it, drawing him in till he felt as though he was falling. "Or a fan to beguile."

Wu Ying coughed and broke eye contact with an exertion of will. That woman... "Yes, well, I do wield a sword for battle. And have other tools for..." He paused, then smiled as he looked back at her. "Beguiling."

"Now, that might be a sight to see." Her voice was filled with mirth, the laughter that followed light and filled with joy.

It was not just Wu Ying but the sailors who stared at the cultivator as she laughed, wind catching her hair and framing her in the afternoon light. Then the wind brushed at Wu Ying's cheek, reminding him it was time to cultivate.

He reluctantly drew a breath and stood, bowing to her. "One day, perhaps. For now, good day, Mistress Yang."

He took to the sky till he reached the crow's nest, where the wind and sway of the mast allowed him to draw more deeply of the formless wind chi. It also put him away from that infuriating and intriguing woman whose eyes sparkled in his memory, over and over again.

Chapter 7

Two weeks and one boat change later, the pair of cultivators landed in the riverside town beside a massive lake. The pair had had a pleasant and quiet trip down south other than a single attack by a Core equivalent fish that Wu Ying had accidentally angered while practicing some blade strikes off the bow of the ship. In the end, they had been forced to slay the slumbering creature and the ship had pulled over for a day to work with the nearby fishermen vessels to debone and harvest the corpse.

Wu Ying kept, of course, the core while happily offering the meat to the fishermen who had aided him in the harvest. The bones themselves he had taken into his World Spirit Ring, leaving them to decompose in one of his many compost piles, knowing their presence would aid the development of his herbs.

Outside of that singular attack, the trip had been so quiet that the captain had made sure to thank the pair of cultivators. Their presence and training had driven off any creature that might normally harass such a vessel. Even the less perceptive river bandits had chosen a different target, though Wu Ying was informed that the current numbers of such individuals were low. Something about an altruistic cultivator having passed by a few months ago.

It was with some minor relief that the pair arrived in the river city, neither wind nor wood cultivator entirely at ease on the ship for such a long period. In quiet agreement, they split apart once accommodation was located and greetings to the local lord offered. Unlike the smaller town they had first visited, the presence of the pair of Core Formation cultivators was of only mild interest to the cadaverous and aged municipal lord, more intent on playing with his numerous grandchildren than passing cultivators.

While Yang Mu retired to her chambers, Wu Ying made his way to the auction house. In short order, he had placed the minor beast stones he had acquired through the trip on sale, along with perusing the full details of their wares. While the auction itself would only be held on the seventh day of the week, the auction house leader was more than happy to allow Wu Ying to browse in hopes of luring him and his coin purse.

Finding only a few minor items of interest, from a spirit level sword and a couple of formation flags and pills, Wu Ying took his leave not long after, carrying the auction house seal with him. The seal would allow him and a guest to bypass the line, a small mark of favor. Along with the seal, Wu Ying also acquired further details of the power structure in the city, and introductions to the trio of families that ruled over the settlement.

For the next two days, Wu Ying met with, spoke with, and undertook minor tasks for these families, acquiring a small bounty of herbs, taels, and manuscripts in return for his aid. Though Wu Ying sensed the presence of at least two Nascent Soul elders in the settlement and suspected at least one other, none of the three sought to treat with him.

Instead, they sent the titular family heads to deal with Wu Ying. It was not an unexpected state of affairs, for most Nascent Soul elders spent their time cultivating when they had the option. After all, the amount of chi required to sustain and feed their newborn spirits was significant. Only powerful pills or cores could help shorten such a process.

On the night before the auction, Wu Ying entered the resplendent inn they were residing within, only to have Yang Mu greet him as he passed through the inner courtyard toward his room.

"Mistress Yang," Wu Ying replied.

"And how goes your ingratiating with the leaders of this city?" Yang Mu said. "Has it bore fruit?"

"Some minor goods and manuals, yes." He walked over to the table where Yang Mu was seated, eyeing the tea set and the extra cups, two of which had been poured and drunk from. A slight sniff spoke of a musky perfume made from the glands of an animal rather than the more flowery ones Yang Mu preferred. He moved the closer cup away from him as he sat. "And yourself? I have not seen much of you since we arrived."

"It would be easier if you did not wake before dawn each day," Yang Mu teased.

"A farmer wakes when the work requires it. And the work never ends," he said.

"No, it doesn't, does it?" She laughed, gesturing at the teapot. At his nod, she poured him a cup, then picked up the second cup and tossed away the tea before setting it on the tea tray for washing later. "But I have been speaking with the factors and merchants my mother has connections with. They offer rumors and dire warnings of the south, complaints about the spoiled spirit stones coming north and the ruining of trade."

"Yes. It has distorted the market a little, for those stones not so corrupted." He extracted the auction house seal from his storage ring and placed it on the table. "The auction house master was quite excited about the stones I brought in. He was fishing to see if I was willing to part with anything more potent than an Energy Storage level stone."

"And did you?"

Wu Ying shook his head. "I might still." He chuckled softly. "Sadly, one of the aspects of my unusual element is the lack of properly suited cultivation aids."

"It has left you quite pure though." The considering look she gave him was very frank, almost to the point that the swordsman wanted to shrink away. Only the madam who ran the army brothel had been more straightforward in her regard of him.

Which, perhaps, tracked. Both cultivators saw him as merchandise. In their own way.

"I intend to visit the auction tomorrow. And then, I think, we have spent long enough here. It is time for us to continue our journey," Wu Ying said, dismissing the earlier discussion. "Did the rumors you were privy to provide a lead of where we should go?"

"Perhaps."

Rather than push her, he picked up the tea and sipped, arching a single eyebrow. Light and complex, with a slight bitterness of an older tea leaf present. A mixed blend then, with some fruit introduced. Or perhaps just the flower of a fruit.

"Good tea," Wu Ying complimented her. He was no tea master, would never be. Still, over the years, he'd learned a little to understand the nuances others might look for. He still would drink anything that was offered to him, but he could enjoy a good drink when it was supplied.

"My contacts did not offer much beyond rumors, as mentioned. But one thread I was able to pick out was that many of the corrupted cores are coming from Liang Soong."

Wu Ying shook his head, not recognizing the name.

"A city further south and west of us. Inland, with no river access. We shall have to cross overland to reach it, though I understand there are a few locations that are safe for us to fly through." A slight smile on Yang Mu's face then. "I have taken the initiative to request a copy of a map of these routes. It will be delivered tomorrow morning."

"Ah…" Wu Ying breathed outward and found himself smiling. "That will be useful."

"I thought so."

Finishing his tea, Wu Ying picked up the seal and made it disappear into his storage ring. "Do you wish to view the auction? If so, we can meet below before we go."

A small smile from Yang Mu. "No need. My family has a standing invitation and seal from these auction houses. I shall see you there, Cultivator Long."

"Ah." Disappointment flickered through him as his invitation was declined. He offered a long nod after a moment. "Of course, Mistress Yang. Till tomorrow then."

"Till tomorrow."

***

The auction was held in a long hall with a single, massive double-doored entrance and a staircase to the left leading toward the second floor. Wooden pillars held the roof aloft with interlocking joists in the *duogong* method, with the second floor built upon these interlocking pillars. Multiple plain wooden benches were arrayed on the lower floor, allowing those present a place to rest while awaiting the start of the auction.

The auction hall was filled with dozens of cultivators. Many moved in groups, dressed in similarly colored clothing to display their association with one of the three families that ruled the city or one of the few martial sects within. Unlike his own kingdom, their current one had few cultivation sects, instead leaning toward powerful families supplemented by secondary martial sects that taught a mixture of martial arts and cultivation techniques.

Sweeping his gaze over the group, Wu Ying guessed that two-thirds of those present were aligned with one of the families, the remainder a mixture of wandering cultivators or the martial sects. Those from the martial sects were less obvious in their alignment, wearing small discreet badges at most, rather than sporting similarly colored robes like the families.

It amused Wu Ying how so many times, even across kingdoms, certain forms repeated themselves. The clothing styles might change, growing tighter or looser, the weave and styles altering. But the signatures of groups that were together—whether in type of clothing, cut, or color—was the same.

More importantly, he noted that few within were above Body Cultivation, the Energy Storage cultivators on the lower floor preening like the little lords that they were among this group. Dressed in his simple green robes, his aura retracted to leak only a small amount of chi, Wu Ying drew few glances from those within as he entered.

However, an attentive attendant spotted him immediately, sweeping over with a smile on her lips and a sway in her hips. Her movements drew appreciative looks from those around for her tight, cloying dress was figure hugging with strategically positioned sashes to pull clothing tighter at bust and waist, while a dangerously tall slit up one leg offered tantalizing glimpses.

"Cultivator Long! Master Woo asked me to watch for you and lead you to the second floor if you chose to attend today," she said, offering him a wide smile. "If you will follow me."

"Of course." Wu Ying ignored the curious looks of the other cultivators, grateful that none chose to block his way or discuss the affront to their dignity his presence might cause. Those kind of tales of arrogant and foolish masters were common enough in the jianghu, though Wu Ying had rarely met such fools. After all, one never knew who was a hidden master. "Have we met before? I fear I do not recall your countenance."

"No, Cultivator Long, we have not. My master and Cultivator Yang were kind enough to describe you." The woman looked over her shoulder as she led the way up the staircase. Each step set her hips swaying, and she seemed to add a little more twist when she met his gaze over her shoulder.

Wu Ying offered her a small smile, knowing that she appreciated the looks, but he kept his gaze fixed on her laughing eyes till she turned around once more to finish their ascent. Upstairs, there were no benches. Instead, it was filled with small wooden tables plated with refreshments and porcelain tea sets as individual chairs were arranged around. Most of the furniture was clustered near the edge of the balcony, allowing the seated to view the raised stage at the end of the hall. The chairs were made of rosewood, shined and glossed such that they gleamed as the reflected light from rice paper windows thrown open glinted off them.

There were significantly fewer cultivators on this level. On the other hand, the quality of those who sat was in direct contrast to their numbers, with the weakest in the latter half of the Energy Storage stage and the leaders of each house or martial sect Core Formation cultivators. Even then, Wu Ying counted nine such figures in the entire room.

A not inconsiderable number for such a city. Certainly the majority of those in power. Though the missing municipal lord was noteworthy in itself.

More to his surprise, Wu Ying found himself led toward a pair of familiar faces at the rightmost edge of the second floor. Once she had done her job, the attendant excused herself to return to the front of the house, leaving Wu Ying with the pair. Yang Mu finished her murmured conversation with the Auction House Leader, Master Woo, before greeting him, followed soon after by her companion.

"I am surprised to find you here before me, Mistress Yang," Wu Ying replied after finishing his greeting. "I had thought you were planning to attend later."

"I had, but Master Woo mentioned that he was supplying these lovely almond cookies." Yang Mu lifted the plate that held a trio of the pale brown, tantalizingly aromatic delicacies. "I would recommend you acquire some before they are finished."

Wu Ying chuckled as he noted how few were left in comparison to the other snacks available. Before he could answer, a new attendant appeared with a teacup that she added to the table before pouring tea into it.

"Ah, good. Get Cultivator Long some of our refreshments as well," Master Woo said firmly to the attendant. Then, glancing at the smiling Yang Mu, he added, "The almond cookies from Han house in particular."

"It really is not necessary," Wu Ying demurred.

"That's fine. I'll eat yours," Yang Mu said quickly.

He could not help but roll his eyes as Master Woo watched their interactions with interest. When he saw that they were done, Master Woo gestured down toward the stage and the cultivators who were now taking a seat as the auction master called for order.

"Thank you again, Cultivator Long, for your additions. I am sure that the younger cultivators will be quite excited over your offerings."

"There's no need for such formalities," Wu Ying said, waving away the thanks.

"On the topic of offerings, you hinted you might have other items to add…?" Master Woo bobbed his head low. "I only bring it up so that we are suitably prepared for the second portion of the auction."

Wu Ying hesitated, considering his offer once again. Before he could answer, Yang Mu interrupted.

"If we were to supply an untainted Core Formation core, aquatic and water-aligned, would you be willing to allow certain restrictions be put in place?"

"Cultivator Yang?" Master Woo sounded perplexed before he answered. "Well, it would depend on the restrictions."

"Cultivator Long has quite the unusual element, as you probably guessed. So he will require unaspected Core Formation pills to aid him. Or cores derived from the wood, fire, or wind elements. The last, of course, being the preference," Yang Mu said. "I believe he also has interest in any Saint-level jian, or materials and use of an enchanter to supplement the expansion of such a weapon."

"Those…" Master Woo grimaced. "Those are rather restrictive guidelines."

"Yes. But his needs are rather restrictive. All of ours are at these levels, but his more so. After all, he should acquire enough of his other needs from what he has already offered you."

Yang Mu smiled at Wu Ying, who was mildly bemused by her taking over the negotiation without asking. "If you aren't willing to, we can always keep the core for another time."

"Well…" Master Woo bit his lower lip, eyes narrowing in thought before he gave a firm nod. "It will be as you say. If you could perhaps allow me to view this core now? And then if you will, I shall inform our premier members of your requirements. Many might need to verify such expense beforehand."

Wu Ying conjured the core from the fish, handing it over to Master Woo. A discreet motion by the auction master had a pair of Energy Storage cultivators step close to guard him as he let his senses and chi techniques play across the offered core.

A few more questions were asked and points clarified before Master Woo disappeared down the stairs, having stored the core in a spirit storage item of his own. As he left, he gave orders to attendants who fanned out, speaking with each of the Core Formation cultivators and leaders on the second floor as promised, bringing further attention to the pair.

Not that Wu Ying, nor Yang Mu from the looks of it, cared. She was secure in the respect and prestige offered by her illustrious parentage. He, on the other hand, had assessed those within. In his estimation, even together, the entire hall was of little threat to him. Even including the trio of cultivators who hid—badly—their true cultivation levels. He knew, in the worst-case scenario, he could escape.

After all, he had fled more than one sect or auction hall before.

"Thank you for speaking with Master Woo," Wu Ying said, after sending the wind down to tease out the secrets of the hidden masters below. "I did not think he'd be so accommodating."

"The lack of proper, untainted cores has grown worrisome. While formations can be used to cleanse the taint, it reduces the potency of those cores by a third at least."

"Well, hopefully they do have some items of interest." He smiled as the attendant arrived with the plate of snacks, then she refilled his and Yang Mu's tea before drifting away to give them privacy.

Of course, the moment the plate was set down, Yang Mu stole a crumbly almond cookie from it.

"Really?" Wu Ying said.

In reply, she took a large bite and only forestalled an unladylike moan by sheer force of will.

Supplied with more tea and refreshments, the pair watched the auction, interrupted by the occasional city Core Formation cultivator. Little of import was discussed, though Wu Ying had to fend off more than one offer to purchase his core directly. Yang Mu too, though she adroitly made a few connections to sell the minerals she acquired in the future or other items directly, rather than at the auction house as in this instance.

For a price, of course.

In the meantime, he enjoyed the spectacle of the auction. While the majority of the items being sold were of little interest to him, he was watching the drama amongst the other cultivators instead. The tension, the surprise and disappointment as much needed and valued resources were purchased and distributed. The enmity that grew from resources bought or sold.

Of the three cultivators below who had cloaked themselves, Wu Ying ascertained one was no more than a Peak Energy Storage cultivator using an enchantment that hid his aura. Not his scent though, like so many others.

Just like the false second, in fact. That one was a Core Formation cultivator who purchased a number of Body Cleansing resources at the most basic level, casting his greater resources ahead of him and nearly destroying his attempts at privacy. More than one cultivator eyed the man who hid his face behind a scarf and a big hat, even as he was profligate with his funds.

"You think he seeks a new path?" Yang Mu asked, nodding toward the man below after the eighth such bid he had pre-empted with his greater wallet.

"Likely. He is old, for a Core Formation cultivator," Wu Ying muttered, the pair of them shaping their words behind chi and their auras to ensure none could hear. A focused probing told Wu Ying the other had no more than a few layerings in his core but had the smell of the elderly hanging around him deeply.

"Body Cleansing. At his age." She shook her head. "A fool's hope."

"But we are all fools." Wu Ying smiled, leaning back. "Some of us just in different ways."

An eyebrow arched in interrogation, but the wind cultivator chose not to continue that conversation.

After all, there was something even more interesting below in the third master who hid his cultivation. He, Wu Ying watched, for there was something about the man who sat there, a massive hat over his head, hunched low in the back of the hall. Hiding his features was a trivial matter, for privacy was sought by some. Rude, but understandable. It was the fact that he did not bid on any of the items in the first half, yet stared avariciously at each item that went by, his greed spiking his scent with each new item.

"Problem?" Yang Mu asked.

"Just a potential troublemaker." Wu Ying shook his head, noting the auctioneer was calling an end to the first portion of the event. "It's probably nothing."

"Do not get involved," Yang Mu murmured. "It is not your role."

"I would never."

"Mmm, of course not. It's not as though the Verdant Gatherer is known for acting like a hero of justice." Her voice was all too dry, contradicting her words and forcing Wu Ying to grimace. "Now, I do hope the next portion is more interesting." Yang Mu stood and stretched a little, looking at her teacup and empty plate. "My mother always said the Woo Auction Houses had decent events. Thus far, I might call her a liar."

Only she could make so light of a Nascent Soul cultivator.

Wu Ying shook his head, even as he answered, "I'm sure it will."

In fact, the auction hall was now even more crowded. This time, of course, with gawkers rather than actual buyers. For what came next, those below could only hunger for. Now, the stage was set for those above.

Chapter 8

"This set of paired *ge* was purchased from a wandering cultivator two months ago from a branch department over a thousand li away," the auctioneer announced, waving at the dagger-axe polearms that the two young and willowy female attendants displayed as they walked up and down the stage. "As you can tell, they are unenchanted and of the Saint-level of quality, with a maker mark from the infamous Brother Dan of the Five Gorges."

At his last pronouncement, whispers broke out from those below. The auctioneer smiled, allowing the audience to speak for a moment before he began the bidding process. Of course, he set it high enough that the majority below were immediately locked out, though a few groups quickly put their funds together to attempt to acquire the polearms.

On the second floor, Wu Ying noted the quiet discussion amongst one family as they considered the purchase. Not so far away, one of the martial sect leaders was watching the family as well, his fingers caressing his storage ring. All this, Wu Ying sensed via the shift of the winds, the gentle murmurs of his spiritual sense in the background while he stared at the stage.

"So, you like them shorter and curvier, do you?" Yang Mu said by his side.

"What?" Wu Ying frowned, bringing his attention back to the present and her.

She jerked her chin to indicate downstairs and the young attendant Wu Ying's eyes had been idly tracking as he paid attention to the winds.

"No," Wu Ying said, slightly offended. "That ge's haft is damaged. There's a minor structural fault that will have the weapon give way soon enough if it is not reinforced. Or replaced."

Yang Mu raised an eyebrow at Wu Ying's quick correction, though she proceeded to extend her senses and sharpen them. After a moment, ascertaining the truth of his words, she gave him a nod and sat back, picking at the cookies on her plate.

The second half of the auction continued to bore them. While the pair placed the occasional bid, nothing that appeared was of great interest to the well-equipped pair. Yang Mu had the best equipment available, gifted to her by her parents or taken from their stores. Wu Ying had traded for the majority of what he needed from her very mother, only his weapons and the skin-tight scaled armor he wore beneath his robes coming from his travels before.

On occasion, other items like the dagger-axes appeared, but for them, the items were of little use. That was the truth all over, weapons or pills or herbs that had little utility for the pair. Thankfully, the event was coming to an end with Wu Ying's final core gift holding pride of place.

"And finally, the item you have all been waiting for… a pristine, high grade Core Formation equivalent spirit beast stone. Water-aspected from a Deep River Golden Carp," the auctioneer announced, waving to the young lady who walked forward, opening the jade box that contained the core's energy. She tilted the box, showcasing the stone for all to see as it drew environmental chi toward it, droplets condensing in the air as they neared the core. Beside the young lady, a pair of mid-grade Energy Storage guards stood, glowering at the audience and any who might have any ideas.

Of course, Wu Ying knew those guards were mostly for show. None of the Core Formation cultivators above would be foolish enough to act. Such a theft would set the others against them, begin a series of retaliatory actions until a new balance was achieved, where face and standing was confirmed.

Funny, how so many things in life could be settled if people were willing to talk and play by the rules—spoken or unspoken. He could see now, to some extent, why his earlier stumbling in the Sect, unknowing of the rules that many played by, had caused such irritation and trouble. He better understood their perspective.

But he also understood how so often those rules could be bent to crush those below. When rules triumphed over empathy and compassion, a tyranny of the petty and cruel arose.

As he had too once experienced.

"The auction is going well," Yang Mu murmured, breaking Wu Ying's idle musings.

He smiled agreeably, listening to the others bid upon the core. It had easily passed what he would have considered a reasonable amount. His eyes glittered with amusement as a jian, a dao, a magnificent guan dao were offered, a Black Faced, Heaven Sundering, Ghost Beating Formation was put up. That one had him leaning over.

"What is that?" he whispered.

"Ghost banishing formation. Works against the soul so it will affect even spirits and cultivators at this strength. I would assume it's in the Saint-stage, much like the others," Yang Mu murmured. "I would need to read the inscriptions themselves and run a few tests to verify, of course."

"Of course."

Other, stranger artifacts were offered. An enchanted war flag that would instill confidence and strength in those standing beneath its banner. It would drive the chi within those who fought underneath, boosting the overall strength of the unit.

An enchanted jade flute, streaks of white and green running through its body alongside the gold inscriptions that calmed the natural chi flows in the surroundings and made the flow of the dao more apparent. It encouraged moments of enlightenment when played, the instrument valuable even for those in the Nascent Soul stage.

A movement technique based upon the hottest part of a flame, the portion that one could not see. The Hidden Flame movement technique was explosive and blisteringly quick, though it could only be used in short bursts. A technique for combat rather than longer travels.

And, of course, the surplus amounts of pills, lower grade cores, taels, and low-grade equipment that would make up the equivalent value, though at their level, such things were only ancillary additions to round out an offer.

"Any that interest you?" Yang Mu murmured, noting how the auctioneer kept an eye on them.

The auction house master had spoken with them, given Wu Ying a small fan and small movements to indicate his preference or disinclination toward items. Of course, he was only to make his wishes known when something was truly objectionable. Or of great interest.

"That movement technique. And perhaps the flute," Wu Ying murmured. In truth, neither were of direct use to him, but perhaps he might derive some further alterations to the Wind Steps if he studied the Hidden Flame.

"So, nothing then."

Wu Ying shrugged.

No sooner had she said that than one of the family elders, eavesdropping on the pair, spoke up. "I have a Clear Mind, Immortal Soul pill. Meant for a Core Formation cultivator on the cusp of breaking through to the next stage," the older man said, leaning forward to stare at the auctioneer. He angled his body a little such that the box he conjured on his lap could be seen by Wu Ying, though the small formations on the wooden inlaid box hid direct spiritual review.

Silence greeted the man's words as the auctioneer stared at the speaker then looked at the other three families. When none made a move to speak, the auctioneer finally called the auction to a close. Immediately, the young lady closed the jade box, retreating to the end of the stage with her guards.

At the same time, Wu Ying ambled over to the Elder, bowing a little in greeting. "Elder Eng. I was surprised that you were willing to provide such a valuable pill."

"Not as valuable as you might think." Wu Ying's conversation was interrupted as another family leader walked over, answering. "That pill has been in their family for nearly a hundred years. It is likely losing efficacy."

"It has not," Elder Eng said coldly. "The pill is in a state of suspension still, and the formation will hold for another decade." Holding the pill up to Wu Ying, he continued. "I believe that the Verdant Gatherer will be able to make use of the pill before then, if rumors of his meteoric ascent are anything to go by. A true dragon among men."

Wu Ying smiled a little at the praise, offering a bow and accepting the offered pill. While he was uncertain if he would be at the stage of ascending so soon, the elder was not wrong that Wu Ying could likely find uses for the pill. If nothing else, he could allow it to degrade a little and use it to build another layer of his core.

"Elder Eng is most generous." He discreetly drew a breath, filtering the man's scent as he double-checked his earlier assessment. Water Core cultivator, on the cusp of another layer it seemed. Likely the spirit stone would be used to aid the next step of his cultivation, allowing him to step smoothly into it. Hard to tell the number of layers, but Wu Ying would guess at least five or six in.

The number of layers in a core varied for each individual, based off both the soul cultivation method they utilized and the size of their dantian. Those with smaller dantians to begin with could not build a thickly layered core, leaving their Nascent Soul undersized for when it was time to birth themselves. On the other hand, too many layers in a core allowed a soul to grow but took significant time to form and made it harder for the Nascent Soul within to break free. As souls were fed not just by chi but the dao understandings one gained, it was not always advantageous to attempt to grow a soul to the maximum size. After all, if one layered one's core too thickly, the soul would be unable to ascend.

Wu Ying's attention was drawn from the polite conversation to the auctioneer, the attendant, and their guards moving through the slowly dispersing crowd toward the second floor. He was not the only one watching their approach, for the hidden cultivator acted at last.

He flickered over the intervening distance just before the attendant started up the stairs, catching the bodyguard with an elbow to the chest before snatching the box from her hands. The auctioneer turned, his mouth opening in a shout, only to freeze as lightning danced between the group of four as a series of talismans were discarded by the attacker.

Then, even as cultivators from the second floor stretched out their auras to intervene, chi flooding through bodies, the figure flickered out the doors. Moments after he left, leaving a trail of lightning and the smell of ozone behind him, the guard formations around the auction house triggered, sealing off the building and those within.

"Did he just steal my core?" Elder Eng said, his voice filled with surprise and disbelief.

Wu Ying, having watched the entire action play out in wonder like the others, discreetly made the pill box disappear into his storage ring.

Shock gave way to action as voices rose, calling for action and for others to catch the thief. On her own, Yang Mu could not help but laugh discreetly, hiding her amusement behind one of her fans.

Chapter 9

Wu Ying and Yang Mu rode through the hinterlands on their way south, leading a pair of pack horses. The pair of cultivators were not alone on the road, for it was often used by merchants and other travelers as one of the main arteries of commerce south. Still, most of the other travelers gave the pair a wide berth, unconsciously grasping the difference in cultivation and social standing.

"I do not believe you refused to help calm them," Wu Ying complained once more. "It was you who pushed for me to include the spirit stone in the first place!"

"You did well enough," Yang Mu said easily.

"It doesn't matter if I did eventually get Elder Eng to stop asking for his pill back, you could have helped. Unless you wanted me to fight my way out…"

"It would not come to that," Yang Mu said. "Once they calmed down, they would have realized we had nothing to do with the matter." A slight smile then. "Anyway, I had to make sure I was ready to run. After all, the Verdant Gatherer is well known for his ability to flee from even Nascent Soul cultivators. A poor cultivator like myself requires more preparation."

"Really?" Wu Ying said, surprise registering at that note.

"Oh yes." Her tone grew singsong as she quoted, "'The Verdant Gatherer. He moves like the wind that precedes his presence, as formless as the air, as dangerous as a typhoon, and as swift as a gale. If he chooses to run, none may catch him.'" Her eyes twinkled with humor. "Or so the stories say."

"Those stories are going to cause me problems in the future, I just know it," he grumbled.

Another laugh, as she guided her horse around a deep pool on the road they rode upon. She waited till the two beasts were close together before picking up the thread of their conversation. "I am surprised that you chose to take the main road and agreed to the horses though. After all, the stories all speak of your travels on foot."

Wu Ying glanced at the horse he rode upon, stroking the creature's neck. The unconscious ability to move with his mount ensured he looked like an experienced rider, though he was nowhere near as comfortable as his companion. After all, she was not wrong.

"It's true that I normally pass through the wilds. Horses are a liability there, as you probably understand now." Wu Ying shrugged. "But I'm not opposed to taking it easy when necessary."

Anyway, he had no further insights into his movement techniques to practice in the wild. He had not managed to purchase the Hottest Flame movement technique at a price he was willing to pay, the family wanting a significant fee for what he felt was no better than a mid-grade technique at best. Without additional inspiration, he was certain he had achieved the best variation in the Wind Steps.

Oh, there were certainly some minor alterations that could be done, but the adjustments would see only the most modest of changes. On the other hand, he did have a technique—

the modified Never Empty Wine Pot method, renamed the Cyclone's Breath—that he could spend time practicing and familiarizing himself with. Here, on the main road, where a mistake in a refinement was unlikely to draw a Nascent Soul spirit, seemed the best time to do so.

And, of course, in this way, they could journey together without Yang Mu having to expend her chi to keep up with him. Even if she had access to the same moving cultivation method, she was neither trained nor interested in studying it. She'd blithely cast it aside, mentioning a conflict with her cultivation techniques but refusing to elaborate.

"Though I would not have appeased them by letting them make me responsible for their deliveries," Yang Mu said, patting the saddle horn and the reins tied to it for the pack mare she led. Wu Ying led a similarly burdened creature, voluminous furs and bags piled upon the backs.

"It was a simple enough compromise. Liang Soong is a busy trade city, and coming in with goods for the families will give us another set of contacts," Wu Ying replied.

"It'll make things slower."

"True, but you don't get to criticize if you don't help."

She chuckled and bowed her head in acknowledgement. After a short break, she could not help but ask, "I do wonder though, why did you not offer to help catch the thief? Surely you could have caught him?"

"It's nice that you're so confident in me, but I would not be so certain." Wu Ying frowned. "Did you not hear the rumors while they took down the safeguard formations?"

"The Lightning Thief?" Yang Mu said. "A wandering cultivator who has plagued the south, a genius wielding the rare aspect of lightning. Extremely fast, his attacks shocking and lethal for many. Hunted by a half-dozen families and the government. A hero among the general populace though, for he has struck down more than one corrupt sect leader."

"Exactly."

"Reminds me a little of another wandering cultivator, in fact."

"Mmmhmmm…." And hadn't that been a fun accusation thrown at him. That he was working with the other, in cahoots. After all, feckless individuals without a home were all the same, to the provincial cultivators who might never travel farther than the nearest capital.

She grinned at his reply, then asked, "Were you scared to face him?"

"The Lightning Thief was at minimum a Peak Energy Storage cultivator. He's known to have beaten Core Formation cultivators before, with a lightning aspect and the soul of the dao of lightning." Wu Ying sighed. "Individuals like that, they will become peerless prodigies. Or legendary lessons as they stumble and fall. Either way, I can sense the workings of fate around him. And as my Master would say, it is best not to get entangled."

"What of the trouble he caused you? The stone he stole?" Yang Mu asked.

"What of it?" Wu Ying said. "It is a single spirit stone. Let him play the rascal of the south. Why feel affront over such a minor thing?" His lips turned up wryly. "If we treat it as no more of an annoyance than the falling rain, as quick to fade as the water on our skin, it will not sink within and nourish the festering weeds of jealousy, anxiety, and anger. Better to let it roll off, than be forced to bend over and weed our very soul of such concerns."

As he spoke, the wind danced, catching at his hair and tugging on it. His horse let out a low nicker, having caught a scent in the wind and shying to the side. A hand pressed against its neck calmed the creature, even as the distant demonic spirit chose to leave the pair of cultivators alone.

"Is that how you hold all individuals, all organizations who cross you then? You discard their existence as no more than the passing rain?" Yang Mu asked.

"Not all individuals, not all organizations." A soft smile tugged at his lips as he recalled friends and family. "Some linger in the heart and the soul. Warming it with their generous actions." Then he grew grimmer, as darker thoughts intruded. "And others, for the harm they have caused. Though most of those no longer survive."

Yang Mu tilted her head, regarding the wind cultivator. A soft smile crossed her lips, and she placed a hand on his arm. He blinked, drawn away from darker thoughts, even as she withdrew her hand as his aura shifted. A moment later, she kicked her mare to bypass a wagon, leading them past the slow-moving transportation.

Leaving Wu Ying to watch her swaying back and lustrous hair in quiet thought.

***

Much to Wu Ying's delight, the remaining journey to Liang Soong was uneventful. Of course, there were demonic spirits to contend with, especially after the pair retracted their auras such that they were an attractive target for the creatures—to supplement their income and clear the surroundings. It cost them little but time and provided a nice supplement to their food stores and resources while adding to the safety of the roadway as they dealt with the threats.

Often, Wu Ying would disappear early in the mornings and late at night, searching the surroundings for new and interesting spirit herbs and vegetation to add to his World Spirit Ring and his stores. Many hours were spent adding to his notes, drawing new images and recording notes while expanding on the maps of the region. He spent daylight hours riding in idle conversation with Yang Mu, the pair building a quiet friendship over the long days.

Conversations flowed across a wide variety of topics, ranging from esoteric debates about the Dao to tales of Wu Ying's journeys and Yang Mu's life in the inn, an existence that was just as exciting, since visitors of all forms and strengths paid homage and did commerce with Yang Mu's parents.

More, Wu Ying basked in the quiet warmth of her stories, the familial and domestic nature of life. He laughed at the pranks played between sisters and sympathized over the long, grueling hours of training that were enforced by their parents.

Slowly, he understood her reasons, her need to leave. Though her parents wielded a light hand, still, their ever-present presence, their watchful eyes had stymied their children's growth.

Yang Mu was a contrast of perspectives, cynical Nascent Soul wisdom pasted on sheltered princess. It led to her delighting in the most mundane of things, while passing cynical judgment on cultivators and their cultivation base when the pair were alone.

Interspersed between their conversations and meals were long periods of cultivation and practice, where Wu Ying refined his understanding of the altered Cyclone's Breath method.

Yang Mu, on the other hand, kept herself entertained by speaking with their fellow travelers when Wu Ying was training. The roadway was busy and the pair often joined passing merchants, nobles, and the occasional farmer. The gregarious woman made acquaintances with ease, sharing meals and wine with her new friends, along with gossip and tall tales. That the majority were mortals seemed not to concern her, her easy grace and charm crossing the gulf between cultivator and mortals with ease.

Only when the pair were forced to showcase their abilities to deal with the occasional demonic beast was the gap widened again. Even then, many times, she was able to set her new friends at ease with a few well-placed jokes and sharing the largesse.

Wu Ying, to his amusement, was brought into such discussions more often than not. It was not a situation he despised. It reminded him much of his time with the Pan clan or the Dorben in the north, where the distance between mortal and cultivator was bridged by bonds of familiarity, family, and feudal responsibilities. It was also an engineered opportunity to practice the new dialects they came across, most especially the dialect of the south and their eventual destination.

One aspect that interested the pair was the slow increase of true mortals—individuals who had never trained in even the basic forms of the Yellow Emperor cultivation technique—and cultivators who had chosen a different path to begin with. For Yang Mu, this was both fascinating and somewhat unique as she encountered a wider variety of basic Body Cleansing techniques. The wider traveled Wu Ying only took time to take notes, acquiring copies for his own library to donate to his sect later on.

As they left the central heartland of the former emperor's domain, the spread of knowledge and the emperor's initial direction faded, leaving clusters of villages and cities filled with offshoot cultivation techniques.

Days and weeks passed, the pair always traveling west and south. Packages were dropped off and others picked up, the string of pack horses increasing and decreasing. With each li, the changes in language, customs, dress, vegetation, and meals increased.

Rice continued to be the dominant food type, with everything from congee to simple glutinous rice meals cooked while on the road, unlike the north where millet had been just as—if not more—common. Each dish utilized a greater degree of sugar and soya sauce than the cleaner, lightly seasoned meals of the coastline. Dry spice rubs for the meats and marinades combined with a preponderance of deep frying and roasting for the meats with separate steamed or fried vegetables gracing their tables.

As the undergrowth grew denser, with clear land hard won through the immense working of the mortals fading away, so did the disappearance of animals that required much grazing space. Rather than sheep or goats or even the occasional cow, pigs and chicken and fish dominated the cuisine. Of course, with the influx of demonic spirits and other beasts from the deep forest, such cuisine also added more diverse meat sources—like snake, lizard, and the occasional massive spider.

Delightful as the changes in their daily meals might have been, the alterations in the ecosystem were even more intriguing to Wu Ying. Gone were the bamboo forests and their swaying trunks, replaced by hardier—and thornier—trees. Along with the warmer climate came denser undergrowth. The muddy wetlands filled with mists and the cloying, barbed shrubs that grew under the shade of broad-leaved trees had never felt the touch of snow.

The land grew hillier, mountains slowly appearing in the distance as the weeks wended on. Rain fell upon the group periodically, for they were entering the peak of summer as hot oceans released their liquid captives to the sky, where they scattered themselves across parched earth. Sheltered—for now—in the lee of the mountains and hills, the broken remnants of monsoon rains and minor thunderstorms still soaked the weary travelers.

More than once, Wu Ying triggered the Earth's Embrace protective formation to form the earthen shelter for himself and his companions as a pounding storm swept away roadways and formed flash streams. Within, the cultivators and whichever lucky mortals would dry off while waiting for the storms to pass.

On such humid and sweltering days, sometimes Wu Ying would look upward and spot the glint of scale or the flicker of motion in the clouds and shudder, memories of a long, storm-tossed day returning. He would pull his aura in tight and step into the shadows, as fingers interlaced with his and offered comfort from old memories.

South and west, they traveled, and the world changed around them.

Dialects switched and altered as they passed clay-and-earth-made villages and a new, predominant language formed upon tongues. Under the guidance of Yang Mu, Wu Ying's linguistic capability strengthened, aided by his cultivator's mind and prior experience. By the time they were close to the border, he was passably fluent.

Each step was a slog, yet the flow of travelers never stopped. More than once, the cultivators passed army patrols tirelessly cutting down trees, clearing blockages and replacing washed out roads. The occasional earth and wood cultivator lieutenant was safeguarded by the army units, their greater cultivation and focus allowing them to utilize chi-techniques to do the work of dozens of unaspected cultivators.

Yet for all the slow-going of the route itself, for all that the environment sought to impede their travel, each day saw them closer to their objective. No monsoon, no physical impediment could stop the pair, and even after crossing the mountain range that demarcated the true Middle Kingdom from the outlying provinces, they persisted with dogged determination.

"Are you certain you cannot shift the winds a little?" Yang Mu grumbled, one hand idly holding the reins of her steed.

The creature knew to pick its way around deeper puddles, though it kept its head hung low as the wind and rain of another rainstorm battered the pair. For once, they were alone, their former companions having elected to stay at a roadside waystop rather than risk nature's fury.

"I am certain. These winds are not for me to control." His lips curled up a little in sardonic amusement. "If nothing else, I would not anger the lords of the skies who dictate the movements of these clouds."

A slight hesitation, as Yang Mu tilted her head upward. There was nothing to see in this cloud-darkened day, heavy rain barring the sight of the clouds themselves. Occasional lightning flashes above and the continual rumble of thunder marked the day, mixing with the constant drum of droplets against her aura.

"Are they up there then?" she said softly.

"Not see. Sense." And only because the wind carried their scent. "They fly high today and are few enough." He offered her a quick smile, placating her concern for him. He drew another deep breath, cycling the Thousand Miseries. Along with the smell of dragons, hints of exotic spices and an acrid, burnt oil and diseased meat stench filled the air. Those, he chose not to bring up again. "I will not draw their attention, intruding. Just be thankful they do not bother to turn their attention to the earth."

"Easy for you to say," Yang Mu said, arms crossed. "But keeping the water off my clothes is tiring."

"Then, do not," Wu Ying offered. "The rain is warm and soothing on the skin."

"And cold."

"Not to me. And it shouldn't be, for you." He inclined his head to the side with a slight smile. "It'd take a lot less energy to warm yourself from the inside than protect your clothing from the rain entirely." He stroked his horse's neck. "Anyway, everyone else is enjoying the rain."

"Or quietly suffering it."

"Yes."

Silence, before Yang Mu let out a long sigh. She twitched her hand, withdrawing a large straw hat from her storage ring, and placed it upon her head, a light silk veil lowered to aid with the gusting rain. Then she added an overcoat, flexing her aura so that it covered her and her mare in a bubble that the rain battered. In that shelter, she dressed quickly to change into something a little thicker before allowing her aura to relax.

Eyes closed, hands gripping the reins, her oil-slicked silk raincoat and veil kept Yang Mu mostly warm, even as she brushed her fingers along her saddle.

"The water *is* warm," Yang Mu commented after a while.

Wu Ying could only smile in agreement, and the pair continued their journey in pleasant silence. Gone was the earlier discomfort, the arguments. Now, they rode companionably.

Till one day, as they turned the corner and ascended the latest hill. They came across the jade green and grey stone walls of the barrier to their destination. Liang Soong stood in the distance, the shimmering barrier of the city's formation flickering as it protected the city from the occasional lightning strike while allowing the rain to fall.

"We're here," Wu Ying said, guiding his steed to a stop with practiced ease.

"Finally." Yang Mu rolled her neck and shoulders. Though her words were laced with fatigue, there was anticipation in her voice.

"Now, we can really begin." Fingers touched the hilt of his sword, brushed against the Coral Dragon Scale armor under his robes, and traced the outlines of his storage rings. He mentally verified the escape talismans he carried, the single Nascent Soul slaughter formation he had been sold, and the extra Saint sword he stored.

Then, satisfied, Wu Ying looked at his companion to verify her own preparedness. When she offered him a single curt nod, he smiled. A click of his tongue sent his steed down the slope to the massive barrier blocking the entrance to the city. The city where, even now, traces of something twisted and rotten wafted toward him.

Chapter 10

Liang Soong. Gateway to the southern kingdom of Nanyue[51], a city made of jade and grey stone. The city was positioned behind the largest passage through the hills and mountains that blocked off the valley the city resided within and the north. To safeguard the passage, a massive stone wall had been built, blocking off access and watched over by the infamous fortress of Liang Soong, a brooding monolith that hung off the walls of a nearby mountain.

The wall blocking the passage stood nearly a hundred feet high, the grey blocks streaked with jade green stone and crawling ivy, while massive siege weapons could be spotted as tiny dots on top of even taller towers. Guards patrolled on top of the obstacle and looked out from the towers, even as the massive gates stood open to allow the continual passage of commerce.

Under the on-going deluge from the heavens, grey spouts from the walls released a steady stream of collected water. So tall were the walls that some of that water dispersed through the air, creating a light mist that coated merchants and farmers alike as they waited in line to be inspected.

Light as the sprinkling of liquid today might be, it was obviously not always so. Vast divots in the ground, formed from the falling water, helped deepen the trench beside the massive wall. Cut perpendicular along the walls, the stream of water was carried into the limestone cliff itself, while glimpses of reinforced earth and stone blocks safeguarded the foundations of the wall.

From their position overlooking all this, Wu Ying spotted the exit of that stream as it joined the snaking river that bisected Liang Soong. Nearby, directly behind the wall, Wu Ying could sense the military outpost, a miniature city in itself. The entire complex likely housed ten thousand soldiers and their counterparts, so large that they could not all stay within the massive fortress. And even so, the military outpost was dwarfed by the city that lay behind.

Liang Soong was a city of a few hundred thousand mortals, hundreds of cultivators, and an uncounted—and possibly uncountable—variety of beasts. The cultural and mercantile hub of the northern region of Nanyue, it also controlled the flow of trade with the Middle Kingdom. As such, alongside the civilian population were the populous army and city guards that maintained order.

All this Wu Ying took in as the pair descended to join the throng awaiting entry through those same massive gates. Farmland sprawled across both sides of the fortress, enterprising farmers accepting the greater safety from proximity to the walls and their guards against the future danger of a battle fought between two kingdoms.

---

[51] While I'm basing some of the aspects of the city and Nanyue on ancient Vietnam and the Lạc Việt or Luoyue, I am not hewing closely to either. So, inconsistencies are either by mistake or made for plot purposes. The entire period and area are fascinating to study, but this is not a historical fantasy.

Wu Ying understood that rationale. He had wielded the same logic when he had re-established his parents and their village beneath the Verdant Green Waters. Assurance of on-going safety brought by the strength of those one sheltered beneath—but the on-going fear that when such security failed, it would come with an all-encompassing wave of destruction.

Yet...

There was no true security in this world.

Fate might overturn the most secure of fortresses or see to the destruction of the most prestigious of sects. For the mortals who sheltered under such aegis, only the strength to bear the consequences of the actions of those above them could be said to be a virtue.

"A long line," Yang Mu said, standing up on the stirrups of her beast to peer ahead. What greeted her was a snaking line of oxen-drawn wagons, pack horses, and laden coolie backs. Her lips compressed as she let herself fall back. "It will be at least an hour or two before we are through."

Wu Ying nodded amiably, wiping his forehead to discard the gathered moisture. The clouds had chosen to let up a little, leaving only a small splattering of rain behind, a fine mist that kept everyone soaked to the bone.

"I hate waiting," Yang Mu said when the silence stretched out.

Wu Ying tugged at the environmental chi as he sat there, feeling it answer him with a lustrous laughter. The southern wind danced to his commands, playful and primal, bringing with it the combined scents of thousands of mortals. Cooking fires, smelting forges, printing presses, and unwashed bodies alike danced on the wings of his unseen companion.

Finding him unresponsive, she growled. "We could just use our rank and bypass all this."

Her words made the man standing behind the pair frown. He let his gaze run over them, stopping on Wu Ying's sheathed weapon, pausing at the lack of the same on Yang Mu's figure. Then it tracked upward, eyeing the bundled lustrous long hair on both of them, before he ran his hand through his own short-cut hair. Conclusions were drawn, and as Wu Ying guided his horse ahead, the man allowed additional space to form between them.

All this Wu Ying noted through his spiritual senses, spoken to by the laughing wind. He felt it tug at his hair, beckoning him to do as the woman said. To bypass the foolish fortress and enter the city proper.

For what was a stone fortress to the insubstantial wind? What point to an earthen line raised across the land, one used to declare ownership, when the wind contained all that was above it anyway? What meaning did a wall have, beyond a physical reminder of man's ego and greed?

Almost. Almost, Wu Ying acquiesced to the wind and Yang Mu.

"Were you not the one who enjoyed mixing with them before?" Wu Ying said instead. "An hour or two, it will make little difference to our objectives. And there is much to be learnt, while we wait."

"We are so close though…" Yang Mu ran a hand through her hair, flexed her will to shed the water aside, and expanded it to keep the fine mist away again.

"Patience."

"We could learn as much, if not more, in the city itself." A wry smile twisted her lips. "Not all of us speak to the elements like you do, Cultivator Long. And it has been a long few weeks. A hot bath and a decent meal not cooked by myself would be much appreciated."

"True enough, Mistress Yang. But these goods must be checked in properly." Wu Ying tapped the reins he had tied off, before tugging on them gently to move the pack horse closer. He scratched the creature's ear as it neared him. "I would be loath to have spent all this extra time for no reason."

"We can still check the goods through, if we rode ahead." She added, using spirit speech, directly to his ears, "I do believe our presence has made others uncomfortable."

Wu Ying sighed. "If you didn't use my title…"

All he received was a big smile.

They moved another dozen or so feet before he let out a long, aggrieved breath and guided his horse around the wagon ahead of them. He relaxed his aura at the same time, causing those around to glance back at them before they politely looked away and shuffled to the side of the road.

Soon enough, the pair were at the front of the line, the gate guards eyeing the approaching cultivators with not a little caution. One of the leaders, clad in the heavy-duty linen scale they wore, hurried out from the gatehouse, smiling congenially as they approached.

"Honored Cultivators. Welcome." Even as he spoke, he was glancing at the gold bracelet he wore, watching as various gems lit up as their auras washed over it. There were four gems, with the first two brightened and glowing.

"Cultivation sensor?" Wu Ying said curiously. "Crude working."

"My apologies, Honored Cultivators. It is routine," the guard lieutenant said, smiling obsequiously.

"It is no concern at all," Yang Mu cut in, edging her horse forward. "My companion can often be a little blunt in his opinions. Such enchantments are rare further north, where we come from. Often, cultivators are used instead."

"Yes, Honored Cultivator. We have heard that. The cultivator in charge…" He flicked his gaze back the way he'd come, hesitated, and shook his head. "May I inquire of why you are here?"

"Trade." Wu Ying gestured backward to the beast of burden he led. "We have items to sell and more to purchase." He touched his storage ring with one thumb, running it over the simple band. "I am also a Gatherer and have some rarer herbs to sell."

"Of course. And the Honored Cultivators know of the taxes imposed on all trade arriving into the city, yes?" The man offered a consoling smile. "For cultivators, the price is three Core Formation equivalent stones."

"What?" Wu Ying nearly shouted in surprise, only calmed when Yang Mu put a hand on his arm.

"Surely you joke. How could trade continue at those rates?" Yang Mu said. "I knew of the taxes—any major city would have them—but the last I heard, it was but three Energy Storage equivalent spirit stones or their equivalent."

"It is a recent change, Honored Cultivator." A deep bow from the man, even as he sweated in apprehension. "The change was directed by the City Lord."

"City Lord?" Wu Ying asked, noting the way the man seemed to emphasize the last two words. "Not a magistrate?"

"No, Honored Cultivator. The City Lord is the ultimate law of the city, with the local government and cultivators answering to her."

"Now that is interesting," Yang Mu said. "That is, I believe, a change too, is it not? Were the cultivators not answerable to the general?"

"I… well… yes." The guard gulped, casting a look back toward the gate. Wu Ying wondered if he regretted exiting now. If he should have, perhaps, refused the order of the one within.

"Another change. So many in such a short period," Yang Mu whispered. "It seems that Liang Soong is in a state of flux."

Tendrils of chi extended from the gatehouse. Wu Ying noticed them, the flexing of power as the one within spoke to the guard. Another cultivator might not have required as much energy put into the working, but to speak to a mortal required more energy. If nothing else, to ensure they heard.

"Honored Cultivators, my apologies." Another gulp, as the guard worked up his courage. "Will you be paying the toll? If not, we would ask that you not hold up the line."

Beside them, the passage of merchants and farmers continued. None were required to offer anything more than a handful of coins or taels, sometimes naught more than the provision of the traveling pass or their residency card.

No cultivators though. Wu Ying sensed none of them along the main line, none behind them. Had others of their kind already been driven away by the high prices? Or had they all entered and refused to exit the city, considering how much it cost to return? After all, for most cultivators, spending a few months or years cultivating while the latest foolishness passed by was simple enough.

The best cure for temporary foolishness was often patience.

"What line?" Wu Ying gestured behind him.

His answer was a strained smile on the guard's face.

"Surely we can come to some arrangement," Yang Mu said, leaning down from her horse to bring herself closer to the other man, her voice heavy with suggestion. It extended her neck gracefully and allowed her raincloak to fall open a little.

"I... Honored Cultivator!" Sounding a little shocked, the guard stepped back. "I am married!"

Yang Mu blinked, then looked affronted. "You! You dare insult me like that? Do you take me for a common strumpet?"

"I..." The guard looked flustered now. "But you suggested..."

"An arrangement for the entry fee. A reduction perhaps, or a payment plan. Or perhaps a favor we could do for the City Lord."

"My apologies..."

"Silence." She straightened further, her gaze turning to the guard house. "Bring out your supervisor. I will not be insulted like this again."

Now, she let her aura unfurl. Not far, but she let the full strength of her Core Formation cultivation beat upon the air. Nearby mortals shrank back, one of the farmers fainting and a pair of horses stilling in fright. Wu Ying frowned but extended his own aura to block hers from all but the guards.

Silence now, as the bracelet on the lieutenant's arm flared into brilliant light across three gems, with the fourth glowing dimly too. Yet even as the bracelet burned on his arm, the man was frozen, his legs and body shaking under the force of her displeasure.

For a few long moments, her displeasure beat upon the air. Then another presence asserted itself. A man strode out from the gates, his aura preceding him and pushing back Yang Mu's. Another Core Formation cultivator, this one with the stolidity of the earth aspect.

"Enough, Honored Cultivator. My man meant no disrespect by his words." He came to a standstill before the pair. Unlike the solid presence of his earth-filled aura, the man was straight and thin like a bamboo pole. Between his thin, upright body and his presence, Wu Ying could not help but recall the hoodoos he had seen in the west, spires of rock that reached the sky, unconnected to anything but the ground itself. "Let us begin again perhaps. I am Ky Be Long, Captain of the Guards under our august lord Xam Minh Chau."

A female city lord. How fascinating.

"Long Wu Ying, of the Verdant Green Waters sect." Offering the man a clasped hand greeting, Wu Ying bowed a little in his saddle. Surreptitiously, he drew a deeper breath, cycling the man's chi through his technique.

Earth aspect, in the middle stages of Core Formation. At least four or five layers, it seemed. More than that though, outside of the slightly dry and dusty smell of his cultivation, there was a rotten tinge to it, distasteful like spilled oil. It was but a touch, but the presence was concerning.

"Yang Mu."

Be Long stared at Yang Mu, waiting for further details. When she failed to give any, he visibly hesitated as he looked between the pair. Wu Ying could see him doing the social mathematics of the situation. Whether he knew of the Verdant Green Waters or not—and the sect was two kingdoms and thousands of li away—that Wu Ying came from a sect placed him at a higher standing than a simple wandering cultivator.

On the other hand, Yang Mu was the one who had been insulted. Furthermore, she had shown herself to be easily offended. In addition, the Luo Yue was a matrilineal society[52], with women bearing the highest status in the kingdom. Everything from legislation to inheritance laws passed through the female line.

All of which meant that discerning who had the higher status and who to speak to in this matter was now but an educated guess. Something Yang Mu understood and likely a situation she had engineered on purpose.

"Honored Cultivators, I understand that the cost of entry is surprising and high. It is, unfortunately, necessary due to the increased cost of guarding our borders. There has been a significant increase in attacks from strong demonic spirits." Be Long let out a long, theatrical sigh. "It has cost our men many lives. For one with such strength, if you were to exert yourselves—"

"One," Yang Mu said, cutting him off.

"Cultivator Yang, a single core—"

"And we will provide it after we have been allowed in. My companion and I will 'exert' ourselves and deal with a single threat for you, providing you its core in payment."

"Madam—" Be Long sounded offended at her insistence, but she was not done.

"Otherwise, we shall turn around and leave. The provisions and deliveries we have brought can be accepted by the factors outside your city walls and we will complete our own purchasing elsewhere."

"You will not find another entrance to Nanyue within a thousand li."

"As though I care. We can find proper jade for my mother in the north. And acquire untainted cores at the same time." Her lips curled up in a sneer now.

Be Long stepped closer and lowered his voice, anger thrumming through each word. "What do you know of the taint?"

"Nothing, other than that it seems to be originating from your city. A fact that I intend to inform everyone else of." She dropped her voice as well, adding, "I'll also inform them that if one uses such cores without filtering them out, it will stain one's own chi. Or is it because this entire country is tainted too?"

"You, you, you infuriating woman…" Be Long's hand dropped to the dao by his side, clutching the handle tightly. "How dare you insult my city and my country!"

"Not an insult when it is the truth."

"And you think you can do better against the taint?" he snarled. "I would like to see you try."

---

[52] Yes, this was a historical fact too.

"Then let us try," Wu Ying said, cutting in. He had watched her insult and push Be Long, all under the eyes of the massive, heavily armed wall. If the man chose to ask for their death, even Wu Ying would find it hard to escape the multiple crossbows and siege weapons aimed at them, alongside the formations that they had readied.

"A single tainted monster, for us to dispose of, in return for entry. Surely you don't think anyone else will pay your outrageous price?" Once more, Wu Ying turned and gestured behind him at the road empty of cultivators. "Or is the price nothing more than a sham to keep others out? To hide what is happening behind those impressive walls?"

"It is no sham. If you people think you can deal with the taint that easily, then I expect a core in a day!"

"Three days," Yang Mu corrected immediately. "It is late today, and we will have to ensure our goods are properly stored. After which I shall require a proper bath before venturing into the wilderness again."

"You do not get to dictate the terms of your entry," Be Long said.

"End of the day tomorrow," Wu Ying said before things could degenerate further. "I shall, however, need to know where I am to send this core. And preferably some information about recent troubles. After all, it would be a shame to go out and not find any such creatures because of a simple mistake."

The man hesitated then nodded, reaching sideways to pull out a small seal. He flexed his aura, imprinting information on the seal before throwing it at Wu Ying. Catching the seal with his off-hand, Wu Ying bit back a curse at the meaty impact. Sending his aura into the seal, he read over the details and reviewed the simple map provided.

Unlike the overly structured cities of the north, Liang Soong was a city bisected by a serpentine river that ran from east to west, and the city was hemmed in by steep cylindrical hills. The northern edge of the city, right after the army encampment, was dominated by a mixture of rice paddy fields and the occasional building. On the southern end, the much more built-out city was enclosed by high walls. On each of those hills, Wu Ying noted tiny buildings and markings indicating the residence of the local cultivation schools.

More importantly, the residence of the city lord—located on one of those many hills on the southern side of the city and enclosed by the city walls—and the local government offices were marked. Detailed information of where to acquire further details about beast sightings as well as instructions of how to deposit the retrieved core were included in the seal.

"Thank you," Wu Ying said after perusing the information, depositing the seal in his storage ring.

Yang Mu sniffed but chose not to antagonize Be Long further. Wu Ying knew by now her irritation was more act than reality, a negotiating tactic wielded for his benefit.

Even if he never asked her to do so.

Be Long stepped aside, arms crossing as the pair led their small train inward. As they passed through the massive gatehouse, Wu Ying could not help but look upward, only relaxing when they passed the murderholes and massive doubled gates to the land before them.

Finally, they were within Nanyue proper.

Chapter 11

Once they had passed out of sight of the gate, Yang Mu clicked her tongue and guided her horse beside Wu Ying. Around them, the soldiers who trained, cared for the fortification, and stood guard watched the pair and other travelers with bored interest. Wu Ying scanned all around, allowing the wind to whisper secrets into his ears—tales of fornication, dirty dealings, and shrill orders alike.

For all that, he still had enough attention to pay to Yang Mu when she spoke to him. "You did well, following my lead."

"It would have been easier if I'd known your purpose." Wu Ying's lips twitched in wry humor. "I doubt you chose to create that scene over some Core Formation stones."

"A merchant should never take the first offer in a negotiation," Yang Mu said. "Furthermore, when pressed, Be Long was quite informative."

"And what did you learn?"

"The city is under attack. The need for cores is high, and their ability to cleanse the cores is failing them. I cannot think of any other reason for a cultivator to taint their core with such energy," Yang Mu explained.

"I can." After all, Wu Ying had once met a demonic cultivator. A man whose scent was all too similar to the one Be Long carried. In generalities, though not in specificity.

"They are worried about word escaping, though they are not stopping those leaving. Yet," Yang Mu said. "However, that they are requesting such a high entrance amount speaks of the powerful beasts they face."

"Nascent Soul level then?" Wu Ying said curiously. It would explain why they'd set entrance payments at Core Formation. An Energy Storage cultivator could do little against a Nascent Soul level creature but delay their progress briefly. Core Formation cultivators working together could fight such a monster. They might even win.

"Possibly. Still, one would think they would need more cultivators, rather than less. After all, those cannot be the only threat they face."

Wu Ying guided his horse around a bickering couple who stood in the middle of the roadway, gesturing at an overturned cart of cabbages. He extended his senses a little farther, feeling the light drizzle of rain wash against his skin, so many scents muted by the constant drum of falling water. Hard to call forth details, but it mattered not for what he was sensing.

"They have enough. Their armies are strong. A lot of Body Cultivators, a decent number in the Energy Storage stage. At least a few hundred," Wu Ying said, turning his head to eye the simple stone barracks and storage buildings that they bypassed. "Bringing so many upward, paying for their resources, feeding and training them…"

"You're thinking there is a shortage of cores," Yang Mu said. "To keep the current supply for their army. But surely they are used to managing such numbers." She gestured at the permanent buildings they passed.

"Unless the roadway and supply from other cities are cut off," Wu Ying guessed. "Or the city has had to raise even more soldiers to guard against the attacks."

"And if they are trying not to feed their soldiers tainted stones…"

"They might have reduced their internal stockpiles such that they are looking to constrain the demand among those of a lower level too," Wu Ying said. "Though… why demand so many Core Formation cores? Is it just to restrict entrance to Core Formation cultivators? Or are they attempting to empower their current batch further, such that they might do battle with what assails them?"

To this, Yang Mu had no answer.

The pair eventually made their way out of the encampment, leaving behind the simply built cube-designed official buildings and crossing the open ground between the city proper and the fortress. Most of this land, as Wu Ying had already noticed, was made up of rice fields. It not only forced an invading force to make use of the lone road to approach the city or risk getting bogged down in the undulating, uneven earth of the farmland in between, but the fields also helped feed the settlement.

Occasional buildings broke up the landscape, storage buildings and residences for the farmers, along with the necessary supplementary buildings that eased life. In most cases, they were small inns or restaurants, providing alcohol and ready-made meals for tired personnel, combined with a small trading outpost that carried everyday needs. Nothing too elaborate of course, since passing merchants and the city itself were a short distance away.

Well, short in a sense. It was still a half a day's fast walk, or longer if one was burdened by produce. No surprise then that there were merchants and wagon drivers who transported goods between the farmland and city, taking only a small cut of the profit in payment for the convenience.

Watching farmers wade through waterlogged fields to tend rice stalks and extract weeds, to care for the fish and prawns that grew within the fields, Wu Ying could not help but feel a pang of nostalgia. His life had been hard as a farmer, long hours with always the fear of a marauding demonic beast or a long drought in the future.

And yet…

These days, he was a leaf on the wind, detached from his former residence. He drifted through life but was no longer tied to any location. As a farmer, he had been bound to his village, to the community and his family. Now, the threads that held him tight were more ephemeral, a suggestion rather than the strictures of his life before.

Maudlin thoughts, and foolish ones. Life had not been better in the past, just different. He could not forget how his entire existence had been upset by another's choice, by the demands of war and the nobles above. It was a fool's game to regret a past that had never been, casually dismissing the pains of yesteryear.

He remembered those early spring days when the snow had yet to leave and winter stores were bereft, eating a meal of watery *chuk* and wanting more. Only to have to hide those hunger pangs or risk his parents offering him their meals. He remembered ducking his head and accepting the abuse and harsh words offered by Yin Xue as he strutted around, lord of it all. Muscles aching, hands bleeding, as Wu Ying worked a hoe through dry ground, turning it over properly.

Ridiculous to pine for a time that never was.

"You're quiet," Yang Mu said, moving easily to the rhythm of her mare. "Problem?"

"Just thinking." At her raised eyebrow, he gestured at the farmers working in the fields. "Remembering a past."

"Ah, yes. You were one of them once. How far you've progressed. Do you regret it, the path you've taken and the one you forsook?"

Wu Ying blinked, surprised at how closely her words paralleled his thoughts. "I miss my friends, my parents." He grimaced, recalling the few letters that had passed between them. So many years now, and the never-ending worry. Would they still live when he returned? Were his friends well? How about his martial sister? "That life was simpler in some ways. But I also had less control. The world pushed me around, and I could only endure."

"And now?"

"Now, I change the world." He grinned suddenly, puffing up his chest. "I am the storm that rages, the typhoon that washes away the debris, the cyclone that destroys."

She burst out laughing in surprise at the sudden change in tone, conjuring a fan to lightly smack his arm. "You are a fool, Cultivator Long."

"But a good-looking one."

In answer, Yang Mu waggled her fan side to side in a horizontal manner.

Then she kicked her horse, spurring it ahead and leaving Wu Ying to call plaintively behind her, "I'm good-looking, right?"

***

Still smiling, the pair entered the southern city, crossing the gated and fortified bridge area with no more than a nod at the guards who watched it all. Now that they were in the city itself, Yang Mu led them as she consulted a small document she had extracted from her storage ring. Twice, she bent low to speak with a passing mortal, tipping them a coin as they provided updated directions.

The city was frustrating to guide oneself through, for unlike the organized cities of the north, Liang Soong's roads wound about like the serpentine river. More than once, Wu Ying noted alleyways ending in walls, wide streets narrowing without rhyme or reason, and multiple roads intersecting one another in a small square, causing untold chaos.

Liang Soong had grown organically rather than being planned in its construction, and though there was some reasoning for its roads, more such thoroughfares had just been added or blocked on the whims of the mortals that resided within.

Between helpful locals and Yang Mu's directions, the pair finally managed to locate their temporary abode as the light drizzle came to a halt. The pair had traveled quite a distance by then, pushing away from the river edge toward the inner walls, nearly two-thirds of their way there. The neighborhood they stood within reminded Wu Ying of the structures he was familiar with in the north, where high exterior walls ensured privacy for those that resided within.

The inn held a roadside entrance and a separate stable beside it. Even as he dismounted, the wind swirled around him, returning reassurance that the outer building entrance was naught but a front for the much more expansive series of connected buildings behind.

Yang Mu was in her element as she entered, giving orders in rapid fire to the innkeeper and her servants, sending some to ready their rooms and set aside their—minimal—personal belongings, while others unloaded their beasts of burden and set them in one of the many meeting rooms. Another servant scurried out of the inn itself, on the way to carry a series of messages that Yang Mu had already penned to the final recipients of the goods.

The portly female innkeeper was all smiles, even under the barrage of orders, adding her additional commentary to the instructions till Yang Mu finally ran down. Then she guided Yang Mu to their waiting room to freshen up while Wu Ying chose to retire to his room.

He had little enough to do with the final delivery, though he assumed he would receive some small share of the fee when all was done. If not, it was a small enough price to pay to grasp another facet of his companion. Yet he doubted it would be a concern. For all her mercantile upbringing, Yang Mu was not greedy.

At least, not for taels.

One long, hot bath later, Wu Ying found himself bereft of immediate projects. Tomorrow, he would learn more about the tainted cores. Even face one of those creatures, as he left the city to do battle. Alone, for the most part, for it had been agreed that Yang Mu would continue to ascertain details and play the part of merchant. Today though, even though the day was late and the sun would set in a bell, he had little direction.

Lips pursed, he hovered near the door, debating if he should join Yang Mu, as a memory rose. Himself, sprawled on the ground after tripping over a bundle of wood, sword tip pointed at his heart. Breathing hard, leg throbbing, as merciless dark eyes stared down at his frail body.

"Always know the terrain you fight upon. Never assume that land you've treaded upon has stayed the same. Balance is everything in battle and life."

Wryly smiling, his father's words still ringing through his mind, he turned aside from the door and approached the window. A simple movement threw him outward, a grip on the windowsill allowing him to fling his body onto the roof.

He landed soundlessly and moved to the peak to view the city from his new vantage point. Wu Ying had spotted not a single flying cultivator, even around the hills and the cultivation sects, and assumed that either a formation kept such activity contained or common courtesy disallowed such modes of travel. Not an uncommon rule in most cities.

He had wondered before about such regulations. Inquiry had led him to conversations about safety concerns, about duels fought high above that destroyed buildings and killed mortals alike. And, quieter asides, about saving face for magistrates and lords who often were unable to take to the skies themselves.

Wu Ying could not help but wonder which reason it was for Liang Soong's ban.

In the end, it mattered not. His placement on the roof was the best vantage that he could achieve unless he traveled to one of the few temples. The tallest was a seven-story pagoda that overlooked the surroundings, but was in the southeastern part of the city, near the river. A trip, especially across the labyrinth of streets of the city that Wu Ying chose to avoid for now.

In any case, Wu Ying sought the roof not just for the greater visual vantage point, but so that the winds might reach him more easily. Crossing his legs, he breathed deeply and let his soul perception permeate the air, dancing on the breeze across rooftops and down alleyways, to rattle closed windows and chase hungry cats.

The winds returned eventually with the scents and smells of the city. Wu Ying filtered out the offensive aromas after sampling them, even as he allowed his mind to build a map of the surroundings. He did not need to see the settlement to understand its size and shape.

A crowded road, filled with mortal food stalls and vendors, ran straight and long, the air choked with scents and the wind slowed. A walled courtyard, where the air was trapped and a slowly dying mortal lay with his window open, staring at the gardens outside. Another twisting street, empty of inhabitants but the pair of beggars who curled up in the corner, seeking a moment's rest while they feasted on the rat they had caught.

Again and again, the wind flowed, curling around and over Wu Ying, expanding and painting a picture of the city. Scents, smells, the pressure and flow of the air around him as he sat on the rooftop.

Mortal, cultivator, spirit beast, and even the occasional tiny demonic rat impinged upon his consciousness. Burning spirit lamps and tightly woven formations kept him out of some locations. Fewer than most would expect. After all, who could truly hide from the very air itself?

Hours passed and the sun set, bringing with it a chill that the muggy air had lacked thus far. In time, Wu Ying's eyes flew open at the scent of a familiar fiery and calm aura.

Wu Ying stood abruptly, turning in the direction of the surprising presence. A wide smile broke upon his face as he darted across rooftops to his new destination. Guards, stationed to watch for trespassers, called out warnings.

Not that Wu Ying cared, for it was time to meet an old friend.

Chapter 12

Wu Ying dropped silently from the rooftop into the courtyard. Cotton shoes made not a sound on the rounded paving stones, even as he bent his knees and ankles a little to take the shock. His arrival drew the attention of those in the food court, numerous tables scattered between the bordering food stalls selling a variety of succulent dishes. Dark eyes regarded Wu Ying, a few city and merchant guards letting their hands fall to their sheathed weapons by reflex, even as the cultivator searched for his prey.

The moment he found him, Wu Ying strode over, a wide grin threatening to pull his cheeks apart. Back to Wu Ying, the seated presence looked no different from all outward appearances. Bald head, black robes trimmed with green, sleeves rolled up so that the skewer of meat clutched in one hand did not stain his clothing, chopsticks in the other hand.

"You! What are you doing here?" Wu Ying said.

In answer, a foot shifted, pushing a stool as an invitation for Wu Ying. Tou He took one last bite from the meat skewer, letting the sizzling meat disappear down his lips before he discarded the wooden skewer and turned to his friend.

Mouth still full, he answered. "My duty. And you?"

"You weren't looking for me then?" Wu Ying said, remembering the letter that had arrived for him months ago. Forecasters and those who could tell the future were unreliable, but with the right incentive and sufficient time, they could find anyone.

"Why would I be?" Tou He said, sounding puzzled. "Now, sit down and order some food. I recommend the thịt nướng."

Wu Ying rolled his eyes as he sat down. "Which one?" To punctuate his point, he gestured at the numerous stalls that included everything from the fragrant skewered meat—pork and chicken among them—to the roast duck, soya chicken and even pots of soya sauce marinated, stewed meat.

"All of them, of course!" Tou He said. "What's the point of being in Core Formation if you cannot indulge?"

"Is that why you ascended then?" Wu Ying teased. "To have more space to put all that food?"

"It's a good reason, isn't it?"

"Good enough."

Wu Ying swiftly ordered from the attendant who brought over Tou He's meal, then tipped her a coin to inform the others stalls of his order. At the same time, he stole from the man's fried fish, wielding his chopstick to remove one long strip of meat, the white flesh glistening as it was brought over. He chewed on the garlic-and-sesame-oil-flavored meal, the small explosion of spice when he bit into a chili causing his eyebrow to rise.

When he finished his mouthful, Wu Ying continued his earlier line of questioning. "What brought you south?"

"An assignment."

"One worthy of an Elder?"

"Yes. You do know even Elders have to contribute. Troubling rumors from the south, and the Sect has chosen to take a more active role in seeking out potential problems," Tou He said. "After the war, that is."

"I assumed that was the change."

"Now, stop that." The ex-monk smacked Wu Ying's hand as he reached for more of the fish. "You have your own."

"Are we so estranged that you will not share with me?" Wu Ying put on a hurt look.

"I'll pay for your meal. But this is mine."

"Greedy."

"Needy." Tou He finished stripping one side of the fish with his chopsticks, scooped more rice into his mouth, then flipped the fish over. He dug into the flensed flesh on this side, though most had been removed already prior to frying; the strips left on the side dish where they had been deep-fried to coat both sides of the flesh after dredging.

His friend's attention turned to the meal, Wu Ying probed the other with his aura, curiously. Tou He had learned additional aura control techniques while Wu Ying had been away, the glow around the other controlled and tight. There was barely a leak of the flame that was buried within. Even so, spending months discerning the difference between Body, Soul, and Spirit cultivation alone had ensured Wu Ying's senses had leapt forward by multiple li.

As such, obscured or not, Tou He was an open book to him. And what Wu Ying found was startling.

It should not have been, if Wu Ying had considered the matter at all. Tou He had been changed by the fire dragon blood Wu Ying had offered the man, allowing him to leapfrog progress as an Energy Storage cultivator. It had improved Tou He's connection to the fire element but had, inadvertently, altered his bloodline as well.

In addition, his friend had both the lower and middle dantian opened. Creating two cores was significantly more complex, prone to failure, and thus, rare compared to the single dantian method. While the Nascent Soul was not, physically, represented in a core—or so it was believed—it was easier to link a single dantian to the growing immortal soul than two cores while managing the flow of energy from both such cores.

Even so, Tou He had had no other choice but to open both dantians if he meant to continue his progression. His lower dantian was smaller than normal, too small to properly nourish the growth and development of a Nascent Soul. If he had progressed with a single dantian, he would have been destined to stay in Core Formation forever.

And a weak one at that.

Now though, he had a multi-layered core within his body, located in the lower dantian. It pressed against the edges of its storage space, allowing no place for unrefined chi to be stored.

Thankfully, the middle dantian was sufficient for this, but Wu Ying wondered how Tou He would grow the core further. Would he, eventually, build a second core in his dantian, as Wu Ying would assume? Or was there another plan?

Likely some painful and challenging technique. It always was with cultivation techniques that were meant to overcome a limitation.

None of that, of course, had anything to do with his friend's ravenous appetite. On the other hand, Wu Ying was sensing something even stranger in the man's body. Lowering his voice, Wu Ying asked, "Did you study a cultivation technique that derives chi from the food you consume?"

"Yes," Tou He said quite proudly. Then, lowering his voice and flexing his aura to help cut off noise around them, an act that Wu Ying mirrored a moment later, he continued. "The fire dragon blood changed my body. Refined it a bit, especially when I broke through. Between that and my dantians, I have to cultivate a lot more chi than most." He waved at the meal before him. "This is one way to supplement my consumption of pills."

"Wouldn't spirit beast or demonic beast meat be better?"

"Of course. Have any left?" A slight pause, then he added, "That isn't tainted?"

Wu Ying nodded. Of course, the meat would be tainted too, would it not? It'd make it difficult to consume such meat without first cleansing it. As it was, Wu Ying could sense traces of the taint in all those around, the mortals unable to wipe it from them. It was tiny traces, but he could not help but wonder what, if the taint was not removed, would happen to these mortals.

"I actually do." Then he let the bubble of silence drop as the first of his dishes arrived— skewers of meat on a large plate that would have fed a family. "But we can discuss that later. As well as your presence here."

Tou He nodded, copying his friend. "Agreed. Right now, I want to hear about your exploits."

"And I, yours!" A slight pause, then he added, "And of my parents and my martial sister."

"They are well." Then Tou He blinked, grinning as he flicked a hand sideways, extracting and offering Wu Ying two scrolls. "On the off-chance that I met you."

Wu Ying took the scrolls, noting the seals on them. No surprise they were from Fairy Yang and his parents. "Thank you. But don't think that lets you off from telling me about what you've been up to!"

Tou He laughed, snagging a skewer from Wu Ying. Waving the thinly cut, marinated pork belly in one hand, he began. "Well, when you left, you should know, it upset quite a few people. Yin Xue was grumbling, a lot, about how he was looking forward to beating you with his new fist…"

***

It was not Wu Ying's wisest course of action. Staying up late into the night, speaking with his friend till even the late-night street stalls had closed, booting the pair out to wander the streets till they found a diner that catered to early risers. They had spoken for hours on end, taking turns relating the important events in their lives and the minor significant truths of their existence. They touched only lightly upon cultivation matters, with Tou He holding forth in the majority. After all, they had many friends in common.

"I still don't believe you all managed to hear so much about my travels," Wu Ying said, shaking his head. "There's barely any news about the Verdant Green Waters sect—and most of it, the usual."

"The usual?" Tou He said curiously.

"The Verdant Green Waters sect has swept the Shou kingdom cultivation tournament again. There's a genius apothecarist who can make any kind of pill you want in the Verdant Green Waters, but you must pay with blood, taels, or cores. The Verdant Green Waters has released a new formation technique. You know, the usual. Oh, and of course, numerous poems, paintings, and long discussions about the beauty and grace of one Fairy Yang."

Tou He laughed at the mocking tone Wu Ying used for the last line, even as the pair strolled away from their latest meal toward the municipal guards' office. Dawn had broken and the streets were crowded, though the pair deftly manipulated their presence such that a small but noticeable bubble was created around them. No need for jostling for these immortal cultivators. Wu Ying almost felt a little guilty at doing so, as mortals shifted away from the cultivators subconsciously, only to stare and point and whisper as they passed.

Yet, it was also for their own good. Bumping into either cultivator would likely see the mortal falling and injuring themselves, as though running into a wall. Even Wu Ying with his wind cultivation was still more solid than most mortals.

"Well, part of the reason is that your martial sister kept an on-going assignment active, such that any verifiable news about you would be brought back. It was quite a popular assignment actually. It seems the new Gatherer Elder—"

"Senior Goh? He managed to make his Core?" Wu Ying interrupted.

"No. Another that the Sect had poached from a smaller sect. The Fertile Saplings, I believe. They actually disbanded not so long after."

"Horrid name."

"I believe that's part of the reason for their dissolution," Tou He said. "Anyway, Elder Kim aided your martial sister in that, because it saw an increase in the number of applicants to the program. Even some men, some of which were being trained to be wandering gatherers in your image."

"Huh."

The pair came to a stop before the guards' administrative building. Wu Ying swept his spiritual sense over it, noting the lack of anyone above Energy Storage stage within. "Are you sure you want to come with me? Surely you have other things to do."

"It will not hurt my own mission to come along."

"We still need to discuss that."

Still, taking his friend's words as agreement, Wu Ying ascended the steps into the building. After offering the seal and informing the attendant of his requirements, the pair were directed to a small waiting room off the main hall. In short order, an officious-looking bureaucrat arrived, his hands hidden within his voluminous robes as he bowed.

"Honored Cultivators. We have been informed of what you will be doing by Captain Ky." The bureaucrat extracted his hands from his sleeves, offering Wu Ying a seal. "This will allow you entry into the city once again after you have acquired the core. You may leave the core with the gate guards or deposit it with us here." He then lifted his other hand, where a bamboo scroll lay. "Here is a map with markings indicating the presence of Core Formation equivalent beasts that have been troubling our city."

"Beasts. So there have been more than one," Wu Ying said, just to confirm.

"There have been a herd of elephants blocking the use of the forest to the east, what we believe to be a cloud leopard to the direct south along the roadway leading out from the city, and to the west, a pack of dhole."

"And they're all Core Formation equivalent?"

"At least a few in the herds or packs," the bureaucrat said. "They are… different of course."

"What do you mean different?"

Before the bureaucrat could answer Wu Ying's question, Tou He said grimly, "The taint that infects the beasts forces their cores to grow. It provides greater strength, as all larger cores do, but the cores themselves are flawed. Jagged and twisted, the cultivation of the creatures corrupted. The monsters act as though they are in pain, even formerly peaceful creatures aggressive."

"I… see."

"Do the Honored Cultivators have any further questions?" the bureaucrat said.

Wu Ying held up a hand before he unrolled the map to review its contents. Once he was satisfied that the map was sufficiently detailed to guide him, he dismissed the man. To Tou He, he said, "Your mission, it is about the tainted cores, is it not?"

"In a way."

When Wu Ying raised an eyebrow, Tou He shook his head, obviously looking around to indicate the reason for caution.

"Well, the day is not getting any longer. And this map seems to indicate we have far to travel, if we are to find these monsters," Wu Ying said. "I do hope you've kept up with your qinggong techniques."

Matching his friend's light tone, Tou He stood and walked to the door. "I'm sure I'll be able to keep up."

Even worried about what might make his friend hesitant of speaking his concerns in a well-guarded building, Wu Ying could not help but grin. It would be good to show off his techniques. After all, the wind would always be faster than the flame.

Chapter 13

Wu Ying came to a stop as they neared the edge of the forest to the east, wind flaring out before him and throwing stones and sticks all around. He reached out with his senses and the wind, searching for the herd of elephants they had decided to deal with. Not only were they more dangerous to the mortals who needed to work amongst the vast trees, Wu Ying was curious. He had read of these creatures in passing but had never met one in person. Doing so would scratch his curiosity and provide safety. It did not, of course, hurt that the additional numbers meant that the pair of them could acquire additional tainted core samples for their own use.

"Did you choose that qinggong method just to continue to be lazy?" Wu Ying crossed his arms and glared, watching as Tou He landed beside him as the wind died down. The ex-monk hopped off the staff he had been standing upon and snatched it before the chi he imbued into the weapon faded.

"I'm not lazy. Just smart," Tou He said.

"What is it called anyway?"

"The Flickering Flame."

"It borrows my wind to move. Does it do that with all chi?" Wu Ying asked.

"It does," Tou He replied. "So long as another is nearby, it consumes the energy they leave behind to aid in movement."

"Like a flame, burning away a wick to fuel itself, allowing another's chi to power your technique." Wu Ying frowned. "What happens when there are no others going in your direction?"

"Then I must provide the chi, of course," Tou He said. "I must say, your wind chi is much simpler to follow than other forms. Earth chi is the worst."

"I can guess." Wu Ying could not help but remember the elemental chart and their interactions. Air as an element derived from wood and fire after all, with fire having a greater control over wind than he liked to admit. Not as bad as fire would dominate wood, though not much better. And both wind and fire would struggle with metal and earth. "So, what do these *elephants* look like?"

"Big. And strange. Similar to oxen but with large ears and bigger."

"Bigger than an ox?" Wu Ying said, not too surprised. After all, he had once fought a massive, multi-story snake that had dwarfed a hill. Spirit beasts had a tendency to grow as they increased in cultivation strength. "How much bigger?"

"The normal ones are at least twice the size," Tou He replied.

Even as they spoke, the pair blanketed the area to pick up traces of their prey. Wu Ying's wind was the first to provide clues of what was to come, as he pointed farther north.

Wu Ying picked up the threads of the conversation as they flew low to the earth. "Normal ones? You mean the creatures are the size of a... a house, normally?"

"Maybe a small hut," Tou He replied, holding his hand upward as though trying to measure invisible elephants and buildings. "You'll see."

Wu Ying shook his head. He knew elephants had been described as big, but he recalled dismissing the descriptions as exaggerations. All too many explorers tended to take poetic license in their writing, rather than providing factual details of the wonders they encountered. As though reality needed to be adjusted, rather than just accepted.

Still, if the wind that spoke to him was clear, perhaps in this case, the writers had not been exaggerating. They might have been underselling these elephants a little. It spoke of feet that struck with the strength of a rockfall. It murmured of ground crushed, trees cracked and broken, branches stripped from the tallest treetops. Of air shifted by simple movements and massive fans in the shape of ears that created breezes, tongues that twisted in the air ahead of them, and trumpet calls that set bird and predator aflight.

Through the forest, the pair skimmed across the earth, staying low beneath the overhanging branches and yet higher than the dense undergrowth. Wu Ying shaped the wind before him, pushing aside branches and thorns that grasped at clothing, armoring his aura to deflect and break when necessary. Behind, Tou He flew higher and hunched, choosing a less destructive route as he followed his friend.

They flew in haste, deeper toward one of the many lakes that littered the northeast. This land was wet, the river dominating the landscape, but it was insufficient to soak up the spring deluge. And so, lakes formed in the valleys between hills, fed from flowing water and blocked by fallen timber.

At one such lake, the herd rested, drawing in liquid nourishment and stripping nearby trees. Wu Ying floated into the branches of a nearby tree to watch the creatures even as his friend alighted nearby, taking a moment to marvel at the sight.

A dozen elephants, the smallest standing five feet tall, the majority around ten feet at the shoulders. They were broad, easily double the width of an ox, and grey-brown in coloration. Their feet were not the dainty hooves of horses or goats, but tree trunks that reached deep into the earth to bear their massive weight. Their nose—hah, not tongue—was the strangest thing, like a living snake resting between paired trunks.

The herd was made up of a child, about eight adults, and the massive trio of creatures that dominated the surroundings. These were no stone turtles of the north, large enough to carry a small village on their backs, but they were still massive. Easily twenty to thirty feet tall each and about two-thirds as wide. Their path through the undergrowth from deeper within the forest was clear, shattered trees and torn up earth marking their route.

Most of all, Wu Ying felt the solidity of the group, their connection to the very earth they traveled. Not just their elemental connection was present to his spiritual senses, but also the marking of the changes on their body, the brownish coloration, the toughened hide that spoke of a defensive addition not just in their aura but flesh as well.

On top of that was the smell, the twisted, burnt energy scent of their chi. It was mixed with the wet, pain-filled acrid odor the creatures gave off—a burnt earthen spirit and something familiar and twisted in it.

"This will be difficult," Wu Ying said, shaping the wind so that their words and scent would not reach the herd. "Those three, the largest ones, they're all in Core Formation or close to it. The biggest is mid-grade or so, for a beast. The other two are early Core Formation or peak Energy Storage."

"I concur," Tou He said.

"This is going to cause a lot of damage when we fight."

"Good thing we're a distance away from the loggers," Tou He said. "Though we might want to angle our attacks from the northwest."

"Easy enough to do." Wu Ying touched the blade by his side, two fingers on the hilt. "I can deal with the biggest three. Can you help with the rest?"

"Just the biggest three?" Tou He said, slightly mocking. Then, more seriously, he added, "Of the remainder, only four are tainted. The others don't need to die."

"I'll leave you to it."

Tou He smiled at his friend's trust. "On you, then."

A slow nod, as Wu Ying's hand wrapped around the sword. There were many options for his opening strike, from a blade draw to a lunge. There was quite the distance between the two groups, though it would not be that difficult for him to cover the ground.

Wu Ying quickly reviewed his goals in the battle. Minimize damage to himself, his friend, and the environment. That meant finishing the fight fast, in particular targeting the most powerful Core Formation creature. The problem was that it was earth-aspected with a preponderance of the endurance and stability that the element was known for.

"Choices, choices, choices…"

Inhale, exhale. Decision made, Wu Ying drew the saint-jian from his sheath. He brought it up then down, positioning his feet. He focused, eyeing the swaying branches in the way, the distance between them. Turning his head to Tou He, he noted the cultivator had his staff out too.

A single nod, and a heartbeat's pause to ensure that the area behind the attack was clear. Wu Ying ran, feet touching upon swaying branches and leaves, the wind guiding a few recalcitrant wooden limbs into the correct position. At the same time, the northern wind gathered at his back, pushing him onward as the cultivator gained speed.

The last distance between Wu Ying and his target was bare of trees and impediments. Feet touching upon wooden branch, he flexed his energy downward, sending chi through his feet with such force that he shattered his launch point and the branches around it.

Sword leveled into a straight line, Wu Ying extended his body and lengthened his form such that he became an arrow in flight, wind chi and sword intent forming a corona of energy around his body as he launched himself into the second cut of the Wandering Dragon.

Bestial instincts had the massive elephant begin its turn, Wu Ying's attack meant to catch it in the side and blast through the massive body foiled. Earth rose up from the ground to form a secondary protective layer, even as the elephant's aura darkened and tightened.

Impact.

Dao and killing intent warred against earthen element and creature's toughened hide. Wu Ying pierced through the layers of aura reinforcement and risen earth, his attack slowed a little before he struck hardened skin. Metal pierced toughened hide and muscle, blood spurting outward as flesh and muscles tore before he met hardened bone. There the tip of his weapon skidded off, his strike angling downward as the combined energy shattered the reinforced skeletal front hip.

Dropping from above, Wu Ying was forced further down, tearing a furrow that opened even further as the cyclone of wind and sword energy parted skin and flesh. Shards of bone were pulled from the body as well, moments before Wu Ying slammed into the ground. The creature's foot now hung on tendrils of flesh and muscles, limb contained and held together by the monster's massive aura.

Retracting his sword and sword chi moments before crashing, Wu Ying extended his opposite hand, taking the impact with it even as he bent hand and elbow, dispersing the energy of his fall. It was not something he would have chosen to do as a mortal, the amount of force and speed outside the bounds of a mortal limit. Now, with his wind body and Core Formation soul, it was a simple matter.

Rolling over and over before springing upward, Wu Ying twisted through the air and around, releasing a blade strike as he spun like a top, robes flaring out behind him. As the arc of sword energy impacted the earth elephant, he noticed that the creature was still standing, its damaged foot and chest covered by earth to replace the destroyed flesh.

He watched as his attacks struck, but now the elephants acted.

Environmental chi flooded from the elephant's core, entering the soil below Wu Ying. From the earth, shards of black stone, jagged and twisted, rose to attack Wu Ying's back. Only his sense of the shifting chi and the disrupted air informed him of the attack.

A surge of wind chi sent him higher, his spin ending as he landed upon the jagged spikes. A moment later he hissed as additional spikes birthed from the completed spikes tore into the foot he had landed upon. A flex of will tore him free from the earth, even as the newly shifted soil drank in his shed blood.

Another flexing of his chi had the open wound seal, blood vessels closing and the skin tightening around his foot. In the air, floating far above the ground through manipulation of the wind, Wu Ying darted sideways as he dealt with his injury. Around him, stone spikes targeted him as the elephants cast them into the air.

A small push of his chi and Wu Ying danced, darting from side to side as he dodged the attacks.

From the trees, Tou He joined the fight, his staff swung downward. Body coated in flames, the bald cultivator struck hard against one of the tainted Energy Storage level elephants, crushing its head and dropping the creature with a single strike. Rather than follow up though, Tou He slowed for a moment to whisper a prayer over the body, barely escaping as the nearest elephant swung its trunk in retaliation.

Brightening with each moment he was in battle, such that it was hard to even look in Tou He's direction, the cultivator darted across the ground, battling the monsters while leaving Wu Ying to handle his own problems.

And problems there were.

Realizing that the fast-moving cultivator floating above them was not going to be struck down by the thrown stone spikes, the other elephants had begun to embed chi into the projectiles. Upon nearing him, the embedded chi made the spikes explode, pelting Wu Ying with sharpened obsidian and granite shrapnel.

In retaliation, Wu Ying lashed out, sending blade strikes of sword and killing intent into the scrum of five elephants that had focused on him. The others were at the edges of the battle, one of the larger elephants having chosen to leave the leader to take on Tou He rather than cluster around him.

Like the thrown shards though, Wu Ying's attacks were doing little damage. Even fast moving as the wind and blade chi was, the lead earth elephant had time to reinforce its brethren, protecting them with walls of dirt or just hardening their auras with its own. All Wu Ying's attacks had done was leave shallow wounds across bodies and scatter blood across the surroundings, staining water and mud below.

Now, with stones shattering around him, Wu Ying conjured a globe of wind that caught the shards and redirected them around himself. The smallest pieces and those coming in at an acute angle were easily deflected, though the larger projectiles and those thrown with greatest force required more effort. Even then, not all were caught, leaving the attacks to pepper his body and tear his robes.

Beneath his robes, the magical scaled armor protected his vitals, allowing Wu Ying to ignore the attacks for now. Yet the battlefield stalemate would not hold forever, and already the clearing and lake they had been fighting next to was torn apart, scattered stoney projectiles and sudden dips in the earth lowering the lake level and leaving behind churned mud.

He had failed in his goal of finishing the battle quickly. Now, it was a test to see if he could finish the fight at all.

"Right. The big one's not going to be finished anytime soon," Wu Ying said, twisting energy to speak to his friend. He floated higher as another large stone spear exploded beneath him, borrowing the wind and energy to do so. As he did so, he let the wind grab the shards and shrapnel and continued to build the wind shield around him, creating a shield three layers thick. "I'm going in close now."

Swinging wide and around as additional shards exploded, he dove low. As Wu Ying neared the ground, he unleashed the various layers of earthen shards at his opponents, imbuing earth and wind chi to strike at the monsters.

His target was no longer the massive cow[53] that led the herd. Instead, he directed the rain of shards at the smaller creatures. Even as he fell, Wu Ying could sense how the matriarch wielded its command of earth chi, the twisted and tar-like feel of its energy clotting and cloying on his skin as it took control of the falling earth. Unable to control the direction or speed of the falling projectiles, it instead broke them apart, creating a choking cloud that swept over the herd.

It was no real surprise to the cultivator that his initial gambit had failed. That didn't stop him from releasing the rest of the earth and his wind shield at the elephants though, wary of keeping the creatures' element so close to him.

More importantly, he was now below and amongst the monsters. The second jian appeared in his hands as he darted between monsters, ducking underneath, above, and behind the creatures as he imbued his weapons with wind and killing intent. Metal blades pierced toughened flesh, flensing skin and tearing into veins and arteries with impunity. The elephants twisted and wielded their trunks, tusks, and bodies, attempting to strike the flying gnat that struck at them and failing again and again.

Viscera and blood swirled in the air, mixing with the cloud of dirt and stone even as it choked sight and breathing, muffling the growls and cries and snorts of anger all around him. Rather than striking individually and expecting to end the fight in a single blow, Wu Ying tore into the group to distract them, bleeding out his opponents. A single, immediately fatal strike would slow him down too much as the matriarch elephant reinforced her brethren, so he attacked with the intent to bleed them out while waiting for an opportunity.

Within minutes, three of the creatures were staggering around, bleeding from deep wounds or already collapsed, hamstrung and unable to empower their bodies via their earth aspects any longer. Even the matriarch was worse for wear, the massive wound down its side still leaking blood, its core drained of energy.

On the other hand, Tou He had only one opponent left, having chased off the other non-tainted elephants. Those monsters were retreating, leaving the fire cultivator the last Core Formation elephant to deal with.

As Wu Ying spun and sought to return to battle, another explosion of stone blocked his way. Again and again, stone slabs rose and exploded, pushing him over the lake from the water's edge where they had fought.

For a moment, floating over the water, Wu Ying was safe. Close by, his friend had been forced to retreat as well, a rolling column of muddy earth rising above the water to shove back the fire cultivator. Only when the pair were floating over the water did the attacks stop, Wu

---

[53] Not a mistake. Cow is the term for a female elephant.

Ying taking higher to the sky as his senses were attenuated by the liquid below. Moments later, hanging onto his staff, his friend joined him.

"I thought you'd deal with the three largest," Tou He teased, dimming the flames and light that surrounded him.

"I thought you were dealing with the smaller ones," Wu Ying replied.

"You were too fast."

"You're too slow."

"That was a nice attack though. Second form of the Wandering Dragon?"

"Yes," Wu Ying confirmed. "What's with the bright light?"

"Sun Form." Tou He added, softer, "Chi-intensive. So we should end this fast."

"I've been trying, but that cow is tough. I need to get close and strike at her properly."

Before his friend could answer, the earth chi that had surrounded them and permeated the entire clearing flexed. It caused the pair to stumble in the air, dropping a few feet before they reasserted their control.

At the same time, a dome of earth formed, rising throughout the edges of the clearing, blocking off the sun and clouds. It moved so fast, the pair already trapped over the lake had not the time to flee before it enclosed their surroundings, leaving the only source of light the brightly burning Tou He.

"*Hun dan*," Wu Ying cursed. "That's new."

"Now what?" Tou He muttered, moments before the dome of earth shrank, more earth pulled upward to reinforce the dome as the entire structure collapsed inward.

"You had to ask," Wu Ying replied.

Chapter 14

Wu Ying flexed his aura, sending the wind to contest the falling earth dome. It shrieked through the surroundings, gale force winds pounding earthen walls, a cyclone forming as it scoured and diminished the barriers that enclosed them. The air filled with dust, the water beneath their feet churning.

To no one's surprise, it was a losing proposition, though he managed to slow the rate of shrinkage. However, each moment saw more earth pulled from the ground into the dome itself, adding to the weight that his wind had to press against.

Meanwhile, Tou He used his staff to bat aside incoming earthen spikes, extending the size and length of the staff and loosing a concentrated beam of fire from the end at times. As the only source of illumination in the dark, the pair were easy targets for the remaining earth elephants.

"They're going to kill themselves!" Tou He grunted out, forming a shield of flame moments before the shrapnel from an exploding earthen spear reached them. Fire was a poor shield, especially against earth. The superheated fluid landed on the pair, burning through enchanted silk robes to their flesh.

Wu Ying flicked the blobs off his body, hissing a little at the pain, rivulets of sweat forming on his forehead. As they were further constrained, his ability to call upon the wind was decreased, the strength of his connection cut off from the world.

"I figure they know they can survive this," Wu Ying replied. "Or perhaps they are truly mad. We won't be alive to find out if we don't find a solution."

"Kill the matriarch?"

Wu Ying glanced over to where the matriarch was. The cow had been smart and shifted its location when the dome had enclosed them. But the cow was not the only one with a spiritual and elemental sense, and even with the dirt clogging the wind, its large size was easy to track. In fact, it was so large, they could have stood under its feet and been protected from the shrinking dome.

"I have an idea." Wu Ying hesitated, then added, "You'll need to stay close to me and follow everything I do without hesitation."

"Of course."

If he called upon the winds from outside, utilized them to punch a hole through… perhaps. Wind against earth was not a winning battle, not in the short term. He could wear the monster away, tear the dome apart with a howling cyclone over time.

But not in time. Already, he felt the energy within his core drop as he poured it into the surroundings to keep him aloft, to battle the shrinking dome. The amount of space between them dwindled, even as the elephants moved toward the deepening water.

"Then follow me."

Wu Ying released his hold on the winds, throwing himself and Tou He into a direct attack. No time to utilize and empower his sword for the second cut of the Wandering Dragon, but the Sword's Truth was more than sufficient. He exited the nearest body in a welter of gore, Tou He flickering along behind him.

The shrinking dome collapsed inward ever faster, catching one of the elephants on the edges by surprise. The earth seemed to suck the creature into the dome itself, swallowing it whole. Only a small, startled trumpet shook the surroundings before it was gone, elephants rushing in closer to one another.

Tou He, behind Wu Ying, swung his staff at an elephant. He caught the smaller creature in its chest, sending the middle-aged calf spinning through the air with a deep burn across its body. Off the ground, the grey-brown figure lost its connection to the earth and the environmental chi it manipulated, allowing a gust of wind to send it higher into the sky.

The dome continued to strengthen, the pair dancing amidst the herd and laying into them with sword and staff. Wu Ying had sheathed his secondary weapon, having to concentrate and manipulate the wind and control his sword, all while watching the thickening dome. Cracks appeared across it as the hastily constructed structure came apart, portions collapsing into the churning water they fought nearby.

The lake had diminished in circumference, the earth beneath its waves pulled away from it. The matriarch raised its head, releasing a trumpet growl of command. Immediately, the elephants sank into the ground, smaller globes of earth forming around them in defense. All the remaining creatures, even the only tiny calf, had a dome created for it.

All but the matriarch, whose attention was split between the dome it had created and the sphere it had created for the calf.

"Follow me!" Wu Ying commanded his friend, sheathing his sword as he darted under the matriarch elephant.

Tou He followed, the pair taking shelter beneath the creature. Moments later, the dome gave way, the massive unstable structure unable to be stabilized by the creature's chi any longer.

A jagged portion struck the water, sending waves rolling. Moments later, the water exploded. It was not the only section of earth that released its energy in this manner, filling the dome in a constant drumroll of explosions that deafened them all and made ears throb.

The matriarch, sensing their presence beneath it as it released control of the structure, sought to deal with them. At first, it bent its head to swipe at them with its trunk, only to jerk away as Tou He's burning staff battered it aside. Then earth bubbled upward, seeking to pull them down. That failed too, as Wu Ying formed a flowing current of air beneath the pair to stand upon. The earth bubbling beneath forced the two to crouch a little between bulging belly and burping earth.

All the while, the dome collapsed but the matriarch stood unharmed. It had formed a small patch of loose earth directly above itself, such that the thinned earth that crashed into its body could be shrugged off.

At the same time, angered that the pests had ducked underneath it, it took the most viable route dealing with them. It lowered its bulk, intent on squishing the pair. Wu Ying flew with his sword upward, bracing himself as she squatted, only for the sharpened tip of his blade to enter her belly and doing little to stop her movement. After all, the dao of the jian was not one of bracing or protection but of piercing and sharpness.

Thankfully, there was another who had studied a protective technique and wielded a staff. Burning weapon thrust into the ground, the staff took the weight of the massive creature as Wu Ying was forced down.

Body tented, the matriarch screamed as the flame-imbued staff caught on her belly. Wu Ying smelled the charring meat, blood dribbling down his arm from his embedded jian. Where jian was insufficient to deter, burning flesh and unyielding staff forced the matriarch to stand again. Her aura flexed at the same time, pushing earth and the pair away as she sent waves of earth rolling to crush them.

If she could have jumped, Wu Ying assumed she would have. Instead, the pair were crushed to the earth by the creature's aura, his flowing wind flooring broken by the surge of energy. High above, earth flowed away at the same time, clearing the air around her.

Trapped in sticky, muddy earth, the matriarch's own elemental dao holding them tight, Wu Ying and Tou He were helpless. Rather than strike them, the elderly cow backed off, bleeding and burned as it trumpeted its agony to the sky, and the earth shook, covering their faces.

Fear surged through Wu Ying as he was held tight, but struggle as he might, the wet earth offered no grip for him, no stability to exert his strength. A slight burning around his lungs had begun, the lack of air a reminder of the exertion of the day already. He had not prepared for being entombed, so even his prior training at diving was of less use than normal.

Focusing within, Wu Ying gathered his chi to throw himself out, only to feel another cultivation base surge. Tou He flared his chi, burning and drying the soil all around them, muddy earth cleansed of tainted earth chi.

Dry now, Wu Ying threw himself to the side, exploding out of the soil and tumbling sideways. Moments later, Tou He followed even as Wu Ying's connection to the wind reformed. As they escaped, the matriarch returned, legs pounding toward them in an attempt to finish the fight.

A little too late. The falling foot clipped Tou He and the cultivator spun away, his staff lost as he was cast aside. Wu Ying on the other hand, more used to being thrust around by tumultuous wind, rolled and came to his feet. One sword was lost, embedded in the creature's body, so he conjured his other.

The matriarch's eyes glowed with fury and hate, large ears flapping as she turned tiny eyes to regard the destruction. Rocks and dirt continued to settle, the sliding of rocks and the groaning of earth echoing as the massive fallen dome rippled. Within all this earth, the remnants of the herd were hidden.

Wu Ying felt the matriarch's core as it throbbed, jagged and twisted and hurting the elephant. He could sense it sucking in chi in desperate need, reserves depleted from the reckless use of energy. The matriarch was exhausted, injured, barely able to output the energy required to keep its remnant earthen foot and side covered.

If he left the matriarch, it might die here and now.

Wu Ying considered retreating with Tou He. Combating and slowing down the earthen dome had required a significant amount of his resources, his core throbbing at the pull of energy it had experienced. The Cyclone's Breath method helped refill his stores, but it was never meant to be anything but an ongoing supplement. In the dust-choked surroundings, wind chi was mixed and corrupted, forcing Wu Ying to expand more focus and energy than ever to keep the cultivation technique working.

Good sense suggested they run.

But this battle was nearly over, in one way or the other.

As though the thought was the signal flag, the matriarch moved. At first, its steps were slow and plodding, the ground trembling with each footfall. As it picked up speed, the earth before them shifted and twisted, smoothing out to make the elephant's charge easier. It bucked and heaved under each step, throwing the creature forward as it moved faster than Wu Ying would have thought possible.

Sword held in the low guard on his right, the cultivator focused, pouring his energy and killing intent into the blade. He felt the dao intentions of the Heart of the Sword filling it, ideas and concepts of sharpness and swiftness, the need to cut and part, to flow elegantly while doing so. At the same time, he wrapped the cutting edge of the northern wind, the strength of the tropical storms of the east, and the flexibility of the central wind into the attack.

Staring down the charging earth elephant, feeling the earth jump and twist with each movement, Wu Ying rode the shifts with ease. He lifted himself off the ground a little to reduce the shocks, his legs bending as he ran. The wind picked up behind him, carrying him on wings of flame as he neared the other.

Two implacable forces, approaching one another. Corona of energy, grey and brown from the earth elephant, white and silver from Wu Ying formed between the pair. But Wu Ying was the wind, not hard-bodied metal or unrelenting earth.

It was but a question of timing for when he would dodge. When his opponent would react to his all-too-predictable movement.

An eyeblink, an extra gust of wind and dust between the pair.

There.

He spun sideways like a top, his feet placing and rotating as he swung around. The central wind's movement techniques influenced his footwork as he whirled around the creature's charge. At the same time, his sword rose, the ring of metal striking earthen tusk shaking the air.

Up in a block, imparting energy to the turn, then down in a sideways cut. Chi engorged the blade, extending its length. Wind and sword intent bit into the flesh along unprotected neck, finding a tiny gap in earthen armor that allowed the creature to turn its head.

Blood fountained as the attack struck deep, but energy unleashed and caught by stubborn earthen chi ran rampant through the weapon. Metal stressed to the maximum, dao intent and chi embedding insufficient to strengthen the weapon, the jian exploded. Metal shards were left within the earthen elephant, sinking deeper into flesh and organs, tearing veins and arteries.

Other metal splinters pelted Wu Ying as he spun away, one fragment leaving a gaping wound in his arm where the scale armor was missing. Another shard tore through the sky, clipping his ear and leaving it bleeding.

Then Wu Ying was away and back in the sky, the elephant stumbling a few further steps. It turned its body to follow Wu Ying, forward momentum and the sudden loss of footing all combining to set the creature tumbling. Earth was gorged apart, a deep trench forming as the beast bled out its life, its massive endurance and strength finally giving way, reinforced earthen limb shattering with suddenness as will finally gave way.

The wind cultivator panted, wringing out his aching hand. The Third Cut of the Wandering Dragon was incomplete, a concept given form and tested in battle but a failure. An explosive, excruciating, and expensive failure it seemed.

Dismissing the hilt of the weapon back into his storage ring, Wu Ying let out a low breath as he flexed numb fingers. Tou He stumbled closer, climbing the trench to stare at the dying matriarch. He offered Wu Ying a nod, and the man smiled.

The matriarch was down.

Finally.

Around the destroyed clearing, earth trembled and twisted. Grey elephant heads poked out of the ground, pushing apart their shielding domes, fury in their tiny eyes as they sensed the loss of their leader. Trunks were raised as they trumpeted their anger and loss.

Wu Ying sighed. "Oh, come on!"

Chapter 15

Thankfully, dealing with the last few elephants was significantly simpler. Many had expended their energy to protect themselves, with Tou He able to send the weakest fleeing with a concentrated burst of his aura and killing intent. After that, the rest of the fight was unsurprising, if a little difficult.

"These tainted cores. It makes them strong. Stronger than what you'd expect, with the amount of energy contained within them," Wu Ying commented as he finished extracting the massive core from the matriarch earth elephant's corpse. He shook his hand clean, withdrawing an insulated jade box to store the jagged spirit stone. Even holding the spirit stone whilst shielded, Wu Ying felt like he needed to give his hand a good wash.

"It does. It's what made keeping these creatures contained such a problem for the city," Tou He replied. The monk was seated on the nearby rise, keeping watch for scavengers while Wu Ying worked.

"I can sense how the taint has entered the bones and meat," Wu Ying commented, prodding the hardened flesh. "I'd consider skinning it, but can it even be used?"

"Some would," Tou He said.

"But you don't suggest it?"

"Even the best cleansing rituals leave a trace behind."

"Ah…." Wu Ying imagined trying to move around in such tainted leather, or even eating the meat or consuming a pill made from this. He could not help but shudder a little. The thought was similar to eating rancid pork. You could wash the meat and the slime away, cook it as best you could, but the taste and the memory would always be there. Never mind the stomach troubles it could cause. And if you mixed it with good herbs or other sources…

"Let's drag the bodies over. I'll extract the other stones, and you can burn it all away." Wu Ying could not help but grin. "I'm assuming your flames can do that?"

"Oh, yes."

Wu Ying stretched, stepping away from the corpse and glancing at the torn and beaten-up robes he wore. If there was one aspect he missed most of all about the Sect, it was the easy surplus of clothing one could acquire at a discount. Not that he had been able to afford the robes initially, but now, as an Elder and a rather successful Gatherer, minor expenses like purchasing multiple sets of robes were a small thing. In truth, robes even now were not that expensive, but his parsimonious nature made him wince at the ongoing expense.

"Watch out!"

A quick hop sideways had Wu Ying cross a dozen feet, removing himself from the point of impact. Moments later, the limp elephant corpse slammed into the ground, raising a cloud of dirt and squirting blood into the air as Tou He lobbed it over.

Wind rose defensively, sending away the droplets and clearing the air around the body. To little use, for moments later, another body landed near the first.

"Someone was holding back, it seems," Wu Ying muttered to himself, watching as his friend heaved the massive corpses around as if they were no heavier than the bags of rice he'd once carried up the mountain. Then, as Tou He paused to locate more corpses, Wu Ying raised his voice. "Stop throwing them if you want me to do any harvesting!"

"Fine, fine. If the great wind gatherer needs me to be *careful*…"

***

The pair watched the flames catch on the corpses, burning merrily and brighter. A small nudge of Wu Ying's will had the winds carry the stench upward and away from the pair, such that they were spared from the noxious fumes. Well, beyond the occasional times when the wind felt playful, shifting to send a puff or a rolling cloud over the two.

After one such gust, Tou He retreated further and glared at his friend, who followed him. He waved the meat bun he'd extracted in front of Wu Ying in agitation. "Why is your control so poor?"

"It's not so much control as a partnership. I can't tell them what to do so much as strongly request it. The wind will, however, do what it wants."

"Dangerous. If I tried that with the flames, they'd consume me. I am the one in control of the fire, not the other way around."

"A difference in dao or element?" Wu Ying asked, curious to hear his friend's opinion.

"Maybe a little of both," Tou He said. "I know some others—not of the fire element, but water and wood in particular—who espouse your views. Where the elements are a partnership. Others view the elements as a portion of themselves, no more required to be dominated than you would dominate your heart or lungs. Control perhaps, but not dominate.

"The fire that you gifted me though. It is not inherently a part of me. It is an element I must battle constantly or risk it consuming me entirely."

Wu Ying winced. "Ah… I'm sorry."

"For what? I knew taking the dragon's blood was dangerous. It was my choice," Tou He said. "And I have gained much from it."

Wu Ying turned his attention then to the fiery depression where the corpses were being consumed. The fire that lit the lakeside was brighter and hotter than any he had seen, outside of the blacksmith's forge. It burnt so hot that portions of it were green and other parts were entirely clear, as though color itself had been consumed.

Fat, flesh, muscle, and even bone transformed to ash and fuel for the flame. The massive corpses shrank visibly, the chi within either dispersed back into metal and earth chi or transformed into fire chi. Wood chi, already fading as the creatures died, became fuel for the flames while all liquid in the bodies hissed and escaped into the air. Most of all, the taint that had marred the corpses was devoured, destroyed, and cleansed.

As he watched the flames do so, Wu Ying was struck with the obvious. Between his earlier upbringing, his dao path, and the dragon flames he now controlled, it was easy to see why Tou He had been selected to come down.

"You were sent down to deal with the taint, weren't you? Is there anything you can tell me about it?" Wu Ying said as the pair continued to watch the fire.

"I was sent to find and deal with the source," Tou He confirmed. Having finished his snack, he conjured another bun, peeling the wrapping off the bottom. "If I could, that is. There was some belief that I would be more of an external aid to local efforts."

"And there have been none?" Wu Ying said worriedly.

"None what?"

"Local efforts to stop the taint."

"None that have survived or continued." Tou He turned and gestured back to the city. "The local government has kept details closely held, but it seems that at least two expeditions have been sent to locate and deal with the problem. Both have not been heard from. The last expedition was a month and a half ago. Since then, the government has pulled back their people, concentrating on shoring up their defenses while further aid is requested."

"Because of the increasing number of tainted Core Formation monsters."

"Exactly."

"And this taint, the source, it creates demonic beasts at a faster rate than ever," Wu Ying said. "Makes them stronger than they should be, maybe even damages spirit beasts who have managed to escape the fate of becoming a demonic beast. Or am I wrong?"

"No, not wrong. That is what I believe too."

"Then pulling back is a fool's move," Wu Ying said firmly. "Hiding away just allows the taint to increase. The source must be dealt with."

"Agreed." Tou He fell silent for a time, staring at the fire before he added, almost as an afterthought, "The last expedition contained a mixture of the city's martial elders and a division from the army holding the fortification. A half-dozen Core Formation elders. And none returned."

"Ah…" Wu Ying's indignation at the foolishness of the locals faded. It was not that they did not see the problem. It was that they did not feel as though they could change their destiny anyway. Or perhaps, a little of that and a little politics. "Are there not more elders in their schools?"

"They're not martial schools, Ah Ying. That one"—he gestured at the largest hill a distance from them, where multiple buildings were situated along the hill—"focuses on teaching cultivation techniques to their bureaucrats." His finger tracked to the right. "That school is one you might want to visit. They're gatherers—though really, they're just farmers. Wood and earth elements mostly. That one is a spirit beast sanctuary.

"Their schools focus more on elements, guiding people to the professions that suit their elements and their inclinations. Martial sects are almost non-existent, with the army taking their place. You know of how they run their armies?"

"Mass conscription at an early age. Everyone is forced to train locally, with current or retired army personnel organizing the training," Wu Ying said.

"Exactly. They have fewer villages, because of the forest and spirit beasts. They're more concentrated in their cities or the areas around their cities, with travel between settlements more difficult than farther north. Travel is vouchsafed by the army." Tou He shook his head. "To do that, the army receives a large stipend of the budget, and every long-term member of the army is stuffed with cores to be pushed to a higher cultivation level if possible."

"How do they afford that?" Wu Ying said with a frown.

One of the problems that cultivators faced in general was the lack of resources at the lower level. While prodigies and those who ran into significant amounts of beneficial events could skip many of the impediments to cultivation, most stalled due to a lack of resources to provide aid when an obstacle occurred.

Wu Ying had been lucky, having encountered more than his share of beneficial events and dao inspiration. Yet, he had also utilized a much larger proportion of resources than your average cultivator to reach the heights he had. If not for the fact that he was a Gatherer, an individual able to acquire these rare resources directly, he would have not progressed as far or as fast.

"Look around you," Tou He said. "We import a portion of the beast stones we need from the south. Do you think they'd sell them to us if they had not filled their demand? The southern jungles are filled with beasts galore."

"And so, they intend to wait then? Until the army is able to send additional aid? Maybe a dedicated team?" Wu Ying mused. "How long has this been going on?"

"The taint? A few years."

"Then they think they have time?"

Tou He shrugged.

"Do you know anything else?" Wu Ying said, a little frustrated.

"Know? No."

"But you suspect something."

"You do too." Lips thinned. "It is not the same, but this smell, this taint. We have experienced it before, once."

"Demonic chi."

Tou He nodded and Wu Ying winced. That it was invading spirit beasts in the wild meant there was a source, possibly uncontrolled, possibly created to infect these creatures. A fount or a spring, a gate between the demonic realm and the middle kingdom.

A travesty against the Dao.

Demons were not, inherently, bad. It was a matter of phrasing and definition.

A spirit beast who broke from their natural path of ascension had to tread a careful path or see the spirit core it built twist and break, driving it insane. In that, they were unnatural and no longer in sync with the Dao and were thus named demonic beasts.

On the other hand, other creatures gained strength or sentience, their very nature—like the taotei, the hundun, the qionggi—destructive, chaotic, and vicious. Though peasant and cultivator alike called them demons, they were not in opposition to their dao. In fact, by embodying these aspects further, they were able to grow in strength along a "true" path.

Both were common events in the Middle Kingdom, and while unfortunate in some cases, like a mortal damaging their own meridians, it was not unusual. Even a common demonic beast was still intrinsically part of the Dao, though they might have left the path to greater heights.

On the other hand, this taint, this corruption was wrong. It forcibly altered the natural world, attempting to subvert nature and beasts in an alien way. The dao that it espoused was not the dao of the Middle Kingdom, their dao originating from another location. It was why such fonts, such breaches or gates that were left open to the demonic plain were not allowed. Each moment it was allowed to exist, it weakened and ate away at the foundations of the greater Dao and realm.

A bone cracked, shattering as the heat weakened it, showering the surroundings with sparks. Wu Ying checked the fire again, but like before, Tou He's control of the flame was spectacular. Outside a ring of around a foot from the corpses, the flames refused to burn, dying off as soon as the sparks landed. Though the heat from the fire should have created lava and slag, crisped the earth and made it liquid, somehow Tou He had kept the flame and heat contained.

The pair fell into a companionable silence, Wu Ying turning over their conversation in his mind. It seemed his objective would not be as easy to complete as he'd first believed. Even so, as smoke and flames rose, he heard the whisper of the southern wind. The promise of secrets of heaven and hell to be exposed.

If he dared to walk this path.

Chapter 16

By the time the fire had consumed the tainted bodies, late evening had fallen. Their return to the city was uneventful, with only a minor argument arising when Wu Ying offered the smallest core as payment. It took the intervention of the southern gate lieutenant before the argument was complete to the dissatisfaction of everyone, leaving Wu Ying less two more beast cores but still holding onto the massive Core Formation matriarch's core.

"I still wouldn't recommend using it," Tou He said as the pair sauntered along the busy city streets.

"The core?"

"Yes."

"Wasn't thinking of it." Wu Ying cocked his head, gesturing in one direction as they reached an intersection. Mortals streamed around the uncaring pair of cultivators as they ran their own errands. "Are you free?"

"If you're paying, certainly."

"Why…" Wu Ying shook his head. "No, you stomach-obsessed fool. Not food. There's someone I want to introduce you to." Then, having been reminded of his own hunger, he added, "Well, we can do dinner too."

Tou He grinned. "Then of course. I even know a place that'll cook up all that untainted spirit beast meat you have."

"Still remember that, do we?"

Another, wider grin from his friend. Wu Ying chuckled, swinging by a roadside stall to pick up some leaf-wrapped glutinous rice meals. He purchased a half-dozen for his friend and one for himself. Tou He murmured his thanks, digging into the meal almost immediately.

As they walked, Wu Ying let the winds out to play, relaxing his control such that wind swirled around the pair without his conscious intent. It tugged at robes, skirted under wagons, and picked at leaves, banging open shutters and carrying snatches of conversation and scents to the wind cultivator. Higher above, the slow swirl of wind chi covered the many li that made up the city, filtering the energy such that his Cyclone's Breath method never stopped refilling his dantian.

Just as importantly, the slow flow of air also brought with it notes and impressions of the schools that arrayed those hills. As Tou He had noted, each of those mountain schools were specialized colleges where promising cultivators were trained in a specific profession. Numerous scents came to him, from the farmlands filled with spirit herbs to herbal-scented apothecarist halls, to the dry smell of old parchment and the musky scent of animals held close together.

"What do you think?" Wu Ying asked his friend as they kept walking. "About their heresy?"

Tou He rolled his eyes, for a few passersby had given Wu Ying a hard look when they caught his last sentence. "There's nothing wrong with not seeking to ascend." The ex-monk flicked his hand upward, indicating the sky. "Their rationale about cultivation also seems quite convincing, if you're willing to look at it emotionlessly."

"What do you mean?"

"The Nanyue believe that cultivation was not given to us mortals to make us gods, but to make our lives easier. A gift, to allow us to contend against the spirit and demonic beasts that lurk at the edges of civilization."

Wu Ying nodded, having learned that much thus far from Yang Mu.

"If you consider the story of the Yellow Emperor and the time before him, humanity struggled, always at the mercy of such creatures till he spread the knowledge of cultivation."

"And because our lives were made easier, we should only use it for that purpose?" Wu Ying said doubtfully.

"Yes. Look at the Heavenly Tribulation," Tou He replied. "We know it is wielded by the Heavens to block ascension. The Nanyue believe even attempting to step further along the path to immortality is inherently wrong."

"Ah, but some believe that the Heavenly Tribulation is not a punishment, but instead an opportunity and a test at once. That one cannot ascend or achieve the next step without the lightning and chi from Heaven itself," Wu Ying pointed out.

"Perhaps. It's not what the Nanyue believe though."

The wind cultivator turned the corner, mulling over his friend's words before finding a gap in the logic. "If they believe that cultivation—and Heavenly Tribulations—are wrong, then why do they even have Core Formation cultivators? After all, are they not then actively defying the 'correct' usage?"

Tou He opened his mouth to answer, then paused and frowned in thought.

"It's because, Cultivator Long, of us." Yang Mu's voice cut in, catching the pair by surprise.

Wu Ying turned smoothly, an eyebrow rising at the fact that the wind had not told him of her presence. Or that he'd even missed her approach through his spiritual sense. Yang Mu had a small smile of satisfaction when she saw his face.

"What do you mean, Lady Cultivator?" Tou He asked. His eyes darted between the pair as he assessed them.

"The other nations, who have Core Formation cultivators," Yang Mu replied. "No nation can afford to be that weak. As it is, Nanyue only shook off northern ownership a bare hundred and eighty years ago."

"Conquest," Tou He idly corrected. "I doubt ownership is a term they'd prefer."

Yang Mu inclined her head, before looking at Wu Ying, who had failed to introduce them. At her pointed glance, he shook off his thoughts and introduced the pair before gesturing up the road to their residence.

"I was about to introduce you two anyway. And afterward, we were planning on sustenance. Would you care to join us?"

Yang Mu shook her head, making Wu Ying frown. "I have matters to attend to for my mother. But perhaps a drink, later tonight?" She gestured at the inn. "They have quite a marvelous garden at night."

Wu Ying glanced at Tou He, who shrugged.

"Tonight then, Mistress Yang," Wu Ying said.

Offering the pair one last smile, she sauntered off to her meeting, leaving Wu Ying wondering what it was that she had to deal with. And what, if any, news she might bring about their objective.

***

Later that evening, the pair stood to greet Yang Mu as she finally returned, the gong having rung for the second time[54] just before she arrived. As it was, the attendant who served the pair looked exhausted, though happy for the generous tips Tou He had provided. As such, food and drink had continuously flowed to their table within the garden of the inn.

Around them, their cultured green surroundings had been illuminated by paper lanterns hoisted onto nearby trees. The lanterns had been artfully arranged such that the few tables in the smaller garden received sufficient illumination while darkening the areas in-between. At the same time, the carefully trimmed vegetation provided privacy, while flowing water features throughout the gardens helped to mask conversations.

Under the cheerful, flickering lights, under clear skies for once, the garden was both friendly and just a little eerie. It attempted to mimic the wild growth of a real forest, and yet was too manufactured to one who had spent much of his life within. Instead, it felt artificial and strange, a child's nighttime painting of the real thing.

Yang Mu smiled at the pair, her hips swaying ever so gently, her long, lustrous hair glinting in the dark. There was a slight flush to her cheeks, a redness that marked the consumption of alcohol in dubious quantities. She slipped into a seat, followed by the pair soon after, and inclined her head in thanks as Tou He poured her a cup of wine.

"Are you sure you should still be drinking?" Wu Ying said doubtfully as she picked up the cup.

"Is this wine enhanced?" Yang Mu said.

"No."

---

[54] Traditional time-telling in China was a little different. There were two methods of speaking of time, depending on whether it was night or day. At night, the "geng dian" system was used, where the night was made of five geng, each of which was $1/10^{th}$ of a day, or two hours and 24 minutes. As such, the second geng would be roughly 21:36 (minus shifting of start time due to setting of sun, as the first geng is technically at sundown). During the day, the "shi-ke" system which divided the day into 12 segments, roughly two hours long each, was used to tell the time. For obvious reasons, I mostly don't get into specific times or use traditional timings.

"Then I shall be fine." She sipped on the wine, nodding appreciatively. "Excellent wine." She looked at Tou He. "A good choice."

"Hey! I could have picked it," Wu Ying protested.

Tou He and Yang Mu exchanged knowing looks, before Tou He spoke up, ignoring his friend who fumed in silence. "So how is it that you know my tasteless friend?"

"Oh, he's got a decent tongue for food. But wine and tea…" She let out a long sigh. "We met at my parents' inn."

Tou He made an encouraging sound, and Yang Mu happily chose to answer in detail, relating how they'd met and who her parents were.

"Twinned dao progression, all the way to Nascent Soul. Incredibly rare. And then choosing to raise their children, all of which have progressed well." Tou He shook his head in wonder. "You, my lady, are a rare creature indeed."

She laughed. "Is that not the case with most who have managed to achieve Core Formation? And even more so at the stage above. Enlightenment, privilege, or dedication, those are the hallmarks of our peers and betters."

"Talent too," Wu Ying added.

"Talent without dedication is like a beautiful girl who hides in her room. If not exploited early, it wastes away, leaving naught but the ashes of regret," Yang Mu said.

Tou He hummed in thought, turning the wine cup in hand as he stared at the reflections of light in the clear liquid. "Yet talent does not waste away in the same manner as beauty."

"But it is not coin to be hoarded for a rainy day. Its value is in its application and growth, not inherent in itself," Yang Mu said.

"Coin can be spent today or a year from now. It is still coin. But someone who is talented in the sword cannot pick up the jian and beat another who has trained for years, just because they were once talented," Wu Ying said. "An appropriate metaphor then."

"Then is talent no longer a concern at later stages of cultivation?" Tou He asked.

"Of course not." Wu Ying stared at his friend rather pointedly. He remembered how Tou He had breezed through the martial and physical portions of their training early on.

That his friend had not achieved the Heart of the Staff was clear, but that was perhaps a decision to avoid certain aspects of the weapon. For all that Tou He had left the monastery, certain aspects of his Buddhist upbringing still held true. Embracing the violent, crushing, and fatal nature of the weapon might be something he could not do.

Pushing aside those musings, Wu Ying continued. "Talent nurtured from the start and brought to our level would still provide an advantage. If anything, I would think that advantage is greater than before, as the continual progression of the talented allowed them to specialize and increase their advantage."

"Only if they concentrated on that which they were talented within," Yang Mu said, a secretive smile on her lips.

Wu Ying considered asking her, then chose not to. If she meant it as a barb against him, he deserved it. He had some small talent with the sword, but while he studied and practiced, he had numerous interests. And all of them took time and effort to exploit.

"Was your dinner fruitful, Lady Yang?" Tou He asked to cover his friend's silence.

"Very much so, Cultivator Liu. I was able to better grasp the city's current predicament."

At the pair's urging, she detailed her findings after speaking with her merchant contacts. There was little new to either party, though Yang Mu was able to elaborate on the actions taken by the army for both expeditions, along with the resources utilized and their future plans.

"A special team from their capital is on the way?" Wu Ying said, leaning back in his chair with a smile. "That'll complicate things, perhaps."

"Oh?" Tou He said, raising an eyebrow.

"Well, you're here to cleanse the source. I've been charged with learning more about it." While Wu Ying could have stayed behind and just received a report when the special team was done, the wind pressing upon him demanded he play a more active role. "And Mistress Yang…"

"And Mistress Yang what?" A single, graceful eyebrow arched, daring him to complete his sentence.

"Will do what she wants."

"Exactly." She shrugged. "In this case, it'll be to accompany the team when they depart."

Once more, Wu Ying wondered about her objectives. Yang Mu took great pleasure, it seemed, in their travels, in seeing the world and making new connections for herself and her parents. While she had amassed a princely fortune via her acquisitions, trade did not seem the focused passion that it was for her mother. It was, like his own Gathering, a profession that supported and gave direction to her travels but was not the objective in itself.

Swapping wine cup for rice bowl, Tou He ladled more of the spicy tofu hotpot onto it. As he prepped another bowl, he mused out loud. "It seems that we need to find reason to have the army commander or the lord magistrate to allow our presence."

"And I'm assuming an extra blade would be insufficient," Wu Ying said as he touched the hilt of his weapon. He'd retrieved the saint jian from the corpse after the battle, though now he needed to acquire a second or third as backup.

Good thing they were in Nanyue, fabled land of weaponry. In the northern kingdoms, weapons from Nanyue were highly prized for their quality and beauty. As he'd walked, Wu Ying had noted that the reputation of the weapons had been somewhat overblown. There were still weapons of shoddy make, mortal weaponry that was no better than farm tools.

But not entirely.

He'd noted a few weapons of great beauty and sturdiness in passing, and the wind carried the noise of hammering and production to him on occasion, speaking of forges that worked late into the night.

"Perhaps one wielded by you," Tou He said. "A prodigy of the jian is still a prodigy. But it might be a safer matter to ingratiate ourselves with the city lord."

"If we can speak with her."

"If we can speak with her," Tou He concurred.

"Well, Cultivator Long knows at least one direct report, no?" When Wu Ying looked confused by Yang Mu's words, she added, "The Guard Captain."

"Oh!" Then a slow nod. That might be a good introduction. Perhaps he might even be able to use Be Long to avoid speaking with the city lord entirely, if he could direct them to the correct individual.

"And yourself, Lady Yang?" Tou He muttered before consuming his bowl of rice.

Bemused, Yang Mu watched as Tou He finished the bowl within moments.

Wu Ying smirked as he added, "And that's after he's eaten. Took us nearly three hours before they were done cooking all the spirit meat I gave them. We also have a meal being prepped for tomorrow. Some of the cuts needed more time."

"Ah, I shall be sure to join you then." She considered, then added, "I'll invite some of my contacts, if that is acceptable."

Wu Ying glanced at his friend, who just shrugged. "I do not see why not," Wu Ying said.

"Good." Then, turning to the ex-monk, she answered his question. "I have some small skill with formations. I intend to visit the nearby school to review the formations they are using to cleanse the cores. My mother helped me work upon the formations we used for those cores that arrived at her village, and from my experience, we have a better solution than what is being utilized now. Certainly, our methods leave less taint behind."

"They are rather messy," Tou He confirmed. He set down his bowl and refilled it once more, checking with the pair if they wished eighths.

"That reminds me." Wu Ying extracted the earth elephant matriarch's core from his ring, opening the jade box to present the item to Yang Mu. "When you've integrated whatever you might learn from the schools here, I'd like to be present when you cleanse this one. I think there might be something to learn in that act."

"For the core?" Yang Mu widened her eyes in impish delight. "Of course!"

"Not for the core," Wu Ying said grumpily. He pulled back the box, closing it. "I do have some other lesser cores that can be used as payment."

"Well, will you at least sell it to me?" She fluttered her eyelids.

Wu Ying snorted at her overt games, though he was uncomfortable as well with exactly how well it worked. He was no blushing teenager. He should not find her as alluring. And yet...

He muttered his agreement. It was quite likely the wood cultivator could make good use of the earth core. It was not as though it would be highly efficient for him to use it to aid his cultivation, what with the clash between earth and wind.

She offered him a brilliant smile in thanks, and Tou He, watching the pair, smirked.

Missing the fire cultivator's silent regard, Yang Mu stood, downing her cup swiftly. "It is late, and there is much to do. Tomorrow. Dinner, yes?"

Receiving their agreement, she sauntered away.

Only when she had retreated far enough away that she could not overhear, did Wu Ying ask, "What?"

"Nothing, nothing at all." Then, before Wu Ying could demand further answers, Tou He pointed at the dishes before him. "Help me finish this, will you? I should rest too, but wasting all this food is a crime."

"You're the one who kept ordering!" Still, Wu Ying picked up his chopsticks, snagging some of the deep-fried pork before his friend took it all.

Chapter 17

Plans thwarted by the simple fact that Captain Ky would not be available till later in the day, Wu Ying left the gate. The smell of early morning congee and buns, fresh produce rolling in from the surrounding farmland, and breakfast consumed by laborers hurrying to work filled the morning, along with the underlying taint that Wu Ying had come to realize was becoming part of the city's makeup.

Concerning, in many ways. It was not something most would notice, not if they had not both the enhanced senses of a cultivator and the training and cultivation technique to sift through the myriad scents. He did, and he could tell that the taint had permeated the city in spots. The occasional guard, a mortal who smelled rank to him.

A beggar child, staring up at him, his clothing threadbare and his meridians clogged. The smell of old, badly cooked rat meat wafting from him, dripped oil and shreds of meat caught in unbrushed gums. Wu Ying paused for a long time, staring at the boy.

He could not save them all. It was not his place. His master would have spoken of altering fates and twisting karmic destinies, of threads that bound one tightly to this earth and curtailed one's rise to the heavens. His martial sister would have spoken of balance and the duty of bureaucracies and nobles.

But a letter read late at night echoed the most.

Your father takes the supplements provided by your friends, as do I, though not as often as he should. He thinks I do not notice, but he often passes them on to the children who clog the village now, many whom call him Master. He spends more time teaching them the jian than he does farming these days. If not for your largesse and that of your friends and the village's understanding, I fear they would have taken our farmland from us long ago.

He sees in them, you. Their excitement, their youth, their optimism. He sees a future beyond the village for them, among the sect and perhaps even in the lands your occasional letters speak of. He sees a future that he did not have and seeks to provide.

And I, I see grandchildren I fear I will never have. Perhaps we both do. It is strange, is it not, that cultivators seeking immortality are often the end of their line? It is an irony of the Heavens, and perhaps why they are so displeased by those seeking to ascend.

If all were to become immortal, what would become of earth and its mortal existence?

Do the gods truly care about mortals? Are cultivators walking the path to immortality forced to give up all mortal ties and mortal feelings?

Or is there another way?

Never mind me. I find that with your father busy teaching and you gone, I have taken to reading and knitting more to pass the time. It leaves me with long periods to contemplate matters of little importance.

Children who were the future, who he might never have. These were not his, it was not his place to interact and change their fate. And yet, his mother's questions rang through his mind.

Before he knew it, Wu Ying found himself buying out a stall, then another, sending the owners to offer the meal to those beggar children this day. And to that single child with his big eyes and missing tooth, for the rest of the year. A largesse that would have beggared him years ago.

Now, barely a consideration.

"And master…" Wu Ying waited for the steam bun maker to meet his gaze, allowing just a trace of killing intent as the wind played and tugged at both their robes. "I would remember that both good deeds and bad are seen by the wind."

And so speaking, he let the wind take him away. For a moment, he joined it, disappearing from mortal sight to drift over to another street before reforming. Dramatic, but sometimes, points needed to be made.

Small mercies, small changes.

In contrast to the larger changes enacted. Every step he took, he felt the massive cleansing formations spread throughout the city. Other, smaller ones were concentrated in the industrial quarter, upon the hill that he knew to house the formation master school. But there was a single larger one too. Limited by the city walls, enacted to cleanse the air and block the taint; to slowly draw it from one and all.

Incredibly inefficient, but at least, a step in the right direction.

Stopping at a roadside stall to purchase a sugar cane and hibiscus drink, Wu Ying debated his next steps. He could, of course, return to training or cultivating. A man could never have enough of either. Then, of course, the city was still an unknown factor. Spending the morning wandering the streets to learn its secrets, listening to the wind and mortals alike might glean unusual and unexpected benefits.

Almost, Wu Ying chose to do so. He might, perhaps, visit a blacksmith or ten to search for a replacement blade.

Then the wind blew again, tugging at a lock of his hair and bringing with it the smell of overturned soil and fresh-cut herbs. It was the smell of ripening fruit and flowering plants, a location filled with wood and earth chi. A gentle reminder.

"My thanks," he murmured, to himself, to the wind.

He downed the last of the drink, returned the cup, and turned aside to exit the city. The journey to the school would require him to traverse open land once more, but it was a small matter for the wind cultivator.

Barely an inconvenience.

He arrived at the green-and-gold paifang that denoted the start of *The School of Bountiful Sustenance*, stone staircases ascending in the distance. Wu Ying smiled at the majestic name, felt the slight touch of dao inspiration in the stroke of the lines on the plaque, a worldly infusion of intent in them. Looking at the words, one was bound to understand the writer's intent, to experience the feel of the earth beneath one's feet, the smell of herbs freshly cut or rice newly threshed.

The hill itself was unlike the others, all of which were left untouched but for the scattering of buildings meant to house their students. No, the School of Bountiful Sustenance's hill was altered, the earth cut away to create the stepped rice fields. Earth berms rose between the fields, closing off the land while drainage ditches and bamboo pipes guided water from wells and springs above.

Figures dotted the hill, moving through the routine of care and tending that were part and parcel of farming. With his spiritual sense unfurled around himself, Wu Ying could feel multiple formations twisting the environmental chi, amplifying earth chi to provide and conserve nutrients, adjusting the flow of wood chi to promote growth and healthy saplings. Water chi was drawn and converted to help sustain the various aquaculture stocks within the fields, while robust ground cover helped ensure firm footing upon the numerous paths ascending and descending.

Of particular interest were the farmers themselves. Most were in the higher grades of Body Cultivation, with a few standout individuals—often the overseers and teachers—in the middle grade of Energy Storage. He sensed no Core Formation cultivators among this group, though it was no surprise they might be higher.

After all, he felt the subtle pull of chi that concentrated toward the peak. Up there, where more than plain rice was grown, would be where those with the strength and expertise to handle more powerful and concentrated spirit herbs lived. He began to ascend, intent on meeting them.

"Are you lost, honored visitor?"

Wu Ying turned smoothly, offering a placating smile for the cultivator clad in a simple brown peasant tunic who'd greeted him. He carried nothing, though Wu Ying could sense a minor fluctuation in space around the man's fingers, a surefire indicator of a storage ring.

"No. I was but observing the fine school." Wu Ying gestured to the hill. "We do not have such an establishment where I come from."

"Of course. Nanyue continues to lead the world in our understanding and exploitation of cultivation techniques for the greater good," the man said.

Wu Ying made a noise to indicate that he had heard the man, though he felt no desire to confirm the other's statement.

Eyes twinkling, as though he understood Wu Ying's silent disagreement, the man put two hands together and bowed. "But my apologies for my rudeness. I am Thich Tuan Sy."

"Long Wu Ying of the Verdant Green Waters Sect. Are you a teacher here, by any chance?"

"I am." Tuan Sy inclined his head. "How did you tell?"

"You're very strongly wood aligned." Wu Ying gestured at the man's hands. "I can also see the hands of a farmer there." Never mind the darkness in his skin, even for a cultivator in the peak Energy Storage stage. Much like Wu Ying's own coloration in fact, though the man seemed to be more naturally tanned and less protected by his continued progress as a cultivator.

"And I yours." Gesturing to the path leading up, Tuan Sy said, "I assume that the famed Verdant Gatherer has questions about our facilities and training methods? Perhaps he wishes to peruse our library and trade some of his rarer stock?"

Wu Ying did not startle. He was beginning—reluctantly—to realize that to some people, his name would be known. He was no unremarkable farmer any longer, even if he might have preferred that. It was also not too surprising that a school dedicated to his profession would know of him.

In any case, it was to his benefit.

"I do, actually. Would Teacher Thich be able to provide some assistance in this matter?" Wu Ying said, following the man as they ascended the hill. He noted idly the way Tuan Sy flexed his chi, using a subtle qinggong method that connected him with the ground and let him rise up the hill at the pace of a swiftly cantering horse.

"I can. I am, however, only a small individual in our illustrious school. For much of what you desire, the principal or vice principal would be more suitable."

"Of course."

Wearing a small smile, Tuan Sy regaled Wu Ying with details about the school, slowing to a stop at times to point out areas of particular interest. A new irrigation method, a breed of rice they were testing that yielded more grains per stalk, a cultivator who had found enlightenment.

Enlightenment. How often Wu Ying noticed it, ascending the hill. It reminded him of the Sect, where individuals could be found seated in silence, caught in the middle of an action or flowing through a form before stilling as a glimpse of the greater Dao arrived. Moments when they would freeze and receive a Heavenly benediction for their insight.

He had forgotten how often that occurred in his own sect, having traversed the wider world for so long. A world where opportunities to embrace the greater Dao were overshadowed by the needs of daily life, the struggle for sustenance, a shelter over one's head and security against demonic spirits.

Here, in the safety of a school that catered to their needs, that taught and broke open preconceptions, these low-ranked cultivators found their first glimpses into the Dao. Wu Ying only sensed three such individuals on his walk up the hill, but even three was more than what he normally experienced in months living in a city.

Rare was the individual who found enlightenment among the press of humanity. An interesting commentary upon civilization and society, if one were willing to focus upon such a matter. Or perhaps a discussion on the natural state of mortals.

"As you probably noticed, we only have a few buildings," Tuan Sy was saying, as Wu Ying brought his attention back to the present as they neared the first of the major structures halfway up the hill.

"If one does not include the warehouses and greenhouses," Wu Ying said.

"If one does not include the warehouses and greenhouses," Tuan Sy echoed in agreement. "These are the residence halls for our newer members, who work the lower fields, as well as the local library for their use and the classrooms. Nothing in there that would be of interest to Cultivator Long."

"Oh?"

"Mortal rice, mortal fish," Tuan Sy said. "We teach cultivators the necessary skills to feed our population." A shrug. "Necessary, but not of interest to one as illustrious as you. Those students who progress far though, who have shown significant skill, are brought higher to more challenging works."

"Spirit herbs."

"Exactly."

"How do you handle those herbs that are impossible, or incredibly difficult, to cultivate domestically?" Wu Ying asked. That was, after all, the entire reason he had a profession. Some plants did not work well with others in near proximity, others took too long to grow, and some just died when domestic cultivation was attempted.

"Mmm… the same way your sects do, of course," Tuan Sy said.

A raised eyebrow greeted his non-answer.

Smiling, Tuan Sy said, "By making wandering gatherers quite welcome."

Wu Ying could not help but chuckle a little. "A good strategy that."

"It is."

Exiting the small mid-stage village, Tuan Sy carried on detailing the fields and the worlds they crossed, carefully probing for Wu Ying's knowledge and interest. The wind cultivator did not mind, for he knew that providing such information would smooth their trades later.

***

There were three things that a Gatherer prized above all. The first were the skills they utilized, whether it was the kinds of formations they could build, the methodology for extracting the most value out of a harvest, or even their ability to spot such plants in the wild. These were hard-won skills, requiring long hours of training, repetition, and often, a talent that had been polished.

The second was knowledge. Whether it was the information contained within their minds or kept within the numerous treatises and volumes they owned, whether base descriptions of various plants and their elements as well as their natural habitat or more complicated details about substitute herbs that might provide similar effects, without knowledge, a Gatherer was nothing.

Lastly, the third aspect a Gatherer prized were heirloom plants and gardens. The seedlings and cuttings, the plants that had been bred over years, germinated and cross-pollinated to provide greater harvest or to survive in unusual environments. Whether it was as simple as a Spirit Grass blend that flourished in the warmer months, sacrificing hardiness from cold, or a complex Fire Orchid graft that flowered seasonally, these heirloom domesticated plants were hoarded by Gatherers of the more sedentary variety.

After all, if one could not just wander into the wilds to acquire what one required, then it was only the unique strains one brought to the table that could bolster one's reputation. Wu Ying, of course, knew of such games of reputation and prestige, of favors and coin that were played by sect Gatherers. Even if, for himself, these games were of less import. His value, as a Wild Gatherer, lay in the first and second areas.

Still, it was not that he did not cultivate his own strains of herbs. The World Spirit Ring allowed him constant access to land, even while traveling. He grew fields of Spirit Grass, worked upon golden rice fields of the highest quality, and had entire orchards filled with plums, many infused with a variety of elemental chi. Over time, small living creatures had come to make his World Spirit Ring their residence—earthworms, flies, bees, and more.

Their flourishing had, of course, created its own issues. Larger mammals still could not exist within his World Spirit Ring. Their existence would strain the ring too greatly, for their greater souls would strain the dao inscriptions and increase the chi burden on Wu Ying. For a time, only the web of formation flags and constant pruning allowed the cultivator to alleviate the insect problem, till a balance was achieved. Even now, Wu Ying had to constantly pay attention as he introduced a variety of more complex but simple organisms, like frogs, to his ring.

For all his success in developing fields of spiritual herbs, Wu Ying was still one person. The variety that he grew was constrained by time and effort, his harvest benefiting more from benign neglect than studied care.

There were many herbs and plants he just could not grow. The amount of effort required to care for certain finnicky plants was enormous. Many of these plants were former wild gathered herbs, domesticated but still prone to failure without constant attention.

A small matter for a sect or a family or a school dedicated to such matters. Impossible for Wu Ying, who had multiple draws upon his time, who had not just a single greenhouse but entire fields and hills and rivers to watch. Such plants could only be thrown into the wild landscape of his own World Spirit Ring and wished the best before he moved on.

Even more importantly, Wu Ying lacked one aspect that these institutions contained— that depth of institutional knowledge and time that allowed multiple variations to sprout. An inheritance of past efforts that allowed one to test on trees and plants that might take years to sprout.

All of which meant that Wu Ying was at a disadvantage in certain kinds of negotiations with other Gatherers.

"We cannot trade the Divine Wind Ivy for such a small sampling of stock," Principal Nguyen said. "Surely you understand how rare such breeds are."

"I do, but at the same time, your Divine Wind Ivy has little demand." Wu Ying gestured at the table and its contents. Between the pair were the samples he had brought forth, breeds of plants that did not grow this far south. Some were seeds, lain dormant and safeguarded in jade boxes, others cuttings that had been preserved for grafting, or even newly sprouted plants, held in stasis by formations in the boxes they had been stored within. Each sample pulsed with the power contained with them, even as the wind danced in the lushly appointed hardwood room they sat within. "There are few cultivators who have need of such plant, even fewer apothecarists."

Principal Nguyen was already shaking his head when Wu Ying was half-done speaking. "Surely not. If anything, I am being overly generous to the Verdant Gatherer due to his prodigious reputation and with the expectations of further trades in the immediate future."

He gestured at the small cutting of ivy that floated above the table, the wind coursing around the still green leaves. "Caring for the wind ivy is quite taxing on our disciples. The fact that we continue to do so with so few customers is an argument that arises each year when allocating resources. Why bother, when we might not sell a cutting or even the leaves? Could we not put such resources to better use growing more fire or wood ivies? Dedicate precious student time to another?"

Now the principal let out a long sigh. "Such arguments continue, and so when a customer arrives, we must make them pay for all the resources already spent to some extent. In this way, we can justify the cost for the future again."

"And yet, if I purchase nothing today, then all those resources are wasted," Wu Ying said.

"Yes. A hard dilemma, for both of us. But I say again, we cannot sell you a cutting—a cutting no less—for such meager returns. Surely the great Verdant Gatherer has more to offer."

"I do, of course. But as the honored principal suggested, we have much to discuss. I would not want to trade all that I have immediately." Wu Ying gestured to the side, in the direction of the library that the pair had visited—briefly—before he had been ushered over to the tearoom to discuss his presence with the principal. "Access to your library and copies of your records among them."

"Then, perhaps, let us discuss that," Principal Nguyen said. "A simple trade, that will include all that you have offered and what you desire along with access to all but the highly restricted works of our library for a period of a week."

"And those works…?"

"Number eight manuals," the principal replied, cutting down sideways as if dismissing the topic. "All for plants and findings that we would not trade with you at all."

Wu Ying raised an eyebrow but received no further answer from the unspoken prompt. In the meantime, he reached for the teacup, light floral notes reaching his nose as he raised it to his lips. He was content to wait till he received further explanation.

Eventually, the principal sighed. "We have restricted plants and other herbs gathered from poison practitioners and other dark sect practitioners. Plantings watered with the blood of innocents, yin-infused corpse flowers, or poisonous roots. Forbidden practices and cuttings, but knowledge that is still important to keep. Though not distribute."

Wu Ying grimaced. "I see. Then I am happy with that exception to our trade. Such things are of little interest or use to me. Still, we have not discussed price for such expansive access."

"A copy—a full copy—of your notes."

"A big request."

"It's a big library," Principal Nguyen said, eyes twinkling.

"Which perhaps might make it less useful for myself," Wu Ying said. "After all, I am but one person. Finding the pearls among the dirt would be difficult."

"We can dedicate one of our senior librarians to you."

"For the whole week," Wu Ying said. "That way, they can copy what works are of interest to me."

"No," the principal said immediately. "This deal favors you much more then."

"Do you think so?" Wu Ying cocked his head. "Your school is vast, its lineage deep. I will not have access to most of your plants after I leave. Much of your findings will have to be replicated by those I might trade with, and even then..." He gestured around him. "Few would have the environment or resources to duplicate your work."

"Mmmm... we would ask that you not trade such learnings within a kingdom of ours," Principal Nguyen said. "There is, of course, little worry within our kingdom, as we share such information freely, but would not give our enemies such an advantage so freely."

"You have many?" Wu Ying said, slightly amused. He nodded to the quiet attendant, who glided forward and refilled his teacup and placed a small snack plate of semi-spherical cookies before them. The wind cultivator had tasted the cookie before, the soft crumbly texture of the dessert pairing with the sweet sesame paste within quite delightfully.

"Many what?" Principal Nguyen said, pushing the plate of sweets toward Wu Ying when he spotted the man's eyes drifting downward.

"Enemies." Giving in to temptation, Wu Ying took another.

"None right now," the principal said. "All hostilities have ceased at the moment. But a man as traveled as you are is cognizant of such political concerns, and the future."

Chewing upon the slightly sticky central filling, careful to wield his wind to send crumbly flakes of pastry to his plate, Wu Ying considered what had been said. And not.

His notes, for theirs. He could, of course, shortchange them, hold back certain volumes since they would not know the full extent of his wanderings or what he had gained. Allowing them to take his work and make copies would certainly benefit the school, see more Wild Gatherers in competition perhaps. But…

It would not be by much. Many of his notes were for environments unlike the ones the Gatherers of Nanyue lived within. The geography, the plants, the animals, and the mix of elements dictated a unique set of collectable herbs—and the pills that supported the growth of the cultivators within that environment. Like him, they too would struggle to make use of his notes of the everlasting, wintry north without access to the plants that grew there.

In the end, what tipped his decision was a simpler moment of understanding. Were he to pass away, all his notes, everything that he had ever gathered would be lost. And mortal as he was now, that might still happen. In the spread of knowledge, he would gain a degree of immortality over and above the stories told of him.

"If you promise to make a second set to be delivered to the Verdant Green Waters if I fall," Wu Ying said, "then we have a deal."

Seeming surprised, Principal Nguyen leaned forward. "Are you expecting to pass away soon, Cultivator Long?"

"The taint affecting much of your city and the spirit beasts. I seek to deal with them."

"You alone?" More surprise.

Wu Ying tried not to take offense at the tone. "There is an expedition arriving soon that will set out to complete the task. I shall join them, if I can."

"A special unit, yes." Principal Nguyen's lips thinned. "Our special units are quite prideful. I fear they will not accept your presence so easily."

"Surely they would not turn down another blade," Wu Ying said. "Or an individual whose experience in the wilds likely compares to theirs at the least."

"Ah, but in our lands? With our beasts?" the principal said. "Surely you know that much can change."

"Of course." Wu Ying turned over one of his hands, revealing a cloth laced with simple enchantments sewn into them. Flipping the cloth open, the smell of tainted chi immediately burst forth as he revealed the beast core within. "And who but me has more experience dealing with a changing environment? Surely a taint that could alter the spiritual core of a magnificent animal like this must have seen changes in the nearby environment."

A smile crossed the principal's face as he interlaced his fingers. "You want my recommendation as well, then?"

"It would not hurt."

The principal fell silent, considering the request. Meanwhile, Wu Ying chose to enjoy the snacks, allowing his wind to drift in from the open window, bringing with it whispered secrets great and small. That the occasional seed or spore drifted into his ring to be planted and grown, well…

The wind blew where it willed.

Eventually, the principal met Wu Ying's gaze firmly, resolve anchored deep within. "Your terms are acceptable. Let us begin then, for I believe there is much to do if we are to have you suitably prepared."

Chapter 18

The rest of the day saw Wu Ying browsing the stacks after their negotiations were complete. He had eventually managed to purchase the cutting at a price that was acceptable, if a little painful. When he was certain none were watching, he replanted the cutting in his World Spirit Ring, watering and tamping the ground down gently amidst a sprawling trellis, before turning his attention to the library.

As good as his word, the principal had been quick to assign Wu Ying a senior librarian. Their intimate knowledge of the library guided Wu Ying to works and treatises that could supplement his own stores of knowledge, the pair flipping through numerous scrolls and manuals together.

Over time, their focus turned to a few specifics, the first a simple overview of mundane plants and spirit herbs in the surrounding countryside to bolster Wu Ying's local knowledge.

The second area of focus was additional works detailing the ecology of neighboring countries and lands. Such treatises would allow Wu Ying to prepare himself should he choose to travel even farther afield from Nanyue—now or in the future.

The third category of work was the notes about grafts, cuttings, and other spliced breeds the school had undertaken. This section took up two entire floors of the massive school library, and only after judicious questioning and narrowing of interest to spirit herbs that Wu Ying had access to or could grow farther north—or in his own World Spirit Ring—were they able to narrow the massive amount of information available to a manageable workload.

For the first two category of works, Wu Ying was able to outright purchase directly reproduced manuals. That saved reproduction time and would allow him to read the works at his leisure while the enormous amount of information he had requested was recopied by the senior librarian.

Reluctant as he might be, Wu Ying chose to leave the library as dusk fell. His head buzzed with images and words, sketches and even samples, for some portions of the library had included dried and pressed herbs where appropriate. As much as he wished to stay, he had an appointment with his companions.

Leaving the senior librarian to his work, Wu Ying spotted a tainted avian predator in the distance as he returned to the city, a creature filled with rage and greed. It swooped from the sky to dive at a farmer, wings tucked in and its claws extended to snatch the man from the ground. Within moments, it tore off, leaving behind a fallen hat and a screaming populace, with neither Wu Ying nor the nearby patrol able to do more but watch from a distance as the creature hastened away.

Under that grim portent, Wu Ying strode to the restaurant Tou He and he had made arrangements with for their spirit beast meat. He found the restaurant owner waiting, effusively grateful that his establishment had been chosen for such a momentous undertaking.

Yet after a series of politely worded thanks, the proprietor nervously shifted from foot to foot rather than leading Wu Ying to their private room upstairs.

"Yes, *laoban*? Is there something else?" Wu Ying asked, knowing there must be.

"I said nothing, Honored Cultivator. I told my people not to speak either but…" He ducked his head low in embarrassment.

"Others have learnt of the feast?" Wu Ying said, the wind whispering of what it had seen above.

"Yes, Honored Cultivator. I fear that a number of missives and young lords and ladies have arrived, seeking to umm… introduce themselves to you and your guest." With his head lowered, Wu Ying had a good view of the sweat upon the balding proprietor's scalp, the man's nervousness all too apparent in both his actions and scent.

Wu Ying understood. The proprietor was caught between angering a pair of cultivators who had sufficient strength to acquire massive amounts of untainted meat and the powers that resided within the city. Displease one and they might level his establishment—or refuse to pay for the work undertaken. But if he chose not to speak with Wu Ying, life in the city would be impossible.

"Show me these missives," Wu Ying said curiously.

He considered what meats they had left, how much had been made. He knew it was too much for the three of them to consume, even with Tou He's massive appetite. Of course, much of the food could have been stored away for a later date, which had been the initial plan.

Still… "We have space for how many?"

"Eight others, Honored Cultivator." Gesturing, the proprietor called for his servants.

Seven then, since the man knew not of Yang Mu. Moments later, the servants arrived, carrying with them plates of invitations. Wu Ying's eyebrow twitched as he stared at the numerous scrolls, simple invitations or declarations of intent.

"How many of those are in the Core Formation stage? Or of equivalent rank within the government or army?" Wu Ying asked.

"Uhh…" The proprietor hesitated, clearly not wanting to answer.

"Let me review that." Yang Mu's voice cut in, a fan coming up to gently push Wu Ying aside from behind.

He shifted to allow the young lady to approach the documents, the fan snapping shut and disappearing a moment later as she plucked and sorted the scrolls. Seals were glanced at, many set aside with only a few held for further examination. Wu Ying shook his head at the proprietor who had moved to object to Yang Mu's actions. Realizing that Wu Ying was not objecting to the matter, the proprietor relaxed and stepped back, casting worried glances into his dining room now.

Curious, the wind cultivator allowed his spiritual sense to turn that way. While he had it running passively in the city, it was entirely defensive. There was no reason to focus that sense upon others, for courtesy's sake if naught else.

Eight individuals, the good majority women with only two men seated within. Differences in clothing and perfumes spoke of different sexes and tastes, from floral to masculine notes. At the same time, he prodded at their auras, noting that not a single cultivator within was above Energy Storage. Most were in the peak or near peak stage of the second stage though, a good showing for the city.

A spiritual whisper slipped through the air from Yang Mu, alerting Wu Ying of her focus. "What is your goal here?"

Calling forth the wind to hide their words, Wu Ying carried on the discreet conversation. "To have dinner."

"Well, this is no longer a simple dinner, Cultivator Long. So, what is your goal here?"

He could not help but grimace. When she was right, she was right. So… "We have but one goal, do we not?"

Yang Mu broke into a wide smile. Moments later, she had discarded all but four of the scrolls, rolling each of them up and offering them to the proprietor.

"Inform the owners of these documents that we would be pleased to see them in an hour." She tilted her head upward, looking through the wooden flooring with her spiritual sense before she added, "I will need that time to adjust the chi in your rooms."

"Madam Cultivator…"

She turned her gaze on him and the proprietor ended up bobbing low in acquiescence. As she started up the stairs, Wu Ying patted the proprietor on the shoulder in sympathy. He too understood not wishing to deal with Yang Mu when she was intent on a task.

"We have two more seats and some local prodigies," Wu Ying said. "What do you wish to do with them?"

"Ask your friend. I care not." Her answer drifted down the stairs.

The proprietor glanced at Wu Ying, only to be dismissed with a wave. Together, he and his servants hurried after Yang Mu as the messages were relayed via runners, her voice already rising as she barked out new orders.

True to her words, moments later, Tou He arrived. Spotting an opportunity, Wu Ying grinned at the bald cultivator, who instantly looked wary.

"Why are you smiling like that? It scares me."

"Oh, no. Nothing scary at all. Just a small problem. You see…"

***

Wu Ying strode up the stairs, well pleased with himself as he left his friend. He stopped at the landing where the hapless proprietor stood, watching Yang Mu command his servants. On the second floor, through an open door, Wu Ying saw her stalking the edges of their private room, a chi compass in hand, taking readings and muttering to herself. Occasionally she shoved a chair sideways or moved the table an inch one way or the other or ordered the servants to remove a piece of furniture and look for a mirror or painting.

Meanwhile, Wu Ying sensed Tou He being mobbed by the Energy Storage cultivators. More than a few of the ladies were plying their wiles against him, as was one of the men, much to the horror of the ex-monk. Better him than Wu Ying.

Yang Mu paused, slippered foot tapping on the floor before she pointed at Wu Ying. "You. Come here and take out that sword of yours. I need you to carve some formations on the walls."

"I do not think the proprietor will enjoy you defacing his building," Wu Ying said even as he followed her orders.

"He'll be fine. I'm adding a permanent cleansing formation in here. It'll remove the impurities from the air and ensure any that might have seeped into our food since he has begun cooking is dispersed. It'll make dining in this room—and his establishment in general— much more agreeable for cultivators."

Even as she spoke, she extracted a series of yellow talisman paper. Using her chi to hold them aloft and wielding two outstretched fingers like a brush, she burnt words and formations into the paper before flicking her hand sideways, letting the papers plaster themselves to the wall.

"Why not just use the talismans?" Wu Ying asked.

"They would not last our dinner." She snapped her fingers and pointed. "Well, get to it."

Wu Ying frowned but ambled over to the nearest document. He had a lot of questions, like the depth he should carve the formations, the order of words to begin carving. All were answered, he soon realized, as he stared at the talisman stuck to the wall. Somehow, Yang Mu had managed to infuse a degree of her own dao understanding of formations into the talismans, such that the inscribed characters were an instruction manual that he need only follow.

Much like a child might follow an outline on a wooden block to learn to draw.

He marveled at the ability she had so casually demonstrated before another snap of her fingers reminded him of her request. Drawing his jian, he raised the weapon and carved into the wooden posts and walls. Sword intent flickered from the tip of his weapon, sharpening and thinning, deepening and twisting as per her instructions, the metal never touching wood.

As he worked, more and more talismans dotted the room, sometimes appearing even on top of previously carved locations. Wu Ying followed the order of the talismans as they appeared, the formation whorls and words forming all across the room as he traversed walls and ceiling, the wind picking at the falling wood to gather it in a corner.

Together, they wove a delicate dance of chi, sword intent, and formation creation. As he worked, flashes of errant chi would spark, swiftly drowned out by the smoothing application of Yang Mu's aura. It was a reassuring presence, a scent that reminded him of peaceful glades and bubbling hot springs amidst lush greenery. A heady presence that comforted and invigorated at the same time.

Time became immaterial, only the next formation to be carved, the next talisman that intruded upon his serenity. Movements became rote, Wu Ying fallen into a trance where time no longer had meaning.

And then, time crashed into existence once more.

No more yellow talismans hovered in the air, each carved piece of yellow paper discarded and gathered by the winds in a corner beside Yang Mu. As Wu Ying reasserted his sense of self, the formation master retrieved the papers and wood shavings to deal with them later.

Floating in mid-air in the room, sensing the formation beginning its work, Wu Ying commanded the wind to lower him. He gently floated to the floor as he tasted the altered chi, the pull of the runes surrounding them. The introduction of cleansed chi, like a refreshing breeze where before, a slightly rancid smell had hung around them all.

"My lady…" The proprietor wrung his hands, staring at the glowing runes, the lady, and Wu Ying in trepidation. He kept his head bowed, speaking to the floor. "I cannot pay you for this."

"Who spoke of payment?" Yang Mu snorted. "I did this myself."

"But this is too much."

"It is done, laoban. It is too late to worry about payment. Consider it a gift."

The man flinched at her abrupt tone, lowering his head further. Curiously, Wu Ying walked over, stopping a short distance from the man. Now that he was present once more, he could smell the cold, rank sweat of fear arising from the other.

"What worries you?" Wu Ying said.

At first the man would not speak. Then, he whispered hesitantly, "I cannot keep this. We do not have the backing to have something so grand. It will be taken from us. This building, this business. It will be taken from us. It's too much for me."

Yang Mu frowned. "Go on."

"There is nothing more to say." The proprietor drew a deep breath, straightened himself, and put on a smile like a prisoner going to the executioner. "I apologize for my unseemly behavior. Your gift, it is generous. I shall ensure you have the most magnificent meal tonight."

Turning, he hurried away, swiping at his eyes as he turned the corner.

"I do not understand," Yang Mu muttered.

Wu Ying could only smile sadly as he watched the man leave. "I do. I should have thought of it."

"Then explain it," Yang Mu said. "Why would he fear this working? It is magnificent, if I say so myself."

"Exactly."

"He did not object when I told him what I intended!"

"He might not have understood all that you meant to do. Did not understand what it would mean, till it was too late. How can any mortal comprehend the differences between a temporary formation and a permanent one?" Wu Ying sighed. "I did not till now."

"Surely the city lord will not allow such a thing?"

Wu Ying considered pointing out they knew nothing of the city lord. Whether she was corrupt or incompetent. But instead, he chose to say, "The individuals who would take action would likely be friends of the city lord. Or otherwise know her."

"Then he needs a protector. Someone who will help stop this from happening."

"I'm sure the proprietor knows that too. However, such connections are not so easily made and always come with a cost."

He understood the man better than Yang Mu did. She had never grown up fearing for her life. Fearing that everything she had struggled for, everything she'd made would be taken away by the whims of the powerful. She had been the powerful, even if humble.

Voices came from the staircase, interrupting their conversation. From below, Tou He led their guests, two young ladies gliding upward proud as peacocks. When Tou He met his friend's gaze, it was with heat and a dare for Wu Ying to comment.

The wind cultivator declined.

In short order, both women were introduced, followed soon after by those Yang Mu had invited. Those who came were not alone, though the majority of their various entourages were left below. As each new guest arrived, the proprietor was sure to announce them.

"Principal Le Khac Duy of the beast-rearing school." Muscular, stocky, and bearing a morose visage, the man was clad in dark browns even during this evening's festivities.

"Nguyen Chi Hieu of the Eight Spiral Arms trading house." Surprisingly a younger man. Like most of the Nanyue, he forewent wearing his hair long, keeping it close-cut with bangs falling over the front of his face. He hunched over a little as he walked, as though attempting to hide his presence.

"Captain Ky Be Long." The proprietor looked surprised at the appearance of the guardsman, who also looked somewhat bemused to be here.

"Captain Ky, a pleasure to see you again," Wu Ying said. He did not twitch when Yang Mu sent a missive to him via spiritual talk for his ears alone.

"I invited him directly, since gaining his support is important."

"Thank you. I must say, this is an unusual gathering," Captain Ky said, offering a nod to Wu Ying. "And Lady Yang Mu, it is a pleasure as always." This time, his smile became more genuine even as he stepped closer. "You are as radiant as the sun, as always."

She smiled, twisting her hand to call forth a fan to cover her lips. "Oh, my. Captain Ky, you're such a flatterer. Such a change from before."

"I was on duty before," Be Long said. "Now, I may pursue my own pleasure and not my lord's wishes."

"Pleasure is it..." She fluttered her eyelashes at him.

Wu Ying frowned, even as Be Long stepped closer and guided Yang Mu toward the table with just his presence. A flash of annoyance ran through Wu Ying as she laughed at another of Be Long's jokes, her fan lowered to show gleaming teeth.

Then the proprietor was speaking again, making another announcement. "Abbess Pham Thu Giang." When he said this, the proprietor dropped into a deep bow for the woman who entered, flanked by two of her nuns. The group were all clad in the typical orange robes of their order, their heads shaved entirely clean. "You honor me by gracing my poor establishment."

Wu Ying frowned then. "I… Abbess. I am uncertain if we have sufficient foodstuff that would suit your palate."

"I am sure it will be fine, will it not, Laoban Sai?" Thu Giang said with a smile. "My nuns have brought some minor gifts as well, to aid with that."

The laoban looked stricken, before Wu Ying gestured for him to take care of the matter. Nodding firmly, the proprietor scurried off with the two nuns following him, heading down the stairs to the kitchen to deal with the sudden change in the meal plan.

"I am surprised to see you here, abbess," Wu Ying commented as he gestured for her to follow him.

Tou He was casting wide-eyed looks at Wu Ying and the abbess, and taking pity on his friend, Wu Ying guided the abbess to a seat away from the ex-monk.

Teasing was one thing, but Wu Ying knew that his friend had quiet misgivings about leaving the monastery early on. Though it was said to be over diet, Wu Ying knew that there were deeper considerations than just whether meat was bad. But disagreement or not, Tou He was still deeply religious. After all, even now, he kept his head shaved, held to many of the principles of Buddhism, sought peace, and offered aid when he could rather than harm.

"I'd heard rumors of a powerful ex-monk from the north arriving in my city, seeking to provide aid with our most recent troubles." Staring at Tou He, who looked away, the older lady added, "Regretfully, I have not been able to speak with him." Wu Ying noted a slight flush appearing on his friend's cheeks. "When I received such a generous invitation, I could not decline."

"Ah…" Wu Ying's lips pursed. It seemed that his minor dinner had caused more of an occasion than he had expected.

"These formations…" Abbess Pham looked around, peering at the walls and the ceiling. "Freshly carved and empowered. And quite adroitly made. It is like stepping into a spring meadow. Your work, Cultivator Long?"

"No," Wu Ying said. "Or, only peripherally. I am but the carver. The formation mistress is Lady Yang." He gestured to where she stood, scandalously close to that oily captain. "Did you want to speak with her?"

Now, the abbess had to force her lips still at his tone of voice. He might have sounded a little too eager with that last sentence. "Over dinner perhaps. But I fear you have another guest. And no one to introduce her."

Wu Ying took his leave with a smile, stopping at the edge of the staircase. The woman who was ascending had an aura of power that had nothing to do with cultivation but of mortal authority and presence. In fact, she was barely a middling Body Cleansing cultivator, but the pair of guards standing behind her spoke of her importance.

"Who is this arriving?" Wu Ying muttered, using the wind to send the words to Yang Mu.

"Oh! She did come," Yang Mu exclaimed out loud. Ignoring the puzzled look from the captain, she excused herself to join Wu Ying. "Cultivator Long Wu Ying of the Verdant Green Waters Sect, known far and wide as the famed Verdant Gatherer, may I present to you Mistress Quach Thuy Ngan."

"Mistress Quach," Wu Ying said, bowing to the woman. He could sense that she was stuck at the peak of Body Cultivation, a deplorable lack of progress considering her age and the resources she likely had. Even looking at the gold and jade that surrounded her fingers and neck spoke of significant wealth, and yet, nothing.

"The Verdant Gatherer." A finger rose, tapping her lip in thought. "Prodigy of the sword. Wandering hero of justice at times, a thief at others. Supposedly disgraced and banished from his own sect, and yet he stands here next to an Elder of that very same sect. How interesting."

"Mistress Quach is too kind in her estimation," Wu Ying murmured as he stepped aside for the woman. Her bodyguards followed, one splitting to guard the door, the other to stand behind her chair. "I fear you have me at a disadvantage."

"Yes. I've heard that too. A man who rarely bothers to do his proper research before his travels, instead choosing to let the wind take him where it will."

"Fate wills us where it will."

"If I ran my family the way you do your life, it would be a failure within three years." Thuy Ngan looked at the chairs beside her, placed as she was next to the abbess, then pointed at the empty seat. "Cultivator Yang, you will sit with me."

"Of course, Mistress Quach."

That left Wu Ying on the other side of the abbess, Tou He almost opposite him, and the others seating themselves soon after. The captain, he noticed, had managed to place himself a seat over from Yang Mu, though the merchant—Nguyen Chi Hieu—was between them. That, of course, meant the principal of the beast-rearing academy was on Wu Ying's other side.

"Do not take offense at Mistress Quach. She has always been that way," the abbess said, patting Wu Ying's hand. "She was a horrible student as a child, impatient to forge ahead even when she had not mastered the classics. Too smart, I fear, for her own good." A small smile. "It is a wonder that she has managed to grow her clan so well, even with her shortcomings."

"Shortcomings…" Mistress Quach sniffed. "You are still looking well. Are you eating the herbs I have sent to the monastery?"

"The temple is grateful for your generosity. Many of my nuns have progressed well because of that generosity."

"You know I meant it for you." Thuy Nyan's eyes narrowed. "Why do you insist on being so troublesome?"

"*Om Amideva Hrih.*"

Sniffing, Thuy Nyan spoke to Yang Mu. "I have heard much of your recent exploits and the goods you have brought south. Numerous core formation stones, untainted. Do you have more?"

"I do, Mistress," Yang Mu replied. "Though I'm not surprised that there are not more arriving. The journey south was a little hazardous."

In short order, the pair were discussing the trip to Liang Soong, Thuy Nyan ignoring the rest. Yang Mu had a glint in her eyes, one that told Wu Ying she was plotting something. The way she cast a glance at the proprietor as he came by spoke perhaps of what she might be planning. He wished her the best of it, knowing that it was her mess to solve.

Meanwhile, Wu Ying offered the abbess a grateful nod for elucidating on Mistress Quach's place in the city before turning to his other companion.

"Principal Le, I have heard that Nanyue takes beast-rearing in a somewhat different direction from the kingdoms I hail from. Both in the kinds of beasts you have and the methodology," Wu Ying remarked.

"Oh, yes," Principal Le said. "We have quite a variety of beasts, including some monkeys and other companions that are not common in your kingdom. In addition, because of our surplus of beast cores, we are able to raise more such creatures than the north." A darkness shadowed the man's face. "Or it used to be. This new taint has made things difficult for us."

"How so?"

"We cleanse the cores we receive as best we can, but eventually, for those beasts we have to feed, some grow tainted. The taint in the air, of course, does little good." He let out a long sigh, looking down. "More than one promising creature has had to be put down, as their forms and dao twisted."

"A tragedy."

"Very much so. We can only hope that the special unit can solve the problem."

"Mmmm…" Wu Ying hesitated, considering if he should mention his desires.

Before he could resolve his thoughts, the abbess cut in. "Cultivator Long, will you join your Elder in the expedition then? I understand you have some skill with your sword. And of course, as a wild gatherer, much knowledge of the backwoods."

"Oh, you're intending to join the special unit?" the principal said, sounding surprised.

"If they will allow us."

"Interesting." He cocked his head. "I must admit, I know little of yourself or the Elder." A nod to where Tou He continued to hold court with the young ladies, even as the servants arrived to place the first of the dishes on the table. "I wonder what you think you might bring in addition to your martial skills."

For a moment, Wu Ying lamented his peaceful meal. It seemed that dinner was going to be less about their meal and more about growing support for their inclusion in the upcoming expedition.

"Well, Principal Le, did you ever hear the story of the time Tou He and I fought a demonic cultivator…?"

Chapter 19

One dinner, a couple of frank conversations, and numerous visits to the various schools around the city and the arrival of the special unit later, and Wu Ying and his friends found themselves summoned to a meeting with the city lord, army command, and the head of the special unit itself.

The meeting was held in the central residence of the city lord, a building that stood multiple floors above the surroundings and where numerous buildings, garden, and walls set it apart from the rest of the city itself. Each of those buildings housed members of the municipal government, everything from the bureau of records and granaries to the bureau of education and enlightenment.

Dark clothed figures scurried between paved walkways, arms clutching stacks of paper as they traversed the ground, similar in appearance and demeanor to the buzzing insects that sought to feast upon blood or processed paper. Wu Ying had learned that there was an entire department whose purpose was nothing more than the reproduction of older works as the ongoing heat and humidity saw to their eventual destruction.

Yang Mu led the trio on foot, seeming to know their destination. No wheeled conveyances were allowed within the bounds of the municipal grounds, and the trio had declined the use of the palanquin that had been offered, even though the grounds were awash with mud, leaving the paved walkways dirtied. Numerous workers cleared the muddy ground, using brooms and shovels galore.

Perhaps regretting the choice to walk, Yang Mu strode ahead, her lips curled up in disgust. Only the exertion of her aura kept the mud from dirtying her robes as she marched onward, mud flung from the soles of her feet to be caught on the winds and discarded.

Behind, Wu Ying, floated above the entire issue. In doing so, he barely disturbed the mud, and the little that was caught by the gusting wind was sent away to splatter behind him or to the side.

Tou He, on the other hand, ignored the dirt, happily tromping over the paved, if muddy, paths. Each splatter of mud showed on the green-trimmed, black robes in stark relief, though it seemed to bother not the man. As he passed, his fiery aura dried the mud on his robes, leaving dry footprints and shavings of earth behind.

"I'm certain they're going to try to bully us out of the expedition," Yang Mu said—again. "So you both need to be careful not to give them an excuse. In addition, if we bow to their authority at all, they'll attempt to place us under their command. And that, we cannot accept."

"Why?" Tou He said innocently. "Surely it is their expedition."

"Their third expedition, after two failures," Yang Mu said. "I do not trust them to succeed this time either."

"Then why join them and not go alone?" Wu Ying said. If she was this doubtful, why had she not raised her concerns before?

"Because there is safety in numbers," Yang Mu said. "And I have picked up hints that the previous expeditions were not complete failures. They have gleaned information of our opponent, and that might be the difference between success and failure."

"So we need them," Wu Ying said.

"And they us." Yang Mu tilted her chin upward. "Even if they do not know it."

They crossed another dozen steps before Tou He muttered to Wu Ying, "She's quite confident, isn't she?"

Wu Ying could only smile. In truth, he dreaded the idea of working for the army. The few times he had been involved with the army or army personnel he had been gravely injured. And while he understood that the circumstances were different, old scars rarely healed cleanly.

"Shall we let you lead the conversation then, Cultivator Yang?" Tou He said.

Yang Mu turned to Tou He, searching the ex-monk's face. Suspicion died upon his innocently beaming face. Turning to Wu Ying, she raised a single, inquiring eyebrow.

"He's just like that," Wu Ying replied to her unasked question.

A slight moment of hesitation, then she nodded firmly. "Yes. Let's do it that way. After all, they're more used to women leading the way here."

Wu Ying had to agree. The city lord was female, their current queen was the same. In fact, the entirety of their inheritance laws were matrilineal—though they had some complexities that Wu Ying was still attempting to understand. Belatedly and lackadaisically admittedly, as he had more than a few subjects to study. Ranging from expanding his command of the language, translating the documents offered to him by the school of Harvesting and Gathering, and amusingly, exploring a new avenue of research.

Spirit beast and spiritual herb coexistence and mixture. Of course, he knew and applied aquaculture to his own rice fields. But the Nanyue had taken the mixing of spirit beasts and spiritual herbs to a whole new level. They raised spirit beasts just for their manure, had them consume certain herbs to enhance the byproducts, allowed them to dig and otherwise till soil to enhance the side effects, and even improved the distribution and growth of wild cultivated plants by adding digestion and dispersal by spirit beasts to the equation.

Fascinating area of study and one that Wu Ying was enacting even as he walked, wielding his will and chi in the bounds of his World Spirit Ring.

The trio were shown into the meeting room, cups of tea and small snacks already distributed. Captain Ky was a familiar face, and by clothing and personality was Lord Xam. Which meant that the colonel of the special unit, Huynh Bich Trang, was the last member.

Bich Trang was, surprisingly, short. If she was even five feet tall, it was because of the hair that had been piled upon her head and tied off in a tight bun. Yet for all her lack of stature, she had an air that drew the eye, a quiescent tiger rather than a slumbering ox.

She was also impatient to get started, for once introduction had been made, she leaned forward and thumped a hand on the table. "Why exactly are you three forcing your way onto my expedition?"

As agreed, the pair glanced at Yang Mu, who sat forward, her hands turning over to show her palms. "The concerns of Nanyue are the concerns of the world, for yours is the beating heart of cultivation. Without the spirit stones that flow northward, progression becomes significantly more difficult for cultivators in the Middle Kingdom."

"And why should we care if you progress?" Bich Trang sneered. "The entire act of immortal cultivation as practiced by the Middle Kingdom is an affront to the heavens itself."

"Yet the trade between the two kingdoms is a guarantee of peace," Yang Mu said. "Constant and consistent trade is a boon to Nanyue. From the north, you receive supplementary rice and meat shipments, from the south, fruits and vegetables. The Middle Kingdom provides Nanyue the majority of the iron it needs for the creation of its famed weapons, along with the various storage vessels and formations that allow you to exploit the land around your city to its fullest. In addition, mercenaries from the north arrive regularly, seeking fame and fortune in your cities, helping do battle against the demonic beasts that assail your cities. And yet…"

"Yet?" Captain Ky asked.

"I noted few coming south during our travels. Few in the city itself," Yang Mu said. "The tainted cores are not in demand, not by the mercenaries."

"Did you know all that?" Tou He sent to Wu Ying through spirit communication, his lips barely moving.

"I did." Only because Yang Mu had told him on their trip south, but Tou He did not need to know that. "Shush now. She's working."

"We do not need mercenaries to protect our cities," Captain Ky objected.

Wu Ying raised a single, elegant eyebrow. He recalled their first meeting, the demand of three Core Formation stones to allow their entrance. The captain chose to ignore Wu Ying's pointed look.

"In the short term, certainly. But the beasts grow stronger, and Nanyue lacks the numbers of Core Formation cultivators to fight them all off," Yang Mu stated.

The city lord shifted in her seat, looking unhappy at the bluntly put situation. Yet she chose not to contradict Yang Mu or even speak at all, waiting to see what the commander had to say before she intervened.

"You speak endlessly about why dealing with the taint is important, but nothing about why you three are pushing to join me," Bich Trang said.

"Is it not clear? We are a significant increase in strength to your expedition," Yang Mu said. "I have skill with formations that can be useful depending on the source of the taint. Containing it, closing it, filtering it further… all of it might be necessary." A gesture at Tou He. "The Verdant Green Waters Elder is a strong fighter who carries a cleansing element in his flames. He can directly do what my formations might fail at. And I'm certain his Sect did not send him down without additional external aid."

Tou He offered a bright smile but chose not to explain. The city lord gained a considering expression at the mention of the sect and additional external aid.

Finally, Yang Mu gestured at Wu Ying. "And the Verdant Gatherer has more experience with the deep wilds than most. His knowledge of plants and changing environments will be useful, if the taint has spread far and wide. Nor should his skill with the sword be underestimated."

Bich Trang shook her head. "I have members in my unit who can do all that you have spoken of and more. I have trackers and formation masters, a physician and pill apothecarist who can aid with dispelling the taint, multiple individuals with skills in weapon arts. You people bring nothing to the table."

Yang Mu nodded before raising a finger. "Perhaps. But we also are not members of your unit. Nanyue has always lacked high-level cultivators. Losing more on an expedition would be a greater loss to you than us."

Tou He and Wu Ying shared a startled glance, neither having been expected to be offered as warm bodies.

Yet for once, Bich Trang looked pleased by what Yang Mu had said. "Then you are offering to face the dangers ahead of my people?"

"We are offering to face them with you." Yang Mu leaned back. "Or you can go ahead without us. And we'll follow after."

Bich Trang snorted. "Lord Xam could have you kept back. Thrown into jail even. Endangering a military exercise is a serious offense."

"She could." Yang Mu inclined her head. "But I believe she sees the wisdom of including us in your expedition. Already the schools have seen significant losses from the taint, as have the harvest of your farmlands. It can only grow worse. If you fail—"

"We will not fail," Bich Trang said.

"—the next unit to arrive might take months. Already, the city's resources are strained." She gestured to the north as she continued. "Never mind the fact that a weakened Liang Soong is a tempting target. Once Nanyue loses the gateway to the north…"

"Are you threatening us?" Now Lord Xam spoke up, coldly.

"Not at all," Yang Mu said. "Just detailing the dangers that Colonel Huynh might not understand. The military are not always cognizant of such greater concerns."

"The military is what holds the fortress of Liang Soong," Bich Trang said. "We are well aware of any designs on Nanyue." Changing tact, she smiled grimly at the trio. "Which is why your addition is concerning. After all, what is to say you three are not looking to sabotage our successful completion of the mission? As you said, a weakened Liang Soong is a tempting target."

Tou He spoke now, brows drawing down over shaved head. "The abbess will speak of my motives and character. And I, in turn, can vouch for Cultivator Long. He has risked much for the greater good of cultivators, whether in the State of Shen or otherwise."

"And my parents are well known to Lord Xam," Yang Mu said. "They have no interest in such greater politics."

"And yet, you are here."

"Curiosity drives my own journey now. Though aiding them in understanding the damage done to their spirit core supply is something I, a filial daughter, can do."

Still Bich Trang looked unconvinced.

Recalling what Yang Mu had hinted at earlier, Wu Ying spoke up. "Your danger is not from any of us. The taint is not something a member of the orthodox sects—or even a heretical sect member—would indulge in. What I have sensed, it is demonic in nature. Left too long, this tear or rupture will eventually draw powerful demonic creatures from their realm. It will twist the Dao of those that exist nearby and empower them in ways that are anathema to our existence. Perhaps its presence is even a precursor to an invasion of demons to this plane."

A demon, without the strict controls of the immortals of hell, would wreak havoc upon all that it encountered. Hungry, angry, vengeful, or vicious, it mattered not. They would savage all they came across, and in so doing, cause untold destruction.

"So, you do know something of our true problems," Bich Trang said quietly. There was new consideration in her eyes, one that set the hair on the back of Wu Ying's neck aright. It was not, he would say, hungry but cold. Calculating. Then he blinked and it was gone.

"Only in small degrees. Let us help," Wu Ying answered. "Or see your land corrupted and see the heavens take action. And watch as such action causes untold damage to your charges."

The room waited with bated breath for Bich Trang after that pronouncement. Her face was unmoving, a carved rock of sullen regard, but one hand clenched tightly beneath the table, unseen to mortal eye but all too clear to the Core Formation cultivators in the room.

Slowly, she nodded acquiescence. The city lord pursed her lips, then nodded back before turning to regard the trio. And the real negotiations began.

Chapter 20

With the expedition leaving the next morning, Wu Ying hurried through the streets on a final errand. Yang Mu was handling the last-minute negotiations with the unit, and there were, surprisingly, a significant amount. It amazed him how much talk there was for such a small expedition, but the military had their way of doing things and it involved a lot of paperwork.

Spending so much time discussing matters, ingratiating himself, and learning over the past few days had driven the thought of purchasing a proper backup weapon from his mind. Now, Wu Ying sought to remedy that failing, seeking to purchase a new Saint-sword.

It would be a shame anyway, to come all the way to Nanyue and fail to buy a weapon. Working through the metalwork district, he caught sight of well-crafted weaponry all around him, the master works of each shop displayed prominently to attract the public.

The quality of such work ranged, the minimum showcased reaching at least the Spirit level. On occasion, he spotted a Saint-level weapon on display and those caused him to slow down. A massive guan dao, placed prominently beneath the sign of a shop displaying the polearm. A paired set of short, handled axes sat farther within another blacksmith's shop, their sides inlaid with polished gems and precious metals. The blades themselves were of the highest quality, infused with a light enchantment whose intent Wu Ying could not grasp fully. A Dao of the Home? Homecoming?

He shook his head, turned on his heel, and hurried on before the blacksmith could spot him. He had no use for a pair of axes. Their brutal techniques were anathema to his elegant jian. And while he understood the wielding of the weapon on a base level—all short melee weapons, to some extent, were similar—he had no true skill in their use.

Hurrying deeper into the warren nest that was the metal-working district, Wu Ying soon found himself outside a massive three-story building that marked his journey's end. On the bottom floor, the building was open on three sides to allow heat and fumes to escape, careful flues and chimneys aiding in that process. Additional enchantments glowed along high ceiling beams, helping to contain the warmth as a dozen blacksmiths worked hard under the aegis of a trio of overseers.

"Cultivator Long." A young female clad in a tight dress that hugged her body in a way that was beyond scandalous greeted him. "If you would follow me, the master of the house awaits you above."

"How did you know who I am?" Wu Ying asked. He did not sense any danger from her or the house itself, so his question was more out of curiosity.

"There are few enough individuals with the Heart of a weapon that even a single one is of interest to our master," the saleswoman said. "One whose Heart is that of a weapon my master specializes in? He knew you would visit us soon enough."

Wu Ying smiled as he admitted she was not wrong.

At her welcome, he entered the building, taking the stairs to the next level. She directed him past the open retail center of the second floor, where numerous weapons were displayed, to a second staircase. Even as he crossed to head above, Wu Ying spotted polearms and butterfly swords, triple staves and axes and knives galore. However, the majority of the space was dominated by the dao and jians that the few customers within perused, all overseen by attentive salespeople.

"The Single Blade Armory specializes in the jian, does it not?" Wu Ying said, getting a confirming nod from the young lady. "Then why the numerous other weapons?"

"Master Vu feels that a solid base in understanding of all weaponry is required for a blacksmith to call himself a proper smith." The answer came easily and smoothly, as though it was an often-repeated answer. Which, Wu Ying assumed, was likely the case. "It is only later, when their base skills have approached an adequate level, that Master Vu feels it is appropriate for an apprentice to specialize."

The third floor consisted of a large waiting room and a trio of enclosed rooms opposite the entrance. It was to the middle room that Wu Ying was guided, the saleswoman knocking on the door before being called within. As Wu Ying waited on the doorstep, he allowed his spiritual sense and wind to dance across the surroundings.

Both doors on either side were connected to the middle room, with the door on the right leading to a simple washroom. The one on the left, however, rebuffed both his aura and wind, formations locking down the space. While Wu Ying could not sense within, minor fluctuations in the environmental chi and the dao spoke of a space dao in play.

An extradimensional storage room, one that likely safeguarded the most precious equipment. After all, Wu Ying had not noted a single Immortal or even Saint weapon on his journey to this floor, a stark contrast to the other blacksmiths.

"Cultivator Long Wu Ying greets Grandmaster Vu of the Single Blade Armory," Wu Ying said, bowing low as he stepped into the office. The wind cultivator was only mildly surprised when his guide stepped in as well, moving to take position on his side of the table and readying refreshments for him.

The room was a simple box, bereft of window or fresh air. A series of cabinets lay at the back wall, a large and dented desk before him, and the owner sat behind it. Perhaps of most interest was the scarring exhibited along the hardwood, reinforced walls, as though numerous men had taken weapons to them.

The man who sat behind the desk, awaiting his arrival, had looked to be sleeping, his eyes shut tightly as he rested. Grandmaster Vu had the hallmarks of an older athlete—or blacksmith in this case—one whose body had long ago betrayed him. The once-bulky frame had shrunken on broad shoulders, while liver-spotted hands rested, clasped on his lap. At Wu Ying's greeting, he leaned forward to sip his drink, eyes still closed. Fingers trembled as they touched the teacup, the cup shaking a little as it was brought to parched lips.

"Cultivator Long. You took your time coming to see me," Grandmaster Vu said.

"My apologies, Senior. I had many tasks to fulfill." Wu Ying glanced at the seat before him and, at the older man's nod, took it. He thanked the young lady as she offered him the cup of tea, even as he turned his full attention to the older man.

Something about him set Wu Ying's senses on edge. He was but a Body Cultivator, not even a peak one, but the wind spoke of danger and a cutting edge to the man. His very aura brought with it a taste of metal and a sharpness like a razor, leaving Wu Ying sitting lightly on his edge of his seat.

"Hmmphff. I'm inclined to send you away rather than sell my babies to you," Grandmaster Vu said.

"That would be unfortunate. I have heard many tales about the Senior's great skills. How there is no greater swordsmith in the entirety of Nanyue."

"Don't think idle praise will help you." Grandmaster Vu sniffed. "I know my standing and it is not the greatest. Old Yue in the south still outshines me. But good luck getting a sword from him." The old man smacked the table with amusement. "He only makes weapons for the Imperial Court. Utter waste, for most of those fools could not cut a bound pig to save their lives."

"I bow to your greater wisdom." Mimicking action to words, Wu Ying inclined his body a little. "Would it be possible, at least, to see your creations?"

"See them, he says. As though they are fish in a market." Grandmaster Vu waved dismissively.

The motion, so languid, so relaxed, put Wu Ying's hair on edge almost immediately. His aura hardened reflexively, and the wind cultivator flicked a finger that gripped the teacup upward as he wielded his own aura. It clashed with the blade projection the old man had directed at him, only for Wu Ying's to shatter upon clashing with the Grandmaster's.

Only when the attack struck his aura did it dissipate, the winds surrounding him swirling in agitation. Wu Ying's hair was blown back, for sharp as the attack might have been, it had only the strength of a Body Cleansing cultivator behind it.

Yet as fast as Wu Ying had destroyed the blade projection, it was not enough. Grandmaster Vu continued to move. Each movement poured chi and blade intent into the action, sending blade energy at Wu Ying.

Lips pursed in annoyance, the wind cultivator shifted his aura. The wind whipped up around them, gaining an edge that cracked against the grandmaster's attacks. At the same time, he swirled his teacup, using the motion to generate additional wind chi, lacing his understanding of the sword into his aura to form a tiny cyclone of blade energy and chi above his teacup.

The motion caught the attacks flying at him from below, no longer directly contesting the attacks but pushing them upward. The conflicting attacks met above Wu Ying's arm, pushing them away. Rather than facing the dense attacks of the grandmaster, Wu Ying sent them away, letting them further scar the wood.

"Are we done?" Wu Ying asked as he allowed the cyclone of blade energy to die away, lifting the teacup the rest of his way to his lips.

"Not a complete lie then," Grandmaster Vu muttered.

"A lie?"

"You have no heft to your blade, boy."

Wu Ying felt realization click into place at the man's words as he placed the teacup down. "That's what is embedded in your Heart of the Blade, isn't it? Your dao understanding of metal, of blacksmithing, and the heaviness of a strike." He frowned a little. "You gained the Heart of the Dao via swordsmithing then?"

"Not just that." The old man snorted. "As though one could truly understand a blade without wielding it."

Curiously, Wu Ying tilted his head. "Are all your blacksmiths swordsmen then? Are all masters and grandmasters swordsmen who've gained the Sense or Heart of the jian?"

"Are all martial cultivators able to Sense or delve into the Heart of their weapons? Or are as many of them naught more but base thugs?"

Wu Ying considered for a moment before he shook his head. The majority were not, though… "The strongest often are."

"Often is not always. And martial art knowledge is intrinsic to the work. Understanding a sword and how it is wielded is required to create a remarkable weapon. Some might even argue that the time spent learning the weapon to this extent detracts from the actual process of creation," Grandmaster Vu said. "I disagree, but that is my belief. And my Armory's."

"Have I passed your test then?" Wu Ying said. "Or shall we destroy more of your office and disrupt your granddaughter's hair?"

Now, Grandmaster Vu looked surprised. "You can see the similarity?"

Wu Ying turned to the silent girl whose plump, baby fat cheeks and sparkling eyes, along with the neat bun, were nothing like the old man's before him. Neither jawline nor nose were similar, and her slim and plentiful build was too soft for the current shrunken figure or the formerly muscular aspect of the blacksmith. He smiled and touched his nose in answer, knowing the stories that were told to him.

"I smelled it."

"Like a bloodhound."

Wu Ying chose not to answer nor elaborate on his skill. If not for the minor thread of metal in both their auras, more prominent in the peak Energy Storage young lady, he might have missed it. Of course, the fact that she carried a pair of blades in the small of her back, hidden by careful cuts of the cloth, had drawn his attention in the first place.

"The swords?" Wu Ying asked.

The old man slumped in his seat, the minor explosion of energy seeming to desert him suddenly. "Go, child. Bring in the three."

"The three?" Surprise now, from the granddaughter.

"Did I stutter? Or do you think I'm senile already?"

"I… yes, Ong Ong[55]." She bowed, then hurried toward the silk cloth that blocked sight of the doorway that led to the dimensional space.

Wu Ying noted the small enchantments on the cloth that sought to divert his attention and make him look anywhere but the doorway itself.

"Stop peeking. It's rude," Grandmaster Vu snapped. "She's not for sale anyway."

"I was more curious about your armory."

"Neither is that."

"Such a large dimensional space. Are you not worried of it breaking down?" Wu Ying asked, locking eyes with the old man.

"What's the use of a big clan and all this coin if you don't spend it, eh?" Grandmaster Vu shook his head. "My useless third son-in-law is at least able to do something useful, if not give me more grandchildren to spoil."

"I find the idea of you as a doting grandfather difficult to imagine."

"Heh. That's because I'm not. Beat them till they learn how to hold a hammer and strike steel properly, that's what I do!"

Wu Ying shook his head at the image that brought to mind. Yet there was enough of a twinkle in the man's eyes that Wu Ying felt that perhaps he was not as harsh as he made himself out to be. Even his earlier test, dangerous as it might have been, was guarded, for he had never targeted a lethal location. Furthermore, interacting with the heavier sword strike had allowed Wu Ying to grasp a different form of the Heart of the Sword. A concept that he might be able to incorporate into his own understanding.

Eventually.

His thoughts were interrupted as the granddaughter returned bearing a trio of sheathed jian. She placed them on the table between the pair, then gently extracted the blades from their sheaths, laying the weapons alongside their coverings in parallel to one another.

The moment the blades were released, Wu Ying could only stare open-mouthed. The difference between these weapons and the ones a floor below… no, even the other Saint-level weapons he had spotted while walking through the streets was night and day.

The tales of the talent of Nanyue swordsmiths all paled before the truth displayed before him. Wu Ying reached for the sword, his hand hovering over the nearest weapon but not yet daring to touch them. Instead, he sensed the weapons, noting how their presence warped the environmental chi around them.

"These are enchanted," Wu Ying said quietly.

"Bah! Enchantments are a waste of a good weapon," Grandmaster Vu said distastefully. "Used only by those who are unable to wield a hammer properly or control their fire." At the

---

[55] Grandfather in Vietnamese

wind cultivator's frown, the old man pointed at the weapons. "Do you see any markings, any etchings on my blades? Anything that would weaken them?"

"No."

"Exactly! Why would I do such a thing?"

"But then…" Wu Ying gestured at the swords.

Each of them had twisted the environment around themselves, with differing aspects being showcased. Around the leftmost weapon, its hilt and sheath wrapped in dyed and bleached white leather, frost had gathered. Not upon the blade itself, but on the table and the air above it, such that tiny snowflakes formed and fell.

The middle weapon seemed to drink up the light, such that it was hard to see the blade amidst the shadows it seemed to draw into itself. The black-wrapped blade spoke of the promise of a silent death under its sharpened edge, a merciless passing of ignoble ends.

Compared to the first two, the final blade was the least showy. No external effects were visible, not on the blade nor their surroundings. Instead, the blade was but itself, silent, deadly, razor-sharp. Yet Wu Ying's gaze kept drifting to it, a part of his soul and dao resonating with the weapon.

"You see it too then." There was a satisfied tone in Grandmaster Vu's voice as he spoke. "What all my time and effort managed."

"Yes." A hesitation, then Wu Ying said, on instinct that there was more, "And no."

"You don't think these are worthy of you?"

"I don't see the final results of your efforts."

Silence greeted his words, and Wu Ying tore his eyes away from the weapon to regard the old blacksmith. Lines deepened on the man's face, such that he looked more prune than man, before an errant breeze tickled the old man's nose. He let out a loud sneeze, not bothering to cover his mouth, and rubbed his nose afterward.

A minor exertion of will ensured that none of his expelled air ever reached Wu Ying, though hazy droplets intensified the snowfall around the leftmost blade. Wu Ying barely caught the long-suffering sigh from the granddaughter, as she regarded the newly dirtied weapons.

"Damn wind." Grandmaster Vu thumped the arm of his chair. "Damn child. Don't even think about trying to wield mu masterpiece. That one is meant for a better man than you." A whisper then, so soft that Wu Ying was not certain he was even expected to hear it. "If I ever find someone with the Soul of the Sword."

"And you'd gift this weapon to one who did have it?" Wu Ying said, cocking an eyebrow.

"Why, you know one?" Grandmaster Vu said peevishly. Before Wu Ying could answer, he waved dismissively. "What kind of fool do you think I am, to give away my wares? If they truly had the Soul of the Jian, they would pay everything they owned for *that* weapon."

"Really."

"Do not sound so doubtful. It is everything I have learnt and understood, the pinnacle of my skill and talent. I poured my heart and soul into its making." Another gesture at the three swords. "These are but mere playthings to it."

"I see." Then remembering their earlier topic, Wu Ying prodded. "Playthings that don't require enchantments."

"You won't give it up, will you?"

"A customer who buys a weapon without understanding it fully is a fool," Wu Ying said. "I am no fool."

"Could have fooled me." Silence, before the Grandmaster shrugged. "It's simple. There are no enchantments because it is the sword itself that calls these effects into being. Enchantments are but the external imposition of a dao and will upon the world, shaping it by their swirls and runes and formations. These swords require none of that—for they are the imposition of such concepts into the world."

"Their very being is an enchantment," Wu Ying said, understandingly.

"And more powerful for that."

"Of course."

One could not forcibly increase the energy or strength of such an enchantment, not empower them with a spirit stone like with a formation flag. Enchantments were even less flexible than carved formations or environmental hazards embedded in the earth. Yet they also required the least amount of upkeep, these swords turned enchantments. For their very being had been turned to their purpose.

"Shuang. Ying. Ren.[56]" The names came to Wu Ying, unbidden.

The blacksmith regarded the wind cultivator with a degree more respect. "You see, child? This is what you want from a customer. Someone who can perceive the weapons for what they are, truly. He might be ignorant, but he sees true."

"I understand, Ong Ong."

"Which will you choose?" Grandmaster Vu asked.

"I'm allowed to choose?"

"Do you want me to pick for you?"

Wu Ying smiled wryly at the man's prodding, his gaze darting over the three blades. In the end though, he reached for Ren. Something within him called to the weapon, called for it. However, before he could touch it, the old man slapped a hand on the table.

"Oy! You pay before you take," Grandmaster Vu said, leaning forward. "What kind of city did you grow up in, that you take what is not yours?"

---

[56] Frost, shadow, and edge of blade respectively

"No city," Wu Ying said. "I'm just a simple farmer. And we mostly traded among friends and village members."

He leaned back in his chair, even as the granddaughter stepped forward to sheathe the other weapons. She went to store them, leaving Wu Ying and her grandfather to negotiate over the remaining weapon.

Which, Wu Ying noticed, the old man had already made him express a strong desire for, removing at least one tool of negotiation. Damn merchants and their tricks. From the predatory gaze that the formerly sleepy old man turned on him, he realized he was in for quite the bargaining session.

Still, he had no intention of leaving this room without the jian. One way or the other.

Chapter 21

"How much did he take you for?" Yang Mu pressed, the next day.

The trio were on horses, waiting near the southern gate for the arrival of the special unit members. By internal agreement, the trio had chosen to arrive earlier than their scheduled departure time on the off chance the colonel would attempt to leave without them.

"Too much," Wu Ying replied, his hand drifting once more to the hilt of the sword by his side. Sheathed as it was, the intensity of the blade was hidden. Yet even a glimpse at the scabbard and hilt had been sufficient to inform Yang Mu of its origins and price, after which she had interrogated him.

"You should not have gone negotiating without me," she said. "Or at least asked me beforehand. I could have told you he was a wily merchant. How do you think he came to own the largest shop in Liang Soong?"

"I would think his obvious mastery as a swordsmith," Wu Ying replied.

"Oh, please! As though the best craftsmen are the best merchants." She sniffed. "It's thinking like that allows us to thrive."

"It's thinking like yours that makes everything more complicated and expensive than it has to be."

"Ah, so you think craftsmen should just give away whatever they have, or that the time and skill they've put into learning their art should be discounted?" She snorted. "Did you give away your rice then?"

"When a family was hungry, we shared what we had."

"But swords aren't rice."

"Though they can save lives too."

She nodded. "Yet not every sword is the same. Rice might taste different, but the end results are the same."

"Final result?" Tou He, listening to the two of them argue, a wrapped steamed bun with a slice of meat in one hand, mumbled through his full mouth.

"For most people." Yang Mu's gaze rolled down to Tou He's handful of buns.

Wu Ying added. "Final being to be shat out."

Yang Mu twitched, glaring at the wind cultivator. "I was about to say to provide sustenance. I would never be that crude."

"You forget, I was there when you fell into that mud pit during the leech swarm," Wu Ying said.

"You were never to bring that incident up again!" She shook her head. "Now I'm glad he took you for all you were worth."

"Not all," he replied.

A flicker of a memory, of being forced to wield his final card in the negotiations. The name of a boy who had achieved the Soul of the Sword. Being forced to scribe a letter to him, to inform him of the weapon that awaited his hands, if he ever sought one that suited his skill.

That it might be years before Pan Chen was old enough to take hold of the weapon or dare the journey, Wu Ying had not informed Grandmaster Vu. Some things, some secrets and individuals were best served by being mysteries. Even if he had confirmed that his own progress to the Heart of the Sword had come from studying under the sword saint.

For all that, for the jian that he now carried, Wu Ying found himself once more nearly penniless. Having to divest himself of nearly all his coin, precious stones, and hoarded spirit stones had barely been enough to satisfy the old man. The wealth that had served him well before, the spirit herbs and rare pills formed from surplus product offered to him by apothecarists, were of little interest to the other.

"Bah! Then he obviously isn't as good as he's rumored to be, what with the way you keep stroking that sword." Yang Mu sniffed.

Tou He suddenly laughed.

"What?" they asked in unison.

"Just remembering a friend of ours," Tou He said, gesturing with the half-eaten bun between Wu Ying and himself. "She'd have made the same joke about sword stroking, but unintentionally."

Yang Mu's eyes narrowed. "And you think I'm talking of his other sword?" She sniffed. "Why would I ever discuss that?"

Tou He raised a single, skeptical eyebrow. She met his gaze, but slowly a blush crept up her cheeks before she turned away. Whether she blushed because of the impertinence or just her blatant falsehood, who could say?

Wu Ying could only smile a little. Whatever he and Yang Mu were—and they still had not spoken of it directly—it was more than friends. Perhaps, one day, more? It was a different relationship, for sure. Slow-growing, friendship coming before lust. A rather nice change.

Silence fell between the group, the wash of passing mortals filling in the surroundings.

Finally though, the special unit arrived. A group of five, the army unit all dressed in similar, armored outfits. Each of the light, hardened leather plates they wore were subtly different in design and significantly varied in format from the uniforms of the regular army personnel.

"Are you ready?" Colonel Huynh Bich Trang said as she arrived, astride her own horse.

"We are. Though perhaps we could be introduced to your companions?" Yang Mu answered, her gaze flicking over the other four. An even split among the others, two men and two women.

"We can talk on the road. We have delayed long enough," Bich Trang said, clicking her tongue.

Her horse pushed ahead at her command, through the open city gates. When they were nearly a hundred feet from the exit and the hubbub around the gates had subsided, they sensed a disturbance behind them. Wu Ying kept track of who noticed it first, his head bent low. The army unit's scout was the first to sense the disturbance, his head turning all the way around. Whether alerted by the movement of her man or sensing it herself, Bich Trang was next to shift.

Then almost simultaneously, two others in the army unit, leaving the scholar who rode with a book open before her as the last to realize something new was happening. And even then, only because a companion grabbed the reins of her horse to stop it from riding into Tou He's.

"Who is that?" Yang Mu asked, standing a little on the stirrups of her horse to peer at the growing dust cloud. She gave up as her steed shifted beneath her, annoyed at her movements and agitated by the crowd of other mares around it. Placing a hand on the neck of the horse and stroking it to calm her mare, she looked at Wu Ying for an answer.

"Why ask me?" he said.

"You're telling me the wind hasn't told you already?"

Wu Ying offered her a guilty grin, eliciting a series of strange looks from the new members of their group. He shrugged to them all. "I speak with the wind. Sometimes, it even answers."

As though to contradict his words, a breeze woke up, sending leaves and dust swirling around them all and startling their steeds, who shifted and tossed their heads. All but Tou He's, for his horse was just as placid as its rider. In fact, while waiting, the ex-monk had removed another bun from the bag tied to the side of his saddle.

"So, who is it?"

"Captain Ky." Wu Ying cocked his head as the wind drifted around him, whispering secrets. Eventually he nodded. "It seems he is packed for travel."

"What is this?" Colonel Huynh snarled, spurring her horse to intercept the captain. The pair slowed when they met, the mortals on the road moving aside to give the pair of cultivators room.

Wu Ying waved, dismissing the winds who insisted on bringing their words. He needed not the details of their conversation to know the gist of it. Instead, he spoke to the four other members of the army unit, offering them a friendly smile.

"I am Long Wu Ying of the Verdant Green Waters Sect. It is a pleasure to meet you all, fellow cultivators. May the heavens smile upon our expedition."

"You should have come on time," one of the men said, eyes narrowed, his face thin and sallow and pinched. "If I had not noticed your earlier presence, it would have caused trouble with the fates, your early arrival. As it stood, we had to adjust our departure for you. Now that one…" He sighed, touching his belt. "Do you think I should start calculating the adjustments to our star charts?"

"I do not think—" Yang Mu began.

"I was not asking you," the other man snapped. "I do not need an amateur to tell me how to do my job."

Yang Mu's lips compressed white at being cut off.

"My apologies, Lady Yang. Minh Trac has not been sleeping well," said the other male in the group, the portly scout offering the trio a friendly smile as he clutched his strung bow with his other hand. "Being our formation master and fortune-teller, Sargent Minh has not had much sleep since our assignment. Fortunes keep changing, he says. I am Bui Dinh Don."

"There's still no reason to be rude," Tou He noted.

"That wasn't rude. If I was being rude, you'd know it," Minh Trac said waspishly.

"Then perhaps you need a lesson in proper manners, if you did not think that was rude," Wu Ying said.

"Picking on our weakest members already." Moving her horse with just the touch of her feet, the speaker shoved back Minh Trac's mare and put herself between him and Wu Ying. Her massive guan dao was a little different. The wide, heavy metal shaft suited her overly large hands, but it had a shortened shaft to make it easier to wield in the forest. The weapon rose and pointed at Wu Ying as the woman spoke. "Suits me well. I have wanted to test your blade."

"Oh, Wu Ying…" Tou He said with a mournful note in his voice. "What is it with these women and your sword? You were such a quiet, respectful gentleman before. Now, look."

"What are you implying… monk?" The polearm-wielder said that last word with a sneer, the tip of her weapon changing direction toward Tou He.

"I am Liu Tou He, Elder of the Verdant Green Waters Sect. And I am no monk," Tou He said genially. "Though I once treaded that path, it was, in the end, not mine." He raised his hand to offer the vine-woven bag to her. "Buns?"

"I will show you buns!"

Guiding his horse between the two, blocking off his own unit member, Dinh Don stuck his hand in the bag to extract three of the steamed buns. He threw one to the fighter, forcing her to lower her polearm as she caught it rather than let it bounce off her chest. "Eat, Thien Giang. You're always so angry when you haven't eaten."

"I'm angry because these fools dare threaten us—"

"And you too, Phuong Vy." Dinh Don's voice grew softer, more considerate as he offered the bun to the last member of the unit.

At her name, the scholar looked up from the manual she had been reading, frowning at the food offered to her. "That'll stain the pages."

"Only if you don't pay attention."

"It'll stain the pages."

Dinh Don rolled his eyes in a good-natured way. "You didn't eat breakfast. Or dinner. Or lunch yesterday. You cannot subsist on chi alone. And we're on a mission. So put the book away and eat."

Phuong Vy closed the book with a snap, rolling it up and tucking it in her robes before taking the offered bun. "Fine. Only because we're on a mission and the colonel will be angry otherwise."

Grinning in triumph, Dinh Don took a bite of the one he had kept for himself, letting out an appreciative moan. "Good bun. Where did you find it?"

Tou He was more than happy to try to describe the location, though not knowing the name of the streets, he was forced to rely on remembered landmarks and vague directions. The pair fell into a loud and robust conversation about food, even as the other members of the unit fell back.

Eventually, a cantering noise alerted them of the returning colonel and captain, both of which looked entirely unhappy.

Rather than explain, the colonel waved down the road. "Let's go. We have a lot of ground to cover."

"Is he joining us?" Minh Trac asked, a scroll propped up on a small traveling case that sat precariously on his saddle.

"He is."

"I'm going to have recalculate all our fortunes again," Minh Trac growled as he extracted the I Ching compass. "You. What's your birth date and sign?"

"I… what?" Captain Ky said.

"Birthdate and sign. Hurry up!"

Shaking his head, Wu Ying guided his horse to follow Bich Trang, murmuring a little command for the wind to help keep track of the aggressive Thien Giang. After all, he doubted their minor conflict was over yet. And while Minh Trac seemed like the kind to be rude, the woman was the kind who spoiled for a fight.

In truth, he was not willing to let it go either.

As for why he was so furious, well, that was his problem.

Chapter 22

The rest of the day passed in relative peace—if you called warding off intrusive personal questions from Minh Trac peaceful. The fortune-teller seemed to not understand why anyone would be unwilling to discuss their personal details, muttering about the lack of accuracy in his forecasts. Be Long had no choice, and Tou He was content to divulge his information with only the mildest of prompts, but neither Yang Mu nor Wu Ying cared to indulge the man.

In fact, it had gotten so bad that Wu Ying had left his horse behind with Yang Mu while he took to scouting ahead, flitting from tree to tree and branch to ground with ease. All the while, the wind swirled around him, providing him details.

Dinh Don followed along more sedately, the scout staying a bare couple hundred feet ahead of the rest of the team. Wu Ying understood his reluctance to travel too far, for the dense woods shrank the range of an individual's spiritual sense. What use was a scout that could not report back?

On the other hand, Wu Ying cared little for such concerns. The entire group was slow-moving on their horses, even if Bich Trang seemed to exude a low-grade wood aura whose focus was less on plants but creatures, benefiting the steeds they rode upon such that they were able to travel without slowing.

Even suppressed, the combined auras of the group exerted a subtle pressure upon the world. External chi swirled, drawn in by Wu Ying's Cyclone's Breath method and, on a more localized basis, the studious bookworm Phuong Vy.

Wu Ying had been surprised when he recognized the gentle touch of a fellow moving cultivator in play, though her method seemed more localized, the chi she drew upon more general. Unlike his technique that drew exclusively upon wind chi, she took in everything but strained it through her meridians to alter it to suit her needs.

That was not the only surprise the army unit had brought with it. It had taken Wu Ying nearly the entire day before he'd noticed the bird that had been watching them high above. It was because of its constant presence that Wu Ying finally noticed it gliding high above them. No bigger than a small dot in the beginning, when the creature landed at night, its true size was apparent.

Wings flaring wide, the bird—a raptor of some form, Wu Ying assumed from the turn of its beak—opened its massive wings, landing on a nearby fallen tree trunk light as a feather as the group prepped for the night in their chosen clearing. Seated with its wings folded, it looked only half the size of one of their horses, though its wingspan easily dwarfed the beast. In fact, if not for the gentle pull and pulse of the colonel's aura, their steeds would have bolted at the new, predatory presence.

"Yours?" Tou He asked as Bich Trang approached the bird, a hand fishing in a storage pouch by her side to extract strips of meat to feed the raptor.

"Yes. My bonded beast companion," Bich Trang said. "As I told you before, we do not rely on a single point of failure."

"Beasts…" Wu Ying shook his head, walking closer. The bird turned its head, slow-blinking eyes regarding him with a predatory gaze that set the hairs on the back of his neck alight. "I understand only a little about them. They're not common among my sect or kingdom."

"Raising a spirit beast requires a significant amount of beast meat, along with access to beast cores. Worse, tamed spirit beast meat isn't sufficient, or it is required in very large quantities. Beast bonding is very expensive and difficult for those without our resources," Bich Trang said. "Even for us, our numbers are constrained by similar considerations. Maybe one in fifty cultivators are able to raise such a creature, and few of those ever ascend."

Yang Mu crouched to stare the raptor in the eye. It returned her regard with the placid calm of a predator, as though its consideration for swallowing her whole was just a small facet of its life.

"On the other hand, Nanyue has been raising spirit beasts for so long, they have quite the variety in the upper echelons. They age even slower than mortal man does as they grow in strength, do they not?" Yang Mu said.

"We do. They are a strategic reserve, one of the pillars of our kingdom's independence. Families from all across the country pass on the beast bond as needed," Bich Trang confirmed. "Sao Choi is my family's contribution."

"Nascent Soul bird," Wu Ying said, understanding at last what he had been feeling for so long and not been able to grasp. The bird controlled not the wind but something close to it, a higher concept. Air, instead of wind, or a portion of that air. He could not grasp it, but he felt deep in his soul the symmetry between their daos. "High level birds are rare. They're more fragile in the early stages. Dragons can be touchy about sharing the skies. Even more so when it's a creature they see as lesser to begin with."

"Yes." The colonel smiled as she stroked the bird. "We are fortunate to have managed to raise Sao Choi as well as we have."

"How do you pass on the bond?" Wu Ying asked. "I understand such a bond between spirit beast and cultivator is one of the most important aspects. Too lax a control, and the beast will consume the cultivator. Too strong, and they will flee. And such bonds must be rebuilt for each new owner."

"You understand well, for one who has not trained in the arts," Bich Trang said.

Wu Ying shrugged. He read a lot, and his time with various cultivating clans had spread his knowledge far and wide.

"We begin the bonding process at a young age, designating heirs by family line. In this way, the bond is like steel when the time comes for a change," Bich Trang replied, offering a genial smile at Sao Choi even as it continued to eat.

"And it didn't think you were prey as a child?" Wu Ying said.

No answer, Bich Trang smiling. No surprise there. Some techniques were meant to be kept secret.

Tou He, having finished caring for his mare, ambled over. "Almost makes us seem superfluous then, having a Nascent Soul spirit beast with you."

"So I said, and yet you all insisted."

Yang Mu shot the ex-monk a glare, to which the man shrugged before wandering back toward the center of their clearing. Tou He dug a fire pit, then a couple of metal rods were withdrawn from his ring and embedded into the ground before he started looking for rocks to line the edge of the pit.

"What are we eating?" Tou He asked. "And did we discuss cooking rotations? Because I think we should discuss cooking rotations. And dinner."

Dinh Don wandered over, armfuls of wood in hand that he deposited next to Tou He. "I completely agree. We should discuss dinner. But I'll be cooking."

"Are you a good cook then?" Tou He said. "Because Wu Ying really isn't."

"Hey!" Wu Ying protested. "You haven't seen me in ten years. I could have gotten better." Then, frowning, he added, "I'm not a bad cook either!"

"You're not a good one though." Tou He lowered his head and faux whispered to Dinh Don, "He uses the same five spices all the time. The only thing he varies is his vegetables, and even then, with access to the whole forest, he falls back on his favorites."

"I like what I like," Wu Ying said, crossing his arms. It hadn't been that bad—and it was not as though they'd had much time to cook or he had been relegated to that role solely. So what if he wanted to go back to the meals that he enjoyed regularly?

"See? I bet he hasn't changed in ten years," Tou He said. "For the wind, my friend can be quite steadfast at times."

Wu Ying chose to ignore his friend gossiping about him. Instead, he watched the bird and the colonel as she fed it a massive carcass that Bich Trang had taken from her ring, a fond look in her eyes. Now that he watched both more closely and with more context, he realized that she looked less like one who watched a pet and more a familiar granduncle.

With a shake of her head, Bich Trang turned away to speak to them all. "The monk is correct. We should speak more about our duties and go over the plan again."

Yang Mu let out an unhappy groan, having left to put up her tent. Still, the group gathered around the makeshift campfire, lit already by the simple expedience of Tou He using a touch of his fire chi, and the colonel took the lead on this discussion. Mostly though, she was reiterating what Yang Mu had agreed to, though more details were offered.

***

It took three days before the newly formed group ran into trouble they could not avoid. They had agreed to stay away from any demonic beasts they could, as constant battles would only wear them down. Every night, the two formation masters interlaid new formation flags around their resting place to help cleanse them, hide their presence, and also purify the corpses for Sao Choi to consume.

Dinh Don had reined his horse in along the deer track they had been following, waiting for the group to arrive before he lowered his head to speak. Wu Ying had drifted back not long before the rest of the group arrived, having sensed the scout's intentions.

"We're being stalked," Dinh Don said without preamble.

"Who and how many?" Bich Trang asked.

Be Long, near the back, flinched. Wu Ying had noted his growing unease as signs of civilization fell by the wayside. Yang Mu, recognizing the discomfort that she too had experienced when she first traveled with Wu Ying, had taken to riding beside the city dweller, engaging him with conversation as a distraction. Too often, as far as Wu Ying was concerned. The captain would not learn to handle the wild if he was distracted by a woman. Especially not Yang Mu.

"I've spotted five so far, but I expect there to be more," Dinh Don hesitated, then looked at Wu Ying for confirmation.

"Seven in total. There might be one more whose ability eludes me, but I believe it is a beast companion instead. One deeply steeped in the dao of shadows," Wu Ying said. "The rest are all earth-aligned."

"What are they?" Bich Trang asked.

"Earth-creature. Unusual looking. Front legs of a bird, back legs of a cat, and a simian face," Dinh Don added. "I have not seen their like before. Something from the deep wilds."

"Then what are they doing out here?" Be Long frowned, the Captain of the Guard sounding entirely unhappy. "Driven out this way by the taint?"

"Or sent," Minh Trac muttered. "The corruption is causing fortunes to change on a constant basis. Clouding the future, hiding us from the sight of the heavens."

"Sight of heavens? Is not everything part of the Dao?" Wu Ying said.

"The heavens are not the Dao, they are just part of it. And though the greatest of the gods might see the Dao in its entirety, my ability to perceive is limited," Minh Trac admitted reluctantly.

"In other words, foretelling the future is useless," Yang Mu said. "A waste of time."

"Understanding the flow of time is important to understand the proper placement of flags in a formation! How can one build proper formations that will last the centuries if one does not understand the changes brought about by the passing of the ages!" Minh Trac replied heatedly.

"The ages? Your formations wouldn't last a week as—"

"Enough!" Bich Trang cut off the pair before the conversation could devolve into another argument. The entire party had listened to them bicker more than enough. "We have a fight to prepare for."

"What is there to ready? Five or seven beasts, it is the same," Thien Giang said, swinging her guan dao down with one motion, slicing through a branch and watching it crash. "They come, I'll kill them all."

"And attract more attention," Wu Ying said. "Not a good thing, if we want to sneak up on the corruption."

"A tear does not care if we stride in or sneak. It is still broken and unthinking," Thien Giang said.

"We don't know it's a tear. Or who made it," Wu Ying replied.

The polearm wielder shook her head under her heavy helm.

Again, Bich Trang cut in before another argument could continue. "I agree with the wind cultivator. We should attempt to finish the fight quickly. If they stalk us, we should pick the location of the battle and end it fast. I see no point in additional risk."

Her words forced reluctant agreement from the group.

"Now, here's what we're going to do."

***

Wu Ying floated high above the group, eyeing the bird that held position with the occasional stroke of its wings. He could almost feel it mocking him with the way it moved, for Sao Choi needed no physical aid to fly. It controlled the very air itself and its position in it with an innate flexing of will. In the meantime, Wu Ying's understanding of the dao was neither as deep nor as broad as the bird's, requiring him to float and spin about in small degrees as the wind bore him aloft.

From their position, the pair could sense the movements of the grounded. The way the earth-chimeras had turned aside, leaving the group alone as they sensed a change in pattern. Hanging back just far enough that they could continue tracking but allowing the creatures the ability to continue their silent surveillance.

Except, of course, Dinh Don was masking the true movements of the team while paper talisman figurines took the place of the group. The simple talismans had been supplied by Yang Mu, shaped to copy the chi flows of the group even as the paper bait sat upon their horses and picked their way forward. Without a direct connection to the earth below, the paper bait could easily trick the earth-chimeras.

It helped, of course, that not all of the team had left for the fight. Tou He, the bookish Phuong Vy, and Be Long stayed behind, imbuing the surroundings with their auras to further mess with the distant chi signatures.

In the meantime, the other group intended to narrow the distance and strike at their stalkers, taking them by surprise. Once the group was engaged, Wu Ying and Sao Choi were to swoop down and finish the battle and deal with any that tried to run.

A simple plan. It should have been a simple battle.

If not for the danger he sensed coming toward him. Wu Ying knew how rare it was for a single bird to rise to Nascent Soul stage, but one exception was not the single avian but a flock. A grouping of spirit beasts taking to the sky could easily chase away or tear down a single powerful creature, utilizing their greater number to peck away at their prey. After all, in the sky, a single injury to the wing could lend to true tragedy.

"Everything's complicated," Wu Ying muttered.

He raised his hand a little, calling the wind to him and sending it toward the incoming flock. He poured an iota of chi into the wind, forcing it to blow brisker and colder, forcing the creatures to push even harder and expend energy to approach him and Sao Choi. At the same time, he turned the wind as it passed the flock, circling the scents to him, such that he might smell their intentions more fully.

A squawk by the side made Wu Ying turn to the bird. He was not sure how intelligent Sao Choi was, but its cultivation stage and that it had a name lent credence to the idea that the bird was no less clever than any human cultivator.

Dangerous to treat it otherwise, even as it was hazardous to assign entirely human motivations to it.

"We can drop into the trees before they arrive," Wu Ying said. Avoid the coming fight.

Another squawk.

"Yeah, I know you can win. I might be able to too." He certainly could unless there were a few Core Formation cultivators among that flock, and he doubted there were. They probably did not even realize the threat they truly faced, not as distant as the pair were and with their auras shrouded. "But we're supposed to be keeping a low profile."

The bird shuddered, raised its beak, and let out one long flap of its wings. It turned its gaze to the struggling flock then back down to the monsters below, seeming to make up its mind. Wings tucked in, it dove. Leaving the startled wind cultivator alone in the skies, Sao Choi sheared through the air, heading for the earth elementals by itself.

"That's not the plan, damn it!" Wu Ying cried.

He felt his control of the wind holding him aloft slip as Sao Choi dragged all the wind toward itself, causing him to fall for tens of feet. The creature contained the air, building up its attack and yanking the wind cultivator along behind it. On purpose or not, Wu Ying was uncertain as he fought to control his fall and not shatter against wooden obstacles ahead.

Dropping like a stone—no, faster than a stone—the pair descended upon the monsters. Wooden trees were blasted apart by the wind spear the raptor had formed ahead of itself, the shards of wood and broken branches pelting the monsters below.

Hardened earth defenses met the initial attack, reflexive use of chi forming to protect the creatures. Sufficient to save them from dire injury, insufficient to stop Sao Choi as it snatched up one of its victims, wings flaring as it banked and rose.

Wu Ying, forced to fall along behind, had drawn his own sword. He guided the wind at the last moment, letting himself skim across the ground even as he struck and rolled, slicing sideways at two of the figures he passed. The attack cracked through the first defense, drawing blood and lopping off a limb, but was deflected on the second stone bulwark that rose in defense.

Then he was past the group. He tucked his feet, twisting as he impacted a tree, the trunk creaking and breaking before breaking free of the earth and tilting precariously. He rode the falling tree trunk down, a light cushion of air stabilizing him as he did so.

In the meantime, Sao Choi had returned, banking in a way that would have been impossible for a mortal bird. Its beak twisted, cracking tainted rock arm before the beak plunged into flesh. Snapping its head, Sao Choi tore free a chunk of its prey's torso. The earth bubbled upward to grab at clawed feet, but Sao Choi levitated directly upward, ignoring the attack contemptuously.

Wu Ying pushed off the tree, returning to the battle even as his feet and limbs ached. His jian swung forward and sideways, bloodying his newest weapon. No fancy enchantments, no special techniques. Just a blade whose heart, whose very being was embodied with a single idea.

Cut.

Sword intent tore through muscular, furred arm and met bone beneath. Arm fell, but the blade strike continued, opening up chest and lungs, continuing onward and letting the two halves of the monster fall apart. Behind, additional trees fell as Wu Ying's empowered attack continued farther than even he had expected.

As Wu Ying reoriented to the new reality of his weapon, the increased deadliness of it, he recognized additional voices and chi flows. The team was on the way, hurrying to catch them.

Too slow.

All too slow.

By the time they arrived, the monsters were dead; even the shadow creature that had attempted to slink away caught in a bubble of constricting air, its control of the Dao subsumed under the greater enlightenment of the raptor.

Bich Trang snarled as she stalked up to Wu Ying, sheathing her sword once she had judged the danger had passed. "What was that? We had a plan, Verdant Gatherer. Disobeying orders is grounds for punishment and dismissal from this party!"

Wu Ying waited for her to end her tirade before he gestured at Sao Choi. "Speak to your companion, colonel. I was but drawn along, unwillingly, when it chose to attack."

The group, as one, turned to regard the Nascent Soul bird that had taken to tearing into the meat of its former prey. It threw back its head, meat sliding down its gullet, white bone of broken ribs marred by blood before it disappeared. Then its head dipped again, beak opening to tear free additional strips of chimerical meat. Tainted meat.

"Should it be eating that?" Yang Mu asked hesitantly.

"No," Thien Giang said.

"Right. I thought so." Yang Mu hesitated as she looked at Bich Trang. "Should you not stop it?"

"You do it," Bich Trang said wryly. For all the lightness in her tone, there was worry in her eyes as she watched Sao Choi consume the creatures. "No? Then let's find the cores from the ones Cultivator Long killed." Lowering her voice a little, she added to Wu Ying, "Put away the ones you killed before Sao Choi consumes them too."

"Yes, colonel," Wu Ying muttered, sheathing his sword and regarding the deadly raptor.

Seven monsters, half of them in the Core Formation stage. The bird had destroyed them within moments. Exactly how powerful was Sao Choi, why was it not further utilized and what kind of control did Bich Trang really have over it?

Wu Ying was uncertain, but it seemed there were depths to this relationship that he had not plumbed.

Chapter 23

Day after day, encounter after encounter. Battles became routine as they delved farther into the humid wilderness, going from every few days to every other day to a daily occurrence. The team took turns doing battle, Bich Trang taking the opportunity to understand how the new additions to her group fought as well as integrating the team into the unit itself.

Wu Ying watched and learned as well, gaining an understanding of the special unit and their tactics. As expected, Thien Giang, Dinh Don, and Bich Trang were the ones who handled the monsters directly while the others hung back and offered support. Surprisingly, Minh Trac, with his formations and talismans, contributed more to the battles, while the bookish Phuong Vy rarely took action. On the other hand, when she did so, it was via poisoned throwing knives that sank into exposed flesh and caused fast-spreading numbness through limbs.

It took Wu Ying only a single battle to understand that the special unit was holding back during the battles. A certain degree of wariness existed between the groups that time together had yet to abate, so trump cards were hidden by all but Captain Ky.

On their side, Wu Ying kept to the modified forms of the Long family style, choosing not to wield the various cuts of the Wandering Dragon in front of his "allies." Yang Mu never activated the advanced inscriptions on her fans during the battles, only allowing them to grow and shrink and return as she fought the creatures. As for Tou He…

Wu Ying knew not what his friend kept hidden. His staff technique had in itself been modified, no longer the mostly defensive form of the Mountain Abides. He utilized a more aggressive blend of attacks and defenses, the flames that were part of his makeup flaring to life and lighting the weapon with each movement. Even so, the ex-monk restrained his fire aura such that the flames he left behind were quickly smothered. Not that setting fire to the humid, damp jungle would have been easy.

Of them all, it was the bronze-based Captain Ky who struggled. While his metal aura provided him with a powerful defensive technique, he struggled in the forest, seeming to never be looking in the right location when surprise attacks appeared.

The captain's dao was difficult to pin down, though Wu Ying was certain it held strains of duty, fortitude, and protection. It reinforced his aura technique which, in itself, built upon his metal element. Unlike Elder Po of the Verdant Green Waters, who transformed his very being into metal itself, Be Long hardened the domain of his aura against attacks. It was more subtle, easier to manipulate and discard, and less effective at the same time.

On the other hand, Wu Ying watched as Be Long extended his metal aura in a spike from the back of his left shoulder, impaling the falling fist-sized leech before it reached him, and had to admit, it did have its advantages. Even as Be Long finished the leech above, another jumped from the ground, attempting to latch onto his leg, where another metal-aura spike caught it.

The leeches were the latest assault, the team of Core Formation cultivators dealing with them in their own ways. Minh Trac had a floating series of talisman inscriptions that burned out one after the other, each of them providing a moving defense for himself and the scholar. Tou He, riding ahead of them, flared his aura in a controlled manner, shriveling those assaulting him and sending them squirming away in search of easier prey.

Yang Mu had subsumed her aura, and that of her horse, such that the leeches themselves were unable to differentiate her from the trees, thus leaving her alone. It was a similar method to Dinh Don, whose passage and scouting ahead of them had picked this route as the least troublesome, threading their way between swamps on the left and a group of ferocious demonic deer on the right.

Most interesting to Wu Ying was the colonel's method, similar to the minor whirlwind that he utilized to cast aside the leeches. In effect, if not specifics. There was no swirling air about her, no movement at all. It seemed as though the leeches falling toward her were gripped and thrown by some force, swatted out of the air violently to splatter against trunks. Even after days of careful observation, Wu Ying could not penetrate the dense layer of defenses surrounding the colonel to ascertain her actual elemental attachment.

As the team finally left the leech-ridden trees, Bich Trang waved them over to a small rise free of vegetation. Sao Choi landed on a nearby rock, taking with grace the meal that Bich Trang offered, even as its beak tore into the corpse with glee. The team took the moment to dismount, providing water and food for their horses and resting them while inspecting for any parasites their spiritual senses might have missed.

"How much longer?" Bich Trang asked Minh Trac, the formation master already having handed his reins to Phuong Vy while he drew out his compass.

"Future is cloudy, it's hard to see—"

"I did not ask for excuses. I asked how much longer," Bich Trang cut the man off impatiently.

"I'm trying to tell you." Receiving her glare, he sighed. "A few days, I believe. Then the cloud of demonic energy grows too close, and my ability to foretell disappears entirely. I will no longer be of use then."

"As if you've been of any use now," muttered Yang Mu.

"I foretold that night attack two days ago!" Minh Trac said. "The one that bypassed your formations, if you forget."

"Just the first layer," Yang Mu replied, lifting her chin. "The Stalking Dragonfly would never have made it through the secondary defenses."

"Not all of us sleep in enchanted tents," Thien Giang said, sneering. "Some of us aren't the spoiled princesses of powerful parents."

"Or perhaps they just don't consider you all worth investing in," Yang Mu replied.

"You—"

"Enough." Bich Trang commanded. The colonel took off her helmet for a moment to wipe her face, the humidity and heat of the jungle causing even the cultivators to sweat a little. "I've told you before, antagonizing one another aids no one. Be like the monk."

"Ex-monk." Tou He waved a banana-leaf-wrapped ball of glutinous rice at them. "But eating is a good idea, I concur."

"That wasn't what I meant." Bich Trang looked upward, eyeing the sun, then shrugged. "But now is as good a time as any for lunch. Unless there are other dangers to be wary of?"

Dinh Don, riding up on his horse from ahead, body slumped over the saddle like a rice sack, straightened at her words. "Always. But if we take our usual precautions, we should be safe enough." He pointed to the southwest. "We'll have to head that way afterward. There's an abandoned village ahead that's now filled with Than Vong."

"Than Vong?" Wu Ying asked as he peeled apart the wrapping on the glutinous rice cake he'd extracted from his storage ring.

"Ma Than Vong[57]. Hanged ghosts," Dinh Don clarified. "Folk tales say they are the vengeful spirits of suicide victims. In truth, they are but a common Middle Kingdom demon whose favorite method of warding off trespassers is to hang their victims from nearby trees. They leave the bodies to be picked apart by vermin and insects."

"That explains what the wind has been telling me," Wu Ying muttered in surprised acknowledgement. "Flying bones and rotting corpses in trees indeed." He cocked his head, eyes going distant as he communed with the wind. A moment later, he frowned.

"Problem, Cultivator Long?" Bich Trang asked. She had learned that his ability with the wind gave him a much broader sense of the world, unlike her own scout. While Dinh Don recognized and was able to ascertain threats low to the earth—including guiding them around dangerous plants and a man-eating Nascent Soul trap door spider—his range was severely limited compared to Wu Ying's wind techniques.

"There's another encampment down that way." Wu Ying gestured in the direction that Dinh Don had pointed. "It's a distance away, and it looks more newly built. Maybe an off shoot from the original?" He shrugged, not knowing the answer. "The bones are hung all along the way till…" His hand traced the air, following the guidance of the wind and stopped nearly all the way due east.

"Too far. We can't afford to go that far off our course," Bich Trang said.

"We need to go to the village," Minh Trac said, waving a piece of paper at the colonel. He had been writing upon it since they stopped, reading the wind and stars and flow of chi. "There's a lingering stain of disaster hovering over the village. It grows with each passing of the moon and will cause great misfortune in the future if it is not dealt with."

Bich Trang was already shaking her head. "No. We can send a missive back to the city lord telling her of the danger on her border, but our objective does not lie in the village."

---

[57] Real Vietnamese ghosts, though I'm changing them for this story.

"My duty does though!" Be Long stepped forward, his body hunching inward a little as he readied himself for an argument. "It sounds like dealing with the village now would be less troublesome than in the future. Especially with such a contingent of heroes gathered here."

"It is not our mission," Bich Trang repeated.

"It is your duty though. To support the city and the people," Be Long said. "We must act for the greater good."

"Dealing with the creeping corruption is the greater good."

"Not if we leave behind an infection like this to spread."

"My vision might be clouded, but I tell you truth, colonel. This is a danger that must be dealt with," Minh Trac said urgently. "It affects not just the city but could become a problem for the country."

"It is that dire?"

Minh Trac nodded soberly. "I see the rise of a demonic kingdom, one where humans are ruled by demons."

Now it was time for Thien Giang to scoff. "Oh, come on. Another demonic kingdom? How many can there be?" She shook her head. "That's the third one you've seen."

"I see possibilities, not certainties!" Minh Trac snapped. "The flow of time and fortune changes systematically as we interact with it. Yet you forget our history if you think it cannot happen."

"I forget nothing!"

"Enough," Bich Trang held up her hand, quieting the two. "Minh Trac and his brethren have served the kingdom well. It was a predecessor of his that freed us from the clutches of the Mo Wang, and it is their vision that allows us to foresee attacks from the north." A hard gaze landed upon the northerners, though it had little effect on the eating Tou He. Minh Trac was smiling, only for Bich Trang to continue. "But I still do not believe that our best choice is to deal with the matter now. We could come by after we have dealt with our primary mission."

That mollified Thien Giang a little and even Minh Trac seemed satisfied with that suggestion. It was clear that whatever disaster his compass and runes might forecast, it was much in the future. Be Long was the only unhappy individual, but the captain was not about to risk his life on an all-out assault by himself.

Satisfied that everyone was handled, Bich Trang waved them away, commanding them to finish taking care of their horses and sustenance. It was a short rest, and within ten minutes, the group was ready to leave.

Dinh Don led the way, headed in the same direction he had indicated, under orders to weave their way through the Ma Than Vong clan lands as best as possible. In aid of this, Minh Trac had distributed a series of talismans to reduce their presence further.

The entire group was halfway down the hill when Bich Trang noticed that Phuong Vy, book before her, was not moving with the rest of the team. Instead, she was absentmindedly guiding her horse toward the main settlement, angling away from the group.

"Private La, what are you doing?" Bich Trang said wearily.

"Huh?" Phuong Vy looked up from her book, looked toward the voice, and then realizing she was separated, checked around her. "I'm going to the disturbance of course."

"What disturbance?" Bich Trang said.

"Why, the one in the center of the encampment. The corruption splinter, torn from its true resting place."

Silence greeted her statement, before voices rose in agitation and anger. Eventually though, Phuong Vy was encouraged to explain herself.

"Can you not sense it? The splinter is a flame that has been brought to the center of the village. They use it to cook with, to prepare their foods and thus cleanse their meat, leaving them untouched." Phuong Vy shook her head in admiration and horror. "It's both their savior and their doom."

"Why do you say that?" Yang Mu asked.

"The flame is fed from the corruption in the meat they consume, the very essence of the twisted chi dripping into the splinter to act as fuel. It burns the flesh clean, allowing them to safely consume the meat for the moment, but because it burns constantly, it infuses the surroundings with demonic chi." She opened her hands and turned them sideways. "It chokes them out slowly, rather than twisting them quickly. In the end, all will fall. It is likely this very splinter that Minh Trac sees in the future. Growing stronger with each meal, becoming a lingering rash on the skin of the earth."

Wu Ying frowned, holding up his hand. A small whirlwind formed as the winds danced in his palm, whispering to him. He shuddered, dismissing the winds after confirming her words. Yet it was no surprise that Captain Ky sought clarity after such a dire pronouncement.

"How do you know all this?" he said. "Neither our scouts nor the soothsayer saw this."

"I know fire," Phuong Vy said simply.

"That explains nothing."

"The fire in the village, it is something I understand. Just like I understand the fire within you, as I understand the fire within you all. Some burn hot"—a nod to Tou He—"others are cooler"—that brought a shy smile from Dinh Don—"and many are between. But that flame is within all living things, all but the coldest of corpses that are becoming naught but earth. I understand flame. And this flame is corrupt and twisted, staining the fire within everything around."

Be Long's lips thinned, but he shook his head a moment later, causing his horse to shift and kick a little. "What a muddled mix of fish and dragons. But it is decided. We are going to the village then?"

"It seems so." Bich Trang turned her hand sideways, conjuring her helmet and slipping it on. "It seems we will have to do this the hard way."

Wu Ying winced a little, and even Yang Mu looked doubtful at Bich Trang's rather casual pronouncement. Tou He was perfectly serene as always, mouth-stuffed like a chipmunk. The rest of the team shifted their rides, joining the scholar as they headed for the village.

How, exactly, taking on an entire settlement of demons was easier than what was to come, Wu Ying knew not. But, it seemed, they were going to find out.

Chapter 24

It took the group almost an hour to make it nearly two-thirds of the way to the ghost village. Wu Ying and Dinh Don had pushed ahead of the group, searching for enemy scouts. As he traveled, the wind whispered a warning to Wu Ying and the wind cultivator drifted over from high above. An open-handed palm strike, coming from above toward the crown of the head, was sufficient, the creature's vertebrae crushed downward into its spine.

Wu Ying spun and caught the falling figure as it slipped to the ground, blood and brain fluid leaking from the ears. He gently placed the body against a nearby tree trunk and knelt, listening. The noise of its pair of hearts slowed as the body caught up to the demon's death.

Long of limb, with elongated bat ears, elongated fingers that jutted from thick knuckles that folded over strangely to form a third knuckle. Gripping hands for clambering through the forest and swinging through the air, rather than a human's. A long tail that moved like a serpent while its shorter, thicker torso hid its gender features under dense fur. Elongated snout, with teeth meant to bite and rend flesh.

Wu Ying frowned at the body, then looked upward to where the creature had crouched in the foliage. Its marked fur, brown and black splotches across coarse hair, had helped hide it in the canopy, the creature almost invisible to the naked eye. Some minor twisting of the dao, a warping of shadows and space had aided its camouflage.

"Dangerous," Wu Ying said softly to Dinh Don as the portly scout rode up on his horse, the pair almost bouncing through the forest as the scout warped the surroundings to fit the two. "Are you even able to sense them in the trees?"

Dinh Don snorted. "My senses might be connected to the earth, but I am not entirely without skill in the woods."

"My apologies," Wu Ying said. "I only noticed this one because the wind spoke of it to me. He eluded my spiritual sense at first."

"You rely too greatly on the wind, spread it out too far," the scout said. "Concentrate your focus and your senses, sweep it before you like a brush, and you will find that you are able to discern much more with your aura."

"A brush?"

The scout grinned. "The Bristled Sense. That's the name of the art I use."

Wu Ying had no answer to the man's obvious pride at his ability. Instead, he gestured at the body beside their feet. "What should we do with this?"

"I'll take care of it. But we should let your people see what they are up against." Dinh Don hesitated, then flicked his hand forward. "It would help if we dealt with some of the closer scouts before the others arrive."

"Not worried they might realize some are missing?"

"The Ma Than Vong might be smart demons, but they are still demons. Discipline is something they struggle with." The man chuckled. "I'd be surprised if they remembered to send out relief on time."

Wu Ying nodded, eyeing the creature's long snout. "Is blood a concern?"

"A little. Their sense of smell is supposedly decent. Though they also have a connection to the woods that often tells them of others arriving. I'd watch your aura."

Wu Ying nodded and suppressed his aura further. He drew it deeper and deeper within him such that it was right beside his skin. Within moments, he became nothing more than another background item, no more of import than a tree or a twig or a breeze.

"Wild Gatherer indeed." Then, as though he refused to be outdone, Dinh Don did the same, fading away from Wu Ying's senses even as he stared right at the other. In a display of control, Dinh Don also extended his control such that his horse was suppressed as well.

Smiling a little, Wu Ying took to the sky, allowing the wind to lift him. Already, his friends were coming back with whispered answers of lurking dangers. A snake lying in wait there. Branches filled with cobwebs and an agitated spider scuttling across thrumming threads to deal with a spirit bird that sought escape. Unseen and unnoticed by many, a colony of red ants waged war with a colony of black ants, their prize a rotting tree.

More.

A scout, another of the hanged ghost demons. Lurking in the tree, behind one of the rotting figures of a long dead body. Only string tied to the bones kept the grisly prize together, and even then, those strings were fraying, remnants scattered across the ground.

A good thing that there were no nearly new corpses. The group was too deep, the locals having drawn back for too long for the hanged ghosts to keep taking humans. In their stead, other demonic beasts were strung up, their bodies fresh, the smell redolent and their bodies bloated.

This scout had chosen a human body to hide behind. To watch for the inevitable reaction when another mortal came across the desecrated body. A chance to launch a surprise attack perhaps, or to scuttle away and alert its friends.

It mattered not to Wu Ying.

He flitted through the trees, a ghost that barely touched the leaves as he neared the creature. He kept his blade in its sheath, remembering the warning about scents, and struck with his hand only. Flying almost directly from below the creature, he rose on the wind that carried his scent at the last moment, causing the creature to flinch backward. Right into the knife ridge of his hand.

Wu Ying felt cartilage crumble as he crushed its trachea. Another hand blocked flailing arm, gripping it tightly as he used the leverage to keep the body from falling as formerly tightened tail and toes relaxed. He spun in the air, pivoting with the wind to kick the creature in the ribs, shattering bone and crushing hearts and lungs to add to the fatal injuries.

Once he was certain it would not move again, he lowered the dying creature to the ground for Dinh Don and the others to deal with. Fighting the Ma Than Vong was simple, a trivial exertion of his skills. No noise escaped, not with his control of the wind, nor was locating them and narrowing the gap before they learned of his presence barely more difficult.

Like a green ghost flowing through the shadowed undergrowth, Wu Ying struck at the scouts, opening a narrow gap in their curtain of paranoia. Through that gap, the rest of the team slipped, Dinh Don manipulating the earth to bury the corpses.

Eventually, however, the easy part was over. Wu Ying was forced to halt his actions and await the team, for the village was but a short distance away. Lounging on a tree limb, he listened to the wind as it spoke of corruption in the air and the burning splinter within the village, even as he listened to the screams of beast and demon alike and felt the stirrings of insanity.

***

The group convened below a short rise that obstructed their view of the village below, though a crafting by Minh Trac over the surrounding area bent light to allow them to see the village without exposing themselves.

The village—really, the ruins of an ancient city which the Ma Than Vong had moved into—sprawled across a significant area of land. It reached all the way to where the group hid, buildings and roads fallen apart and broken down by the never-ending encroachment of the jungle. Where they stood, only minor signs of the previously magnificent civilization stood. A remnant green stone block there, a paved path that had yet to be completely torn down here.

Closer to the village, the jungle had been beaten back on a more regular basis, leaving remnant walls and buildings still standing. Many of those walls were vine-choked, easily mistaken for a standing shrub or tree if not for the regularity of their lines and placement along the curving streets leading to the new village walls.

And what walls they were. Massive stone blocks torn from older buildings and glittering green-grey. The walls rose up around the much smaller portion of the hanged ghosts' village, enclosing the demons within. They stretched for a good li in either direction from the main gates, and another couple of li away from the team, overlooking the stream that ran through their center before being enclosed again.

Within the walls of the city, many buildings had been patched together with stone torn from other buildings or filled in with simple clay and reed. The existing buildings were a diverse mixture of reinforced remnants and still pristine works, all of them stained with splashes of mud, soot, and a mixture so dark red, it was nearly black.

Through the winding streets, fires were built and tended, offering warmth and light to the darkening day, even as a pale shadow seemed to hang over the entire settlement, adding to the shadows that shrouded the location. It was this shadow that Wu Ying and the other cultivators eyed, for their spiritual senses spoke of a twisted corruption that emanated from the towering stepped pyramid in the center.

"So, you were not wrong in that the corruption is spreading," Bich Trang said. "This miasma… it hangs in the air."

"But is not part of it," Wu Ying said, shaking his head. "Or not intrinsically so." The wind tugged at his robes, pushing at him gently as it whispered further advice and histrionics. "And my dao, my grasp is of the wind, not the air. The wind cares not about the smell or corruption, not as much as a dao of the air might."

"Excuses," Thien Giang sniffed.

"Oh, and you've been at all helpful during this expedition," Yang Mu said. "Remind me again what you've done beyond eat and shit?" She tapped her lips. "You've done a lot of both though."

"Better than a prissy princess who acts as though she doesn't do either but leaves the largest turds of us all."

"Oh, I didn't know you were checking."

"Anyone with a nose could—"

"Enough!" Bich Trang said. "You are professionals. Nervous as you might be, bickering is unacceptable."

Thien Giang lowered her head, her cheeks a little red as she kept her gaze downward. At the same time, Yang Mu raised her chin.

"Nervous? Why would we be nervous about assaulting a city?" Tou He said. "Not as though we'd be outnumbered by hundreds, maybe thousands. And while most are no stronger than Body Cleansing, I can sense at least a half dozen that burn with the intensity of a Core Formation cultivator."

"I'm more concerned about the Nascent Soul level one that is near the splinter. I cannot but think that we will have to confront them to acquire the splinter." Be Long hesitated, then added, "We are trying to acquire the splinter, are we not?"

"Acquire or destroy," Phuong Vy said, the diminutive scholar looking up briefly as she finished dipping another set of knives into a pot of scentless poisons. "I believe I have the right equipment to contain the corruption so that we can study it further and make the destruction of the true source easier. But if not, destroying it immediately will be necessary."

"A Nascent Soul demon is dangerous. Not as dangerous as a Spirit Beast of the same rank, of course." Be Long nodded to Bich Trang, whose bird had joined them by perching on a branch high above, glaring at the group in silent disapproval. It was still worrying how something so big and powerful could be so stealthy, hiding its strength and arrival with disturbing ease. "But dangerous nonetheless."

"Sao Choi will not take direct action during the battle," Bich Trang said. "There are a number of aerial scouts that can be dealt with, but otherwise, it will not enter the city."

"Why?" Wu Ying could not help but ask.

Bich Trang shook her head, refusing to answer his question. The wind cultivator frowned, as did his friends, all of them looking unhappy at the sudden loss of one of their most powerful trump cards. Though, Wu Ying noted, none of the special unit members looked surprised at all.

"If that is the case, can we do this?" Be Long said, the guard captain looking nervous now.

"You were the one pushing for us to deal with the village originally," Thien Giang said, sounding annoyed.

"I might have been overenthusiastic."

"It doesn't matter. We can deal with a Nascent Soul demon, if necessary. Hold it off long enough, at least, for the others to handle." Bich Trang looked at both Minh Trac and Thien Giang as she said this, her gaze heavy with unspoken meaning.

"Do you want me to use them now?" Minh Trac said, looking surprised.

"We have a spare, do we not?" Bich Trang said.

"We do. But—"

"It's necessary. If a single splinter can do this much damage, we need to know what we're likely to face. If we can contain it, destroy it from a distance, or even close the tear, it can only benefit us. Entering a battle with so little knowledge is a failure of planning of the most basic level."

Wu Ying cocked his head. "You might want to look closer at the temple before you make a final decision. Front gates."

As one, the group turned their attention to the view. Minh Trac sighed audibly, but then manipulated the formation to magnify the projected vision around the temple in the center of the city. A small gasp escaped Yang Mu's lips, a hand rising to cover them. Thien Giang's hands tightened on her halberd, but she did not take her gaze off the projection, much like the rest of the group who were locked in shared, silent horror.

Four figures, their corpses significantly fresher than the majority of bodies they'd passed. These four were varied in their damage, most missing limbs, one bearing a large hole in the center of their chest where the heart would have been, the last one its head crushed, the skin peeling from the remnants of its skull.

"I guess we know where the rest of the expeditions ended at least." Tou He placed his hands together, bowing his head and chanting, "*Namo Amitoufo*. May they rest in peace and their families find release from suffering."

"We should send a message back," Be Long said into the silence.

"When we enter. Ready yourselves. We will make them pay for their desecration," Bich Trang said firmly.

Wu Ying cast one last look at the corpses, their twisted and bulging cheeks, their swinging bodies, and inclined his head to the colonel in agreement.

Hanged ghosts indeed.

Chapter 25

Of course it was not as simple as that. Where the sect cultivators might have undertaken a simpler series of tactics to deal with the village, perhaps even pushing forward with fierce determination and only a single plan for retreat, the special unit undertook more elaborate preparations.

Almost immediately, Bich Trang barked orders to the two utility cultivators, Minh Trac moving away to begin placement of formation flags to provide a defensive redoubt for the team in the event of a withdrawal. At the same time, Phuong Vy handed Dinh Don the knives she had poisoned, along with a series of wrapped powders. The scout left then, laying out a series of trails and traps for those that might follow them back or for the group to retreat toward, bolstering Minh Trac's efforts.

In the meantime, Bich Trang and Thien Giang were reviewing the routes through the city, highlighting roads and potential resistance points. Wu Ying was of great use there, his winds able to provide details of numbers even within buildings. They discussed tactics, specifically around which of the Core Formation opponents they sensed were best dealt with immediately, while including the non-special unit cultivators in the discussion.

Even overly elaborate as the entire planning session seemed to Wu Ying, it took less than half an hour before the group was ready to move. Bich Trang looked somewhat unhappy at the speed and lack of preparation, but with the loss of the enemies' scouts and the fading light, the need to take action before suspicions were raised trumped further preparations.

Pushing ahead of the group, Wu Ying and Dinh Don traversed the ground to the city, flitting between the crumbling walls in search of stragglers and watchers. Something they had noticed early on was the presence of smaller groups of the Ma Than Vong in the outskirts, almost all in the lower grade of Body Cleansing. Scrawny, hungry-looking creatures that had all the earmarks of the discards of society.

The decision had been made to avoid them if at all possible, so the pair charted a way through the low-burning fires and the fitfully sleeping outcasts. Only twice did the pair have to act. The first time to kill a trio of hanged demons that had stumbled out from an underground passage right into the path of the pair. The second time, Dinh Don collapsed the stone walls of a building upon its inhabitants, causing some minor ruckus but opening a gap which the rest of the team managed to slip through.

Eventually, the group found themselves before the main walls of the settlement, staring at the crude but powerful enchantments carved into them to block easy access. Yang Mu took action then, utilizing a series of talismans to split the formation that bolstered the strength of the wall without destroying the formation itself. Once it had been complete, the team ascended the wall with quick jumps.

A single, unlucky guard was dispatched at the top of the wall by Thien Giang, her polearm landing flat side down and crushing the creature before it could speak. After that, Phuong Vy utilized a series of metallic strings to hang the creature over the wall, shrouded in shadows and out of the line of sight of any passing guard before the group traveled deeper into the city.

In the shadowed, muggy light that filtered through soiled air and fading sunset, the group moved through the city. The few fires that dotted the intersections to offer illumination or that peeked out from open windows were avoided when possible. When not, the group struck quickly and efficiently, falling into a routine that had become common during the journey.

After the second such battle, while Dinh Don sucked the bodies into the earth, Wu Ying brought his concern to light. Finding Bich Trang, he spoke softly.

"You will need to be careful about relying on my senses for the rest of this incursion." Seeing the colonel's perplexed expression, he continued. "The corruption in the air is significant. The longer I am in here, the longer I interact with it and the fallen air, the worse my control. My sense of the winds has declined appreciably."

"What do you mean?"

"What I'm learning is not reliable," Wu Ying said simply. After all, he was not certain he could explain the disjointed conversations the winds were having with him. The conversations that regularly contradicted one another.

Of hanged demons in the rooms ahead and above, of beings that were—visibly—not there, and of past—and perhaps future—atrocities to come. Again and again, he heard the wind whisper of monsters approaching or leaving their vicinity, of creatures eighty-feet tall that sucked upon the marrow of humans and moving swarms of flesh maggots that threatened to swallow the world.

"Then we'll have you take your place in the front line and have Don take over the scouting," Bich Trang decided. She issued the orders in quick clipped conversation, leaving Wu Ying to trail after the other scout.

Tou He drifted over to Wu Ying, lowering his voice as he said, "Are you okay?"

"Just the corruption. It's... staining the wind."

"And the flames itself," Tou He murmured.

Looking at his friend, Wu Ying realized that he had missed the growing strain on the ex-monk's face, the lines that creased his brows.

Seeing his friend looking him over, Tou He shrugged. "Phuong Vy is sensing it too. The splinter is a flame, and it is corrupting everything. My own dao is not of the fire, but..." He shrugged, then as they came to a stop near a wall while waiting for a signal, he raised his hand. For a moment, his aura brightened a little and Wu Ying realized that his friend's flames were reacting constantly to the corruption around them. Burning it away.

"How are you containing it?" Wu Ying asked.

"With difficulty." Turning his hand over, Tou He allowed soot to fall from his hand and body, a small mound forming around him. "My aura and dao is not meant to do this, but..." He shrugged. "Needs must."

"Needs must indeed."

"This splinter… Amitabha, but it is bad. My flames are struggling to contain themselves, for they seek to consume it."

"We'll deal with it. And its guardian." Wu Ying's lips thinned as he thought of the Nascent Soul demon that lay at the center of the temple.

Before Tou He could answer, Bich Trang held up a hand. She gave the signal that they'd been waiting for, and the group tensed, the pair joining Thien Giang in front of the target building. Together, the three burst into the room, followed by Bich Trang and Yang Mu. For the trio, their target was the Core Formation demon at the far end of the room. The other two would deal with the remainder.

Wu Ying led the attack even though he was a step behind Thien Giang on entering, thrusting his sword into a single, focused blade strike that combined sword intent and wind. The attack punctured the creature's upper chest even as it stood up, forcing it back and disrupting the chi it drew from its core. Even so, a wave of water drawn from a pot beside it blocked Thien Gian's cut with the polearm.

As the cultivator swept her weapon around for a return attack, the globe of water clung to her weapon, impacting her movements. No matter, for there was a third member of the group and Tou He finished the fight by bringing his staff down on the creature's skull.

For a moment, just before the staff impacted, Wu Ying could have sworn he saw a burst of flames interacting with the creature's aura as it cleansed the impurities. It happened so fast that he was uncertain he had seen it, but the crushing impact was sufficient to put an end to the fight, their opponent off-guard and overwhelmed by the trio.

In the meantime, the rest of the team within the building finished the battle with the quartet of hanged demons that had accompanied the Core Formation monster. The fight was over fast, though not before one of the creatures managed to stumble over a hanging pot. The sound of the pot cracking open reverberated through the room, making everyone wince.

The group stood still as they strained their hearing and spiritual senses, alert for danger and awareness after the last of the demons were dispatched, breathing slowing as they searched for additional enemies. Sensing nothing, they relaxed, pausing only long enough for Dinh Don to extract the Core Formation demon's beast stone and bury the remaining bodies before moving onward.

There were two other targets to take out before they reached the temple, the remaining Core Formation cultivators too far out of the way for the group to dare test their subterfuge. This entire incursion was a delicate balance as the colonel weighed the varying needs of stealth, security, and terror.

The two targets were dealt with as quickly and efficiently as the first, so much so that Wu Ying felt the tension in his shoulders increase with each death and battle that went their way. In his experience, no plan ever went as well as this. Each success, each fight that resulted in the alarm still not being raised only put him further on edge. He was not the only one, for he saw it in the movements of the others too. All but Yang Mu, who had neither the experience nor wisdom to know that good fortune always preceded bad.

No surprise then that when the alarm was finally raised, by chance encounter rather than planned counter, Wu Ying felt deep relief.

The bucket of dung, thrown out of the window, had been tossed without looking, without conscious intent to cause harm. It was a routine chore, one laced with boredom, such that even the sensitive spiritual auras of the cultivators were unable to pick out the action until it was all too late. Wu Ying's winds, reacting on instinct, caught the sloppy contents as it approached him, throwing it aside at Thien Giang, who was standing beside him. Her startled cry of disgust was loud and shrill and all too human.

A beat of startled silence as the group took in the disruption, even as Thien Giang quieted herself and shook herself clean. Tou He launched himself toward the window, one hand reaching the lower level to haul himself upward.

Too late, for the demon within, still gripping the bucket, screamed. Once, before the ex-monk's staff crushed life and noise alike as he swung it sideways, still hanging from the windowsill. Commotion grew as the bucket fell to the floor inside the room and figures awakened.

"Leave them!" Bich Trang snapped at Tou He as he began to haul himself into the room and Yang Mu turned to the door, her fan ready to crack it open. "Speed is our friend now."

So saying, she ran forward, the colonel leading the way. Dinh Don, crouched ahead of the group, offered her a single nod, raising his crossbow and forging onward. He fired the crossbow moments later, reloading it as he ran, the soft thump of the bolt entering a body and the dying gurgle soon followed by additional voices crying for help.

Confusion still held true as demons were slow to awaken and orient themselves to the assault. The group made the most of it, following Bich Trang and the scout. The group moved swiftly, burning chi and triggering their various movement techniques. Wu Ying took the front once more, even as Tou He briefly laid a hand on Thien Giang, flooding her body and aura with his cleansing flame to purify her of the mess.

A group of late-night revelers boiled out of an alleyway, makeshift weapons including a kitchen cleaver in hand. They shouted in their demonic tongue, harsh and broken and unknowable, as they emerged, only to face Wu Ying's blades. He tore through them like a whirling dervish, leaving the group dying and crippled as he kept running, gesturing with one hand to blow an archer off a balcony. The archer landed with a crushing thump, a spike emerging from the road moments later to end his life.

And on they ran, chaos and the dead left behind. An entire village came alive, lights blooming through buildings and spreading like a rash. Soon enough, everyone would be awake and the Core Formation level demons they had missed would be alerted.

Even as they approached a town square, the fountain that used to dominate it now dried and collapsed, a massive spiritual pressure descended upon them all. The Nascent Soul level demon had awoken and was seeking them, sweeping his spiritual aura through the city in an effort to locate their presence and guide his forces.

Wu Ying shrugged off the pressure with ease, shunting it aside without alerting the other. Even Yang Mu—after her experience with him in the deep wilds—managed to do the same, and the special unit were easily able to avoid suspicion by utilizing their own techniques. Unfortunately, not all of them had the methods nor experience to avoid such scrutiny.

The guard captain, Be Long, was much more used to being on the opposite side of an aura search. Never having needed to hide his aura before, his aura suppression techniques had been supplemented with enchantments and talismans. Those were overcome and destroyed within moments as the Nascent Soul aura pressured them, cracking the jade bracelet he wore and setting alight the talisman papers that hovered beside him.

But it was Tou He's aura, the purifying flames of the fire dragon contained within him, that reacted the most inappropriately. Under pressure, his aura burst to life and tore into the extended spiritual sense, savaging it and sending flames licking outward into the visual spectrum even as spiritually, it chased its way back toward the demon in the temple. It only reached a dozen feet before the flames were snuffed out and the spiritual pressure retracted.

Moments later, a roar of immense anger born of insult and hostility echoed through the abandoned city, causing the group to regard one another in trepidation.

"Well, that really is the end of any kind of stealth," Minh Trac said. "Orders, colonel?"

Bich Trang hesitated, glancing around the abandoned square. She took in Yang Mu, who swung her fan down one side, sending an arc of energy to catch and bowl over a dozen charging demons, many exploding as the attack tore through them. To Phuong Vy, who had just finished throwing a series of daggers with thin wires strung across them at the walls of the alleyway, trapping it for those that might follow them directly.

Then she nodded. "So be it. We take him here."

Chapter 26

Minh Trac immediately extracted formation flags from his ring, casting his gaze around the square and muttering to himself. The ground in the square had been crushed down, few weeds growing from the cracked paving stones, a testament of a better period in the city and square's existence. Moonlight from a waning moon shone upon the group, its angle low and occasionally clouded, even as the ever-increasing number of flames stoked from awakening demons lit up the horizon.

Phuong Vy was the first to disagree, stating simply, "That's not our objective."

"No, it isn't. You said you have a containment method?" At her nod, Bich Trang continued. "Take the wind cultivator and his companion with you. They'll help you break in and take the splinter."

Phuong Vy frowned, turning toward Wu Ying and Yang Mu, then nodded. Together, the trio gathered at the exit Wu Ying had chosen, knowing this was no time to object.

"I'd like to go with them," Tou He said.

"No. You're the bait for this trap," Bich Trang said. "You angered him, you stay here. Your job is to last until the formation is ready, then we'll finish this fight."

Wu Ying felt a thrill of fear run through him at this pronouncement. He still did not trust the colonel and the special unit, but he could not see a way to object without disrupting the chain of command. And she was right, Tou He had angered the creature.

He could only hope that they were honorable and unlikely to abandon his friend.

"And myself?" Be Long asked, the captain looking a little mystified.

"Keep Minh Trac safe. The rest of us will support the monk."

"Ex-monk."

Bich Trang ignored the man, frowning at Wu Ying and his group who had yet to leave. "Go! Before he arrives."

Wu Ying took off down the road, closely followed by the other two. As he ran, he lashed out with his jian, cutting down a trio of demons that stepped outside of their residence. He turned down a road soon after, a road that ran parallel to the one they had been on previously and that twisted away from the temple.

Phuong Vy hurried to catch up with Wu Ying. "Where are you going? This is not the way to the temple!"

"Exactly. The demon is rushing toward us. Best not to meet him, or the roadblocks that are forming," Wu Ying replied.

Yang Mu in the back let out a little grunt of agreement, her fans held by her sides, one half open and the other closed. Occasionally she'd throw one, blocking off an alleyway before she would recall it, catching the weapon before they turned the corner.

Even so, the numbers and the creatures they fought continued to grow.

"How far do you intend to run?" Phuong Vy said, ripping a dagger from a skull as they disengaged from another quick skirmish.

Rather than answer, Wu Ying stepped toward a ramshackle door, striking it with the edge of his hand. His dao-imbued knife strike cut into the side of the door, causing it to swing open as he shouldered inside. An older demon, struggling to his feet, was struck with the backend of a pommel, causing him to crumple to the ground senseless. Then after the pair had followed him in, Wu Ying shoved the wobbly table in the way of the door, blocking it.

"Why are we here?" Phuong Vy snapped.

Again, Wu Ying held up his hand. His head cocked, he listened to the winds, filtering through their declarations of animosity, their shrieks of bloodlust and hunger, their descriptions of threats lurking in the trees above. He listened and waited until the impact of the flying Nascent Soul demon landing in the square they had left finally reverberated through the room, throwing plates and feet into the air.

"That."

"What?"

"We were waiting for that," Wu Ying reiterated before he ducked through the hallway and headed for the front door.

He ignored the child demon lurking in the stairs, clutching a doll made of bones and dried skin, ignored the mother who held a knife pointed at them while she blocked the way upward. Ignored even the shadow beetle that might or might not be upstairs, feasting on the corpse of its latest prey.

Instead, he exited the front door and leapt upward, almost stumbling as the foothold of air he had expected to appear never did so until he had begun to fall. He righted himself and sprang sideways onto the roof, ignoring the curious and worried look Yang Mu sent him as she joined him moments later.

"Now we go to the temple. Straight and fast as we can," he said.

"Finally!" Phuong Vy cried, joining them.

The scholar ran ahead and was easily caught by Wu Ying, the wind cultivator taking the lead once again. All around him, the winds stirred and blew, offering him glimpses of the world around. Yet for once, the wind was not reliable.

In the gloom, the group was hard to spot, as were the archers that had taken to the roofs. More than once, Wu Ying found the wind was too slow to inform him of a crouching watcher, their arrows and javelins thrown at them and blocked only by Yang Mu's fans or the occasional floating talisman.

Those he did spot, he utilized the wind to cast down, sending them crashing to the earth. There were more than sufficient targets, for as their enemies realized their location, they took to the crumbling skyline too, chasing after the trio.

Yet this was where the well-trained cultivators shined. Qinggong methods allowed them to lighten their bodies, allowed them to step on precarious footing and not send crumbling mortar breaking or rotting beams crashing. No such luck for the heavy-footed demons, who raced across the ancient city only to collapse through rotten tiles or fall as they leapt massive gaps between streets, only to find footing too slick or in too great disrepair.

It did not, of course, help that the wind had picked up in the strangest ways. Tugging at robes, sending dislodged clay tiles spinning through the air at incredible—and deadly—speeds, or pulling demons and cultivators aside at the slightest provocation.

"Control your winds, false dragon!" Phuong Vy snarled as she was sent stumbling by a gust that caught her just before she fell, only Yang Mu's sudden grip on her elbow keeping her from being thrown aside. Of the three, the scholar was struggling the hardest in their race across the moonlit rooftops. It was she that the wind seemed to target the most.

"I cannot. Like I told your colonel, the corruption has infected the air here. The wind is but a portion of the air, and with the corruption, my control has lessened. I can only stir it awake and let it dance through the night," Wu Ying said. "I assume we are better able to handle some chaos than our enemies."

And chaos there was. He could sense it already, as the modified Cyclone's Breath method formed a nexus point farther south of them on the other side of the city. A whirlwind was forming there, gusting in circular fashion and in its initial stages. None of the others might sense it, but given time, it would come roaring through the city, bringing with it additional danger.

"Idiotic, chaotic fool…" Phuong Vy cursed, but she did not ask again, instead lowering her head to concentrate on their journey. She did deploy another half dozen yellow talisman papers around her, each of them floating about her body as she ran, working to intercept attacks that sought their lives.

Each moment, they neared the stepped pyramid that dominated the center of this abandoned city. They were nearly at the temple grounds, the massive edifice having a clear space all around.

On the steps leading up, they noticed a pair of figures awaiting them, standing under the rotting corpses of the previous expedition. Without verbal signal, the trio slowed their approach. Neither of their opponents were attempting to hide their auras, unlike the trio.

"Trouble," Yang Mu muttered as they jogged across slick tiles. "They look strong. Stronger than the ones we fought."

"They do," Wu Ying said, eyeing the massive hammer the creature on the left wielded. Its long fingers were entirely wrapped around the massive shaft, the head nearly twice as big as its already elongated width.

The other Ma Than Vong held a pair of serrated blades low to its body, the weapons curved backward over the guards of the hilts, offering a crescent-shaped, jagged moon for attacking with. It kept its body low, hunched over unlike its proud companion, eyes hooded as it eyed the trio as they approached.

"We cannot stay long. Your friend might be doing well, but their leader is stronger than we expected," Phuong Vy said, drawing a pair of small daggers which she hid beneath her palms.

In the background, the pulse and flare of battle between cultivators and Nascent Soul demon could be felt. It caused the very air to tremble and shriek, the repeated noises of weapons clashing and the crack of massive strikes that tore up the ground and sent gouts of flame and debris flinging through the air lighting up the sky. No wonder the roused villagers had chosen to chase the three rather than join a battle where they were nothing but minor obstacles.

The glow from the battle, where Tou He had unleashed the full strength of the fire dragon blood that coursed through his body, was clear across a third of the city. It lit up the night's sky like a beacon of the gods, and the heat and its effects had created an updraft that threw Wu Ying's command of the wind in further disarray. Yet the air freed at the top of that growing cyclone was clean and clear, singing to his senses like a cup of water after a day's march through the desert.

"Then we finish this quickly. I'll take the hammer," Wu Ying said flatly. He buried the worry for his friend beneath action as he sped up once more. Sword held by his side, his eyes narrowed as he approached, searching for the opening.

With each step, the wind gathered around him as he flexed an iron control he rarely utilized. No longer friend but subservient to his demands, forced to work as he demanded as his wind chi poured out from his dantian. He formed a domain where even the corrupted energies had no choice but to accede to his iron control.

He would not fail, he would not stop, and he would not allow his friend to fall.

Killing intent bled into his aura, the long dormant wind dragon's blood thrashing awake at the presence of a nearby cousin. The air around him bled energy, a corona of wind and light forming around him as he outpaced his friends with each step, his sword pointed at his foe.

Second form of the Wandering Dragon, the Dragon's Truth.

Consume.

The modified lunge tore through the air, the last hundred feet covered in the blink of an eye. His opponent turned, feet braced under the incoming gale, timing the swing of the hammer he held over his head. He timed it perfectly, swinging downward when Wu Ying crossed under the ponderous attack, the hammerhead targeted to crush the cultivator's neck and spine.

Perfectly timed, but an utter misjudgment of the strength of Wu Ying's strike.

The leading trail of the attack was not the sword point, but the killing intent and energy that bled outward from Wu Ying. Those tore into the muscular hanged demon long before Wu Ying's tip struck. Then winds along the edges and around Wu Ying cut into exposed muscles and tendons, killing intent laced through the motion as the hammer began its descent.

As it neared, underneath the glowing light of shed chi, the swirling cyclone of wind that wrapped the wind cultivator tugged the attack off course.

Even the ponderous attack, filled with its own form of dao and the full killing intent of the demon, could not stop Wu Ying. His attack tore through the monster's side, even as the sharpened tip of killing intent entered the demon's body, expanding wider as winds burst into the body. The hammer head twisted away, torn from numbed fingers, the weapon never even reaching Wu Ying as he continued moving all the way through.

Chunks of the body, torn apart by shredding winds and blade intent, exploded, leaving Wu Ying to skim across the ground as he bled off momentum. He turned around, robes flaring out behind him, not a touch of blood or viscera on him.

Surprise registered on his other opponent's face, the creature awaiting Wu Ying's friends, confident in his ally's ability to deal with the wind cultivator. For a moment more, it stared at Wu Ying before it began to fade into the shadow pooled around its feet.

Wu Ying raised his weapon, throwing a blade strike he knew would never reach the creature.

But both parties had forgotten he was not the only one in battle.

Yang Mu's fan opened, flaring bright green and white as the inscriptions on the fan triggered. Light flowed through the surroundings, spreading out in a formation beneath her feet and catching the creature as it sank halfway through the ground, trapping it.

Surprise registered on its face as it leaned away from Wu Ying's blade strike that finally caught up, carving a deep trench in its flesh. Moments later, poisoned throwing knives from Phuong Vy sank into its back.

Then the fan's light guttered out, the massive configuration disappearing. The creature finished sinking into the ground as the pair of cultivators hurried over to Wu Ying.

"Thousand hells, where did it go?" Wu Ying said, casting his senses outward and finding no sign of the creature. It sat ill with him, to leave behind what was an obvious assassin.

"Do not worry, it is dead." Phuong Vy grinned savagely as she hurried by him. She called over her shoulder, "It just doesn't know it yet."

Wu Ying shook his head, turning away from the scholar. He stared at the hanging corpses, many missing limbs and bones after the fury and suddenness of their battle. Rather than leave them to hang, he sliced sideways, parting the rope holding the last corpse above and sending it clattering to the ground. "She scares me sometimes."

"Only sometimes?" Yang Mu said. "My father always said women with books are the most dangerous, for they know too many things."

"Aren't you and your sisters and your mother all well read?" Wu Ying asked.

"Yes, yes, we are."

Even as they spoke, bones were pulled toward them by simple chi strings, Yang Mu utilizing the wood chi in the ropes to do so. In short order, they had the corpses gathered in a storage ring to be taken back. The actions by the pair were done by unspoken accord, neither willing to leave the bodies behind.

Task complete, the pair ran after Phuong Vy, scanning the surroundings for additional guards. There were some, but most lay on the ground, gurgling their lifeblood or twitching as Phuong Vy cleared the way with her poisoned knives.

She might not be a martial cultivator, but she was still a Core Formation cultivator. And these poor demons were nothing beneath their eyes.

Chapter 27

They caught up with Phuong Vy as she stood before the massive doors of the temple, the way closed and barred. A deep hand imprint in the center of the doors indicated an attempt to enter once already, and now the woman was standing back, glaring at the doors while she pulled pouches from her storage ring before putting them back.

"What, exactly, are you thinking of doing?" Yang Mu asked, obviously scandalized as she stared at the tiny scholar.

"Finding a poison that'll eat through those doors, of course." Phuong Vy hefted a pouch consideringly, then hung it off one finger with another pair she had already drawn out. "I've not seen this kind of stone before, but I'm sure I can work something out."

"You… it's a formation! Just let me break the formation." Giving her head a hard shake, Yang Mu turned to eye the doors before frowning more and more.

Wu Ying briefly looked over the glistening inscriptions and runes, understanding just enough about the flows of energy that passed through the doors to accept that he had no purpose looking at it. He recognized at least one portion of the energy signature to be a reflective attack, which saw off brute forcing their entrance.

On the other hand, waiting around for more enemies to arrive sat ill with him. He stepped back, raising his hand and enforcing his will on the winds again. He pushed his chi outward, feeling his core drain further as he sent the wind scurrying around the building, searching for another way within.

One, two, three entrances were found in quick order. Each were barred, though none as powerfully as the front doors. Still, they were inconveniently placed and two were inappropriately sized for normal cultivators. He might be able to bypass the physical restrictions with his qinggong methods, but it was unlikely the pair could fit.

More, he assumed that such weakness in the formation was a ruse. It seemed likely, though overconfidence could not be ruled out. After all, when one had a Nascent Soul level guardian, few enough were worried about such things.

Which reminded him…

"What is Sao Choi doing?" he muttered.

Phuong Vy glanced at Wu Ying, then shook her head a little as though dissuading him from pursuing that conversation. It was concerning, this lack of information, especially amongst his erstwhile allies. Especially when his friend was battling for his life.

He could only hope that the absence of the Nascent Soul beast was not something he should concern himself about. Did Bich Trang lack control over the creature, as he his winds, in this environment? If so, how did the cultivator know this beforehand? How much information had really been communicated backward, before the previous expeditions fell?

Or was there another reason for the bird's lack of effort during this battle? Were they that certain they could handle matters in the village with their current resources? Was Sao Choi more fragile than it looked? Certainly birds were powerful allies, but weak in many ways. Their thin bones were easy to crush and break, their greater speed and maneuverability useless in a long, drawn-out battle.

Mostly.

Wu Ying had memories about one particular Nascent Soul bird that had beaten him bloody not that long ago. The right combination of dao and elements could allay many natural disadvantages after all.

A sharp cry drew Wu Ying's attention back to the immediate surroundings. He was not concerned about the guards or the incoming mob, many of whom had come across their champion's body and slowed down, gathering together at the far edges of his perception as they sought courage in numbers.

"There!" With a clap of Yang Mu's hands and flooding of her chi, the massive double doors shattered.

Or they seemed to, in Wu Ying's vision, before suddenly reforming. Or perhaps it was an image of the door that had shattered and the real ones had always been there? He shook his head, the dueling visions that clouded his senses throwing him off for a moment.

He could not help but wonder if the corruption that was invading the wind was taking its toll on him too. And if so, what could he do about it? Something to discuss with Tou He and Yang Mu later, it seemed.

Phuong Vy was not caught in idle musings like him, already setting tiny hands against the door. She put her strength into the push, levering the doors apart before she jerked backward, twisting as she did so. Too slow to avoid the trap entirely as bolts fired from within. Some of the pre-set crossbow bolts clattered uselessly against the massive doors that were still swinging open, others flew by and caught naught but air. One was deflected at the last minute by a fan snapped open, and Wu Ying swayed aside as two seemed to home in on him, one seemingly blown his way by an errant gust of wind.

Another snap of a fan and a blast of energy was thrown outward from the enchanted accessory. The racks of crossbows were blown over, the remaining weapons meant to fire a second volley sent clattering to the floor, launching their deadly payload upward and away.

Not without cost though.

Phuong Vy tumbled backward, clutching her side where it had begun to stain the area under her rosebud breasts, a grimace of pain across her visage.

"Are you well, Cultivator La?" Wu Ying said, hurrying over.

He stopped as she waved him away, the scholar muttering curses as she straightened. "I shall live. Go, deal with whatever traps there might be. We must get the splinter before they move it or bring more reinforcements."

Wu Ying's lips pursed, but he chose to not pursue the matter. He did recall, after all, that there were still a number of Core Formation demons unaccounted for. Not all of them were martial combatants of course, or were unlikely to be, but these were demons. Who knew how much of a martial tradition they truly held? In any case, the scholar was already extracting a compress to press to her side, and her being more experienced in the physicking arts than he, he saw no point in pressing the matter.

Striding in with his sword drawn, Wu Ying dealt with the half dozen guards waiting for him in short order, along with the four traps he located in as many steps. He stopped after that, anger rolling through his body as he took in the insides of the temple.

It seemed that the Ma Than Vong took their name and traditions to the extreme within this sacred place. Corpses of beasts and men and even their own people littered the insides, many strung high into the massive, empty ceiling of the sloped pyramid. The bodies rotted slowly, festering and decaying and staining the air, while large hunks of fresh meat hung near the center of the building around a central fire, a fire that burned a twisted, sickly greenish yellow.

The tainted flame.

And the splinter itself, that which fueled the fire, drew the eye and senses, twice the size of a slim man's torso as it beat within the flame. If the reek of corruption and decay that filled the building, the one made of voided bowels and decomposing corpses and rotting meat, was not enough to turn the stomach, the sight of the pulsing heart in the center of the flame would have emptied a lesser man's innards. Even Wu Ying, who had seen much in his travels, found himself recoiling, a deep sense of wrongness rising within him.

"I cannot spot every trap in here," Yang Mu said, her voice high and a little desperate as she sought a topic other than the still-beating heart, the thundering rhythm filling the air now that the formation had been torn aside. The noise was all too present, all too… wrong. "Too many shadows. Too many… bodies."

"Neither can I. Not this near that… thing." Wu Ying made a quick decision, twisting his hand and cutting, first to the right then left. The blade strikes tore through the air, shattering unseen wires and cutting down corpses. When traps, magical and mechanical, were triggered by his actions, he grinned. "But my father used to say, if you could not be smarter than your opponent, you could always just work harder."

Yang Mu matched the vicious smile on Wu Ying's face, turning to one side. She raised her fans and swung them, slicing sideways with the edges of the metal implements, sending chi blades through the air with each motion. Unlike with a sword, her movements took on a slight flutter as she made the cuts, causing a wind to rise with each movement such that living snakes of power and intent traversed the air in search of prey.

Wu Ying swung his jian in short, sharp movements. He tore into the temple and the traps all around, making sure to gouge not just the walls and pillars but the floor and ceiling as well. All around them, stone cracked and exploded, wires and ropes were cut, and corpses tumbled, entrails and bones tumbling.

Traps triggered, one after the other, most misfiring and targeting other portions of the empty building. Some, however, were more widespread, throwing lit oil and releasing flying blades through the air. Rather than stay still, Wu Ying strode forward through the attacks, closing the distance toward the beating heart, beating aside attacks that came for him or slipping past them with the barest of movements.

Yang Mu let out a low laugh, joining Wu Ying in his approach. Unlike his—mostly—straight line approach, she took a more circuitous route, the steps of a drunken fairy both unpredictable and inefficient. Yet not once did the traps touch her, and the fans that never stopped moving cut again and again, picking up discarded bodies and tearing through traps that had been missed by Wu Ying.

Between the two of them, they took apart the temple, the storm of white and brown energy throwing corpses and limbs, flames and rope askew, even as the sickly green flames continued to thrum through the air.

Far behind and safe from the ongoing storm, Phuong Vy walked inside, a series of new talismans floating around her in protection. They formed interconnecting triangles, the sharp-edged formation beating aside the occasional bone or bolt cast in her direction.

It took the group only a short time to cover the rest of the ground, the few attendants who streamed out to stop falling to the flurry of power. In another time, in another place, Wu Ying might have been disturbed by the casual ending of their lives. But here, in this desecrated temple of corruption and decay where the beating heart of an infernal creature rested, he found such sensibilities muted.

No.

More than that, they were washed away by a righteous anger that saw him take deep satisfaction in the destruction of the temple and the ending of the Ma Than Vong.

"How are we to douse that fire?" Yang Mu said as the pair of them stopped a healthy distance from the heart.

Neither of them desired to near it, for an instinctive revulsion ran through them, along with a strong desire for the destruction of the infernal object.

"It does not seem to mind my wind," Wu Ying noted idly. "Even the hardest gales barely shifted the flames."

"And wood is of no use. I do have a water barrel in my ring…" Yang Mu said.

"You have a water barrel in your storage ring?" Wu Ying repeated, surprised. "Why?"

"A woman needs to keep herself clean and presentable. You never know what circumstances one might find oneself within," Yang Mu said primly.

"I really want a ring that large," Wu Ying grumbled.

"Of course you do. But the fire?"

"I'll handle that. And the heart. You two, watch for trouble," Phuong Vy said, coming up to the two.

The pair stepped aside, allowing the diminutive scholar to approach the heart and stop a few feet from it. The flames reflected off the glowing talismans that hovered around her, the yellow paper smoking at the edges as the chi devoted to their creation burnt out.

"First, to quench the flames, remove the air." Phuong Vy threw her hands sideways, casting a formation flag out of both hands, then slammed a third into the floor before her feet.

The trio of flags shimmered, twisting the space caught between them and locking it away. Wu Ying cocked his head curiously, watching the fractured vision of the heart as the flame guttered and died, idly noting that such a formation could be used against him too. He regarded it with some minor trepidation, searching for flaws even as he attempted to enforce his will on the air around them, pulling fresher air from the broken entrance.

Yang Mu barely even eyed the formation, instead walking around the temple. She had stored one of her fans, leaving her with a staff that she used to prod and push at the wreckage, as though searching for treasures.

"Find anything?" Wu Ying asked.

"Nothing yet. But you never know."

He shook his head, surprised at her optimism. This was not a place he would have expected anything of value, and he certainly had no desire to dirty his hands searching among the offal and rotting corpses.

Which was an interesting change from his earlier years, if he thought about it. Once he would have scrabbled through corpses for the meanest amount of coin. Now, he was rich enough – at least in theory – that he would turn up his nose at the thought of some advantage, when it came to pushing through all this mess.

Was he, dare he think it, becoming an effete noble?

Shuddering a little at the thought, Wu Ying eyed the surroundings more religiously. No. He had been tasked with watching for danger and that was what he was doing. He was not shirking such efforts just because he did not want to get his hands dirty—or at least, not only that. Though there was certainly a difference between good dirt and compost and the tainted, rotting remains around them.

"If you two will be quiet, I'm working here." Phuong Vy snapped. "This is taking too long…" And it was, for the flames, while dying, were doing so slowly. "I'll need to cool it further. The Nine Buddha Palms Void Formation or the Ice Jade Mountain Formation?" Muttering to herself, she stalked sideways then back, lips thin.

"The Buddha Palms will damage your formation and the heart. The Ice Jade will take longer, but it will likely cause the least amount of damage to both," Yang Mu offered. "Truly depends on what you need."

"I knew that!" Phuong Vy said, then hesitated before extracting the Ice Jade flags. These formation flags, enscripted and enchanted with runes all along the cloth, were blue and white, in contrast to the more common yellow or cream-colored flags.

She inserted the flags into the floor, this time there being a total of nine that she had to carefully position around the randomly inserted flags of before. Yang Mu took to watching the scholar work with pursed lips in between poking at the wreckage.

In the meantime, Wu Ying eyed the numerous entrances scattered throughout the four-sided pyramid, noting hallways running parallel to the base of the pyramid and disappearing into shadowed alcoves within that defied easy perception. With so much to be seen, he felt himself a little exposed, especially as the wind continued to shriek their misery and twisted visions in equal measure.

Without his usual flighty companions, with his senses seriously curtailed by the presence of the infernal heart that continued to beat—perhaps even more strongly now that the fire that had consumed it was guttering—and with so many entrances to watch, Wu Ying never noticed the attack until it was nearly too late.

For some, it was entirely tardy.

Chapter 28

"'Ware, above!" Wu Ying roared, the flicker of a descending shadow catching his attention as demonic beasts dropped from the tall chimney at the peak of the pyramid. They descended without warning, falling through the smoke while holding their weapons. A dozen descending figures, but Wu Ying only had eyes for one—the Core Formation cultivator that sought Phuong Vy's life.

Controlling the building power of the formation as she planted the flags, the scholar was slow to react and even slower to defend. She barely brought the pair of formation flags in her hand above her head when the hanged demon arrived, his massive sword leading the way in the attack. It tore through her protective talismans with ease, struck her upraised defenses, and parted the flags and their staves with equal ease before the attack plunged into her chest via her shoulder.

Formed and controlled energies exploded, released after being twisted and held together by the placement of the flags the moment the flags she held were destroyed. They tore the first three emplaced out of the floor, sent the remainder of the Ice Jade flags away, and covered the entire area in a wave of unrestricted cold.

The explosion was what saved Phuong Vy's life, the released energies casting her back even as she shrank away, the blade cutting deeper into her body with each moment. Thrown to the floor, her entire body was covered in fast-forming ice as her attacker was cast upward by the very same explosion.

Wu Ying's retaliatory attack was cast aside by the same explosion, the released energies sending him tumbling through the air like a sapling amongst an avalanche. Frost covered the temple innards within moments, the temperature dropping below freezing as demons and cultivators were beset by the contained energies.

The entirety of the area was a winter wasteland but the still-beating heart. That froze for a second, the flames around it guttering out before it began beating again, more furiously than ever. The hellish beating caused frost nearby to shatter and bones to thrum as the infernal heart sought to impose a synchronicity to even the cultivator's life beat.

A low cry from Yang Mu, one that had Wu Ying's gut tightening in concern. He could not lose her. Not yet, not when they had not decided upon what they were to one another. Yet he could do nothing as he was assailed too by the infernal heart.

Wu Ying was pressed against the edge of the building, his breathing hard and tight as he pushed against the energy that threatened to overtake his control. He found his vision fuzzing, his focus wavering, and, worst of all, his dao understandings crumbling.

What was wind but moving air, and the air here had already been corrupted. He was nothing, not even as encompassing as the five winds he so desperately sought to understand. Traces of the wind of heaven, that he had sought for so long and that had led him here, dissipated as the heart thundered, driving something as paltry as wind aside with each beat.

Surprise then, that a wind, another wind he had only glimpsed and understood in the barest, rose within. A thread of understanding that he had gripped while learning of its counterpart pushed back against this tyrannical imposition from outside. The heavens might bow to tyrants, but hell would always be filled with rebels.

Hell—the hundred hells—was a place of suffering, a place of punishment and despair. There was never a doubt in that. But it was also a place of due process, of justice and understanding. Of redemption and cleansing before an individual's rebirth.

Heaven might judge, but hell offered justice.

The infernal heart was anathema to the very understanding of what the hells offered, a place to regain one's lost humanity, to set right the wrongs created in the foolish heat of mortal life. To rob another of their ability to choose, to strip free will and impose one's dictates was not justice. For that, governments—heavenly or not—were required, in seeking governance for all they lacked nuance.

As the heart beat, as will eroded, that singular thread of hellish enlightenment fought against such an imposition. It freed Wu Ying from the noise, emerged from his core to create a barrier of howling wind. Hell itself gave the wind cultivator an opportunity to strengthen his resolve and firm his mind, closing off the aura that had left him vulnerable.

Gripping his sword, he levelled it toward the pedestal and the heart it held, only to spot Phuong Vy already there, blood dripping freely from her wounds. A hand raised and plunged downward, an obsidian knife gripped tightly, green and black light from glowing enchantments appearing around her as she struck.

Blade entered beating heart, and the heart stuttered. It beat once before it stilled.

Blessed silence rolled through the surroundings, broken only by the groans and moans of the living.

Her task done, Phuong Vy slumped to the floor. The Core Cultivator hanged demon rose too, its gaze flicking from Wu Ying, who was in the midst of finishing off its brethren to the silent heart, the senseless scholar, and the slowly recovering Yang Mu. The creature hesitated, claws flexing.

Wu Ying turned toward the hanged demon, sword raised and firm with resolution. The creature met Wu Ying's glare with its own before it inclined its head a little, turning and bounding away, disappearing out an exit. The wind cultivator sagged in relief, his mind and energy still in disarray. A fight against the demon might have been more risky than he would have preferred, but he assumed the creature had done much the same math.

Perhaps, even, been grateful for them removing such a cursed object from their lives. Wu Ying could hope, at least.

He strode past the few hanged demons still alive, many staring senselessly into the horizon. He cut them down mercilessly, remembrance of the temple decorations still fresh. Yang Mu, unsteady on her feet, was doing the same as the pair approached Phuong Vy's body.

The tiny scholar let out a long groan. "Owww…"

"You live," Wu Ying said, surprised.

"Box it…" A twitch of her hand and a massive crate appeared next to her, crashing to the floor and shaking up dust and bones.

Wu Ying hesitated, but since Yang Mu was extracting bandages and pills, he chose to follow the scholar's words. Except when he turned to the heart, he stopped. He had no desire to touch it or use anything of his own to touch it. Eventually, he shoved the crate over and opened its top before using the wreckage to lever the heart, floor stones propped against still flesh as he dropped the infernal organ into the crate. Listening to the fleshy thud, Wu Ying almost swore he heard the echo of that infernal heartbeat begin again. He shuddered, his soul quailing, but it was but an echo.

Then the lid closed, and it was over, the heart hidden from them.

"Activate it," Phuong Vy croaked softly.

Frowning, Wu Ying looked at her before he turned away immediately. Yang Mu had stripped the scholar of her outer clothing, leaving only the thin silk underlayer to cover her modesty, an underlayer that clung tightly from spilled blood. There was nothing erotic about such a sight, but courtesy was an iron law in such situations.

"Right. Umm… how?" Wu Ying scanned the surroundings just in case, idly noting his control of the wind was strengthening with the source of the taint removed.

Phuong Vy rattled off the instructions and, following the intricate motions and flow of chi required, he managed to activate the inscriptions on the box. Immediately, the beast stone set in the top glowed, imbuing the box with its strength and locking away the heart.

Tension left Wu Ying's body, the sense of wrongness that had existed beside him all this time disappearing. The sighs of relief from the pair behind him informed him that they felt similarly.

Finally, it was over.

At least, this portion of their infiltration. Now, they just had to leave.

***

Exiting the temple with the box gripped in one hand, Wu Ying eyed the destroyed exterior of the temple and the empty square around it, searching for the enemies he knew had been gathering outside. He was carrying the box rather than storing it in a ring because Phuong Vy had scolded him for even attempting that. It seemed that certain containment runes on the wooden box required access to the Dao of the Heavens to function and placing them within a storage ring would cut the box off. An act that could lead to untold disasters.

Of course, the other reason he was carrying the box was because Yang Mu had flatly refused to go near it at all, muttering about them destroying the thing immediately rather than leaving it to fester.

The badly injured scholar was of no use. They were lucky she was on her feet and lucid. As it was, she was bolstered by a series of apothecary pills and enchanted bandages that stopped her bleeding while increasing the production of blood and fluids. Now, in one hand, she held a bottle of tea laced with honey and sugar cane that she quaffed habitually, riding after them on a moving cauldron. Even so, each shift of the cauldron made her lips compress and her face pale while blood leaked from the bandages.

"The fight is over, it seems." Wu Ying eyed the distance where a flame had once burnt, surprised that they had missed the ending. He would have thought the formation the other team had been emplacing would have been destructive in its activation, but the Nascent Soul demon's end had been understated.

Now, the only sign of the battle and the activation of the formation was the extensive destruction to entire blocks of the ancient city. Stone walls and buildings were shattered, pavement that had survived the weathering of time broken and scattered across multiple li. Fires burned fitfully across the swath of destruction, concentrated where the group had fought but also scattered as though thrown by an impetuous immortal hand.

Wu Ying relaxed a little as he stared about, noting a column of flame and wind that moved forward, a blaze that burned hot and cleansed the very air it lit.

"Are you done staring? Because it might be time to go. Our 'friends' are recovering, if slowly."

Following Yang Mu's gesture, Wu Ying noted the mass of demons that had gathered at the steps of the temple. The strongest and hardiest of the creatures were already standing and shaking their heads and bodies, dark fur rippling as the attack and control exerted by the demonic heart faded. Others—the weakest of mind and soul—were still senseless. A few, Wu Ying sensed, had entirely expired from the whiplash of effects.

Perhaps the heart had done them some good, for if the massed army had launched their attack while Wu Ying and the other cultivators were still in battle with the Core Formation demon within, the danger would have escalated.

Funny, how some circumstances, upon first blush a disaster, might instead be a blessing.

Though perhaps Phuong Vy might disagree with that thought.

"Lead the way," Wu Ying answered, gesturing with his sword. "My winds are still hampered, even if Tou He is cleansing the air."

Yang Mu moved down the stairs at an angle so that they would not have to face the majority of the gathered demons. Even in the short period they had been speaking, the demons were shifting up the stairs, though none chose to attack.

Not yet, at least.

Phuong Vy took to the middle of the group. She had her legs crossed, the central handle of the top of the cauldron poking upward from the center of her legs as she meditated, attempting to extract the full strength of the pills she had consumed as quickly as possible.

Additional protective talismans floated around her, replacing the ones shattered by the Core Formation demon.

Descending, they moved through the demons who parted at their presence, the few in the corner unwilling to face the trio, injured and tired as they might be. Wu Ying kept an eye on the column of flame as he brought up the rear, noting that it was closing on them too, if slowly.

Concerning, that their speed was so low. A thread of worry that had faded wormed its way into Wu Ying's gut once more. Was Tou He injured? Was another of the group, such that they could not approach quickly?

In contrast, other than Phuong Vy, they had managed to emerge from the battles with few enough injuries. Some bruises, a few minor cuts, but their defenses and skills had held. Considering the number of enemies they had faced, Wu Ying considered their entire fight to have gone well, even if his stores of energy were significantly lower than he wished.

Enforcing his domain over the winds was taxing, an almost polar opposite to his normal methods of utilizing the wind. It drew greatly from his stores to impose his will. In addition, he had to cut his body's natural connection to the surroundings. After all, while his body might—usually—draw in ambient wind chi, the corrupted energy around him was not normal.

If nothing else, subsuming the taint would intensify the agonizing cleansing baths he had to take.

Farther south, the massive tornado that had formed from the interaction between Wu Ying's cultivation techniques, the twisted air of the city, and the elemental fury of the winds raged. It tore through the city, causing further destruction and hampering any travel in that direction.

Tension ratcheted up as they traversed the city, casting around for potential enemies and opponents. Though a small group followed the trio at a distance, it seemed the hanged demons had retreated for the moment as their leaders were vanquished. The farther the group got from the temple, the lesser the effects of the taint and the greater the number of hanged demons.

Wu Ying's wind continued to whisper secrets as they traveled, of creatures hiding in damp basements or sweaty palms clutching weapons tightly, breathing harsh and fearful.

A demonic female, a toddler hanging off her body and latched onto one ponderous breast, gripped the hands of two other children as they exited a building, only to freeze upon encountering the violent winds that surrounded Wu Ying. She hunkered down with her children, realization crossing an all-too-human face that she'd left her departure too long. Grief, resignation, then fierce resolve and resolution as she gripped her children tightly. Dark eyes followed their motion as they passed by.

Yang Mu ignored the demon, having discarded her as a potential threat. Instead, her fans swung sideways to strike at an archer farther ahead, loosed arrow skittering into the night before the cut struck, leaving the bisected body to fall to earth.

Meeting the gaze of the mother, Wu Ying offered the most minor of nods before moving on. She was thin, as were her children, as were the majority of the tribe. Whatever meat that splinter heart had cleansed, it was insufficient for the needs of such a large settlement.

For a moment, his sense of self and place lurched as a recollection of himself as a child, worried about raiders, tore through him.

Who here was the monster?

He had come into their home, murdered their leaders, torn apart their most sacred place, and stolen what they required to survive. Now, he escaped with his people, unharmed and with the spoils of their raid clutched over one shoulder.

Yet…

He could find little to regret, upon recalling the temple and its innards. Perhaps, sometimes, certain races and individuals could not coexist in peace. Perhaps the Dao of existence between two such groups was of never-ending conflict.

The tiger ate the lamb. The worm ate the tiger. Neither was wrong to do so.

For a moment, the wind brushed his senses, whispering unintelligible words. Enlightenment passed, as did the benediction of heaven. In this place, neither was available.

Disappointed, Wu Ying shoved those thoughts aside. Time enough later.

They turned the corner and found their friends at last. There, the reason for their sluggish arrival was revealed. And once more, Wu Ying found concern rising for his old friend.

Chapter 29

Tou He was on his feet and moving under his own volition. While he might have been injured, the injuries were mostly superficial—at least for a cultivator at their rank. A few long cuts down one side, a limp from a bloody cut on a thigh on the other. Healing pills and a few days' rest were sufficient to repair that.

No, what caused Wu Ying's concern were the unconstrained flames that erupted from his aura. The ex-monk moved jerkily and ponderously, more living flame than man, an elemental that might consume the very world if left unattended. A cleansing flame to set the world aright, that swept through a forest and in its passing, allowed new growth and new life to emerge.

Much like what was happening now.

Around him, the rest of the unit moved, each of them bearing a formation flag. They strained as they walked, their faces deeply troubled as they contained the heat from the cultivator, allowing the inflow of air and the occasional burst of energy outward, but also mitigating the damage to the surroundings.

"How is he not exhausted already?" Yang Mu asked, cocking her head to the side. While Wu Ying had to strain to control his own winds here, she had not faced the same level of issues. And yet, even Wu Ying could sense that she was low in the chi within her dantian.

"Fire feeds on itself and others," Wu Ying said. "You need only offer it a spark and it burns continually."

"Except it is not just plain fire, is it?" Yang Mu said. "And I know how fire works."

Fire, one of the more common elements for those in the martial side of cultivation. It was the element of destruction and cleansing. It was also the most directly damaging of the elements. It was a question that philosophers debated endlessly: whether fire cultivators ended up as martial cultivators because fire lent itself best to martial methods, or martial cultivators were fire based because the element was destructive.

"Of course you do." Wu Ying glanced at the floating and silent Phuong Vy. He knew why his friend had lasted so long, above and beyond the propensity of fire to spread. Tou He's journey to Core Formation had been difficult, requiring him to open and utilize a second dantian. It gave him a much larger store of energy than one would expect. Even if he might trust Yang Mu enough to discuss his friend's secrets, it was not his secret to tell. "Even a cleansing fire like this, I'm sure."

"One taken from a fire dragon." Yang Mu's lips rose in a wry smile. "What is it with you and dragons? Most cultivators spend their entire lives never interacting with a single Heavenly beast, whether it be golden carp, regal phoenix, or majestic dragon. You…"

Wu Ying shrugged. "Maybe like calls to like?"

"It's just a name."

Wu Ying grinned, and she rolled her eyes, sticking out her tongue. He understood that she was distracting him as they closed the last few feet to join the group. Wu Ying stopped near his friend, Tou He's eyes empty as he jerked onward.

"What is wrong with him?" Wu Ying asked.

The team continued to strain as they imbued the formation with their chi, containing the flames, but Wu Ying could see that the flags were failing. The air howled inward to be consumed with each passing moment, molten lava footprints left behind as Tou He trudged onward.

"The demon realized what we were about to do and sought to escape. Rather than allow it, your friend met it headlong, doing battle with his aura and that thing that lives in him," Dinh Don replied.

"A fire dragon."

"A fire demon perhaps," Thien Giang replied. "He injured that hanged demon when he unleashed it, doing half the job for us before the formation activated. If we'd known…" She shook her head. "But afterward, the flames continued to burn. It kept attacking, destroying the buildings, the hanged demons all around."

"You?" Yang Mu asked.

"No." The polearm wielder shook her head, long hair swishing in disarray. Rather than the helmet that the team normally wore, hers had been knocked free at some point, such that they could observe the sweat and strain of holding the formation together. "He avoided attacking us, thankfully."

"Then he's still in there," Wu Ying said.

"Why did you stop him anyway?" Yang Mu asked. "I cannot see you caring for the Ma Than Vong."

"We don't. But we worried you might be caught by his flames if we let it run amok," Be Long replied. Surprisingly, the captain was holding up well. "If you're ready to leave, we'll drop it and let the monk do what he wants."

Phuong Vy, raising her head and opening her eyes, gestured at Wu Ying's arms where he held the box. "We have it. I had to damage the specimen, but it should do well enough."

"Good. Then, on my command…" Minh Trac said.

Wu Ying's lips pursed, then he ducked to the corner of the street, dropping the box before moving to place himself before his friend.

"What are you doing?" Yang Mu asked.

"Get the box, go. I'll deal with him," Wu Ying said.

"Let them burn, boy. They're demons," Dinh Don said. "No less to us what the monk does. In fact, it'll probably save lives in the long run if we wipe them out."

"Probably," Wu Ying said. "But that's not my decision to make. Or yours." He nodded toward the blank-eyed cultivator before him, whose flame seemed to roar and beat the air.

"It's him who should decide and who has to live with the consequences. And it's not what he would want."

All life was important. All life sacred. Demon or human, Tou He would regret taking it, especially in the state that he was in. So the monk believed.

And if that was the case, Wu Ying would not let his friend mar his soul and karma like this.

"Fool," Dinh Don said.

"Leave them," Bich Trang commanded. "If he wishes to die with his friend, so be it. We have what we need. On Guardsman Thi's command."

Yang Mu looked back and forth, indecision warring on her face. Wu Ying caught her gaze and shook his head, flicking his gaze toward the group and narrowing his eyes, trying to communicate his desire for her to watch over their unsteady allies. Whether she understood the unspoken pantomime or just came to a decision, she nodded in return.

Fingers dipped then came up, Yang Mu flicking a half dozen talismans at him. Wu Ying watched as they took position around his body, much like Phuong Vy's protective formation, though he caught sight of the words fire and protection in the inscriptions around him.

"Be careful," she said.

"Always."

That elicited a snort. Then Yang Mu left, joining the already fleeing Phuong Vy on her floating cauldron.

One more command, a quiet countdown by the formation master. At the end, like sugar candy dissolving in a puddle of water, the formation came apart as the cultivators stopped feeding it power. They ran immediately, long before the edges of the wall came down, Dinh Don pausing only to collect the wooden box and its contents.

Leaving Wu Ying alone to face Tou He.

His friend, his ally, his brother.

As the fires burnt, as the winds howled and demons watched.

Chapter 30

The formation failed and fire exploded outward, fed by Wu Ying's winds. The air had never stopped moving, from the cyclone in the south, from the column of fire above Tou He, from Wu Ying's ministrations. Now, a second massive cyclone arose in the city, one made of flame and smoke as Tou He's aura was no longer contained.

Under Wu Ying's control, the air pulled the heat that was radiating off Tou He away from the wind cultivator, aiding his survival. Protective talismans glowed, dark ink crisping on yellow paper as the enchantments empowered themselves from flame chi and provided the protection required for survival near the flaming vortex.

Even through all these defenses, even with the hardened, resistant, and empowered skin of a Body Cultivator, Wu Ying roasted. The purifying flames of his friend's aura crisped his skin and dried it out while nearby pavement stones cracked like thunder.

"Tou He!" Wu Ying roared. "Wake up, you old fool."

Silence.

"You meat-loving greedy idiot. You third-rate monk. Wake!" he shouted again, his words barely audible under the roar of the winds. "UP!"

Each word was empowered by chi embedded in his voice and air, into the breath exiting his lungs. The last word was so loud that stones rattled and glass broke, even as wind buffeted the flames and pressed them back upon the senseless cultivator.

A minor twitch, a flutter of an eyelid and shift of expression. Then once more, Tou He's face went blank. Unshaken from his stupor, from his senseless progress onward.

"Damn you." Wu Ying eyed the talismans, clenching his fist. This was going to hurt. He had to wake the man, and he could only think of one way of doing so. On the other hand, perhaps he did not have to be entirely foolish while doing so.

Left hand rose, fist clenched. He focused his attention, his full understanding of the blade and wind. He solidified his aura, compressing the swirling texture and edges, ensured the countless whorls and gullies that made up the outer boundaries of his aura spun at full strength.

Ready as he could ever be, Wu Ying approached his senseless friend. Each step increased the temperature he was facing, sweat beading upon his forehead and skin. Another step and sweat stopped forming, drying the moment it appeared on his skin. Talismans glowed brighter and brighter, coming closer to his body in an attempt to shield him. Robes crisped and frayed, edging disappearing and armor beneath robes growing unbearably hot.

Another step, nearly within reach, and Wu Ying was forced to close his eyes. He could not stare at Tou He, not anymore. His eyes hurt from the brightness and lack of moisture. Skin crisped, blisters forming across exposed skin, threads of silk from his robes lighting up and dying in fitful gasps.

Close enough.

Wu Ying lunged.

Left hand, concentrated chi within, reached for his friend. The last few cun was blistering pain, as though Wu Ying had thrust his untamed hand into boiling oil. Skin crisped, blood boiled, nerves lit, and a scream erupted from his mouth as he backhanded his friend.

The ex-monk staggered from the blow, his aura reacting reflexively to protect himself. Wu Ying found himself thrown away, boiling air and flame sending him skipping down the hard road like a stone over still water. He tumbled through a trio of buildings, shattering walls and leaving behind wrecked structures till he fetched up against a fourth building, half inside the wall that now leaned precariously.

Tou He slowly straightened. A trickle of blood from his mouth rolled down his lips, the surprising attack having bypassed a number of reflexive defenses. However, his eyes had lost the blankness of before, confusion warring with anger. Then the ex-monk drew a deep breath of superheated air.

And screamed.

It was a primal shout, one bereft of words. It was a scream of loss and rage, of sorrow at loss of control and pain at the deaths he had caused. The monk screamed and screamed, as though he might never run out of breath, even as the flames in his aura guttered and died.

Eventually, he collapsed, breath and energy exhausted. Silent, on his knees, in a circle of molten rock and ashen air. Robes burnt to ashes, ash slowly falling to cover his nude body.

Then inch by inch, the ex-monk collapsed within himself, gripping his body as though he were afraid he would fall apart or shatter if he clutched not at all or too hard. Racking sobs, dry of tears—for what tears could be shed and not evaporate in the center of his loss of control?—were wrung from his body.

Wu Ying stumbled out of the building, stepping gingerly across rubble, compassion in his eyes. He understood his friend's grief, for once Tou He had promised not to harm even a fly. In an attempt to serve and escape the confines of this grief-ridden mortal plain, monks chose to offer no harm. And now, and now, his friend had walked further than ever from that pacific path.

Deserving or not, it was not Tou He's place to judge. No true monk would choose to bear such a burden, to accept the karmic threads and lock themselves away from nirvana. No true monk, but Tou He had left that path many years ago.

Here and now was the final measure of that choice.

Violence enacted upon the world without care or consideration. Death served wholesale to creatures– big and small, demon and insect–alike. Karma piled upon a single soul, to revibrate through eternity till payment was complete.

Wu Ying wiped his eyes, finding them bleary. His heart ached for his friend, for the choices made and the final result. The path to immortality was treacherous, filled with gullies and twists, the way above littered with the fallen.

Slowly, Wu Ying limped over to his friend, his body bruised and aching, a rib grating in his chest. One of his legs had popped back into the hip socket when he had tried to stand. He had taken more damage from his friend than the enemy. And yet, that pain was nothing compared to what Tou He suffered.

As much as heart desired, body refused, and Wu Ying sank to a stop twenty feet away from his friend. Somewhere along the way, the talismans had been destroyed and he could no longer approach his friend without suffering additional burns. The residual heat was too much for one not on the flaming path.

And so he stopped. His left arm and hand throbbed, burnt skin and white bone showing beneath his hand from where he'd backhanded the fire cultivator. What was not burnt, blistered. What was not blistered, was crisped and red.

Legs crossed, eyes half-lidded, Wu Ying extracted a healing pill and swallowed it. Then he sat, meditating and watching his friend.

Waiting.

Even as the demons that made up this city stirred, fear giving way to righteous anger.

Soon enough, righteous rage would take over.

Soon enough, a penance would be paid.

And still, he stayed.

***

"Your hand." Tou He's voice was rough, cracked and hoarse. The ex-monk walked over to the meditating wind cultivator, gaze locked on his friend's injured appendage. "I hurt you."

"Pretty sure I was the one who struck you." Wu Ying fully opened his eyes, then comically shut them immediately, raising a hand in front of his face too. "Oh gods, I'm blind."

"What? No! The fire?" Tou He said, panicked.

"No. It's too bright and white."

The ex-monk seemed puzzled, rather than grieving. He looked around, searching for something white and bright. If anything, without his aura flaring anymore, with only the occasional fire in the distance lingering, it was much darker than before. "I don't understand."

"You. You need to get a proper tan. I mean, really. It's so pale!" Head turned away, Wu Ying gestured with his uninjured hand up and down in the direction of his friend's body. His still naked body.

It took Tou He a few moments to understand, a fraction of the time to get offended, and then embarrassed. It was not as though, having lived and trained together, they had not caught sight of one another in the nude before. Hot baths and accidents during battle—and the occasional joke while training—had seen to that. But still, accidental nudity was a different matter.

"You… I… aargh. Just…" Flustered, Tou He conjured a set of robes and dressed. The black robes with green edging with a small badge of their Sect suited him, the protective enchantments woven into the robes themselves protecting him from damage. "You can open your delicate eyes now, you idiot."

Grinning, Wu Ying stood and regarded his friend. Tou He looked better, less focused upon the damage he had done, the deaths he had caused. In the corner of his friend's eyes, the way they darted sideways to fires and destroyed buildings, Wu Ying could tell it was not done. But for now at least, he was focused.

"Good. I'd already been injured once, you know," Wu Ying said. "Didn't need a second injury."

"You deserved that."

"Probably." Then, sobering, Wu Ying cocked his head. "We should go."

"Trouble?" Tou He flexed his hands, made to conjure his weapon, then chose against doing so. His lips thinned, the slight tremble in one hand all too apparent to Wu Ying's concerned regard.

"The corruption has significantly lessened. My control has returned somewhat." Wu Ying gestured down the way they'd come, where shadowy movement spoke of gathered demons. "Let's get going, before they find their courage."

Tou He nodded, then looked upward. "Can we fly?"

A slight hesitation as they both searched for additional trouble. Flying would be the safest method out, though Wu Ying disliked how low his energy stores were at present. He could sense that his friend was not much better, that last explosion and the wresting of control back having drained him of chi.

Still…

"Yes. Let's go." Wu Ying took to the air, the wind kicking up around him.

He guided it to help Tou He, who had extracted his staff, balancing on it as he followed. Together, they ascended and retraced their steps.

Overhead, clouds continued to gather and the cyclone that Wu Ying had inadvertently created raged through the city. Hot air generated by Tou He's actions combined to increase the flow rate, such that the cyclone had increased in size. The constant roar of swirling air, the occasional flung stone as it was released from the confines of the grip, and the occasional scream that pierced the roar of the wind chased the pair as they fled.

Along with two Core Formation demons, their bodies shadows on this ill-spent night. The final two? Wu Ying was not certain. He'd lost count of those that they had killed and fought.

"Trouble," Wu Ying warned his friend.

"I sense them," Tou He said. It was clear they would not escape the pair chasing them. "I'm not sure I can fight them."

Wu Ying chose not to ask if that was because of the most recent tragedy or because he lacked the energy to win. The answer would not matter in this case. Instead, he cast his mind and senses ahead, searching for the team and finding no trace of them.

"We might be alone on this." Might be, sensing that, those demons had chosen to pursue them. Or perhaps they had just grown so enraged, they cared not for their lives any longer. Wu Ying cast a glance back one last time, eyeing their pursuers directly rather than using the still-flickering wind sense and his attenuated spirit sense. "Good thing we have some surprises left for them, no?"

"Can we not run from them?" Tou He asked softly.

"If this was the start of the evening, certainly. Now?" Wu Ying shook his head. "I'm sorry. I will not risk our lives for theirs."

"I should not have asked."

Wu Ying shrugged. The pair fell silent for a time, the city dwindling beneath their feet, city walls disappearing as they entered the outer, barren lands. Even so, the demons chased them, passing over the city walls. All hope that they might stop, gaining some degree of sanity, was lost. Each moment, they came closer. Occasionally, they would release one strike or another, but the pair easily dodged the attacks of chi or twisted killing intent.

A slight adjustment of the wind and Wu Ying dropped lower, letting them skim across broken buildings and cowering demons beneath. He ignored their screams even as he sought to pull away from their pursuers who, seeing them leave the city, had sped up even more.

"Thank you. If I don't get a chance to say it. For bringing me back to myself," Tou He said.

"This cleansing flame. It's not just the dragon blood, is it?" Wu Ying said, shaping the wind channels so that they could speak easily.

"No. When I ascended, during the ascension, I was struck by heavenly lightning." A laugh then, one filled with bitterness. "I thought it offered peace, enlightenment when it came pouring down. Instead, it twisted my dao to that of the heavens, warped my flame and turned my anger into something that it wanted. This flame is mine to wield, except when it isn't. The heavens command, and I am but an instrument."

Wu Ying's brows furrowed. He had known the Heavens were imperious, uncaring in some ways of the wants of the humans below. Or they cared, but in an abstract way. At least, some of them. And the Dao itself, of course, cared—or accepted. It got confusing, when the immortals about were of the heavens, but heaven itself had its own objectives, being part of the greater Dao. And the Dao itself was not necessarily merciful—no more than a typhoon could be merciful. It just was.

But…

"That seems wrong," Wu Ying snarled. "You are more than a tool."

"Not for the Heavens, it seems."

"And what of your dao? Of your path? This is tearing you away from it."

Silence greeted his words and stretched so long that Wu Ying thought his friend might have chosen to not answer him. Then, when he finally replied, it was softly. "Humanity must adapt, must they not? To the winds of fate and to the demands of Heaven? If my dao can be twisted so easily, perhaps it was the wrong dao in the first place. Or perhaps I just did not understand it well enough."

More silence as they finally reached the edge of the forest. Wu Ying had to focus on controlling the wind, guiding the pair through the reaching branches. He stayed low, ducking between tree trunks and underneath long limbs to eke out more space between them and their pursuers. Under the shadows of the tall canopy, the darkness of the night deepened to an extent that Wu Ying was relying on his spiritual sense and his feel of the winds ahead rather than his eyes.

Still, he had to ask. "What was it that you saw, old friend? What path did you find that night?"

That night when they had battled an Elder dark sect member, who had transformed in his desperation. When a song had played, and in the gap of time between demonic transformation and ending, Tou He had ascended.

"A middle path. Not *the* Middle Path, but a middle path. One balanced between the Heavens and the Hells, one that was intrinsic to our current world and that embraced all that was before us, rather than abandoning it for the Heavens above or reincarnation," Tou He replied.

Wu Ying almost crashed into a tree, jerking away only at the last moment as he took in what his friend had said. That path was a very mortal path, one dedicated to this world and existence in a way that Buddhism lacked. Even among the Daoist immortals, few chose to sully themselves amongst mankind to that extent. Guan Yin, the Twelve Immortals, and Hoi An were a few notables.

Most others, they stood above, making judgments upon humanity and dealing with demonic incursions or just tending to the significant celestial bureaucracy required to ensure the proper running of the Thousand Hells and celestial alignments. Like the Kitchen Gods who watched all that happened, but only reported upon wrongdoings once a year. Beyond that, they did not involve themselves.

"Careful there!" Tou He said, a light flare of his aura burning away a branch and shattering it as he, too slow to follow Wu Ying, had to go through the tree.

"Sorry!" Wu Ying answered then focused. He would speak about this later with his friend. Or perhaps, not at all. After all, the monk already had enough trouble with his dao. He did not need Wu Ying prodding on the topic.

A building of energy behind them. Twisted and sharp. Wu Ying guided the pair to the right with a sudden burst of wind, running almost parallel for a second, moments before the explosion of energy. He watched as chi—corrupted and twisted and without a guiding principle or element or even a style behind—tore through the undergrowth, destroying foliage and the occasional sleeping creature in its way.

"Whoa!" Tou He cried, eyeing the destruction. "Who was that?"

"No idea. What I want to know is why he didn't do that before?" Wu Ying replied. He could not look behind to spy upon their pursuers, so fast were they moving and so tricky was his control of the winds. Dragging his friend along and making judgments that ensured Tou He could follow was taking more attention than he cared for.

"Incoming. I have this one," Tou He said.

Wu Ying could sense it, though only briefly. Water droplets moving at a high speed were thrown forward at them, like pebbles snatched from the ground and slung ahead. Then a flare of energy as his friend concentrated his aura, creating a shield of fire. The two opposing elements combatted one another before the water dispersed as proximity and strength won out.

Letting out a pained grunt, Tou He asked, "How much further?"

"Soon."

And it would be. Wu Ying could sense the clearing they had trapped coming ahead. He just had to get the two demons to follow them in without becoming suspicious. Turning his mind to flying, Wu Ying concentrated on plotting their escape, even as the occasional attack from behind lashed out. Tou He did his best to deal with the water cultivator while the raw chi attacker was easier to dodge, his massive attack only releasing once more.

Then, they were there.

Wu Ying cut the flow of wind, releasing his hold of the energy that held him aloft, and lightened his form. He hit the ground with a slight thump, allowing his sturdier body to take some of the burden of impact rather than utilize even more of his already low reserves.

Spinning about, Wu Ying took position on the far side of the clearing, his sword drawn. Tou He landed not long after, having chosen to fly the remainder of the way and brake using his staff before dropping around and sending the spinning staff backward, deflecting a half dozen fist-sized balls of water. Those globes exploded as they came into contact with the staff, releasing clouds of steam before Tou He jerked his hand backward, bringing the staff back into his hands.

Moments later, the pair of hanged demons arrived, one of them bounding across the branches to crash onto the ground with branches and leaves still caught in her hair. To Wu Ying's surprise, surrounding her body and seeming to have grown into her body was a plant, the series of peach flowers—the *hoa doa*—hanging from her body via a single branch. Two of the peach flowers were dead, their petals falling down though another three still glowed, energy forming around them.

As for the second demonic cultivator, he was just as strange, swirling bands of water running along his furred body. He wielded no weapons, though long claws were curled before him as they stared at the pair of cultivators.

For a moment, the opponents regarded one another, weapons held before them. Breaths were stabilized, as the headlong rush had drained energy. Wu Ying's body was turned toward his opponents, his jian held before him, other injured hand hidden by long sleeves as he used his fingers to gently guide the tendrils of air to do his bidding.

Watching the demons, Wu Ying felt they normally could have taken them without an issue. Neither seemed to have a martial bent. In normal times, they might have drawn out the fight, but it would not be a difficult one. But these were not regular times, for he and Tou He were exhausted from their earlier battles.

Nor was there a point to bringing them here, all this way, if not to cheat. Fair fights filled with honor were for nobles and fools. Wu Ying was neither.

A snarl, a shout, and the pair scattered. Water demon went left, the other bounced backward. A flower wilted, the energy from it pulled to an untouched one. As a distraction, Tou He thrust his staff at them, a gout of flame broad and wide sweeping toward both. The pair reacted, one by releasing a wave of water to combat Tou He's attack, the other by channeling a touch of the energy going into the flower into its own aura.

More importantly, it gave Wu Ying time to finish his preparations. Triggering the formation was simple enough in theory, but he had chosen to attempt to modify it further such that the effects were more focused. A few moments of concentration, if he was uninjured and his fingers were moving properly. Right now, it was all he could do to keep them from trembling and flicking at inopportune moments. With a slight tug of energy, light filled the clearing again and the pair of demons stumbled to a halt.

More yips, more shouts, calls of surprise and dismay between the pair. Laced across the ground, in glittering walls of light and power, were strands of energy. From outside the illusion formation, it looked no more than gossamer strands of energy, while within the illusion formation, the pair were in worlds of the creator's making, driving them to distraction.

A motion, a twist, a jerk of a head. Then the water demon stumbled backward, blood streaming from his nose. Illusion the formation might be, but with chi coursing through their bodies and affecting their motions, a mental attack could cause damage too.

"Well, that worked," Tou He said, slamming the edge of his staff into the ground and leaning on it. He let out a long, thready exhale as he did so, his gaze never leaving the pair.

Wu Ying lowered his sword arm, the killing intent he had gathered fading with each moment. He shifted his stance so that he was not as bladed to his opponents. "So it seems."

Perhaps he should not have said that, for at that time, the energy that had gathered across the flower burst forth. It tore through the air, shattering the delicate strands of energy that the formation had woven. Wu Ying cast himself aside, thankful that the formation had trapped and turned their opponents around such that the attack had mostly been aimed away from them.

Yet aimed away or not, the attack shattered the formation, destroying the frame of energy that supported the illusion as well as one of the formation flags. Without the necessary preconditions holding forth the illusion, it freed the pair of Ma Than Vong.

"I've got the water demon." Tou He suited motion to words, launching himself forth with his staff tip leading the way.

Fire-heated metal cap sank deep into flesh, even as the water vines attempted to block the attack. The pair disappeared out the back of the clearing, a tree shattering as they passed.

Wu Ying snorted, but he was also moving, cutting sideways with his blade. To his surprise, the flower demon ducked, dodging his attack even while shaking off the lingering effects of the illusion. At the same time, one flower had begun to glow, power consolidating again. He was on a timer, it seemed, before another blast of energy.

"Well then, let's do this," Wu Ying whispered, gusting forward. He led with his sword, choosing not to commit to a pure lunge on instinct. Long honed battle instincts stood him well, for moments later, a forest of branches exploded upward, intent on pinning the wind cultivator.

He cut apart a couple while dodging the rest, idly noting that these branches were less corrupted. Almost completely free of the taint, in fact. Outside of the demon city, it seemed, the corruption was fading quickly—from both the demon and the surroundings.

Good.

Closing in, he threw a blade strike that poured energy through the motion. To his surprise, additional roots crawled upward, blocking the attack as it formed a buckler that was then snatched away by the demon. A twist of his feet broke him free from grass that had suddenly grown upward, grabbing at his feet even as he slowed for a moment.

If he had more energy, he would have flown. But the battles had taxed even his stores, and he was uncertain how much more fighting he would have to do. Even newborn demons could be trouble, if they came in sufficient numbers.

No flying, just staying grounded then. If that was the case, he would have to be careful, for the roots that speared upward were coming too close for comfort. Another lunge to the side, a touch too slow, the root bouncing off hardened spirit robes and leaving him bruised beneath. Unfortunately, that attack had done one other, more dangerous thing.

It had pushed him back.

Throwing his spiritual sense at the ground, Wu Ying sought clarity. Just because he was the wind did not mean he could not feel the earth with his aura. However, to his surprise and shock, his senses were repelled immediately.

In his shock, Wu Ying stumbled. Roots grabbed at his feet then his sword arm, trapping him before he could move. Straining, the cultivator felt one of the roots give way, the demonic cultivator letting out a grunt of pain; only for additional roots to erupt and trap his body and arm further.

"Fool!" cackled the demon.

Suddenly, Wu Ying understood. The demon had been expecting—planning—for him to push his senses into the ground. The entire fight, from the roots to the energy blast that she was going to use to finish him, had been planned. Even now, Wu Ying felt the energy in the flower growing at a pace that was triple the speed of earlier.

Like a fool, he had fallen for the demonic cultivator's trap. It might not have his direct martial experience or skills, but it had chosen to wield its power well.

"Hun dan!" Cursing, Wu Ying focused deep. He had one other technique he could utilize, but the timing would be tricky. Too early and he would take the attack anyway. Too late and he would definitely be struck. More worrying was what would happen after he utilized his wind technique.

How would he finish the fight?

"You know, I'm a Gatherer. Why don't we put down our weapons and talk some plants or something? Maybe trade some around?"

Silence. Well, it was worth a shot.

More energy built up, and the cultivator narrowed his eyes as he forced his breathing to lengthen, as he attempted to calm his racing heart. His world became nothing more than the glowing energy around the flower, the red petals and the long stamen the focus of his being. As it seemed was the case for the demonic cultivator, for no further attacks sought Wu Ying's life.

Not at that moment.

Power building, budding, then finally, ready to fruit—before the explosion. A shriek of the wind kicked up around the pair, reacting to Wu Ying's emotions, churning up dust and leaves. A shriek that pierced the air and went deep into a primal center.

Except that shriek was no wind.

Fractions of a second before the blast arrived, Sao Choi—Nascent Soul raptor and beast companion of Colonel Huynh Bich Trang—arrived. Hunting claws pierced unprotected back, destroying the delicate balance of power in vine and body, closing on flesh and skin and cracking bone. Wings flared open wide even as body was crushed and torn from the ground, the demon taken into the sky.

Leaving Wu Ying to stare after the fast-departing demon and bird through the slowly lightening night air. His limbs were still trapped, his jaw hanging open in shock. And alive. Most importantly, alive.

Chapter 31

By the time Tou He returned, Wu Ying had managed to extract himself from the roots holding him down. He had just begun to walk toward the clearing when his friend returned, looking exhausted and sodden but gratified at the same time.

"Your opponent?" Wu Ying asked.

"Will not be bothering us further."

The wind cultivator frowned, cocking his head. The wind spoke of mud and earth, dried ground and a still struggling demon. Talismans stood around the demon, draining it of power and reinforcing the earth, such that the demon's greater strength could not be utilized. The wind also spoke of a bird feasting on the remnants of a wily opponent three li to the east.

"Very well," Wu Ying said. If his friend wanted to avoid killing again at this moment, he would not gainsay him. It might be a concern in the future, if he kept to that reticence. After all, theirs was not a kind world and a cultivator—a martial cultivator in particular—who chose not to kill was a danger on the field. At the very least, Wu Ying would want to know his friend's decision before they took to the field of battle. "Shall we find our companions then?"

Tou He nodded. He took a couple of steps, then paused. "Umm, which way?"

"I thought you knew," Wu Ying said.

"How would I know?" Tou He said, sounding exasperated. "You're the scout with the wind and all that."

"Yeah, but they have formations hiding them. Aren't you the one who pays attention to all the details of the plans."

"And you don't anymore?"

Wu Ying shrugged. "I've not really worked in teams much recently. And if I did, they worked to my needs, not theirs. Or worse, I just let the wind let me know where they are."

"Really?" Tou He sighed. "You've gotten lazy."

"Or more efficient." The wind cultivator cocked his head again, listening to the wind. "I could try to find them, but I'm dangerously low on chi. I need to spend some time refining more soon."

"What, all your usual methods of restoring energy not sufficient?" Tou He said, smirking. "Where's the continually energized cultivator who cultivates even when he sleeps?"

Touching his ring, which Wu Ying noted was made of a red crystal of some form, the fire cultivator extracted a pill bottle. He swallowed a pill from it, the opening of the bottle releasing a fragrant and spicy tinge to the air before he recapped it.

"Not offering me anything?" Wu Ying said grumpily. Not that he didn't have a few pills of his own, but none of them were geared toward a wind cultivator and their needs. Unlike Tou He, it seemed, whose pill was obviously meant for a fire cultivator.

"Not unless you want heartburn."

"I'll pass. Thanks." Giving in and copying his friend, Wu Ying swallowed a pill too. He felt the large marble-sized pill enter his stomach and break apart as the acrid and bitter taste lingered in his mouth and threatened to make him vomit.

Focusing on the growing chi, Wu Ying set himself to the task of breaking down the energy, utilizing his older techniques to do so. Even now, the Cyclone's Breath method was not working, the winds co-opted to continue wrecking the ruined ancient city. He felt a little guilty about that, since the destruction was entirely accidental.

"Any suggestions?" Wu Ying asked.

"We could ask the bird." Tou He inclined his head to the side, where at some point, Sao Choi had returned and was perched on a branch high above the pair.

Wu Ying started, eyes narrowing. Damn beast. He hadn't even sensed it arriving. As though noticing his regard and thoughts, the raptor opened its mouth and let out a short, sharp call. Then flapping its wings once, it flew a short distance away, stopping on a tree to look back at the pair.

If a bird could mock, Wu Ying was sure this one was.

***

One moment they were passing through regular jungle filled with hanging branches, sleeping snakes, and heavy vines amidst the omnipresent buzzing of insects and beneath the silent gaze of the Nascent Soul raptor. The next, noise deadened and the quintet of cultivators appeared, scholar still seated upon her brazier even if it no longer floated.

"Oh, very good concealment formation," Tou He said, head turning from side to side as he took in the dome of earth that been formed with only a single approach available. Outside of the dome, vegetation had crept over the loosened earth, mixing with the enchantments to deaden their spiritual marks.

"It really is… oof!" Wu Ying let out a grunt as Yang Mu threw herself at him into a tight hug. She nearly bore him over, holding him tightly before she suddenly released the hug.

"Sorry…" Still, her hands had not left his body and trailed down his arms as she did so, going so far as to grip both hands. That brought a startled cry of pain from Wu Ying, causing the wood cultivator to release him before snatching up the injured arm again, causing another grunt of pain to escape. "What happened?"

Wu Ying could not tell if she was outraged at him for getting injured or over the fact that he was injured. Perhaps a little of both, since the way she stared at him had him wincing. "Just a little accident."

"Accident?" She lifted the cooked and charred hand, staring at the burn and the way Wu Ying's fingers were trembling a little. "What kind of accident involved you getting burnt to a crisp like this?" Then, turning to Tou He, she narrowed her eyes as she noted the bruising along one side of his face. She put two and two together swiftly. "You fought him? I thought you were going to convince him to calm down."

"I did. A real man learns to speak with his fist!" Wu Ying puffed out his chest as he spoke, only to deflate as Yang Mu smacked it with the edge of her fan, the weapon and tool surprisingly heavy. He coughed, rubbing at what he swore would likely bruise, even as he noted that she never let go of his injured hand.

"You idiot. It's not time to boast."

"I wasn't…" Eyeing the fan that she raised, he chuckled. "Sorry. I deserved that."

"You did," Tou He said, a small smile on his lips as he watched the two, his gaze resting on their joined hands.

Wu Ying did not blush. He was no teenager worried about showing his feelings. More importantly, he noted that Yang Mu was no longer looking at him or his antics, her focus on his injured arm. Even his increased healing factor as a cultivator and Body Cultivator had not covered it yet, leaving the crisped skin, the significant number of boils, and the exposed bones.

"Did you wash this?"

Wu Ying shook his head.

"Why isn't this at least wrapped?" she hissed. "Did you even bother to take care of it?"

"Not exactly. We were in a little bit of a hurry to get out because we had company."

"We know," she muttered as she continued to inspect his hand. "Colonel Huynh sent her spirit beast to aid you when we realized you were being chased. Seems like she's able to watch things through Sao Choi's eyes."

"Interesting."

"Yes." She tugged on his arm, bringing him over to where a makeshift stone table had been created and a tea set had been extracted. A pointed look at Minh Trac and Thien Giang sent the formation master and fighter off their seats. When Minh Trac moved to take the hot water kettle, Yang Mu said firmly, "Leave it."

The formation master let out a long sigh but did as she asked.

"Can you fight, boy?" Bich Trang asked, walking over to the pair when they were seated.

Wu Ying hissed as Yang Mu poured the near boiling water on his hand, a brush appearing in her hand before she scoured his skin. If he was not a Body Cultivator, he would have been burned. But because he was, the heat was no more than hot oil poured on sensitive skin.

"It's not my sword hand," Wu Ying panted when he managed to gain control of his senses once more.

He willed himself to accept the pain as she finished debriding his hand, removing dirt, twigs, and burnt skin. In doing so, she had burst a couple of the boils, which caused her to click her tongue. At the same time, Yang Mu stared at the damaged skin, some of which was still hanging on, the exposed muscle, tendons, and white bone beneath.

"Can you still flex that hand?" Yang Mu demanded.

"With effort." Wu Ying showed her, opening and shutting it, his fingers trembling a little when he was done.

"Well, you have the night. We'll stay hidden for the evening, wait for our pursuers to give up, and start again in the morning."

Wu Ying whispered a quiet acknowledgement to the colonel before taking in the rest of the group. Having been removed from their table, Minh Trac and Thien Giang had unrolled their bedrolls and taken a corner of the dome to sleep within, while Tou He was propped up against one corner, his staff resting on his shoulder as he meditated and worked through the cultivation pill he had swallowed. Already, Wu Ying could sense that the fires that burned within his friend had strengthened, the chi within his body refilling at a prodigious rate.

"Stop moving, you idiot," Yang Mu muttered. After placing his hand on the table, she extracted a mortar and pestle and a series of pills, roots, and leaves. "We're going to have to put a paste on that to keep it moist and speed up your healing." She pondered. "If we have a day, perhaps we can have you rest in one of your medicinal baths. It would speed your healing."

"And hurt more," Wu Ying pointed out.

"Says the man who plunged his hand into heavenly fire." She waved at his body. "I don't have enough paste for all of you, so having you refresh your body in the medicinal bath is the best we can do."

"There's not much space here," Wu Ying continued to protest.

Rather than answer him, she looked around till she caught sight of Dinh Don who, unlike the others, had already fallen asleep. Somehow, even asleep, he seemed to blend right into the earth he slept upon, such that Wu Ying had missed his presence entirely.

"Wait here." She stalked over to the sleeping scout to harangue him into building Wu Ying an earthen bath.

While she did that, Wu Ying eyed Bich Trang, who continued to hover close by. Gesturing to the now-free seat, Wu Ying waited for the soldier to sit. "You wanted to know something."

She glanced between him and Tou He, something like disappointment and envy flicking through her gaze before it shuttered. "Your friend and yourself. Are you two typical of your sect?"

"In what way?" Wu Ying said, brow furrowed in honest confusion. "The Verdant Green Waters is a large sect. Typical is a hard word to use."

"Ah. My apologies, I will try to be a little clearer." Bich Trang hesitated, then glanced at Tou He and Yang Mu, who still attempting to get Dinh Don to do her bidding. "You are both exceptional martial cultivators with rare elemental influences. I am wondering if that is usual."

"Not at all," Wu Ying replied. "Martial cultivators are only a small number of our members. Just like the army is but a small number in your kingdom." A considering look in her eyes as he said that. He offered a half-smile that was all falsely modest next. "Anyway, you are wrong."

"Wrong?" she repeated, looking puzzled.

"I'm not a martial cultivator. I'm a Wild Gatherer." He touched the blade on the other side of his hip with his uninjured hand, before placing his hand back on the table. "I just have some small talent with the sword."

"Small talent." A snort of disbelief.

"Oh yes. My Master, you might have heard of him. He was a true Master of the blade."

"I have not heard this story."

"Master Cheng Zhao Wan, the Sundering Blade." Wu Ying sighed. "He was a true Master, and a martial cultivator, unlike me."

"Your Master was the Sundering Blade?" Bich Trang worked her jaw, eyeing Wu Ying anew now with more caution. "The tales of his near heretical dao have reached even us. Along with his deadly sword style." A slight hesitation before she added, "Your martial style, is it similar?"

"Some aspects," Wu Ying said. "I do not claim to be near as talented as he is, but I have derived portions of mine from his and my family's forms."

"The Long family style, you said?" Bich Trang said. "The Dragon's Style."

"Yes."

"Interesting." The colonel shook her head bemusedly, sending the edges of the bob cut shifting behind her. "So, the Verdant Green Waters is filled with heroes."

The wind cultivator shrugged "We are but what we have to be, to stand against Dark Sects and encroaching kingdoms."

"And expansion?"

"The Shen are far away from Nanyue."

"Today."

Wu Ying shrugged, because he had nothing to offer that. What may come in the future, only fortune-tellers could say. And perhaps mortal emperors. He was but a mere cultivator.

"Humble heroes…" Bich Trang muttered as she stood. She bade him a good night's rest as she left him to take a seat beside Sao Choi once more.

A short while later, when Wu Ying had managed to pour himself a cup of tepid, over-brewed tea without jostling his arm, Yang Mu returned. She began the process of sorting out his arm, even as Wu Ying sensed the heating stones she had tossed into the newly created bath warming the water slowly.

"What was that about?" Yang Mu murmured, weaving a simple chi formation with her aura to block eavesdropping.

"Just someone attempting to learn more about my sect and my kingdom."

"Ah… information gathering."

Wu Ying nodded, watching as she expertly combined roots and herbs, grinding them in the mortar to form a wet poultice. She threw in some flower petals then pills, her brow furrowed in concentration. He just watched, noting the way a stray lock fell across her brow that she would swipe at ineffectively, utterly concentrated on the tendrils of wood chi she wove into the poultice.

When she was done, she looked up and caught him watching her, then blushed deeply. "What?"

"Just thinking that being a wood cultivator must make such things easier," Wu Ying said.

"Making poultices and being a physician?" Yang Mu chuckled darkly. "My mother always said I should concentrate on that. Made me learn all the various methods, partly to sell better but also because she wanted me to be all that I could be. And then, of course, she punished me when I chose to study formations instead of more boring physician works."

"But you still learned something, right?" Wu Ying eyed the poultice she was applying to the bandage before raising the dark-green mixture and pressing it upon his hand. He did not move away from her actions.

"Of course. At least enough to deal with something as simple as a burn." Yang Mu's movements hesitated a little before she continued winding the bandage around his hand, drawing a little hiss from him as she worked. "And this is mostly a burn. No dao conceptions in it to block healing, no lingering heat or flame. The cleanest martial burn I've ever come across in fact."

"Purifying flame," Wu Ying said. "Though it seems Tou He might have drawn some of it back just before I struck him."

"Good," Yang Mu said, mildly mollified. She finished with the cleaning and bandages, the compress tightened over his arm. She pointed at the medicinal bath next, her face still stern. "I don't have your herbs, but I'm sure you can do what you need to."

"I can." He stood and bowed to her a little, offering thanks. Wu Ying hesitated, glancing over to the group, to the exhausted cultivators. He reflected, briefly, on the way they had been treated and how quick the group had been to abandon him and Tou He. How Sao Choi had looked at them, almost as though considering them for food.

"What is it?" she asked, seeing the look in his eyes.

Wu Ying frowned, then turning away from the others, quickly extracted and deposited some of his herbs and other collected items into a storage ring. As he extracted the formation flags offered to him by Yang Mu's mother, he slowed down long enough for her to see what he did, before he deposited them within the ring. After which, he pulled the small ring off and handed it to her.

"What's this for?"

"Use. After your display, I figured you'd have better use for those herbs, formations, and talismans." Wu Ying kept his voice light and level, though he made sure to look directly into her eyes as he spoke. "There's little point in having such things if they're not put to use, you know?"

"Preparation is everything for many such formations."

"Exactly."

She smiled grimly, inclining her head and slipping the ring onto her finger. As he turned away, he noted that she was washing the mortar and pestle rather than storing it. It seemed she intended to make another compress with different properties, from the array of different herbs she had set out.

Stepping into the medicinal bath after adding the necessary herbs to it was a pain. His skin, crispy at the least damaged parts, overly sensitive and burned on much of his left side, flared with pain as he slipped within. The astringent herbs and scouring chi within the bath took effect almost immediately, stripping damaged skin and releasing fluids. Old scabs and wounds reopened, the fluids and caustic energy entering his body ever faster.

Wu Ying hissed, his breathing coming in short, sharp breaths for a time. For long minutes, he struggled to control the energy within before he was able to regain control of his senses. Idly, he noted that the Cyclone's Breath method had reestablished itself around him, wind energy reentering his body and churning through his meridians. Already, he was pulling wind chi and embedding his dao in it before condensing the energy further in his dantian, a portion of that energy entering his near-empty core while the rest seeped into his body.

Once he'd established the flow of chi that was necessary through his meridians and his body to handle the caustic, dissolution chi that sought to destroy his body and the reinforcing nutrients that would bolster him, Wu Ying turned his mind to the winds and the moments of enlightenment he had experienced.

Perhaps enlightenment was not the right word, for he'd had no stream of Heavenly energy, no benediction from above or below. Yet facing the corruption of the heart, the purifying fire of Tou He, and the whispered, twisted winds, Wu Ying found himself coming ever closer to understanding. Not of the corruption and the twisted demonic realm, but of the Heavens, their decrees, their requirements, and their unflinching resolve.

Turning those thoughts over and over, weighing the experiences and finding within them an aspect that he could imbue within his body, he sought understanding as he took another step closer to becoming one with the winds.

Chapter 32

Days later, the team had finally left behind the Ma Than Vong, the abandoned city and the angry demons within but a memory. Even so, the danger to the group only increased as the number of creatures corrupted and forcibly strengthened increased in number as the group moved toward the origin of the corruption. Each day, the team found themselves forced to do battle, often utilizing overwhelming force in combined attacks to finish the battle quickly before moving on.

It was the only method to ensure their continued safety as battles that lasted too long attracted attention. Wu Ying found himself utilizing his World Spirit Ring more often, pulling corpses into the ring to store them. He, thankfully, had managed to acquire an altered formation at the same time to cleanse the bodies inside his ring, though even then, he would never have allowed their presence if not for the dangers they faced.

The more he learned of the splinter—the heart—that had been brought and the corruption it had generated, the more concerned he grew. The special unit, along with Yang Mu, had taken to studying the staked heart during the night under multiple formations, slicing off portions of it to test new concoctions, formations, and dao inscriptions in an attempt to more quickly deal with the corruption.

It was almost immediately clear that the heart contained a dao that was anathema to the mortal ones they held. It was a twisted, encompassing dao that sought to dominate and control and corrupt, but it was strong, and it was stubborn. Formations without the influence of an individual's dao could not break down the corruption very quickly. As such, only Tou He's purifying flame had managed to tear through the heart, influenced by the dao contained within the ex-monk himself.

It was his dao they used as a benchmark, checking how fast he could cleanse a sliver against the various methods they utilized. It was his dao they used to understand how many contaminants were released into the atmosphere, to guide their own research. It was his dao that burned pure and clean and that made Wu Ying's hand ache each time he neared the other.

After emerging from the medicinal bath, the majority of the simple wounds—the dry skin, the crisped and sunburned mien—had disappeared. His body, trained to replace and fix damage, borrowing the power contained within his dantian and aided by the medicinal herbs and pills he consumed, had fixed those minor wounds easily.

His hand though, the damaged skin there, wasn't healing at the appropriate rate. If Wu Ying did not know better, he would have sworn that he was healing at a normal cultivator's speed. Swift, impressive for a mortal—but nothing like what a Body Cultivator at his level should have experienced. Even if Tou He had drawn back his dao upon contact, it seemed that some lingering effects of the flame had removed all trace of his Wind Body.

Such a dangerous, dangerous flame and dao.

Because of his injury, Wu Ying was relegated to watching the group's back. As they neared the source of corruption, his control over the winds around them had grown ever more tenuous. Speaking with Dinh Don, training with him and studying the manual the other scout had offered, Wu Ying had managed to progress the strength of his own spiritual sense, but it helped little with the winds.

Those no longer spoke to him in the same way, the southern wind twisted by the corrupted flow of energy. In time, Wu Ying almost felt that the winds in their entirety might be corrupted; but for now, it was but a marring of the local atmosphere.

As they journeyed, the land became hotter and more humid. More than once, Yang Mu utilized a small talisman to cool the air around her, even the enchanted silk robes she wore insufficient to deal with the oppressive heat and humidity. She also kept close to Wu Ying, checking on his hand and benefitting from the constant swirl of air around him.

Captain Ky suffered as well, the soldier refusing to remove his armor even as the days grew longer. Rivulets of sweat dripped from his brow, though he plodded on stolidly without complaint. Only late into the evenings, when the group camped, would he remove his armor for a short period while seated by the wind cultivator.

The special unit members, on the other hand, all managed to make their way through the jungle with minimal issues. It had puzzled Wu Ying at first, only for Yang Mu to point out that embedded enchantments in their armor offered the group a degree of comfort that the captain's armor did not.

For all their expertise and skills, injuries accumulated further. There was no hiding their presence entirely, and the demonic beasts they faced grew in strength with each moment. The team found themselves beset at all hours, once even during the morning as insects—missed until that moment—emerged in the early morning light to swarm the group.

Wounds accumulated, and even the massive chi resources and speedy healing of cultivators were unable to keep up. Healing pills were continuously consumed, and the group stopped the moment light began to fade, not daring to risk attacks at night. Sao Choi, the Nascent Soul companion of the colonel, kept a closer watch over the group, no longer venturing far afield of his companion.

In this way, the group slogged through the corrupted forest, trees and bushes tainted, flowers and vermin infected to release noxious gasses or to aggressively strip local, uncorrupted flora, damaging the plants. Every day saw the group cross further ground, knowing that each li brought them closer to an answer and, likely, an even more difficult battle.

***

"Do you have an updated estimate for me?" Bich Trang asked Minh Trac, hunched over beside the fitfully burning, smokeless fireplace in the center of their camp. After multiple night attacks, the group had chosen to keep multiple small fires—their flames imbued with Tou He's purifying flame—lit throughout their encampments. If the illusion and deception formations failed, they would be ready, rather than groping in the dark.

"The bones say two days from now. Maybe three, if we have to fight as much as today," the fortune-teller and formation master said, brows furrowed. "I cannot offer more. The strands of fate here are corrupted beyond belief."

"So are the winds. I can barely hold onto them within close proximity of us. Worse, I expect that if not for the formations we are utilizing at night to cleanse the atmosphere, it would begin corrupting us too eventually."

"It has tried. Sending those without a clear understanding of their dao beforehand was a mistake." Bich Trang grimaced, lines deepening across her face. "Energy Storage and weaker cultivators would have drawn in the energy and been unable to erode the corruptive dao with their own understanding. They would never have made it this far. It is clear we must deal with this immediately before it reaches the city."

"As I've said, numerous times," Captain Ky said, jutting out his chin. "As my lord mentioned in his communiques. And yet, army command took forever to arrive. And even then, they only send one single unit."

"This is not the only crisis that the kingdom faces," Bich Trang snapped. "Our resources are stretched thin, especially during the growing months."

"Damn your harvests. We are the rice fields of the kingdom!" Be Long said. "We should have been the first priority."

"We had our orders," Bich Trang replied coolly. "As you had yours."

"Enough. You two complain like Minh Trac," Thien Giang cut off the pair before they could continue the argument. The formation master made a face, but eyeing the size of the warrior's biceps, he kept his mouth shut. "Go, cool off somewhere."

"Like there's anywhere cool with the furnace in here." Be Long glared at Tou He, who sat in one corner at the edge of the formation and clearing, his aura flicking outward on occasion.

Around Tou He, a light heat haze shimmered as his aura reacted to the corruption in the air and sought to cleanse it. Concerns about the ex-monk giving them away had been raised numerous times, but neither Tou He's control nor their need for his dao and flames had changed, so the team had chosen to ignore the matter.

"Just go," Thien Giang said.

Standing, Be Long stalked off, wiping his face with a silk cloth and grimacing at the streaks of dirt on it. He flopped down on his bedroll a short distance away, crossing his legs after a moment and cultivating. Those not currently engaged in experimenting, like Phuong Vy, were cultivating too, desperate to replace the lost energy.

"Do we have any further clue of what the cause of this corruption is? A twisted demonic beast? A herd of them?" Wu Ying asked, glancing over to where Phuong Vy was pouring a liquid over a slice of the heart, watching the silvery liquid react. A stray gust of wind caught the released smoke, bringing it toward them before another breeze, stronger than the first, sent it upward and away. "Or something else?"

"The amount of corruption flowing through, it can only be a doorway." Minh Trac tapped the ground. "The energy flows are all twisted in the surroundings, as a formation pries open the gates of our realm. I believe what we face is a deliberate act."

"Someone opened a gate to a demonic realm and left it open," Wu Ying said slowly. "A demonic realm so twisted, it is destroying ours by being in contact with it." After a moment, he shook his head. "How can it be so strong?"

"Strong?" Bich Trang repeated.

"Yes. It corrupts everything it touches here. Why not the other way?"

Minh Trac gave Wu Ying a pitying look, as though the simplicity of the question and answering it was almost beneath him. However, as Bich Trang shot Minh Trac a look, he sighed and explained. "It's not a matter of just strength of daos. But the kind and its interaction." He scooped up some earth, then reached over to Wu Ying's cup and dropped the earth into his tea. "Is the earth stronger than the tea? No. But the tea is still soiled, is it not? Poison is not stronger than your body, but it can still kill it. So is this dao. It corrupts because it is anathema to the dao and the living in our world. In time, it would be dealt with by those above. But—"

"No one wants to see that," Bich Trang said before she stood. "If we are to see a fight soon, you should all rest and recuperate."

"Yes, colonel." Minh Trac and Thien Giang echoed each other's acknowledgment.

Contrary to her words though, the colonel did not cultivate but extracted a writing table and paper, beginning the process of grinding ink so she could write a note. Wu Ying cocked his head. It was not the first time she had done so.

"Reporting to her commanders?" Wu Ying asked. "We have not received a reply as yet though."

"That, and writing to her family. You should do the same," Thien Giang said.

"Family?" Wu Ying paused, then smiled wryly. "I don't think your spirit messengers have the ability to carry my messages."

"I'm sure they'd be willing to pass it on northward." Thien Giang looked serious as she continued. "It is one of the things they promise us when we volunteer for these units. That they will ensure all our messages, as best they can, are passed on to our loved ones."

"That, and they will be supported in the future if we cannot," Minh Trac said. "Only reason the colonel and I continue this. Not unlike some orphans."

Thien Giang grinned. "My pension will go to the orphanage. It's a better use than your money going to your pair of wives and your six squabbling children. Or going to prop up your family's failing fortune-telling business."

"It's not failing," Minh Trac growled. "We just have had some bad luck recently."

"Hah! Telling a prince—crowned or not—that their favorite concubine is cheating on them is not bad luck, it's foolishness. Even when you're right, you're in the wrong."

Minh Trac shrugged. "My family has always told the truth. Always."

"And see where that's brought you."

"Yes, a family and children. Just like the colonel. And what about you? You don't even have a husband or a lover."

"I do not lower myself to see just anyone. I am looking for a man who values more than my position, my money," Thien Giang said. "Someone with a good heart."

"A good heart, you say. That's another way of saying your face is as appealing as rotten tofu."

Wu Ying barely noticed Thien Giang move, though the crack of the strike and the flying body that followed it was easy enough to spot. Minh Trac arced through the air and crashed into the ground a short distance away, rolling over and over, his robes tangling up around him before he came to a stop against a nearby tree.

"Ass," Thien Giang said.

Well, it was clear someone had issues around her looks. And as Minh Trac popped right back up, nursing his chest she had punched him, he obviously knew that for he was smirking. Wu Ying made no move to intervene, noting that the colonel hadn't even lifted her head from where she was working. Obviously, this was not the first time.

Though there was something that had caught his attention.

"You and the colonel have children as well?" Wu Ying said to Thien Giang when he was certain she was calm. Unusual, up north, for cultivators to have many children unless they had given up on the pursuit of immortality. Strange that this entire group had so many parents. Was that because of the differing philosophies.

"Three for me. She only has one. Eight months old," Thien Giang said. "She got into it late."

"Eight months?" Wu Ying whispered, horrified. So young.

"Yes. When you reach her level, you can't turn down orders as much." Thien Giang gestured at the group. "Units are sent out as a group, so we're forced to go along too. It's not ideal, but as we said, the army takes good care of us." She gestured toward Tou He, head cocked. "Isn't that the same for you and your Sects? You go where they tell you?"

"I wouldn't know," Wu Ying said. "At least, not at our level." He chuckled, a little self-conscious. "I left as an Energy Storage cultivator and have not been back yet."

She nodded, knowing the story.

"But it seemed that there were more options, mostly, to do what you wanted as an Elder. Except occasionally," Wu Ying added.

"That's because you people pursue the dao more vigorously, don't you?"

"We do."

Her gaze turned down, tracing to where his hand lay bandaged, and muttered, "So, are you going to be able to fight?"

"We'll find out, won't we?" Wu Ying flexed his injured hand, wincing as the growing flesh pulled tight and the scabbed skin broke apart. He could feel a little wetness, but it was important to keep moving it no matter the pain less it become stiff. "But I won't slow you down at least."

Chapter 33

The group was up early the next morning, stress and anticipation drawing each member from slumber. Wu Ying eyed the others, many dressed and ready with their full armaments for the first time. Even people like Yang Mu, who had storage rings that she used to keep her weapons, were sporting weapons this time. He glimpsed, beneath the robe of her dress, the flash of dark steel.

Yang Mu cocked her head, the motion drawing his gaze upward. Then she raised a single, graceful eyebrow, a little mocking smile on her lips. Realizing what it might look like, staring at her dress and chest so intently, Wu Ying let out an awkward chuckle.

"You could just ask…" she murmured, sending the words directly to his ears.

Her smirk grew even wider as he smiled, but her attention snapped to the colonel as the diminutive woman strode up. Sao Choi landed beside Bich Trang and flapped its wings a few times to draw everyone's attention.

"Sao Choi says there is no more hiding. When we exit, we will not have much time before we are beset by more demonic beasts. Any fighting is likely going to draw even more opponents to us," Bich Trang said. "We have two options then. Fight them all, deplete the forces we are facing. Or…"

"Or?" Tou He said, taking the bait.

Minh Trac smirked at the ex-monk's foolishness, though he said nothing directly.

"Or we hurry. Push right into the battle, hold off our enemies, and close the gate."

"And you're sure it's a gate," Tou He said. When she nodded, he looked at Yang Mu and Minh Trac. "It'll be easy enough to close then, will it not? Just find the formation flags and destroy them? If I can see it, I could probably burn it all down."

"Let's keep that as a backup plan," Bich Trang said. "My orders are not just to close the gate, but to find the reason for the corruption. Burning it all to ashes will not allow me to do so."

Tou He shrugged, looking unrepentant even as more than a few people eyed the wannabe arsonist.

Yang Mu, having edged over to Wu Ying, leaned in close to whisper, "Don't worry. I've been setting up an escape formation in case your friend gets too enthusiastic."

"He's not that bad."

"Of course he is not."

Somehow, Wu Ying was not sure he believed her reassurance. He regarded the group and the risks they were about to undertake. He added, slowly. "Did you add your mother's formation to it?"

"Yes." Such a simple answer, laced with meaning.

"We could combine the two options," Thien Giang said. "Rush in, find out what caused this, gather whatever evidence we need, set a formation to destroy it all, then retreat." She shifted a little, looking farther south, her gaze resting past the trees that blocked their view. Even so, all of them could sense the powerful spirits that moved through the woods, lurking at the edge of their perception. Creatures in the Core Formation realm, and a few even stronger than that. "If there're multiple Nascent Soul beasts who attack us…"

"Then would it not be better to wait?" Phuong Vy said. The scholar touched her side where she had mostly healed, though the occasional hitch in her stride indicated she was not completely fine. "If we draw them to us, we could prepare our formations beforehand."

"But can we even win against the forces arrayed against us?" Dinh Don said. "We already used one of our formations. With the number of Nascent Soul opponents we face…"

"We are not turning back," Bich Trang said firmly, glaring at the scout. He raised his hands in supplication and she continued. "The danger is real. I am willing to listen to any suggestions others might have."

"I don't think we should try to fight them all," Yang Mu said. "Nor should we try to break through directly. It leaves too many monsters behind us, and our best formations have taken hours to break the corruption down."

"If it's a gate, it matters not," Wu Ying said. "We just destroy the formation."

"Unless the gate is anchored by a splinter," Minh Trac said. "If it is anchored and protected by the energy, we might have to break down the energy and splinter itself first. That would be the way I would create a self-replicating and lasting formation."

The wind cultivator grimaced, then shot a look at Tou He. The ex-monk shrugged, for this level of discussion about formations and enchantments was over his head. He had even less knowledge than Wu Ying.

"I don't like splitting up," Be Long replied. "Our best fighters are the ones who need to be at the opening anyway."

"And aren't we quite far from it, a few days away minimum?" Phuong Vy said. "Are there really that many beasts that we will be wading through them for days on end?"

Dinh Don was the one to answer, his face grim. "There is no carpet of monsters before us, but each of those are so powerful, their senses so widespread that we cannot help but lure them toward us. The first battle we begin will be enough to alert the rest."

"Can we not anger them?" Wu Ying said. "Demonic beasts do not normally stay together, so if we can aggravate them against one another…"

"These are staying quiescent, soaking in the corrupted chi. They are happy with the current status. Those beasts who might have chosen to fight are dead or driven away. Though there might be some fighting when they near us," Dinh Don said. "But I would not count on it."

Yang Mu pulled out her fan, waving it in front of her face and generating a little wind. Wu Ying cocked his head, noting a look in her eyes, the way she was thinking. The others were talking, arguing with one another about the plan, but Wu Ying was waiting.

His patience was rewarded soon enough. "We don't split ourselves. We split the enemy."

"What rubbish do you speak of?" Minh Trac said.

"We have lures, ways to bring the enemy to us. We have illusion and confoundment formations, and we can, with the right kind of adjustment, anger the demon beasts when they near one another. If they are fighting one another here, we can thin their ranks. And put distance between us and them," Yang Mu said, snapping her fan closed and waving it around with her words. "We don't fight them all. We let them fight each other. And if we move fast enough, we never have to worry about them catching up."

"That's… not a bad idea," Minh Trac reluctantly agreed.

Yang Mu snorted, but her gaze was locked on the colonel. She was silent, obviously considering the outlined strategy.

In the end, Bich Trang nodded. "It's a start. But there're details to be dealt with."

"We'll need to work fast," Dinh Don said. "The Night Shadow formation is beginning to fail."

"Then let us not waste time."

***

Saying and doing was, of course, two different things. The special unit was, if nothing else, thorough in their planning. With an overall strategy in mind, Bich Trang was swift to deploy the specialists, everyone contributing to the plan.

Dinh Don would lure creatures toward them, targeting—if possible—the swifter and closer demonic creatures. Destroying them beforehand would mean the group reduced the risk as they ran. At the same time, the faster creatures would likely be the first to disengage in battle and chase them, so killing them was paramount.

Minh Trac was building formations with the aid of Yang Mu. The pair were using formation plates—metallic discs the size of a large serving plate—with adjusted runic formations, working calculations into the plates for their use in the surroundings while being buried deep in the earth. It would reduce their effectiveness overall, but it would also ensure that accidental attacks would not see the flags destroyed.

The pair were arguing viciously, throwing occasional barbed insults at one another while their hands flew across the metal, etching directly into the plates, dribbling gold dust or jade or other enchanted mixtures to seal the newly reformed works. At the same time, for all their bickering, the pair was working well together.

Theirs was the most important aspect of this entire procedure, for they were forming the entrapment and illusion formations that would contain the monsters. Preferably without the demonic beasts knowing they were trapped.

At the same time, the pair had to add an escape formation that would allow the group to exit the clearing when it was time to flee. Since they needed to contain the creatures, the illusion formation would trigger first, trapping everyone within. Without the escape formation, there would be no escape.

"Focus. You have to grind those pills down to a fine dust, but not release too much of it into the wind," Phuong Vy snapped, drawing Wu Ying's attention back to his own task. With only one functioning hand, the wind cultivator had been relegated to helping the other pillar of their plan, the alchemist and scholar.

Looking at the pestle in his hand, he eyed the pills he was slowly grinding apart, his motions carefully measured. Using the Three Star, Six Pulses method of grinding as had been taught to him by Liu Tsong, he was crushing the alchemist's pills and dried herbs to create an enraging concoction. The dust was to be used to lower the inhibitions of the demonic beasts and increase their rage while adding a small level of irritant—the equivalent of itching powder—to the air. In this way, they would keep the monsters within fighting one another.

That was his job, since he still had some minor control over his winds and could guide any dust into the air to be dispersed.

Phuong Vy was standing beside her alchemical cauldron, chi flowing from her hand as she brewed up a series of enticements for the demonic beasts. While the alchemist had a wide range of stores for numerous scenarios, she had never envisioned one that required her to lure such a vast quantity of creatures to them and keep them close. As such, rather than make do—something Wu Ying was relegated to—she had elected to make the concoction directly.

Thankfully for Wu Ying's ego, he had been able to help Phuong Vy with the addition of various herbs she had been missing, offering substitutes when neither party had the required optimal item. The resulting concoction would likely be significantly reduced in effectiveness, but the group was betting on the innate aggressiveness of these creatures to cover any shortcomings.

In the meantime, the rest of the team was preparing the surroundings for battle. Traps and simple blood and death talismans were being laid, pits dug and trees cut and branches sharpened so that they could utilize the surroundings to their best effects.

Time passed quickly, the sun rising and the last of the Night Shadow formation breaking apart as the lingering traces of yin energy and moonlight-infused chi disappeared. The formation flags were left where they were, their energies drained and the material already half-consumed by the energies coursing through them through the night. Forced to combat the early morning yang energies, they had broken down entirely.

Still, their use in this way had offered the team a few extra precious hours, sufficient for the team to have completed most of their tasks.

Pouring the powder into clay urns via a funnel, a silk covering over his face, Wu Ying cocked his head. His damaged hand wavered for a moment before he clamped iron will onto it and forced the funnel he held to still. The reason for his distraction made itself known to the rest of the team soon enough, as Dinh Don released a shout of surprise and fear, the thunder of skittering feet preceding his desperate dash.

Time was up.

Chapter 34

Wu Ying moved as quickly as he could, sweat gathering on his brow that even the cooling flow of the winds constantly surrounding him could do little to relieve. He capped the clay bottle, pushing it aside before moving to the final container, cursing as his injured off-hand trembled again. Overuse was making it less reliable than ever, causing some of the dust to spill as he tried to insert the funnel spout into the bottle.

"Give it here, you idiot." Phuong Vy snatched spout and scoop from Wu Ying's hands, pushing him aside with her hip. "Go use your blade. All you're really good for after all."

"I…" The wind cultivator shook his head, stepping aside and gripping his still shaking hand at the wrist. Under his fingers, he felt the cool metal of the Coral Dragon Scales, the emerald scale mail that he had taken as payment ages ago. Even here, in the heat of Nanyue, it provided protection and a cooling effect on his torso and arms. "Fine."

Striding away from the scholar, he cast his gaze about. Neither Yang Mu nor Minh Trac were to be seen. He knew the pair were busy planting the last of the formation flags, burying them as deep as was viable. In any other time or place, he would have been informed of their presence by the wind.

Now, he was reliant on his stunted spiritual sense, and even that was truncated by the corruptive energies coursing through the air. More to the point, he had trained Yang Mu too well—she knew how to hide her aura, unlike the other formation master. A lapse of concentration pierced Wu Ying's spiritual sense like the jab of a pin and he oriented in that direction.

"I hope he intends to use another talisman before we leave…" Wu Ying muttered, mostly to himself. That was the way Minh Trac had managed to keep his overall presence hidden till now, even in the deep woods they traveled within.

"What?" Tou He, resting against his staff nearby, asked Wu Ying.

When his friend looked over, the ex-monk offered him a meat stick that he had somehow managed to cook while busy with his own tasks. By the curl of smoke and the warmth of the meat, the entire thing had been freshly barbecued too.

"How?" Wu Ying said around a mouthful of juicy meat. "Why?"

"My aura," Tou He said without shame. He even extracted another thin, pre-marinated slice from his ring and held out his other hand, letting his aura concentrate on the skewer. The flame chi intensified around his hand, the smell of roasting meat filling the air. "My Master suggested it as a training method early on. Not long after you left, in fact. Useful for focusing my energies."

Thien Giang, standing with her guan dao resting on one shoulder, let out a loud snort. When the pair looked at her, she explained. "Unorthodox training method, but smart. Keep him interested and his stomach full."

"Oh yes. No one wants to eat burnt meat," Tou He said, making a face. "Such a waste."

"I'm sure I'd like to eat some meat right now." She looked straight at Tou He, then let her gaze drift down. Then up.

Wordlessly, Tou He offered her the newly cooked skewer before turning away, ignoring her blatant suggestion. She did not seem to mind, biting into the skewer with gusto as they waited for Dinh Don to finally arrive.

Bich Trang was further back, helping set up the last of the dispersal mechanisms—clay urns and pots with talismans situated upon them and tied to trees high above—while Phuong Vy finished her preparations.

It left the three as the front line for what was incoming, even as Dinh Don's cries of warning and pain drifted toward them, the crack of broken branches and the thunder of thousands of feet filling the air.

"You know, he was supposed to bring the fastest to us," Wu Ying said idly. He felt his heartbeat speeding up, but he kept his breathing slow and controlled. The pulses of energy, the contained chi bundles that were the beast stones of the creatures approaching were offering conflicting information to his spiritual sense. It rocketed up and down constantly, from as low as nothing stronger than a Body Cleansing cultivator to all the way to Core Formation, mixing and twisting as though the bundles of energy kept reforming and parting. "Not a herd."

"Nest," Thien Giang said, shifting her feet. "It's a nest."

"Of what?" Tou He asked as he took a defensive stance like hers. His aura flared a little brighter, reacting to his emotions, and his companions edged away reflexively.

"Ants. He brought a nest of fire ants," she answered.

"Thousand hells…" Wu Ying whispered. Then there was no more time to prepare, for Dinh Don emerged from the vegetation into the clearing, leaping high to dodge a bite from a particularly fast ant and loosing a half dozen bolts from his crossbow in that single motion, his hand blurring as he twisted around in mid-air. "Here we go."

***

Fire ants. Except these weren't just the big, red, overly aggressive invertebrates that made sitting down in the jungle without checking a foolish idea. No, these were fire ants that had been warped by the corruptive forces to grow significantly larger while gaining additional traits. Amongst them, every tenth or so monster had a squirting attack, unleashing fiery liquid from their behind that struck at Wu Ying as he floated in the air. That kept the wind cultivator moving even as he unleashed blade strikes at the living crimson carpet beneath him.

On the ground, unable to fly and fight at the same time, the pair of polearm users held back the living wave with long sweeping attacks of their weapons. Individually, each invertebrate was weak. Some as weak as a Body Cleansing cultivator, though many stood at the peak of that stage or low Energy Storage. Of course, being beasts, the comparison was only approximate at best. Even so, they were no threat to the Core Formation martial artists below.

Except in their quantity. For each monster that they struck aside, for each sweep of burning staff or bisected body created by a guan dao, another half dozen monsters clambered closer. If not for the fact that the creatures lacked a single guiding mind, the pair would have been overwhelmed immediately.

As it stood, they held the wave back by dint of stubbornness, skill, and large expenditures of chi. And the occasional wind blade from above, as Wu Ying cut and crippled the monsters still pouring out of the jungle, clambering up trees and falling to the ground without care.

Dinh Don, having retreated to the edge of the clearing, was loosing more bolts from his handheld crossbow, striking at the ants that wandered to the sides. Each attack tore clear wide swaths of vegetation, widening the clearing and opening even more to their view. While the majority of the beasts concentrated on the pair below, the disparate nature of the ants themselves lent them to a disjointed approach, forcing the scout to pick off those few he could lest the team be surrounded.

Yet, each moment saw more and more of the creatures pour out, trampling and destroying vegetation. Auras that had been leashed exploded forth, blackening earth and withering greenery, contending with the ants' merging aura. A disturbing trend began to show as the intensity of their combined aura climbed.

It strengthened further with each passing moment, the amalgamated aura building upon itself. The strengthened aura meant that chi attacks like Wu Ying's wind blades or the waves of flame that Tou He released did less damage, blunted by the creatures' protective life force. Thankfully, the sharpened edge of Thien Giang's metallic dao and the killing intent that she and Wu Ying wielded still cut through the defenses of the invertebrates with ease, even as the earth churned and the battle drew even more enemies to them.

All in all, they were doing well.

So far.

"You done yet?" Wu Ying cried, left hand flicking upward automatically, fingers splayed open. He caught a burst of acidic liquid squirted at him in a ball of wind, then threw it back, a last-minute spasm by his hand sending the wind attack off course. Luckily, the ground was so covered by monsters it still struck something.

"Done!" Bich Trang roared. She hopped to the side, extracting her dao and cutting down some of the ants there. With the ants on the edge not part of the main aura combination, they were much simpler to finish off.

Phuong Vy was floating at the back, choosing not to waste her energy. Her knives were utterly useless on the chitin-covered ants, and rather than attempt to poison them slowly, she let the cultivators better suited to the fight deal with them.

Thien Giang screamed as pincers closed on her arm. She reached sideways and tore the ant off her body, the head still attached to her upper arm. Then she hopped back, booting aside a leaping ant before she swung her weapon again.

"Where are the other two?" she said.

No answer, even as the living carpet of insects neared them. The two polearm fighters backed off reluctantly, step by step, weapons swinging as the sheer volume overwhelmed them. Chi strikes no longer budged the buildup, as converged aura contested theirs. They had retreated across nearly half the clearing when Wu Ying heard something different, something louder.

A creature with a single horn, glowing black and dangerous, came charging in. It crushed and shattered ant after ant as it approached, tiny beady eyes set in thick grey hide searching for more victims. Something was off around the creature too, something subtle that Wu Ying instinctively understood to be wrong, twisted, but could not pin down.

Before he could call out a warning, the rhinoceros spotted Wu Ying's friends. The creature was bulky, the size of a wagon and so much heavier. It lowered its head even as ants, taking that moment of its inactivity to clamber or fall upon it, assaulted the creature. Mandibles tore at tough hide, thin legs dug into body as the creature finished reorienting and charged.

Watching a falling ant, Wu Ying was caught off guard by the shift in the ant's trajectory as it entered the creature's sphere of influence. Understanding blossomed, but all too late. The rhinoceros was headed straight for Thien Giang, the cultivator set to attack and leap aside at the last moment. The rhinoceros's sphere of influence affected her upon contact, making her movements, her reactions slower than ever. Timing that was so important to avoid injury was sabotaged and her leap and swing started all too late.

A horned head dipped and twisted, catching the woman in mid-air. The tusk shone with solidified energy, but in reaction, Thien Giang concentrated her metal aura around the impact point. Sparkling dust motes drew together, blunting and slowing the impact even as her aura pulsed in an attempt to protect the cultivator.

By the spray of blood and the scream, attenuated and then sped up as she was thrown clear of the monster's aura, it had failed. She blasted through the air, taking out trees and bushes, bouncing out of the clearing to disappear from sight.

"The beast has a slowing aura!" Wu Ying cried. "A time dao of some sort." Had to be, since it had even affected the fall of the ant. Maybe space? Sometimes, the difference between daos was difficult to comprehend.

"Then he's mine!" Waves of emerald crescent energy preceded the cry, slicing into hidebound flesh and drawing the creature's attention away from the two martial cultivators. In the western corner of the clearing, emerging from the forest, Yang Mu wielded her fans, slicing sideways and cutting air, skin, and chitin alike.

The rhinoceros, coming to a stop in its charge, snorted and regarded Yang Mu with its beady eyes.

Wu Ying would have objected, for the creature they fought was at mid-Core Formation at least by the pulsing energy of its center. But he now had his own problems.

From the sky, a couple of birds swooped down upon him, long, hooked beaks and white tufts of feathers on their heads speaking of their scavenger status. To his surprise, one bird launched a series of water orbs as it flew, swinging upward long before it came close to Wu Ying's blade and forcing him to dodge the marble-sized attacks that tore through ants and ground alike when they impacted.

Its partner was much more traditional in its attack, flames coursing through its body as it swept toward Wu Ying. Blade met claw as he battered the creature away, unable to cut it and finding his face and hands scorched by proximity. Even the quick impact sent him careening toward the earth, his control over the winds tenuous as it was.

Bare feet from crashing to the ground, Wu Ying caught a sudden updraft that cast him and a half dozen ants into the sky. Reorienting himself, Wu Ying bounced between ants as he created footing in the air to allow him to boot the monsters at his flying opponents.

A quick series of wind blades followed the attack, before the wind gave way beneath him suddenly, dropping him amongst the ants. Surprised as they were, the creatures were quick to converge on Wu Ying, forcing the wind cultivator to employ sword and sheath alike in defense. The Dragon turns in Slumber formed a whirlwind of steel and leather to beat back the invertebrates before the wind threw him into the sky once more.

One bird was down, the fire bird screeching its dismay as it winged around. Not from his kicked ants, Wu Ying was certain, but the bird was still gone. No idea where, not exactly, though he assumed the fact that Sao Choi was nowhere to be seen had something to do with it.

Without another target, the fire bird focused its ire on Wu Ying, tucking in its wing to dive. Cursing under his breath and hoping his friends had the other creatures—rhinoceros, ants, and was that a warthog? When did that arrive?—handled, he focused on his own battle.

Already, the clash between Core Formation cultivators had widened the initial clearing by half a li. Auras contested one another below, a rainbow lightshow of competing energies and daos that lit the sky and split the earth, where vegetation was torn down and bloomed under separate influences. From his height, Wu Ying saw Thien Giang returning to the battle, a mutated cat hanging off one upraised arm that she used to batter through trees as she sped over.

No more time to focus on others. His opponent—no, opponents now as another trio of birds joined, smaller than the raptors—was winging back. He would need to concentrate as he fought birds and the wind.

After all, this was just the start of a long day. Until enough of the corrupted beasts arrived, they had to hold.

Chapter 35

"Time!" Bich Trang's voice echoed through the clearing. "To me!"

No reason to concern themselves over the demonic beasts understanding what they said. Instead, clarity was of greatest import. After all, the cultivators only had one chance to get away.

Upon the command, the cultivators broke apart, streaming toward Minh Trac and Bich Trang, who were standing in a cleared portion of the clearing, a single hastily built blood formation draining any beast that came near it and using their blood and chi to power the escape formation. Such blood and death formations were considered dark and heretical in the kingdoms to the north, but it seemed the rules were different here.

In either case, none of the cultivators were slow in ducking through the opening that had been created, Yang Mu utilizing the spatial portion of her enchanted fan to slow the rhinoceros she had been battling all this time. Not just a spatial or time dao suffused it, but a remarkable level of endurance and defense.

Of all the creatures that had piled into the clearing and were fighting at the edges, only the rhinoceros and the ants still survived from the start of the day. The ants by sheer virtue of their numbers, though most now scuttled around the edges, with few reinforcements coming to the battle.

"Wu Ying, come on!" Yang Mu cried, turning around just before she ducked under an invisible line, entering the formation sigils that had begun to glow.

He was the slowest to disengage, being the busiest of them all. Where before the air had been clear of monsters, now it was filled with flying enemies. Everything from squirrels that glided, buffeted by the chaotic winds that filled the airspace, to monkeys leaping and swinging, generating vines of wood chi energy to aid their attacks, to a veritable smorgasbord of lurid birds and insects, all seeking to end the wind cultivator.

The only member of the group in the air, Wu Ying contended with them all. If not for the occasional appearance of Sao Choi, the raptor diving down from high above before returning to the skies as rapidly as it had arrived, he would have been overwhelmed. Well, that and the beasts' distracted attacks upon one another at times and the chaotic nature of the winds.

"I'm. Trying!" Wu Ying replied.

Two swords held in hand, swinging them as he cast about and struck his opponents, legs twisting and kicking, Wu Ying could not help but recall another chaotic flight. Except that time, it had been with the true lords of the skies, the dragons.

Like then, he was but a leaf in the wind, cast from one end to another of the clearing at the behest of forces outside of his control. He could only allow himself to embrace the chaos, lashing out and defending himself in turn.

"Get down here or we're leaving!" Bich Trang shouted. She darted a glance sideways, eyeing Tou He and Yang Mu, cold calculation flicking through her gaze.

Wu Ying wondered if she was considering if the others would stand with the unit if she left him behind or if his loss now would fit her plans.

Tou He was at the opening, holding it against all comers, his staff flicking and dancing with improbable grace. He struck, beat, and smashed with impunity, the wooden staff smoldering with contained flame, each of his victims left with deep burns. And yet even the mountain wore down under the tide of time and water and wind. This human mountain too was ground down, blood running from light wounds, energy streaming from cores with each moment.

"You can't leave him!" Yang Mu cried, then flinched backward as something moved past her. Her eyes widened a little when she realized it was Sao Choi. The bird carried a monster in its claws, having landed at the far end of the small circle they were standing within, its head dipping and tearing at the still-twitching body.

"The formation cannot hold much longer. You know that!" Minh Trac cried, head buried in his compass, fingers of his dominant hand moving above it as he adjusted the flow of chi via thin, almost invisible strings of energy.

"We can't leave him," Yang Mu said again, searching for support amongst the others.

There was none, even Be Long looking away from her. Tou He was too busy holding the line to answer, the crack of wooden staff on flesh continuing to echo through the domain.

Wu Ying heard all this and understood what was happening. He saw them grab Yang Mu as she struggled forward, Thien Giang's muscular arms snaking around the other woman's waist. Dangerous to exit the circle, to disrupt Tou He's desperate defense. Not that Wu Ying's situation was any less desperate, as he was struck again by a flying insect, the creature bouncing off hidden armor.

"Three seconds!" Bich Trang roared. "Three."

Energy built up within Wu Ying's core, controlled and careful. He let it churn, focusing the flow even as he let chaos take over the surroundings. Without even the modicum of energy passed to it earlier, the chaotic winds gleefully cast him about, sending him careening into monsters and flipping him around and down.

"Two!"

"Wu Ying!"

Energy built churning through his body at ever-growing speed. He felt it push against the constraints of his mortal form, soaking into each inch of it. His cells hummed, his tendons sang, and his heart beat with the secrets of the air. Body Cultivator of the Seven Winds, he encompassed the energies, going so far as to put away his weapons as he was thrown around and struck. A bird latched onto his shoulder, strong talons piercing his mail and a beak aiming to tear off an eye.

"One!"

Seven Winds. One dao. Chaos.

A canyon of stone where air, forced to push against itself, sped up and compressed into a wind tunnel. Where the gentlest of breezes became a roaring gale. Wu Ying formed the canyon walls with his chi, a pulse of energy. Then his body, filled to the brim with wind chi, sublimated into it.

He was no longer man, no longer cultivator but the element itself. Vicious bird striking toward his face fell, flapping its wings in surprise as its perch disappeared beneath its talons. Insects winging through the air felt something blow past them, flung projectiles flowing through a figure that was and wasn't there. Pushing apart semi-corporeal form.

Tou He, a mountain in the gap, felt the flow of energy as it passed through him. He anchored his feet, locking himself in place. Hair was tossed about amongst those within the circle, dust thrown into the air. Most of the other cultivators crashed to the ground as a body formed within the circle, still moving.

"NOW!"

Energy surged, the gap in the formation closed. Bright light grew, and the connection between their location and another, multiple li away, was strengthened. For a moment, two realities cojoined as the formation connected them. A moment later, the contents of both places swapped, leaving the cultivators woozy and off-balance as their connection to the greater Dao was momentarily displaced.

Moments later, the formation protecting their corner of the clearing collapsed and their enemies landed within. An enraged rhinoceros charged over, knocking aside a massive simian with its horn, snorting its disdain at the fled cultivators.

At the same time, blood and death formations drew upon the released chi energies of the creatures slain and empowered the illusion formation. Beneath the ground, buried formation plates glowed as they were triggered. Layers of illusions were created in a spiral that trapped all within. Even space was twisted and expanded, leading the fleeing back to the center and allowing even more monsters within.

Step one of their plan had been enacted. And all it took was the bloodying of cultivators, the lives of dozens of corrupted creatures, and the exhaustion of half their stores.

***

Chivied on by an impatient Bich Trang, the group hurried away from their landing spot in short order. Limping and with multiple stealth and concealment talismans in use, the group scurried deeper into the deep wilds.

As they wobbled onward, Wu Ying could not help but take stock of the team. Minh Trac was exhausted, his face pale and drawn, the core energy within him guttering low. As the main formation master—by his insistence—the energy of the formations enacted had drawn from his core. Already seriously depleted from previous battles, he now rested on the moving cauldron as he cultivated with the aid of a series of pills.

The alchemist and scholar was similarly resting with him, the pair propping one another up back-to-back. While the creation of pills was less energy intensive, the stress of the hurried morning and the accumulated injuries from the battle had Phuong Vy resting again. Once more, the woman's lack of martial ability had taken its toll.

On the opposite end, Dinh Don and Tou He seemed to have emerged from the fight less damaged, though a little low on energy. The scout had stayed away from the frontlines during the battle, utilizing his crossbow and enchanted bolts to the maximum. Wu Ying noted the nervous way the scout's fingers played over the quiver, counting feathered ends over and over. A necessary disadvantage of reliance upon a consumable.

As for Tou He… Wu Ying frowned and limped over to his friend, elbowing him in the side as the ex-monk watched their surroundings.

"What?" Tou He said, rubbing his ribs.

"Your chi. It seems to be replenishing faster the closer we get to the corruption," Wu Ying said. "How?"

"All is Fuel."

Wu Ying could hear the emphasis in his friend's words, but emphasis or not, it was no explanation.

Seeing the frown, the fire cultivator explained. "It's a cultivation technique. A sort of moving one—but it's more that it is located within my dantian." A slight hand movement, touching the center of his chest told Wu Ying which dantian he meant. Unlike the usual, the ex-monk had two dantians opened, due to the smaller than normal size of his original base one. "It takes chi—all kinds of chi, the more concentrated and ummm…. synergetic, the better, and burns it. Creating the fuel for me."

"Huh." Wu Ying was a little jealous, he had to admit. Unlike his friend, who was growing strong here, he was struggling. His Cyclone's Breath method no longer functioned. He could only passively sift energy into his dantian and even that was failing because of the level of corruption within the air.

For the first time, Wu Ying found himself unable to rely on anything but what he had stored in his dantian. Even when he was underwater, he had never expected to be out of energy for a long period, so he had been profligate with his chi while battling that Nascent Soul octopus.

Now, he had to be careful, had to watch every use of his chi. He walked rather than flew, moved with the most modicum of chi in his qinggong methods to keep up with everyone else. It helped that no one was on a horse any longer, the beasts released to return if they could. The energy requirements to transport their equine companions had been more than anything they could have conceivably charged, not without exhausting Minh Trac entirely.

More than that, Wu Ying was utilizing the pills he had hoarded, the Twice Cooked Kidney and Liver Pills that he had been reserving for the times when he needed to compress his core.

Unfortunately, this was not the time to conserve resources, even if he had thus far not found more useful pills.

Perhaps when he got back, he might speak with Liu Tsong and beg her aid once more. She had been well on the way to becoming the right hand of Elder Wei as the apothecarist head when he'd left, though he knew she faced some stiff competition from other apprentices, many who had been away or in closed door cultivation when he had been around.

When he had been around.

Strange to think of how long he had been gone. Wu Ying had spent more years as a wandering gatherer, making a name for himself, than he ever had in the Sect itself. More time outside the Sect, it felt, than he had actually been in it.

Strange to think that he still felt some form of loyalty to it, even after all these years. But perhaps not so strange, for without the initial push, the opportunity offered to him by Master Cheng, he would have stayed in the army, perhaps returned to his village, and worked the field with his father and mother. Married someone and maybe even had children.

If he had not died, nameless, on some unnamed farmer's field.

Strange, what alternate lives there might have been.

"What has you frowning so hard?" Yang Mu asked. She had moved up to the pair, her gaze never resting on any single spot. Nor did it stay at eye level, dipping to the ground to verify footing and hidden threats before sweeping upward, searching for monsters that might wing or swing at them.

Even with Sao Choi on guard, flying ahead in short bursts, they had learned their lessons well. Never trust a Nascent Soul beast to properly gauge what is a threat to everyone else.

"My Sect. My place in it." Wu Ying gestured around him. "My place here."

"A little late to be worried about why you're here, no?" she said.

"To change my mind, certainly. But to think about it?" Wu Ying shrugged. "It seems questioning one's place can lead to further enlightenment. Understanding the decisions one makes and the reasons why we make them can lead to wisdom." Then he grinned, nodding toward Tou He. "Anyway, I have to keep an eye on this fool."

"Fool? At least I'm getting contribution points for this," Tou He said. "What are you getting?"

"Me? Why, the most precious coin of all." Wu Ying waited a beat for Tou He to inquire. "Friendship!"

Yang Mu chuckled at Tou He's grimace.

"Seriously, why did you choose to do this?" Tou He said.

"Enlightenment." Wu Ying raised his hand, feeling the flow of air that cut through it with each step, that caught at his hair and sent it spinning. "Knowledge of my path is hard to find, and I must go where the wind beckons."

"Then what of you, Cultivator Yang?" Tou He followed up, eyes narrowed a little. Not in suspicion per se, but certainly in something more focused than honest and innocent inquiry.

Yang Mu's eyes flickered sideways to Wu Ying. "Why, adventure of course. It's why I left my family. That, and making sure this is dealt with will help my mother's business. Being down here has also allowed me to form new relationships, new contacts."

"For your family?" Tou He asked curiously.

"For myself." She shook her head. "I do not expect to be returning home in the near future."

"Another wanderer. That's why you two get along so well." Tou He chuckled. "And here I was worried about Wu Ying."

"Worried about me?" Wu Ying glared at his friend, debated smacking him, and settled for the glare. "Worry about yourself. Monk."

Tou He snorted. "Some of us have progressed past simple carnal desires."

"Carnal desires?" Wu Ying said, scandalized. "I'll let you know—"

"I really would prefer you didn't," Tou He said, cutting off his friend.

"Me too," Yang Mu added on the other side.

That had Wu Ying turning, surprised at the betrayal. She laughed a little, leaning over, and gave him a quick peck on the cheek, an act that made Wu Ying raise an eyebrow.

"Oh, my dear, I don't mind carnal desires, but this is not the time. Nor, really, is discussing it with your friends and in public something that is very… courteous." Eyes glittering with amusement, she stopped, letting the wind cultivator and his friend leave her behind. She, in turn, fell in beside Thien Giang, the older melee fighter looking highly amused at their actions.

"She's a handful, is she not?" Tou He said.

"You have no idea," Wu Ying muttered, but then his frown softened. "Still, worth it, I think."

Tou He nodded, sobering up as Dinh Don returned. He waved the group to the left, crossbow raised at a danger he sensed ahead. Levity aside, they were still in the middle of a corrupted jungle and Wu Ying's inability to sense such dangers was a problem.

A deep problem he had no answer for.

Chapter 36

It was a battered and weary group that managed to make it to their destination two days later. Rather than stop in the evening and be beset by demonic beasts not drawn into the major conflict they had staged, the group had chosen to forge ahead. As cultivators, ignoring the effects of sleeplessness was simple. Between bodies that had transcended the limits of normal humanity, practice after years of constant cultivation, and the refined chi within their cores, such pesky exhaustion was simple enough to ignore.

Even so, the constant battles and the struggle through the undergrowth that grew more tangled and twisted as they neared their destination taxed the group. Even the vegetation struck at them, entangling feet, dipping to bat at faces and rip at clothing. Wu Ying knew it would be years before some of the damage done here was healed. The full effects of such wide-ranging pollution, the wind cultivator dared not guess.

No surprise then that they had to keep a constant state of vigilance, their auras hardened against the corruptive influences that resided within the air and earth. Even so, Wu Ying understood, they would all require time purifying themselves later. No mere Energy Storage cultivator could have survived this trek.

As it stood, even the Core Formation cultivators were finding their energy levels dangerously depleted. All but Tou He, whose aura no longer stayed quiescent but flared and burnt rhythmically. The ex-monk was forced to control that aura constantly, ensuring that it stayed benign around the cultivators even as it hungrily consumed the tainted air, earth, and vegetation.

Of the rest, Minh Trac and Be Long were the most depleted, the formation master having utilized too much of his energy in the initial escape and Be Long due to a lack of training.

On the other hand, Yang Mu seemed the most upbeat of the group, utilizing the vast stores of alchemical pills that she owned—each tailored to her constitution—to ensure she was alert and filled with energy.

Wu Ying too was worn, a constant pounding headache making him grouchy, as did the indignity of having to trek through the forest without his winds. The pressure of the corrupted air pressed upon him constantly, the whispering of the winds he had so grown used to muted. Now, a darker whisper surrounded him, offering him great strength if only he would accept their shackles.

Only the occasional murmur of the winds could be heard near his friend, though the Heavenly cleansing flame and its resultant purified wind offered naught but an insistent refrain that he continue this journey.

In the end, when they stumbled from the choked and twisted jungle into a clearing, not a single cultivator failed to react with joy at reaching their destination. That moment of delight quickly soured, as the reason for the clearing and a clear sight of their objective came to them.

What had to be an abandoned monastery or temple lay before them, situated upon a slight rise in the surroundings. Around it, Wu Ying's trained eyes picked out the remnants of fallow fields, left untended for years—perhaps decades—where the occasional young tree dominated the otherwise flat land. Drainage ditches and earth embankments to separate the fields cut the ground ahead, the earth lying twisted with low-lying bushes and twisted shrubbery. Even the occasional stalk of old rice could be noted, though none of the plants were vegetation that the gatherer would willingly introduce to his World Spirit Ring.

Outside the nearby twisted vegetation, closer to the abandoned, multi-walled, stepped temple that rose above with its green stone walls, was the blasted and shriveled land. No vegetation, twisted or not, lay along those steps and hill. As though the corruptive forces that seeped out from the monastery was anathema to life itself.

"It's inside," Minh Trac said unnecessarily. Holding his compass upward, he stared at the twitching arrow and the myriad glowing runes around it. "I can't see the formation from here. But it's definitely a formation."

"I still say we should destroy it without approaching further," Be Long said, lips curling up. "We have enough formations to do that, do we not? The City Lord even gave me something in case…"

"She did what?" Bich Trang turned now, eyes narrowing. "You have not mentioned this in all this time?"

Be Long blinked, realizing the mistake he had made. He wilted under her demanding gaze until the Captain of the Guards admitted, "It was not meant to be used unless necessary. Ha Jin's Mirror of Infinite Reflections never stood up to its name, though perhaps if the City Lord's ancestor had not caught the Coqui Frog's cry and contained it, it might have lasted longer."

"A sound attack trapped in an enchanted mirror." Bich Trang repeated slowly. "And you carried that fragile item with you, through all this?"

"It's in a special storage pouch." Be Long patted his chest, on the opposite side of his heart. "It will not be damaged by mere travel."

Still looking furious, Bich Trang turned away from the captain. Her words were so low that in any other company, none would have heard them. Amongst a group of Core Formation cultivators, she might as well have shouted. "This is why I hate working with outsiders."

Be Long did not reply, though he did hunch in a little more.

"We go in?" Dinh Don said, cutting through the tension with his usual cheer. "If we can deal with the guardians, of course."

"Guardians?" Wu Ying said, peering closer. He saw nothing, though he knew better than to trust his impaired senses.

"Two within." Dinh Don pointed toward the temple, then shifted his finger to point at the ground ahead of them, about halfway across the distance. "And one there. I can barely sense one of those within and the one under the ground is completely hidden to my spiritual sense. If not for its displacement of the earth…"

"How strong?" Bich Trang asked.

"And why are they not coming for us?" Yang Mu asked. "Surely they can sense us."

"They are guardians. Tasked to stay here," Phuong Vy replied. "I doubt they will bother us if we choose not to engage them."

At the same time, Dinh Don was answering Bich Trang, "Nascent Soul."

"All of them?" Thien Giang asked, eyebrow rising in surprise as she unconsciously shifted her guan dao to place it between her and the temple.

"I believe so."

"Three." Be Long licked his lips. "Three Nascent Soul guardians. How can there be so many?"

"One of them, the one I can sense within the mansion… it feels strange. Its aura trembles, shifting in strength," Dinh Don said. "If it was a cultivator, I would say they'd just broke through and are reinforcing their cultivation."

"But spirit beasts—even demonic beasts—are not like that," Wu Ying said. "They just grow into their strength. There are no stages for them, just a progression of strength and understanding."

"Yes," Dinh Don said. "That's why I said strange."

"It matters not," Bich Trang said firmly. "We have a job, and we shall finish it. Striking at them now, with three Nascent Soul guardians in place, is not going to work. We shall have to deal with our enemies."

"A formation?" Minh Trac said slowly. "For the one out here?"

"That seems best."

Now the formation master hesitated. Phuong Vy, who was beside Minh Trac, leaned over, whispering something into his ear, twisting the threads of chi so no one else could hear her. He angrily brushed her away.

He did, however, reluctantly add, "I cannot do it. Not and help analyze the formation within and take it down for Private Vy."

"Then it is a good thing we have a second formation master, is it not? One who insisted on coming with us," Bich Trang said, turning to Yang Mu.

"It is. What formation would you have me emplace?" She looked right at Minh Trac, holding out a hand as though expecting him to supply it.

The formation master looked unhappy, but after receiving a firm nod from Bich Trang, extracted a number of flags and plates from his storage ring. The pair moved a short distance away to discuss details, even as Dinh Don kept an eye on the temple.

"She'll need protection." Thien Giang muttered. "I don't trust that beast to not attack once she begins."

"Or the ones within," Wu Ying added. "Even if the formation can handle a single Nascent Soul beast, that leaves two."

"Three. The formation we have left will trap it indefinitely," Bich Trang said. "We were to utilize other formations and our skills to finish the fight if necessary. Or bring back the culprit."

Wu Ying nodded. He understood why the other had clarified the point. Still… "Two is still two too many. We barely handled one the last time."

"Sao Choi has been conserving its energy," the colonel said, looking upward. Somewhere up there, the raptor flew, unseen. "It will act when we need it to."

"Fine. One." Wu Ying shook his head. "Still too much, if we have to protect her and fight it off." He hesitated, then added, "And there's no telling what else is in there. Charging in is a bad idea."

"Yet here we are," Bich Trang said. "We must do this. We must finish this battle. The monk must come with us. The best I can do is offer you Thien Giang and Dinh Don. You will have to hold this time, while we do the job."

"Hold," Wu Ying said flatly. "Why not just fight them together?"

"Because there are three Nascent Soul demonic beasts."

Wu Ying stared into the colonel's eyes and realized that her focus, her dedication was unwavering. She had a job to do and that meant learning what was within and destroying it, even if she had to sacrifice most of their lives. All of them, perhaps.

He wanted to object, to suggest a return at a later date with greater reinforcements. But he knew, seeing the resolve in her gaze, that she would brook no argument. They would go on, with or without him and his friends.

For that matter, looking at Tou He, whose gaze had gone adrift, whose aura flickered and twitched, listening to the flames of the heavens that burned through him and the resolute nature of its dictates, that his friend was of the same mind.

"So we split up and try to hold them off," Wu Ying said softly.

He looked up again, searching for the bird. Hoping that it was up there. Three Core Formation cultivators against a Nascent Soul beast, two if they attacked immediately. There was just no way this was going to work.

Not without some finagling.

***

"We're ready," Yang Mu said, returning moments later.

Minh Trac followed her, wringing his hands and muttering last-minute admonishments about the use of the formation flag. The rest of the group kept close together, resting and ingesting food and pills. They kept casting worried glances toward the temple, but thus far, no movement had occurred. The quiet pressure from three Nascent Soul beasts kept the surroundings quiet, and now that Wu Ying knew to look for it, he too sensed the low-level dread that permeated the air.

Wu Ying had clamped down so hard on his aura that he had numbed himself to such sensations, and even the minor flexing and relaxation had almost made him want to retch. An unpleasant aspect of being a Body Cultivator, of being so intensely tied on a physical level to the Dao. Almost immediately, he had to contain his aura, pushing back the corrupted chi and disallowing its continued infiltration.

"How long will you need?" Wu Ying asked. "How far do you need to go?"

"This is a seven-star formation, so I'll first need to emplace fifty-six flags across the surroundings," Yang Mu said.

"It should be one hundred and twelve," Minh Trac muttered.

"Those fifty-six will be the guiding flags of the formation. The control formation itself requires another seven." She flicked her hand upward, and the fan appeared in her hand. "The initial guiding flags do not need to be placed by myself and it would be better if I was aided in their emplacement." She gestured at her feet. "So long as the placement is within the approximately correct location, I can adjust for it in the control formation."

"It'll be slipshod and inefficient and make the entire thing weaker."

"And if we did it your way, it'd take nearly two hours to emplace everything properly," Yang Mu snapped, spinning to glare at Minh Trac and his interruptions. "Now, are you going to let me do this, or am I and my friends going in instead?"

"Peace. Minh Trac will be quiet." Bich Trang held up her hand, offering a consoling smile at the same time.

Yang Mu huffed then gestured at their feet. "The formation will hold for at least an hour, probably closer to two. If you cannot discern the cause and how to destroy the taint and the portal within that time, that's your problem."

"An hour should be sufficient," Phuong Vy said easily. She had a book open, index finger holding her place in it as she waited impatiently for the conversation to be over. Wu Ying could not help but note that she had extracted the well-worn book the moment they had paused.

"If we want to do a slipshod, wasted-ink survey, sure..." Minh Trac muttered.

This time, Phuong Vy was the one who shut down the formation master with a flat look that made him duck his head in chagrin.

"Thien Giang, I'll want you with me and placing the closest flags. Dinh Don and Wu Ying can place the others," Yang Mu continued. "We must get these in the ground before our opponents attack, so speed is of the utmost importance."

The named trio muttered their agreement, though Wu Ying frowned.

"It'll still take time. If the worm attacks before the flags are emplaced..." Wu Ying trailed off.

"That's where the captain comes in. You must delay it." Yang Mu stared at Be Long, then glanced at his belt where a pair of manacles had hung before. "Your skills and techniques are good at that, are they not?"

"What? Fighting worms?" Be Long said.

"Delaying and hampering a cultivator's movements," Yang Mu said.

"Well, yes. But this is a Nascent Soul beast. And you want me to fight it. Alone."

"Delay, not kill."

The man hesitated, looking away. Only to find the colonel staring at him expectantly. In the end, the captain sighed. "I'll do my best. But I guarantee nothing."

Yang Mu nodded. "I can utilize some basic talismans to help distract it further, while I wait for the flags to be emplaced."

"Thank you."

Bich Trang gestured at herself and Tou He before waving to the side to encompass the others. "Our team will attempt to enter the temple once the worm has been captured. We believe that will draw at least one, if not both of the demonic cultivators to attack." She inclined her head upward. "Sao Choi will distract the next demonic beast that exits the building. It will stay outside, dealing with it, and if it finishes its task quickly, it will aid the rest of you."

"That still leaves one more," Tou He said. "Depending on the timing of this…"

"It's why we must wait to take action," Bich Trang said firmly. "So we must hold, even if it is difficult. It is why the captain is the only one who will take on the worm when it comes."

"And what if they choose not to follow your plan?" Wu Ying asked. "What if all three attack at once?"

"Then we will adapt. But my team has to enter the temple, no matter what. If the captain must unleash his mirror, if you must show the techniques you have hidden, then do so." Bich Trang glared, waiting for Wu Ying to duck his head before she looked around one last time. "Any other questions?"

There were, of course, a few more, but they were quickly dealt with. Soon, the group was splitting apart, given their marching orders. A series of simple defensive formations were added a short distance away, talismans floating in the air to help shield the infiltration group from attacks and collateral damage.

As Tou He was about to join them, Yang Mu's long-fingered hand dropped on his arm. He automatically took the red jade bracelet she pressed on him.

"What is this?" Tou He said, holding up the bracelet and turning it over.

"Protective bracelet. Fire aspected, so it should survive your aura. Wear it," Yang Mu said.

"Thank you." The ex-monk wiggled his hand a little, getting the jade bracelet across his knuckles. Minor enchantments on it allowed it to flex and slip on. He smirked a little when he saw that Wu Ying already sported a similar bracelet, though his was made of white jade, the wind cultivator having had a much simpler time putting his on.

"Take care of yourself, you meat-loving fool." Wu Ying dropped his voice, twisting the chi around the trio to hide his words. "Don't trust them to keep you alive."

"Of course," Tou He said. The monk hesitated before he extracted a four-foot-wide scroll and handed the large document to Yang Mu. The pressed bamboo paper was tied off by a simple red cord, keeping the document closed. "If you're in danger, open this and point it at your enemy. Infuse chi through your heart seven, small intestine three, and lung five meridians as well as the inner gate while connecting to your target. It will ensure you have control."

"Control?" Yang Mu said, raising an eyebrow.

"Yes. Best of luck, friends." Putting his hands together, Tou He bowed. "Amitabha."

Wu Ying watched the man leave, then touched the bracelet Yang Mu had handed him. It was obvious she was taking precautions too. Now it was time to see if it was sufficient.

Chapter 37

Wu Ying had twenty-one flags on him, the majority stored in a ring on one hand and the other three already planted. The rest he held in one hand as he ran along the earth from point to point. Yang Mu had cast a flurry of yellow talismans into the air, which had shot off toward the edges of the clearing, grounding themselves as markers. These were the targets the cultivators were to strike.

Each time he drew close to one, Wu Ying threw a flag at the location, guiding its movement with a tendril of chi and his wind dao to land on the marker. Dinh Don was doing the same, though he was both less accurate and slower than Wu Ying. On the other hand, what Dinh Don lacked in accuracy, he made up for by shifting the flags to their appropriate location with a pulse of his chi, the flags bobbing up and down as they rode the wave of energy and shifting earth.

In the meantime, Thien Giang had the fewest to emplace and was taking careful steps to her targets, stabbing the flags deeply before moving on. Each time a flag was planted, it unrolled and flapped in an unseen wind, drawing in chi from the surroundings as the enchantments woven into the material activated.

No movement yet, not from the creatures in the temple.

Wet earth, slightly musky. Damp grass, twisted and corrupt as though it was rotting within. Each footstep sank into the ground, feet digging in with difficulty and balance threatening to disrupt Wu Ying's movements if not for his qinggong methods.

Twenty flags.

Wu Ying breathed slowly, cycling air through his lungs. Funny how, even after all this time, all the changes, breathing and the act of breathing, of eating and sleeping, were important to him. Perhaps at some point, such acts might no longer be necessary, but Wu Ying thought that such a change would be a true loss.

Every path to immortality was different, but he would miss being human if his path up the mountain required him to discard such mundane things. Even the flicker of pain from stubbing a toe or a stretch held too long would be missed, for such moments were a contrast to everyday existence.

Flap of robes, twisting in the air as his arms shifted and threw flags. The surge of chi and the displacement of air as flags appeared in his hand.

Fourteen.

He was halfway through his path, for the next set of talismans were placed close together. He threw them, guiding them with the barest of touches, only to fall short with one as his attention was forcibly pulled away.

An aura, cloying and sticky, repugnant in the way it crept and stuck to his own, unfolded across the surroundings. It emanated from the worm under the ground, the slumbering creature awoken. The stretching of its aura was a reflex action, but under its pressure, Wu Ying felt his own buckle.

Instinctively, Wu Ying stopped fighting it, allowing himself and his aura to be displaced. Such was the strength that he found his path in the physical world shifted. Wu Ying quickly readjusted his plans for emplacing the flags, hands snapping out as more were drawn from the ring.

Eleven.

Removing his hand from the flag he had buried, he extracted three more and immediately tossed one at another target. Another flexing of energy by the creature and Wu Ying struggled to keep the flag flying in the right direction. He managed it, barely, the top swaying from side to side.

A muffled curse from behind as Yang Mu adjusted her formation again.

Ten.

Now the worm was moving. Surging under the ground. Moving as though angered by their actions, its aura intensified. Each moment was a struggle, as though Wu Ying was moving through deep water. No, not water. Mud. The aura clung to him, refused to let him go. Offered no escape.

A momentary flashback of being gripped by a creature whose arms were filled with suction cups. A creature that had sought his life by crushing and eating him. Then memory faded as reality reasserted itself, feet digging into the ground even as he forced himself to breathe.

He was not underwater.

He was not even under the ground or mired in mud.

Or…

"It's making the earth muddy!" Wu Ying cursed, kicking off the ground and using his wind to lift him. "'Ware!"

"Hun dan! The flags are shifting," Yang Mu cursed. "Get the rest in now."

Wu Ying, in the air, stopped concentrating on getting exact placement. Instead, he threw the flags he held into the sky and extracted the others, repeating the motion as the wind sent the flags to their targets. Thank the gods for cultivator memory, for he knew roughly where they had to go and not where the new talismans were. Also, thankfully, as a wind cultivator, as he was hovering, he found himself significantly less affected by the aura that rose from the ground to choke him.

The wind cultivator was not the only one who had recognized the weakness in the earth worm's attack. Be Long had jumped high, his hands moving in arcane gestures as he triggered a series of cultivation techniques. Light glowed around the metal cultivator, digging deep into the earth and connecting him to the worm. Bands of copper stretched and wrapped around the monster, stopping its motion and holding it still.

Briefly.

A surge of concentrated energy was enough to shatter the bands and send Be Long plummeting to the ground. Even as he fell, the earth surged upward as muddy soup engulfed the copper cultivator. He was swallowed within moments and the worm pulsed its aura to constrict and crush.

On the other side, Dinh Don was having the least trouble with the aura. Perhaps because this was his element, he skated across the muddy ground with admirable ease, using the slick earth to help him complete placement faster than before.

Thien Giang took to leaping to emplace her flags, sending still forming mud splattering all around her with each explosive leap and landing. The earth beneath was still solid, though each landing sank her a foot or more deep. Even so, it was a small matter for the cultivator to bunch her legs again and jump, a metal frog flinging itself through the air.

Five. Four. Three. Two.

"Done," Wu Ying shouted.

Moments later, Dinh Don repeated it on his side. The moment he was finished, his hands dipped to the ground as he sent energy into the earth as well.

"Almost!" Thien Giang bunched her feet again and jumped.

However, in a movement too fast to catch, only sensory impressions lasting, something emerged from the temple and slammed into her. The fast-moving demon took the metal cultivator out of the air, sending her into the woods behind and shattering trees and scattering leaves.

Somehow, the woman had managed to throw the flag into the air, perhaps reflexively or by accident. Wu Ying caught it before it landed, guiding the winds to cast the flag into its final resting spot. Moments later, another explosion happened as Be Long was vomited from the ground, the bronze cultivator's chest heaving as he exited the earth.

Dinh Don cried out in triumph, hands still plunged in the earth.

"Finally!" Yang Mu spun about and slammed the flags in around her.

Casting about for their enemies, Wu Ying blinked. As the pressure from the worm's aura continued to pulse through the surroundings, turning earth to mud, its very presence beneath the ground had faded. He opened his mouth to shout a warning, only to watch as the worm reared up in front of Yang Mu, its massive mouth open and hungry.

In contrast to all around them, the earth around the talisman master's feet was solid, the plug of earth rocking to the side and forcing her to her knees as she held the last flag in one hand and a pulsing, enchanted fan in the other.

"Too late," Yang Mu cried in triumph as she plunged the flag into the ground.

It never reached it as another tainted demonic beast took action.

***

The pulse of energy, a twisting cone of corrupted chi with tendrils of dao enlightenment within flew from the entrance of the temple. A single furred bipedal creature stood there, a hand extended as the energy it had drawn and released tore through the air, piercing the worm through and through and enveloping Yang Mu. Wu Ying found himself screaming her name as he watched the attack wash over the surroundings.

"The formation! The corruption. It's all in its body!" Minh Trac shouted, waving his hand from their formerly sheltered site a short distance away from Yang Mu. The incursion formation flags had been torn apart from the backlash of the attack that had struck Yang Mu.

Wu Ying's eyes were locked on the spot Yang Mu had been, the breeze already carrying him over to the location. The massive worm that had reared upward, the revealed portion of its body the size of his family house before the attack, was now damaged. It hung in the air dangerously, slumping sideways slowly.

A hole the size of a man's torso had been blasted through one side, fluids and tainted flesh hanging and running from the wound. Grievous as the wound looked, flesh and muscle knitted visibly together. Empowered by earth and the corruption, it would take more than a single attack—even by another Nascent Soul creature—to kill the worm.

The body finally crashed sideways, throwing up mud and dirt and showering Wu Ying in it as he flew through without a care. His wind aura took the debris and flung it away from him as he emerged on the other side. Dreading what he expected to see, his heart clenched tightly and his lungs refusing to expand.

Only to find Yang Mu alive. Unharmed.

The glimmering portals that her fans had created were fading, and the energy of the attack passed through to exit a short distance behind. The glow around the fans were diming, the enchanted energy stored within consumed in that single moment of expenditure. Worse, the formation Yang Mu had been in the midst of creating was gone, formation flags destroyed.

None of that, he cared about.

Wu Ying landed beside Yang Mu, pulling her into his arms. He hugged her tightly then released her, searching for injury. She offered him a weak, exhausted smile, though the wood cultivator was fast recovering.

"You're alive."

"I am." She grimaced. "Not for lack of trying on our enemies' part."

"Where is Sao Choi!" Wu Ying snarled.

Even as he spoke, the incursion team was acting, launching attacks on the biped Nascent Soul demon with its twisted arm. No, more than its arm was twisted.

Now that Wu Ying was paying attention, he sensed the defilement.

Someone had taken the dark-furred ape with streaks of white hair and hammered metallic formation spikes into its body. Each of those spikes were engraved with formation words, though at the ends of each metal rod was a single, familiar character—chaos.

That was not the only dishonor enacted upon the creature. Its left arm had been removed and another attached. That arm was hairless, dense enchanted runes and characters carved into the pale flesh, runes that bled and wept greenish fluid. Light shimmered around the arm, the air twisted and spiraling away as the arm was anathema to this world.

In its entirety, the creature was a rupture in this world. What had been done to it was a savage and heretical action. The chi pulsing from the monster was corrupted but in such plentiful supply, it was clear that it was no plain Nascent Soul monster.

As it stood there, glowing eldritch green and sickly yellow, blood-red runes made of flesh and blood tore free from its body. They hovered in a sphere of twisted chi that warded off the combined attacks of the others, runes peeling from the alien arm as the infernal formation was worn away.

Now, in its other hand, the untainted one, a new attack built.

"I saw it go after Thien Giang," Yang Mu said, casting aside the useless flag. The formation they had planned to wield was gone now, destroyed. There was no recovering it, not without time. "We have to help them."

"Agree—"

Wu Ying's only warning was the worm as it burrowed into the earth again, submerging the portion of its body still above the ground as it sensed the upcoming attack.

Chi formed in untainted hand was unleashed, corrupt energy seeking the pair of still targets. Intent on finishing what it had started. Time slowed for the wind cultivator as he sought a solution. Instinct had him step in front of Yang Mu, hand reaching for his sword. He could not face this attack directly, he had not the strength. If he was his Master, perhaps…

But he was not Master Cheng, and he had his own techniques.

Time sped up as Wu Ying moved. He took a step to the right, opening his hips with the motion as his foot landed at an angle. His right hand brought the Saint-jian out of its sheath, turning sideways and upward as he cut. Robes rose and gusted in the wind that followed his motion, the Cyclone's Breath burning through the air, joining him to the corrupted air all around.

He followed the motion of his foot, turning the rest of the way with his body as he pivoted. Foot, hip, shoulder, arm, other foot touching down not just once but three times in quick succession as he pivoted. Spinning himself and the world around him, revolving like a top.

Or a cyclone.

Wind, beckoned by the application of dao and chi, rushed in to fulfill his command. Air surged forward, a looping gust that caught the twisted dao and chi-empowered attack and threw it sideways as a sixth, stronger wind joined the five that Wu Ying had threaded through his attack.

Wu Ying's understanding of the world, his sword, and wind dao combined and a torrent of his chi met the attack. For a moment, he feared it would not be enough.

But it is always easier to divert rather than challenge, to bend rather than stand strong. If you turn and turn enough, sometimes you come back to the place you started, the calamity that had come bearing down upon you having passed by.

Corrupted chi tore through the world and twisted feet away from the pair to strike the ground, to burrow deep after the hiding worm. The earth shook and thundered, and the pair rode the bucking mud with each moment.

When the attack finally guttered out, Wu Ying and Yang Mu still stood. Smoke rose from their robes, protective enchantments pushed to the brink. Their hair was in disarray, ends frayed from the passing energy. Wu Ying's uninjured sword arm had a cherry blossom glow to it, the energy that had been cast aside leaking through. His breathing was hard, his mind in disarray, his aura shredded.

Still, they stood.

The Third Cut of the Wandering Dragon.

The Dragon Turns.

Chapter 38

No backlash, no condemnation of the Heavens. Wu Ying could have sworn that the Heavens themselves had aided him, pressing enlightenment and understanding upon him as he faced their enemy. As though a guiding hand had pushed the necessary knowledge such that he had known what to change, how to change his own technique. Helped him perfect the third cut when he most needed it.

He would be grateful. Later.

"Move. Take care of the worm, finish it!" Wu Ying ordered Yang Mu as he moved away, eyes fixed on the tainted ape.

The redirected attack had injured the worm and exposed it, the attack having burned away more flesh and widened the wound. Blood flowed freely from the gaping injury and around the edges of the flesh. Healing that had begun had shifted, cancerous growths and tumors appearing, bubbling forth and displacing healthy flesh.

Acting on Wu Ying's orders, Yang Mu pushed forward, her fans gone. Instead, a bow appeared in her hand, enchanted arrows fitting to the bowstring. She loosed them at the giant worm with smooth efficiency, sinking barbed arrows deep into the flesh. Each arrow was part of a formation, lightning crackling between each embedded shaft and growing in strength with each addition.

Dinh Don turned back to aid Yang Mu, having recovered from freeing Be Long. He added his paltry attacks to hers. Crossbow bolts, both enchanted and chi-charged and plain, sank into the elongated body with impunity. The worm sought to escape, to twist and catch the pair, but the elusive drunken fairy and the swift-moving, mud-skating scout evaded the massive creature while leading it farther east and away from the main battle.

As Wu Ying rushed forward, he sensed further commotion behind from an ongoing battle between Thien Giang, the other Nascent Soul enemy, and Sao Choi. Wu Ying cursed under his breath, wishing the bird was here, taking part in the real battle. Then again, he was beginning to realize that bird had likely grown strong and old in this way—avoiding the dangerous fights.

Perhaps there was a lesson there that he should learn.

Later.

The corrupted ape howled, head thrown back, fur standing on end. The cry of anger shook the leaves of nearby plants and sent stones tumbling from the abandoned temple. It struck its own chest, the rapid drum beat of its challenge causing Wu Ying's teeth to ache and his ears to hurt as the metallic spikes embedded within its body rung in resonance.

More than anger or frustration, the energy it had gathered to unleash—twice now—had drained the ape. The flow of energy within its body had decreased significantly, the lights on the metallic spikes dimming. The glowing eldritch runes around it had faded a little from the attack and faded again even as the other members of the team attacked, runes flickering through different colors and diminishing in order as the attacks landed.

All but two cultivators attacked, distracting the monster.

One was his friend.

Tou He had stopped assaulting the ape when it had unleashed the second pulse of energy from its arm. The ex-monk had placed his staff low against his hip, the tip pointed a little high and above his sternum. His breathing had slowed, his aura churning and concentrating, beginning at the outer edges of his body and flowing through his hands into the tip of his weapon. Not a single other motion did he make, standing there as he focused fiery chi into a singular strike.

Wu Ying wondered what that attack was called.

The second fighter who chose not to participate was Be Long. The captain was half-sunk and on his side, smoke rising from his armor and a rictus of pain on his face. Propped up on his splayed open legs, kept out of the churning mud was a mirror, lights ticking off one after the other along its gilded edge.

Moments. It had taken Wu Ying moments to assess the fight anew, dart out of the way of the next expected attack which hadn't come, take to the air to avoid being sucked into the slowly firming mud, and unleash a half dozen wind blades of his own.

None of which had pierced the protective shielding around the infernal ape. He saw maybe a couple of the runes switch and fade, but they were soon replaced as more flesh, more runes tore free from the creature's body.

As though it was mocking him, the ape stopped striking its chest, dropped down to its knuckles, body twisted in a lopsided manner as the grotesque, perverse, and oversized arm touched the ground first. Still ignoring its other attackers, it fixed its gaze on Wu Ying.

"Why me? What did I do to you?" the wind cultivator muttered.

A spiral of water, rising from the churning mud, clean and pure, struck the glowing energy cloud around the ape. It hissed and disappeared in a rolling cloud of steam, and Wu Ying watched as a single rune, taking the brunt of the attack, faded and fell to the ground.

Phuong Vy continued to lob small spheres of poisonous smoke and powder, but none penetrated, the attacks disappearing as quickly as they appeared. Mostly, however, she was peering at the runes, muttering under her breath.

"I nearly have it!" she said.

"Be quick about it!" Bich Trang snarled, her hands moving through the motions as she dragged more moisture from the surroundings to form another stream to attack the beast.

A beast that had chosen to lift its corrupted arm outward, even as a new rune peeled off it and joined the swirling mass. Doing so dimmed the spikes further, the energy pulsing within dimming further. Another buildup of power in the corrupted arm, the creature readying another attack.

"Again? Do you not have any other tricks?" Wu Ying muttered.

Wu Ying focused his energy, hard as it was, and pushed himself higher. No fancy techniques this time. If he was going to avoid that attack, he'd best have his full mobility. In the sky, he waited, drifting in the wind as he felt the energy grow.

As he waited to see who acted next.

***

"There!" Phuong Vy cried. A single knife flew out, glowing white as it struck a blood red and yellow rune.

Tou He, in his green-edged black robes, took a single step and thrust with the tip of his staff. It moved faster than a striking serpent, leaving a trail of blazing energy that ignited the air in its wake. He was too far for the metal staff to strike the ape, but not the bar of energy that he wielded.

Purifying flame, concentrated into a single attack, struck with the strength of a falling boulder. Once it touched the flesh rune that formed part of the shield, the corrupted flesh blackened and shriveled, the energy around the runic web rushing to concentrate in a point around the striking ape.

At the same time, all that energy that had been built up exploded outward too, unable to penetrate the shield. That threw back Phuong Vy, burnt away the hastily constructed sphere of water that protected the colonel, and threw chaotic but clean winds into the air to buffet Wu Ying.

Yet Tou He's bar of flame was not without cost to the corrupted ape. One after the other of the flesh runes failed, their eldritch green and yellow light fading. The shield around it shattered, the ex-monk's attack progressing another half-inch before the impetus of his attack ended.

"NOW!" Bich Trang, smoking but still on her feet, cried out in command.

The wind cultivator thrust his sword lower, pouring energy and sword intent into a killing strike. At the same time, he knew he was not the one she had spoken to.

Instead, it was Be Long and his mirror that unleashed the energy of the captured attack. From within the mirror, rather than a beam of concentrated chi or compressed killing and blade intent, what emerged was a torrent of choking ash and smoke. It flowed down the surroundings in a stream of twisted grey and black smoke, moving even more swiftly than the compressed air blades Wu Ying swung.

The corrupted ape raised its grafted arm, the massive limb turned sideways such that the attack struck the back of the limb. Smoke splashed like water and flowed around the limb, clinging to it even as hot ash burned and filled the air with choking corruption.

Forced back by the strike, the other Core Formation cultivators retreated. Wu Ying's attack was absorbed into the cloud, disappearing with barely any sign but a rippling in the cloud. The sound of whistling gale winds, the hiss of burning flesh, and the cry of pain from the smoke were all the sounds that arose from their clearing, even as the noise of ongoing battles continued from the other two locations where the remaining Nascent Soul beasts survived.

In the meantime, none of the cultivators—barring Be Long, who strained to keep the attack aimed and targeted at their opponent—were taking a break. Bich Trang, who had retreated to the farthest location, was drawing forth groundwater and moisture from the air and the mud as she built up a globe of water.

Phuong Vy, at the edge of the clearing, was scribbling on a floating piece of paper, creating a formation on the spot. Wu Ying knew not its purpose, but with a glance at the sheet of paper she wielded, twice the height of herself, he knew it would be fiendishly complex in creation and execution.

As for Tou He, he had retreated far enough away that he could unleash his aura such that the ambient temperature rose. Small patches of fire appeared in the air and on the ground as the purifying flames consumed the corruption all around them, reducing the environmental advantage their opponent fought under.

Above them all, Wu Ying floated, straining his aura to sense what was going on under the ongoing onslaught from the mirror. His weapon was held by his side as he sought calm and silence within his mind, sharpening the killing edge of his intent as he waited to strike. No hasty outpouring, no built-up attack for him. That was not the way of the Wandering Dragon.

No. He would strike quickly and sharply, without warning.

As suddenly as it had begun, the outpouring of ash and flame ceased. A half dozen breaths since it began, the torrent ended. Be Long's mirror shattered, showering the surroundings with slivers of glass and metal.

Within the cloud, only silence at first. Straining his hearing, his spiritual sense, Wu Ying noticed it then. Harsh, irregular breathing, a huffing and snarling noise. He opened his mouth to cry a warning to the others, but was once more, too late.

It was always too late when one fought a Nascent Soul creature.

Too fast, too smart, too instinctive. Each fighter had to look out for themselves, for a moment's inattention was all it took. Stone and dirt sprayed outward as the monster leapt across the distance between it and its target in a single explosive motion.

It reached, snatched, tore, and turned around, the earth parting in a deep gouge that reached nearly the end of the clearing as the ape attempted to stop. The monster hooted and hollered, holding up its still-dripping prize as the body left behind slowly slumped onto muddy earth. Blood gushed and dribbled, coming from the remaining stump of a body.

Headless.

In burned and hairless twisted arm, metal rods embedded within half melted and other rods all across the nearly hairless body glowing a deep cherry red, Be Long's head hung. Its eyes wide in surprise, mouth moving a touch as soul and mind caught up with its abrupt end.

Then the light faded, and the beast moved again.

Chapter 39

The wind saved Wu Ying. It threw him high, high above the trees and into the realm of birds and dragons. Not that there were either—thankfully—for the mortal avian companions had fled in good wisdom and the dragons had yet to seek out the disturbance. After all, no papers had been burned, no gifts offered to the Heavens. The cultivators below knew better than to attract the attention of those above.[58]

No, this was a mortal problem. A very obvious mortal problem, for who but a mortal could have chosen such inhumane action against another living creature? Or done so while utilizing such an inventive and civilized form of torture?

Wu Ying was no sheltered nobleman or effete cultivator who had never left the city. He had walked through the deep forests and hidden from creatures of great cruelty and playfulness. Seen great cats strike and exhaust their prey, watched boars savage birds and rabbits for no greater reason than savagery. Pulled corpses of mortal and cultivator alike from the webbing of massive, semi-sapient spiders that had paralyzed them and injected the bodies with venom to eat later.

Nature was cruel, and only a fool would think it not.

But its cruelty was not civilized, was not without point.

Below him, the corrupted ape reached the apex of its jump and thrust a hand upward. Energy flooded out in a wide band, loosed upon Wu Ying as he sought to flee. In his failure, he was forced to control the winds around him to form a shield even as he darted sideways, feeling the corruption burn aura and wind alike.

Energy drained from Wu Ying swiftly, exhaustion greying out the edges of his vision. He felt the corruption seep into his skin, his bones, and he gritted his teeth, for its presence was like a blade taken to his skin, flaying it apart.

But pain was an old companion, and the monster found itself drawn down by the remorseless advance of gravity. Leaping for Wu Ying was a mistake as well, for in the air, it could not change its landing spot. And Bich Trang was waiting, her sphere of water interposed to accept the monster's descent and keep it from the earth.

Submerging into the sphere with barely a ripple, the monster thrashed and attempted to break free. Outside, hands held upward, Bich Trang moved the sphere with the swimming corrupted ape, keeping it trapped in the center.

"Help me!" Bich Trang cried.

A moment later, a handful of folded sachets struck the sphere. They broke apart within the water, dissolving as they came into contact with it. Streaks of green and blue mixed,

---

[58] "May you be recognized by powerful people / attract the attention of the government"—supposedly one of three Chinese curses (its more famous brethren is "May you live in interesting times") isn't an actual Chinese curse. There's no evidence of it being used in ancient China beyond some journals by Western diplomats in the early 20th century.

muddying the sphere and darkening it as the corruptive elements of the creature's body twisted the very nature of the water itself. The poisonous sachets mixed with the chi within, turning even more vicious and eating into the monster's flesh and the runes carved into its body, runes that had begun to peel away to protect it.

No more.

As the water altered its form and function, it increased the strain upon Bich Trang. She began to sweat blood, leaking from pores all across her body as she struggled to contain the monster and the working. Her body trembled as she fought on, though her hands were never anything but swift and certain.

Floating down, Wu Ying's lips compressed. He had no attacks that could penetrate the sphere without disrupting the working. He had formation flags, but none of those were workable here. He had neither the understanding nor expertise to emplace a formation at speed—certainly not one that could harm the creature. And the few talismans he carried were not meant to deal with a Nascent Soul beast, never mind one that was further empowered by elaborate rituals and enchanted spikes driven into its body.

Once again, Wu Ying felt a degree of helplessness. He had climbed so far, struggled and fought and trained to hone himself into a powerful cultivator. A man who wielded not just a rare element but who had the combined strength of soul and body cultivation at his fingertips and one who had grasped the Heart of the Jian.

He was no weakling.

And yet here he was, helpless.

Unable to change the fate of the one struggling below. Even as he watched, Tou He strode up to Bich Trang and placed a hand in the center of her back. He flooded her body with unaspected chi, empowering her and drawing the burden of holding forth the sphere toward himself.

It was a technique the monk must have learned while in the sect, a technique meant for those who worked with others. A technique that Wu Ying had never studied.

Cursing—whether himself, his friend, or his fate—the wind cultivator looked aside. Searching for signs of the other battles. He found them soon enough. And, to his surprise, Thien Giang returning. Even as Sao Choi, the bird, cried and struck, tearing into its prey that still struggled weakly beneath its claw, the polearm wielding cultivator returned to the main battle.

Good.

Dinh Don and Yang Mu continued their fight, though the worm had grown sluggish. To his surprise, Wu Ying noticed a dozen creatures made of ink and shadows that moved around the great worm, tearing into it. A dozen creatures, a rat, a tiger, a pig, even an ink dragon. Fabled creatures from the calendar, released to do battle from a scroll carried across kingdoms from a sect that saw all too well into the future.

No last-minute aid coming from that direction.

Another twitch, a surge of energy. Wu Ying's head lowered, eyes widening as the sphere below changed in color, darkening as blood—dark and tainted—flooded the sphere. It trembled, bulging like a cancerous pustule. At the same time, erupting from the sphere was a metal rod. It fell to the ground as the limb it had been connected to grew, mutated, rotted and twisted, expelling the rod from the constantly changing limb.

"Grab that!" snarled Bich Trang.

Wu Ying gestured downward, but the wind balked at his command. It refused to move toward the metal rod, leaving the wind cultivator to extend his chi in tendrils. Even so, accessing the wind and the energy of the world in this way was a struggle as he neared the piece.

"Hun dan," Wu Ying snarled. He let himself fall, knowing he would have to grasp the rod directly.

At the same time, the bulging water sphere exploded, showering the surroundings with poisonous, bloodied, and corrupted water. Without thought, Wu Ying called forth a wind wall, sending the slurry away from him. Tou He did the same, his fire aura triggering and sweeping outward to create a cloud of steam when the water struck his expanding sphere of influence.

Bich Trang reeled backward as her control disappeared, blood fountaining from her mouth as she suffered the backlash of her technique being forcibly torn apart. She fell to the ground as the fire cultivator twisted his aura to help deal with the current threat.

The other cultivators were less fortunate. Phoung Vy staggered backward, crying in pain as she clutched her neck where a fast-moving glob of water had scalded her skin. Flesh peeled and poured from the wound, even as the formation paper she had protected instead of herself floated away from her body as her control and aura slipped, nearly falling to the ground.

Minh Trac, the formation master who was scurrying on the edges of the fight, was similarly struck. He had been hiding under numerous enchanted talismans, using the battle and the distraction of others to emplace a slaughter formation. However, the explosion tore through his meager defenses and sent him sprawling to the ground, piercing his clothing in a wave of poisonous water. Screaming in pain, he managed to strip his outer robes and slip a bottle of pills into his mouth—whole—to help stem the damage.

Thankfully, the corrupted ape was not attacking.

Having landed on its feet, it was searching the ground with its demonic arm, seeking the twisted bar of metal through mud and dirt. Its energy had grown chaotic, fluctuating as arcs of green energy and white lightning raced across its core. Energies contained by the corrupt formation burned across its body, unstable with the loss.

No time to worry about the lightning, the sudden surge of heavenly chi all around, the twisted smell of rotten meat and new cut flowers that surrounded Wu Ying now. No time to worry about the crash of blades in the distance or the screams of the dying Nascent Soul monsters. No time but to drop like a stooping bird, hands tucked close to him, and pray that his still tenuous control of the wind held.

Wu Ying led the way with his jian, dropping with each moment. Holding the wind as he neared the ape was like gripping an oiled, living eel about to be submerged in a vat of heated cooking oil. The closer he grew, the greater the struggle. He had no time to launch a proper attack, to pour all his energy into a blow, not when he was holding onto the element with all his might.

Instead, he could only sharpen the edge of his intent, allow the blade to do what it was made for. It cut deep into the side of the monster. It cut, carving a long furrow along the ape's torso, hardened fur like steel parting beneath the dao-inspired edge. It cut and a fountain of blood exploded forth, some of it striking Wu Ying as he passed beside tree-trunk legs.

Already curving upward and rising to harass it as he sought the metal spike, the wind cultivator was surprised when his control failed utterly. Once the blood touched him, breaching his aura shield, the wind no longer answered him, growing chaotic.

He struck the muddy earth, a wave of soil, burnt grass, and poisonous water washing ahead of him and into the folds of his clothing. Poison and corruption invaded his body, seeking entrance even as the strength of his Body Cultivation and his dao battled back. Disoriented and injured, muscles along one leg cramping as he struggled upright, Wu Ying sought to rejoin the battle. He was not the only one, as Tou He engaged the beast, his staff and aura striking the creature again and again, attempting to push it back.

No more enchanted shielding to block attacks. The twisted formation that had given the ape strength had been broken, and now the creature only had the strength of its arms and its twisted dao to wield against them, the energy it had contained slowly fading.

But it was more than enough.

Even on the defensive, the ex-monk could barely hold on as each blow sent nearby mud and water jumping. The volume of their clashes was like a dozen bells being struck at once, a thousand drums played during the new year to scare away demons and hungry taotei.

The few standing trees were blown aside, leaving only the half-built formation that Minh Trac had been attempting to build standing. With each blow, the ex-monk was driven a step back, even the Resolute Mountain unable to bear up against the attacks, feet skidding on muddy earth and bringing him ever closer to the insensate colonel.

A flicker of movement in the corner, Thien Giang had gathered as much speed as she could in her headlong return. She was battered and exhausted, reckless in her actions, furious at being removed from the initial battle by the other monster. Her attack was without plan, led only by surging emotion and the intent to injure and rejoin battle.

Her guan dao, sweeping downward at the last moment, was caught on upraised, corrupted arm. It dug in deep, shearing portions of twisted skin apart only for cancerous flesh to grow around the guan dao. Surprise registered on her face as her attack came to a sudden stop. Still, experienced fighter that she was, the cultivator threw herself backward, tugging on the weapon to free it.

Only to find it unwilling to free itself entirely.

A momentary stoppage. A fatal one.

Guan dao was pulled toward body, the cultivator drawn toward ape. The ape's other hand, moving in simultaneous and opposite direction, thrust forward. It emerged from her back, clawed fingers clutching her still-beating heart.

So died Thien Giang. So ended another cultivator.

And then, the monster turned to Tou He.

Chapter 40

"Together!" Wu Ying snarled, forcing himself to charge the creature. He no longer utilized the adjusted Wind Steps, no longer borrowed the wind to do his bidding. He could not afford to battle for control of the environment. Not and save his friend in time.

Already, the monster had struck. Wu Ying watched wide-eyed as the staff, reinforced and enchanted, bent under an open palm attack that his friend caught as it descended. Fingers hooked and gripped metal body, threatening to tear away the staff.

Gripping tightly, Tou He was lifted and pulled forward, flipping himself over the kick that followed and planting his feet on the exposed face, double kicking the monster. The attack tore his staff from the hand and sent him spinning backward as the explosive contact between the pair sent a wave of purifying flame washing outward. The smell of scorched hair and flesh intensified, even as Wu Ying was forced to squint against the glare.

More and more of the creature's fur had caught fire, flames racing across exposed skin and burning at the cursed glyphs. Lightning rushed back and forth across the monster's body, the lightning never having touched Tou He. As though the heavens themselves were attempting to punish the monster, even as pulses of eldritch energy poured from the metal spikes in contention.

Wu Ying felt his spiritual sense recoil as he approached the pair, feet sinking into muddy earth with each movement. No hesitation, he twisted in mid-air, throwing himself into the sky to stab downward. Dao-infused jian sank through decaying metal like butter, piercing the leftover spike.

The moment he made contact, he felt corruptive energy rush up his jian along his extended aura, attempting to intrude upon his understanding of the blade and his dao. Sinking to one knee, Wu Ying clutched his sword arm with his other hand feeling the corruption push upward with each moment. Joined together, blood and fluids weeping from the cracked open wound of his injured hand, Wu Ying poured chi down the blade. Forcing down the energy, the corruptive dao.

Not enough, the five winds. Not enough, the mortal understanding of this world. And though this energy had echoes of the wind of hell, it was spoiled, having wandered off the true path. He could not take this dao into his being, not and stay true. It would taint him, no matter the power it promised—and so much power it did promise—for it was not of this world.

It was not his path.

Could not be.

And yet, struggle as he might, he was losing. The only good fortune there was that his attack had disrupted the creature's focus on his friend. Now, it was Tou He who defended him.

If it had been his arm instead of sword that he had used…

No time for possibilities or further thought.

Head bent low, Wu Ying poured energy and understanding down his weapon, the innate stubbornness of a peasant who never knew where his next meal might arise coming to the fore. The arrogance that any cultivator held was tested as energy slowly forced itself upward against his efforts. And finally, as it reached his guard, the obstinance to keep moving forward, no matter the examples of failures, of deaths and injuries that littered the mountain of immortality all around.

Each moment, he lost ground, cun[59] by cun. Energy drawn from his core, energy required to feed the burgeoning Nascent Immortal soul was drained. He refused to let the energy have its way, but even so, he lost.

Moment by moment, the corruption won and a little more of who he was lost.

***

"Cleanse through the liver meridian, push through the large intestine and stomach meridians your chi in the eight and eleventh part. Concentrate the winds through that, rather than fourth meridian." Phuong Vy's voice was urgent, demanding as she jogged over to Wu Ying. The ground had firmed, mud having faded as the chi that had initially created the slurry drained away, the water drawn into a sphere wielded by another.

"What?" Wu Ying said, muzzily.

She repeated herself, even as she flicked a dozen hastily scribbled talismans onto the ground around Wu Ying's sword point. The air warmed and smoke arose, the cleansing formation triggering and purifying the tainted energy that escaped the metal rod.

A slight moment of hesitation preceded another wave of corruptive energy forcing its way past the guard, touching the knuckles of his hand. Wu Ying poured energy as she recommended, cleansing and twisting his chi before it was guided into his hand. Almost immediately, the corruption shrank back. The altered flow of chi made the fire element of the winds more prominent and reduced the wood element, splitting his energy apart and making it hotter.

Instinct guided his next action, as he recalled the warm winds of the south. He guided energy based off that aspect through the meridians further, pulling cold chi from the north from his arm, pouring warmth from the south down the sword. It helped as he pushed back the energy from the rod, though soon enough a balance of power formed.

Balance was not enough, for he could not extract his hand. Balance was not enough, for Tou He battled for his life. Balance was important, but it was also stasis. It was equilibrium

---

[59] A traditional Chinese measurement, measured as the width of a person's thumb at knuckle. It is—in current, standardized measurement—3 1/3 cm or approximately 1.312 inches.

that threatened to tip into failure. It was the man on the cliff's ledge, ready to fall through the air. Or a plant, freshly cut. Dead and no longer growing but poised for the end.

Life—existence—was not about balance. It was about growth and change, about fall and failure and subsequent rise and success. It was about learning when one won or lost. A churning whirlwind of the future and uncertainty, of regret from the past and that ever-present, ever-passing moment of the current.

Five winds from the corners of the earth held back the ever-encroaching power of corruption, the alien dimensional energy, and Wu Ying found balance. It was not enough. But there was a sixth wind, one that he had followed on its behest down south that had yet to act.

Balanced between success and failure, the tiny thread of heavenly wind that he had grasped tipped the scales. Enlightenment, the barest thread of understanding and beneficence from a realm that demanded obedience, offered him success.

He clutched at it, bent to their demands and allowed himself to be the tool they required. He fell into the wind, no longer fighting heavenly dictates, no longer seeking to impose his own goals. Heaven had no time for disobedience, brooked no argument. Wu Ying was but a soldier bound to their whims, fighting a celestial battle for the worlds below.

Cold.

Heaven's wind was cold. He knew it was not truly freezing. It was not the frigid, bone-aching chill of the north, where the snow never left and greenery was but an ancient memory.

No, this was the chill of a disappointed parent, the reserve of unfeeling rules and regulations applied to one and all without concern for circumstances. It was imposed order that had created canals across the entirety of the south, linking cities and reducing flood plains, such that farmers could survive turbulent rainy months. It was the logical progression of civilization, the building of roads between settlements and the construction of walls to provide protection.

It was neither good nor bad, just like the true hell winds were neither weal nor woe. It was a factor of life that saw the imposition of order and the perfection of civilization, that provided guidance and wisdom and judgment in equal order.

And the pitiless heavens did not, could not, accept the corruption, for that brought chaos.

Roaring through Wu Ying's body, straining muscles and bones and skin, Heavens' winds roared. It drew from his understanding and now, offered a true channel to this world, arrived in force. It tore apart his body even as the corrupted energy was pushed all the way back into the metal rod.

The wind cultivator glowed, white light emanating from his body, and gale-force winds picked up around him, pushing against the scholar who had stood beside him and bringing forth damp earth and scattered foliage.

Greenish-yellow energy frosted over, turned white and sky blue all around him. In the distance, Wu Ying heard the ape scream as heavenly chi flooded the flesh runes engraved on the creature's body. Straining energies coursed through the monster's body, cracking it apart as a weakness was exploited. Now, the monster suffered, torn apart as energies warred within its form from two dimensions. Now, the heavens acted.

A door went both ways.

Where it had flooded Wu Ying's world before, now the Heavens invaded their realm. Sought the breach and imposed their own demands upon the world from the other side. In so doing, they put a strain upon the monster and the gate formation.

"Yes! This will work." Phuong Vy flicked her hand sideways and cast it upward. The large slip of paper that had hovered beside her flew into the sky, inked words ripping free from the paper to hang above them all. Instructions for another.

In the distance, Minh Trac's eyes widened as he staggered to his feet. Looking from instructions to the flags he held, he grinned and ran, yanking some flags out of the ground, slipping others in as he sought to finish the formation. So many flags, some from the earlier stasis formation, others from the slaughter formation, and now, newer ones that utilized other elements were added.

"I have the north!" Yang Mu, returned at last, cried out.

She dashed from corner to corner, gripping and tossing formation flags as she aided the formation master. Dinh Don was already there, hands plunged into the still-hardening earth, roots reaching from the ground to grip the ape that thrashed about in pain and fury, hampering its movement.

In the meantime, Tou He fought the creature directly, his flames wrapping around himself and the colonel. The small woman clutched her weapon tightly, exhausted and weaving on her feet but stubbornly joining the battle. Together, they held off the distracted ape as the formation masters worked.

All this, Wu Ying sensed peripherally. Yet it was unimportant. For in the grip of heavenly orders, in the midst of healing a tortured barrier, he could do naught but stand, hands gripping sword and sword hand, a conduit for those above.

One way or the other, the heavens would have their way. No matter what it cost him.

Chapter 41

"Hold on. Just hold on…" The words were urgent, sent through threads of spirit chi. Her words were a whisper on the wind, barely heard by the recipient for he was no longer a person alone but a conduit. A pathway for a higher power that poured its wrath and orders.

Caught between worlds, sword embedded in carved and corrupted iron rod that was the gateway to another dimension, Wu Ying's form wavered at the edges. Wisps of smoky wind floated away from him, drawn back by iron will before reforming as mortal flesh and blood. His skin dissolved and split, flesh and skin and bone disappearing and reforming as his mortal form was sublimated into his element to better carry the demands of those above.

The Seven Winds cultivation technique that Wu Ying studied was incomplete. Its creator had never managed to reach the Heavens, even with the understanding that he had wielded. And Wu Ying was but a poor student.

For he was missing enlightenment on the hell wind entirely, barely grasped the heavenly wind that overrode him now. He could not balance the demands of those above with the stubbornness of those below, and so he was but a puppet. Rather than making the element part of him and thus subject to his commands, he was becoming the wind, a portion of the greater Dao itself.

What then was the need for a human form? What need for human wants and needs? The seductive whisper of enlightenment and nature itself threatened to unmoor Wu Ying. Each moment, his ego and self were robbed of their edge, their true form. He could become the wind, and in so doing, achieve his ultimate goal.

Immortality.

Of sorts.

In becoming the wind, the man known as Wu Ying, farmer once before, mere peasant at one time, now cultivator, gatherer, swordmaster would vanish. The wind had no need for past nor future, no necessity for mortal demands or goals. It blew and it changed the world, but it was also as immutable as the sun, as formless as water. By joining the wind, Wu Ying would end.

Wu Ying fought on to hold onto himself, pitting his will against the heavens now.

In the meantime, a new formation was built; a new method to achieve victory was created. The ape raged and burnt, Wu Ying wavered and faded, and the formation was implanted. But formations took time to create, time to adjust.

A blow sank Tou He half into the earth, his staff bending again. A deep cut from a dao, crossing one leg and traveling up the thigh, opened a wound near a metal rod. Lightning jumped, striking the blade, rushing upward to shock the colonel, its demands for purity indiscriminate. The cultivator struck the dirt and lay a distance away, lightning racing across her body and through her core.

Dinh Don was by their side, wielding two shorter machete-like blades made not of metal but wood. He cut into the creature, the blades humming with infused dao understanding and his chi, and where they struck, they parted scorched flesh and iron-tipped fur with equal ease. Blood flew through the air, poisonous and caustic and left the ground smoking and tainted. An acrid, nauseating aroma arose from the earth and the rotting flesh and open wounds of the ape, choking the fighters if not for Tou He's aura.

A shriek from above, a flicker of movement passing by all too fast. Blood blossomed in the air in its passing. Sao Choi acted now, its previous opponent consumed, the creature wielding wind and compressed air against the ape but never seeking to touch it.

Beset on all sides, the ape was still acting. Blows were exchanged between opponents, cultivators and beast alike striving for victory even as lightning arced between all, fire burned and cleansed, and gale winds swept the surroundings. In the distance, vegetation burned and was uprooted, the very earth scoured from the ground and bedrock found, the temple half-destroyed by attacks that were dodged or deflected.

A backhand blow was narrowly avoided, Dinh Don ducking, a breeze ruffling his hair as he did so. Realization arrived too late for the scout as the swinging backhand was but a set up for the foot that followed. It caught him in the chest and lower body, throwing him away as bones cracked under the assault and his body catapulted out of the clearing.

"Nearly there. Just hold the monster!" Minh Trac cried.

He no longer tried to emplace the formation flags exactly, instead dodging from side to side to cast them into the ground. Dozens of them already sprouted across the clearing, an inner line forming a simple casing to protect the true formation on the outside as the battle continued.

Yang Mu mirrored his actions on the other side, though alterations in chi flow, the lay of the land, and even the ambient magic required her to emplace formation flags in different places. Unlike Minh Trac, who carried the formation flags in his hand, she only pulled them forth when required, wielding a fan in the other to deflect the occasional glob of earth that the monstrous ape managed to cast in her direction.

Most of those were intercepted by Phuong Vy as she floated in the sky in a circle of talismans. From one storage ring, a continual flow of yellow talisman papers appeared. Waving, she orchestrated the movement of the talismans, intercepting attacks of opportunity the creature wielded and occasionally sweeping the monster back to the center of the formation in a flood of quick-burning talisman papers.

All this, Wu Ying sensed and more.

He felt the billowing in the creature's lungs, the thread of air as it breathed. He felt the shift of space and air as the group battled, the concussive effects of blows that threw up mud and leaves all around. He knew if he could just grasp the edges of understanding of wind and air and space, he could wield it like a weapon.

Form gale-strength winds to throw the monster aside, create a spiral of wind that could lift it into the edges of the heavens, even bring a stillness to its lungs and choke it to death.

Wu Ying knew if he could just grasp it, he could aid his friends.

And they needed it.

The last remaining cultivator, Tou He, fought on. A mistimed dodge saw a leg break. Only stubbornness and a cultivator's ability to control their bodies kept the broken bones together. A successful block saw the creature shift its aim as it rebounded, crushing fingers of one hand as it passed.

He fought with valiance, with courage and skill. With the obstinate stubbornness of the unyielding mountain. But he was losing against the ape, even beset by lightning and heavenly chi, by talismans and gripping roots and rising water.

He fought on, alone.

And the formation masters Yang Mu, Minh Trac, they would not finish in time.

Clarity returned to Wu Ying amidst the chaos and agony of existence as he glimpsed an upcoming future. His friend would slip, miss a block, be crushed.

Without anyone to stop it, the ape would ignore the talismans that were but a distraction, it would reach Wu Ying and scoop up the missing diabolical metal rod. Free his jian from it, return it to his body, and finish the battle.

For all their efforts, for everything they had done, the creature was still too strong.

They would lose.

And knowing that future, knowing that his friends would fail and fall, it was the simplest thing in the world to give in. To allow the heavens control. For his body to go from mortal to immortal, to breach the gap of formless wind.

It was the easiest thing in the world, no more difficult than changing one's mind and heart.

***

A sword clattered to the ground. A body disappeared. A woman screamed.

Wind swept around a burning flame, growing in strength and speed, swirling around and around in a cyclone as it approached the target. It caught the ape as it swung meaty hands, corrupted and alien limb leaving trails of eldritch greenish light behind.

If the formless could scream, it would have.

Instead, the wind sped up, slowing limbs, energy torn from the skies and borrowed from the flames. Debris caught in the storm tore at exposed limbs, wind filled with ice and shards of frost with an edge like a sword's blade flensed skin and eyes and fur alike.

High above, corrupted skies and air was peeled apart as the cyclone grew ever wider, as the flames taken from dragonkin cultivator were poured into them, forming a cyclone of fire. In so doing, it opened a gap such that the heavens could finally see without hindrance. A column of flame and wind that signaled those above and guided their actions.

Heavenly disapproval arrived.

It struck, tearing through cyclone and flame, through sentient wind to corrupted being. It struck without mercy, without hesitation, enforcing its dictates. Lightning, blue and white and yellow, brighter even than the heavenly disapproval of ascension. Burning away that which did not belong.

Once, twice, thrice.

Bolts of lightning the size of a tree trunk launched downward, white light so bright that those mortal cultivators could only shield themselves. The lightning tore through it all, and a mortal-being taken immortal form was torn free from its mooring and cast aside, chastised for daring to be so forward. Nearby, another mortal whose flames had fed the cyclone was blasted away as well, collateral damage now that he was no longer needed.

Under heavenly assault, the corrupted ape roared defiance. Skin burned and bones crisped, metal rods melting under the intense heat. The creature was driven to its knees and collapsed, a charred corpse filled with metal attached to an alien arm.

As suddenly as heavenly disapproval had arrived, it faded. Human channeler no longer present, the clouds of corrupted chi rolled back, hiding those below. Silence descended on the surroundings as stunned cultivators stared at the fallen body.

Silence so deep that the fall of leaves, the cracking of cooling sand, and the slow, heavy beat of a heart reinforced by demonic dimensional energy could be heard. Stuttering, stopping, but slowly regaining strength.

Not done, not finished, not yet.

Even as the fighters lay on the ground, senseless.

Chapter 42

Wu Ying woke to the sense of chi rushing inward, concentrating. Every cell in his body ached, bones and muscles conducting a deep sense of wrongness within. He rolled to the side as a racking cough took him, forcing blood and phlegm from his mouth and lungs. Bits of pieces, portions of his body that should have stayed within came with it, even as his vision swam and the world rung.

When the cough finally ended, Wu Ying struggled to pull his legs under him. Dizziness swam through his body and the commands were disjointed, as though his body was reacting a fraction of a moment later. The hesitation created a strange sense of unreality as he struggled to his swaying feet. Instinctively, he sought a weapon, casting around for his jian and not finding it anywhere nearby.

Confusion still warred with pain in his mind as the wind cultivator sought to understand what had happened. He recalled them losing, the monster beating down his friend, a decision. Then separation. Being pulled upward, his body, his sense of self separated and cradled in the arms of the world itself.

Wu Ying had belonged in a way he had never before. A sense of peace, of connection that had stretched his soul and being not just across the clearing or the multiple li his senses allowed but further, to the heavens above and the earth below. He had been one, and in becoming that one, he had felt himself dissolving. Even now, a sense of unease sat within him, as though the world was but an illusion, no more real than a paper doll house. Just as fragile to his whims.

Another shudder ran through his body, dampness in his robes enhancing the shivers that prickled his skin. Pain coursed through his body with each movement, each breath. Pain that Wu Ying found himself grateful for, for it anchored him in the present, provided him a prop to lean upon in the tides of unreality that his mind floated upon.

Focus came with that anchoring, and he let his hazy gaze trace across the blasted, twisted ground of burned grass, blackened earth, and melted sand to spot the withered, seared body of the corrupted ape. He could sense the flow of heavenly chi that poured into the corpse now, tearing at the edges of corruption that it attempted to exude. At the same time, he saw its effects in the real world, as it stripped away the flesh and bones that kept attempting to regrow, breaking them down even as cancerous mutations bubbled forth.

Wu Ying's stomach lurched a little at the sight. He turned away, moving too fast, and felt his nausea heighten. He emptied his stomach, sinking to his knees near the vomit, his body pulsing with waves of agony that made him more nauseated, sending him in a cycle of pain and nausea.

A hand pressed upon his back. He felt it stroke his back, helped to ease his pain as calming wood chi entered his body.

"It's okay. You're okay. Just breathe. Just breathe."

Looking sideways, he spotted a worried-looking Yang Mu, her lower lip caught between her teeth as she stroked his back. Wu Ying could not help but notice that her hair was still almost perfectly coiffed, other than a single lock that fell over her left eye. Not that she was without injury, for a trail of blood ran down her scalp from a crusted wound on the same side. Yet it was her hazel eyes that were filled with concern that had him mastering himself by sheer will, to shrug off the hurt rather than increase her concern.

"I'm fine. I'm here." And how close that was, how easily he felt he could have slipped away entirely, he would never say. That he might have joined the winds themselves, not as an immortal but just as another passing spirit, he shuddered to consider.

Or perhaps that was the fried nerves, the arcing pain that ran through him constantly from the tips of his toes to the ends of his hair.

"Idiot. What were you thinking?"

"That we were losing."

Wu Ying's gaze drifted away, searching. He found his target, the still body of his friend. He found himself limping over, one foot dragging, stumbling over unseen rocks. Eyes narrowed, he tried to spot a moving chest, his spiritual sense buzzing and warping, at times narrowing down to no more than his own skin, at other times flaring outward across multiple li. Too much and too little information, all at once.

"Tou He... how..."

"He's alive," Yang Mu comforted Wu Ying. "The lightning that struck, it was not targeted at him. I think his fire, it helped protect him a little."

"Is that... smoke?" Wu Ying muttered, squinting. He felt his lips crack as he spoke, a tooth a little too loose in his mouth. For that matter, now that he stared at the body, that robe was not his usual one, being a little too green and embroidered for the monk.

"He was still struck. I had to cover him because of the damage done." Without a word, she took his arm, helping him limp closer. "It's surprising your own stayed with you. Along with your armor."

"Yeah..."

Wu Ying had no explanation for that. He vaguely recalled pulling them with him when he had chosen to give up. Instinct that he could not explain, like catching a teacup that fell from a table or breathing. It had been natural, just an extension of his modified Wind Steps. He had done it before, this passing through, but only in short bursts. Now, perhaps, he might be able to do the same for longer.

The pair shuffled over to Tou He in silence, the flow of chi thrumming through the clearing. Minh Trac was crouched on one side, lifting an exhausted Phuong Vy. Dinh Don was taking a more active part in the proceedings, laboriously loading his crossbow and sending bolts into the twitching ape, each attack sending a spurt of blood anew.

As for the colonel...

"Where's Bich Trang?" Wu Ying asked. Where was Sao Choi for that matter?

"Over there."

A nod of Yang Mu's head guided Wu Ying's gaze. Through the haze and darkness, the wavering lines of his own vision, he struggled to see what she indicated. Eventually, the figures resolved, though each time he blinked, he found his attention drawn away and a headache building.

"The bird is doing something to the air around them," Wu Ying said, tearing his gaze away at last.

"It is. A camouflage of some form."

Wu Ying grimaced, recalling how the Nascent Soul creature had sneaked up on him multiple times.

"I think it's worried about the colonel," Yang Mu said.

"I'm worried about us," Tou He said, wrapping the robes around himself like a towel rather than putting on the entire thing. He worked the sleeves over his shoulders, making a makeshift monk robe and covering himself modestly. As his friend turned to face them fully, Wu Ying spotted scars tracing down one side of Tou He's body; lightning scars that played across the top of his skin and reached upward to cross over one eye and three quarters of his shaved scalp.

"Are you okay?"

Tou He touched his face with the injured hand, wincing as he did so. Eventually, he answered slowly. "I believe so. My flames are subdued, and I ache, but the pain was worth the final blow. More importantly, how are you?" He eyed Wu Ying dubiously. "You look like you've spent a year fighting your Master and Elder Koh, getting cut and grappled to death."

"I..." Wu Ying coughed again, wincing as a gob of darkened blood flew from his lips. "I have been better." Then he smiled wryly. "And worse."

"You really need to learn how to finish a fight without coming out of it half alive."

"Said the crispy Elder..."

"Commented the bleeding Gatherer."

"Boys." Yang Mu let the word out with a huff, drawing their attention to her. "If you're done, perhaps it's time to do what we came for?"

She tilted her head toward the ape, the blackened skin a hedgehog of crossbow bolts and burned flesh that struggled to reform before bursting apart, leaking fluids staining the earth. Tou He grunted, gesturing and bringing forth a new staff. This was a familiar weapon, wood rather than the bent metal of his other weapon. That one, he stored away. Wu Ying could not help but push his own senses out a little, hoping to find his own jian.

Using his staff, Tou He stood carefully on his splinted leg, testing it before nodding thanks to Yang Mu. Slowly, the trio limped over to the beating heart.

"I thought when we destroyed the formation, it would be over. Yet the creature's heart beats still, and the corruption is still in the air," Tou He commented.

"We had to change our plans," Phuong Vy said weakly as she was brought along on her brazier. Minh Trac had joined her on it, looking nearly as exhausted as she was. He had one arm cradled in a sling, the broken limb carefully tucked into his robes. "The formation was anchored by the metal rods, but the actual gate is the beast's body. To close it, we must drain the creature of all its strength then kill it."

"You said anchored." Tou He frowned. "What happens when it's not?"

Phuong Vy gestured at the body that kept attempting to grow and heal, cancerous tumors and cysts forming on various parts of its body, weeping fluids causing vegetation to burst from the ground before they died under the influx of clean chi. "That."

"Not pretty," Wu Ying muttered. "Do we have any indication of who did this?"

He nodded idly to Dinh Don, who had ambled over to the group, a bolt loaded in the crossbow but the scout no longer releasing them. The man took position a short distance away, just a little behind Yang Mu, and had forced Wu Ying to turn to greet him. Phuong Vy and Minh Trac were both nearly opposite the man, just off a little.

"Also, anyone seen my sword?" Wu Ying asked.

"I have it," Yang Mu muttered softly.

"Some," Minh Trac said. "We had to kill it fast, so we never had a chance to study the metal rods. If someone had stolen a rod rather than stabbing it…" He sighed. "The temple, on the other hand, might offer further clues."

Reflexively, Wu Ying turned his blurry gaze to the temple. The abandoned building was mostly rubble now, the battle having destroyed the walls and taken down the roof such that only the massive stone blocks lay in the distance. As he squinted, Wu Ying's spiritual sense flared and narrowed, his sense of the wind and the surroundings expanding in a pulse of uncontrolled energy that left him reeling and Yang Mu steadying him more forcefully.

"You are not looking very well," Minh Trac said idly. "That wind form you took, it took a lot out of you, did it?"

When Tou He noticed Wu Ying was too tired and disoriented to answer, the monk did so for him. "It was not easy, facing the beast. It was closer to immortal than Nascent Soul, I would have said. At least in terms of chi concentration." Turning his head, Tou He peered about the surroundings. "We were lucky to win."

"We were," Dinh Don confirmed. "As it stood…" His gaze tracked over to where Thien Giang had fallen, her body already stored away, and it grew heavy with grief.

Yang Mu frowned. She tilted her head up, her voice growing a little light as she spoke. "What happened to Sao Choi?"

"Probably out scouting, now that the Colonel's awake." As Dinh Don spoke, the scout played with the crossbow, a flickering at the edge of his aura making Wu Ying's vision swim as energy pulsed back and forth.

"You think the formation is enough? To finish the ape?" Tou He asked.

"It should be," Yang Mu said, eyeing Minh Trac as though waiting for him to confirm her words.

The man offered a sharp nod, even as he cocked his head toward where the colonel had propped herself up on one arm.

"We couldn't have done this without you three," Minh Trac said suddenly, turning back to them and pacing a little to the side. "So, you know, thank you."

Wu Ying, his head clearing a little as his senses were drawn inward, muttered, "There's a formation inside the building. A circle, with words scribbled on the ground. It feels familiar but…" He shook his head, trying to remove the clouds that sat within him. "I can't remember where."

"It's okay. Just relax. You'll remember soon enough," Yang Mu murmured.

"Cultivator Yang," Dinh Don said softly, "thank you for using the scroll. If you had not, I believe that worm would have survived all our efforts."

"That's what equipment is for, is it not?" Yang Mu replied, offering the man a half-smile. "To be used. But all this gratitude, it is making me blush."

"I did not want to leave it unsaid," the scout said.

Minh Trac was still pacing, his chi compass out. He was staring at the group, at the formation, at the flow of chi, frowning so much so that a deep line had creased the area between his eyebrows.

Wu Ying blinked again, touching his head. He felt the dampness from a cut, wiped it away, frowned at his fingers that felt numb. Something was going on here, something that his friends and those surrounding them understood. His thoughts were muddy, every moment a struggle. His mind struggled to understand relevance, for there was an ant over there that had survived the storm of battle. Now, it had found a beetle corpse, one that had elevated itself. Bringing the tiny core back to its nest would see their fate change.

Over there, a branch threatened to break. Leaves on it would spill, and somehow, Wu Ying knew, depending on where it fell and how, lives thousands of li away would change. A storm would form, or not, from a single branch.

The sun shone, baking the earth, drying it out. The rotting smell was slowly giving way as the purifying chi from the heavens, pure yang energy burned away at the edges. The wind stirred, dispersing the scent further, and all around them, slowly, the true world reasserted itself.

All so important. But here, now, something was happening. Yet thinking was like wading through heavy mud after a hard rainfall. It should have been obvious. He knew it should have been. After all, Tou He clearly got it.

"No," Tou He said, head rising a little. "I didn't think you would want to do so. Bad fortune, leaving such karma behind. Worse karma, of course, in other actions." His hand twitched by his side, then he raised his arm and frowned. A bracelet that had been given to him was missing.

For that matter, the one Wu Ying had worn was gone too. Obviously not everything had transferred when the wind cultivator had transformed.

For a moment, the wind cultivator panicked. He looked at his fingers, only relaxing when he noticed his World Spirit Ring was still there. He relaxed, almost laughing at his actions, the others all eyeing him carefully.

"Problem?" Phuong Vy said carefully.

"No. It's nothing."

Yang Mu sighed and pulled Wu Ying a step closer to his friend. She cocked her head, eyeing the surroundings before she placed a hand on Tou He's arm too. She turned his wrist over, the monk looking bemused as she took his pulse.

"What do you think you're doing?" Phuong Vy said suspiciously. "You're no physician."

"No. And your trap isn't very good," Yang Mu said. "It's a good thing we planned for betrayal anyway."

Wu Ying felt the energy pulling at him, the twisting of power as Yang Mu activated the charm on her hand, expanding the escape formation she had laid across each of the campsites they had used. At the same time, Wu Ying felt the sudden spike of killing intent, masked until now, as the raptor dove, blurring across intervening distance in an attempt to finish them before they could escape.

Simultaneously, Dinh Don raised and released the crossbow bolt while the formation Minh Trac had been marking with his aura snapped into place, glowing. Phuong Vy's brazier opened, the cauldron expelling a poisonous mixture toward them.

All too late. All but the stooping raptor.

Sao Choi, having contained its strength, now poured it into its movement. It crossed intervening space, claws extended, in the blink of an eye. As the energy from the escape formation swept over the group and tore them from the clearing, Wu Ying felt a deep impact that shook him to the core as chi wrapped itself around them all and blasted them clear.

Chapter 43

Yang Mu had created these escape formations all through their journey since the appearance of the Ma Than Vong. Each night, she had planted the formations guarding them and embedded the escape formation within the very same formation to ensure their safety. Now, the group skipped across space, each campsite a beacon for the energy that threw them forth.

At the same time, Yang Mu screamed. The power required for their transportation was greater than ever. Though much of it was drawn from the environment, the necessary extension of the bracelet that she wore to envelop both Wu Ying and Tou He—and now, Sao Choi—drew directly from her core.

The wood-and-earth escape formation was meant to be a short-range enchantment, transferring their bodies through the ground and connecting trees to the next location. The added energy and the modifications Yang Mu had completed allowed them to extend it across multiple li, each of the campsites pulling energy from the formation flags that had been slowly gathering the energy while the team was away.

Yet the passage of wind and air aspected cultivator and spirit beast through wood and earth was draining. Their bodies, unused to the transformation, instinctively fought against the change, for their very daos were anathema to this act.

Dragged along through the ground, Wu Ying felt as though his body and soul were being scoured. As though he was an ill-kept pot once utilized by an inattentive cook, the rice meant to cook left too long over the fire such that it burnt itself into blackened charcoal. The earth was the cleanser, soil and rough stone rubbed over and over again.

Fortune and misfortune all in one. Remnant wounds and blood clots, leftover debris from when he had reformed were pulled from his body, left behind as they jumped from camp to camp. His body was purified by the enchantment in a way that he would have been grateful for if not for the indescribable agony of the act.

Wu Ying was no stranger to pain, to the slow ache of being boiled alive and having poisons and corruption drawn from his form. He had soaked in baths for days on end, had his very cells broken down repeatedly before being reformed, sometimes multiple times during a single session.

The wind cultivator was no stranger to agony.

And yet, this journey transcended each of his previous experiences. Old wounds that had just finished clotting were reopened. His body, hastily rebuilt and only kept together by grace of the Dao, was damaged once more. His mind rode the waves of unending pain, his sanity tested. A sense of self that had nearly exhausted itself on the winds of existence was pinned to earthly body, and Wu Ying longed for those moments of serenity and inexistence he had approached.

But it was not to be.

The earth did not offer such solace, just more agony.

A pouring of energy, one last twist of power along a guided route, and the quartet were vomited out into an encampment near the hanged ghosts' settlement. The formation itself burst into flame moments later as its energy was exhausted.

Tou He rolled, coming to his uninjured knee in a half-crouch with broken leg splayed out behind him. A wound along the left arm he had used to block the raptor's claw dribbled blood, the staff he held in his other hand bearing long claw marks.

Yang Mu was not much better, having crashed into a tree and through it to fetch against another towering tree trunk. She lay still, her core exhausted as she struggled to stay awake. Passing tens of li within moments with an extra passenger had drained the wood cultivator of every dreg of power within her, and only the fact that the wood-and-earth escape formation had been so appropriately entwined with her own element had made it possible.

All this, Wu Ying was informed of by the winds that had returned to him. It spoke to him as he lay on the ground, nearly senseless. It blew from afar, sweeping corrupted energy away now that the source was fading, a massive makeshift formation draining the corruption with each moment. Heavenly wind even returned, grumbling about mortal concerns, powerful cultivators, and the plottings of mortal kingdoms.

For all that, it was the slowly wakening bird, a creature whose magnificent feathers had been half- plucked from its body, that concerned Wu Ying most of all. The wind cultivator struggled to put energy into his injured body to force himself to stand, only for the energy to bleed out of him through myriad damaged meridians and body parts.

"Amithaba, great one. We have no desire to fight." Tou He limped, dragging one foot, his flame guttering. He swallowed another alchemical pill in hopes of providing fuel as he approached the raptor, passing by Wu Ying's lolling head and his field of vision. "This need not end in tragedy. We were friends, were we not?"

No answer of course. What kind of answer could they expect from a spirit beast? Certainly not from one that had been silent through the entire journey. Yet the ex-monk had to try, Wu Ying knew. And he… he had to do his best too.

Voice cracked once then again, as Wu Ying swallowed around dry mouth. "Yang Mu. Slaughter formation."

Tou He turned a little at Wu Ying's words. Only to sway to the side, blocking an attack with his wooden staff. The Mountain Abides stance was not as resolute as before, its roots chipped and mined by battle and exhaustion, such that when struck even by the weightless attacks of a crippled god of the sky, it shifted.

"Great one, this need not be this way," Tou He repeated, even as he blocked another attack. Not at him this time, but at Wu Ying.

Even threatened with the loss of his life, Wu Ying found himself unable to shift away, so robbed of energy was he. Yet slowly, a trickle of energy was returning to him as the Cyclone's Breath stirred within his core, winds from multiple li pouring their energy into him. From the look in the raptor's eyes, such action had not gone unnoticed.

"Yang Mu. Get up," Wu Ying muttered, hoping she would do so. Hoping that she could find the energy to waken. He had given her the killing formation he had bargained for from her mother, knowing she could make use of it better.

Treachery had always been a concern. Their presence had been unwanted, the threat the trio showcased as powerful additions to the kingdoms that had previously threatened Nanyue clear. That they had learned of a weakness in the fortress of Liang Soong, a weakness that could be exploited by an expansionist kingdom to the north...

Well, sometimes, it was better to close off such threats beforehand. Especially if the reason for the corrupted ape, for the portal that had been opened was a secret that needed to be kept.

All those thoughts flickered through Wu Ying's mind as energy trickled into his dantian through dried out meridians. Now that he had energy, his body ached even further, blood seeping from his robes and dripping from the edges of his armor to stain the earth.

In the meantime, Tou He had shifted to block the raptor. He struck again and again with his staff, driving back the hopping bird. If not for Sao Choi's own injuries, its inability to fly beyond short hops aided by its control of the air, the fight might have been over already. As it stood, Tou He had long, bleeding wounds across his body, the robe he wore torn and bloodied.

"Great One... please..." Tou He's voice was a little desperate now.

One moment he was raising his left hand in a block, the next the staff was spinning away, a trail of blood arcing through the air and the Nascent Soul bird a short distance away, letting out a long happy cry even as it swallowed the pair of fingers it had taken from the cultivator.

No more time. Unable to delay any longer, Wu Ying forced the little energy he had gathered through his meridians. He poured it into his World Spirit Ring, his soul tearing apart as he wielded it to manipulate the storage ring and extract the formation flag. A secondary command flag that he had kept.

Trust, but plan for the worst.

Then Wu Ying sank the formation flag into the ground beside him and released the last of his energy, powering it with a touch of his lifeblood. Insufficient energy meant that the formation took what it required to start from his very body.

Energy coursed through Wu Ying, and once again, he rode the waves of pain. Except this time, no longer caught outside the realm of mortal form, consciousness was robbed from him even as lifeblood poured from his hands into the formation itself.

***

"You idiot," Tou He ranted at him even as he finished bandaging Wu Ying. He did so adroitly, only occasionally fumbling the passing of the bandages between one hand to another as he adapted to the loss of his last two fingers. "You used lifeblood to power the formation. What kind of fool does that?"

Too tired to answer him directly, Wu Ying just stared at his friend. After all, he could recall one such idiot.

"I was young and headstrong then. I did not know the importance of it," Tou He replied, finishing the bandage around his friend's leg and moving on. "You are no longer young. There was no need for that. If you'd just handed me the flag…"

In reply, Wu Ying looked at his friend's damaged hand. He could not help but smirk a little, causing the ex-monk to growl in exasperation.

"Already? I only lost my fingers a few hours ago," he said.

Working his lips, Wu Ying tried to speak, only to fail. His throat was raw and lacking in moisture. Seeing his friend struggle, Tou He extracted a wine gourd and allowed a low trickle to enter his friend's throat before continuing his haranguing.

"Don't try to speak, you should rest." Tou He nodded to the side, where Yang Mu still lay senseless. "Follow her example."

"You… too…" Wu Ying finally croaked.

"After I deal with the corpse."

Wu Ying's gaze returned to the corpse of Sao Choi, a part of him rising in disappointment as he saw the mangled and bloody body. He knew that it was important for Tou He to deal with the corpse, to extract the spirit core within and even butcher the body for meat and resources. Yet Wu Ying found himself deeply saddened as he stared at it.

Not just for the loss of a magnificent creature, one that had lived for hundreds of years, but also the betrayal. It did not have to happen that way. If they had but trusted one another, spoken to one another, this final betrayal might not have occurred.

But greed and paranoia had driven the actions of others. And now the trio was here, trapped in the wilderness, wounded and exhausted and with enemies not far behind.

There would be no talking, not anymore. Not now, perhaps not for a very long time. Too much had been lost on both sides.

All Wu Ying could hope was that it had been worth it.

Chapter 44

Wu Ying took the lead the day after. As much as the team had wanted to immediately leave, to escape and put further ground between them and their pursuers, they had only stumbled a short distance away from the battle location before slipping into a deep earthen depression created by a sloping hill and a fallen tree.

Their sleep was fitful, the constant use of alchemical pills to restore body and energy reserves filling the surroundings with the stink of alchemical impurities. Only Wu Ying's returning control of the wind kept the odors drifting upward and away, leaving them hidden.

Over the course of the next few days, the group swung north and east, seeking to bypass the village and the angered hanged demons while also leaving minimal traces for their pursuers. Wu Ying was all too aware that Dinh Don had survived the battle and the scout's method of tracking them was one that the wind cultivator would struggle to combat.

More often than not, the group waded through streams, trading the discomfort of cold feet and water-logged shoes for the opportunity to throw off the earth cultivator. While other modes of travel would normally be available, the significant drain on their chi of the multiple battles forbade such methods. When the group finally regained a portion of their chi, sufficient enough that Wu Ying believed it worth the risk, they took to the skies, flitting from tree branch to tree branch.

Their paranoia increased as knowledge of their enemies was blocked on the first day of travel, the wind no longer able to provide further details. It was no surprise that the other team had methods to hide their presence, not after weeks of travel and study of the wind cultivator's abilities.

That they did not know or understand the extent of damage Wu Ying had suffered was probably for the best. Even now, the wind cultivator found his control and awareness slipping at the most inopportune times. His awareness and connection with the winds would grow stronger than ever, allowing the wind cultivator to sense the fall of a leaf or the tremble of a spider's web over a falling waterfall tens of li away.

At other times, the wind that carried him across the ground, that allowed him to brush past tree trunks or send aggressive insects away, would fail him. He would tumble to the ground or into trunks, hardened skin becoming as soft and pliable as a mortal's. Wounds and injuries accumulated, adding to the plethora that he sported and that he suffered in silence.

When night fell, Yang Mu offered cold compresses and rewrapped bandages for the pair. She would often sit by Wu Ying's side, offering silent comfort as fevers and shivers racked his body before he fell asleep, only to bolt upright as nightmares took him. A sense of fading, a splitting of his consciousness, and the memory of pain kept him up.

Long conversations would result as the moon rose and set, the humid jungle forcing sweat down necks and reminding the pair of all-too-mortal frailties.

For all their difficulties, the trio traversed the land experiencing few enough encounters. The corrupted Core Formation beasts had scattered. Some traveled outward to spread their corruption and destroy and consume other, weaker members of their kind. In their passing, they would spread additional taint, destroy the balance of the Dao, and pollute their surroundings before they were finally destroyed and purified.

At the same time, others were drawn to the cleansing formation around the ape's body. They sought to consume the most potent source of energy that had empowered them. Some might ravage the very land around the heart itself, for the taint still lingered in soil and vegetation.

In such an environment, a trio of weak and injured Core Formation cultivators who sought no trouble and did their best to avoid it were of little consequence. Occasionally they found themselves forced to do battle with demonic beasts, their minds and bodies twisted by the corruptive forces, and dispatched these weakened creatures as quickly and mercifully as possible. Most times, they left the cores and bodies behind rather than bring the taint with them.

Days passed, and as they traveled, the number of attacks decreased. The number of tainted creatures grew fewer, the surroundings normalized and the normal flow of life returned.

It was nearly three weeks later, the group having traversed hundreds of li across deep and treacherous rivers and boggy marshes, that they began to relax. No sign had been seen of their former allies and erstwhile attackers, and the tense silence bled out of them with each quiet day.

When the trio located a shaded clearing with a pond reflecting the waning moon, by unspoken agreement, the group chose to settle in for a longer period. Formation flags—illusion, deception, and slaughter—were emplaced and a merry fire was set alight. Yet for all their preparations, within an hour, Tou He had crashed, a forearm-long hunk of roasted meat still clutched in his hand as he slept.

By the banked fire, coals still glowing under a bubbling stew pot, Wu Ying and Yang Mu took seats near one another. She leaned against him, resting her head on his shoulder in serene silence. Eventually though, Yang Mu shifted her weight off his arm and turned to the wind cultivator. Sensing the change in atmosphere, Wu Ying met her gaze and raised an eyebrow in inquiry.

"Don't do that. You have something on your mind, I know it. Is it your injuries?" Yang Mu's lips thinned in distress. "If it's worse than we thought, I can ask my parents. They know people."

"I'm sure they do." Wu Ying smiled a little at her easy declaration. "But it's not that. I can feel myself healing slowly. The dizziness grows less, the disorientation. I feel more mortal, more constrained each day."

"And that is good?"

"When you were the wind all across the land, yes." Wu Ying shook his head. "I don't know if I can explain it, but even now…" He looked into the distance. Sensing the fingertip brushes of breezes, the exhalation of a thousand creatures, both big and small. The flutter of insect wings, the ruffling of air through leaves and grass, the mixing of aromas as they rose from night-wakened flowers. How the air hung differently over the river or the marsh they had journeyed through compared to the soil and rock of other locations. Rising and falling, in slow ponderous nature. The play of sunlight and individuals and a memory of mountains worn away and rivers turned… "It's everything, the past and the present and the future. The wind is everywhere and yet, I am nothing in it. A mortal amongst immortal forces. It's too much."

Her hand gripped his, squeezing tightly. He traced the back of her hand, the smooth pale skin that covered tendons and veins, the subtle strength contained within them, and the warmth of a human body. He felt her aura push against his, not in conflict but in reassurance. The vitality of her presence, the pressing need of it, the exploration of new sensations and new experiences required for healthy growth…

It anchored him, once more, in the here and now. The pain of his body, the coldness of the stone he sat upon, the warmth radiating from the coals—all a reminder of his mortality. A mortality that he had discarded in its entirety.

"Then what is the problem?" Her voice was low, insistent without being intruding. Empathetic inquiry that left him with the option of answering or not.

"When I was the wind, when the Heavens passed on their decree and wielded their strength directly, I sensed them, sensed what they saw… their actions, sometimes, I thought were mistakes. But I can see it now, oh so clearly…"

Silence greeted his words, even as he trailed off. She took his left hand with both of hers, squeezing it gently in encouragement, fingers running across scabbed flesh.

"The Heavens care not for us." Then before she could object, he continued. "Not individually." He gestured with his right hand, waving at the tree. "How can they? A farmer does not weep for the branch he must trim, the stalk of rice he must extract. He cannot mourn the weeds that must be pulled for the greater good of the crop.

"And we, we are no more important than a blade of grass. The Heavens must watch and care for all, from the mosquito that lands on our skin, seeking sustenance, to the mighty dragon that soars above, bringing rain."

She inclined her head a little, her voice coming softly now. "And that has left a shadow in your heart?"

"A shadow, yes. Because to progress further, to become one with the Seven Winds… to join with it all, I must accept the Heavens." Wu Ying laughed softly. "It's funny. I know I have an inkling of the Hells winds. They burn, they punish, they renew. That is the role of our hells, to see the refinement and betterment of souls. And that… that I can accept."

"But you rail against a heaven that sees not the individual but only the greater."

"Yes. A heaven that would flood a valley to drown a demon, that allows the fall of storms in one region and drought in another; all to ensure a balance that only they can—barely—understand." Wu Ying's voice grew wry, aggrieved. "And barely it is."

"What do you mean?"

"Perhaps the Jade Emperor is different, but the others… from what I sensed, they're like us, except a little stronger and a little wiser. But they are embodiments of a sliver of the Dao. They cannot encompass it. Perhaps it's not even viable to be everything in a sliver of the Dao. I couldn't handle being the wind, not really." Wu Ying exhaled threadedly. "Immortals cannot be the Dao, for the Dao is endless. To be the Dao, we too would have to be everything. But when you are everything, you are also nothing."

"Yet to be so close to the Dao…" It was her turn now to trail off. It was not a path she had taken, not a path she could walk. Yet the cultivator could not help but imagine what that might be like, the strength, the power, the wisdom that might encompass one. "What wonder."

He looked down at his hand gripped in hers and offered Yang Mu a little half-smile. "Wonder, yes. But I think there is wisdom too in finding that wonder in the smaller, mortal things. To marvel at the fortune one might gain in the present, if one is willing to accept it."

Now it was Yang Mu's turn to look surprised. She began to retract her hand, only for him to squeeze his shut, trapping her. She stilled, eyes searching his.

"I do not remember much of my time as the wind. Of the rejection of the heavens, though a part of me fears that the path I walk might be the wrong one. But what I do remember is that when I was the wind, when all that was mortal in me began to fray and come apart… I had a rock to stand upon, and a smile to remember."

"A rock?" Yang Mu said.

"Is that what you heard through all that?" Now Wu Ying was amused, though neither party let go of the other's hand.

"Well, maybe I don't like to share."

"He has my friendship. You have my heart." Wu Ying cocked one shoulder upward. "Is that not enough?"

Now she smiled, leaning forward. She crossed the space between them, lips inches from his as she answered him. "Yes."

Neither party knew who closed the final distance. Perhaps they both did. Lips met lips, and for a time, the aches of battle and the fears of the future faded away, as arms released only to wrap around one another. One around the waist, another to cradle head and body. Breath mingled, and for a time, there was no fear of the future or debate over the dao.

For a time, there was just two mortals hanging onto one another in a turbulent, changing world. And that was enough.

Epilogue

They came by boat, traversing churning river water. It was no massive merchant vessel they rode, but a sleek nobleman's craft that took them upriver, its sails filled with a wind that carried them—and them alone.

The crew of other vessels had stared at the ship enviously, eyeing the beautiful female who lounged on the foredeck or watching with awe the pair of battling cultivation masters who danced across the deck and on the water itself in an ongoing test of martial ability.

Yet now, today, neither party fought. Over a year and a half had passed since one of the passengers had left on a mission. Over a decade since the other had been banished. Yet similar feelings arose in the breasts of the pair as they watched the looming mountain range approach and the massive waterfall that earmarked the end of the river. Beside the waterfall stood the city harbor, filled to bursting with merchants plying their trade, and the city behind that.

"That path, over there?" Wu Ying said, gesturing with his right hand, his left gripped in Yang Mu's. His left hand no longer bled, though a white scar marked the skin that had been lost to a purifying flame and, on occasion, a deep ache would arise within, making his hand tremble without stop. Perhaps one day it would disappear, along with the other wounds— most unseen—that dotted his body.

"I see it." Yang Mu smiled a little. "Is that the one you used to climb?"

"A few times a day, as an outer sect member," Wu Ying confirmed. "Bags of rice on my back as training and for contribution points."

"And there's an inner and outer sect, right?" Yang Mu said to clarify.

"Inner, outer, and core." Tou He was not far from the pair, leaning on his old wooden staff. His right hand was bandaged tightly, the missing stubs of his bottom two fingers healed over. "Though the core members are rarely seen by the general populace. They are busy training or consuming their pills."

"Speaking of that…" Yang Mu cocked her head. "You finished all of yours?"

"Two nights ago. I pray I never have to consume something as disgusting in my life. Why anyone would think to make the original Wolf Heart, Dog Kidney pill—and make it more effective even—I cannot understand. I couldn't eat properly for days," Tou He said.

"But it refilled your energy levels, did it not?" Wu Ying smirked. "You even managed to add another layer to your core." Something dark flickered across his face as he added, "It's not as though we were lacking in experience and enlightenment at least."

His friends shared a glance, one that they perhaps thought Wu Ying missed. Or perhaps not. Their concern over his health and state of mind had grown more noticeable as he attempted to shake the experience of becoming the wind.

Changing the subject, Yang Mu pointed at the waterfalls. "Your Elder Sister climbed those early on, did she not?"

"She did," Wu Ying confirmed as they slid closer to the docks. He gently turned his hand sideways, and the wind stopped blowing, the sail flapping at the sudden lack of force. "Were you planning to ascend that way?"

"It seems appropriate, do you not think so?" Yang Mu said. "After all, you come back not as a mere Energy Storage cultivator. Let them know that their exiled son has returned. Let them understand you are no mere Gatherer. And that the child who left has returned a man."

Wu Ying shook his head, his natural aversion to making a scene warring with his desire to show off for her. Even as he debated internally, the wind arose once more and shifted direction, pushing the boat toward the waterfall. A startled yelp from the steersmen and the snap of sails being filled were the only signs of the suddenly straining sail.

"It seems we're not the only ones who thinks you should approach with some pride, old friend." Tou He smiled a little as he listened to the flapping sail. "Go. I'll be up, the normal way."

"It seems not." Wu Ying gazed upon the distant, cloud-covered peak, shrouded by the spray of mist and fog, and smiled. "Let's go then."

Lifting Yang Mu's hand, he gave it one more squeeze.

"Back home to the Verdant Green Waters sect."

The End

Check out the Bonus Epilogue!
www.mylifemytao.com/my-book-series/a-thousand-li/bonus-epilogue-for-the-third-cut

Continue following Wu Ying's journey in *The Fourth Stage*.
www.starlitpublishing.com/products/the-fourth-stage

The System Apocalypse Series

What happens when the apocalypse arrives, not via nuclear weapons or a comet but as Levels and monsters? What if you were camping in the Yukon when the world ended?

All John wanted to do was get away from his life in Kluane National Park for a weekend. Hike, camp and chill. Instead, the world comes to an end in a series of blue boxes. Animals start evolving, monsters start spawning and he has a character sheet and physics defying skills. Now, he has to survive the apocalypse, get back to civilisation and not lose his mind.

The System has arrived and with it, aliens, monsters and a reality that draws upon past legends and game-like reality. John will need to find new friends, deal with his ex and the slavering monsters that keep popping up.

Life in the North is Book 1 of the *System Apocalypse*, a LitRPG Apocalypse series that combines modern day life, science fiction and fantasy elements along with game mechanics. This series contains elements of games like level ups, experience, enchanted materials, a sarcastic spirit, mecha, a beguiling dark elf, monsters, minotaurs, a fiery red head and a semi-realistic view on violence and its effects. Does not include harems.

Read more of the completed System Apocalypse series.
www.starlitpublishing.com/collections/the-system-apocalypse

Author's Note

Thank you for following the story of Wu Ying for nine books so far! We still have an exciting road ahead, and if you can't wait until the next book is published, you can read new chapters as I work on them on my patreon. There are also plenty of short stories set in A Thousand Li universe, you might be interested in. Feel free to check them out on Starlit Publishing's website.

Please do leave a review and check out my many other works if you have time.

As always, for more information of what I'm up to or writing, my newsletter is the best place.

~Tao

For more great information about great LitRPG series, check out the Facebook groups:
- GameLit Society
  www.facebook.com/groups/LitRPGsociety
- LitRPG Books
  www.facebook.com/groups/LitRPG.books

And join my Cultivation Novel Group for more recommendations and to talk about the Thousand Li series:
  www.facebook.com/groups/cultivationnovels/

About the Author

Tao Wong is a Canadian author based in Toronto who is best known for his System Apocalypse post-apocalyptic LitRPG series and A Thousand Li, a Chinese xianxia fantasy series. His work has been released in audio, paperback, hardcover and ebook formats and translated into German, Spanish, Portuguese, Russian and other languages. He was shortlisted for the UK Kindle Storyteller award in 2021 for his work, A Thousand Li: the Second Sect. When he's not writing and working, he's practicing martial arts, reading and dreaming up new worlds.

Tao became a full-time author in 2019 and is a member of the Science Fiction and Fantasy Writers of America (SFWA) and Novelists Inc.

If you'd like to support Tao directly, he has a Patreon page - benefits include previews of all his new books, full access to series short stories, and other exclusive perks.
    www.patreon.com/taowong

Want updates on upcoming deluxe editions and exclusive merch? Follow Tao on Kickstarter to get notifications on all projects.
    www.kickstarter.com/profile/starlitpublishing

For updates on the series and his other books (and special one-shot stories), please visit the author's website.
    www.mylifemytao.com/

Subscribers to Tao's mailing list to receive exclusive access to short stories in the Thousand Li and System Apocalypse universes.

About the Publisher

Starlit Publishing is wholly owned and operated by Tao Wong. It is a science fiction and fantasy publisher focused on the LitRPG & cultivation genres. Their focus is on promoting new, upcoming authors in the genre whose writing challenges the existing stereotypes while giving a rip-roaring good read.

For more information on Starlit Publishing, visit our website!
www.starlitpublishing.com/

You can also join Starlit Publishing's mailing list to learn about new, exciting authors and book releases.
https://starlitpublishing.com/newsletter-signup/

Glossary

Aura Reinforcement Exercise—Cultivation exercise that allows Wu Ying to contain his aura, trapping his chi within himself and making his cultivation more efficient and making him, to most senses, feel like someone of a lower cultivation level.

Blade Energy/Chi—A specific type of energy that is harnessed by cultivators who have gained understanding of their weapon. Can be projected for more damage.

Body Cleansing – First cultivation stage where the cultivator must cleanse their body of the impurities that have accumulated. Has twelve stages.

Cangue — wooden pillory where head and arms are placed, far apart enough that the prisoner may not feed themselves.

Cao – Fuck

Catty - Weight measurement. One cattie is roughly equivalent to one and a half pounds or 604 grams. A tael is $1/16^{th}$ of a catty

Chi (or Qi) – I use the Cantonese pinyin here rather than the more common Mandarin. Chi is life force / energy and it permeates all things in the universe, flowing through living creatures in particular.

Chi points (a.k.a. acupuncture points) – Locations in the body that, when struck, compressed, or otherwise affected, can affect the flow of chi. Traditional acupuncture uses these points in a beneficial manner.

Cì Kè (刺客) - individuals trained in martial arts meant for assassination and spying, including the use of poison, camouflage, blending into the night and more.

Congee — Chinese rice porridge. Best made with stock, though plain water is viable. Eight portions of water or stock to one portion rice, boil until rice is mushy. Meat, fish, and other items may be added to give flavor and nutrients.

Core formation – Third stage of cultivation. Having gathered sufficient chi, the cultivator must form a "core" of compressed chi. The stages in Core formation purify and harden the core.

Cultivation Exercise—A supplementary exercise that improves an individual's handling of chi within their body. Cultivation exercises are ancillary to cultivation styles.

Cultivation Style—A method to manipulate chi within an individual's body. There are thousands of cultivation exercises, suited for various constitutions, meridians, and bloodlines.

Cun - A traditional Chinese measurement, measured as the width of a person's thumb at knuckle. It is—in current, standardized measurement—3 1/3 cm or approximately 1.312 inches.

Dào—Literally translated, the Way (also spelled Tao). The Dao when capitalized speaks of the universal Dao, the one natural Way or Path. When not capitalized, it denotes a lesser way, a lesser truth.

Dāo—Chinese sabre. Closer to a western cavalry sabre, it is thicker, often single-edged, with a curve at the end where additional thickness allows the weapon to be extra efficient at cutting.

Dantian – there are actually three dantians in the human body. The most commonly referred to one is the lower dantian, located right above the bladder and an inch within the body. The other two are located in the chest and forehead, though they are often less frequently used. The dantian is said to be the center of chi.

Dark Sects—These are considered 'evil' Sects. Their cultivation methods and daos tap into darker emotions and often include blood and flesh sacrifice and the stealing of chi from others.

Demonic Sects—Demonic Sects draw power not from the chi in the natural world but from the demonic plane. While not necessarily evil or harmful like Dark Sects, many Demonic Sects are hunted by Orthodox Sects due to the damage their presence can cause to the natural order of the world.

Double Soul, Double Body Sect—an orthodox sect with an unorthodox approach to recruitment, dedicated to the development of individuals with unusual body and soul configurations.

Dragon's Breath—Chi projection attack from the Long family style.

Elements—The Chinese traditionally have five elements—Wood, Fire, Earth, Metal, and Water. Within these elements, additional sub-elements may occur (example—air from Chao Kun, ice from Li Yao).

Energy Storage – Second stage of cultivation, where the energy storage circulation meridians are opened. This stage allows cultivators to project their chi, the amount of chi stored and projected depending on level. There are eight levels.

Heretical Sects—Sects practising unorthodox daos or cultivation methods. These heretical sects might not even focus on cultivation in the same manner as 'orthodox' sects.

Huài dàn – Rotten egg

Hún dàn - Bastard

Jian – A straight, double-edged sword. Known in modern times as a "taichi sword." Mostly a thrusting instrument, though it can be used to cut as well.

Jianghu (Jiāng hú)—Is literally translated as "rivers and lakes" but is a term used for the "martial arts world" in wuxia works (and this one too). In modern parlance, it can also mean the underworld or can be added to other forms of discussion like "school Jianghu" to discuss specific societal bounds.

Li – Roughly half a kilometer per li. Traditional Chinese measurement of distance.

Long family jian style – A family sword form passed on to Wu Ying. Consists of a lot of cuts, fighting at full measure, and quick changes in direction.

Lord Wen—Father of Yin Xue. The Wen family is a branch family of nobles born in the neighboring state of Wei and that defected.

Medicinal Baths— The process of creating a bath in which an individual may steep their body within to strengthen and reinforce the cultivator's body. Uses a variety of different spiritual herbs and recipes, often concocted to specific physiologies.

Meridians – In traditional Chinese martial arts and medicine, meridians are how chi flows through the body. In traditional Chinese medicine, there are twelve major meridian flows and eight secondary energy flows. I've used these meridians for the stages in cultivation for the first two stages.

Mountain Breaking Fist—Fist form that Wu Ying gained in the inner sect library. Focused, single, powerful attacks.

Nascent Soul—The fourth and last known stage of cultivation. Cultivators form a new, untouched soul steeped in the dao they had formed. This new soul must ascend to the heavens, facing heavenly tribulation at each step.

Northern Shen Kicking Style – Kicking form that Wu Ying learned at the sect library. Both a grappling and kicking style, meant for close combat.

Orthodox Sects—The most common type of Sect. Differentiated from other types by the cultivation type conducted.

Qinggong – Literally "light skill." Comes from baguazhang and is basically wire-fu – running on water, climbing trees, gliding along bamboo, etc.

Iron Reinforced Bones—Defensive, physical cultivation technique that Wu Ying trains in that will increase the strength and defense of his body.

Sect – A grouping of like-minded martial artists or cultivators. Generally, Sects are hierarchical. There are often core, inner, and outer disciples in any sect, with Sect Elders above them and the Sect patriarch above all.

Six Jades Sect—Rival sect of the Verdant Green Waters, located in the State of Wei.

Seven Diamond Fist – Verdant Green Water's Sect most basic fist form taught to outer sect members.

State of Shen – Location in which the first book is set. Ruled by a king and further ruled locally by lords. The State of Shen is made up of numerous counties ruled over by local lords and administered by magistrates. It is a temperate kingdom with significant rainfall and a large number of rivers connected by canals.

State of Wei – The antagonistic kingdom that borders the State of Shen. The two states are at war.

Tael – System of money. A thousand copper coins equals one tael.

Tai Kor – Elder brother

Verdant Green Waters Sect – Most powerful sect in the State of Wen. Wu Ying's current sect.

Wu wei—Taoist concept, translates as "inaction" or "non-doing" and relates to the idea of an action without struggle, that is perfectly aligned with the natural world.